THE NORTON ANTHOLOGY OF

WORLD LITERATURE

THIRD EDITION

VOLUME D

THE NORTON ANTHOLOGY OF

WORLD LITERATURE

THIRD EDITION

MARTIN PUCHNER, *General Editor*
HARVARD UNIVERSITY

SUZANNE AKBARI
UNIVERSITY OF TORONTO

WIEBKE DENECKE
BOSTON UNIVERSITY

VINAY DHARWADKER
UNIVERSITY OF WISCONSIN, MADISON

BARBARA FUCHS
UNIVERSITY OF CALIFORNIA, LOS ANGELES

CAROLINE LEVINE
UNIVERSITY OF WISCONSIN, MADISON

PERICLES LEWIS
YALE UNIVERSITY

EMILY WILSON
UNIVERSITY OF PENNSYLVANIA

VOLUME D

W. W. NORTON & COMPANY | New York · London

W. W. Norton & Company has been independent since its founding in 1923, when William Warder Norton and Mary D. Herter Norton first published lectures delivered at the People's Institute, the adult education division of New York City's Cooper Union. The firm soon expanded its program beyond the Institute, publishing books by celebrated academics from America and abroad. By midcentury, the two major pillars of Norton's publishing program—trade books and college texts—were firmly established. In the 1950s, the Norton family transferred control of the company to its employees, and today—with a staff of four hundred and a comparable number of trade, college, and professional titles published each year—W. W. Norton & Company stands as the largest and oldest publishing house owned wholly by its employees.

Editor: Peter Simon
Assistant Editor: Conor Sullivan
Managing Editor, College: Marian Johnson
Manuscript Editors: Barney Latimer, Alice Falk, Katharine Ings, Michael Fleming, Susan Joseph, Pamela Lawson, Diane Cipollone
Electronic Media Editor: Eileen Connell
Print Ancillary Editor: Laura Musich
Editorial Assistant, Media: Jennifer Barnhardt
Marketing Manager, Literature: Kimberly Bowers
Senior Production Manager, College: Benjamin Reynolds
Photo Editor: Patricia Marx
Permissions Manager: Megan Jackson
Permissions Clearing: Margaret Gorenstein
Text Design: Jo Anne Metsch
Art Director: Rubina Yeh
Cartographer: Adrian Kitzinger
Composition: Jouve North America, Brattleboro, VT
Manufacturing: R. R. Donnelley & Sons—Crawfordsville, IN

The text of this book is composed in Fairfield Medium with the display set in Aperto.

Library of Congress Cataloging-in-Publication Data

The Norton anthology of world literature / Martin Puchner, general editor . . . [et al.].—3rd ed.
    p. cm.
    "Volume D."
    Includes bibliographical references and index.
    ISBN 978-0-393-91329-3 (v. A : pbk.)—ISBN 978-0-393-91330-9 (v. B : pbk.)—
ISBN 978-0-393-91331-6 (v. C : pbk.)—**ISBN 978-0-393-91332-3 (v. D : pbk.)**—ISBN
978-0-393-91333-0 (v. E : pbk.)—ISBN 978-0-393-91334-7 (v. F : pbk.) 1. Literature—
Collections. I. Puchner, Martin, 1969– II. Norton anthology of world masterpieces
    PN6014.N66 2012
    808.8—dc23

                                                                    2011047211

W. W. Norton & Company, Inc., 500 Fifth Avenue, New York, NY 10110-0017
wwnorton.com
W. W. Norton & Company Ltd., Castle House, 75/76 Wells Street, London W1T 3QT

1 2 3 4 5 6 7 8 9 0

Contents

PREFACE / ix

ABOUT THE THIRD EDITION / xix

ACKNOWLEDGMENTS / xxiii

I. EAST ASIAN DRAMA 3

ZEAMI MOTOKIYO (ca. 1363–1443) 5
  Atsumori / 8
  (*Translated by Royall Tyler*)

KONG SHANGREN (1648–1718) 16
  From The Peach Blossom Fan / 19
  (*Translated by Stephen Owen*)

CHIKAMATSU MONZAEMON (1653–1725) 45
  From The Love Suicides at Amijima / 48
  (*Translated by Donald Keene*)

FROM THE SONG OF CH'UN-HYANG (eighteenth century) 74
  (*Translated by Richard Rutt and Kim Chong-un*)

II. THE ENLIGHTENMENT IN EUROPE
AND THE AMERICAS 91

WHAT IS ENLIGHTENMENT? / 101
SAMUEL JOHNSON, *FROM* A DICTIONARY OF THE ENGLISH
  LANGUAGE / 104
IMMANUEL KANT, WHAT IS ENLIGHTENMENT? / 105
  (*Translated by Lewis White Beck*)
RENÉ DESCARTES, *FROM* THE DISCOURSE ON METHOD / 110
  (*Translated by Isaac Kramnick*)
DENIS DIDEROT AND JEAN LE ROND D'ALEMBERT, *FROM*
  THE ENCYCLOPÉDIE / 113

BENJAMIN FRANKLIN, LETTER TO JOSEPH PRIESTLEY / 128
DAVID HUME, *FROM* OF NATIONAL CHARACTERS / 129
JAMES BEATTIE, *FROM* AN ESSAY ON TRUTH / 130
MARY WOLLSTONECRAFT, *FROM* A VINDICATION OF THE
    RIGHTS OF WOMAN / 133
MARQUIS DE SADE, *FROM* PHILOSOPHY IN THE BEDROOM / 137
    (*Translated by Richard Seaver and Austryn Wainhouse*)

MOLIÈRE (JEAN-BAPTISTE POQUELIN) (1622–1673)   141
    Tartuffe / 144
    (*Versification by Constance Congdon, from a translation by Virginia Scott*)

APHRA BEHN (1640?–1689)   198
    Oroonoko; or, The Royal Slave / 200

SOR JUANA INÉS DE LA CRUZ (1648–1695)   246
    From The Poet's Answer to the Most Illustrious Sor Filotea
        de la Cruz / 248
    Poem 145 [This object which you see, a painted snare] / 262
    Poem 164 [This afternoon, my darling, when we spoke] / 262
    Philosophical Satire, Poem 92 / 263
    (*Translated by Electa Arenal and Amanda Powell*)

JONATHAN SWIFT (1667–1745)   265
    Gulliver's Travels / 269
        Part IV. A Voyage to the Country of the Houyhnhnms / 269
    A Modest Proposal / 315

ALEXANDER POPE (1688–1744)   321
    The Rape of the Lock / 325
    (*Text and notes by Samuel Holt Monk*)
    An Essay on Man / 344
        Epistle I / 344

VOLTAIRE (FRANÇOIS-MARIE AROUET) (1694–1778)   352
    Candide, or Optimism / 355
    (*Translated and with notes by Robert M. Adams*)

III. EARLY MODERN CHINESE VERNACULAR
LITERATURE   415

WU CHENG'EN (ca. 1500–1582)   421
    From The Journey to the West / 424
    (*Translated by Anthony Yu*)

FENG MENGLONG (1574–1646)   497
    Du Tenth Sinks the Jewel Box in Anger / 499
    (*Translated by Robert Ashmore*)

CAO XUEQIN (ca. 1715–1763)   517
    The Story of the Stone / 521
      From Chapters 1–3, 17 / 523
      (*Translated by David Hawkes*)
      From Chapters 96–98, 119, 120 / 562
      (*Translated by John Minford*)

IV. EARLY MODERN JAPANESE POPULAR LITERATURE   585

IHARA SAIKAKU (1642–1693)   591
    From Life of a Sensuous Woman / 593
    (*Translated by Chris Drake*)

THE WORLD OF HAIKU / 613

KITAMURA KIGIN, *FROM* THE MOUNTAIN WELL / 615
    (*Translated by Haruo Shirane*)
MATSUO BASHŌ, *FROM* THE NARROW ROAD TO THE DEEP
    NORTH / 616
    (*Translated by Haruo Shirane*)
MORIKAWA KYORIKU, *FROM* HAIKAI DIALOGUE / 629
    (*Translated by Haruo Shirane*)
YOSA BUSON
    Preface to Shōha's Haiku Collection / 630
    (*Translated by Jack Stoneman*)
    From New Flower Gathering / 631
      The Badger / 631
    (*Translated by Cheryl Crowley*)

SELECTED BIBLIOGRAPHIES / A1

TIMELINE / A7

PERMISSIONS ACKNOWLEDGMENTS / A19

INDEX / A21

Preface

In 1665, a Turkish nobleman traveled from his native Istanbul to Europe and recorded with disarming honesty his encounter with an alien civilization. Over the course of his life, Evliya Çelebi would crisscross the Ottoman Empire from Egypt all the way to inner Asia, filling volume after volume with his reports of the cities, peoples, and legends he came across. This was his first journey to Vienna, a longtime foe of the Ottoman Empire. Full of confidence about the superiority of his own culture, Evliya was nevertheless impressed by Vienna's technical and cultural achievements. One episode from his *Travels,* a charming moment of self-deprecation, tells us how, during his tour of Vienna's inner city, Evliya sees what he believes to be "captives from the nation of Muhammad" sitting in front of various shops, toiling away at mind-numbing, repetitive tasks. Feeling pity for them, he offers them some coins, only to find that they are in fact mechanical automatons. Embarrassed and amazed at the same time, Evliya ends this tale by embracing the pleasure of seeing something new: "This was a marvelous and wonderful adventure indeed!"

Throughout his travels, Evliya remained good-humored about such disorienting experiences, and he maintained an open mind as he compared the cultural achievements of his home with those of Vienna. The crowning achievement of Vienna is the cathedral, which towers over the rest of the city. But Evliya found that it couldn't compare with the architectural wonders of Istanbul's great mosques. As soon as he was taken to the library, however, he was awestruck: "There are God knows how many books in the mosques of Sultan Barqūq and Sultan Faraj in Cairo, and in the mosques of [Sultan Meḥmed] The Conqueror and Sultan Süleymān and Sultan Bāyezīd and the New Mosque, but in this St. Stephen's Monastery in Vienna there are even more." He admired the sheer diversity and volume of books: "As many nations and different languages as there are, of all their authors and writers in their languages there are many times a hundred thousand books here." He was drawn, naturally enough, to the books that make visible the contours and riches of the world: atlases, maps, and illustrated books. An experienced travel writer, he nonetheless struggled to keep his equilibrium, saying finally that he was simply "stunned."

Opening *The Norton Anthology of World Literature* for the first time, a reader may feel as overwhelmed by its selection of authors and works (from "as many different languages as there are") as Evliya was by the cathedral library. For most students, the world literature course is a semester- or year-long encounter with the unknown—a challenging and rewarding journey, not a stroll down familiar, well-worn paths. Secure in their knowledge of the culture of their upbringing, and perhaps even proud of its accomplishments, most students will discover in world literature a bewildering variety of similarly rich and admirable cultures about which they know little, or nothing. Setting off on an imaginative journey in an unfamiliar text, readers may ask themselves questions similar to those a traveler in a strange land might ponder: How should I orient myself in this unfamiliar culture? What am I not seeing that someone raised in this culture would recognize right away? What can I learn here? How can I relate to the people I meet? Students might imagine the perils of the encounter, wondering if they will embarrass themselves in the process, or simply find themselves "stunned" by the sheer number of things they do not know.

But as much as they may feel anxiety at the prospect of world literature, students may also feel, as Evliya did, excitement at the discovery of something new, the exhilaration of having their horizons expanded. This, after all, is why Evliya traveled in the first place. Travel, for him, became almost an addiction. He sought again and again the rush of the unknown, the experience of being stunned, the feeling of marveling over cultural achievements from across the world. Clearly Evliya would have liked to linger in the cathedral library and immerse himself in its treasures. This experience is precisely what *The Norton Anthology of World Literature* offers to you and your students.

As editors of the Third Edition, we celebrate the excitement of world literature, but we also acknowledge that the encounter with the literary unknown is a source of anxiety. From the beginning of our collaboration, we have set out to make the journey more enticing and less intimidating for our readers.

First, we have made the introductory matter clearer and more informative by shortening headnotes and by following a consistent pattern of presentation, beginning with the author's biography, then moving to the cultural context, and ending with a brief introduction to the work itself. The goal of this approach is to provide students with just enough information to prepare them for their own reading of the work, but not so much information that their sense of discovery is numbed.

The mere presentation of an anthology—page after page of unbroken text—can feel overwhelming to anyone, but especially to an inexperienced student of literature. To alleviate this feeling, and to provide contextual information that words might not be able to convey, we have added hundreds of images and other forms of visual support to the anthology. Most of these images are integrated into the introductions to each major section of the anthology, providing context and visual interest. More than fifty of these images are featured in six newly conceived color inserts that offer pictures of various media, utensils, tools, technologies, and types of writing, as well as scenes of writing and reading from different epochs. The result is a rich visual overview of the material and cultural importance of writing and texts. Recognizing the importance of geography to many of the works in the anthology, the editors have revised the map program so that it complements the literature more directly. Each of the twenty-six maps has been redrawn to help readers orient themselves in the many corners of the world to which this anthology will take them. Finally, newly redesigned timelines at the end of each volume help students see at a glance the temporal relationships among literary works and historical events. Taken together, all of these visual elements make the anthology not only more inviting but also more informative than ever before.

The goal of making world literature a pleasurable adventure also guided our selection of translations. World literature gained its power from the way it reflected and shaped the imagination of peoples, and from the way it circulated outside its original context. For this, it depends on translation. While purists sometimes insist on studying literature only in the original language, a dogma that radically shrinks what one can read, world literature not only relies on translation but actually thrives on it. Translation is a necessity, the only thing that enables a worldwide circulation of literature. It also is an art. One need only think of the way in which translations of the Bible shaped the history of Latin or English. Translations are re-creations of works for new readers. Our edition pays keen attention to translation, and we feature dozens of new translations that make classical texts newly readable and capture the originals in compelling ways. With each choice of translation, we sought a version that would spark a sense of wonder while still being accessible to a contemporary reader. Many of the anthology's most fundamental classics—from *Gilgamesh*, Homer's epics, the Greek dramatists, Virgil, the Bible, the *Bhagavad-Gītā*, and the Qur'an to *The Canterbury Tales*, *The Tale of Genji*, Goethe's *Faust*, Ibsen's *Hedda Gabler*, and Kafka's *Metamorphosis*—are presented in new translations that are both exciting works in English and skillful echoes of the spirit and flavor of the original. In some cases, we commissioned new translations—for instance, for the work of the South Asian poet Kabir, rendered beautifully by our South Asian editor and prize-winning translator Vinay Dharwadker, and for a portion of Çelebi's travels to Vienna by our Ottoman expert Gottfried Hagen that has never before been translated into English.

Finally, the editors decided to make some of the guiding themes of the world literature course, and this anthology, more visible. Experienced teachers know about these major themes and use them to create linked reading assignments, and the anthology has long touched on these topics, but with the Third Edition, these themes rise to the surface, giving all readers a clearer sense of the ties that bind diverse works together. Following is discussion of each of these organizing themes.

Contact and Culture

Again and again, literature evokes journeys away from home and out into the world, bringing its protagonists—and thus its readers—into contact with peoples who are different from them. Such contact, and the cross-pollination it fosters, was crucial for the formation of cultures. The earliest civilizations— the civilizations that invented writing and hence literature—sprang up where they did because they were located along strategic trading and migration routes. Contact was not just something that happened between fully formed cultures, but something that made these cultures possible in the first place.

Committed to presenting the anthology's riches in a way that conveys this central fact of world literature, we have created new sections that encompass broad contact zones—areas of intense trade in peoples, goods, art, and ideas. The largest such zone is centered on the Mediterranean basin and reaches as far as the Fertile Crescent. It is in this large area that the earliest literatures emerged and intermingled. For the Mediterranean Sea was not just a hostile environment that could derail a journey home, as it did for Odysseus, who took ten years to find his way back to Greece from the Trojan War in Asia Minor; it was a connecting tissue as well, allowing for intense contact around its harbors. Medieval maps of the Mediterranean pay tribute to this fact: so-called portolan charts show a veritable mesh of lines connecting hundreds of ports. In the reorganized Mediterranean sections in volumes A and B, we have placed together texts from this broad region, the location of intense conflict as well as friendly exchange, rather than isolating them from each other. In a similar manner, the two major traditions of East Asia, China and Japan, are now presented in the context of the larger region, which means that for the first time the anthology includes texts from Vietnam and Korea.

One of the many ways that human beings have bound themselves to each other and have attempted to bridge cultural and geographic distances is through religion. As a form of cultural exchange, and an inspiration for cultural conflict, religion is an important part of the deep history of contact and encounter presented in the anthology, and the editors have taken every opportunity to call attention to this fact. This is nowhere more visible than in a new section in volume C called "Encounters with Islam," which follows the cultural influence of Islam beyond its point of origin in Arabia and Persia. Here we draw together works from western Africa, Asia Minor, and South Asia, each of them blending the ideas and values of Islam with indigenous folk traditions to create new forms of cultural expression. The original oral stories of the extraordinary Mali epic *Sunjata* (in a newly established version and translation) incorporate elements of Islam much the way the Anglo-Saxon epic *Beowulf* incorporates elements of Christianity. The early Turkish epic *The Book of Dede Korkut* similarly blends Islamic thought and expression with the cultural traditions of the pre-Islamic nomadic tribes whose stories make up the bulk of the book. In a different way, the encounter of Islam with other cultures emerges at the eastern end of its sphere of influence, in South Asia, where a multireligious culture absorbs and transforms Islamic material, as in the philosophical poems of Tukaram and Kabir (both presented in new selections and translations). Evliya Çelebi, with his journey to Vienna, belongs to this larger history as well, giving us another lens through which to view the encounter of Islam and Christianity that is dramatized by so many writers elsewhere in the anthology (most notably, in the *Song of Roland*).

The new emphasis on contact and encounter is expressed not just in the overall organization of the anthology and the selection of material; it is also made visible in clusters of texts on the theme of travel and conquest, giving students access to documents related to travel, contact, trade, and conflict. The greatest story of encounter between peoples to be told in the first half of the anthology is the encounter of Europe (and thus of Eurasia) with the Americas. To tell this story properly, the editors decided to eliminate the old dividing line between the European Renaissance and the New World that had prevailed in previous editions and instead created one broad cultural sphere that combines the two. A (newly expanded) cluster within this section gathers texts immediately relevant to this encounter, vividly chronicling all of its willful violence and its unintended consequences in the "New" World. This section also reveals the ways in which the European discovery of the Americas wrought violence in Europe. Old certainties and authorities overthrown, new worlds imagined, the very concept of being human revised—nothing that happened in the European Renaissance was untouched by the New World. Rarely had contact between two geographic zones had more consequences: henceforth, the Americas would be an important part of the story of Europe.

For a few centuries European empires dominated global politics and economics and accelerated the pace of globalization by laying down worldwide trade routes and communication networks, but old empires, such as China, continued to be influential as well. A new section called "At the Crossroads of Empire" in volume E gathers literature produced in Vietnam, India, and China as Asian and European empires met and collided, vying for control not only of trade routes and raw materials but also of ideas and values. The writers included here felt the pressures of ancient traditions and new imperial powers and resisted both, crafting brave and imaginative responses to repressive conditions. Another new section, "Realism across the World," traces perhaps the first truly global artistic movement, one that found expression in France, Britain, Russia, Brazil, and Japan. And it was not just an effect of European dominance. Representing the daily experiences of people living in gritty urban poverty, for example, the Japanese writer Higuchi Ichiyō developed her own realism without ever having read a European novel.

In the twentieth century, the pace of cultural exchange and contact, so much swifter than in preceding centuries, transformed most literary movements, from modernism to postcolonialism, into truly global phenomena. At the end of the final volume, we encounter Elizabeth Costello, the title character in J. M. Coetzee's novel. A writer herself, Costello has been asked to give lectures on a cruise ship; mobile and deracinated, she and a colleague deliver lectures on the novel in Africa, including the role of geography and oral literature. The scene captures many themes of world literature—and serves as an image of our present stage of globalization. World literature is a story about the relation between the world and literature, and we tell this story partly by paying attention to this geographic dimension.

Travel

The accounts of Evliya Çelebi and other explorers are intriguing because they recount real journeys and real people. But travel has also inspired a rich array of fictional fabulation. This theme lived in past editions of the anthology, as indeed it does in nearly any world literature course in which Homer's *Odyssey*, Chaucer's *Canterbury Tales*, Cervantes' *Don Quixote*, Swift's *Gulliver's Travels*, and many other touchstones of the world literature canon are read. To further develop this theme in the Third Edition, the editors have added several new texts with travel at their center. Among them is the first and most influential Spanish picaresque novel, *Lazarillo de Tormes*, a fast-paced story that shows how fortune has her way with the low-born hero. Lazarillo's resilience and native smarts help him move from master to master, serving a priest, a friar, a chaplain, and an archbishop, all of whom seek to exploit him. The great Vietnamese epic *The Tale of Kiều*, another new selection, features an even greater survival artist. In this tale the heroine, repeatedly abducted and pressed into prostitution and marriage, survives because of her impeccable stoicism, which she maintains in the face of a life that seems shaped by cruel accidents and ill fortune. Even as these tales delight in adventures and highlight the qualities that allow their heroes to survive them, they are invested in something else: the sheer movement from one place to the next. Travel narratives are relentlessly driven forward, stopping in each locale for only the duration of an adventure before forcing their heroes to resume their wanderings. Through such restless wandering, travel literature, both factual and fiction, crisscrosses the world and thereby incorporates it into literature.

Worlds of the Imagination

Literature not only moves us to remote corners of the world and across landscapes; it also presents us with whole imagined worlds to which we as readers can travel. The construction of literary, clearly made-up worlds has always been a theme of world literature, which has suggested answers to fundamental questions, including how the world came into being. The Mayan epic *Popol Vuh*, featured in volume C, develops one of the most elaborate creation myths, including several attempts at creating humans (only the fourth is successful). In the same volume, Milton retells the biblical story of the Fall, but he also depicts the creation of new worlds, including earth, in a manner that is influenced by the discovery of the New World in the Western Hemisphere. For this new edition, the editors have decided to underline this theme, which also celebrates the world-creating power of language and literature, by placing a new cluster of creation myths, called "Creation and the Cosmos," at the very beginning of the anthology. The myths in this cluster resonate throughout the history of world literature, providing imaginative touchstones for later authors (such as Virgil, John Mandeville, Dante, and Goethe) to adapt and use in their own imaginative world-creation.

But world-creation, as highlighted in the new cluster, not only operates on a grand scale. It also occurs at moments when literature restricts itself to small, enclosed universes that are observed with minute attention. The great eighteenth-century Chinese novel *The Story of the Stone* by Cao Xuequin (presented in a new selection) withdraws to a family compound, whose walls it almost never leaves, to depict life in all its subtlety within this restricted space for several thousand pages. Sometimes we are invited into the even more circumscribed space of the narrator's own head, where we encounter strange and surreal worlds, as in the great modernist and postmodernist fictions from Franz Kafka and Jorge Luis Borges. By providing a thematic through-line, the new edition of the anthology reveals the myriad ways in which authors not only seek to explain our world but also compete with it by imagining new and different ones.

Genres

Over the millennia, literature has developed a set of rules and conventions that authors work with and against as they make decisions about subject matter, style, and form. These rules help us distinguish between different types of literature—that is, different genres. The broad view of literature afforded by the anthology, across both space and time, is particularly capable of showing how genres emerge and are transformed as they are used by different writers and for different purposes. The new edition of the anthology underscores this crucial dimension of literature by tracking the movement of genres—of, for example, the frame-tale narration from South Asia to northern Europe. To help readers recognize this theme, we have created ways of making genre visible. Lyric poetry is found everywhere in the anthology, from the foundational poetry anthologies of China to modern experiments, but it is the focus of specially designed clusters that cast light on medieval lyric; on how Petrarch's invention, the sonnet, is adopted by other writers; or, to turn to one of the world's most successful poetic genres, on the haiku. By the same token, a cluster on manifestos highlights modernism's most characteristic invention, with its shrill demands and aggressive layout. Among the genres, drama is perhaps the most difficult to grapple with because it is so closely entangled with theatrical performance. You don't understand a play unless you understand what kind of theater it was intended for, how it was performed, and how audiences watched it. To capture this dimension, we have grouped two of the most prominent regional drama traditions—Greek theater and East Asian drama—in their own sections.

Oral Literature

The relation of the spoken word to literature is perhaps the most important theme that emerges from these pages. All literature goes back to oral storytelling—all the foundational epics, from South Asia via Greece and Africa to Central America, are deeply rooted in oral storytelling; poetry's rhythms are best appreciated when heard; and drama, a form that comes alive in performance, continues to be engaged with an oral tradition. Throughout the anthology, we connect works to the oral traditions from which they sprang and remind readers that writing has coexisted with oral storytelling since the invention of the former. A new and important cluster in volume E on oral literature foregrounds this theme and showcases the nineteenth-century interest in oral traditions such as fairy and folk tales and slave stories. At the same time, this cluster, and the anthology as a whole, shows the importance of gaining literacy.

Varieties of Literature

In presenting everything from the earliest literatures to a (much-expanded) selection of contemporary literature reaching to the early twenty-first century, and from oral storytelling to literary experiments of the avant-garde, the anthology confronts us with the question not just of world literature, but of literature as such. We call attention to the changing nature of literature with new thematic clusters on literature in the early volumes, to give students and teachers access to how early writers from different cultures thought about literature. But the changing role and nature of literature are visible in the anthology as a whole. The world of Greek myth is seen by almost everyone as literary, even though it arose from ritual practices that are different from what we associate with literature. But this is even more the case with other texts, such as the Qur'an or the Bible, which still function as religious texts for many, while others appreciate them primarily or exclusively as literature. Some texts, such as those by Laozi (new addition) or Plato (in a new and expanded selection) or Kant (new addition) belong in philosophy, while others, such as the Declaration of Independence (new addition), are primarily political documents. Our modern conception of literature as imaginative literature, as fiction, is very recent, about two hundred years old. In this Third Edition, we have opted for a much-expanded conception of literature that includes creation myths, wisdom literature, religious texts, philosophy, political writing, and fairy tales in addition to plays, poems, and narrative fiction. This answers to an older definition of literature as writing of high quality. There are many texts of philosophy, or religion, or politics that are not remarkable or influential for their literary qualities and that would therefore have no place in an anthology of world literature. But the works presented here do: in addition to or as part of their other functions, they have acquired the status of literature.

This brings us to the last and perhaps most important question: When we study the world, why study it through its literature? Hasn't literature lost some of its luster for us, we who are faced with so many competing media and art forms? Like no other art form or medium, literature offers us a deep history of human thinking. As our illustration program shows, writing was invented not for the composition of literature, but for much more mundane purposes, such as the recording of ownership, contracts, or astronomical observations. But literature is writing's most glorious side-product. Because language expresses human consciousness, no other art form can capture the human past with the precision and scope of literature. Language shapes our thinking, and literature, the highest expression of language, plays an important role in that process, pushing the boundaries of what we can think, and how we think it. The other great advantage of literature is that it can be reactivated with each reading. The great architectural monuments of the past are now in ruins. Literature, too, often has to be excavated, as with many classical texts. But once a text has been found or reconstructed it can be experienced as if for the first time by new readers. Even though many of the literary texts collected in this anthology are at first strange, because they originated so very long ago, they still speak to today's readers with great eloquence and freshness.

Because works of world literature are alive today, they continue to elicit strong emotions and investments. The epic *Rāmāyana*, for example, plays an important role in the politics of India, where it has been used to bolster Hindu nationalism, just as the *Bhagavad-Gītā*, here in a new translation, continues to be a moral touchstone in the ethical deliberation about war. Saddam Hussein wrote an updated version of the *Epic of Gilgamesh*. And the three religions of the book, Judaism, Christianity, and Islam, make our selections from their scriptures a more than historical exercise. China has recently elevated the sayings of Confucius, whose influence on Chinese attitudes about the state had waned in the twentieth century, creating Confucius Institutes all over the world to promote Chinese culture in what is now called New Confucianism. The debates about the role of the church and secularism, which we highlight through a new cluster and selections in all volumes, have become newly important in current deliberations on the relation between church and state. World literature is never neutral. We know its relevance precisely by the controversies it inspires.

Going back to the earliest moments of cultural contact and moving forward to the global flows of the twenty-first century, *The Norton Anthology of World Literature* attempts to provide a deep history. But it is a special type of history: a literary one. World literature is grounded in the history of the world, but it is

also the history of imagining this world; it is a history not just of what happened, but also of how humans imagined their place in the midst of history.
We, the editors of this Third Edition, can think of no better way to prepare
young people for a global future than through a deep and meaningful exploration of world literature. Evliya Çelebi sums up his exploration of Vienna as a
"marvelous and wonderful adventure"—we hope that readers will feel the same
about the adventure in reading made possible by this anthology and will return
to it for the rest of their lives.

About the Third Edition

New Selections and Translations

This Third Edition represents a thoroughgoing, top-to-bottom revision of the anthology that altered nearly every section in important ways. Following is a list of the new sections and works, in order:

VOLUME A

A new cluster, "Creation and the Cosmos," and a new grouping, "Ancient Egyptian Literature" • Benjamin Foster's translation of *Gilgamesh* • Selections from chapters 12, 17, 28, 29, 31, and 50 of Genesis, and from chapters 19 and 20 of Exodus • All selections from Genesis, Exodus, and Job are newly featured in Robert Alter's translation, and chapter 25 of Genesis (Jacob spurning his birthright) is presented in a graphic visualization by R. Crumb based on Alter's translation • Homer's *Iliad* and *Odyssey* are now featured in Stanley Lombardo's highly regarded translations • A selection of Aesop's *Fables* • A new selection and a new translation of Sappho's lyrics • A new grouping, "Ancient Athenian Drama," gathers together the three major Greek tragedians and Aristophanes • New translations of *Oedipus the King*, *Antigone* (both by Robert Bagg), *Medea* (by Diane Arnson Svarlien), and *Lysistrata* (by Sarah Ruden) • A new cluster, "Travel and Conquest" • Plato's *Symposium* • A new selection of Catullus's poems, in a new translation by Peter Green • *The Aeneid* is now featured in Robert Fagles's career-topping translation • New selections from book 1 of Ovid's *Metamorphoses* join the previous selection, now featured in Charles Martin's recent translation • A new cluster, "Speech, Writing, Poetry," features ancient Egyptian writings on writing • A new tale from the Indian *Jātaka* • New selections from the Chinese *Classic of Poetry* • Confucius's *Analects* now in a new translation by Simon Leys • *Daodejing* • New selections from the Chinese *Songs of the South* • Chinese historian Sima Qian • A new cluster, "Speech, Writing, and Poetry in Early China," features selections by Confucius, Zhuangzi, and Han Feizi.

VOLUME B

Selections from the Christian Bible now featured in a new translation by Richmond Lattimore • A selection from book 3 of Apuleius's *The Golden Ass* • Selections from the Qur'an now featured in Abdel Haleem's translation • A new selection from Abolqasem Ferdowsi's *Shahnameh*, in a new translation by Dick Davis • Avicenna • Petrus Alfonsi • Additional material from Marie de France's *Lais*, in a translation by Robert Hanning and Joan Ferrante • An expanded selection of poems fills out the "Medieval Lyrics" cluster • Dante's *Divine Comedy* now featured in Mark Musa's translation • The Ethiopian

Kebra Nagast • An expanded selection from Boccaccio's *Decameron*, in a new translation by Wayne Rebhorn • A new translation by Sheila Fisher of Chaucer's *Canterbury Tales* • *Sir Gawain and the Green Knight* now featured in a new translation by Simon Armitage • Christine de Pizan's *Book of the City of Ladies* • A new cluster, "Travel and Encounter," features selections from Marco Polo, Ibn Battuta, and John Mandeville • New selections in fresh translations of classical Tamil and Sanskrit lyric poetry • New selections and translations of Chinese lyric poetry • A new cluster, "Literature about Literature," in the Medieval Chinese Literature section • Refreshed selections and new translations of lyric poetry in "Japan's Classical Age" • Selection from Ki No Tsurayuki's *Tosa Diary* • A new translation by Meredith McKinney of Sei Shōnagon's *Pillow Book* • A new, expanded selection from, and a new translation of, Murasaki Shikibu's *The Tale of Genji* • New selections from *The Tales of the Heike*, in Burton Watson's newly included translation.

VOLUME C

A new translation by David C. Conrad of the West African epic *Sunjata* • *The Book of Dede Korkut* • A new selection from Evliya Çelebi's *The Book of Travels*, never before translated into English, now in Gottfried Hagen's translation • New selection of Indian lyric poetry by Basavaṇṇā, Mahādevīyakkā, Kabir, Mīrabāī, and Tukaram, in fresh new translations • Two new clusters, "Humanism and the Rediscovery of the Classical Past" and "Petrarch and the Love Lyric," open the new section "Europe and the New World" • Sir Thomas More's *Utopia* in its entirety • Story 10 newly added to the selection of Marguerite de Navarre's *Heptameron* • *Lazarillo de Tormes* included in its entirety • A new cluster, "The Encounter of Europe and the New World" • Lope de Vega's *Fuenteovejuna* now featured in Gregary Racz's recent translation • A new cluster, "God, Church, and Self."

VOLUME D

A new section, "East Asian Drama," brings together four examples of Asian drama from the fourteenth through nineteenth centuries, including Zeami's *Atsumori*, Kong Shangren's *The Peach Blossom Fan* (in a new translation by Stephen Owen), and two newly included works: Chikamatsu's *Love Suicides at Amijima* and the Korean drama *Song of Ch'un-hyang* • A new cluster, "What Is Enlightenment?" • Molière's *Tartuffe* now featured in a new translation by Constance Congdon and Virginia Scott • Aphra Behn's *Oroonoko; or, The Royal Slave*, complete • New selections by Sor Juana Inés de la Cruz, in a new translation by Electa Arenal and Amanda Powell • An expanded, refreshed selection from Cao Xueqin's *The Story of the Stone*, part of which is now featured in John Minford's translation • Ihara Saikaku's *Life of a Sensuous Woman* • A new cluster, "The World of Haiku," features work by Kitamura Kigin, Matsuo Bashō, Morikawa Kyoriku, and Yosa Buson.

VOLUME E

A new cluster, "Revolutionary Contexts," features selections from the Declaration of Independence, the Declaration of the Rights of Man and of the Citizen, and the Declaration of Sentiments from the Seneca Falls convention, as well as pieces by Olympe de Gouges, Edmund Burke, Jean-Jacques Dessalines, William Wordsworth, and Simón Bólivar • New selection from book 2 of Rousseau's *Confessions* • Olaudah Equiano's *Interesting Narrative* • Goethe's *Faust* now featured in Martin Greenberg's translation • Selections from Domingo Sarmiento's *Facundo* • A new grouping, "Romantic Poets and Their Successors," features a generous sampling of lyric poetry from the period, including new poems by Anna Laetitia Barbauld, William Wordsworth, Samuel Taylor Coleridge, Anna Bunina, Andrés Bello, John Keats, Heinrich Heine, Elizabeth Barrett Browning, Tennyson, Robert Browning, Walt Whitman, Christina Rossetti, Rosalía de Castro, and José Martí, as well as an exciting new translation of Arthur Rimbaud's *Illuminations* by John Ashbery • From Vietnam, Nguyễn Du's *The Tale of Kiều* • A new selection and all new translations of Ghalib's poetry by Vinay Dharwadker • Liu E's *The Travels of Lao Can* • Two pieces by Pandita Ramabai • Flaubert's *A Simple Heart* • Ibsen's *Hedda Gabler*, now featured in a new translation by Rick Davis and Brian Johnston • Machado de Assis's *The Rod of Justice* • Chekhov's *The Cherry Orchard*, now featured in a new translation by Paul Schmidt • Tagore's *Kabuliwala* • Higuchi Ichiyō's *Separate Ways* • A new cluster, "Orature," with German, English, Irish, and Hawaiian folktales; Anansi stories from Ghana, Jamaica, and the United States; as well as slave songs, stories, and spirituals, Malagasy wisdom poetry, and the Navajo Night Chant.

VOLUME F

Joseph Conrad's *Heart of Darkness* • Tanizaki's *The Tattooer* • Selection from Marcel Proust's *Remembrance of Things Past* now featured in Lydia Davis's critically acclaimed translation • Franz Kafka's *The Metamorphosis* now featured in Michael Hofmann's translation • Lu Xun, *Medicine* • Akutagawa's *In a Bamboo Grove* • Kawabata's *The Izu Dancer* • Chapter 1 of Woolf's *A Room of One's Own* newly added to the selections from chapters 2 and 3 • Two new Faulkner stories: "Spotted Horses" and "Barn Burning" • Kushi Fusako, *Memoirs of a Declining Ryukyuan Woman* • Lao She, *An Old and Established Name* • Ch'ae Man-Sik, *My Innocent Uncle* • Zhang Ailing's *Sealed Off* • Constantine Cavafy • Octavio Paz • A new cluster, "Manifestos" • Julio Cortazár • Tadeusz Borowski's *This Way for the Gas, Ladies and Gentlemen*, in a new translation by Barbara Vedder • Paul Celan • Saadat Hasan Manto • James Baldwin • Vladimir Nabokov • Tayeb Salih • Chinua Achebe's *Chike's School Days* • Carlos Fuentes • Mahmoud Darwish • Seamus Heaney • Ama Ata Aidoo • V. S. Naipul • Ngugi Wa Thiong'o • Bessie Head • Ōe Kenzaburō • Salman Rushdie • Mahasweta Devi's *Giribala* • Hanan Al-Shaykh • Toni Morrison • Mo Yan • Niyi Osundare • Nguyen Huy Thiep • Isabel Allende • Chu T'ien-Hsin • Junot Díaz • Roberto Bolaño • J. M. Coetzee • Orhan Pamuk.

Supplements for Instructors and Students

Norton is pleased to provide instructors and students with several supplements to make the study and teaching of world literature an even more interesting and rewarding experience:

Instructor Resource Folder

A new Instructor Resource Folder features images and video clips that allow instructors to enhance their lectures with some of the sights and sounds of world literature and its contexts.

Instructor Course Guide

Teaching with The Norton Anthology of World Literature: *A Guide for Instructors* provides teaching plans, suggestions for in-class activities, discussion topics and writing projects, and extensive lists of scholarly and media resources.

Coursepacks

Available in a variety of formats, Norton coursepacks bring digital resources into a new or existing online course. Coursepacks are free to instructors, easy to download and install, and available in a variety of formats, including Blackboard, Desire2Learn, Angel, and Moodle.

StudySpace (*wwnorton.com/nawol*)

This free student companion site features a variety of complementary materials to help students read and study world literature. Among them are reading-comprehension quizzes, quick-reference summaries of the anthology's introductions, review quizzes, an audio glossary to help students pronounce names and terms, tours of some of the world's important cultural landmarks, timelines, maps, and other contextual materials.

Writing about World Literature

Written by Karen Gocsik, Executive Director of the Writing Program at Dartmouth College, in collaboration with faculty in the world literature program at the University of Nevada, Las Vegas, *Writing about World Literature* provides course-specific guidance for writing papers and essay exams in the world literature course.

For more information about any of these supplements, instructors should contact their local Norton representative.

Acknowledgments

The editors would like to thank the following people, who have provided invaluable assistance by giving us sage advice, important encouragement, and help with the preparation of the manuscript: Sara Akbari, Alannah de Barra, Wendy Belcher, Jodi Bilinkoff, Freya Brackett, Psyche Brackett, Michaela Bronstein, Amanda Claybaugh, Rachel Carroll, Lewis Cook, David Damrosch, Dick Davis, Amanda Detry, Anthony Domestico, Merve Emre, Maria Fackler, Guillermina de Ferrari, Karina Galperín, Stanton B. Garner, Kimberly Dara Gordon, Elyse Graham, Stephen Greenblatt, Sara Guyer, Langdon Hammer, Iain Higgins, Mohja Kahf, Peter Kornicki, Paul Kroll, Lydia Liu, Bala Venkat Mani, Ann Matter, Barry McCrea, Alexandra McCullough-Garcia, Rachel McGuiness, Jon McKenzie, Mary Mullen, Djibril Tamsir Niane, Felicity Nussbaum, Andy Orchard, John Peters, Daniel Taro Poch, Daniel Potts, Megan Quigley, Imogen Roth, Catherine de Rose, Ellen Sapega, Jesse Schotter, Brian Stock, Tomi Suzuki, Joshua Taft, Sara Torres, Lisa Voigt, Kristen Wanner, and Emily Weissbourd.

All the editors would like to thank the wonderful people at Norton, principally our editor Pete Simon, the driving force behind this whole undertaking, as well as Marian Johnson (Managing Editor, College), Alice Falk, Michael Fleming, Katharine Ings, Susan Joseph, Barney Latimer, and Diane Cipollone (Copyeditors), Conor Sullivan (Assistant Editor), Megan Jackson (College Permissions Manager), Margaret Gorenstein (Permissions), Patricia Marx (Art Research Director), Debra Morton Hoyt (Art Director; cover design), Rubina Yeh (Design Director), Jo Anne Metsch (Designer; interior text design), Adrian Kitzinger (cartography), Agnieszka Gasparska (timeline design), Eileen Connell, (Media Editor), Jennifer Barnhardt (Editorial Assistant, Media), Laura Musich (Associate Editor; Instructor's Guide), Benjamin Reynolds (Production Manager), and Kim Bowers (Marketing Manager, Literature) and Ashley Cain (Humanities Sales Specialist).

This anthology represents a collaboration not only among the editors and their close advisors, but also among the thousands of instructors who teach from the anthology and provide valuable and constructive guidance to the publisher and editors. *The Norton Anthology of World Literature* is as much their book as it is ours, and we are grateful to everyone who has cared enough about this anthology to help make it better. We're especially grateful to the more than five hundred professors of world literature who responded to an online survey in early 2008, whom we have listed below. Thank you all.

Michel Aaij (Auburn University Montgomery); Sandra Acres (Mississippi Gulf Coast Community College); Larry Adams (University of North Alabama); Mary Adams (Western Carolina University); Stephen Adams (Westfield State

College); Roberta Adams (Roger Williams University); Kirk Adams (Tarrant County College); Kathleen Aguero (Pine Manor College); Richard Albright (Harrisburg Area Community College); Deborah Albritton (Jefferson Davis Community College); Todd Aldridge (Auburn University); Judith Allen-Leventhal (College of Southern Maryland); Carolyn Amory (Binghamton University); Kenneth Anania (Massasoit Community College); Phillip Anderson (University of Central Arkansas); Walter Anderson (University of Arkansas at Little Rock); Vivienne Anderson (North Carolina Wesleyan College); Susan Andrade (University of Pittsburgh); Kit Andrews (Western Oregon University); Joe Antinarella (Tidewater Community College); Nancy Applegate (Georgia Highlands College); Sona Aronian (University of Rhode Island); Sona Aronian (University of Rhode Island); Eugene Arva (University of Miami); M. G. Aune (California University of Pennsylvania); Carolyn Ayers (Saint Mary's University of Minnesota); Diana Badur (Black Hawk College); Susan Bagby (Longwood University); Maryam Barrie (Washtenaw Community College); Maria Baskin (Alamance Community College); Samantha Batten (Auburn University); Charles Beach (Nyack College); Michael Beard (University of North Dakota); Bridget Beaver (Connors State College); James Bednarz (C. W. Post College); Khani Begum (Bowling Green State University); Albert Bekus (Austin Peay State University); Lynne Belcher (Southern Arkansas University); Karen Bell (Delta State University); Elisabeth Ly Bell (University of Rhode Island); Angela Belli (St. John's University); Leo Benardo (Baruch College); Paula Berggren (Baruch College, CUNY); Frank Bergmann (Utica College); Nancy Blomgren (Volunteer State Community College); Scott Boltwood (Emory & Henry College); Ashley Bonds (Copiah-Lincoln Community College); Thomas Bonner (Xavier University of Louisiana); Debbie Boyd (East Central Community College); Norman Boyer (Saint Xavier University); Nodya Boyko (Auburn University); Robert Brandon (Rockingham Community College); Alan Brasher (East Georgia College); Harry Brent (Baruch College); Charles Bressler (Indiana Wesleyan University); Katherine Brewer; Mary Ruth Brindley (Mississippi Delta Community College); Mamye Britt (Georgia Perimeter College); Gloria Brooks (Tyler Junior College); Monika Brown (University of North Carolina–Pembroke); Greg Bryant (Highland Community College); Austin Busch (SUNY Brockport); Barbara Cade (Texas College); Karen Caig (University of Arkansas Community College at Morrilton); Jonizo Cain-Calloway (Del Mar College); Mark Calkins (San Francisco State University); Catherine Calloway (Arkansas State University); Mechel Camp (Jackson State Community College); Robert Canary (University of Wisconsin–Parkside); Stephen Canham (University of Hawaii at Manoa); Marian Carcache (Auburn University); Alfred Carson (Kennesaw State University); Farrah Cato (University of Central Florida); Biling Chen (University of Central Arkansas); Larry Chilton (Blinn College); Eric Chock (University of Hawaii at West Oahu); Cheryl Clark (Miami Dade College–Wolfson Campus); Sarah Beth Clark (Holmes Community College); Jim Cody (Brookdale Community College); Carol Colatrella (Georgia Institute of Technology); Janelle Collins (Arkansas State University); Theresa Collins (St. John's University); Susan Comfort (Indiana University of Pennsylvania); Kenneth Cook (National Park Community College); Angie Cook (Cisco Junior College); Yvonne Cooper (Pierce College); Brenda Cornell (Central Texas College); Judith Cortelloni (Lincoln College); Robert Cosgrove (Saddleback College); Rosemary Cox (Georgia Perimeter College);

Daniel Cozart (Georgia Perimeter College); Brenda Craven (Fort Hays State University); Susan Crisafulli (Franklin College); Janice Crosby (Southern University); Randall Crump (Kennesaw State University); Catherine Cucinella (California State University San Marcos); T. Allen Culpepper (Manatee Community College–Venice); Rodger Cunningham (Alice Lloyd College); Lynne Dahmen (Purdue University); Patsy J. Daniels (Jackson State University); James Davis (Troy University); Evan Davis (Southwestern Oregon Community College); Margaret Dean (Eastern Kentucky University); JoEllen DeLucia (John Jay College, CUNY); Hivren Demir-Atay (Binghamton University); Rae Ann DeRosse (University of North Carolina–Greensboro); Anna Crowe Dewart (College of Coastal Georgia); Joan Digby (C. W. Post Campus Long Island University); Diana Dominguez (University of Texas at Brownsville); Dee Douglas-Jones (Winston-Salem State University); Jeremy Downes (Auburn University); Denell Downum (Suffolk University); Sharon Drake (Texarkana College); Damian Dressick (Robert Morris University); Clyburn Duder (Concordia University Texas); Dawn Duncan (Concordia College); Kendall Dunkelberg (Mississippi University for Women); Janet Eber (County College of Morris); Emmanuel Egar (University of Arkansas at Pine Bluff); David Eggebrecht (Concordia University of Wisconsin); Sarah Eichelman (Walters State Community College); Hank Eidson (Georgia Perimeter College); Monia Eisenbraun (Oglala Lakota College/Cheyenne-Eagle Butte High School); Dave Elias (Eastern Kentucky University); Chris Ellery (Angelo State University); Christina Elvidge (Marywood University); Ernest Enchelmayer (Arkansas Tech University); Niko Endres (Western Kentucky University); Kathrynn Engberg (Alabama A&M University); Chad Engbers (Calvin College); Edward Eriksson (Suffolk Community College); Donna Estill (Alabama Southern Community College); Andrew Ettin (Wake Forest University); Jim Everett (Mississippi College); Gene Fant (Union University); Nathan Faries (University of Dubuque); Martin Fashbaugh (Auburn University); Donald J. Fay (Kennesaw State University); Meribeth Fell (College of Coastal Georgia); David Fell (Carroll Community College); Jill Ferguson (San Francisco Conservatory of Music); Susan French Ferguson (Mountain View Comumunity College); Robyn Ferret (Cascadia Community College); Colin Fewer (Purdue Calumet); Hannah Fischthal (St. John's University); Jim Fisher (Peninsula College); Gene Fitzgerald (University of Utah); Monika Fleming (Edgecombe Community College); Phyllis Fleming (Patrick Henry Community College); Francis Fletcher (Folsom Lake College); Denise Folwell (Montgomery College); Ulanda Forbess (North Lake College); Robert Forman (St. John's University); Suzanne Forster (University of Alaska–Anchorage); Patricia Fountain (Coastal Carolina Community College); Kathleen Fowler (Surry Community College); Sheela Free (San Bernardino Valley College); Lea Fridman (Kingsborough Community College); David Galef (Montclair State University); Paul Gallipeo (Adirondack Community College); Jan Gane (University of North Carolina–Pembroke); Jennifer Garlen (University of Alabama–Huntsville); Anita Garner (University of North Alabama); Elizabeth Gassel (Darton College); Patricia Gaston (West Virginia University, Parkersburg); Marge Geiger (Cuyahoga Community College); Laura Getty (North Georgia College & State University); Amy Getty (Grand View College); Leah Ghiradella (Middlesex County College); Dick Gibson (Jacksonville University); Teresa Gibson (University of Texas–Brownsville); Wayne Gilbert (Community College of Aurora); Sandra Giles (Abraham Baldwin Agricultural College); Pamela Gist (Cedar Valley College); Suzanne Gitonga (North Lake College); James Glickman (Community College of Rhode Island); R. James Goldstein (Auburn University); Jennifer Golz (Tennessee Tech University); Marian Goodin (North Central Missouri College); Susan Gorman (Massachusetts College of Pharmacy and Health Sciences); Anissa Graham (University of North Alabama); Eric Gray (St. Gregory's University); Geoffrey Green (San Francisco State University); Russell Greer (Texas Woman's University); Charles Grey (Albany State University); Frank Gruber (Bergen Community College); Alfonso Guerriero Jr. (Baruch College, CUNY); Letizia Guglielmo (Kennesaw State University); Nira Gupta-Casale (Kean University); Gary Gutchess (SUNY Tompkins Cortland Community College); William Hagen (Oklahoma Baptist University); John Hagge (Iowa State University); Julia Hall (Henderson State University); Margaret Hallissy (C. W. Post Campus Long Island University); Laura Hammons (Hinds Community College); Nancy Hancock (Austin Peay State University); Carol Harding (Western Oregon University); Cynthia Hardy (University of Alaska–Fairbanks); Steven Harthorn (Williams Baptist College); Stanley Hauer (University of Southern Mississippi); Leean Hawkins (National Park Community College); Kayla Haynie (Harding University); Maysa Hayward (Ocean County College); Karen Head (Georgia Institute of Technology); Sandra Kay Heck (Walters State Community College); Frances Helphinstine (Morehead State University); Karen Henck (Eastern Nazarene College); Betty Fleming Hendricks (University of Arkansas); Yndaleci Hinojosa (Northwest Vista College); Richard Hishmeh (Palomar College); Ruth Hoberman (Eastern Illinois University); Rebecca Hogan (University of Wisconsin–Whitewater); Mark Holland (East Tennessee State University); John Holmes (Virginia State University); Sandra Holstein (Southern Oregon University); Fran Holt (Georgia Perimeter College–Clarkston); William Hood (North Central Texas College); Glenn Hopp (Howard Payne University); George Horneker (Arkansas State University); Barbara Howard (Central Bible College); Pamela Howell (Midland College); Melissa Hull (Tennessee State University); Barbara Hunt (Columbus State University); Leeann Hunter (University of South Florida); Gill Hunter (Eastern Kentucky University); Helen Huntley (California Baptist University); Luis Iglesias (University of Southern Mississippi); Judith Irvine (Georgia State University); Miglena Ivanova (Coastal Carolina University); Kern Jackson (University of South Alabama); Kenneth Jackson (Yale University); M. W. Jackson (St. Bonaventure University); Robb Jackson (Texas A&M University–Corpus Christi); Karen Jacobsen (Valdosta State University); Maggie Jaffe (San Diego State University); Robert Jakubovic (Raymond Walters College); Stokes James (University of Wisconsin–Stevens Point); Beverly Jamison (South Carolina State University); Ymitri Jayasundera-Mathison (Prairie View A&M University); Katarzyna Jerzak (University of Georgia); Alice Jewell (Harding University); Elizabeth Jones (Auburn University); Jeff Jones (University of Idaho); Dan Jones (Walters State Community College); Mary Kaiser (Jefferson State Community College); James Keller (Middlesex County College); Jill Keller (Middlesex Community College); Tim Kelley (Northwest-Shoals Community College); Andrew Kelley (Jackson State Community College); Hans Kellner (North Carolina State); Brian Kennedy (Pasadena City College); Shirin Khanmohamadi (San Francisco State University); Jeremy Kiene (McDaniel College); Mary Catherine Kiliany (Robert Morris University); Sue Kim (University of Alabama–Birmingham); Pam Kingsbury (University of North Alabama); Sharon Kinoshita (University of California, Santa Cruz); Lydia Kualapai (Schreiner University); Rita Kumar (University of Cincinnati); Roger Ladd (University of North Carolina–Pembroke); Daniel Lane (Norwich University); Erica Lara (Southwest Texas Junior College); Leah Larson (Our Lady of the Lake University); Dana Lauro (Ocean County College); Shanon Lawson (Pikes Peak Community College); Michael Leddy (Eastern Illinois University); Eric Leuschner (Fort Hays State University); Patricia Licklider (John Jay College, CUNY); Pamela Light (Rochester College); Alison Ligon (Morehouse College); Linda Linzey (Southeastern University); Thomas Lisk (North Carolina State University); Matthew Livesey (University of Wisconsin–Stout); Vickie Lloyd (University of Arkansas Community College at Hope); Judy Lloyd (Southside Virginia Community College); Mary Long (Ouachita Baptist University); Rick Lott (Arkansas State University); Scott Lucas (The Citadel); Katrine Lvovskaya (Rutgers University); Carolin Lynn (Mercyhurst College); Susan Lyons (University of Connecticut—Avery Point); William Thomas MacCary (Hofstra University); Richard Mace (Pace University); Peter Marbais (Mount Olive College); Lacy Marschalk (Auburn University); Seth Martin (Harrisburg Area Community College–Lancaster); Carter Mathes (Rutgers University); Rebecca Mathews (University of Connecticut); Marsha Mathews (Dalton State College); Darren Mathews (Grambling State University); Corine Mathis (Auburn University); Ken McAferty (Pensacola State College); Jeff McAlpine (Clackamas Community College); Kelli McBride (Seminole State College); Kay McClellan (South Plains College); Michael McClung (Northwest-Shoals Community College); Michael McClure (Virginia State University); Jennifer McCune (University of Central Arkansas); Kathleen McDonald (Norwich University); Charles McDonnell (Piedmont Technical College); Nancy McGee (Macomb Community College); Gregory McNamara (Clayton State University); Abby Mendelson (Point Park University); Ken Meyers (Wilson Community College); Barbara Mezeske (Hope College); Brett Millan (South Texas College); Sheila Miller (Hinds Community College); David Miller (Mississippi College); Matt Miller (University of South Carolina–Aiken); Yvonne Milspaw (Harrisburg Area Community College); Ruth Misheloff (Baruch College); Lamata Mitchell (Rock Valley College); D'Juana Montgomery (Southwestern Assemblies of God University); Lorne Mook (Taylor University); Renee Moore (Mississippi Delta Community College); Dan Morgan (Scott Community College); Samantha Morgan-Curtis (Tennessee State University); Beth Morley (Collin College); Vicki Moulson (College of the Albemarle); L. Carl Nadeau (University of Saint Francis); Wayne Narey (Arkansas State University); LeAnn Nash (Texas A&M University–Commerce); Leanne Nayden (University of Evansville); Jim Neilson (Wake Technical Community College); Jeff Nelson (University of Alabama–Huntsville); Mary Nelson (Dallas Baptist University); Deborah Nester (Northwest Florida State College); William Netherton (Amarillo College); William Newman (Perimeter College); Adele Newson-Horst (Missouri State University); George Nicholas (Benedictine College); Dana Nichols (Gainesville State College); Mark Nicoll-Johnson (Merced College); John Mark Nielsen (Dana College); Michael Nifong (Georgia College & State University); Laura Noell (North Virginia Community College); Bonnie Noonan (Xavier University of Louisiana); Patricia Noone (College of

Mount Saint Vincent); Paralee Norman (Northwestern State University–Leesville); Frank Novak (Pepperdine University); Kevin O'Brien (Chapman University); Sarah Odishoo (Columbia College Chicago); Samuel Olorounto (New River Community College); Jamili Omar (Lone Star College–CyFair); Michael Orlofsky (Troy University); Priscilla Orr (Sussex County Community College); Jim Owen (Columbus State University); Darlene Pagan (Pacific University); Yolanda Page (University of Arkansas–Pine Bluff); Lori Paige (Westfield State College); Linda Palumbo (Cerritos College); Joseph Parry (Brigham Young University); Carla Patterson (Georgia Highlands College); Andra Pavuls (Davenport University); Sunita Peacock (Slippery Rock University); Velvet Pearson (Long Beach City College); Joe Pellegrino (Georgia Southern University); Sonali Perera (Rutgers University); Clem Perez (St. Philip's College); Caesar Perkowski (Gordon College); Gerald Perkus (Collin College); John Peters (University of North Texas); Lesley Peterson (University of North Alabama); Judy Peterson (John Tyler Community College); Sandra Petree (Northwestern Oklahoma State University); Angela Pettit (Tarrant County College NE); Michell Phifer (University of Texas–Arlington); Ziva Piltch (Rockland Community College); Nancy Popkin (Harris-Stowe State University); Marlana Portolano (Towson University); Rhonda Powers (Auburn University); Lisa Propst (University of West Georgia); Melody Pugh (Wheaton College); Jonathan Purkiss (Pulaski Technical College); Patrick Quinn (College of Southern Nevada); Peter Rabinowitz (Hamilton College); Evan Radcliffe (Villanova University); Jody Ragsdale (Northeast Alabama Community College); Ken Raines (Eastern Arizona College); Gita Rajan (Fairfield University); Elizabeth Rambo (Campbell University); Richard Ramsey (Indiana University–Purdue University Fort Wayne); Jonathan Randle (Mississippi College); Amy Randolph (Waynesburg University); Rodney Rather (Tarrant County College Northwest); Helaine Razovsky (Northwestern State University); Rachel Reed (Auburn University); Karin Rhodes (Salem State College); Donald R. Riccomini (Santa Clara University); Christina Roberts (Otero Junior College); Paula Robison (Temple University); Jean Roelke (University of North Texas); Barrie Rosen (St. John's University); James Rosenberg (Point Park University); Sherry Rosenthal (College of Southern Nevada); Daniel Ross (Columbus State University); Maria Rouphail (North Carolina State University); Lance Rubin (Arapahoe Community College); Mary Ann Rygiel (Auburn University); Geoffrey Sadock (Bergen Community College); Allen Salerno (Auburn University); Mike Sanders (Kent State University); Deborah Scally (Richland College); Margaret Scanlan (Indiana University South Bend); Michael Schaefer (University of Central Arkansas); Tracy Schaelen (Southwestern College); Daniel Schenker (University of Alabama–Huntsville); Robyn Schiffman (Fairleigh Dickinson University); Roger Schmidt (Idaho State University); Robert Schmidt (Tarrant County College–Northwest Campus); Adrianne Schot (Weatherford College); Pamela Schuman (Brookhaven College); Sharon Seals (Ouachita Technical College); Su Senapati (Abraham Baldwin Agricultural College); Phyllis Senfleben (North Shore Community College); Theda Shapiro (University of California–Riverside); Mary Sheldon (Washburn University); Donald Shull (Freed-Hardeman University); Ellen Shull (Palo Alto College); Conrad Shumaker (University of Central Arkansas); Sara Shumaker (University of Central Arkansas); Dave Shuping (Spartanburg Methodist College); Horacio Sierra (University of Florida); Scott Simkins (Auburn University); Bruce

Simon (SUNY Fredonia); LaRue Sloan (University of Louisiana–Monroe); Peter Smeraldo (Caldwell College); Renee Smith (Lamar University); Victoria Smith (Texas State University); Connie Smith (College of St. Joseph); Grant Smith (Eastern Washington University); Mary Karen Solomon (Coloardo NW Community College); Micheline Soong (Hawaii Pacific University); Leah Souffrant (Baruch College, CUNY); Cindy Spangler (Faulkner University); Charlotte Speer (Bevill State Community College); John Staines (John Jay College, CUNY); Tanja Stampfl (Louisiana State University); Scott Starbuck (San Diego Mesa College); Kathryn Stasio (Saint Leo University); Joyce Stavick (North Georgia College & State University); Judith Steele (Mid-America Christian University); Stephanie Stephens (Howard College); Rachel Sternberg (Case Western Reserve University); Holly Sterner (College of Coastal Georgia); Karen Stewart (Norwich University); Sioux Stoeckle (Palo Verde College); Ron Stormer (Culver-Stockton College); Frank Stringfellow (University of Miami); Ayse Stromsdorfer (Soldan I. S. H. S.); Ashley Strong-Green (Paine College); James Sullivan (Illinois Central College); Zohreh Sullivan (University of Illinois); Richard Sullivan (Worcester State College); Duke Sutherland (Mississippi Gulf Coast Community College/Jackson County Campus); Maureen Sutton (Kean University); Marianne Szlyk (Montgomery College); Rebecca Taksel (Point Park University); Robert Tally (Texas State University); Tim Tarkington (Georgia Perimeter College); Patricia Taylor (Western Kentucky University); Mary Ann Taylor (Mountain View College); Susan Tekulve (Converse College); Stephen Teller (Pittsburgh State University); Stephen Thomas (Community College of Denver); Freddy Thomas (Virginia State University); Andy Thomason (Lindenwood University); Diane Thompson (Northern Virginia Community College); C. H. Thornton (Northwest-Shoals Community College); Elizabeth Thornton (Georgia Perimeter); Burt Thorp (University of North Dakota); Willie Todd (Clark Atlanta University); Martin Trapp (Northwestern Michigan College); Brenda Tuberville (University of Texas–Tyler); William Tucker (Olney Central College); Martha Turner (Troy University); Joya Uraizee (Saint Louis University); Randal Urwiller (Texas College); Emily Uzendoski (Central Community College–Columbus Campus); Kenneth Van Dover (Lincoln University); Kay Walter (University of Arkansas–Monticello); Cassandra Ward-Shah (West Chester University); Gina Weaver (Southern Nazarene University); Cathy Webb (Meridian Community College); Eric Weil (Elizabeth City State University); Marian Wernicke (Pensacola Junior College); Robert West (Mississippi State University); Cindy Wheeler (Georgia Highlands College); Chuck Whitchurch (Golden West College); Julianne White (Arizona State University); Denise White (Kennesaw State University); Amy White (Lee University); Patricia White (Norwich University); Gwen Whitehead (Lamar State College–Orange); Terri Whitney (North Shore Community College); Tamora Whitney (Creighton University); Stewart Whittemore (Auburn University); Johannes Wich-Schwarz (Maryville University); Charles Wilkinson (Southwest Tennessee Community College); Donald Williams (Toccoa Falls College); Rick Williams (Rogue Community College); Lea Williams (Norwich University); Susan Willis (Auburn University–Montgomery); Sharon Wilson (University of Northern Colorado); J. D. Wireman (Indiana State University); Rachel Wiren (Baptist Bible College); Bertha Wise (Oklahoma City Community College); Sallie Wolf (Arapahoe Community College); Rebecca Wong (James Madison University); Donna

Woodford-Gormley (New Mexico Highlands University); Paul Woodruff (University of Texas–Austin); William Woods (Wichita State University); Marjorie Woods (University of Texas–Austin); Valorie Worthy (Ohio University); Wei Yan (Darton College); Teresa Young (Philander Smith College); Darcy Zabel (Friends University); Michelle Zenor (Lon Morris College); and Jacqueline Zubeck (College of Mount Saint Vincent).

THE NORTON ANTHOLOGY OF

WORLD
LITERATURE

THIRD EDITION

VOLUME D

I

East Asian Drama

ast Asian and European literary traditions developed on different trajectories. Greek literature began with epic poetry and drama, genres that came to enjoy the highest status in later European literatures. Epic poetry and drama played no role in the early literature of East Asia, where instead short lyrical poetry was prized as the supreme vessel for public opinion, moral education, and personal expression. In this environment, dramatic literature emerged late in China, Japan, and Korea, although theatrical rituals and entertainments had existed for a long time. In China, Northern variety plays (*zaju*) were recorded since the thirteenth century and Southern plays (*chuanqi*) matured into a literary genre in the sixteenth century. In Japan, Noh drama received its defining shape under the patronage of military leaders, the shoguns, in the fourteenth century, and kabuki and puppet theater emerged as popular drama for the new urban commoner class in the seventeenth century. Finally, Korean *p'ansori* narrative drama appeared in the eighteenth century as a form of popular theater in a society ruled by a strict Confucian moral code. These are only some of the many traditional performance genres of East

A late nineteenth-century woodblock print from Tsukioka Kōgyo's series "One Hundred Noh Pictures."

Asia, which also include ritual dances, oral storytelling, and regional theater forms.

Although Chinese, Japanese, and Korean dramatic traditions developed under different historical conditions and in different societies they share a number of common features. First, they are all dance dramas, variously combining chant with music, singing, and dancing. Spoken drama, concert music, and ballet became separate genres in the West. They could be combined, like in opera, and therefore the local drama that developed in Beijing since the eighteenth century is often called "Peking Opera." However, unlike Western opera, where each work was authored by musical composers, Chinese "opera" relied on a fixed repertoire of tunes. The basic tunes could be performed in infinite variations, but they were still part of the same shared (and anonymous) repertoire, not an individual score. Second, East Asian drama, like the *Commedia dell'arte* in early modern Italy, relies on role-types such as the beautiful woman, the scoundrel, the fool, the demon, and so on. The types can easily be recognized by the masks live actors wear, their vivid, mask-like face paint or, for puppetry, the puppet type. Third, East Asian drama has, at its most extreme, plays without authors. Aeschylus, Sophocles, and Euripides wrote tragedies that bear their distinctive styles, and generations of European playwrights would later do the same. In contrast, the repertoire of Korean *p'ansori*, for example, consists today of only five anonymous pieces, all products of a longer process of oral transmission. They are reenacted again and again, with archetypal gravity. Other East Asian traditions, especially Chinese drama, developed a rich culture of dramatic authorship; even centuries after Chinese variety plays had disappeared from the

stage, new plays were still being written exclusively for reading (staging these plays would have required considerable adjustments). Fourth, because most East Asian theater is not merely spoken drama, but involves such different skills as dancing, chanting, singing, and playing of music, it often requires lengthy and arduous training. **Zeami**, the most distinguished Noh playwright, once suggested that a Noh actor should spend the first ten years of training—from about age seven to age seventeen—merely practicing the vocabulary of dance movements and voice articulations. Only after this training could he move on to actual acting. Consummate mastery and virtuosity acquired through lifelong practice is central to East Asian theater culture.

Since the twentieth century, traditional drama in East Asia has been facing great challenges. It competes with modernist spoken drama, which playwrights adopted under Western influence, often because they believed that the realistic acting of Western drama could be a better tool for social criticism and allowed them to put on stage themes of contemporary relevance. Also, the long apprenticeship and ultimate devotion required by traditional practice has little appeal to many young people. Because traditional East Asian theater depends largely on the transmission from master to disciple, its survival is endangered as the number of performers dwindles. The national governments of China, Japan, and Korea are therefore supporting traditional drama as a part of national cultural heritage. What started as popular entertainment centuries ago has now become a traditionalist icon of national pride.

While East Asian drama has thus faced challenges in China, Japan, and Korea, it has won new audiences in the West. In particular Chinese theater and Japanese Noh drama mesmerized twentieth-century writers such as the American poet Ezra Pound, who published English adaptations of Noh plays with the scholar Ernest Fenollosa; the Irish author **William Butler Yeats,** who wrote Noh-influenced plays; and the German dramatist **Bertolt Brecht,** who used Chinese and Japanese locales for some of his plays and adopted elements of Chinese and Japanese theater for his aesthetics of "estrangement." The highly stylized theater of East Asia offers an alternative to Western realism and therefore keeps inspiring theater makers throughout the world.

ZEAMI MOTOKIYO
ca. 1363–1443

Imagine a theater without sets and with virtually no props, with no interest in depicting character development or dramatic conflict, a music-drama at the hypnotic pace of solemn ritual. This is Noh, the oldest dramatic form of Japan and one of the world's oldest living professional theater traditions.

Zeami Motokiyo, arguably Noh's foremost practitioner and theorist, did as much as anyone to establish the traditions and aesthetics of this sophisticated art form, which fascinated modern dramatists in the West and which is practiced to this day.

THE BASICS OF NOH

The word *noh* may be translated as "talent," "skill," or "accomplishment." Like many traditional Japanese arts, Noh is hereditary: actors and musicians learn from their parents or masters and undergo strenuous training from early childhood on. True mastery is said to come only with advanced age.

Noh is the most stylized of Japan's dramatic genres, which also include *kyōgen* ("wild words"), comical inter-missions performed between Noh acts. Although Noh emerged in the fourteenth century, its basic elements of dance, music and recitation have older roots. It adapted elements from Buddhist chanting, from the music and dances of the Japanese imperial court (which were imported from China and Korea and are still practiced today) and from "Monkey/comic music" (*sarugaku* or *sangaku*), variety entertainment that included acrobatics and mime. Out of these and other performance traditions Noh emerged, and the playwrights Kan'ami (1333–1384) and his son Zeami gave the genre its defining shape.

Noh plays contain a limited number of actors: the "leading actor" and the opposite, though not antagonistic "supporting actor," with their companions. There is also a chorus, stage attendants, and occasional child actors. Although women played an important role in the development of Japanese dramatic arts, professional actors are traditionally all male. The current repertoire of some 240 plays is divided into five groups depending on their central

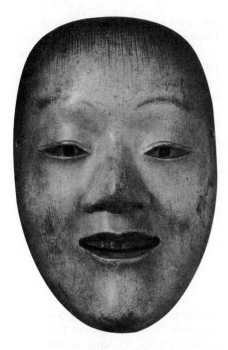

protagonist: plays about gods, warriors, women, and demons, and miscellaneous plays. Most plays extract particular moments from famous literary works. They explore strong, obsessive emotions—grief, despair, anguish, love, devotion. Although today some plays are written on contemporary themes—a Noh play on heart transplants premiered in 1991—traditionally Noh plays are based on old stories and are studded with famous phrases from classical literature.

Noh is performed on an austere, undecorated stage of polished cypress wood, and consists of a main stage and a bridgeway, on which the actors enter the stage. Except for child actors and actors playing living adult characters, actors impersonating ghosts, gods, or demons wear masks. Because most masks have enigmatic expressions they are open to various interpretations. The actors mostly move at an extremely slow pace, and their performance is accompanied by a flutist and three drummers playing a hip, shoulder, and stick drum. The musicians sit along the back of the stage under the lone pine tree painted on the wall, the single and unvarying decoration for all Noh plays.

Stylization is central to Noh. Noh is like a slowly moving tapestry of emotions framed into fixed performance patterns, and every move on stage is precisely choreographed. For example, the act of weeping is suggested by the actor's slow raising of his hand to eye height, followed by an equally poised lowering. It is the vocabulary and grammar of these stylized moves that Noh actors need to master through tireless training not unlike a Western musician practicing typical cadences or trill patterns. The fixity of form and gesture in Noh is enhanced by the fluidity of space, time, and narration: the absence of a set leaves spatial boundaries and distances unclear; the key events belong to the murky realm of memories and dreams, where the boundaries between past and present merge; and narration is fluid because characters do not necessarily speak their own lines and thoughts. For example the chorus does not comment on the action as in Greek plays, but can take the place of a narrator or recite the words or thoughts of a character. In turn, actors can sometimes function as character, opponent, and narrator at the same time, as in a famous scene from Zeami's play *Tadanori*, where the protagonist at the crucial final moment plays both Tadanori and the warrior who kills him. The disjunction among actor, character, and voice gives the text an enthralling autonomy from the action on stage.

NOH PATRONAGE

Zeami was born to a father who was a gifted playwright and headed a *sarugaku* troupe. He attracted the attention of Ashikaga Yoshimitsu (1358–1408), the third shogun of the Muromachi military regime (1338–1573), when performing in his father's troupe as a beautiful boy actor. Although a later shogun shifted his patronage away from Zeami and even exiled him in 1435, Zeami's earlier favor with the shoguns gave a decisive turn to the fate of Noh: it was to become a sophisticated art sponsored by the military rulers for their domain lords and retainers to enjoy. In 1868, when Emperor Meiji abolished the shogunate, Noh lost its greatest patron. That Noh survived this watershed moment was partly thanks to the symbolic power of foreign relations. Mindful of Western opera which was presented to Japanese diplomats during their visits to the West, the Japanese government entertained the American president Ulysses Grant with a Noh performance when he visited Japan in 1879. From an obsolete tradition it became a national art: nowadays the Japanese government sponsors Noh and grants exquisite actors stipends and the honorary title of "Living National Treasures."

THE WARRIOR PLAY ATSUMORI

Atsumori is an example of how Zeami gave the grisly subject matter of battle action and tormented warrior ghosts a new, cultivated form that appealed to the increasingly sophisticated warrior elite. It focuses on the death of the young Heike warrior Atsumori, a famous episode from Tales of the Heike. During the battle at Ichi-no-tani, a decisive moment in the civil wars between the Genji and Heike clans in the 1180s that resulted in the defeat of the Heike, the Genji supporter Naozane catches sight of a Heike warrior alone on the seashore. When Naozane realizes that the soldier, Atsumori, is only a boy the age of his own son, he takes pity, but is in the end forced to kill the boy when fellow Genji warriors suddenly approach the scene. The flute that Naozane finds under the dead boy's armor testifies to his courtly elegance. Plagued by remorse, Naozane soon becomes a monk to pray for Atsumori's salvation.

The Noh play revisits the final encounter between Atsumori, now a ghost, and Naozane, now a monk named Renshō. In the first act, Renshō meets Atsumori's ghost, who is disguised as a reaper. In the second act, the ghost appears in its true form and remembers the pleasures of a banquet held the night before his death. The play ends with a double salvation, as Naozane prays for Atsumori and Atsumori forgives him. Because the episode unfolds at Suma Bay, where Genji, the protagonist of the eleventh-century Tale of Genji, was exiled, Atsumori frequently alludes to Murasaki Shikibu's tale and draws an analogy between its central protagonist Genji and the young Atsumori. (Allusions in Noh plays could be powerful enough to bend history: a later puppet-play version of Atsumori claimed that the historical Atsumori was the son of an emperor, just like the fictional Genji.)

In an age of action movies and fast-paced entertainment, what has Noh to offer? Can we appreciate its ceremonial slowness and minimalist understatement? Measured on the scale of the cosmic significance of Noh themes—death, salvation, obsessive emotions—Noh performances have an eerie power to transform an audience's perception of time and significance. Although the artistry of Noh is fully realized only on stage, reading the rich and allusive text does give an indication of its graceful power.

Atsumori[1]

Persons in order of appearance

> *The monk* RENSHŌ, *formerly the Minamoto warrior Kumagai*
> A YOUTH (*no mask*)
> *Two or three* COMPANIONS *to the* YOUTH
> A VILLAGER
> *The phantom of the Taira warrior* ATSUMORI
> (Atsumori *or* Jūroku *mask*)

ACT I

Enter RENSHŌ, *carrying a rosary. He stands in base square,[2] facing rear of stage.*

RENSHŌ   The world is all a dream, and he who wakes
the world is all a dream, and he who wakes,
casting it from him, may yet know the real.
> *He turns to the audience.*

You have before you one who in his time was Kumagai no Jirō Naozane, a warrior from Musashi province. Now I have renounced the world, and Renshō is my name. It was I, you understand, who struck Atsumori down;[3] and the great sorrow of this deed moved me to become the monk you see. Now I am setting out for Ichi-no-tani, to comfort Atsumori and guide his spirit towards enlightenment.

> The wandering moon,
> issuing from among the Ninefold Clouds[4]
> issuing from among the Ninefold Clouds,
> swings southward by Yodo and Yamazaki,
> past Koya Pond and the Ikuta River,   *Mimes walking.*
> and Suma shore, loud with pounding waves,
> to Ichi-no-tani, where I have arrived
> to Ichi-no-tani, where I have arrived.

Having come so swiftly, I have reached Ichi-no-tani in the province of Tsu. Ah, the past returns to mind as though it were before me now. But what is this? I hear a flute from that upper field. I will wait for the player to come by and question him about what happened here.

> *Enter the* YOUTH *and* COMPANIONS. *Each carries a split bamboo pole with a bunch of mowed grass secured in the cleft. They face each other at front.*

YOUTH *and* COMPANIONS
> The sweet music of the mower's flute
> the sweet music of the mower's flute
> floats, windborne, far across the fields.

YOUTH   Those who gather grass on yonder hill
now start for home, for twilight is at hand.

---

1. Translated by Royall Tyler.
2. Back left corner of the stage.
3. For the passage on which this play is based see Vol. B, *Tales of the Heike*, "The Death of Atsumori."

4. Reference to the capital. The moon suggests Renshō himself, wandering from Kyoto to the Suma shore, the site of the battle of Ichi-no-tani, where Atsumori was killed.

YOUTH *and* COMPANIONS

> They too head back to Suma, by the sea,
> and their way, like mine, is hardly long.
> Back and forth I ply, from hill to shore,
> heart heavy with the cares of thankless toil.
> Yes, should one perchance ask after me,
> my reply would speak of lonely grief.[5]
> On Suma shore
> the salty drops fall fast, though were I known
> the salty drops fall fast, though were I known,
> I myself might hope to have a friend.
> Yet, having sunk so low, I am forlorn,
> and those whom I once loved are strangers now.

While singing, YOUTH *goes to stand in base square,* COMPANIONS *before Chorus.*

> But I resign myself to what life brings,
> and accept what griefs are mine to bear   RENSHŌ *rises.*
> and accept what griefs are mine to bear.

RENSHŌ   Excuse me, mowers, but I have a question for you.

YOUTH   For us, reverend sir? What is it, then?

RENSHŌ   Was it one of you I just heard playing the flute?

YOUTH   Yes, it was one of us.

RENSHŌ   How touching! For people such as you, that is a remarkably elegant thing to do![6] Oh yes, it is very touching.

YOUTH   It is a remarkably elegant thing, you say, for people like us to do? The proverb puts the matter well: 'Envy none above you, despise none below.' Besides,

> the woodman's songs and the mower's flute

YOUTH *and* COMPANIONS

> are called 'sylvan lays' and 'pastoral airs':[7]
> they nourish, too, many a poet's work,
> and ring out very bravely through the world.
> You need not wonder, then, to hear me play.

RENSHŌ   I do not doubt that what you say is right.
Then, 'sylvan lays' or 'pastoral airs'

YOUTH   mean the mower's flute,

RENSHŌ   the woodman's songs:

YOUTH   music to ease all the sad trials of life,

RENSHŌ   singing,

YOUTH   dancing,

RENSHŌ   fluting—

YOUTH   all these pleasures

Below, YOUTH *begins to move and gesture in consonance with the text.*

CHORUS   are pastimes not unworthy of those
who care to seek out beauty: for bamboo,
who care to seek out beauty: for bamboo,

---

5. These and the following three lines allude to a poem by Ariwara no Yukihira (818–893 C.E.), who was also exiled to Suma.
6. Flute playing is associated with the aristocracy.
7. Atsumori and his companions refer here to an elegant line from a Heian poetry collection.

washed up by the sea, yields Little Branch,
Cicada Wing, and other famous flutes;
while this one, that the mower blows,
could be Greenleaf, as you will agree.
Perhaps upon the beach at Sumiyoshi,
one might expect instead a Koma flute;[8]
but this is Suma. Imagine, if you will,
a flute of wood left from saltmakers' fires
a flute of wood left from saltmakers' fires.

Exeunt COMPANIONS. YOUTH, *in base square, turns to* RENSHŌ.

RENSHŌ   How strange! While the other mowers have gone home, you have stayed on, alone. Why is this?

YOUTH   You ask why have I stayed behind? A voice called me here, chanting the Name.[9] O be kind and grant me the Ten Invocations![1]

RENSHŌ   Very gladly. I will give you the Ten Invocations, as you ask. But then tell me who you are.

YOUTH   In truth, I am someone with a tie to Atsumori.

RENSHŌ   One with a tie to Atsumori?
Ah, the name recalls such memories!
Presses his palms together in prayer over his rosary.
'Namu Amida Bu,' I chant in prayer:
YOUTH *goes down on one knee and presses his palms together.*

YOUTH *and* RENSHŌ   'If I at last become a Buddha,
then all sentient beings who call my Name
in all the worlds, in the ten directions,
will find welcome in Me, for I abandon none.'[2]

CHORUS   Then, O monk, do not abandon me!
One calling of the Name should be enough,
but you have comforted me by night and day—
a most precious gift! As to my name,
no silence I might keep could quite conceal
the one you pray for always, dawn and dusk: YOUTH *rises.*
that name is my own. And, having spoken,
he fades away and is lost to view
he fades away and is lost to view.   *Exit* YOUTH.

INTERLUDE

VILLAGER *entered discreetly and sat at villager position.*
He now comes forward to base square.

VILLAGER   You see before you one who lives here at Suma, on the shore. Today I will go down to the beach and pass the time watching the ships

8. Presumably bamboo washed up by the sea yielded particularly fine flutes. "Greenleaf": a legendary flute. "Little Branch": Atsumori's own flute, mentioned in this list of famous flutes. "Sumiyoshi": where ships from Koma (Korea) once used to put in, thus "Koma flute." 9. That of Amida, the "Buddha of Infinite Light." Invoking his name (*Namu Amida Bu*)

saved the believer and was a typical practice of the Pure Land school of Buddhism.
1. Ten callings of the Name for the benefit of another were often requested of holy persons.
2. The canonical vow made by Amida, before he became a Buddha, to save all beings by his grace.

sail by. [*Sees* RENSHŌ.] Well! There's a monk I've not seen before. May I ask you, reverend sir, where you are from?

RENSHŌ I came from Miyako. Do you live nearby?

VILLAGER Yes, I do.

RENSHŌ Then would you please come nearer? I have something to ask of you.

VILLAGER Very well, reverend sir. [*Sits at centre, facing* RENSHŌ.] Now, what is it?

RENSHŌ Something rather unexpected, perhaps. I hear this is where the Minamoto and the Taira fought, and where the young Taira noble, Atsumori, died. Would you tell me all you know of the way he met his end?

VILLAGER That certainly is an unexpected request, reverend sir. I do live here, it is true, but I really know very little about such things. Still, it would be too bad of me, the very first time we meet, to claim I know nothing at all. So I will tell you the story as I myself have heard it told.

RENSHŌ That is very kind of you.

VILLAGER [*Turns to audience.*] It came to pass that in the autumn of the second year of Juei, Minamoto no Yoshinaka drove the Taira clan out of Miyako.[3] This is where they came. Then the Minamoto, bent on destroying the Taira for ever, split their army—sixty thousand and more mounted warriors — into two wings and attacked without mercy. The Taira fled.

Now one among them, a young gentleman of the fifth rank named Atsumori, was the son of Tsunemori, the Director of Palace Repairs. Atsumori was on his way down to the sea, meaning to board the imperial barge,[4] when he realized that back in the camp he had forgotten his flute, Little Branch. He prized this flute very highly and hated to leave it behind for the enemy's taking. So he turned back, fetched the flute, and again went down to the beach. But by this time, the imperial barge and the rest of the fleet had sailed. Just as he was riding into the sea, hoping to swim his horse out to the ships, Kumagai no Jirō Naozane, a warrior from Musashi province, spread his war fan and challenged him to fight.

Atsumori wheeled his horse and closed fiercely with Kumagai. The two crashed to the ground between their mounts. But Kumagai was a very powerful man. He instantly got Atsumori under him and ripped off his helmet, meaning to take his head. He saw a youth of fifteen or sixteen, with powdered face and blackened teeth—a young man of high rank, there was no doubt about that.[5] Kumagai wanted to spare him. Then he glanced behind him and saw Doi and Kajiwara riding up.[6] A good seven or eight other warriors were with them. 'I do not wish to kill you,' said Kumagai, 'but as you can see, there are many men from my own side behind me. I will take your head myself, then, and afterwards pray with all my heart for the peace of your spirit.' So he cut off Atsumori's head. On examining the

---

3. Yoshinaka, a Genji warrior who was later killed by his own clan because of his ambitions for power, conquered Kyoto, the "Miyako," in 1183 during the Genpei Wars (1180–85) recounted in the *Tales of the Heike*.
4. The Taira (or Heike) fled Kyoto with the child emperor Antoku, whose mother belonged to the Taira.
5. Courtiers of both sexes wore white powder and blackened their teeth. Teeth in their natural state (certainly Kumagai's) were considered unsightly by the aristocracy.
6. Warriors, like Renshō, on the Genji side.

body, he found a flute in a brocade bag attached to the waist. When he showed the flute to his commander, all present wet the sleeves of their armour with tears. To think that he had been carrying a flute at a time like that! Even among all those gentlemen from the court, he must have been an especially gentle youth! Eventually, Kumagai found out that his victim had been Atsumori.

I wonder whether it's true, as they say, that Kumagai made himself into a monk to pray for Atsumori. If he was that sort of man, though, he wouldn't have killed Atsumori in the first place. But he did kill him, so the story must be wrong. I'd like to see that Kumagai here now! I'd kill him myself, just to make Atsumori feel better.

Well, that is the way I have heard it told. But why did you ask? I am a bit puzzled.

RENSHŌ   Thank you very much for your kind account. Perhaps there is no harm in my telling you who I am. In my time I was Kumagai no Jirō Naozane, but now I am a monk and my name is Renshō. I came here, you see, to give Atsumori's spirit comfort and guidance.

VILLAGER   *You* are Kumagai, who fought in the battle here? Why, I had no idea! Please excuse all the silly things I said. They say the man mighty in good is mighty, too, in evil. I'm sure it's just as true the other way round. Anyway, do go on comforting Atsumori's spirit.

RENSHŌ   I assure you, I am not in the least offended. Since I came here to comfort Atsumori, I will stay on a while and continue chanting the precious Sutra[7] for him.

VILLAGER   If that is your intention, then please accept lodging at my house.

RENSHŌ   I will do so gratefully.

VILLAGER   Very well.

[*Exit.*]

ACT 2

RENSHŌ   Then it is well: to guide and comfort him
             then it is well: to guide and comfort him,
             I shall do holy rites, and through the night
             call aloud the Name for Atsumori,
             praying that he reach enlightenment
             praying that he reach enlightenment.

Enter ATSUMORI, *in the costume of a warrior. He stops in base square.*

ATSUMORI   Across to Awaji the plovers fly,
             while the Suma barrier guard sleeps on;
             yet one, I see, keeps nightlong vigil here.

---

7. The Lotus Sutra, a central text in certain schools of Buddhism.

O keeper of the pass, tell me your name.[8]
Behold, Renshō: I am Atsumori.

RENSHŌ   Strange! As I chant aloud the Name,
beating out the rhythm on this gong,
and wakeful as ever in broad day,
I see Atsumori come before me.
The sight can only be a dream.

ATSUMORI   Why need you take it for a dream?
For I have come so far to be with you
in order to clear karma that is real.

RENSHŌ   I do not understand you: for the Name
has power to clear away all trace of sin.
Call once upon the name of Amida
and your countless sins will be no more:
so the sutra promises. As for me,
I have always called the Name for you.
How could sinful karma afflict you still?

ATSUMORI   Deep as the sea it runs. O lift me up,

RENSHŌ   that I too may come to Buddhahood!

ATSUMORI   Let each assure the other's life to come,

RENSHŌ   for we, once enemies,

ATSUMORI   are now become,

RENSHŌ   in very truth,

ATSUMORI   fast friends in the Law.

    Below, ATSUMORI *moves and gestures in consonance with the text.*

CHORUS   Now I understand!
'Leave the company of an evil friend,
cleave to the foe you judge a good man':
and that good man is you! O I am grateful!
How can I thank you as you deserve?
Then I will make confession of my tale,
and pass the night recounting it to you
and pass the night recounting it to you.

    ATSUMORI *sits on a stool at centre, facing audience.*
The flowers of spring rise up and deck the trees
to urge all upwards to illumination;
the autumn moon plumbs the waters' depths
to show grace from on high saving all beings.

ATSUMORI   Rows of Taira mansions lined the streets:
we were the leafy branches on the trees.
Like the rose of Sharon, we flowered one day;

CHORUS   but as the Teaching that enjoins the Good

---

8. The barrier on the pass through the hills behind Suma was well known in poetry, which often features its nameless guard, an older man seen at night. Atsumori's words, "O keeper of the pass, tell me your name," are from a 12th-century poem.

is seldom found,[9] birth in the human realm
quickly ends, like a spark from a flint.
This we never knew, nor understood
that vigour is followed by decline.

ATSUMORI   Lords of the land, we were, but caused much grief;
CHORUS   blinded by wealth, we never knew our pride.

ATSUMORI *rises now, and dances through the passage below.*

Yes, the house of Taira ruled the world
twenty years and more: a generation
that passed by as swiftly as a dream.
Then came the Juei years, and one sad fall,
when storms stripped the trees of all their leaves
and scattered them to the four directions,
we took to our fragile, leaflike ships,
and tossed in restless sleep upon the waves.
Our very dreams foretold no return.
We were like caged birds that miss the clouds,
or homing geese that have lost their way.
We never lingered long under one sky,
but travelled on for days, and months, and years,
till at last spring came round again,
and we camped here, at Ichi-no-tani.
So we stayed on, hard by Suma shore,

ATSUMORI   while winds swept down upon us off the hills.
CHORUS   The fields were bitterly cold. At the sea's edge
our ships huddled close, while day and night
the plovers cried, and our own poor sleeves
wilted in the spray that drenched the beach.
Together in the seafolk's huts we slept,
till we ourselves joined these villagers,
bent to their life like the wind-bent pines.
The evening smoke rose from our cooking fires
while we sat about on heaps of sticks
piled upon the beach, and thought and thought
of how we were at Suma, in the wilds,
and we ourselves belonged to Suma now,
even as we wept for all our clan.

ATSUMORI *stands before drums.*

ATSUMORI   Then came the sixth night of the second month.
My father, Tsunemori, summoned us
to play and dance, and sing *imayō.*[1]

RENSHŌ   Why, that was the music I remember!
A flute was playing so sweetly in their camp!
We, the attackers, heard it well enough.

---

9. It is only by great good fortune that a sentient being gets to hear the Buddha's teaching,
and it is only as a human being that one has
the potential to reach enlightenment.
1. Popular songs much appreciated at court
in the late 12th century.

ATSUMORI	It was Atsumori's flute, you see:
	the one I took with me to my death
RENSHŌ	and that you wished to play this final time,
ATSUMORI	while from every throat
CHORUS	rose songs and poems
	sung in chorus to a lively beat.

ATSUMORI *performs a lively dance, ending in base square. Below, be continues dancing and miming in consonance with the text.*

ATSUMORI	Then, in time, His Majesty's ship sailed,
CHORUS	with the whole clan behind him in their own.
	Anxious to be aboard, I sought the shore,
	but all the warships and the imperial barge
	stood already far, far out to sea.
ATSUMORI	I was stranded. Reining in my horse,
	I halted, at a loss for what to do.
CHORUS	There came then, galloping behind me,
	Kumagai no Jirō Naozane,
	shouting, 'You will not escape my arm!'
	At this Atsumori wheeled his mount
	and swiftly, all undaunted, drew his sword.
	We first exchanged a few rapid blows,
	then, still on horseback, closed to grapple, fell,
	and wrestled on, upon the wave-washed strand.
	But you had bested me, and I was slain.
	Now karma brings us face to face again.

'You are my foe!' Atsumori shouts,   *Brandishes sword.*
lifting his sword to strike; but Kumagai   *Drops to one knee.*
with kindness has repaid old enmity,   *Rises, retreats.*
calling the Name to give the spirit peace.
They at last shall be reborn together
upon one lotus throne in paradise.
Renshō, you were no enemy of mine.

He drops his sword and, in base square, turns to RENSHŌ *with palms pressed together.*

Pray for me, O pray for my release!
Pray for me, O pray for my release!

Facing side from base square, stamps the final beat.

KONG SHANGREN

1648–1718

Kong Shangren's *The Peach Blossom Fan* is one of the last and greatest works in the Chinese tradition of Southern drama. Called *chuanqi* ("tales of the marvelous," the same term used for Tang tales in the classical language), drama in the Southern style became prominent during the Ming Dynasty (1368–1644). *The Peach Blossom Fan* is a historical drama devoted to the chaotic events surrounding the fall of the Ming Dynasty and the eventual establishment of the Qing Dynasty (1644–1911). Spinning a romantic love tale around a corrupt counter-regime that attempted to uphold the legitimacy of the Ming Dynasty, Kong Shangren's play is a grand and subtle reflection on the theatricality of all human endeavors, on the power of fiction to speak historical truths, and on the ambivalent nostalgia that draws us to lost causes.

Although there are indications of quasi-dramatic performances in China at an early period, drama grew in sophistication during the Song Dynasty (960–1279). The earliest extant Chinese plays date from the thirteenth century. Chinese theater typically alternates between prose dialogue and arias, which were sung in performance, and the actors' dazzling costumes and bright makeup and the audience's expectation of technical virtuosity, comparable perhaps to Western opera. Originally an act of a play was organized around a suite of arias, all in the same musical mode. In early northern drama, so-called "variety plays" (*zaju*), only one character was allowed to sing in each act. The often very lively dialogue around the arias was given considerably less attention in early works, but when drama matured, the interplay between aria and fully developed dialogue became central to the artistic success of the play.

During the Ming Dynasty, drama reached an unprecedented peak. From the short span of less than three centuries we know of about four hundred playwrights and some fifteen hundred plays, which ranged from one-act skits to bombastic dramatic romances in fifty scenes or more. Chuanqi, also known as "Kunqu Opera," of which *The Peach Blossom Fan* is the best-known example, became prominent. Chuanqi are very long plays, most between thirty and fifty acts, and were performed either piecemeal as single acts or spread out over a number of days. Drama also developed as a literary form with printed editions designed for reading. Chuanqi plots are intricate and sprawling affairs, often weaving together numerous characters and story lines. Although the plots have a degree of linear unity, it is clear that the primary sense of artistic coherence comes from parallel scenes and situations, in which each moment gains significance by echoing corresponding moments in the play (and often in earlier dramatic works). Drama was immensely popular in late imperial China, and audiences developed a high degree of connoisseurship and close knowledge of a wide range of plays. By the same token, only writers of wide-ranging erudition and deep knowledge of various musical traditions could hope to write plays that would satisfy their sophisticated audiences.

A 2006 performance of *The Peach Blossom Fan* in Beijing.

THE PEACH BLOSSOM FAN

Kong Shangren was a remote descendant of Confucius (551–479 B.C.E.), and a well-known expert in Confucian ritual and the interpretation of the Confucian Classics. He wrote *The Peach Blossom Fan* in 1699 in his early fifties when nearing the end of a decade-long service in a mid-level position at the Manchu court of the Qing Dynasty. He had previously written plays, but it was *The Peach Blossom Fan* that made him famous as a playwright. However, it was the last play he wrote, and in the following year he retreated to his home in Qufu, Confucius's birthplace, and took on ritual duties as a clan descendant at the temple complex of Confucius. The pride Kong took in his family lineage and in Confucius both as a moral paragon, but also as a historian and reputed author of *The Spring and Autumn Annals*, a historical chronicle of his home state of Lu in modern-day Shandong Province, shines through in many moments in *The Peach Blossom Fan*.

As a historical drama *The Peach Blossom Fan* re-creates events surrounding the fall of the Ming Dynasty. In 1644 the rebel Li Zicheng captured Beijing whereupon the last Ming Emperor, Chongzhen, hanged himself in the Forbidden City. The rebels were eventually driven back by the armies of the Manchu, a former vassal tribe of the Ming from the northeast, who proceeded to put their tribal chief on the throne and established the last imperial dynasty of China, the Qing. After the Manchu takeover members of the Ming court retreated to the southern capital of Nanjing and various regimes loyal to the Ming emerged, collectively called the "Southern Ming." The last Ming loyalists were not eliminated until 1662, but *The Peach Blossom Fan* focuses only on one earlier abortive regime between 1643–46, when the pleasure-indulgent and theater-addicted Prince Fu was elevated to the position of emperor.

Because strong sympathies for the Ming lingered during the late seventeenth century, when the play was written, the Qing government was highly sensitive to any remnant Ming nostalgia and criticism of the new dynasty. It was thus a most delicate matter for Kong to choose this historical backdrop and put on stage protagonists based on actual historical figures. He drew on a wide variety of historical sources to create a play that would function as a different kind of history. At the center of the plot is the love story between the courtesan Li Xiangjun, "Fragrant Princess," and Hou Fangyu, a dramatic actor in the play who in reality was a famous writer and even wrote a biography of Xiangjun. The meeting, separation, and eventual reunion of the lovers is the frame for this play in forty scenes. The peach blossom fan that gives the play its title is the object onto which their tumultuous story of absolute love, uncompromising devotion, and resistance to the corrupt world around them is gradually inscribed, in poetry, blood, and paint. The selections here, the Prologue and scenes 2, 7, 23, and 40, include the frame of the play and central moments involving the lovers and their emblematic fan.

Scenes of theatricality and performance occur throughout the play, for Kong was interested in the degree to which relationships involve playing roles. Even the frame surrounding the play is performative: the text begins with a prologue set in 1684, during the reign of the powerful Qing emperor Kangxi, where a former ritual officiant at the Ming court, now an old man, gives a preview of the play, eagerly praising the blessed peaceful times under the new dynasty. This old man is many roles in one: an eyewitness of the fall of the incompetent and decadent Southern Ming, an actor in the play and a spectator of the play. He embodies the mysteries of the workings of history on which Kong invites us to reflect with his *Peach Blossom Fan*: what is the relation between history

as lived and history as remembered, reconstructed? How can we reconcile ourselves with the outcomes and forces of history? And how can fiction and drama serve as an alternative, truer history of sorts? As the old man observes in the prologue to the second part of the play (not included in our selection):

> In bygone years, reality was the play;
> The play becomes reality today.
> Twice I have watched its progress:
>   Heaven preserves
> This passive gazer with his cold clear
>   eyes.

Theatricality is also central to the portrayal of the play's arch villain, Ruan Dacheng, who produces immensely popular but vapid romantic comedies in the midst of national disaster (nine plays by the historical Ruan Dacheng are preserved) and who becomes one of the obsequious and dark forces behind the dubitable throne of the Southern Ming regime. The play's romantic plot, too, begins and ends with scenes of theatricality: When in scene 2 we first meet the heroine, Fragrant Princess, she is a young courtesan being taught by her singing master to perform the arias sung by the heroine in another famous play, *The Peony Pavilion*. In the last scene of the play, when the lovers are finally reunited, the act of their changing their robes indicates a fundamental change in roles. In this moment the lovers are enlightened to love's illusion, and they separate, literally a fitting closure to Kong's drama about drama and about the drama of history.

Although Southern dramas continued to be written and performed, the genre was eclipsed toward the end of the eighteenth century by "Peking Opera," a more popular and action-driven form of theater that fostered the cult of virtuoso actors and singers rather than of sophisticated writers and playwrights. Thus, reading Kong's play today is a doubly nostalgic experience, because we can admire the intellectual and literary sophistication of Southern drama at its best and indulge in the bitter and complex nostalgia for lost dreams and causes that pervades every word of *The Peach Blossom Fan*.

From The Peach Blossom Fan[1]

PROLOGUE (1), OCTOBER 1684

Enter an OLD MAN *with a white beard, a felt hat, and Daoist robes.*[2]

OLD MAN
> Is there such an antique as I?—
> antique of neither bronze nor jade,
> but my face gives off an antique gloss.
> The last soul surviving, companions gone—
> why flinch from young men's scorn?
> The outrage that once filled my breast
> > has all been swept away,
> and now I may well linger on, wherever
> > I find drink and song.
> Now children revere their parents,
> > state officers are true,
> > > all things rest secure,
> so yearn no more for the ginseng root
> > that makes a man live long.

The sun shines gloriously on this age of sage-kings, and flowers bloom in the onset of a new cycle of years. There are no bandits in the hills, while gods and immortals fill the earth. I was once an Officiant at the Court of Imperial Sacrifices in Nanjing, a post of no great prestige or pay, so my name may be withheld here. It has been my great good fortune to have escaped disaster, and I have been alive these ninety-seven years, during which I have witnessed much of splendor and ruin. And now I have reached the first year of a new hundred-and-eighty-year cycle. A ruler comparable to Yao and Shun is on the throne, and ministers like Yu and Gao have been installed to aid him.[3] Everywhere the populace is happy, and the harvests have been abundant year after year. This is the twenty-third year of the Kangxi Reign,[4] and twenty-one signs of good luck have appeared.

VOICE [*offstage*]   What are these signs of good luck?

OLD MAN [*counting them off on his fingers*]
> The Yellow River Diagram appeared.
> The Luo River Inscription appeared.
> The Star of Virtue brightened.

---

1. Translated by and with notes adapted from Stephen Owen.
2. A former officer of the state calling out the prescribed actions in Confucian rituals, the old man wears Daoist robes, indicating that he has retired from public office.
3. Flattering comparison of the new Manchu government of the Qing Dynasty to exemplary rulers and ministers of high antiquity.
4. Reign of the Kangxi emperor, the second emperor of the Qing Dynasty.

Auspicious clouds manifested themselves.
A sweet dew fell.
An oily rain came down.
A phoenix roosted.
A unicorn roamed.
The ming plant came out.
The sacred mushroom grew.
There were no waves on the sea.
The Yellow River cleared.

Every single one of these occurred—doesn't that deserve celebration? I'm delighted to have lived to see such glorious times, and I roam about everywhere. In the Taiping Gardens yesterday I saw a new play being put on, entitled *Peach Blossom Fan*, which concerned what happened around Nanjing in the last years of the Ming. It treated the emotions of separation and reunion, and it described how people felt about the splendor and ruin of men and kingdoms. The events really happened and the people were real ones; it was all accurate. I not only heard of these things, I saw them all with my own eyes. Even more amusing, I, now a frail old man, was actually put on the stage as one of the minor characters. This inspired tears, laughter, rage, and condemnation in me. And no one in the whole audience realized that I, just an old man to them, was really one of the persons in the play.

VOICE [*offstage*]   Who wrote this fine play?

OLD MAN   Don't you gentlemen know that the most famous playwrights don't reveal their names. But when you observe how he apportions praise and criticism, it must come from someone with a family tradition in the study of *The Springs and Autumns*; and its suitability for singing shows that the author clearly had family instruction in the *Classic of Poetry*.[5]

VOICE [*offstage*]   In that case it's obviously the Hermit of Yunting Mountain.[6]

OLD MAN   To whom are you referring?

VOICE [*offstage*]   There's going to be a gathering of the upper crust of officialdom, and they're going to have this very play performed. Since you're one of the characters in it and since you've also heard this new version, why don't you give us an outline of the plot beforehand, and we'll all listen carefully.

OLD MAN   It's all in the lyrics to "Fragrance Fills the Yard," sung by the Daoist Zhang Wei.

[*Sings*]

A young gentleman, Hou Fangyu,
sometime resident in Nanjing,
was matched with the Southland's fairest;
Harm worked unseen by vicious lies
in one night split this loving pair.

---

5. Confucian Classics. *The Spring and Autumn Annals* was reputedly written by Confucius, who was also credited with the compilation of the *Classic of Poetry*. Kong Shangren counted himself a descendant of Confucius in the sixty-fourth generation.

6. One of Kong Shangren's sobriquets.

They saw the world turned upside down,
the Jiang-Huai garrisons amok.
Next a blind prince took the throne,
choosing performers, his only concern,
while faction's ills raised wicked ministers.

Their bond of love could not continue:
she in her tower with martyr's ardor,
he in his dungeon, in deep despair.
They owed thanks to Liu and old Su[7]
whose earnest endeavors set them free.
At midnight ruler and minister fled,
who laments a loyal soul in misty waves?
And the peach blossom fan
shredded on the altar lay,
and I shall show you how they strayed.

VOICE [*offstage*]   Excellent! Excellent! But sometimes we couldn't quite understand you because of the ringing quality of the melody. Summarize it again
in a few lines.

OLD MAN   Let me try.

[*Recites*]

The traitors Ma and Ruan[8] lurked with swords
    both inside the court and out;
deft Liu and Su went back and forth
    seeking to tie the secret threads.
Young Hou Fangyu found true love's course
    broken beyond recall,
Zhang Wei the Daoist gave judgment
    on glory and the fall.

But here as I'm talking, Hou Fangyu has already come on stage. Let's all
watch.[9]

* * *

TEACHING THE SONG (II), APRIL 1643

Enter MADAM LI ZHENLI, *elegantly made up.*

LI [*sings*]
With dark-drawn brows, I do not close
the doors of this red mansion.
On Long Plank Bridge thin willow strands
flirt and draw the passing riders.
I tighten up the harp strings
and deftly work the mouth organ's pouch.

7. Su Kunsheng and Liu Jingting, who appear
later in the play.
8. The villains Ma Shiying and Ruan Dacheng.
9. In scene 2 we meet the heroine Xiangjun

("Fragrant Princess") who receives instruction
from her music teacher Su Kungsheng and a
marriage proposal through the painter Yang
Wencong.

[*Recites*]

Blooms of pear are like the snow,
    the grasses like a mist,
springtime comes to the Qin-Huai,
    here on both its shores.
Courtesans' parlors in a row
    look out on the waters,
and from each house reflections cast
    the fetching images of girls.

I am Li Zhenli, and I belong to the finest troupe of singers, to the most famous band of "misty flowers" and "moonlit breeze."[1] I was born and bred in the pleasure quarters, where I have welcomed clients and sent them on their way across Long Bridge. This face, with its powder and paint, has not yet lost its bloom, and ample charms remain to me. I have raised one adopted daughter, a tender and gentle little thing, just now beginning to take part in our elegant soirées; but in her shy grace, she has not yet gone behind the lotus bed curtains. There is hereabouts a retired country magistrate called Yang Wencong, who is the brother-in-law of Ma Shiying, the governor-general of Fengyang, and a sworn friend of Ruan Dacheng, the former head of the Court of Imperial Entertainments. On his frequent visits to my establishment, Yang has often praised my daughter and wants to arrange for a client to "do up her hair."[2] The spring weather is so bright and inviting today, I suspect he'll be here for a visit. [*Calls out*] Maid, open the curtains and sweep up, and keep your eye out to see if any visitors are coming.

VOICE [*offstage*] Yes, ma'am.

Enter YANG WENCONG.

YANG [*recites*]

Triple Mountain's scenery is
    a resource for my paintings,
the flair of Southern Dynasties
    courses through my poems.

I am Yang Wencong, a licentiate and former county magistrate who has retired from my post to live a quiet life. Li Zhenli, the famous courtesan of the Qin-Huai, is an old friend of mine, and I'm taking advantage of the spring weather to pay her a visit and have a chat. Here I am now. I'll be going in. [*Enters*] Where's the lady? [*Greets her*] Splendid! See how the petals of the plum have fallen and the fronds of the willows are turning yellow.

1. Metaphors for romantic love.
2. That is, to deflower her. In the case of a young courtesan-to-be of exceptional beauty and talent—like Fragrant Princess—this was an honor for which young men would eagerly vie. If the process led to a more enduring attachment, there was the possibility that the young man might purchase the girl's freedom from her adoptive mother (the madam of the house) and install her as his wife or secondary wife. This is what indeed happens to Hou Fangyu and Fragrant Princess. The vows of fidelity and plans to marry are to be taken as serious intentions. Their union, however, was not regarded by others as totally binding.

Soft and rich in color, spring's beauty is everywhere in the yard, which makes me wonder how we may best spend these moments.

LI It is lovely indeed. Come to the little room upstairs. I'll burn some incense and put on some tea, and we can read over some poems.

YANG Even better! [*They climb stairs. He recites*]
> Curtain stripes seem to cage the bird on its perch,
> flowers' shadows seem to guard the fish in its bowl.

These are your daughter's apartments. Where is she?

LI She hasn't yet finished dressing; she's still in the bedroom.

YANG Ask her to come out.

LI [*calling out*] Come out, child. Mr. Yang is here.

YANG [*reading the poems on her walls*] How remarkable! These are all poems inscribed to her by well-known figures! [*He clasps his hands behind his back and recites them*]

Enter HEROINE, *splendidly made up.*

HEROINE [*sings*]
> Just now called back from sweetest dreams,
> I threw off red coverlets
>> broidered with mated ducks.
> I put on lipstick and glossy rouge
> and hastily did my hair
>> in a ponytail with straying tresses.
> What relief is there for spring's moodiness?—
> just learning new lyrics for songs.

[*Greets* YANG] Good-day, sir!

YANG You have grown even more stunning in these past few days since I saw you last. These poems are not at all wrong in their praise of you. [*Reads on and registers surprise*] Well, look at this! Such prominent figures as Zhang Pu and Xia Yunyi have both written poems to you. I really must write you a poem of my own, using their rhymes. [LI ZHENLI *brings him a brush and inkstone.* YANG *takes the brush in hand and mulls over it a long time, as if ready to recite*] I can't do as well as them; I might as well hide my weaknesses by decorating your white wall here with a few black-ink drawings of orchids.

LI That's even better!

YANG [*looking at the wall*] Here's a rock like a fist painted by Lan Ying. I can use his painting as a background and draw my orchids over at the side of the rock. [*Paints and sings*]
> The white wall glows
>> like rippling silk,
> Here I sketch the *Lisao's*
>> poetic temper.[3]

---

3. Orchids were associated, in their solitary purity, with Qu Yuan, the virtuous minister who did not find a ruler who would appreciate his worth and in despair committed suicide.

> Tender leaves and scented sheaths,
> rain-burdened, drunk in streaks of mist.
> This rock of Xuanzhou, ink-flowers shattered,
> with several spots of gray moss,
>   tingeing the pavements randomly.

[*Goes back and looks at it*] Not bad!

> No match, of course, for black-ink orchids
>   done by masters of the Yuan,
>   that mood of nonchalance,
> but our own famous beauties should wear
>   Xiang orchids at their waists.

LI   This is truly the brushwork of a master. You have added much beauty to our apartments.

YANG   You're making fun of me. [*To* HEROINE] Tell me your professional name so that I can write it here in the dedication.

HEROINE   I'm still young and don't have a professional name yet.

LI   Why don't you do her the honor of giving her a name?

YANG   There is a passage in *The Zuo Tradition*:[4] "And because [the] orchid has the sweetest smell in all the land, people will wear it in their sashes and be fond of it." Why don't we call her Xiangjun, "Queen of Sweet Fragrance"?

LI   Excellent! Xiangjun, come over and thank Mr. Yang.

XIANGJUN [*bowing*]   Thank you very much, sir.

YANG [*laughing*]   We even have a name for these chambers. [*Writes the dedication*] "In mid-spring, this sixteenth year of the Chongzhen Reign, 1643, I chanced to draw these orchids in ink in the Chambers of Beguiling Fragrance to win a smile from Xiangjun, who is Queen of Sweet Fragrance. Yang Wencong of Guiyang."

LI   Both the paintings and the calligraphy are superb, worthy of acclaim as a double perfection. Thank you so much! [*All sit*]

YANG   As I see it, Xiangjun here may be the most beautiful woman in the land, but I don't know her level of skill in the arts.

LI   She has always been spoiled and allowed to have her own way, so she didn't study anything. But just recently I've asked one of the habitués of the pleasure quarters to give her lessons in singing.

YANG   Who is it?

LI   Someone called Su Kunsheng.

YANG   Yes, Su Kunsheng. His real name is Zhou Rusong, originally from Henan and now a resident of Wuxi. I have known him well for some time— he is a true master. What suites of songs has he taught her?

LI   The "Four Dream Plays" of Tang Xianzu.[5]

YANG   How much of them has she learned?

LI   She's just now learned half of *Peony Pavilion*. [*Calls to* XIANGJUN] Child, Mr. Yang here is no stranger to us. Get out your score and practice some of the songs you know. After your teacher quizzes you, you can try some new tunes.

---

4. Important commentary to the Confucian classic *The Spring and Autumn Annals*.

5. Outstanding dramatist of the preceding Ming Period.

XIANGJUN   How can I practice my singing with a guest present?

LI   Don't be silly! For those of us in the quarter the costume for singing and dancing is the endowment that provides us our food. How are you going to get by if you won't practice singing? [XIANGJUN *looks at her score*]

LI *[sings]*

> When born among bevies of powder and paint,
> and entering blossom and oriole troupes,
> a throat that can carry an aria
> is the place where we find our wealth.
> Don't lightly throw your heart away,
> but study "The early morning wind
>   and dying moonlight sinking";
> then with red clapper's slow beat,
> from Yichun performers you'll steal the glow,[6]
> and tied before your gate will be seen
>   horses of princes.

Enter SU KUNSHENG, *wearing a headband and in informal dress.*

SU *[recites]*

> Idly I come to azure lodges
>   to train my parakeet,
> lazily leaving vermilion gates
>   to see the peonies.

I am Su Kunsheng. I've left Ruan Dacheng's levee to come here to the pleasure quarters. Taking this beautiful girl through her lessons is certainly a lot better than toadying to that foster child of a eunuch. [*Goes in and greets them*] Well, Yang Wencong, fancy meeting you here. It's been some time.

YANG   My compliments, Kunsheng, on taking such a stunning beauty as a pupil.

LI   Your teacher, Mr. Su, is here. Go pay him the proper welcome, child.

XIANGJUN *bows.*

SU   No need for that. Have you memorized thoroughly the song I taught you yesterday?

XIANGJUN   I have.

SU   We'll take advantage of Mr. Yang's presence as our audience to ask him for pointers as you go over it with me.

YANG   I just want you to show me how it should be performed.

XIANGJUN *[seated opposite* SU, *sings]*[7]

> Coy lavenders, fetching reds
>   bloom everywhere, here
>   all given to this broken well

---

6. Yichun Palace was the site of the "Pear Garden Academy" of imperial musicians and singers during the early 8th century of the Tang Dynasty.

7. Aria from Tang Xianzu's most famous play, *The Peony Pavilion.*

and tumbled wall. Fair season,
>fine scene, overwhelming
>weather . . .

SU   Wrong! Wrong! "Fair" gets a beat and "overwhelming" gets a beat; don't
run the two clauses together. Let's try it again.

XIANGJUN

Fair season,
>fine scene—overwhelming
weather. Where
and in whose garden shall we find
pleasure and the heart's delight?
Drifting in at dawn, at twilight
>roll away
clouds and colored wisps
>through azure balustrades
streaming rain, petals in wind . . .

SU   No, that's not right again. "Streaming" carries a special weight in the
melody; it should be sung from the diaphragm.

XIANGJUN

streaming rain, petals in wind,
a painted boat in misty waves,
the girl behind her brocade screen
>has seen but dimly
>such splendor of spring.

SU   Excellent! Excellent! Exactly right! Let's go on.

XIANGJUN

Throughout green hills the nightjar cries
>its tears of blood; and out beyond
the blackberry the threads
>of mist coil drunkenly.
And though the peony be fair,
how can it maintain its sway
>when spring is leaving?

SU   These lines are a bit rough. Try them again.

XIANGJUN

And though the peony be fair,
how can it maintain its sway
>when spring is leaving?
Idly I stare
where twittering swallows crisply speak
>words cut clear,
and from the warbling orioles comes
>a bright and liquid melody.

SU   Fine! Now you've completed another suite of songs.

YANG [to LI ZHENLI]   I'm pleased to see that your daughter is so quick. I have no
doubt she will become a famous courtesan. [To SU] I met young Hou Fangyu

the other day, the son of Hou, the executive in the Ministry of Revenue. He is well provided for, and he also is known for his talent. At present he is looking for a woman of distinguished beauty. Do you know him, Kunsheng?

SU Our families are from the same region. He is, indeed, a young man of great talent.

YANG We'd be making no mistake if we arranged a union between these two.

[Sings]

Fair match for our Sapphire,[8] now sixteen:
she sings charming songs,
he rides a sleek horse.
He will lavish her with turban brocades,[9]
and hand in hand they will drain their cups.
Wedding poems will speed them to bed,
a lacquered coach to greet the bride.
With a rare young noble as her mate,
year after year she will never let
    her Ruan Zhao go away,
by the spring waters of Peach Leaf Ford
    he will buy a cottage and stay.[1]

LI It would be just wonderful if such a young gentleman were willing to come "do up her hair." I hope you will do what you can to help in bringing this match about.

YANG It is on my mind.

LI [sings]

No pearl can compare to this girl of mine,
who mimics the new oriole's sweet cries,
in springtime closed behind many gates,
    never known by man.

We can't waste such a glorious spring day. Let's go have a little wine downstairs.

YANG Sounds good to me. [Recites]
In front of Little Su's[2] curtain,
    flowers fill the meadow,

LI

orioles tipsy, swallows languid
    across the springtime banks.

XIANGJUN

In my red silk handkerchief
    are fruits of cherry,

8. The legendary concubine of a Southern prince during the Period of Disunion.
9. Brocade used for turbans was the standard figure for gifts and payment to a courtesan.
1. The story of Ruan Zhao and Liu Zhen's encounter with two immortals became a standard figure for losing oneself in a love affair.

"Peach Leaf" was a famous concubine during the Period of Disunion; "Peach Leaf Ford" was on the Qin-Huai River, in the area of the pleasure quarters of Nanjing.
2. A famous courtesan during the Period of Disunion.

SU

> waiting for Pan Yue's carriage
> to pass west of the lane.[3]

*   *   *

REFUSING THE TROUSSEAU (VII), MAY 1643

Enter SERVANT, *picking up the nightstools.*

SERVANT

> Tortoise piss, tortoise piss
> spews out little tortoises,
> blood of turtle, blood of turtle
> turns to little turtles fertile.
> Tortoise piss and turtle blood,
> whose is whose I cannot guess;
> turtle blood and tortoise piss,
> can't say if it's that or this.
> Whose is whose I cannot guess,
> can't say who the father is;
> who can tell one from another?—
> can't say who's the father's brother.

[*Laughing*] *Tsk, tsk, tsk.* Last night Miss Xiangjun lost her virginity, and the hoopla went on half the night. I got up early today and have to scrub out the nightstools and empty the chamberpots. There's so much to get done. I wonder how much longer the client and our girl are going to spend in each other's arms. [*Scrubs the nightstools*]

Enter YANG WENCONG.

YANG [*sings*]

> They spend nights deep in willow lanes
> of Pingkang Ward,[4]
> and outside the gate a flower peddler
> wakes them suddenly from dreams.
> The finely wrought door still unopened,
> and the curtain hooks are tinkling,
> with spring blocked off by ten layers
> of hanging lace.

I've come early to offer Hou Fangyu my congratulations, but as you can see, the door to the establishment is closed tight and there's not a sound from the servants. I suppose they haven't gotten up yet. [*Calls out*] You, boy, go over to the newlyweds' window and tell them that I've come to offer my congratulations.

---

3. Pan Yue was a 3rd-century poet renowned for his exceptional handsomeness; women would pelt his carriage with flowers and fruits when he rode in the capital.

4. Pleasure quarter of the Tang Dynasty capital Chang'an.

SERVANT They got to sleep rather late last night, and they may not have gotten up yet. Why don't you come again tomorrow, sir.

YANG [*laughing*] Don't be silly. Quick, now, go find out!

LI [*from within*] Boy, who's that who just came?

SERVANT It's Yang Wencong, who's come to offer his congratulations.

LI [*enters hurriedly, recites*]

> Head rests on pillow, spring nights too brief,
> but good often comes from a knock at the gate.

[*Greets* YANG] Thank you so much for bringing about this lifelong union for my daughter.

YANG Think nothing of it. Have the newlyweds risen yet?

LI They went to sleep late last night and still haven't gotten up yet. [*Gestures to* YANG *to sit*] Please have a seat while I go hurry them up.

YANG There's no need for that.

Exit LI ZHENLI.

YANG [*sings*]

> Young passion is heady like flower wine,
> so fine that they think of nothing else
> but to share that sweet black land of sleep.

Which would have been impossible, of course, failing my help.
> Pearls and kingfisher feathers gleam,
> silks and satins ripple and rustle,
> each and every item of new attire
> is proclamation of love's desire.

Enter LI ZHENLI.

LI It's so charming. They're both in there buttoning each other up and looking in the mirror to see how they look as a pair. They've finished combing and washing up, but they're not through with getting dressed. Let's go into their rooms together and call them out to drink a cup of wine to help their hangover.

YANG It was unforgivable of me to have woken them. [*Exeunt*]

Enter HOU FANGYU *and* XIANGJUN, *fully made up.*

HOU *and* XIANGJUN [*sing*]

> Passion's cloud joining
>   to cloudburst and rain
> scratches a wondrous itch in the heart—
> who now disturbs the sleeping pair
>   of mated ducks?
> Blankets heaved in waves of red,
> as we joyously took full measure
>   of all love's pleasure.
> A lingering scent on the pillow,
> a lingering scent on the handkerchief,
> sensations that melt the rapturous soul
> tasted now as we rise from dream.

Enter YANG WENCONG *and* LI ZHENLI.

YANG   Well, you've gotten up at last. Congratulations. [*He bows, then sits*] Did you like the wedding night verse I wrote for you yesterday evening?

HOU [*bowing*]   Thank you very much. [*Laughs*] It was the height of excellence—except for one little point . . .

YANG   What little point?

HOU   However tiny Xiangjun may be, she deserves to be kept in a chamber of gold, but [*looks in his sleeves*] how would I get her in my sleeves?[5]

All laugh.

YANG   I'm sure you also must have written something fine last night when you two declared your love.

HOU   I just scribbled out something hastily—I wouldn't dare show you.

YANG   And where is the poem?

XIANGJUN   The poem is on the fan.

XIANGJUN *takes the fan out of her sleeve and gives it to*
YANG WENCONG, *who looks it over.*

YANG   It's a white satin palace fan. [*Sniffs it*] And it has a subtle aroma. [*Recites the poem*]
"Blue mansions line the road,
    a single path slants through,
here the prince first drives
    the Count of Fuping's coach.
Everywhere upon Blue Creek
    there are magnolia trees—
no match for blooms of peach and plum
    in the east wind of spring."[6]

Excellent! Only Xiangjun would not be put to shame by this poem. [*Hands it back to* XIANGJUN] Take care of it. [XIANGJUN *puts away the fan.* YANG *sings*]
Scent of peach and scent of plum,
    fragrance at its sweetest,
all written on a satin fan.
Lest they meet the tossing gusts
    of wild winds,
hide it close within your sleeve,
hide it close within your sleeve.

[*Looks at* XIANGJUN] After her wedding night, Xiangjun seems to have an even more sensual beauty. [*To* HOU FANGYU] You're a lucky man to enjoy this splendid creature.

HOU   Xiangjun's natural beauty makes her the fairest in the land, but the pearl and kingfisher ornaments that she wears in her hair today and all her

---

5. The Han Dynasty emperor Wudi said that if he could get Ajiao as his consort, he would keep her in a chamber of gold. Hou Fangyu is referring to a line in Yang's poem in which she would be "hidden in his sleeves," suggesting an embrace rather than Hou Fangyu's joking interpretation.

6. The poem is not repeated in this act, but it is included from scene 6. The poem is, in fact, a variation on one by the historical Hou Fangyu. The praise of "peach and plum" over the magnolia plays on Xiangjun's surname, Li, which is the word for "plum." Peach blossoms will play an even larger role in the play.

silken finery add something extra to her utterly flowerlike beauty. She is entirely lovable.

LI   This is all thanks to Mr. Yang's assistance.

[*Sings*]

> He sent the turbans of brocade,
>   the chests of varied gems,
>   fringed curtains wound with pearls
>   and kingfisher feathers, silver
>   candlesticks, shades of gauze
>   shining through the night,
>   golden cups for offering wine
>   to go along with song at feasts.

> And now he has come to see you so early today.
>   As though you were his very own
>   children he raised himself,
>   first providing the needed trousseau,
>   now also paying this early call.

XIANGJUN   It seems to me, Mr. Yang, that even though you're a close relative of the governor-general, Ma Shiying, you are in rather difficult financial circumstances yourself and live on the goodwill of others; why should you so casually throw away your money into the bottomless pit of the pleasure quarters? For my own part, I am embarrassed to receive it; and on your side, it was given anonymously. Please make things clear to us so that we can plan how to repay such generosity.

HOU   Xiangjun is quite right to ask this. You and I have met like duckweeds drifting on the water; your show of kindness the other day was so generous that I feel uncomfortable.

YANG   Since I have been asked, I can only tell you the truth. The trousseau and the party cost somewhat over two hundred pieces of silver, and all of it came from a gentleman from Huaining.

HOU   Who from Huaining?

YANG   Ruan Yuanhai, who was the head of the Court of Imperial Entertainments.

HOU   Do you mean Ruan Dacheng from Anhui?

YANG   That's right.

HOU   Why has he been so lavish?

YANG   He simply wants to become acquainted with you.

[*Sings*]

> He admires your prospects and panache,
> your name for talent like Luoyang's Zuo Si,
> your writings like those of Sima Xiangru.
> Wherever you go, you find welcome;
> all crowd around the young man in the coach.[7]

---

7. Reference, again, to Pan Yue.

> In the finest spots of the Qin-Huai
> you sought a fair maiden for your side,
> but you lacked the spread for the marriage bed
>   and lotus make-up.

You wonder who did this—
>   the senior Ruan of the southern branch[8]
>   put himself out for your wedding apparel.

HOU   Ruan Dacheng was an acquaintance of my father's, but I despise him and have had nothing to do with him for a long time. I can't understand this unexpected show of generosity to me now.

YANG   Ruan Dacheng has a problem that troubles him and he would like to put it before you.

HOU   Please explain.

YANG   Ruan Dacheng used to be associated with Zhao Nanxing and was one of our own.[9] When he later became associated with the faction of Wei Zhongxian, the eunuch, it was only to protect the East Grove faction.[1] He had no idea that once the Wei Zhongxian faction was defeated, the East Grove faction would treat him like an arch enemy. Members of the Restoration Society have recently advocated attacking him, and they viciously beat up and humiliated him. This is a fight within the same household. Even though Ruan Dacheng has many former associates, no one will try to explain his side of the story because his actions were so dubious. Every day he weeps toward Heaven, saying, "It is painful to be so savaged by one's own group. No one but Hou Fangyu of Henan can save me." This is the reason that he now seeks so earnestly to make your acquaintance.

HOU   Well, in this case I can see why he feels such anguish, and it seems to me that he deserves some pity. Even if he had really been a member of Wei Zhongxian's faction, he's come around again and is sorry for his mistakes. One shouldn't ostracize him so absolutely, and even less if there's an explanation for what he did. Dingsheng and Ciwei are both close friends of mine. I'll go see them tomorrow and try to resolve this.

YANG   It would be a great blessing for us if you would do this.

XIANGJUN [angrily]   What are you saying! Ruan Dacheng rushed to join the corrupt men in power and lost all sense of shame. There is not a grown woman or young girl who would not spit on him and curse him. If you try to save him when others attack him, what camp will you be putting yourself in?

[Sings]

> You aren't thinking
> when you speak like this so frivolously.

---

8. This refers to the 3rd-century poet Ruan Ji, to whom Ruan Dacheng is, somewhat outrageously, compared. Ruan Ji belonged to the "Seven Sages of the Bamboo Grove," an iconoclastic coterie of eccentric poets and drinkers.
9. Zhao Nanxing had been a senior Ming official who was unjustly denounced and sent into exile by the Wei Zhongxian faction.

1. The East Grove Society was a group of late Ming intellectuals dedicated to reforming the Ming government through a revival of ancient learning and literature. They opposed Wei Zhongxian and his secret police. After they were purged, a successor group, the Restoration Society, was formed.

> You want to rescue him from ruin,
> you want to rescue him from ruin,
> but beware lest the judgment fall on you.

The only reason you're going to speak for him is because he provided my trousseau; that is disregarding the common good and selling oneself for private benefit. Don't you realize that I find all these bangles and hairpins and skirts and gowns beneath contempt. [*She pulls out hairpins and takes off gown*]

> I take off these skirts,
> accepting poverty;
> in homespun and simple adornments
> a person's name smells sweet.[2]

YANG You're being far too hot-tempered, Xiangjun.

LI What a pity to throw away such fine things on the floor! [*She picks them up*]

HOU Splendid! Her judgment in this matter is better than mine. I truly stand in awe of her. [*To* YANG] Please don't think ill of me in this. It's not that I wouldn't accept your suggestion, but I fear the scorn of women.

[*Sings*]

> In the pleasure quarters' lanes
> they can lecture on principle and good name;
> while school and court,
> while school and court
> confuse virtue and vice,
>   and cannot tell black from white.

My friends in the Restoration Society have always held me in esteem because of my sense of right. But if I associate myself with someone who is corrupt, they will all rise and attack me; and I won't have a chance to save myself, not to mention someone else.

> Principles and good name
> are no common things;
> one must consider carefully
> what is serious and what is negligible.

YANG Considering Ruan Dacheng's goodwill, you shouldn't act so drastically.

HOU I may be foolish, but I'm not going to throw myself in a well to save someone else.

YANG In that case, I will take my leave.

HOU All these things in the chests belong to Ruan Dacheng. Since Xiangjun has no use for them, there's no point in keeping them, so would you have them taken away?

YANG As the couplet goes:

> One full of feeling finds himself
>   upset by lack of feeling,

---

2. In this line Xiangjun is playing on her name, "Lady of Sweet Fragrance."

> I came here following my whim;
>> the whim done, I return. [*Exit*]

XIANGJUN *shows herself upset.*

HOU [*looking at* XIANGJUN]   When I look at your natural beauty, pulling out a few pearls and feathers and taking off your fine silken gown, your perfect beauty is doubled in its perfection, and I think you are even more lovable.

LI   Whatever you say, it's still too bad to give up so many fine things.

[*Sings*]

> Gold and pearls come to you,
>> you carelessly throw them away;
> these spoiled and childish poses betray
> all my hard efforts to sponsor you.

HOU   These things aren't worth brooding over. I'll make the loss good in kind.

LI   Then it will be all right.

[*Recites*]

> The money spent on powder and paint
>> costs some consideration,

XIANGJUN

>> homespun skirts and hairpins of twig
>> do not bother me.

HOU

>> What matters is our Xiang Princess
>> could take off her pendants,[3]

XIANGJUN

>> the standard of taste does not follow
>> the fashions of the times.

*   *   *

SENDING THE FAN (XXIII), JANUARY 1645

Enter XIANGJUN, *looking ill, her head wrapped with a kerchief as bandage.*

XIANGJUN [*sings*]

> These icy silks pierced through
>> by wind's harsh chill,
> the heart too dull
>> to light the scented brazier.
> The single thread of blood, here
>> at the tip of brow,
> is a more becoming red than red of rouge.
> My lonely shadow stands in fear,

---

3. When ancient goddesses, such as Lady Xiang (*Xiangjun*, punning on Xiangjun's name, though written with different characters), take off their pendants, it is usually the sign of plighting troth with a man; here it seems to refer to Xiangjun's stripping away her ornaments in rejecting the trousseau.

a weak soul tossed about, my life
suspended as by a spring floss strand.
A frosty moonlight fills the upper rooms,
    the nighttime stretches on and on,
and daylight will not melt this pain.

[Sits]   In a moment when I had no other choice, I inflicted wounds on my
own flesh as the only way to save myself. By doing so I managed to keep
my honor intact. But now I lie here, sick and alone in these empty rooms,
under cold blankets within chilly bed curtains, with no companion. It's so
cold and lonely here.

Freezing clouds and patchy snow
    block Long Bridge,
the red mansions are closed up tight,
    and men seeking pleasure, few.
Low beyond the balcony the lines of geese
    write signs in the skies,
and from the curtained windows
    icicles hang;
the charcoal chills, the incense burns away,
and I grow gaunt
    in the sharp evening wind.

Though I live here in the blue mansions of the pleasure quarters, all scenes
of love and passion are finished for me from now on.
Past patterned doors winds wail,
the parrot calls for tea, its skill
    displayed for its pleasure alone;
the chambers are still,
the snow white cat hugs the pillow
    sound asleep.
My skirt, pomegranate red,
    ripped to shreds,
        waist dancing in wind,
and phoenix-decorated boots,
    slit to pieces
        the wave-pacing soles;
with sorrow's increase sickness grows,
never again will these chambers allow
    the turmoil of passion.

I think back on when Hou Fangyu had to flee for his life in such haste, and
now I don't know where he's gone. How can he know that I am living here
alone in this empty house, protecting my honor for his sake?

[Rises and sings]

I recall how in an instant
    all thrill of charming song was swept away,
at midnight passion's flood forsaken;
I look for him at Peach Leaf Ford,

I seek him out by Swallow Jetty—
just hills with roiling clouds
    where winds blow high,
        and wild geese faint and far.
Who would have thought
    that though the plums will bloom again
        reliably,
the man would be still farther away?
I lean on the balcony
    and concentrate my gaze,
but autumn floods from lovely eyes
are frozen hard by sour wind.

It enrages me how the servants of that evil man crowded into my gate and insisted that I get married. How could I ever betray Hou Fangyu?

They took advantage of a courtesan
    whose fate is fragile, not her own;
their awful arrogance depended on
    the Minister's authority.
To keep this alabaster body pure
I could not help rending
these features like flower.

The saddest thing of all is how my mother sacrificed herself for my sake and was whisked away. [*Points*] See her bed there as it always was, but when will she come back?

Just like a petal of peach,
    borne on snow-capped billows,
or floss of willow, tossed in wind;
her sleeves hid a face like the breeze of spring,
as she left the court of Han at dusk.[4]
Such loneliness—the dust
    that covers her quilt
        not brushed away;
a silence where a flower bloomed,
    which I admire alone.

A rush of sourness catches me unawares when I consider this.

It seems to goad me in the heart,
so many teardrops spilled.
No girlfriends call me away
    to idle pastimes,
I listen to the clack of hooks
    hanging from the curtain.

---

4. Li Zhenli's forced marriage (in Xiangjun's place) is here compared to the situation of the Han concubine Wang Zhaojun who was, tragically, sent as a gift to the northern Xiongnu tribes to serve as a bride to their chieftain.

Sitting here with nothing to do, I'll take out the fan with Hou Fangyu's poem and look at it. [*She takes out fan*] Oh no! It's ruined, stained all over with drops of my blood. What am I going to do?

> Look at them—some far apart,
>   some thick together,
> dark spots and pale,
> with fresh blood haphazardly stained.
> Not sprinkled from the nightjar's tears,
> these are the peach blooms of my cheeks
>   turned to a red rain,
> falling speck after speck, splattering
>   the icy silk.

Oh Hou Fangyu! This was all for you.

> You caused me to dishevel
>   hair's cloudy coils
> and mar my slender waist;
> Senseless I lay like the Consort
>   on Mawei's slope interred;[5]
> my blood streamed like the concubine
>   who leapt from tower's heights.[6]
> I feared the shouts of those below
> and left my too frail soul uncalled.
> In silver mirror, afterglow
>   of scarlet cloud,
> and on the lovers' pillow,
>   red tears in spring flood.
> In the heart a rancor sprouts,
> and melancholy sits upon the brows,
> I washed away the rouge,
> that stained the seafolk gauze.

I feel a weariness coming over me. I'll doze here a moment at my dressing table. [*Falls asleep on the fan*]

> Enter YANG WENCONG *in everyday clothes.*

YANG [*recites*]
> I recognize this red mansion
>   that slants on the water's face,
> a row of dying willows
>   bearing the last of the crows.

---

5. Reference to Yang Guifei ("Yang the Prized Consort"), the woman with whom Emperor Xuanzong of the Tang became infatuated and whose death was demanded by the army when rebellion broke out. A riveting account of their tragic love affair—*Song of Lasting Regret*—was written by the Tang poet Bo Juyi.

6. Green Pearl, the concubine of the fabulously wealthy Shi Chong, threw herself from a tower rather than be taken from him by a powerful enemy.

Enter SU KUNSHENG.

SU [*recites*]

> The silver harp and castanets,
>> a lovely maiden's yard,
> now with wind-blown snow the same
>> as the home of a recluse.

YANG [*turning his head and greeting him*]   Ah! Good to see you, Mr. Su.

SU   After Li Zhenli got married, Xiangjun has been living alone. I can't stop worrying about her, so I always come by to visit.

YANG   The day that Li Zhenli had to go, I stayed with Xiangjun the entire night, but I've been so busy at the office these past few days that I haven't been able to get away. Just now I was going to the eastern part of the city to pay a visit, and I thought I'd look in on her.

They enter her apartments.

SU   Xiangjun won't come downstairs, so why don't we go upstairs to talk to her.

YANG   Fine. [*They climb stairs.* YANG *points*] Look how depressed and sickly Xiangjun seems, all worn out dozing there at her dressing table. Let's not wake her up for a while.

SU   Her fan is spread out here by her face. Why does it have so many splotches of red?

YANG   This was Hou Fangyu's wedding gift to her. She has always kept it hidden and wasn't willing to show it. I imagine she's left it out here to dry because it got stained with blood from her face. [*Pulls away fan and looks at it*] These spots of blood are a gorgeous red! I'll add some branches and leaves and decorate it for her. [*Thinks*] But I don't have any green paint.

SU   I'll pick some of these plants in the flowerpots and squeeze fresh sap from them—that can serve in place of paint.

YANG   An excellent idea. [SU KUNSHENG *squeezes plants and* YANG *paints and recites*]

> The leaves share the green of aromatic plants,
> the blooms draw their red from a lady fair.

The painting is finished. SU KUNSHENG *looks at it with delight.*

SU   Superb! It's some broken sprays of peach blossoms.

YANG [*laughing*]   It's a true peach blossom fan.

XIANGJUN [*waking startled*]   Mr. Yang, Mr. Su, I'm glad to see you both. Please forgive me. [*She invites them to sit down*]

YANG   During these past few days when I haven't come to look in on you, the wound on your forehead has gotten better. [*Laughs*] I have a painted fan here that I would like to present to you. [*Hands fan to* XIANGJUN]

XIANGJUN [*looking at it*]   This is my old fan that was ruined by bloodstains! I can't even look at it. [*Puts it in her sleeve*]

SU   But there's some marvelous painting on it—how can you not take a look and admire it?

XIANGJUN   When was this painting done?

YANG   It's my fault. I've just ruined it.

XIANGJUN [*looks at the fan and sighs*]   Ah! The unhappy fate of peach blossoms, tossed and fallen on this fan. Thank you, Mr. Yang, for painting my own portrait in this.

[*Sings*]

Every blossom breaks the heart,
lazily smiling in springtime breeze;
every petal melts the soul,
sadly swirled in the current.
Fetching colors freshly picked,
drawn from nature;
even old masters like Xu Xi[7]
could hardly have painted these.
Vermilion's tint is mixed on cherry lips,
first sketch made on lotus cheeks,
then in a few strokes, red peach blooms,
    depicting the truth within.
You added some azure twigs and leaves,
remarkably fresh and fair,
and of an unfortunate woman
    drew the portrait in blooms of peach.

YANG   Now that you have this peach blossom fan, you need a companion like Zhou Yu to notice you and appreciate you.[8] Do you really mean to live here as a widow in the spring of your life like Chang E in the moon?

XIANGJUN   Don't go on like this. Guan Panpan was also a courtesan, and didn't she stay locked up in Swallow Tower until old age?[9]

SU   If Hou Fangyu were to come back tomorrow, wouldn't you come down from your tower then?

XIANGJUN   In that case I'd have a glorious married life ahead and would enjoy everything. I wouldn't just come down from my tower, I'd want to go roaming everywhere.

YANG   We don't often see such a long-suffering sense of honor these days. [*To* SU KUNSHENG] Mr. Su, I would feel a lot less worried if you would go find Hou Fangyu and bring him back here, out of the affection of a teacher for his student.

SU   Yes, I've had it in mind to go visit him for some time now, and I've found out that he served on the Huai for half a year with Shi Kefa, then from the Huai he came to Nanjing, and from Nanjing he went to Yangzhou. Now he's gone off again with the army of General Gao Jie to defend the Yellow River. I was going to go back to my hometown soon, and on the way I can go look for him when I have the chance. [*To* XIANGJUN] It would be a good idea if I had a letter from you.

7. A famous 10th-century painter of flowers and vegetation.
8. Literally, "a young master Zhou to pay attention to the tune," referring to Zhou Yu, the admiral of the fleet of the state of Wu during the Three Kingdoms Period (220–280 C.E.), who was said to have had a particularly fine ear for music.
9. Panpan, the concubine of a powerful Tang Dynasty military governor, refused to remarry after his death. Although such behavior was considered proper for first wives, it was an unusual sign of devotion on the part of a concubine.

XIANGJUN [*to* YANG WENCONG]   My words come out without literary polish. Would you write for me Mr. Yang?

YANG   Just tell me how to write what is in your heart.

XIANGJUN   Just let me think a moment . . . [*Thinks*] No, no! All my griefs and sufferings are on the fan, so take the fan with you.

SU [*delighted*]   Well, this is a whole new style in personal letters.

XIANGJUN   Wait while I wrap it up. [*Wraps up fan, then sings*]:
> He plied the brush's silvery hairs
>   and will know these lines he wrote before.
> Specks stain the red marks of the dice—
>   newly painted, hold it fast.
> For though the fan be small,
>   it has heart's blood, ten thousand streaks;
> wrapped up in my handkerchief,
>   with hair ribbon wound about,
> saying much more than palindrome brocade.[1]

SU [*taking the fan*]   I'll take good care of it and deliver it for you.

XIANGJUN   When are you going to leave?

SU   I'll get my things ready in the next few days.

XIANGJUN   I just hope that you'll set out soon.

SU   All right.

YANG   Let's go downstairs now. [*To* XIANGJUN] Take good care of yourself. When we tell Hou Fangyu of the hardships you have endured to stay true to him, he will naturally come to get you.

SU   I won't be back before I leave. As they say, [*recites*]
> A new letter sent afar:
>   the peach blossom fan,

YANG [*capping couplet*]
> a yard forever shut up tight:
>   the Tower of the Swallows.[2] [*Exeunt*]

XIANGJUN [*wiping away tears*]   Mama hasn't returned and now my teacher is going away too. It's going to be even more lonely closed up here in my room.

[*Sings*]

> The warbler's throat has done with
>   melodies of North and South,
> the icy strings have given up
>   tunes of Sui and Chen,
> my lips will no more play the pipes,
> the flute is thrown aside,
> the mouth organ is broken,
> and castanets are cast away.
> I wish only the fan's swift delivery,
> that my teacher be ready to set off soon;

---

1. Su Hui famously sent a palindrome woven into brocade to her husband, both to express her love and to call him home.

2. Place where Panpan shut herself up after the death of her lover, the military governor.

Let my young Liu come on the third of May,
then hand in hand we'll come down from the tower,
and eat our fill of peach blossom gruel.[3]

[*Recites*]

The letter will reach the garden of Liang
    ere the snow has melted,
when the path along Blue Creek
    will be blocked by springtime floods.
Peach Root and Peach Leaf
    are visited by none,
by Dingzi Curtain[4]
    there is a broken bridge.

* * *

From "ACCEPTING THE WAY" (XL), SEPTEMBER 1645

Enter BIAN YUJING, *leading* XIANGJUN.

BIAN YUJING   The greatest joy in Heaven and among mortal men comes from doing good. We and a group of Daoist nuns have just strung up votive banners before the altar to Empress Zhou, and now we come to the lecture hall to listen to the abbot's sermon.

XIANGJUN   May I just come along?

BIAN YUJING [*pointing*]   See all the Daoists and laypersons in the two side porches; there are too many to count, so there shouldn't be any problem with you watching. [BIAN *bows before the altar*] Your disciple Bian Yujing prostrates herself. [*Together with* XIANGJUN, *she stands back to one side*]

Enter DING JIZHI.

DING JIZHI   Hard to be born in human form, hard to learn of the Way. [*He bows before the altar*] Your disciple Ding Jizhi prostrates himself. [*Calls out*] Hou Fangyu! This is the lecture hall. To come here will bring you joy.

Enter HOU FANGYU *hurriedly.*

HOU   Here I am. Long weary of the sufferings of the secular world, I now see the path that can lead to immortality. [*Stands back to one side with* DING JIZHI]

ZHANG WEI [*hitting his lectern*]   You good folk listening in the wings, you should abandon your worldly hearts utterly, for only then can you seek the path that will lead you upward. If you still have even a grain of base passion, you will have to endure a thousand more revolutions of the karmic cycle.

HOU [*looks at* XIANGJUN *from behind the fan and is startled*]   That's Xiangjun standing over there. How did she come to be here? [*He pushes forward urgently*]

XIANGJUN [*sees him and is startled*]   Hou Fangyu, I almost died of longing for you.

3. Reference here is to Liu Zhen. This was a custom for the so-called "Cold Food Festival" in the ancient city of Luoyang.

4. A spot in the Nanjing pleasure quarters. "Peach Root": the sister of Peach Leaf, the famous courtesan.

[*Sings*]

I think back on how you abruptly left me,
faint and far
    across the silvery River of Stars
        no bridge could span,
a barrier higher than
    the very edge of sky.
No way to convey a letter,
I struggled in vain to reach you in dream,
and yet the passion did not end;
and when I escaped, the road to you
    seemed even further away.

HOU [*pointing to the fan*]   When I looked at these peach blossoms on the fan, I wondered how I would ever repay your love.

[*Sings*]

See how fresh blood covered the fan
    and bloomed into red blossoms of peach,
as they say flowers fell from Dharma Heaven.[5]

> XIANGJUN *and* HOU FANGYU *examine the fan together.* DING JIZHI *pulls away* HOU FANGYU, *while* BIAN YUJING *pulls away* XIANGJUN.

BIAN YUJING   The abbot is at the altar. You can't go discussing how you feel about one another now!

> HOU FANGYU *and* XIANGJUN *cannot be restrained.* ZHANG WEI *slams his hand on the lectern in fury.*

ZHANG WEI   What sort of young people are you, making love talk in a place like this? [*He comes quickly down from the altar, snatches the fan out of* HOU FANGYU'*s and* XIANGJUN'*s hands, tears it up, and throws it on the ground*] These pure and unsullied precincts of the Way have no room for lecherous young men and loose girls to get together and flirt with one another.

CAI YISUO [*recognizing them*]   Aiya! This is Hou Fangyu of Henan. Your Reverence knew him once.

ZHANG WEI   Who's the girl?

LAN YING   I know her. She's Xiangjun. I used to live in her apartments. She is Hou Fangyu's concubine.

ZHANG WEI   And where have the two of them come from?

DING JIZHI   Hou is staying at my Lodge of Finding the Genuine.

BIAN YUJING   Li Xiangjun is staying at my Retreat of the Genuine Accumulated.

HOU [*bowing to* ZHANG WEI]   This is Master Zhang Wei, who was so merciful to me in the past.

ZHANG WEI   So you're Hou Fangyu. I'm glad you were able to escape from prison. Did you know that it was on account of you that I renounced the world?

HOU   How could I have known?

---

5. When a certain Buddhist abbot reached the best part in his lectures on the holy scriptures, flowers were supposed to have fallen from Heaven.

CAI YISUO I am Cai Yisuo. I also renounced the world on account of you. I'll tell you at leisure how all this came to pass.

LAN YING I am Lan Ying. I brought Xiangjun here looking for you, but I didn't think we would finally meet you.

HOU Xiangjun and I will need lifetimes to repay your kindness in taking us in, Ding Jizhi and Bian Yujing, and to repay the feeling you two showed in guiding us, Cai Yisuo and Lan Ying.

XIANGJUN And don't forget Su Kunsheng, who accompanied me here.

HOU And Liu Jingting, who came with me.

XIANGJUN The way in which Su and Liu stayed with us through everything, without flinching in desperate situations, is even more moving.

HOU When my wife and I get home, we hope to repay you all for everything.

ZHANG WEI In all this babbling and jabbering, what do you think you are talking about? Great upheavals have turned Heaven and Earth upside down, and you're still clinging to the love and passion that has taken root within you. Isn't this ludicrous!

HOU You are wrong in this! A man and a woman founding a household has always been the primary human relationship, a focus for love through separation and reunion, through grief and joy. How can you be concerned about this?

ZHANG WEI [*furiously*] Aaah! Two besotted worms. Just where is your nation, where is your family, where is your prince, where is your father? Is it only this little bit of romantic love you can't cut away?

[*Sings*]

Pathetic trifling of man and maid—
the world turned upside down
    and you don't care;
you babble on
    with wanton phrases, lurid words,
tugging clothes and holding hands, declare
a happily-ever-after to the gods.
Don't you realize that long ago
    your fated wedlock was erased
        from registries in Heaven?
With thudding wingbeats mated ducks
    wake from dream
        and fly apart,
the precious mirror of reunion
    lies in fragments on the ground,
        happy endings proved unsound.
Blush at this bad performance of your scene,
    inspiring bystanders' laughter—
the great path lies before you clear,
    flee on it immediately!

HOU [*bowing*] What you have just said makes a cold sweat run down me, as if suddenly waking up from a dream.

ZHANG WEI Did you understand?

HOU   I understood.

ZHANG WEI   Since you understood, go accept Ding Jizhi as your teacher right here and now.

HOU FANGYU *goes and bows to* DING JIZHI.

XIANGJUN   I also understood.

ZHANG WEI   Since you understood, right here and now go accept Bian Yujing as your teacher.

XIANGJUN *goes and bows to* BIAN YUJING.

ZHANG WEI [*instructing* DING *and* BIAN]   Dress them for the parts of Daoists.

HOU FANGYU *and* XIANGJUN *change clothes.*

DING *and* BIAN   Would Your Reverence please take the seat at the altar so that we can present our disciples to you.

ZHANG WEI *climbs back to the altar and seats himself.* DING JIZHI *leads* HOU FANGYU *and* BIAN YUJING *leads* XIANGJUN *before him; they bow.*

ZHANG WEI [*sings*]
>   Weed out the sprouts of passion,
>   weed out the sprouts of passion
>   and behold
>   jade leaves and boughs of gold
>   wither up and die;
>   cut out the embryo of love,
>   cut out the embryo of love
>   and hear
>   phoenix chick and dragon spawn cry out.
>   Bubble swirling in the water,
>   bubble swirling in the water,
>   a spark struck from flint,
>   a spark struck from flint,
>   half this life adrift remains
>   and now you will learn the Teaching.

[*Pointing*] The male has his proper domain, which lies to the south and corresponds to the trigram Li; go then at once south of the southern mountains, where you will learn the Genuine and study the Way.

HOU   Yes. Now I understand the rightness of the great Way, and feel regret recognizing the strength of my passion. [*Exit* DING JIZHI *to the left, leading* HOU FANGYU]

ZHANG WEI [*pointing*]   The female has her proper domain, which lies to the north and matches the trigram Kan; go then at once north of the northern mountains, where you will learn the Genuine and study the Way.

XIANGJUN   Yes. In the turn of a head everything all proved to be illusion. Who was that man facing me? [*Exit* BIAN YUJING *to the right, leading* XIANGJUN]

ZHANG WEI [*descending from the altar with a loud laugh; sings*]
>   Note that when those two parted
>   no lovelorn glances passed.
>   Thanks to my having ripped

      shred by shred
         the peach blossom fan,
no more may besotted worms
      spin their soft cocoons of thread
         enwrapping themselves a thousand times.

         [Recites]

White bones and blue ashes lie
      forever in the weeds,
the peach blossom fan bids goodbye
      to a southern dynasty.
Never again will come those dreams
      of glory and the fall,
but when will love of man and maid
      melt away once and for all?

CHIKAMATSU MONZAEMON
1653–1725

The early eighteenth century in Japan was perhaps the only period in the history of theater when puppets performing for adult audiences were more popular than real-life actors. Although puppetry exists in many cultures and often has a long history as a folk art, in Japan it became a major literary form with acclaimed playwrights and sophisticated puppeteers. No playwright in this tradition was more popular or influential than Chikamatsu Monzaemon, and his play *The Love Suicides at Amijima* (1721) is considered one of his greatest masterpieces.

THE RISE OF PUPPET
THEATER IN JAPAN

Beginning with the Heian Period (794–1185) puppeteer troupes roamed the capital and the provinces in search for audiences, competing with other low-class entertainers who thrived on the fringes of the aristocratic culture at the court in Kyoto. But puppet theater entered a new stage as a literary art form in 1684, when Takemoto Gidayū, a famous chanter, founded his own puppet theater in Osaka. Gidayū was an acclaimed performer of *jōruri*, popular narrative chanting that took its name from the heroine of a well-known tale and that was accompanied by a banjolike instrument called a *shamisen* ("three flavor strings"). The shamisen had recently been imported from Okinawa, then a kingdom south of Japan, and had become a popular instrument in the demimonde of the pleasure quarters. Gidayū convinced Chikamatsu to collaborate with him. Gidayū's invitation was fortunate: Chikamatsu would become the most brilliant playwright in the history of puppet theater.

Puppet theater thrived in the early modern milieu of the Tokugawa Shogunate (1600–1868), the military regime of the Tokugawa family that ruled from Edo, modern-day Tokyo. Also called the

"Edo Period," this era saw an unprecedented growth of commercial culture. Urbanization accelerated, book printing caught on and fostered various genres of popular literature, while also enabling the spread of education and the flourishing of Confucianism and scholarship. Licensed pleasure quarters thrived, attracting customers of all social classes. Yet Tokugawa society was based on strict status order. Under the symbolic authority of the emperor, who resided in Kyoto, and the Tokugawa shoguns, the de facto power holders in Edo, there were four social classes: samurai (warriors), peasants, artisans, and merchants. Actors and entertainers were considered outcasts, together with prostitutes and beggars. Marriage outside one's class was forbidden, although in practice the boundaries were more fluid. Medieval Noh theater often borrowed themes and language from classical literature and addressed the higher rungs of Edo society, mostly samurai and rich merchants; it was sponsored by the shoguns as official state theater. In contrast to the high-class Noh theater, the new popular theater of the Edo Period—Kabuki and puppet theater—attracted commoners by staging current events and addressing concerns of contemporary society.

THE ELEMENTS OF PUPPET THEATER

Puppet theater performances include three elements: puppets; shamisen music; and jōruri chanting. The puppets are up to three-quarters of life-size. At first they were handled by one person, but they quickly became more complex creatures requiring the manipulation of three men, a head puppeteer in charge of the head and right hand, and two assistants responsible in turn for the left hand and the feet. Unlike puppetry that uses strings or other devices to make the puppeteers invisible to the audience, Japanese puppeteers are in full view on stage, dressed in black. The assistants' heads are covered with black hoods, while the calm face of the main puppeteer is visible above the heads of the puppet. During the eighteenth century the puppets became ever more sophisticated, as the genre competed with other forms of popular theater such as Kabuki, an opulent popular genre of dance-drama with live actors. Crucial technical inventions that enhanced the puppets' appeal were the introduction of movable eyelids and mouths, and prehensile hands that could now wield swords, tissue paper, and other props.

During performance, the shamisen player and the chanter sit on an auxiliary stage protruding into the theater at stage left. Although the puppeteers, the shamisen player, and the chanter usually do not make eye contact, their performance is carefully synchronized and the percussive strumming of the shamisen helps pace the narrative and timing of the action. The central star of puppet theater is the chanter. He intones the entire text of the play, taking in turn the roles of all puppet protagonists and of the narrator. At times he must switch among the voices of a timid child, a swashbuckling warrior, and an enamored lady within a few sentences. A master chanter uttering the last dramatic words of a famed young beauty in utmost despair before taking her life can make an audience forget that he is an old man who is turning the script's pages with his coarse and wrinkled hands.

Although in its heyday, puppet theater had raging success and reached a broad spectrum of early modern Japanese society, it has long since been eclipsed by other forms of mass entertainment. Today the Japanese government sponsors puppet theater as a traditional art form that is struggling in the modern world. But its reputation has spread beyond Japan and it dazzles even those first-time spectators outside Japan who consider

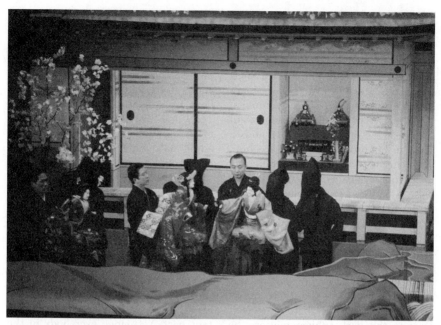

A contemporary puppet-theater performance in Osaka.

themselves immune to the perplexing power of puppets to evoke the deepest human feelings.

THE LOVE SUICIDES AT AMIJIMA

Chikamatsu was born into a provincial samurai family. He served in the households of the imperial aristocracy in Kyoto before moving to Osaka, a bustling commercial hub at the time. He produced his first plays in the 1680s. Although after 1693 he devoted most of his energies to kabuki, in 1703 he reconnected with Gidayū and wrote exclusively for Gidayū's puppet theater during the last two decades of his life.

Chikamatsu wrote about one hundred puppet plays. His earlier plays were mostly historical dramas common at the time, but this subject changed in 1703, when he pioneered a new subgenre: the "contemporary-life play." In that year a shopkeeper from Osaka had

committed double suicide with a prostitute from the Sonezaki pleasure quarters, because at the time people believed that they could be reborn with their lover "on the same lotus" in the Buddhist Pure Land if they committed suicide together. Three weeks after the event Chikamatsu's *The Love Suicides at Sonezaki* premiered with roaring success. It was the first time that such a scandalous contemporary event was depicted on the puppet theater stage. Chikamatsu would write twenty-four contemporary-life plays inspired by contemporary incidents during his lifetime.

The Love Suicides at Amijima, Chikamatsu's masterwork, was first performed in Osaka in 1721, and quickly adapted for the kabuki stage, as happened often with successful plays. In the play the Osaka paper merchant Jihei, with a wife and children, falls desperately in love with Koharu, a prostitute under contract at a Sonezaki establishment.

This situation upsets a complicated network of social relationships and obligations between husband and wife, parent and child, and even among prostitute, madam, and customer. Koharu, a prostitute far below Jihei's social status, refuses other customers, Jihei squanders the sparse resources of his shop, his father-in-law demands a divorce, his brother tries to save him, while his wife develops an admirable bond of loyalty with Koharu. The clashes between social obligations and the desire for personal happiness are irreconcilable. Unlike in other "love suicide" plays, where suicide is the unforeseen final outcome, in *The Love Suicides at Amijima* suicide is on the horizon from the beginning and nobody can in the end avert the tragic end of the lovers, however hard they try. Despite the dark subject matter, the play glistens with moments of social comedy.

The play became so successful that the authorities intervened. While Noh theater was patronized by the shoguns and the warrior elite, popular theater was seen by the elite classes as potentially subversive and incendiary and was often subject to censorship. Some of the prohibitions concerned the actors; for example, women and young boys were banned from the stage in 1629 and 1652, respectively, because of the seductive appeal they had for adult male audiences. Other prohibitions concerned the plays' subject matter: a year after *The Love Suicides at Amijima* premiered, the government prohibited plays on "love suicide" since they seemed to inspire waves of real-live suicides of lovers whose social class and life circumstances forbade their union. Prohibitions fostered inventiveness and playwrights started to disguise their staging of current events by setting the action in the distant past. Yet, since everybody in the audience knew what lay behind the historical veil, these plays remained contemporary-life plays of sorts and thus sustained the immense popularity of puppet theater.

From The Love Suicides at Amijima[1]

CHARACTERS

JIHEI, *a paper merchant, age twenty-eight*
MAGOEMON, *a flour merchant, Jihei's brother*
GOZAEMON, *Jihei's father-in-law*
TAHEI, *Jihei's rival for Koharu*
DEMBEI, *Proprietor of the Yamato House*
SANGORŌ, *Jihei's servant*

KANTARŌ, *Jihei's son, age six*
OSUE, *Jihei's daughter, age four*
KOHARU, *a courtesan belonging to the Kinokuni House in Sonezaki, a pleasure quarter in the northern part of Ōsaka*
OSAN, *Jihei's wife*
OSAN'S MOTHER (*also Jihei's aunt*), *age fifty-six*

1. Translated by Donald Keene. A rarely performed opening scene, omitted here, shows Koharu making her way to the teahouse in Sonezaki to meet a samurai customer (the disguised Magoemon, Jihei's brother). The audience learns that Koharu is in love with Jihei, while Tahei, a man she dislikes, is trying to buy out her contract. When Koharu sees Tahei in the street, she escapes.

ACT I

* * *

SCENE: *The Kawachi House, a Sonezaki teahouse.*

NARRATOR Koharu slips away, under cover of the crowd, and hurries into the Kawachi House.

PROPRIETRESS Well, well, I hadn't expected you so soon.—It's been ages even since I've heard your name mentioned. What a rare visitor you are, Koharu! And what a long time it's been!

NARRATOR The proprietress greets Koharu cheerfully.

KOHARU Oh—you can be heard as far as the gate. Please don't call me Koharu in such a loud voice. That horrible Ri Tōten[2] is out there. I beg you, keep your voice down.

NARRATOR Were her words overheard? In bursts a party of three men.

TAHEI I must thank you first of all, dear Koharu, for bestowing a new name on me, Ri Tōten. I never was called *that* before. Well, friends, this is the Koharu I've confided to you about—the good-hearted, good-natured, good-in-bed Koharu. Step up and meet the whore who's started all the rivalry! Will I soon be the lucky man and get Koharu for my wife? Or will Kamiya Jihei ransom her?

NARRATOR He swaggers up.

KOHARU I don't want to hear another word. If you think it's such an achievement to start unfounded rumors about someone you don't even know, throw yourself into it, say what you please. But I don't want to hear.

NARRATOR She steps away suddenly, but he sidles up again.

TAHEI You may not want to hear me, but the clink of my gold coins will make you listen! What a lucky girl you are! Just think—of all the many men in Temma and the rest of Osaka, you chose Jihei the paper dealer, the father of two children, with his cousin for his wife and his uncle for his father-in-law! A man whose business is so tight he's at his wits' ends every sixty days merely to pay the wholesalers' bills! Do you think he'll be able to fork over nearly ten *kamme* to ransom you? That reminds me of the mantis who picked a fight with an oncoming vehicle![3] But look at me—I haven't a wife, a father-in-law, a father, or even an uncle, for that matter. Tahei the Lone Wolf—that's the name I'm known by. I admit that I'm no match for Jihei when it comes to bragging about myself in the Quarter, but when it comes to money, I'm an easy winner. If I pushed with all the strength of my money, who knows what I might conquer?—How about it, men?—Your customer tonight, I'm sure, is none other than Jihei, but I'm taking over. The Lone Wolf's taking over. Hostess! Bring on the saké! On with the saké!

PROPRIETRESS What are you saying? Her customer tonight is a samurai, and he'll be here any moment. Please amuse yourself elsewhere.

NARRATOR But Tahei's look is playful.

TAHEI A customer's a customer, whether he's a samurai or a townsman. The

---

2. Villain in another puppet play.
3. Allusion to an ancient Chinese text, where it is an image for someone who does not know his

own limitations. "*Kamme*": one *kamme* corresponded to 3.75 kilograms (or 8.3 pounds) of silver. The price is extremely high.

only difference is that one wears swords and the other doesn't. But even if this samurai wears his swords he won't have five or six—there'll only be two, the broadsword and dirk. I'll take care of the samurai and borrow Koharu afterwards. (*To* KOHARU.) You may try to avoid me all you please, but some special connection from a former life must have brought us together. I owe everything to that ballad-singing priest—what a wonderful thing the power of prayer is! I think I'll recite a prayer of my own. Here, this ashtray will be my bell, and my pipe the hammer. This is fun.

> *Chan Chan Cha Chan Chan.*
> *Ei Ei Ei Ei Ei.*
> Jihei the paper dealer—
> Too much love for Koharu
> Has made him a foolscap,
> He wastepapers sheets of gold
> Till his fortune's shredded to confetti
> And Jihei himself is like scrap paper
> You can't even blow your nose on!
> Hail, Hail Amida Buddha!
> *Namaida Namaida Namaida.*

NARRATOR   As he prances wildly, roaring his song, a man appears at the gate, so anxious not to be recognized that he wears, even at night, a wicker hat.[4]

TAHEI   Well, Toilet paper's showed up! That's quite a disguise! Why don't you come in, Toilet paper? If my prayer's frightened you, say a Hail Amida![5] Here, I'll take off your hat!

NARRATOR   He drags the man in and examines him: it is the genuine article, a two-sworded samurai, somber in dress and expression, who glares at Tahei through his woven hat, his eyeballs round as gongs. Tahei, unable to utter either a Hail or an Amida, gasps "Haaa!" in dismay, but his face is unflinching.

TAHEI   Koharu, I'm a townsman. I've never worn a sword, but I've lots of New Silver[6] at my place, and I think that the glint could twist a mere couple of swords out of joint. Imagine that wretch from the toilet paper shop, with a capital as thin as tissue, trying to compete with the Lone Wolf! That's the height of impertinence! I'll wander down now from Sakura Bridge to Middle Street, and if I meet that Wastepaper along the way, I'll trample him under foot. Come on, men.

NARRATOR   Their gestures, at least, have a cavalier assurance as they swagger off, taking up the whole street.

   The samurai customer patiently endures the fool, indifferent to his remarks because of the surroundings, but every word of gossip about Jihei, whether for good or ill, affects Koharu. She is so depressed that she stands there blankly, unable even to greet her guest. Sugi, the maid from the Kinokuni House, runs up from home, looking annoyed.

---

4. Customers visiting the pleasure quarter by day usually wore deep wicker hats, concealing their faces, in order to preserve the secrecy of their visits; this customer wears the hat even at night.

5. A word play on *ami*, part of the name of *Ami*da Buddha (the "Buddha of Infinite Light" promising rebirth in the Western Paradise of the Pure Land) and *ami*gasa, meaning "woven hat."

6. Good-quality coinage common around 1720.

SUGI   When I left you here a while ago, Miss Koharu, your guest hadn't appeared yet, and they gave me a terrible scolding when I got back for not having checked on him. I'm very sorry, sir, but please excuse me a minute.

NARRATOR   She lifts the woven hat and examines the face.

SUGI   Oh—it's not him! There's nothing to worry about, Koharu. Ask your guest to keep you for the whole night, and show him how sweet you can be. Give him a barrelful of nectar![7] Good-by, madam, I'll see you later, honey.

NARRATOR   She takes her leave with a cloying stream of puns. The extremely hard-baked[8] samurai is furious.

SAMURAI   What's the meaning of this? You'd think from the way she appraised my face that I was a tea canister or a porcelain cup! I didn't come here to be trifled with. It's difficult enough for me to leave the Residence even by day, and in order to spend the night away I had to ask the senior officer's permission and sign the register. You can see how complicated the regulations make things. But I'm in love, miss, just from hearing about you, and I wanted very badly to spend a night with you. I came here a while ago without an escort and made the arrangements with the teahouse. I had been looking forward to your kind reception, a memory to last me a lifetime, but you haven't so much as smiled at me or said a word of greeting. You keep your head down, as if you were counting money in your lap. Aren't you afraid of getting a stiff neck? Madam—I've never heard the like. Here I come to a teahouse, and I must play the part of night nurse in a maternity room!

PROPRIETRESS   You're quite right, sir. Your surprise is entirely justified, considering that you don't know the reasons. This girl is deeply in love with a customer named Kamiji. It's been Kamiji today and Kamiji tomorrow, with nobody else allowed a chance at her. Her other customers have scattered in every direction, like leaves in a storm. When two people get so carried away with each other, it often leads to trouble, for both the customer and the girl. In the first place, it inteferes with business, and the owner, whoever he may be, is bound to prevent it. That's why all her guests are examined. Koharu is naturally depressed—it's only to be expected. You are annoyed, which is equally to be expected. But, speaking as the proprietress here, it seems to me that the essential thing is for you to meet each other halfway and cheer up. Come, have a drink.—Act a little more lively, Koharu.

NARRATOR   Koharu, without answering, lifts her tear-stained face.

KOHARU   Tell me, samurai, they say that, if you're going to kill yourself anyway, people who die during the Ten Nights[9] are sure to become Buddhas. Is that really true?

SAMURAI   How should I know? Ask the priest at your family temple.

KOHARU   Yes, that's right. But there's something I'd like to ask a samurai. If you're committing suicide, it'd be a lot more painful, wouldn't it, to cut your throat rather than hang yourself?

---

7. The translator has changed the imagery from puns on saltiness in the original (soy sauce, green vegetables, etc.) to puns on sweetness.
8. Technical term from pottery making, meaning "hard-fired."

9. A period in the Tenth Month when special Buddhist services were conducted in temples of the Pure Land sect. It was believed that people who died during this period immediately became Buddhas.

SAMURAI   I've never tried cutting my throat to see whether or not it hurt. Please ask more sensible questions.—What an unpleasant girl!

NARRATOR   Samurai though he is, he looks nonplussed.

PROPRIETRESS   Koharu, that's a shocking way to treat a guest the first time you meet him. I'll go and get my husband. We'll have some saké together. That ought to liven things a bit.

NARRATOR   The gate she leaves is illumined by the evening moon low in the sky; the clouds and the passers in the street have thinned.

For long years there has lived in Temma, the seat of the mighty god, though not a god himself, Kamiji, a name often bruited by the gongs of worldly gossip, so deeply, hopelessly, is he tied to Koharu by the ropes[1] of an ill-starred love. Now is the tenth moon, the month when no gods will unite them;[2] they are thwarted in their love, unable to meet. They swore in the last letters they exchanged that if only they could meet, that day would be their last. Night after night Jihei, ready for death, trudges to the Quarter, distractedly, as though his soul had left a body consumed by the fires of love.

At a roadside eating stand he hears people gossiping about Koharu. "She's at Kawashō with a samurai customer," someone says, and immediately Jihei decides, "It will be tonight!"

He peers through the latticework window and sees a guest in the inside room, his face obscured by a hood. Only the moving chin is visible, and Jihei cannot hear what is said.

JIHEI   Poor Koharu! How thin her face is! She keeps it averted from the lamp. In her heart she's thinking only of me. I'll signal her that I'm here, and we'll run off together. Then which will it be—Umeda or Kitano?[3] Oh—I want to tell her I'm here. I want to call her.

NARRATOR   He beckons with his heart, his spirit flies to her, but his body, like a cicada's cast-off shell, clings to the latticework. He weeps with impatience.

The guest in the inside room gives a great yawn.

SAMURAI   What a bore, playing nursemaid to a prostitute with worries on her mind!—The street seems quiet now. Let's go to the end room. We can at least distract ourselves by looking at the lanterns. Come with me.

NARRATOR   They go together to the outer room. Jihei, alarmed, squeezes into the patch of shadow under the lattice window. Inside they do not realize that anyone cavesdrops.

SAMURAI   I've been noticing your behavior and the little things you've said this evening. It's plain to me that you intend a love suicide with Kamiji, or whatever his name is—the man the hostess mentioned. I'm sure I'm right. I realize that no amount of advice or reasoning is likely to penetrate the ears of somebody bewitched by the god of death, but I must say that you're exceedingly foolish. The boy's family won't blame him for his recklessness, but they will blame and hate you. You'll be shamed by the public exposure of your body. Your parents may be dead, for all I know, but if they're alive, you'll be

1. The sacred ropes at a Shintō shrine. "Temma . . . god": one of the main districts of Ōsaka, Temma was the site of the Tenjin Shrine, dedicated to the deified poet-official Sugawara no Michizane (845–903). "Kamiji": the word *kami*, for "paper," sounds like *kami*,

"god."
2. The Tenth Month was when the gods were believed to gather at Izumo, an ancient province on Japan's southwestern shore; they thus were absent from the rest of Japan.
3. Both places had well-known cemeteries.

punished in hell as a wicked daughter. Do you suppose that you'll become a Buddha? You and your lover won't even be able to fall smoothly into hell together! What a pity—and what a tragedy! This is only our first meeting but, as a samurai, I can't let you die without trying to save you. No doubt money's the problem. I'd like to help, if five or ten *ryō* would be of service. I swear by the god Hachiman and by my good fortune as a samurai that I will never reveal to anyone what you tell me. Open your heart without fear.

NARRATOR   He whispers these words. She joins her hands and bows.

KOHARU   I'm extremely grateful. Thank you for your kind words and for swearing an oath to me, someone you've never had for a lover or even a friend. I'm so grateful that I'm crying.—Yes, it's as they say, when you've something on your mind it shows on your face. You were right. I have promised Kamiji to die with him. But we've been completely prevented from meeting by my master, and Jihei, for various reasons, can't ransom me at once. My contracts with my former master[4] and my present one still have five years to run. If somebody else claimed me during that time, it would be a blow to me, of course, but a worse disgrace to Jihei's honor. He suggested that it would be better if we killed ourselves, and I agreed. I was caught by obligations from which I could not withdraw, and I promised him before I knew what I was doing. I said, "We'll watch for a chance, and I'll slip out when you give the signal." "Yes," he said, "slip out somehow." Ever since then I've been leading a life of uncertainty, never knowing from one day to the next when my last hour will come.

   I have a mother living in a back alley south of here. She has no one but me to depend on, and she does piecework to eke out a living. I keep thinking that after I'm dead she'll become a beggar or an outcast, and maybe she'll die of starvation. That's the only sad part about dying. I have just this one life. I'm ashamed that you may think me a coldhearted woman, but I must endure the shame. The most important thing is that I don't want to die. I beg you, please help me to stay alive.

NARRATOR   As she speaks the samurai nods thoughtfully. Jihei, crouching outside, hears her words with astonishment; they are so unexpected to his manly heart that he feels like a monkey who has tumbled from a tree. He is frantic with agitation.

JIHEI (*to himself*)   Then was everything a lie? Ahhh—I'm furious! For two whole years I've been bewitched by that rotten she-fox! Shall I break in and kill her with one blow of my sword? Or shall I satisfy my anger by shaming her to her face?

NARRATOR   He gnashes his teeth and weeps in chagrin. Inside the house Koharu speaks through her tears.

KOHARU   It's a curious thing to ask, but would you please show the kindness of a samurai and become my customer for the rest of this year and into next spring? Whenever Jihei comes, intent on death, please interfere and force him to postpone and postpone his plan. In this way our relations can be broken quite naturally. He won't have to kill himself, and my life will also be saved.—What evil connection from a former existence made us promise to die? How I regret it now!

4. The master at the bathhouse where Koharu worked before.

NARRATOR   She weeps, leaning on the samurai's knee.

SAMURAI   Very well, I'll do as you ask. I think I can help you.—But there's a draft blowing. Somebody may be watching.

NARRATOR   He slams shut the latticework *shōji*. Jihei, listening outside, is in a frenzy.

JIHEI   Exactly what you'd expect from a whore, a cheap whore! I misjudged her foul nature. She robbed the soul from my body, the thieving harlot! Shall I slash her down or run her through? What am I to do?

NARRATOR   The shadows of two profiles fall on the *shōji*.

JIHEI   I'd like to give her a taste of my fist and trample her.—What are they chattering about? See how they nod to each other! Now she's bowing to him, whispering and sniveling. I've tried to control myself—I've pressed my chest, I've stroked it—but I can't stand any more. This is too much to endure!

NARRATOR   His heart pounds wildly as he unsheathes his dirk, a Magoroku of Seki. "Koharu's side must be here," he judges, and stabs through an opening in the latticework. But Koharu is too far away for his thrust, and though she cries out in terror, she remains unharmed. Her guest instantly leaps at Jihei, grabs his hands, and jerks them through the latticework. With his sword knot he quickly and securely fastens Jihei's hands to the window upright.

SAMURAI   Don't make any outcry, Koharu. You are not to look at him.

NARRATOR   At this moment the proprietor and his wife return. They exclaim in alarm.

SAMURAI   This needn't concern you. Some ruffian ran his sword through the *shōji*, and I've tied his arms to the latticework. I have my own way of dealing with him. Don't untie the cord. If you attract a crowd, the place is sure to be thrown in an uproar. Let's all go inside. Come with me, Koharu. We'll go to bed.

NARRATOR   Koharu answers, "Yes," but she recognizes the handle of the dirk, and the memory—if not the blade—transfixes her breast.

KOHARU   There're always people doing crazy things in the Quarter when they've had too much to drink. Why don't you let him go without making any trouble? I think that's best, don't you, Kawashō?

SAMURAI   Out of the question. Do as I say—inside, all of you. Koharu, come along.

NARRATOR   Jihei can still see their shadows even after they enter the inner room, but he is bound to the spot, his hands held in fetters which grip him the tighter as he struggles, his body beset by suffering as he tastes a living shame worse than a dog's.[5] More determined than ever to die, he sheds tears of blood, a pitiful sight.

   Tahei the Lone Wolf returns from his carousing.

TAHEI   That's Jihei standing by Kawashō's window. I'll give him a tossing.

NARRATOR   He catches Jihei by the collar and starts to lift him over his back.

JIHEI   Owww!

TAHEI   Owww? What kind of weakling are you? Oh, I see—you're tied here. You must've been pulling off a robbery. You dirty pickpocket! You rotten pickpocket!

NARRATOR   He drubs Jihei mercilessly.

---

5. Allusion to a proverb of Buddhist origin: "Suffering follows one like a dog."

TAHEI   You burglar! You convict!

NARRATOR   He kicks him wildly.

TAHEI   Kamiya Jihei's been caught burgling, and they've tied him up!

NARRATOR   Passersby and people of the neighborhood, attracted by his shouts, quickly gather. The samurai rushes from the house.

SAMURAI   Who's calling him a burglar? You? Tell what Jihei's stolen! Out with it!

NARRATOR   He seizes Tahei and forces him into the dirt. Tahei rises to his feet only for the samurai to kick him down again and again. He grips Tahei.

SAMURAI   Jihei! Trample him to your heart's content!

NARRATOR   He pushes Tahei under Jihei's feet. Bound though he is, Jihei stamps furiously over Tahei's face. Tahei, thoroughly trampled and covered with mire, gets to his feet and glares around him.

TAHEI (to bystander)   How could you fools stand there calmly and let him step on me? I've memorized every one of your faces, and I intend to pay you back. Remember that!

NARRATOR   He makes his escape, still determined to have the last word. The spectators burst out laughing.

VOICES   Listen to him brag, even after he's been trampled on! Let's throw him from the bridge and give him a drink of water! Don't let him get away!

NARRATOR   They chase after him. When the crowd has dispersed, the samurai approaches Jihei and unfastens the knots. He shows his face with his hood removed.

JIHEI   Magoemon! My brother! How shaming!

NARRATOR   He sinks to the ground and weeps, prostrating himself in the dirt.

KOHARU   Are you his brother, sir?

NARRATOR   Koharu runs to them. Jihei, catching her by the front of the kimono, forces her to the ground.

JIHEI   Beast! She-fox! I'd sooner trample on you than on Tahei!

NARRATOR   He raises his foot, but Magoemon calls out.

MAGOEMON   That's the kind of foolishness responsible for all your trouble. A prostitute's business is to deceive men. Have you just now waked up to that? I've seen to the bottom of her heart the very first time I met her, but you're so scatter-brained that in over two years of intimacy with the woman you never discovered what she was thinking. Instead of stamping on Koharu, why don't you use your feet on your own misguided disposition?—It's deplorable. You're my younger brother, but you're almost thirty, and you've got a six-year-old boy and a four-year-old girl, Kantarō and Osue. You run a shop with a thirty-six-foot frontage,[6] but you don't seem to realize that your whole fortune's collapsing. You shouldn't have to be lectured to by your brother. Your father-in-law is your aunt's husband, and your mother-in-law is your aunt. They've always been like real parents to you. Your wife Osan is my cousin too. The ties of marriage are multiplied by those of blood. But when the family has a reunion the only subject of discussion is our mortification over your incessant visits to Sonezaki. I feel sorry for our poor aunt. You know what a stiff-necked gentleman of the old school her husband Gozaemon is. He's forever flying into a rage and saying, "We've been tricked

6. A large shop.

by your nephew. He's deserted our daughter. I'll take Osan back and ruin Jihei's reputation throughout Temma." Our aunt, with all the heartache to bear herself, sometimes sides with him and sometimes with you. She's worried herself sick. What an ingrate, not to appreciate how she's defended you in your shame! This one offense is enough to make you the target for Heaven's future punishment!

I realized that your marriage couldn't last much longer at this rate. I decided, in the hopes of relieving our aunt's worries, that I'd see with my own eyes what kind of woman Koharu was, and work out some sort of solution afterwards. I consulted the proprietor here, then came myself to investigate the cause of your sickness. I see now how natural it was that you should desert your wife and children. What a faithful prostitute you discovered! I congratulate you!

And here I am, Magoemon the Miller,[7] known far and wide for my paragon of a brother, dressed up like a masquerader at a festival or maybe a lunatic! I put on swords for the first time in my life, and announced myself, like a bit player in a costume piece, as an officer at a residence. I feel like an absolute idiot with these swords, but there's nowhere I can dispose of them now.—It's so infuriating—and ridiculous—that it's given me a pain in the chest.

NARRATOR He gnashes his teeth and grimaces, attempting to hide his tears. Koharu, choking the while with emotion, can only say:

KOHARU Yes, you're entirely right.

NARRATOR The rest is lost in tears. Jihei pounds the earth with his fist.

JIHEI I was wrong. Forgive me, Magoemon. For three years I've been possessed by that witch. I've neglected my parents, relatives—even my wife and children—and wrecked my fortune, all because I was deceived by Koharu, that sneak thief! I'm utterly mortified. But I'm through with her now, and I'll never set foot here again. Weasel! Vixen! Sneak thief! Here's proof that I've broken with her!

NARRATOR He pulls out the amulet bag which has rested next to his skin.

JIHEI Here are the written oaths we've exchanged, one at the beginning of each month, twenty-nine in all. I return them. This means our love and affection are over. Take them.

NARRATOR He flings the notes at her.

JIHEI Magoemon, collect from her my pledges. Please make sure you get them all. Then burn them with your own hands. (*To* KOHARU.) Hand them to my brother.

KOHARU As you wish.

NARRATOR In tears, she surrenders the amulet bag. Magoemon opens it.

MAGOEMON One, two, three, four . . . ten . . . twenty-nine. They're all here. There's also a letter from a woman. What's this?

NARRATOR He starts to unfold it.

KOHARU That's an important letter. I can't let you see it.

NARRATOR She clings to Magoemon's arm, but he pushes her away. He holds the letter to the lamplight and examines the address, "To Miss Koharu from

---

7. A dealer in flour (for noodles). His shop name Konaya—"the flour merchant"—is used almost as a surname.

Kamiya Osan." As soon as he reads the words, he casually thrusts the letter into his kimono.

MAGOEMON   Koharu. A while ago I swore by my good fortune as a samurai, but now Magoemon the Miller swears by his good fortune as a businessman that he will show this letter to no one, not even his wife. I alone will read it, then burn it with the oaths. You can trust me. I will not break this oath.

KOHARU   Thank you. You save my honor.

NARRATOR   She bursts into tears again.

JIHEI (*laughs contemptuously*)   Save your honor! You talk like a human being! (*To* MAGOEMON.) I don't want to see her cursed face another minute. Let's go. No—I can't hold so much resentment and bitterness! I'll kick her one in the face, a memory to treasure for the rest of my life. Excuse me, please.

NARRATOR   He strides up to Koharu and stamps on the ground.

JIHEI   For three years I've loved you, delighted in you, longed for you, adored you, but today my foot will say my only farewells.

NARRATOR   He kicks her sharply on the forehead and bursts into tears. The brothers leave, forlorn figures. Koharu, unhappy woman, raises her voice in lament as she watches them go. Is she faithful or unfaithful? Her true feelings are hidden in the words penned by Jihei's wife, a letter no one has seen. Jihei goes his separate way without learning the truth.

ACT 2

SCENE: *The house and shop of Kamiya* JIHEI.

TIME: *Ten days later.*

NARRATOR   The busy street that runs straight to Tenjin Bridge named for the god of Temma, bringer of good fortune, is known as the Street Before the Kami,[8] and here a paper shop does business under the name Kamiya Jihei. The paper is honestly sold, the shop well situated; it is a long established firm, and customers come thick as raindrops.

Outside crowds pass in the street, on their way to the Ten Nights service, while inside the husband dozes in the *kotatsu,*[9] shielded from draughts by a screen at his pillow. His wife Osan keeps solitary, anxious watch over shop and house.

OSAN   The days are so short—it's dinnertime already, but Tama still hasn't returned from her errand to Ichinokawa.[1] I wonder what can be keeping her. That scamp Sangorō isn't back either. The wind is freezing. I'm sure the children will both be cold. He doesn't even realize that it's time for Osue to be nursed. Heaven preserve me from ever becoming such a fool! What an infuriating creature!

NARRATOR   She speaks to herself.

KANTARŌ   Mama, I've come back all by myself.

NARRATOR   Her son, the older child, runs up to the house.

---

8. Again, wordplay on *kami* (god) and *kami* (paper).
9. A low, quilt-covered table under which a charcoal burner is placed as a source of heat.

1. Site of a large vegetable market near the north end of Tenjin Bridge, named, again, after the god "Tenjin," the deified Michizane.

OSAN Kantarō—is that you? What's happened to Osue and Sangorō?

KANTARŌ They're playing by the shrine. Osue wanted her milk and she was bawling her head off.

OSAN I was sure she would. Oh—your hands and feet are frozen stiff as nails! Go and warm yourself at the *kotatsu*. Your father's sleeping there.—What am I to do with that idiot?

NARRATOR She runs out impatiently to the shop just as Sangorō shuffles back, alone.

OSAN Come here, you fool! Where have you left Osue?

SANGORŌ You know, I must've lost her somewhere. Maybe somebody's picked her up. Should I go back for her?

OSAN How could you? If any harm has come to my precious child, I'll beat you to death!

NARRATOR But even as she screams at him, the maid Tama returns with Osue on her back.

TAMA The poor child—I found her in tears at the corner. Sangorō, when you're supposed to look after the child, do it properly.

OSAN You poor dear. You must want your milk.

NARRATOR She joins the others by the *kotatsu* and suckles the child.

OSAN Tama—give that fool a taste of something that he'll remember!²

NARRATOR Sangorō shakes his head.

SANGORŌ No, thanks. I gave each of the children two tangerines just a while ago at the shrine, and I tasted five myself.

NARRATOR Fool though he is, bad puns come from him nimbly enough, and the others can only smile despite themselves.

TAMA Oh—I've become so involved with this half-wit that I almost forgot to tell you, ma'am, that Mr. Magoemon and his aunt³ are on their way here from the west.

OSAN Oh dear! I'll have to wake Jihei in that case. (*To* JIHEI.) Please get up. Mother and Magoemon are coming. They'll be upset again if you let them see you, a businessman, sleeping in the afternoon, with the day so short as it is.

JIHEI All right.

NARRATOR He struggles to a sitting position and, with his abacus in one hand, pulls his account book to him with the other.

JIHEI Two into ten goes five, three into nine goes three, three into six goes two, seven times eight is fifty-six.

NARRATOR His fifty-six-year old aunt enters with Magoemon.

JIHEI Magoemon, aunt. How good of you. Please come in. I was in the midst of some urgent calculations. Four nines makes thirty-six *momme*. Three sixes make eighteen *fun*. That's two *momme* less two *fun*.⁴ Kantarō! Osue! Granny and Uncle have come! Bring the tobacco tray! One times three makes three. Osan,⁵ serve the tea!

NARRATOR He jabbers away.

---

2. A pun on two meanings of *kurawasu*: "to make eat" and "to beat."

3. Magoemon's and Jihei's aunt, who is also Osan's mother.

4. Meaningless calculations. Twenty *fun* made two *momme* (and one *kamme* made one thousand *momme*).

5. The name Osan echoes the word "three" (*san*).

AUNT   We haven't come for tea or tobacco. Osan, you're young I know, but you're the mother of two children, and your excessive forbearance does you no credit. A man's dissipation can always be traced to his wife's carelessness. Remember, it's not only the man who's disgraced when he goes bankrupt and his marriage breaks up. You'd do well to take notice of what's going on and assert yourself a bit more.

MAGOEMON   It's foolish to hope for any results, aunt. The scoundrel even deceives me, his elder brother. Why should he take to heart criticism from his wife? Jihei—you played me for a fool. After showing me how you returned Koharu's pledges, here you are, not ten days later, redeeming her! What does this mean? I suppose your urgent calulations are of Koharu's debts! I've had enough!

NARRATOR   He snatches away the abacus and flings it clattering into the hallway.

JIHEI   You're making an enormous fuss without any cause. I haven't crossed the threshold since the last time I saw you except to go twice to the wholesalers in Imabashi and once to the Tenjin Shrine. I haven't even thought of Koharu, much less redeemed her.

AUNT   None of your evasions! Last evening at the Ten Nights service I heard the people in the congregation gossiping. Everybody was talking about the great patron from Temma who'd fallen in love with a prostitute named Koharu from the Kinokuni House in Sonezaki. They said he'd driven away her other guests and was going to ransom her in the next couple of days. There was all kinds of gossip about the abundance of money and fools even in these days of high prices.

My husband Gozaemon has been hearing about Koharu constantly, and he's sure that her great patron from Temma must be you, Jihei. He told me, "He's your nepbew, but for me he's a stranger, and my daughter's happiness is my chief concern. Once he ransoms the prostitute he'll no doubt sell his wife to a brothel. I intend to take her back before he starts selling her clothes."

He was halfway out of the house before I could restrain him. "Don't get so excited. We can settle this calmly. First we must make sure whether or not the rumors are true."

That's why Magoemon and I are here now. He was telling me a while ago that the Jihei of today was not the Jihei of yesterday—that you'd broken all connections with Sonezaki and completely reformed. But now I hear that you've had a relapse. What disease can this be?

Your father was my brother. When the poor man was on his deathbed, he lifted his head from the pillow and begged me to look after you, as my son-in-law and nephew. I've never forgotten those last words, but your perversity has made a mockery of his request!

NARRATOR   She collapses in tears of resentment. Jihei claps his hands in sudden recognition.

JIHEI   I have it! The Koharu everybody's gossiping about is the same Koharu, but the great patron who's to redeem her is a different man. The other day, as my brother can tell you, Tahei—they call him the Lone Wolf because he hasn't any family or relations—started a fight and was trampled on. He gets all the money he needs from his home town, and he's been trying for a long time to redeem Koharu. I've always prevented him, but I'm sure he's decided that now is his chance. I have nothing to do with it.

NARRATOR   Osan brightens at his words.

OSAN   No matter how forbearing I might be—even if I were an angel—you don't suppose I'd encourage my husband to redeem a prostitute! In this instance at any rate there's not a word of untruth in what my husband has said. I'll be a witness to that, Mother.

NARRATOR   Husband's and wife's words tally perfectly.

AUNT   Then it's true?

NARRATOR   The aunt and nephew clap their hands with relief.

MAGOEMON   Well, I'm happy it's over, anyway. To make us feel doubly reassured, will you write an affidavit which will dispel any doubts your stubborn uncle may have?

JIHEI   Certainly. I'll write a thousand if you like.

MAGOEMON   Splendid! I happen to have bought this on the way here.

NARRATOR   Magoemon takes from the fold of his kimono a sheet of oath-paper from Kumano, the sacred characters formed by flocks of crows.[6] Instead of vows of eternal love, Jihei now signs under penalty of Heaven's wrath an oath that he will sever all ties and affections with Koharu. "If I should lie, may Bonten and Taishaku above, and the Four Great Kings below afflict me!"[7] So the text runs, and to it is appended the names of many Buddhas and gods. He signs his name, Kamiya Jihei, in bold characters, imprints the oath with a seal of blood, and proffers it.

OSAN   It's a great relief to me too. Mother, I have you and Magoemon to thank. Jihei and I have had two children, but this is his firmest pledge of affection. I hope you share my joy.

AUNT   Indeed we do. I'm sure that Jihei will settle down and his business will improve, now that he's in this frame of mind. It's been entirely for his sake and for love of the grandchildren that we've intervened. Come, Magoemon, let's be on our way. I'm anxious to set my husband's mind at ease.—It's become chilly here. See that the children don't catch cold.—This too we owe to the Buddha of the Ten Nights. I'll say a prayer of thanks before I go. Hail, Amida Buddha!

NARRATOR   She leaves, her heart innocent as Buddha's. Jihei is perfunctory even about seeing them to the door. Hardly have they crossed the threshold than he slumps down again at the *kotatsu*. He pulls the checked quilting over his head.

OSAN   You still haven't forgotton Sonezaki, have you?

NARRATOR   She goes up to him in disgust and tears away the quilting. He is weeping; a waterfall of tears streams along the pillow, deep enough to bear him afloat. She tugs him upright and props his body against the *kotatsu* frame. She stares into his face.

OSAN   You're acting outrageously, Jihei. You shouldn't have signed that oath if you felt so reluctant to leave her. The year before last, on the middle day

6. The charms issued by the Shintō shrine at Kumano were printed on the face with six Chinese characters, the strokes of which were in the shape of crows. The reverse side of the charms was used for writing oaths.

7. A formal oath. Bonten (Brahma) and Taishaku (Indra), though Hindu gods, were considered protective deities of the Buddhist law. The four Deva kings served under Indra and were also protectors of Buddhism.

of the Boar of the tenth moon,[8] we lit the first fire in the *kotatsu* and celebrated by sleeping here together, pillow to pillow. Ever since then—did some demon or snake creep into my bosom that night?—for two whole years I've been condemned to keep watch over an empty nest. I thought that tonight at least, thanks to Mother and Magoemon, we'd share sweet words in bed as husbands and wives do, but my pleasure didn't last long. How cruel of you, how utterly heartless! Go ahead, cry your eyes out, if you're so attached to her. Your tears will flow into Shijimi River and Koharu, no doubt, will ladle them out and drink them! You're ignoble, inhuman.

NARRATOR She embraces his knees and throws herself over him, moaning in supplication. Jihei wipes his eyes.

JIHEI If tears of grief flowed from the eyes and tears of anger from the ears, I could show my heart without saying a word. But my tears all pour in the same way from my eyes, and there's no difference in their color. It's not surprising that you can't tell what's in my heart. I have not a shred of attachment left for that vampire in human skin, but I bear a grudge against Tahei. He has all the money he wants, no wife or children. He's schemed again and again to redeem her, but Koharu refused to give in, at least until I broke with her. She told me time and again, "You have nothing to worry about. I'll never let myself be redeemed by Tahei, not even if my ties with you are ended and I can no longer stay by your side. If my master is induced by Tahei's money to deliver me to him, I'll kill myself in a way that'll do you credit!" But think—not ten days have passed since I broke with her, and she's to be redeemed by Tahei! That rotten whore! That animal! No, I haven't a trace of affection left for her, but I can just hear how Tahei will be boasting. He'll spread the word around Osaka that my business has come to a standstill and I'm hard pressed for money. I'll meet with contemptuous stares from the wholesalers. I'll be dishonored. My heart is broken and my body burns with shame. What a disgrace! How maddening! I've passed the stage of shedding hot tears, tears of blood, sticky tears—my tears now are of molten iron!

NARRATOR He collapses with weeping. Osan pales with alarm.

OSAN If that's the situation, poor Koharu will surely kill herself.

JIHEI You're too well bred, despite your intelligence, to understand her likes! What makes you suppose that faithless creature would kill herself? Far from it—she's probably taking moxa treatments and medicine to prolong her life!

OSAN No, that's not true. I was determined never to tell you so long as I lived, but I'm afraid of the crime I'd be committing if I concealed the facts and let her die with my knowledge. I will reveal my great secret. There is not a grain of deceit in Koharu. It was I who schemed to end the relations between you. I could see signs that you were drifting towards suicide. I felt so unhappy that I wrote a letter, begging her as one woman to another to break with you, though I knew how painful it would be. I asked her to save your life. The letter must have moved her. She answered that she would give you up, though you were more precious than life itself, because she could not shirk her duty to me. I've kept her letter with me ever since—it's been like a pro-

---

8. It was customary to light the first fire of the winter on this day.

tective charm. Could such a noble-hearted woman violate her promise and brazenly marry Tahei? When a woman—I no less than another—has given herself completely to a man, she does not change. I'm sure she'll kill herself. I'm sure of it. Ahhh—what a dreadful thing to have happened! Save her, please.

NARRATOR   Her voice rises in agitation. Her husband is thrown into a turmoil.

JIHEI   There was a letter in an unknown woman's hand among the written oaths she surrendered to my brother. It must have been from you. If that's the case, Koharu will surely commit suicide.

OSAN   Alas! I'd be failing in the obligations I owe her as another woman if I allowed her to die. Please go to her at once. Don't let her kill herself.

NARRATOR   Clinging to her husband, she melts in tears.

JIHEI   But what can I possibly do? It'd take half the amount of her ransom in earnest money merely to keep her out of Tahei's clutches. I can't save Koharu's life without administering a dose of 750 *momme* in New Silver.[9] How could I raise that much money in my present financial straits? Even if I crush my body to powder, where will the money come from?

OSAN   Don't exaggerate the difficulties. If that's all you need, it's simple enough.

NARRATOR   She goes to the wardrobe, and opening a small drawer takes out a bag fastened with cords of twisted silk. She unhesitantly tears it open and throws down a packet which Jihei retrieves.

JIHEI   What's this? Money? Four hundred *momme* in New Silver? How in the world—

NARRATOR   He stares astonished at this money he never put there.

OSAN   I'll tell you later where this money came from. I've scraped it together to pay the bill for Iwakuni paper that falls due the day after tomorrow. We'll have to ask Magoemon to help us keep the business from betraying its insolvency. But Koharu comes first. The packet contains 400 *momme*. That leaves 350 *momme* to raise.

NARRATOR   She unlocks a large drawer. From the wardrobe lightly fly kite-colored Hachijō silks;[1] a Kyoto crepe kimono lined in pale brown, insubstantial as her husband's life which flickers today and may vanish tomorrow; a padded kimono of Osue's, a flaming scarlet inside and out—Osan flushes with pain to part with it; Kantarō's sleeveless, unlined jacket—if she pawns this, he'll be cold this winter. Next comes a garment of striped Gunnai silk lined in pale blue and never worn, and then her best formal costume—heavy black silk dyed with her family crest, an ivy leaf in a ring. They say that those joined by marriage ties can even go naked at home, though outside the house clothes make the man she snatches up even her husband's finery, a silken cloak, making fifteen articles in all.

OSAN   The very least the pawnshop can offer is 350 *momme* in New Silver.

9. Koharu's situation is described in terms of the money needed to cure a sickness. If 750 *me* is half the sum needed to redeem Koharu, the total of 1,500 *me* (or 6,000 *me* in Old Silver) is considerably less than the 10 *kamme*, or 10,000 *me* in Old Silver.

1. Woven with a warp of brown and a woof of yellow thread to give a color like that of a kite. "Kite" also suggests that the material "flies" out of the cupboard.

NARRATOR   Her face glows as though she already held the money she needs; she hides in the one bundle her husband's shame and her own obligation, and puts her love in besides.

OSAN   It doesn't matter if the children and I have nothing to wear. My husband's reputation concerns me more. Ransom Koharu. Save her. Assert your honor before Tahei.

NARRATOR   But Jihei's eyes remain downcast all the while, and he is silently weeping.

JIHEI   Yes, I can pay the earnest money and keep her out of Tahei's hands. But once I've redeemed her, I'll either have to maintain her in a separate establishment or bring her here. Then what will become of you?

NARRATOR   Osan is at a loss to answer.

OSAN   Yes, what shall I do? Shall I become your children's nurse or the cook? Or perhaps the retired mistress of the house?

NARRATOR   She falls to the floor with a cry of woe.

JIHEI   That would be too selfish. I'd be afraid to accept such generosity. Even if the punishment for my crimes against my parents, against Heaven, against the gods and the Buddhas fails to strike me, the punishment for my crimes against my wife alone will be sufficient to destroy all hope for the future life. Forgive me, I beg you.

NARRATOR   He joins his hands in tearful entreaty.

OSAN   Why should you bow before me? I don't deserve it. I'd be glad to rip the nails from my fingers and toes, to do anything which might serve my husband. I've been pawning my clothes for some time in order to scrape together the money for the paper wholesalers' bills. My wardrobe is empty, but I don't regret it in the least. But it's too late now to talk of such things. Hurry, change your cloak and go to her with a smile.

NARRATOR   He puts on an under kimono of Gunnai silk, a robe of heavy black silk, and a striped cloak. His sash of figured damask holds a dirk of middle length worked in gold: Buddha surely knows that tonight it will be stained with Koharu's blood.

JIHEI   Sangorō! Come here!

NARRATOR   Jihei loads the bundle on the servant's back, intending to take him along. Then he firmly thrusts the wallet next to his skin and starts towards the gate.

VOICE   Is Jihei at home?

NARRATOR   A man enters, removing his fur cap. They see—good heavens!—that it is Gozaemon.

OSAN *and* JIHEI   Ahhh—how fortunate that you should come at this moment!

NARRATOR   Husband and wife are upset and confused. Gozaemon snatches away Sangorō's bundle and sits heavily. His voice is sharp.

GOZAEMON   Stay where you are, harlot!—My esteemed son-in-law, what a rare pleasure to see you dressed in your finest attire, with a dirk and a silken cloak! Ahhh—that's how a gentleman of means spends his money! No one would take you for a paper dealer. Are you perchance on your way to the New Quarter? What commendable perseverance! You have no need for your wife, I take it—Give her a divorce. I've come to take her home with me.

NARRATOR   He speaks needles and his voice is bitter. Jihei has not a word to reply.

OSAN   How kind of you, Father, to walk here on such a cold day. Do have a cup of tea.

NARRATOR   Offering the teacup serves as an excuse for edging closer.

OSAN   Mother and Magoemon came here a while ago, and they told my husband how much they disapproved of his visits to the New Quarter. Jihei was in tears and he wrote out an oath swearing he had reformed. He gave it to Mother. Haven't you seen it yet?

GOZAEMON   His written oath? Do you mean this?

NARRATOR   He takes the paper from his kimono.

GOZAEMON   Libertines scatter vows and oaths wherever they go, as if they were monthly statements of accounts. I thought there was something peculiar about this oath, and now that I am here I can see I was right. Do you still swear to Bonten and Taishaku? Instead of such nonsense, write out a bill of divorcement!

NARRATOR   He rips the oath to shreds and throws down the pieces. Husband and wife exchange looks of alarm, stunned into silence. Jihei touches his hands to the floor and bows his head.

JIHEI   Your anger is justified. If I were still my former self, I would try to offer explanations, but today I appeal entirely to your generosity. Please let me stay with Osan. I promise that even if I become a beggar or an outcast and must sustain life with the scraps that fall from other people's chopsticks, I will hold Osan in high honor and protect her from every harsh and bitter experience. I feel so deeply indebted to Osan that I cannot divorce her. You will understand that this is true as time passes and I show you how I apply myself to my work and restore my fortune. Until then please shut your eyes and allow us to remain together.

NARRATOR   Tears of blood stream from his eyes and his face is pressed to the matting in contrition.

GOZAEMON   The wife of an outcast! That's all the worse. Write the bill of divorcement at once! I will verify and seal the furniture and clothes Osan brought in her dowry.

NARRATOR   He goes to the wardrobe. Osan is alarmed.

OSAN   My clothes are all here. There's no need to examine them.

NARRATOR   She runs up to forestall him, but Gozaemon pushes her aside and jerks open a drawer.

GOZAEMON   What does this mean?

NARRATOR   He opens another drawer: it too is empty. He pulls out every last drawer, but not so much as a foot of patchwork cloth is to be seen. He tears open the wicker hampers, long boxes, and clothes chests.

GOZAEMON   Stripped bare, are they?

NARRATOR   His eyes set in fury. Jihei and Osan huddle under the striped *kotatsu* quilts, ready to sink into the fire with humiliation.

GOZAEMON   This bundle looks suspicious.

NARRATOR   He unties the knots and dumps out the contents.

GOZAEMON   As I thought! You were sending these to the pawnshop, I take it. Jihei—you'd strip the skin from your wife's and your children's bodies to squander the money on your whore! Dirty thief! You're my wife's nephew, but an utter stranger to me, and I'm under no obligation to suffer for your sake. I'll explain to Magoemon what has happened and ask him to make good whatever inroads you've already made on Osan's belongings. But first, the bill of divorcement!

NARRATOR Even if Jihei could escape through seven padlocked doors, eight thicknesses of chains, and a hundred girdling walls, he could not evade so stringent a demand.

JIHEI I won't use a brush to write the bill of divorcement. Here's what I'll do instead! Good-by, Osan.

NARRATOR He lays his hand on his dirk, but Osan clings to him.

OSAN Father—Jihei admits that he's done wrong and he's apologized in every way. You press your advantage too hard. Jihei may be a stranger, but his children are your grandchildren. Have you no affection for them? I will not accept a bill of divorcement.

NARRATOR She embraces her husband and raises her voice in tears.

GOZAEMON Very well. I won't insist on it. Come with me, woman.

NARRATOR He pulls her to her feet.

OSAN No, I won't go. What bitterness makes you expose to such shame a man and wife who still love each other? I will not suffer it.

NARRATOR She pleads with him, weeping, but he pays her no heed.

GOZAEMON Is there some greater shame? I'll shout it through the town!

NARRATOR He pulls her up, but she shakes free. Caught by the wrist she totters forward when—alas!—her toes brush against her sleeping children. They open their eyes.

CHILDREN Mother dear, why is Grandfather, the bad man, taking you away? Whom will we sleep beside now?

NARRATOR They call out after her.

OSAN My poor dears! You've never spent a night away from Mother's side since you were born. Sleep tonight beside your father. (*To* JIHEI.) Please don't forget to give the children their tonic before breakfast.—Oh, my heart is broken!

NARRATOR These are her parting words. She leaves her children behind, abandoned as in the woods; the twin-trunked bamboo of conjugal love is sundered forever.

ACT 3

SCENE 1: *Sonezaki New Quarter, in front of the Yamato House.*

TIME: *That night.*

NARRATOR This is Shijimi River, the haunt of love and affection. Its flowing water and the feet of passersby are stilled now at two in the morning, and the full moon shines clear in the sky. Here in the street a dim doorway lantern is marked "Yamatoya Dembei" in a single scrawl. The night watchman's clappers take on a sleepy cadence as he totters by on uncertain legs. The very thickness of his voice crying, "Beware of fire! Beware of fire!" tells how far advanced the night is. A serving woman from the upper town comes along, followed by a palanquin. "It's terribly late," she remarks to the bearers as she clatters open the side door of the Yamato House and steps inside.

SERVANT   I've come to take back Koharu of the Kinokuni House.

NARRATOR   Her voice is faintly heard outside. A few moments later, after hardly time enough to exchange three or four words of greeting, she emerges.

SERVANT   Koharu is spending the night. Bearers, you may leave now and get some rest. (*To proprietress, inside the doorway.*) Oh, I forgot to tell you, madam. Please keep an eye on Koharu. Now that the ransom to Tahei has been arranged and the money's been accepted, we're merely her custodians. Please don't let her drink too much saké.

NARRATOR   She leaves, having scattered at the doorway the seeds that before morning will turn Jihei and Koharu to dust.

   At night between two and four even the teahouse kettle rests; the flame flickering in the low candle stand narrows; and the frost spreads in the cold river-wind of the deepening night. The master's voice breaks the stillness.

DEMBEI (*to* JIHEI)   It's still the middle of the night. I'll send somebody with you. (*To servants.*) Mr. Jihei is leaving. Wake Koharu. Call her here.

NARRATOR   Jihei slides open the side door.

JIHEI   No, Dembei, not a word to Koharu. I'll be trapped here till dawn if she hears I'm leaving. That's why I'm letting her sleep and slipping off this way. Wake her up after sunrise and send her back then. I'm returning home now and will leave for Kyoto immediately on business. I have so many engagements that I may not be able to return in time for the interim payment.[2] Please use the money I gave you earlier this evening to clear my account. I'd like you also to send 150 *me* of Old Silver to Kawashō for the moon-viewing party last month. Please get a receipt. Give Saietsubō[3] from Fukushima one piece of silver as a contribution to the Buddhist altar he's bought, and tell him to use it for a memorial service. Wasn't there something else? Oh yes—give Isoichi a tip of four silver coins. That's the lot. Now you can close up and get to bed. Good-by. I'll see you when I return from Kyoto.

NARRATOR   Hardly has he taken two or three steps than he turns back.

JIHEI   I forgot my dirk. Fetch it for me, won't you?—Yes, Dembei, this is one respect in which it's easier being a townsman. If I were a samurai and forgot my sword, I'd probably commit suicide on the spot!

DEMBEI   I completely forgot that I was keeping it for you. Yes, here's the knife with it.

NARRATOR   He gives the dirk to Jihei, who fastens it firmly into his sash.

JIHEI   I feel secure as long as I have this. Good night!

NARRATOR   He goes off.

DEMBEI   Please come back to Osaka soon! Thank you for your patronage!

NARRATOR   With this hasty farewell Dembei rattles the door bolt shut; then not another sound is heard as the silence deepens. Jihei pretends to leave, only to creep back again with stealthy steps. He clings to the door of the Yamato House. As he peeps within he is startled by shadows moving towards him. He takes cover at the house across the way until the figures pass.

   Magoemon the Miller, his heart pulverized with anxiety over his younger

---

2. On the last day of the Tenth Month, one of the times during the year for making payments.

3. Name of a male entertainer in the Fukushima quarter, west of Sonezaki.

brother, comes first, followed by the apprentice Sangorō with Jihei's son Kantarō on his back. They hurry along until they spy the lantern of the Yamato House. Magoemon pounds on the door.

MAGOEMON Excuse me. Kamiya Jihei's here, isn't he? I'd like to see him a moment.

NARRATOR Jihei thinks, "It's my brother!" but dares not stir from his place of concealment. From inside a man's sleep-laden voice is heard.

DEMBEI Jihei left a while ago saying he was going up to Kyoto. He's not here.

NARRATOR Not another sound is heard. Magoemon's tears fall unchecked.

MAGOEMON (*to himself*) I ought to have met him on the way if he'd been going home. I can't understand what takes him to Kyoto. Ahhh—I'm trembling all over with worry. I wonder if he didn't take Koharu with him.

NARRATOR The thought pierces his heart; unable to bear the pain, he pounds again on the door.

DEMBEI Who is it, so late at night? We've gone to bed.

MAGOEMON I'm sorry to disturb you, but I'd like to ask one more thing. Has Koharu of the Kinokuni House left? I was wondering if she mightn't have gone with Jihei.

DEMBEI What's that? Koharu's upstairs, fast asleep.

MAGOEMON That's a relief, anyway. There's no fear of a lovers' suicide. But where is he hiding himself causing me all this anxiety? He can't imagine the agony of suspense that the whole family is going through on his account. I'm afraid that bitterness towards his father-in-law may make him forget himself and do something rash. I brought Kantarō along, hoping he would help to dissuade Jihei, but the gesture was in vain. I wonder why I failed to meet him?

NARRATOR He murmurs to himself, his eyes moist with tears. Jihei's hiding place is close enough for him to hear every word. He chokes with emotion, but can only swallow his tears.

MAGOEMON Sangorō! Where does the fool go night after night? Don't you know anywhere else?

NARRATOR Sangorō imagines that he himself is the fool referred to.

SANGORŌ I know a couple of places, but I'm too embarrassed to mention them.

MAGOEMON You know them? Where are they? Tell me.

SANGORŌ Please don't scold me when you've heard. Every night I wander down below the warehouses by the market.

MAGOEMON Imbecile! Who's asking about that? Come on, let's search the back streets. Don't let Kantarō catch a chill. The poor kid's having a cold time of it, thanks to that useless father of his. Still, if the worst the boy experiences is the cold I won't complain. I'm afraid that Jihei may cause him much greater pain. The scoundrel!

NARRATOR But beneath the rancor in his heart of hearts is profound pity.

MAGOEMON Let's look at the back street!

NARRATOR They pass on. As soon as their figures have gone off a distance Jihei runs from his hiding place. Standing on tiptoes he gazes with yearning after them and cries out in his heart.

JIHEI He cannot leave me to my death, though I am the worst of sinners! I remain to the last a burden to him! I'm unworthy of such kindness!

NARRATOR   He joins his hands and kneels in prayer.

JIHEI   If I may make one further request of your mercy, look after my children!

NARRATOR   These are his only words; for a while he chokes with tears.

JIHEI   At any rate, our decision's been made. Koharu must be waiting.

NARRATOR   He peers through a crack in the side door of the Yamato House and glimpses a figure.

JIHEI   That's Koharu, isn't it? I'll let her know I'm here.

NARRATOR   He clears his throat, their signal. "Ahem, ahem"—the sound blends with the clack of wooden clappers as the watchman comes from the upper street, coughing in the night wind. He hurries on his round of fire warning, "Take care! Beware!" Even this cry has a dismal sound to one in hiding. Jihei, concealing himself like the god of Katsuragi,[4] lets the watchman pass. He sees his chance and rushes to the side door, which softly opens from within.

JIHEI   Koharu?

KOHARU   Were you waiting? Jihei—I want to leave quickly.

NARRATOR   She is all impatience, but the more hastily they open the door, the more likely people will be to hear the casters turning. They lift the door; it gives a moaning that thunders in their ears and in their hearts. Jihei lends a hand from the outside, but his fingertips tremble with the trembling of his heart. The door opens a quarter of an inch, a half, an inch—an inch ahead are the tortures of hell, but more than hell itself they fear the guardian-demon's eyes. At last the door opens, and with the joy of New Year's morn[5] Koharu slips out. They catch each other's hands. Shall they go north or south, west or east? Their pounding hearts urge them on, though they know not to what destination: turning their backs on the moon reflected in Shijimi River, they hurry eastward as fast as their legs will carry them.

SCENE 2: *The farewell journey of many bridges.*

NARRATOR

The running hand in texts of Nō is always Konoe style;
An actor in a woman's part is sure to wear a purple hat.[6]
Does some teaching of the Buddha as rigidly decree
That men who spend their days in evil haunts must end like this?

Poor creatures, though they would discover today their destiny in the Sutra of Cause and Effect, tomorrow the gossip of the world will scatter like blossoms the scandal of Kamiya Jihei's love suicide, and, carved in cherry wood, his story to the last detail will be printed in illustrated sheets.[7]

---

4. The god was so ashamed of his ugliness that he ventured forth only at night.
5. Mention of the New Year is connected with Koharu's name, with *haru* meaning "spring."
6. The Konoe style of calligraphy was used in books with Noh texts. Custom also decreed that young male actors playing the parts of women cover their foreheads with a square of purple cloth to disguise the fact that they were shaven.

7. These sheets mentioned here featured current scandals, such as lovers' suicides. "Cause and Effect": a sacred scripture of Buddhism, which says: "If you wish to know the past cause, look at the present effect; if you wish to know the future effect, look at the present cause." "Cherry wood": the blocks from which illustrated books were printed were often of cherry wood.

Jihei, led on by the spirit of death—if such there be among the gods—is resigned to this punishment for neglect of his trade. But at times—who could blame him?—his heart is drawn to those he has left behind, and it is hard to keep walking on. Even in the full moon's light, this fifteenth night of the tenth moon,[8] he cannot see his way ahead—a sign perhaps of the darkness in his heart? The frost now falling will melt by dawn but, even more quickly than this symbol of human frailty, the lovers themselves will melt away. What will become of the fragrance that lingered when he held her tenderly at night in their bedchamber?

This bridge, Tenjin Bridge, he has crossed every day, morning and night, gazing at Shijimi River to the west. Long ago, when Tenjin, then called Michizane,[9] was exiled to Tsukushi, his plum tree, following its master, flew in one bound to Dazaifu, and here is Plum-field Bridge. Green Bridge recalls the aged pine that followed later, and Cherry Bridge the tree that withered away in grief over parting. Such are the tales still told, bespeaking the power of a single poem.

JIHEI   Though born the parishioner of so holy and mighty a god, I shall kill you and then myself. If you ask the cause, it was that I lacked even the wisdom that might fill a tiny Shell Bridge.[1] Our stay in this world has been short as an autumn day. This evening will be the last of your nineteen, of my twenty-eight years. The time has come to cast away our lives. We promised we'd remain together faithfully, till you were an old woman and I an old man, but before we knew each other three full years, we have met this disaster. Look, here is Ōe Bridge. We follow the river from Little Naniwa Bridge to Funairi Bridge. The farther we journey, the closer we approach the road to death.

NARRATOR   He laments. She clings to him.

KOHARU   Is this already the road to death?

NARRATOR   Falling tears obscure from each the other's face and threaten to immerse even the Horikawa bridges.

JIHEI   A few steps north and I could glimpse my house, but I will not turn back. I will bury in my breast all thoughts of my children's future, all pity for my wife. We cross southward over the river. Why did they call a place with as many buildings as a bridge has piers "Eight Houses"? Hurry, we

---

8. November 14, 1720. In the lunar calendar the full moon occurs on the fifteenth of the month.

9. Sugawara no Michizane, unfairly slandered at court, was exiled to Dazaifu on Japan's southernmost main island of Kyushu. When he was about to depart, he composed a poem of farewell to his favorite plum tree. Legend has it that the tree, moved by his master's poem, flew after him to Kyushu, while the cherry tree in Michizane's garden withered away in grief. Only the pine seemed indifferent, but after Michizane complained in a poem, the pine tree also flew to Kyushu to join his master.

1. The lovers' journey takes them over twelve bridges altogether. They proceed first along the north bank of Shijimi River ("Shell River") to Shijimi Bridge, where they cross to Dōjima. At Little Naniwa Bridge they cross back again to Sonezaki. Continuing eastward, they cross Horikawa, then cross the Temma Bridge over the Ōkawa. At "Eight Houses" (Hakkenya) they journey eastward along the south bank of the river as far as Kyō Bridge (Sutra Bridge). They cross this bridge to the tip of land at Katamachi and then take the Onari Bridge to the final destination, Amijima.

want to arrive before the down-river boat from Fushimi comes—with what happy couples sleeping aboard!

Next is Temma Bridge, a frightening name[2] for us about to depart this world. Here the two streams Yodo and Yamato join in one great river, as fish with water, and as Koharu and I, dying on one blade will cross together the River of Three Fords.[3] I would like this water for our tomb offering!

KOHARU   What have we to grieve about? Though in this world we could not stay together, in the next and through each successive world to come until the end of time we shall be husband and wife. Every summer for my devotions[4] I have copied the All Compassionate and All Merciful Chapter of the Lotus Sutra, in the hope that we may be reborn on one lotus.

NARRATOR   They cross over Kyō Bridge and reach the opposite shore.[5]

KOHARU   If I can save living creatures at will when once I mount a lotus calyx in Paradise and become a Buddha, I want to protect women of my profession, so that never again will there be love suicides.

NARRATOR   This unattainable prayer stems from worldly attachment, but it touchingly reveals her heart.

They cross Onari Bridge.[6] The waters of Noda Creek are shrouded with morning haze; the mountain tips show faintly white.

JIHEI   Listen—the voices of the temple bells begin to boom. How much farther can we go on this way? We are not fated to live any longer—let us make an end quickly. Come this way.

NARRATOR   Tears are strung with the 108 beads of the rosaries in their hands. They have come now to Amijima, to the Daichō Temple; the overflowing sluice gate of a little stream beside a bamboo thicket will be their place of death.

SCENE 3: *Amijima.*

JIHEI   No matter how far we walk, there'll never be a spot marked "For Suicides." Let us kill ourselves here.

NARRATOR   He takes her hand and sits on the ground.

KOHARU   Yes, that's true. One place is as good as another to die. But I've been thinking on the way that if they find our dead bodies together people will say that Koharu and Jihei committed a lovers' suicide. Osan will think then that I treated as mere scrap paper the letter I sent promising her, when she asked me not to kill you, that I would not, and vowing to break all relations. She will be sure that I lured her precious husband into a lovers' suicide. She will despise me as a one-night prostitute, a false woman with no sense of decency. I fear her contempt more than the slander of a thousand or ten

2. The characters used for Temma mean literally "demon."
3. A river in the Buddhist underworld that had to be crossed to reach the world of the dead. One blade plus two people equal "Three Fords."
4. It was customary for Buddhist monks and

some of the laity in Japan to observe a summer retreat to practice austerities.
5. This location implies Nirvana. "Kyō Bridge": called "Sutra Bridge."
6. The word "Onari" implies "to become a Buddha."

thousand strangers. I can imagine how she will resent and envy me. That is the greatest obstacle to my salvation. Kill me here, then choose another spot, far away, for yourself.

NARRATOR   She leans against him. Jihei joins in her tears of pleading.

JIHEI   What foolish worries! Osan has been taken back by my father-in-law. I've divorced her. She and I are strangers now. Why should you feel obliged to a divorced woman? You were saying on the way that you and I will be husband and wife through each successive world until the end of time. Who can criticize us, who can be jealous if we die side by side?

KOHARU   But who is responsible for your divorce? You're even less reasonable than I. Do you suppose that our bodies will accompany us to the afterworld? We may die in different places, our bodies may be pecked by kites and crows, but what does it matter as long as our souls are twined together? Take me with you to heaven or to hell!

NARRATOR   She sinks again in tears.

JIHEI   You're right. Our bodies are made of earth, water, fire, and wind, and when we die they revert to emptiness. But our souls will not decay, no matter how often reborn. And here's a guarantee that our souls will be married and never part!

NARRATOR   He whips out his dirk and slashes off his black locks at the base of the top knot.

JIHEI   Look, Koharu. As long as I had this hair I was Kamiya Jihei, Osan's husband, but cutting it has made me a monk. I have fled the burning house of the three worlds of delusion; I am a priest, unencumbered by wife, children, or worldly possessions. Now that I no longer have a wife named Osan, you owe her no obligations either.

NARRATOR   In tears he flings away the hair.

KOHARU   I am happy.

NARRATOR   Koharu takes up the dirk and ruthlessly, unhesitantly, slices through her flowing Shimada coiffure. She casts aside the tresses she has so often washed and combed and stroked. How heartbreaking to see their locks tangled with the weeds and midnight frost of this desolate field!

JIHEI   We have escaped the inconstant world, a nun and a priest. Our duties as husband and wife belong to our profane past. It would be best to choose quite separate places for our deaths, a mountain for one, the river for the other. We will pretend that the ground above this sluice gate is a mountain. You will die there. I shall hang myself by this stream. The time of our deaths will be the same, but the method and place will differ. In this way we can honor to the end our duty to Osan. Give me your under sash.

NARRATOR   Its fresh violet color and fragrance will be lost in the winds of impermanence; the crinkled silk long enough to wind twice round her body will bind two worlds, this and the next. He firmly fastens one end to the crosspiece of the sluice, then twists the other into a noose for his neck. He will hang for love of his wife like the "pheasant in the hunting grounds."[7]

7. A reference to a poem from the 8th-century anthology *Collection of Myriad Leaves* (*Man'yōshū*): "The pheasant foraging in the fields of spring reveals his whereabouts to man as he cries for his mate."

Koharu watches Jihei prepare for his death. Her eyes swim with tears, her mind is distraught.

KOHARU Is that how you're going to kill yourself?—If we are to die apart, I have only a little while longer by your side. Come near me.

NARRATOR They take each other's hands.

KOHARU It's over in a moment with a sword, but I'm sure you'll suffer. My poor darling!

NARRATOR She cannot stop the silent tears.

JIHEI Can suicide ever be pleasant, whether by hanging or cutting the throat? You mustn't let worries over trifles disturb the prayers of your last moments. Keep your eyes on the westward-moving moon, and worship it as Amida himself.[8] Concentrate your thoughts on the Western Paradise. If you have any regrets about leaving the world, tell me now, then die.

KOHARU I have none at all, none at all. But I'm sure you must be worried about your children.

JIHEI You make me cry all over again by mentioning them. I can almost see their faces, sleeping peacefully, unaware, poor dears, that their father is about to kill himself. They're the one thing I can't forget.

NARRATOR He droops to the ground with weeping. The voices of the crows leaving their nests at dawn rival his sobs. Are the crows mourning his fate? The thought brings more tears.

JIHEI Listen to them. The crows have come to guide us to the world of the dead. There's an old saying that every time somebody writes an oath on the back of a Kumano charm, three crows of Kumano die on the holy mountain. The first words we've written each New Year have been vows of love, and how often we've inscribed oaths at the beginning of the month! If each oath has killed three crows, what a multitude must have perished! Their cries have always sounded like "beloved, beloved," but hatred for our crime of taking life makes their voices ring tonight "revenge, revenge!"[9] Whose fault is it they demand revenge? Because of me you will die a painful death. Forgive me!

NARRATOR He takes her in his arms.

KOHARU No, it's my fault!

NARRATOR They cling to each other, face pressed to face; their sidelocks, drenched with tears, freeze in the winds blowing over the fields. Behind them echoes the voice of the Daichō Temple.

JIHEI Even the long winter night seems short as our lives.

NARRATOR Dawn is already breaking, and matins can be heard. He draws her to him.

JIHEI The moment has come for our glorious end. Let there be no tears on your face when they find you later.

KOHARU There won't be any.

NARRATOR She smiles. His hands, numbed by the frost, tremble before the pale vision of her face, and his eyes are first to cloud. He is weeping so profusely that he cannot control the blade.

---

8. Amida's Western Paradise of the Pure Land lies in the west. The moon is frequently used as a symbol of Buddhist enlightenment.

9. The cries have always sounded like *kawai, kawai* ("beloved"), but now they sound like *mukui, mukui* ("revenge").

KOHARU   Compose yourself—but be quick!

NARRATOR   Her encouragement lends him strength; the invocations to Amida carried by the wind urge a final prayer. *Namu Amida Butsu.* He thrusts in the saving sword.[1] Stabbed, she falls backwards, despite his staying hand, and struggles in terrible pain. The point of the blade has missed her windpipe, and these are the final tortures before she can die. He writhes with her in agony, then painfully summons his strength again. He draws her to him, and plunges his dirk to the hilt. He twists the blade in the wound, and her life fades away like an unfinished dream at dawning.

He arranges her corpse head to the north, face to the west, lying on her right side,[2] and throws his cloak over her. He turns away at last, unable to exhaust with tears his grief over parting. He pulls the sash to him and fastens the noose around his neck. The service in the temple has reached the closing section, the prayers for the dead. "Believers and unbelievers will equally share in the divine grace," the voices proclaim, and at the final words Jihei jumps from the sluice gate.

JIHEI   May we be reborn on one lotus! Hail Amida Buddha!

NARRATOR   For a few moments he writhes like a gourd swinging in the wind, but gradually the passage of his breath is blocked as the stream is dammed by the sluice gate, where his ties with this life are snapped.

Fishermen out for the morning catch find the body in their net.[3]

FISHERMEN   A dead man! Look, a dead man! Come here, everybody!

NARRATOR   The tale is spread from mouth to mouth. People say that they who were caught in the net of Buddha's vow immediately gained salvation and deliverance, and all who hear the tale of the Love Suicides at Amijima are moved to tears.

1. The invocations of Amida's name freed one from spiritual obstacles, just as a sword freed one from physical obstacles.
2. The dead were arranged in this manner because the historical Buddha, Shakyamuni Buddha, chose this position when he died and passed into Nirvana.
3. The vow of the Buddha to save all sentient beings is likened to a net that catches people in its meshes. "Net" (*ami*) is echoed a few lines later in the name "Amijima."

THE SONG OF CH'UN-HYANG

eighteenth century

The most famous work of traditional Korea, *The Song of Ch'un-hyang*, is also the most widely performed and best-loved example of Korea's indigenous *p'ansori* narrative drama, wrapping a stunning indictment of the corruption of Korea's elites within a compelling tale of romantic love, heroism, and fidelity. Tracing its roots to shaman songs, folktales, and folksongs, *p'ansori* drama has much in common with other narrative forms that were sung or chanted by a single actor, such as the rhapsodic performances of ancient Greek epic poetry. When *p'ansori* first appeared in the early eighteenth century, it was mostly performed in the open air, but in the twentieth century it became customary to perform shows on a Western-style theater stage. *P'ansori* drama remains one of Korea's foremost cultural forms.

P'ansori was shaped by the social changes that took place during the Chosŏn Dynasty (1392–1910). Chosŏn rulers adopted Confucianism as the basic ideology for the state and society. The ruling class, the so-called *yangban* ("two orders," referring to the civilian and military elites), was recruited through a Chinese-style system of civil service examinations, which required extensive study of the Confucian Classics. Although in principle the examination system rewarded academic merit, access to the exams became increasingly limited to the sons of yangban families. To further enhance the power of the leading yangban families, sons of concubines were excluded from the exams. The adoption of Confucianism had a profound impact on women.

Whereas during the previous dynasty women could continue their family lineage and young couples were often living with the wife's family before finding their own home, Chosŏn Confucianism emphasized inheritance through the male lineage of descendants and daughters were often erased from the family registers when they got married. Also, Confucian ancestor worship and attention to the values of filial piety and one's duties towards superiors, such as ruler and husband, became prominent.

The interplay between resistance to and adoption of Confucian values is particularly prevalent in *p'ansori*, a form that explores Confucian sensibility in contact with the popular culture of commoners. *P'ansori* has always been a communal act. While the male *p'ansori* performer, accompanied only by a drummer, tells his riveting tales about the suffering of the common people, alternating between singing and speaking, all in verse, the audience responds spontaneously to the story and cheers on the performer with encouraging shouts. A form of vernacular literature and popular oral storytelling, *p'ansori* often attacked the values of the ruling elite. Thus *p'ansori* offers an alternately critical, tragicomic and often sarcastic portrait of the Chosŏn ruling elite. However, as Confucianism gradually spread to all classes of society and as commoners aspired to raise their social status through education, even popular genres such as *p'ansori* came to embrace those values, although often in surprising and indirect ways.

P'ansori is a traditional performance art with a set repertoire. As the art form became increasingly popular in Chosŏn society, a series of master performers emerged, and a repertoire of twelve *p'ansori* works was established. This number dropped to six by the end of the Chosŏn Dynasty in the early twentieth century, and today five works are regularly performed, namely *The Song of Ch'un-hyang*, *The Song of Shim Ch'ŏng*, *The Song of Hŭngbu*, *The Song of the Water Palace*, and *The Song of the Red Cliff*.

THE SONG OF CH'UN-HYANG

The oral narrative on which *The Song of Ch'un-hyang* is based probably emerged in the early eighteenth century. The first-known text version, a long poem written in Chinese style, dates to 1754 and was written by an otherwise unknown man named Yu Chin-han. The other extant texts are woodblock prints, all from the nineteenth century.

Set in Chŏlla Province, *The Song of Ch'un-hyang* tells the story of Ch'un-hyang, the daughter of a *yangban* aristocrat and a *kisaeng* (a female entertainer or courtesan), and Master Yi Mong-ryŏng (or Yi To-ryŏng), son of the local magistrate. When Master Yi's father is reassigned to a position in Seoul, Master Yi leaves Ch'un-hyang, promising to come back for her once he succeeds in the all-important civil service examinations. Ch'un-hyang vows to wait for him. Her faithfulness is soon put to the test when the new magistrate arrives and wants to make Ch'un-hyang his concubine. Determined to bend her to his will, the magistrate has her jailed and tortured. In the sections presented here, Ch'un-hyang rejects the magistrate's advances. In the end, Master Yi, recently gradu-ated with honors, returns to Chŏlla, rescues Ch'un-hyang, and we are told they go on to live a happy, prosperous life together.

The traditional happy ending of the drama should not undermine the explosive message underlying *The Song of Ch'un-hyang*. Ch'un-hyang directly contradicts the values of the elite by claiming that her love for Master Yi transcends societal hierarchies and that even the daughter of a lowly *kisaeng* can aspire to a respectable union with the son of a high-ranking official. Even more subversive are the lessons Ch'un-hyang teaches the torturers who try to force her to become the incoming magistrate's concubine: she instructs them in the Confucian values of virtue, female chastity, and fidelity, shows her erudition in Chinese history by evoking series of Chinese examples to make her points, and to illustrate her own plight cites the names of Chinese rulers and sages who suffered unjustly. While she is beaten close to death and blood streams over her "jade-white body" she lectures the magistrate with every single stroke of beating on Confucian duties and her way of upholding them. Her hauntingly beautiful lament in prison marks her as one of the strongest heroines in all of Korean literature.

The story of Ch'un-hyang has been told not only in *p'ansori* but in a variety of other genres, including plays, novels, and films. At least thirteen films about the story exist, including one from North Korea. The most recent film version, by the renowned Korean director Im Kwon-taek, which incorporates traditional elements of *p'ansori* performance, appeared in 2001, bringing this story, which holds an incriminatory mirror to the corrupt values of elites and their enforcement of a rigid class society, into the twenty-first century.

From The Song of Ch'un-hyang[1]

* * *

Ch'un-hyang could do nothing but return to her room: 'Hyang-dan! Pull down the blind, lay the pillow and cushions out for me, and shut the door. I don't know whether I'll ever see him again in this life, so I'll try to sleep and perhaps I'll see him in a dream. There's an old saying that a lover seen in dreams will be unfaithful. I know, but if I don't see him in a dream how shall I see him? Come, my dreams, come to me. My sorrows are piled up so deeply, what shall I do if I cannot dream? Oh dear, it's all my fault.

'Mankind is born for partings, but how can I bear this empty room? Who can understand how desperately I want to see him again? I am so distraught and bewildered that whether I lie down to sleep, or wake and try to eat, I feel choked by my longings. I yearn to see his handsome face and hear his voice ringing in my ears. Oh, I want to see him again! I want to see him! I want to hear him again! I want to hear him!

'What enemy from a former life arranged that we should be born like this, to love one another, to vow that we should never forget one another but live together till death, a vow more precious than gold or jewels—why should the world come between us? A spring should grow into a stream: how could I know that our love, piled high like mountains upon mountains, would crumble like this? Some evil spirit has harmed us, or creation envies us. When shall I see again the husband I parted from this morning? I have plumbed the depths of a thousand griefs and ten thousand sorrows.

'My face and hair will grow old and useless, and the sun and moon will give me no joy. On autumn nights the moon will shine through the paulownia branches and make me sad. The sunshine on the summer leaves will only make me miserable. Even if he knows how much I love him, and he loves me too. I shall still be lying alone in this empty room with no company save my sighs and tears wrung from my tortured heart. I will collect my tears to make a sea, and my sighs to make a breeze, and sail a little boat to Seoul to seek my love. In the sadness of the moonlit nights I will pray for him with tears—and he will shine in my dreams.

'The cuckoo crying in the moonlight may reach the ears of my beloved, but only I shall know my sorrows. In the gloom of the night, the fireflies gleam outside the windows: I sit up at midnight wondering whether he shall come. Even though I lie down, shall I be able to sleep? Neither sleep nor my lover shall come. What can I do? Fate is cruel.

'*After joy comes sorrow; after the bitter, the sweet,*' is an old saying, but there seems no end to waiting, and who can unravel the sorrows of my heart except my own beloved?

'High heaven, look down kindly and let me see him soon. Let us meet again to complete our love, and never part till the white hairs of old age fall in death. Green waters and blue hills. I beg of you! I was suddenly deprived of my love, and no news comes; he must be made of wood or stone. Oh dear, the pity of it!'

She passed her time praying and grieving. Meanwhile the boy, as he stopped for the night on his way to Seoul, could not sleep: 'I want to see her, I want to

---

1. Translated by Richard Rutt and Kim Chong-un.

see my love. Day and night the thought of her never leaves me. She is longing for me, let me see her soon and satisfy her.'

So the day and months passed, and he looked forward to his name appearing in the list of examination successes.

After some months a new governor was appointed to Namwŏn, Pyŏn Hak-to, of Chaha-dong, in Seoul. He was a famous author and a fine figure of a man, well-versed in music and widely respected, but he had one fault: he sometimes behaved irresponsibly, forgot his morals and made errors of judgment. So it was commonly said of him that he was unusually stubborn.

The officials of his new post presented themselves:

'The staff are all present, sir.'

'The chief clerk.'

'The steward.'

'The chamberlain.'

'Call the chief clerk forward.'

'Chief clerk here, sir.'

'Is there anything to report from your district?'

'Everything is in good order, sir.'

'I hear that the men in your department are the best in the three southern provinces.'

'Yes, sir, they work well.'

'They say there's a very pretty girl there, called Ch'un-hyang.'

'Yes, sir.'

'Is she well?'

'She is very well, sir.'

'How far is Namwŏn from here?'

'Six hundred and thirty *li*,[2] sir.'

Pyŏn grew impatient: 'Let's get started quickly.'

The staff withdrew, saying to each other: 'Things are going to happen when we get home.'

It was soon time for the new governor's departure, and he set off in magnificent array. He was surrounded by litters and palanquins; banners fluttered in the wind: the yamen[3] servants, dressed in brightly-colored coats with bandoliers of white cloth, and wide-brimmed felt hats, decorated with tortoiseshell ornaments, worn low on their brows, carried the banners: 'Make way, make way!'

The bodyguard was formidable; on either side were servants leading bridled horses. Two men in military felt hats carried whips, and followed behind the cavalcade with the chamberlain, the steward, the officer of works and the chief clerk of the new post. A pair of yamen slaves and two servants carried the great ceremonial parasol, supporting it from before and behind, and sometimes from the sides. It was made of white flowered silk, with a broad border of indigo brocade, and the metal rings around the edge tinkled as it moved. The noise of the guard echoed through the hills, and the shouts of the grooms resounded from the clouds. When they arrived at Chŏnju, he reported at the Kyŏnggi-jŏn of the official guest-house and paid his respects to the garrison. He passed quickly through the hills to the south of the city, crossed the pass at Manmagwan,

2. A Chinese *li* is about a third of a mile.   3. Headquarters of a government official.

passed the Nogu rock and did not stop as he went through Imsil. At Osu he stopped for lunch. When he arrived at Namwŏn later in the day all the men of the garrison and the servants of the local government came out to meet him at the Ori pavilion. As he passed through the garnished streets there was a great din from the two men who swept the path in front of him, two carriers of the Red Gate banners, the two bearers of the Banner of the Scarlet Bird, made of red silk with indigo flowers, the two bearers of the Azure Dragon banner of blue silk, the two bearers of the black banner with red flowers of the Sable Tortoise, the two banners of the watch, the two banners of the garrison, the two officers of the guard, two color-sergeants, and twenty-four military slaves. The fanfares of the trumpeters shook the city, and the air rang with the music of the band and the shouts of the grooms.

They stopped at the Kwanghal-lu to marshal the procession, while the governor changed his clothes. He paid his respects at the guest-house and mounted an open carriage so that all the people could see him. He rolled his eyes fiercely as he left the guest-house and went to his official residence, where he sat down to his meal of welcome. When it was over the officials came to greet him: the officers of the garrison, the master of the rites, and the officials of the six departments. The governor ordered them: 'Call the master of the slaves, and tell him to muster the kisaeng.'

The chief secretary, when he received this command, brought out the register of kisaeng and called their names in order, with a verse of poetry for each:

'After the rain on the eastern hills: Full Moon!'

Full Moon came in, her gauze skirts rustling as her slender form moved daintily to report before the governor: 'I am here!'

'The fisherman's boat follows the stream
Through the flowering hills of spring: Peach Blossom!'

Peach Blossom walked daintily in, clutching the edge of her crimson skirt, and presented herself before the governor: 'I am here!'

'The phoenix of Danshan has lost its mate
And roosts in the paulownia tree:
A spirit of the hills.
A wraith among birds.
It starves, but cannot eat millet.
A bird of eternal loyalty: Painted Phoenix!'

Painted Phoenix came in, her gauze skirt gracefully gathered around her slender body, walking with mincing steps to present herself before the governor: 'I am here!'

'The purity of the lotus never changes,
Is not this the loveliest of flowers? Lotus Heart!'

Lotus Heart came in trailing her gauze skirt and moving slowly in her embroidered shoes as she walked before the governor: 'I am here!'

'Like a peerless moon over the sapphire sea
The white stone of Jingshan, Bright Jade!'

Bright Jade came in dressed in misty gauze, moving gracefully before the governor to present herself: 'I am here!'

'The clouds are light, the breezes gentle.
No one is near.
Gold shines among the willows; Oriole!'

Oriole came in trailing her crimson skirt as her slender form moved daintily to report before the governor: 'I am here!'

The governor said: 'Call them more quickly!'

'Yes, sir.'

The secretary, in response to this command, called each of them with brief couplets:

'*The fairy girl who offered peaches*
In the palace of the moon: Cinnamon Fragrance!'

'Here I am.'

'*Little boy under the pine-tree, tell me*
What news of the master among the green hills: Misty Deep!'

'Here I am.'

'*Going up to the moon-palace*
To pluck a cinnamon flower: Love-token!'

'Here I am.'

'*I ask where the wine-shop is;*
The herdboy points to the Apricot Blossom!'

'Here I am.'

'*Half-moon of autumn on Emei Mountain:*
The shadows follow the flowing stream. Water Fairy!'

'Here I am.'

'*Playing on a lute of paulownia wood.* Lutanist!'

'Here I am.'

'*Noble lotus of the eighth moon,*
Fill the autumn pool with color, Pink Lotus!'

'Here I am.'

'*Knotted with cords of vermilion silk.* Embroidered Purse!'

'Here I am.'

The governor spoke again: 'Call a dozen or so at once.'

The secretary began to call them more quickly: 'Sun-terrace Fairy, Moon Fairy, Flower Fairy!'

'Here we are.'

'Embroidered Fairy, Embroidered Jade, Embroidered Lotus!'

'Here we are.'

'Toy Jade, Orchid Jade, Crimson Jade!'

'Here we are.'

'*The breezes fail in* Fading Spring!'

'Here I am, I'm coming!'

When Fading Spring came in, it was clear that she thought she was very beautiful. Because she had heard that she was pretty, she had plastered her hair away from her forehead, well back behind her ears; and because she had heard about powder and rouge she had bought four *yang* and seventy cents' worth of coarse powder and spread it all over her face as though she were plastering a wall. She was as tall and lanky as a man, had gathered far too much of her skirt in her hand and was holding it so high that it nearly touched her chin. She walked like a swan on dry land, waddling forward to report before the governor: 'Here I am!'

Many of the kisaeng were very pretty, but the governor had heard a great deal about Ch'un-hyang, and was surprised that her name was not on the list. He called the master of the slaves and asked him: 'The roll of kisaeng has been called, but Ch'un-hyang was not called. Has she retired?'

The man replied: 'Ch'un-hyang's mother was a kisaeng, but Ch'un-hyang herself is not.'

The governor asked him again: 'If she is not a kisaeng, but has been brought up at home in the women's quarters, how has she become so well-known?'

The man answered: 'She is a kisaeng's daughter. She is so beautiful that when great gentlemen and writers and such-like come this way, they ask to see her, but both mother and daughter refuse. Not only the gentry, but even the men who live in the household, have not seen her once in ten years, much less spoken to her. However, it seems that by a strange dispensation of heaven your predecessor's son met her and was betrothed to her. When he left Namwŏn, he said that he would come to fetch her after he had been appointed to public office, and Ch'un-hyang believes this and is staying faithful to him.'

The governor was very angry: 'You fool! What sort of a gentleman would he be if, while he was still living under his father's care, and before he was married, he took a concubine from a kisaeng family? If you say such a thing again I will have you punished. Do you think you will put me off by talking like that? Stop prevaricating and fetch her.'

When the yamen guards who were to fetch Ch'un-hyang appeared, the chief clerk and the secretary said to the governor: 'Ch'un-hyang is not a kisaeng, but that's not all. Her betrothal to the former governor's son is a solemn matter. Although your ages are very different, please summon her as though she were of the same social rank as yourself. Otherwise we fear you may damage your reputation.'

The governor flew into a rage: 'If you delay any longer in fetching Ch'un-hyang, I will have every one of you demoted. Are you unable to fetch her?'

There was consternation in the yamen offices. They all began to say to one another: 'Sergeant Kim, Sergeant Yi, something dreadful is afoot.' 'Poor Ch'un-hyang will find it hard to stay faithful.' 'The governor is in a rage.' 'Go quickly....' 'Hasten!'

The servants and the yamen slaves went in a body to Ch'un-hyang's house. Ch'un-hyang knew nothing about their arrival; she was thinking night and day of nothing but her husband. Her crying could be heard through the blinds. The voice of the deserted girl was compulsively raised in sad moans and wails, and anybody who saw or heard her was wounded in his own heart. Her longing for her husband took the taste from her food, and robbed her rest of sleep; yearning for him drew her skin tightly over her bones and made her weak. She sang a mournful dirge:

> I want to go, I want to go,
> I want to follow my love;
> I will go a thousand *li*,
> I will go ten thousand *li*,
> I want to go to him.
>
> I will go through storm and rains,
> I will go over the high peaks,
> Where sparrow-hawks and peregrines fly,
> Beyond the Tongsŏl Pass.
> If he will come to find me,
> I will take off my shoes
> And carry them in my hands,
> To run to him faster.

My husband is in Seoul
And does he think of me?
Has he forgotten me completely?
Has he taken another love?

She was crying like this when the yamen servants heard her moaning. Since they were not wood and stone, how could they not be moved? All the joints of their bodies melted like spring ice on the Naktong River: 'How pitiful! What sort of men are we, who can do nothing to help a girl like that!'

Then one of the servants shouted: 'Come on out!'

Ch'un-hyang was surprised by the noise and peeped through the crack of the door. She saw the soldiers and servants gathering: 'Oh, I had forgotten! Today is three days after the arrival of the new governor, and they are doing the third-day inspection. What a row they are making!'

She opened the sliding door: 'Hey, guards, come here, come here! We weren't expecting you. Aren't you tired after your journey with the new governor? How is he doing? Did none of you go to the old governor's house, and bring me a letter from the young master? When he was with me. I was very unwelcoming to you because I had to respect his position, but I didn't forget you. Come in, come in!'

She took Kim, Yi and several of the others by the hand, pulled them into the room and made them sit down. Then she called Hyang-dan: 'Bring in a table of wine!'

When they had drunk and were slightly tipsy, she opened a box and took out five *yang*: 'Please take this and buy yourselves something to drink on the way, and don't say anything about it afterward.'

The men were fuddled with the wine. They said: 'You mustn't give us money. Do you think we came for money? Put it away again.'

'Kim, you take it.'

'It's against the rules, but there are a lot of us. . . .' He took the money; but as they were turning to go, the chief kisaeng came along clapping her hands: 'Come on, Ch'un-hyang, do as you are told! I'm as constant as you are! I'm as chaste as you are! Why are you making such a fuss about being chaste and faithful? Just for the sake of your virtue, you pretty little miss, the whole yamen is in trouble and everybody is likely to lose his job. Come on quickly! Get along fast!'

Ch'un-hyang came reluctantly out of the gate, leaving her retirement: 'Don't treat me like this, madam. You have your position and I have mine. We must all die once, and no one can die twice.' So they hobbled along together to the yamen.

'Ch'un-hyang's here.'

When the governor saw her, he was delighted: 'This is Ch'un-hyang, for sure. Come up on the dais.'

She went up and sat down meekly. The governor, entirely bewitched, gave an order: 'Go to the office and tell the treasurer to come here.' The little treasurer was already on his way in. The happy governor said: 'Look at her now. That's Ch'un-hyang.'

'M-m ... She's a pretty little piece. Very well formed. When we were in Seoul you kept talking about Ch'un-hyang. She's worth looking at.'

The governor laughed: 'Will you play the marriage-broker?'

The treasurer sat down: 'Oh, you shouldn't have called her yourself first. It would have been more proper to send a go-between. Things have been done a little carelessly. But now you have gone so far, there's really nothing you can do but marry her.'

The governor enjoyed the joke, and then said to Ch'un-hyang: 'From today you must dress yourself properly and start to attend on me in the yamen.'

'Your commands must be respected, but since I am married I cannot do as you say.'

The governor laughed: 'A pretty girl, a pretty girl! And a virtuous woman too! Your chastity is wonderful. You are quite right to reply like that. But young Yi is the eldest son of a famous family in Seoul, and do you think he regards you as anything more than a flower he plucked in passing? You are a faithful child and while you keep faith the bloom will fade from your face, your hair will grow white and lose its lustre. As you bewail the vain passing of the years, who will there be to blame but yourself? However faithful you remain, who will recognize it? Forget all that. Is it better to belong to your governor or to be tied to a child? Let me hear what you have to say.'

Ch'un-hyang replied: '*A subject cannot serve two kings, and a wife cannot belong to two husbands*: that is my principle. I would rather die than do as you say, however many times you ask me. Please allow me to hold to my ideal: I cannot have more than one husband.'

The treasurer spoke to her then: 'Look here, now; that lad is fickle. Life is no more than a mayfly, and men are all the same. Why should you take so much trouble? His Excellency proposes to lift you up in the world. What do you singing girls know about faithfulness and chastity? The old governor has gone and the new governor has arrived: it's proper for you to obey him. Stop talking strangely. What have loyalty and faithfulness to do with people of your sort?'

Ch'un-hyang was amazed. She relaxed her posture and said: 'A woman's virtue is the same for high ranks and low. If you listen I will explain. Let's speak of kisaeng. There are no virtuous ones, you say; but I will tell them to you one by one: Nong-sŏn of Haesŏ died at Tongsŏn Pass; there was a child kisaeng of Sŏnch'ŏn who learned all about the Seven Reasons for divorce: Non-gae is so famous as a patriot that a memorial was erected to her and sacrifices are offered there; Hwa-wŏl of Ch'ŏngju had a three-storied pavilion raised in her memory: Wŏl-sŏn of P'yŏng'yang has a memorial; Il-chi-hong of Andong had a memorial erected in her lifetime, and was raised to the nobility; so do not belittle kisaeng.'

Then she turned to the governor again: 'Even a mighty man like Meng Ben[4] could not wrest from me my determination to stay a faithful wife and keep the oath, high as the mountains and deep as the sea, that I made to young master Yi. The eloquence of Su Qin or Zhang Yi[5] could not move my heart. Zhuge Liang[6] was so clever that he could restrain the southeast wind, but he could not change my heart. Xu You would not bend his will to Yao;[7] Bo Yi and

---

4. Famous man endowed with legendary strength from early China.
5. Famous political strategists and persuaders from early China.
6. Astute Chinese general of the Three King-

doms Period (220–280 C.E.).
7. The Chinese emperor Yao of high antiquity offered Xu You the throne, but Xu You, a sage recluse, refused.

Shu Qi[8] would not eat the grain of Zhou. Were it not for Xu You there would be no high-principled ministers; were it not for Bo Yi and Shu Qi there would be many more criminals and robbers. I may be of humble birth, but I know these examples. If I forsook my husband and became a concubine, it would be treason as much as it is for a minister to betray his king. But the decision is yours.'

The governor was furious: 'Listen, girl: treason is a capital offence, and insulting royal officers is equally serious. Refusing to obey a governor meets the same punishment. Don't put yourself in danger of death.'

Ch'un-hyang burst out: 'If the rape of a married woman is not a crime, what is?'

The governor in his fury pounded the writing-desk with such force that his hat-band snapped and his top-knot came undone. His voice grew harsh: 'Take this girl away;' he shouted. The yamen guards and servants answered: 'Yes, sir,' and ran forward to catch Ch'un-hyang by the hair and drag her away.

'Slaves!'

'Yes, sir!'

'Take this girl away.'

Ch'un-hyang trembled: 'Let go of me!'

She had come halfway down the steps when the slaves rushed up: 'You stupid woman, if you talk to the officers like that, you'll never save your life.'

They pulled her down to the ground of the courtyard. The fearsome soldiers and yamen servants swarmed around her like bees and grabbed her hair, black as black seaweed, coiled like a kite-string on its reel in springtime, like a lantern on Buddha's birthday, coiled tightly. They threw her down on the ground. It was pitiful. Her white jade body was crumpled up like a figure six: she was surrounded by grim soldiers holding spears, clubs, paddles and red cudgels.

'Call the executioner.'

'Bow your heads, the executioner comes!'

The governor had recovered a little, but he was still trembling and panting: 'Executioner, there is no need for any interrogation of this girl. Bind her to the frame immediately. Break her shin-bones and prepare the writ of execution.'

See what the jailers do while he binds her to the frame: the noise they make as they pile the paddles and clubs in armfuls beside the frame makes Ch'un-hyang faint.

Watch the executioner: he tries the paddles one by one, tests them for strength and suppleness, chooses one that will break easily and raises it over his right shoulder waiting for the governor's order.

'Receive your orders: if you pretend to beat her harder than you do, because you pity her, you will be punished on the spot. Beat her hard.'

The executioner replied loudly: 'Your orders will be obeyed. Why should we pity her? Now, girl, don't move your legs; if you do, your bones will break.'

He yelled as he danced about her brandishing the paddle. Then he stood still and said to her quietly: 'Just stand a couple of blows. I can't avoid it, but thrash your legs about wildly, as though it were hurting more than it does.'

'Beat her hard.'

'Yes, sir. I'll beat her!'

---

8. Virtuous sons of a local ruler under the Shang Dynasty (ca. 1600–1045 B.C.E.) who retreated into the mountains and starved themselves to death out of loyalty when the Shang Dynasty was overthrown by the Zhou Dynasty (1045–256 B.C.E.).

At the first stroke the broken pieces of the paddle flew through the air and fell in front of the governor. Ch'un-hyang tried to bear the pain but ground her teeth and flung her head back, screaming: 'What have I done?'

During the practice strokes, the executioner stood alone, but from the time he took the paddle to give the legal punishment, a servant stood facing him. Like a pair of fighting-cocks, as one stooped to beat, the other stooped to mark the tally, in the same way that ignorant penniless fellows in the wine-shop mark on the wall the number of cups they have drunk. He drew a line for the first stroke. Ch'un-hyang cried unrestrainedly:

> One heart undivided,
> Faithful to one husband,
> One punishment before one year is over,
> But for one moment I will not change.

All the townsfolk of Namwŏn, old and young, were gathered to watch what was going on: 'It's cruel! Our governor is cruel! Why should he punish a girl like that? Why should she be beaten so? Look at the executioner! When he comes out, we'll kill him!'

Everybody who saw and heard was weeping. Then came the second stroke:

> Two spouses are faithful,
> Two husbands there cannot be:
> Though my body is beaten,
> Though I die for ever,
> I'll never forget master Yi.

The third stroke came:

> Three rules for a woman's life,
> Three principles of behavior, and five relationships:
> Though I am punished three times,
> I will never forget my husband,
> Master Yi of Samch'ŏng-dong, the Three Springs Vale.

Then came the fourth stroke:

> The governor is father of the people,
> But he ignores the four social classes:
> He rules by force and power
> And has no love for the people
> In the forty-eight quarters of Namwŏn.
> Though my four limbs are severed.
> Alike in life and death
> I'll never forget young master Yi,
> My husband.

The fifth stroke came:

> The five relationships remain unbroken:
> Husband and wife both have their station:
> Our fate was sealed by the five elements,

And, sleeping or waking, I cannot forget my husband.
When the autumn moon shines on the paulownia where he is,
Will he send a letter to me?
Will there be a message tomorrow?
My innocent body does not deserve death.
Don't convict me unjustly.
Oh, oh, the pity of it!

The sixth stroke came:

Six times six is thirty-six,
And though I die sixty thousand times,
The body has six thousand joints,
All bound in love.
How can I change my heart?

The seventh stroke came:

If I have not broken one of the Seven Rules
Why should I receive seven punishments?
Take a seven-foot sword,
Cut me up and kill me quickly.
Executioner, do not spare me.
The seven jewels of my face must be destroyed.

The eighth stroke came:

The eight characters of my horoscope
Brought the governors of the Eight Provinces to meet me.
Are the governors of the Eight Provinces sent to rule the people well,
Or are they sent to do them evil?

The ninth stroke came:

In the nine organs of my body
My tears have made a nine-years flood.
The tall pine-trees of the nine hills
Are cut and loaded on a river-boat
To go quick to Seoul
And lay my case before the King
In the ninefold palace.
When I leave the nine courts
I will go to the Vale of the Three Springs and meet my love,
To relieve my heart and refresh my soul.

The tenth stroke came:

Though I live the tenth time
   After escaping death nine times,
My mind is made up for the rest of my days
   And a hundred thousand deaths will not change it,
But I cannot escape.

> Ch'un-hyang at six and ten,
> Poor devil under the cudgels,
>   Is hardly alive.

Ten strokes were expected, but she was beaten fifteen times:

> The moon shines bright on the fifteenth night,
>   But is hidden in the clouds.
> My beloved now in Seoul is hidden in Samch'ŏng-dong.
> Moon, bright moon, do you see him?
> Why can I not see where he has gone?

Twenty strokes would have been enough, but they went on to twenty-five:

> Playing the lute of twenty-five strings,
> In the moonlight I cannot restrain my sorrow.
> Wild goose, where are you flying to?
> If you go to Seoul,
> Take a message to my beloved,
> Who lives in Samch'ŏng-dong:
> See what I look like now;
> Take care you don't forget.

Her young mind craved to flee above the thirty-three heavens to the throne of the heavenly emperor. Her jade-white body was covered with blood, and she was bathed in tears. The blood and the tears flowed together, like peach-petals in the water when the man of Wuling found the hidden vale.[9]

Ch'un-hyang cried in her bitterness: 'Do not treat a girl like this. Better kill me quickly, and when I am dead my soul will become a cuckoo like the bird of Chu, crying in the empty hills on moonlit nights and breaking the dreams of young master Yi after he has gone to sleep.'

She could not finish her words before she fainted. The officers and servants turned their heads and wiped their tears. The executioner who had beaten her also turned away, wiping his eyes: 'No son of man should do such things.'

All the onlookers and officials standing round also wiped their eyes and looked away, unable to hear the sight. 'We shall never see anyone who takes a beating like Ch'un-hyang. Oh, it's cruel, it's cruel! Her chastity is cruel; her virtue is from heaven.'

Men and women, young and old, all alike were weeping, and the governor was displeased: 'Now, girl, you have been beaten for insulting the governor. What good has it done you? Will you persist in your disobedience?'

Half dead and half alive, Ch'un-hyang answered proudly: 'Listen to me, governor: don't you understand an oath that binds till death? A faithless woman brings frost in summer weather. My soul will fly to the king and present its petitions. You will not escape; please let me die.'

The governor was exasperated: 'The girl is beyond reason. Put her in a cangue and send her to the prison.'

---

9. Allusion to the man who found a blissful utopian land described in *Peach Blossom Spring* by the Chinese poet Tao Qian (365–427 C.E.).

The big cangue was fastened round her neck and sealed. The jailer took the weight of it and as they came out of the third gate the group of kisaeng saw it: 'Poor Ch'un-hyang! Keep hold on your senses! Oh, how piteous!' They stroked her limbs and offered her soothing drugs. They wept to see her. Just then the tall and stupid Fading Spring appeared: 'What on earth is going on? It looks as though the board for a memorial gate is being brought in.'

When she came closer and saw what it really was, she said: 'Poor Ch'un-hyang! How awful!'

While the commotion was going on, Ch'un-hyang's mother heard these words, and rushed wildly forward to throw her arms round her daughter: 'Oh! Why should this happen? What is her crime, and why was she beaten? Jailers! Chief clerk! What has my daughter done wrong? Officers! Executioners! What enemy has ordered this? Oh dear, it's all my fault! I'm nearly seventy, and I've no support. I have no sons and I brought up my only daughter so carefully and properly. I taught her to read and to study the rules of propriety for women, and she said to me: "Don't cry, mother, don't cry. Don't be sad because you have no son. Can't my children offer sacrifices for you when you die?" Her great devotion to her mother was not surpassed even by Guo Zhu or Meng Zong.[1] Does social class make any difference to love for one's children? My soul will never rest. My sighs are wasting my heart away. Sergeant Kim! Sergeant Yi! Even though your orders were strict, why did you beat her so cruelly? Look at my poor daughter's wounds! Her legs were as white as snow, and now they are red with blood. If she had been the daughter of a well-born family, even a blind girl ...! But she is only the daughter of the kisaeng Wŏl-mae. How can such things happen? Ch'un-hyang, keep hold on your senses! Oh dear, oh dear, the pity of it!'

'Hyang-dan, go outside the yamen and hire two runners. I am going to send them to Seoul.'

When Ch'un-hyang heard that the runners were being hired, she said: 'Mother, don't do it. What are you thinking of? If the runners go to Seoul and Mong-nyong sees them but does not know what to do about it, the worry will make him ill, which will make matters worse. Don't send them: I will go to the jail.'

She was carried on the jailer's back to the prison house, with Hyang-dan bearing the weight of the cangue. Her mother walked behind. When they got to the door of the jail: 'Keeper, open the gate. Are the keepers asleep?'

This is what the jail was like: the wooden bars were rotten, and a piercing wind came through them: through the cracks in the crumbling walls lice and fleas came in and attacked the whole of her body.

This is the lament of Ch'un-hyang in the prison-house:

What was my crime?
I have not stolen government grain.
   Why was I beaten so fiercely?
   I am not a murderer.
Why am I put in the cangue and the stocks?
I have not broken the laws.
   Why have I been bound hand and foot?

1. Chinese figures famous for filial piety.

I have not committed adultery.
What is this punishment for?
  I will take the waters of the rivers for ink
  And the blue sky for my paper;
  And protest my innocence,
  A petition to the heavenly king.
My heart burns with longing for my husband,
My sighs are a wind that fans those flames,
I shall die with my love unrequired.
  The chrysanthemum stands alone in the wind
  In holy faithfulness.
  The green pine amid the snow
  Has kept faith for a thousand years.
  The green pine is just as I am,
  My husband is a gold chrysanthemum.
My sad thoughts and the tears I shed
Soak my sighs.
I will use my sighs as a wind,
My tears will turn to rain.
The wind will drive the rain before it,
Blown and splashed on my beloved's window to wake him.
  Stars of the Herdboy and the Weaving Maid,
  When they meet on the seventh night,[2]
  Though the Milky Way divides them,
  Yet they never fail to meet.
  What waters divide me
  From the place where my beloved is?
I never hear anything from him.
Rather than live in longing,
I would die and forget it all.
Better this body should die
And be a cuckoo in the empty hills.
When the moon shines on the pear-blossom at night,
To sing in my husband's ears;
Or become a mandarin duck on the river,
Calling in search of its mate.
  I long to see the light of love
  In my husband's eyes.
  Shall I become a butterfly in spring
  Gathering fragrance on my wings?
  Glorying in the sunshine
  And settling on his clothes?
I will be the bright moon in the sky.
When night comes, I will rise
And shed my bright beams
On my beloved's face.
  I will draw blood from my veins
  And paint a portrait of my lord.
  Hang it as a scroll beside my door,

2. Legendary Chinese lovers (and star constellations) who could meet only one night of the year, on the seventh day of the seventh month.

And see it when I go out and in.
Because I am chaste and faithful
I have been treated thus cruelly:
Like fine white jade of Jingshan
Buried in the dust.
Like fragrant plants of Shangshan
Buried in the weeds,
Like a phoenix that played in paulownias
Making its nest in a thorn-patch. . . . .
    In ancient days the virtuous sages
    Lived free from fault,
    Yao, Shun, Yu and Tang were good kings,
    Jie and Zhou were tyrants:
Tang was imprisoned at Xiatai;
But he became a holy king
Who ruled the people virtuously.
    King Wen of Zhou
    Was hurt by Zhou of Shang,
    Imprisoned in the jail of Youli;
    But he became a holy king.[3]
The greatest of all sages, Confucius,
Because he resembled Yanghou
Was imprisoned at Kuangye;
But he became the light of China.
    When I think of all these things
    My innocence gives me hope
    That I may live to see the world again.
Oh the stifling sorrow of it!
Who will come to rescue me?
Will my husband, now in Seoul,
Come here as an officer?
Here I am now close to dying—
Will he come and save my life?
    The summer clouds flock round the peaks:
    Do the high hills bar his way?
    If the peaks of the Diamond Mountains
    Could be flattened, would he come?
    If the golden cockerel painted on the screen
    Flaps his wings and crows at dawn,
    Will my beloved come?
    Alas, alas, the pity of it!

    The bamboo slats let in the tranquil moonlight, and the girl, sitting there alone, implored the moon: 'Bright moon, do you see us? Lend me your light, for I too want to see the place where he is. Is he lying, is he sitting? Tell me what you see and relieve my sorrows.'

* * *

3. List of virtuous Chinese rulers of high antiquity who suffered unjustly.

II

The Enlightenment in Europe and the Americas

I s the latest thing always the best? On the whole, our society assumes that progress is likely and desirable. We move and communicate ever faster; we pursue the newest and shiniest things—our appetite for the modern knows no bounds. Yet we also indulge in moments of nostalgia, worrying that things are no longer what they used to be, that something has been lost in our tremendous rush. Before, we tell ourselves, there were standards; now all is confusion. Although the pace of change is now swifter, this ambivalence is nothing new.

The quarrel between "ancients" and "moderns"—those who believed, respectively, that old ideas or new ones were likely to prove superior to any alternatives—proved especially virulent in France and England during the late seventeenth and eighteenth centuries. Those who espoused the cause of the ancients feared—understandably—that the new commitment to individualism promoted by the moderns might lead to social alienation, unscrupulous self-seeking, and lack of moral responsibility. Believing in the universality of truth, they wished to uphold established values, not to invent new ones. On the other side, the moderns upheld the importance of individual autonomy, broad education for

A Philosopher Giving a Lecture in the Orrery, 1766, by Joseph Wright of Derby.

This engraving by J. Zucchi, a copy of a painting by Angelica Kauffmann, depicts Urania, the classical muse of astronomy.

women, and intellectual and geographical exploration. They stood for the new and are the recognizable forebears of what we even now call "modernity."

On both sides of the ancient/modern divide, thinkers believed in reason as a dependable guide. Both sides insisted that one should not take any assertion of truth on faith, blindly following the authority of others; instead, one should think skeptically about causes and effects, subjecting all truth-claims to logic and rational inquiry. **Dr. Johnson's** famous *Dictionary* defined reason as "the power by which man deduces one proposition from another, or proceeds from premises to consequences." By this definition, illumination occurs not by divine inspiration or by order of kings but by the reasoning powers of the ordinary human mind. Reason, some people argued, would lead human beings back to eternal truths. For others, reason provided a means for discovering fresh solutions to scientific, philosophical, and political questions.

In the realm of philosophy, thinkers turned their attention to defining what it meant to be human. "I think, therefore I am," **René Descartes** pronounced, declaring the mind the source of truth and meaning. But this idea proved less reassuring than it initially seemed. Subsequent philosophers, exploring the concept's implications, realized the possibility of the mind's isolation in its own constructions. Perhaps, Wilhelm Leibniz suggested, no real communication can take place between one consciousness and another. Possibly, according to **David Hume**, the idea of individual identity is a fiction constructed by our minds to make discontinuous experiences and memories seem continuous and whole. Philosophers pointed out the impossibility of knowing for sure even the reality of the external world: the only certainty is that we think it exists.

If contemplating the nature of human reason led philosophic skeptics to doubt our ability to know anything with certainty, other thinkers insisted on the existence, beyond ourselves, of an entirely rational physical and moral universe. Isaac Newton's demonstrations of the order of natural law greatly encouraged this line of thought, leading many to believe that the fullness and complexity of the perceived physical world testified to the sublime rationality of a divine plan. The Planner, however, did not necessarily supervise the day-to-day operations of His arrangements; He might rather, as a popular analogy had it, resemble the watchmaker who winds the watch and leaves it running.

God as a watchmaker was the central image for thinkers known as deists, who justified evil in the world by arguing that God never interfered with nature or with human action. Deism encouraged the separation of ethics from religion, as ethics was increasingly understood as a matter of reason.

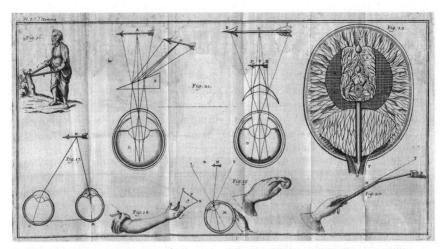

An illustration from an early eighteenth-century edition of the French philosopher René Descartes's unfinished book on the human body. Descartes saw the body as a machine whose operations could be understood mathematically.

Human beings, Enlightenment thinkers argued, could rely on their own authority—rather than looking to priests or princes—to decide how to act well in the world. Yet no one could fail to recognize that men and women embodied a capacity for passion as well as reason: "On life's vast ocean diversely we sail, / Reason the card, but Passion is the gale," **Alexander Pope's** *Essay on Man* (1733) pointed out. One could hope to steer with reason as guide, but one had to face the omnipresence of unreasonable passions. Life could be understood as a struggle between rationality and emotion, with feeling frequently exercising controlling force. Those who believed in the desirability of reason's governance often worried that it rarely prevailed over feelings of greed, lust, or the desire for power. For them as for us, the gap between the ideal and the actual caused frustration and often despair.

The questions raised by Enlightenment thinkers about human powers and limitations have left a legacy so lasting that it is hard to imagine our world without the Enlightenment. They are the ones who urged us to trust our own judgments and our own senses—while insisting on the need to think skeptically and critically—and they were the ones who shifted the dominant model of truth from divine revelation to human forms of knowledge: science, statistics, history, literature. They imagined conquering nature with ever-increasing knowledge—allowing humans to control their environment and harness nature's power for their own gain. And they ushered in a new sense of the equality of all human beings, launching the demand for universal human rights.

SOCIETY

The late seventeenth century, when the Enlightenment began, was a period of great turmoil, which persisted at intervals throughout the succeeding century. Reason had led many thinkers to the conclusion that kings and queens were ordinary mortals, and that conclusion implied new kinds of uncertainty. Civil war in England had ended in the king's execution in 1649; the French would guillotine their ruler before the end of the eighteenth century. The notion of divine right, the belief that monarchs governed with authority from God, had been effectively destroyed. God seemed to be moving further away. Religion still figured as a political reality, as it did in the struggle of Cavaliers and Puritans in England, which ended with the restoration of Charles II to the throne in 1660. But the most significant social divisions were now those of class and of political conviction—divisions no less powerful for lacking any claim of God-given authority. To England, the eighteenth century brought two unsuccessful but bitter rebellions on behalf of the deposed Stuart monarchs as well as the cataclysmic American Revolution. Throughout the eighteenth century, wars erupted over succession to

European thrones and over nationalistic claims. In Europe, internal divisions often assumed greater importance than struggles between nations. In the Americas, meanwhile, the ideas of the Enlightenment and the example of the American Revolution spread widely, leading to the revolts of creole elites against their European masters and to the birth of new nations.

Although revolution, civil war, and other forms of social instability dominated this period, the idea of civil society retained great power during the Enlightenment. Seventeenth-century English philosopher Thomas Hobbes, who believed that human life before the formation of societies was inevitably "nasty, mean, brutish, and short," thought that men and women had originally banded together for the sake of preservation and progress. By the late seventeenth century in Europe as in the Americas, social organization had evolved into elaborate hierarchical

The Topsy-Turvy World, 1663, by the Dutch genre painter Jan Steen, presents a satirical picture of the disarray in the household of a newly wealthy middle-class family.

structures with the aristocracy at the top. Just below the aristocrats were the educated gentry—clergymen, lawyers, men of leisure with landed property. Below them were masses of workers of various kinds, many of them illiterate, and, in the Americas, the large populations of indigenous or *mestizo* (mixed-race) peoples, as well as slaves of African descent. Although literacy rates grew dramatically during the eighteenth century, those who wrote (and, for a long time, those who read) belonged almost entirely to the two upper classes. As new forms of commerce generated new wealth, and with it, newly wealthy people who felt entitled to their share of social power, the traditional social order faced increasing challenges. In the Americas, white creoles chafed at European entitlements while insisting on their own privilege over other races. By the eighteenth century, the abolitionist movement would begin to question whether slavery could be ethical, a challenge anticipated by **Aphra Behn's Oroonoko**, the story of an African prince tricked into slavery and spirited to the New World.

Among the privileged classes, men had many opportunities: for education, for service in government or diplomacy, for the exercise of political and economic power. Both men and women generally accepted as necessary the subordination of women, who, even in the upper classes, had few opportunities for education and occupation beyond the household. But the increasing value attached to individualism had implications for women as well as men. In the late seventeenth century, **Sor Juana Inés de la Cruz**, a Mexican nun, articulated her own passion for thought and reading, and became an eloquent advocate of the right of women to education and a life of the mind. During the next century, a number of women and an occasional man made the same case. It became increasingly common to argue that limiting women solely to

childbearing and childrearing might not conform to the dictates of reason. If God had given all human beings reason, then women were just as entitled to develop and exercise their minds as their male counterparts. The emphasis on education in virtually all of the period's tracts about women provides proof that the concept of rational progress offered a device that could be used to gain at least some rights for women—if not civil rights, which were long in coming, at least the right to thought and knowledge.

Women of the upper classes occupied an important place in Enlightenment society, presiding over "salons," gatherings whose participants engaged in intellectual as well as frivolous conversation. In France as in England, by the late seventeenth century women also began writing novels, their books widely read by men and women alike. Although novels by women often focused attention on the domestic scene, they also ranged further, as in Behn's *Oroonoko*. Women published translations from the Greek as well as volumes of literary criticism, and were the most prolific writers in certain genres, such as Gothic fiction. Even if society as a whole did not acknowledge their full intellectual and moral capacities, individual women were beginning to claim for themselves more rights than those of motherhood.

Society in this period operated, as societies always do, by means of well-defined codes of behavior. Commentators at the time frequently showed themselves troubled by the possibility of sharp discrepancies between social appearance and the "truth" of human nature: **Molière's Tartuffe** provides a vivid example, with its exposé of religious sham. **Jonathan Swift**, lashing the English for institutionalized hypocrisy; Pope, calling attention to ambiguous sexual mores; **Voltaire** and Johnson, sending naive fictional protagonists to find that moralists don't always practice

Molière reading Tartuffe *at the home of Ninon de L'Enclos*, by Nicolas Andre Monsiau. This eighteenth-century painting of the seventeenth-century playwright is a tribute both to Molière and to L'Enclos, an author, courtesan, and patron of the arts who was host to some of the era's most celebrated literary salons.

what they preach—all of these writers call attention to the deceptiveness and the possible misuses of social norms as well as to their necessity. While the social codes may themselves not be at fault, people fail to live up to what they profess. The world would be a better place, these writers suggest, if people examined not only their standards of behavior but also their tendency to hide behind them.

In fiction, drama, poetry, and prose satire, writers of the Enlightenment in one way or another make society their subject. On occasion, they use domestic situations to provide microcosms of a wider social universe. Molière focuses on a private family to suggest how professed sentiment can obscure the operations of ambition; marriage comes to represent a society in miniature, not merely a structure for the fulfillment of personal desire. Marriage, an institution at once social and personal, provides a useful image for human re-

lationship as social and emotional fact. The developing eighteenth-century novel would assume marriage as the normal goal for men and women.

Other writers focus on a broader panorama. In *The Rape of the Lock*, Pope pokes fun at social structures by treating petty social squabbles in an epic form. Swift imagines idealized forms of social institutions ranging from marriage to Parliament, contrasting the ideals with their actual English counterparts. Johnson's and Voltaire's world travelers witness and participate in a vast range of sobering experiences. In general, women fill subordinate roles in the harsh social environments evoked by these satiric works: erotic love plays a less important part and the position of women becomes increasingly insignificant as the public life is privileged over the home. It is perhaps relevant to note that no literary work in this section (with the horrifying exception of Swift's *A Modest Proposal*) describes or evokes children, an omission that the generation of writers to follow—the Romantics—were eager to correct. But for the thinkers of the Enlightenment, it was only in adulthood that people assumed social responsibility; and so it was only then that they could provide interesting substance for social commentary.

HUMANITY AND NATURE

If the subject of human beings' relation to society occupied many writers, the problem of humankind's relation to the universe also perplexed them. Deism assumed the existence of a God who provided evidence of Himself only in His created works. Studying the natural world, therefore, might be seen as a religious act; the powers of reason would enable fruitful study. But how, exactly, should humanity's position in the created universe be understood? Alexander Pope, who in *An Essay on Man* investigates his subject in relation both to society and to the universe, understood creation as a great continuum, with man at the apex of the animal world. This view, sometimes described as belief in a Great Chain of Being, was widely shared. But if one turned the eye of reason on generic man himself, his dominance might seem questionable. Pope describes the inner life of human beings as a "Chaos of Thought and Passion, all confused," and sums up man as "the glory, jest, and riddle of the world." Glory? Perhaps. But when one adds jest and riddle, human preeminence seems less obvious.

Yet the natural order—however incomplete our grasp of it—remains a comfort. It suggests a *system*, a structure of relationships that makes sense at least in theory; rationality thus lies below all apparently irrational experience. It supplies a means of evaluating the natural world: every flower, every minnow, has meaning beyond itself as part of the great pattern. The passion with which the period's thinkers cling to belief in such a system suggests anxiety about what human reason could not do.

The notion of a permanent natural order corresponds to the notion of a permanent human nature, as conceived in the eighteenth century. It was generally believed that human nature remains in all times and places the same: all people hope and fear, are envious and lustful, and possess the capacity to reason. All suffer loss, all face death. Thinkers of the Enlightenment emphasized these common aspects of humanity far more than they considered cultural dissimilarities. Readers and writers alike could draw on this conviction about universality. It provided a test of excellence: if an author's imagining of character failed to conform to what eighteenth-century readers understood as human nature, a work might be securely judged inadequate. Conversely, the idea of a constant human nature held out the hope of longevity for writers who successfully evoked it. Moral philosophers could define human obligation and possibility, convinced that they, too, wrote for all time; ethical standards would never change. Like the vision of order in the physical universe, the notion of constancy in human nature provided bedrock.

CONVENTION AND AUTHORITY

Guides to manners proliferated in the eighteenth century, emphasizing the idea that commitment to decorum helped preserve society's standards. Literary conventions—agreed-on systems of verbal behavior—served comparable purposes in their own sphere, providing continuity between present and past. While these conventions may strike modern readers as antiquated and artificial, to contemporary readers they seemed both natural and proper, much as the plaintive lyrics of current country music or the extravagances of rap operate within restrictive conventions that appear "natural" only because they are familiar to us. Eighteenth-century writers had at their disposal an established set of conventions for every traditional literary genre. As the repetitive rhythms of the country ballad tell listeners what to expect, these literary conventions provided readers with clues about the kind of experience they could anticipate in a given poem or play.

Underlying all the conventions of this era was the classical assumption that literature existed to delight and instruct its readers. The various genres of this period embody such belief in literature's dual function. Stage comedy and tragedy, the early novel, satire in prose and verse, didactic poetry, the philosophical tale: each form developed its own set of devices for creating pleasure as well as for involving audiences and readers in situations requiring moral choice. The insistence in drama on unity of time and place (stage action occupying no more time than its

representation, with no change of scene) exemplifies one such set of conventions, intended to produce in their audiences the maximum emotional and moral effect. The elevated diction of the *Essay on Man* ("Mark how it mounts, to Man's imperial race, / From the green myriads in the peopled grass"), like the mannered but less dignified language of *The Rape of the Lock* ("Here thou, great Anna! whom three realms obey, / Dost sometimes counsel take—and sometimes tea"), and the two-dimensional characters of Johnson's and Voltaire's tales all provide clues about whether the author intends us to read "straight" or to recognize a satirical intention.

One dominant convention of twenty-first-century poetry and prose is something we call "realism." In fiction, verse, and drama, writers often attempt to convey the literal feel of experience, the shape in which events actually occur in the world, the way people really talk. Behn, Pope, and Voltaire pursued no

Chiswick House in London, an early eighteenth-century villa modeled on the Renaissance architect Palladio's Villa Rotunda outside Vicenza. The Villa Rotunda itself was designed to hearken back to classical ideals.

such goal. Despite their concern with permanent patterns of thought and feeling, they employed deliberate and obvious forms of artifice as modes of emphasis and of indirection. The sonorous lines in which Behn's characters reflect on their passions ("Since I have sacrificed Imoinda to my revenge, shall I lose that Glory which I have purchased so dear, as at the Price of the fairest, dearest, softest Creature that ever Nature made?") embodies a characteristic form of stylization. Artistic transformation of life, the period's writers believed, involves the imposition of formal order on the endless flux of event and feeling. The formalities of this literature constitute part of its meaning: its statement that what experience shows as unstable, art makes stable.

By relying on convention, eighteenth-century writers attempted to control an unstable world. The classical past, for many, provided an emblem of that stability, a standard of permanence. But some felt that overvaluing the past was problematic, the problem epitomized by the quarrel of ancients versus moderns in England and France. At stake in this controversy was, among other things, the value of permanence as opposed to the value of change. Proponents of the ancients believed that the giants of Greece and Rome had not only established standards applicable to all future works but had provided models of achievement never to be excelled. Homer wrote the first great epics; subsequent epics could only imitate him. When innovation came, it came by making the old new, as Pope makes a woman's dressing for conquest new by comparing it to the arming of Achilles. Moderns who valued originality for its own sake, who claimed significance for worthless publications that time had not tested, thereby testified to their own inadequacies and their foolish pride.

Those proud to be moderns, on the other hand, held that men (possibly even women) standing on the shoulders of the ancients could see further than their predecessors. The new was conceivably more valuable than the old. One might discover flaws even in revered figures of the classic past, and not everything had yet been accomplished. This view, of course, corresponds to one widely current since the eighteenth century, but it did not triumph easily: many powerful thinkers of the late seventeenth and early eighteenth centuries adhered to the more conservative position.

Also at issue in this debate was the question of authority, which was to prove so perilous in the political sphere. What position should be assumed by one who hoped to write and be read? Did authority reside only in tradition? If so, must one write in classical forms, rely on classical allusions? Until late in the eighteenth century, virtually all important writers attempted to ally themselves with the authority of tradition, declaring themselves part of a community extending through time as well as space. The problems of authority became particularly important in connection with satire, a popular Enlightenment form. Satire involves criticism of vice and folly; Molière, Pope, Swift, Voltaire, and Johnson at least on occasion wrote in the satiric mode. The fact that satire flourished so richly in this period suggests another version of the central conflict between reason and passion: that of the forces of stability and of instability. In its heightened description of the world (people eating babies, young women initiating epic battles over the loss of a lock of hair), satire calls attention to the powerful presence of the irrational, opposing that presence with the clarity of the satirist's own claim to reason and tradition. As it chastises human beings for their eruptions of passion, urging resistance and control, satire reminds its readers of the universality of the irrational as well as of opposition to it.

WHAT IS ENLIGHTENMENT?

One of the central goals of an education in our own time is the development of critical thinking. Rather than simply taking conventional wisdom on faith, we learn to stop and reflect on the arguments we hear, analyzing them for gaps and errors, exposing their unstated assumptions and evaluating their evidence. Instead of relying on external authorities, we put our own intelligence to work to distinguish between persuasive and misleading claims. Ideally, we learn to cultivate these habits in our everyday lives so that we become independent and skeptical adults, never carried away by mere prejudice or habit, and willing to examine all beliefs, including our own.

Critical thinking is a legacy of the Enlightenment. According to the great eighteenth-century French *Encyclopédie*, the enlightened person is one who "dares to think for himself . . . trampling on prejudice, tradition, conventional wisdom, authority, in a word, all that enslaves most minds." This was a bold new ideal, but one that had been in the works for a couple of centuries, as the principle of individualism had gained ground across Europe. By the seventeenth and eighteenth centuries, many educated people had begun to believe that they had a right to think and act for themselves, and to cast a critical eye on the pronouncements of priests and princes who had turned

out, after all, to be merely human like themselves.

But what did it mean to be human? Enlightenment thinkers typically distinguished humans by the particular faculty of reason: unlike animals, they argued, humans had the capacity to think through relationships between objects or events. They could establish cause and effect, and follow logical arguments. **Mary Wollstonecraft**, the founder of modern feminism, made the case that women had as much right to freedom and authority as men because they too had been given the faculty of reason by God. While many, like Wollstonecraft, assumed that reason was a divine endowment, a commitment to thoroughgoing rationalism could also lead people to reject established religions. Determined to resist superstition and prejudice, some influential voices of the Enlightenment asked searching questions about Christianity: if God had given human beings the capacity to understand cause and effect, for example, then miracles seemed to make no sense. Why would God violate his own rules? The French writer **Voltaire** went further. Christianity for him was fundamentally corrupt and unreasonable and should therefore be altogether destroyed. "Écrasez l'infâme!" he is famous for saying, "Wipe out the infamous thing!" Although there was by no means a consensus about religion among Enlightenment thinkers, almost all of them urged people to look not to divine or priestly authority but to their own experience— human perception, human intelligence, and human reason—to guide them to

An illustrated plate, *Anatomie*, from Diderot and D'Alembert's eighteenth-century *Encyclopédie*.

truth and action in the world. In an intellectual revolution that has left a lasting mark on our world, humans started to see themselves, rather than gods or spirits, as the sole sources of experience, knowledge, and judgment.

While Enlightenment thinkers were upending what they saw as irrational and self-serving religions, scientific knowledge provided them with a new ideal. Guided by human reason, scientists claimed to take nothing on faith: they turned assertions into hypotheses, performing rigorous experiments that could be verified by others. And science also lent human beings an exciting and perilous new prospect of supremacy, the capacity to conquer nature and harness its forces for human ends: "the power of man over matter," as **Benjamin Franklin** called it, as he forecast endless new capabilities, enabled by scientific discovery, that would keep improving the lives of human beings for a thousand years and more. His own discovery of electricity in lightning certainly fit this image of science. Putting this natural form of energy to human use has transformed the world in countless ways since Franklin's breakthrough.

With its potential for endless technological advancement, science promised a bright future. Perhaps all human problems could be solved: sickness could be eradicated, natural disasters averted, human emotion fully understood. A vast optimistic prospect opened up. It was important to many Enlightenment thinkers to leave the past behind and to focus on a future made possible not only by scientific knowledge but by a thoroughgoing insistence on improving human conditions. The very metaphor of enlightenment rested on an idea of progress. People were moving from an immature darkness—superstition, ignorance, error—into the mature light of knowledge and reason. Advances would come from rationalizing life, making it more efficient and thereby increasing the store of human happiness. Enlightened governments were supposed to work not for a few privileged families but for the common good, committing themselves to maximizing the well-being of the people as a whole.

To be sure, there was a lot of debate about what the common good should be. The German philosopher **Immanuel Kant** argued that debate was itself crucial to the process of enlightenment. He claimed that societies would make progress only if they opened all questions to public deliberation, inviting a full discussion of alternatives. This insistence on rational public argument gained strength as literacy rates rose, and more and more people eagerly entered into debates about law, politics, and science. Newspapers and magazines reached a growing swathe of society, making it possible to envision a genuinely open public sphere. Two new kinds of reference book—the comprehensive dictionary and the grand encyclopedia—were also meant to foster progress by disseminating information widely: "to collect all the knowledge scattered over the face of the earth, to present its general outlines and structure to the men with whom we live, and to transmit this to those who will come after us, so that the work of past centuries may be useful to the following centuries, that our children, by becoming more educated, may at the same time become more virtuous and happier" (*Encyclopédie*).

The promise of future happiness began to shape the political landscape. Many thinkers, eager to hurry along the path of social progress, made the case for sweeping social reforms—such as new legal systems to protect natural and inalienable human rights. Others, disgusted at the corruption of traditional aristocracies and clerics, saw no possibility of genuine progress without revolution. And in fact Enlightenment thinking would help to inspire the dramatic political revolutions that broke out in the Americas and in France in the late eighteenth and early nineteenth centuries. Thomas Jefferson, for one, was very much a man of the Enlightenment. "We are not afraid to follow truth wherever it may lead," he wrote, "nor to tolerate any error so long as reason is left free to combat it."

Freedom was an Enlightenment watchword. Aside from the freedom to use one's own reason against traditional authorities, the new science of economics, whose most famous exponent was the Scottish thinker Adam Smith, argued that money worked according to rational laws just like physics, and that the marketplace, left free, would produce ever-increasing wealth. No government need interfere with its workings. The free market became an influential model for thinking about human liberty.

But the Enlightenment faith in freedom only went so far. Few writers at the time believed in a fully fledged democracy, where anyone—male or female, rich or poor, white or non-white—could participate equally, and as they set limits on political rights and liberties, they often concluded that enlightened monarchs were more trustworthy when it came to acting with reason than the mass of people, who were too likely to be swayed by prejudice and superstition. Though Kant favored open public discussion, for example, he actively argued against republicanism, praising King Frederick the Great of Prussia for imposing a rigid order and keeping a "well-disciplined army." It was only under such restrictive conditions, Kant argued, that enlightened discussion could occur. He, like many other thinkers of his time, rationalized arbitrary authority and so helped to legitimate distinctly undemocratic regimes.

There was a grim side to the Enlightenment embrace of progress as well. Europeans saw themselves as having emerged from a dark age—one they associated with immaturity and ignorance—and now, civilized and guided by reason, they were the only people who could understand and govern the world rationally. As Europeans set off from their native lands to find new markets for their products and new luxuries and natural resources to bring back, they increasingly encountered peoples whose lives were governed not by reason but by a great variety of traditions and faiths. All of these, according to numerous spokesmen for the Enlightenment, were primitive and unreasonable. What Europeans had begun as commercial interests overseas increasingly turned into imperial conquests, justified as the proper dominion of rational peoples over unreasonable and childlike ones. One had an obligation, it was argued, to bring the light of reason to those who lived in darkness.

What justified this worldview was a widespread faith in the universality of reason. Enlightenment was not only good for France or for Europe: it was what every nation needed. Enlightenment thinkers tended to be cosmopolitan in their outlook—imagining themselves as citizens of the world. Often they were travelers: Voltaire, for example, spent time in Britain, Switzerland, and Prussia; Wollstonecraft lived in Portugal and Ireland as well as her native Britain; and Benjamin Franklin was the American ambassador to France. And this international vantage point helped them to imagine that the light of reason would bring truth and understanding everywhere. Some even suggested that individual nations be abolished in favor of a single world state.

But others argued that reason could not be exported to everyone. It was during the Enlightenment that scientific theories of natural differences between the races emerged. Thus Thomas Jefferson argued that black slaves in the

United States were naturally inferior when it came to reason because they could not follow Euclidean geometry, and **David Hume**, the Scottish philosopher, could not think of any Africans who had shown "ingenuity." Others hotly disagreed. **James Beattie** criticized Hume's logic on the grounds of evidence gathered from around the world. "The Africans and Americans are known to have many ingenious manufactures and arts among them, which even Europeans would find it no easy matter to imitate," he wrote, pointing to the great civilizations of Mexico and Peru.

The question of racial difference was no matter of mere theoretical interest. The eighteenth century saw the height of the slave trade, as millions of Africans were forcibly taken to work land in the Americas, and Enlightenment thinkers had to defend their own theories of human rationality and progress in this charged context. As reports of cruelty and exploitation reached them, most of the leading figures of the Enlightenment—even Hume—found slavery abhorrent and argued fiercely against it. The French *Encyclopédie* put it simply: the slave trade is a "business that violates religion, morality, natural laws, and all the rights of human nature." When it comes to global justice, the Enlightenment left us a double legacy. While its thinkers were responsible for the harmful new science of race and helped to justify European imperial domination, Enlightenment ideas would also support struggles for universal human rights down to our own day.

SAMUEL JOHNSON

"Dr. Johnson," as he was known in his own time (1709–1784), was a British novelist, poet, essayist, biographer, and most famously, the sole author of the 40,000 definitions in his *Dictionary of the English Language*, first published in 1755. As the market for printed books and newspapers expanded dramatically in the early eighteenth century, demand grew for a standardization of spelling and word usage. Dr. Johnson's was not the first English dictionary, but it remained the standard until the *Oxford English Dictionary* appeared a century and a half later. It included many scientific and technical terms as a way of disseminating knowledge widely.

From A Dictionary of the English Language[1]

To ENLI'GHTEN. *v. a.* [from *light.*] 1. To illuminate; to supply with light. 2. To quicken in the faculty of vision. 3. To instruct; to furnish with encrease of knowledge. 4. To cheer; to exhilarate; to gladden. 5. To illuminate with divine knowledge.

---

1. From the 4th edition, 1777.

IMMANUEL KANT

One of the most influential thinkers in the Western tradition, Kant (1724–1804) made an impact that is still being felt among philosophers, who continue to debate the substance and implications of his thought. He spent his whole life in Königsberg, then in Prussia. In 1784, he responded to a monthly magazine that had posed the question: "What Is Enlightenment?" Kant's answer, which makes the case for a critical, skeptical, reflective approach to the world, has become a classic definition of what it means to be enlightened. He argues that people have slavishly followed the opinions of authorities, rather than having the courage to seek truth for themselves, and adopts the motto: "Dare to know!" Kant also dwells here on the ideal form of government for fostering enlightenment, and concludes that it is not democracy but enlightened monarchy.

What Is Enlightenment?[1]

Enlightenment is man's release from his self-incurred tutelage. Tutelage is man's inability to make use of his understanding without direction from another. This tutelage is self-incurred when its cause lies not in lack of reason but in lack of resolution and courage to use it without direction from another. *Sapere aude!*[2] "Have courage to use your own reason!"—that is the motto of enlightenment.

Laziness and cowardice are the reasons why so great a portion of mankind, after nature has long since discharged them from external direction (*naturaliter maiorennes*),[3] nevertheless remains under lifelong tutelage, and why it is so easy for others to set themselves up as their guardians. It is so easy not to be of age. If I have a book which understands for me, a pastor who has a conscience for me, a physician who decides my diet, and so forth, I need not trouble myself. I need not think, if I can only pay—others will readily undertake the irksome work for me.

That the step to competence is held to be very dangerous by the far greater portion of mankind (and by the entire fair sex)—quite apart from its being arduous—is seen to by those guardians who have so kindly assumed superintendence over them. After the guardians have first made their domestic cattle dumb and have made sure that these placid creatures will not dare take a single step without the harness of the cart to which they are confined, the guardians then show them the danger which threatens if they try to go alone. Actually, however, this danger is not so great, for by falling a few times they would finally learn to walk alone. But an example of this failure makes them timid and ordinarily frightens them away from all further trials.

1. Translated by Lewis White Beck.
2. Dare to know! (Latin; a quotation from the Roman poet Horace [65 B.C.E.–8 B.C.E.]).
3. Those who come of age naturally (Latin).

For any single individual to work himself out of the life under tutelage which has become almost his nature is very difficult. He has come to be fond of this state, and he is for the present really incapable of making use of his reason, for no one has ever let him try it out. Statutes and formulas, those mechanical tools of the rational employment or rather misemployment of his natural gifts, are the fetters of an everlasting tutelage. Whoever throws them off makes only an uncertain leap over the narrowest ditch because he is not accustomed to that kind of free motion. Therefore, there are only few who have succeeded by their own exercise of mind both in freeing themselves from incompetence and in achieving a steady pace.

But that the public should enlighten itself is more possible; indeed, if only freedom is granted, enlightenment is almost sure to follow. For there will always be some independent thinkers, even among the established guardians of the great masses, who, after throwing off the yoke of tutelage from their own shoulders, will disseminate the spirit of the rational appreciation of both their own worth and every man's vocation for thinking for himself. But be it noted that the public, which has first been brought under this yoke by their guardians, forces the guardians themselves to remain bound when it is incited to do so by some of the guardians who are themselves capable of some enlightenment—so harmful is it to implant prejudices, for they later take vengeance on their cultivators or on their descendants. Thus the public can only slowly attain enlightenment. Perhaps a fall of personal despotism or of avaricious or tyrannical oppression may be accomplished by revolution, but never a true reform in ways of thinking. Rather, new prejudices will serve as well as old ones to harness the great unthinking masses.

For this enlightenment, however, nothing is required but freedom, and indeed the most harmless among all the things to which this term can properly be applied. It is the freedom to make public use of one's reason at every point. But I hear on all sides, "Do not argue!" The officer says: "Do not argue but drill!" The tax-collector: "Do not argue but pay!" The cleric: "Do not argue but believe!" Only one prince in the world says, "Argue as much as you will, and about what you will, but obey!"[4] Everywhere there is restriction on freedom.

Which restriction is an obstacle to enlightenment, and which is not an obstacle but a promoter of it? I answer: The public use of one's reason must always be free, and it alone can bring about enlightenment among men. The private use of reason, on the other hand, may often be very narrowly restricted without particularly hindering the progress of enlightenment. By the public use of one's reason I understand the use which a person makes of it as a scholar before the reading public. Private use I call that which one may make of it in a particular civil post or office which is intrusted to him. Many affairs which are conducted in the interest of the community require a certain mechanism through which some members of the community must passively conduct themselves with an artificial unanimity, so that the government may direct

---

4. King Frederick II of Prussia (1712–1786), called "the Great," was an enlightened despot who expanded Prussia into a major European power; he was inspired by French philosophical ideas, including religious toleration.

them to public ends, or at least prevent them from destroying those ends. Here argument is certainly not allowed—one must obey. But so far as a part of the mechanism regards himself at the same time as a member of the whole community or of a society of world citizens, and thus in the role of a scholar who addresses the public (in the proper sense of the word) through his writings, he certainly can argue without hurting the affairs for which he is in part responsible as a passive member. Thus it would be ruinous for an officer in service to debate about the suitability or utility of a command given to him by his superior; he must obey. But the right to make remarks on errors in the military service and to lay them before the public for judgment cannot equitably be refused him as a scholar. The citizen cannot refuse to pay the taxes imposed on him; indeed, an impudent complaint at those levied on him can be punished as a scandal (as it could occasion general refractoriness). But the same person nevertheless does not act contrary to his duty as a citizen when, as a scholar, he publicly expresses his thoughts on the inappropriateness or even the injustice of these levies. Similarly a clergyman is obligated to make his sermon to his pupils in catechism and his congregation conform to the symbol of the church which he serves, for he has been accepted on this condition. But as a scholar he has complete freedom, even the calling, to communicate to the public all his carefully tested and well-meaning thoughts on that which is erroneous in the symbol and to make suggestions for the better organization of the religious body and church. In doing this, there is nothing that could be laid as a burden on his conscience. For what he teaches as a consequence of his office as a representative of the church, this he considers something about which he has no freedom to teach according to his own lights; it is something which he is appointed to propound at the dictation of and in the name of another. He will say, "Our church teaches this or that; those are the proofs which it adduces." He thus extracts all practical uses for his congregation from statutes to which he himself would not subscribe with full conviction but to the enunciation of which he can very well pledge himself because it is not impossible that truth lies hidden in them, and, in any case, there is at least nothing in them contradictory to inner religion. For if he believed he had found such in them, he could not conscientiously discharge the duties of his office; he would have to give it up. The use, therefore, which an appointed teacher makes of his reason before his congregation is merely private, because this congregation is only a domestic one (even if it be a large gathering); with respect to it, as a priest, he is not free, nor can he be free, because he carries out the orders of another. But as a scholar, whose writings speak to his public, the world, the clergyman in the public use of his reason enjoys an unlimited freedom to use his own reason and to speak in his own person. That the guardians of the people (in spiritual things) should themselves be incompetent is an absurdity which amounts to the eternalization of absurdities.

But would not a society of clergymen, perhaps a church conference or a venerable classis (as they call themselves among the Dutch), be justified in obligating itself by oath to a certain unchangeable symbol in order to enjoy an unceasing guardianship over each of its members and thereby over the people as a whole, and even to make it eternal? I answer that this is altogether impossible. Such a contract, made to shut off all further enlightenment from the human race, is absolutely null and void even if confirmed by the supreme power, by parliaments, and by the most ceremonious of peace treaties. An age cannot bind itself and ordain to put the succeeding one into such a condition that it cannot extend its (at best very occasional) knowledge, purify itself of errors, and progress in general enlightenment. That would be a crime against human nature, the proper destination of which lies precisely in this progress; and the descendants would be fully justified in rejecting those decrees as having been made in an unwarranted and malicious manner.

The touchstone of everything that can be concluded as a law for a people lies in the question whether the people could have imposed such a law on itself. Now such a religious compact might be possible for a short and definitely limited time, as it were, in expectation of a better. One might let every citizen, and especially the clergyman, in the role of scholar, make his comments freely and publicly, i.e., through writing, on the erroneous aspects of the present institution. The newly introduced order might last until insight into the nature of these things had become so general and widely approved that through uniting their voices (even if not unanimously) they could bring a proposal to the throne to take those congregations under protection which had united into a changed religious organization according to their better ideas, without, however, hindering others who wish to remain in the order. But to unite in a permanent religious institution which is not to be subject to doubt before the public even in the lifetime of one man, and thereby to make a period of time fruitless in the progress of mankind toward improvement, thus working to the disadvantage of posterity—that is absolutely forbidden. For himself (and only for a short time) a man can postpone enlightenment in what he ought to know, but to renounce it for himself and even more to renounce it for posterity is to injure and trample on the rights of mankind.

And what a people may not decree for itself can even less be decreed for them by a monarch, for his lawgiving authority rests on his uniting the general public will in his own. If he only sees to it that all true or alleged improvement stands together with civil order, he can leave it to his subjects to do what they find necessary for their spiritual welfare. This is not his concern, though it is incumbent on him to prevent one of them from violently hindering another in determining and promoting this welfare to the best of his ability. To meddle in these matters lowers his own majesty, since by the writings in which his subjects seek to present their views he may evaluate his own governance. He can do this when, with deepest understanding, he lays upon himself the reproach, *Caesar non est supra grammaticos.*[5] Far more does he injure his own majesty when he degrades his supreme power by supporting the ecclesiastical despotism of some tyrants in his state over his other subjects.

If we are asked, "Do we now live in an *enlightened age?*" the answer is, "No," but we do live in an *age of enlightenment*. As things now stand, much is lacking which prevents men from being, or easily becoming, capable of correctly using their own reason in religious matters with assurance and free from outside

---

5. Caesar is not above the grammarians (Latin); in other words, even an emperor has to abide by grammatical rules.

direction. But, on the other hand, we have clear indications that the field has now been opened wherein men may freely deal with these things and that the obstacles to general enlightenment or the release from self-imposed tutelage are gradually being reduced. In this respect, this is the age of enlightenment, or the century of Frederick.

A prince who does not find it unworthy of himself to say that he holds it to be his duty to prescribe nothing to men in religious matters but to give them complete freedom while renouncing the haughty name of *tolerance*, is himself enlightened and deserves to be esteemed by the grateful world and posterity as the first, at least from the side of government, who divested the human race of its tutelage and left each man free to make use of his reason in matters of conscience. Under him venerable ecclesiastics are allowed, in the role of scholars, and without infringing on their official duties, freely to submit for public testing their judgments and views which here and there diverge from the established symbol. And an even greater freedom is enjoyed by those who are restricted by no official duties. This spirit of freedom spreads beyond this land, even to those in which it must struggle with external obstacles erected by a government which misunderstands its own interest. For an example gives evidence to such a government that in freedom there is not the least cause for concern about public peace and the stability of the community. Men work themselves gradually out of barbarity if only intentional artifices are not made to hold them in it.

I have placed the main point of enlightenment—the escape of men from their self-incurred tutelage—chiefly in matters of religion because our rulers have no interest in playing the guardian with respect to the arts and sciences and also because religious incompetence is not only the most harmful but also the most degrading of all. But the manner of thinking of the head of a state who favors religious enlightenment goes further, and he sees that there is no danger to his lawgiving in allowing his subjects to make public use of their reason and to publish their thoughts on a better formulation of his legislation and even their open-minded criticisms of the laws already made. Of this we have a shining example wherein no monarch is superior to him whom we honor.

But only one who is himself enlightened, is not afraid of shadows, and has a numerous and well-disciplined army to assure public peace can say: "Argue as much as you will, and about what you will, only obey!" A republic could not dare say such a thing. Here is shown a strange and unexpected trend in human affairs in which almost everything, looked at in the large, is paradoxical. A greater degree of civil freedom appears advantageous to the freedom of mind of the people, and yet it places inescapable limitations upon it; a lower degree of civil freedom, on the contrary, provides the mind with room for each man to extend himself to his full capacity. As nature has uncovered from under this hard shell the seed for which she most tenderly cares—the propensity and vocation to free thinking—this gradually works back upon the character of the people, who thereby gradually become capable of managing freedom; finally, it affects the principles of government, which finds it to its advantage to treat men, who are now more than machines, in accordance with their dignity.

RENÉ DESCARTES

A mathematician, scientist, and philosopher, the French thinker René Descartes (1595–1650) wrote a book that transformed European thinking. *The Discourse on Method* (1637) asks how it is possible for human beings to know anything at all. It puts its emphasis not on what we know, but on the critical and rational methods by which we arrive at knowledge. The philosopher begins by resolving to strip away all claims to truth that cannot be grounded in certainty. Little remains apart from the fact that he is thinking. From this Descartes deduces that he himself exists: *Cogito ergo sum*, or "I think, therefore I am." With this conclusion he affirms that the mind is separate from the body, and more important than mere physical experience. Descartes believed that his own rational conclusions proved the existence of God, but others worried that his skeptical questioning might lead to atheism. Either way, Western thought has grappled ever since with the Cartesian "mind-body problem."

From The Discourse on Method[1]

Like a man who walks alone and in darkness, I resolved to go so slowly, and to use so much circumspection in everything, that if I did not advance speedily, at least I should keep from falling. I would not even have desired to begin by entirely rejecting any of the opinions which had formerly been able to slip into my belief without being introduced there by reason, had I not first spent much time in projecting the work which I was to undertake, and in seeking the true method of arriving at a knowledge of everything of which my understanding should be capable.

When I was younger, I had devoted a little study to logic, among philosophical matters, and to geometrical analysis and to algebra, among mathematical matters—three arts or sciences which, it seemed, ought to be able to contribute something to my design. But on examining them I noticed that the syllogisms of logic and the greater part of the rest of its teachings serve rather for explaining to other people the things we already know, or even, like the art of Lully,[2] for speaking without judgment of things we know not, than for instructing us of them. And although they indeed contain many very true and very good precepts, there are always so many others mingled therewith that it is almost as difficult to separate them as to extract a Diana or a Minerva[3] from a

---

1. Translated by Isaac Kramnick.
2. Ramón Llull (1232–1315), a medieval Catalán philosopher who tried to prove the existence of a Christian God by means of logic

machines; his reasoning was circular.
3. Roman goddesses often represented by sculptors in marble.

block of marble not yet rough hewn. Then, as to the analysis of the ancients and the algebra of the moderns, besides that they extend only to extremely abstract matters and appear to have no other use, the first is always so restricted to the consideration of figures that it cannot exercise the understanding without greatly fatiguing the imagination, and in the other one is so bound down to certain rules and ciphers that it has been made a confused and obscure art which embarrasses the mind, instead of a science which cultivates it. This made me think that some other method must be sought, which, while combining the advantages of these three, should be free from their defects. And as a multitude of laws often furnishes excuses for vice, so that a state is much better governed when it has but few, and those few strictly observed, so in place of the great number of precepts of which logic is composed, I believed that I should find the following four sufficient, provided that I made a firm and constant resolve not once to omit to observe them.

The first was, never to accept anything as true when I did not recognize it clearly to be so, that is to say, to carefully avoid precipitation and prejudice, and to include in my opinions nothing beyond that which should present itself so clearly and so distinctly to my mind that I might have no occasion to doubt it.

The second was, to divide each of the difficulties which I should examine into as many portions as were possible, and as should be required for its better solution.

The third was, to conduct my thoughts in order, by beginning with the simplest objects, and those most easy to know, so as to mount little by little, as if by steps, to the most complex knowledge, and even assuming an order among those which do not naturally precede one another.

And the last was, to make everywhere enumerations so complete, and surveys so wide, that I should be sure of omitting nothing.

The long chains of perfectly simple and easy reasons, which geometers are accustomed to employ in order to arrive at their most difficult demonstrations, had given me reason to believe that all things which can fall under the knowledge of man succeed each other in the same way, and that provided only we abstain from receiving as true any opinions which are not true, and always observe the necessary order in deducing one from the other, there can be none so remote that they may not be reached, or so hidden that they may not be discovered. And I was not put to much trouble to find out which it was necessary to begin with, for I knew already that it was with the simplest and most easily known; and considering that of all those who have heretofore thought truth in the sciences it is the mathematicians alone who have been able to find demonstrations, that is to say, clear and certain reasons, I did not doubt that I must start with the same things that they have considered, although I hoped for no other profit from them than that they would accustom my mind to feed on truths and not to content itself with false reasons. But I did not therefore design to try to learn all those particular sciences which bear the general name of mathematics: and seeing that although their objects were different they nevertheless all agree, in that they consider only the various relations or proportions found therein, I thought it would be better worth while if I merely examined these proportions in general, supposing them only in subjects which would serve to render the knowledge of them more easy to me, and even, also, without in any wise restricting them thereto, in order to be the better able to apply them subsequently to every other subject to which they should be suitable. Then, having remarked that in order to know them I should sometimes need to consider each separately, I had to suppose them in lines, because I found nothing more simple, or which I could more distinctly represent to my imagination and to my senses; but to retain them, or to comprehend many of them together, it was necessary that I should express them by certain ciphers as short as possible, and in this way I should borrow all the best in geometrical analysis, and in algebra, and correct all the faults of the one by means of the other.

I do not know whether I ought to discuss with you the earlier of my meditations, for they are so metaphysical and so out of the common that perhaps they would not be to everyone's taste; and yet, in order that it may be judged whether the bases I have taken are sufficiently firm, I am in some measure constrained to speak of them. I had remarked for long that, in conduct, it is sometimes necessary to follow opinions known to be very uncertain, just as if they were indubitable, as has been said above; but then, because I desired to devote myself only to the research of truth, I thought it necessary to do exactly the contrary, and reject as absolutely false all in which I could conceive the least doubt, in order to see if afterwards there did not remain in my belief something which was entirely indubitable. Thus, because our senses sometimes deceive us, I wanted to suppose that nothing is such as they make us imagine it; and because some men err in reasoning, even touching the simplest matters of geometry, and make paralogisms, and judging that I was as liable to fail as any other, I rejected as false all the reasons which I had formerly accepted as demonstrations; and finally, considering that all the thoughts which we have when awake can come to us also when we sleep, without any of them then being true, I resolved to feign that everything which had ever entered into my mind was no more true than the illusions of my dreams. But immediately afterwards I observed that while I thus desired everything to be false, I, who thought, must of necessity be something; and remarking that this truth, *I think, therefore I am*, was so firm and so assured that all the most extravagant suppositions of the skeptics were unable to shake it, I judged that I could unhesitatingly accept it as the first principle of the philosophy I was seeking.

Then, examining attentively what I was, and seeing that I could feign that I had no body, and that there was no world or any place where I was, but that nevertheless I could not feign that I did not exist, and that, on the contrary, from the fact that I thought to doubt of the truth of other things, it followed very evidently that I was; while if I had only ceased to think, although all else which I had previously imagined had been true I had no reason to believe that I might have been, therefore I knew that I was a substance whose essence or nature is only to think, and which, in order to be, has no need of any place, and depends on no material thing; so that this I, that is to say, the soul by which I am what I am, is entirely distinct from the body, and even easier to know than the body, and although the body were not, the soul would not cease to be all that it is.

After that I considered generally what is requisite to make a proposition true and certain; for since I had just found one which I knew to be so, I thought that I ought also to know in what this certainly consisted. And having remarked that there is nothing at all in this, *I think, therefore I am*, which assures me that I speak the truth, except that I see very clearly that in order to think it is necessary to exist, I judged that I might take it as a general rule that the things which we conceive very clearly and very distinctly are all true, and that there is difficulty only in seeing plainly which things they are that we conceive distinctly.

After this, and reflecting upon the fact that I doubted, and that in consequence my being was not quite perfect (for I saw clearly that to know was a greater perfection than to doubt), I bethought myself to find out from whence I had learned to think of something more perfect than I; and I knew for certain that it must be from some nature which was in reality more perfect. For as regards the thoughts I had of many other things outside myself, as of the sky, the earth, light, heat, and a thousand more, I was not so much at a loss to know whence they came, because, remarking nothing in them which seemed to make them superior to me, I could believe that if they were true they were dependencies of my nature, inasmuch as it had some perfection, and if they were not true that I derived them from nothing—that is to say, that they were in me because I had some defect. But it could not be the same with the idea of a Being more perfect than my own, for to derive it from nothing was manifestly impossible; and since it is no less repugnant to me that the more perfect should follow and depend on the less perfect than that out of nothing should proceed something, I could not derive it from myself; so that it remained that it had been put in me by a nature truly more perfect than I, which had in itself all perfections of which I could have any idea; that is, to explain myself in one word, God.

DENIS DIDEROT / JEAN LE ROND D'ALEMBERT

It may come as a surprise to learn that an encyclopedia could be considered one of the most dangerous books of its time. Edited by Denis Diderot (1713–1784) and Jean le Rond D'Alembert (1717–1783), two French thinkers, the thirty-volume illustrated *Encyclopédie* (1751–1777) broke with established knowledge and religious authority to affirm the kinds of knowledge that could be gained through human experience and human reason. A hundred and forty authors collaborated on the finished product, putting together more than 70,000 entries, starting with *asparagus* and ending with *zodiac*. Often considered the quintessential creation of the Enlightenment, it was written in French, rather than Latin, and intended to be accessible to a wide audience.

Diderot, who was especially interested in biology, and D'Alembert, who was an important mathematician, worked from an unshakable confidence in science, and deliberately inserted views unsettling to established religion in minor articles, which they cross-referenced with more orthodox articles on major topics. But it was not only unsettling, it was also useful: a collection of the latest scientific and technological advances that could be put to use for industrial development. The *Encyclopédie* proved enormously popular across Europe, reprinted in cheap editions to meet the demands of an ever-expanding readership. It helped to circulate the central values of the Enlightenment—universalism, reason, progress, and a thoroughgoing skepticism about authority—on an unprecedented new scale.

From The Encyclopédie

AFRICA,[1] one of the four principal parts of the Earth. It measures approximately 800 leagues from Tangiers to Suez; 1420 from Cape Verde to Cape Guardafui; and 1450 from the Cape of Good Hope to Bone. Long. 1-71. Lat. (southern) 1-35 and (northern) 1-37.30.

There is little trading on the *African* coasts; the interior of this part of the world is still insufficiently known, and Europeans began trading only around the middle of the XIVth century. There is little trade between the Kingdoms of Morocco and Fez and the area near Cape Verde. Trading posts can be found around Cape Verde and between the Senegal and the Sierra Leone rivers. The coast of Sierra Leone has been explored by the four Nations, but only the Portuguese and the English have established posts. Only the English have a trading post near Cape Miserado. We do some trading along the Melegueta and Greve Coasts: we trade even more along "little Dieppe" and the grand Sestre. The Ivory (or Tusk) Coast is frequented by all Europeans; they almost all have Settlements and Forts along the Gold Coast. The Cape of Corsica is the main settlement of the English; there is little trade at Asdres. Many Negroes are taken from Benin and Angola. There is no activity in Kafir country. The Portuguese are established in Sofala, in Mozambique, in Madagascar. They also handle all the Malindi trade. We will follow the branches of this trade in the different articles CAPE VERDE, SENEGAL, etc.

BEAST, ANIMAL, BRUTE.[2] People use *beast* in contradistinction to *man*; thus one says: "man has a soul, but some philosophers do not concede that beasts have any at all." *Brute* is a term of contempt applied to *beasts* and to man only in a bad sense. *He surrenders himself to all the fury of his inclinations like a brute. Animal* is a generic term suitable to all organic and living beings: *the animal lives, acts, and moves by itself, etc.* If we consider the animal as thinking, wanting, acting, reflecting, etc., then the sense of the word would be restricted to the human race. If we consider the animal to be limited in all the functions

---

1. Translated by Lauren Yoder.　　　2. Translated by Stephen J. Gendzier.

that indicate intelligence and will, but seem to have them in common with the human race, then it is restricted to the *beast*. If we consider the *beast* in its lowest depths of stupidity, released from the laws of reason and honesty according to which we must regulate our conduct, then we call it a *brute*. We do not know if *beasts* are governed by the general laws of motion or by a particular impulse. Both of these opinions present difficulties. If they act out of a particular impulse, if they think, if they have a soul, etc., then what is that soul? We cannot suppose that it is material in nature, but could it be spiritual? To declare that they do not have souls and do not think would reduce animals to the level of machines, which we hardly seem any more authorized to do than to maintain that a man whose speech we do not hear is an automaton. The argument based on the perfection of their works is strong, for it would seem, if we judge from their first steps, that they should go rather far. Nevertheless, they all stop at the same point, which is almost the character of machines. But the argument based on the uniformity of their productions does not appear quite as well-founded to me. The nests of swallows and the dwellings of beavers do not resemble each other any more than do the houses of men. If a swallow places its nest in an angle, the only circumference will be the arc covered between the sides of the angle. On the other hand, if the nest is set against a wall, it will measure half a circumference. If you dislodge beavers from their homes, and they go settle in another location, as it is not possible for them to find the same piece of ground, there will necessarily be variety in the techniques they use and the dwellings they construct.

However that may be, one cannot imagine that beasts have a much more intimate relationship with God than the other parts of the material world, otherwise, which one of us would dare to lay a hand on them and shed their blood without any qualms? Who would be able to kill a lamb with an easy conscience? The feelings they have, whatever their nature, are only useful in communicating with each other or with other creatures. With the incentive of pleasure they conserve their own being; and with the same incentive, they conserve their species. I have said *incentive of pleasure* for lack of a more precise expression, for if *beasts* were capable of the same feeling which we call *pleasure*, to cause them any harm would be an act of unprecedented cruelty. They have their own natural laws because they are united by common needs, interests, etc., but they do not have any positive ones because they are not united by any intellectual understanding. However, they do not seem to follow their natural laws in an invariable manner; and plants which we assume have neither understanding nor feeling are even more subject to these laws.

Beasts do not have the supreme advantage of human beings. However, they have some that we do not have: they do not have our hopes, but they do not have our fears. They suffer death as we do, but it is without knowing it. Most of them take better care of themselves and do not misuse their passions as much as we do. *See* the articles SOUL and ANIMAL.

EDUCATION[3] is the care one takes of feeding, bringing up and instructing children; thus education has as goals, 1) the health and good constitution of

---

3. Translated by Carolina Armenteros.

the body; 2) what regards the rectitude and the instruction of the mind; 3) manners, that is the conduct of life, and social qualities.

Of *education* in general. Children who come into the world, must form one day the society in which they will live. Their *education* is thus the most interesting subject, 1) for themselves, whom *education* must fashion such that they will be useful to that society, obtain its esteem, and find in it their well-being; 2) for their families, whom they must support and honor; 3) for the state itself, which must reap the fruits of the good *education* that the citizens that compose it receive.

All children who come into the world must be subjected to the care of *education*, for there is none who is born completely instructed and completely *educated*. So what advantage does not accrue everyday to a state whose head has had his mind cultivated early, who has learned in History that the most stable empires are exposed to revolutions; who has been as much instructed in what he owes his subjects, as in what his subjects owe to him; to whom the source, the motive, the extent and the limits of his authority have been made known; to whom it has been taught that the sole certain means of conserving it and making it be respected, is to make good use of it? *Erudimini qui judicatis terram* [be wise, you rulers of the earth] Psalm II, 10. What happiness that of a state in which magistrates have early learned their duties, and have manners; where each citizen is warned that in coming into the world he has received a talent to render valuable; that he is member of a political body, and that in this capacity he must contribute to the common good, search for everything that can procure true advantages to society, and avoid what can disrupt its harmony, and disturb tranquility and good order! It is evident that there is no order of citizens in a state, for whom some kind of *education* is not proper; *education* for the children of sovereigns; *education* for the children of the great, for those of magistrates, etc; *education* for the children of the countryside, where, in the same way that there are schools for learning the truths of religion, there should be also those in which the exercises, the practices, the duties and the virtues of their social state could be shown to them, so that they might act with greater knowledge.

If every kind of *education* were imparted with enlightenment and perseverance, the motherland would be well constituted, well governed, and protected from the insults of its neighbors.

Education is the greatest good that fathers can leave to their children. One finds only too frequently fathers who do not know their true interests, refuse to spend what is necessary for a good *education*, and who save nothing afterwards to provide an occupation for their children, or to lend to them an honorable office: yet what duty is more useful than a good *education*, which commonly does not cost so much, although it is the good whose product is the greatest, the most honorable and the most sensible? It pays back every day: other goods are often dissipated; but one cannot get rid of a good *education*, nor, unfortunately, of a bad one, which often is such because one has not wanted to defray the expenses of a good one:

* * *

You give your son to be *educated* by a slave, said one day an ancient philosopher to a rich father, very well, instead of one slave you shall have two.

There is much analogy between the cultivation of plants and the education of children; in one and in the other nature must furnish the base. The owner of a field cannot make it be usefully cultivated, unless the terrain is proper to what he wants to produce in it; likewise, an enlightened father, and a master who has discernment and experience, must observe their student; and after a certain period of observation, they must disentangle his penchants, his inclinations, his taste, his character, and know what he is good for, and what role, so to speak, he must play in the concert of society.

Do not force the inclinations of your children, but also do not allow them to choose lightly a station for which you foresee that they will realize in time they were not suitable. One must, as much as one can, spare them bad initiatives. Happy those children who have experienced parents capable of conducting them well in the choice of a station! A choice on which depends happiness or evil—without considering the rest of life.

*　*　*

With regard to the mind, the first years of childhood require much more care than is commonly given to them, so that it is often very difficult afterwards to erase the bad impressions that a young man has had through the discourses and the examples of people of little sense and little enlightenment, who were near him in those first years.

From the moment that a child lets it be known by his look and by his gestures that he understands what is said to him, he should be regarded as a subject proper to be submitted to the jurisdiction of *education*, whose goal is to form the mind, and set aside what can lead it astray. It would be desirable for him to be approached only by sensible people, and for him to see and hear nothing but good. The first instances of sensible acquiescence in our mind, or, to speak in common parlance, the first knowledge or the first ideas that form within us during the first years of our life, are as many models that it is difficult to refashion, and which later serve us as rules in the use that we make of our reason. Thus it is extremely important for a young man to acquiesce only to what is true, that is to what is, as soon as he has judgment. So keep him away from all fabulous stories, from all puerile tales of Fairies, of werewolves, of wandering Jews,[4] of goblins, of ghosts, of wizards, of spells, told by those makers of horoscopes, those fortune-tellers male and female, those interpreters of dreams, and so many other superstitious practices that serve only to lead astray children's reason, to frighten their imagination, and often even to make them regret having come into the world.

Persons who amuse themselves by frightening children are very reprehensible. It has often happened that the weak organs of children's brains have been deranged for the rest of their lives, besides their mind being filled with ridiculous prejudices, etc. The more these chimerical ideas are extraordinary, the more deeply ingrained they become in the brain.

One must not blame less those who amuse themselves by tricking children, leading them into error, deluding them into believing things, and who congratulate themselves instead of being ashamed. In such instances it is the

4. German legend of a Jew who insulted Jesus on his way to be crucified and was therefore doomed to wander the earth.

young man who has the good part; he does not yet know that there are persons whose soul is low enough to speak against their thought, and who affirm shameful falsehoods in the same tone in which honest people say the most certain truths; he has not yet learned to suspect; he puts himself in your hands, and you trick him: all those false ideas become as many exemplary ideas, which lead children's reason astray. I would have it that instead of thus taming the mind of young people with charm and lies, one never told them anything but the truth.

ENCYCLOPEDIA[5] (*Philosophy*). This word means the *interrelation of all knowledge*; it is made up of the Greek prefix *en*, in, and the nouns *kyklos*, circle, and *paideia*, instruction, science, knowledge. In truth, the aim of an *encyclopedia* is to collect all the knowledge scattered over the face of the earth, to present its general outlines and structure to the men with whom we live, and to transmit this to those who will come after us, so that the work of past centuries may be useful to the following centuries, that our children, by becoming more educated, may at the same time become more virtuous and happier, and that we may not die without having deserved well of the human race.

* * *

We have seen that our *Encyclopedia* could only have been the endeavor of a philosophical century; that this age has dawned, and that fame, while raising to immortality the names of those who will perfect man's knowledge in the future, will perhaps not disdain to remember our own names. We have been heartened by the ever so consoling and agreeable idea that people may speak to one another about us, too, when we shall no longer be alive; we have been encouraged by hearing from the mouths of a few of our contemporaries a certain voluptuous murmur that suggests what may be said of us by those happy and educated men in whose interests we have sacrificed ourselves, whom we esteem and whom we love, even though they have not yet been born. We have felt within ourselves the development of those seeds of emulation which have moved us to renounce the better part of ourselves to accomplish our task, and which have ravished away into the void the few moments of our existence of which we are genuinely proud. Indeed, man reveals himself to his contemporaries and is seen by them for what he is: a peculiar mixture of sublime attributes and shameful weaknesses. But our weaknesses follow our mortal remains into the tomb and disappear with them; the same earth covers them both, and there remains only the total result of our attributes immortalized in the monuments we raise to ourselves or in the memorials that we owe to public respect and gratitude—honors which a proper awareness of our own deserts enables us to enjoy in anticipation, an enjoyment that is as pure, as great, and as real as any other pleasure and in which there is nothing imaginary except, perhaps, the titles on which we base our pretensions. Our own claims are deposited in the pages of this work, and posterity will judge them.

5. Translated by Stephen J. Gendzier.

I have said that it could only belong to a philosophical age to attempt an *encyclopedia*; and I have said this because such a work constantly demands more intellectual daring than is commonly found in ages of pusillanimous taste. All things must be examined, debated, investigated without exception and without regard for anyone's feelings. . . . We must ride roughshod over all these ancient puerilities, overturn the barriers that reason never erected, give back to the arts and sciences the liberty that is so precious to them. . . . We have for quite some time needed a reasoning age when men would no longer seek the rules in classical authors but in nature, when men would be conscious of what is false and true about so many arbitrary treatises on aesthetics: and I take the term *treatise on aesthetics* in its most general meaning, that of a system of given rules to which it is claimed that one must conform in any genre whatsoever in order to succeed.

* * *

It would be desirable for the government to authorize people to go into the factories and shops, to see the craftsmen at their work, to question them, to draw the tools, the machines, and even the premises.

There are special circumstances when craftsmen are so secretive about their techniques that the shortest way of learning about them would be to apprentice oneself to a master or to have some trustworthy person do this. There would be few secrets that one would fail to bring to light by this method, and all these secrets would have to be divulged without any exception.

I know that this feeling is not shared by everyone. These are narrow minds, deformed souls, who are indifferent to the fate of the human race and who are so enclosed in their little group that they see nothing beyond its special interest. These men insist on being called good citizens, and I consent to this, provided that they permit me to call them *bad men*. To listen to them talk, one would say that a successful *encyclopedia*, that a general history of the mechanical arts, should only take the form of an enormous manuscript that would be carefully locked up in the king's library, inaccessible to all other eyes but his, an official document of the state, not meant to be consulted by the people. What is the good of divulging the knowledge a nation possesses, its private transactions, its inventions, its industrial processes, its resources, its trade secrets, its enlightenment, its arts, and all its wisdom? Are not these the things to which it owes a part of its superiority over the rival nations that surround it? This is what they say; and this is what they might add: would it not be desirable if, instead of enlightening the foreigner, we could spread darkness over him or even plunge all the rest of the world into barbarism so that we could dominate more securely over everyone? These people do not realize that they occupy only a single point on our globe and that they will endure only a moment in its existence. To this point and to this moment they would sacrifice the happiness of future ages and that of the entire human race.

They know as well as anyone that the average duration of empires is not more than two thousand years and that in less time, perhaps, the name *Frenchman*, a name that will endure forever in history, will be sought after in vain over the surface of the earth. These considerations do not broaden their point of view; for it seems that the word *humanity* is for them a word without meaning. All the same, they should be consistent! For they also fulminate against the impenetrability of the Egyptian sanctuaries;[6] they deplore the loss of the knowledge of the ancients; they accuse the writers of the past for having been silent or negligent in writing so badly on an infinite number of important subjects; and these illogical critics do not see that they demand of the writers of earlier ages something they call a crime when it is committed by a contemporary, that they are blaming others for having done what they think it honorable to do.

* * *

LYRIC POETRY.[7] * * * It is a type of *poetry* totally devoted to sentiment; that's its substance, its essential object. Whether it rises like a trembling flame; whether it seeps in, little by little, and excites us without noise; whether it is an eagle, a butterfly, a bee, it is always sentiment that guides it or carries it along.

In general, *lyric poetry* is destined to be set to music; it is for this that it is called *lyric*, and because, in times past, when it was sung, the lyre accompanied the voice. The word ode has the same origin; it means, song, hymn or canticle.

Thence, *lyric poetry* and music have an intimate connection between them, founded on things themselves, since they both have the same object to express; and if this is so, music being an expression of sentiments from the heart through inarticulate sound, musical or *lyric poetry* will be the expression of sentiments through articulate sound, that is to say, through words.

So, one can define *lyric poetry* as that which expresses sentiment in verse that is melodic; but as sentiments are hot, passionate and powerful, warmth must dominate in this genre of work. Thence are born all the rules of *lyric poetry*, as well as its privileges: that is what allows for the boldness of beginnings, the deviations, the energy of unconventional moments; it is from here that it derives this sublimity, which so specifically belongs to it, and this enthusiasm that brings it close to the divine.

Lyric poetry is as ancient as the world. When man had opened his eyes on to the universe, on the agreeable impressions that he received from all his senses, on the marvels that surrounded him, he raised his voice to pay the tribute of glory that he owed to the supreme benefactor. And that is the origin of hymns, odes, in a word, *lyric poetry*.

At the base of their holidays, the pagans had the same principle as the worshippers of the true God. It was joy and gratitude that made them institute solemn games to celebrate the gods to whom they believed they were indebted for their harvest. From there came the songs of joy that they devoted to the god of the harvest, and to that of love. If the beneficent gods were the natural material of lyric poetry, heroes, children of the gods naturally had to have their part in this sort of tribute, without counting that their virtue, their courage, or their favors either to a particular people or to the whole human race, made them resemble divinity. * * *

---

6. The holiest, innermost parts of ancient Egyptian temples.　　7. Translated by Helen O'Connor.

We will only point out here that it is particularly to *lyric poets* that it is given to instruct with dignity and agreement. Dramatic and fable poetry rarely bring together these two advantages; the ode brings respect to a moral divinity by the sublimity of thoughts, the majesty of cadences, the boldness of figures, the force of expressions; at the same time it wards off distaste by brevity, by the variety of its turns, and by the choice of the embellishments that a skillful poet knows how to use at the right time.

POLITICAL AUTHORITY.[8] No man has received from nature the right to command others. Liberty is a gift from heaven, and each individual of the same species has the right to enjoy it as soon as he enjoys the use of reason. If nature has established any *authority*, it is paternal control; but paternal control has its limits, and in the state of nature it would terminate when the children could take care of themselves. Any other *authority* comes from another origin than nature. If one seriously considers this matter, one will always go back to one of these two sources: either the force and violence of an individual who has seized it, or the consent of those who have submitted to it by a contract made or assumed between them and the individual on whom they have bestowed *authority*.

Power that is acquired by violence is only usurpation and only lasts as long as the force of the individual who commands can prevail over the force of those who obey; in such a way that if the latter become in their turn the strongest party and then shake off the yoke, they do it with as much right and justice as the other who had imposed it upon them. The same law that made *authority* can then destroy it; for this is the law of might.

Sometimes *authority* that is established by violence changes its nature; this is when it continues and is maintained with the express consent of those who have been brought into subjection, but in this case it reverts to the second case about which I am going to speak; and the individual who had arrogated it then becomes a prince, ceasing to be a tyrant.

Power that comes from the consent of the people necessarily presupposes certain conditions that make its use legitimate, useful to society, advantageous to the republic, and set and restrict it between limits: for man must not nor cannot give himself entirely and without reserve to another man, because he has a master superior to everything, to whom he alone belongs in his entire being. It is God, whose power always has a direct bearing on each creature, a master as jealous as absolute, who never loses his rights and does not transfer them. He permits for the common good and for the maintenance of society that men establish among themselves an order of subordination, that they obey one of them, but he wishes that it be done with reason and proportion and not by blindness and without reservation, so that the creature does not arrogate the rights of the creator. Any other submission is the veritable crime of idolatry. To bend one's knee before a man or an image is merely an external ceremony about which the true God, who demands the heart and the mind, hardly cares and which he leaves to the institution of men to do with as they please

8. Translated by Stephen J. Gendzier.

the tokens of civil and political devotion or of religious worship. Thus it is not these ceremonies in themselves, but the spirit of their establishment that makes their observance innocent or criminal. An Englishman has no scruples about serving the king on one knee; the ceremonial only signifies what people wanted it to signify. But to deliver one's heart, spirit, and conduct without any reservation to the will and caprice of a mere creature, making him the unique and final reason for one's actions, is assuredly a crime of divine lese majesty[9] of the highest degree. Otherwise this power of God about which one speaks so much would only be empty noise that human politics would use out of pure fantasy and which the spirit of irreligion could play with in its turn; so that all ideas concerning power and subordination coming to the point of merging, the prince would trifle with God, and the subject with the prince.

*   *   *

The prince owes to his very subjects the *authority* that he has over them; and this *authority* is limited by the laws of nature and the state. The laws of nature and the state are the conditions under which they have submitted or are supposed to have submitted to its government. One of these conditions is that, not having any power or *authority* over them but by their choice and consent, he can never employ this *authority* to break the act or the contract by which it was transferred to him. From that time on he would work against himself, since his authority could only subsist by virtue of the right that established it. Whoever annuls one, destroys the other. The prince cannot therefore dispose of his power and his subjects without the consent of the nation and independently of the option indicated in the contract of allegiance. If he proceeded otherwise, everything would be nullified, and the laws would relieve him of the promises and the oaths that he would have been able to make, as a minor who would have acted without full knowledge of the facts, since he would have claimed to have at his disposal that which he only had in trust and with a clause of entail, in the same way as if he had had it in full ownership and without any condition.

Moreover the government, although hereditary in a family and placed in the hands of one person, is not private property, but public property that consequently can never be taken from the people, to whom it belongs exclusively, fundamentally, and as a freehold. Consequently it is always the people who make the lease or the agreement: they always intervene in the contract that adjudges its exercise. It is not the state that belongs to the prince, it is the prince who belongs to the state: but it does rest with the prince to govern in the state, because the state has chosen him for that purpose: he has bound himself to the people and the administration of affairs, and they in their turn are bound to obey him according to the laws. The person who wears the crown can certainly discharge himself of it completely if he wishes, but he cannot replace it on the head of another without the consent of the nation who has placed it on his. In a word, the crown, the government, and the public *authority* are possessions owned by the body of the nation, held as a usufruct by

---

9. An offense against God.

princes and as a trust by ministers. Although heads of state, they are nonetheless members of it; as a matter of fact the first, the most venerable, and the most powerful allowed everything in order to govern, allowed nothing legitimately to change the established government or to place another head in their place. The sceptre of Louis XV[1] necessarily passes to his eldest son, and there is no power who can oppose this; nor any nation because it is the condition of the contract; nor his father for the same reason.

The depository of *authority* is sometimes only for a limited time, as in the Roman republic. It is sometimes for the life of only one man, as in Poland; sometimes for all the time a family exists, as in England; sometimes for the time a family exists only through its male descendants, as in France.[2]

This depository is sometimes entrusted to a certain class in society, sometimes to several people chosen by all the classes, and sometimes to one man.

The conditions of this pact are different in different states. But everywhere the nation has a right to maintain against all forces the contract that they have made; no power can change it; and when it is no longer valid, the nation recovers its rights and full freedom to enter into a new one with whomever and however it pleases them. This is what would happen in France if by the greatest of misfortunes the entire reigning family happened to die out, including the most remote descendants; then the sceptre and the crown would return to the nation.

It seems that only slaves whose minds are as limited as their hearts are debased could think otherwise. Such men are born neither for the glory of the prince nor for the benefit of society; they have neither virtue nor greatness of soul. Fear and self-interest are the motives of their conduct. Nature only produces them to improve by contrast the worth of virtuous men; and Providence uses them to make tyrannical powers, with which it chastises as a rule the people and the sovereigns who offend God; the latter for usurping, the former for granting too much to man of supreme power, that the Creator reserved for Himself over the created being.

The observation of laws, the conservation of liberty, and the love of country are the prolific sources of all great things and of all beautiful actions. Here we can find the happiness of people, and the true luster of princes who govern them. Here obedience is glorious, and command august. On the contrary, flattery, self-interest, and the spirit of slavery are at the root of all the evils that overpower a state and of all the cowardice that dishonor it. There the subjects are miserable, and the princes hated; there the monarch has never heard himself proclaimed *the beloved*; submission is hateful there, and domination cruel. If I view France and Turkey[3] from the same perspective, I perceive on the one hand a society of men united by reason, activated by virtue, and governed by a head of state equally wise and glorious according to the laws of justice; on the other, a herd of animals assembled by habit, driven by the law of the rod, and led by an absolute master according to his caprice.

1. King of France (1710–1774).
2. The Roman Republic (ca. 509 B.C.E.–49 B.C.E.) limited its dictators to six-month terms; Mieszko I (ca. 930–992) founded and ruled Poland before dividing the nation among his sons at his death; the unwritten Salic law in France excluded women from inheriting the throne.
3. Eighteenth-century Europeans frequently associated Turkey with despotism.

SAVAGES.[4] Barbarous peoples who live without law, without governance, without religion, and who have no fixed habitation.

This word comes from the Italian *salvagio*, derived from *salvaticus*, *selvaticus* and *silvaticus*, which signifies the same thing as *sylvestris*—*rustic*, or that which concerns woods and forests, because savages ordinarily dwell in forests.

A large part of America is peopled by *savages*, the majority of whom are still fierce and feed upon human flesh.

* * *

THE SLAVE TRADE[5] (*Commerce of Africa*) is the buying of unfortunate Negroes by Europeans on the coast of Africa to use as slaves in their colonies. This buying of Negroes, to reduce them to slavery, is one business that violates religion, morality, natural laws, and all the rights of human nature.

Negroes, says a modern Englishman full of enlightenment and humanity, have not become slaves by the right of war; neither do they deliver themselves voluntarily into bondage, and consequently their children are not born slaves. Nobody is unaware that they are bought from their own princes, who claim to have the right to dispose of their liberty, and that traders have them transported in the same way as their other goods, either in their colonies or in America, where they are displayed for sale.

If commerce of this kind can be justified by a moral principle, there is no crime, however atrocious it may be, that cannot be made legitimate. Kings, princes, and magistrates are not the proprietors of their subjects: they do not, therefore, have the right to dispose of their liberty and to sell them as slaves.

On the other hand, no man has the right to buy them or to make himself their master. Men and their liberty are not objects of commerce; they can be neither sold nor bought nor paid for at any price. We must conclude from this that a man whose slave has run away should only blame himself, since he had acquired for money illicit goods whose acquisition is prohibited by all the laws of humanity and equity.

There is not, therefore, a single one of these unfortunate people regarded only as slaves who does not have the right to be declared free, since he has never lost his freedom, which he could not lose and which his prince, his father, and any person whatsoever in the world had not the power to dispose of. Consequently the sale that has been completed is invalid in itself. This Negro does not divest himself and can never divest himself of his natural right; he carries it everywhere with him, and he can demand everywhere that he be allowed to enjoy it. It is, therefore, patent inhumanity on the part of judges in free countries where he is transported, not to emancipate him immediately by declaring him free, since he is their fellow man, having a soul like them.

There are authors who, posing as political jurists, come to tell us confidently that the questions relative to the state of persons must be decided by the laws of the countries in which they belong and that therefore a man who is declared a slave in America and who is transported from there to Europe must be regarded there as a slave. But this is to decide the rights of humanity by the

---

4. Translated by Richard Weyhing.   **5.** Translated by Stephen J. Gendzier.

civil laws of a gutter, as Cicero says.[6] Must the magistrates of a nation, out of consideration for another nation, have no regard for their own people? Must their deference to a law that binds them in no way make them trample underfoot the law of nature that binds all men at all times and in all places? Is there any law as obligatory as the eternal laws of equity? What problem is created if a judge is bound to observe them more than to respect the arbitrary and inhuman practices of the colonies?

One will say perhaps that these colonies will soon be ruined if the slavery of Negroes were abolished there. But if this were true, should we conclude from this that the human race must be horribly injured to enrich us and to provide us with luxuries? It is true that the pockets of highwaymen would be empty if robbery were to be entirely suppressed, but do men have the right to enrich themselves by cruel and criminal acts? What right has a bandit to rob travelers? Who is allowed to become opulent by making his fellow men unfortunate? Can it be legitimate to rob mankind of its most sacred rights solely to satisfy one's avarice, one's vanity, or one's particular passions? No . . . therefore let the European colonies be destroyed rather than make so many unfortunate people.

But I believe it is false that the suppression of slavery would entail its ruin. Commerce would suffer for some time, I agree; this is the effect of all new arrangements, because in this case new trade relations could not be readily found to follow another economic system; but out of this suppression other advantages would arise.

It is this *slave trade*, this practice of slavery, that has prevented America from being populated as promptly as it would have been. Let them free the Negroes, and in a few generations this vast and fertile country will have innumerable inhabitants. The arts and talent will flourish there, and instead of a land populated almost entirely by savages and wild beasts there will soon be a country of industrious men. It is freedom, it is industry that are the real sources of abundance. As long as a nation conserves this industry and this freedom, it has nothing to fear. Industry as well as necessity is ingenious and inventive: it finds a thousand different ways to procure riches for itself; and if one of the channels to opulence is blocked, a hundred others immediately open up.

Sensible and generous souls will without doubt applaud these reasons in favor of humanity; but avarice and greed which dominate the earth will never wish to hear them.

WIFE,[7] in Latin *uxor*, female of man, considered such when she is united to him by ties of marriage. See therefore Marriage [MARRIAGE (NATURAL LAW), MARRIAGE (JURISPRUDENCE), MARRIAGE (THEOLOGY)] and HUSBAND.

The Supreme Being having judged that it was not good for man to be alone, conceived a desire to unite him in close society with a companion, and this society is made through a voluntary accord between the parties. As this society has as its principal goal the procreation and protection of the children it produces, the father and mother of necessity devote all their energies to nourishing and

---

6. Marcus Tullius Cicero (106–43 B.C.E.), Roman philosopher, politician, and legal theo- rist who argued against despotism.
7. Translated by Naomi Andrews.

properly rearing the fruits of their love up until the time when they are able to care and judge for themselves.

But although the husband and the *wife* have fundamentally the same interests in their marriage, it is nevertheless essential that governing authority belong to one or the other: now the affirmative right of civilized nations, the laws and the customs of Europe give this authority unanimously to the male, being the one endowed with the greatest strength of mind and body, contributing more to the common good in matters of sacred and human things; such that the woman must necessarily be subordinated to her husband and obey his orders in all domestic affairs. This is the belief of the ancient and modern jurists and the formal decision of legislators.

In addition, the Frederician code,[8] which appeared first in 1750 and which seems to have attempted to introduce definitive and universal rights, declares that the husband is according to nature itself the master of the house, the chief of the family; and that it therefore follows that the *wife* resides there at his leave, she is in all regards under the power of the husband, from which fact devolve diverse prerogatives which pertain personally to him. Finally, holy scripture commands the wife to submit to him as to her master.[9]

However the reasons we've just listed for marital power are not without rejoinder, humanely speaking; and the character of this work allows us to boldly enunciate them.

It appears first of all that it would be difficult to demonstrate that the authority of the husband comes from nature; because this principle is contrary to the natural equality of men; and just because one is suited for commanding doesn't mean that it is actually one's right to do so: 2. man does not always have greater strength of body, wisdom, spirit or conduct than woman: 3. Scriptural precepts being established in punitive terms, indicates as well that there is only a positive right. One can therefore claim that there is no other type of subordination in marital relations than that of the civil law, and as a consequence, the only things preventing change in the civil law are particular conventions, and that natural law and religion do not determine anything to the contrary.

We do not deny that in a society composed of two people, it is necessary that the deliberative laws of one or the other carry the day; and since ordinarily men are more capable than women of ably governing particular matters, it is wise to establish as a general rule, that the voice of the man will carry more weight as long as the two have not made any agreement to the contrary, because general law results from human institutions, and not from natural right. In this way, a woman who knows the basis of civil law and who contracts her marriage purely and simply, has by law submitted, tacitly, to this civil law.

But if this woman, persuaded that she has more judgment and direction, or knowing that she has greater fortune or is of a higher station than that of the man who asks her to marry him, stipulates the contrary of that which the law implies, and with the consent of this husband, should she not have, by virtue

---

8. A body of laws drafted for King Frederick II of Prussia (1712–1786). The code combined ancient Roman traditions with Enlightenment theories of sociability.

9. Ephesians 5.22: "Wives, submit yourselves unto your own husbands, as unto the Lord."

of natural law, the same power her husband has by virtue of the law of the realm? The case of a queen, who, being sovereign in her own right, marries a prince below her rank, or if she likes, one of her subjects, is enough to show that the authority of a woman over her husband, even in matters concerning the governance of the family, is not incompatible with the nature of the marital contract.

In effect, we have seen among the most civilized nations, marriages which submit the husband to the domain of the *wife*; we have seen a princess, heir to the realm, reserve to herself, while marrying, the sovereign power of the state. Everyone knows the conventions of marriage which were made between Philip II and Mary Queen of England; those of Mary Queen of Scots and those of Ferdinand and Isabel, in order to govern the kingdom of Castile together.[1] * * *

The examples of England and of Muscovy[2] make evident that women can succeed equally, both in moderate and despotic government; and if it is not against reason and nature that they rule an empire, then it would seem that it is no more contradictory that they should be mistresses in a family.

When Lacedaemonian[3] marriages were ready to be consummated, the woman took the dress of a man; and it was a symbol of the equal power that she would share with her husband. On this subject we know what Gorgo, the wife of Leonidas, king of Sparta,[4] said to a foreign woman who was extremely surprised by this equality: Don't you know, responded the queen, that we bring men into the world? In other times, even in Egypt, marriage contracts between individuals, as much as those of the king and the queen, gave authority over the husband to the wife.

It makes no difference (because it is not a matter here of exploiting unique examples which prove too much); it makes no difference, I say, if the authority of a woman in marriage cannot exist within conventional bounds, between people of equal stature, at least let the legislature refrain from prohibiting exceptions to the law, made with the free consent of the parties.

Marriage is by its nature a contract; and as a result, in all things not expressly prohibited by natural law, the contractual engagements between the husband and the wife determine reciprocal rights.

Finally, why should the ancient maxim, *provisio hominis tollit provisionem legis*,[5] not be accepted in this case, such as one allows it in dowries, in the division of goods, and in several other things, where the law does not rule except when the parties have not stipulated provisions different from those prescribed by law?

---

1. Philip II of Spain (1527–1598) married Mary I of England (1516–1558), but she denied him the right to rule England and inherit the throne upon her death; Mary, Queen of Scots (1542–1587) refused monarchical power to her husband, Henry Stewart, Lord Darnley; Ferdinand II (1452–1516) and Isabella I (1451–1504) of Spain shared their powers of governance.

2. Catherine the Great (1729–1796) assumed control of Russia, called Muscovy, after her husband Peter III was dethroned.

3. From ancient Sparta.

4. Gorgo and Leonidas ruled Sparta in the early sixth and late fifth centuries B.C.E.

5. The provision made by an individual does not take away the provision made by the law (Latin).

BENJAMIN FRANKLIN

Few people have ever boasted the immense and various talents shown by Benjamin Franklin (1706–1790). This American started his adult life as a printer, moving to Philadelphia from his birthplace in Boston as a young man, and went on to become a successful businessman, inventor, scientist, writer, musician, diplomat, and signatory to the Declaration of Independence and the United States Constitution. He invented swimming fins and bifocal glasses and discovered new sources of electricity. Always looking for solutions to improve human life, he founded or improved libraries, hospitals, insurance companies, and volunteer fire departments. At first a slaveholder, Franklin eventually converted to the antislavery cause and freed the slaves he owned. In this letter to the Englishman Joseph Priestley (1733–1804), the discoverer of oxygen and one of the Enlightenment's most important scientists, Franklin articulates the belief that scientific knowledge will give rise to endless progress.

Letter to Joseph Priestley[1]

PASSY, Feb. 8, 1780.

DEAR SIR,

Your kind letter of September 27 came to hand but very lately, the bearer having stayed long in Holland. I always rejoice to hear of your being still employed in experimental researches into nature, and of the Success you meet with. The rapid Progress *true* Science now makes, occasions my regretting sometimes that I was born so soon. It is impossible to imagine the height to which may be carried, in a thousand years, the power of man over matter. We may perhaps learn to deprive large masses of their gravity, and give them absolute levity, for the sake of easy transport. Agriculture may diminish its labor and double its produce; all diseases may by sure means be prevented or cured, not excepting even that of old age, and our lives lengthened at pleasure even beyond the antediluvian standard. O that moral science were in as fair a way of improvement, that men would cease to be wolves to one another, and that human beings would at length learn what they now improperly call humanity!

I am glad my little paper on the *Aurora Borealis* pleased. If it should occasion further enquiry, and so produce a better hypothesis, it will not be wholly useless. I am ever, with the greatest and most sincere esteem, dear sir, yours very affectionately

B. FRANKLIN.

1. An English chemist (1733–1804) who experimented with electricity and discovered a range of gases; also a close friend of Franklin.

DAVID HUME

The Scottish-born philosopher David Hume (1711–1776) rejected the quest for abstract and theoretical truths. He favored an empirical approach, that is, the demand to "reject every system . . . however subtle or ingenious, which is not founded on fact and observation," and to "hearken to no arguments but those which are derived from experience." This insistence on trusting only the evidence of observable facts led readers to assume that he was an atheist, though in fact he refused to deny the existence of God, preferring rather to suspend judgment on what seemed to him an insoluble mystery.

While Hume stands for the quintessential Enlightenment values of skepticism and critical questioning, and was known to be a gentle and tolerant person, his work shows the more brutal side of the Enlightenment too: the belief that only Europeans were fully rational, human subjects. Always committed to empirical evidence, he makes a distinction between white and black races supposedly based on observed fact, though his own experience of African people was in fact exceptionally limited. While affirming a natural racial hierarchy, Hume also opposes slavery as disgusting and corrupting.

From Of National Characters

* * *

I am apt to suspect the negroes to be naturally inferior to the whites. There scarcely ever was a civilized nation of that complexion, nor even any individual eminent either in action or speculation. No ingenious manufactures amongst them, no arts, no sciences. On the other hand, the most rude and barbarous of the whites, such as the ancient GERMANS, the present TARTARS, have still something eminent about them, in their valour, form of government, or some other particular. Such a uniform and constant difference could not happen, in so many countries and ages, if nature had not made an original distinction between these breeds of men. Not to mention our colonies, there are NEGROE slaves dispersed all over EUROPE, of whom none ever discovered any symptoms of ingenuity; though low people, without education, will start up amongst us, and distinguish themselves in every profession. In JAMAICA, indeed, they talk of one negroe as a man of parts and learning; but it is likely he is admired for slender accomplishments, like a parrot, who speaks a few words plainly.

* * *

The chief difference between the *domestic* economy of the ancients and that of the moderns consists in the practice of slavery, which prevailed among the former, and which has been abolished for some centuries throughout the greater part of EUROPE. Some passionate admirers of the ancients, and zealous partizans of civil liberty, (for these sentiments, as they are, both of them, in the main, extremely just, are found to be almost inseparable) cannot forbear regretting the loss of this institution; and whilst they brand all submission to the government of a single person with the harsh denomination of slavery, they would gladly reduce the greater part of mankind to real slavery and subjection. But to one who considers coolly on the subject it will appear, that human nature, in general, really enjoys more liberty at present, in the most arbitrary government of EUROPE, than it ever did during the most flourishing period of ancient times. As much as submission to a petty prince, whose dominions extend not beyond a single city, is more grievous than obedience to a great monarch; so much is domestic slavery more cruel and oppressive than any civil subjection whatsoever. The more the master is removed from us in place and rank, the greater liberty we enjoy; the less are our actions inspected and controled; and the fainter that cruel comparison becomes between our own subjection, and the freedom, and even dominion of another. The remains which are found of domestic slavery, in the AMERICAN colonies, and among some EUROPEAN nations, would never surely create a desire of rendering it more universal. The little humanity, commonly observed in persons, accustomed, from their infancy, to exercise so great authority over their fellow-creatures, and to trample upon human nature, were sufficient alone to disgust us with that unbounded dominion. Nor can a more probable reason be assigned for the severe, I might say, barbarous manners of ancient times, than the practice of domestic slavery; by which every man of rank was rendered a petty tyrant, and educated amidst the flattery, submission, and low debasement of his slaves.

According to ancient practice, all checks were on the inferior, to restrain him to the duty of submission; none on the superior, to engage him to the reciprocal duties of gentleness and humanity. In modern times, a bad servant finds not easily a good master, nor a bad master a good servant; and the checks are mutual, suitably to the inviolable and eternal laws of reason and equity.

* * *

JAMES BEATTIE

James Beattie (1735–1803) read **David Hume**'s work and burned with anger. He was a Scottish philosopher, too, who made quite a reputation for himself by refuting Hume. In his *Essay on Truth* (1770), Beattie disputes claims about racial difference on Hume's own grounds— empirical evidence—and argues that such assertions of inferiority and superiority necessarily legitimate the practice of slavery. He thus exposes contradictions in Hume's own logic, using Enlightenment methods against one of the period's great philosophical heroes.

From An Essay on Truth

* * *

That I may not be thought a blind admirer of antiquity, I would here crave the reader's indulgence for one short digression more, in order to put him in mind of an important error in morals, inferred from partial and inaccurate experience, by no less a person than Aristotle himself.[1] He argues, "That men of little genius, and great bodily strength, are by Nature destined to serve, and those of better capacity to command; that the natives of Greece, and of some other countries, being superior in genius, have a natural right to empire; and that the rest of mankind, being naturally stupid, are destined to labour and slavery." This reasoning is now, alas! of little advantage to Aristotle's countrymen, who have for many ages been doomed to that slavery which, in his judgment, Nature had destined them to impose on others; and many nations whom he would have consigned to everlasting stupidity, have shown themselves equal in genius to the most exalted of human kind. It would have been more worthy of Aristotle, to have inferred man's natural and universal right to liberty, from that natural and universal passion with which men desire it, and from the salutary consequences to learning, to virtue, and to every human improvement, of which it never fails to be productive. He wanted, perhaps, to devise some excuse for servitude; a practice which to their eternal reproach, both Greeks and Romans tolerated even in the days of their glory.

Mr. Hume argues nearly in the same manner in regard to the superiority of white men over black. "I am apt to suspect," says he, "the negroes, and in general all the other species of men (for there are four or five different kinds), to be naturally inferior to the whites. There *never was* a civilized nation of any other complexion than white, *nor even any individual* eminent either in action or speculation. *No* ingenious manufactures among them, *no* arts, *no* sciences.— There are negro-slaves dispersed all over Europe, of which *none* ever discovered any symptoms of ingenuity." These assertions are strong; but I know not whether they have any thing else to recommend them.—For, first, though true, they would not prove the point in question, except it were also proved, that the Africans and Americans, even though arts and sciences were introduced among them, would still remain unsusceptible of cultivation. The inhabitants of Great Britain and France were as savage two thousand years ago, as those of Africa and America are at this day. To civilize a nation, is a work which requires long time to accomplish. And one may as well say of an infant, that he can never become a man, as of a nation now barbarous, that it never can be civilized.— Secondly, of the facts here asserted, no man could have sufficient evidence, except from a personal acquaintance with all the negroes that now are, or ever were, on the face of the earth. These people write no histories; and all the reports of all the travellers that ever visited them, will not amount to any thing like a proof of what is here affirmed.—But, thirdly, we know that these assertions are not true. The empires of Peru and Mexico could not have been governed, nor the metropolis of the latter built after so singular a manner, in the middle of a lake, without men eminent both for action and speculation. Every

1. Ancient Greek philosopher (384–322 B.C.E.).

body has heard of the magnificence, good government, and ingenuity, of the ancient Peruvians. The Africans and Americans are known to have many ingenious manufactures and arts among them, which even Europeans would find it no easy matter to imitate. Sciences indeed they have none, because they have no letters; but in oratory, some of them, particularly the Indians *of the Five Nations*,[2] are said to be greatly our superiors. It will be readily allowed, that the condition of a slave is not favourable to genius of any kind; and yet the negro-slaves dispersed over Europe, have often discovered symptoms of ingenuity, notwithstanding their unhappy circumstances. They become excellent handicraftsmen, and practical musicians, and indeed learn every thing their masters are at pains to teach them, perfidy and debauchery not excepted. That a negro-slave, who can neither read nor write, nor speak any European language, who is not permitted to do any thing but what his master commands, and who has not a single friend on earth, but is universally considered and treated as if he were of a species inferior to the human;—that such a creature should so distinguish himself among Europeans, as to be talked of through the world as a man of genius, is surely no reasonable expectation. To suppose him of an inferior species, because he does not thus distinguish himself, is just as rational, as to suppose any private European of an inferior species, because he has not raised himself to the condition of royalty.

Had the Europeans been destitute of the arts of writing, and working in iron, they might have remained to this day as barbarous as the natives of Africa and America. Nor is the invention of these arts to be ascribed to our superior capacity. The genius of the inventor is not always to be estimated according to the importance of the invention. Gunpowder, and the mariner's compass, have produced wonderful revolutions in human affairs, and yet were accidental discoveries. Such, probably, were the first essays in writing, and working in iron. Suppose them the effect of contrivance, they were at least contrived by a few individuals; and if they required a superiority of understanding, or of species, in the inventors, those inventors, and their descendants, are the only persons who can lay claim to the honour of that superiority.

That every practice and sentiment is barbarous which is not according to the usages of modern Europe, seems to be a fundamental maxim with some of our philosophers. Their remarks often put us in mind of the fable of the man and the lion.[3] If negroes or Indians were disposed to recriminate; if a Lucian or a Voltaire,[4] from the coast of Guinea, or from *the Five Nations*, were to pay us a visit; what a picture of European manners might he present to his countrymen at his return! Nor would caricature, or exaggeration be necessary to render it hideous. A plain historical account of some of our most fashionable duellists, gamblers, and adulterers (to name no more), would exhibit specimens of brutish barbarity and sottish infatuation, such as might vie with any that ever appeared in Kamschatka, California, or the land of Hottentots.[5]

---

2. A confederacy of American Indian tribes: the Mohawk, Oneida, Onondaga, Cayuga, and Seneca peoples.
3. Story told by Aesop (620–564 B.C.E.) about a man and a lion, each of whom boasts of being superior to the other.

4. A French philosopher and satirist (1694–1778); Lucian (ca. 125–180), a Syrian satirist who wrote in Greek.
5. A southwest African people today better known as the Khoikhoi. "Kamschatka": a Russian peninsula that juts into the Pacific Ocean.

The natural inferiority of negroes is a favourite topic with some modern writers. They mean perhaps to invalidate the authority of that Book, which declares, that "Eve was the mother of all living," and that "God hath made of one blood all nations of men, for to dwell on all the face of the earth." And perhaps some of them may have it in view to vindicate a certain barbarous piece of policy, which, though it does no honour to the Christian world, and is not, I believe, attended with pecuniary advantage to the commercial, has notwithstanding many patrons even in this age of light and liberty.—But Britons are famous for generosity; a virtue in which it is easy for them to excel both the Romans and the Greeks. Let it never be said, that slavery is countenanced by the bravest and most generous people on earth; by a people who are animated with that heroic passion, the love of liberty, beyond all nations ancient or modern; and the fame of whose toilsome, but unwearied perseverance, in vindicating, at the expence of life and fortune, the sacred rights of mankind, will strike terror into the hearts of sycophants and tyrants, and excite the admiration and gratitude of all good men to the latest posterity.

MARY WOLLSTONECRAFT

Consorting with radicals in England who favored the French Revolution, with its overthrow of traditional authority and its embrace of universal principles of equality and reason, Mary Wollstonecraft (1759–1797) launched a powerful argument for inalienable human rights in her essay *A Vindication of the Rights of Men* (1791). Here she relied on rational principles to attack justifications for traditional privilege and power. She followed this essay in 1792 with the even more radical *A Vindication of the Rights of Woman*, where she argued that marriage was no better than prostitution, and that education and unequal laws for women at the time subjected them to a condition similar to slavery. For these political views, Wollstonecraft was widely mocked in her own lifetime. And when it emerged after her death that she had had a child out of wedlock, her reputation sank so low that few readers were willing to open her "immoral" books for more than a century. It was only in the 1960s that she became known as the great founder of feminism. Wollstonecraft also left a legacy of a different kind: her second daughter, Mary, the only legitimate child of Wollstonecraft and fellow radical writer William Godwin, grew up to write *Frankenstein*, one of the most influential works of nineteenth-century literature.

From A Vindication of the Rights of Woman

* * *

Men and women must be educated, in a great degree, by the opinions and manners of the society they live in. In every age there has been a stream of popular opinion that has carried all before it, and given a family character, as it were, to the century. It may then fairly be inferred, that, till society be differently constituted, much cannot be expected from education. It is, however, sufficient for my present purpose to assert, that, whatever effect circumstances have on the abilities, every being may become virtuous by the exercise of its own reason; for if but one being was created with vicious inclinations, that is positively bad, what can save us from atheism? or if we worship a God, is not that God a devil?

Consequently, the most perfect education, in my opinion, is such an exercise of the understanding as is best calculated to strengthen the body and form the heart. Or, in other words, to enable the individual to attain such habits of virtue as will render it independent. In fact, it is a farce to call any being virtuous whose virtues do not result from the exercise of its own reason. This was Rousseau's opinion[1] respecting men: I extend it to women, and confidently assert that they have been drawn out of their sphere by false refinement, and not by an endeavour to acquire masculine qualities. Still the regal homage which they receive is so intoxicating, that till the manners of the times are changed, and formed on more reasonable principles, it may be impossible to convince them that the illegitimate power, which they obtain, by degrading themselves, is a curse, and that they must return to nature and equality, if they wish to secure the placid satisfaction that unsophisticated affections impart. But for this epoch we must wait—wait, perhaps, till kings and nobles, enlightened by reason, and, preferring the real dignity of man to childish state, throw off their gaudy hereditary trappings: and if then women do not resign the arbitrary power of beauty—they will prove that they have *less* mind than man.

I may be accused of arrogance; still I must declare what I firmly believe, that all the writers who have written on the subject of female education and manners from Rousseau to Dr. Gregory,[2] have contributed to render women more artificial, weak characters, than they would otherwise have been; and, consequently, more useless members of society. I might have expressed this conviction in a lower key; but I am afraid it would have been the whine of affectation, and not the faithful expression of my feelings, of the clear result, which experience and reflection have led me to draw. When I come to that division of the subject, I shall advert to the passages that I more particularly disapprove of, in the works of the authors I have just alluded to; but it is first necessary to observe, that my objection extends to the whole purport of those books, which tend, in my opinion, to degrade one half of the human species, and render women pleasing at the expense of every solid virtue.

1. Jean-Jacques Rousseau (1712–1778), philosopher from Geneva whose ideas about human equality and freedom inspired many revolutionaries; he also wrote about education.

2. John Gregory (1724–1773), Scottish physician who wrote an influential book on educating girls called *A Father's Legacy to his Daughters* (1774).

Though, to reason on Rousseau's ground, if man did attain a degree of perfection of mind when his body arrived at maturity, it might be proper, in order to make a man and his wife *one*, that she should rely entirely on his understanding; and the graceful ivy, clasping the oak that supported it, would form a whole in which strength and beauty would be equally conspicuous. But, alas! husbands, as well as their helpmates, are often only overgrown children; nay, thanks to early debauchery, scarcely men in their outward form—and if the blind lead the blind, one need not come from heaven to tell us the consequence.

Many are the causes that, in the present corrupt state of society, contribute to enslave women by cramping their understandings and sharpening their senses. One, perhaps, that silently does more mischief than all the rest, is their disregard of order.

To do every thing in an orderly manner, is a most important precept, which women, who, generally speaking, receive only a disorderly kind of education, seldom attend to with that degree of exactness that men, who from their infancy are broken into method, observe. This negligent kind of guess-work, for what other epithet can be used to point out the random exertions of a sort of instinctive common sense, never brought to the test of reason? prevents their generalizing matters of fact—so they do to-day, what they did yesterday, merely because they did it yesterday.

This contempt of the understanding in early life has more baneful consequences than is commonly supposed; for the little knowledge which women of strong minds attain, is, from various circumstances, of a more desultory kind than the knowledge of men, and it is acquired more by sheer observations on real life, than from comparing what has been individually observed with the results of experience generalized by speculation. Led by their dependent situation and domestic employments more into society, what they learn is rather by snatches; and as learning is with them, in general, only a secondary thing, they do not pursue any one branch with that persevering ardour necessary to give vigor to the faculties, and clearness to the judgment. In the present state of society, a little learning is required to support the character of a gentleman; and boys are obliged to submit to a few years of discipline. But in the education of women, the cultivation of the understanding is always subordinate to the acquirement of some corporeal accomplishment; even while enervated by confinement and false notions of modesty, the body is prevented from attaining that grace and beauty which relaxed half-formed limbs never exhibit. Besides, in youth their faculties are not brought forward by emulation; and having no serious scientific study, if they have natural sagacity it is turned too soon on life and manners. They dwell on effects, and modifications, without tracing them back to causes; and complicated rules to adjust behaviour are a weak substitute for simple principles.

As a proof that education gives this appearance of weakness to females, we may instance the example of military men, who are, like them, sent into the world before their minds have been stored with knowledge or fortified by principles. The consequences are similar; soldiers acquire a little superficial knowledge, snatched from the muddy current of conversation, and, from continually mixing with society, they gain, what is termed a knowledge of the world; and this acquaintance with manners and customs has frequently been confounded with a knowledge of the human heart. But can the crude fruit of casual observation, never brought to the test of judgment, formed by comparing speculation and experience, deserve such a distinction? Soldiers, as well as women, practice the minor virtues with punctilious politeness. Where is then the sexual difference, when the education has been the same? All the difference that I can discern, arises from the superior advantage of liberty, which enables the former to see more of life.

It is wandering from my present subject, perhaps, to make a political remark; but, as it was produced naturally by the train of my reflections, I shall not pass it silently over.

Standing armies can never consist of resolute, robust men; they may be well disciplined machines, but they will seldom contain men under the influence of strong passions, or with very vigorous faculties. And as for any depth of understanding, I will venture to affirm, that it is as rarely to be found in the army as amongst women; and the cause, I maintain, is the same. It may be further observed, that officers are also particularly attentive to their persons, fond of dancing, crowded rooms, adventures, and ridicule.[3] Like the *fair* sex, the business of their lives is gallantry.—They were taught to please, and they only live to please. Yet they do not lose their rank in the distinction of sexes, for they are still reckoned superior to women, though in what their superiority consists, beyond what I have just mentioned, it is difficult to discover.

The great misfortune is this, that they both acquire manners before morals, and a knowledge of life before they have, from reflection, any acquaintance with the grand ideal outline of human nature. The consequence is natural; satisfied with common nature, they become a prey to prejudices, and taking all their opinions on credit, they blindly submit to authority. So that, if they have any sense, it is a kind of instinctive glance, that catches proportions, and decides with respect to manners; but fails when arguments are to be pursued below the surface, or opinions analyzed.

May not the same remark be applied to women? Nay, the argument may be carried still further, for they are both thrown out of a useful station by the unnatural distinctions established in civilized life. Riches and hereditary honours have made cyphers of women to give consequence to the numerical figure;[4] and idleness has produced a mixture of gallantry and despotism into society, which leads the very men who are the slaves of their mistresses to tyrannize over their sisters, wives, and daughters. This is only keeping them in rank and file, it is true. Strengthen the female mind by enlarging it, and there will be an end to blind obedience; but, as blind obedience is ever sought for by power, tyrants and sensualists are in the right when they endeavour to keep women in the dark, because the former only want slaves, and the latter a plaything. The sensualist, indeed, has been the most dangerous of tyrants, and women have been duped by their lovers, as princes by their ministers, whilst dreaming that they reigned over them.

3. Why should women be censured with petulant acrimony, because they seem to have a passion for a scarlet coat? Has not education placed them more on a level with soldiers than any other class of men? [Wollstonecraft's note].

4. Wealth and hereditary privilege have made women into "cyphers"—zeroes—which are nothing in themselves but valuable when added to the end of numbers.

MARQUIS DE SADE

The French aristocrat Donatien-Alphonse-François, the Marquis de Sade (1740–1814) is best known for his erotic writings, which are marked by an appetite for violence and cruelty (the word *sadism* is derived from his name). Not one of the standard figures of Enlightenment philosophy, he nonetheless represents a provocative extreme on the spectrum of Enlightenment thought. Like other influential thinkers of the period, he favored freedom—but in his case it was a freedom so complete that he saw no need for laws of any kind. Like others he asked how there could be a God when evil existed in the world, but rather than denying God's existence or justifying God's goodness in the face of evil, de Sade argued that God must be cruel and malicious himself. Humans therefore have the natural right to act as cruelly as they choose. In *Philosophy in the Bedroom* (1795), de Sade writes in a conventional philosophical form—the dialogue—and pursues a debate governed by the reasoned pursuit of truth. But his characters conclude that the only right way to act in the world involves rejecting modesty, compassion, and all moral and religious rules in favor of their own pleasure. In the selection included here, a libertine aristocrat asks whether murder is a crime in the eyes of nature and uses the eminently enlightened tools of logic and observed fact to reason through to his startling conclusions.

From Philosophy in the Bedroom[1]

* * *

Thus, my dear Eugénie, is the manner of these persons' arguing, and from my experience and studies I may add thereunto that cruelty, very far from being a vice, is the first sentiment Nature injects in us all. The infant breaks his toy, bites his nurse's breast, strangles his canary long before he is able to reason; cruelty is stamped in animals, in whom, as I think I have said, Nature's laws are more emphatically to be read than in ourselves; cruelty exists amongst savages, so much nearer to Nature than civilized men are; absurd then to maintain cruelty is a consequence of depravity. I repeat, the doctrine is false. Cruelty is natural. All of us are born furnished with a dose of cruelty education later modifies; but education does not belong to Nature, and is as deforming to Nature's sacred effects as arboriculture is to trees. In your orchards compare the tree abandoned to Nature's ministry with the other your art cares for, and you will see which is the more beautiful, you will discover from which you will pluck the superior fruit. Cruelty is simply the energy in a man civilization has not yet altogether corrupted: therefore it is a virtue, not a vice. Repeal your laws, do away with your constraints, your chastisements, your habits, and cruelty will have dangerous effects no more, since it will never manifest itself save

1. Translated by Richard Seaver and Austryn Wainhouse.

when it meets with resistance, and then the collision will always be between competing cruelties; it is in the civilized state cruelty is dangerous, because the assaulted person nearly always lacks the force or the means to repel injury; but in the state of uncivilization, if cruelty's target is strong, he will repulse cruelty; and if the person attacked is weak, why, the case here is merely that of assault upon one of those persons whom Nature's law prescribes to yield to the strong—'tis all one, and why seek trouble where there is none?

* * *

Have we not acquired the right to say anything? The time has come for the ventilation of great verities; men today will not be content with less. The time has come for error to disappear; that blindfold must fall beside the heads of kings. From Nature's point of view, is murder a crime? That is the first question posed.

It is probable that we are going to humiliate man's pride by lowering him again to the rank of all of Nature's other creatures, but the philosopher does not flatter small human vanities; ever in burning pursuit of truth, he discerns it behind stupid notions of pride, lays it bare, elaborates upon it, and intrepidly shows it to the astonished world.

What is man? and what difference is there between him and other plants, between him and all the other animals of the world? None, obviously. Fortuitously placed, like them, upon this globe, he is born like them; like them, he reproduces, rises, and falls; like them he arrives at old age and sinks like them into nothingness at the close of the life span Nature assigns each species of animal, in accordance with its organic construction. Since the parallels are so exact that the inquiring eye of philosophy is absolutely unable to perceive any grounds for discrimination, there is then just as much evil in killing animals as men, or just as little, and whatever be the distinctions we make, they will be found to stem from our pride's prejudices, than which, unhappily, nothing is more absurd. Let us all the same press on to the question. You cannot deny it is one and the same, to destroy a man or a beast; but is not the destruction of all living animals decidedly an evil, as the Pythagoreans believed, and as they who dwell on the banks of Ganges[2] yet believe? Before answering that, we remind the reader that we are examining the question only in terms of Nature and in relation to her; later on, we will envisage it with reference to men.

Now then, what value can Nature set upon individuals whose making costs her neither the least trouble nor the slightest concern? The worker values his work according to the labor it entails and the time spent creating it. Does man cost Nature anything? And, under the supposition that he does, does he cost her more than an ape or an elephant? I go further: what are the regenerative materials used by Nature? Of what are composed the beings which come into life? Do not the three elements of which they are formed result from the prior destruction of other bodies? If all individuals were possessed of eternal life,

2. River in India that is sacred to the Hindu religion, which encourages a vegetarian diet. "Pythagoreans": followers of the Greek philosopher Pythagoras (ca. 570 B.C.E.–ca. 490 B.C.E.), who claimed that after death the soul migrated to a new human or animal body; Pythagoreans often espoused vegetarianism.

would it not become impossible for Nature to create any new ones? If Nature denies eternity to beings, it follows that their destruction is one of her laws. Now, once we observe that destruction is so useful to her that she absolutely cannot dispense with it, and that she cannot achieve her creations without drawing from the store of destruction which death prepares for her, from this moment onward the idea of annihilation which we attach to death ceases to be real; there is no more veritable annihilation; what we call the end of the living animal is no longer a true finis, but a simple transformation, a transmutation of matter, what every modern philosopher acknowledges as one of Nature's fundamental laws. According to these irrefutable principles, death is hence no more than a change of form, an imperceptible passage from one existence into another, and that is what Pythagoras called metempsychosis.

These truths once admitted, I ask whether it can ever be proposed that destruction is a crime? Will you dare tell me, with the design of preserving your absurd illusions, that transmutation is destruction? No, surely not; for, to prove that, it would be necessary to demonstrate matter inert for an instant, for a moment in repose. Well, you will never detect any such moment. Little animals are formed immediately a large animal expires, and these little animals' lives are simply one of the necessary effects determined by the large animal's temporary sleep. Given this, will you dare suggest that one pleases Nature more than another? To support that contention, you would have to prove what cannot be proven: that elongated or square are more useful, more agreeable to Nature than oval or triangular shapes; you would have to prove that, with what regards Nature's sublime scheme, a sluggard who fattens in idleness is more useful than the horse, whose service is of such importance, or than a steer, whose body is so precious that there is no part of it which is not useful; you would have to say that the venomous serpent is more necessary than the faithful dog.

Now, as not one of these systems can be upheld, one must hence consent unreservedly to acknowledge our inability to annihilate Nature's works; in light of the certainty that the only thing we do when we give ourselves over to destroying is merely to effect an alteration in forms which does not extinguish life, it becomes beyond human powers to prove that there may exist anything criminal in the alleged destruction of a creature, of whatever age, sex, or species you may suppose it. Led still further in our series of inferences proceeding one from the other, we affirm that the act you commit in juggling the forms of Nature's different productions is of advantage to her, since thereby you supply her the primary material for her reconstructions, tasks which would be compromised were you to desist from destroying.

Well, let *her* do the destroying, they tell you; one ought to let her do it, of course, but they are Nature's impulses man follows when he indulges in homicide; it is Nature who advises him, and the man who destroys his fellow is to Nature what are the plague and famine, like them sent by her hand which employs every possible means more speedily to obtain of destruction this primary matter, itself absolutely essential to her works.

Let us deign for a moment to illumine our spirit by philosophy's sacred flame; what other than Nature's voice suggests to us personal hatreds, revenges, wars, in a word, all those causes of perpetual murder? Now, if she incites us to murderous acts, she has need of them; that once grasped, how may we suppose ourselves guilty in her regard when we do nothing more than obey her intentions?

But that is more than what is needed to convince any enlightened reader, that for murder ever to be an outrage to Nature is impossible.

Is it a political crime? We must avow, on the contrary, that it is, unhappily, merely one of policy's and politics' greatest instruments. Is it not by dint of murders that France is free today? Needless to say, here we are referring to the murders occasioned by war, not to the atrocities committed by plotters and rebels; the latter, destined to the public's execration, have only to be recollected to arouse forever general horror and indignation. What study, what science, has greater need of murder's support than that which tends only to deceive, whose sole end is the expansion of one nation at another's expense? Are wars, the unique fruit of this political barbarism, anything but the means whereby a nation is nourished, whereby it is strengthened, whereby it is buttressed? And what is war if not the science of destruction? A strange blindness in man, who publicly teaches the art of killing, who rewards the most accomplished killer, and who punishes him who for some particular reason does away with his enemy! Is it not high time errors so savage be repaired?

Is murder then a crime against society? But how could that reasonably be imagined? What difference does it make to this murderous society, whether it have one member more, or less? Will its laws, its manners, its customs be vitiated? Has an individual's death ever had any influence upon the general mass? And after the loss of the greatest battle, what am I saying? after the obliteration of half the world—or, if one wishes, of the entire world—would the little number of survivors, should there be any, notice even the faintest difference in things? No, alas. Nor would Nature notice any either, and the stupid pride of man, who believes everything created for him, would be dashed indeed, after the total extinction of the human species, were it to be seen that nothing in Nature had changed, and that the stars' flight had not for that been retarded. Let us continue.

What must the attitude of a warlike and republican state be toward murder?

Dangerous it should certainly be, either to cast discredit upon the act, or to punish it. Republican mettle calls for a touch of ferocity: if he grows soft, if his energy slackens in him, the republican will be subjugated in a trice. A most unusual thought comes to mind at this point, but if it is audacious it is also true, and I will mention it. A nation that begins by governing itself as a republic will only be sustained by virtues because, in order to attain the most, one must always start with the least. But an already old and decayed nation which courageously casts off the yoke of its monarchical government in order to adopt a republican one, will only be maintained by many crimes; for it is criminal already, and if it were to wish to pass from crime to virtue, that is to say, from a violent to a pacific, benign condition, it should fall into an inertia whose result would soon be its certain ruin.

*   *   *

MOLIÈRE
(JEAN-BAPTISTE POQUELIN)
1622–1673

Jean-Baptiste Molière, one of the great comic dramatists in the Western tradition, wrote both broad farce and comedies of character in which he caricatured some form of vice or folly by embodying it in a single figure. His targets included the miser, the aspiring but vulgar middle class, female would-be intellectuals, the hypochondriac, and in *Tartuffe*, the religious hypocrite. Yet Molière's questioning goes far beyond witty farce: his works suggest not only the fallibility of specific types, but also the foolishness of trusting reason to arrange human affairs.

LIFE AND TIMES

Son of a prosperous Paris merchant, Molière (originally named Poquelin) devoted his entire adult life to the creation of stage illusion, as playwright and as actor. He was educated at a prestigious Jesuit school and seems to have studied law for some time, though without taking a degree. At about the age of twenty-five, he took his stage name and abandoned the comfortable life of a bourgeois to join the Illustre Théâtre, a company of traveling players established by the Béjart family. With them he toured the provinces for about twelve years, and, in 1662, he married Armande Béjart. Molière's lengthy experience as an actor doubtless honed his dramatic writing skills, although he first became known not for the tragedies that he preferred but for the short farces that he appended to them. Molière's particular talents, it would soon become clear, lay in satirizing an overly sophisticated society that was heavily invested in fashion, appearances, and proper behavior. Molière's skepticism about religious devotion, which he exposed as hypocrisy, would prove hugely controversial in a France that had recently been led by the powerful Cardinal Mazarin, chief minister while Louis XIV was a young boy, and where the Catholic Church still wielded considerable power.

Over the course of his long reign, Louis XIV, the "Sun King," consolidated royal power by upholding the divine right of kings, and became an important patron of the visual and literary arts. In Louis's France, the true measure of cultural worth was the approval of the court and the Paris stage. After years of courting noble patrons, in 1658 Molière's theatrical company was finally ordered to perform for the king in Paris; a year later, the playwright's first great success, *The High-Brow Ladies* (*Les Précieuses ridicules*), was produced. The company, now patronized by the king, became increasingly successful, developing finally (1680) into the Comédie Française. With success came opposition: the *parti des Devots* (party of the faithful) banded together to protest Molière's irreverence, as he took on more and more of his society's sacred cows. Yet the king continued to protect him, granting him a pension and allowing Molière to evade the censorship often demanded by the Church or the more conservative voices in society.

Molière became increasingly famous—and infamous—as his works met with increasing resistance, culminating in the furor over *Tartuffe*, discussed below. Over the course of his years in Paris, Molière wrote over thirty plays and produced many more on his stage. Ever the man of the theater, he died a few hours after performing in the lead role of his own play *The Imaginary Invalid*.

TARTUFFE

In *Tartuffe* (1664), as in his other plays, Molière employs classic comic devices of plot and character—here, a foolish, stubborn father blocking the course of young love; an impudent servant commenting on her superiors' actions; a happy ending involving a marriage facilitated by implausible means. He often uses such devices, however, to comment on his own immediate social scene, imagining how universal patterns play themselves out in a specific historical context. *Tartuffe* targeted the hypocrisy of piety so directly and transparently that the Catholic Church forced the king to ban it, although Molière managed to have it published and produced once more by 1669.

The play's emotional energy derives not from the simple discrepancy of man and mask in Tartuffe ("Is not a face quite different from a mask?" inquires Cléante, who has no trouble making such distinctions) but from the struggle for erotic, psychic, and economic power in which people employ their masks. Orgon, an aging man with grown children, seeks ways to preserve control and instead falls for the ploys of the hypocritical Tartuffe. A domestic tyrant, Orgon insists on submission from the women in the play, even when they prove far more perceptive than he about Tartuffe's deceptions. Tartuffe's lust, one of those passions forever eluding human mastery, dis-

turbs Orgon's arrangements; in the end, the will of the offstage king orders everything, as though a benevolent god had intervened.

To make Tartuffe a specifically religious hypocrite is an act of inventive daring. Although one may easily accept Molière's defense of his intentions (not to mock faith but to attack its misuse), it is not hard to see why the play might trouble religious authorities. Molière suggests how readily religious faith lends itself to misuse, how high-sounding pieties allow men and women to evade self-examination and immediate responsibilities. Tartuffe deceives others by his grand gestures of mortification ("Hang up my hair shirt") and charity; he encourages his victims in their own grandiosities. Religion offers ready justification for a course as destructive as it is self-seeking.

Throughout the play, Orgon's brother-in-law Cléante speaks in the voice of wisdom, counseling moderation, common sense, and self-control, calling attention to folly. More important, he emphasizes how the issues Molière examines in this comedy relate to dominant late seventeenth-century themes:

> Ah, Brother, man's a strangely
>   fashioned creature
> Who seldom is content to follow
>   Nature,
> But recklessly pursues his inclination
> Beyond the narrow bounds of
>   moderation,
> And often, by transgressing Reason's
>   laws,
> Perverts a lofty aim or noble cause.

To follow Nature means to act appropriately to the human situation in the created universe, recognizing the limitations inherent in the human condition. As Cléante's observations suggest, "to follow Nature," given the rationality of the universe, implies adherence to "Reason's laws." All transgression involves failure to submit to reason's dictates, a point that Molière's stylized comic plot makes insistently.

Although the comedy suggests a social world in which women exist in utter subordination to fathers and husbands, in the plot, two women bring about the unmasking of the villain. The virtuous wife, Elmire, object of Tartuffe's lust, and the clever servant girl, Dorine, confront the immediate situation with pragmatic inventiveness. Both women have a clear sense of right and wrong, although they express it in less resounding terms than does Cléante. Their concrete insistence on facing what is really going on, cutting through all obfuscation, rescues the men from entanglement in their own abstract formulations.

Molière achieves comic effects above all through style and language. Devoted to exposing the follies of his society, his plays use a number of devices that have become the gold standard of comic writing. His characters are often in the grip of a fixed idea, rigidly following a single principle of action, such as extreme religious devotion or sexual rejuvenation. These fixed ideas also manifest themselves in the characters' speech patterns, which are full of ticks and repetitions. Adhering to single abstractions, Molière's comic protagonists often seem like marionettes, whose rigid bearing, behavior and language is controlled by an outside force as if by a puppet master. Yet despite their singlemindedness, his characters are also recognizable portraits of human folly, closely observed and humorously rendered.

Comedies conventionally end in the restoration of order, declaring that good inevitably triumphs; rationality renews itself despite the temporary deviations of the foolish and the vicious. Although at the end of *Tartuffe* order is restored, the arbitrary intervention of the king leaves a disturbing emotional residue. The play has demonstrated that Tartuffe's corrupt will to power can ruthlessly aggrandize itself. Money speaks, in this society as in ours; possession of wealth implies total control over others. In the benign world of comedy, the play reminds its readers of the extreme precariousness with which reason finally triumphs. Tartuffe's monstrous lust, for women, money, power, genuinely endangers the social structure. The play forces us to recognize the constant threats to rationality, and how much we have at stake in trying to use reason as a principle of action.

Tartuffe[1]

CHARACTERS

MADAME PERNELLE, *mother of Orgon*
ORGON, *husband of Elmire*
ELMIRE, *wife of Orgon*
DAMIS, *son of Orgon*
MARIANE, *daughter of Orgon*
VALÈRE, *fiancé of Mariane*
CLÉANTE, *brother-in-law of Orgon*

TARTUFFE,[2] *a religious hypocrite*
DORINE, *lady's maid to Mariane*
MONSIEUR LOYAL, *a bailiff*
THE EXEMPT, *an officer of the king*
FLIPOTE, *lady's maid to Madame
    Pernelle*
LAURENT, *a servant of Tartuffe*

The scene is Paris, in ORGON's *house.*

1.1

[MADAME PERNELLE, FLIPOTE, ELMIRE,
MARIANE, DORINE, DAMIS, CLÉANTE]

MADAME PERNELLE[3] Flipote, come on! My visit here is through!
ELMIRE You walk so fast I can't keep up with you!
MADAME PERNELLE Then stop! That's your last step! Don't take another.
  After all, I'm just your husband's mother.
ELMIRE And, as his wife, I have to see you out—   5
  Agreed? Now, what is this about?
MADAME PERNELLE I cannot bear the way this house is run—
  As if I don't know how things should be done!
  No one even thinks about my pleasure,
  And, if I ask, I'm served at someone's leisure.   10
  It's obvious—the values here aren't good
  Or everyone would treat me as they should.
  The Lord of Misrule here has his dominion—
DORINE But—
MADAME PERNELLE See? A servant with an opinion.
  You're the former nanny, nothing more.   15
  Were I in charge here, you'd be out the door.
DAMIS If—
MADAME PERNELLE —You—be quiet. Now let Grandma spell
  Her special word for you: "F-O-O-L."
  Oh yes! Your dear grandmother tells you that,

---

1. Versification by Constance Congdon, from a translation by Virginia Scott.
2. The name Tartuffe is similar both to the Italian word *tartufo*, meaning "truffle," and to the French word for truffle, *truffe*, from which is derived the French verb *truffer*—one meaning of which in Molière's day was "to deceive or cheat."
3. The role of Madame Pernelle was originally played by a male actor, a practice that was already a comic convention in Molière's time.

Just as I told my son, "Your son's a brat.   20
He won't become a drunkard or a thief,
And yet, he'll be a lifetime full of grief."
MARIANE   I think—
MADAME PERNELLE   —Oh, don't do that, my dear grandchild.
You'll hurt your brain. You think that we're beguiled
By your quietude, you fragile flower,   25
But as they say, still waters do run sour.
ELMIRE   But Mother—
MADAME PERNELLE   —Daughter-in-law, please take this well—
Behavior such as yours leads straight to hell.
You spend money like it grows on trees
Then wear it on your back in clothes like these.   30
Are you a princess? No? You're dressed like one!
One wonders whom you dress for—not my son.
Look to these children whom you have corrupted
When their mama's life was interrupted.
She spun in her grave when you were wed;   35
She's still a better mother, even dead.
CLÉANTE   Madame, I do insist—
MADAME PERNELLE   —You do? On what?
That we live life as you do, caring not
For morals? I hear each time you give that speech
Your sister memorizing what you teach.   40
I'd slam the door on you. Forgive my frankness.
That is how I am! And it is thankless.
DAMIS   Tartuffe would, from the bottom of his heart,
If he had one, thank you.
MADAME PERNELLE   Oh, now you start.
Grandson, it's "Monsieur Tartuffe" to you.   45
And he's a man who should be listened to.
If you provoke him with ungodly chat,
I will not tolerate it, and that's that.
DAMIS   Yet I should tolerate this trickster who
Has become the voice we answer to.   50
And I'm to be as quiet as a mouse
About this tyrant's power in our house?
All the fun things lately we have planned,
We couldn't do. And why? Because they're banned—
DORINE   By him! Anything we take pleasure in   55
Suddenly becomes a mortal sin.
MADAME PERNELLE   Then "he's here just in time" is what I say!
Don't you see? He's showing you the way
To heaven! Yes! So follow where he leads!
My son knows he is just what this house needs.   60
DAMIS   Now Grandmother, listen. Not Father, not you,
No one can make me follow this man who
Rules this house, yet came here as a peasant.
I'll put him in his place. It won't be pleasant.

DORINE   When he came here he wasn't wearing shoes.   65
  But he's no village saint—it's all a ruse.
  There was no vow of poverty—he's poor!
  And he was just some beggar at the door
  Whom we should have tossed. He's a disaster!
  To think this street bum now plays the master.   70
MADAME PERNELLE   May God have mercy on me. You're all blind.
  A nobler, kinder man you'll never find.
DORINE   So you think he's a saint. That's what he wants.
  But he's a hypocrite and merely flaunts
  This so-called godliness.   75
MADAME PERNELLE   Will you be quiet!?
DORINE   And that man of his—I just don't buy it—
  He's supposed to be his servant? No.
  They're in cahoots, I bet.
MADAME PERNELLE   How would you know?
  When, clearly, you don't understand, in fact,
  How a servant is supposed to act?   80
  This holy man you think of as uncouth,
  Tries to help by telling you the truth
  About yourself. But you can't hear it.
  He knows what heaven wants and that you fear it.
DORINE   So "heaven" hates these visits by our friends?   85
  I see! And that's why Tartuffe's gone to any ends
  To ruin our fun? But it is he who's zealous
  About "privacy"—and why? He's jealous.
  You can't miss it, whenever men come near—
  He's lusting for our own Madame Elmire.   90
MADAME PERNELLE   Since you, Dorine, have never understood
  Your place, or the concepts of "should"
  And "should not," one can't expect you to see
  Tartuffe's awareness of propriety.
  When these men visit, they bring noise and more—   95
  Valets and servants planted at the door,
  Carriages and horses, constant chatter.
  What must the neighbors think? These things matter.
  Is something going on? Well, I hope not.
  You know you're being talked about a lot.   100
CLÉANTE   Really, Madame, you think you can prevent
  Gossip? When most human beings are bent
  On rumormongering and defamation,
  And gathering or faking information
  To make us all look bad—what can we do?   105
  The fools who gossip don't care what is true.
  You would force the whole world to be quiet?
  Impossible! And each new lie—deny it?
  Who in the world would want to live that way?
  Let's live our lives. Let gossips have their say.   110

DORINE   It's our neighbor, Daphne. I just know it.
 They don't like us. It's obvious—they show it
 In the way they watch us—she and her mate.
 I've seen them squinting at us, through their gate.
 It's true—those whose private conduct is the worst   115
 Will mow each other down to be the first
 To weave some tale of lust, so hearts are broken
 Out of a simple kiss that's just a token
 Between friends—just friends and nothing more.
 See—those whose trysts are kept behind a door   120
 Yet everyone finds out? Well, then, they need
 New stories for the gossip mill to feed
 To all who'll listen. So they must repaint
 The deeds of others, hoping that a taint
 Will color others' lives in darker tone   125
 And, by this process, lighten up their own.
MADAME PERNELLE   Daphne and her mate are not the point.
 But when Orante says things are out of joint,
 There's a problem. She's a person who
 Prays every day and should be listened to.   130
 She condemns the mob that visits here.
DORINE   This good woman shouldn't live so near
 Those, like us, who run a bawdy house.
 I hear she lives as quiet as a mouse—
 Devout, though. Everyone applauds her zeal.   135
 She needed that when age stole her appeal.
 Her passion is policing—it's her duty.
 And compensation for her loss of beauty.
 She's a reluctant prude. And now, her art,
 Once used so well to win a lover's heart,   140
 Is gone. Her eyes, that used to flash with lust,
 Are steely from her piety. She must
 Have seen that it's too late to be a wife,
 And so she lives a plain and pious life.
 This is a strategy of old coquettes.   145
 It's how they manage once the world forgets
 Them. First, they wallow in a dark depression,
 Then see no recourse but in the profession
 Of a prude. They criticize the lives of everyone.
 They censure everything, and pardon none.   150
 It's envy. Pleasures that they are denied
 By time and age, now, they just can't abide.
MADAME PERNELLE   You do go on and on. [To ELMIRE] My dear Elmire,
 This is all your doing. It's so clear
 Because you let a servant give advice.   155
 Just be aware—I'm tired of being nice.
 It's obvious to anyone with eyes
 That what my son has done is more than wise

In welcoming this man who's so devout;
His very presence casts the devils out.   160
Or most of them—that's why I hope you hear him.
And I advise all of you to stay near him.
You need his protection and advice.
Your casual attention won't suffice.
It's heaven sent him here to fill a need,   165
To save you from yourselves—oh yes, indeed.
These visits from your friends you seem to want—
Listen to yourselves! So nonchalant!
As if no evil lurks in these events.
As if you're blind to what Satan invents.   170
And dances! What are those but food for slander!
It's to the worst desires these parties pander.
I ask you now, what purpose do they serve?
Where gossip's passed around like an hors-d'oeuvre.
A thousand cackling hens, busy with what?   175
It takes a lot of noise to cover smut.
It truly is the tower of Babylon,[4]
Where people babble on and on and on.
Ah! Case in point—there stands Monsieur Cléante,
Sniggering and eyeing me askant,   180
As if this has nothing to do with him,
And nothing that he does would God condemn.
And so, Elmire, my dear, I say farewell.
Till when? When it is a fine day in hell.
Farewell, all of you. When I pass through that door,   185
You won't have me to laugh at anymore.
Flipote! Wake up! Have you heard nothing I have said?
I'll march you home and beat you till you're dead.
March, slut, march.

1.2[5]

[DORINE, CLÉANTE]

CLÉANTE   I'm staying here. She's scary,
   That old lady—
DORINE   I know why you're wary.
   Shall I call her back to hear you say,
   "That *old* lady"? That would make her day.

---

4. That is, the biblical Tower of Babel (the Hebrew equivalent of the Akkadian Bab-ilu, or Babylon—a name explained by the similar sounding but unrelated Hebrew verb *balal*, "confuse"), described in Genesis 11.1–9; to prevent it from being constructed and reaching heaven, God scattered all the people and confused their language, creating many tongues where there had been only one.
5. In classical French drama, a new scene begins whenever a character enters or leaves the stage, even if the action continues without interruption; this convention has become known as "French scenes." Characters remaining on-stage are listed; others from the previous scene can be assumed to have exited.

CLÉANTE   She's lost her mind, she's—now we have the proof—   5
    Head over heels in love with whom? Tartuffe.
DORINE   So here's what's worse and weird—so is her son.
    What's more—it's obvious to everyone.
    Before Tartuffe and he became entwined,
    Orgon once ruled this house in his right mind.   10
    In the troubled times,[6] he backed the prince,
    And that took courage. We haven't seen it since.
    He is intoxicated with Tartuffe—
    A potion that exceeds a hundred proof.
    It's put him in a trance, this devil's brew.   15
    And so he worships this imposter who
    He calls "brother" and loves more than one—
    This charlatan—more than daughter, wife, son.
    This charlatan hears all our master's dreams,
    And all his secrets. Every thought, it seems,   20
    Is poured out to Tartuffe, like he's his priest!
    You'd think they'd see the heresy, at least.
    Orgon caresses him, embraces him, and shows
    More love for him than any mistress knows.
    Come for a meal and who has the best seat?   25
    Whose preferences determine what we eat?
    Tartuffe consumes enough for six, is praised,
    And to his health is every goblet raised,
    While on his plate are piled the choicest bites.
    Then when he belches, our master delights   30
    In that and shouts, "God bless you!" to the beast,
    As if Tartuffe's the reason for the feast.
    Did I mention the quoting of each word,
    As if it's the most brilliant thing we've heard?
    And, oh, the miracles Tartuffe creates!   35
    The prophecies! We write while he dictates.
    All that's ridiculous. But what's evil
    Is seeing the deception and upheaval
    Of the master and everything he owns.
    He hands him money. They're not even loans—   40
    He's giving it away. It's gone too far.
    To watch Tartuffe play him like a guitar!
    And this Laurent, his man, found some lace.
    Shredded it and threw it in my face.
    He'd found it pressed inside *The Lives of Saints*,[7]   45
    I thought we'd have to put him in restraints.
    "To put the devil's finery beside

---

6. That is, during the Fronde (literally, "sling"; 1648–53), a civil war that took place while France was being ruled by a regent for Louis XIV—"the prince" whom Orgon supported—as various factions of the nobility sought to limit the growing authority of the monarchy.
7. A text (*Flos Sanctorum*, 1599–1601) by the Spanish Jesuit Pedro de Ribadeneyra, available in French translation by 1646.

The words and lives of saintly souls who died—
Is action of satanical transgression!"
And so, of course, I hurried to confession.   50

1.3

[ELMIRE, MARIANE, DAMIS, CLÉANTE, DORINE]

ELMIRE [*to* CLÉANTE]   Lucky you, you stayed. Yes, there was more,
    And more preaching from Grandma, at the door.
    My husband's coming! I didn't catch his eye.
    I'll wait for him upstairs. Cléante, good-bye.
CLÉANTE   I'll see you soon. I'll wait here below,   5
    Take just a second for a brief hello.
DAMIS   While you have him, say something for me?
    My sister needs for Father to agree
    To her marriage with Valère, as planned.
    Tartuffe opposes it and will demand   10
    That Father break his word, and that's not fair;
    Then I can't wed the sister of Valère.
    Listening only to Tartuffe's voice,
    He'd break four hearts at once—
DORINE   He's here.

1.4

[ORGON, CLÉANTE, DORINE]

ORGON   Rejoice!
    I'm back.
CLÉANTE   I'm glad to see you, but I'm on my way.
    Just stayed to say hello.
ORGON   No more to say?
    Dorine! Come back! And Cléante, why the hurry?
    Indulge me for a moment. You know I worry.   5
    I've been gone two days! There's news to tell.
    Now don't hold back. Has everyone been well?
DORINE   Not quite. There was that headache Madame had
    The day you left. Well, it got really bad.
    She had a fever—   10
ORGON   And Tartuffe?
DORINE   He's fine—
    Rosy-nosed and red-cheeked, drinking your wine.
ORGON   Poor man!
DORINE   And then, Madame became unable
    To eat a single morsel at the table.
ORGON   Ah, and Tartuffe?
DORINE   He sat within her sight,
    Not holding back, he ate with great delight,   15

A brace of partridge, and a leg of mutton.
In fact, he ate so much, he popped a button.
ORGON   Poor man!
DORINE   That night until the next sunrise,
Your poor wife couldn't even close her eyes.
What a fever! Oh, how she did suffer!   20
I don't see how that night could have been rougher.
We watched her all night long, worried and weepy.
ORGON   Ah, and Tartuffe?
DORINE   At dinner he grew sleepy.
After such a meal, it's not surprising.
He slept through the night, not once arising.   25
ORGON   Poor man!
DORINE   At last won over by our pleading,
Madame agreed to undergo a bleeding.[8]
And this, we think, has saved her from the grave.
ORGON   Ah, and Tartuffe?
DORINE   Oh, he was very brave.
To make up for the blood Madame had lost   30
Tartuffe slurped down red wine, all at your cost.
ORGON   Poor man!
DORINE   Since then, they've both been fine, although
Madame needs me. I'll go and let her know
How anxious you have been about her health,
And that you prize it more than all your wealth.   35

1.5

[ORGON, CLÉANTE]

CLÉANTE   You know that girl was laughing in your face.
I fear I'll make you angry, but in case
There is a chance you'll listen, I will try
To say that you are laughable and why.
I've never known of something so capricious   5
As letting this man do just as he wishes
In your home and to your family.
You brought him here, relieved his poverty,
And, in return—
ORGON   Now you listen to me!
You're just my brother-in-law, Cléante. Quite!   10
You don't know this man. And don't deny it!
CLÉANTE   I don't know him, yes, that may be so,
But men like him are not so rare, you know.

---

8. Bloodletting (whether by leeches or other means), for centuries a standard medical treatment
for a wide range of diseases.

ORGON   If you only could know him as I do,
    You would be his true disciple, too.   15
    The universe, your ecstasy would span.
    This is a man . . . who . . . ha! . . . well, such a man.
    Behold him. Let him teach you profound peace.
    When first we met, I felt my troubles cease.
    Yes, I was changed after I talked with him.   20
    I saw my wants and needs as just a whim!
    Everything that's written, all that's sung,
    The world, and you and me, well, it's all dung!
    Yes, it's crap! And isn't that a wonder!
    The real world—it's just some spell we're under!   25
    He's taught me to love nothing and no one!
    Mother, father, wife, daughter, son—
    They could die right now, I'd feel no pain.
CLÉANTE   What feelings you've developed, how humane.
ORGON   You just don't see him in the way I do,   30
    But if you did, you'd feel what I feel, too.
    Every day he came to church and knelt,
    And from his groans, I knew just what he felt.
    Those sounds he made from deep inside his soul,
    Were fed by piety he could not control.   35
    Of the congregation, who could ignore
    The way he humbly bowed and kissed the floor?
    And when they tried to turn away their eyes,
    His fervent prayers to heaven and deep sighs
    Made them witness his deep spiritual pain.   40
    Then something happened I can't quite explain.
    I rose to leave—he quickly went before
    To give me holy water at the door.
    He knew what I needed, so he blessed me.
    I found his acolyte, he'd so impressed me,   45
    To ask who he was and there I learned
    About his poverty and how he spurned
    The riches of this world. And when I tried
    To give him gifts, in modesty, he cried,
    "That is too much," he'd say, "A half would do."   50
    Then gave a portion back, with much ado.
    "I am not worthy. I do not deserve
    Your gifts or pity. I am here to serve
    The will of heaven, that and nothing more."
    Then takes the gift and shares it with the poor.   55
    So heaven spoke to me inside my head.
    "Just bring him home with you" is what it said
    And so I did. And ever since he came,
    My home's a happy one. I also claim
    A moral home, a house that's free of sin,   60
    Tartuffe's on watch—he won't let any in.
    His interest in my wife is reassuring,

She's innocent of course, but so alluring,
He tells me whom she sees and what she does.
He's more jealous than I ever was.   65
It's for my honor that he's so concerned.
His righteous anger's all for me, I've learned,
To the point that just the other day,
A flea annoyed him as he tried to pray,
Then he rebuked himself, as if he'd willed it—   70
His excessive anger when he killed it.
CLÉANTE   Orgon, listen. You're out of your mind.
   Or you're mocking me. Or both combined.
   How can you speak such nonsense without blinking?
ORGON   I smell an atheist! It's that freethinking!   75
   Such nonsense is the bane of your existence.
   And that explains your damnable resistance.
   Ten times over, I've tried to save your soul
   From your corrupted mind. That's still my goal.
CLÉANTE   You have been corrupted by your friends,   80
   You know of whom I speak. Your thought depends
   On people who are blind and want to spread it
   Like some horrid flu, and, yes, I dread it.
   I'm no atheist. I see things clearly.
   And what I see is loud lip service, merely,   85
   To make exhibitionists seem devout.
   Forgive me, but a prayer is not a shout.
   Yet those who don't adore these charlatans
   Are seen as faithless heathens by your friends.
   It's as if you think you'd never find   90
   Reason and the sacred intertwined.
   You think I'm afraid of retribution?
   Heaven sees my heart and their pollution.
   So we should be the slaves of sanctimony?
   Monkey see, monkey do, monkey phony.   95
   The true believers we should emulate
   Are not the ones who groan and lay prostrate.
   And yet you see no problem in the notion
   Of hypocrisy as deep devotion.
   You see as one the genuine and the spurious.   100
   You'd extend this to your money? I'm just curious.
   In your business dealings, I'd submit,
   You'd not confuse the gold with counterfeit.
   Men are strangely made, I'd have to say.
   They're burdened with their reason, till one day,   105
   They free themselves with such force that they spoil
   The noblest of things for which they toil.
   Because they must go to extremes. It's a flaw.
   Just a word in passing, Brother-in-law.
ORGON   Oh, you are the wisest man alive, so   110
   You know everything there is to know.

You are the one enlightened man, the sage.
You are Cato the Elder[9] of our age.
Next to you, all men are dumb as cows.
CLÉANTE I'm not the wisest man, as you espouse,   115
Nor do I know—what—all there is to know?
But I do know, Orgon, that quid pro quo
Does not apply at all to "false" and "true,"
And I would never trust a person who
Cannot tell them apart. See, I revere   120
Everyone whose worship is sincere.
Nothing is more noble or more beautiful
Than fervor that is holy, not just dutiful.
So nothing is more odious to me
Than the display of specious piety   125
Which I see in every charlatan
Who tries to pass for a true holy man.
Religious passion worn as a facade
Abuses what's sacred and mocks God.
These men who take what's sacred and most holy   130
And use it as their trade, for money, solely,
With downcast looks and great affected cries,
Who suck in true believers with their lies,
Who ceaselessly will preach and then demand
"Give up the world!" and then, by sleight of hand,   135
End up sitting pretty at the court,
The best in lodging and new clothes to sport.
If you're their enemy, then heaven hates you.
That's their claim when one of them berates you.
They'll say you've sinned. You'll find yourself removed   140
And wondering if you'll be approved
For anything, at all, ever again.
Because so heinous was this fictional "sin."
When these men are angry, they're the worst,
There's no place to hide, you're really cursed.   145
They use what we call righteous as their sword,
To coldly murder in the name of the Lord.
But next to these imposters faking belief,
The devotion of the true is a relief.
Our century has put before our eyes   150
Glorious examples we can prize.
Look at Ariston, and look at Periandre,
Oronte, Alcidamas, Polydore, Clitandre:[1]
Not one points out his own morality,
Instead they speak of their mortality.   155

---

9. Roman statesman and author (234–149
B.C.E.), famous as a stern moralist devoted to
traditional Roman ideals of honor, courage,
and simplicity.
1. Made-up names.

They don't form cabals,[2] they don't have factions,
They don't censure other people's actions.
They see the flagrant pride in such correction
And know that humans can't achieve perfection.
They know this of themselves and yet their lives   160
Good faith, good works, all good, epitomize.
They don't exhibit zeal that's more intense
Than heaven shows us in its own defense.
They'd never claim a knowledge that's divine
And yet they live in virtue's own design.   165
They concentrate their hatred on the sin,
And when the sinner grieves, invite him in.
They leave to others the arrogance of speech.
Instead they practice what others only preach.
These are the men who show us how to live.   170
Their lives, the best example I can give.
These are my men, the ones whom I would follow.
Your man and his life, honestly, are hollow.
I believe you praise him quite sincerely,
I also think you'll pay for this quite dearly.   175
He's a fraud, this man whom you adore.
ORGON   Oh, you've stopped talking. Is there any more?
CLÉANTE   No.
ORGON   I am your servant, sir.
CLÉANTE   No! wait!
There's one more thing—no more debate—
I want to change the subject, if I might.   180
I heard that you said the other night,
To Valère, he'd be your son-in-law.
ORGON   I did.
CLÉANTE   And set the date?
ORGON   Yes.
CLÉANTE   Did you withdraw?
ORGON   I did.
CLÉANTE   You're putting off the wedding? Why?
ORGON   Don't know.   185
CLÉANTE   There's more?
ORGON   Perhaps.
CLÉANTE   Again I'll try:
You would break your word?
ORGON   I couldn't say.
CLÉANTE   Then, Orgon, why did you change the day?
ORGON   Who knows?

---

2. A possible allusion to the Compagnie de Saint-Sacrement, a tightly knit group of prominent French citizens known for public works as well as strict morality; they were pejoratively referred to as the *cabale*.

CLÉANTE   But we need to know, don't we now?
  Is there a reason you would break your vow?
ORGON   That depends.
CLÉANTE   On what? Orgon, what is it?   190
  Valère was the reason for my visit.
ORGON   Who knows? Who knows?
CLÉANTE   So there's some mystery there?
ORGON   Heaven knows.
CLÉANTE   It does? And now, Valère—
  May he know, too?
ORGON   Can't say.
CLÉANTE   But, dear Orgon,
  We have no information to go on.   195
  We need to know—
ORGON   What heaven wants, I'll do.
CLÉANTE   Is that your final answer? Then I'm through.
  But your pledge to Valère? You'll stand by it?
ORGON   Good-bye.

                              [ORGON *exits.*]

CLÉANTE   More patience, yes, I should try it.
  I let him get to me. Now I confess   200
  I fear the worst for Valère's happiness.

                              2.1

                         [ORGON, MARIANE]

ORGON   Mariane.
MARIANE   Father.
ORGON   Come. Now. Talk with me.
MARIANE   Why are you looking everywhere?
ORGON   To see
  If everyone is minding their own business.
  So, Child, I've always loved your gentleness.
MARIANE   And for your love, I'm grateful, Father dear.   5
ORGON   Well said. And so to prove that you're sincere,
  And worthy of my love, you have the task
  Of doing for me anything I ask.
MARIANE   Then my obedience will be my proof.
ORGON   Good. What do you think of our guest, Tartuffe?   10
MARIANE   Who, me?
ORGON   Yes, you. Watch what you say right now.
MARIANE   Then, Father, I will say what you allow.
ORGON   Wise words, Daughter. So this is what you say:
  "He is a perfect man in every way;
  In body and soul, I find him divine."   15
  And then you say, "Please Father, make him mine."
  Huh?

MARIANE   Huh?
ORGON   Yes?
MARIANE   I heard . . .
ORGON   Yes.
MARIANE   What did you say?
  Who is this perfect man in every way,
  Whom in body and soul I find divine
  And ask of you, "Please, Father, make him mine?"   20
ORGON   Tartuffe.
MARIANE   All that I've said, I now amend
  Because you wouldn't want me to pretend.
ORGON   Absolutely not—that's so misguided.
  Have it be the truth, then. It's decided.
MARIANE   What?! Father, you want—   25
ORGON   Yes, my dear, I do—
  To join in marriage my Tartuffe and you.
  And since I have—

2.2

[DORINE, ORGON, MARIANE]

ORGON   Dorine, I know you're there!
  Any secrets in this house you don't share?
DORINE   "Marriage"—I think, yes, I heard a rumor,
  Someone's failed attempt at grotesque humor,
  So when I heard the story, I said, "No!   5
  Preposterous! Absurd! It can't be so."
ORGON   Oh, you find it preposterous? And why?
DORINE   It's so outrageous, it must be a lie.
ORGON   Yet it's the truth and you will believe it.
DORINE   Yet as a joke is how I must receive it.   10
ORGON   But it's a story that will soon come true.
DORINE   A fantasy!
ORGON   I'm getting tired of you.
  Mariane, it's not a joke—
DORINE   Says he,
  Laughing up his sleeve for all to see.
ORGON   I'm telling you—   15
DORINE   —more make-believe for fun.
  It's very good—you're fooling everyone.
ORGON   You have made me really angry now.
DORINE   I see the awful truth across your brow.
  How can a man who looks as wise as you
  Be such a fool to want—   20
ORGON   What can I do
  About a servant with a mouth like that?
  The liberties you take! Decorum you laugh at!
  I'm not happy with you—

DORINE   Oh sir, don't frown.
  A smile is just a frown turned upside down.
  Be happy, sir, because you've shared your scheme,   25
  Even though it's just a crazy dream.
  Because, dear sir, your daughter is not meant
  For this zealot—she's too innocent.
  She'd be alarmed by his robust desire
  And question heaven's sanction of this fire   30
  And then the gossip! Your friends will talk a lot,
  Because you're a man of wealth and he is not.
  Could it be your reasoning has a flaw—
  Choosing a beggar for a son-in-law?
ORGON   You, shut up! If he has nothing now   35
  Admire that, as if it were his vow,
  This poverty. His property was lost
  Because he would not pay the deadly cost
  Of daily duties nibbling life away,
  Leaving him with hardly time to pray.   40
  The grandeur in his life comes from devotion
  To the eternal, thus his great emotion.
  And at those moments, I can plainly see
  What my special task has come to be:
  To end the embarrassment he feels   45
  And the sorrow he so nobly conceals
  Of the loss of his ancestral domain.
  With my money, I can end his pain.
  I'll raise him up to be, because I can,
  With my help, again, a gentleman.   50
DORINE   So he's a gentleman. Does that seem vain?
  Then what about this piety and pain?
  Those with "domains" are those of noble birth.
  A holy man's domain is not on earth.
  It seems to me a holy man of merit   55
  Wouldn't brag of what he might inherit—
  Even gifts in heaven, he won't mention.
  To live a humble life is his intention.
  Yet he wants something back? That's just ambition
  To feed his pride. Is that a holy mission?   60
  You seem upset. Is it something I said?
  I'll shut up. We'll talk of her instead.
  Look at this girl, your daughter, your own blood.
  How will her honor fare covered with mud?
  Think of his age. So from the night they're wed,   65
  Bliss, if there is any, leaves the marriage bed,
  And she'll be tied unto this elderly person.
  Her dedication to fidelity will worsen
  And soon he will sprout horns,[3] your holy man,

---

3. The traditional sign of the cuckold.

And no one will be happy. If I can 70
Have another word, I'd like to say
Old men and young girls are married every day,
And the young girls stray, but who's to blame
For the loss of honor and good name?
The father, who proceeds to pick a mate, 75
Blindly, though it's someone she may hate,
Bears the sins the daughter may commit,
Imperiling his soul because of it.
If you do this, I vow you'll hear the bell,
As you die, summoning you to hell. 80
ORGON   You think that you can teach me how to live.
DORINE   If you'd just heed the lessons that I give.
ORGON   Can heaven tell me why I still endure
    This woman's ramblings? Yet, of this I'm sure,
    I know what's best for you—I'm your father. 85
    I gave you to Valère, without a bother.
    But I hear he gambles and what's more,
    He thinks things that a Christian would abhor.
    It's from free thinking that all evils stem.
    No wonder, then, at church, I don't see him. 90
DORINE   Should he race there, if he only knew
    Which Mass you might attend, and be on view?
    He could wait at the door with holy water.
ORGON   Go away. I'm talking to my daughter.
    Think, my child, he is heaven's favorite! 95
    And age in marriage? It can flavor it,
    A sweet comfit suffused with deep, deep pleasure.
    You will be loving, faithful, and will treasure
    Every single moment—two turtledoves—
    Next to heaven, the only thing he loves. 100
    And he will be the only one for you.
    No arguments or quarrels. You'll be true,
    Like two innocent children, you will thrive,
    In heaven's light, thrilled to be alive.
    And as a woman, surely you must know 105
    Wives mold husbands, like making pies from dough.
DORINE   Four and twenty cuckolds baked in a pie.
ORGON   Ugh! What a thing to say!
DORINE   Oh, really, why?
    He's destined to be cheated on, it's true.
    You know he'd always question her virtue. 110
ORGON   Quiet! Just be quiet. I command it!
DORINE   I'll do just that, because you do demand it!
    But your best interests—I will protect them.
ORGON   Too kind of you. Be quiet and neglect them.
DORINE   If I weren't fond of you— 115
ORGON   —Don't want you to
DORINE   I will be fond of you in spite of you.

ORGON   Don't!

DORINE   But your honor is so dear to me,
  How can you expose yourself to mockery?

ORGON   Will you never be quiet!

DORINE   Oh, dear sir,
  I can't let you do this thing to her,   120
  It's against my conscience—

ORGON   You vicious asp!

DORINE   Sometimes the things you call me make me gasp.
  And anger, sir, is not a pious trait.

ORGON   It's your fault, girl! You make me irate!
  I am livid! Why won't you be quiet!   125

DORINE   I will. For you, I'm going to try it.
  But I'll be thinking.

ORGON   Fine. Now, Mariane,
  You have to trust—your father's a wise man.
  I have thought a lot about this mating.
  I've weighed the options—   130

DORINE   It's infuriating
  Not to be able to speak.

ORGON   And so
  I'll say this. Of up and coming men I know,
  He's not one of them, no money in the bank,
  Not handsome.

DORINE   That's the truth. Arf! Arf! Be frank.
  He's a dog!   135

ORGON   He has manly traits.
  And other gifts.

DORINE   And who will blame the fates
  For failure of this marriage made in hell?
  And whose fault will it be? Not hard to tell.
  Since everyone you know will see the truth:
  You gave away your daughter to Tartuffe.   140
  If I were in her place, I'd guarantee
  No man would live the night who dared force me
  Into a marriage that I didn't want.
  There would be war with no hope of détente.

ORGON   I asked for silence. This is what I get?   145

DORINE   You said not to talk to *you*. Did you forget?

ORGON   What do you call what you are doing now?

DORINE   Talking to myself.

ORGON   You insolent cow!
  I'll wait for you to say just one more word.
  I'm waiting . . .   150

      [ORGON *prepares to give* DORINE *a smack but each time he looks*
      over at her, she stands silent and still.]
           Just ignore her. Look at me.
  I've chosen you a husband who would be,
  If rated, placed among the highest ranks.

[*To* DORINE]   Why don't you talk?

DORINE   Don't feel like it, thanks.

ORGON   I'm watching you.

DORINE   Do you think I'm a fool?

ORGON   I realize that you may think me cruel.   155
   But here's the thing, child, I will be obeyed,
   And this marriage, child, will not be delayed.

DORINE [*running from* ORGON, DORINE *throws a line to* MARIANE]
   You'll be a joke with Tartuffe as a spouse.
      [ORGON *tries to slap her but misses.*]

ORGON   What we have is a plague in our own house!
   It's her fault that I'm in the state I'm in,   160
   So furious, I might commit a sin.
   She'll drive me to murder. Or to curse.
   I need fresh air before my mood gets worse.   [ORGON *exits.*]

2.3

[DORINE, MARIANE]

DORINE   Tell me, have you lost the power of speech?
   I'm forced to play your role and it's a reach.
   How can you sit there with nothing to say
   Watching him tossing your whole life away?

MARIANE   Against my father, what am I to do?   5

DORINE   You want out of this marriage scheme, don't you?

MARIANE   Yes.

DORINE   Tell him no one can command a heart.
   That when you marry, you will have no part
   Of anyone unless he pleases you.
   And tell your father, with no more ado,   10
   That you will marry for yourself, not him,
   And that you won't obey his iron whim.
   Since he finds Tartuffe to be such a catch,
   He can marry him himself. There's a match.

MARIANE   You know that fathers have such sway   15
   Over our lives that I've nothing to say.
   I've never had the strength.

DORINE   Let's think. All right?
   Didn't Valère propose the other night?
   Do you or don't you love Valère?

MARIANE   You know the answer, Dorine—that's unfair.   20
   Just talking about it tears me apart.
   I've said a hundred times, he has my heart.
   I'm wild about him. I know. And I've told you.

DORINE   But how am I to know, for sure, that's true?

MARIANE   Because I told you. And yet you doubt it?   25
   See me blushing when I speak about it?

DORINE   So you do love him?

MARIANE   Yes, with all my might.
DORINE   He loves you just as much?
MARIANE   I think that's right.
DORINE   And it's to the altar you're both heading?
MARIANE   Yes.
DORINE   So what about this other wedding?   30
MARIANE   I'll kill myself. That's what I've decided.
DORINE   What a great solution you've provided!
   To get out of trouble, you plan to die!
   Immediately? Or sometime, by and by?
MARIANE   Oh, really, Dorine, you're not my friend,   35
   Unsympathetic—
DORINE   I'm at my wit's end,
   Talking to you whose answer is dying,
   Who, in a crisis, just gives up trying.
MARIANE   What do you want of me, then?
DORINE   Come alive!
   Love needs a resolute heart to survive.   40
MARIANE   In my love for Valère, I'm resolute.
   But the next step is his.
DORINE   And so, you're mute?
MARIANE   What can I say? It's the job of Valère,
   His duty, before I go anywhere,
   To deal with my father—
DORINE   —Then, you'll stay.   45
   "Orgon was born bizarre" is what some say.
   If there were doubts before, we have this proof—
   He is head over heels for his Tartuffe,
   And breaks off a marriage that he arranged.
   Valère's at fault if your father's deranged?   50
MARIANE   But my refusal will be seen as pride
   And, worse, contempt. And I have to hide
   My feelings for Valère, I must not show
   That I'm in love at all. If people know,
   Then all the modesty my sex is heir to   55
   Will be gone. There's more: how can I bear to
   Not be a proper daughter to my father?
DORINE   No, no, of course not. God forbid we bother
   The way the world sees you. What people see,
   What other people think of us, should be   60
   Our first concern. Besides, I see the truth:
   You really want to be Madame Tartuffe.
   What was I thinking, urging opposition
   To Monsieur Tartuffe! This proposition,
   To merge with him—he's such a catch!   65
   In fact, for you, he's just the perfect match.
   He's much respected, everywhere he goes,
   And his ruddy complexion nearly glows.
   And as his wife, imagine the delight

Of being near him, every day and night.   70
And vital? Oh, my dear, you won't want more.
MARIANE   Oh, heaven help me!
DORINE   How your soul will soar,
Savoring this marriage down to the last drop,
With such a handsome—
MARIANE   All right! You can stop!
Just help me. Please. And tell me there's a way   75
To save me. I'll do whatever you say.
DORINE   Each daughter must choose always to say yes
To what her father wants, no more and no less.
If he wants to give her an ape to marry,
Then she must do it, without a query.   80
But it's a happy fate! What is this frown?
You'll go by wagon to his little town,
Eager cousins, uncles, aunts will greet you
And will call you "sister" when they meet you,
Because you're family now. Don't look so grim.   85
You will so adore chatting with them.
Welcomed by the local high society,
You'll be expected to maintain propriety
And sit straight, or try to, in the folding chair
They offer you, and never, ever stare   90
At the wardrobe of the bailiff's wife
Because you'll see her every day for life.[4]
Let's not forget the village carnival!
Where you'll be dancing at a lavish ball
To a bagpipe orchestra of locals,   95
An organ grinder's monkey doing vocals—
And your husband—
MARIANE   —Dorine, I beg you, please,
Help me. Should I get down here on my knees?
DORINE   Can't help you.
MARIANE   Please, Dorine, I'm begging you!
DORINE   And you deserve this man.   100
MARIANE   That just not true!
DORINE   Oh yes? What changed?
MARIANE   My darling Dorine . . .
DORINE   No.
MARIANE   You can't be this mean.
I love Valère. I told you and it's true.
DORINE   Who's that? Oh. No, Tartuffe's the one for you.
MARIANE   You've always been completely on my side.   105
DORINE   No more. I sentence you to be Tartuffified!
MARIANE   It seems my fate has not the power to move you,
So I'll seek my solace and remove to

---

4. Dorine's description reflects the stereotypes associated with rural pretensions to culture.

A private place for me in my despair.
To end the misery that brought me here.   110
    [MARIANE *starts to exit.*]
DORINE   Wait! Wait! Come back! Please don't go out that door.
I'll help you. I'm not angry anymore.
MARIANE   If I am forced into this martyrdom,
You see, I'll have to die, Dorine.
DORINE   Oh come,
Give up this torment. Look at me—I swear.   115
We'll find a way. Look, here's your love, Valère.
    [DORINE *moves to the side of the stage.*]

2.4

[VALÈRE, MARIANE, DORINE]

VALÈRE   So I've just heard some news that's news to me,
And very fine news it is, do you agree?
MARIANE   What?
VALÈRE   You have plans for marriage I didn't know.
You're going to marry Tartuffe. Is this so?
MARIANE   My father has that notion, it is true.   5
VALÈRE   Madame, your father promised—
MARIANE   —me to you?
He changed his mind, announced this change to me,
Just minutes ago . . .
VALÈRE   Quite seriously?
MARIANE   It's his wish that I should marry this man.
VALÈRE   And what do you think of your father's plan?   10
MARIANE   I don't know.
VALÈRE   Honest words—better than lies.
You don't know?
MARIANE   No.
VALÈRE   No?
MARIANE   What do you advise?
VALÈRE   I advise you to . . . marry Tartuffe. Tonight.
MARIANE   You advise me to . . .
VALÈRE   Yes.
MARIANE   Really?
VALÈRE   That's right.
Consider it. It's an obvious choice.   15
MARIANE   I'll follow your suggestion and rejoice.
VALÈRE   I'm sure that you can follow it with ease.
MARIANE   Just as you gave it. It will be a breeze.
VALÈRE   Just to please you was my sole intent.
MARIANE   To please you, I'll do it and be content.   20
DORINE   I can't wait to see what happens next.
VALÈRE   And this is love to you? I am perplexed.
Was it a sham when you—

MARIANE   That's in the past
  Because you said so honestly and fast
  That I should take the one bestowed on me.   25
  I'm nothing but obedient, you see,
  So, yes, I'll take him. That's my declaration,
  Since that's your advice and expectation.
VALÈRE   I see, you're using me as an excuse,
  Any pretext, so you can cut me loose.   30
  You didn't think I'd notice—I'd be blind
  To the fact that you'd made up your mind?
MARINE   How true. Well said.
VALÈRE   And so it's plain to see,
  Your heart never felt a true love for me.
MARIANE   If you want to, you may think that is true.   35
  It's clear this thought has great appeal for you.
VALÈRE   If I want? I will, but I'm offended
  To my very soul. But your turn's ended,
  And I can win this game we're playing at:
  I've someone else in mind.   40
MARIANE   I don't doubt that.
  Your good points—
VALÈRE   Oh, let's leave them out of this.
  I've very few—in fact, I am remiss.
  I must be. Right? You've made that clear to me.
  But I know someone, hearing that I'm free,
  To make up for my loss, will eagerly consent.   45
MARIANE   The loss is not that bad. You'll be content
  With your new choice, replacement, if you will.
VALÈRE   I will. And I'll remain contented still,
  In knowing you're as happy as I am.
  A woman tells a man her love's a sham.   50
  The man's been fooled and his honor blighted.
  He can't deny his love is unrequited,
  Then he forgets this woman totally,
  And if he can't, pretends, because, you see,
  It is ignoble conduct and weak, too,   55
  Loving someone who does not love you.
MARIANE   What a fine, noble sentiment to heed.
VALÈRE   And every man upholds it as his creed.
  What? You expect me to keep on forever
  Loving you after you blithely sever   60
  The bond between us, watching as you go
  Into another's arms and not bestow
  This heart you've cast away upon someone
  Who might welcome—
MARIANE   I wish it were done.
  That's exactly what I want, you see.   65
VALÈRE   That's what you want?
MARIANE   Yes.

VALÈRE   Then let it be.
    I'll grant your wish.
MARIANE   Please do.
VALÈRE   Just don't forget,
    Whose fault it was when you, filled with regret,
    Realize that you forced me out the door.
MARIANE   True.   70
VALÈRE   You've set the example and what's more,
    I'll match you with my own hardness of heart.
    You won't see me again, if I depart.
MARIANE   That's good!
       [VALÈRE *goes to exit, but when he gets to the door, he returns.*]
VALÈRE   What?
MARIANE   What?
VALÈRE   You said . . . ?
MARIANE   Nothing at all.
VALÈRE   Well, I'll be on my way, then.
       [*He goes, stops.*]
                  Did you call?
MARIANE   Me? You must be dreaming.   75
VALÈRE   I'll go away.
    Good-bye, then.
MARIANE   Good-bye.
DORINE   I am here to say,
    You both are idiots! What's this about?
    I left you two alone to fight it out,
    To see how far you'd go. You're quite a pair
    In matching tit for tat—Hold on, Valère!   80
    Where are you going?
VALÈRE   What, Dorine? You spoke?
DORINE   Come here.
VALÈRE   I'm upset and will not provoke
    This lady. Do not try to change my mind.
    I'm doing what she wants.
DORINE   You are so blind.
    Just stop.   85
VALÈRE   No. It's settled.
DORINE   Oh, is that so?
MARIANE   He can't stand to look at me, I know.
    He wants to go away, so please let him.
    No, I shall leave so I can forget him.
DORINE   Where are you going?
MARIANE   Leave me alone.
DORINE   Come back here at once.   90
MARIANE   No. Even that tone
    Won't bring me. I'm not a child, you see.
VALÈRE   She's tortured by the very sight of me.
    It's better that I free her from her pain.

DORINE   What more proof do you need? You are insane!
  Now stop this nonsense! Come here both of you.   95
VALÈRE   To what purpose?
MARIANE   What are you trying to do?
DORINE   Bring you two together! And end this fight.
  It's so stupid! Yes?
VALÈRE   No. It wasn't right
  The way she spoke to me. Didn't you hear?
DORINE   Your voices are still ringing in my ear.   100
MARIANE   The way he treated me—you didn't see?
DORINE   Saw and heard it all. Now listen to me.
  The only thing she wants, Valère, is you.
  I can attest to that right now. It's true.
  And Mariane, he wants you for his wife,   105
  And only you. On that I'll stake my life.
MARIANE   He told me to be someone else's bride!
VALÈRE   She asked for my advice and I replied!
DORINE   You're both impossible. What can I do?
  Give your hand—   110
VALÈRE   What for?
DORINE   Come on, you.
  Now yours, Mariane—don't make me shout.
  Come on!
MARIANE   All right. But what is this about?
DORINE   Here. Take each other's hand and make a link.
  You love each other better than you think.
VALÈRE   Mademoiselle, this is your hand I took,   115
  You think you could give me a friendly look?
      [MARIANE *peeks at* VALÈRE *and smiles.*]
DORINE   It's true. Lovers are not completely sane.
VALÈRE   Mariane, haven't I good reason to complain?
  Be honest. Wasn't it a wicked ploy?
  To say—   120
MARIANE   You think I told you that with joy?
  And you confronted me.
DORINE   Another time.
  This marriage to Tartuffe would be a crime,
  We have to stop it.
MARIANE   So, what can we do?
  Tell us.
DORINE   All sorts of things involving you.   125
  It's all nonsense and your father's joking.
  But if you play along, say, without choking,
  And give your consent, for the time being,
  He'll take the pressure off, thereby freeing
  All of us to find a workable plan   130
  To keep you from a marriage with this man.
  Then you can find a reason every day

To postpone the wedding, in this way;
One day you're sick and that can take a week.
Another day you're better but can't speak, 135
And we all know you have to say "I do,"
Or the marriage isn't legal. And that's true.
Now bad omens—would he have his daughter
Married when she's dreamt of stagnant water,
Or broken a mirror or seen the dead? 140
He may not care and say it's in your head,
But you will be distraught in your delusion,
And require bed rest and seclusion.
I do know this—if we want to succeed,
You can't be seen together. [*To* VALÈRE] With all speed, 145
Go, and gather all your friends right now,
Have them insist that Orgon keep his vow.
Social pressure helps. Then to her brother.
All of us will work on her stepmother.
Let's go. 150

VALÈRE   Whatever happens, can you see?
My greatest hope is in your love for me.

MARIANE   Though I don't know just what Father will do,
I do know I belong only to you.

VALÈRE   You put my heart at ease! I swear I will . . .

DORINE   It seems that lovers' tongues are never still. 155
Out, I tell you.

VALÈRE [*taking a step and returning*]   One last—

DORINE   No more chat!
You go out this way, yes, and you go that.

3.1

[DAMIS, DORINE]

DAMIS   May lightning strike me dead, right here and now,
Call me a villain, if I break this vow:
Forces of heaven or earth won't make me sway
From this my—

DORINE   Let's not get carried away.
Your father only said what he intends 5
To happen. The real event depends
On many things and something's bound to slip,
Between this horrid cup and his tight lip.

DAMIS   That this conceited fool Father brought here
Has plans? Well, they'll be ended—do not fear. 10

DORINE   Now stop that! Forget him. Leave him alone.
Leave him to your stepmother. He is prone,
This Tartuffe, to indulge her every whim.
So let her use her power over him.
It does seem pretty clear he's soft on her, 15
Pray God that's true. And if he will concur

That this wedding your father wants is bad,
That's good. But he might want it, too, the cad.
She's sent for him so she can sound him out
On this marriage you're furious about,   20
Discover what he feels and tell him clearly
If he persists that it will cost him dearly.
It seems he can't be seen while he's at prayers,
So I have my own vigil by the stairs
Where his valet says he will soon appear.   25
Do leave right now, and I'll wait for him here.

DAMIS   I'll stay to vouch for what was seen and heard.

DORINE   They must be alone.

DAMIS   I won't say a word.

DORINE   Oh, right. I know what you are like. Just go.
You'll spoil everything, believe me, I know.   30
Out!

DAMIS   I promise I won't get upset.
          [DORINE *pinches* DAMIS *as she used to do when he was a child.*]
                                        Ow!

DORINE   Do as I say. Get out of here right *now!*

3.2

[TARTUFFE, LAURENT, DORINE]

TARTUFFE [*noticing* DORINE]   Laurent, lock up my scourge and
    hair shirt,[5] too.
And pray that our Lord's grace will shine on you.
If anyone wants me, I've gone to share
My alms at prison with the inmates there.

DORINE   What a fake! What an imposter! What a sleaze!   5

TARTUFFE   What do you want?

DORINE   To say—

TARTUFFE [*taking a handkerchief from his pocket*]   Good heavens, please,
    Do take this handkerchief before you speak.

DORINE   What for?

TARTUFFE   Cover your bust. The flesh is weak.
Souls are forever damaged by such sights,
When sinful thoughts begin their evil flights.   10

DORINE   It seems temptation makes a meal of you—
To turn you on, a glimpse of flesh will do.
Inside your heart, a furnace must be housed.
For me, I'm not so easily aroused.
I could see you naked, head to toe—   15
Never be tempted once, and this I know.

TARTUFFE   Please! Stop! And if you're planning to resume
This kind of talk, I'll leave the room.

---

5. Implements to mortify his flesh (penitential practices of religious ascetics).

DORINE If someone is to go, let it be me.
    Yes, I can't wait to leave your company.   20
    Madame is coming down from her salon,
    And wants to talk to you, if you'll hang on.
TARTUFFE Of course. Most willingly.
DORINE [*aside*]   Look at him melt.
    I'm right. I always knew that's how he felt.
TARTUFFE Is she coming soon?   25
DORINE   You want me to leave?
    Yes, here she is in person, I believe.

3.3

[ELMIRE, TARTUFFE]

TARTUFFE Ah, may heaven in all its goodness give
    Eternal health to you each day you live,
    Bless your soul and body, and may it grant
    The prayerful wishes of this supplicant.
ELMIRE Yes, thank you for that godly wish, and please,   5
    Let's sit down so we can talk with ease.
TARTUFFE Are you recovered from your illness now?
ELMIRE My fever disappeared, I don't know how.
TARTUFFE My small prayers, I'm sure, had not the power,
    Though I was on my knees many an hour.   10
    Each fervent prayer wrenched from my simple soul
    Was made with your recovery as its goal.
ELMIRE I find your zeal a little disconcerting.
TARTUFFE I can't enjoy my health if you are hurting,
    Your health's true worth, I can't begin to tell.   15
    I'd give mine up, in fact, to make you well.
ELMIRE Though you stretch Christian charity too far,
    Your thoughts are kind, however strange they are.
TARTUFFE You merit more, that's in my humble view.
ELMIRE I need a private space to talk to you.   20
    I think that this will do—what do you say?
TARTUFFE Excellent choice. And this is a sweet day,
    To find myself here tête-à-tête with you,
    That I've begged heaven for this, yes, is true,
    And now it's granted to my great relief.   25
ELMIRE Although our conversation will be brief,
    Please open up your heart and tell me all.
    You must hide nothing now, however small.
TARTUFFE I long to show you my entire soul,
    My need for truth I can barely control.   30
    I'll take this time, also, to clear the air—
    The criticisms I have brought to bear
    Around the visits that your charms attract,
    Were never aimed at you or how you act,

But rather were my own transports of zeal,   35
Which carried me away with how I feel,
Consumed by impulses, though always pure,
Nevertheless, intense in how—
ELMIRE   I'm sure
That my salvation is your only care.
TARTUFFE [*grasping her fingertips*]   Yes, you're right, and   40
     so my fervor there—
ELMIRE   Ouch! You're squeezing too hard.
TARTUFFE   —comes from this zeal . . .
     I didn't mean to squeeze. How does this feel?
     [*He puts his hand on* ELMIRE's *knee.*]
ELMIRE   Your hand—what is it doing . . . ?
TARTUFFE   So tender,
     The fabric of your dress, a sweet surrender
     Under my hand—   45
ELMIRE   I'm quite ticklish. Please, don't.
     [*She moves her chair back, and* TARTUFFE *moves his forward.*]
TARTUFFE   I want to touch this lace—don't fret, I won't,
     It's marvelous! I so admire the trade
     Of making lace. Don't tell me you're afraid.
ELMIRE   What? No. But getting back to business now,
     It seems my husband plans to break a vow   50
     And offer you his daughter. Is this true?
TARTUFFE   He mentioned it, but I must say to you,
     The wondrous gifts that catch my zealous eye,
     I see quite near in bounteous supply.
ELMIRE   Not earthly things for which you would atone.   55
TARTUFFE   My chest does not contain a heart of stone.
ELMIRE   Well, I believe your eyes follow your soul,
     And your desires have heaven as their goal.
TARTUFFE   The love that to eternal beauty binds us
     Doesn't stint when temporal beauty finds us.   60
     Our senses can as easily be charmed
     When by an earthly work we are disarmed.
     You are a rare beauty, without a flaw,
     And in your presence, I'm aroused with awe
     But for the Author of All Nature, so,   65
     My heart has ardent feelings, even though
     I feared them at first, questioning their source.
     Had I been ambushed by some evil force?
     I felt that I must hide from this temptation:
     You. My feelings threatened my salvation.   70
     Yes, I found this sinful and distressing,
     Until I saw your beauty as a blessing!
     So now my passion never can be wrong,
     And, thus, my virtue stays intact and strong.
     That is how I'm here in supplication,   75
     Offering my heart in celebration

Of the audacious truth that I love you,
That only you can make this wish come true,
That through your grace, my offering's received,
And accepted, and that I have achieved   80
Salvation of a sort, and by your grace,
I could be content in this low place.
It all depends on you, at your behest—
Am I to be tormented or be blest?
You are my welfare, solace, and my hope,   85
But, whatever your decision, I will cope.
Will I be happy? I'll rely on you.
If you want me to be wretched, that's fine, too.

ELMIRE   Well, what a declaration! How gallant!
But I'm surprised you want the things you want.   90
It seems your heart could use a talking to—
It's living in the chest of someone who
Proclaims to be pious—

TARTUFFE   —And so I am.
My piety's a true thing—not a sham,
But I'm no less a man, so when I find   95
Myself with you, I quickly lose my mind.
My heart is captured and, with it, my thought.
Yet since I know the cause, I'm not distraught.
Words like these from me must be alarming,
But it is your beauty that's so charming,   100
I cannot help myself, I am undone.
And I'm no angel, nor could I be one.
If my confession earns your condemnation,
Then blame your glance for the annihilation
Of my command of this: my inmost being.   105
A surrender of my soul is what you're seeing.
Your eyes blaze with more than human splendor,
And that first look had the effect to render
Powerless the bastions of my heart.
No fasting, tears or prayers, no pious art   110
Could shield my soul from your celestial gaze
Which I will worship till the End of Days.[6]
A thousand times my eyes, my sighs have told
The truth that's in my heart. Now I am bold,
Encouraged by your presence, so I say,   115
With my true voice, will this be the day
You condescend to my poor supplication,
Offered up with devout admiration,
And save my soul by granting this request:
Accept this love I've lovingly confessed?   120
Your honor has, of course, all my protection,
And you can trust my absolute discretion.

---

6. That is, the final days before human history ends and the Kingdom of God is established.

For those men that all the women die for,
Love's a game whose object is a high score.
Although they promise not to talk, they will.   125
They need to boast of their superior skill,
Receive no favors not as soon revealed,
Exposing what they vowed would be concealed.
And in the end, this love is overpriced,
When a woman's honor's sacrificed.   130
But men like me burn with a silent flame,
Our secrets safe, our loves we never name,
Because our reputations are our wealth,
When we transgress, it's with the utmost stealth.
Your honor's safe as my hand in a glove,   135
So I can offer, free from scandal, love,
And pleasure without fear of intervention.
ELMIRE   Your sophistry does not hide your intention.
In fact, you know, it makes it all too clear.
What if, through me, my husband were to hear   140
About this love for me you now confess
Which shatters the ideals you profess?
How would your friendship fare, then, I wonder?
TARTUFFE   It's your beauty cast this spell I suffer under.
I'm made of flesh, like you, like all mankind.   145
And since your soul is pure, you will be kind,
And not judge me harshly for my brashness
In speaking of my love in all its rashness.
I beg you to forgive me my offense,
I plead your perfect face as my defense.   150
ELMIRE   Some might take offense at your confession,
But I will show a definite discretion,
And keep my husband in the dark about
These sinful feelings for me that you spout.
But I want something from you in return: 155
There's a promised marriage, you will learn,
That supersedes my husband's recent plan—
The marriage of Valère and Mariane.
This marriage you will openly support,
Without a single quibble, and, in short,   160
Renounce the unjust power of a man
Who'd give his own daughter, Mariane,
To another when she's promised to Valère.
In return, my silence—

3.4

[ELMIRE, DAMIS, TARTUFFE]

DAMIS [*jumping out from where he had been hiding*]
            —Hold it right there!
No, no! You're done. All this will be revealed.
I heard each word. And as I was concealed,

Something besides your infamy came clear:
Heaven in its great wisdom brought me here,   5
To witness and then give my father proof
Of the hypocrisy of his Tartuffe,
This so-called saint anointed from above,
Speaking to my father's wife of love!
ELMIRE   Damis, there is a lesson to be learned,   10
  And there is my forgiveness to be earned.
  I promised him. Don't make me take it back.
  It's not my nature to see as an attack
  Such foolishness as this, or see the need
  To tell my husband of the trivial deed.   15
DAMIS   So, you have your reasons, but I have mine.
  To grant this fool forgiveness? I decline.
  To want to spare him is a mockery,
  Because he's more than foolish, can't you see?
  This fanatic in his insolent pride,   20
  Brought chaos to my house, and would divide
  Me and my father—unforgivable!
  What's more, he's made my life unlivable,
  As he undermines two true love affairs,
  Mine and Valère's sister, my sister and Valère's!   25
  Father must hear the truth about this man.
  Heaven helped me—I must do what I can
  To use this chance. I'd deserve to lose it,
  If I dropped it now and didn't use it.
ELMIRE   Damis—
DAMIS   No, please, I have to follow through.
  I've never felt as happy as I do
  Right now. And don't try to dissuade me—
  I'll have my revenge. If you forbade me,
  I'd still do it, so you don't have to bother.
  I'll finish this for good. Here comes my father.   35

3.5

[ORGON, DAMIS, TARTUFFE, ELMIRE]

DAMIS   Father! You have arrived. Let's celebrate!
  I have a tale that I'd like to relate.
  It happened here and right before my eyes,
  I offer it to you—as a surprise!
  For all your love, you have been repaid   5
  With duplicity. You have been betrayed
  By your dear friend here, whom I just surprised
  Making verbal love, I quickly surmised,
  To your wife. Yes, this is how he shows you
  How he honors you—he thinks he knows you.   10
  But as your son, I know you much better—
  You demand respect down to the letter.

Madame, unflappable and so discreet,
Would keep this secret, never to repeat.
But, as your son, my feelings are too strong,   15
And to be silent is to do you wrong.
ELMIRE   One learns to spurn without being unkind,
And how to spare a husband's peace of mind.
Although I understood just what he meant,
My honor wasn't touched by this event.   20
That's how I feel. And you would have, Damis,
Said nothing, if you had listened to me.

3.6

[ORGON, DAMIS, TARTUFFE]

ORGON   Good heavens! What he said? Can it be true?
TARTUFFE   Yes, my brother, I'm wicked through and through.
The most miserable of sinners, I.
Filled with iniquity, I should just die.
Each moment of my life's so dirty, soiled,   5
Whatever I come near is quickly spoiled.
I'm nothing but a heap of filth and crime.
I'd name my sins, but we don't have the time.
And I see that heaven, to punish me,
Has mortified my soul quite publicly.   10
What punishment I get, however great,
I well deserve so I'll accept my fate.
Defend myself? I'd face my own contempt,
If I thought that were something I'd attempt.
What you've heard here, surely, you abhor,   15
So chase me like a criminal from your door.
Don't hold back your rage, please, let it flame,
For I deserve to burn, in my great shame.
ORGON [to DAMIS]   Traitor! And how dare you even try
To tarnish this man's virtue with a lie?   20
DAMIS   What? This hypocrite pretends to be contrite
And you believe him over me?
ORGON   That's spite!
And shut your mouth!
TARTUFFE   No, let him have his say.
And don't accuse him. Don't send him away.
Believe his story—why be on my side?   25
You don't know what motives I may hide.
Why give me so much loyalty and love?
Do you know what I am capable of?
My brother, you have total trust in me,
And think I'm good because of what you see?   30
No, no, by my appearance you're deceived,
And what I say you think must be believed.
Well, believe this—I have no worth at all.

The world sees me as worthy, yet I fall
Far below. Sin is so insidious. 35
[*To* DAMIS] Dear son, do treat me as perfidious,
Infamous, lost, a murderer, a thief.
Speak on, because my sins, beyond belief,
Can bring this shameful sinner to his knees,
In humble, paltry effort to appease. 40
ORGON [*to* TARTUFFE]   Brother, there is no need . . .

[*To* DAMIS] Will you
    relent?
DAMIS   He has seduced you!
ORGON   Can't you take a hint?
    Be quiet! [*To* TARTUFFE] Brother, please get up. [*To* DAMIS] Ingrate!
DAMIS   But father, this man
ORGON   —whom you denigrate.
DAMIS   But you should— 45
ORGON   Quiet!
DAMIS   But I saw and heard—
ORGON   I'll slap you if you say another word.
TARTUFFE   In the name of God, don't be that way.
    Brother, I'd rather suffer, come what may,
    Than have this boy receive what's meant for me.
ORGON [*to* DAMIS]   Heathen! 50
TARTUFFE   Please! I beg of you on bended knee.
ORGON [*to* DAMIS]   Wretch! See his goodness?!
DAMIS   But—
ORGON   No!
DAMIS   But—
ORGON   Be still!
    And not another word from you until
    You admit the truth. It's plain to see
    Although you thought that I would never be
    Aware and know your motives, yet I do. 55
    You all hate him. And I saw today, you,
    Wife, servants—everyone beneath my roof—
    Are trying everything to force Tartuffe
    Out of my house—this holy man, my friend.
    The more you try to banish him and end 60
    Our sacred brotherhood, the more secure
    His place is. I have never been more sure
    Of anyone. I give him as his bride
    My daughter. If that hurts the family pride,
    Then good. It needs humbling. You understand? 65
DAMIS   You're going to force her to accept his hand?
ORGON   Yes, traitor, and this evening. You know why?
    To infuriate you. Yes, I defy
    You all. I am master and you'll obey.
    And you, you ingrate, now I'll make you pay 70
    For your abuse of him—kneel on the floor,

And beg his pardon, or go out the door.
DAMIS   Me? Kneel and ask the pardon of this fraud?
ORGON   What? You refuse? Someone get me a rod!
A stick! Something! [*To* TARTUFFE] Don't hold me.   75
[*To* DAMIS] Here's your whack!
Out of my house and don't ever come back!
DAMIS   Yes, I'll leave, but—
ORGON   Get out of my sight!
I disinherit you, you traitor, you're a blight
On this house. And you'll get nothing now
From me, except my curse!   80

3.7

[ORGON, TARTUFFE]

ORGON   You have my vow,
He'll never more question your honesty.
TARTUFFE [*to heaven*]   Forgive him for the pain he's given me.
[*To* ORGON] How I suffer. If you could only see
What I go through when they disparage me.   5
ORGON   Oh no!
TARTUFFE   The ingratitude, even in thought,
Tortures my soul so much, it leaves me fraught
With inner pain. My heart's stopped. I'm near death,
I can barely speak now. Where is my breath?
ORGON [*running in tears to the door through which he chased* DAMIS]
You demon! I held back, you little snot   10
I should have struck you dead right on the spot!
[*To* TARTUFFE] Get up, Brother. Don't worry anymore.
TARTUFFE   Let us end these troubles, Brother, I implore.
For the discord I have caused, I deeply grieve,
So for the good of all, I'll take my leave.   15
ORGON   What? Are you joking? No!
TARTUFFE   They hate me here.
It pains me when I see them fill your ear
With suspicions.
ORGON   But that doesn't matter.
I don't listen.
TARTUFFE   That persistent chatter
You now ignore, one day you'll listen to.   20
Repetition of a lie can make it true.
ORGON   No, my brother. Never.
TARTUFFE   A man's wife
Can so mislead his soul and ruin his life.
ORGON   No, no.
TARTUFFE   Brother, let me, by leaving here,
Remove any cause for doubt or fear.   25
ORGON   No, no. You will stay. My soul is at stake.

TARTUFFE   Well, then, a hefty penance I must make.
  I'll mortify myself, unless . . .
ORGON   No need!
TARTUFFE   Then we will never speak of it, agreed?
  But the question of your honor still remains,   30
  And with that I'll take particular pains
  To prevent rumors. My absence, my defense—
  I'll never see your wife again, and hence—
ORGON   No. You spend every hour with her you want,
  And be seen with her. I want you to flaunt,   35
  In front of them, this friendship with my wife.
  And I know how to really turn the knife
  I'll make you my heir, my only one,
  Yes, you will be my son-in-law and son.[7]
  A good and faithful friend means more to me   40
  Than any member of my family.
  Will you accept this gift that I propose?
TARTUFFE   Whatever heaven wants I can't oppose.
ORGON   Poor man! A contract's what we need to write.
  And let all the envious burst with spite.   45

4.1

[CLÉANTE, TARTUFFE]

CLÉANTE   Yes, everyone is talking and each word
  Diminishes your glory, rest assured.
  Though your name's tainted with scandal and shame,
  I'm glad I ran across you, all the same,
  Because I need to share with you my view   5
  On this disaster clearly caused by you.
  Damis, let's say for now, was so misguided,
  He spoke before he thought. But you decided
  To just sit back and watch him be exiled
  From his own father's house. Were he a child,   10
  Then, really, would you dare to treat him so?
  Shouldn't you forgive him, not make him go?
  However, if there's vengeance in your heart,
  And you act on it, tell me what's the part
  That's Christian in that? And are you so base,   15
  You'd let a son fall from his father's grace?
  Give God your anger as an offering,
  Bring peace and forgive all for everything.
TARTUFFE   I'd do just that, if it were up to me.
  I blame him for nothing, don't you see?   20
  I've pardoned him already. That's my way.

---

7. In fact, French laws governing inheritance would have made such a change extremely difficult to accomplish.

And I'm not bitter, but have this to say:
Heaven's best interests will have been served,
When wrongdoers have got what they deserved.
In fact, if he returns here, I would leave,   25
Because God knows what people might believe.
Faking forgiveness to manipulate
My accuser, silencing the hate
He has for me could be seen as my goal,
When I would only wish to save his soul.   30
What he said to me, though unforgivable,
I give unto God to make life livable.

CLÉANTE   To this conclusion, sir, I have arrived:
Your excuses could not be more contrived.
Just how did you come by the opinion   35
Heaven's business is in your dominion,
Judging who is guilty and who is not?
Taking revenge is heaven's task, I thought.
And if you're under heaven's sovereignty,
What human verdict would you ever be   40
The least bit moved by. No, you wouldn't care—
Judging other's lives is so unfair.
Heaven seems to say "live and let live,"
And our task, I believe, is to forgive.

TARTUFFE   I said I've pardoned him. I take such pains   45
To do exactly what heaven ordains.
But after his attack on me, it's clear,
Heaven does not ordain that he live here.

CLÉANTE   Does it ordain, sir, that you nod and smile,
When taking what is not yours, all the while?   50
On this inheritance you have no claim
And yet you think it's yours. Have you no shame?

TARTUFFE   That this gift was, in any way, received
Out of self-interest, would not be believed
By anyone who knows me well. They'd say,   55
"The world's wealth, to him, holds no sway."
I am not dazzled by gold nor its glitter,
So lack of wealth has never made me bitter.
If I take this present from the father,
The source of all this folderol and bother,   60
I am saving, so everyone understands,
This wealth from falling into the wrong hands,
Waste of wealth and property's a crime,
And that is what would happen at this time.
But I would use it as part of my plan: 65
For glory of heaven, and the good of man.

CLÉANTE   Well, sir, I think these small fears that plague you,
In fact, may cause the rightful heir to sue.
Why trouble yourself, sir—couldn't you just
Let him own his property, if he must?   70

Let others say his property's misused
By him, rather than have yourself accused
Of taking it from its rightful owner.
Wouldn't a pious man be a donor
Of property? Unless there is a verse   75
Or proverb about how you fill your purse
With what's not yours, at all, in any part.
And if heaven has put into your heart
This obstacle to living with Damis,
The honorable thing, you must agree,   80
As well as, certainly, the most discreet,
Is pack your bags and, quickly, just retreat.
To have the son of the house chased away,
Because a guest objects, is a sad day.
Leaving now would show your decency,   85
Sir . . .
TARTUFFE   Yes. Well, it is half after three;
Pious duties consume this time of day,
You will excuse my hurrying away.
CLÉANTE   Ah!

4.2

[ELMIRE, MARIANE, DORINE, CLÉANTE]

DORINE   Please, come to the aid of Mariane.
She's suffering because her father's plan
To force this marriage, impossible to bear,
Has pushed her from distress into despair.
Her father's on his way here. Do your best,   5
Turn him around. Use subtlety, protest,
Whatever way will work to change his mind.

4.3

[ORGON, ELMIRE, MARIANE, CLÉANTE, DORINE]

ORGON   Ah! Here's everyone I wanted to find!
[To MARIANE] This document I have here in my hand
Will make you very happy, understand?
MARIANE   Father, in the name of heaven, I plead
To all that's good and kind in you, concede   5
Paternal power, just in this sense:
Free me from my vows of obedience.
Enforcing that inflexible law today
Will force me to confess each time I pray
My deep resentment of my obligation.   10
I know, father, that I am your creation,
That you're the one who's given life to me.
Why would you now fill it with misery?

If you destroy my hopes for the one man
I've dared to love by trying now to ban   15
Our union, then I'm kneeling to implore,
Don't give me to a man whom I abhor.
To you, Father, I make this supplication:
Don't drive me to some act of desperation,
By ruling me simply because you can.   20

ORGON [*feeling himself touched*]   Be strong! Human weakness
   shames a man!

MARIANE   Your affection for him doesn't bother me—
Let it erupt, give him your property,
And if that's not enough, then give him mine.
Any claim on it, I do now decline.   25
But in this gifting, don't give him my life.
If I must wed, then I will be God's wife,
In a convent, until my days are done.

ORGON   Ah! So you will be a holy, cloistered nun,
Because your father thwarts your love affair.   30
Get up! The more disgust you have to bear,
The more of heaven's treasure you will earn,
And the heaven will bless you in return.
Through this marriage, you'll mortify your senses.
Don't bother me with any more pretenses.   35

DORINE   But . . . !

ORGON   Quiet, you! I see you standing there.
Don't speak a single word! don't even dare!

CLÉANTE   If you permit, I'd like to say a word . . .

ORGON   Brother, the best advice the world has heard
Is yours—its reasoning, hard to ignore.   40
But I refuse to hear it anymore.

ELMIRE [*to* ORGON]   And now, I wonder, have you lost your mind?
Your love for this one man has made you blind.
Can you stand there and say you don't believe
A word we've said? That we're here to deceive?   45

ORGON   Excuse me—I believe in what I see.
You, indulging my bad son, agree
To back him up in this terrible prank,
Accusing my dear friend of something rank.
You should be livid if what you claim took place,   50
And yet this look of calm is on your face.

ELMIRE   Because a man says he's in love with me,
I'm to respond with heavy artillery?
I laugh at these unwanted propositions.
Mirth will quell most ardent ambitions.   55
Why make a fuss over an indiscretion?
My honor's safe and in my possession.
You say I'm calm? Well, that's my constancy—
It won't need a defense, or clemency.
I know I'll never be a vicious prude   60

Who always seems to hear men being rude,
And then defends her honor tooth and claw,
Still snarling, even as the men withdraw.
From honor like that heaven preserve me,
If that's what you want, you don't deserve me,   65
Besides, you're the one who has been betrayed.
ORGON   I see through this trick that's being played.
ELMIRE   How can you be so dim? I am amazed
How you can hear these sins and stay unfazed.
But what if I could show you what he does?   70
ORGON   Show?
ELMIRE   Yes.
ORGON   A fiction!
ELMIRE   No, the truth because
I am quite certain I can find a way
To show you in the fullest light of day . . .
ORGON   Fairy tales!
ELMIRE   Come on, at least answer me.
I've given up expecting you to be   75
My advocate. What have you got to lose,
By hiding somewhere, anyplace you choose,
And see for yourself. And then we can
Hear what you say about your holy man.
ORGON   Then I'll say nothing because it cannot be.   80
ELMIRE   Enough. I'm tired. You'll see what you see.
I'm not a liar, though I've been accused.
The time is now and I won't be refused.
You'll be a witness. And we can stop our rants.
ORGON   All right! I call your bluff, Miss Smarty Pants.   85
ELMIRE [to DORINE]   Tell Tartuffe to come.
DORINE   Watch out. He's clever.
Men like him are caught, well, almost never.
ELMIRE   Narcissism is a great deceiver,
And he has lots of that. He's a believer
In his charisma. [To CLÉANTE and MARIANE] Leave us for a bit.   90

4.4

[ELMIRE, ORGON]

ELMIRE   See this table? Good. Get under it.
ORGON   What!
ELMIRE   You are hiding. Get under there and stay.
ORGON   Under the table?
ELMIRE: Just do as I say.
I have a plan, but for it to succeed,
You must be hidden. So are we agreed?   5
You want to know? I'm ready to divulge it.
ORGON   This fantasy of yours—I'll indulge it.
But then I want to lay this thing to rest.

ELMIRE Oh, that'll happen. Because he'll fail the test.
    You see, I'm going to have a conversation   10
    I'd never have—just as an illustration
    Of how this hypocrite behaved with me.
    So don't be scandalized. I must be free
    To flirt. Clearly, that's what it's going to take
    To prove to you your holy man's a fake.   15
    I'm going to lead him on, to lift his mask,
    Seem to agree to anything he'll ask,
    Pretend to respond to his advances.
    It's for you I'm taking all these chances.
    I'll stop as soon as you have seen enough;   20
    I hope that comes before he calls my bluff.
    His plans for me must be circumvented,
    His passion's strong enough to be demented,
    So the moment you're convinced, you let me know
    That I've revealed the fraud I said I'd show.   25
    Stop him so I won't have a minute more
    Exposure to your friend, this lecherous boor.
    You're in control. I'm sure I'll be all right.
    And . . . here he comes—so hush, stay out of sight.

4.5

[TARTUFFE, ELMIRE, ORGON (*under the table*)]

TARTUFFE I'm told you want to have a word with me.
ELMIRE Yes. I have a secret but I'm not free
    To speak. Close that door, have a look around,
    We certainly do not want to be found
    The way we were just as Damis appeared.   5
    I was terrified for you and as I feared,
    He was irate. You saw how hard I tried
    To calm him down and keep him pacified.
    I was so upset; I never had the thought
    "Deny it all," which might have helped a lot,   10
    But as it turns out, we've nothing to fear,
    My husband's not upset, it would appear.
    Things are good, to heaven I defer,
    Because they're even better than they were.
    I have to say I'm quite amazed, in fact,   15
    His good opinion of you is intact.
    To clear the air and quiet every tongue,
    And to kill any gossip that's begun—
    You could've pushed me over with a feather—
    He wants us to spend all our time together!   20
    That's why, with no fear of a critical stare,
    I can be here with you or anywhere.
    Most important, I am completely free

To show my ardor for you, finally.
TARTUFFE   Ardor? This is a sudden change of tone   25
From the last time we found ourselves alone.
ELMIRE   If thinking I was turning you away
Has made you angry, all that I can say
Is that you do not know a woman's heart!
Protecting our virtue keeps us apart,   30
And makes us seem aloof, and even cold.
But cooler outside, inside the more bold.
When love overcomes us, we are ashamed,
Because we fear that we might be defamed.
We must protect our honor—not allow   35
Our love to show. I fear that even now,
In this confession, you'll think ill of me.
But now I've spoken, and I hope you see
My ardor that is there. Why would I sit
And listen to you? Why would I permit   40
Your talk of love, unless I had a notion
Just like yours, and with the same emotion?
And when Damis found us, didn't I try
To quiet him? And did you wonder why,
In speaking of Mariane's marriage deal,   45
I not only asked you, I made an appeal
That you turn it down? What was I doing?
Making sure I'd be the one you'd be wooing.
TARTUFFE   It is extremely sweet, without a doubt,
To watch your lips as loving words spill out.   50
Abundant honey there for me to drink,
But I have doubts. I cannot help but think,
"Does she tell the truth, or does she lie,
To get me to break off this marriage tie?
Is all this ardor something she could fake,   55
And just an act for her stepdaughter's sake?"
So many questions, yet I want to trust,
But need to know the truth, in fact, I must.
Pleasing you, Elmire, is my main task,
And happiness, and so I have to ask   60
To sample this deep ardor felt for me
Right here and now, in blissful ecstasy.
ELMIRE [coughing to alert ORGON]
You want to spend this passion instantly?
I've been opening my heart consistently,
But for you, it's not enough, this sharing.   65
Yet for a woman, it is very daring.
So why can't you be happy with a taste,
Instead of the whole meal consumed in haste?
TARTUFFE   We dare not hope, all those of us who don't
Deserve a thing. And so it is I won't   70
Be satisfied with words. I'll always doubt,
Assume my fortune's taken the wrong route

On its way to me. And that is why
I don't believe in anything till I
Have touched, partaken until satisfied.   75
ELMIRE   So suddenly, your love can't be denied.
It wants complete dominion over me,
And what it wants, it wants violently.
I know I'm flustered, I know I'm out of breath—
Your power over me could be the death   80
Of my reason. Does this seem right to you?
To use my weakness against me, just to
Conquer? No one's gallant anymore.
I invite you in. You break down the door.
TARTUFFE   If your passion for me isn't a pretense,   85
Then why deny me its best evidence?
ELMIRE   But, heaven, sir, that place that you address
So often, would judge us both if we transgress.
TARTUFFE   That's all that's in the way of my desires?
These judgments heaven makes of what transpires?   90
All you fear is heaven's bad opinion.
ELMIRE   But I am made to fear its dominion.
TARTUFFE   And I know how to exorcise these fears.
To sin is not as bad as it appears
If, and stay with me on this, one can think   95
That in some cases, heaven gives a wink
    [*It is a scoundrel speaking.*][8]
When it comes to certain needs of men
Who can remain upright but only when
There is a pure intention. So you see,
If you just let yourself be led by me,   100
You'll have no worries, and I can enjoy
You. And you, me. Because we will employ
This way of thinking—a real science
And a secret, thus, with your compliance,
Fulfilling my desires without fear,   105
Is easy now, so let it happen here.
    [ELMIRE *coughs.*]
That cough, Madame, is bad.
ELMIRE   I'm in such pain.
TARTUFFE   A piece of licorice might ease the strain.
ELMIRE [*directed to* ORGON]   This cold I have is very obstinate.
It stubbornly holds on. I can't shake it.   110
TARTUFFE   That's most annoying.
ELMIRE   More than I can say.
TARTUFFE   Let's get back to finding you a way,
Finally, to get around your scruples:
Secrecy—I'm one of its best pupils
And practitioners. Responsibility   115

---

8. This stage direction, inserted by Molière himself, supports the playwright's assertion that he took pains to demonstrate Tartuffe's true nature.

For any evil—you can put on me,
I will answer up to heaven if I must,
And give a good accounting you can trust.
There'll be no sins for which we must atone,
'Cause evil exists only when it's known.   120
Adam and Eve were public in their fall.
To sin in private is not to sin at all.

ELMIRE [*after coughing again*]   Obviously, I must give in to you,
Because, it seems, you are a person who
Refuses to believe anything I say.   125
Live testimony only can convey
The truth of passion here, no more, no less.
That it should go that far, I must confess,
Is such a pity. But I'll cross the line,
And give myself to you. I won't decline   130
Your offer, sir, to vanquish me right here.
But let me make one point extremely clear:
If there's a moral judgment to be made,
If anyone here feels the least betrayed,
Then none of that will be my fault. Instead,   135
The sin weighs twice as heavy on your head.
You forced me to this brash extremity.

TARTUFFE   Yes, yes, I will take all the sin on me.

ELMIRE   Open the door and check because I fear
My husband—just look—might be somewhere near.   140

TARTUFFE   What does it matter if he comes or goes?
The secret is, I lead him by the nose.
He's urged me to spend all my time with you.
So let him see—he won't believe it's true.

ELMIRE   Go out and look around. Indulge my whim.   145
Look everywhere and carefully for him.

4.6

[ORGON, ELMIRE]

ORGON [*coming out from under the table*]
I swear that is the most abominable man!
How will I bear this? I don't think I can.
I'm stupefied!

ELMIRE   What? Out so soon? No, no.
You can't be serious. There's more to go.
Get back under there. You can't be too sure.   5
It's never good relying on conjecture.

ORGON   That kind of wickedness comes straight from hell.

ELMIRE   You've turned against this man you know so well?
Good lord, be sure the evidence is strong
Before you are convinced. You might be wrong.
[*She steps in front of* ORGON.]

4.7

[TARTUFFE, ELMIRE, ORGON]

TARTUFFE Yes, all is well; there's no one to be found,
    And I was thorough when I looked around.
    To my delight, my rapture, at last . . .
ORGON [*stopping him*]   Just stop a minute there! You move too fast!
    Delight and rapture? Fulfilling desire?   5
    Ah! Ah! You are a traitor and a liar!
    Some holy man you are, to wreck my life,
    Marry my daughter? Lust after my wife?
    I've had my doubts about you, but kept quiet,
    Waiting for you to slip and then deny it.   10
    Well, now it's happened and I'm so relieved,
    To stop pretending that I am deceived.
ELMIRE [*to* TARTUFFE]   I don't approve of what I've done today,
    But I needed to do it, anyway.
TARTUFFE What? You can't think . . .   15
ORGON   No more words from you.
    Get out of here, you. . . . You and I are through.
TARTUFFE But my intentions . . .
ORGON   You still think I'm a dunce?
    You shut your mouth and leave this house at once!
TARTUFFE You're the one to leave, you, acting like the master.
    Now I'll make it known, the full disaster: 20
    This house belongs to me, yes, all of it,
    And I'll decide what's true, as I see fit.
    You can't entrap me with demeaning tricks,
    Yes, here's a situation you can't fix.
    Here nothing happens without my consent.   25
    You've offended heaven. You must repent.
    But I know how to really punish you.
    Those who harm me, they know not what they do.

4.8

[ELMIRE, ORGON]

ELMIRE What was that about? I mean, the latter.
ORGON I'm not sure, but it's no laughing matter.
ELMIRE Why?
ORGON   I've made a mistake I now can see,
    The deed I gave him is what troubles me.
ELMIRE The deed?   5
ORGON   And something else. I am undone.
    I think my troubles may have just begun.
ELMIRE What else?
ORGON   You'll know it all. I have to race,
    To see if a strongbox is in its place.

5.1

[ORGON, CLÉANTE]

CLÉANTE   Where are you running to?
ORGON   Who knows.
CLÉANTE   Then wait.
  It seems to me we should deliberate,
  Meet, plan, and have some family talks.
ORGON   I can't stop thinking about the damned box
  More than anything, that's the loss I fear.   5
CLÉANTE   What about this box makes it so dear?
ORGON   I have a friend whom I felt sorry for,
  Because he chose the wrong side in the war;[9]
  Before he fled, he brought it to me,
  This locked box. He didn't leave a key.   10
  He told me it has papers, this doomed friend,
  On which his life and property depend.
CLÉANTE   Are you saying you gave the box away?
ORGON   Yes, that's true, that's what I'm trying to say.
  I was afraid that I would have to lie,   15
  If I were confronted. That is why
  I went to my betrayer and confessed
  And he, in turn, told me it would be best
  If I gave him the box, to keep, in case
  Someone were to ask me to my face   20
  About it all, and I might lie and then,
  In doing so, commit a venial sin.[1]
CLÉANTE   As far as I can see, this is a mess,
  And with a lot of damage to assess.
  This secret that you told, this deed you gave,   25
  Make the situation hard to save.
  He's holding all the cards, your holy man,
  Because you gave them to him. If you can,
  Restrain yourself a bit and stay away.
  That would be best. And do watch what you say.   30
ORGON   What? With his wicked heart and corrupt soul,
  Yet I'm to keep my rage under control?
  Yes, me who took him in, right off the street?
  Damn all holy men! They're filled with deceit!
  I now renounce them all, down to the man,   35
  And I'll treat them worse than Satan can.
CLÉANTE   Listen to yourself! You're over the top,
  Getting carried away again. Just stop.
  "Moderation." Is that a word you know?
  I think you've learned it, but then off you go.   40

9. That is, he opposed Louis in the Fronde (see 1.2.11 and note). Although Orgon supported the king, this act left him open to the charge of being a traitor to the throne—a capital offense.

1. A "pardonable" or relatively minor sin. Because Tartuffe had possession of the box, Orgon could deny that he had it without lying.

Always ignoring the strength in reason,
Flinging yourself from loyalty to treason.
Why can't you just admit that you were swayed
By the fake piety that man displayed?
But no. Rather than change your ways, you turned   45
Like that. [*Snaps fingers*] Attacking holy men who've earned
The right to stand among the true believers.
So now all holy men are base deceivers?
Instead of just admitting your delusion,
"They're all like that!" you say—brilliant conclusion.   50
Why trust reason, when you have emotion?
You've implied there is no true devotion.
Freethinkers are the ones who hold that view,
And yet, you don't agree with them, do you?
You judge a man as good without real proof.   55
Appearances can lie—witness: Tartuffe.
If your respect is something to be prized,
Don't toss it away to those disguised
In a cloak of piety and virtue.
Don't you see how deeply they can hurt you?   60
Look for simple goodness—it does exist.
And just watch for imposters in our midst,
With this in mind, try not to be unjust
To true believers, sin on the side of trust.

5.2

[DAMIS, ORGON, CLÉANTE]

DAMIS   Father, what? I can't believe it's true,
　　That scoundrel has the gall to threaten you?
　　And use the things you gave him in his case
　　'Gainst you? To throw you out? I'll break his face.
ORGON   My son, I'm in more pain than you can see.   5
DAMIS   I'll break both his legs. Leave it to me.
　　We must not bend under his insolence.
　　I'll finish this business, punish his offense,
　　I'll murder him and do it with such joy.
CLÉANTE   Damis, you're talking like a little boy.   10
　　Tantrums head the list of your main flaws.
　　We live in modern times, with things called "laws."
　　Murder is illegal. At least for us.

5.3

[MADAME PERNELLE, MARIANE, ELMIRE, DORINE,
DAMIS, ORGON, CLÉANTE]

MADAME PERNELLE   It's unbelievable! Preposterous!
ORGON   Believe it. I've seen it with my own eyes.
　　He returned kindness with deceit and lies.

I took in a man, miserable and poor,
Brought him home, gave him the key to my door,   5
I loaded him with favors every day,
To him, my daughter, I just gave away,
My house, my wealth, a locked box from a friend.
But to what depths this devil would descend.
This betrayer, this abomination,   10
Who had the gall to preach about temptation,
And know in his black heart he'd woo my wife.
Seduce her! Yes! And then to steal my life.
Using my property, which I transferred to him,
I know, I know—it was a stupid whim.   15
He wants to ruin me, chase me from my door,
He wants me as he was, abject and poor.

DORINE   Poor man!

MADAME PERNELLE   I don't believe a word, my son,
  This isn't something that he could have done.

ORGON   What?   20

MADAME PERNELLE   Holy men always arouse envy.

ORGON   Mother, what are you trying to say to me?

MADAME PERNELLE   That you live rather strangely in this house;
  He's hated here, especially by your spouse.

ORGON   What has this got to do with what I said?

MADAME PERNELLE   Heaven knows, I've beat into your head: 25
  "In this world, virtue is mocked forever;
  Envious men may die, but envy never."

ORGON   How does that apply to what's happened here?

MADAME PERNELLE   Someone made up some lies; it's all too clear.

ORGON   But I saw it myself, you understand.   30

MADAME PERNELLE   "Whoever spreads slander has a soiled hand."

ORGON   You'll make me, Mother, say something not nice.
  I saw it for myself; I've told you twice.

MADAME PERNELLE   "No one can trust what gossips have to say,
  Yet they'll be with us until Judgment Day."   35

ORGON   You're talking total nonsense, Mother!
  I said I saw him, this man I called Brother!
  I saw him with my wife, with these two eyes.
  The word is "saw," past tense of "see." These "lies"
  That you misnamed are just the truth.   40
  I saw my wife almost beneath Tartuffe.

MADAME PERNELLE   Oh, is that all? Appearances deceive.
  What we think we see, we then believe.

ORGON   I'm getting angry.

MADAME PERNELLE   False suspicions, see?
  We are subject to them, occasionally,   45
  Good deeds can be seen as something other.

ORGON   So I'm to see this as a good thing, Mother,
  A man trying to kiss my wife?

MADAME PERNELLE   You must.
  Because, to be quite certain you are just,

You should wait until you're very, very sure 50
And not rely on faulty conjecture.
ORGON   Goddammit! You would have me wait until . . . ?
And just be quiet while he has his fill,
Right before my very eyes, Mother, he'd—
MADAME PERNELLE   I can't believe that he would do this "deed" 55
Of which he's been accused. There is no way.
His soul is pure.
ORGON   I don't know what to say!
Mother!
DORINE   Just deserts, for what you put us through.
You thought we lied, now she thinks that of you.
CLÉANTE   Why are we wasting time with all of this? 60
We're standing on the edge of the abyss.
This man is dangerous! He has a plan!
DAMIS   How could he hurt us? I don't think he can.
ELMIRE   He won't get far, complaining to the law—
You'll tell the truth, and he'll have to withdraw. 65
CLÉANTE   Don't count on it; trust me, he'll find a way
To use these weapons you gave him today.
He has legal documents, and the deed.
To kick us out, just what else does he need?
And if he's doubted, there are many ways 70
To trap you in a wicked legal maze.
You give a snake his venom, nice and quick,
And after that you poke him with a stick?
ORGON   I know. But what was I supposed to do?
Emotions got the best of me, it's true. 75
CLÉANTE   If we could placate him, just for a while,
And somehow get the deed back with a smile.
ELMIRE   Had I known we had all this to lose,
I never would have gone through with my ruse.
I would've— 80
        [*A knock on the door.*]
ORGON   What does that man want? You go find out.
But I don't want to know what it's about.

5.4

[MONSIEUR LOYAL, MADAME PERNELLE, ORGON,
DAMIS, MARIANE, DORINE, ELMIRE, CLÉANTE]

MONSIEUR LOYAL [*to* DORINE]   Dear sister, hello. Please, I beg of you,
Your master is the one I must speak to.
DORINE   He's not receiving visitors today.
MONSIEUR LOYAL   I bring good news so don't send me away.
My goal in coming is not to displease; 5
I'm here to put your master's mind at ease.
DORINE   And you are . . . who?
MONSIEUR LOYAL   Just say that I have come

For his own good and with a message from
Monsieur Tartuffe.
DORINE [*to* ORGON]   It's a soft-spoken man,
Who says he's here to do just what he can   10
To ease your mind. Tartuffe sent him.
CLÉANTE   Let's see
What he might want.
ORGON   Oh, what's my strategy?
He's come to reconcile us, I just know.
CLÉANTE   Your strategy? Don't let your anger show,
For heaven's sake. And listen for a truce.   15
MONSIEUR LOYAL   My greetings, sir. I'm here to be of use.
ORGON   Just what I thought. His language is benign.
For the prospect of peace, a hopeful sign.
MONSIEUR LOYAL   Your family's dear to me, I hope you know.
I served your father many years ago.   20
ORGON   I humbly beg your pardon, to my shame,
I don't know you, nor do I know your name.
MONSIEUR LOYAL   My name's Loyal. I'm Norman by descent.
My job of bailiff is what pays my rent.
Thanks be to heaven, it's been forty years   25
I've done my duty free of doubts or fear.
That you invited me in, I can report,
When I serve you with this writ from the court.
ORGON   What? You're here . . .
MONSIEUR LOYAL   No upsetting outbursts, please.
It's just a warrant saying we can seize,   30
Not me, of course, but this Monsieur Tartuffe—
Your house and land as his. Here is the proof.
I have the contract here. You must vacate
These premises. Please, now, don't be irate.
Just gather up your things now, and make way   35
For this man, without hindrance or delay.
ORGON   Me? Leave my house?
MONSIEUR LOYAL   That's right, sir, out the door.
This house, at present, as I've said before,
Belongs to good Monsieur Tartuffe, you see,
He's lord and master of this property   40
By virtue of this contract I hold right here.
Is that not your signature? It's quite clear.
DAMIS   He's so rude, I do almost admire him.
MONSIEUR LOYAL   Excuse me. Is it possible to fire him?
My business is with you, a man of reason,   45
Who knows resisting would be seen as treason.
You understand that I must be permitted
To execute the orders as committed.
DAMIS   I'll execute him, Father, to be sure.
His long black nightgown won't make him secure.   50

MONSIEUR LOYAL   He's your son! I thought he was a servant.
  Control the boy. His attitude's too fervent,
  His anger is a bone of contention—
  Throw him out, or I will have to mention
  His name in this, my official report.   55
DORINE   "Loyal" is loyal only to the court.
MONSIEUR LOYAL   I have respect for all God-fearing men,
  So instantly I knew I'd come here when
  I heard your name attached to this assignment.
  I knew you'd want a bailiff with refinement.   60
  I'm here for you, just to accommodate,
  To make removal something you won't hate.
  Now, if I hadn't come, then you would find
  You got a bailiff who would be less kind.
ORGON   I'm sorry, I don't see the kindness in   65
  An eviction order.
MONSIEUR LOYAL   Let me begin:
  I'm giving you time. I won't carry out
  This order you are so upset about.
  I've come only to spend the night with you,
  With my men, who will be coming through.   70
  All ten of them, as quiet as a mouse,
  Oh, you must give me the keys to the house.
  We won't disturb you. You will have your rest—
  You need a full night's sleep—that's always best.
  There'll be no scandal, secrets won't be bared;   75
  Tomorrow morning you must be prepared,
  To pack your things, down to the smallest plate,
  And cup, and then these premises vacate.
  You'll have helpers; the men I chose are strong,
  And they'll have this house empty before long.   80
  I can't think of who would treat you better
  And still enforce the law down to the letter,
  Just later with the letter is my gift.
  So, no resistance. And there'll be no rift.
ORGON   From that which I still have, I'd give this hour,   85
  One hundred coins of gold to have the power
  To sock this bailiff with a punch as great
  As any man in this world could create.
CLÉANTE   That's enough. Let's not make it worse.
DAMIS   The nerve
  Of him. Let's see what my right fist can serve.   90
DORINE   Mister Loyal, you have a fine, broad back,
  And if I had a stick, you'd hear it crack.
MONSIEUR LOYAL   Words like that are punishable, my love—
  Be careful when a push becomes a shove.
CLÉANTE   Oh, come on, there's no reason to postpone.   95
  Just serve your writ and then leave us alone.

MONSIEUR LOYAL   May heaven keep you, till we meet again!
ORGON   And strangle you, and him who sent you in!

5.5

[ORGON, CLÉANTE, MARIANE, ELMIRE, MADAME
PERNELLE, DORINE, DAMIS]

ORGON   Well, Mother, look at this writ. Here is proof
  Of treachery supreme by your Tartuffe.
  Don't jump to judgment—that's what you admonished.
MADAME PERNELLE   I'm overwhelmed, I'm utterly astonished.
DORINE   I hear you blaming him and that's just wrong.   5
  You'll see his good intentions before long.
  "Just love thy neighbor" is here on this writ,
  Between the lines, you see him saying it.
  Because men are corrupted by their wealth,
  Out of concern for your spiritual health.   10
  He's taking, with a pure motivation,
  Everything that keeps you from salvation.
ORGON   Aren't you sick of hearing "Quiet!" from me?
CLÉANTE   Thoughts of what to do now? And quickly?
ELMIRE   Once we show the plans of that ingrate,   15
  His trickery can't get him this estate.
  As soon as they see his disloyalty,
  He'll be denied, I hope, this property.

5.6

[VALÈRE, ORGON, CLÉANTE, ELMIRE, MARIANE, etc.]

VALÈRE   I hate to ruin your day—I have bad news.
  Danger's coming. There's no time to lose.
  A good friend, quite good, as it turns out,
  Discovered something you must know about,
  Something at the court that's happening now.   5
  That swindler—sorry, if you will allow,
  That holy faker—has gone to the king,
  Accusing you of almost everything.
  But here's the worst: he says that you have failed
  Your duty as a subject, which entailed   10
  The keeping of a strongbox so well hidden,
  That you could deny knowledge, if bidden,
  Of a traitor's whereabouts. What's more,
  That holy fraud will come right through that door,
  Accusing you. You can't do anything.   15
  He had this box and gave it to the king.
  So there's an order out for your arrest!
  And evidently, it's the king's behest,
  That Tartuffe come, so justice can be done.

CLÉANTE   Well, there it is, at last, the smoking gun.   20
  He can claim this house, at the very least.
ORGON   The man is nothing but a vicious beast.
VALÈRE   You must leave now, and I will help you hide.
  Here's ten thousand in gold. My carriage is outside.
  When a storm is bearing down on you   25
  Running is the best thing one can do.
  I have a place where both of us can stay.
ORGON   My boy, I owe you more than I can say.
  I pray to heaven that, before too long,
  I can pay you back and right the wrong   30
  I've done to you. [*To* ELMIRE] Good-bye. Take care, my dear.
CLÉANTE   We'll plan. You go while the way is still clear.

5.7

[THE EXEMPT, TARTUFFE, VALÈRE, ORGON, ELMIRE,
MARIANE, DORINE, *etc.*[2]]

TARTUFFE   Easy, just a minute, you move too fast.
  Your cowardice, dear sir, is unsurpassed.
  What I have to say is uncontested.
  Simply put, I'm having you arrested.
ORGON   You villain, you traitor, your lechery   5
  Is second only to your treachery.
  And you arrest me—that's the crowning blow.
TARTUFFE   Suffering for heaven is all I know,
  So revile me. It's all for heaven's sake.
CLÉANTE   Why does he persist when we know it's fake?   10
DAMIS   He's mocking heaven. What a loathsome beast.
TARTUFFE   Get mad—I'm not bothered in the least.
  It is my duty, what I'm doing here.
MARIANE   You really think that if you persevere
  In this lie, you'll keep your reputation?   15
TARTUFFE   My honor is safeguarded by my station,
  As I am on a mission from the king.
ORGON   You dog, have you forgotten everything?
  Who picked you up from total poverty?
TARTUFFE   I know that there were things you did for me.   20
  My duty to our monarch is what stifles
  Memory, so your past gifts are trifles.
  My obligations to him are so rife,
  That I would give up family, friends, and life.
ELMIRE   Fraud!   25
DORINE   Now there's a lie that beats everything,
  His pretended reverence for our king!

2. Molière himself added "etc." to the list of speaking characters. Thus Laurent and Flipote may
return to the stage for this final scene.

CLÉANTE This "duty to our monarch," as you say,
 Why didn't it come up before today?
 You had the box, you lived here for some time,
 To say the least, and yet this crime   30
 That you reported—why then did you wait?
 Orgon caught you about to desecrate
 The holy bonds of marriage with his wife.
 Suddenly, your obligations are so "rife"
 To our dear king, that you're here to turn in 35
 Your former friend and "brother" and begin
 To move into his house, a gift, but look,
 Why would you accept gifts from a crook?
TARTUFFE [to THE EXEMPT] Save me from this whining! I have had my fill!
 Do execute your orders, if you will.   40
THE EXEMPT I will. I've waited much too long for that.
 I had to let you have your little chat.
 It confirmed the facts our monarch knew,
 That's why, Tartuffe, I am arresting you.[3]
TARTUFFE Who, me?   45
THE EXEMPT   Yes, you.
TARTUFFE   You're putting me in jail?
THE EXEMPT Immediately. And there will be no bail.
 [To ORGON] You may compose yourself now, sir, because
 We're fortunate in leadership and laws.
 We have a king who sees into men's hearts,
 And cannot be deceived, so he imparts   50
 Great wisdom, and a talent for discernment,
 Thus frauds are guaranteed a quick internment.
 Our Prince of Reason sees things as they are,
 So hypocrites do not get very far.
 But saintly men and the truly devout,   55
 He cherishes and has no doubts about.
 This man could not begin to fool the king
 Who can defend himself against the sting
 Of much more subtle predators. And thus,
 When this craven pretender came to us,   60
 Demanding justice and accusing you,
 He betrayed himself. Our king could view
 The baseness lurking in his coward's heart.
 Evil like that can set a man apart,
 And so divine justice nodded her head,   65
 The king did not believe a word he said.
 It was soon confirmed, he has a crime
 For every sin, but why squander the time
 To list them or the aliases he used.
 For the king, it's enough that he abused   70

---

3. In his capacity as officer of the king, The Exempt becomes both Louis's representative and his surrogate.

Your friendship and your faith. And though we knew
Each accusation of his was untrue,
Our monarch himself, wanting to know
Just how far this imposter planned to go,
Had me wait to find this out, then pounce,   75
Arrest this criminal, quickly denounce
The man and all his lies. And now, the king
Orders delivered to you, everything
This scoundrel took, the deed, all documents,
This locked box of yours and all its contents,   80
And nullifies the contract giving away
Your property, effective today.
And finally, our monarch wants to end
Your worries about aiding your old friend
Before he went into exile because,   85
In that same way, and in spite of the laws,
You openly defended our king's right
To his throne. And you were prepared to fight.
From his heart, and because it makes good sense
That a good deed deserves a recompense,   90
He pardons you. And wanted me to add:
He remembers good longer than the bad.
DORINE   May heaven be praised!
MADAME PERNELLE   I am so relieved.
ELMIRE   A happy ending!
MARIANE   Can it be believed?
ORGON [*to* TARTUFFE]   Now then, you traitor . . .   95
CLÉANTE   Stop that, Brother, please.
You're sinking to his level. Don't appease
His expectations of mankind. His fate
Is misery. But it's never too late
To take another path, and feel remorse.
So let's wish, rather, he will change his course,   100
And turn his back upon his life of vice,
Embrace the good and know it will suffice.
We've all seen the wisdom of this great king,
Whom we should go and thank for everything.
ORGON   Yes, and well said. So come along with me,   105
To thank him for his generosity.
And then once that glorious task is done,
We'll come back here for yet another one—
I mean a wedding for which we'll prepare,
To give my daughter to the good Valère.   110

APHRA BEHN
1640?–1689

Poised between Africa and the New World, *Oroonoko* follows the heroic prince of that name into captivity, slavery, and desperate violence. The novella tantalizes us with the fiction of a narrator who personally witnesses much of Oroonoko's story, and whose close friendship with the hero makes her both sympathetic to his plight and complicit in his fate. *Oroonoko* itself is similarly ambiguous: it makes a powerful case against slavery, long before the actual birth of abolitionism, yet it also presents the prince as an exceptional victim whose enslavement is tragic only because of his exalted, aristocratic nature.

As the first professional woman writer in England, Aphra Behn gave women "the right to speak their minds," as **Virginia Woolf** put it. She wrote popular plays, longer epistolary fiction, novellas such as *Oroonoko*, and occasional poetry. Early in her career, she probably served as a spy for the English in Holland, and in later years was associated with libertines and freethinkers. Both in her personal and in her professional life she showed a pronounced disregard for convention and for the limits imposed on women's behavior in her time.

Little is known about Behn's early life, though it seems likely that her father was a barber in Canterbury. In *Oroonoko* she creates a more exalted parentage for herself, claiming to be the daughter of the "lieutenant-general of six and thirty islands, besides the continent of Surinam." This purely fictional genealogy was repeated by her first biographer and has confused readers ever since. Behn did visit the English colony of Surinam, on the northern edge of South America, with her mother and siblings in 1663, and became involved in the political infighting there. On her return to London in 1664, she apparently married a German merchant, Johannes Behn, but the marriage did not last long, either because of his death or their separation.

In 1660, London playhouses reopened after an eighteen-year hiatus that coincided with Puritan control of England following the English Civil War. The restoration to the English throne of Charles II, an avid enthusiast of the theater, virtually guaranteed that the period later called "the Restoration" would witness a flowering of theatrical innovation and creativity. It also provided women with new opportunities to participate in the cultural life of London. For example, actresses, not actors, now routinely played female roles.

In this environment, Behn forged her writing career. It didn't hurt that her political sympathies would always lie with the king: in a time of continuing political turmoil, she supported first Charles and then James II. As political parties developed in England she consistently sided with the more conservative Tories, who supported a strong monarchy. Her ties to the monarchy were so strong that at one point, Behn was sent by the king to Holland as a spy. Her code name during this stint in espionage was "Astrea," the Greek goddess associated with purity and renewal, one of the many names given to another exceptional early modern Englishwoman, Elizabeth I. Behn would later adopt this name in her literary pursuits whenever she needed to conceal her identity. By 1670 she had become a playwright, writing for the Duke's Company in London. Uniquely for her time, she had at least nineteen plays staged, and probably contributed to many more. In keeping with the fashion of the times, Behn wrote tragicomedies on love and political restoration, as well as city comedies full of incorrigible rakes, duped husbands, and pert heroines. The most famous of these, *The Rover* (1677), is still produced regularly.

Behn was associated with the circle of the Earl of Rochester, the most famous libertine of a libertine time. She wrote a number of explicit poems on sexual matters, which led to many accusations of indecency, both from her contemporaries and especially during the Victorian era, when her work was dismissed for its "coarseness." Yet Behn was a famous and successful writer in her own time, whose work paved the way for playwrights and novelists, both male and female, in the eighteenth century. Today, her reputation rests primarily on *Oroonoko* and her city comedies, while her wider oeuvre is increasingly read and studied.

First published in 1688, *Oroonoko* describes the triangular trade in manufactured goods, slaves, and sugar among Europe, Africa, and the Caribbean. English slave traders picked up their human cargo on the west coast of Africa, transported them to the West Indies, where those who survived the cruel passage were sold to work on the sugar plantations, and then returned to England with a cargo of sugar to complete their profitable, if brutal, trajectory. Behn's novella is partly a frame narrative: it opens in the English sugar colony of Surinam, where the first-person narrator, who identifies herself as Behn, has traveled with her father, the new governor, and her sister. There the narrator befriends the imposing slave Oroonoko, who shares his story. His fantastic narrative takes us back to an exotic West Africa of harems and vulnerable virgins, a place overcivilized in its luxury, in contrast to the supposedly innocent New World. As the tale unfolds, we learn that Oroonoko, a prince in his own land, had managed to save his beloved Imoinda from his lecherous grandfather, only to be tricked into captivity by a greedy English slave trader.

In denouncing Oroonoko's fate, the narrator insists on Oroonoko's status as a virtual European and an aristocrat, as evinced by his elegant physique and European education. These claims underscore the text's ambivalence about slavery and race. The text leaves us wondering: Is Oroonoko meant to be a representative victim, or an exalted exception? How is he different from other Africans, who, in the world of the text, can be enslaved unproblematically? As Oroonoko and Imoinda's prolonged slavery becomes unbearable to the dignified hero, he leads his fellow slaves in a revolt, bringing down upon himself the fury of the slave-owning establishment and destroying the supposed harmony that the text relates. Are Oroonoko's violent acts justified? Does the text encourage us to see his resistance as necessary but unfortunate, or instead as evidence of his ultimate savagery?

Oroonoko's first-person narrator, closely identified with the author, raises for the reader basic questions of narrative authority and omniscience: what is this narrator privy to, and what are the limits of her power? What can she and can she not do for the enslaved prince, beyond narrating his story? Ultimately, how can we read her framed and partial account of him? In its short span, Behn's novella probes the dilemmas of personal versus political morality, of the legitimacy of government in a violent colonial space, and of the true nature of heroism.

Whatever its ambiguities, *Oroonoko* resonated profoundly with opponents of slavery and was repeatedly adapted both in prose and on the stage, from Thomas Southerne's 1695 tragicomedy through several tragic versions over the course of the eighteenth century, as the abolitionist movement in England found its voice.

Oroonoko; or, The Royal Slave

The Epistle Dedicatory

To The
Right Honourable
The
Lord MAITLAND.[1]

*   *   *

My Lord, the Obligations I have to some of the Great Men of your Nation, particularly to your Lordship, gives me an Ambition of making my Acknowledgments, by all the Opportunities I can; and such humble Fruits, as my Industry produces, I lay at your Lordship's Feet. This is a true Story, of a Man Gallant enough to merit your Protection; and, had he always been so Fortunate, he had not made so Inglorious an end: The Royal Slave I had the Honour to know in my Travels to the other World; and though I had none above me in that Country, yet I wanted power to preserve this Great Man. If there be any thing that seems Romantick, I beseech your Lordship to consider, these Countries do, in all things, so far differ from ours, that they produce unconceivable Wonders; at least, they appear so to us, because New and Strange. What I have mention'd I have taken care shou'd be Truth, let the Critical Reader judge as he pleases. 'Twill be no Commendation to the Book, to assure your Lordship I writ it in a few Hours, though it may serve to Excuse some of its Faults of Connexion; for I never rested my Pen a Moment for Thought: 'Tis purely the Merit of my Slave that must render it worthy of the Honour it begs; and the Author of that of Subscribing herself,

My Lord,
Your Lordship's most oblig'd
and obedient Servant,
A. BEHN.

The History of the Royal Slave

I do not pretend, in giving you the History of this *Royal Slave*, to entertain my Reader with the Adventures of a feign'd *Hero*, whose Life and Fortunes Fancy may manage at the Poet's Pleasure; nor in relating the Truth, design to adorn it with any Accidents, but such as arriv'd in earnest to him: And it shall come simply into the World, recommended by its own proper Merits, and natural Intrigues; there being enough of Reality to support it, and to render it diverting, without the Addition of Invention.

I was my self an Eye-Witness to a great part, of what you will find here set down; and what I cou'd not be Witness of, I receiv'd from the Mouth of the

---

1. Richard Maitland (1635–1695) held important posts in Scotland and was noted for his fine library.

chief Actor in this History, the *Hero* himself, who gave us the whole Transactions of his Youth; and though I shall omit, for Brevity's sake, a thousand little Accidents of his Life, which, however pleasant to us, where History was scarce, and Adventures very rare; yet might prove tedious and heavy to my Reader, in a World where he finds Diversions for every Minute, new and strange: But we who were perfectly charm'd with the Character of this great Man, were curious to gather every Circumstance of his Life.

The Scene of the last part of his Adventures lies in a Colony in *America*, called *Surinam*,[2] in the *West-Indies*.

But before I give you the Story of this *Gallant Slave*, 'tis fit I tell you the manner of bringing them to these new *Colonies*; for those they make use of there, are not *Natives* of the place; for those we live with in perfect Amity, without daring to command 'em; but on the contrary, caress 'em with all the brotherly and friendly Affection in the World; trading with 'em for their Fish, Venison, Buffilo's,[3] Skins, and little Rarities; as Marmosets, a sort of *Monkey* as big as a Rat or Weasel, but of a marvellous and delicate shape, and has Face and Hands like an Humane Creature: and *Cousheries*,[4] a little Beast in the form and fashion of a Lion, as big as a Kitten; but so exactly made in all parts like that noble Beast, that it is it in *Miniature*. Then for little *Parakeetoes*, great Parrots, *Muckaws*, and a thousand other Birds and Beasts of wonderful and surprizing Forms, Shapes, and Colours. For Skins of prodigious Snakes, of which there are some threescore Yards in length; as is the Skin of one that may be seen at His Majesty's *Antiquaries*: Where are also some rare Flies,[5] of amazing Forms and Colours, presented to 'em by my self; some as big as my Fist, some less; and all of various Excellencies, such as Art cannot imitate. Then we trade for Feathers, which they order into all Shapes, make themselves little short Habits of 'em, and glorious Wreaths for their Heads, Necks, Arms and Legs, whose Tinctures are unconceivable. I had a Set of these presented to me, and I gave 'em to the King's Theatre, and it was the Dress of the *Indian Queen*,[6] infinitely admir'd by Persons of Quality; and were unimitable. Besides these, a thousand little Knacks, and Rarities in Nature, and some of Art; as their Baskets, Weapons, Aprons, &c. We dealt with 'em with Beads of all Colours, Knives, Axes, Pins and Needles; which they us'd only as Tools to drill Holes with in their Ears, Noses and Lips, where they hang a great many little things; as long Beads, bits of Tin, Brass, or Silver, beat thin; and any shining Trincket. The Beads they weave into Aprons about a quarter of an Ell long, and of the same breadth;[7] working them very prettily in Flowers of several Colours of Beads; which Apron they wear just before 'em, as *Adam* and *Eve* did the Figleaves; the Men wearing a long Stripe of Linen, which they deal with us for. They thread these Beads also on long Cotton-threads, and make Girdles to tie their Aprons to, which come twenty times, or more, about the Waist; and then

2. An English colony in the region of Guiana, on the coast of South America east of Venezuela, now Suriname. It was settled by planters from Barbados seeking more land.
3. Buffalo or wild oxen.
4. A lion-headed marmoset.
5. Butterflies. "*Antiquaries*": the new Royal Society museum.
6. A play by Robert Howard and John Dryden, set in Mexico, first performed at the Theatre Royal in 1664.
7. About one foot square. "Ell": old English measure, about forty-five inches.

cross, like a Shoulder-belt, both ways, and round their Necks, Arms and Legs. This Adornment, with their long black Hair, and the Face painted in little Specks or Flowers here and there, makes 'em a wonderful Figure to behold. Some of the Beauties which indeed are finely shap'd, as almost all are, and who have pretty Features, are very charming and novel; for they have all that is called Beauty, except the Colour, which is a reddish Yellow; or after a new Oiling, which they often use to themselves, they are of the colour of a new Brick, but smooth, soft and sleek. They are extream modest and bashful, very shy, and nice[8] of being touch'd. And though they are all thus naked, if one lives for ever among 'em, there is not to be seen an indecent Action, or Glance; and being continually us'd to see one another so unadorn'd, so like our first Parents before the Fall, it seems as if they had no Wishes; there being nothing to heighten Curiosity, but all you can see, you see at once, and every Moment see; and where there is no Novelty, there can be no Curiosity. Not but I have seen a handsom young *Indian*, dying for Love of a very beautiful young *Indian* Maid; but all his Courtship was, to fold his Arms, pursue her with his Eyes, and Sighs were all his Language: While she, as if no such Lover were present; or rather, as if she desired none such, carefully guarded her Eyes from beholding him; and never approach'd him, but she look'd down with all the blushing Modesty I have seen in the most severe and cautious of our World. And these People represented to me an absolute *Idea* of the first State of Innocence, before Man knew how to sin: And 'tis most evident and plain, that simple Nature is the most harmless, inoffensive and vertuous Mistress. 'Tis she alone, if she were permitted, that better instructs the World, than all the Inventions of Man: Religion wou'd here but destroy that Tranquillity, they possess by Ignorance; and Laws wou'd but teach 'em to know Offence, of which now they have no Notion. They once made Mourning and Fasting for the Death of the *English* Governor, who had given his Hand to come on such a Day to 'em, and neither came, nor sent; believing, when once a Man's Word was past, nothing but Death cou'd or shou'd prevent his keeping it: And when they saw he was not dead, they ask'd him, what Name they had for a Man who promis'd a thing he did not do? The Governor told them, Such a man was a *Lyar*, which was a Word of Infamy to a Gentleman. Then one of 'em reply'd, *Governor, you are a Lyar, and guilty of that Infamy.* They have a Native Justice, which knows no Fraud; and they understand no Vice, or Cunning, but when they are taught by the *White Men*. They have Plurality of Wives, which, when they grow old, they serve those that succeed 'em, who are young; but with a Servitude easie and respected; and unless they take Slaves in War, they have no other Attendants.

Those on that *Continent* where I was, had no King; but the oldest War-Captain was obey'd with great Resignation.

A War-Captain is a Man who has led them on to Battel with Conduct,[9] and Success; of whom I shall have Occasion to speak more hereafter, and of some other of their Customs and Manners, as they fall in my way.

With these People, as I said, we live in perfect Tranquillity, and good Understanding, as it behooves us to do; they knowing all the places where to seek the best Food of the Country, and the Means of getting it; and for very small and

---

8. Fastidious, careful.　　　　　9. Good leadership.

unvaluable Trifles, supply us with what 'tis impossible for us to get; for they do not only in the Wood, and over the *Sevana's*,[1] in Hunting, supply the parts of Hounds, by swiftly scouring through those almost impassable places; and by the meer Activity of their Feet, run down the nimblest Deer, and other eatable Beasts: But in the water, one wou'd think they were Gods of the Rivers, or Fellow-Citizens of the Deep; so rare an Art they have in Swimming, Diving, and almost Living in Water; by which they command the less swift Inhabitants of the Floods. And then for Shooting; what they cannot take, or reach with their Hands, they do with Arrows; and have so admirable an Aim, that they will split almost an Hair; and at any distance that an Arrow can reach, they will shoot down Oranges, and other Fruit, and only touch the Stalk with the Dart's Point, that they may not hurt the Fruit. So that they being, on all Occasions, very useful to us, we find it absolutely necessary to caress 'em as Friends, and not to treat 'em as Slaves; nor dare we do other, their Numbers so far surpassing ours in that *Continent*.

Those then whom we make use of to work in our Plantations of Sugar, are *Negro's*, *Black*-Slaves altogether; which are transported thither in this manner.

Those who want Slaves, make a Bargain with a Master, or a Captain of a Ship, and contract to pay him so much a-piece, a matter of twenty Pound a Head for as many as he agrees for, and to pay for 'em when they shall be deliver'd on such a Plantation: So that when there arrives a Ship laden with Slaves, they who have so contracted, go a-board, and receive their Number by Lot;[2] and perhaps in one Lot that may be for ten, there may happen to be three or four Men; the rest, Women and Children: Or be there more or less of either Sex, you are oblig'd to be contented with your Lot.

Coramantien,[3] a Country of *Blacks* so called, was one of those places in which they found the most advantageous Trading for these Slaves; and thither most of our great Traders in that Merchandice traffick'd; for that Nation is very war-like and brave; and having a continual Campaign, being always in Hostility with one neighbouring Prince or other, they had the fortune to take a great many Captives; for all they took in Battel, were sold as Slaves; at least, those common Men who cou'd not ransom themselves. Of these Slaves so taken, the General only has all the profit; and of these Generals, our Captains and Masters of Ships buy all their Freights.

The King of *Coramantien* was himself a Man of a Hundred and odd Years old, and had no Son, though he had many beautiful *Black*-Wives; for most certainly, there are Beauties that can charm of that Colour. In his younger Years he had had many gallant Men to his Sons, thirteen of which died in Battel, conquering when they fell; and he had only left him for his Successor, one Grand-Child, Son to one of these dead Victors; who, as soon as he cou'd bear a Bow in his Hand, and a Quiver at his Back, was sent into the Field, to be trained up by one of the oldest Generals, to War; where, from his natural Inclination to Arms, and the Occasions given him, with the good Conduct of the

---

1. I.e., savannas, tropical and subtropical grasslands.
2. Groups.
3. An English fort and slave trading station in West Africa, in what is today Ghana. Slaves shipped out of this region were mainly Fante, Ashante, and other Akan-speaking peoples, whom the English referred to as Cormantines. They were known for their beauty and dignity, and their fierceness in war.

old General, he became, at the Age of Seventeen, one of the most expert Captains, and bravest Soldiers, that ever saw the Field of *Mars*:[4] So that he was ador'd as the Wonder of all that World, and the Darling of the Soldiers. Besides, he was adorn'd with a native Beauty so transcending all those of his gloomy Race, that he strook an Awe and Reverence, even in those that knew not his Quality; as he did in me, who beheld him with Surprize and Wonder, when afterwards he arriv'd in our World.

He had scarce arriv'd at his Seventeenth Year, when fighting by his Side, the General was kill'd with an Arrow in his Eye, which the Prince *Oroonoko* (for so was this gallant *Moor*[5] call'd) very narrowly avoided; nor had he, if the General, who saw the Arrow shot, and perceiving it aim'd at the Prince, had not bow'd his Head between, on purpose to receive it in his own Body rather than it shou'd touch that of the Prince, and so saved him.

'Twas then, afflicted as *Oroonoko* was, that he was proclaim'd General in the old Man's place; and then it was, at the finishing of that War, which had continu'd for two Years, that the Prince came to Court; where he had hardly been a Month together, from the time of his fifth Year, to that of Seventeen; and 'twas amazing to imagine where it was he learn'd so much Humanity; or, to give his Accomplishments a juster Name, where 'twas he got that real Greatness of Soul, those refin'd Notions of true Honour, that absolute Generosity, and that Softness that was capable of the highest Passions of Love and Gallantry, whose Objects were almost continually fighting Men, or those mangl'd, or dead; who heard no Sounds, but those of War and Groans: Some part of it we may attribute to the Care of a *French*-Man of Wit and Learning; who finding it turn to very good Account to be a sort of Royal Tutor to this young *Black*, & perceiving him very ready, apt, and quick of Apprehension, took a great pleasure to teach him Morals, Language and Science; and was for it extreamly belov'd and valu'd by him. Another Reason was, He lov'd, when he came from War, to see all the *English* Gentlemen that traded thither; and did not only learn their Language, but that of the *Spaniards* also, with whom he traded afterwards for Slaves.

I have often seen and convers'd with this great Man, and been a Witness to many of his mighty Actions; and do assure my Reader, the most Illustrious Courts cou'd not have produc'd a braver Man, both for Greatness of Courage and Mind, a Judgment more solid, a Wit more quick, and a Conversation more sweet and diverting. He knew almost as much as if he had read much: He had heard of, and admir'd the *Romans*; he had heard of the late Civil Wars in *England*, and the deplorable Death of our great Monarch;[6] and wou'd discourse of it with all the Sense, and Abhorrence of the Injustice imaginable. He had an extream good and graceful Mien, and all the Civility of a well-bred great Man. He had nothing of Barbarity in his Nature, but in all Points address'd himself, as if his Education had been in some *European* Court.

This great and just Character of *Oroonoko* gave me an extream Curiosity to see him, especially when I knew he spoke *French* and *English*, and that I cou'd talk with him. But though I had heard so much of him, I was as greatly surpriz'd

---

4. Battlefield, after the Roman god of war.
5. Variously used in the period for Muslims or for dark-skinned peoples.

6. Charles I, tried and executed in 1649 during the civil war between Royalists and Parliamentarians.

when I saw him, as if I had heard nothing of him; so beyond all Report I found him. He came into the Room, and address'd himself to me, and some other Women, with the best Grace in the World. He was pretty tall, but of a Shape the most exact that can be fancy'd: The most famous Statuary[7] cou'd not form the Figure of a Man more admirably turn'd from Head to Foot. His Face was not of that brown, rusty Black which most of that Nation are, but a perfect Ebony, or polish'd Jett. His Eyes were the most awful that cou'd be seen, and very piercing; the White of 'em being like Snow, as were his Teeth. His Nose was rising and *Roman*, instead of *African* and flat. His Mouth, the finest shap'd that cou'd be seen; far from those great turn'd Lips, which are so natural to the rest of the *Negroes*. The whole Proportion and Air of his Face was so noble, and exactly form'd, that bating[8] his Colour there cou'd be nothing in Nature more beautiful, agreeable and handsome. There was no one Grace wanting, that bears the Standard of true Beauty: His Hair came down to his Shoulders, by the Aids of Art; which was, by pulling it out with a Quill, and keeping it comb'd; of which he took particular Care. Nor did the Perfections of his Mind come short of those of his Person; for his Discourse was admirable upon almost any Subject; and who-ever had heard him speak, wou'd have been convinc'd of their Errors, that all fine Wit is confin'd to the *White* Men, especially to those of *Christendom*; and wou'd have confess'd that *Oroonoko* was as capable even, of reigning well, and of governing as wisely, had as great a Soul, as politick[9] Maxims, and was as sensible of Power as any Prince civiliz'd in the most refin'd Schools of Humanity and Learning, or the most Illustrious Courts.

This Prince, such as I have describ'd him, whose Soul and Body were so admirably adorn'd, was (while yet he was in the Court of his Grandfather) as I said, as capable of Love, as 'twas possible for a brave and gallant Man to be; and in saying that, I have nam'd the highest Degree of Love; for sure, great Souls are most capable of that Passion.

I have already said, the old General was kill'd by the shot of an Arrow, by the Side of this Prince, in Battel; and that *Oroonoko* was made General. This old dead *Hero* had one only Daughter left of his Race; a Beauty that, to describe her truly, one need say only, she was Female to the noble Male; the beautiful *Black Venus*,[1] to our young *Mars*; as charming in her Person as he, and of delicate Vertues. I have seen an hundred *White* Men sighing after her, and making a thousand Vows at her Feet, all vain, and unsuccessful: And she was, indeed, too great for any, but a Prince of her own Nation to adore.

Oroonoko coming from the Wars, (which were now ended) after he had made his Court to his Grand-father, he thought in Honour he ought to make a Visit to *Imoinda*, the Daughter of his Foster-father, the dead General; and to make some Excuses to her, because his Preservation was the Occasion of her Father's Death; and to present her with those Slaves that had been taken in this last Battel, as the Trophies of her Father's Victories. When he came, attended by all the young Soldiers of any Merit, he was infinitely surpriz'd at the Beauty of this fair Queen of Night, whose Face and Person was so exceeding all he had ever beheld, that lovely Modesty with which she receiv'd him, that Softness in her

7. Sculptor.
8. Except for.
9. Prudent, shrewd.

1. Roman goddess of love; lover of Mars, the god of war.

Look, and Sighs, upon the melancholy Occasion of this Honour that was done by so great a Man as *Oroonoko*, and a Prince of whom she had heard such admirable things; the Awfulness[2] wherewith she receiv'd him, and the Sweetness of her Words and Behaviour while he stay'd, gain'd a perfect Conquest over his fierce Heart, and made him feel, the Victor cou'd be subdu'd. So that having made his first Compliments, and presented her an hundred and fifty Slaves in Fetters, he told her with his Eyes, that he was not insensible of her Charms; while *Imoinda*, who wish'd for nothing more than so glorious a Conquest, was pleas'd to believe, she understood that silent Language of new-born Love; and from that Moment, put on all her Additions to Beauty.

The Prince return'd to Court with quite another Humour than before; and though he did not speak much of the fair *Imoinda*, he had the pleasure to hear all his Followers speak of nothing but the Charms of that Maid; insomuch that, even in the Presence of the old King, they were extolling her, and heightning, if possible, the Beauties they had found in her: So that nothing else was talk'd of, no other Sound was heard in every Corner where there were Whisperers, but *Imoinda! Imoinda!*

'Twill be imagin'd *Oroonoko* stay'd not long before he made his second Visit; nor, considering his Quality, not much longer before he told her, he ador'd her. I have often heard him say, that he admir'd by what strange Inspiration he came to talk things so soft, and so passionate, who never knew Love, nor was us'd to the Conversation of Women; but (to use his own Words) he said, Most happily, some new, and till then unknown Power instructed his Heart and Tongue in the Language of Love, and at the same time, in favour of him, inspir'd *Imoinda* with a Sense of his Passion. She was touch'd with what he said, and return'd it all in such Answers as went to his very Heart, with a Pleasure unknown before: Nor did he use those Obligations[3] ill, that Love had done him; but turn'd all his happy Moments to the best advantage; and as he knew no Vice, his Flame aim'd at nothing but Honour, if such a distinction may be made in Love; and especially in that Country, where Men take to themselves as many as they can maintain; and where the only Crime and Sin with Woman is, to turn her off, to abandon her to Want, Shame and Misery: Such ill Morals are only practis'd in *Christian*-Countries, where they prefer the bare Name of Religion; and, without Vertue or Morality, think that's sufficient. But *Oroonoko* was none of those Professors; but as he had right Notions of Honour, so he made her such Propositions as were not only and barely such; but, contrary to the Custom of his Country, he made her Vows, she shou'd be the only woman he wou'd possess while he liv'd; that no Age or Wrinkles shou'd incline him to change, for her Soul wou'd be always fine, and always young; and he shou'd have an eternal *Idea* in his Mind of the Charms she now bore, and shou'd look into his Heart for that *Idea*, when he cou'd find it no longer in her Face.

After a thousand Assurances of his lasting Flame, and her eternal Empire[4] over him, she condescended to receive him for her Husband; or rather, receiv'd him, as the greatest Honour the Gods cou'd do her.

---

2. Awe, reverence.
3. Benefits.

4. Rule, power.

There is a certain Ceremony in these Cases to be observ'd, which I forgot to ask him how perform'd; but 'twas concluded on both sides, that, in Obedience to him, the Grand-father was to be first made aequainted with the Design; for they pay a most absolute Resignation[5] to the Monarch, especially when he is a Parent also.

On the other side, the old King, who had many Wives, and many Concubines, wanted not Court-Flatterers to insinuate in his Heart a thousand tender Thoughts for this young Beauty; and who represented her to his Fancy, as the most charming he had ever possess'd in all the long Race of his numerous Years. At this Character his old Heart, like an extinguish'd Brand, most apt to take Fire, felt new Sparks of Love, and began to kindle; and now grown to his second Childhood, long'd with Impatience to behold this gay thing, with whom, alas! he cou'd but innocently play. But how he shou'd be confirm'd she was this *Wonder*, before he us'd his Power to call her to Court (where Maidens never came, unless for the King's private Use) he was next to consider; and while he was so doing, he had Intelligence brought him, that *Imoinda* was most certainly Mistress to the Prince *Oroonoko*. This gave him some *Shagrien*[6] however, it gave him also an Opportunity, one Day, when the Prince was a-hunting, to wait on a Man of Quality, as his Slave and Attendant, who shou'd go and make a Present to *Imoinda*, as from the Prince; he shou'd then, unknown, see this fair Maid, and have an Opportunity to hear what Message she wou'd return the Prince for his Present; and from thence gather the state of her Heart, and degree of her Inclination. This was put in Execution, and the old Monarch saw, and burnt: He found her all he had heard, and wou'd not delay his Happiness, but found he shou'd have some Obstacle to overcome her Heart; for she express'd her Sense of the Present the Prince had sent her, in terms so sweet, so soft and pretty, with an Air of Love and Joy that cou'd not be dissembl'd; insomuch that 'twas past doubt whether she lov'd *Oroonoko* entirely. This gave the old King some Affliction: but he salv'd[7] it with this, that the Obedience the People pay their King, was not at all inferior to what they pay'd their Gods: And what Love wou'd not oblige *Imoinda* to do, Duty wou'd compel her to.

He was therefore no sooner got to his Apartment, but he sent the Royal Veil to *Imoinda*; that is, the Ceremony of Invitation: he sends the Lady, he has a Mind to honour with his Bed, a Veil, with which she is cover'd, and secur'd for the King's Use; and 'tis Death to disobey; besides, held a most impious Disobedience.

'Tis not to be imagin'd the Surprize and Grief that seiz'd this lovely Maid at this News and Sight. However, as Delays in these Cases are dangerous, and Pleading worse than Treason; trembling, and almost fainting, she was oblig'd to suffer her self to be cover'd, and led away.

They brought her thus to Court; and the King, who had caus'd a very rich Bath to be prepar'd, was led into it, where he sate under a Canopy, in State, to receive this long'd for Virgin; whom he having commanded shou'd be brought to him, they (after dis-robing her) led her to the Bath, and making fast the Doors, left her to descend. The King, without more Courtship, bad her throw

---

5. Deference, submission.
6. I.e., chagrin.

7. Salved: soothed or remedied a wound.

off her Mantle, and come to his Arms. But *Imoinda*, all in Tears, threw her self on the Marble, on the Brink of the Bath, and besought him to hear her. She told him, as she was a Maid, how proud of the Divine Glory she should have been of having it in her power to oblige her King: but as by the Laws, he cou'd not; and from his Royal Goodness, wou'd not take from any Man his wedded Wife: So she believ'd she shou'd be the Occasion of making him commit a great Sin, if she did not reveal her State and Condition; and tell him, she was anothers, and cou'd not be so happy to be his.

The King, enrag'd at this Delay, hastily demanded the Name of the bold Man, that had marry'd a Woman of her Degree, without his Consent. *Imoinda*, seeing his Eyes fierce, and his Hands tremble; whether with Age, or Anger, I know not; but she fancy'd the last, almost repented she had said so much, for now she fear'd the Storm wou'd fall on the Prince; she therefore said a thousand things to appease the raging of his Flame, and to prepare him to hear who it was with Calmness; but before she spoke, he imagin'd who she meant, but wou'd not seem to do so, but commanded her to lay aside her Mantle, and suffer her self to receive his Caresses; or, by his Gods, he swore, that happy Man whom she was going to name shou'd die, though it were even *Oroonoko* himself. *Therefore* (said he) *deny this Marriage, and swear thy self a Maid. That* (reply'd *Imoinda*) *by all our Powers I do; for I am not yet known to my Husband. 'Tis enough* (said the King); *'tis enough to satisfie both my Conscience, and my Heart.* And rising from his Seat, he went, and led her into the Bath; it being in vain for her to resist.

In this time the Prince, who was return'd from Hunting, went to visit his *Imoinda*, but found her gone; and not only so, but heard she had receiv'd the Royal Veil. This rais'd him to a Storm; and in his Madness, they had much ado to save him from laying violent Hands on himself. Force first prevail'd, and then Reason: They urg'd all to him, that might oppose his Rage; but nothing weigh'd so greatly with him as the King's Old Age uncapable of injuring him with *Imoinda*.[8] He wou'd give way to that Hope, because it pleas'd him most, and flatter'd best his Heart. Yet this serv'd not altogether to make him cease his different Passions, which sometimes rag'd within him, and sometimes softned into Showers. 'Twas not enough to appease him, to tell him, his Grand-father was old, and cou'd not that way injure him, while he retain'd that awful[9] Duty which the young Men are us'd there to pay to their grave Relations. He cou'd not be convinc'd he had no Cause to sigh and mourn for the Loss of a Mistress, he cou'd not with all his Strength and Courage retrieve. And he wou'd often cry, *O my Friends! were she in wall'd Cities, or confin'd from me in Fortifications of the greatest Strength; did Inchantments or Monsters detain her from me, I wou'd venture through any Hazard to free her: But here, in the Arms of a feeble old Man, my Youth, my violent Love, my Trade in Arms, and all my vast Desire of Glory, avail me nothing: Imoinda is as irrecoverably lost to me, as if she were snatch'd by the cold Arms of Death: Oh! she is never to be retrive'd. If I wou'd wait tedious Years, till Fate shou'd bow the old King to his Grave; even that wou'd not leave me Imoinda free; but still that Custom that makes it so vile a Crime for a Son to marry his Father's Wives or Mistresses, wou'd hinder my Happiness;*

8. The king's great age suggests he is impotent. 9. Reverent.

unless I wou'd either ignobly set an ill President[1] to my Successors, or abandon
my Country, and fly with her to some unknown World, who never heard our
Story.

But it was objected to him, that his Case was not the same; for *Imoinda*
being his lawful Wife, by solemn Contract, 'twas he was the injur'd Man, and
might, if he so pleas'd, take *Imoinda* back, the Breach of the Law being on his
Grand-father's side; and that if he cou'd circumvent him, and redeem her from
the *Otan*,[2] which is the Palace of the King's Women, a sort of *Seraglio*, it was
both just and lawful for him so to do.

This Reasoning had some force upon him, and he shou'd have been entirely
comforted, but for the Thought that she was possess'd by his Grand-father.
However, he lov'd so well, that he was resolv'd to believe what most favour'd
his Hope; and to endeavour to learn from *Imoinda's* own Mouth, what only she
cou'd satisfie him in; whether she was robb'd of that Blessing, which was only
due to his Faith and Love. But as it was very hard to get a Sight of the Women,
for no Men ever enter'd into the *Otan*, but when the King went to entertain
himself with some one of his Wives, or Mistresses; and 'twas Death at any
other time, for any other to go in; so he knew not how to contrive to get a Sight
of her.

While *Oroonoko* felt all the Agonies of Love, and suffer'd under a Torment
the most painful in the World, the old King was not exempted from his share
of Affliction. He was troubl'd for having been forc'd by an irresistable Passion,
to rob his Son[3] of a Treasure, he knew, cou'd not but be extreamly dear to him,
since she was the most beautiful that ever had been seen; and had besides, all
the Sweetness and Innocence of Youth and Modesty, with a Charm of Wit
surpassing all. He found that, however she was forc'd to expose her lovely Person to his wither'd Arms, she cou'd only sigh and weep there, and think of
Oroonoko; and oftentimes cou'd not forbear speaking of him, though her Life
were, by Custom, forfeited by owning her Passion. But she spoke not of a
Lover only, but of a Prince dear to him, to whom she spoke; and of the Praises
of a Man, who, till now, fill'd the old Man's Soul with Joy at every Recital of his
Bravery, or even his Name. And 'twas this Dotage on our young *Hero*, that gave
Imoinda a thousand Privileges to speak of him, without offending; and this
Condescention in the old King, that made her take the Satisfaction of speaking
of him so very often.

Besides, he many times enquir'd how the Prince bore himself; and those of
whom he ask'd, being entirely Slaves to the Merits and Vertues of the Prince,
still answer'd what they thought conduc'd best to his Service; which was, to
make the old King fancy that the Prince had no more Interest in *Imoinda*, and
had resign'd her willingly to the Pleasure of the King; that he diverted himself
with his Mathematicians, his Fortifications, his Officers, and his Hunting.

This pleas'd the old Lover, who fail'd not to report these things again to
Imoinda, that she might, by the Example of her young Lover, withdraw her
Heart, and rest better contented in his Arms. But however she was forc'd to
receive this unwelcome News, in all Appearance, with Unconcern, and Con-

---

1. Precedent, example.
2. *Odan* is the Fante word for house or apartment; *oda*, in Turkish, is a room in a harem or

seraglio.
3. I.e., grandson.

tent, her Heart was bursting within, and she was only happy when she cou'd get alone, to vent her Griefs and Moans with Sighs and Tears.

What Reports of the Prince's Conduct were made to the King, he thought good to justifie as far as possibly he cou'd by his Actions; and when he appear'd in the Presence of the King, he shew'd a Face not at all betraying his Heart: So that in a little time the old Man, being entirely convinc'd that he was no longer a Lover of *Imoinda*, he carry'd him with him, in his Train, to the *Otan*, often to banquet with his Mistress. But as soon as he enter'd, one Day, into the Apartment of *Imoinda*, with the King, at the first Glance from her Eyes, notwithstanding all his determin'd Resolution, he was ready to sink in the place where he stood; and had certainly done so, but for the Support of *Aboan*, a young Man, who was next to him; which, with his Change of Countenance, had betray'd him, had the King chanc'd to look that way. And I have observ'd, 'tis a very great Error in those, who laugh when one says, A Negro *can change Colour*; for I have seen 'em as frequently blush, and look pale, and that as visibly as ever I saw in the most beautiful *White*. And 'tis certain that both these Changes were evident, this Day, in both these Lovers. And *Imoinda*, who saw with some Joy the Change in the Prince's Face, and found it in her own, strove to divert the King from beholding either, by a forc'd Caress, with which she met him; which was a new Wound in the Heart of the poor dying Prince. But as soon as the King was busy'd in looking on some fine thing of *Imoinda*'s making, she had time to tell the Prince with her angry, but Love-darting Eyes, that she resented his Coldness, and bemoan'd her own miserable Captivity. Nor were his Eyes silent, but answer'd hers again, as much as Eyes cou'd do, instructed by the most tender, and most passionate Heart that ever lov'd: And they spoke so well, and so effectually, as *Imoinda* no longer doubted, but she was the only Delight, and the Darling of that Soul she found pleading in 'em its Right of Love, which none was more willing to resign than she. And 'twas this powerful Language alone that in an Instant convey'd all the Thoughts of their Souls to each other; that they both found, there wanted[4] but Opportunity to make them both entirely happy. But when he saw another Door open'd by *Onahal*, a former old Wife of the King's, who now had Charge of *Imoinda*; and saw the Prospect of a Bed of State made ready, with Sweets and Flowers for the Dalliance of the King; who immediately led the trembling Victim from his Sight, into that prepar'd Repose; What Rage! what wild Frenzies seiz'd his Heart! which forcing to keep within Bounds, and to suffer without Noise, it became the more insupportable, and rent[5] his Soul with ten thousand Pains. He was forc'd to retire, to vent his Groans; where he fell down on a Carpet, and lay struggling a long time, and only breathing now and then,—O *Imoinda!* When *Onahal* had finish'd her necessary Affair within, shutting the Door, she came forth to wait, till the King call'd; and hearing some one sighing in the other Room, she pass'd on, and found the Prince in that deplorable Condition, which she thought needed her Aid: She gave him Cordials, but all in vain; till finding the nature of his Disease, by his Sighs, and naming *Imoinda*. She told him, he had not so much Cause as he imagin'd, to afflict himself; for if he knew the King so well as she did, he wou'd not lose a Moment in Jealousie, and that she was confident that *Imoinda* bore, at this Minute, part in his Affliction.

4. So that; wanted: lacked.   5. Tore apart.

Aboan was of the same Opinion; and both together, perswaded him to re-assume his Courage; and all sitting down on the Carpet, the Prince said so many obliging things to *Onahal*, that he half perswaded her to be of his Party. And she promis'd him, she wou'd thus far comply with his just Desires, that she wou'd let *Imoinda* know how faithful he was, what he suffer'd, and what he said.

This Discourse lasted till the King call'd, which gave *Oroonoko* a certain Satisfaction; and with the Hope *Onahal* had made him conceive, he assum'd a Look as gay as 'twas possible a Man in his Circumstances cou'd do; and presently after, he was call'd in with the rest who waited without. The King commanded Musick to be brought, and several of his young Wives and Mistresses came all together by his Command, to dance before him; where *Imoinda* perform'd her Part with an Air and Grace so passing all the rest, as her Beauty was above 'em; and receiv'd the Present, ordain'd as a Prize. The Prince was every Moment more charm'd with the new Beauties and Graces he beheld in this fair One: And while he gaz'd, and she danc'd, *Onahal* was retir'd to a Window with *Aboan*.

This *Onahal*, as I said, was one of the Cast-Mistresses of the old King; and 'twas these (now past their Beauty) that were made Guardians, or Governants[6] to the new, and the young Ones; and whose Business it was, to teach them all those wanton Arts of Love, with which they prevail'd and charm'd heretofore in their Turn; and who now treated the triumphing happy Ones with all the Severity, as to Liberty and Freedom, that was possible, in revenge of those Honours they rob them of; envying them those Satisfactions, those Gallantries and Presents, that were once made to themselves, while Youth and Beauty lasted, and which they now saw pass regardless by, and were pay'd only to the Bloomings.[7] And certainly, nothing is more afflicting to a decay'd Beauty, than to behold in it self declining Charms, that were once ador'd; and to find those Caresses paid to new Beauties, to which once she laid a Claim; to hear 'em whisper as she passes by, *That once was a delicate[8] Woman*. These abandon'd Ladies therefore endeavour to revenge all the Despights,[9] and Decays of Time, on these flourishing happy Ones. And 'twas this Severity, that gave *Oroonoko* a thousand Fears he shou'd never prevail with *Onahal*, to see *Imoinda*. But, as I said, she was now retir'd to a Window with *Aboan*.

This young Man was not only one of the best Quality, but a Man extreamly well made, and beautiful; and coming often to attend the King to the *Otan*, he had subdu'd the heart of the antiquated *Onahal*, which had not forgot how pleasant it was to be in Love: And though she had some decays in her Face, she had none in her Sense and Wit; she was there agreeable still, even to *Aboan*'s Youth, so that he took pleasure in entertaining her with Discourses of Love. He knew also, that to make his Court to these She-Favourites, was the way to be great; these being the Persons that do all Affairs and Business at Court. He had also observ'd that she had given him Glances more tender and inviting, than she had done to others of his Quality: And now, when he saw that her Favour cou'd so absolutely oblige the Prince, he fail'd not to sigh in her Ear,

6. Female caretakers or instructors. "Cast": cast-off, with a pun on chaste.
7. I.e., the younger women.
8. Delightful, lovely.
9. Insults.

and to look with Eyes all soft upon her, and give her Hope that she had made some Impressions on his Heart. He found her pleas'd at this, and making a thousand Advances to him; but the Ceremony ending, and the King departing, broke up the Company for that Day, and his Conversation.

Aboan fail'd not that Night to tell the Prince of his Success, and how advantageous the Service of *Onahal* might be to his Amour[1] with *Imoinda*. The Prince was overjoy'd with this good News, and besought him, if it were possible, to caress her so, as to engage her entirely; which he cou'd not fail to do, if he comply'd with her Desires: *For then* (said the Prince) *her Life lying at your Mercy, she must grant you the Request you make in my Behalf. Aboan* understood him; and assur'd him, he would make Love so effectually[2] that he wou'd defie the most expert Mistress of the Art, to find out whether he dissembl'd it, or had it really. And 'twas with Impatience they waited the next Opportunity of going to the *Otan*.

The Wars came on, the Time of taking the Field approach'd, and 'twas impossible for the Prince to delay his going at the Head of his Army, to encounter the Enemy: So that every Day seem'd a tedious Year, till he saw his *Imoinda*; for he believ'd he cou'd not live, if he were forc'd away without being so happy. 'Twas with Impatience therefore, that he expected the next Visit the King wou'd make; and, according to his Wish, it was not long.

The Parley of the Eyes of these two Lovers had not pass'd so secretly, but an old jealous Lover cou'd spy it; or rather, he wanted not Flatterers, who told him, they observ'd it: So that the Prince was hasten'd to the Camp, and this was the last Visit he found he shou'd make to the *Otan*; he therefore urg'd *Aboan* to make the best of this last Effort, and to explain himself so to *Onahal*, that she, deferring her Enjoyment of her young Lover no longer, might make way for the Prince to speak to *Imoinda*.

The whole Affair being agreed on between the Prince and *Aboan*, they attended the King, as the Custom was, to the *Otan*; where, while the whole Company was taken up in beholding the Dancing, and antick Postures the Women Royal made, to divert the King, *Onahal* singl'd out *Aboan*, whom she found most pliable to her Wish. When she had him where she believ'd she cou'd not be heard, she sigh'd to him, and softly cry'd, *Ah,* Aboan! *When will you be sensible of my Passion? I confess it with my Mouth, because I wou'd not give my Eyes the Lye; and you have but too much already perceiv'd they have confess'd my Flame: Nor wou'd I have you believe, that because I am the abandon'd Mistress of a King, I esteem my self altogether divested of Charms. No,* Aboan; *I have still a Rest of Beauty enough engaging, and have learn'd to please too well, not to be desirable. I can have Lovers still, but will have none but* Aboan. *Madam* (reply'd the half-feigning Youth) *you have already, by my Eyes, found, you can still conquer; and I believe 'tis in pity of me, you condescend to this kind Confession. But, Madam, Words are us'd to be so small a part of our Country-Courtship, that 'tis rare one can get so happy an Opportunity as to tell one's Heart; and those few Minutes we have are forc'd to be snatch'd for more certain Proofs of Love, than speaking and sighing; and such I languish for.*

He spoke this with such a Tone, that she hop'd it true, and cou'd not forbear believing it; and being wholly transported with Joy, for having subdu'd the finest

---

1. Love (French).   2. Diligently, thoroughly.

of all the King's Subjects to her Desires, she took from her Ears two large Pearls, and commanded him to wear 'em in his. He wou'd have refus'd 'em, *crying, Madam, these are not the Proofs of your Love that I expect; 'tis Opportunity, 'tis a Lone-hour only, that can make me happy.* But forcing the Pearls into his Hand, she whisper'd softly to him, *Oh! Do not fear a Woman's Invention, when Love sets her a-thinking.* And pressing his Hand, she cry'd, *This Night you shall be happy. Come to the Gate of the Orange-Groves, behind the* Otan; *and I will be ready, about Mid-night, to receive you.* 'Twas thus agreed, and she left him, that no notice might be taken of their speaking together.

The Ladies were still dancing, and the King, laid on a Carpet, with a great deal of pleasure, was beholding them, especially *Imoinda*; who that Day appear'd more lovely than ever, being enliven'd with the good Tidings *Onahal* had brought her of the constant Passion the Prince had for her. The Prince was laid on another Carpet, at the other end of the Room, with his Eyes fix'd on the Object of his Soul; and as she turn'd, or mov'd, so did they; and she alone gave his Eyes and Soul their Motions: Nor did *Imoinda* employ her Eyes to any other Use, than in beholding with infinite Pleasure the Joy she produc'd in those of the Prince. But while she was more regarding him, than the Steps she took, she chanc'd to fall; and so near him, as that leaping with extream force from the Carpet, he caught her in his Arms as she fell; and 'twas visible to the whole Presence, the Joy wherewith he receiv'd her: He clasp'd her close to his Bosom, and quite forgot that Reverence that was due to the Mistress of a King, and that Punishment that is the Reward of a Boldness of this nature; and had not the Presence of Mind of *Imoinda* (fonder of his Safety, than her own) befriended him, in making her spring from his Arms, and fall into her Dance again, he had, at that Instant, met his Death; for the old King, jealous to the last degree, rose up in Rage, broke all the Diversion, and led *Imoinda* to her Apartment, and sent out Word to the Prince, to go immediately to the Camp; and that if he were found another Night in Court, he shou'd suffer the Death ordain'd for disobedient Offenders.

You may imagine how welcome this News was to *Oroonoko*, whose unseasonable Transport and Caress of *Imoinda* was blam'd by all Men that lov'd him; and now he perceiv'd his Fault, yet cry'd, *That for such another Moment, he wou'd be content to die.*

All the *Otan* was in disorder about this Accident; and *Onahal* was particularly concern'd, because on the Prince's Stay depended her Happiness; for she cou'd no longer expect that of *Aboan.* So that, e'er the departed, they contriv'd it so, that the Prince and he shou'd come both that Night to the Grove of the *Otan*, which was all of Oranges and Citrons; and that there they shou'd wait her Orders.

They parted thus, with Grief enough, till Night; leaving the King in possession of the lovely Maid. But nothing cou'd appease the Jealousie of the old Lover: He wou'd not be impos'd on, but wou'd have it, that *Imoinda* made a false Step on purpose to fall into *Oroonoko*'s Bosom and that all things look'd like a Design on both sides, and 'twas in vain she protested her Innocence: He was old and obstinate, and left her more than half assur'd that his Fear was true.

The King going to his Apartment, sent to know where the Prince was, and if he intended to obey his Command. The Messenger return'd, and told him, he found the Prince pensive, and altogether unpreparing for the Campaign; that he lay negligently on the Ground, and answer'd very little. This confirm'd the Jealousie of the King, and he commanded that they shou'd very narrowly and privately watch his Motions; and that he shou'd not stir from his Apartment, but one Spy or other shou'd be employ'd to watch him: So that the Hour approaching, wherein he was to go to the Citron-Grove; and taking only *Aboan* along with him, he leaves his Apartment, and was watch'd to the very Gate of the *Otan*; where he was seen to enter, and where they left him, to carry back the Tidings to the King.

Oroonoko and *Aboan* were no sooner enter'd, but *Onahal* led the Prince to the Apartment of *Imoinda*; who, not knowing any thing of her Happiness, was laid in Bed. But *Onahal* only left him in her Chamber, to make the best of his Opportunity, and took her dear *Aboan* to her own; where he shew'd the heighth of Complaisance for his Prince, when, to give him an Opportunity, he suffer'd himself to be caress'd in Bed by *Onahal*.

The Prince softly waken'd *Imoinda*, who was not a little surpriz'd with Joy to find him there; and yet she trembl'd with a thousand Fears. I believe, he omitted saying nothing to this young Maid, that might perswade her to suffer him to seize his own, and take the Rights of Love; and I believe she was not long resisting those Arms, where she so long'd to be; and having Opportunity, Night and Silence, Youth, Love and Desire, he soon prevail'd; and ravish'd in a Moment, what his old Grand-father had been endeavouring for so many Months.

'Tis not to be imagin'd the Satisfaction of these two young Lovers; nor the Vows she made him, that she remain'd a spotless Maid, till that Night; and that what she did with his Grand-father, had robb'd him of no part of her Virgin-Honour, the Gods, in Mercy and Justice, having reserv'd that for her plighted Lord, to whom of Right it belong'd. And 'tis impossible to express the Transports he suffer'd, while he listen'd to a Discourse so charming, from her lov'd Lips; and clasp'd that Body in his Arms, for whom he had so long languish'd; and nothing now afflicted him, but his suddain Departure from her; for he told her the Necessity, and his Commands; but shou'd depart satisfy'd in this, That since the old King had hitherto not been able to deprive him of those Enjoyments which only belong'd to him, he believ'd for the future he wou'd be less able to injure him; so that, abating the Scandal of the Veil, which was no otherwise so, than that she was Wife to another: He believ'd her safe, even in the Arms of the King, and innocent; yet wou'd he have ventur'd at the Conquest of the World, and have given it all, to have had her avoided that Honour of receiving the *Royal Veil*. 'Twas thus, between a thousand Caresses, that both bemoan'd the hard Fate of Youth and Beauty, so liable to that cruel Promotion: 'Twas a Glory that cou'd well have been spar'd here, though desir'd, and aim'd at by all the young Females of that Kingdom.

But while they were thus fondly employ'd, forgetting how Time ran on, and that the Dawn must conduct him far away from his only Happiness, they heard a great Noise in the *Otan*, and unusual Voices of Men; at which the Prince, starting from the Arms of the frighted *Imoinda*, ran to a little Battle-Ax he us'd to wear by his Side; and having not so much leisure, as to put on his Habit, he oppos'd himself against some who were already opening the Door; which they did with so much Violence, that *Oroonoko* was not able to defend it; but was forc'd to cry out with a commanding Voice, *Whoever ye are that have the Boldness to attempt to approach this Apartment thus rudely, know, that I, the Prince*

Oroonoko, *will revenge it with the certain Death of him that first enters: There-*
fore stand back, and know, this place is sacred to Love, and me this Night; to
Morrow 'tis the King's.

This he spoke with a Voice so resolv'd and assur'd, that they soon retir'd from
the Door, but cry'd, *'Tis by the King's Command we are come; and being satisfy'd*
by thy Voice, O Prince, as much as if we had enter'd, we can report to the King
the Truth of all his Fears, and leave thee to provide for thy own Safety, as thou art
advis'd by thy Friends.

At these Words they departed, and left the Prince to take a short and sad
Leave of his *Imoinda*; who trusting in the strength of her Charms, believ'd she
shou'd appease the Fury of a jealous King, by saying, She was surpriz'd, and
that it was by force of Arms he got into her Apartment. All her Concern now
was for his Life, and therefore she hasten'd him to the Camp; and with much
a-do, prevail'd on him to go: Nor was it she alone that prevail'd, *Aboan* and
Onahal both pleaded, and both assur'd him of a Lye that shou'd be well enough
contriv'd to secure *Imoinda*. So that, at last, with a Heart sad as Death, dying
Eyes, and sighing Soul, *Oroonoko* departed and took his way to the Camp.

It was not long after the King in Person came to the *Otan*; where beholding
Imoinda with Rage in his Eyes, he upbraided her Wickedness and Perfidy, and
threatning her Royal Lover, she fell on her Face at his Feet, bedewing the
Floor with her Tears, and imploring his Pardon for a Fault which she had not
with her Will committed; as *Onahal*, who was also prostrate with her, cou'd
testifie: That, unknown to her, he had broke into her Apartment, and ravish'd
her. She spoke this much against her Conscience; but to save her own Life,
'twas absolutely necessary she shou'd feign this Falsity. She knew it cou'd not
injure the Prince, he being fled to an Army that wou'd stand by him, against
any Injuries that shou'd assault him. However, this last Thought of *Imoinda's*
being ravish'd, chang'd the Measures of his Revenge; and whereas before he
design'd to be himself her Executioner, he now resolv'd she shou'd not die. But
as it is the greatest Crime in nature amongst 'em to touch a Woman, after having been possess'd by a Son, a Father, or a Brother; so now he look'd on
Imoinda as a polluted thing, wholly unfit for his Embrace; nor wou'd he resign
her to his Grand-son, because she had receiv'd the *Royal Veil*. He therefore
removes her from the *Otan*, with *Onahal*; whom he put into safe Hands, with
Order they should be both sold off, as Slaves, to another Country, either *Chris-*
tian, or *Heathen*; 'twas no matter where.

This cruel Sentence, worse than Death, they implor'd, might be revers'd; but
their Prayers were vain, and it was put in Execution accordingly, and that with
so much Secrecy, that none, either without, or within the *Otan*, knew any
thing of their Absence, or their Destiny.

The old King, nevertheless, executed this with a great deal of Reluctancy;
but he believ'd he had made a very great Conquest over himself, when he had
once resolv'd, and had perform'd what he resolv'd. He believ'd now, that his
Love had been unjust; and that he cou'd not expect the Gods, or Captain of the
Clouds (as they call the unknown Power) shou'd suffer a better Consequence
from so ill a Cause. He now begins to hold *Oroonoko* excus'd; and to say, he
had Reason for what he did: And now every Body cou'd assure the King, how
passionately *Imoinda* was belov'd by the Prince; even those confess'd it now,
who said the contrary before his Flame was abated. So that the King being old,

and not able to defend himself in War, and having no Sons of all his Race[3] remaining alive, but only this, to maintain him on his Throne; and looking on this as a Man disoblig'd, first by the Rape of his Mistress, or rather, Wife; and now by depriving of him wholly of her, he fear'd, might make him desperate, and do some cruel thing, either to himself, or his old Grand-father, the Offender; he began to repent him extreamly of the Contempt he had, in his Rage, put on *Imoinda*. Besides, he consider'd he ought in Honour to have kill'd her, for this Offence, if it had been one: He ought to have had so much Value and Consideration for a Maid of her Quality, as to have nobly put her to death; and not to have sold her like a common Slave, the greatest Revenge, and the most disgraceful of any; and to which they a thousand times prefer Death, and implore it; as *Imoinda* did, but cou'd not obtain that Honour. Seeing therefore it was certain that *Oroonoko* wou'd highly resent this Affront, he thought good to make some Excuse for his Rashness to him; and to that End he sent a Messenger to the Camp, with Orders to treat with him about the Matter, to gain his Pardon, and to endeavour to mitigate his Grief; but that by no means he shou'd tell him, she was sold, but secretly put to death; for he knew he shou'd never obtain his Pardon for the other.

When the Messenger came, he found the Prince upon the point of Engaging with the Enemy; but as soon as he heard of the Arrival of the Messenger, he commanded him to his Tent, where he embrac'd him, and receiv'd him with Joy; which was soon abated, by the downcast Looks of the Messenger, who was instantly demanded the Cause by *Oroonoko*, who, impatient of Delay, ask'd a thousand Questions in a Breath; and all concerning *Imoinda*: But there needed little Return, for he cou'd almost answer himself of all he demanded, from his Sighs and Eyes. At last, the Messenger casting himself at the Prince's feet, and kissing them, with all the Submission of a Man that had something to implore which he dreaded to utter, he besought him to hear with Calmness what he had to deliver to him, and to call up all his noble and Heroick Courage, to encounter with his Words, and defend himself against the ungrateful[4] things he must relate. *Oroonoko* reply'd, with a deep Sigh, and a languishing voice,—*I am arm'd against their worst Efforts*——; *for I know they will tell me,* Imoinda *is no more*——; *and after that, you may spare the rest.* Then, commanding him to rise, he laid himself on a Carpet, under a rich Pavillion, and remain'd a good while silent, and was hardly heard to sigh. When he was come a little to himself, the Messenger ask'd him leave to deliver that part of his Embassy, which the Prince had not yet divin'd: And the Prince cry'd, *I permit thee*——. Then he told him the Affliction the old King was in, for the Rashness he had committed in his Cruelty to *Imoinda*; and how he deign'd to ask Pardon for his Offence, and to implore the Prince wou'd not suffer that Loss to touch his Heart too sensibly, which now all the Gods cou'd not restore him, but might recompence him in Glory, which he begg'd he wou'd pursue; and that Death, that common Revenger of all Injuries, wou'd soon even the Account between him, and a feeble old Man.

Oroonoko bad him return his Duty to his Lord and Master; and to assure him, there was no Account of Revenge to be adjusted between them; if there

---

3. Kin.   4. Offensive.

were, 'twas he was the Aggressor, and that Death wou'd be just, and, maugre[5] his Age, wou'd see him righted; and he was contented to leave his Share of Glory to Youths more fortunate, and worthy of that Favour from the Gods. That henceforth he wou'd never lift a Weapon, or draw a Bow; but abandon the small Remains of his Life to Sighs and Tears, and the continual Thoughts of what his Lord and Grand-father had thought good to send out of the World, with all that Youth, that Innocence, and Beauty.

After having spoken this, whatever his greatest Officers, and Men of the best Rank cou'd do, they cou'd not raise him from the Carpet, or perswade him to Action, and Resolutions of Life; but commanding all to retire, he shut himself into his Pavillion all that Day, while the Enemy was ready to engage; and wondring at the Delay, the whole Body of the chief of the Army then address'd themselves to him, and to whom they had much a-do to get Admittance. They fell on their Faces at the Foot of his Carpet; where they lay, and besought him with earnest Prayers and Tears, to lead 'em forth to Battel, and not let the Enemy take Advantages of them; and implor'd him to have regard to his Glory, and to the World, that depended on his Courage and Conduct. But he made no other Reply to all their Supplications but this. That he had now no more Business for Glory; and for the World, it was a Trifle not worth his Care. *Go,* (continu'd he, sighing) *and divide it amongst you; and reap with Joy what you so vainly prize, and leave me to my more welcome Destiny.*

They then demanded what they shou'd do, and whom he wou'd constitute in his Room[6] that the Confusion of ambitious Youth and Power might not ruin their Order, and make them a Prey to the Enemy. He reply'd, He wou'd not give himself the Trouble—; but wish'd 'em to chuse the bravest Man amongst 'em, let his Quality or Birth be what it wou'd: *For, O my Friends!* (said he) *it is not Titles make Men brave, or good; or Birth that bestows Courage and Generosity, or makes the Owner happy. Believe this, when you behold* Oroonoko, *the most wretched, and abandon'd by Fortune, of all the Creation of the Gods.* So turning himself about, he wou'd make no more Reply to all they cou'd urge or implore.

The Army beholding their Officers return unsuccessful, with sad Faces, and ominous Looks, that presag'd no good Luck, suffer'd a thousand Fears to take Possession of their Hearts, and the Enemy to come even upon 'em, before they wou'd provide for their Safety, by any Defence; and though they were assur'd by some, who had a mind to animate 'em, that they shou'd be immediately headed by the Prince, and that in the mean time *Aboan* had Orders to command as General; yet they were so dismay'd for want of that great Example of Bravery, that they cou'd make but a very feeble Resistance; and at last, downright, fled before the Enemy, who pursu'd 'em to the very Tents, killing 'em: Nor cou'd all *Aboan's* Courage, which that Day gain'd him immortal Glory, shame 'em into a Manly Defence of themselves. The Guards that were left behind, about the Prince's Tent, seeing the Soldiers flee before the Enemy, and scatter themselves all over the Plain, in great Disorder, made such Outcries as rouz'd the Prince from his amorous Slumber, in which he had remain'd bury'd for two Days, without permitting any Sustenance to approach him: But, in spite of all his Resolutions, he had not the Constancy of Grief to that Degree, as to make him insensible of the Danger of his Army; and in that

---

5. Despite. Oroonoko hopes to die first.   **6.** I.e., in his place.

Instant he leap'd from his Couch, and cry'd,—*Come, if we must die, let us meet Death the noblest Way; and 'twill be more like* Oroonoko *to encounter him at an Army's Head, opposing the Torrent of a conquering Foe, than lazily, on a Couch, to wait his lingering Pleasure, and die every Moment by a thousand wrecking[7] Thoughts; or be tamely taken by an Enemy, and led a whining, Love-sick Slave, to adorn the Triumphs of* Jamoan, *that young Victor, who already is enter'd beyond the Limits I had prescrib'd him.*

While he was speaking, he suffer'd his People to dress him for the Field; and sallying out of his Pavillion, with more Life and Vigour in his Countenance than ever he shew'd, he appear'd like some Divine Power descended to save his Country from Destruction; and his People had purposely put on him all things that might make him shine with most Splendor, to strike a reverend Awe into the Beholders. He flew into the thickest of those that were pursuing his Men; and being animated with Despair, he fought as if he came on purpose to die, and did such things as will not be believ'd that Humane Strength cou'd perform; and such as soon inspir'd all the rest with new Courage, and new Order: And now it was, that they began to fight indeed; and so, as if they wou'd not be out-done, even by their ador'd *Hero*; who turning the Tide of the Victory, changing absolutely the Fate of the Day, gain'd an entire Conquest; and *Oroonoko* having the good Fortune to single out *Jamoan*, he took him Prisoner with his own Hand, having wounded him almost to death.

This *Jamoan* afterwards became very dear to him, being a Man very gallant, and of excellent Graces, and fine Parts; so that he never put him amongst the Rank of Captives, as they us'd to do, without distinction, for the common Sale, or Market; but kept him in his own Court, where he retain'd nothing of the Prisoner, but the Name, and return'd no more into his own Country, so great an Affection he took for *Oroonoko*; and by a thousand Tales and Adventures of Love and Gallantry, flatter'd[8] his Disease of Melancholy and Languishment; which I have often heard him say, had certainly kill'd him, but for the Conversation of this Prince and *Aboan*, and the *French* Governor[9] he had from his Childhood, of whom I have spoken before, and who was a Man of admirable Wit, great Ingenuity and Learning; all which he had infus'd into his young Pupil. This *French*-Man was banish'd out of his own Country, for some Heretical Notions he held; and though he was a Man of very little Religion, he had admirable Morals, and a brave Soul.

After the total Defeat of *Jamoan's* Army, which all fled, or were left dead upon the Place, they spent some time in the Camp; *Oroonoko* chusing rather to remain a while there in his Tents, than enter into a Place, or live in a Court where he had so lately suffer'd so great a Loss. The Officers therefore, who saw and knew his Cause of Discontent, invented all sorts of Diversions and Sports, to entertain their Prince: So that what with those Amuzements abroad, and others at home, that is, within their Tents, with the Perswasions, Arguments and Care of his Friends and Servants that he more peculiarly priz'd, he wore off in time a great part of that *Shagrien*, and Torture of Despair, which the first Efforts of *Imoinda's* Death had given him: Insomuch as having receiv'd a thousand kind Embassies from the King, and Invitations to return to Court, he

---

7. Racking.
8. Soothed.

9. Tutor.

obey'd, though with no little Reluctancy; and when he did so, there was a visible Change in him, and for a long time he was much more melancholy than before. But Time lessens all Extreams, and reduces 'em to *Mediums* and Unconcern; but no Motives or Beauties, though all endeavour'd it, cou'd engage him in any sort of Amour, though he had all the Invitations to it, both from his own Youth, and others Ambitions and Designs.

Oroonoko was no sooner return'd from this last Conquest, and receiv'd at Court with all the Joy and Magnificence that cou'd be express'd to a young Victor, who was not only return'd triumphant, but belov'd like a Deity, when there arriv'd in the Port an *English* Ship.

This Person[1] had often before been in these Countries, and was very well known to *Oroonoko*, with whom he had traffick'd for Slaves, and had us'd to do the same with his Predecessors.

This Commander was a Man of a finer sort of Address, and Conversation, better bred, and more engaging, than most of that sort of Men are; so that he seem'd rather never to have been bred out of a Court, than almost all his Life at Sea. This Captain therefore was always better receiv'd at Court, than most of the Traders to those Countries were; and especially by *Oroonoko*, who was more civiliz'd, according to the *European* Mode, than any other had been, and took more Delight in the *White* Nations; and, above all, Men of Parts and Wit. To this Captain he sold abundance of his Slaves; and for the Favour and Esteem he had for him, made him many Presents, and oblig'd him to stay at Court as long as possibly he cou'd. Which the Captain seem'd to take as a very great Honour done him, entertaining the Prince every Day with Globes and Maps, and Mathematical Discourses and Instruments; eating, drinking, hunting and living with him with so much Familiarity, that it was not to be doubted, but he had gain'd very greatly upon the Heart of this gallant young Man. And the Captain, in Return of all these mighty Favours, besought the Prince to honour his Vessel with his Presence, some Day or other, to Dinner, before he shou'd set Sail; which he condescended to accept, and appointed his Day. The Captain, on his part, fail'd not to have all things in a Readiness, in the most magnificent Order he cou'd possibly: And the Day being come, the Captain, in his Boat, richly adorn'd with Carpets and Velvet-Cushions, row'd to the shore to receive the Prince; with another Long-Boat, where was plac'd all his Musick and Trumpets, with which *Oroonoko* was extreamly delighted; who met him on the shore, attended by his *French* Governor, *Jamoan*, *Aboan*, and about an hundred of the noblest of the Youths of the Court: And after they had first carry'd the Prince on Board, the Boats fetch'd the rest off; where they found a very splendid Treat, with all sorts of fine Wines; and were as well entertain'd, as 'twas possible in such a place to be.

The Prince having drunk hard of Punch, and several Sorts of Wine, as did all the rest (for great Care was taken, they shou'd want nothing of that part of the Entertainment) was very merry, and in great Admiration of the Ship, for he had never been in one before; so that he was curious of beholding every place, where he decently might descend. The rest, no less curious, who were not quite overcome with Drinking, rambl'd at their pleasure *Fore* and *Aft*, as their Fancies guided 'em: So that the Captain, who had well laid his Design before,

1. The captain of the ship.

gave the Word, and seiz'd on all his Guests; they clapping great Irons suddenly on the Prince, when he was leap'd down in the Hold, to view that part of the Vessel; and locking him fast down, secur'd him. The same Treachery was us'd to all the rest; and all in one Instant, in several places of the Ship, were lash'd fast in Irons, and betray'd to Slavery. That great Design over, they set all Hands to work to hoise[2] Sail; and with as treacherous and fair a Wind, they made from the Shore with this innocent and glorious Prize, who thought of nothing less than such an Entertainment.

Some have commended this Act, as brave, in the Captain; but I will spare my sense of it, and leave it to my Reader, to judge as he pleases.

It may be easily guess'd, in what manner the Prince resented this Indignity, who may be best resembl'd to a Lion taken in a Toil[3] so he rag'd, so he struggl'd for Liberty, but all in vain; and they had so wisely manag'd his Fetters, that he cou'd not use a Hand in his Defence, to quit himself of a Life that wou'd by no Means endure Slavery; nor cou'd he move from the Place, where he was ty'd, to any solid part of the Ship, against which he might have beat his Head, and have finish'd his Disgrace that way: So that being depriv'd of all other means, he resolved to perish for want of Food: And pleased at last with that Thought, and toil'd and tired by Rage and Indignation, he laid himself down, and sullenly resolved upon dying, and refused all things that were brought him.

This did not a little vex the Captain, and the more so, because, he found almost all of 'em of the same Humour; so that the loss of so many brave Slaves, so tall and goodly to behold, wou'd have been very considerable: He therefore order'd one to go from him (for he wou'd not be seen himself) to *Oroonoko*, and to assure him he was afflicted for having rashly done so unhospitable a Deed, and which cou'd not be now remedied, since they were far from shore; but since he resented it in so high a nature, he assur'd him he wou'd revoke his Resolution, and set both him and his Friends a-shore on the next Land they shou'd touch at; and of this the Messenger gave him his Oath, provid'd he wou'd resolve to live: And *Oroonoko*, whose Honour was such as he never had violated a Word in his Life himself, much less a solemn Asseveration, believ'd in an instant what this Man said, but reply'd, He expected for a Confirmation of this, to have his shameful Fetters dismiss'd. This Demand was carried to the *Captain*, who return'd him answer, That the Offence had been so great which he had put upon the Prince, that he durst not trust him with Liberty while he remained in the Ship, for fear lest by a Valour natural to him, and a Revenge that would animate that Valour, he might commit some Outrage fatal to himself and the *King* his Master, to whom his Vessel did belong. To this *Oroonoko* replied, he would engage his Honour to behave himself in all friendly Order and Manner, and obey the Command of the *Captain*, as he was Lord of the *King*'s Vessel, and General of those Men under his Command.

This was deliver'd to the still doubting *Captain*, who could not resolve to trust a *Heathen*, he said, upon his Parole,[4] a Man that had no Sense or notion of the God that he Worshipp'd. *Oroonoko* then replied. He was very sorry to hear that the *Captain* pretended to the Knowledge and Worship of any *Gods*,

---

2. Hoist. Early accounts report the abduction of Africans who visited ships. Those of high rank were ransomed or returned to prevent the end of the slave trade.
3. Trap.
4. Word of honor.

who had taught him no better Principles, than not to Credit as he would be Credited: but they told him the Difference of their Faith occasion'd that Distrust: For the *Captain* had protested to him upon the Word of a *Christian*, and sworn in the Name of a Great G O D; which if he shou'd violate, he would expect eternal Torment in the World to come. *Is that all the Obligation he has to be Just to his Oath?* replied Oroonoko. *Let him know I Swear by my Honour, which to violate, wou'd not only render me contemptible and despised by all brave and honest Men, and so give my self perpetual pain, but it wou'd be eternally offending and diseasing all Mankind, harming, betraying, circumventing and outraging all Men; but Punishments hereafter are suffer'd by ones self; and the World takes no cognizances whether this God have revenged 'em, or not, 'tis done so secretly, and deferr'd so long: While the Man of no Honour, suffers every moment the scorn and contempt of the honester World, and dies every day ignominiously in his Fame, which is more valuable than Life: I speak not this to move Belief, but to shew you how you mistake, when you imagine, That he who will violate his Honour, will keep his Word with his Gods.* So turning from him with a disdainful smile, he refused to answer him, when he urg'd him to know what Answer he shou'd carry back to his *Captain*; so that he departed without saying any more.

The *Captain* pondering and consulting what to do, it was concluded that nothing but *Oroonoko*'s Liberty wou'd encourage any of the rest to eat, except the *French*-man, whom the *Captain* cou'd not pretend to keep Prisoner, but only told him he was secured because he might act something in favour of the Prince, but that he shou'd be freed as soon as they came to Land. So that they concluded it wholly necessary to free the Prince from his Irons, that he might show himself to the rest; that they might have an Eye upon him, and that they cou'd not fear a single Man.

This being resolv'd, to make the Obligation the greater, the Captain himself went to *Oroonoko*; where, after many Compliments, and Assurances of what he had already promis'd, he receiving from the Prince his *Parole*, and his Hand, for his good Behaviour, dismiss'd his Irons, and brought him to his own Cabin; where, after having treated and repos'd him a while, for he had neither eat nor slept in four Days before, he besought him to visit those obstinate People in Chains, who refus'd all manner of Sustenance, and intreated him to oblige 'em to eat, and assure 'em of their Liberty the first Opportunity.

Oroonoko, who was too generous, not to give Credit to his Words, shew'd himself to his People, who were transported with Excess of Joy at the sight of their Darling Prince; falling at his Feet, and kissing and embracing 'em; believing, as some Divine Oracle, all he assured 'em. But he besought 'em to bear their Chains with that Bravery that became those whom he had seen act so nobly in Arms; and that they cou'd not give him greater Proofs of their Love and Friendship, since 'twas all the Security the Captain (his Friend) cou'd have, against the Revenge, he said, they might possibly justly take, for the Injuries sustain'd by him. And they all, with one Accord, assur'd him, they cou'd not suffer enough, when it was for his Repose and Safety.

After this they no longer refus'd to eat, but took what was brought 'em, and were pleas'd with their Captivity, since by it they hop'd to redeem the Prince, who, all the rest of the Voyage, was treated with all the Respect due to his Birth, though nothing cou'd divert his Melancholy; and he wou'd often sigh for

Imoinda, and think this a Punishment due to his Misfortune, in having left that noble Maid behind him, that fatal Night, in the *Otan*, when he fled to the Camp.

Possess'd with a thousand Thoughts of past Joys with this fair young Person, and a thousand Griefs for her eternal Loss, he endur'd a tedious Voyage, and at last arriv'd at the Mouth of the River of *Surinam*, a Colony belonging to the King of *England*, and where they were to deliver some part of their Slaves. There the Merchants and Gentlemen of the Country going on Board, to demand those Lots of Slaves they had already agreed on; and, amongst those, the Over-seers of those Plantations where I then chanc'd to be, the Captain, who had given the Word, order'd his Men to bring up those noble Slaves in Fetters, whom I have spoken of; and having put 'em, some in one, and some in other Lots, with Women and Children (which they call *Pickaninies*), they sold 'em off, as Slaves, to several Merchants and Gentlemen; not putting any two in one Lot, because they wou'd separate 'em far from each other; not daring to trust 'em together, lest Rage and Courage shou'd put 'em upon contriving some great Action, to the Ruin of the Colony.

Oroonoko was first seiz'd on, and sold to our Over-seer, who had the first Lot, with seventeen more of all sorts and sizes, but not one of Quality with him. When he saw this, he found what they meant; for, as I said, he understood *English* pretty well; and being wholly unarm'd and defenceless, so as it was in vain to make any Resistance, he only beheld the Captain with a Look all fierce and disdainful, upbraiding him with Eyes, that forc'd Blushes on his guilty Cheeks, he only cry'd, in passing over the Side of the Ship, *Farewel, Sir: 'Tis worth my Suffering, to gain so true a Knowledge both of you, and of your Gods by whom you swear.* And desiring those that held him to forbear their pains, and telling 'em he wou'd make no Resistance, he cry'd, *Come, my Fellow-Slaves; let us descend, and see if we can meet with more Honour and Honesty in the next World we shall touch upon.* So he nimbly leap'd into the Boat, and shewing no more Concern, suffer'd himself to be row'd up the River, with his seventeen Companions.

The Gentleman that bought him was a young *Cornish* Gentleman, whose Name was *Trefry*; a Man of great Wit, and fine Learning, and was carry'd into those Parts by the Lord—— Governor,[5] to manage all his Affairs. He reflecting on the last Words of *Oroonoko* to the Captain, and beholding the Richness of his Vest,[6] no sooner came into the Boat, but he fix'd his Eyes on him; and finding something so extraordinary in his Face, his Shape and Mien, a Greatness of Look, and Haughtiness in his Air, and finding he spoke *English*, had a great mind to be enquiring into his Quality and Fortune; which, though *Oroonoko* endeavour'd to hide, by only confessing he was above the Rank of common Slaves, *Trefry* soon found he was yet something greater than he confess'd; and from that Moment began to conceive so vast an Esteem for him, that he ever after lov'd him as his dearest Brother, and shew'd him all the Civilities due to so great a Man.

Trefry was a very good Mathematician, and a Linguist; cou'd speak *French* and *Spanish*; and in the three Days they remain'd in the Boat (for so long were

5. Francis, Lord Willoughby of Parham, held a royal grant as coproprietor of Surinam. John

Trefry was his plantation overseer.
6. Robe.

they going from the Ship, to the Plantation) he entertain'd *Oroonoko* so agreeably with his Art and Discourse, that he was no less pleas'd with *Trefry*, than he was with the Prince; and he thought himself, at least, fortunate in this, that since he was a Slave, as long as he wou'd suffer himself to remain so, he had a Man of so excellent Wit and Parts for a Master: So that before they had finish'd their Voyage up the River, he made no scruple of declaring to *Trefry* all his Fortunes, and most part of what I have here related, and put himself wholly into the Hands of his new Friend, whom he found resenting all the Injuries were done him, and was charm'd with all the Greatness of his Actions; which were recited with that Modesty, and delicate Sense, as wholly vanquish'd him, and subdu'd him to his Interest. And he promis'd him on his Word and Honour, he wou'd find the Means to reconduct him to his own Country again: assuring him, he had a perfect Abhorrence of so dishonourable an Action; and that he wou'd sooner have dy'd, than have been the Author of such a Perfidy. He found the Prince was very much concern'd to know what became of his Friends, and how they took their Slavery; and *Trefry* promis'd to take care about the enquiring after their Condition, and that he shou'd have an Account of 'em.

Though, as *Oroonoko* afterwards said, he had little Reason to credit the Words of a *Backearary*,[7] yet he knew not why; but he saw a kind of Sincerity, and awful Truth in the Face of *Trefry*; he saw an Honesty in his Eyes, and he found him wise and witty enough to understand Honour; for it was one of his Maxims, *A Man of Wit cou'd not be a Knave or Villain.*

In their passage up the River, they put in at several Houses for Refreshment; and ever when they landed, numbers of People wou'd flock to behold this Man; not but their Eyes were daily entertain'd with the sight of Slaves, but the Fame of *Oroonoko* was gone before him, and all People were in Admiration of his Beauty. Besides, he had a rich Habit on, in which he was taken, so different from the rest, and which the Captain cou'd not strip him of, because he was forc'd to surprize his Person in the Minute he sold him. When he found his Habit made him liable, as he thought, to be gaz'd at the more, he begg'd *Trefry* to give him something more befitting a Slave; which he did, and took off his Robes. Nevertheless, he shone through all; and his *Osenbrigs* (a sort of brown *Holland*[8] Suit he had on) cou'd not conceal the Graces of his Looks and Mien; and he had no less Admirers, than when he had his dazzling Habit on: The Royal Youth appear'd in spite of the Slave, and People cou'd not help treating him after a different manner, without designing it: As soon as they approach'd him, they venerated and esteem'd him; his Eyes insensibly commanded Respect, and his Behaviour insinuated it into every Soul. So that there was nothing talk'd of but this young and gallant Slave, even by those who yet knew not that he was a Prince.

I ought to tell you, that the *Christians* never buy any Slaves but they give 'em some Name of their own, their native ones being likely very barbarous, and hard to pronounce; so that Mr. *Trefry* gave *Oroonoko* that of *Caesar*;[9] which

---

7. Master or white person, from *backra*, an Ibo or Efik word brought to Surinam by slaves.
8. A coarse linen or cotton cloth used to clothe slaves, also called *osnaburg* after a German town where it was made.
9. Slaves often received classical names. Julius Caesar was a famous Roman general and ruler.

Name will live in that Country as long as that (scarce more) glorious one of the great *Roman;* for 'tis most evident, he wanted no part of the Personal Courage of that *Caesar,* and acted things as memorable, had they been done in some part of the World replenish'd with People, and Historians, that might have given him his due. But his Misfortune was, to fall in an obscure World, that afforded only a Female Pen to celebrate his Fame; though I doubt not but it had liv'd from others Endeavours, if the *Dutch,* who, immediately after his Time, took that Country,[1] had not kill'd, banish'd and dispers'd all those that were capable of giving the World this great Man's Life, much better than I have done. And Mr. *Trefry,* who design'd it, dy'd before he began it; and bemoan'd himself for not having undertook it in time.

For the future therefore, I must call *Oroonoko, Caesar,* since by that Name only he was known in our Western World, and by that Name he was receiv'd on Shore at *Parham-House,* where he was destin'd a Slave. But if the King himself (God bless him) had come a-shore, there cou'd not have been greater Expectations by all the whole Plantation, and those neighbouring ones, than was on ours at that time; and he was receiv'd more like a Governor, than a Slave. Notwithstanding, as the Custom was, they assign'd him his Portion of Land, his House, and his Business, up in the Plantation. But as it was more for Form, than any Design, to put him to his Task, he endur'd no more of the Slave but the Name, and remain'd some Days in the House, receiving all Visits that were made him, without stirring towards that part of the Plantation where the *Negroes* were.

At last, he wou'd needs go view his Land, his House, and the Business assign'd him. But he no sooner came to the Houses of the Slaves, which are like a little Town by it self, the *Negroes* all having left Work, but they all came forth to behold him, and found he was that Prince who had, at several times, sold most of 'em to these Parts; and, from a Veneration they pay to great Men, especially if they know 'em, and from the Surprize and Awe they had at the sight of him, they all cast themselves at his Feet, crying out, in their Language, *Live, O King! Long Live, O King!* And kissing his Feet, paid him even Divine Homage.

Several *English* Gentlemen were with him; and what Mr. *Trefry* had told 'em, was here confirm'd; of which he himself before had no other Witness than *Caesar* himself: But he was infinitely glad to find his Grandure confirm'd by the Adoration of all the Slaves.

Caesar troubl'd with their Over-Joy, and Over-Ceremony, besought 'em to rise, and to receive him as their Fellow-Slave; assuring them, he was no better. At which they set up with one Accord a most terrible and hidious Mourning and condoling, which he and the *English* had much a-do to appease; but at last they prevail'd with 'em, and they prepar'd all their barbarous Musick, and every one kill'd and dress'd something of his own Stock (for every Family has their Land a-part, on which, at their leisure-times they breed all eatable things); and clubbing it together, made a most magnificent Supper, inviting their *Grandee*[2] *Captain,* their *Prince,* to honour it with his Presence; which he did, and several *English* with him; where they all waited on him, some playing, others dancing

---

1. The Dutch attacked and conquered Surinam in 1667, and the British exchanged it for

New York in the treaty of Breda.
2. Eminent or noble.

before him all the time, according to the Manners of their several Nations; and with unwearied Industry, endeavouring to please and delight him.

While they sat at Meat Mr. *Trefry* told *Caesar*, that most of these young *Slaves* were undone in Love, with a fine she-*Slave*, whom they had had about Six Months on their Land; the *Prince*, who never heard the Name of *Love* without a Sigh, nor any mention of it without the Curiosity of examining further into that tale, which of all Discourses was most agreeable to him, asked, how they came to be so Unhappy, as to be all undone for one fair *Slave*? *Trefry*, who was naturally Amorous, and lov'd to talk of Love as well as any body, proceeded to tell him, they had the most charming Black that ever was beheld on their *Plantation*, about Fifteen or Sixteen Years old, as he guess'd; that, for his part, he had done nothing but Sigh for her ever since she came; and that all the white Beautys he had seen, never charm'd him so absolutely as this fine Creature had done; and that no Man, of any Nation, ever beheld her, that did not fall in Love with her; and that she had all the *Slaves* perpetually at her Feet; and the whole Country resounded with the Fame of *Clemene*, for so, said he, we have Christ'ned her: But she denys us all with such a noble Disdain, that 'tis a Miracle to see, that she, who can give such eternal Desires, shou'd herself be all Ice, and all Unconcern. She is adorn'd with the most Graceful Modesty that ever beautifyed Youth; the softest Sigher—that, if she were capable of Love, one would swear she languish'd for some absent happy Man; and so retir'd, as if she fear'd a Rape even from the God of Day,[3] or that the Breezes would steal Kisses from her delicate Mouth. Her Task of Work some sighing Lover every day makes it his Petition to perform for her, which she accepts blushing, and with reluctancy, for fear he will ask her a Look for a Recompence, which he dares not presume to hope; so great an Awe she strikes into the Hearts of her Admirers. *I do not wonder*, replied the Prince, *that* Clemene *shou'd refuse Slaves, being as you say so Beautiful, but wonder how she escapes those who can entertain her as you can do; or why, being your Slave, you do not oblige her to yield. I confess*, said *Trefry, when I have, against her will, entertain'd her with Love so long, as to be transported with my Passion; even above Decency, I have been ready to make use of those advantages of Strength and Force Nature has given me. But oh! she disarms me, with that Modesty and Weeping so tender and so moving, that I retire, and thank my Stars she overcame me.* The Company laugh'd at his Civility to a *Slave*, and *Caesar* only applauded the nobleness of his Passion and Nature; since that Slave might be Noble, or, what was better, have true Notions of Honour and Vertue in her. Thus pass'd they this Night, after having received, from the *Slaves*, all imaginable Respect and Obedience.

The next Day *Trefry* ask'd *Caesar* to walk, when the heat was allay'd, and designedly carried him by the Cottage of the *fair Slave*; and told him, she whom he spoke of last Night liv'd there retir'd. *But*, says he, *I would not wish you to approach, for, I am sure, you will be in Love as soon as you behold her.* *Caesar* assur'd him, he was proof against all the Charms of that Sex; and that if he imagin'd his Heart cou'd be so perfidious to Love again, after *Imoinda*, he believ'd he shou'd tear it from his Bosom: They had no sooner spoke, but a little shock Dog, that *Clemene* had presented[4] her, which she took great Delight

---

3. The sun.
4. Clemene had presented to her a long-haired

dog or poodle, associated with fashionable women.

in, ran out; and she, not knowing any body was there, ran to get it in again, and bolted out on those who were just Speaking of her: When seeing them, she wou'd have run in again; but *Trefry* caught her by the Hand, and cry'd, *Clemene, however you fly a Lover, you ought to pay some Respect to this Stranger* (pointing to *Caesar*). But she, as if she had resolv'd never to raise her Eyes to the Face of a Man again, bent 'em the more to the Earth, when he spoke, and gave the *Prince* the leisure to look the more at her. There needed no long Gazing, or Consideration, to examin who this fair Creature was; he soon saw *Imoinda* all over her; in a Minute he saw her Face, her Shape, her Air, her Modesty, and all that call'd forth his Soul with Joy at his Eyes, and left his Body destitute of almost Life; it stood without Motion, and, for a Minute, knew not that it had a Being; and, I believe, he had never come to himself, so opprest he was with over-Joy, if he had not met with this Allay,[5] that he perceiv'd *Imoinda* fall dead in the Hands of *Trefry*: this awaken'd him, and he ran to her aid, and caught her in his Arms, where, by degrees, she came to herself; and 'tis needless to tell with what transports, what extasies of Joy, they both a while beheld each other, without Speaking; then Snatcht each other to their Arms; then Gaze again, as if they still doubted whether they possess'd the Blessing: They Graspt; but when they recovered their Speech, 'tis not to be imagin'd, what tender things they exprest to each other; wondering what strange Fate had brought 'em again together. They soon inform'd each other of their Fortunes, and equally bewail'd their Fate; but, at the same time, they mutually protested, that even Fetters and Slavery were Soft and Easy; and wou'd be supported with Joy and Pleasure, while they cou'd be so happy to possess each other, and to be able to make good their Vows. *Caesar* swore he disdain'd the Empire of the World, while he cou'd behold his *Imoinda*; and she despis'd Grandure and Pomp, those Vanities of her Sex, when she cou'd Gaze on *Oroonoko*. He ador'd the very Cottage where she resided, and said, That little Inch of the World wou'd give him more Happiness than all the Universe cou'd do; and she vow'd, It was a Pallace, while adorn'd with the Presence of *Oroonoko*.

Trefry was infinitely pleas'd with this Novel,[6] and found this *Clemene* was the Fair Mistress of whom *Caesar* had before spoke; and was not a little satisfied, that Heaven was so kind to the *Prince*, as to sweeten his Misfortunes by so lucky an Accident; and leaving the Lovers to themselves, was impatient to come down to *Parham House*, (which was on the same *Plantation*) to give me an Account of what had hapned. I was as impatient to make these Lovers a Visit, having already made a Friendship with *Caesar*; and from his own Mouth learn'd what I have related, which was confirm'd by his *French*-man, who was set on Shore to seek his Fortunes; and of whom they cou'd not make a Slave, because a Christian; and he came daily to *Parham Hill* to see and pay his Respects to his Pupil *Prince*: So that concerning and intresting myself, in all that related to *Caesar*, whom I had assur'd of Liberty, as soon as the Governor arriv'd, I hasted presently to the Place where the Lovers were, and was infinitely glad to find this Beautiful young *Slave* (who had already gain'd all our Esteems, for her Modesty and be extraordinary Prettyness) to be the same I had heard *Caesar*

---

5. Intrusion.   6. New event.

speak so much of. One may imagine then, we paid her a treble Respect; and though from her being carv'd in fine Flowers and Birds all over her Body, we took her to be of Quality before, yet, when we knew *Clemene* was *Imoinda*, we cou'd not enough admire her.

I had forgot to tell you, that those who are Nobly born of that Country, are so delicately Cut and Rac'd all over the fore-part of the Trunk of their Bodies, that it looks as if it were Japan'd; the Works being raised like high Poynt[7] round the Edges of the Flowers: Some are only Carv'd with a little Flower, or Bird, at the Sides of the Temples, as was *Caesar* and those who are so Carv'd over the Body, resemble our Ancient *Picts*[8] that are figur'd in the Chronicles, but these Carvings are more delicate.

From that happy Day *Caesar* took *Clemene* for his Wife, to the general Joy of all People; and there was as much Magnificence as the Country wou'd afford at the Celebration of this Wedding: and in a very short time after she conceiv'd with Child; which made *Caesar* ever adore her, knowing he was the last of his Great Race. This new Accident made him more Impatient of Liberty, and he was every Day treating with *Trefry* for his and *Clemene*'s Liberty; and offer'd either Gold or a vast quantity of Slaves, which shou'd be paid before they let him go, provided he cou'd have any Security that he shou'd go when his Ransom was paid: They fed him from Day to Day with Promises, and delay'd him, till the Lord Governor shou'd come; so that he began to suspect them of falshood, and that they wou'd delay him till the time of his Wives delivery, and make a Slave of that too, for all the Breed is theirs to whom the Parents belong: This Thought made him very uneasy, and his Sullenness gave them some Jealousies[9] of him; so that I was oblig'd, by some Persons, who fear'd a Mutiny (which is very Fatal sometimes in those Colonies, that abound so with Slaves, that they exceed the Whites in vast Numbers) to discourse with *Caesar*, and to give him all the Satisfaction I possibly cou'd; they knew he and *Clemene* were scarce an Hour in a Day from my Lodgings; that they eat with me, and that I oblig'd 'em in all things I was capable of: I entertain'd him with the Lives of the Romans,[1] and great Men, which charm'd him to my Company; and her, with teaching her all the pretty Works that I was Mistress of; and telling her Stories of Nuns, and endeavouring to bring her to the knowledge of the true God. But of all Discourses *Caesar* lik'd that the worst, and wou'd never be reconcil'd to our Notions of the Trinity, of which he ever made a Jest; it was a Riddle, he said, wou'd turn his Brain to conceive, and one cou'd not make him understand what Faith was. However, these Conversations fail'd not altogether so well to divert him, that he lik'd the Company of us Women much above the Men; for he cou'd not Drink; and he is but an ill Companion in that Country that cannot: So that obliging him to love us very well, we had all the Liberty of Speech with him, especially my self, whom he call'd his *Great Mistress*; and indeed my Word wou'd go a great way with him. For these Reasons, I had Opportunity to take notice to him, that he was not well pleas'd of late, as he us'd to be; was more retir'd and thoughtful; and told him, I took it Ill he shou'd

---

7. An elaborate type of lace. "Rac'd": traced, incised. "Japan'd": like lacquerwork in the Japanese style.
8. Ancient British people, named *Picti* (painted or tattooed) by the Romans.
9. Suspicions.
1. Plutarch's biographies of famous men, from the late first century.

Suspect we wou'd break our Words with him, and not permit both him and *Clemene* to return to his own Kingdom, which was not so long a way, but when he was once on his Voyage he wou'd quickly arrive there. He made me some Answers that shew'd a doubt in him, which made me ask him, what advantage it wou'd be to doubt? it would but give us a Fear of him, and possibly compel us to treat him so as I shou'd be very loath to behold: that is, it might occasion his Confinement. Perhaps this was not so Luckily spoke of me, for I perceiv'd he resented that Word, which I strove to Soften again in vain: However, he assur'd me, that whatsoever Resolutions he shou'd take, he wou'd Act nothing upon the White-People; and as for my self, and those upon that *Plantation* where he was, he wou'd sooner forfeit his eternal Liberty, and Life it self, than lift his Hand against his greatest Enemy on that Place: He besought me to suffer no Fears upon his Account, for he cou'd do nothing that Honour shou'd not dictate; but he accus'd himself for having suffer'd Slavery so long; yet he charg'd that weakness on Love alone, who was capable of making him neglect even Glory it self; and, for which, now he reproaches himself every moment of the Day. Much more to this effect he spoke, with an Air impatient enough to make me know he wou'd not be long in Bondage; and though he suffer'd only the Name of a Slave, and had nothing of the Toil and Labour of one, yet that was sufficient to render him Uneasy; and he had been too long Idle, who us'd to be always in Action, and in Arms: He had a Spirit all Rough and Fierce, and that cou'd not be tam'd to lazy Rest; and though all endeavors were us'd to exercise himself in such Actions and Sports as this World afforded, as Running, Wrastling, Pitching the Bar, Hunting and Fishing, Chasing and Killing *Tigers*[2] of a monstrous Size, which this Continent affords in abundance; and wonderful *Snakes*, such as *Alexander* is reported to have incounter'd at the River of *Amazons*,[3] and which *Caesar* took great Delight to overcome; yet these were not Actions great enough for his large Soul, which was still panting after more renown'd Action.

Before I parted that Day with him, I got, with much ado, a Promise from him to rest yet a little longer with Patience, and wait the coming of the Lord Governor, who was every Day expected on our Shore; he assur'd me he wou'd, and this Promise he desired me to know was given perfectly in Complaisance to me, in whom he had an intire Confidence.

After this, I neither thought it convenient to trust him much out of our View, nor did the Country who fear'd him; but with one accord it was advis'd to treat him Fairly, and oblige him to remain within such a compass, and that he shou'd be permitted, as seldom as cou'd be, to go up to the Plantations of the Negroes; or, if he did, to be accompany'd by some that shou'd be rather in appearance Attendants than Spys. This Care was for some time taken, and *Caesar* look'd upon it as a Mark of extraordinary Respect, and was glad his discontent had oblig'd 'em to be more observant to him; he received new assurance from the Overseer, which was confirmed to him by the Opinion of all the Gentlemen of the Country, who made their court to him. During this time that we had his Company more frequently than hitherto we had had, it may not be unpleasant to relate to you the Diversions we entertain'd him with, or rather he us.

---

2. Jaguars. "Pitching the bar": a game of distance throwing.

3. Alexander the Great supposedly encountered Amazons (and snakes) in India.

My stay was to be short in that Country, because my Father dy'd at Sea, and never arriv'd to possess the Honour was design'd him, (which was Lieutenant-General of Six and thirty Islands, besides the Continent of *Surinam*) nor the advantages he hop'd to reap by them;[4] so that though we were oblig'd to continue on our Voyage, we did not intend to stay upon the Place: Though, in a Word, I must say thus much of it, That certainly had his late Majesty, of sacred Memory, but seen and known what a vast and charming World he had been Master of in that Continent, he would never have parted so Easily with it to the *Dutch*. 'Tis a Continent whose vast Extent was never yet known, and may contain more Noble Earth than all the Universe besides; for, they say, it reaches from East to West; one Way as far as *China*, and another to *Peru*: It affords all things both for Beauty and Use; 'tis there Eternal Spring, always the very Months of *April*, *May* and *June*; the Shades are perpetual, the Trees, bearing at once all degrees of Leaves and Fruit, from blooming Buds to ripe Autumn; Groves of Oranges, Limons, Citrons, Figs, Nutmegs, and noble Aromaticks, continually bearing their Fragrancies. The Trees appearing all like Nosegays adorn'd with Flowers of different kinds; some are all White, some Purple, some Scarlet, some Blue, some Yellow; bearing, at the same time, Ripe Fruit and Blooming Young, or producing every Day new. The very Wood of all these Trees have an intrinsick Value above common Timber; for they are, when cut, of different Colours, glorious to behold; and bear a Price considerable, to inlay withal. Besides this, they yield rich Balm, and Gums; so that we make our Candles of such an Aromatick Substance, as does not only give a sufficient Light, but, as they Burn, they cast their Perfumes all about. Cedar is the common Firing, and all the Houses are built with it. The very Meat we eat, when set on the Table, if it be Native, I mean of the Country, perfumes the whole Room; especially a little Beast call'd an *Armadilly*, a thing which I can liken to nothing so well as a *Rhinoceros*; 'tis all in white Armor so joynted, that it moves as well in it, as if it had nothing on; this Beast is about the bigness of a Pig of Six Weeks old. But it were endless to give an Account of all the divers Wonderfull and Strange things that Country affords, and which we took a very great Delight to go in search of; though those adventures are oftentimes Fatal and at least Dangerous: But while we had *Caesar* in our Company on these Designs we fear'd no harm, nor suffer'd any.

As soon as I came into the Country, the best House in it was presented me, call'd *St. John's Hill*.[5] It stood on a vast Rock of white Marble, at the Foot of which the River ran a vast depth down, and not to be descended on that side; the little Waves still dashing and washing the foot of this Rock, made the softest Murmurs and Purlings in the World; and the Opposite Bank was adorn'd with such vast quantities of different Flowers eternally Blowing,[6] and every Day and Hour new, fenc'd behind 'em with lofty Trees of a Thousand rare Forms and Colours, that the Prospect was the most ravishing that fancy can create. On the Edge of this white Rock, towards the River, was a Walk or Grove of Orange and Limon Trees, about half the length of the *Mall*[7] here,

---

4. There is no record of Willoughby appointing anyone to the position of lieutenant-governor. "Continent": land joined to other lands.
5. A plantation near Willoughby's Parham Hill.
6. Blooming.
7. A fashionable park walk in London.

whose Flowery and Fruit-bearing Branches meet at the top, and hinder'd the Sun, whose Rays are very fierce there, from entering a Beam into the Grove; and the cool Air that came from the River made it not only fit to entertain People in, at all the hottest Hours of the Day, but refresh'd the sweet Blossoms, and made it always Sweet and Charming; and sure the whole Globe of the World cannot show so delightful a Place as this Grove was: Not all the Gardens of boasted *Italy* can produce a Shade to out-vie this, which Nature had joyn'd with Art to render so exceeding Fine; and 'tis a marvel to see how such vast Trees, as big as English Oaks, cou'd take footing on so solid a Rock, and in so little Earth, as cover'd that Rock; but all things by Nature there are Rare, Delightful and Wonderful. But to our Sports.

Sometimes we wou'd go surprizing,[8] and in search of young *Tigers* in their Dens, watching when the old Ones went forth to forage for Prey; and oftentimes we have been in great Danger, and have fled apace for our Lives, when surpriz'd by the Dams. But once, above all other times, we went on this Design, and *Caesar* was with us, who had no sooner stol'n a young *Tiger* from her Nest, but going off, we incounter'd the Dam, bearing a Buttock of a Cow, which he[9] had torn off with his mighty Paw, and going with it towards his *Den*; we had only found Women, *Caesar*, and an English Gentleman, Brother to *Harry Martin*,[1] the great *Oliverian*; we found there was no escaping this inrag'd and ravenous Beast. However, we Women fled as fast as we cou'd from it; but our Heels had not sav'd our Lives, if *Caesar* had not laid down his *Cub*, when he found the *Tiger* quit her Prey to make the more speed towards him; and taking Mr. *Martin*'s Sword desir'd him to stand aside, or follow the Ladies. He obey'd him, and *Caesar* met this monstrous Beast of might, size, and vast Limbs, who came with open Jaws upon him; and fixing his Awful stern Eyes full upon those of the Beast, and putting himself into a very steddy and good aiming posture of Defence, ran his Sword quite through his Breast down to his very Heart, home to the Hilt of the Sword; the dying Beast stretch'd forth her Paw, and going to grasp his Thigh, surpriz'd with Death in that very moment, did him no other harm than fixing her long Nails in his Flesh very deep, feebly wounded him, but cou'd not grasp the Flesh to tear off any. When he had done this, he hollow'd to us to return; which, after some assurance of his Victory, we did, and found him lugging out the Sword from the Bosom of the *Tiger*, who was laid in her Bloud on the Ground; he took up the *Cub*, and with an unconcern, that had nothing of the Joy or Gladness of a Victory, he came and laid the Whelp at my Feet: We all extreamly wonder'd at his Daring, and at the Bigness of the Beast, which was about the highth of an Heifer, but of mighty, great, and strong Limbs.

Another time, being in the Woods, he kill'd a *Tiger*, which had long infested that part, and born away abundance of Sheep and Oxen, and other things, that were for the support of those to whom they belong'd; abundance of People assail'd this Beast, some affirming they had shot her with several Bullets quite through the Body, at several times; and some swearing they shot her through the very Heart, and they believ'd she was a Devil rather than a Mortal thing.

---

8. Mounting sudden raids.
9. The tiger is alternatively she, he, and it.
1. Henry Martin had been one of judges who signed Charles I's death warrant. His younger brother George, a Barbados planter, moved to Surinam in 1658.

Caesar had often said, he had a mind to encounter this Monster, and spoke with several Gentlemen who had attempted her; one crying, I shot her with so many poyson'd Arrows, another with his Gun in this part of her, and another in that; so that he remarking all these Places where she was shot, fancy'd still he shou'd overcome her, by giving her another sort of a Wound than any had yet done; and one day said (at the Table) *What Trophies and Garlands, Ladies, will you make me, if I bring you home the Heart of this Ravenous Beast, that eats up all your Lambs and Pigs?* We all promis'd he shou'd be rewarded at all our Hands. So taking a Bow, which he chus'd out of a great many, he went up in the Wood, with two Gentlemen, where he imagin'd this Devourer to be; they had not past very far in it, but they heard her Voice, growling and grumbling, as if she were pleas'd with something she was doing. When they came in view, they found her muzzling in the Belly of a new ravish'd Sheep, which she had torn open; and seeing herself approach'd, she took fast hold of her Prey, with her fore Paws, and set a very fierce raging Look on *Caesar*, without offering to approach him; for fear, at the same time, of losing what she had in Possession. So that *Caesar* remain'd a good while, only taking aim, and getting an opportunity to shoot her where he design'd; 'twas some time before he cou'd accomplish it, and to wound her, and not kill her, wou'd but have enrag'd her more, and indanger'd him: He had a Quiver of Arrows at his side, so that if one fail'd he cou'd be supply'd; at last, retiring a little, he gave her opportunity to eat, for he found she was Ravenous, and fell to as soon as she saw him retire; being more eager of her Prey than of doing new Mischiefs. When he going softly to one side of her, and hiding his Person behind certain Herbage that grew high and thick, he took so good aim, that, as he intended, he shot her just into the Eye, and the Arrow was sent with so good a will, and so sure a hand, that it stuck in her Brain, and made her caper, and become mad for a moment or two; but being seconded by another Arrow, he fell dead upon the Prey: *Caesar* cut him Open with a Knife, to see where those Wounds were that had been reported to him, and why he did not Die of 'em. But I shall now relate a thing that possibly will find no Credit among Men, because 'tis a Notion commonly receiv'd with us, That nothing can receive a Wound in the Heart and Live; but when the Heart of this courageous Animal was taken out, there were Seven Bullets of Lead in it, and the Wounds seam'd up with great Scars, and she liv'd with the Bullets a great while, for it was long since they were shot: This Heart the Conqueror brought up to us, and 'twas a very great Curiosity, which all the Country came to see; and which gave *Caesar* occasion of many fine Discourses; of Accidents in War, and Strange Escapes.

At other times he wou'd go a Fishing; and discoursing on that Diversion, he found we had in that Country a very Strange Fish, call'd a *Numb Eel*,[2] (an *Eel* of which I have eaten) that while it is alive, it has a quality so Cold, that those who are Angling, though with a Line of never so great a length, with a Rod at the end of it, it shall, in the same minute the Bait is touched by this *Eel*, seize him or her that holds the Rod with benumb'dness, that shall deprive 'em of Sense, for a while; and some have fall'n into the Water, and others drop'd as dead on the Banks of the Rivers where they stood, as soon as this Fish touches the Bait. *Caesar* us'd to laugh at this, and believ'd it impossible a Man cou'd

2. Electric eel.

lose his Force at the touch of a Fish; and cou'd not understand that Philosophy,[3] that a cold Quality should be of that Nature: However, he had a great Curiosity to try whether it wou'd have the same effect on him it had on others, and often try'd, but in vain; at last, the sought for Fish came to the Bait, as he stood Angling on the Bank; and instead of throwing away the Rod, or giving it a sudden twitch out of the Water, whereby he might have caught both the *Eel*, and have dismiss'd the Rod, before it cou'd have too much Power over him; for Experiment sake, he grasp'd it but the harder, and fainting fell into the River; and being still possest of the Rod, the Tide carry'd him senseless as he was a great way, till an *Indian* Boat took him up; and perceiv'd, when they touch'd him, a Numbness seize them, and by that knew the Rod was in his Hand; which, with a Paddle (that is, a short Oar) they struck away, and snatch'd it into the Boat, *Eel* and all. If *Caesar* were almost Dead, with the effect of this Fish, he was more so with that of the Water, where he had remain'd the space of going a League; and they found they had much a-do to bring him back to Life: But, at last, they did, and brought him home, where he was in a few Hours well Recover'd and Refresh'd; and not a little Asham'd to find he shou'd be overcome by an *Eel*; and that all the People, who heard his Defiance, wou'd Laugh at him. But we cheared him up; and he, being convinc'd, we had the *Eel* at Supper; which was a quarter of an Ell about, and most delicate Meat; and was of the more Value, since it cost so Dear, as almost the Life of so gallant a Man.

About this time we were in many mortal Fears, about some Disputes the *English* had with the *Indians*; so that we cou'd scarce trust our selves, without great Numbers, to go to any *Indian* Towns, or Place, where they abode; for fear they shou'd fall upon us, as they did immediately after my coming away; and that it was in the possession of the *Dutch*, who us'd 'em not so civilly as the *English*; so that they cut in pieces all they cou'd take, getting into Houses, and hanging up the Mother, and all her Children about her; and cut a Footman, I left behind me, all in Joynts, and nail'd him to Trees.

This feud began while I was there; so that I lost half the satisfaction I propos'd, in not seeing and visiting the *Indian* Towns. But one Day, bemoaning of our Misfortunes upon this account, *Caesar* told us, we need not Fear; for if we had a mind to go, he wou'd undertake to be our Guard: Some wou'd, but most wou'd not venture; about Eighteen of us resolv'd, and took Barge; and, after Eight Days, arriv'd near an *Indian* Town: But approaching it, the Hearts of some of our Company fail'd, and they wou'd not venture on Shore; so we Poll'd who wou'd, and who wou'd not: For my part, I said, If *Caesar* wou'd, I wou'd go; he resolv'd, so did my Brother, and my Woman, a Maid of good Courage. Now none of us speaking the Language of the People, and imagining we shou'd have a half Diversion in Gazing only; and not knowing what they said, we took a Fisherman that liv'd at the Mouth of the River, who had been a long Inhabitant there, and oblig'd him to go with us: But because he was known to the *Indians*, as trading among 'em; and being, by long Living there, become a perfect *Indian* in Colour, we, who resolv'd to surprize 'em, by making 'em see something they never had seen, (that is, White People) resolv'd only my self, my Brother, and Woman shou'd go; so *Caesar*, the Fisherman, and the rest, hiding behind some thick Reeds and Flowers, that grew on the Banks, let

3. Principle or system.

us pass on towards the Town, which was on the Bank of the River all along. A little distant from the Houses, or Huts, we saw some Dancing, others busy'd in fetching and carrying of Water from the River: They had no sooner spy'd us, but they set up a loud Cry, that frighted us at first; we thought it had been for those that should Kill us, but it seems it was of Wonder and Amazement. They were all Naked, and we were Dress'd, so as is most comode,[4] for the hot Countries, very Glittering and Rich; so that we appear'd extreamly fine; my own Hair was cut short, and I had a Taffaty Cap, with Black Feathers, on my Head; my Brother was in a Stuff[5] Suit, with Silver Loops and Buttons, and abundance of Green Ribon; this was all infinitely surprising to them, and because we saw them stand still, till we approach'd 'em, we took Heart and advanc'd; came up to 'em, and offer'd 'em our Hands; which they took, and look'd on us round about, calling still for more Company; who came swarming out, all wondering, and crying out *Tepeeme*;[6] taking their Hair up in their Hands, and spreading it wide to those they call'd out to; as if they would say (as indeed it signify'd) *Numberless Wonders*, or not to be recounted, no more than to number the Hair of their Heads. By degrees they grew more bold, and from gazing upon us round, they touch'd us; laying their Hands upon all the Features of our Faces, feeling our Breasts and Arms, taking up one Petticoat, then wondering to see another; admiring our Shoes and Stockings, but more our Garters, which we gave 'em; and they ty'd about their Legs, being Lac'd with Silver Lace at the ends, for they much Esteem any shining things: In fine, we suffer'd 'em to survey us as they pleas'd, and we thought they wou'd never have done admiring us. When *Caesar*, and the rest, saw we were receiv'd with such wonder, they came up to us; and finding the *Indian* Trader whom they knew, (for 'tis by these Fishermen, call'd *Indian* Traders, we hold a Commerce with 'em; for they love not to go far from home, and we never go to them) when they saw him therefore they set up a new Joy; and cry'd, in their Language, *Oh! here's our* Tiguamy, *and we shall now know whether those things can speak*: So advancing to him, some of 'em gave him their Hands, and cry'd, *Amora Tiguamy*, which is as much as, *How do you*, or *Welcome Friend*; and all, with one din, began to gabble to him, and ask'd, If we had Sense, and Wit? if we cou'd talk of affairs of Life, and War, as they cou'd do? if we cou'd Hunt, Swim, and do a thousand things they use? He answer'd 'em, We cou'd. Then they invited us into their Houses, and dress'd Venison and Buffelo for us; and, going out, gathered a Leaf of a Tree, call'd a *Sarumbo* Leaf, of Six Yards long, and spread it on the Ground for a Table-Cloth; and cutting another in pieces instead of Plates, setting us on little bow *Indian* Stools, which they cut out of one intire piece of Wood, and Paint, in a sort of Japan Work: They serve every one their Mess[7] on these pieces of Leaves, and it was very good, but too high season'd with Pepper. When we had eat, my Brother, and I, took out our Flutes, and play'd to 'em, which gave 'em new Wonder; and I soon perceiv'd, by an admiration, that is natural to these People, and by the extream Ignorance and Simplicity of 'em, it were not difficult to establish any unknown or extravagant Religion among them; and to impose any Notions or Fictions upon 'em. For seeing a Kinsman

---

4. Appropriate.
5. Woven fabric. "Taffaty": taffeta.
6. *Tapouimé* (a modern transcription of the

word Behn transcribed as *Tepeeme*) is the word for "many" in the indigenous Galibi language.
7. Serving.

of mine set some Paper a Fire, with a Burning-glass, a Trick they had never before seen, they were like to have Ador'd him for a God; and beg'd he wou'd give them the Characters or Figures of his Name, that they might oppose it against Winds and Storms; which he did, and they held it up in those Seasons, and fancy'd it had a Charm to conquer them; and kept it like a Holy Relique. They are very Superstitious, and call'd him the Great *Peeie*, that is, *Prophet*. They show'd us their *Indian Peeie*, a Youth of about Sixteen Years old, as handsom as Nature cou'd make a Man. They consecrate a beautiful Youth from his Infancy, and all Arts are us'd to compleat him in the finest manner, both in Beauty and Shape: He is bred to all the little Arts and cunning they are capable of; to all the Legerdemain Tricks, and Sleight of Hand, whereby he imposes upon the Rabble; and is both a Doctor in Physick and Divinity. And by these Tricks makes the Sick believe he sometimes eases their Pains; by drawing from the afflicted part little Serpents, or odd Flies, or Worms, or any Strange thing; and though they have besides undoubted good Remedies, for almost all their Diseases, they cure the Patient more by Fancy than by Medicines; and make themselves Fear'd, Lov'd, and Reverenc'd. This young *Peeie* had a very young Wife, who seeing my Brother kiss her, came running and kiss'd me; after this, they kiss'd one another, and made it a very great Jest, it being so Novel; and new Admiration and Laughing went round the Multitude, that they never will forget that Ceremony, never before us'd or known. *Caesar* had a mind to see and talk with their War *Captains*, and we were conducted to one of their Houses; where we beheld several of the great *Captains*, who had been at Councel: But so frightful a Vision it was to see 'em no Fancy can create; no such Dreams can represent so dreadful a Spectacle. For my part I took 'em for Hobgoblins, or Fiends, rather than Men; but however their Shapes appear'd, their Souls were very Humane and Noble; but some wanted their Noses, some their Lips, some both Noses and Lips, some their Ears, and others Cut through each Cheek, with long Slashes, through which their Teeth appear'd; they had other several formidable Wounds and Scars, or rather Dismemberings; they had *Comitias*, or little Aprons before 'em; and Girdles of Cotton, with their Knives naked, stuck in it; a Bow at their Backs, and a Quiver of Arrows on their Thighs; and most had Feathers on their Heads of divers Colours. They cry'd, *Amora Tigame* to us, at our entrance, and were pleas'd we said as much to 'em; they seated us, and gave us Drink of the best Sort; and wonder'd, as much as the others had done before, to see us. *Caesar* was marvelling as much at their Faces, wondering how they shou'd all be so Wounded in War; he was Impatient to know how they all came by those frightful Marks of Rage or Malice, rather than Wounds got in Noble Battel: They told us, by our Interpreter, That when any War was waging, two Men chosen out by some old *Captain*, whose Fighting was past, and who cou'd only teach the Theory of War, these two Men were to stand in Competition for the Generalship, or Great War Captain; and being brought before the old Judges, now past Labour, they are ask'd, What they dare do to shew they are worthy to lead an Army? When he, who is first ask'd, making no Reply, Cuts off his Nose, and throws it contemptably[8] on the Ground; and the other does something to himself that he thinks surpasses him, and perhaps deprives himself of Lips and an Eye; so they Slash on till one gives

---

8. With contempt.

out, and many have dy'd in this Debate. And 'tis by a passive Valour they shew and prove their Activity; a sort of Courage too Brutal to be applauded by our Black Hero; nevertheless he express'd his Esteem of 'em.

In this Voyage *Caesar* begot so good an understanding between the *Indians* and the *English*, that there were no more Fears, or Heart-burnings during our stay; but we had a perfect, open, and free Trade with 'em: Many things Remarkable, and worthy Reciting, we met with in this short Voyage; because *Caesar* made it his Business to search out and provide for our Entertainment, especially to please his dearly Ador'd *Imoinda*, who was a sharer in all our Adventures; we being resolv'd to make her Chains as easy as we cou'd, and to Compliment the Prince in that manner that most oblig'd him.

As we were coming up again, we met with some *Indians* of strange Aspects; that is, of a larger Size, and other sort of Features, than those of our Country: Our *Indian Slaves*, that Row'd us, ask'd 'em some Questions, but they cou'd not understand us; but shew'd us a long Cotton String, with several Knots on it;[9] and told us, they had been coming from the Mountains so many Moons as there were Knots; they were habited in Skins of a Strange Beast, and brought along with 'em Bags of Gold Dust; which, as well as they cou'd give us to understand, came streaming in little small Chanels down the high Mountains, when the Rains fell; and offer'd to be the Convoy to any Body, or Persons, that wou'd go to the Mountains. We carry'd these Men up to *Parham*, where they were kept till the Lord Governour came: And because all the Country was mad to be going on this Golden Adventure, the Governour, by his Letters, commanded (for they sent some of the Gold to him) that a Guard shou'd be set at the Mouth of the River of *Amazons*, (a River so call'd, almost as broad as the River of *Thames*) and prohibited all People from going up that River, it conducting to those Mountains of Gold.[1] But we going off for *England* before the Project was further prosecuted, and the Governour being drown'd in a Hurricane[2] either the Design dy'd, or the *Dutch* have the Advantage of it: And 'tis to be bemoan'd what his Majesty lost by losing that part of *America*.

Though this digression is a little from my Story, however since it contains some Proofs of the Curiosity and Daring of this great Man, I was content to omit nothing of his Character.

It was thus, for some time we diverted him; but now *Imoinda* began to shew she was with Child, and did nothing but Sigh and Weep for the Captivity of her Lord, her Self, and the Infant yet Unborn; and believ'd, if it were so hard to gain the Liberty of Two, 'twou'd be more difficult to get that for Three. Her Griefs were so many Darts in the great Heart of *Caesar*; and taking his Opportunity one *Sunday*, when all the Whites were overtaken in Drink, as there were abundance of several Trades, and *Slaves* for Four Years, that Inhabited among the *Negro* Houses; and *Sunday* was their Day of Debauch, (otherwise they were a sort of Spys upon Caesar); he went pretending out of Goodness to 'em, to Feast amongst 'em; and sent all his Musick, and order'd a great Treat for the whole Gang, about Three Hundred *Negros*; and about a Hundred and Fifty were able to bear Arms, such as they had, which were sufficient to do Execution

---

9. A *quipu*, used by the Incas of Peru for keeping records and accounts.
1. Spanish as well as English explorers had

searched for the mythical golden city of El Dorado in Guiana.
2. Willoughby died in a storm in 1666.

with Spirits accordingly: For the *English* had none but rusty Swords, that no Strength cou'd draw from a Scabbard; except the People of particular Quality, who took care to Oyl 'em and keep 'em in good Order: The Guns also, unless here and there one, or those newly carry'd from *England*, wou'd do no good or harm; for 'tis the Nature of that Country to Rust and Eat up Iron, or any Metals, but Gold and Silver. And they are very Unexpert at the Bow, which the *Negros* and *Indians* are perfect Masters off.

Caesar, having singl'd out these Men from the Women and Children, made an Harangue to 'em of the Miseries, and Ignominies of Slavery; counting up all their Toyls and Sufferings, under such Loads, Burdens, and Drudgeries, as were fitter for Beasts than Men; Senseless Brutes, than Humane Souls. He told 'em it was not for Days, Months, or Years, but for Eternity; there was no end to be of their Misfortunes: They suffer'd not like Men who might find a Glory, and Fortitude in Oppression; but like Dogs that lov'd the Whip and Bell, and fawn'd the more they were beaten: That they had lost the Divine Quality of Men, and were become insensible Asses, fit only to bear; nay worse: and Ass, or Dog, or Horse having done his Duty, cou'd lye down in Retreat, and rise to Work again, and while he did his Duty indur'd no Stripes; but Men, Villanous, Senseless Men, such as they, Toyl'd on all the tedious Week till Black *Friday*; and then, whether they Work'd or not, whether they were Faulty or Meriting, they promiscuously, the Innocent with the Guilty, suffer'd the infamous Whip, the sordid Stripes, from their Fellow *Slaves* till their Blood trickled from all Parts of their Body; Blood, whose every drop ought to be Reveng'd with a Life of some of those Tyrants, that impose it; *And why,* said he, *my dear Friends and Fellow-sufferers, shou'd we be Slaves to an unknown People? Have they Vanquish'd us Nobly in Fight? Have they Won us in Honourable Battel? And are we, by the chance of War, become their Slaves? This wou'd not anger a Noble Heart, this wou'd not animate a Souldiers Soul; no, but we are Bought and Sold like Apes, or Monkeys, to be the Sport of Women, Fools and Cowards; and the Support of Rogues, Runagades,*[3] *that have abandon'd their own Countries, for Rapin, Murders, Thefts and Villanies: Do you not hear every Day how they upbraid each other with infamy of Life, below the Wildest Salvages; and shall we render Obedience to such a degenerate Race, who have no one Humane Vertue left, to distinguish 'em from the vilest Creatures? Will you, I say, suffer the Lash from such Hands?* They all Reply'd, with one accord, *No, no, no; Caesar has spoke like a Great Captain; like a Great King.*

After this he wou'd have proceeded, but was interrupted by a tall *Negro* of some more Quality than the rest, his Name was *Tuscan*; who Bowing at the Feet of *Caesar*, cry'd, *My Lord, we have listen'd with Joy and Attention to what you have said; and, were we only Men, wou'd follow so great a Leader through the World: But oh! consider, we are Husbands and Parents too, and have things more dear to us than Life; our Wives and Children unfit for Travel, in these unpassable Woods, Mountains and Bogs; we have not only difficult Lands to overcome, but Rivers to Wade, and Monsters to Incounter; Ravenous Beasts of Prey——*. To this, *Caesar* Reply'd, *That Honour was the First Principle in Nature, that was to be Obey'd; but as no Man wou'd pretend to that, without all the Acts of Vertue, Compassion, Charity, Love, Justice and Reason; he found it not*

3. Renegades.

inconsistent with that, to take an equal Care of their Wives and Children, as they wou'd of themselves; and that he did not Design, when he led them to Freedom, and Glorious Liberty, that they shou'd leave that better part of themselves to Perish by the Hand of the Tyrant's Whip: But if there were a Woman among them so degenerate from Love and Vertue to chuse Slavery before the pursuit of her Husband, and with the hazard of her Life, to share with him in his Fortunes; that such an one ought to be Abandon'd, and left as a Prey to the common Enemy.

To which they all Agreed,—and Bowed. After this, he spoke of the Impassable Woods and Rivers; and convinc'd 'em, the more Danger, the more Glory. He told them that he had heard of one *Hannibal* a great Captain, had Cut his Way through Mountains of solid Rocks; and shou'd a few Shrubs oppose them; which they cou'd Fire before 'em?[4] No, 'twas a trifling Excuse to Men resolv'd to die, or overcome. As for Bogs, they are with a little Labour fill'd and harden'd; and the Rivers cou'd be no Obstacle, since they Swam by Nature; at least by Custom, from their First Hour of their Birth: That when the Children were Weary they must carry them by turns, and the Woods and their own Industry wou'd afford them Food. To this they all assented with Joy.

Tuscan then demanded, What he wou'd do? He said, they wou'd Travel towards the Sea; Plant a New Colony, and Defend it by their Valour; and when they cou'd find a Ship, either driven by stress of Weather, or guided by Providence that way, they wou'd Seize it, and make it a Prize, till it had Transported them to their own Countries; at least, they shou'd be made Free in his Kingdom, and be Esteem'd as his Fellow-sufferers, and Men that had the Courage, and the Bravery to attempt, at least, for Liberty; and if they Dy'd in the attempt it wou'd be more brave, than to Live in perpetual Slavery.

They bow'd and kiss'd his Feet at this Resolution, and with one accord Vow'd to follow him to Death. And that Night was appointed to begin their March; they made it known to their Wives, and directed them to tie their Hamaca[5] about their Shoulder, and under their Arm like a Scarf; and to lead their Children that cou'd go, and carry those that cou'd not. The Wives, who pay an intire Obedience to their Husbands, obey'd, and stay'd for 'em, where they were appointed: The Men stay'd but to furnish themselves with what defensive Arms they cou'd get; and All met at the Rendezvous, where *Caesar* made a new incouraging Speech to 'em, and led 'em out.

But, as they cou'd not march far that Night, on Monday early, when the Overseers went to call 'em all together, to go to Work, they were extreamly surpris'd, to find not one upon the Place, but all fled with what Baggage they had. You may imagine this News was not only suddenly spread all over the *Plantation*, but soon reach'd the Neighbouring ones; and we had by Noon about Six hundred Men, they call the *Militia* of the Country, that came to assist us in the pursuit of the Fugitives: But never did one see so comical an Army march forth to War. The Men, of any fashion, wou'd not concern themselves, though it were almost the common Cause; for such Revoltings are very ill Examples, and have very fatal Consequences oftentimes in many Colonies: But they had a Respect for *Caesar*, and all hands were against the *Parhamites*, as they call'd those of *Parham Plantation*; because they did not, in the

---

4. Roman accounts relate how the Carthaginian general and his army hacked through the Alps on their way to attack Rome.
5. Hammock.

first place, love the Lord Governor; and secondly, they wou'd have it, that *Caesar* was Ill us'd, and Baffl'd with;[6] and 'tis not impossible but some of the best in the Country was of his Council in this Flight, and depriving us of all the *Slaves;* so that they of the better sort wou'd not meddle in the matter. The Deputy Governor,[7] of whom I have had no great occasion to speak, and who was the most Fawning fair-tongu'd Fellow in the World, and one that pretended the most Friendship to *Caesar*, was now the only violent Man against him; and though he had nothing, and so need fear nothing, yet talk'd and look'd bigger than any Man: He was a Fellow, whose Character is not fit to be mention'd with the worst of the *Slaves.* This Fellow wou'd lead his Army forth to meet *Caesar*, or rather to pursue him; most of their Arms were of those sort of cruel Whips they call *Cat with Nine Tayls;* some had rusty useless Guns for show; others old Basket-hilts,[8] whose Blades had never seen the Light in this Age; and others had long Staffs, and Clubs. Mr. *Trefry* went along, rather to be a Mediator than a Conqueror, in such a Battel; for he foresaw, and knew, if by fighting they put the Negroes into despair, they were a sort of sullen Fellows, that wou'd drown, or kill themselves, before they wou'd yield; and he advis'd that fair means was best: But *Byam* was one that abounded in his own Wit, and wou'd take his own Measures.

It was not hard to find these Fugitives; for as they fled they were forc'd to fire and cut the Woods before 'em, so that Night or Day they pursu'd 'em by the light they made, and by the path they had clear'd: But as soon as *Caesar* found he was pursu'd, he put himself in a Posture of Defence, placing all the Women and Children in the Rear; and himself, with *Tuscan* by his side, or next to him, all promising to Dye or Conquer. Incourag'd thus, they never stood to Parley, but fell on Pell-mell upon the *English*, and kill'd some, and wounded a good many; they having recourse to their Whips, as the best of their Weapons: And as they observ'd no Order, they perplex'd the Enemy so sorely, with Lashing 'em in the Eyes; and the Women and Children, seeing their Husbands so treated, being of fearful Cowardly Dispositions, and hearing the *English* cry out, *Yield and Live, Yield and be Pardon'd;* they all run in amongst their Husbands and Fathers, and hung about 'em, crying out, *Yield, yield; and leave* Caesar *to their Revenge;* that by degrees the Slaves abandon'd *Caesar*, and left him only *Tuscan* and his Heroick *Imoinda;* who, grown big as she was, did nevertheless press near her Lord, having a Bow, and a Quiver full of poyson'd Arrows, which she manag'd with such dexterity, that she wounded several, and shot the *Governor* into the Shoulder; of which Wound he had like to have Dy'd, but that an *Indian* Woman, his Mistress, suck'd the Wound, and cleans'd it from the Venom: But however, he stir'd not from the Place till he had Parly'd with *Caesar*, who he found was resolv'd to dye Fighting, and wou'd not be Taken; no more wou'd *Tuscan*, or *Imoinda.* But he, more thirsting after Revenge of another sort, than that of depriving him of Life, now made use of all his Art of talking, and dissembling; and besought *Caesar* to yield himself upon Terms, which he himself should propose, and should be Sacredly assented to and kept by him: He told him, It was not that he any longer fear'd him, or cou'd believe the force of Two Men, and a young Heroine, cou'd overcome all them, with all

6. Cheated.
7. William Byam, a Royalist exile from England and Barbados.
8. Swords with hilt guards.

the Slaves now on their side also; but it was the vast Esteem he had for his Person; the desire he had to serve so Gallant a Man; and to hinder himself from the Reproach hereafter, of having been the occasion of the Death of a *Prince*, whose Valour and Magnanimity deserv'd the Empire of the World. He protested to him, he look'd upon this Action, as Gallant and Brave; however tending to the prejudice of his Lord and Master, who wou'd by it have lost so considerable a number of *Slaves*; that this Flight of his shou'd be look'd on as a heat of Youth, and rashness of a too forward Courage, and an unconsider'd impatience of Liberty, and no more; and that he labour'd in vain to accomplish that which they wou'd effectually perform, as soon as any Ship arriv'd that wou'd touch on his Coast. *So that if you will be pleas'd*, continued he, *to surrender your self, all imaginable Respect shall be paid you; and your Self, your Wife, and Child, if it be here born, shall depart free out of our Land.* But *Caesar* wou'd hear of no Composition,[9] though *Byam* urg'd, If he pursu'd, and went on in his Design, he wou'd inevitably Perish, either by great *Snakes*, wild Beasts, or Hunger; and he ought to have regard to his Wife, whose Condition required ease, and not the fatigues of tedious Travel; where she cou'd not be secur'd from being devoured. But *Caesar* told him, there was no Faith in the White Men, or the Gods they Ador'd; who instructed 'em in Principles so false, that honest Men cou'd not live amongst 'em; though no People profess'd so much, none perform'd so little; that he knew what he had to do, when he dealt with Men of Honour; but with them a Man ought to be eternally on his Guard, and never to Eat and Drink with *Christians* without his Weapon of Defence in his Hand; and, for his own Security, never to credit one Word they spoke. As for the rashness and inconsiderateness of his Action he wou'd confess the Governor is in the right; and that he was asham'd of what he had done, in endeavoring to make those Free, who were by Nature *Slaves*, poor wretched Rogues, fit to be us'd as *Christians* Tools; Dogs, treacherous and cowardly, fit for such Masters; and they wanted only but to be whipt into the knowledge of the *Christian Gods* to be the vilest of all creeping things; to learn to Worship such Deities as had not Power to make 'em Just, Brave, or Honest. In fine, after a thousand things of this Nature, not fit here to be recited, he told *Byam*, he had rather Dye than Live upon the same Earth with such Dogs. But *Trefry* and *Byam* pleaded and protested together so much, that *Trefry* believing the *Governor* to mean what he said; and speaking very cordially himself, generously put himself into *Caesar*'s Hands, and took him aside, and perswaded him, even with Tears, to Live, by Surrendring himself, and to name his Conditions. *Caesar* was overcome by his Wit and Reasons, and in consideration of *Imoinda*; and demanding what he desir'd, and that it shou'd be ratify'd by their Hands in Writing, because he had perceiv'd that was the common way of contract between Man and Man, amongst the Whites: All this was perform'd, and *Tuscan*'s Pardon was put in, and they Surrender to the Governor, who walked peaceably down into the *Plantation* with 'em, after giving order to bury their dead. *Caesar* was very much toyl'd with the bustle of the Day; for he had fought like a Fury, and what Mischief was done he and *Tuscan* perform'd alone; and gave their Enemies a fatal Proof that they durst do any thing, and fear'd no mortal Force.

9. Settlement.

But they were no sooner arriv'd at the Place, where all the Slaves receive their Punishments of Whipping, but they laid Hands on *Caesar* and *Tuscan*, faint with heat and toyl; and, surprising them, Bound them to two several Stakes, and Whipt them in a most deplorable and inhumane Manner, rending the very Flesh from their Bones; especially *Caesar*, who was not perceiv'd to make any Moan, or to alter his Face, only to roul his Eyes on the Faithless *Governor*, and those he believ'd Guilty, with Fierceness and Indignation; and, to compleat his Rage, he saw every one of those *Slaves*, who, but a few Days before, Ador'd him as something more than Mortal, now had a Whip to give him some Lashes, while he strove not to break his Fetters; though, if he had, it were impossible: But he pronounced a Woe and Revenge from his Eyes, that darted Fire, that 'twas at once both Awful and Terrible to behold.

When they thought they were sufficiently Reveng'd on him, they unty'd him, almost Fainting, with loss of Blood, from a thousand Wounds all over his Body; from which they had rent his Cloaths, and led him Bleeding and Naked as he was; and loaded him all over with Irons; and then rubbed his Wounds, to compleat their Cruelty, with *Indian Pepper*, which had like to have made him raving Mad; and, in this Condition, made him so fast to the Ground that he cou'd not stir, if his Pains and Wounds wou'd have given him leave. They spar'd *Imoinda*, and did not let her see this Barbarity committed towards her Lord, but carry'd her down to *Parham*, and shut her up; which was not in kindness to her, but for fear she shou'd Dye with the Sight, or Miscarry; and then they shou'd lose a young *Slave*, and perhaps the Mother.

You must know, that when the News was brought on Monday Morning, that *Caesar* had betaken himself to the Woods, and carry'd with him all the *Negroes*, we were possess'd with extream Fear, which no perswasions cou'd Dissipate, that he wou'd secure himself till Night; and then, that he wou'd come down and Cut all our Throats. This apprehension made all the Females of us fly down the River, to be secur'd; and while we were away, they acted this Cruelty: For I suppose I had Authority and Interest enough there, had I suspected any such thing, to have prevented it; but we had not gone many Leagues, but the News overtook us that *Caesar* was taken, and Whipt like a common *Slave*. We met on the River with Colonel *Martin*, a Man of great Gallantry, Wit, and Goodness, and whom I have celebrated in a Character of my New *Comedy*,[1] by his own Name, in memory of so brave a Man: He was Wise and Eloquent; and, from the fineness of his Parts, bore a great Sway over the Hearts of all the *Colony*: He was a Friend to *Caesar*, and resented this false Dealing with him very much. We carried him back to *Parham*, thinking to have made an Accommodation; when we came, the First News we heard was, that the *Governor* was Dead of a Wound *Imoinda* had given him; but it was not so well; But it seems he wou'd have the Pleasure of beholding the Revenge he took on *Caesar*; and before the cruel Ceremony was finish'd, he drop'd down; and then they perceiv'd the Wound he had on his Shoulder, was by a venom'd Arrow; which, as I said, his *Indian* Mistress heal'd, by Sucking the Wound.

We were no sooner Arriv'd, but we went up to the *Plantation* to see *Caesar*, whom we found in a very Miserable and Unexpressable Condition; and I have

---

1. Behn's *The Younger Brother, or The Amorous Jilt*, produced in 1696.

a Thousand times admired how he liv'd, in so much tormenting Pain. We said all things to him, that Trouble, Pitty, and Good Nature cou'd suggest; Protesting our Innocency of the Fact, and our Abhorance of such Cruelties; making a Thousand Professions of Services to him, and Begging as many Pardons for the Offenders, till we said so much, that he believ'd we had no Hand in his ill Treatment; but told us, he cou'd never Pardon *Byam*; as for *Trefry*, he confess'd he saw his Grief and Sorrow, for his Suffering, which he cou'd not hinder, but was like to have been beaten down by the very *Slaves*, for Speaking in his Defence: But for *Byam*, who was their Leader, their Head;——and shou'd, by his Justice, and Honor, have been an Example to 'em,——For him, he wish'd to Live, to take a dire Revenge of him, and said, *It had been well for him, if he had Sacrific'd me, instead of giving me the contemptable Whip.* He refus'd to Talk much, but Begging us to give him our Hands, he took 'em, and Protested never to lift up his, to do us any Harm. He had a great Respect for Colonel *Martin*, and always took his Counsel, like that of a Parent; and assur'd him, he wou'd obey him in any thing, but his Revenge on *Byam*. *Therefore*, said he, *for his own Safety, let him speedily dispatch me; for if I cou'd dispatch my self, I wou'd not, till that Justice were done to my injur'd Person, and the contempt of a Souldier: No, I wou'd not kill my self, even after a Whipping, but will be content to live with that Infamy, and be pointed at by every grinning Slave, till I have compleated my Revenge; and then you shall see that* Oroonoko *scoms to live with the Indignity that was put on* Caesar. All we cou'd do cou'd get no more Words from him; and we took care to have him put immediately into a healing Bath, to rid him of his Pepper; and order'd a Chirurgeon to anoint him with healing Balm, which he suffer'd, and in some time he began to be able to Walk and Eat; we fail'd not to visit him every Day, and, to that end, had him brought to an apartment at *Parham*.

The *Governor* was no sooner recover'd, and had heard of the menaces of *Caesar*, but he call'd his Council; who (not to disgrace them, or Burlesque the Government there) consisted of such notorious Villains as *Newgate*[2] never transported; and possibly originally were such, who understood neither the Laws of *God* or *Man*; and had no sort of Principles to make 'em worthy the Name of Men: But, at the very Council Table, wou'd Contradict and Fight with one another; and Swear so bloodily that 'twas terrible to hear, and see 'em. (Some of 'em were afterwards Hang'd, when the *Dutch* took possession of the place; others sent off in Chains.) But calling these special Rulers of the Nation together, and requiring their Counsel in this weighty Affair, they all concluded, that (Damn 'em) it might be their own Cases; and that *Caesar* ought to be made an Example to all the *Negroes*, to fright 'em from daring to threaten their Betters, their Lords and Masters; and, at this rate, no Man was safe from his own *Slaves*; and concluded, *nemine contradicente*,[3] that *Caesar* shou'd be Hang'd.

Trefry then thought it time to use his Authority; and told *Byam* his Command did not extend to his Lord's *Plantation*; and that *Parham* was as much exempt from the Law as *White-hall*,[4] and that they ought no more to touch the Servants of the Lord——— (who there represented the King's Person) than they cou'd

2. The main prison in London, from where criminals were transported to the colonies.
3. With no one disagreeing (Latin).

4. The king's palace in London. Trefry is Willoughby's deputy in Parham, Byam in the colony.

those about the King himself; and that *Parham* was a Sanctuary; and though his Lord were absent in Person, his Power was still in Being there; which he had intrusted with him, as far as the Dominions of his particular *Plantations* reach'd, and all that belong'd to it; the rest of the *Country*, as *Byam* was Lieutenant to his Lord, he might exercise his Tyrany upon. *Trefry* had others as powerful, or more, that int'rested themselves in *Caesar*'s Life, and absolutely said, He shou'd be Defended. So turning the *Governor*, and his wise Council, out of Doors, (for they sate at *Parham-house*) they set a Guard upon our Landing Place, and wou'd admit none but those we call'd Friends to us and *Caesar*.

The *Governor* having remain'd wounded at *Parham*, till his recovery was compleated, *Caesar* did not know but he was still there; and indeed, for the most part, his time was spent there; for he was one that lov'd to Live at other Peoples Expence; and if he were a Day absent, he was Ten present there; and us'd to Play, and Walk, and Hunt, and Fish, with *Caesar*. So that *Caesar* did not at all doubt, if he once recover'd Strength, but he shou'd find an opportunity of being Reveng'd on him: Though, after such a Revenge, he cou'd not hope to Live; for if he escap'd the Fury of the English *Mobile*,[5] who perhaps wou'd have been glad of the occasion to have kill'd him, he was resolv'd not to survive his Whipping; yet he had, some tender Hours, a repenting Softness, which he called his fits of Coward; wherein he struggl'd with Love for the Victory of his Heart, which took part with his charming *Imoinda* there; but, for the most part, his time was past in melancholy Thought, and black Designs; he consider'd, if he shou'd do this Deed, and Dye, either in the Attempt, or after it, he left his lovely *Imoinda* a Prey, or at best a *Slave*, to the inrag'd Multitude; his great Heart cou'd not indure that Thought. *Perhaps*, said he, *she may be first Ravished by every Brute; exposed first to their nasty Lusts, and then a shameful Death.* No; he could not Live a Moment under that Apprehension, too insupportable to be born. These were his Thoughts, and his silent Arguments with his Heart, as he told us afterwards; so that now resolving not only to kill *Byam*, but all those he thought had inrag'd him; pleasing his great Heart with the fancy'd Slaughter he shou'd make over the whole Face of the *Plantation*; he first resolv'd on a Deed, that (however Horrid it at first appear'd to us all) when we had heard his Reasons, we thought it Brave and Just: Being able to Walk, and, as he believ'd, fit for the Execution of his great Design, he beg'd *Trefry* to trust him into the Air, believing a Walk wou'd do him good; which was granted him, and taking *Imoinda* with him, as he us'd to do in his more happy and calmer Days, he led her up into a Wood, where, after (with a thousand Sighs, and long Gazing silently on her Face, while Tears gusht, in spite of him, from his Eyes) he told her his Design first of Killing her, and then his Enemies, and next himself, and the impossibility of Escaping, and therefore he told her the necessity of Dying; he found the Heroick Wife faster pleading for Death than he was to propose it, when she found his fix'd Resolution; and, on her Knees, besought him, not to leave her a Prey to his Enemies. He (griev'd to Death) yet pleased at her noble Resolution, took her up, and imbracing her, with all the Passion and Languishment of a dying Lover, drew his Knife to kill this Treasure of his Soul, this Pleasure of his Eyes; while Tears trickl'd down his Cheeks, hers were Smiling with Joy she shou'd dye by so noble a Hand, and be

5. Mob.

sent in her own Country, (for that's their Notion of the next World) by him she so tenderly Lov'd, and so truly Ador'd in this; for Wives have a respect for their Husbands equal to what any other People pay a Deity; and when a Man finds any occasion to quit his Wife, if he love her, she dyes by his Hand; if not, he sells her, or suffers some other to kill her. It being thus, you may believe the Deed was soon resolv'd on; and 'tis not to be doubted, but the Parting, the eternal Leave taking of Two such Lovers, so greatly Born, so Sensible,[6] so Beautiful, so Young, and so Fond, must be very Moving, as the Relation of it was to me afterwards.

All that Love cou'd say in such cases, being ended; and all the intermitting Irresolutions being adjusted, the Lovely, Young, and Ador'd Victim lays her self down, before the Sacrificer; while he, with a Hand resolv'd, and a Heart breaking within, gave the Fatal Stroke; first, cutting her Throat, and then severing her yet Smiling Face from that Delicate Body, pregnant as it was with Fruits of tend'rest Love. As soon as he had done, he laid the Body decently on Leaves and Flowers; of which he made a Bed, and conceal'd it under the same cover-lid of Nature; only her Face he left yet bare to look on: But when he found she was Dead, and past all Retrieve, never more to bless him with her Eyes, and soft Language; his Grief swell'd up to Rage; he Tore, he Rav'd, he Roar'd, like some Monster of the Wood, calling on the lov'd Name of *Imoinda*; a thousand times he turn'd the Fatal Knife that did the Deed, toward his own Heart, with a Resolution to go immediately after her; but dire Revenge, which now was a thousand times more fierce in his Soul than before, prevents him; and he wou'd cry out, *No; since I have sacrificed* Imoinda *to my Revenge, shall I lose that Glory which I have purchas'd so dear, as at the Price of the fairest, dearest, softest Creature that ever Nature made? No, no!* Then, at her Name, Grief wou'd get the ascendant of Rage, and he wou'd lye down by her side, and water her Face with showers of Tears, which never were wont to fall from those Eyes: And however bent he was on his intended Slaughter, he had not power to stir from the Sight of this dear Object, now more Belov'd, and more Ador'd than ever.

He remain'd in this deploring Condition for two Days, and never rose from the Ground where he had made his sad Sacrifice; at last, rousing from her side, and accusing himself with living too long, now *Imoinda* was dead; and that the Deaths of those barbarous Enemies were deferr'd too long, he resolv'd now to finish the great Work; but offering to rise, he found his Strength so decay'd, that he reel'd to and fro, like Boughs assail'd by contrary Winds; so that he was forced to lye down again, and try to summons all his Courage to his Aid; he found his Brains turn round, and his Eyes were dizzy; and Objects appear'd not the same to him they were wont to do; his Breath was short; and all his Limbs surprised with a Faintness he had never felt before: He had not Eat in two Days, which was one occasion of this Feebleness, but excess of Grief was the greatest; yet still he hop'd he shou'd recover Vigour to act his Design; and lay expecting it yet six Days longer; still mourning over the dead Idol of his Heart, and striving every Day to rise, but cou'd not.

In all this time you may believe we were in no little affliction for *Caesar*, and his Wife; some were of Opinion he was escap'd never to return; others thought

6. Sensitive.

some Accident had hap'ned to him: But however, we fail'd not to send out an hundred People several ways to search for him; a Party, of about forty, went that way he took; among whom was *Tuscan*, who was perfectly reconcil'd to *Byam*; they had not go very far into the Wood, but they smelt an unusual Smell, as of a dead Body; for Stinks must be very noisom that can be distinguish'd among such a quantity of Natural Sweets, as every Inch of that Land produces. So that they concluded they shou'd find him dead, or some-body that was so; they past on towards it, as Loathsom as it was, and made such a rustling among the Leaves that lye thick on the Ground, by continual Falling, that *Caesar* heard he was approach'd; and though he had, during the space of these eight Days, endeavor'd to rise, but found he wanted Strength, yet looking up, and seeing his Pursuers, he rose, and reel'd to a Neighbouring Tree, against which he fix'd his Back; and being within a dozen Yards of those that advanc'd, and saw him, he call'd out to them, and bid them approach no nearer, if they wou'd be safe: So that they stood still, and hardly believing their Eyes, that wou'd perswade them that it was *Caesar* that spoke to 'em, so much was he alter'd, they ask'd him, What he had done with his Wife? for they smelt a Stink that almost struck them dead. He, pointing to the dead Body, sighing, cry'd, *Behold her there*; they put off the Flowers that cover'd her with their Sticks, and found she was kill'd; and cry'd out, *Oh monster! that hast murther'd thy Wife*: Then asking him, Why he did so cruel a Deed? He replied, he had no leasure to answer impertinent Questions; *You may go back*, continued he, *and tell the Faithless Governor, he may thank Fortune that I am breathing my last; and that my Arm is too feeble to obey my Heart, in what it had design'd him*: But his Tongue faultering, and trembling, he cou'd scarce end what he was saying. The *English* taking Advantage by his Weakness, cry'd, *Let us take him alive by all means*: He heard 'em; and, as if he had reviv'd from a Fainting, or a Dream, he cry'd out, *No, Gentlemen, you are deceiv'd; you will find no more Caesars to be Whipt; no more find a Faith in me: Feeble as you think me, I have Strength yet left to secure me from a second Indignity*. They swore all a-new, and he only shook his Head, and beheld them with Scorn; then they cry'd out, *Who will venture on this single Man? Will no body?* They stood all silent while *Caesar* replied, *Fatal will be the Attempt to the first Adventurer; let him assure himself*, and, at that Word, held up his Knife in a menacing Posture, *Look ye, ye faith-less Crew*, said he, *'tis not Life I seek, nor am I afraid of Dying*; and, at that Word, cut a piece of Flesh from his own Throat, and threw it at 'em, *yet still I wou'd Live if I cou'd, till I had perfected my Revenge. But oh! it cannot be; I feel Life gliding from my Eyes and Heart; and, if I make not haste, I shall yet fall a Victim to the shameful Whip*. At that, he rip'd up his own Belly; and took his Bowels and pull'd 'em out, with what Strength he cou'd; while some, on their Knees imploring, besought him to hold his Hand. But when they saw him tot-tering, they cry'd out, *Will none venture on him?* A bold *English* cry'd, *Yes, if he were the Devil*; (taking Courage when he saw him almost Dead) and swearing a horrid Oath for his farewell to the World, he rush'd on; *Caesar*, with his Arm'd Hand met him so fairly, as stuck him to the Heart, and he fell Dead at his Feet. *Tuscan* seeing that, cry'd out, *I love thee, oh Caesar; and therefore will not let thee Dye, if possible*: And, running to him, took him in his Arms; but, at the same time, warding a Blow that *Caesar* made at his Bosom, he receiv'd it quite through his Arm; and *Caesar* having not the Strength to pluck the Knife forth, though he attempted it, *Tuscan* neither pull'd it out himself, nor suffer'd it to be pull'd out; but came down with it sticking in his Arm; and the reason he gave for it was, because the Air shou'd not get into the Wound: They put their Hands a-cross, and carried *Caesar* between Six of 'em, fainted as he was; and they thought Dead, or just Dying; and they brought him to *Parham*, and laid him on a Couch, and had the Chirurgeon immediately to him, who drest his Wounds, and sew'd up his Belly, and us'd means to bring him to Life, which they effected. We ran all to see him; and, if before we thought him so beautiful a Sight, he was now so alter'd, that his Face was like a Death's Head black'd over; nothing but Teeth, and Eyeholes: For some Days we suffer'd no body to speak to him, but caused Cordials to be poured down his Throat, which sustained his Life; and in six or seven Days he recover'd his Senses: For, you must know, that Wounds are almost to a Miracle cur'd in the *Indies*; unless Wounds in the Legs, which rarely ever cure.

When he was well enough to speak, we talk'd to him; and ask'd him some Questions about his Wife, and the Reasons why he kill'd her; and he then told us what I have related of that Resolution, and of his Parting; and he besought us, we would let him Dye, and was extreamly Afflicted to think it was possible he might Live; he assur'd us, if we did not Dispatch him, he wou'd prove very Fatal to a great many. We said all we cou'd to make him Live, and gave him new Assurances; but he begg'd we wou'd not think so poorly of him, or of his love to *Imoinda*, to imagine we cou'd Flatter him to Life again; but the Chirurgeon assur'd him, he cou'd not Live, and therefore he need not Fear. We were all (but *Caesar*) afflicted at this News; and the Sight was gashly;[7] his Discourse was sad; and the earthly Smell about him so strong, that I was perswaded to leave the Place for some time (being my self but Sickly, and very apt to fall into Fits of dangerous Illness upon any extraordinary Melancholy); the Servants, and *Trefry*, and the Chirurgeons, promis'd all to take what possible care they cou'd of the Life of *Caesar*; and I, taking Boat, went with other Company to Colonel *Martin*'s, about three Days Journy down the River; but I was no sooner gon, but the *Governor* taking *Trefry*, about some pretended earnest Business, a Days Journy up the River; having communicated his Design to one *Banister*,[8] a wild *Irish* Man, and one of the Council; a Fellow of absolute Barbarity, and fit to execute any Villany, but was Rich. He came up to *Parham*, and forcibly took *Caesar*, and had him carried to the same Post where he was Whip'd; and causing him to be ty'd to it, and a great Fire made before him, he told him, he shou'd Dye like a Dog, as he was. *Caesar* replied, this was the first piece of Bravery that ever *Banister* did; and he never spoke Sense till he pronounc'd that Word; and, if he wou'd keep it, he wou'd declare, in the other World, that he was the only Man, of all the Whites, that ever he heard speak Truth. And turning to the Men that bound him, he said, *My Friends, am I to Dye, or to be Whip'd?* And they cry'd, *Whip'd! no; you shall not escape so well:* And then he replied, smiling, *A Blessing on thee*; and assur'd them, they need not tye him, for he wou'd stand fixt, like a Rock; and indure Death so as shou'd encourage them to Dye. *But if you Whip me*, said he, *be sure you tye me fast.*

---

7. Ghastly.
8. James Banister was the deputy governor in

1688, when Surinam was turned over to the Dutch.

He had learn'd to take Tobaco; and when he was assur'd he should Dye, he desir'd they would give him a Pipe in his Mouth, ready Lighted, which they did; and the Executioner came, and first cut off his Members[9] and threw them into the Fire; after that, with an ill-favoured Knife, they cut his Ears, and his Nose, and burn'd them; he still Smoak'd on, as if nothing had touch'd him; then they hack'd off one of his Arms, and still he bore up, and held his Pipe; but at the cutting off the other Arm, his Head sunk, and his Pipe drop'd; and he gave up the Ghost, without a Groan, or a Reproach. My Mother and Sister were by him all the while, but not suffer'd to save him; so rude and wild were the Rabble, and so inhumane were the Justices, who stood by to see the Execution, who after paid dearly enough for their Insolence. They cut *Caesar* in Quarters, and sent them to several of the chief *Plantations*: One Quarter was sent to Colonel *Martin*, who refus'd it; and swore, he had rather see the Quarters of *Banister*, and the *Governor* himself, than those of *Caesar*, on his *Plantations*; and that he cou'd govern his *Negroes* without Terrifying and Grieving them with frightful Spectacles of a mangl'd King.

Thus Dy'd this Great Man; worthy of a better Fate, and a more sublime Wit than mine to write his Praise; yet, I hope, the Reputation of my Pen is considerable enough to make his Glorious Name to survive to all Ages; with that of the Brave, the Beautiful, and the Constant *Imoinda*.

FINIS.

9. Genitals.

SOR JUANA INÉS DE LA CRUZ
1648–1695

Sor (Sister) Juana, a nun from New Spain (colonial Mexico), was one of the most famous writers of her time, celebrated as the "Tenth Muse" in Europe and the Americas. She is best known for her spirited defense of women's intellectual rights in *The Poet's Answer to the Most Illustrious Sor Filotea de la Cruz*. While ostensibly declaring her humility and her religious subordination in this text, Sor Juana also manages to advance claims for her sex that are more far-reaching and profound than any previously offered. At the same time, she paints a passionate yet nuanced picture of the life of the mind that combines rhetorical precision and intense emotion.

Born illegitimate to an upper-class creole woman and a Spanish captain, Sor Juana learned to read in her grandfather's library. Despite ongoing tensions among Spaniards, creoles, and the indigenous population, Sor Juana's Mexico was a huge metropole with a lively artistic and intellectual scene centered around the viceregal court. As a young girl, Juana served as lady-in-waiting at the court before entering the Convent of Saint Jerome when she was eighteen. Her *Answer* suggests that she became a nun in search of a safe environment in which to pursue her intellectual interests, and her religious vocation did not prevent her from writing in secular forms—lyric poetry and drama—for which she became known throughout the Spanish-speaking world. She wrote sixty-five sonnets, over sixty *romances* (ballads), and a profusion of poems in other metrical forms. She also wrote for the stage, producing everything from comedies and farces to *autos sacramentales*, religious plays that marked Catholic holidays.

Because her religious superiors rebuked her worldly interests, however, she struggled to continue writing secular literature without abandoning her faith. The natural disturbances and disasters that plagued Mexico City in the 1690s—a solar eclipse, storms, and famine—and the departure of some of her key supporters rekindled her religious passions and led her in 1694 to formally reaffirm her faith in a statement that she signed in her own blood with the words, "I, Sor Juana Inés de la Cruz, the worst of all." She died soon after, while nursing the convent sick during an epidemic.

The *Answer* stems directly from Sor Juana's venture into theological polemic. In 1690 she wrote a commentary on a sermon delivered forty years earlier, on the nature of Christ's love toward humanity. Her commentary, in the form of a letter, was published without her consent by the bishop of Puebla. The bishop provided the title, *Athenagoric Letter*, or "letter worthy of the wisdom of Athena," and also prefixed his own letter to Sor Juana, signed with the pseudonym "Filotea de la Cruz." In the letter, one "nun" advises the other to focus her attention and her talents on religious matters. In her *Answer* (1691), Sor Juana nominally accepts the bishop's rebuke; the smooth surface of her elegant prose, however, conceals both rage and determination to assert her right—and that of other women—to a fully realized life of the mind.

The artistry of this piece of self-defense demonstrates Sor Juana's powers and thus constitutes part of her justification. While asserting her own unimportance, she illustrates the range of her knowledge and of her rhetorical skill. The sheer abundance of her biblical allusions and quotations from theological texts, for instance, proves that she has mastered a large body of religious material and that she has not sacrificed religious for secular study. Her elaborate protestations of deference, her vocabulary of insignificance, and her narrative of subservience all show the verbal dexterity that enables her to achieve her own rhetorical ends even as she denies her commitment to purely personal goals. No matter how often Sor Juana admits that her intellectual longings amount to a form of "vice," she embodies in her prose the energy and the vividness that they generate.

Her larger argument depends on her utter denial that intelligence or a thirst for knowledge should be attributed to only one gender. While she draws on history for evidence of female intellectual power, even more forceful is the testimony of her own experience: her account of how, deprived of books, she finds matter for intellectual inquiry everywhere—in the yolk of an egg, the spinning of a top, the reading of the Bible. If she arouses uneasiness when she implicitly equates herself, as object of persecution, with Christ, she also makes one feel directly the horror of women's official exclusion, in the past, from intellectual pursuits.

Sor Juana's sonnets offer a different perspective on this versatile writer. By turns playful and passionate, they often have a satiric edge that recalls the artful arguments of the *Answer*. In poem 145, she takes up the Spanish Baroque tradition of *desengaño* or disillusion, in which the poet finds behind the surface of things the emptiness and vanity of earthly existence. But instead of revealing the impermanence of a person or a building, as her models often do, Sor Juana writes about a portrait, so that her sonnet dismantles one piece of art as it makes another. Poem 164 is a passionate, intimate plea to end a lover's quarrel, reminding us of the remarkable poetic range available to this scholarly nun. In "Philosophical Satire," perhaps her most famous poem, Sor Juana methodically analyzes the contradictions in men's expectations of women, in a devastating anatomy of sexual hypocrisy that reverberates far beyond her own sophisticated milieu.

From The Poet's Answer to the Most Illustrious Sor Filotea de la Cruz[1]

Most illustrious Lady, my Lady:

It has not been my will, but my scant health and a rightful fear that have delayed my reply for so many days. Is it to be wondered that, at the very first step, I should meet with two obstacles that sent my dull pen stumbling? The first (and to me the most insuperable) is the question of how to respond to your immensely learned, prudent, devout, and loving letter. For when I consider how the Angelic Doctor, St. Thomas Aquinas, on being asked of his silence before his teacher Albertus Magnus,[2] responded that he kept quiet because he could say nothing worthy of Albertus, then how much more fitting it is that I should keep quiet—not like the Saint from modesty, but rather because, in truth, I am unable to say anything worthy of you. The second obstacle is the question of how to render my thanks for the favor, as excessive as it was unexpected, of giving my drafts and scratches to the press[3] a favor so far beyond all measure as to surpass the most ambitious hopes or the most fantastic desires, so that as a rational being I simply could not house it in my thoughts. In short, this was a favor of such magnitude that it cannot be bounded by the confines of speech and indeed exceeds all powers of gratitude, as much because it was so large as because it was so unexpected. In the words of Quintilian:[4] *"They produce less glory through hopes, more glory through benefits conferred."* And so much so, that the recipient is struck dumb.

---

1. Translated by Electa Arenal and Amanda Powell.
2. Thomas Aquinas (1225–1274), scholastic philosopher and theologian who held that faith and reason existed in harmony. The great thinker Albertus Magnus (ca. 1206?–1280) defended his student Thomas from criticisms.
3. "Sor Filotea" (from the Greek, lover of God) was the pseudonym used by Manuel Fernández de Santa Cruz, bishop of Puebla, who had published Sor Juana's commentary on a sermon without her consent.
4. Marcus Fabius Quintilianus (35–100), Roman orator and rhetorician from Hispania.

When the mother of [John] the Baptist—felicitously barren, so as to become miraculously fertile—saw under her roof so exceedingly great a guest as the Mother of the Word, her powers of mind were dulled and her speech was halted; and thus, instead of thanks, she burst out with doubts and questions: "*And whence is this to me . . . ?*" The same occurred with Saul when he was chosen and anointed[5] King of Israel: "*Am not I a son of Jemini of the least tribe of Israel, and my kindred the last among all the families of the tribe of Benjamin? Why then hast thou spoken this word to me?*"[6] Just so, I too must say: Whence, O venerable Lady, whence comes such a favor to me? By chance, am I something more than a poor nun, the slightest creature on earth and the least worthy of drawing your attention? Well, *why then hast thou spoken this word to me? And whence is this to me?*

I can answer nothing more to the first obstacle than that I am entirely unworthy of your gaze. To the second, I can offer nothing more than amazement, instead of thanks, declaring that I am unable to thank you for the slightest part of what I owe you. It is not false humility, my Lady, but the candid truth of my very soul, to say that when the printed letter reached my hands— that letter you were pleased to dub "Worthy of Athena"[7]—I burst into tears (a thing that does not come easily to me), tears of confusion. For it seemed to me that your great favor was nothing other than God's reproof aimed at my failure to return His favors, and while He corrects others with punishments, He wished to chide me through benefits. A special favor, this, for which I acknowledge myself His debtor, as I am indebted for infinitely many favors given by His immense goodness; but this is also a special way of shaming and confounding me. For it is the choicest form of punishment to cause me to serve, knowingly, as the judge who condemns and sentences my own ingratitude. And so when I consider this fully, here in solitude, it is my custom to say: Blessed are you, my Lord God, for not only did you forbear to give another creature the power to judge me, nor have you placed that power in my hands. Rather, you have kept that power for yourself and have freed me of myself and of the sentence I would pass on myself, which, forced by my own conscience, could be no less than condemnation. Instead you have reserved that sentence for your great mercy to declare, because you love me more than I can love myself.

My Lady, forgive the digression wrested from me by the power of truth; yet if I must make a full confession of it, this digression is at the same time a way of seeking evasions so as to flee the difficulty of making my answer. And therefore I had nearly resolved to leave the matter in silence; yet although silence explains much by the emphasis of leaving all unexplained, because it is a negative thing, one must name the silence, so that what it signifies may be understood. Failing that, silence will say nothing, for that is its proper function: to say nothing. The holy Chosen Vessel was carried off to the third Heaven and, having seen the arcane secrets of God, he says: "*That he was caught up into paradise, and heard secret words, which it is not granted to man to utter.*"[8] He

5. Luke 1.43.
6. I Samuel 9.21.
7. Fernández had entitled Sor Juana's commentary "Athenagoric Letter," letter worthy of Athena, after the Greek goddess of wisdom.

8. 2 Corinthians 12.4. "Chosen Vessel": in Acts 9.15, Christ describes St. Paul as his "chosen vessel" to carry his message to the Gentiles.

does not say what he saw, but he says that he cannot say it. In this way, of those things that cannot be spoken, it must be said that they cannot be spoken, so that it may be known that silence is kept not for lack of things to say, but because the many things there are to say cannot be contained in mere words. St. John says that if he were to write all of the wonders wrought by Our Redeemer, the whole world could not contain all the books.[9] Vieira says of this passage that in this one phrase the Evangelist says more than in all his other writings; and indeed how well the Lusitanian Phoenix[1] speaks (but when is he not well-spoken, even when he speaks ill?), for herein St. John says all that he failed to say and expresses all that he failed to express. And so I, my Lady, shall answer only that I know not how to answer; I shall thank you only by saying that I know not how to give thanks; and I shall say, by way of the brief label placed on what I leave to silence, that only with the confidence of one so favored and with the advantages granted one so honored, do I dare speak to your magnificence. If this be folly, please forgive it; for folly sparkles in good fortune's crown, and through it I shall supply further occasion for your good-will, and you shall better arrange the expression of my gratitude.

Moses, because he was a stutterer,[2] thought himself unworthy to speak to Pharaoh. Yet later, finding himself greatly favored by God, he was so imbued with courage that not only did he speak to God Himself, but he dared to ask of Him the impossible: "*Shew me thy face.*"[3] And so it is with me, my Lady, for in view of the favor you show me, the obstacles I described at the outset no longer seem entirely insuperable. For one who had the letter printed, unbeknownst to me, who titled it and underwrote its cost, and who thus honored it (unworthy as it was of all this, on its own account and on account of its author), what will such a one not do? What not forgive? Or what fail to do or fail to forgive? Thus, sheltered by the assumption that I speak with the safe-conduct granted by your favors and with the warrant bestowed by your goodwill, and by the fact that, like a second Ahasuerus,[4] you have allowed me to kiss the top of the golden scepter of your affection as a sign that you grant me kind license to speak and to plead my case in your venerable presence, I declare that I receive in my very soul your most holy admonition to apply my study to Holy Scripture; for although it arrives in the guise of counsel, it shall have for me the weight of law. And I take no small consolation from the fact that it seems my obedience, as if at your direction, anticipated your pastoral insinuation, as may be inferred from the subject matter and arguments of that very Letter. I recognize full well that your most prudent warning touches not on the letter, but on the many writings of mine on humane matters that you have seen.[5] And thus, all that

9. John 21.25.

1. Lusitania is the Roman name for Portugal; the phoenix was a mythical bird reborn from its own ashes, used as a term of praise for writers in the period. Sor Juana was herself called the Mexican Phoenix. Antonio Vieira (1608–1697), author of the sermon that Sor Juana had criticized in her commentary, was a Jesuit Portuguese priest, diplomat, and orator who served as a missionary in Brazil.

2. In Exodus 4.10, Moses complains to God that he lacks the eloquence to approach Pharaoh.

3. Exodus 33.13.

4. King Xerxes of Persia, 486–465 B.C.E. In Esther 5.2–3, Ahasuerus holds out his scepter to his queen, Esther, and promises to grant her whatever she wishes, an opportunity that the wise queen uses to save the Jews from destruction.

5. Sor Juana had published secular poetry and drama.

I have said can do no more than offer that letter to you in recompense for the failure to apply myself which you must have inferred (and reasonably so) from my other writings. And to speak more specifically, I confess, with all the candor due to you and with the truth and frankness that are always at once natural and customary for me, that my having written little on sacred matters has sprung from no dislike, nor from lack of application, but rather from a surfeit of awe and reverence toward those sacred letters, which I know myself to be so incapable of understanding and which I am so unworthy of handling. For there always resounds in my ears the Lord's warning and prohibition to sinners like me, bringing with it no small terror: *"Why does thou declare my justices, and take my convenant in thy mouth?"*[6] With this question comes the reflection that even learned men were forbidden to read the Song of Songs, and indeed Genesis[7] before they reached the age of thirty: the latter text because of its difficulty, and the former so that with the sweetness of those epithalamiums, imprudent youth might not be stirred to carnal feelings. My great father St. Jerome confirms this, ordering the Song of Songs to be the last text studied, for the same reason: *"Then at last she may safely read the Song of Songs: if she were to read it at the beginning, she might be harmed by not perceiving that it was the song of a spiritual bridal expressed in fleshly language."*[8] And Seneca[9] says, *"In early years, faith is not yet manifest."* Then how should I dare take these up in my unworthy hands, when sex, and age, and above all our customs oppose it? And thus I confess that often this very fear has snatched the pen from my hand and has made the subject matter retreat back toward that intellect from which it wished to flow; an impediment I did not stumble across with profane subjects, for a heresy against art is not punished by the Holy Office[1] but rather by wits with their laughter and critics with their censure. And this, *"just or unjust, is not to be feared,"* for one is still permitted to take Communion and hear Mass, so that it troubles me little if at all. For in such matters, according to the judgment of the very ones who slander me, I have no obligation to know how nor the skill to hit the mark, and thus if I miss it is neither sin nor discredit. No sin, because I had no obligation; no discredit, because I had no possibility of hitting the mark, and *"no one is obliged to do the impossible."* And truth to tell, I have never written save when pressed and forced and solely to give pleasure to others, not only without taking satisfaction but with downright aversion, because I have never judged myself to possess the rich trove of learning and wit that is perforce the obligation of one who writes. This, then, is my usual reply to those who urge me to write, and the more so in the case of a sacred subject: What understanding do I possess, what studies, what subject matter, or what instruction, save four profundities of a superficial scholar? They can leave such things to those who understand them; as for me,

6. Psalms 50.16.
7. First book of the Old Testament. "Song of Songs": Old Testament praise poem, uses erotic imagery.
8. St. Jerome (ca. 342–420), ascetic and scholar, learned Church Father, and founder of the Jeronymite order. He wrote this advice for the education of the Roman girl Paula, who would eventually collaborate with Jerome

and become a saint in her own right. Sor Juana's convent, St. Paula's of the Order of St. Jerome, was named after both figures.
9. Roman playwright, philosopher, and orator (ca. 3 B.C.E.–63 C.E.).
1. The Holy Office of the Inquisition, founded by the papacy in the 13th century to root out heresy and suppress challenges to religious orthodoxy.

I want no trouble with the Holy Office, for I am but ignorant and tremble lest I utter some ill-sounding proposition or twist the true meaning of some passage. I do not study in order to write, nor far less in order to teach (which would be boundless arrogance in me), but simply to see whether by studying I may become less ignorant. This is my answer, and these are my feelings.

My writing has never proceeded from any dictate of my own, but a force beyond me; I can in truth say, "*You have compelled me.*"[2] One thing, however, is true, so that I shall not deny it (first because it is already well known to all, and second because God has shown me His favor in giving me the greatest possible love of truth, even when it might count against me). For ever since the light of reason first dawned in me, my inclination to letters was marked by such passion and vehemence that neither the reprimands of others (for I have received many) nor reflections of my own (there have been more than a few) have sufficed to make me abandon my pursuit of this native impulse that God Himself bestowed on me. His Majesty knows why and to what end He did so, and He knows that I have prayed that He snuff out the light of my intellect, leaving only enough to keep His Law. For more than that is too much, some would say, in a woman; and there are even those who say that it is harmful. His Majesty knows too that, not achieving this, I have attempted to entomb my intellect together with my name and to sacrifice it to the One who gave it to me; and that no other motive brought me to the life of religion, despite the fact that the exercises and companionship of a community were quite opposed to the tranquillity and freedom from disturbance required by my studious bent. And once in the community, the Lord knows—and in this world only he who needs must know it, does[3]—what I did to try to conceal my name and renown from the public; he did not, however, allow me to do this, telling me it was temptation, and so it would have been. If I could repay any part of my debt to you, my Lady, I believe I might do so merely by informing you of this, for these words have never left my mouth save to that one to whom they must be said. But having thrown wide the doors of my heart and revealed to you what is there under seal of secrecy, I want you to know that this confidence does not gainsay the respect I owe to your venerable person and excessive favors.

To go on with the narration of this inclination of mine, of which I wish to give you a full account: I declare I was not yet three years old when my mother sent off one of my sisters, older than I, to learn to read in one of those girls' schools that they call *Amigas*.[4] Affection and mischief carried me after her; and when I saw that they were giving her lessons, I so caught fire with the desire to learn that, deceiving the teacher (or so I thought), I told her that my mother wanted her to teach me also. She did not believe this, for it was not to be believed; but to humor my whim she gave me lessons. I continued to go and she continued to teach me, though no longer in make-believe, for the experience undeceived her. I learned to read in such a short time that I already knew how by the time my mother heard of it. My teacher had kept it from my mother to give delight with a thing all done and to receive a prize for a thing done well. And I had kept still, thinking I would be whipped for having done this without

---

2. 1 Corinthians 12.11.
3. Presumably her confessor, Father Antonio Núñez.

4. Informal schools set up by cultured women in their homes to teach girls.

permission. The woman who taught me (may God keep her) is still living, and she can vouch for what I say.

I remember that in those days, though I was as greedy for treats as children usually are at that age, I would abstain from eating cheese, because I heard tell that it made people stupid, and the desire to learn was stronger for me than the desire to eat—powerful as this is in children. Later, when I was six or seven years old and already knew how to read and write, along with all the other skills like embroidery and sewing that women learn, I heard that in Mexico City there were a University and Schools where they studied the sciences. As soon as I heard this I began to slay my poor mother with insistent and annoying pleas, begging her to dress me in men's clothes and send me to the capital, to the home of some relatives she had there, so that I could enter the University and study. She refused, and was right in doing so; but I quenched my desire by reading a great variety of books that belonged to my grandfather, and neither punishments nor scoldings could prevent me. And so when I did go to Mexico City, people marveled not so much at my intelligence as at my memory and the facts I knew at an age when it seemed I had scarcely had time to learn to speak.

I began to study Latin, in which I believe I took fewer than twenty lessons. And my interest was so intense, that although in women (and especially in the very bloom of youth) the natural adornment of the hair is so esteemed, I would cut off four to six fingerlengths of my hair, measuring how long it had been before. And I made myself a rule that if by the time it had grown back to the same length I did not know such and such a thing that I intended to study, then I would cut my hair off again to punish my dull-wittedness. And so my hair grew, but I did not yet know what I had resolved to learn, for it grew quickly and I learned slowly. Then I cut my hair right off to punish my dull-wittedness, for I did not think it reasonable that hair should cover a head that was so bare of facts—the more desirable adornment. I took the veil because, although I knew I would find in religious life many things that would be quite opposed to my character (I speak of accessory rather than essential matters), it would, given my absolute unwillingness to enter into marriage, be the least unfitting and the most decent state I could choose, with regard to the assurance I desired of my salvation. For before this first concern (which is, at the last, the most important), all the impertinent little follies of my character gave way and bowed to the yoke. These were wanting to live alone and not wanting to have either obligations that would disturb my freedom to study or the noise of a community that would interrupt the tranquil silence of my books. These things made me waver somewhat in my decision until, being enlightened by learned people as to my temptation, I vanquished it with divine favor and took the state I so unworthily hold. I thought I was fleeing myself, but—woe is me!—I brought myself with me, and brought my greatest enemy in my inclination to study, which I know not whether to take as a Heaven-sent favor or as a punishment. For when snuffed out or hindered with every [spiritual] exercise known to Religion, it exploded like gunpowder; and in my case the saying *"privation gives rise to appetite"* was proven true.

I went back (no, I spoke incorrectly, for I never stopped)—I went on, I mean, with my studious task (which to me was peace and rest in every moment left over when my duties were done) of reading and still more reading, study and still more study, with no teacher besides my books themselves. What a hardship it is to learn from those lifeless letters, deprived of the sound of a teacher's voice and explanations; yet I suffered all these trials most gladly for the love of learning. Oh, if only this had been done for the love of God, as was rightful, think what I should have merited! Nevertheless I did my best to elevate these studies and direct them to His service, for the goal to which I aspired was the study of Theology. Being a Catholic, I thought it an abject failing not to know everything that can in this life be achieved, through earthly methods, concerning the divine mysteries. And being a nun and not a laywoman, I thought I should, because I was in religious life, profess the study of letters—the more so as the daughter of such as St. Jerome and St. Paula: for it would be a degeneracy for an idiot daughter to proceed from such learned parents. I argued in this way to myself, and I thought my own argument quite reasonable. However, the fact may have been (and this seems most likely) that I was merely flattering and encouraging my own inclination, by arguing that its own pleasure was an obligation.

I went on in this way, always directing each step of my studies, as I have said, toward the summit of Holy Theology; but it seemed to me necessary to ascend by the ladder of the humane arts and sciences in order to reach it; for who could fathom the style of the Queen of Sciences without knowing that of her handmaidens? Without Logic, how should I know the general and specific methods by which Holy Scripture is written? Without Rhetoric, how should I understand its figures, tropes, and locutions? Or how, without Physics or Natural Science, understand all the questions that naturally arise concerning the varied natures of those animals offered in sacrifice, in which a great many things already made manifest are symbolized, and many more besides? How should I know whether Saul's cure at the sound of David's harp was owing to a virtue and power that is natural in Music or owing, instead, to a supernatural power that God saw fit to bestow on David?[5] How without Arithmetic might one understand all those mysterious reckonings of years and days and months and hours and weeks that are found in Daniel[6] and elsewhere, which can be comprehended only by knowing the natures, concordances, and properties of numbers? Without Geometry, how could we take the measure of the Holy Ark of the Covenant or the Holy City of Jerusalem, each of whose mysterious measurements forms a perfect cube uniting their dimensions, and each displaying that most marvelous distribution of the proportions of every part?

Without the science of Architecture, how understand the mighty Temple of Solomon—where God Himself was the Draftsman who set forth His arrangement and plan, and the Wise King was but the overseer who carried it out; where there was no foundation without its mystery, nor column without its symbol, nor cornice without its allusion, nor architrave without its meaning, and likewise for every other part, so that even the very least fillet served not only for the support and enhancement of Art, but to symbolize greater things? How, without a thorough knowledge of the order and divisions by which History is composed, is one to understand the Historical Books[7]—as in those summaries, for example, which often postpone in the narration what happened

---

5. 1 Samuel 16.23.
6. The book of Daniel includes the numerical interpretation of complex visions (Daniel

9.21–27).
7. The sections of the Old Testament that recount history rather than law or prophecies.

first in fact? How, without command of the two branches of Law, should one understand the Books of Law?[8] Without considerable erudition, how should we understand the great many matters of profane history that are mentioned by Holy Scripture: all the diverse customs of the Gentiles, all their rituals, all their manners of speech? Without knowing many precepts and reading widely in the Fathers of the Church, how could one understand the obscure sayings of the Prophets? Well then, and without being expert in Music, how might one understand those musical intervals and their perfections that occur in a great many passages—especially in Abraham's petitions to God on behalf of the Cities,[9] beseeching God to spare them if there were found fifty righteous people within? And the number fifty Abraham reduced to forty-five, which is sesquinonal [10 to 9] or like the interval from mi to re; this in turn he reduced to forty, which is the sesquioctave [9 to 8] or like the interval from re to mi; thence he went down to thirty, which is sesquitertia, or the interval of the diatessaron [the perfect fourth]; thence to twenty, the sesquialtera or the diapente [the fifth]; thence to ten, the duple, which is the diapason [the interval and consonance of the octave]; and because there are no more harmonic intervals, Abraham went no further. How could all this be understood without knowledge of music?[1] Why, in the very Book of Job, God says to him: "*Shalt thou be able to join together the shining stars the Pleiades, or canst thou stop the turning about of Arcturus? Canst thou bring forth the day star in its time, and make the evening star to rise upon the children of the earth?*"[2] Without knowledge of Astronomy, these terms would be impossible to understand. Nor are these noble sciences alone represented; indeed, not one of the mechanical arts escapes mention. In sum, we see how this Book contains all books, and this Science[3] includes all sciences, all of which serve that She may be understood. And once each science is mastered (which we see is not easy, or even possible), She demands still another condition beyond all I have yet said, which is continual prayer and purity of life, to entreat God for that cleansing of the spirit and illumination of the mind required for an understanding of such high things. And if this be lacking, all the rest is useless.

The Church says these words of the Angelic Doctor, St. Thomas Aquinas: "*At the difficult passages of Holy Scripture, he added fasting to prayer. And he used to say to his companion Brother Reginald that he owed all his knowledge not so much to study or hard work, but rather he had received it from God.*" How then should I, so far from either virtue or learning, find the courage to write? And so, to acquire a few basic principles of knowledge, I studied constantly in a variety of subjects, having no inclination toward any one of them in particular but being drawn rather to all of them generally. Therefore, if I have studied some things more than others it has not been by my choice, but because by chance the books on certain subjects came more readily to hand, and this gave preference to those topics, without my passing judgment in the matter. I held

---

8. The sections of the Old Testament that give laws. "Two branches of law": canon and civil laws, or the codes for church and state.
9. Sodom and Gomorrah. Abraham beseeches God to save Sodom from destruction for the sake of its just inhabitants (Genesis 18.22–23).

1. Sor Juana refers here to the intervals of classical music theory.
2. Job 38.31–32. "Pleiades": a constellation. "Arcturus": a star in the Great Bear.
3. Theology, here feminized. "This Book": the Bible.

no particular interest to spur me, nor had I any limit to my time compelling me to reduce the continuous study of one subject, as is required in taking a degree. Thus almost at one sitting I would study diverse things or leave off some to take up others. Yet even in this I maintained a certain order, for some subjects I called my study and others my diversion, and with the latter I would take my rest from the former. Hence, I have studied many things but know nothing, for one subject has interfered with another. What I say is true regarding the practical element of those subjects that require practice, for clearly the compass must rest while the pen is moving, and while the harp is playing the organ is still, *and likewise with all things.* Much bodily repetition is needed to form a habit, and therefore a person whose time is divided among several exercises will never develop one perfectly. But in formal and speculative arts the opposite is true, and I wish I might persuade everyone with my own experience: to wit, that far from interfering, these subjects help one another, shedding light and opening a path from one to the next, by way of divergences and hidden links—for they were set in place so as to form this universal chain by the wisdom of their great Author.

*   *   *

I confess that I am far indeed from the terms of Knowledge and that I have wished to follow it, though *"afar off."* But all this has merely led me closer to the flames of persecution, the crucible of affliction; and to such extremes that some have even sought to prohibit me from study.

They achieved this once, with a very saintly and simple mother superior who believed that study was an affair for the Inquisition and ordered that I should not read. I obeyed her (for the three months or so that her authority over us lasted) in that I did not pick up a book. But with regard to avoiding study absolutely, as such a thing does not lie within my power, I could not do it. For although I did not study in books, I studied all the things that God created, taking them for my letters, and for my book all the intricate structures of this world. Nothing could I see without reflecting upon it, nothing could I hear without pondering it, even to the most minute, material things. For there is no creature, however lowly, in which one cannot recognize the great *"God made me"*; there is not one that does not stagger the mind if it receives due consideration. And so, I repeat, I looked and marveled at all things, so that from the very persons with whom I spoke and from what they said to me, a thousand speculations leapt to my mind: Whence could spring this diversity of character and intelligence among individuals all composing one single species? What temperaments, what hidden qualities could give rise to each? When I noticed a shape, I would set about combining the proportions of its lines and measuring it in my mind and converting it to other proportions. I sometimes walked back and forth along the forewall of one of our dormitories (which is a very large room), and I began to observe that although the lines of its two sides were parallel and the ceiling was flat, yet the eye falsely perceived these lines as though they approached each other and the ceiling as though it were lower in the distance than close by; from this I inferred that visual lines run straight, but not parallel, and that they form a pyramidal figure. And I conjectured whether this might be the reason the ancients were obliged to question whether the world is spherical or not. Because even though it seems so, this could be a delusion of the eye, displaying concavities where there were none.

This kind of observation has been continual in me and is so to this day, without my having control over it; rather, I tend to find it annoying, because it tires my head. Yet I believed this happened to everyone, as with thinking in verse, until experience taught me otherwise. This trait, whether a matter of nature or custom, is such that nothing do I see without a second thought. Two little girls were playing with a top in front of me, and no sooner had I seen the motion and shape than I began, with this madness of mine, to observe the easy movement of the spherical form and how the momentum lasted, now fixed and set free of its cause; for even far from its first cause, which was the hand of the girl, the little top went on dancing. Yet not content with this, I ordered flour to be brought and sifted on the floor, so that as the top danced over it, we could know whether its movement described perfect circles or no. I found they were not circular, but rather spiral lines that lost their circularity as the top lost its momentum. Other girls were playing at spillikins (the most frivolous of all childhood games). I drew near to observe the shapes they made, and when I saw three of the straws by chance fall in a triangle, I fell to intertwining one with another, recalling that this was said to be the very shape of Solomon's mysterious ring[4] where distantly there shone bright traces and representations of the Most Blessed Trinity, by virtue of which it worked great prodigies and marvels. And they say David's harp had the same shape, and thus was Saul cured by its sound; to this day, harps have almost the same form.

Well, and what then shall I tell you, my Lady, of the secrets of nature that I have learned while cooking? I observe that an egg becomes solid and cooks in butter or oil, and on the contrary that it dissolves in sugar syrup. Or again, to ensure that sugar flow freely one need only add the slightest bit of water that has held quince or some other sour fruit. The yolk and white of the very same egg are of such a contrary nature that when eggs are used with sugar, each part separately may be used perfectly well, yet they cannot be mixed together. I shall not weary you with such inanities, which I relate simply to give you a full account of my nature, and I believe this will make you laugh. But in truth, my Lady, what can we women know, save philosophies of the kitchen? It was well put by Lupercio Leonardo [sic][5] that one can philosophize quite well while preparing supper. I often say, when I make these little observations, "Had Aristotle[6] cooked, he would have written a great deal more." And so to go on with the mode of my cogitations: I declare that all this is so continual in me that I have no need of books. On one occasion, because of a severe stomach ailment, the doctors forbade me to study. I spent several days in that state, and then quickly proposed to them that it would be less harmful to allow me my books, for my cogitations were so strenuous and vehement that they consumed more vitality in a quarter of an hour than the reading of books could in four days. And so the doctors were compelled to let me read. What is more, my Lady, not even my sleep has been free of this ceaseless movement of my imagination. Rather, my mind operates in sleep still more freely and unobstructedly, ordering with greater clarity and ease the events it has preserved

4. It may, like Solomon's seal, have contained a Star of David, composed of triangles.
5. Sor Juana actually refers to his brother, Bernardo Leonardo de Argensola, Spanish poet and satirist (1562–1631).
6. Greek philosopher (384–322 B.C.E.) who studied with Plato and wrote on logic, politics, ethics, natural science, and poetics.

from the day, presenting arguments and composing verses. I could give you a very long catalogue of these, as I could of certain reasonings and subtle turns I have reached far better in my sleep than while awake; but I leave them out in order not to weary you. I have said enough for your judgment and your surpassing eminence to comprehend my nature with clarity and full understanding, together with the beginnings, the methods, and the present state of my studies.

If studies, my Lady, be merits (for indeed I see them extolled as such in men), in me they are no such thing: I study because I must. If they be a failing, I believe for the same reason that the fault is none of mine. Yet withal, I live always so wary of myself that neither in this nor in anything else do I trust my own judgment. And so I entrust the decision to your supreme skill and straightway submit to whatever sentence you may pass, posing no objection or reluctance, for this has been no more than a simple account of my inclination to letters.

I confess also that, while in truth this inclination has been such that, as I said before, I had no need of exemplars, nevertheless the many books that I have read have not failed to help me, both in sacred as well as secular letters. For there I see a Deborah[7] issuing laws, military as well as political, and governing the people among whom there were so many learned men. I see the exceedingly knowledgeable Queen of Sheba[8] so learned she dares to test the wisdom of the wisest of all wise men with riddles, without being rebuked for it; indeed, on this very account she is to become judge of the unbelievers. I see so many and such significant women: some adorned with the gift of prophecy, like an Abigail; others, of persuasion, like Esther; others, of piety, like Rahab; others, of perseverance, like Anna [Hannah] the mother of Samuel;[9] and others, infinitely more, with other kinds of qualities and virtues.

If I consider the Gentiles, the first I meet are the Sibyls,[1] chosen by God to prophesy the essential mysteries of our Faith in such learned and elegant verses that they stupefy the imagination. I see a woman such as Minerva,[2] daughter of great Jupiter and mistress of all the wisdom of Athens, adored as goddess of the sciences. I see one Polla Argentaria, who helped Lucan, her husband, to write the *Battle of Pharsalia*.[3] I see the daughter of the divine Tiresias,[4] more learned still than her father. I see, too, such a woman as Zenobia,[5] queen of the Palmyrians, as wise as she was courageous. Again, I see an Arete,[6] daughter of Aristippus, most learned. A Nicostrata,[7] inventor of Latin letters and most erudite in

7. Prophetess who judged the Israelites (Judges 4.4–14).
8. Sheba tested King Solomon with her questions (1 Kings 10.1–3).
9. Abigail saved her husband's life by prophesying for King David (1 Samuel 25.2–35). Esther persuaded King Ahasuerus to protect the Jews (Esther 5–9). The harlot Rahab protected two Israelites from the King of Jericho (Joshua 2.1–7). Anna persevered in her prayers until granted the birth of her son (1 Samuel 1.1–20).
1. Female prophets of the ancient world.

2. Roman name for Athena, goddess of wisdom.
3. Epic poem on the civil war between Caesar and Pompey.
4. A blind seer in ancient Thebes, whose daughter Manto was known for her skill in divination.
5. Matriarchal warrior queen of Palmyra (ruled 266–72 C.E.), much admired for her learning.
6. Founder of a Greek school of philosophy (4th century B.C.E.).
7. Mythical healer and teacher who adapted Greek characters into the Roman alphabet.

the Greek. An Aspasia Miletia,[8] who taught philosophy and rhetoric and was the teacher of the philosopher Pericles. An Hypatia, who taught astrology and lectured for many years in Alexandria. A Leontium, who won over the philosopher Theophrastus and proved him wrong. A Julia, a Corinna, a Cornelia;[9] and, in sum, the vast throng of women who merited titles and earned renown: now as Greeks, again as Muses, and yet again as Pythonesses.[1] For what were they all but learned women, who were considered, celebrated, and indeed venerated as such in Antiquity? Without mentioning still others, of whom the books are full; for I see the Egyptian Catherine,[2] lecturing and refuting all the learning of the most learned men of Egypt. I see a Gertrude[3] read, write, and teach. And seeking no more examples far from home, I see my own most holy mother Paula, learned in the Hebrew, Greek, and Latin tongues and most expert in the interpretation of the Scriptures. What wonder then can it be that, though her chronicler was no less than the unequaled Jerome, the Saint found himself scarcely worthy of the task, for with that lively gravity and energetic effectiveness with which only he can express himself, he says: "If all the parts of my body were tongues, they would not suffice to proclaim the learning and virtues of Paula." Blessilla, a widow, earned the same praises, as did the luminous virgin Eustochium, both of them daughters of the Saint herself [Paula][4] and indeed Eustochium was such that for her knowledge she was hailed as a World Prodigy. Fabiola,[5] also a Roman, was another most learned in Holy Scripture. Proba Falconia, a Roman woman, wrote an elegant book of centos[6] joining together verses from Virgil, on the mysteries of our holy Faith. Our Queen Isabella,[7] wife of Alfonso X, is known to have written on astrology—without mentioning others, whom I omit so as not merely to copy what others have said (which is a vice I have always detested): Well then, in our own day there thrive the great Christina Alexandra, Queen of Sweden,[8] as learned as she is brave and generous; and too those most excellent ladies, the Duchess of Aveyro and the Countess of Villaumbrosa.

*   *   *

My Lady, I have not wished to reply, though others have done so without my knowledge. It is enough that I have seen certain papers, among them one I send to you because it is learned, and because reading it will restore to you a portion of your time that I have wasted with what I am writing. If by your wisdom and sense, my Lady, you should be pleased for me to do other than what I propose, then as is only right, to the slightest motion of your pleasure I shall cede my own decision, which was as I have told you to keep still. For although

8. Reputed teacher of eloquence in ancient Athens.

9. Julia Domna (second century C.E.), wife of the Roman emperor Septimius Severus, known for her learning as Julia the Philosopher. Corinna (ca. 500? B.C.E.), a lyric poet of Tanagra who wrote for a female audience. Cornelia (2nd century B.C.E.), noted for her devotion to her children's education.

1. Seers.

2. St. Catherine of Alexandria (4th century?), allegedly so wise she could refute fifty philoso-

phers at once.

3. St. Gertrude (d. 1302), Benedictine nun and mystic.

4. Blessilla and Eustochium, daughters of St. Paula, also taught by St. Jerome.

5. Another member of St. Jerome's circle.

6. Poems made up of verses from other authors.

7. Wife of Alfonso X of Spain (1221–1284), also known as Alfonso the Wise.

8. She attracted many scholars and writers to her court (1626–1689).

St. John Chrysostom[9] says, "*One's slanderers must be proven wrong, and one's questioners must be taught,*" I see too that St. Gregory[1] says, "*It is no less a victory to tolerate one's enemies than to defeat them,*" and that patience defeats by tolerance and triumphs by suffering. Indeed, it was the custom among the Roman Gentiles, for their captains at the very height of glory—when they entered triumphing over other nations, clothed in purple and crowned with laurel; with their carts drawn by the crowned brows of vanquished kings rather than by beasts of burden; accompanied by the spoils of the riches of all the world, before a conquering army decorated with the emblems of its feats; hearing the crowd's acclaim in such honorable titles and epithets as Fathers of the Fatherland, Pillars of the Empire, Ramparts of Rome, Refuge of the Republic, and other glorious names—it was the custom, at this supreme apex of pride and human felicity, that a common soldier should cry aloud to the conqueror, as if from his own feeling and at the order of the Senate: "Behold, how you are mortal; behold, for you have such and such a failing." Nor were the most shameful excused; as at the triumph of Caesar, when the most contemptible soldiers shouted in his ears, "*Beware, Romans, for we bring before you the bald adulterer.*" All of this was done so that in the midst of great honor the conqueror might not puff up with pride, and that the ballast of these affronts might prove a counterweight to the sails of so much praise, so that the ship of sound judgment should not founder in the winds of acclaim. If, as I say, all this was done by mere Gentiles, guided only by the light of Natural Law, then for us as Catholics, who are commanded to *love* our enemies, is it any great matter for us to tolerate them? For my part, I can testify that these detractions have at times been a mortification to me, but they have never done me harm. For I think that man very foolish who, having the opportunity to earn due merit, undertakes the labor and then forfeits the reward. This is like people who do not want to resign themselves to death. In the end they die all the same, with their resistance serving not to exempt them from dying, but only to deprive them of the merit of conformity to God's will, and thus to give them an evil death when it could have been blessed. And so, my Lady, I think these detractions do more good than harm. I maintain that a greater risk to human frailty is worked by praise, which usually seizes what does not belong to it, so that one must proceed with great care and have inscribed in one's heart these words of the Apostle: "*Or what hast thou that thou hast not received? And if thou hast received, why dost thou glory, as if thou hadst not received it?*"[2] For these words should serve as a shield to deflect the prongs of praises, which are spears that, when not attributed to God to whom they belong, take our very lives and make us thieves of God's honor and usurpers of the talents that He bestowed on us, and of the gifts He lent us, for which we must one day render Him a most detailed account. And so, good Lady, I fear applause far more than slander. For the slander, with just one simple act of patience, is turned to a benefit, whereas praise requires many acts of reflection and humility and self-knowledge if it is not to cause harm. And so, for myself I know and own that this knowledge is a

---

9. Syrian prelate (ca. 347–407), known as a great orator.
1. Gregory the Great (ca. 540–604), pope from 590.
2. Corinthians 11.4.

special favor from God, enabling me to conduct myself in the face of one as in the other, following that dictum of St. Augustine.[3] *One must believe neither the friend who speaks praises nor the enemy who reviles.*" Although I am such a one as most times must either let the opportunity go to waste, or mix it with such failings and flaws that I spoil what left to itself would have been good. And so, with the few things of mine that have been printed, the appearance of my name—and, indeed, permission for the printing itself—have not followed my own decision, but another's liberty that does not lie under my control, as was the case with the "Letter Worthy of Athena." So you see, only some little *Exercises for the Annunciation* and certain *Offerings for the Sorrows* were printed at my pleasure for the prayers of the public, but my name did not appear. I submit to you a few copies of the same, so that you may distribute them (if you think it seemly) among our sisters the nuns of your blessed community and others in this City. Only one copy remains of the *Sorrows*, because they have all been given away and I could find no more. I made them only for the prayers of my sisters, many years ago, and then they became more widely known. Their subjects are as disproportionate to my lukewarm ability as to my ignorance, and I was helped in writing them only by the fact that they dealt with matters of our great Queen; I know not why it is that in speaking of the Most Blessed Mary, the most icy heart is set aflame. It would please me greatly, my venerable Lady, to send you works worthy of your virtue and wisdom, but as the Poet[4] remarked:

> *Even when strength is lacking, still the intention must be praised.*
> *I surmise the gods would be content with that.*

If ever I write any more little trifles, they shall always seek haven at your feet and the safety of your correction, for I have no other jewel with which to repay you. And in the opinion of Seneca, he who has once commenced to confer benefits becomes obliged to continue them. Thus you must be repaid by your own generosity, for only in that way can I be honorably cleared of my debt to you, lest another statement, again Seneca's, be leveled against me: "*It is shameful to be outdone in acts of kindness.*" For it is magnanimous for the generous creditor to grant a poor debtor some means of satisfying the debt. Thus God behaved toward the world, which could not possibly repay Him: He gave His own Son, that He might offer Himself as a worthy amends.

If the style of this letter, my venerable Lady, has been less than your due, I beg your pardon for its household familiarity or the lack of seemly respect. For in addressing you, my sister, as a nun of the veil, I have forgotten the distance between myself and your most distinguished person, which should not occur were I to see you unveiled. But you, with your prudence and benevolence, will substitute or emend my terms; and if you think unsuitable the familiar terms of address I have employed—because it seems to me that given all the reverence I owe you, "Your Reverence" is very little reverence indeed—please alter it to whatever you think suitable. For I have not been so bold as to exceed

---

3. North African philosopher and theologian, one of the Latin Church Fathers (354–430).

4. Generally used to refer to Virgil, but this citation is from Ovid.

the limits set by the style of your letter to me, nor to cross the border of your modesty.

And hold me in your own good grace, so as to entreat divine grace on my behalf; of the same, may the Lord grant you great increase, and may He keep you, as I beg of Him and as I am needful. Written at the Convent of our Father St. Jerome in Mexico City, this first day of March of the year 1691. Receive the embrace of your most greatly favored,

Sor Juana Inés de la Cruz

Poem 145

[*She endeavors to expose the praises recorded in a portrait of the poetess by truth, which she calls passion.*]

> This object which you see—a painted snare
> exhibiting the subtleties of art
> with clever arguments of tone and hue—
> is but a cunning trap to snare your sense;
>   this object, in which flattery has tried   5
> to overlook the horrors of the years
> and, conquering the ravages of time,
> to overcome oblivion and age:
>   this is an empty artifice of care,
> a flower, fragile, set out in the wind,   10
> a letter of safe-conduct sent to Fate;
>   it is a foolish, erring diligence,
> a palsied will to please which, clearly seen,
> is a corpse, is dust, is shadow, and is gone.

Poem 164

[*In which she answers a suspicion with the eloquence of tears.*]

> This afternoon, my darling, when we spoke,
> and in your face and gestures I could see
> that I was not persuading you with words,
> I wished you might look straight into my heart;
>   and Love, who was assisting my designs,   5
> succeeded in what seemed impossible:
> for in the stream of tears which anguish loosed
> my heart itself, dissolved, dropped slowly down.
>   Enough unkindness now, my love, enough;
> don't let these tyrant jealousies torment you   10
> nor base suspicions shatter your repose
>   with foolish shadows, empty evidence:
> in liquid humor you have seen and touched
> my heart undone and passing through your hands.

Philosophical Satire

Poem 92

[*The poet proves illogical both the whim and the censure of men who accuse, in women, that which they cause.*]

You foolish and unreasoning men
who cast all blame on women,
not seeing you yourselves are cause
of the same faults you accuse:

if, with eagerness unequaled,   5
you plead against women's disdain,
why require them to do well
when you inspire them to fall?

You combat their firm resistance,
and then solemnly pronounce   10
that what you've won through diligence
is proof of women's flightiness.

What do we see, when we see you
madly determined to see us so,
but the child who makes a monster appear   15
and then goes trembling with fear?

With ridiculous conceit
you insist that woman be
a sultry Thais while you woo her;
a true Lucretia[1] once she's won.   20

Whose behavior could be odder
than that of a stubborn man
who himself breathes on the mirror,
and then laments it is not clear?

Women's good favor, women's scorn   25
you hold in equal disregard:
complaining, if they treat you badly;
mocking, if they love you well.

Not one can gain your good opinion,
for she who modestly withdraws   30
and fails to admit you is ungrateful;
yet if she admits you, too easily won.

---

1. A noble Roman woman (d. ca. 508 B.C.E.) who killed herself after being raped; a symbol of chastity. "Thais": a celebrated courtesan in ancient Greece.

So downright foolish are you all
that your injurious justice claims
to blame one woman's cruelty   35
and fault the other's laxity.

How then can she be moderate
to whom your suit aspires,
if, ingrate, she makes you displeased,
or, easy, prompts your ire?   40

Between such ire and such anguish
—the tales your fancy tells—
lucky is she who does not love you;
complain then, as you will!

Your doting anguish feathers the wings   45
of liberties that women take,
and once you've caused them to be bad,
you want to find them as good as saints.

But who has carried greater blame
in a passion gone astray: 50
she who falls to constant pleading,
or he who pleads with her to fall?

Or which more greatly must be faulted,
though either may commit a wrong:
she who sins for need of payment,   55
or he who pays for his enjoyment?

Why then are you so alarmed
by the fault that is your own?
Wish women to be what you make them,
or make them what you wish they were.   60

Leave off soliciting her fall
and then indeed, more justified,
that eagerness you might accuse
of the woman who besieges you.

Thus I prove with all my forces   65
the ways your arrogance does battle:
for in your offers and your demands
we have devil, flesh, and world: a man.

JONATHAN SWIFT

1667–1745

Jonathan Swift was such a thorough-going satirist that his definition of the genre was itself satirical. "Satire," he wrote, "is a sort of glass wherein beholders do generally discover everybody's face but their own; which is the chief reason for that kind reception it meets with in the world, and that so very few are offended with it." He was not wrong: his own brilliant, often bitter satirical writings were immensely popular in his own time, and have remained so for centuries, despite the fact that he pokes fun at all of us in some way or other, mocking political ambitions, religious convictions, scientific knowledge, war, power, lust, vanity, and greed. His derisive wit in fact takes in so much of the world that readers have had trouble figuring out whether he held any affirmative beliefs or values at all. But for Swift, that may not have been the point. What he said he most wanted was to "vex" his readers with an uncomfortable awareness of the follies of the world.

LIFE

Early in the seventeenth century, the English monarchy had seized great parcels of Irish land and sold them to loyal English families. These wealthy and powerful families were Protestants, and they struggled to prevent the Catholic majority from gaining power in Ireland: they officially barred Catholics from holding public office, joining the military, and teaching children. Jonathan Swift belonged to this small Protestant minority, born to English parents in 1667 in Dublin. His lawyer father died before he was born, and his mother moved to England when he was a small child. He was raised by a cold and unsympathetic uncle in Ireland, who had him educated at Trinity College in Dublin. A rebellious student, Swift was punished more than once for failing to attend religious services and carousing in the city. During a Catholic uprising in 1688, he left for England, and went to work for a powerful aristocrat and statesman named William Temple. There he made contact with influential writers and politicians, and he tutored a young girl named Esther Johnson, whom he nicknamed "Stella." He began as her teacher and mentor, but became her friend, and remained on close terms with her for the rest of his life.

In 1694, after earning his M.A. at Oxford, Swift was ordained a priest in the Protestant Church of England and was offered a position in Northern Ireland. Dissatisfied, he moved back and forth between England and Ireland, staying at the Temple household on and off for years. It was in this period that he began to develop a reputation as a witty writer, producing a comic picture of literary disputes called *The Battle of the Books* (1704) and in the same year, a clever satire of religious controversy called *The Tale of a Tub*. "What a genius I had when I composed that book!" he said later in life. He befriended **Alexander Pope** and other noted writers of the day, who together formed a club of satirists called the Scriblerians.

Swift hoped for church advancement in England, but in 1713 he was named dean of St. Patrick's Cathedral in Dublin and remained there for the rest of his life. "I reckon no man is thoroughly miserable unless he be condemned to live in Ireland," he wrote. And yet, he was to become an Irish national hero. For the rest of his life, he wrote passionately against the British government's treatment of Ireland, including his essay on economic policy called *Irish Manufacture*, later banned by the British government. "By the Laws of God, of Nature, of Nations, and of your Country," he urged Irish readers, "you are, and ought to be, as free a people as your brethren in England."

Swift's personal life in this period was both mysterious and complicated. "Stella" moved to Ireland, and spent a great deal of time with him. People have occasionally speculated that they were secretly married, but there is no evidence for this. Meanwhile, Swift made the acquaintance of one Esther Vanhomrigh, who fell passionately in love with him and moved to Ireland to pursue him, jealously demanding to know more about his relationship with Stella. She died shortly after Swift rejected her, some said of a broken heart.

In 1726, Swift published *Gulliver's Travels* anonymously. It sold out immediately. A friend in London wrote to tell him that the book was "the conversation of the whole town. . . . From the highest to the lowest it is universally read, from the Cabinet-council to the nursery." The next year Stella died, plunging him into misery. His last great work, the fiercely satirical *Modest Proposal*, appeared in 1729. In a touching and witty poem about his own demise called "The Death of Doctor Swift," Swift predicted madness and senility for his final years. Sadly, he guessed well. As he declined, guardians were appointed to take care of his finances and keep him from injuring himself. He died at the age of seventy-eight and was buried not far from Stella.

TIMES

Swift was a great coffee drinker, and this small fact points to a turning point in the history of English literature. In the late seventeenth century, English literary life began to shift away from its old status as a courtly culture, centered on the monarchy and its great palaces, to a more diffuse and democratic urban culture that revolved around coffeehouses. These establishments were not only places to eat and drink: one could see scientific experiments there, debate politics, attend lectures on religion, and gossip and share information. Altogether, there may have been as many as three thousand coffeehouses in London alone. Books and pamphlets were sold there, and as the reading public grew, so too did the printed matter available for reading. "Runners" appeared frequently to announce the latest news, making coffeehouses great places to catch up on what was current. In fact, they became the engine of an increasingly powerful new political force—public opinion. Thus coffeehouses helped to move the weight of political authority from the old aristocracy into the hands of the urban middle class. Most coffeehouses charged a penny for those who wanted to enter, but beyond the entrance fee, there were few barriers. They therefore gathered a wide range of men (women were not expected to patronize them), including journalists, artisans, merchants, aspiring writers, and powerful politicians. Only the very poorest could not pass through the doors. And coffeehouses became the sites for new institutions. A coffeehouse in London called Jonathan's was a meeting ground for stockbrokers, which eventually became the London Stock Exchange; while Lloyd's coffeehouse was to become the most important British insurance company. Button's was the coffeehouse for the "Wits" during Swift's time, a hub where young writers struggled to make the right contacts and begin their careers.

As journalists, businesspeople, artisans, and aristocrats gathered in coffeehouses, they argued over the political affairs of their time. Governing England were two main political parties, the Whigs and the Tories. In 1688, the British Isles had deposed James II, a Catholic king, and put a new pair of Protestant rulers, William and Mary, in his place. The Whigs worried about monarchical tyranny and the return of the Catholic Church, and they favored a constitutional monarchy. The Tories believed in the divine right of kings, and feared the growing power of Parliament and the people. The two parties shared power until 1714, when the Protestant Queen Anne died. Her most immediate heir was a foreigner—he came from the German land of Hanover—and spoke no English. The Tories saw him as a break with the proper line of English kings who had been deposed in 1688, and many showed support for bringing back a Catholic king, the direct heir of James II, then in exile. The new King George suppressed this pro-Catholic uprising and expressed gratitude to his supporters by installing the Whigs in positions of power. Thus began a long period of Whig rule. Swift and his friend Alexander Pope, who were Tories, found that many of their supporters fled England or were imprisoned, and that they were on the losing side.

In this political context, satirical writing flourished. On the one hand, in an atmosphere of fierce political debate, persuasive writers were in great demand: Swift and Pope found they had great support from powerful politicians who wanted the best writers on their side. On the other hand, it could be dangerous to launch direct political challenges. After 1714, Tory writers often resorted to indirections such as innuendos and masks to avoid prosecution. And so satire seemed a perfect solution: veiled enough never to seem outright oppositional, it could still be pointed enough to hit political targets, including the king.

WORK

Gulliver's Travels and *A Modest Proposal* are two of the most famous satires in the English language. *Gulliver* is in part a parody of travel books, such as those of William Dampier (1651–1715), who published hugely popular descriptions of his three circumnavigations of the globe. Like Dampier, Gulliver seems intent on giving us precise facts: he offers exact dates and statistics and describes in copious detail the strange customs, flora, and fauna of the far-flung islands he happens to encounter. But the places where Gulliver alights carry uncanny echoes of his native England: in Lilliput, for example, he finds a people six inches tall whose pettiness and grandiose ambitions offer a recognizable commentary on political debates raging in England at the time. Opportunities for satire also emerge when Gulliver is asked to explain the customs of his own land to the inhabitants of the islands he visits. The covetousness, belligerence, and factionalism he describes at home in Britain horrify his audiences.

Gulliver typically fails to notice the ironies he generates. Swift deliberately opts for a naive narrator, allowing us to identify with him at times but also to distance ourselves from him to draw out the larger implications of his stories for ourselves. (Not all of Swift's readers got the point of this; one bishop reported "that the book was full of improbable lies, and for his part, he hardly believed a word of it.") One advantage of the gullible perspective is that it allows Swift to make his readers see themselves from an outsider's perspective: the writer thus makes ordinary life seem strange and prompts us to question what we might otherwise take for granted. More descriptive than contemplative, the language of the text is quite plain, and in fact *Gulliver's Travels* has long been read by children as well as adults.

Gulliver makes three voyages before we reach the fourth and final book, included here. After his first journey to Lilliput, he goes to a land of giants, Brobdingnag, whose benevolent king, after hearing Gulliver's patriotic account of England, comments, "I cannot but conclude the bulk of your natives, to be the most pernicious race of odious little vermin that nature ever suffered to crawl upon the surface of the earth." In the third book, Gulliver aims at some intellectual targets: philosophers so deep in abstract thought they have to be attended by "flappers"—servants who flap them into an awareness of their immediate surroundings—and ghosts from the past who stress the lies of historians. The most terrifying group he meets are the Struldbrugs, who live forever but grow old and infirm like humans, surviving decrepit and senile into eternity.

On his fourth voyage, Gulliver finds himself on an island inhabited by Houyhnhnms—horses—and Yahoos, who are uncomfortably similar to human beings. But Swift turns the conventional distinction between humans and animals upside-down. On this island, the horses are the rational, clean, and articulate ones, and they keep the island under peaceful control, while the humans are greedy, filthy, violent, and irrational. As the Houyhnhnms ask Gulliver questions about his homeland, they are shocked by the depravity of the Yahoos of England. Gulliver offers a bitter indictment of British colonialism in this section and also comes to see his fellow Yahoos—including his own wife and children—with disgust.

Despite Gulliver's revulsion against British Yahoos, readers have long wondered whether the Houyhnhnms really are a model society, or whether there is something chilling in their cool, entirely rational resistance to close ties of affection and loyalty. In seventeenth-century England, Protestant philosophers had begun to put forward the notion that human beings, rather than being corrupt and fallen, were inherently rational and virtuous. This notion of a benevolent human nature gathered strength over the course of the eighteenth century. Swift, however, seems determined to keep alive the older belief in a naturally conceited, vain, greedy, lustful human nature. This sometimes made him seem misanthropic to his contemporaries. But understanding human beings as imperfect allowed him to make fun of all utopian projects and to cast his satirical eye on schemes for social improvement.

One such satire takes shape brilliantly in A Modest Proposal. Imitating the voice of rational social planners, who for the first time were depending on statistics and economic laws, Swift takes an extreme position and follows it to its logical conclusion. If the point of social reform is to produce solutions to social problems, maximizing profits along the way, then why not sell the infants of the poor as food for the rich? Surely this is a rational solution for the wealthy Protestant minority in England, since they want to cut down on the number of Catholics in any case. Charges of cannibalism, so often used against non-European peoples, take on figurative force as Swift suggests that the English are in many ways feeding off Irish flesh.

In much of his work, Swift takes a particularly satirical look at the production of knowledge: while Gulliver's Travels satirizes travel narratives, with their detailed descriptions of exotic cultures, and mocks historians, clergymen, and philosophers along the way, A Modest Proposal explicitly relies on demographic facts and scientific rationality to come to its outrageous conclusions. These satires therefore ask us to reflect on the relationship between what we know and how we choose to act. Do facts and reason help us to make good decisions in the world? And if not, where should we turn instead? Swift leaves it up to us to develop solutions. For him, it is enough to make us confront the unsettling questions.

From Gulliver's Travels[1]

Part IV

A Voyage to the Country of the Houyhnhnms[2]

CHAPTER I

The Author sets out as Captain of a ship. His men conspire against him, confine him a long time to his cabin, set him on shore in an unknown land. He travels up into the country. The Yahoos, a strange sort of animal, described. The Author meets two Houyhnhnms.

I continued at home with my wife and children about five months in a very happy condition, if I could have learned the lesson of knowing when I was well. I left my poor wife big with child, and accepted an advantageous offer made me to be Captain of the *Adventure*, a stout merchantman of 350 tons; for I understood navigation well, and being grown weary of a surgeon's employment at sea, which however I could exercise upon occasion, I took a skillful young man of that calling, one Robert Purefoy, into my ship. We set sail from Portsmouth upon the 7th day of September, 1710; on the 14th we met with Captain Pocock of Bristol, at Tenariff, who was going to the Bay of Campeachy[3] to cut logwood. On the 16th he was parted from us by a storm; I heard since my return that his ship foundered and none escaped, but one cabin boy. He was an honest man and a good sailor, but a little too positive in his own opinions, which was the cause of his destruction, as it hath been of several others. For if he had followed my advice, he might at this time have been safe at home with his family as well as myself.

I had several men died in my ship of calentures,[4] so that I was forced to get recruits out of Barbadoes and the Leeward Islands,[5] where I touched by the direction of the merchants who employed me; which I had soon too much cause to repent, for I found afterwards that most of them had been buccaneers. I had fifty hands on board; and my orders were that I should trade with the Indians in the South Sea, and make what discoveries I could. These rogues whom I had picked up debauched my other men, and they all formed a con-

1. Swift's full title for this work was *Travels into Several Remote Nations of the World. In Four Parts. By Lemuel Gulliver, First a Surgeon, and then a Captain of several Ships.* The text is based on the Dublin edition of Swift's work (1735).
2. The word suggests the sound of a horse neighing.
3. Probably Campeche, in southeast Mexico, on the western side of the Yucatán Peninsula. Tenariff (now Tenerife) is the largest of the Canary Islands, off northwest Africa in the Atlantic.
4. Tropical fever.
5. The northern group of the Lesser Antilles in the West Indies, extending southeast from Puerto Rico. Barbados is the easternmost of the West Indies.

spiracy to seize the ship and secure me; which they did one morning, rushing into my cabin, and binding me hand and foot, threatening to throw me overboard, if I offered to stir. I told them, I was their prisoner, and would submit. This they made me swear to do, and then unbound me, only fastening one of my legs with a chair near my bed, and placed a sentry at my door with his piece charged, who was commanded to shoot me dead if I attempted my liberty. They sent me down victuals and drink, and took the government of the ship to themselves. Their design was to turn pirates and plunder the Spaniards, which they could not do, till they got more men. But first they resolved to sell the goods in the ship, and then go to Madagascar for recruits, several among them having died since my confinement. They sailed many weeks, and traded with the Indians; but I knew not what course they took, being kept close prisoner in my cabin, and expecting nothing less than to be murdered, as they often threatened me.

Upon the 9th day of May, 1711, one James Welch came down to my cabin; and said he had orders from the Captain to set me ashore. I expostulated with him, but in vain; neither would he so much as tell me who their new Captain was. They forced me into the longboat, letting me put on my best suit of clothes, which were as good as new, and a small bundle of linen, but no arms except my hanger;[6] and they were so civil as not to search my pockets, into which I conveyed what money I had, with some other little necessaries. They rowed about a league, and then set me down on a strand. I desired them to tell me what country it was; they all swore, they knew no more than myself, but said that the Captain (as they called him) was resolved, after they had sold the lading, to get rid of me in the first place where they discovered land. They pushed off immediately, advising me to make haste, for fear of being overtaken by the tide, and bade me farewell.

In this desolate condition I advanced forward, and soon got upon firm ground, where I sat down on a bank to rest myself, and consider what I had best to do. When I was a little refreshed, I went up into the country, resolving to deliver myself to the first savages I should meet, and purchase my life from them by some bracelets, glass rings, and other toys, which sailors usually provide themselves with in those voyages, and whereof I had some about me. The land was divided by long rows of trees, not regularly planted, but naturally growing; there was great plenty of grass, and several fields of oats. I walked very circumspectly for fear of being surprised, or suddenly shot with an arrow from behind, or on either side. I fell into a beaten road, where I saw many tracks of human feet, and some of cows, but most of horses. At last I beheld several animals in a field, and one or two of the same kind sitting in trees. Their shape was very singular, and deformed, which a little discomposed me, so that I lay down behind a thicket to observe them better. Some of them coming forward near the place where I lay, gave me an opportunity of distinctly marking their form. Their heads and breasts were covered with a thick hair, some frizzled and others lank; they had beards like goats, and a long ridge of hair down their backs, and the fore parts of their legs and feet; but the rest of their bodies were bare, so that I might see their skins, which were of a brown buff color. They had no tails, nor any hair at all on their buttocks, except about the anus; which,

6. A small sword.

I presume Nature had placed there to defend them as they sat on the ground; for this posture they used, as well as lying down, and often stood on their hind feet. They climbed high trees, as nimbly as a squirrel, for they had strong extended claws before and behind,[7] terminating in sharp points, and hooked. They would often spring, and bound, and leap with prodigious agility. The females were not so large as the males; they had long lank hair on their heads, and only a sort of down on the rest of their bodies, except about the anus, and pudenda. Their dugs hung between their forefeet, and often reached almost to the ground as they walked. The hair of both sexes was of several colors, brown, red, black, and yellow. Upon the whole, I never beheld in all my travels so disagreeable an animal; or one against which I naturally conceived so strong an antipathy. So that thinking I had seen enough, full of contempt and aversion, I got up and pursued the beaten road, hoping it might direct me to the cabin of some Indian: I had not gone far when I met one of these creatures full in my way, and coming up directly to me. The ugly monster, when he saw me, distorted several ways every feature of his visage, and stared as at an object he had never seen before; then approaching nearer, lifted up his forepaw, whether out of curiosity or mischief, I could not tell; but I drew my hanger, and gave him a good blow with the flat side of it; for I durst not strike him with the edge, fearing the inhabitants might be provoked against me, if they should come to know that I had killed or maimed any of their cattle. When the beast felt the smart, he drew back, and roared so loud, that a herd of at least forty came flocking about me from the next field, howling and making odious faces; but I ran to the body of a tree, and leaning my back against it, kept them off, by waving my hanger. Several of this cursed brood getting hold of the branches behind, leaped up into the tree, from whence they began to discharge their excrements on my head; however, I escaped pretty well, by sticking close to the stem of the tree, but was almost stifled with the filth, which fell about me on every side.

In the midst of this distress, I observed them all to run away on a sudden as fast as they could; at which I ventured to leave the tree, and pursue the road, wondering what it was that could put them into this fright. But looking on my left hand, I saw a horse walking softly in the field; which my persecutors having sooner discovered, was the cause of their flight. The horse started a little when he came near me, but soon recovering himself, looked full in my face with manifest tokens of wonder; he viewed my hands and feet, walking round me several times. I would have pursued my journey, but he placed himself directly in the way, yet looking with a very mild aspect, never offering the least violence. We stood gazing at each other for some time; at last I took the boldness, to reach my hand towards his neck, with a design to stroke it; using the common style and whistle of jockies when they are going to handle a strange horse. But, this animal seeming to receive my civilities with disdain, shook his head, and bent his brows, softly raising up his left forefoot to remove my hand. Then he neighed three or four times, but in so different a cadence, that I almost began to think he was speaking to himself in some language of his own.

While he and I were thus employed, another horse came up; who applying himself to the first in a very formal manner, they gently struck each other's right hoof before, neighing several times by turns, and varying the sound,

---

7. Concealed, or sheathed by flesh.

which seemed to be almost articulate. They went some paces off, as if it were to confer together, walking side by side, backward and forward, like persons deliberating upon some affair of weight; but often turning their eyes towards me, as it were to watch that I might not escape. I was amazed to see such actions and behavior in brute beasts; and concluded with myself that if the inhabitants of this country were endued with a proportionable degree of reason, they must needs be the wisest people upon earth. This thought gave me so much comfort, that I resolved to go forward until I could discover some house or village, or meet with any of the natives, leaving the two horses to discourse together as they pleased. But the first, who was a dapple grey, observing me to steal off, neighed after me in so expressive a tone that I fancied myself to understand what he meant; whereupon I turned back, and came near him, to expect his farther commands; but concealing my fear as much as I could; for I began to be in some pain, how this adventure might terminate; and the reader will easily believe I did not much like my present situation.

The two horses came up close to me, looking with great earnestness upon my face and hands. The grey steed rubbed my hat all round with his right fore hoof, and discomposed it so much that I was forced to adjust it better, by taking it off, and settling it again; whereat both he and his companion (who was a brown bay) appeared to be much surprised; the latter felt the lappet of my coat, and finding it to hang loose about me, they both looked with new signs of wonder. He stroked my right hand, seeming to admire the softness, and color; but he squeezed it so hard between his hoof and his pastern,[8] that I was forced to roar; after which they both touched me with all possible tenderness. They were under great perplexity about my shoes and stockings, which they felt very often, neighing to each other, and using various gestures, not unlike those of a philosopher, when he would attempt to solve some new and difficult phenomenon.

Upon the whole, the behavior of these animals was so orderly and rational, so acute and judicious, that I at last concluded, they must needs be magicians, who had thus metamorphosed themselves upon some design; and seeing a stranger in the way, were resolved to divert themselves with him; or perhaps were really amazed at the sight of a man so very different in habit, feature, and complexion from those who might probably live in so remote a climate. Upon the strength of this reasoning, I ventured to address them in the following manner: "Gentlemen, if you be conjurers, as I have good cause to believe, you can understand any language; therefore I make bold to let your worships know that I am a poor distressed Englishman, driven by his misfortunes upon your coast; and I entreat one of you, to let me ride upon his back, as if he were a real horse, to some house or village, where I can be relieved. In return of which favor, I will make you a present of this knife and bracelet" (taking them out of my pocket). The two creatures stood silent while I spoke, seeming to listen with great attention; and when I had ended, they neighed frequently towards each other, as if they were engaged in serious conversation. I plainly observed, that their language expressed the passions very well, and the words might with little pains be resolved into an alphabet more easily than the Chinese.

8. The part of a horse's foot between the joint at the rear and the hoof.

I could frequently distinguish the word *Yahoo*, which was repeated by each of them several times; and although it was impossible for me to conjecture what it meant, yet while the two horses were busy in conversation, I endeavored to practice this word upon my tongue; and as soon as they were silent, I boldly pronounced "Yahoo" in a loud voice, imitating, at the same time, as near as I could, the neighing of a horse; at which they were both visibly surprised, and the grey repeated the same word twice, as if he meant to teach me the right accent, wherein I spoke after him as well as I could, and found myself perceivably to improve every time, although very far from any degree of perfection. Then the bay tried me with a second word, much harder to be pronounced; but reducing it to the English orthography, may be spelt thus, *Houyhnhnm*. I did not succeed in this so well as the former, but after two or three farther trials, I had better fortune; and they both appeared amazed at my capacity.

After some farther discourse, which I then conjectured might relate to me, the two friends took their leaves, with the same compliment of striking each other's hoof; and the grey made me signs that I should walk before him; wherein I thought it prudent to comply, till I could find a better director. When I offered to slacken my pace, he would cry, "Hhuun, Hhuun"; I guessed his meaning, and gave him to understand, as well as I could that I was weary, and not able to walk faster; upon which, he would stand a while to let me rest.

CHAPTER II

The Author conducted by a Houyhnhnm to his house. The house described. The Author's reception. The food of the Houyhnhnms. The Author in distress for want of meat is at last relieved. His manner of feeding in that country.

Having traveled about three miles, we came to a long kind of building, made of timber, stuck in the ground, and wattled across; the roof was low, and covered with straw. I now began to be a little comforted, and took out some toys, which travelers usually carry for presents to the savage Indians of America and other parts, in hopes the people of the house would be thereby encouraged to receive me kindly. The horse made me a sign to go in first; it was a large room with a smooth clay floor, and a rack and manger extending the whole length on one side. There were three nags, and two mares, not eating, but some of them sitting down upon their hams, which I very much wondered at; but wondered more to see the rest employed in domestic business; the last seemed but ordinary cattle; however this confirmed my first opinion, that a people who could so far civilize brute animals must needs excel in wisdom all the nations of the world. The grey came in just after, and thereby prevented any ill treatment, which the others might have given me. He neighed to them several times in a style of authority, and received answers.

Beyond this room there were three others, reaching the length of the house, to which you passed through three doors, opposite to each other, in the manner of a vista; we went through the second room towards the third; here the grey walked in first, beckoning me to attend; I waited in the second room, and got ready my presents, for the master and mistress of the house; they were two knives, three bracelets of false pearl, a small looking-glass and a bead necklace.

The horse neighed three or four times, and I waited to hear some answers in a human voice, but I heard no other returns than in the same dialect, only one or two a little shriller than his. I began to think that this house must belong to some person of great note among them, because there appeared so much ceremony before I could gain admittance. But, that a man of quality should be served all by horses, was beyond my comprehension. I feared my brain was disturbed by my sufferings and misfortunes; I roused myself, and looked about me in the room where I was left alone; this was furnished as the first, only after a more elegant manner. I rubbed my eyes often, but the same objects still occurred. I pinched my arms and sides, to awake myself, hoping I might be in a dream. I then absolutely concluded that all these appearances could be nothing else but necromancy and magic. But I had no time to pursue these reflections; for the grey horse came to the door, and made me a sign to follow him into the third room; where I saw a very comely mare, together with a colt and foal, sitting on their haunches, upon mats of straw, not unartfully made, and perfectly neat and clean.

The mare soon after my entrance, rose from her mat, and coming up close, after having nicely observed my hands and face, gave me a most contemptuous look; then turning to the horse, I heard the word Yahoo often repeated betwixt them; the meaning of which word I could not then comprehend, although it were the first I had learned to pronounce; but I was soon better informed, to my everlasting mortification: for the horse beckoning to me with his head, and repeating the word, "Hhuun, Hhuun," as he did upon the road, which I understood was to attend him, led me out into a kind of court, where was another building at some distance from the house. Here we entered, and I saw three of those detestable creatures, which I first met after my landing, feeding upon roots, and the flesh of some animals, which I afterwards found to be that of asses and dogs, and now and then a cow dead by accident or disease. They were all tied by the neck with strong withes,[9] fastened to a beam; they held their food between the claws of their forefeet, and tore it with their teeth.

The master horse ordered a sorrel nag, one of his servants, to untie the largest of these animals, and take him into a yard. The beast and I were brought close together; and our countenances diligently compared, both by master and servant; who thereupon repeated several times the word "Yahoo." My horror and astonishment are not to be described, when I observed, in this abominable animal, a perfect human figure; the face of it indeed was flat and broad, the nose depressed, the lips large, and the mouth wide; but these differences are common to all savage nations, where the lineaments of the countenance are distorted by the natives suffering their infants to lie groveling on the earth, or by carrying them on their backs, nuzzling with their face against the mother's shoulders. The forefeet of the Yahoo differed from my hands in nothing else but the length of the nails, the coarseness and brownness of the palms, and the hairiness on the backs. There was the same resemblance between our feet, with the same differences, which I knew very well, although the horses did not, because of my shoes and stockings; the same in every part of our bodies, except as to hairiness and color, which I have already described.

9. Fibers braided into rope.

The great difficulty that seemed to stick with the two horses, was to see the rest of my body so very different from that of a Yahoo, for which I was obliged to my clothes, whereof they had no conception; the sorrel nag offered me a root, which he held (after their manner, as we shall describe in its proper place) between his hoof and pastern; I took it in my hand, and having smelled it, returned it to him again as civilly as I could. He brought out of the Yahoo's kennel a piece of ass's flesh, but it smelled so offensively that I turned from it with loathing; he then threw it to the Yahoo, by whom it was greedily devoured. He afterwards showed me a wisp of hay, and a fetlock[1] full of oats; but I shook my head, to signify that neither of these were food for me. And indeed, I now apprehended that I must absolutely starve, if I did not get to some of my own species; for as to those filthy Yahoos, although there were few greater lovers of mankind, at that time, than myself, yet I confess I never saw any sensitive being so detestable on all accounts; and the more I came near them, the more hateful they grew, while I stayed in that country. This the master horse observed by my behavior, and therefore sent the Yahoo back to his kennel. He then put his forehoof to his mouth, at which I was much surprised, although he did it with ease, and with a motion that appeared perfectly natural; and made other signs to know what I would eat; but I could not return him such an answer as he was able to apprehend; and if he had understood me, I did not see how it was possible to contrive any way for finding myself nourishment. While we were thus engaged, I observed a cow passing by; whereupon I pointed to her, and expressed a desire to let me go and milk her. This had its effect; for he led me back into the house, and ordered a mare-servant to open a room, where a good store of milk lay in earthen and wooden vessels, after a very orderly and cleanly manner. She gave me a large bowl full, of which I drank very heartily, and found myself well refreshed.

About noon I saw coming towards the house a kind of vehicle, drawn like a sledge by four Yahoos. There was in it an old steed, who seemed to be of quality; he alighted with his hind feet forward, having by accident got a hurt in his left forefoot. He came to dine with our horse, who received him with great civility. They dined in the best room, and had oats boiled in milk for the second course, which the old horse eat warm, but the rest cold. Their mangers were placed circular in the middle of the room, and divided into several partitions, round which they sat on their haunches upon bosses of straw. In the middle was a large rack with angles answering to every partition of the manger. So that each horse and mare eat their own hay, and their own mash of oats and milk, with much decency and regularity. The behavior of the young colt and foal appeared very modest; and that of the master and mistress extremely cheerful and complaisant to their guest. The grey ordered me to stand by him; and much discourse passed between him and his friend concerning me, as I found by the stranger's often looking on me, and the frequent repetition of the word Yahoo.

I happened to wear my gloves; which the master grey observing, seemed perplexed; discovering signs of wonder what I had done to my forefeet; he put his hoof three or four times to them, as if he would signify, that I should reduce

---

1. The joint at the back of a horse's foot, just above the hoof, in which the Houyhnhnm holds the oats.

them to their former shape, which I presently did, pulling off both my gloves, and putting them into my pocket. This occasioned farther talk, and I saw the company was pleased with my behavior, whereof I soon found the good effects. I was ordered to speak the few words I understood; and while they were at dinner, the master taught me the names for oats, milk, fire, water, and some others which I could readily pronounce after him, having from my youth a great facility in learning languages.

When dinner was done, the master horse took me aside, and by signs and words made me understand the concern he was in that I had nothing to eat. Oats in their tongue are called *hlunnh*. This word I pronounced two or three times; for although I had refused them at first, yet upon second thoughts, I considered that I could contrive to make a kind of bread, which might be sufficient with milk to keep me alive, till I could make my escape to some other country, and to creatures of my own species. The horse immediately ordered a white mare-servant of his family to bring me a good quantity of oats in a sort of wooden tray. These I heated before the fire as well as I could, and rubbed them till the husks came off, which I made a shift to winnow from the grain; I ground and beat them between two stones, then took water, and made them into a paste or cake, which I toasted at the fire, and eat warm with milk. It was at first a very insipid diet, although common enough in many parts of Europe, but grew tolerable by time; and having been often reduced to hard fare in my life, this was not the first experiment I had made how easily nature is satisfied. And I cannot but observe that I never had one hour's sickness, while I staid in this island. It is true, I sometimes made a shift to catch a rabbit, or bird, by springes made of Yahoos' hairs; and I often gathered wholesome herbs, which I boiled, or ate as salads with my bread; and now and then, for a rarity, I made a little butter, and drank the whey. I was at first at a great loss for salt; but custom soon reconciled the want of it; and I am confident that the frequent use of salt among us is an effect of luxury, and was first introduced only as a provocative to drink; except where it is necessary for preserving of flesh in long voyages, or in places remote from great markets. For we observe no animal to be fond of it but man;[2] and as to myself, when I left this country, it was a great while before I could endure the taste of it in anything that I eat.

This is enough to say upon the subject of my diet, wherewith other travelers fill their books, as if the readers were personally concerned whether we fare well or ill. However, it was necessary to mention this matter, lest the world should think it impossible that I could find sustenance for three years in such a country, and among such inhabitants.

When it grew towards evening, the master horse ordered a place for me to lodge in; it was but six yards from the house, and separated from the stable of the Yahoos. Here I got some straw, and covering myself with my own clothes, slept very sound. But I was in a short time better accommodated, as the reader shall know hereafter, when I come to treat more particularly about my way of living.

---

2. Gulliver's error; many animals are very fond of salt.

CHAPTER III

The Author studious to learn the language, the Houyhnhnm his master
assists in teaching him. The language described. Several Houyhnhnms of
quality come out of curiosity to see the Author. He gives his master a
short account of his voyage.

My principal endeavor was to learn the language, which my master (for so I shall henceforth call him) and his children, and every servant of his house were desirous to teach me. For they looked upon it as a prodigy, that a brute animal should discover such marks of a rational creature. I pointed to everything, and enquired the name of it, which I wrote down in my journal book when I was alone, and corrected my bad accent, by desiring those of the family to pronounce it often. In this employment, a sorrel nag, one of the under servants, was very ready to assist me.

In speaking, they pronounce through the nose and throat, and their language approaches nearest to the High Dutch or German, of any I know in Europe; but is much more graceful and significant. The Emperor Charles V made almost the same observation, when he said, that if he were to speak to his horse, it should be in High Dutch.[3]

The curiosity and impatience of my master were so great, that he spent many hours of his leisure to instruct me. He was convinced (as he afterwards told me) that I must be a Yahoo, but my teachableness, civility, and cleanliness astonished him; which were qualities altogether so opposite to those animals. He was most perplexed about my clothes, reasoning sometimes with himself whether they were a part of my body; for I never pulled them off till the family were asleep, and got them on before they waked in the morning. My master was eager to learn from whence I came; how I acquired those appearances of reason, which I discovered in all my actions; and to know my story from my own mouth, which he hoped he should soon do by the great proficiency I made in learning and pronouncing their words and sentences. To help my memory, I formed all I learned into the English alphabet, and writ the words down with the translations. This last, after some time, I ventured to do in my master's presence. It cost me much trouble to explain to him what I was doing; for the inhabitants have not the least idea of books or literature.

In about ten weeks time I was able to understand most of his questions; and in three months could give him some tolerable answers. He was extremely curious to know from what part of the country I came, and how I was taught to imitate a rational creature; because the Yahoos (whom he saw I exactly resembled in my head, hands, and face, that were only visible) with some appearance of cunning, and the strongest disposition to mischief, were observed to be the most unteachable of all brutes. I answered that I came over the sea, from a far place, with many others of my own kind, in a great hollow vessel made of the bodies of trees; that my companions forced me to land on this coast, and then left me to shift for myself. It was with some difficulty, and by the help of many signs, that I brought him to understand me. He replied that I must needs be mistaken, or that I *said the thing which was not*. (For they have no words in

---

3. Charles was reputed to have said he would address God in Spanish, women in Italian, men in French, and his horse in German.

their language to express lying or falsehood.) He knew it was impossible that there could be a country beyond sea, or that a parcel of brutes could move a wooden vessel whither they pleased upon water. He was sure no Houyhnhnm alive could make such a vessel, or would trust Yahoos to manage it.

The word Houyhnhnm, in their tongue, signifies a Horse; and in its etymology, the Perfection of Nature. I told my master that I was at a loss for expression, but would improve as fast as I could; and hoped in a short time I should be able to tell him wonders; he was pleased to direct his own mare, his colt, and foal, and the servants of the family to take all opportunities of instructing me; and every day for two or three hours, he was at the same pains himself; several horses and mares of quality in the neighborhood came often to our house, upon the report spread of a wonderful Yahoo, that could speak like a Houyhnhnm, and seemed in his words and actions to discover some glimmerings of reason. These delighted to converse with me; they put many questions, and received such answers as I was able to return. By all which advantages, I made so great a progress, that in five months from my arrival, I understood whatever was spoke, and could express myself tolerably well.

The Houyhnhnms who came to visit my master, out of a design of seeing and talking with me, could hardly believe me to be a right Yahoo, because my body had a different covering from others of my kind. They were astonished to observe me without the usual hair or skin, except on my head, face, and hands; but I discovered that secret to my master, upon an accident, which happened about a fortnight before.

I have already told the reader, that every night when the family were gone to bed, it was my custom to strip and cover myself with my clothes; it happened one morning early, that my master sent for me, by the sorrel nag, who was his valet; when he came, I was fast asleep, my clothes fallen off on one side, and my shirt above my waist. I awaked at the noise he made, and observed him to deliver his message in some disorder; after which he went to my master, and in a great fright gave him a very confused account of what he had seen; this I presently discovered; for going as soon as I was dressed, to pay my attendance upon his honor, he asked me the meaning of what his servant had reported; that I was not the same thing when I slept as I appeared to be at other times; that his valet assured him, some part of me was white, some yellow, at least not so white, and some brown.

I had hitherto concealed the secret of my dress, in order to distinguish myself as much as possible, from that cursed race of Yahoos; but now I found it in vain to do so any longer. Besides, I considered that my clothes and shoes would soon wear out, which already were in a declining condition, and must be supplied by some contrivance from the hides of Yahoos, or other brutes; whereby the whole secret would be known. I therefore told my master, that in the country from whence I came, those of my kind always covered their bodies with the hairs of certain animals prepared by art, as well for decency, as to avoid inclemencies of air both hot and cold; of which, as to my own person I would give him immediate conviction, if he pleased to command me; only desiring this excuse, if I did not expose those parts that nature taught us to conceal. He said, my discourse was all very strange, but especially the last part; for he could not understand why Nature should teach us to conceal what Nature had given. That neither himself nor family were ashamed of any parts of their bodies; but however

I might do as I pleased. Whereupon, I first unbuttoned my coat, and pulled it off. I did the same with my waistcoat; I drew off my shoes, stockings, and breeches. I let my shirt down to my waist, and drew up the bottom, fastening it like a girdle about my middle to hide my nakedness.

My master observed the whole performance with great signs of curiosity and admiration. He took up all my clothes in his pastern, one piece after another, and examined them diligently; he then stroked my body very gently, and looked round me several times; after which he said, it was plain I must be a perfect Yahoo; but that I differed very much from the rest of my species, in the whiteness and smoothness of my skin, my want of hair in several parts of my body, the shape and shortness of my claws behind and before, and my affectation of walking continually on my two hinder feet. He desired to see no more; and gave me leave to put on my clothes again, for I was shuddering with cold.

I expressed my uneasiness at his giving me so often the appellation of Yahoo, an odious animal, for which I had so utter an hatred and contempt. I begged he would forbear applying that word to me, and take the same order in his family, and among his friends whom he suffered to see me. I requested likewise, that the secret of my having a false covering to my body might be known to none but himself, at least as long as my present clothing should last; for as to what the sorrel nag his valet had observed, his honor might command him to conceal it.

All this my master very graciously consented to; and thus the secret was kept till my clothes began to wear out, which I was forced to supply by several contrivances, that shall hereafter be mentioned. In the meantime, he desired I would go on with my utmost diligence to learn their language, because he was more astonished at my capacity for speech and reason, than at the figure of my body, whether it were covered or no; adding that he waited with some impatience to hear the wonders which I promised to tell him.

From thenceforward he doubled the pains he had been at to instruct me; he brought me into all company, and made them treat me with civility, because, as he told them privately, this would put me into good humor, and make me more diverting.

Every day when I waited on him, beside the trouble he was at in teaching, he would ask me several questions concerning myself, which I answered as well as I could; and by those means he had already received some general ideas, although very imperfect. It would be tedious to relate the several steps, by which I advanced to a more regular conversation, but the first account I gave of myself in any order and length was to this purpose:

That, I came from a very far country, as I already had attempted to tell him, with about fifty more of my own species; that we traveled upon the seas, in a great hollow vessel made of wood, and larger than his honor's house. I described the ship to him in the best terms I could; and explained by the help of my handkerchief displayed, how it was driven forward by the wind. That, upon a quarrel among us, I was set on shore on this coast, where I walked forward without knowing whither, till he delivered me from the persecution of those execrable Yahoos. He asked me who made the ship, and how it was possible that the Houyhnhnms of my country would leave it to the management of brutes? My answer was that I durst proceed no farther in my relation, unless he would give me his word and honor that he would not be offended; and then

I would tell him the wonders I had so often promised. He agreed; and I went on by assuring him, that the ship was made by creatures like myself, who in all the countries I had traveled, as well as in my own, were the only governing, rational animals; and that upon my arrival hither, I was as much astonished to see the Houyhnhnms act like rational beings, as he or his friends could be in finding some marks of reason in a creature he was pleased to call a Yahoo; to which I owned my resemblance in every part, but could not account for their degenerate and brutal nature. I said farther, that if good fortune ever restored me to my native country, to relate my travels hither, as I resolved to do; everybody would believe that I *said the thing which was not*; that I invented the story out of my own head; and with all possible respect to himself, his family, and friends, and under his promise of not being offended, our countrymen would hardly think it probable, that a Houyhnhnm should be the presiding creature of a nation, and a Yahoo the brute.

CHAPTER IV

The Houyhnhnms' notion of truth and falsehood. The author's discourse disapproved by his master. The author gives a more particular account of himself, and the accidents of his voyages.

My master heard me with great appearances of uneasiness in his countenance; because *doubting* or *not believing* are so little known in this country, that the inhabitants cannot tell how to behave themselves under such circumstances. And I remember in frequent discourses with my master concerning the nature of manhood, in other parts of the world, having occasion to talk of *lying* and *false representation*, it was with much difficulty that he comprehended what I meant; although he had otherwise a most acute judgment. For he argued thus: that the use of speech was to make us understand one another, and to receive information of facts; now if anyone *said the thing which was not*, these ends were defeated; because I cannot properly be said to understand him; and I am so far from receiving information, that he leaves me worse than in ignorance; for I am led to believe a thing *black* when it is *white*, and *short* when it is *long*. And these were all the notions he had concerning that faculty of *lying*, so perfectly well understood, and so universally practiced among human creatures.

To return from this digression; when I asserted that the Yahoos were the only governing animals in my country, which my master said was altogether past his conception, he desired to know, whether we had Houyhnhnms among us, and what was their employment; I told him we had great numbers; that in summer they grazed in the fields, and in winter were kept in houses, with hay and oats, where Yahoo servants were employed to rub their skins smooth, comb their manes, pick their feet, serve them with food, and make their beds. "I understand you well," said my master; "it is now very plain from all you have spoken, that whatever share of reason the Yahoos pretend to, the Houyhnhnms are your masters; I heartily wish our Yahoos would be so tractable." I begged his honor would please to excuse me from proceeding any farther, because I was very certain that the account he expected from me would be highly displeasing. But he insisted in commanding me to let him know the best and the worst; I told him he should be obeyed. I owned that the Houyhnhnms among us, whom we called Horses, were the most generous[4] and comely animal we had; that they excelled in strength and swiftness; and when they belonged to persons of quality, employed in traveling, racing, and drawing chariots, they were treated with much kindness and care, till they fell into diseases, or became foundered in the feet; but then they were sold, and used to all kind of drudgery till they died; after which their skins were stripped and sold for what they were worth, and their bodies left to be devoured by dogs and birds of prey. But the common race of horses had not so good fortune, being kept by farmers and carriers, and other mean people, who put them to greater labor, and fed them worse. I described as well as I could, our way of riding; the shape and use of a bridle, a saddle, a spur, and a whip; of harness and wheels. I added, that we fastened plates of a certain hard substance called iron at the bottom of their feet, to preserve their hoofs from being broken by the stony ways on which we often traveled.

My master, after some expressions of great indignation, wondered how we dared to venture upon a Houyhnhnm's back; for he was sure, that the weakest servant in his house would be able to shake off the strongest Yahoo; or by lying down, and rolling upon his back, squeeze the brute to death. I answered that our horses were trained up from three or four years old to the several uses we intended them for; that if any of them proved intolerably vicious, they were employed for carriages; that they were severely beaten while they were young for any mischievous tricks; that the males, designed for the common use of riding or draught, were generally castrated about two years after their birth, to take down their spirits, and make them more tame and gentle; that they were indeed sensible of rewards and punishments; but his honor would please to consider that they had not the least tincture of reason any more than the Yahoos in this country.

It put me to the pains of many circumlocutions to give my master a right idea of what I spoke; for their language doth not abound in variety of words, because their wants and passions are fewer than among us. But it is impossible to express his noble resentment at our savage treatment of the Houyhnhnm race; particularly after I had explained the manner and use of castrating horses among us, to hinder them from propagating their kind, and to render them more servile. He said, if it were possible there could be any country where Yahoos alone were endued with reason, they certainly must be the governing animal, because reason will in time always prevail against brutal strength. But, considering the frame of our bodies, and especially of mine, he thought no creature of equal bulk was so ill-contrived for employing that reason in the common offices of life; whereupon he desired to know whether those among whom I lived resembled me or the Yahoos of his country. I assured him that I was as well shaped as most of my age; but the younger and the females were much more soft and tender, and the skins of the latter generally as white as milk. He said I differed indeed from other Yahoos, being much more cleanly, and not altogether so deformed; but in point of real advantage, he thought I differed for the worse. That my nails were of no use either to my fore or hinder feet; as to my forefeet, he could not properly call them by that name, for he never observed me to walk upon them; that they were too soft to bear the

---

4. Noble.

ground; that I generally went with them uncovered, neither was the covering I sometimes wore on them of the same shape, or so strong as that on my feet behind. That I could not walk with any security; for if either of my hinder feet slipped, I must inevitably fall. He then began to find fault with other parts of my body; the flatness of my face, the prominence of my nose, my eyes placed directly in front, so that I could not look on either side without turning my head; that I was not able to feed myself without lifting one of my forefeet to my mouth; and therefore nature had placed those joints to answer that necessity. He knew not what could be the use of those several clefts and divisions in my feet behind; that these were too soft to bear the hardness and sharpness of stones without a covering made from the skin of some other brute; that my whole body wanted a fence against heat and cold, which I was forced to put on and off every day with tediousness and trouble. And lastly, that he observed every animal in his country naturally to abhor the Yahoos, whom the weaker avoided, and the stronger drove from them. So that supposing us to have the gift of reason, he could not see how it were possible to cure that natural antipathy which every creature discovered against us; nor consequently, how we could tame and render them serviceable. However, he would (as he said) debate the matter no farther, because he was more desirous to know my own story, the country where I was born, and the several actions and events of my life before I came hither.

I assured him how extremely desirous I was that he should be satisfied in every point; but I doubted much whether it would be possible for me to explain myself on several subjects whereof his honor could have no conception, because I saw nothing in his country to which I could resemble them. That however, I would do my best, and strive to express myself by similitudes, humbly desiring his assistance when I wanted proper words; which he was pleased to promise me.

I said, my birth was of honest parents, in an island called England, which was remote from this country, as many days journey as the strongest of his honor's servants could travel in the annual course of the sun. That I was bred a surgeon, whose trade it is to cure wounds and hurts in the body, got by accident or violence. That my country was governed by a female man, whom we called a queen.[5] That I left it to get riches, whereby I might maintain myself and family when I should return. That in my last voyage, I was Commander of the ship and had about fifty Yahoos under me, many of which died at sea, and I was forced to supply them by others picked out from several nations. That our ship was twice in danger of being sunk; the first time by a great storm, and the second, by striking against a rock. Here my master interposed, by asking me, how I could persuade strangers out of different countries to venture with me, after the losses I had sustained, and the hazards I had run. I said, they were fellows of desperate fortunes, forced to fly from the places of their birth, on account of their poverty or their crimes. Some were undone by lawsuits; others spent all they had in drinking, whoring, and gambling; others fled for treason; many for murder, theft, poisoning, robbery, perjury, forgery, coining false money; for committing rapes or sodomy; for flying from their colors, or deserting to the enemy; and most of them had broken prison. None of these durst

5. Queen Anne (1665–1714), the last Stuart ruler.

return to their native countries for fear of being hanged, or of starving in a jail; and therefore were under a necessity of seeking livelihood in other places.

During this discourse, my master was pleased often to interrupt me. I had made use of many circumlocutions in describing to him the nature of the several crimes, for which most of our crew had been forced to fly their country. This labor took up several days conversation before he was able to comprehend me. He was wholly at a loss to know what could be the use or necessity of practicing those vices. To clear up which I endeavored to give him some ideas of the desire of power and riches; of the terrible effects of lust, intemperance, malice, and envy. All this I was forced to define and describe by putting of cases, and making suppositions. After which, like one whose imagination was struck with something never seen or heard of before, he would lift up his eyes with amazement and indignation. Power, government, war, law, punishment, and a thousand other things had no terms, wherein that language could express them; which made the difficulty almost insuperable to give my master any conception of what I meant; but being of an excellent understanding, much improved by contemplation and converse, he at last arrived at a competent knowledge of what human nature in our parts of the world is capable to perform; and desired I would give him some particular account of that land, which we call Europe, especially, of my own country.

CHAPTER V

The Author, at his master's commands, informs him of the state of England. The causes of war among the princes of Europe. The Author begins to explain the English Constitution.

The reader may please to observe that the following extract of many conversations I had with my master contains a summary of the most material points, which were discoursed at several times for above two years; his honor often desiring fuller satisfaction as I farther improved in the Houyhnhnm tongue. I laid before him, as well as I could, the whole state of Europe; I discoursed of trade and manufactures, of arts and sciences; and the answers I gave to all the questions he made, as they arose upon several subjects, were a fund of conversation not to be exhausted. But I shall here only set down the substance of what passed between us concerning my own country, reducing it into order as well as I can, without any regard to time or other circumstances, while I strictly adhere to truth. My only concern is that I shall hardly be able to do justice to my master's arguments and expressions; which must needs suffer by my want of capacity, as well as by a translation into our barbarous English.

In obedience therefore to his honor's commands, I related to him the Revolution under the Prince of Orange; the long war with France entered into by the said Prince, and renewed by his successor the present queen; wherein the greatest powers of Christendom were engaged, and which still continued. I computed at his request, that about a million of Yahoos might have been killed in the whole progress of it; and perhaps a hundred or more cities taken, and five times as many ships burned or sunk.[6]

6. Gulliver relates recent English history: the Glorious Revolution of 1688 and the War of the Spanish Succession (1703–14). He greatly exaggerates the casualties in the war.

He asked me what were the usual causes or motives that made one country to go to war with another. I answered, they were innumerable; but I should only mention a few of the chief. Sometimes the ambition of princes, who never think they have land or people enough to govern; sometimes the corruption of ministers, who engage their master in a war in order to stifle or divert the clamor of the subjects against their evil administration. Difference in opinions hath cost many millions of lives; for instance, whether flesh be bread, or bread be flesh; whether the juice of a certain berry be blood or wine; whether whistling be a vice or a virtue; whether it be better to kiss a post, or throw it into the fire; what is the best color for a coat, whether black, white, red, or grey; and whether it should be long or short, narrow or wide, dirty or clean;[7] with many more. Neither are any wars so furious and bloody, or of so long continuance, as those occasioned by difference in opinion, especially if it be in things indifferent.

Sometimes the quarrel between two princes is to decide which of them shall dispossess a third of his dominions, where neither of them pretend to any right. Sometimes one prince quarreleth with another, for fear the other should quarrel with him. Sometimes a war is entered upon, because the enemy is too strong, and sometimes because he is too weak. Sometimes our neighbors want the things which we have, or have the things which we want; and we both fight, till they take ours or give us theirs. It is a very justifiable cause of war to invade a country after the people have been wasted by famine, destroyed by pestilence, or embroiled by factions amongst themselves. It is justifiable to enter into a war against our nearest ally, when one of his towns lies convenient for us, or a territory of land, that would render our dominions round and compact. If a prince send forces into a nation, where the people are poor and ignorant, he may lawfully put half of them to death, and make slaves of the rest, in order to civilize and reduce them from their barbarous way of living. It is a very kingly, honorable, and frequent practice, when one prince desires the assistance of another to secure him against an invasion, that the assistant, when he hath driven out the invader, should seize on the dominions himself, and kill, imprison, or banish the prince he came to relieve. Alliance by blood or marriage is a sufficient cause of war between princes; and the nearer the kindred is, the greater is their disposition to quarrel; poor nations are hungry, and rich nations are proud; and pride and hunger will ever be at variance. For these reasons, the trade of a soldier is held the most honorable of all others: because a soldier is a Yahoo hired to kill in cold blood as many of his own species, who have never offended him, as possibly he can.

There is likewise a kind of beggarly princes in Europe, not able to make war by themselves, who hire out their troops to richer nations for so much a day to each man; of which they keep three fourths to themselves, and it is the best part of their maintenance; such are those in many northern parts of Europe.

"What you have told me," said my master, "upon the subject of war, doth indeed discover most admirably the effects of that reason you pretend to; however, it is happy that the shame is greater than the danger; and that Nature hath left you utterly uncapable of doing much mischief; for your mouths lying

7. Gulliver refers to the religious controversies of the Reformation and Counter-Reformation: the doctrine of transubstantiation, the use of music in church services, the veneration of the Crucifix, and the wearing of priestly vestments.

flat with your faces, you can hardly bite each other to any purpose, unless by consent. Then, as to the claws upon your feet before and behind, they are so short and tender, that one of our Yahoos would drive a dozen of yours before him. And therefore in recounting the numbers of those who have been killed in battle, I cannot but think that you have *said the thing which is not.*"

I could not forebear shaking my head and smiling a little at his ignorance. And, being no stranger to the art of war, I gave him a description of cannons, culverins, muskets, carabines, pistols, bullets, powder, swords, bayonets, battles, sieges, retreats, attacks, undermines, countermines, bombardments, sea fights; ships sunk with a thousand men; twenty thousand killed on each side; dying groans, limbs flying in the air; smoke, noise, confusion, trampling to death under horses' feet; flight, pursuit, victory; fields strewed with carcasses left for food to dogs, and wolves, and birds of prey; plundering, stripping, ravishing, burning, and destroying. And, to set forth the valor of my own dear countrymen, I assured him that I had seen them blow up a hundred enemies at once in a siege, and as many in a ship; and beheld the dead bodies drop down in pieces from the clouds, to the great diversion of all the spectators.

I was going on to more particulars, when my master commanded me silence. He said, whoever understood the nature of Yahoos might easily believe it possible for so vile an animal, to be capable of every action I had named, if their strength and cunning equaled their malice. But, as my discourse had increased his abhorrence of the whole species, so he found it gave him a disturbance in his mind, to which he was wholly a stranger before. He thought his ears being used to such abominable words, might by degrees admit them with less detestation. That, although he hated the Yahoos of this country, yet he no more blamed them for their odious qualities, than he did a *gnnayh* (a bird of prey) for its cruelty, or a sharp stone for cutting his hoof. But, when a creature pretending to reason could be capable of such enormities, he dreaded lest the corruption of that faculty might be worse than brutality itself. He seemed therefore confident, that instead of reason, we were only possessed of some quality fitted to increase our natural vices; as the reflection from a troubled stream returns the image of an ill-shapen body, not only larger, but more distorted.

He added that he had heard too much upon the subject of war, both in this and some former discourses. There was another point which a little perplexed him at present. I had said that some of our crew left their country on account of being ruined by law: that I had already explained the meaning of the word; but he was at a loss how it should come to pass, that the law which was intended for every man's preservation, should be any man's ruin. Therefore he desired to be farther satisfied what I meant by law, and the dispensers thereof, according to the present practice in my own country; because he thought nature and reason were sufficient guides for a reasonable animal, as we pretended to be, in showing us what we ought to do, and what to avoid.

I assured his honor that law was a science wherein I had not much conversed, further than by employing advocates, in vain, upon some injustices that had been done me. However, I would give him all the satisfaction I was able.

I said there was a society of men among us, bred up from their youth in the art of proving by words multiplied for the purpose, that white is black, and black is white, according as they are paid. To this society all the rest of the people are slaves.

"For example. If my neighbor hath a mind to my cow, he hires a lawyer to prove that he ought to have my cow from me. I must then hire another to defend my right; it being against all rules of law that any man should be allowed to speak for himself. Now in this case, I who am the true owner lie under two great disadvantages. First, my lawyer being practiced almost from his cradle in defending falsehood is quite out of his element when he would be an advocate for justice, which as an office unnatural, he always attempts with great awkwardness, if not with ill-will. The second disadvantage is that my lawyer must proceed with great caution, or else he will be reprimanded by the judges, and abhorred by his breathren, as one who would lessen the practice of the law. And therefore I have but two methods to preserve my cow. The first is to gain over my adversary's lawyer with a double fee; who will then betray his client, by insinuating that he hath justice on his side. The second way is for my lawyer to make my cause appear as unjust as he can; by allowing the cow to belong to my adversary; and this if it be skillfully done, will certainly bespeak the favor of the bench.

"Now, your honor is to know that these judges are persons appointed to decide all controversies of property, as well as for the trial of criminals; and picked out from the most dextrous lawyers who are grown old or lazy; and having been biased all their lives against truth and equity, lie under such a fatal necessity of favoring fraud, perjury, and oppression, that I have known some of them to have refused a large bribe from the side where justice lay, rather than injure the faculty,[8] by doing anything unbecoming their nature or their office.

"It is a maxim among these lawyers, that whatever hath been done before may legally be done again; and therefore they take special care to record all the decisions formerly made against common justice and the general reason of mankind. These, under the name of *precedents*, they produce as authorities to justify the most iniquitous opinions; and the judges never fail of directing accordingly.

"In pleading, they studiously avoid entering into the merits of the cause; but are loud, violent, and tedious in dwelling upon all circumstances which are not to the purpose. For instance, in the case already mentioned, they never desire to know what claim or title my adversary hath to my cow; but whether the said cow were red or black; her horns long or short; whether the field I graze her in be round or square; whether she were milked at home or abroad; what diseases she is subject to, and the like. After which they consult precedents, adjourn the cause, from time to time, and in ten, twenty, or thirty years come to an issue.

"It is likewise to be observed, that this society hath a peculiar cant and jargon of their own, that no other mortal can understand, and wherein all their laws are written, which they take special care to multiply; whereby they have wholly confounded the very essence of truth and falsehood, of right and wrong; so that it will take thirty years to decide whether the field, left me by my ancestors for six generations, belong to me, or to a stranger three hundred miles off.

"In the trial of persons accused for crimes against the state, the method is much more short and commendable: the judge first sends to sound the disposition of those in power; after which he can easily hang or save the criminal, strictly preserving all the forms of law."

---

8. Profession.

Here my master interposing said it was a pity that creatures endowed with such prodigious abilities of mind as these lawyers, by the description I gave of them must certainly be, were not rather encouraged to be instructors of others in wisdom and knowledge. In answer to which, I assured his honor that in all points out of their own trade, they were usually the most ignorant and stupid generation among us, the most despicable in common conversation, avowed enemies to all knowledge and learning; and equally disposed to pervert the general reason of mankind, in every other subject of discourse as in that of their own profession.

CHAPTER VI

A continuation of the state of England, under Queen Anne. The character of a first minister in the courts of Europe.

My master was yet wholly at a loss to understand what motives could incite this race of lawyers to perplex, disquiet, and weary themselves by engaging in a confederacy of injustice, merely for the sake of injuring their fellow animals; neither could he comprehend what I meant in saying they did it for hire. Whereupon I was at much pains to describe to him the use of money, the materials it was made of, and the value of the metals; that when a Yahoo had got a great store of this precious substance, he was able to purchase whatever he had a mind to; the finest clothing, the noblest houses, great tracts of land, the most costly meats and drinks; and have his choice of the most beautiful females. Therefore since money alone was able to perform all these feats, our Yahoos thought they could never have enough of it to spend or to save, as they found themselves inclined from their natural bent either to profusion or avarice. That the rich man enjoyed the fruit of the poor man's labor, and the latter were a thousand to one in proportion to the former. That the bulk of our people was forced to live miserably, by laboring every day for small wages to make a few live plentifully. I enlarged myself much on these and many other particulars to the same purpose, but his honor was still to seek, for he went upon a supposition that all animals had a title to their share in the productions of the earth; and especially those who presided over the rest. Therefore he desired I would let him know what these costly meats were, and how any of us happened to want[9] them. Whereupon I enumerated as many sorts as came into my head, with the various methods of dressing them, which could not be done without sending vessels by sea to every part of the world, as well for liquors to drink, as for sauces, and innumerable other conveniencies. I assured him, that this whole globe of earth must be at least three times gone round, before one of our better female Yahoos could get her breakfast, or a cup to put it in. He said, "That must needs be a miserable country which cannot furnish food for its own inhabitants." But what he chiefly wondered at, was how such vast tracts of ground as I described, should be wholly without fresh water, and the people put to the necessity of sending over the sea for drink. I replied that England (the dear place of my nativity) was computed to produce three times the quantity of food, more than its inhabitants are able to consume, as well as

9. Lack.

liquors extracted from grain, or pressed out of the fruit of certain trees, which made excellent drink; and the same proportion in every other convenience of life. But, in order to feed the luxury and intemperance of the males, and the vanity of the females, we sent away the greatest part of our necessary things to other countries, from whence in return we brought the materials of diseases, folly, and vice, to spend among ourselves. Hence it follows of necessity, that vast numbers of our people are compelled to seek their livelihood by begging, robbing, stealing, cheating, pimping, foreswearing, flattering, suborning, forging, gaming, lying, fawning, hectoring, voting, scribbling, star gazing, poisoning, whoring, canting, libeling, freethinking, and the like occupations; every one of which terms, I was at much pains to make him understand.

That, wine was not imported among us from foreign countries, to supply the want of water or other drinks, but because it was a sort of liquid which made us merry, by putting us out of our senses; diverted all melancholy thoughts, begat wild extravagant imaginations in the brain, raised our hopes, and banished our fears; suspended every office of reason for a time, and deprived us of the use of our limbs, until we fell into a profound sleep; although it must be confessed, that we always awaked sick and dispirited; and that the use of this liquor filled us with diseases, which made our lives uncomfortable and short.

But beside all this, the bulk of our people supported themselves by furnishing the necessities or conveniencies of life to the rich, and to each other. For instance, when I am at home and dressed as I ought to be, I carry on my body the workmanship of an hundred tradesmen; the building and furniture of my house employ as many more; and five times the number to adorn my wife.

I was going on to tell him of another sort of people, who get their livelihood by attending the sick; having upon some occasions informed his honor that many of my crew had died of diseases. But here it was with the utmost difficulty that I brought him to apprehend what I meant. He could easily conceive that a Houyhnhnm grew weak and heavy a few days before his death; or by some accident might hurt a limb. But that nature, who worketh all things to perfection, should suffer any pains to breed in our bodies, he thought impossible; and desired to know the reason of so unaccountable an evil. I told him, we fed on a thousand things which operated contrary to each other; that we eat when we were not hungry, and drank without the provocation of thirst; that we sat whole nights drinking strong liquors without eating a bit, which disposed us to sloth, enflamed our bodies, and precipitated or prevented digestion. That, prostitute female Yahoos acquired a certain malady, which bred rottenness in the bones of those who fell into their embraces; that this and many other diseases were propagated from father to son; so that great numbers come into the world with complicated maladies upon them; that it would be endless to give him a catalogue of all diseases incident to human bodies; for they could not be fewer than five or six hundred, spread over every limb, and joint; in short, every part, external and intestine, having diseases appropriated to each. To remedy which, there was a sort of people bred up among us, in the profession or pretense of curing the sick. And because I had some skill in the faculty, I would in gratitude to his honor let him know the whole mystery and method by which they proceed.

Their fundamental is that all diseases arise from repletion; from whence they conclude, that a great evacuation of the body is necessary, either through the natural passage, or upwards at the mouth. Their next business is, from herbs, minerals, gums, oils, shells, salts, juices, seaweed, excrements, barks of trees, serpents, toads, frogs, spiders, dead men's flesh and bones, birds, beasts and fishes, to form a composition for smell and taste the most abominable, nauseous, and detestable, that they can possibly contrive, which the stomach immediately rejects with loathing, and this they call a vomit. Or else from the same storehouse, with some other poisonous additions, they command us to take in at the orifice above or below (just as the physician then happens to be disposed) a medicine equally annoying and disgustful to the bowels; which relaxing the belly, drives down all before it; and this they call a purge, or a clyster. For nature (as the physicians allege) having intended the superior anterior orifice only for the intromission of solids and liquids, and the inferior posterior for ejection, these artists ingeniously considering that in all diseases nature is forced out of her seat; therefore to replace her in it, the body must be treated in a manner directly contrary, but interchanging the use of each orifice; forcing solids and liquids in at the anus, and making evacuations at the mouth.

But, besides real diseases, we are subject to many that are only imaginary, for which the physicians have invented imaginary cures; these have their several names, and so have the drugs that are proper for them; and with these our female Yahoos are always infested.

One great excellency in this tribe is their skill at prognostics, wherein they seldom fail; their predictions in real diseases, when they rise to any degree of malignity, generally portending death, which is always in their power, when recovery is not, and therefore, upon any unexpected signs of amendment, after they have pronounced their sentence, rather than be accused as false prophets, they know how to approve[1] their sagacity to the world by a seasonable dose.

They are likewise of special use to husbands and wives, who are grown weary of their mates; to eldest sons, to great ministers of state, and often to princes.

I had formerly upon occasion discoursed with my master upon the nature of government in general, and particularly of our own excellent constitution, deservedly the wonder and envy of the whole world. But having here accidentally mentioned a minister of state, he commanded me some time after to inform him what species of Yahoo I particularly meant by that appellation.

I told him that a first or chief minister of state, whom I intended to describe, was a creature wholly exempt from joy and grief, love and hatred, pity and anger; at least makes use of no other passions but a violent desire of wealth, power, and titles; that he applies his words to all uses, except to the indication of his mind; that he never tells a truth, but with an intent that you should take it for a lie; nor a lie, but with a design that you should take it for a truth; that those he speaks worst of behind their backs are in the surest way to preferment; and whenever he begins to praise you to others or to yourself, you are from that day forlorn. The worst mark you can receive is a promise, especially when it is confirmed with an oath; after which every wise man retires, and gives over all hopes.

There are three methods by which a man may rise to be chief minister: the first is by knowing how with prudence to dispose of a wife, a daughter, or a

1. Prove.

sister; the second, by betraying or undermining his predecessor; and the third is by a furious zeal in public assemblies against the corruptions of the court. But a wise prince would rather choose to employ those who practice the last of these methods; because such zealots prove always the most obsequious and subservient to the will and passions of their master. That, these ministers having all employments at their disposal, preserve themselves in power by bribing the majority of a senate or great council; and at last by an expedient called an Act of Indemnity (whereof I described the nature to him) they secure themselves from after-reckonings, and retire from the public, laden with the spoils of the nation.

The palace of a chief minister is a seminary to breed up others in his own trade; the pages, lackies, and porter, by imitating their master, become ministers of state in their several districts, and learn to excel in the three principal ingredients, of insolence, lying, and bribery. Accordingly, they have a subaltern court paid to them by persons of the best rank; and sometimes by the force of dexterity and impudence, arrive through several gradations to be successors to their lord.

He is usually governed by a decayed wench, or favorite footman, who are the tunnels through which all graces are conveyed, and may properly be called, in the last resort, the governors of the kingdom.

One day, my master, having heard me mention the nobility of my country, was pleased to make me a compliment which I could not pretend to deserve: that, he was sure, I must have been born of some noble family, because I far exceeded in shape, color, and cleanliness, all the Yahoos of his nation, although I seemed to fail in strength, and agility, which must be imputed to my different way of living from those other brutes; and besides, I was not only endowed with the faculty of speech, but likewise with some rudiments of reason, to a degree, that with all his acquaintance I passed for a prodigy.

He made me observe, that among the Houyhnhnms, the white, the sorrel, and the iron grey were not so exactly shaped as the bay, the dapple grey, and the black; nor born with equal talents of mind, or a capacity to improve them; and therefore continued always in the condition of servants, without ever aspiring to match out of their own race, which in that country would be reckoned monstrous and unnatural.

I made his honor my most humble acknowledgements for the good opinion he was pleased to conceive of me; but assured him at the same time, that my birth was of the lower sort, having been born of plain, honest parents, who were just able to give me a tolerable education; that, nobility among us was altogether a different thing from the idea he had of it; that, our young noblemen are bred from their childhood in idleness and luxury; that, as soon as years will permit, they consume their vigor, and contract odious diseases among lewd females; and when their fortunes are almost ruined, they marry some woman of mean birth, disagreeable person, and unsound constitution, merely for the sake of money, whom they hate and despise. That, the productions of such marriages are generally scrofulous, rickety or deformed children; by which means the family seldom continues above three generations, unless the wife take care to provide a healthy father among her neighbors, or domestics, in order to improve and continue the breed. That a weak diseased body, a meager countenance, and sallow complexion are the true marks of noble blood; and a healthy robust appearance is so disgraceful in a man of quality, that the world concludes his real father to have been a groom or a coachman. The imperfections of his mind run parallel with those of his body; being a composition of spleen, dullness, ignorance, caprice, sensuality, and pride.

Without the consent of this illustrious body, no law can be enacted, repealed, or altered, and these nobles have likewise the decision of all our possessions without appeal.

CHAPTER VII

The Author's great love of his native country. His master's observations
upon the constitution and administration of England, as described by the
Author, with parallel cases and comparisons. His master's observations
upon human nature.

The reader may be disposed to wonder how I could prevail on myself to give so free a representation of my own species, among a race of mortals who were already too apt to conceive the vilest opinion of humankind, from that entire congruity betwixt me and their Yahoos. But I must freely confess that the many virtues of those excellent quadrupeds placed in opposite view to human corruptions had so far opened my eyes, and enlarged my understanding, that I began to view the actions and passions of man in a very different light; and to think the honor of my own kind not worth managing; which, besides, it was impossible for me to do before a person of so acute a judgment as my master, who daily convinced me of a thousand faults in myself, whereof I had not the least perception before, and which with us would never be numbered even among human infirmities. I had likewise learned from his example an utter detestation of all falsehood or disguise; and truth appeared so amiable to me, that I determined upon sacrificing everything to it.

Let me deal so candidly with the reader as to confess that there was yet a much stronger motive for the freedom I took in my representation of things. I had not been a year in this country, before I contracted such a love and veneration for the inhabitants, that I entered on a firm resolution never to return to humankind, but to pass the rest of my life among these admirable Houyhnhnms in the contemplation and practice of every virtue; where I could have no example or incitement to vice. But it was decreed by fortune, my perpetual enemy, that so great a felicity should not fall to my share. However, it is now some comfort to reflect that in what I said of my countrymen, I extenuated their faults as much as I durst before so strict an examiner; and upon every article, gave as favorable a turn as the matter would bear. For, indeed, who is there alive that will not be swayed by his bias and partiality to the place of his birth?

I have related the substance of several conversations I had with my master, during the greatest part of the time I had the honor to be in his service; but have indeed for brevity sake omitted much more than is here set down.

When I had answered all his questions, and his curiosity seemed to be fully satisfied; he sent for me one morning early, and commanding me to sit down at some distance (an honor which he had never before conferred upon me), he said he had been very seriously considering my whole story, as far as it related both to myself and my country; that, he looked upon us as a sort of animal to whose share, by what accident he could not conjecture, some small pittance of reason had fallen, whereof we made no other use than by its assistance to aggravate our natural corruptions, and to acquire new ones which nature had not given us. That we disarmed ourselves of the few abilities she had bestowed; had been very successful in multiplying our original wants, and seemed to spend our whole lives in vain endeavors to supply them by our own inventions. That, as to myself, it was manifest I had neither the strength or agility of a common Yahoo; that I walked infirmly on my hinder feet; had found out a contrivance to make my claws of no use or defense, and to remove the hair from my chin, which was intended as a shelter from the sun and the weather. Lastly, that I could neither run with speed, nor climb trees like my brethren (as he called them) the Yahoos in this country.

That our institutions of government and law were plainly owing to our gross defects in reason, and by consequence, in virtue; because reason alone is sufficient to govern a rational creature; which was therefore a character we had no pretense to challenge, even from the account I had given of my own people; although he manifestly perceived, that in order to favor them, I had concealed many particulars, and often *said the thing which was not.*

He was the more confirmed in this opinion, because he observed that I agreed in every feature of my body with other Yahoos, except where it was to my real disadvantage in point of strength, speed, and activity, the shortness of my claws, and some other particulars where nature had no part; so, from the representation I had given him of our lives, our manners, and our actions, he found as near a resemblance in the disposition of our minds. He said the Yahoos were known to hate one another more than they did any different species of animals; and the reason usually assigned was the odiousness of their own shapes, which all could see in the rest, but not in themselves. He had therefore begun to think it not unwise in us to cover our bodies, and by that invention, conceal many of our deformities from each other, which would else be hardly supportable. But he now found he had been mistaken; and that the dissentions of those brutes in his country were owing to the same cause with ours, as I had described them. For, if (said he) you throw among five Yahoos as much food as would be sufficient for fifty, they will, instead of eating peaceably, fall together by the ears, each single one impatient to have all to itself; and therefore a servant was usually employed to stand by while they were feeding abroad, and those kept at home were tied at a distance from each other. That, if a cow died of age or accident, before a Houyhnhnm could secure it for his own Yahoos, those in the neighborhood would come in herds to seize it, and then would ensue such a battle as I had described, with terrible wounds made by their claws on both sides, although they seldom were able to kill one another, for want of such convenient instruments of death as we had invented. At other times the like battles have been fought between the Yahoos of several neighborhoods without any visible cause; those of one district watching all opportunities to surprise the next before they are prepared. But if they find their project hath miscarried, they return home, and for want of enemies, engage in what I call a civil war among themselves.

That, in some fields of his country, there are certain shining stones of several colors, whereof the Yahoos are violently fond; and when part of these stones are fixed in the earth, as it sometimes happeneth, they will dig with their claws for whole days to get them out, and carry them away, and hide them by heaps in their kennels; but still looking round with great caution, for fear their comrades should find out their treasure. My master said he could never discover the reason of this unnatural appetite, or how these stones could be of any use to a Yahoo; but now he believed it might proceed from the same principle of avarice, which I had ascribed to mankind. That he had once, by way of experiment, privately removed a heap of these stones from the place where one of his Yahoos had buried it, whereupon, the sordid animal missing his treasure, by his loud lamenting brought the whole herd to the place, there miserably howled, then fell to biting and tearing the rest; began to pine away, would neither eat nor sleep, nor work, till he ordered a servant privately to convey the stones into the same hole, and hide them as before; which when his Yahoo had found, he presently recovered his spirits and good humor; but took care to remove them to a better hiding place; and hath ever since been a very serviceable brute.

My master farther assured me, which I also observed myself; that in the fields where these shining stones abound, the fiercest and most frequent battles are fought, occasioned by perpetual inroads of the neighboring Yahoos.

He said it was common when two Yahoos discovered such a stone in a field, and were contending which of them should be the proprietor, a third would take the advantage, and carry it away from them both; which my master would needs contend to have some resemblance with our suits at law; wherein I thought it for our credit not to undeceive him; since the decision he mentioned was much more equitable than many decrees among us; because the plaintiff and defendant there lost nothing beside the stone they contended for; whereas our courts of equity would never have dismissed the cause while either of them had anything left.

My master continuing his discourse said there was nothing that rendered the Yahoos more odious, than their undistinguished appetite to devour everything that came in their way, whether herbs, roots, berries, corrupted flesh of animals, or all mingled together; and it was peculiar in their temper, that they were fonder of what they could get by rapine or stealth at a greater distance, than much better food provided for them at home. If their prey held out, they would eat till they were ready to burst, after which nature had pointed out to them a certain root that gave them a general evacuation.

There was also another kind of root very juicy, but something rare and difficult to be found, which the Yahoos fought for with much eagerness, and would suck it with great delight; it produced the same effects that wine hath upon us. It would make them sometimes hug, and sometimes tear one another; they would howl and grin, and chatter, and reel, and tumble, and then fall asleep in the mud.

I did indeed observe that the Yahoos were the only animals in this country subject to any diseases; which however, were much fewer than horses have among us, and contracted not by any ill treatment they meet with, but by the nastiness and greediness of that sordid brute. Neither has their language any more than a general appellation for those maladies; which is borrowed from the name of the beast, and called *Hnea Yahoo*, or the Yahoo's Evil; and the cure prescribed is a mixture of their own dung and urine, forcibly put down the Yahoo's throat. This I have since often known to have been taken with success, and do here freely recommend it to my countrymen, for the public good, as an admirable specific against all diseases produced by repletion.

As to learning, government, arts, manufactures, and the like, my master confessed he could find little or no resemblance between the Yahoos of that country and those in ours. For he only meant to observe what parity there was in our natures. He had heard indeed some curious Houyhnhnms observe that in most herds there was a sort of ruling Yahoo (as among us there is generally some leading or principal stag in a park) who was always more deformed in body, and mischievous in disposition, than any of the rest. That this leader had usually a favorite as like himself as he could get, whose employment was to lick his master's feet and posteriors, and drive the female Yahoos to his kennel; for which he was now and then rewarded with a piece of ass's flesh. This favorite is hated by the whole herd; and therefore to protect himself, keeps always near the person of his leader. He usually continues in office till a worse can be found; but the very moment he is discarded, his successor, at the head of all the Yahoos in that district, young and old, male and female, come in a body, and discharge their excrements upon him from head to foot. But how far this might be applicable to our courts and favorites, and ministers of state, my master said I could best determine.

I durst make no return to this malicious insinuation, which debased human understanding below the sagacity of a common hound, who hath judgment enough to distinguish and follow the cry of the ablest dog in the pack, without being ever mistaken.

My master told me there were some qualities remarkable in the Yahoos, which he had not observed me to mention, or at least very slightly, in the accounts I had given him of humankind. He said, those animals, like other brutes, had their females in common; but in this differed, that the she-Yahoo would admit the male while she was pregnant; and that the hes would quarrel and fight with the females as fiercely as with each other. Both which practices were such degrees of infamous brutality, that no other sensitive creature ever arrived at.

Another thing he wondered at in the Yahoos was their strange disposition to nastiness and dirt; whereas there appears to be a natural love of cleanliness in all other animals. As to the two former accusations, I was glad to let them pass without any reply, because I had not a word to offer upon them in defense of my species, which otherwise I certainly had done from my own inclinations. But I could have easily vindicated humankind from the imputation of singularity upon the last article, if there had been any swine in that country (as unluckily for me there were not) which although it may be a sweeter quadruped than a Yahoo, cannot I humbly conceive in justice pretend to more cleanliness; and so his honor himself must have owned, if he had seen their filthy way of feeding, and their custom of wallowing and sleeping in the mud.

My master likewise mentioned another quality, which his servants had discovered in several Yahoos, and to him was wholly unaccountable. He said, a fancy would sometimes take a Yahoo, to retire into a corner, to lie down and howl, and groan, and spurn away all that came near him, although he were young and fat, and wanted neither food nor water; nor did the servants imagine what could possibly ail him. And the only remedy they found was to set him to hard work, after which he would infallibly come to himself. To this I was silent out of partiality to my own kind; yet here I could plainly discover the true seeds of spleen,[2] which only seizeth on the lazy, the luxurious, and the rich; who, if they were forced to undergo the same regimen, I would undertake for the cure.

His Honor had farther observed, that a female Yahoo would often stand behind a bank or a bush, to gaze on the young males passing by, and then appear, and hide, using many antic gestures and grimaces; at which time it was observed, that she had a most offensive smell; and when any of the males advanced, would slowly retire, looking back, and with a counterfeit show of fear, run off into some convenient place where she knew the male would follow her.

At other times, if a female stranger came among them, three or four of her own sex would get about her, and stare and chatter, and grin, and smell her all over; and then turn off with gestures that seemed to express contempt and disdain.

Perhaps my master might refine a little in these speculations, which he had drawn from what he observed himself, or had been told by others; however, I could not reflect without some amazement, and much sorrow, that the rudiments of lewdness, coquetry, censure, and scandal, should have place by instinct in womankind.

I expected every moment that my master would accuse the Yahoos of those unnatural appetites in both sexes, so common among us. But nature it seems hath not been so expert a school-mistress; and these politer pleasures are entirely the productions of art and reason, on our side of the globe.

CHAPTER VIII

The Author relateth several particulars of the Yahoos. The great virtues of the Houyhnhnms. The education and exercises of their youth. Their general assembly.

As I ought to have understood human nature much better than I supposed it possible for my master to do, so it was easy to apply the character he gave of the Yahoos to myself and my countrymen; and I believed I could yet make farther discoveries from my own observation. I therefore often begged his honor to let me go among the herds of Yahoos in the neighborhood; to which he always very graciously consented, being perfectly convinced that the hatred I bore those brutes would never suffer me to be corrupted by them; and his honor ordered one of his servants, a strong sorrel nag, very honest and good-natured, to be my guard; without whose protection I durst not undertake such adventures. For I have already told the reader how much I was pestered by those odious animals upon my first arrival. I afterwards failed very narrowly three or four times of falling into their clutches, when I happened to stray at any distance without my hanger. And I have reason to believe, they had some imagination that I was of their own species, which I often assisted myself, by stripping up my sleeves, and shewing my naked arms and breast in their sight, when my protector was with me; at which times they would approach as near as they durst, and imitate my actions after the manner of monkeys, but ever

2. Hypochondria.

with great signs of hatred; as a tame jackdaw with cap and stockings is always persecuted by the wild ones, when he happens to be got among them.

They are prodigiously nimble from their infancy; however, I once caught a young male of three years old, and endeavored by all marks of tenderness to make it quiet; but the little imp fell a squalling, scratching, and biting with such violence, that I was forced to let it go; and it was high time, for a whole troop of old ones came about us at the noise; but finding the cub was safe (for away it ran) and my sorrel nag being by, they durst not venture near us. I observed the young animal's flesh to smell very rank, and the stink was somewhat between a weasel and a fox, but much more disagreeable. I forgot another circumstance (and perhaps I might have the reader's pardon, if it were wholly omitted) that while I held the odious vermin in my hands, it voided its filthy excrements of a yellow liquid substance, all over my clothes; but by good fortune there was a small brook hard by, where I washed myself as clean as I could; although I durst not come into my master's presence until I were sufficiently aired.

By what I could discover, the Yahoos appear to be the most unteachable of all animals, their capacities never reaching higher than to draw or carry burdens. Yet I am of opinion, this defect ariseth chiefly from a perverse, restive disposition. For they are cunning, malicious, treacherous and revengeful. They are strong and hardy, but of a cowardly spirit, and by consequence insolent, abject, and cruel. It is observed that the red-haired of both sexes are more libidinous and mischievous than the rest, whom yet they much exceed in strength and activity.

The Houyhnhnms keep the Yahoos for present use in huts not far from the house; but the rest are sent abroad to certain fields, where they dig up roots, eat several kinds of herbs, and search about for carrion, or sometimes catch weasels and *luhimuhs* (a sort of wild rat) which they greedily devour. Nature hath taught them to dig deep holes with their nails on the side of a rising ground, wherein they lie by themselves; only the kennels of the females are larger, sufficient to hold two or three cubs.

They swim from their infancy like frogs, and are able to continue long under water, where they often take fish, which the females carry home to their young. And upon this occasion, I hope the reader will pardon my relating an odd adventure.

Being one day abroad with my protector the sorrel nag, and the weather exceeding hot, I entreated him to let me bathe in a river that was near. He consented, and I immediately stripped myself stark naked, and went down softly into the stream. It happened that a young female Yahoo standing behind a bank, saw the whole proceeding; and inflamed by desire, as the nag and I conjectured, came running with all speed, and leaped into the water within five yards of the place where I bathed. I was never in my life so terribly frighted; the nag was grazing at some distance, not suspecting any harm; she embraced me after a most fulsome manner; I roared as loud as I could, and the nag came galloping towards me, whereupon she quitted her grasp, with the utmost reluctancy, and leaped upon the opposite bank, where she stood gazing and howling all the time I was putting on my clothes.

This was matter of diversion to my master and his family, as well as of mortification to myself. For now I could no longer deny that I was a real Yahoo, in every limb and feature, since the females had a natural propensity to me as one of their own species; neither was the hair of this brute of a red color (which might have been some excuse for an appetite a little irregular) but black as a sole, and her countenance did not make an appearance altogether so hideous as the rest of the kind; for I think, she could not be above eleven years old.

Having already lived three years in this country, the reader I suppose will expect that I should, like other travelers, give him some account of the manners and customs of its inhabitants, which it was indeed my principal study to learn.

As these noble Houyhnhnms are endowed by Nature with a general disposition to all virtues, and have no conceptions or ideas of what is evil in a rational creature; so their grand maxim is to cultivate reason, and to be wholly governed by it. Neither is reason among them a point problematical as with us, where men can argue with plausibility on both sides of a question; but strikes you with immediate conviction; as it must needs do where it is not mingled, obscured, or discolored by passion and interest. I remember it was with extreme difficulty that I could bring my master to understand the meaning of the word "opinion," or how a point could be disputable; because reason taught us to affirm or deny only where we are certain; and beyond our knowledge we cannot do either. So that controversies, wranglings, disputes, and positiveness in false or dubious propositions are evils unknown among the Houyhnhnms. In the like manner when I used to explain to him our several systems of natural philosophy, he would laugh that a creature pretending to reason should value itself upon the knowledge of other people's conjectures, and in things, where that knowledge, if it were certain, could be of no use. Wherein he agreed entirely with the sentiments of Socrates, as Plato delivers them, which I mention as the highest honor I can do that prince of philosophers. I have often since reflected what destruction such a doctrine would make in the libraries of Europe; and how many paths to fame would be then shut up in the learned world.

Friendship and benevolence are the two principal virtues among the Houyhnhnms; and these not confined to particular objects, but universal to the whole race. For a stranger from the remotest part is equally treated with the nearest neighbor, and wherever he goes, looks upon himself as at home. They preserve decency and civility in the highest degrees, but are altogether ignorant of ceremony. They have no fondness for[3] their colts or foals; but the care they take in educating them proceedeth entirely from the dictates of reason. And I observed my master to show the same affection to his neighbor's issue that he had for his own. They will have it that nature teaches them to love the whole species, and it is reason only that maketh a distinction of persons, where there is a superior degree of virtue.

When the matron Houyhnhnms have produced one of each sex, they no longer accompany with their consorts, except they lose one of their issue by some casualty, which very seldom happens; but in such a case they meet again; or when the like accident befalls a person whose wife is past bearing, some other couple bestows on him one of their own colts, and then go together a second time, until the mother be pregnant. This caution is necessary to prevent the

---

3. Attachment to.

country from being overburdened with numbers. But the race of inferior Houyh-nhnms bred up to be servants is not so strictly limited upon this article; these are allowed to produce three of each sex, to be domestics in the noble families.

In their marriages they are exactly careful to choose such colors as will not make any disagreeable mixture in the breed. Strength is chiefly valued in the male, and comeliness in the female; not upon the account of love, but to preserve the race from degenerating; for, where a female happens to excel in strength, a consort is chosen with regard to comeliness. Courtship, love, presents, jointures, settlements, have no place in their thoughts, or terms whereby to express them in their language. The young couple meet and are joined, merely because it is the determination of their parents and friends; it is what they see done every day; and they look upon it as one of the necessary actions in a reasonable being. But the violation of marriage, or any other unchastity, was never heard of; and the married pair pass their lives with the same friendship and mutual benevolence that they bear to all others of the same species who come in their way, without jealousy, fondness, quarreling, or discontent.

In educating the youth of both sexes, their method is admirable, and highly deserveth our imitation. These are not suffered to taste a grain of oats, except upon certain days, till eighteen years old; nor milk, but very rarely; and in summer they graze two hours in the morning, and as many in the evening, which their parents likewise observe; but the servants are not allowed above half that time; and a great part of the grass is brought home, which they eat at the most convenient hours, when they can be best spared from work.

Temperance, industry, exercise, and cleanliness are the lessons equally enjoined to the young ones of both sexes; and my master thought it monstrous in us to give the females a different kind of education from the males, except in some articles of domestic management; whereby, as he truly observed, one half of our natives were good for nothing but bringing children into the world; and to trust the care of their children to such useless animals, he said was yet a greater instance of brutality.

But the Houyhnhnms train up their youth to strength, speed, and hardiness, by exercising them in running races up and down steep hills, or over hard stony grounds; and when they are all in a sweat, they are ordered to leap over head and ears into a pond or a river. Four times a year the youth of certain districts meet to show their proficiency in running, and leaping, and other feats of strength or agility; where the victor is rewarded with a song made in his or her praise. On this festival the servants drive a herd of Yahoos into the field, laden with hay, and oats, and milk for a repast to the Houyhnhnms; after which these brutes are immediately driven back again, for fear of being noisome to the assembly.

Every fourth year, at the vernal equinox, there is a representative council of the whole nation, which meets in a plain about twenty miles from our house, and continueth about five or six days. Here they inquire into the state and condition of the several districts; whether they abound or be deficient in hay or oats, or cows or Yahoos? And wherever there is any want (which is but seldom) it is immediately supplied by unanimous consent and contribution. Here likewise the regulation of children is settled: as for instance, if a Houyhnhnm hath two males, he changeth one of them with another who hath two females, and when a child hath been lost by any casualty, where the mother is past breeding, it is determined what family in the district shall breed another to supply the loss.

CHAPTER IX

A grand debate at the general assembly of the Houyhnhnms, and how it was determined. The learning of the Houyhnhnms. Their buildings. Their manner of burials. The defectiveness of their language.

One of these grand assemblies was held in my time, about three months before my departure, whither my master went as the representative of our district. In this council was resumed their old debate, and indeed, the only debate that ever happened in their country; whereof my master after his return gave me a very particular account.

The question to be debated was whether the Yahoos should be exterminated from the face of the earth. One of the members for the affirmative offered several arguments of great strength and weight, alleging that, as the Yahoos were the most filthy, noisome, and deformed animal which nature ever produced, so they were the most restive and indocile, mischievous, and malicious; they would privately suck the teats of the Houyhnhnms' cows; kill and devour their cats, trample down their oats and grass, if they were not continually watched; and commit a thousand other extravagancies. He took notice of a general tradition, that Yahoos had not been always in their country, but that many ages ago, two of these brutes appeared together upon a mountain; whether produced by the heat of the sun upon corrupted mud and slime, or from the ooze and froth of the sea, was never known. That these Yahoos engendered, and their brood in a short time grew so numerous as to overrun and infest the whole nation. That the Houyhnhnms to get rid of this evil, made a general hunting, and at last enclosed the whole herd; and destroying the older, every Houyhnhnm kept two young ones in a kennel, and brought them to such a degree of tameness as an animal so savage by nature can be capable of acquiring, using them for draft and carriage. That there seemed to be much truth in this tradition, and that those creatures could not be *ylnhniamshy* (or aborigines of the land) because of the violent hatred the Houyhnhnms as well as all other animals bore them; which although their evil disposition sufficiently deserved, could never have arrived at so high a degree, if they had been aborigines, or else they would have long since been rooted out. That the inhabitants taking a fancy to use the service of the Yahoos, had very imprudently neglected to cultivate the breed of asses, which were a comely animal, easily kept, more tame and orderly, without any offensive smell, strong enough for labor, although they yield to the other in agility of body; and if their braying be no agreeable sound, it is far preferable to the horrible howlings of the Yahoos.

Several others declared their sentiments to the same purpose, when my master proposed an expedient to the assembly, whereof he had indeed borrowed the hint from me. He approved of the tradition, mentioned by the honorable member, who spoke before; and affirmed, that the two Yahoos said to be first seen among them, had been driven thither over the sea; that coming to land, and being forsaken by their companions, they retired to the mountains, and degenerating by degrees, became in process of time much more savage than those of their own species in the country from whence these two originals came. The reason of his assertion was that he had now in his possession a certain wonderful Yahoo (meaning myself) which most of them had heard of, and many of them had seen. He then related to them how he first found me; that my body was all covered with an artificial composure of the skins and hairs of other animals; that I spoke in a language of my own, and had thoroughly learned theirs; that I had related to him the accidents which brought me thither; that when he saw me without my covering, I was an exact Yahoo in every part, only of a whiter color, less hairy and with shorter claws. He added how I had endeavored to persuade him that in my own and other countries the Yahoos acted as the governing, rational animal, and held the Houyhnhnms in servitude; that he observed in me all the qualities of a Yahoo, only a little more civilized by some tincture of reason, which however was in a degree as far inferior to the Houyhnhnm race as the Yahoos of their country were to me; that among other things, I mentioned a custom we had of castrating Houyhnhnms when they were young, in order to render them tame; that the operation was easy and safe; that it was no shame to learn wisdom from brutes, as industry is taught by the ant, and building by the swallow (for so I translate the word *lyhannh*, although it be a much larger fowl). That this invention might be practiced upon the younger Yahoos here, which, besides rendering them tractable and fitter for use, would in an age put an end to the whole species without destroying life. That in the meantime the Houyhnhnms should be exhorted to cultivate the breed of asses, which, as they are in all respects more valuable brutes, so they have this advantage, to be fit for service at five years old, which the others are not till twelve.

This was all my master thought fit to tell me at that time, of what passed in the grand council. But he was pleased to conceal one particular, which related personally to myself, whereof I soon felt the unhappy effect, as the reader will know in its proper place, and from whence I date all the succeeding misfortunes of my life.

The Houyhnhnms have no letters, and consequently, their knowledge is all traditional. But there happening few events of any moment among a people so well united, naturally disposed to every virtue, wholly governed by reason, and cut off from all commerce with other nations, the historical part is easily preserved without burdening their memories. I have already observed that they are subject to no diseases, and therefore can have no need of physicians. However, they have excellent medicines composed of herbs, to cure accidental bruises and cuts in the pastern or frog of the foot by sharp stones, as well as other maims and hurts in the several parts of the body.

They calculate the year by the revolution of the sun and the moon, but use no subdivisions into weeks. They are well enough acquainted with the motions of those two luminaries, and understand the nature of eclipses; and this is the utmost progress of their astronomy.

In poetry they must be allowed to excel all other mortals; wherein the justness of their similes, and the minuteness, as well as exactness of their descriptions, are indeed inimitable. Their verses abound very much in both of these, and usually contain either some exalted notions of friendship and benevolence, or the praises of those who were victors in races and other bodily exercises. Their buildings, although very rude and simple, are not inconvenient, but well contrived to defend them from all injuries of cold and heat. They have a kind of tree, which at forty years old loosens in the root, and falls with the first storm; it grows very straight, and being pointed like stakes with a sharp stone (for the Houyhnhnms know not the use of iron), they stick them erect in the ground about ten inches asunder, and then weave in oat straw, or sometimes wattles, betwixt them. The roof is made after the same manner, and so are the doors.

The Houyhnhnms use the hollow part between the pastern and the hoof of their forefeet as we do our hands, and this with greater dexterity than I could at first imagine. I have seen a white mare of our family thread a needle (which I lent her on purpose) with that joint. They milk their cows, reap their oats, and do all the work which requires hands in the same manner. They have a kind of hard flints, which by grinding against other stones they form into instruments that serve instead of wedges, axes, and hammers. With tools made of these flints, they likewise cut their hay, and reap their oats, which there groweth naturally in several fields; the Yahoos draw home the sheaves in carriages, and the servants tread them in certain covered huts, to get out the grain, which is kept in stores. They make a rude kind of earthen and wooden vessels, and bake the former in the sun.

If they can avoid casualties, they die only of old age, and are buried in the obscurest places that can be found, their friends and relations expressing neither joy nor grief at their departure; nor does the dying person discover the least regret that he is leaving the world, any more than if he were upon returning home from a visit to one of his neighbors; I remember my master having once made an appointment with a friend and his family to come to his house upon some affair of importance; on the day fixed, the mistress and her two children came very late; she made two excuses, first for her husband, who, as she said, happened that very morning to *lhnuwnh*. The word is strongly expressive in their language, but not easily rendered into English; it signifies, *to retire to his first Mother*. Her excuse for not coming sooner was that her husband dying late in the morning, she was a good while consulting her servants about a convenient place where his body should be laid; and I observed she behaved herself at our house, as cheerfully as the rest; she died about three months after.

They live generally to seventy or seventy-five years, very seldom to four-score; some weeks before their death they feel a gradual decay, but without pain. During this time they are much visited by their friends, because they cannot go abroad with their usual ease and satisfaction. However, about ten days before their death, which they seldom fail in computing, they return the visits that have been made by those who are nearest in the neighborhood, being carried in a convenient sledge drawn by Yahoos; which vehicle they use, not only upon this occasion, but when they grow old, upon long journeys, or when they are lamed by any accident. And therefore when the dying Houyhnhnms return those visits, they take a solemn leave of their friends, as if they were going to some remote part of the country, where they designed to pass the rest of their lives.

I know not whether it may be worth observing, that the Houyhnhnms have no word in their language to express anything that is evil, except what they borrow from the deformities or ill qualities of the Yahoos. Thus they denote the folly of a servant, an omission of a child, a stone that cuts their feet, a continuance of foul or unseasonable weather, and the like, by adding to each the epithet of Yahoo. For instance, *hhnm Yahoo, whnaholm Yahoo, ynlhmndwihlma Yahoo*, and an ill-contrived house, *ynholmhnmrohlnw Yahoo*.

I could with great pleasure enlarge farther upon the manners and virtues of this excellent people; but intending in a short time to publish a volume by itself expressly upon that subject, I refer the reader thither. And in the meantime, proceed to relate my own sad catastrophe.

CHAPTER X

The Author's economy, and happy life among the Houyhnhnms. His great improvement in virtue, by conversing with them. Their conversations. The Author hath notice given him by his master that he must depart from the country. He falls into a swoon for grief, but submits. He contrives and finishes a canoe, by the help of a fellow servant, and puts to sea at a venture.

I had settled my little economy to my own heart's content. My master had ordered a room to be made for me after their manner, about six yards from the house; the sides and floors of which I plastered with clay, and covered with rush mats of my own contriving; I had beaten hemp, which there grows wild, and made of it a sort of ticking; this I filled with the feathers of several birds I had taken with springes made of Yahoos' hairs, and were excellent food. I had worked two chairs with my knife, the sorrel nag helping me in the grosser and more laborious part. When my clothes were worn to rags, I made myself others with the skins of rabbits, and of a certain beautiful animal about the same size, called *nnuhnoh*, the skin of which is covered with a fine down. Of these I likewise made very tolerable stockings. I soled my shoes with wood which I cut from a tree, and fitted to the upper leather, and when this was worn out, I supplied it with the skins of Yahoos, dried in the sun. I often got honey out of hollow trees, which I mingled with water, or eat it with my bread. No man could more verify the truth of these two maxims, that *Nature is very easily satisfied*; and, that *Necessity is the mother of invention*. I enjoyed perfect health of body, and tranquility of mind; I did not feel the treachery or inconstancy of a friend, nor the inquiries of a secret or open enemy. I had no occasion of bribing, flattering, or pimping to procure the favor of any great man, or of his minion. I wanted no fence against fraud or oppression; here was neither physician to destroy my body, nor lawyer to ruin my fortune; no informer to watch my words and actions, or forge accusations against me for hire; here were no gibers, censurers, backbiters, pickpockets, highwaymen, housebreakers, attorneys, bawds, buffoons, gamesters, politicians, wits, splenetics, tedious talkers, controvertists, ravishers, murderers, robbers, virtuosos; no leaders or followers of party and faction; no encouragers to vice, by seducement or examples; no dungeons, axes, gibbets, whipping posts, or pillories; no cheating shopkeepers or mechanics; no pride, vanity or affectation; no fops, bullies, drunkards, strolling whores, or poxes; no ranting, lewd, expensive wives; no stupid, proud pedants; no importunate, overbearing, quarrelsome, noisy, roaring, empty, conceited, swearing companions; no scoundrels raised from the dust upon the merit of their vices; or nobility thrown into it on account of their virtues; no lords, fiddlers, judges, or dancing masters.

I had the favor of being admitted to several Houyhnhnms, who came to visit or dine with my master; where his honor graciously suffered me to wait in the room, and listen to their discourse. Both he and his company would often descend to ask me questions, and receive my answers. I had also sometimes the honor of attending my master in his visits to others. I never presumed to speak, except in answer to a question; and then I did it with inward regret, because it was a loss of so much time for improving myself; but I was infinitely delighted with the station of an humble auditor in such conversations, where nothing passed but what was useful, expressed in the fewest and most significant words; where (as I have already said) the greatest decency was observed, without the least degree of ceremony; where no person spoke without being pleased himself, and pleasing his companions; where there was no interruption, tediousness, heat, or difference of sentiments. They have a notion, that when people are met together, a short silence doth much improve conversation; this I found to be true; for during those little intermissions of talk, new ideas would arise in their minds, which very much enlivened the discourse. Their subjects are generally on friendship and benevolence; on order and economy; sometimes upon the visible operations of nature, or ancient traditions; upon the bounds and limits of virtue; upon the unerring rules of reason; or upon some determinations, to be taken at the next great assembly; and often upon the various excellencies of poetry. I may add, without vanity, that my presence often gave them sufficient matter for discourse, because it afforded my master an occasion of letting his friends into the history of me and my country, upon which they were all pleased to discant in a manner not very advantageous to human kind; and for that reason I shall not repeat what they said; only I may be allowed to observe that his honor, to my great admiration, appeared to understand the nature of Yahoos much better than myself. He went through all our vices and follies, and discovered many which I had never mentioned to him; by only supposing what qualities a Yahoo of their country, with a small proportion of reason, might be capable of exerting; and concluded, with too much probability, how vile as well as miserable such a creature must be.

I freely confess, that all the little knowledge I have of any value was acquired by the lectures I received from my master, and from hearing the discourses of him and his friends; to which I should be prouder to listen, than to dictate to the greatest and wisest assembly in Europe. I admired the strength, comeliness, and speed of the inhabitants; and such a constellation of virtues in such amiable persons produced in me the highest veneration. At first, indeed, I did not feel that natural awe which the Yahoos and all other animals bear towards them; but it grew upon me by degrees, much sooner than I imagined, and was mingled with a respectful love and gratitude, that they would condescend to distinguish me from the rest of my species.

When I thought of my family, my friends, my countrymen, or human race in general, I considered them as they really were, Yahoos in shape and disposition, perhaps a little more civilized, and qualified with the gift of speech; but making no other use of reason than to improve and mutiply those vices, whereof their brethren in this country had only the share that nature allotted them. When I happened to behold the reflection of my own form in a lake or fountain, I turned away my face in horror and detestation of myself, and could better endure the sight of a common Yahoo than of my own person. By conversing with the Houyhnhnms, and looking upon them with delight, I fell to imitate their gait and gesture, which is now grown into a habit; and my friends often tell me in a blunt way, that I trot like a horse; which, however, I take for a great compliment; neither shall I disown, that in speaking I am apt to fall into the voice and manner of the Houyhnhnms, and hear myself ridiculed on that account without the least mortification.

In the midst of this happiness, when I looked upon myself to be fully settled for life, my master sent for me one morning a little earlier than his usual hour. I observed by his countenance that he was in some perplexity, and at a loss how to begin what he had to speak. After a short silence, he told me, he did not know how I would take what he was going to say; that, in the last general assembly, when the affair of the Yahoos was entered upon, the representatives had taken offense at his keeping a Yahoo (meaning myself) in his family more like a Houyhnhnm than a brute animal. That he was known frequently to converse with me, as if he could receive some advantage of pleasure in my company; that such a practice was not agreeable to reason or nature, or a thing ever heard of before among them. The assembly did therefore exhort him, either to employ me like the rest of my species, or command me to swim back to the place from whence I came. That the first of these expedients was utterly rejected by all the Houyhnhnms who had ever seen me at his house or their own; for, they alleged, that because I had some rudiments of reason, added to the natural pravity of those animals, it was to be feared, I might be able to seduce them into the woody and mountainous parts of the country, and bring them in troops by night to destroy the Houyhnhnms' cattle, as being naturally of the ravenous kind, and averse from labor.

My master added that he was daily pressed by the Houyhnhnms of the neighborhood to have the assembly's exhortation executed, which he could not put off much longer. He doubted[4] it would be impossible for me to swim to another country; and therefore wished I would contrive some sort of vehicle resembling those I had described to him, that might carry me on the sea; in which work I should have the assistance of his own servants, as well as those of his neighbors. He concluded that for his own part he could have been content to keep me in his service as long as I lived; because he found I had cured myself of some bad habits and dispositions, by endeavoring, as far as my inferior nature was capable, to imitate the Houyhnhnms.

I should here observe to the reader, that a decree of the general assembly in this country is expressed by the word *hnhloayn*, which signifies an exhortation, as near as I can render it; for they have no conception how a rational creature can be compelled, but only advised, or exhorted; because no person can disobey reason without giving up his claim to be a rational creature.

I was struck with the utmost grief and despair at my master's discourse; and being unable to support the agonies I was under, I fell into a swoon at his feet; when I came to myself, he told me that he concluded I had been dead (for these people are subject to no such imbecilities of nature). I answered, in a faint voice, that death would have been too great an happiness; that although I could not blame the assembly's exhortation, or the urgency of his friends; yet in my weak and corrupt judgment, I thought it might consist with reason to have been less rigorous. That I could not swim a league, and probably the nearest land to theirs might be distant above an hundred; that many materials, necessary for making a small vessel to carry me off, were wholly wanting in this country, which, however, I would attempt in obedience and gratitude to his honor, although I concluded the thing to be impossible, and therefore looked on myself as already devoted[5] to destruction. That the certain prospect of an

---

4. Suspected. 5. Doomed.

unnatural death was the least of my evils; for, supposing I should escape with life by some strange adventure, how could I think with temper[6] of passing my days among Yahoos, and relapsing into my old corruptions, for want of examples to lead and keep me within the paths of virtue. That I knew too well upon what solid reasons all the determinations of the wise Houyhnhnms were founded, not to be shaken by arguments of mine, a miserable Yahoo; and therefore after presenting him with my humble thanks for the offer of his servants' assistance in making a vessel, and desiring a reasonable time for so difficult a work, I told him I would endeavor to preserve a wretched being; and, if ever I returned to England, was not without hopes of being useful to my own species by celebrating the praises of the renowned Houyhnhnms, and proposing their virtues to the imitation of mankind.

My master in a few words made me a very gracious reply, allowed me the space of two months to finish my boat, and ordered the sorrel nag, my fellow servant (for so at this distance I may presume to call him), to follow my instructions, because I told my master that his help would be sufficient, and I knew he had a tenderness for me.

In his company my first business was to go to that part of the coast where my rebellious crew had ordered me to be set on shore. I got upon a height, and looking on every side into the sea, fancied I saw a small island towards the northeast; I took out my pocket glass, and could then clearly distinguish it about five leagues off, as I computed; but it appeared to the sorrel nag to be only a blue cloud; for, as he had no conception of any country besides his own, so he could not be as expert in distinguishing remote objects at sea, as we who so much converse in that element.

After I had discovered this island, I considered no farther; but resolved, it should, if possible, be the first place of my banishment, leaving the consequence to fortune.

I returned home, and consulting with the sorrel nag, we went into a copse at some distance, where I with my knife, and he with a sharp flint fastened very artificially,[7] after their manner, to a wooden handle, cut down several oak wattles about the thickness of a walking staff, and some larger pieces. But I shall not trouble the reader with a particular description of my own mechanics; let it suffice to say, that in six weeks time, with the help of the sorrel nag, who performed the parts that required most labor, I finished a sort of Indian canoe; but much larger, covering it with the skins of Yahoos, well stitched together, with hempen threads of my own making. My sail was likewise composed of the skins of the same animal; but I made use of the youngest I could get, the older being too tough and thick; and I likewise provided myself with four paddles. I laid in a stock of boiled flesh, of rabbits and fowls; and took with me two vessels, one filled with milk, and the other with water.

I tried my canoe in a large pond near my master's house, and then corrected in it what was amiss, stopping all the chinks with Yahoo's tallow, till I found it staunch, and able to bear me and my freight. And when it was as complete as I could possibly make it, I had it drawn on a carriage very gently by Yahoos, to the seaside, under the conduct of the sorrel nag and another servant.

6. Equanimity.   7. Adroitly.

When all was ready, and the day came for my departure, I took leave of my master and lady, and the whole family, my eyes flowing with tears and my heart quite sunk with grief. But his honor, out of curiosity, and perhaps (if I may speak it without vanity) partly out of kindness, was determined to see me in my canoe; and got several of his neighboring friends to accompany him. I was forced to wait above an hour for the tide, and then observing the wind very fortunately bearing towards the island to which I intended to steer my course, I took a second leave of my master; but as I was going to prostrate myself to kiss his hoof, he did me the honor to raise it gently to my mouth. I am not ignorant how much I have been censured for mentioning this last particular. Detractors are pleased to think it improbable that so illustrious a person should descend to give so great a mark of distinction to a creature so inferior as I. Neither have I forgot how apt some travelers are to boast of extraordinary favors they have received. But, if these censurers were better acquainted with the noble and courteous disposition of the Houyhnhnms, they would soon change their opinion. I paid my respects to the rest of the Houyhnhnms in his honor's company; then getting into my canoe, I pushed off from shore.

CHAPTER XI

The Author's dangerous voyage. He arrives at New Holland, hoping to settle there. Is wounded with an arrow by one of the natives. Is seized and carried by force into a Portuguese ship. The great civilities of the Captain. The Author arrives at England.

I began this desperate voyage on February 15, 1714/5,[8] at 9 o'clock in the morning. The wind was very favorable; however, I made use at first only of my paddles; but considering I should soon be weary, and that the wind might probably chop about, I ventured to set up my little sail; and thus, with the help of the tide, I went at the rate of a league and a half an hour, as near as I could guess. My master and his friends continued on the shore, till I was almost out of sight; and I often heard the sorrel nag (who always loved me) crying out, *"Hnuy illa nyha maiah Yahoo"* ("Take care of thyself, gentle Yahoo").

My design was, if possible, to discover some small island uninhabited, yet sufficient by my labor to furnish me with necessaries of life, which I would have thought a greater happiness than to be first minister in the politest court of Europe, so horrible was the idea I conceived of returning to live in the society and under the government of Yahoos. For in such a solitude as I desired, I could at least enjoy my own thoughts, and reflect with delight on the virtues of those inimitable Houyhnhnms, without any opportunity of degenerating into the vices and corruptions of my own species.

The reader may remember what I related when my crew conspired against me, and confined me to my cabin, how I continued there several weeks, without knowing what course we took; and when I was put ashore in the longboat, how the sailors told me with oaths, whether true or false, that they knew not in what part of the world we were. However, I did then believe us to be about 10 degrees southward of the Cape of Good Hope, or about 45 degrees southern latitude, as I gathered from some general words I overheard among them,

8. I.e., 1714. The year began on March 25.

being I supposed to the southeast in their intended voyage to Madagascar. And although this were but little better than conjecture, yet I resolved to steer my course eastward, hoping to reach the southwest coast of New Holland, and perhaps some such island as I desired, lying westward of it. The wind was full west, and by six in the evening I computed I had gone eastward at least eighteen leagues; when I spied a very small island about half a league off, which I soon reached. It was nothing but a rock with one creek,[9] naturally arched by the force of tempests. Here I put in my canoe, and climbing a part of the rock, I could plainly discover land to the east, extending from south to north. I lay all night in my canoe; and repeating my voyage early in the morning, I arrived in seven hours to the southeast point of New Holland.[1] This confirmed me in the opinion I have long entertained, that the maps and charts place this country at least three degrees more to the east than it really is; which thought I communicated many years ago to my worthy friend Mr. Herman Moll,[2] and gave him my reasons for it, although he hath rather chosen to follow other authors.

I saw no inhabitants in the place where I landed; and being unarmed, I was afraid of venturing far into the country. I found some shellfish on the shore, and eat them raw, not daring to kindle a fire, for fear of being discovered by the natives. I continued three days feeding on oysters and limpets, to save my own provisions; and I fortunately found a brook of excellent water, which gave me great relief.

On the fourth day, venturing out early a little too far, I saw twenty or thirty natives upon a height, not above five hundred yards from me. They were stark naked, men, women, and children round a fire, as I could discover by the smoke. One of them spied me, and gave notice to the rest; five of them advanced towards me, leaving the women and children at the fire. I made what haste I could to the shore, and getting into my canoe, shoved off; the savages observing me retreat, ran after me; and before I could get far enough into the sea, discharged an arrow, which wounded me deeply on the inside of my left knee. (I shall carry the mark to my grave.) I apprehended the arrow might be poisoned; and paddling out of the reach of their darts (being a calm day) I made a shift to suck the wound, and dress it as well as I could.

I was at a loss what to do, for I durst not return to the same landing place, but stood to the north, and was forced to paddle; for the wind, although very gentle, was against me, blowing northwest. As I was looking about for a secure landing place, I saw a sail to the north northeast, which appearing every minute more visible, I was in some doubt whether I should wait for them or no; but at last my detestation of the Yahoo race prevailed; and turning my canoe, I sailed and paddled together to the south, and got into the same creek from whence I set out in the morning, choosing rather to trust myself among these barbarians than live with European Yahoos. I drew up my canoe as close as I could to the shore, and hid myself behind a stone by the little brook, which, as I have already said, was excellent water.

The ship came within half a league of this creek, and sent out her longboat with vessels to take in fresh water (for the place it seems was very well known),

---

9. A bay.
1. Present-day Republic of South Africa.
2. A famous contemporary mapmaker.

but I did not observe it until the boat was almost on shore; and it was too late to seek another hiding place. The seamen at their landing observed my canoe, and rummaging it all over, easily conjectured that the owner could not be far off. Four of them well armed searched every cranny and lurking hole, till at last they found me flat on my face behind the stone. They gazed a while in admiration at my strange uncouth dress; my coat made of skins, my wooden-soled shoes, and my furred stockings; from whence, however, they concluded I was not a native of the place, who all go naked. One of the seamen in Portuguese bid me rise, and asked who I was. I understood that language very well, and getting upon my feet, said I was a poor Yahoo, banished from the Houyh-nhnms, and desired they would please to let me depart. They admired to hear me answer them in their own tongue, and saw by my complexion I must be an European; but were at a loss to know what I meant by Yahoos and Houyh-nhnms, and at the same time fell a laughing at my strange tone in speaking, which resembled the neighing of a horse. I trembled all the while betwixt fear and hatred; I again desired leave to depart, and was gently moving to my canoe; but they laid hold on me, desiring to know what country I was of? whence I came? with many other questions. I told them I was born in England, from whence I came about five years ago, and then their country and ours was at peace. I therefore hoped they would not treat me as an enemy, since I meant them no harm, but was a poor Yahoo, seeking some desolate place where to pass the remainder of his unfortunate life.

When they began to talk, I thought I never heard or saw any thing so unnatural; for it appeared to me as monstrous as if a dog or a cow should speak in England, or a Yahoo in Houyhnhnmland. The honest Portuguese were equally amazed at my strange dress, and the odd manner of delivering my words, which however they understood very well. They spoke to me with great humanity, and said they were sure their Captain would carry me *gratis* to Lisbon, from whence I might return to my own country; that two of the seamen would go back to the ship, to inform the Captain of what they had seen, and receive his orders; in the meantime, unless I would give my solemn oath not to fly, they would secure me by force. I thought it best to comply with their proposal. They were very curious to know my story, but I gave them very little satisfaction; and they all conjectured, that my misfortunes had impaired my reason. In two hours the boat, which went laden with vessels of water, returned with the Captain's commands to fetch me on board. I fell on my knees to preserve my liberty; but all was in vain, and the men having tied me with cords, heaved me into the boat, from whence I was taken into the ship, and from thence into the Captain's cabin.

His name was Pedro de Mendez; he was a very courteous and generous person; he entreated me to give some account of myself, and desired to know what I would eat or drink; said I should be used as well as himself, and spoke so many obliging things, that I wondered to find such civilities from a Yahoo. However, I remained silent and sullen; I was ready to faint at the very smell of him and his men. At last I desired something to eat out of my own canoe; but he ordered me a chicken and some excellent wine, and then directed that I should be put to bed in a very clean cabin. I would not undress myself, but lay on the bedclothes; and in half an hour stole out, when I thought the crew was at dinner; and getting to the side of the ship, was going to leap into the sea, and swim for my life, rather than continue among Yahoos. But one of the seamen prevented me, and having informed the Captain, I was chained to my cabin.

After dinner Don Pedro came to me, and desired to know my reason for so desperate an attempt; assured me he only meant to do me all the service he was able; and spoke so very movingly, that at last I descended to treat him like an animal which had some little portion of reason. I gave him a very short relation of my voyage; of the conspiracy against me by my own men; of the country where they set me on shore, and of my five years residence there. All which he looked upon as if it were a dream or a vision; whereat I took great offense; for I had quite forgot the faculty of lying, so peculiar to Yahoos in all countries where they preside, and consequently the disposition of suspecting truth in others of their own species. I asked him whether it were the custom of his country to *say the thing that was not?* I assured him I had almost forgot what he meant by falsehood; and if I had lived a thousand years in Houyhnhnmland, I should never have heard a lie from the meanest servant. That I was altogether indifferent whether he believed me or no; but however, in return for his favors, I would give so much allowance to the corruption of his nature, as to answer any objection he would please to make; and he might easily discover the truth.

The Captain, a wise man, after many endeavors to catch me tripping in some part of my story, at last began to have a better opinion of my veracity. But he added that since I professed so inviolable an attachment to truth, I must give him my word of honor to bear him company in this voyage without attempting anything against my life; or else he would continue me a prisoner till we arrived at Lisbon. I gave him the promise he required; but at the same time protested that I would suffer the greatest hardships rather than return to live among Yahoos.

Our voyage passed without any considerable accident. In gratitude to the Captain I sometimes sat with him at his earnest request, and strove to conceal my antipathy against humankind, although it often broke out; which he suffered to pass without observation. But the greatest part of the day, I confined myself to my cabin, to avoid seeing any of the crew. The Captain had often entreated me to strip myself of my savage dress, and offered to lend me the best suit of clothes he had. This I would not be prevailed on to accept, abhorring to cover myself with anything that had been on the back of a Yahoo. I only desired he would lend me two clean shirts, which having been washed since he wore them, I believed would not so much defile me. These I changed every second day, and washed them myself.

We arrived at Lisbon, Nov. 5, 1715. At our landing, the Captain forced me to cover myself with his cloak, to prevent the rabble from crowding about me. I was conveyed to his own house; and at my earnest request, he led me up to the highest room backwards.[3] I conjured him to conceal from all persons what I had told him of the Houyhnhnms; because the least hint of such a story would not only draw numbers of people to see me, but probably put me in danger of being imprisoned, or burned by the Inquisition. The Captain persuaded me to accept a suit of clothes newly made; but I would not suffer the tailor to take my measure; however, Don Pedro being almost of my size, they fitted me

3. At the rear.

well enough. He accoutred me with other necessaries, all new, which I aired for twenty-four hours before I would use them.

The Captain had no wife, nor above three servants, none of which were suffered to attend at meals; and his whole deportment was so obliging, added to very good human understanding, that I really began to tolerate his company. He gained so far upon me, that I ventured to look out of the back window. By degrees I was brought into another room, from whence I peeped into the street, but drew my head back in a fright. In a week's time he seduced me down to the door. I found my terror gradually lessened, but my hatred and contempt seemed to increase. I was at last bold enough to walk the street in his company, but kept my nose well stopped with rue, or sometimes with tobacco.

In ten days, Don Pedro, to whom I had given some account of my domestic affairs, put it upon me as a point of honor and conscience that I ought to return to my native country, and live at home with my wife and children. He told me there was an English ship in the port just ready to sail, and he would furnish me with all things necessary. It would be tedious to repeat his arguments, and my contradictions. He said it was altogether impossible to find such a solitary island as I had desired to live in; but I might command in my own house, and pass my time in a manner as recluse as I pleased.

I complied at last, finding I could not do better. I left Lisbon the 24th day of November, in an English merchantman, but who was the Master I never inquired. Don Pedro accompanied me to the ship, and lent me twenty pounds. He took kind leave of me, and embraced me at parting; which I bore as well as I could. During this last voyage I had no commerce with the Master, or any of his men; but pretending I was sick kept close in my cabin. On the fifth of December, 1715, we cast anchor in the Downs about nine in the morning, and at three in the afternoon I got safe to my house at Redriff.

My wife and family received me with great surprise and joy, because they concluded me certainly dead; but I must freely confess, the sight of them filled me only with hatred, disgust, and contempt; and the more, by reflecting on the near alliance I had to them. For, although since my unfortunate exile from the Houyhnhnm country, I had compelled myself to tolerate the sight of Yahoos, and to converse with Don Pedro de Mendez; yet my memory and imaginations were perpetually filled with the virtues and ideas of those exalted Houyhnhnms. And when I began to consider that by copulating with one of the Yahoo species, I had become a parent of more, it struck me with the utmost shame, confusion, and horror.

As soon as I entered the house, my wife took me in her arms, and kissed me; at which, having not been used to the touch of that odious animal for so many years, I fell in a swoon for almost an hour. At the time I am writing, it is five years since my last return to England; during the first year I could not endure my wife or children in my presence, the very smell of them was intolerable; much less could I suffer them to eat in the same room. To this hour they dare not presume to touch my bread, or drink out of the same cup; neither was I ever able to let one of them take me by the hand. The first money I laid out was to buy two young stone-horses,[4] which I keep in a good stable, and next to

4. Stallions.

them the groom is my greatest favorite; for I feel my spirits revived by the smell he contracts in the stable. My horses understand me tolerably well; I converse with them at least four hours every day. They are strangers to bridle or saddle; they live in great amity with me, and friendship to each other.

CHAPTER XII

The Author's veracity. His design in publishing this work. His censure of those travelers who swerve from the truth. The Author clears himself from any sinister ends in writing. An objection answered. The method of planting colonies. His native country commended. The right of the crown to those countries described by the Author is justified. The difficulty of conquering them. The Author takes his last leave of the reader; proposeth his manner of living for the future; gives good advice, and concludeth.

Thus, gentle reader, I have given thee a faithful history of my travels for sixteen years, and above seven months; wherein I have not been so studious of ornament as of truth. I could perhaps like others have astonished thee with strange improbable tales; but I rather chose to relate plain matter of fact in the simplest manner and style; because my principal design was to inform, and not to amuse thee.

It is easy for us who travel into remote countries, which are seldom visited by Englishmen or other Europeans, to form descriptions of wonderful animals both at sea and land. Whereas a traveler's chief aim should be to make men wiser and better, and to improve their minds by the bad as well as good example of what they deliver concerning foreign places.

I could heartily wish a law were enacted, that every traveler, before he were permitted to publish his voyages, should be obliged to make oath before the Lord High Chancellor that all he intended to print was absolutely true to the best of his knowledge; for then the world would no longer be deceived as it usually is, while some writers, to make their works pass the better upon the public, impose the grossest falsities on the unwary reader. I have perused several books of travels with great delight in my younger days; but, having since gone over most parts of the globe, and been able to contradict many fabulous accounts from my own observation, it hath given me a great disgust against this part of reading, and some indignation to see the credulity of mankind so impudently abused. Therefore, since my acquaintance were pleased to think my poor endeavors might not be unacceptable to my country; I imposed on myself as a maxim, never to be swerved from, that I would *strictly adhere to truth*; neither indeed can I be ever under the least temptation to vary from it, while I retain in my mind the lectures and example of my noble master, and the other illustrious Houyhnhnms, of whom I had so long the honor to be an humble hearer.

> ——*Nec si miserum Fortuna Sinonem*
> *Finxit, vanum etiam, mendacemque improba finget.*[5]

---

5. Fortune has made a derelict of Sinon / but the bitch won't make an empty liar of him, too (Latin; Virgil's *Aeneid* 2).

I know very well how little reputation is to be got by writings which require neither genius nor learning, nor indeed any other talent, except a good memory, or an exact *Journal*. I know likewise, that writers of travels, like dictionary-makers, are sunk into oblivion by the weight and bulk of those who come last, and therefore lie uppermost. And it is highly probable that such travelers who shall hereafter visit the countries described in this work of mine, may be detecting my errors (if there be any) and adding many new discoveries of their own, jostle me out of vogue, and stand in my place, making the world forget that ever I was an author. This indeed would be too great a mortification if I wrote for fame; but, as my sole intention was the PUBLIC GOOD, I cannot be altogether disappointed. For, who can read the virtues I have mentioned in the glorious Houyhnhnms, without being ashamed of his own vices, when he considers himself as the reasoning, governing animal of his country? I shall say nothing of those remote nations where Yahoos preside; amongst which the least corrupted are the Brobdingnagians, whose wise maxims in morality and government it would be our happiness to observe. But I forbear descanting further, and rather leave the judicious reader to his own remarks and applications.

I am not a little pleased that this work of mine can possibly meet with no censurers; for what objections can be made against a writer who relates only plain facts that happened in such distant countries, where we have not the least interest with respect either to trade or negotiations? I have carefully avoided every fault with which common writers of travels are often too justly charged. Besides, I meddle not the least with any party, but write without passion, prejudice, or ill-will against any man or number of men whatsoever. I write for the noblest end, to inform and instruct mankind, over whom I may, without breach of modesty, pretend to some superiority, from the advantages I received by conversing so long among the most accomplished Houyhnhnms. I write without any view towards profit or praise. I never suffer a word to pass that may look like reflection, or possibly give the least offense even to those who are most ready to take it. So that, I hope, I may with justice pronounce myself an Author perfectly blameless; against whom the tribes of answerers, considerers, observers, reflectors, detecters, remarkers will never be able to find matter for exercising their talents.

I confess it was whispered to me that I was bound in duty as a subject of England, to have given in a memorial to a secretary of state, at my first coming over; because, whatever lands are discovered by a subject, belong to the Crown. But I doubt whether our conquests in the countries I treat of would be as easy as those of Ferdinando Cortez[6] over the naked Americans. The Lilliputians, I think, are hardly worth the charge of a fleet and army to reduce them; and I question whether it might be prudent or safe to attempt the Brobdingnagians; or, whether an English army would be much at their ease with the Flying Island over their heads. The Houyhnhnms, indeed, appear not to be so well prepared for war, a science to which they are perfect strangers, and especially against missive weapons. However, supposing myself to be a minister of state, I could never give my advice for invading them. Their prudence, unanimity, unacquaintedness with fear, and their love of their country would amply supply

---

6. Hernán Cortés (1485–1547), who destroyed the Aztec Empire.

all defects in the military art. Imagine twenty thousand of them breaking into the midst of an European army, confounding the ranks, overturning the carriages, battering the warriors' faces into mummy, by terrible yerks[7] from their hinder hoofs: for they would well deserve the character given to Augustus, *Recalcitrat undique tutus*.[8] But instead of proposals for conquering that magnanimous nation, I rather wish they were in a capacity or disposition to send a sufficient number of their inhabitants for civilizing Europe; by teaching us the first principles of Honor, Justice, Truth, Temperance, Public Spirit, Fortitude, Chastity, Friendship, Benevolence, and Fidelity. The names of all which Virtues are still retained among us in most languages, and are to be met with in modern as well as ancient authors, which I am able to assert from my own small reading.

But I had another reason which made me less forward to enlarge his majesty's dominions by my discoveries: to say the truth, I had conceived a few scruples with relation to the distributive justice of princes upon those occasions. For instance, a crew of pirates are driven by a storm they know not whither; at length a boy discovers land from the topmast; they go on shore to rob and plunder; they see an harmless people, are entertained with kindness, they give the country a new name, they take formal possession of it for the king, they set up a rotten plank or a stone for a memorial, they murder two or three dozen of the natives, bring away a couple more by force for a sample, return home, and get their pardon. Here commences a new dominion acquired with a title by Divine Right. Ships are sent with the first opportunity; the natives driven out or destroyed, their princes tortured to discover their gold; a free license given to all acts of inhumanity and lust; the earth reeking with the blood of its inhabitants: and this execrable crew of butchers employed in so pious an expedition is a *modern colony* sent to convert and civilize an idolatrous and barbarous people.

But this description, I confess, doth by no means affect the British nation, who may be an example to the whole world for their wisdom, care, and justice in planting colonies; their liberal endowments for the advancement of religion and learning; their choice of devout and able pastors to propagate Christianity; their caution in stocking their provinces with people of sober lives and conversations from this the Mother Kingdom; their strict regard to the distribution of justice, in supplying the civil administration through all their colonies with officers of the greatest abilities, utter strangers to corruption: and to crown all, by sending the most vigilant and virtuous governors, who have no other views than the happiness of the people over whom they preside, and the honor of the king their master.

But, as those countries which I have described do not appear to have any desire of being conquered, and enslaved, murdered, or driven out by colonies, nor abound either in gold, silver, sugar, or tobacco, I did humbly conceive they were by no means proper objects of our zeal, our valor, or our interest. However, if those whom it may concern, think fit to be of another opinion, I am ready to depose, when I shall be lawfully called, that no European did ever visit these countries before me. I mean, if the inhabitants ought to be believed.

---

7. Kicks. "Mummy": pulp.
8. He kicks backward, at every point on his guard (Latin; Horace's *Satires* 2.20).

But, as to the formality of taking possession in my sovereign's name, it never came once into my thoughts; and if it had, yet as my affairs then stood, I should perhaps in point of prudence and self-preservation have put it off to a better opportunity.

Having thus answered the only objection that can be raised against me as a traveler, I here take a final leave of my courteous readers, and return to enjoy my own speculations in my little garden at Redriff; to apply those excellent lessons of virtue which I learned among the Houyhnhnms; to instruct the Yahoos of my own family as far as I shall find them docible animals; to behold my figure often in a glass, and thus if possible habituate myself by time to tolerate the sight of a human creature; to lament the brutality of Houyhnhnms in my own country, but always treat their persons with respect, for the sake of my noble master, his family, his friends, and the whole Houyhnhnm race, whom these of ours have the honor to resemble in all their lineaments, however their intellectuals came to degenerate.

I began last week to permit my wife to sit at dinner with me, at the farthest end of a long table; and to answer (but with the utmost brevity) the few questions I ask her. Yet the smell of a Yahoo continuing very offensive, I always keep my nose well stopped with rue, lavender, or tobacco leaves. And although it be hard for a man late in life to remove old habits, I am not altogether out of hopes in some time to suffer a neighbor Yahoo in my company, without the apprehensions I am yet under of his teeth or his claws.

My reconcilement to the Yahoo kind in general might not be so difficult, if they would be content with those vices and follies only which nature hath entitled them to. I am not in the least provoked at the sight of a lawyer, a pickpocket, a colonel, a fool, a lord, a gamester, politician, a whoremonger, a physician, an evidence, a suborner, an attorney, a traitor, or the like: this is all according to the due course of things. But when I behold a lump of deformity, and diseases both in body and mind, smitten with pride, it immediately breaks all the measures of my patience; neither shall I be ever able to comprehend how such an animal and such a vice could tally together. The wise and virtuous Houyhnhnms, who abound in all excellencies that can adorn a rational creature, have no name for this vice in their language, which hath no terms to express anything that is evil, except those whereby they describe the detestable qualities of their Yahoos, among which they were not able to distinguish this of pride, for want of thoroughly understanding human nature, as it showeth itself in other countries, where that animal presides. But I, who had more experience, could plainly observe some rudiments of it among the wild Yahoos.

But the Houyhnhnms, who live under the government of reason, are no more proud of the good qualities they possess, than I should be for not wanting a leg or an arm, which no man in his wits would boast of, although he must be miserable without them. I dwell the longer upon this subject from the desire I have to make the society of an English Yahoo by any means not insupportable; and therefore I here entreat those who have any tincture of this absurd vice, that they will not presume to appear in my sight.

A Modest Proposal[1]

for Preventing the Children of poor People in Ireland, from being a Burden to their Parents or Country; and for making them beneficial to the Publick.

Written in the year 1729

It is a melancholy object to those who walk through this great town,[2] or travel in the country, when they see the streets, the roads, and cabin-doors crowded with beggars of the female sex, followed by three, four, or six children, all in rags, and importuning every passenger for an alms. These mothers, instead of being able to work for their honest livelihood, are forced to employ all their time in strolling to beg sustenance for their helpless infants: who, as they grow up, either turn thieves for want of work, or leave their dear native country to fight for the Pretender in Spain, or sell themselves to the Barbadoes.[3]

I think it is agreed by all parties, that this prodigious number of children in the arms, or on the backs, or at the heels of their mothers, and frequently of their fathers, is, in the present deplorable state of the kingdom, a very great additional grievance; and, therefore, whoever could find out a fair, cheap, and easy method of making these children sound and useful members of the commonwealth, would deserve so well of the public, as to have his statue set up for a preserver of the nation.

But my intention is very far from being confined to provide only for the children of professed beggars; it is of a much greater extent, and shall take in the whole number of infants at a certain age, who are born of parents in effect as little able to support them as those who demand our charity in the streets.

As to my own part, having turned my thoughts for many years upon this important subject, and maturely weighed the several schemes of other projectors,[4] I have always found them grossly mistaken in their computation. It is true, a child, just dropped from its dam, may be supported by her milk for a solar year with little other nourishment; at most, not above the value of two shillings, which the mother may certainly get, or the value in scraps, by her lawful occupation of begging; and it is exactly at one year old that I propose to provide for them in such a manner, as, instead of being a charge upon their parents or the parish, or wanting food and raiment for the rest of their lives, they shall, on the contrary, contribute to the feeding, and partly to the clothing, of many thousands.

There is likewise another advantage in my scheme, that it will prevent those voluntary abortions, and that horrid practice of women murdering their bastard children, alas, too frequent among us, sacrificing the poor innocent babes, I doubt more to avoid the expense than the shame, which would move tears and pity in the most savage and inhuman breast.

The number of souls in this kingdom being usually reckoned one million and a half, of these I calculate there may be about two hundred thousand couple

---

1. The complete text edited by Herbert Davis.
2. Dublin.
3. At this time a British possession, with a prosperous sugar industry. Workers were needed in the sugar plantations. "The Pretender": James Edward (1688–1766), son of the Catholic king James II of England, called the "Old Pretender" (in distinction to his son Charles, nine years old at the time of this work, called the "Young Pretender"). Many thought him a legitimate claimant to the throne.
4. Planners.

whose wives are breeders; from which number I subtract thirty thousand couple, who are able to maintain their own children (although I apprehend there cannot be so many, under the present distresses of the kingdom); but this being granted, there will remain an hundred and seventy thousand breeders. I again subtract fifty thousand for those women who miscarry, or whose children die by accident or disease within the year. There only remain a hundred and twenty thousand children of poor parents annually born. The question therefore is how this number shall be reared and provided for? which, as I have already said, under the present situation of affairs, is utterly impossible by all the methods hitherto proposed. For we can neither employ them in handicraft or agriculture; we neither build houses (I mean in the country) nor cultivate land: they can very seldom pick up a livelihood by stealing until they arrive at six years old, except where they are of towardly parts;[5] although I confess they learn the rudiments much earlier; during which time they can, however, be properly looked upon only as probationers; as I have been informed by a principal gentleman in the county of Cavan, who protested to me, that he never knew above one or two instances under the age of six, even in a part of the kingdom so renowned for the quickest proficiency in that art.

I am assured by our merchants that a boy or a girl before twelve years old is no saleable commodity; and even when they come to this age they will not yield above three pounds or three pounds and half-a-crown at most, on the exchange; which cannot turn to account either to the parents or kingdom, the charge of nutriment and rags having been at least four times that value.

I shall now, therefore, humbly propose my own thoughts, which I hope will not be liable to the least objection.

I have been assured by a very knowing American of my acquaintance in London, that a young healthy child, well nursed, is, at a year old, a most delicious, nourishing, and wholesome food, whether stewed, roasted, baked, or boiled; and I make no doubt that it will equally serve in a fricassee or a ragout.

I do therefore humbly offer it to public consideration, that of the hundred and twenty thousand children already computed, twenty thousand may be reserved for breed, whereof only one-fourth part to be males; which is more than we allow to sheep, black cattle, or swine; and my reason is, that these children are seldom the fruits of marriage, a circumstance not much regarded by our savages, therefore one male will be sufficient to serve four females. That the remaining hundred thousand may, at a year old, be offered in sale to the persons of quality and fortune through the kingdom; always advising the mother to let them suck plentifully in the last month, so as to render them plump and fat for a good table. A child will make two dishes at an entertainment for friends; and when the family dines alone, the fore or hind quarter will make a reasonable dish, and, seasoned with a little pepper or salt, will be very good boiled on the fourth day, especially in winter.

I have reckoned, upon a medium,[6] that a child just born will weigh twelve pounds, and in a solar year, if tolerably nursed, increaseth to twenty-eight pounds.

---

5. Particularly talented, unusually gifted.   6. Average.

I grant this food will be somewhat dear,[7] and therefore very proper for land-lords, who, as they have already devoured most of the parents, seem to have the best title to the children.

Infants' flesh will be in season throughout the year, but more plentifully in March, and a little before and after: for we are told by a grave author, an emi-nent French physician,[8] that fish being a prolific diet, there are more children born in Roman Catholic countries about nine months after Lent than at any other season; therefore, reckoning a year after Lent, the markets will be more glutted than usual, because the number of popish infants is at least three to one in this kingdom; and therefore it will have one other collateral advantage, by lessening the number of papists among us.

I have already computed the charge of nursing a beggar's child (in which list I reckon all cottagers, labourers, and four-fifths of the farmers) to be about two shillings per annum,[9] rags included; and I believe no gentleman would repine to give ten shillings for the carcass of a good fat child, which, as I have said, will make four dishes of excellent nutritive meat, when he has only some par-ticular friend, or his own family, to dine with him. Thus the squire will learn to be a good landlord, and grow popular among his tenants; the mother will have eight shillings net profit, and be fit for work till she produces another child.

Those who are more thrifty (as I must confess the times require) may flay the carcass; the skin of which, artificially dressed, will make admirable gloves for ladies, and summer-boots for fine gentlemen.

As to our city of Dublin, shambles[1] may be appointed for this purpose in the most convenient parts of it, and butchers we may be assured will not be want-ing; although I rather recommend buying the children alive, and dressing them hot from the knife, as we do roasting pigs.

A very worthy person, a true lover of his country, and whose virtues I highly esteem, was lately pleased, in discoursing on this matter, to offer a refinement upon my scheme. He said, that many gentlemen of this kingdom, having of late destroyed their deer, he conceived that the want of venison might be well sup-plied by the bodies of young lads and maidens, not exceeding fourteen years of age, nor under twelve; so great a number of both sexes in every country being now ready to starve for want of work and service; and these to be disposed of by their parents, if alive, or otherwise by their nearest relations. But, with due deference to so excellent a friend, and so deserving a patriot, I cannot be alto-gether in his sentiments; for as to the males, my American acquaintance assured me from frequent experience, that their flesh was generally tough and lean, like that of our schoolboys, by continual exercise, and their taste dis-agreeable; and to fatten them would not answer the charge. Then as to the females, it would, I think, with humble submission, be a loss to the public, because they soon would become breeders themselves: and besides, it is not improbable that some scrupulous people might be apt to censure such a prac-tice (although indeed very unjustly) as a little bordering upon cruelty; which, I confess hath always been with me the strongest objection against any project, how well soever intended.

7. Expensive.
8. François Rabelais (1494?–1553), French satirist and author of Gargantua and Pan-tagruel (1532–52).
9. Per year (Latin).
1. Slaughterhouses.

But in order to justify my friend, he confessed that this expedient was put into his head by the famous Psalmanazar,[2] a native of the island Formosa, who came from thence to London above twenty years ago; and in conversation told my friend, that in his country, when any young person happened to be put to death, the executioner sold the carcass to persons of quality as a prime dainty; and that in his time the body of a plump girl of fifteen, who was crucified for an attempt to poison the emperor, was sold to his Imperial Majesty's prime minister of state, and other great mandarins of the court, in joints from the gibbet,[3] at four hundred crowns. Neither indeed can I deny, that if the same use were made of several plump young girls in this town, who, without one single groat to their fortunes, cannot stir abroad without a chair,[4] and appear at playhouse and assemblies in foreign fineries which they never will pay for, the kingdom would not be the worse.

Some persons of a desponding spirit are in great concern about the vast number of poor people who are aged, diseased, or maimed; and I have been desired to employ my thoughts what course may be taken to ease the nation of so grievous an encumbrance. But I am not in the least pain upon that matter, because it is very well known, that they are every day dying, and rotting, by cold and famine, and filth and vermin, as fast as can be reasonably expected. And as to the younger labourers, they are now in almost as hopeful a condition: they cannot get work, and consequently pine away for want of nourishment, to a degree, that if at any time they are accidentally hired to common labour, they have not strength to perform it; and thus the country and themselves are happily delivered from the evils to come.

I have too long digressed, and therefore shall return to my subject. I think the advantages by the proposal which I have made are obvious and many, as well as of the highest importance.

For first, as I have already observed, it would greatly lessen the number of papists, with whom we are yearly overrun, being the principal breeders of the nation as well as our most dangerous enemies; and who stay at home on purpose with a design to deliver the kingdom to the Pretender, hoping to take their advantage by the absence of so many good Protestants, who have chosen rather to leave their country than stay at home and pay tithes against their conscience to an idolatrous Episcopal curate.

Secondly, the poorer tenants will have something valuable of their own, which by law may be made liable to distress,[5] and help to pay their landlord's rent; their corn and cattle being already seized, and money a thing unknown.

Thirdly, whereas the maintenance of an hundred thousand children, from two years old and upwards, cannot be computed at less than ten shillings a piece per annum, the nation's stock will be thereby increased fifty thousand pounds per annum; besides the profit of a new dish introduced to the tables of all gentlemen of fortune in the kingdom who have any refinement in taste. And

---

2. George Psalmanazar (1679?–1763), a literary impostor born in southern France who claimed to be a native of Formosa and a recent Christian convert. He published a catechism in an invented language that he called Formosan, as well as a description of Formosa with an introductory autobiography.

3. The post from which the bodies of criminals were hung in chains after execution. "Joints": portions of a carcass carved up by a butcher.

4. I.e., a sedan chair, an enclosed seat carried on poles by men.

5. The legal seizing of goods to satisfy a debt, particularly for unpaid rent.

the money will circulate among ourselves, the goods being entirely of our own growth and manufacture.

Fourthly, the constant breeders, besides the gain of eight shillings sterling per annum by the sale of their children, will be rid of the charge of maintaining them after the first year.

Fifthly, this food would likewise bring great custom to taverns; where the vinters will certainly be so prudent as to procure the best receipts[6] for dressing it to perfection, and, consequently, have their houses frequented by all the fine gentlemen, who justly value themselves upon their knowledge in good eating: and a skilful cook, who understands how to oblige his guests, will contrive to make it as expensive as they please.

Sixthly, this would be a great inducement to marriage, which all wise nations have either encouraged by rewards, or enforced by laws and penalties. It would increase the care and tenderness of mothers towards their children, when they were sure of a settlement for life to the poor babes, provided in some sort by the public, to their annual profit instead of expense. We should soon see an honest emulation among the married women, which of them could bring the fattest child to the market. Men would become as fond of their wives during the time of their pregnancy, as they are now of their mares in foal, their cows in calf, or sows when they are ready to farrow; nor offer to beat or kick them (as is too frequent a practice) for fear of a miscarriage.

Many other advantages might be enumerated. For instance, the addition of some thousand carcasses in our exportation of barrelled beef; the propagation of swine's flesh, and improvement in the art of making good bacon, so much wanted among us by the great destruction of pigs, too frequent at our tables, which are no way comparable in taste or magnificence to a well-grown, fat yearling child, which, roasted whole, will make a considerable figure at a Lord Mayor's feast, or any other public entertainment. But this, and many others, I omit, being studious of brevity.

Supposing that one thousand families in this city would be constant customers for infants' flesh, besides others who might have it at merry meetings, particularly weddings and christenings. I compute that Dublin would take off annually about twenty thousand carcasses; and the rest of the kingdom (where probably they will be sold somewhat cheaper) the remaining eighty thousand.

I can think of no one objection that will possibly be raised against this proposal, unless it should be urged, that the number of people will be thereby much lessened in the kingdom. This I freely own, and it was indeed one principal design in offering it to the world. I desire the reader will observe that I calculate my remedy *for this one individual kingdom of Ireland, and for no other that ever was, is, or I think ever can be, upon earth.* Therefore let no man talk to me of other expedients: *of taxing our absentees at five shillings a pound: of using neither clothes nor household-furniture except what is of our own growth and manufacture: of utterly rejecting the materials and instruments that promote foreign luxury: of curing the expensiveness of pride, vanity, idleness, and gaming in our women; of introducing a vein of parsimony, prudence, and temperance: of learning to love our country, wherein we differ even from Laplanders, and the inhabitants of Topinamboo:*[7] of quitting our animosities and factions, nor act

6. Recipes.   7. In Brazil.

any longer like the Jews, who were murdering one another at the very moment their city was taken: of being a little cautious not to sell our country and consciences for nothing: of teaching landlords to have at least one degree of mercy towards their tenants: lastly, of putting a spirit of honesty, industry, and skill into our shopkeepers; who, if a resolution could now be taken to buy only our native goods, would immediately unite to cheat and exact upon us in the price, the measure, and the goodness, nor could ever yet be brought to make one fair proposal of just dealing, though often and earnestly invited to it.[8]

Therefore I repeat, let no man talk to me of these and the like expedients, till he hath at least some glimpse of hope that there will ever be some hearty and sincere attempts to put them in practice.

But, as to myself, having been wearied out for many years with offering vain, idle, visionary thoughts, and at length utterly despairing of success, I fortunately fell upon this proposal; which, as it is wholly new, so it hath something solid and real, of no expense and little trouble, full in our own power, and whereby we can incur no danger in disobliging England. For this kind of commodity will not bear exportation, the flesh being of too tender a consistence to admit a long continuance in salt, although perhaps I could name a country[9] which would be glad to eat up our whole nation without it.

After all, I am not so violently bent upon my own opinion as to reject any offer proposed by wise men which shall be found equally innocent, cheap, easy, and effectual. But before something of that kind shall be advanced in contradiction to my scheme, and offering a better, I desire the author, or authors, will be pleased maturely to consider two points. First, as things now stand, how they will be able to find food and raiment for a hundred thousand useless mouths and backs? And, secondly, there being a round million of creatures in human figure throughout this kingdom, whose whole subsistence put into a common stock would leave them in debt two millions of pounds sterling, adding those who are beggars by profession, to the bulk of farmers, cottagers, and labourers, with the wives and children who are beggars in effect; I desire those politicians who dislike my overture, and may perhaps be so bold as to attempt an answer, that they will first ask the parents of these mortals, whether they would not at this day think it a great happiness to have been sold for food at a year old, in the manner I prescribe, and thereby have avoided such a perpetual scene of misfortunes as they have since gone through, by the oppression of landlords, the impossibility of paying rent without money or trade, the want of common sustenance, with neither house nor clothes to cover them from the inclemencies of weather, and the most inevitable prospect of entailing the like, or greater miseries, upon their breed for ever.

I profess, in the sincerity of my heart, that I have not the least personal interest in endeavouring to promote this necessary work, having no other motive than the public good of my country, by advancing our trade, providing for infants, relieving the poor, and giving some pleasure to the rich. I have no children by which I can propose to get a single penny; the youngest being nine years old, and my wife past child-bearing.

---

8. The italicized proposals are Swift's serious   9. England.
suggestions for remedying Ireland's situation.

ALEXANDER POPE

1688–1744

Socially marginal and physically disabled, Alexander Pope might seem an unlikely candidate for celebrity, but he won great wealth and fame through his writing. Crowds parted when he entered a room, and people rushed to shake his hand. In 1741, the renowned actor David Garrick heard that Pope was in the audience: "I instantaneously felt a palpitation at my heart. . . . His look shot, and thrilled, like lightning through my frame; and I had some hesitation in proceeding, from anxiety, and from joy." What made Pope so celebrated in his own time? His writing did not strive to be innovative; he proudly turned backward to ancient Greek and Roman traditions of literature and morality—especially Homer, Virgil, and Horace—and borrowed from them to make critical and satirical commentaries on his own society. But his witty, graceful, often bitingly comic poetic lines, coupled with his deep sense of moral and philosophical authority, marked him as both the most respected and the most popular poet of his time.

LIFE

Born to Roman Catholic parents in a year when the last Catholic king of England, James II, was deposed in favor of the Protestant regime of William and Mary, Pope lived when repressive measures against Catholics restricted his freedom. He could not attend a university or hold public office. He was even forbidden to live within ten miles of London. Sickly and undersized in childhood, he never reached more than four feet six inches tall, and had a hunchback for his whole life. In his youth, he was educated sporadically at illegal Catholic schools and at home, learning Latin, Greek, French, and Italian. He began to write epic poetry at the age of twelve. He taught himself a great deal, and developed his understanding of the world through literary friendships that remained important to him throughout his career.

Pope first came to the attention of the literary world with his *Essay on Criticism*, an ambitious piece of writing for a twenty-three year old, since it offered advice to rising writers when he had not yet established himself. This work earned him as many attackers as defenders, and he entered into a lively, sometimes acrimonious, literary debate about whether the ancient writers could be surpassed by modern innovations. *The Rape of the Lock*, Pope's most popular work from his time to ours, appeared in 1714. It sold three thousand copies in the first week of its publication. Then, in the ten years that followed, he produced little new poetry of his own, instead translating Homer's *Iliad* and *Odyssey*, and editing the works of Shakespeare to make both newly accessible to English readers. A rival translation of Homer appeared around the same time, and debate about the two versions reached a fever pitch, with newspapers reporting on both sides. But Pope's translations soon won the field, establishing him as a literary representative of the whole nation. They also earned him substantial sums of money, making him perhaps the first English writer to make a fortune from his work.

Pope never married, but he had some notable friendships with women.

For some time he was on close terms with Lady Mary Wortley Montagu, a fellow writer, but they fell out, and she satirized him in print. His closest relationship was with a woman named Martha Blount, whom he had known since adolescence. He wrote her serious letters and for a period saw her every day, giving rise to some scandalous gossip about the pair. When he died he left her his estate.

In his later years, Pope was best known for two works: a philosophical poem that reflects on the role of human beings in the universe, called *The Essay on Man* (1733–34) and *The Dunciad* (completed in 1742), a satirical poem he wrote in response to criticisms of his edition of Shakespeare. Here he condemned almost all of his intellectual contemporaries, scientists, critics, and writers—with the notable exception of his friend **Jonathan Swift**—as hacks and dunces. This work earned him so many enemies that he refused to leave his house without a pair of loaded pistols. The money Pope made from his translations had allowed him to retire to Twickenham, where he built a small villa and a famous garden and grotto. He died there at the age of fifty-six.

TIMES

Although he was the richest poet of his era, Pope frequently condemned writers who wrote for monetary gain. This might make him seem hypocritical, but in fact his whole culture was feeling a new and profound ambivalence about money, which underwent a major transformation during his lifetime. In the eighteenth century European economies for the first time began to produce paper currencies rather than relying on exchanges of gold and silver, and people started to write checks. Lottery tickets went on sale as a new thrill. Among the most important new financial instruments of the period was the joint stock company—where an individual investor could advance a small sum that would be lumped in with money from others. It became popular to buy shares in these companies, and this wave of enthusiasm enabled large-scale economic projects that would never have been possible before.

The most famous—and ill-fated—of the new joint stock ventures was the South Sea Company. In the early eighteenth century, the British government found itself deep in debt, and in 1711, they sold a substantial portion of the debt to the South Sea Company, promising a return of 6 percent interest. The company publicized the fact that they had bought the rights to all new trading opportunities in South America, since Spain had just opened up access to British ships. Having heard about gold and silver mines in Mexico and Peru, people rushed to buy shares in the company, and the price of stocks rose precipitously. The South Sea Company abruptly failed in 1720. It turned out that many of the glowing rumors about it had been false. The directors wanted to sell and get out quickly. "And thus," wrote a historian looking back in 1803, "were seen, in the space of eight months, the rise, progress, and fall of that mighty fabric, which, being wound up by mysterious springs to a wonderful height, had fixed the eyes and expectations of all Europe, but whose foundation, being fraud, illusion, credulity, and infatuation, fell to the ground as soon as the artful management of its directors was discovered."

Intangible and sometimes illusory, the new paper economy often seemed simply immoral. Pope saw the crash as "God punishing the avaritious." But it was also hugely tempting, since it was clearly now possible to amass a great fortune from very little. As Pope himself put it, "'Tis ignominious (in this Age of Hope and Golden Mountains) not to Venture." The poet had in fact invested in the South Sea Company, but on the advice of a wise broker, he got much of his money out before the crash, losing only a part of his growing fortune. Torn between excitement at a fast-growing economy where ordinary people could accumulate riches, and alarm at the greed, deception, and catastrophic failure that the new financial world made possible, the whole of Europe was caught up in wonder and uncertainty at the new, strange fact of wealth on paper.

Pope was particularly shrewd about putting the changing marketplace to use for his own writing career. Since he was a Catholic outsider, he could not depend on powerful patrons in the Anglican Church or the court, and he suffered particular hardships when new anti-Catholic laws diminished his family's property in 1714. But like Jonathan Swift he figured out how to exploit a growing democratic and urban market for books and pamphlets. Pope retained his own copyright and acted as his own publisher. He also borrowed a trick out of the book of the new joint stock companies. That is, he sold subscriptions to his translation of Homer's *Iliad* before it appeared. Subscribers therefore "invested" in a promise rather than a concrete object, just as they bought stocks in new companies, and Pope could live on the cash that flowed in before the publication was complete. Unlike the South Sea Bubble, this turned out to be a good investment for his readers—and excellent for Pope's own finances. Where many contemporary writers might make a total £10 or £20 on a book they sold to a publisher, Pope made more than £800 on his *Iliad*, roughly equivalent to about $200,000 today. Thus he brought about his independence. As he put it proudly: "South-sea subscriptions take who please, / Leave me but Liberty and Ease!"

WORK

Alexander Pope wrote *The Rape of the Lock* in response to a real event. Arabella Fermor, the most famous beauty of her time, was deeply insulted one evening when a young aristocrat, Lord Petre, snipped off a lock of her hair without her permission. He bragged about the event, acting as if the young lady were the kind of person who invited such advances. Her family was outraged, and friends turned to the most celebrated poet of the time to intervene. Pope's poem pretends to belong to the genre of dignified epic poetry— traditionally poetry that commemorates heroic warriors—to describe this trifling social quarrel. His work is a "mock epic," one that relies on epic conventions while also poking fun at them. Thus Pope, like Homer and Virgil before him, stages the event as an elaborate military encounter, including the careful arming of the hero—which in this case involves the protagonist seated at her cosmetics table.

Part of the great wit of the poem lies in constant juxtaposition of two radically dissimilar worlds. Not only does Pope employ the conventions of epic for a high-society squabble, but he repeatedly joins the trivial and the serious in the fabric of the poem. Among the jumble of things on Belinda's dressing table, for example, are "Puffs, powders, patches, Bibles, billet-doux," and we are invited to wonder whether she "will stain her honor or her new brocade." In bringing the grave and the petty close together, Pope manages to move beyond mere comic lightness: he opens up questions about the relationship between femininity and masculinity, between private and public, and between sacred and secular. Criticism of social inequality appears on the margins ("wretches hang that jurymen may dine"), and the society Pope mocks revolves around tensions between the sexes. Most searchingly, he investigates the question of beauty, the target of much contemplation in the poem: is it a superficial quality, to be cast in with puffs and powders, or does it belong to the realms of timeless and even spiritual grandeur, like art itself? Reaching great heights and shallow depths, Pope also manages to take aim at the monarchy itself: the court is a place where Queen Anne, "whom three realms obey, / Dost sometimes counsel take—and sometimes tea." Thus the queen becomes at once powerful and domestic.

This idea of pairing suits the poetic form Pope was most famous for—pairs of lines called rhyming couplets. Although this form often seemed mechanical and forced in the hands of other poets, Pope used it with astonishing dexterity and variety: sometimes he follows a cheerful couplet with a solemn one; sometimes the two lines connect to one another thematically, while at other times he uses their closeness to accentuate opposition or difference; occasionally the line pairing makes a neat, self-enclosed whole, but Pope most often built his couplets into larger conceptual or thematic units. The pair of scissors used to cut Belinda's hair in *The Rape of the Lock* echoes the ways that the couplet form can both bring together and separate—"now joins it, to divide."

Pope used the couplet equally effectively for a very different kind of poem. His *Essay on Man* ambitiously sets out to consider humanity in relation to the universe, to itself, to society, and to happiness. He draws on a number of intellectual traditions—Catholic and Protestant theology, Platonic and Stoic philosophy, his own period's interest in a natural order—to reinforce the assumption of a timeless and universal human nature. Above all, the text is, like **Milton's *Paradise Lost***, a theodicy— a genre that asks how, if God is good,

there can be evil in the world. The first section of the poem, included here, begins by insisting on the necessary limitations of human judgment: we see only parts, not the whole. And yet, our ignorance of future events and our hope for eternal life give us the possibility of happiness. He explores the nature of human pride and the place of humans in the Great Chain of Being that stretches from God down to the minutest living things, suggesting that this order extends farther than we can know and that any attempt to interfere with it will destroy the whole.

Pope draws us into the poem by addressing us directly, reminding us of our own tendencies to presumption. "In Pride, in reas'ning Pride, our error lies": we all share bewilderment at our situation, we all need to interpret it, we all face, every day, our necessary limitations. The poet rapidly shifts tone and perspective, sometimes berating his readers, sometimes reminding us (and himself) of his own participation in the universal dilemma, sometimes assuming a godlike perspective and suggesting his superior knowledge. And as he moves among voices and viewpoints, he comes to the conclusion that although we cannot see it, the universe works according to a design that is good, and thus demands "our absolute submission . . . to Providence."

Pope conceded that it was difficult to write a philosophical argument in poetic form, but he defended his choice. "This I might have done in prose," he wrote, "but I chose verse, and even rhyme, for two reasons. The one will appear obvious; that principles, maxims, or precepts, so written, both strike the reader more strongly at first, and are more easily retained by him afterwards: the other may seem odd, but it is true: I found I could express them more shortly this way than in prose itself; and nothing is more certain than that much of the force as well as grace of arguments or instructions depends on their conciseness." Forceful and concise, Pope's lines also offer concrete imagery—such as the Indian looking up at the clouds to find God or the eye of the fly, which sees more minutely than the human eye. And his perfectly turned couplets remind us of the complex dualities of humankind, at once godlike and animal, fallen and saved, capable of happy triviality and grim seriousness.

In the later eighteenth century, Pope's writing came under attack. Romantic poets such as **William Wordsworth** saw Pope's elegant verse couplets as artificial, mechanical, lacking "soul." But he remained a well-loved poet for his moral wisdom and his remarkable technical skill. Most famous today for lines we may not even recognize as his—such as "A little learning is a dangerous thing" and "Hope springs eternal in the human breast"—Pope embodies a whole literary era in England, which has come to be known as the "age of Pope."

The Rape of the Lock[1]

An Heroi-Comical Poem

Nolueram, Belinda, tuos violare capillos;
sed juvat hoc precibus me tribuisse tuis.[2]
—MARTIAL

TO MRS. ARABELLA FERMOR

MADAM,

It will be in vain to deny that I have some regard for this piece, since I dedicate it to you. Yet you may bear me witness, it was intended only to divert a few young ladies, who have good sense and good humor enough to laugh not only at their sex's little unguarded follies, but at their own. But as it was communicated with the air of a secret, it soon found its way into the world. An imperfect copy having been offered to a bookseller, you had the good nature for my sake to consent to the publication of one more correct; this I was forced to, before I had executed half my design, for the machinery was entirely wanting to complete it.

The machinery, Madam, is a term invented by the critics, to signify that part which the deities, angels, or demons are made to act in a poem; for the ancient poets are in one respect like many modern ladies: let an action be never so trivial in itself, they always make it appear of the utmost importance. These machines I determined to raise on a very new and odd foundation, the Rosicrucian[3] doctrine of spirits.

1. Text and notes by Samuel Holt Monk.
2. "I was unwilling, Belinda, to ravish your locks; but I rejoice to have conceded this to your prayers" (Martial, *Epigrams* 12.84.1–2). Pope substituted his heroine for Martial's Polytimus. The epigraph is intended to suggest that the poem was published at Miss Fermor's request.
3. A system of arcane philosophy introduced into England from Germany in the 17th century.

I know how disagreeable it is to make use of hard words before a lady; but 'tis so much the concern of a poet to have his works understood, and particularly by your sex, that you must give me leave to explain two or three difficult terms.

The Rosicrucians are a people I must bring you acquainted with. The best account I know of them is in a French book called *Le Comte de Gabalis*,[4] which both in its title and size is so like a novel, that many of the fair sex have read it for one by mistake. According to these gentlemen, the four elements are inhabited by spirits, which they call Sylphs, Gnomes, Nymphs, and Salamanders. The Gnomes or Demons of earth delight in mischief; but the Sylphs, whose habitation is in the air, are the best-conditioned creatures imaginable. For they say, any mortals may enjoy the most intimate familiarities with these gentle spirits, upon a condition very easy to all true adepts, an inviolate preservation of chastity.

As to the following cantos, all the passages of them are as fabulous as the vision at the beginning, or the transformation at the end; (except the loss of your hair, which I always mention with reverence). The human persons are as fictitious as the airy ones; and the character of Belinda, as it is now managed, resembles you in nothing but in beauty.

If this poem had as many graces as there are in your person, or in your mind, yet I could never hope it should pass through the world half so uncensured as you have done. But let its fortune be what it will, mine is happy enough, to have given me this occasion of assuring you that I am, with the truest esteem,

MADAM,
Your most obedient, humble servant,

A. POPE

CANTO I

What dire offense from amorous causes springs,
What mighty contests rise from trivial things,
I sing—This verse to Caryll,[5] Muse! is due:
This, even Belinda may vouchsafe to view:
Slight is the subject, but not so the praise,   5
If she inspire, and he approve my lays.
　　Say what strange motive, Goddess! could compel
A well-bred lord t' assault a gentle belle?
Oh, say what stranger cause, yet unexplored,
Could make a gentle belle reject a lord?   10
In tasks so bold can little men engage,
And in soft bosoms dwells such mighty rage?
　　Sol through white curtains shot a timorous ray,
And oped those eyes that must eclipse the day.
Now lapdogs give themselves the rousing shake,   15

---

4. By the Abbé de Montfaucon de Villars, published in 1670.
5. John Caryll (1666?–1736), a close friend of Pope's who suggested that he write this poem.

And sleepless lovers just at twelve awake:
Thrice rung the bell, the slipper knocked the ground,
And the pressed watch[6] returned a silver sound.
Belinda still her downy pillow pressed,
Her guardian Sylph prolonged the balmy rest: 20
'Twas he had summoned to her silent bed
The morning dream that hovered o'er her head.
A youth more glittering than a birthnight beau[7]
(That even in slumber caused her cheek to glow)
Seemed to her ear his winning lips to lay,   25
And thus in whispers said, or seemed to say:
    "Fairest of mortals, thou distinguished care
Of thousand bright inhabitants of air!
If e'er one vision touched thy infant thought,
Of all the nurse and all the priest have taught,   30
Of airy elves by moonlight shadows seen,
The silver token, and the circled green,[8]
Or virgins visited by angel powers,
With golden crowns and wreaths of heavenly flowers,
Hear and believe! thy own importance know,   35
Nor bound thy narrow views to things below.
Some secret truths, from learned pride concealed,
To maids alone and children are revealed:
What though no credit doubting wits may give?
The fair and innocent shall still believe.   40
Know, then, unnumbered spirits round thee fly,
The light militia of the lower sky:
These, though unseen, are ever on the wing,
Hang o'er the box,[9] and hover round the Ring.
Think what an equipage thou hast in air,   45
And view with scorn two pages and a chair.[1]
As now your own, our beings were of old,
And once enclosed in woman's beauteous mold
Thence, by a soft transition, we repair
From earthly vehicles to these of air.   50
Think not, when woman's transient breath is fled,
That all her vanities at once are dead:
Succeeding vanities she still regards,
And though she plays no more o'erlooks the cards.
Her joy in gilded chariots, when alive,   55
And love of ombre,[2] after death survive.

---

6. A watch that chimes the hour and the quarter hour when the stem is pressed down. "Thrice rung the bell": Belinda thus summons her maid.

7. Courtiers wore especially fine clothes on the sovereign's birthday.

8. According to popular belief, fairies skim off the cream from jugs of milk left standing overnight and leave a coin in payment. "The circled green": rings of bright green grass, which are common in England even in winter, were held to be due to the round dances of fairies.

9. "Box" in the theater and the fashionable circular drive ("Ring") in Hyde Park.

1. Sedan chair.

2. The popular card game. See III.27ff. and note.

For when the Fair in all their pride expire,
To their first elements[3] their souls retire:
The sprites of fiery termagants in flame
Mount up, and take a Salamander's name.[4]   60
Soft yielding minds to water glide away,
And sip, with Nymphs, their elemental tea.[5]
The graver prude sinks downward to a Gnome,
In search of mischief still on earth to roam.
The light coquettes in Sylphs aloft repair,   65
And sport and flutter in the fields of air.
    "Know further yet; whoever fair and chaste
Rejects mankind, is by some Sylph embraced:
For spirits, freed from mortal laws, with ease
Assume what sexes and what shapes they please.   70
What guards the purity of melting maids,
In courtly balls, and midnight masquerades,
Safe from the treacherous friend, the daring spark,
The glance by day, the whisper in the dark,
When kind occasion prompts their warm desires,   75
When music softens, and when dancing fires?
'Tis but their Sylph, the wise Celestials know,
Though Honor is the word with men below.
    "Some nymphs there are, too conscious of their face,
For life predestined to the Gnomes' embrace.   80
These swell their prospects and exalt their pride,
When offers are disdained, and love denied:
Then gay ideas[6] crowd the vacant brain,
While peers, and dukes, and all their sweeping train,
And garters, stars, and coronets appear,   85
And in soft sounds, 'your Grace' salutes their ear.
'Tis these that early taint the female soul,
Instruct the eyes of young coquettes to roll,
Teach infant cheeks a bidden blush to know,
And little hearts to flutter at a beau.   90
    "Oft, when the world imagine women stray,
The Sylphs through mystic mazes guide their way,
Through all the giddy circle they pursue,
And old impertinence expel by new.
What tender maid but must a victim fall   95
To one man's treat, but for another's ball?
When Florio speaks what virgin could withstand,
If gentle Damon did not squeeze her hand?
With varying vanities, from every part,

3. The four elements out of which all things were believed to have been made were fire, water, earth, and air. One or another of these elements was supposed to be predominant in both the physical and psychological makeup of each human being. In this context they are spoken of as "humors."

4. Pope borrowed his supernatural beings from Rosicrucian mythology. Each element was inhabited by a spirit, as the following lines explain. The salamander is a lizardlike animal, in antiquity believed to live in fire.
5. Pronounced *tay*.
6. Images.

They shift the moving toyshop[7] of their heart; 100
Where wigs with wigs, with sword-knots sword-knots strive,
Beaux banish beaux, and coaches coaches drive.
This erring mortals levity may call;
Oh, blind to truth! the Sylphs contrive it all.
  "Of these am I, who thy protection claim, 105
A watchful sprite, and Ariel is my name.
Late, as I ranged the crystal wilds of air,
In the clear mirror of thy ruling star
I saw, alas! some dread event impend,
Ere to the main this morning sun descend, 110
But Heaven reveals not what, or how, or where:
Warned by thy Sylph, O pious maid, beware!
This to disclose is all thy guardian can:
Beware of all, but most beware of Man!"
  He said; when Shock,[8] who thought she slept too long, 115
Leaped up, and waked his mistress with his tongue.
'Twas then, Belinda, if report say true,
Thy eyes first opened on a billet-doux;
Wounds, charms, and ardors were no sooner read,
But all the vision vanished from thy head. 120
  And now, unveiled, the toilet stands displayed,
Each silver vase in mystic order laid.
First, robed in white, the nymph intent adores,
With head uncovered, the cosmetic powers.
A heavenly image in the glass appears; 125
To that she bends, to that her eyes she rears.
The inferior priestess, at her altar's side,
Trembling begins the sacred rites of Pride.
Unnumbered treasures ope at once, and here
The various offerings of the world appear; 130
From each she nicely culls with curious toil,
And decks the goddess with the glittering spoil.
This casket India's glowing gems unlocks,
And all Arabia breathes from yonder box.
The tortoise here and elephant unite, 135
Transformed to combs, the speckled and the white.
Here files of pins extend their shining rows,
Puffs, powders, patches, Bibles, billet-doux.
Now awful Beauty puts on all its arms;
The fair each moment rises in her charms, 140
Repairs her smiles, awakens every grace,
And calls forth all the wonders of her face;
Sees by degrees a purer blush arise,
And keener lightnings quicken in her eyes.
The busy Sylphs surround their darling care, 145
These set the head, and those divide the hair,

7. A shop stocked with baubles and trifles.   8. Belinda's lapdog.

Some fold the sleeve, whilst others plait the gown;
And Betty's[9] praised for labors not her own.

CANTO II

    Not with more glories, in the ethereal plain,
The sun first rises o'er the purpled main,
Than, issuing forth, the rival of his beams
Launched on the bosom of the silver Thames.
Fair nymphs and well-dressed youths around her shone,   5
But every eye was fixed on her alone.
On her white breast a sparkling cross she wore,
Which Jews might kiss, and infidels adore.
Her lively looks a sprightly mind disclose,
Quick as her eyes, and as unfixed as those: 10
Favors to none, to all she smiles extends;
Oft she rejects, but never once offends.
Bright as the sun, her eyes the gazers strike,
And, like the sun, they shine on all alike.
Yet graceful ease, and sweetness void of pride,   15
Might hide her faults, if belles had faults to hide:
If to her share some female errors fall,
Look on her face, and you'll forget 'em all.
    This nymph, to the destruction of mankind,
Nourished two locks which graceful hung behind   20
In equal curls, and well conspired to deck
With shining ringlets the smooth ivory neck.
Love in these labyrinths his slaves detains,
And mighty hearts are held in slender chains.
With hairy springes we the birds betray,   25
Slight lines of hair surprise the finny prey,
Fair tresses man's imperial race ensnare,
And beauty draws us with a single hair.
    The adventurous Baron the bright locks admired,
He saw, he wished, and to the prize aspired.   30
Resolved to win, he meditates the way,
By force to ravish, or by fraud betray;
For when success a lover's toil attends,
Few ask if fraud or force attained his ends.
    For this, ere Phoebus rose, he had implored   35
Propitious Heaven, and every power adored,
But chiefly Love—to Love an altar built,
Of twelve vast French romances, neatly gilt.
There lay three garters, half a pair of gloves,
And all the trophies of his former loves.   40
With tender billet-doux he lights the pyre,
And breathes three amorous sighs to raise the fire.

---

9. Belinda's maid, the "inferior priestess" mentioned in line 127.

Then prostrate falls, and begs with ardent eyes
Soon to obtain, and long possess the prize:
The powers gave ear, and granted half his prayer,   45
The rest the winds dispersed in empty air.
   But now secure the painted vessel glides,
The sunbeams trembling on the floating tides,
While melting music steals upon the sky,
And softened sounds along the waters die.   50
Smooth flow the waves, the zephyrs gently play,
Belinda smiled, and all the world was gay.
All but the Sylph—with careful thoughts oppressed,
The impending woe sat heavy on his breast.
He summons straight his denizens of air;   55
The lucid squadrons round the sails repair:
Soft o'er the shrouds aërial whispers breathe
That seemed but zephyrs to the train beneath.
Some to the sun their insect-wings unfold,
Waft on the breeze, or sink in clouds of gold.   60
Transparent forms too fine for mortal sight,
Their fluid bodies half dissolved in light,
Loose to the wind their airy garments flew,
Thin glittering textures of the filmy dew,
Dipped in the richest tincture of the skies,   65
Where light disports in ever-mingling dyes,
While every beam new transient colors flings,
Colors that change whene'er they wave their wings.
Amid the circle, on the gilded mast,
Superior by the head was Ariel placed;   70
His purple[1] pinions opening to the sun,
He raised his azure wand, and thus begun:
   "Ye Sylphs and Sylphids, to your chief give ear!
Fays, Fairies, Genii, Elves, and Daemons, hear!
Ye know the spheres and various tasks assigned   75
By laws eternal to the aërial kind.
Some in the fields of purest ether play,
And bask and whiten in the blaze of day.
Some guide the course of wandering orbs on high,
Or roll the planets through the boundless sky.   80
Some less refined, beneath the moon's pale light
Pursue the stars that shoot athwart the night,
Or suck the mists in grosser air below,
Or dip their pinions in the painted bow,
Or brew fierce tempests on the wintry main,   85
Or o'er the glebe distill the kindly rain.
Others on earth o'er human race preside,
Watch all their ways, and all their actions guide:
Of these the chief the care of nations own,
And guard with arms divine the British Throne.   90

---

1. In 18th-century poetic diction, the word might mean "blood-red," "purple," or simply (as is likely here) "brightly colored." The word derives from Virgil, *Eclogue* 9.40, *pupureus*.

"Our humbler province is to tend the Fair,
Not a less pleasing, though less glorious care:
To save the powder from too rude a gale,
Nor let the imprisoned essences exhale;
To draw fresh colors from the vernal flowers 95
To steal from rainbows e'er they drop in showers
A brighter wash;[2] to curl their waving hairs,
Assist their blushes, and inspire their airs;
Nay oft, in dreams invention we bestow,
To change a flounce, or add a furbelow. 100
    "This day black omens threat the brightest fair,
That e'er deserved a watchful spirit's care;
Some dire disaster, or by force or slight,
But what, or where, the Fates have wrapped in night:
Whether the nymph shall break Diana's[3] law, 105
Or some frail china jar receive a flaw,
Or stain her honor or her new brocade,
Forget her prayers, or miss a masquerade,
Or lose her heart, or necklace, at a ball;
Or whether Heaven has doomed that Shock must fall. 110
Haste, then, ye spirits! to your charge repair:
The fluttering fan be Zephyretta's care;
The drops[4] to thee, Brillante, we consign;
And, Momentilla, let the watch be thine;
Do thou, Crispissa,[5] tend her favorite Lock; 115
Ariel himself shall be the guard of Shock.
    "To fifty chosen Sylphs, of special note,
We trust the important charge, the petticoat;
Oft have we known that sevenfold fence to fail,
Though stiff with hoops, and armed with ribs of whale. 120
Form a strong line about the silver bound,
And guard the wide circumference around.
    "Whatever spirit, careless of his charge,
His post neglects, or leaves the fair at large,
Shall feel sharp vengeance soon o'ertake his sins, 125
Be stopped in vials, or transfixed with pins,
Or plunged in lakes of bitter washes lie,
Or wedged whole ages in a bodkin's eye;[6]
Gums and pomatums shall his flight restrain,
While clogged he beats his silken wings in vain, 130
Or alum styptics with contracting power
Shrink his thin essence like a riveled[7] flower:
Or, as Ixion fixed,[8] the wretch shall feel
The giddy motion of the whirling mill,

2. Cosmetic lotion.
3. Diana was the goddess of chastity.
4. Diamond earrings.
5. From Latin *crispere*, to curl.
6. A blunt needle with a large eye, used for drawing ribbon through eyelets in the edging
of women's garments.
7. To "rivel" is to "contract into wrinkles and corrugations" (Johnson's *Dictionary*).
8. In the Greek myth Ixion was punished in the underworld by being bound on an ever-turning wheel.

In fumes of burning chocolate shall glow,   135
And tremble at the sea that froths below!"
   He spoke; the spirits from the sails descend;
Some, orb in orb, around the nymph extend;
Some thread the mazy ringlets of her hair;
Some hang upon the pendants of her ear: 140
With beating hearts the dire event they wait,
Anxious, and trembling for the birth of Fate.

CANTO III

   Close by those meads, forever crowned with flowers,
Where Thames with pride surveys his rising towers,
There stands a structure of majestic frame,
Which from the neighboring Hampton[9] takes its name.
Here Britain's statesmen oft the fall foredoom   5
Of foreign tyrants and of nymphs at home;
Here thou, great Anna! whom three realms obey,
Dost sometimes counsel take—and sometimes tea.
   Hither the heroes and the nymphs resort,
To taste awhile the pleasures of a court;   10
In various talk the instructive hours they passed,
Who gave the ball, or paid the visit last;
One speaks the glory of the British Queen,
And one describes a charming Indian screen;
A third interprets motions, looks, and eyes;   15
At every word a reputation dies.
Snuff, or the fan, supply each pause of chat,
With singing, laughing, ogling, and all that.
   Meanwhile, declining from the noon of day,
The sun obliquely shoots his burning ray;   20
The hungry judges soon the sentence sign,
And wretches hang that jurymen may dine;
The merchant from the Exchange returns in peace,
And the long labors of the toilet cease.
Belinda now, whom thirst of fame invites,   25
Burns to encounter two adventurous knights,
At ombre[1] singly to decide their doom
And swells her breast with conquests yet to come.
Straight the three bands prepare in arms to join,
Each band the number of the sacred nine.   30
Soon as she spreads her hand, the aërial guard

---

9. Hampton Court, the royal palace, about fifteen miles up the Thames from London.
1. The game that Belinda plays against the baron and another young man is too complicated for complete explication here. Pope has carefully arranged the cards so that Belinda wins. The baron's hand is strong enough to be a threat, but the third player's is of little account.

The hand is played exactly according to the rules of ombre, and Pope's description of the cards is equally accurate. Each player holds nine cards (line 30). The "Matadores" (line 33), when spades are trumps, are "Spadillio" (line 49), the ace of spades; "Manillio" (line 51), the two of spades; "Basto" (line 53), the ace of clubs; Belinda holds all three of these.

Descend, and sit on each important card:
First Ariel perched upon a Matadore,
Then each according to the rank they bore;
For Sylphs, yet mindful of their ancient race,   35
Are, as when women, wondrous fond of place.
   Behold, four Kings in majesty revered,
With hoary whiskers and a forky beard;
And four fair Queens whose hands sustain a flower,
The expressive emblem of their softer power;   40
Four Knaves in garbs succinct,[2] a trusty band,
Caps on their heads, and halberts in their hand;
And parti-colored troops, a shining train,
Draw forth to combat on the velvet plain.
The skillful nymph reviews her force with care;   45
"Let Spades be trumps!" she said, and trumps they were.
   Now move to war her sable Matadores,
In show like leaders of the swarthy Moors.
Spadillio first, unconquerable lord!
Led off two captive trumps, and swept the board.   50
As many more Manillio forced to yield,
And marched a victor from the verdant field.
Him Basto followed, but his fate more hard
Gained but one trump and one plebeian card.
With his broad saber next, a chief in years,   55
The hoary Majesty of Spades appears,
Puts forth one manly leg, to sight revealed,
The rest his many-colored robe concealed.
The rebel Knave, who dares his prince engage,
Proves the just victim of his royal rage.   60
Even mighty Pam,[3] that kings and queens o'erthrew
And mowed down armies in the fights of loo,
Sad chance of war! now destitute of aid,
Falls undistinguished by the victor Spade.
   Thus far both armies to Belinda yield;   65
Now to the Baron fate inclines the field.
His warlike amazon her host invades,
The imperial consort of the crown of Spades.
The Club's black tyrant first her victim died,
Spite of his haughty mien and barbarous pride.   70
What boots the regal circle on his head,
His giant limbs, in state unwieldy spread?
That long behind he trails his pompous robe,
And of all monarchs only grasps the globe?
   The Baron now his Diamonds pours apace;   75
The embroidered King who shows but half his face,
And his refulgent Queen, with powers combined
Of broken troops an easy conquest find.

---

2. Girded up.
3. The knave of clubs, the highest trump in the game of loo.

Clubs, Diamonds, Hearts, in wild disorder seen,
With throngs promiscuous strew the level green.   80
Thus when dispersed a routed army runs,
Of Asia's troops, and Afric's sable sons,
With like confusion different nations fly,
Of various habit, and of various dye,
The pierced battalions disunited fall   85
In heaps on heaps; one fate o'erwhelms them all.
    The Knave of Diamonds tries his wily arts,
And wins (oh, shameful chance!) the Queen of Hearts.
At this, the blood the virgin's cheek forsook,
A livid paleness spreads o'er all her look;   90
She sees, and trembles at the approaching ill,
Just in the jaws of ruin, and Codille,[4]
And now (as oft in some distempered state)
On one nice trick depends the general fate.
An Ace of Hearts steps forth: the King unseen   95
Lurked in her hand, and mourned his captive Queen.
He springs to vengeance with an eager pace,
And falls like thunder on the prostrate Ace.
The nymph exulting fills with shouts the sky,
The walls, the woods, and long canals reply.   100
    O thoughtless mortals! ever blind to fate,
Too soon dejected, and too soon elate:
Sudden these honors shall be snatched away,
And cursed forever this victorious day.
    For lo! the board with cups and spoons is crowned,   105
The berries crackle, and the mill turns round;[5]
On shining altars of Japan[6] they raise
The silver lamp; the fiery spirits blaze:
From silver spouts the grateful liquors glide,
While China's earth receives the smoking tide.   110
At once they gratify their scent and taste,
And frequent cups prolong the rich repast.
Straight hover round the fair her airy band;
Some, as she sipped, the fuming liquor fanned,
Some o'er her lap their careful plumes displayed,   115
Trembling, and conscious of the rich brocade.
Coffee (which makes the politician wise,
And see through all things with his half-shut eyes)
Sent up in vapors to the Baron's brain
New stratagems, the radiant Lock to gain.   120
Ah, cease, rash youth! desist ere 'tis too late,
Fear the just Gods, and think of Scylla's fate![7]

4. The term applied to losing a hand at cards.
5. That is, coffee is roasted and ground.
6. That is, small, lacquered tables. The word "altars" suggests the ritualistic character of coffee drinking in Belinda's world.
7. Scylla, daughter of Nisus, was turned into a sea bird because, for the sake of her love for Minos of Crete, who was besieging her father's city of Megara, she cut from her father's head the purple lock on which his safety depended. She is not the Scylla of the "Scylla and Charybdis" episode in the Odyssey.

Changed to a bird, and sent to flit in air,
She dearly pays for Nisus' injured hair!
But when to mischief mortals bend their will,   125
How soon they find fit instruments of ill!
Just then, Clarissa drew with tempting grace
A two-edged weapon from her shining case:
So ladies in romance assist their knight,
Present the spear, and arm him for the fight.   130
He takes the gift with reverence, and extends
The little engine on his fingers' ends;
This just behind Belinda's neck he spread,
As o'er the fragrant steams she bends her head.
Swift to the Lock a thousand sprites repair,   135
A thousand wings, by turns, blow back the hair,
And thrice they twitched the diamond in her ear,
Thrice she looked back, and thrice the foe drew near.
Just in that instant, anxious Ariel sought
The close recesses of the virgin's thought;   140
As on the nosegay in her breast reclined,
He watched the ideas rising in her mind,
Sudden he viewed, in spite of all her art,
An earthly lover lurking at her heart.
Amazed, confused, he found his power expired,   145
Resigned to fate, and with a sigh retired.
    The Peer now spreads the glittering forfex[8] wide,
T' enclose the Lock; now joins it, to divide.
Even then, before the fatal engine closed,
A wretched Sylph too fondly interposed;   150
Fate urged the shears, and cut the Sylph in twain
(But airy substance soon unites again):
The meeting points the sacred hair dissever
From the fair head, forever, and forever!
    Then flashed the living lightning from her eyes,   155
And screams of horror rend the affrighted skies.
Not louder shrieks to pitying heaven are cast,
When husbands, or when lapdogs breathe their last;
Or when rich china vessels fallen from high,
In glittering dust and painted fragments lie!   160
"Let wreaths of triumph now my temples twine,"
The victor cried, "the glorious prize is mine!
While fish in streams, or birds delight in air,
Or in a coach and six the British Fair,
As long as Atalantis[9] shall be read,   165
Or the small pillow grace a lady's bed,
While visits shall be paid on solemn days,
When numerous wax-lights in bright order blaze,
While nymphs take treats, or assignations give,

8. Scissors.
9. Mrs. Manley's *New Atalantis* (1709) was

notorious for its thinly concealed allusions to
contemporary scandals.

So long my honor, name, and praise shall live!   170
What Time would spare, from Steel receives its date,
And monuments, like men, submit to fate!
Steel could the labor of the Gods destroy,
And strike to dust the imperial towers of Troy;
Steel could the works of mortal pride confound,   175
And hew triumphal arches to the ground.
What wonder then, fair nymph! thy hairs should feel,
The conquering force of unresisted Steel?"

CANTO IV

But anxious cares the pensive nymph oppressed,
And secret passions labored in her breast.
Not youthful kings in battle seized alive,
Not scornful virgins who their charms survive,
Not ardent lovers robbed of all their bliss,   5
Not ancient ladies when refused a kiss,
Not tyrants fierce that unrepenting die,
Not Cynthia when her manteau's[1] pinned awry,
E'er felt such rage, resentment, and despair,
As thou, sad virgin! for thy ravished hair.   10
For, that sad moment, when the Sylphs withdrew
And Ariel weeping from Belinda flew,
Umbriel,[2] a dusky, melancholy sprite
As ever sullied the fair face of light,
Down to the central earth, his proper scene,   15
Repaired to search the gloomy Cave of Spleen.[3]
Swift on his sooty pinions flits the Gnome,
And in a vapor[4] reached the dismal dome.
No cheerful breeze this sullen region knows,
The dreaded east is all the wind that blows.   20
Here in a grotto, sheltered close from air,
And screened in shades from day's detested glare,
She sighs forever on her pensive bed,
Pain at her side, and Megrim[5] at her head.
Two handmaids wait the throne: alike in place,   25
But differing far in figure and in face.
Here stood Ill-Nature like an ancient maid,
Her wrinkled form in black and white arrayed;
With store of prayers for mornings, nights, and noons,
Her hand is filled; her bosom with lampoons.   30
There Affectation, with a sickly mien,
Shows in her cheek the roses of eighteen,
Practiced to lisp, and hang the head aside,
Faints into airs, and languishes with pride,

---

1. Negligee, or loose robe.
2. The name suggests shade and darkness.
3. Ill humor.
4. Punning on *vapor* as (1) mist and (2) an excessively emotional (even peevish) state of mind, appropriate to the realm of "spleen."
5. Headache.

On the rich quilt sinks with becoming woe,   35
Wrapped in a gown, for sickness and for show.
The fair ones feel such maladies as these,
When each new nightdress gives a new disease.
   A constant vapor[6] o'er the palace flies,
Strange phantoms rising as the mists arise;   40
Dreadful as hermit's dreams in haunted shades,
Or bright as visions of expiring maids.
Now glaring fiends, and snakes on rolling spires,[7]
Pale specters, gaping tombs, and purple fires;
Now lakes of liquid gold, Elysian scenes,   45
And crystal domes, and angels in machines.[8]
   Unnumbered throngs on every side are seen
Of bodies changed to various forms by Spleen.
Here living teapots stand, one arm held out,
One bent; the handle this, and that the spout: 50
A pipkin[9] there, like Homer's tripod, walks;
Here sighs a jar, and there a goose pie talks;
Men prove with child, as powerful fancy works,
And maids, turned bottles, call aloud for corks.
   Safe passed the Gnome through this fantastic band,   55
A branch of healing spleenwort[1] in his hand.
Then thus addressed the Power: "Hail, wayward Queen!
Who rule the sex to fifty from fifteen:
Parent of vapors and of female wit,
Who give the hysteric or poetic fit,   60
On various tempers act by various ways,
Make some take physic, others scribble plays;
Who cause the proud their visits to delay,
And send the godly in a pet to pray.
A nymph there is that all your power disdains,   65
And thousands more in equal mirth maintains.
But oh! if e'er thy Gnome could spoil a grace,
Or raise a pimple on a beauteous face,
Like citron-waters[2] matrons' cheeks inflame,
Or change complexions at a losing game;   70
If e'er with airy horns[3] I planted heads,
Or rumpled petticoats, or tumbled beds,
Or caused suspicion when no soul was rude,
Or discomposed the headdress of a prude,

---

6. Emblematic of "the vapors"—hypochondria, melancholy, peevishness, often affected by fashionable women.
7. Coils.
8. Mechanical devices used in the theaters for spectacular effects. The fantasies of neurotic women here merge with the sensational stage effects popular with contemporary audiences.
9. An earthen pot. In *Iliad* 18.434–40, Vulcan furnishes the gods with self-propelling "tripods" (three-legged stools).

1. An herb, efficacious against the spleen. Pope alludes to the golden bough that Aeneas and the Cumaean sybil carry with them for protection into the underworld in *Aeneid* 6.
2. Brandy flavored with orange or lemon peel.
3. The symbol of the cuckold; here "airy," because they exist only in the jealous suspicions of the husband, the victim of the mischievous Umbriel.

Or e'er to costive lapdog gave disease,   75
Which not the tears of brightest eyes could ease,
Hear me, and touch Belinda with chagrin:[4]
That single act gives half the world the spleen."
    The Goddess with a discontented air
Seems to reject him though she grants his prayer.   80
A wondrous bag with both her hands she binds,
Like that where once Ulysses held the winds;[5]
There she collects the force of female lungs,
Sighs, sobs, and passions, and the war of tongues.
A vial next she fills with fainting fears,   85
Soft sorrows, melting griefs, and flowing tears.
The Gnome rejoicing bears her gifts away,
Spreads his black wings, and slowly mounts to day.
    Sunk in Thalestris'[6] arms the nymph he found,
Her eyes dejected and her hair unbound.   90
Full o'er their heads the swelling bag he rent,
And all the Furies issued at the vent.
Belinda burns with more than mortal ire,
And fierce Thalestris fans the rising fire.
"O wretched maid!" she spread her hands, and cried   95
(While Hampton's echoes, "Wretched maid!" replied),
"Was it for this you took such constant care
The bodkin, comb, and essence to prepare?
For this your locks in paper durance bound,
For this with torturing irons wreathed around?   100
For this with fillets strained your tender head,
And bravely bore the double loads of lead?[7]
Gods! shall the ravisher display your hair,
While the fops envy, and the ladies stare!
Honor forbid! at whose unrivaled shrine   105
Ease, pleasure, virtue, all, our sex resign.
Methinks already I your tears survey,
Already hear the horrid things they say,
Already see you a degraded toast,
And all your honor in a whisper lost!   110
How shall I, then, your helpless fame defend?
'Twill then be infamy to seem your friend!
And shall this prize, the inestimable prize,
Exposed through crystal to the gazing eyes,
And heightened by the diamond's circling rays,   115
On that rapacious hand forever blaze?
Sooner shall grass in Hyde Park Circus grow,

---

4. Ill humor.

5. Aeolus (later conceived of as god of the winds) gave Ulysses a bag containing all the winds adverse to his voyage home. When his ship was in sight of Ithaca, his companions opened the bag and the storms that ensued drove Ulysses far away (*Odyssey* 10.19ff.).

6. The name is borrowed from a queen of the Amazons, hence a fierce and warlike woman. Thalestris, according to legend, traveled thirty days in order to have a child by Alexander the Great. Plutarch denies the story.

7. The frame on which the elaborate coiffures of the day were arranged.

And wits take lodgings in the sound of Bow;[8]
Sooner let earth, air, sea, to chaos fall,
Men, monkeys, lapdogs, parrots, perish all!"   120
    She said; then raging to Sir Plume repairs,
And bids her beau demand the precious hairs
(Sir Plume of amber snuffbox justly vain,
And the nice conduct of a clouded cane).
With earnest eyes, and round unthinking face,   125
He first the snuffbox opened, then the case,
And thus broke out—"My Lord, why, what the devil!
Z—ds! damn the lock! 'fore Gad, you must be civil!
Plague on't! 'tis past a jest—nay prithee, pox!
Give her the hair"—he spoke, and rapped his box.   130
    "It grieves me much," replied the Peer again,
"Who speaks so well should ever speak in vain.
But by this Lock, this sacred Lock I swear
(Which never more shall join its parted hair;
Which never more its honors shall renew,   135
Clipped from the lovely head where late it grew),
That while my nostrils draw the vital air,
This hand, which won it, shall forever wear."
He spoke, and speaking, in proud triumph spread
The long-contended honors[9] of her head.   140
    But Umbriel, hateful Gnome, forbears not so;
He breaks the vial whence the sorrows flow.
Then see! the nymph in beauteous grief appears,
Her eyes half languishing, half drowned in tears;
On her heaved bosom hung her drooping head,   145
Which with a sigh she raised, and thus she said:
    "Forever cursed be this detested day,
Which snatched my best, my favorite curl away!
Happy! ah, ten times happy had I been,
If Hampton Court these eyes had never seen!   150
Yet am not I the first mistaken maid,
By love of courts to numerous ills betrayed.
Oh, had I rather unadmired remained
In some lone isle, or distant northern land;
Where the gilt chariot never marks the way,   155
Where none learn ombre, none e'er taste bohea![1]
There kept my charms concealed from mortal eye,
Like roses that in deserts bloom and die.
What moved my mind with youthful lords to roam?
Oh, had I stayed, and said my prayers at home!   160
'Twas this the morning omens seemed to tell,
Thrice from my trembling hand the patch box[2] fell;

---

8. A person born within sound of the bells of St. Mary-le-Bow in Cheapside is said to be a cockney. No fashionable wit would have so vulgar an address.
9. Ornaments, hence locks; a Latinism.

1. A costly sort of tea.
2. A box to hold the ornamental patches of court plaster worn on the face by both sexes. Cf. *Spectator* 81.

The tottering china shook without a wind,
Nay, Poll sat mute, and Shock was most unkind!
A Sylph too warned me of the threats of fate,   165
In mystic visions, now believed too late!
See the poor remnants of these slighted hairs!
My hands shall rend what e'en thy rapine spares.
These in two sable ringlets taught to break,
Once gave new beauties to the snowy neck;   170
The sister lock now sits uncouth, alone,
And in its fellow's fate foresees its own;
Uncurled it hangs, the fatal shears demands,
And tempts once more thy sacrilegious hands.
Oh, hadst thou, cruel! been content to seize   175
Hairs less in sight, or any hairs but these!"

CANTO V

She said: the pitying audience melt in tears.
But Fate and Jove had stopped the Baron's ears.
In vain Thalestris with reproach assails,
For who can move when fair Belinda fails?
Not half so fixed the Trojan[3] could remain,   5
While Anna begged and Dido raged in vain.
Then grave Clarissa graceful waved her fan;
Silence ensued, and thus the nymph began:
  "Say why are beauties praised and honored most,
The wise man's passion, and the vain man's toast?   10
Why decked with all that land and sea afford,
Why angels called, and angel-like adored?
Why round our coaches crowd the white-gloved beaux,
Why bows the side box from its inmost rows?
How vain are all these glories, all our pains,   15
Unless good sense preserve what beauty gains;
That men may say when we the front box grace,
'Behold the first in virtue as in face!'
Oh! if to dance all night, and dress all day,
Charmed the smallpox, or chased old age away,   20
Who would not scorn what housewife's cares produce,
Or who would learn one earthly thing of use?
To patch, nay ogle, might become a saint,
Nor could it sure be such a sin to paint.
But since, alas! frail beauty must decay,   25
Curled or uncurled, since locks will turn to gray;
Since painted, or not painted, all shall fade,
And she who scorns a man must die a maid;
What then remains but well our power to use,
And keep good humor still whate'er we lose?   30
And trust me, dear, good humor can prevail

---

3. A reference to Aeneas, the epic hero of *The Aeneid*, by the Roman poet Virgil (70–19 B.C.E). Aeneas abandons his lover Dido at the bidding of the gods, despite her reproaches; Virgil compares him to a steadfast oak that withstands a storm (*Aeneid* 4.427–43).

When airs, and flights, and screams, and scolding fail.
Beauties in vain their pretty eyes may roll;
Charms strike the sight, but merit wins the soul."
      So spoke the dame, but no applause ensued;   35
Belinda frowned, Thalestris called her prude.
"To arms, to arms!" the fierce virago cries,
And swift as lightning to the combat flies.
All side in parties, and begin the attack;
Fans clap, silks rustle, and tough whalebones crack;   40
Heroes' and heroines' shouts confusedly rise,
And bass and treble voices strike the skies.
No common weapons in their hands are found,
Like Gods they fight, nor dread a mortal wound.
      So when bold Homer makes the Gods engage,   45
And heavenly breasts with human passions rage;
'Gainst Pallas, Mars; Latona, Hermes arms;
And all Olympus rings with loud alarms:
Jove's thunder roars, heaven trembles all around,
Blue Neptune storms, the bellowing deeps resound: 50
Earth shakes her nodding towers, the ground gives way,
And the pale ghosts start at the flash of day!
      Triumphant Umbriel on a sconce's height
Clapped his glad wings, and sat to view the fight:
Propped on their bodkin spears, the sprites survey   55
The growing combat, or assist the fray.
      While through the press enraged Thalestris flies,
And scatters death around from both her eyes,
A beau and witling perished in the throng,
One died in metaphor, and one in song.   60
"O cruel nymph! a living death I bear,"
Cried Dapperwit, and sunk beside his chair.
A mournful glance Sir Fopling upwards cast,
"Those eyes are made so killing"—was his last.
Thus on Maeander's flowery margin lies   65
The expiring swan, and as he sings he dies.
      When bold Sir Plume had drawn Clarissa down,
Chloe stepped in, and killed him with a frown;
She smiled to see the doughty hero slain,
But, at her smile, the beau revived again.   70
Now Jove suspends his golden scales in air,
Weighs the men's wits against the lady's hair;
The doubtful beam long nods from side to side;
At length the wits mount up, the hairs subside.
      See, fierce Belinda on the Baron flies,   75
With more than usual lightning in her eyes;
Nor feared the chief the unequal fight to try,
Who sought no more than on his foe to die.
      But this bold lord with manly strength endued,
She with one finger and a thumb subdued: 80
Just where the breath of life his nostrils drew,
A charge of snuff the wily virgin threw;

The Gnomes direct, to every atom just,
The pungent grains of titillating dust.
Sudden, with starting tears each eye o'erflows, 85
And the high dome re-echoes to his nose.
  "Now meet thy fate," incensed Belinda cried,
And drew a deadly bodkin[4] from her side.
(The same, his ancient personage to deck,
Her great-great-grandsire wore about his neck, 90
In three seal rings; which after, melted down,
Formed a vast buckle for his widow's gown:
Her infant grandame's whistle next it grew,
The bells she jingled, and the whistle blew;
Then in a bodkin graced her mother's hairs, 95
Which long she wore, and now Belinda wears.)
  "Boast not my fall," he cried, "insulting foe!
Thou by some other shalt be laid as low.
Nor think to die dejects my lofty mind:
All that I dread is leaving you behind! 100
Rather than so, ah, let me still survive,
And burn in Cupid's flames—but burn alive."
  "Restore the Lock!" she cries; and all around
"Restore the Lock!" the vaulted roofs rebound.
Not fierce Othello in so loud a strain 105
Roared for the handkerchief that caused his pain.[5]
But see how oft ambitious aims are crossed,
And chiefs contend till all the prize is lost!
The lock, obtained with guilt, and kept with pain,
In every place is sought, but sought in vain: 110
With such a prize no mortal must be blessed,
So Heaven decrees! with Heaven who can contest?
  Some thought it mounted to the lunar sphere,
Since all things lost on earth are treasured there.
There heroes' wits are kept in ponderous vases, 115
And beaux' in snuffboxes and tweezer cases.
There broken vows and deathbed alms are found,
And lovers' hearts with ends of riband bound,
The courtier's promises, and sick man's prayers,
The smiles of harlots, and the tears of heirs, 120
Cages for gnats, and chains to yoke a flea,
Dried butterflies, and tomes of casuistry.
  But trust the Muse—she saw it upward rise,
Though marked by none but quick, poetic eyes
(So Rome's great founder[6] to the heavens withdrew, 125
To Proculus alone confessed in view);
A sudden star, it shot through liquid air,
And drew behind a radiant trail of hair.

---

4. An ornamental pin shaped like a dagger, to be worn in the hair.
5. A reference to Shakespeare's tragedy *Othello* (Act 3, Scene 4).

6. Romulus, the "founder" and first king of Rome, was snatched to heaven in a storm cloud while reviewing his army in the Campus Martius (Livy 1.16).

Not Berenice's[7] locks first rose so bright,
The heavens bespangling with disheveled light.   130
The Sylphs behold it kindling as it flies,
And pleased pursue its progress through the skies.
    This the beau monde shall from the Mall[8] survey,
And hail with music its propitious ray.
This the blest lover shall for Venus take,   135
And send up vows from Rosamonda's Lake.[9]
This Partridge soon shall view in cloudless skies,
When next he looks through Galileo's eyes;[1]
And hence the egregious wizard shall foredoom
The fate of Louis, and the fall of Rome.   140
    Then cease, bright nymph! to mourn thy ravished hair,
Which adds new glory to the shining sphere!
Not all the tresses that fair head can boast,
Shall draw such envy as the Lock you lost.
For, after all the murders of your eye,   145
When, after millions slain, yourself shall die:
When those fair suns shall set, as set they must,
And all those tresses shall be laid in dust,
This Lock the Muse shall consecrate to fame,
And 'midst the stars inscribe Belinda's name.   150

An Essay on Man

To Henry St. John, Lord Bolingbroke

EPISTLE I

ARGUMENT OF THE NATURE AND STATE OF MAN, WITH RESPECT TO THE UNIVERSE.
Of man in the abstract—I. That we can judge only with regard to our own system, being ignorant of the relations of systems and things, ver. 17, &c.—II. That man is not to be deemed imperfect, but a being suited to his place and rank in the creation, agreeable to the general order of things, and conformable to ends and relations to him unknown, ver. 35, &c.—III. That it is partly upon his ignorance of future events, and partly upon the hope of a future state, that all his happiness in the present depends, ver. 77, &c.—IV. The pride of aiming at more knowledge, and pretending to more perfection, the cause of man's error and misery. The impiety of putting himself in the place of God, and judging of the fitness or unfitness, perfection or imperfection, justice or injustice of his dispensations, ver. 113, &c.—V. The absurdity of conceiting himself the

---

7. Queen Berenice II of Egypt, wife of Ptolemy III in the 3rd century B.C.E; she promised the goddess Aphrodite that she would sacrifice her beautiful long hair if her husband returned safely from war; Aphrodite was so pleased that she turned the hair into a constellation of stars.
8. A walk laid out by Charles II in St. James's

Park, a resort for strollers of all sorts.
9. In St. James's Park; associated with unhappy lovers.
1. A telescope. John Partridge was an astrologer whose annually published predictions had been amusingly satirized by Swift and other wits in 1708.

final cause of the creation, or expecting that perfection in the moral world which is not in the natural, ver. 131, &c.—VI. The unreasonableness of his complaints against Providence, while on the one hand he demands the perfections of the angels, and on the other the bodily qualifications of the brutes; though, to possess any of the sensitive faculties in a higher degree, would render him miserable, ver. 173, &c.—VII. That throughout the whole visible world, an universal order and gradation in the sensual and mental faculties is observed, which causes a subordination of creature to creature, and of all creatures to man. The gradations of sense, instinct, thought, reflection, reason: that reason alone countervails all the other faculties, ver. 207.—VIII. How much further this order and subordination of living creatures may extend, above and below us; were any part of which broken, not that part only, but the whole connected creation must be destroyed, ver. 233—IX. The extravagance, madness, and pride of such a desire, ver. 259.—X. The consequence of all, the absolute submission due to Providence, both as to our present and future state, ver. 281, &c., to the end.

> Awake, my St. John![1] leave all meaner things
> To low ambition, and the pride of Kings.
> Let us (since Life can little more supply
> Than just to look about us and to die)
> Expatiate free o'er all this scene of Man;   5
> A mighty maze! but not without a plan;
> A Wild, where weeds and flowers promiscuous shoot;
> Or Garden, tempting with forbidden fruit.
> Together let us beat this ample field,
> Try what the open, what the covert yield;   10
> The latent tracts, the giddy heights, explore
> Of all who blindly creep, or sightless soar;
> Eye Nature's walks, shoot Folly as it flies,
> And catch the Manners living as they rise;
> Laugh where we must, be candid where we can;   15
> But vindicate the ways of God to man.[2]
>
>   I. Say first, of God above, or Man below,
> What can we reason, but from what we know?
> Of Man, what see we but his station here,
> From which to reason, or to which refer?   20
> Through worlds unnumbered though the God be known,
> 'Tis ours to trace him only in our own.
> He, who through vast immensity can pierce,
> See worlds on worlds compose one universe,
> Observe how system into system runs,   25
> What other planets circle other suns,
> What varied Being peoples every star,

1. Henry St. John, Viscount Bolingbroke, Pope's friend, who had thus far neglected to keep his part of their friendly bargain: Pope was to write his philosophical speculations in verse; Bolingbroke was to write his in prose.

2. Cf. Milton's *Paradise Lost* 1.26. Pope's theme is essentially the same as Milton's, and even the opening image of the garden reminds one of the earlier poet's Paradise.

May tell why Heaven has made us as we are.
But of this frame the bearings, and the ties,
The strong connections, nice dependencies,   30
Gradations just, has thy pervading soul
Looked through? or can a part contain the whole?
   Is the great chain,[3] that draws all to agree,
And drawn supports, upheld by God, or thee?

   II. Presumptuous Man! the reason wouldst thou find,   35
Why formed so weak, so little, and so blind?
First, if thou canst, the harder reason guess,
Why formed no weaker, blinder, and no less?
Ask of thy mother earth, why oaks are made
Taller or stronger than the weeds they shade?   40
Or ask of yonder argent fields above,
Why Jove's satellites are less than JOVE?
   Of Systems possible, if 'tis confest.
That Wisdom infinite must form the best,
Where all must full[4] or not coherent be,   45
And all that rises, rise in due degree;
Then, in the scale of reasoning life, 'tis plain,
There must be, somewhere, such a rank as Man:
And all the question (wrangle e'er so long)
Is only this, if God has placed him wrong?   50
   Respecting Man, whatever wrong we call,
May, must be right, as relative to all.
In human works, though laboured on with pain,
A thousand movements scarce one purpose gain;
In God's, one single can its end produce;   55
Yet serves to second too some other use.
So Man, who here seems principal alone,
Perhaps acts second to some sphere unknown,
Touches some wheel, or verges to some goal;
'Tis but a part we see, and not a whole.   60
   When the proud steed shall know why Man restrains
His fiery course, or drives him o'er the plains;
When the dull Ox, why now he breaks the clod,
Is now a victim, and now Egypt's God:
Then shall Man's pride and dullness comprehend   65
His actions', passions', being's use and end;
Why doing, suffering, checked, impelled; and why
This hour a slave, the next a deity.
   Then say not Man's imperfect, Heaven in fault;
Say rather, Man's as perfect as he ought: 70
His knowledge measured to his state and place;
His time a moment, and a point his space.
If to be perfect in a certain sphere,

3. A reference to the popular 18th-century notion of the Great Chain of Being, in which elements of the universe took their places in a hierarchy ranging from the lowest matter to God.
4. Theorists of the Great Chain of Being believed that there must be no gaps in the chain.

What matter, soon or late, or here or there?
The blest to-day is as completely so,   75
As who began a thousand years ago.

    III. Heaven from all creatures hides the book of Fate,
All but the page prescribed, their present state:
From brutes what men, from men what spirits know:
Or who could suffer Being here below?   80
The lamb thy riot dooms to bleed to-day,
Had he thy Reason, would he skip and play?
Pleased to the last, he crops the flowery food,
And licks the hand just raised to shed his blood.
Oh blindness to the future! kindly given,   85
That each may fill the circle marked by Heaven:
Who sees with equal eye, as God of all,
A hero perish, or a sparrow fall,
Atoms or systems into ruin hurled,
And now a bubble burst, and now a world.   90
  Hope humbly then; with trembling pinions soar;
Wait the great teacher Death; and God adore.
What future bliss, he gives not thee to know,
But gives that Hope to be thy blessing now.
Hope springs eternal in the human breast: 95
Man never Is, but always To be blest:
The soul, uneasy and confined from home,
Rests and expatiates in a life to come.
  Lo, the poor Indian! whose untutored mind
Sees God in clouds, or hears him in the wind;   100
His soul, proud Science never taught to stray
Far as the solar walk, or milky way;
Yet simple Nature to his hope has given,
Behind the cloud-topt hill, an humbler heaven;
Some safer world in depth of woods embraced,   105
Some happier island in the watery waste,
Where slaves once more their native land behold,
No fiends torment, no Christians thirst for gold.
To Be, contents his natural desire,
He asks no Angel's wing, no Seraph's fire;   110
But thinks, admitted to that equal sky,
His faithful dog shall bear him company.

    IV. Go, wiser thou! and, in thy scale of sense,
Weigh thy Opinion against Providence;
Call imperfection what thou fanciest such,   115
Say, here he gives too little, there too much:
Destroy all Creatures for thy sport or gust,
Yet cry, If Man's unhappy, God's unjust;
If Man alone engross not Heaven's high care,
Alone made perfect here, immortal there: 120
Snatch from his hand the balance and the rod,
Re-judge his justice, be the GOD of GOD.

In Pride, in reasoning Pride, our error lies;
All quit their sphere, and rush into the skies.
Pride still is aiming at the blest abodes, 125
Men would be Angels, Angels would be Gods.
Aspiring to be Gods, if Angels fell,
Aspiring to be Angels, Men rebel:
And who but wishes to invert the laws
Of ORDER, sins against the Eternal Cause. 130

    V. Ask for what end the heavenly bodies shine,
Earth for whose use? Pride answers, " 'Tis for mine:
For me kind Nature wakes her genial Power,
Suckles each herb, and spreads out ev'ry flower;
Annual for me, the grape, the rose, renew, 135
The juice nectareous, and the balmy dew;
For me, the mine a thousand treasures brings;
For me, health gushes from a thousand springs;
Seas roll to waft me, suns to light me rise;
My footstool earth, my canopy the skies." 140
    But errs not Nature from this gracious end,
From burning suns when livid deaths descend,
When earthquakes swallow, or when tempests sweep
Towns to one grave, whole nations to the deep?
"No," 'tis replied, "the first Almighty Cause 145
Acts not by partial, but by general laws;
The exceptions few; some change since all began:
And what created perfect?"—Why then Man?
If the great end be human happiness,
Then Nature deviates; and can man do less? 150
As much that end a constant course requires
Of showers and sunshine, as of man's desires;
As much eternal springs and cloudless skies,
As Men forever temperate, calm, and wise.
If plagues or earthquakes break not Heaven's design, 155
Why then a Borgia, or a Catiline?[5]
Who knows but He whose hand the lightning forms,
Who heaves old Ocean, and who wings the storms;
Pours fierce Ambition in a Caesar's mind,
Or turns young Ammon[6] loose to scourge mankind? 160
From pride, from pride, our very reasoning springs;
Account for moral, as for natural things:
Why charge we Heaven in those, in these acquit?
In both, to reason right is to submit.
    Better for Us, perhaps, it might appear, 165
Where there all harmony, all virtue here;
That never air or ocean felt the wind;
That never passion discomposed the mind.

---

5. Roman who conspired against the state in 63 B.C.E. Cesare Borgia (1476–1507), an Italian prince notorious for his crimes.

6. Alexander the Great, who when he visited the oracle of Zeus Ammon in Egypt was hailed by the priest there as son of the god.

But ALL subsists by elemental strife;
And Passions are the elements of Life.   170
The general ORDER, since the whole began,
Is kept in Nature, and is kept in Man.

    VI. What would this Man? Now upward will he soar,
And little less than Angel, would be more;
Now looking downwards, just as grieved appears   175
To want the strength of bulls, the fur of bears.
Made for his use all creatures if he call,
Say what their use, had he the powers of all?
Nature to these, without profusion, kind,
The proper organs, proper powers assigned;   180
Each seeming want compénsated of course,
Here with degrees of swiftness, there of force;
All in exact proportion to the state;
Nothing to add, and nothing to abate.
Each beast, each insect, happy in its own: 185
Is Heaven unkind to Man, and Man alone?
Shall he alone, whom rational we call,
Be pleased with nothing, if not blessed with all?
    The bliss of Man (could Pride that blessing find)
Is not to act or think beyond mankind;   190
No powers of body or of soul to share,
But what his nature and his state can bear.
Why has not Man a microscopic eye?
For this plain reason, Man is not a Fly.
Say what the use, were finer optics[7] given,   195
T' inspect a mite, not comprehend the heaven?
Or touch, if tremblingly alive all o'er,
To smart and agonize at every pore?
Or quick effluvia[8] darting through the brain,
Die of a rose in aromatic pain?   200
If nature thundered in his opening ears,
And stunned him with the music of the spheres,[9]
How would he wish that Heaven had left him still
The whispering Zephyr, and the purling rill?
Who finds not Providence all good and wise,   205
Alike in what it gives, and what it denies?

    VII. Far as Creation's ample range extends,
The scale of sensual, mental powers ascends:
Mark how it mounts, to Man's imperial race,
From the green myriads in the peopled grass: 210
What modes of sight betwixt each wide extreme,
The mole's dim curtain, and the lynx's[1] beam:

---

7. Eyes.
8. Stream of minute particles.
9. The old notion that the movement of the planets created a "higher" music.

1. According to legend, one of the keenest sighted animals. "Dim curtain": the mole's poor vision.

Of smell, the headlong lioness between,
And hound sagacious[2] on the tainted green:
Of hearing, from the life that fills the Flood,   215
To that which warbles through the vernal wood:
The spider's touch, how exquisítely fine!
Feels at each thread, and lives along the line:
In the nice bee, what sense so subtly true
From poisonous herbs extracts the healing dew?   220
How Instinct varies in the grovelling swine,
Compared, half-reasoning elephant, with thine!
'Twixt that, and Reason, what a nice barriér,
For ever separate, yet for ever near!
Remembrance and Reflection how allied;   225
What thin partitions Sense from Thought divide:
And Middle natures,[3] how they long to join,
Yet never pass the insuperable line!
Without this just gradation, could they be
Subjected, these to those, or all to thee?   230
The powers of all subdued by thee alone,
Is not thy Reason all these powers in one?

    VIII. See, through this air, this ocean, and this earth,
All matter quick, and bursting into birth.
Above, how high, progressive life may go!   235
Around, how wide! how deep extend below!
Vast chain of Being! which from God began,
Natures ethereal, human, angel, man,
Beast, bird, fish, insect, what no eye can see,
No glass can reach; from Infinite to thee,   240
From thee to Nothing.—On superior powers
Were we to press, inferior might on ours:
Or in the full creation leave a void,
Where, one step broken, the great scale's destroyed:
From Nature's chain whatever link you strike,   245
Tenth or ten thousandth, breaks the chain alike.
    And, if each system in gradation roll
Alike essential to the amazing Whole,
The least confusion but in one, not all
That system only, but the Whole must fall.   250
Let Earth unbalanced from her orbit fly,
Planets and Suns run lawless through the sky;
Let ruling angels from their spheres be hurled,
Being on Being wrecked, and world on world;
Heaven's whole foundations to their center nod,   255
And Nature tremble to the throne of God.
All this dread ORDER break—for whom? for thee?
Vile worm!—oh Madness! Pride! Impiety!

---

2. Here, exceptionally quick of scent.
3. Animals that seem to share the characteris-

tics of several different classes, e.g., the duck-
billed platypus.

IX. What if the foot, ordained the dust to tread,
Or hand, to toil, aspired to be the head?   260
What if the head, the eye, or ear repined
To serve mere engines to the ruling Mind?
Just as absurd for any part to claim
To be another, in this general frame:
Just as absurd, to mourn the tasks or pains,   265
The great directing MIND of ALL ordains.
All are but parts of one stupendous whole,
Whose body Nature is, and God the soul;
That, changed through all, and yet in all the same;
Great in the earth, as in the ethereal frame;   270
Warms in the sun, refreshes in the breeze,
Glows in the stars, and blossoms in the trees,
Lives through all life, extends through all extent,
Spreads undivided, operates unspent;
Breathes in our soul, informs our mortal part,   275
As full, as perfect, in a hair as heart;
As full, as perfect, in vile Man that mourns,
As the rapt Seraph that adores and burns:
To him no high, no low, no great, no small;
He fills, he bounds, connects, and equals all.   280

X. Cease then, nor ORDER imperfection name:
Our proper bliss depends on what we blame.
Know thy own point: this kind, this due degree
Of blindness, weakness, Heaven bestows on thee.
Submit.—In this, or any other sphere,   285
Secure to be as blest as thou canst bear:
Safe in the hand of one disposing Power,
Or in the natal, or the mortal hour.
All Nature is but Art, unknown to thee;
All Chance, Direction, which thou canst not see;   290
All Discord, Harmony not understood;
All partial Evil, universal Good:
And, spite of Pride, in erring Reason's spite,
One truth is clear, WHATEVER IS, IS RIGHT.[4]

---

4. Epistle II deals with "the Nature and State of Man with respect to himself, as an Individual"; Epistle III examines "the Nature and State of Man with respect to Society"; and the last epistle concerns "the Nature and State of Man with Respect to Happiness."

VOLTAIRE

(FRANÇOIS-MARIE AROUET)

1694–1778

Imagine a writer so outspoken and so fearless that although his work landed him in prison and in exile—more than once—he never stopped writing defiantly. If he could not publish his work openly, he would have it printed secretly and smuggled across borders. If he could not circulate it by the post, he would have it hand-carried in suitcases and distributed by trusted friends. He seized freedom of speech even when it was not granted to him, and he used it to mock corrupt priests and self-regarding kings. The sheer gutsiness of Voltaire is breathtaking. In an atmosphere of stern censorship and absolute power, he managed to live to the ripe age of eighty-three, writing lively denunciations of dominant orthodoxies and powerful authorities almost every day. And his darkly comic imagination propelled him to enormous fame. He was so successful that he grew richer than many kings in Europe. His witty, light prose, and his clear and accessible style allowed him to popularize many of the revolutionary goals of the Enlightenment—human rights, the value of freedom and tolerance, the hope for progress through reasoned debate, and the urgent desire to end human suffering where we can. It is in no small part thanks to Voltaire that these ideals shape our own political landscape today.

LIFE AND TIMES

Bold, witty, and rebellious, François-Marie Arouet was a trouble to his parents as a child and became a trouble to the authorities for the rest of his life. He was born near Paris in 1694 to a middle-class family. At the age of ten he went to a boarding school run by Jesuits, where he developed an enthusiasm for literature and a passionate opposition to organized religion. His father wanted him to pursue a career in law, but he soon gave it up to write poetry and plays. So sparkling and brilliant was his conversation that he won powerful friends, but his propensity for satire also brought him enemies, and an attack on the acting head of state got him locked in the Bastille prison in Paris for almost a year. While there, he committed himself to writing, and his first play, *Oedipus*, turned into a huge success, bringing him considerable wealth and establishing his reputation.

The young writer, who was now known by his pen name, "Voltaire," spent three years in exile in England after a quarrel with a French nobleman. There he met the writers **Jonathan Swift** and **Alexander Pope**. He enjoyed the freedom from censorship and punishment allowed to writers in England, and returned to France with an even stronger sense of his right to dissent and oppose authority. His many subversive writings, called by the authorities "most dangerous to religion and civil order," earned him another spell of exile from Paris, which he spent with his longtime mistress and intellectual companion Madame du Châtelet. In 1750, Voltaire moved to Potsdam, in Prussia, where he joined the court of the young King Frederick, later to be known as Frederick the

Great, who loved the arts and wanted philosophy and literature to flourish. Voltaire, like many other Enlightenment thinkers, did not see democracy as the best form of government. The masses seemed to him to impede reason, freedom, and progress (he said he would "rather obey one lion than 200 rats"). The regime he idealized was the enlightened despot—a sensitive, rational king who welcomed dissent and sought the counsel of philosophers like himself. Early on, Frederick promised to live up to that ideal, but Voltaire was soon to be disappointed. He and Frederick argued; Frederick waged violent warfare and asserted power high-handedly. Voltaire was invited to leave.

He took up residence for the rest of his life at Ferney, a town on the border between France and Switzerland, so that he could escape from France easily if necessary. It was here that he wrote the best-selling *Candide*—and a great deal more. Travelers and visitors brought suitcases filled with Voltaire's "scandal-sheets" back with them to Paris where the public eagerly gobbled them up. He repeatedly attacked religious extremism and stultifying tradition and argued for universal human rights. And he refused the traditional literary goal of immortality, casting his writing as a response to current debates and events.

Voltaire was no atheist (he once said that "if God did not exist it would be necessary to invent him"). His own religion is usually known as Deism; that is, faith in a God who created the world and then stands back, allowing nature to follow its own laws and never intervening. The Deists' signature metaphor was God as a watchmaker: the world he made was a mechanism, which then ticked away on its own. As far as human beings were concerned, God gave them reason, and then left them free to use it. Deists disagreed about whether God had instilled human beings with a love of virtue, and whether there was an afterlife of rewards and punishments. Voltaire claimed that it was impossible for humans to know anything beyond their senses—so God's will must remain mysterious—and he believed that humans should use their senses and their reason to understand how the world works and, to the best of our ability, to make it better.

By the time of Voltaire's death, he had become a national hero. In all, he had produced enough work to fill 135 volumes, in a range of genres including tragedy, epic, philosophy, history, fiction, and journalism. In death as in life, he continued to generate scandal and division. Clergy in Paris refused to let him be buried in hallowed ground, so friends smuggled his body out of the city—propping it up on the journey like a sleeping passenger—and brought it to a monastery to be laid to rest. Later, leaders of the French Revolution, who had been inspired by Voltaire's attacks on authority and religion, had his body exhumed and reburied in Paris to huge national fanfare.

WORK

Voltaire wrote *Candide* in part as a response to a piece of news that shook him, and many of his contemporaries, badly. On November 1, 1755, a devastating earthquake hit Lisbon, in Portugal. Upwards of thirty thousand people died. Voltaire, writing almost obsessively about this tragedy in his letters, wondered how anyone could make a case for an optimistic philosophy in light of it. He worried over Alexander Pope's assertion in his ***Essay on Man*** that "Whatever is, is right." Could anyone really believe that this was God's will—that a just and rational God had created this world and that it was, in the words of the German philosopher Gottfried Wilhelm Leibniz, "the best of all possible worlds"? Voltaire's absurd philosopher Pangloss ("all-tongue") is a caricature of Leibniz.

Though philosophical, *Candide* is so brief and so easy to read that it was immediately popular with a wide range of readers. Voltaire deliberately opted for short, cheap, excitingly readable texts. Long works "will never make a revolution," he argued, and wrote that "if the New Testament had cost 4,200 sesterces, the Christian religion would never have taken root." Thus *Candide's* brevity may be seen as part of its power.

It is also deliberately entertaining. Voltaire combines a lively appetite for humor with a horrifying sense of the real existence of evil. The exuberance and extravagance of the sufferings characters undergo may even prompt us to laugh: the plight of the old woman whose buttock has been cut off to make rump steak for her starving companions, the weeping of two girls whose monkey-lovers have been killed, the glum circumstances of six exiled, poverty-stricken kings. But Voltaire also manages to keep his readers off balance. Raped, cut to pieces, hanged, stabbed in the belly, the central characters of *Candide* keep coming back to life at opportune moments, as though no disaster could have permanent effects. Such reassuring fantasy at first suggests that it is all a joke, designed to ridicule an outmoded philosophical system. And yet, reality keeps intruding. An admiral really did face a firing squad and die for failing to engage an enemy ferociously enough. Those six hungry kings were actual historical figures who were dispossessed. The Lisbon earthquake was so real that it haunted Voltaire for years. And his satirical pen attacks genuine social problems as various as military discipline, class hierarchy, greed, religious extremism, slavery, and even the publishing industry. The extravagances of the story are therefore uncomfortably matched by the extravagances of real life, and despite the comic lightness of the telling, Voltaire demands that the reader confront these horrors.

The fantastic and exaggerated nature of the events stands out against the simplicity of the narrative style. Candide is a naive traveler, like Jonathan Swift's Gulliver, who does not grasp the ironies he witnesses. He travels widely, taking in Europe, South America, and the Ottoman Empire, where Catholics, Protestants, and Muslims all emerge as cruel and hypocritical. The only exception is the mythical Eldorado, which takes place almost exactly at the halfway point of the text, where corruption, crime, malice, and poverty do not exist. Candide nonetheless insists on leaving Eldorado to find his beloved Cunégonde. Readers have often wondered about the role of this paradise in an otherwise bleak picture of human experience: does Eldorado suggest that human beings are capable of virtue, and if so, then why does Voltaire compel his protagonist to leave? Is it too stagnant, too isolated, too dull? Is it like the Garden of Eden, a paradise no longer home to fallen humanity? The fact that Candide admires **Milton's *Paradise Lost*** and that the novella concludes with the protagonist cultivating a garden suggests that Voltaire may have been rethinking the story of Adam and Eve in his own imaginative way.

Candide encapsulated the many problems that stoked Voltaire's anger and fed his satire: absolutism and religious bigotry, unnecessary bloodshed, restrictions on freedom of speech and religion, and the intolerable reality of human suffering. This story has always been the most famous work of its author's incalculably influential career. Voltaire inspired leaders of the American Revolution—**Thomas Jefferson**, Thomas Paine, and **Benjamin Franklin**—and helped to shape the United States Constitution. The French Revolutionaries held Voltaire up as a hero, as did generations fighting against religious intolerance. He was hotly reviled by those who wanted to maintain the

A late Ming Dynasty (ca. seventeenth century) ink-on-paper illustration of Dushi Huang, one of the "Yama" kings of the ten courts of the underworld. The concept of layers and courts of hell appears to have arisen from a blending of ideas from Daoism, Buddhism, and Chinese folk religion. In this image, Dushi Huang appears as a divine record-keeper, with a scroll and writing implements laid out before him.

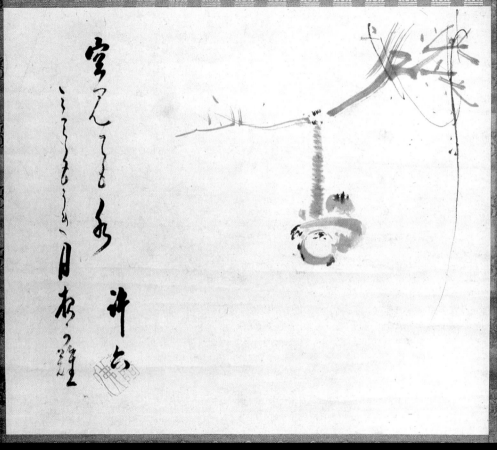

Calligraphy by the hand of the haiku poet Matsuo Bashō (1644–1694), accompanied by a

The Indian plant being withered
Grows in y[e] merne cut downe ere night
Showes thy decay all flesh is clay
Thus thinke

The pipe of cley being lily white
Showes thou art but a mortall wight
Even such gon w[th] a touch
Thus thinke. then drinke Tobacco

The smoke ascends on high
Showes y[t] all is but vanity
A world of stuffe gon w[th] a puffe
Thus thinke

The pipe being foule w[th]in
And the soule defild w[th] sin
To be purg'd w[th] fire it doth require
Thus

quite
Byes th[e] ashes left behind
Still to put thee in mind
That vnto duct returne y[u] must
Thus thinke then drinke

Tobacco.

When thus [...]

TRAVELS

INTO SEVERAL

Remote Nations

OF THE

WORLD.

In FOUR PARTS.

By *LEMUEL GULLIVER*,
First a SURGEON, and then a CAPTAIN of several SHIPS.

VOL. I.

LONDON:

Printed for BENJ. MOTTE, *at the*
Middle Temple-Gate *in* Fleet-street.
MDCCXXVI.

Frontispiece and title page of *Travels Into Several Remote Nations of the World. In Four Parts. By Lemuel Gulliver, First a Surgeon, and then a Captain of Several Ships,* later known as *Gulliver's Travels,* by Jonathan Swift. Especially in its early history in English, much prose fiction was presented in a nonfiction guise, as a memoir or, as here, a travel journal of a real person.

Daytime in the Gay Quarters (ca. 1739), a woodblock color print by Okumura Masanobu (1686–1764), a prolific Japanese print designer, painter, and publisher. The geisha in the foreground is about to use a brush to render calligraphy on paper.

A posthumous portrait, by Miguel Cabrera (1695–1768), of Sor Juana Inés de la Cruz (1648–1695), a pioneering writer and thinker in New Spain. Sor Juana is revered as a major figure in Mexican literature, and as a brave and eloquent advocate of formal education for women.

This medallion, designed in 1787 by the English potter and ceramicist Josiah Wedgwood (1730–1795), features an inscription, "Am I not a man and a brother?" that became one of the most recognizable mottoes of the abolitionist movement. The medallion became a wildly popular fashion accessory among people sympathetic to the abolitionist cause, and thus raised public awareness of the issue.

authority of established churches, and some went so far as to call him the Antichrist. But in the centuries that have followed, Voltaire's ideas have become part of the common fabric of our ideals.

Candide, or Optimism[1]

translated from the German of Doctor Ralph with the additions which were found in the Doctor's pocket when he died at Minden in the Year of Our Lord 1759

CHAPTER I

How Candide Was Brought up in a Fine Castle and How He Was Driven Therefrom

There lived in Westphalia,[2] in the castle of the Baron of Thunder-Ten-Tronckh, a young man on whom nature had bestowed the perfection of gentle manners. His features admirably expressed his soul; he combined an honest mind with great simplicity of heart; and I think it was for this reason that they called him Candide. The old servants of the house suspected that he was the son of the Baron's sister by a respectable, honest gentleman of the neighborhood, whom she had refused to marry because he could prove only seventy-one quarterings,[3] the rest of his family tree having been lost in the passage of time.

The Baron was one of the most mighty lords of Westphalia, for his castle had a door and windows. His great hall was even hung with a tapestry. The dogs of his courtyard made up a hunting pack on occasion, with the stable-boys as huntsmen; the village priest was his grand almoner. They all called him "My Lord," and laughed at his stories.

The Baroness, who weighed in the neighborhood of three hundred and fifty pounds, was greatly respected for that reason, and did the honors of the house with a dignity which rendered her even more imposing. Her daughter Cunégonde,[4] aged seventeen, was a ruddy-cheeked girl, fresh, plump, and desirable. The Baron's son seemed in every way worthy of his father. The tutor Pangloss was the oracle of the household, and little Candide listened to his lectures with all the good faith of his age and character.

1. Translated and with notes by Robert M. Adams.
2. A province of western Germany, near Holland and the lower Rhineland. Flat, boggy, and drab, it is noted chiefly for its excellent ham. In a letter to his niece, written during his German expedition of 1750, Voltaire described the "vast, sad, sterile, detestable countryside of Westphalia."

3. Genealogical divisions of one's family tree. Seventy-one of them is a grotesque number to have, representing something over 2,000 years of uninterrupted nobility.
4. Cunégonde gets her odd name from Kunigunda (wife to Emperor Henry II) who walked barefoot and blindfolded on red-hot irons to prove her chastity; Pangloss gets his name from Greek words meaning "all-tongue."

Pangloss gave instruction in metaphysico-theologico-cosmoloonigology.[5] He proved admirably that there cannot possibly be an effect without a cause and that in this best of all possible worlds the Baron's castle was the best of all castles and his wife the best of all possible Baronesses.

—It is clear, said he, that things cannot be otherwise than they are, for since everything is made to serve an end, everything necessarily serves the best end. Observe: noses were made to support spectacles, hence we have spectacles. Legs, as anyone can plainly see, were made to be breeched, and so we have breeches. Stones were made to be shaped and to build castles with; thus My Lord has a fine castle, for the greatest Baron in the province should have the finest house; and since pigs were made to be eaten, we eat pork all year round.[6] Consequently, those who say everything is well are uttering mere stupidities; they should say everything is for the best.

Candide listened attentively and believed implicitly; for he found Miss Cunégonde exceedingly pretty, though he never had the courage to tell her so. He decided that after the happiness of being born Baron of Thunder-Ten-Tronckh, the second order of happiness was to be Miss Cunégonde; the third was seeing her every day, and the fourth was listening to Master Pangloss, the greatest philosopher in the province and consequently in the entire world.

One day, while Cunégonde was walking near the castle in the little woods that they called a park, she saw Dr. Pangloss in the underbrush; he was giving a lesson in experimental physics to her mother's maid, a very attractive and obedient brunette. As Miss Cunégonde had a natural bent for the sciences, she watched breathlessly the repeated experiments which were going on; she saw clearly the doctor's sufficient reason, observed both cause and effect, and returned to the house in a distracted and pensive frame of mind, yearning for knowledge and dreaming that she might be the sufficient reason of young Candide—who might also be hers.

As she was returning to the castle, she met Candide, and blushed; Candide blushed too. She greeted him in a faltering tone of voice; and Candide talked to her without knowing what he was saying. Next day, as everyone was rising from the dinner table, Cunégonde and Candide found themselves behind a screen; Cunégonde dropped her handkerchief, Candide picked it up; she held his hand quite innocently, he kissed her hand quite innocently with remarkable vivacity and emotion; their lips met, their eyes lit up, their knees trembled, their hands wandered. The Baron of Thunder-Ten-Tronckh passed by the screen and, taking note of this cause and this effect, drove Candide out of the castle by kicking him vigorously on the backside. Cunégonde fainted; as soon as she recovered, the Baroness slapped her face; and everything was confusion in the most beautiful and agreeable of all possible castles.

5. The "looney" buried in this burlesque word corresponds to a buried *nigaud*—"booby" in the French. Christian Wolff, disciple of Leibniz, invented and popularized the word "cosmology." The catch phrases in the following sentence, echoed by popularizers of Leibniz, make reference to the determinism of his system, its linking of cause with effect, and its optimism.

6. The argument from design supposes that everything in this world exists for a specific reason; Voltaire objects not to the argument as a whole, but to the abuse of it.

CHAPTER 2

What Happened to Candide Among the Bulgars[7]

Candide, ejected from the earthly paradise, wandered for a long time without knowing where he was going, weeping, raising his eyes to heaven, and gazing back frequently on the most beautiful of castles which contained the most beautiful of Baron's daughters. He slept without eating, in a furrow of a plowed field, while the snow drifted over him; next morning, numb with cold, he dragged himself into the neighboring village, which was called Waldberghoff-trarbk-dikdorff; he was penniless, famished, and exhausted. At the door of a tavern he paused forlornly. Two men dressed in blue[8] took note of him:

—Look, chum, said one of them, there's a likely young fellow of just about the right size.

They approached Candide and invited him very politely to dine with them.

—Gentlemen, Candide replied with charming modesty, I'm honored by your invitation, but I really don't have enough money to pay my share.

—My dear sir, said one of the blues, people of your appearance and your merit don't have to pay; aren't you five feet five inches tall?

—Yes, gentlemen, that is indeed my stature, said he, making a bow.

—Then, sir, you must be seated at once; not only will we pay your bill this time, we will never allow a man like you to be short of money; for men were made only to render one another mutual aid.

—You are quite right, said Candide; it is just as Dr. Pangloss always told me, and I see clearly that everything is for the best.

They beg him to accept a couple of crowns, he takes them, and offers an I.O.U.; they won't hear of it, and all sit down at table together.

—Don't you love dearly . . . ?

—I do indeed, says he, I dearly love Miss Cunégonde.

—No, no, says one of the gentlemen, we are asking if you don't love dearly the King of the Bulgars.

—Not in the least, says he, I never laid eyes on him.

—What's that you say? He's the most charming of kings, and we must drink his health.

—Oh, gladly, gentlemen; and he drinks.

—That will do, they tell him; you are now the bulwark, the support, the defender, the hero of the Bulgars; your fortune is made and your future assured.

Promptly they slip irons on his legs and lead him to the regiment. There they cause him to right face, left face, present arms, order arms, aim, fire, doubletime, and they give him thirty strokes of the rod. Next day he does the drill a little less awkwardly and gets only twenty strokes; the third day, they give him only ten, and he is regarded by his comrades as a prodigy.

Candide, quite thunderstruck, did not yet understand very clearly how he was a hero. One fine spring morning he took it into his head to go for a walk, stepping straight out as if it were a privilege of the human race, as of animals in general, to

7. Voltaire chose this name to represent the Prussian troops of Frederick the Great because he wanted to make an insinuation of pederasty against both the soldiers and their master. Cf. French *bougre*, English "bugger."

8. The recruiting officers of Frederick the Great, much feared in 18th-century Europe, wore blue uniforms. Frederick had a passion for sorting out his soldiers by size; several of his regiments would accept only six-footers.

use his legs as he chose.[9] He had scarcely covered two leagues when four other heroes, each six feet tall, overtook him, bound him, and threw him into a dungeon. At the court-martial they asked which he preferred, to be flogged thirty-six times by the entire regiment or to receive summarily a dozen bullets in the brain. In vain did he argue that the human will is free and insist that he preferred neither alternative; he had to choose; by virtue of the divine gift called "liberty" he decided to run the gauntlet thirty-six times, and actually endured two floggings. The regiment was composed of two thousand men. That made four thousand strokes, which laid open every muscle and nerve from his nape to his butt. As they were preparing for the third beating, Candide, who could endure no more, begged as a special favor that they would have the goodness to smash his head. His plea was granted; they bandaged his eyes and made him kneel down. The King of the Bulgars, passing by at this moment, was told of the culprit's crime; and as this king had a rare genius, he understood, from everything they told him of Candide, that this was a young metaphysician, extremely ignorant of the ways of the world, so he granted his royal pardon, with a generosity which will be praised in every newspaper in every age. A worthy surgeon cured Candide in three weeks with the ointments described by Dioscorides.[1] He already had a bit of skin back and was able to walk when the King of the Bulgars went to war with the King of the Abares.[2]

CHAPTER 3

How Candide Escaped from the Bulgars, and What Became of Him

Nothing could have been so fine, so brisk, so brilliant, so well-drilled as the two armies. The trumpets, the fifes, the oboes, the drums, and the cannon produced such a harmony as was never heard in hell. First the cannons battered down about six thousand men on each side; then volleys of musket fire removed from the best of worlds about nine or ten thousand rascals who were cluttering up its surface. The bayonet was a sufficient reason for the demise of several thousand others. Total casualties might well amount to thirty thousand men or so. Candide, who was trembling like a philosopher, hid himself as best he could while this heroic butchery was going on.

Finally, while the two kings in their respective camps celebrated the victory by having *Te Deum*s sung, Candide undertook to do his reasoning of cause and effect somewhere else. Passing by mounds of the dead and dying, he came to a nearby village which had been burnt to the ground. It was an Abare village, which the Bulgars had burned, in strict accordance with the laws of war. Here old men, stunned from beatings, watched the last agonies of their butchered wives, who

9. This episode was suggested by the experience of a Frenchman named Courtilz, who had deserted from the Prussian army and been bastinadoed for it. Voltaire intervened with Frederick to gain his release. But it also reflects the story that Wolff, Leibniz's disciple, got into trouble with Frederick's father when someone reported that his doctrine denying free will had encouraged several soldiers to desert. "The argument of the grenadier," who was said to have pleaded preestablished harmony to justify his desertion, so infuriated the king that he had Wolff expelled from the country.

1. Dioscorides' treatise on *materia medica*, dating from the 1st century C.E., was not the most up to date.

2. A tribe of semicivilized Scythians, who might be supposed at war with the Bulgars; allegorically, the Abares are the French, who opposed the Prussians in the Seven Years' War (1756–63). According to the title page of 1761, "Doctor Ralph," the dummy author of *Candide*, himself perished at the battle of Minden (Westphalia) in 1759.

still clutched their infants to their bleeding breasts; there, disemboweled girls, who had first satisfied the natural needs of various heroes, breathed their last; others, half-scorched in the flames, begged for their death stroke. Scattered brains and severed limbs littered the ground.

Candide fled as fast as he could to another village; this one belonged to the Bulgars, and the heroes of the Abare cause had given it the same treatment. Climbing over ruins and stumbling over corpses, Candide finally made his way out of the war area, carrying a little food in his knapsack and never ceasing to dream of Miss Cunégonde. His supplies gave out when he reached Holland; but having heard that everyone in that country was rich and a Christian, he felt confident of being treated as well as he had been in the castle of the Baron before he was kicked out for the love of Miss Cunégonde.

He asked alms of several grave personages, who all told him that if he continued to beg, he would be shut up in a house of correction and set to hard labor.

Finally he approached a man who had just been talking to a large crowd for an hour on end; the topic was charity. Looking doubtfully at him, the orator demanded:

—What are you doing here? Are you here to serve the good cause?

—There is no effect without a cause, said Candide modestly; all events are linked by the chain of necessity and arranged for the best. I had to be driven away from Miss Cunégonde, I had to run the gauntlet, I have to beg my bread until I can earn it; none of this could have happened otherwise.

—Look here, friend, said the orator, do you think the Pope is Antichrist?[3]

—I haven't considered the matter, said Candide; but whether he is or not, I'm in need of bread.

—You don't deserve any, said the other; away with you, you rascal, you rogue, never come near me as long as you live.

Meanwhile, the orator's wife had put her head out of the window, and, seeing a man who was not sure the Pope was Antichrist, emptied over his head a pot full of————Scandalous! The excesses into which women are led by religious zeal!

A man who had never been baptized, a good Anabaptist[4] named Jacques, saw this cruel and heartless treatment being inflicted on one of his fellow creatures, a featherless biped possessing a soul;[5] he took Candide home with him, washed him off, gave him bread and beer, presented him with two florins, and even undertook to give him a job in his Persian-rug factory—for these items are widely manufactured in Holland. Candide, in an ecstasy of gratitude, cried out:

—Master Pangloss was right indeed when he told me everything is for the best in this world; for I am touched by your kindness far more than by the harshness of that black-coated gentleman and his wife.

Next day, while taking a stroll about town, he met a beggar who was covered with pustules, his eyes were sunken, the end of his nose rotted off, his mouth twisted, his teeth black, he had a croaking voice and a hacking cough, and spat a tooth every time he tried to speak.

---

3. Voltaire is satirizing extreme Protestant sects that have sometimes seemed to make hatred of Rome the sum and substance of their creed.

4. Holland, as the home of religious liberty, had offered asylum to the Anabaptists, whose radical views on property and religious discipline had made them unpopular during the 16th century. Granted tolerance, they settled down into respectable burghers. Since this behavior confirmed some of Voltaire's major theses, he had a high opinion of contemporary Anabaptists.

5. Plato's famous minimal definition of man, which he corrected by the addition of a soul to distinguish man from a plucked chicken.

CHAPTER 4

How Candide Met His Old Philosophy Tutor, Doctor Pangloss, and What Came of It

Candide, more touched by compassion even than by horror, gave this ghastly beggar the two florins that he himself had received from his honest Anabaptist friend Jacques. The phantom stared at him, burst into tears, and fell on his neck. Candide drew back in terror.

—Alas, said one wretch to the other, don't you recognize your dear Pangloss any more?

—What are you saying? You, my dear master! you, in this horrible condition? What misfortune has befallen you? Why are you no longer in the most beautiful of castles? What has happened to Miss Cunégonde, that pearl among young ladies, that masterpiece of Nature?

—I am perishing, said Pangloss.

Candide promptly led him into the Anabaptist's stable, where he gave him a crust of bread, and when he had recovered:—Well, said he, Cunégonde?

—Dead, said the other.

Candide fainted. His friend brought him around with a bit of sour vinegar which happened to be in the stable. Candide opened his eyes.

—Cunégonde, dead! Ah, best of worlds, what's become of you now? But how did she die? It wasn't of grief at seeing me kicked out of her noble father's elegant castle?

—Not at all, said Pangloss; she was disemboweled by the Bulgar soldiers, after having been raped to the absolute limit of human endurance; they smashed the Baron's head when he tried to defend her, cut the Baroness to bits, and treated my poor pupil exactly like his sister. As for the castle, not one stone was left on another, not a shed, not a sheep, not a duck, not a tree; but we had the satisfaction of revenge, for the Abares did exactly the same thing to a nearby barony belonging to a Bulgar nobleman.

At this tale Candide fainted again; but having returned to his senses and said everything appropriate to the occasion, he asked about the cause and effect, the sufficient reason, which had reduced Pangloss to his present pitiful state.

—Alas, said he, it was love; love, the consolation of the human race, the preservative of the universe, the soul of all sensitive beings, love, gentle love.

—Unhappy man, said Candide, I too have had some experience of this love, the sovereign of hearts, the soul of our souls; and it never got me anything but a single kiss and twenty kicks in the rear. How could this lovely cause produce in you such a disgusting effect?

Pangloss replied as follows:—My dear Candide! you knew Paquette, that pretty maidservant to our august Baroness. In her arms I tasted the delights of paradise, which directly caused these torments of hell, from which I am now suffering. She was infected with the disease, and has perhaps died of it. Paquette received this present from an erudite Franciscan, who took the pains to trace it back to its source; for he had it from an elderly countess, who picked it up from a captain of cavalry, who acquired it from a marquise, who caught it from a page, who had received it from a Jesuit, who during his novitiate got it directly from one of the companions of Christopher Columbus. As for me, I shall not give it to anyone, for I am a dying man.

—Oh, Pangloss, cried Candide, that's a very strange genealogy. Isn't the devil at the root of the whole thing?

—Not at all, replied that great man; it's an indispensable part of the best of worlds, a necessary ingredient; if Columbus had not caught, on an American island, this sickness which attacks the source of generation and sometimes prevents generation entirely—which thus strikes at and defeats the greatest end of Nature herself—we should have neither chocolate nor cochineal. It must also be noted that until the present time this malady, like religious controversy, has been wholly confined to the continent of Europe. Turks, Indians, Persians, Chinese, Siamese, and Japanese know nothing of it as yet; but there is a sufficient reason for which they in turn will make its acquaintance in a couple of centuries. Meanwhile, it has made splendid progress among us, especially among those big armies of honest, well-trained mercenaries who decide the destinies of nations. You can be sure that when thirty thousand men fight a pitched battle against the same number of the enemy, there will be about twenty thousand with the pox on either side.

—Remarkable indeed, said Candide, but we must see about curing you.

—And how can I do that, said Pangloss, seeing I don't have a cent to my name? There's not a doctor in the whole world who will let your blood or give you an enema without demanding a fee. If you can't pay yourself, you must find someone to pay for you.

These last words decided Candide; he hastened to implore the help of his charitable Anabaptist, Jacques, and painted such a moving picture of his friend's wretched state that the good man did not hesitate to take in Pangloss and have him cured at his own expense. In the course of the cure, Pangloss lost only an eye and an ear. Since he wrote a fine hand and knew arithmetic, the Anabaptist made him his bookkeeper. At the end of two months, being obliged to go to Lisbon on business, he took his two philosophers on the boat with him. Pangloss still maintained that everything was for the best, but Jacques didn't agree with him.

—It must be, said he, that men have corrupted Nature, for they are not born wolves, yet that is what they become. God gave them neither twenty-four-pound cannon nor bayonets, yet they have manufactured both in order to destroy themselves. Bankruptcies have the same effect, and so does the justice which seizes the goods of bankrupts in order to prevent the creditors from getting them.[6]

—It was all indispensable, replied the one-eyed doctor, since private misfortunes make for public welfare, and therefore the more private misfortunes there are, the better everything is.

While he was reasoning, the air grew dark, the winds blew from all directions, and the vessel was attacked by a horrible tempest within sight of Lisbon harbor.

CHAPTER 5

Tempest, Shipwreck, Earthquake, and What Happened to Doctor Pangloss, Candide, and the Anabaptist, Jacques

Half of the passengers, weakened by the frightful anguish of seasickness and the distress of tossing about on stormy waters, were incapable of noticing their danger. The other half shrieked aloud and fell to their prayers, the sails were ripped to shreds, the masts snapped, the vessel opened at the seams. Everyone worked who could stir, nobody listened for orders or issued them. The Anabaptist was lending a hand in the after part of the ship when a frantic sailor struck him

---

6. Voltaire had suffered losses from various bankruptcy proceedings.

and knocked him to the deck; but just at that moment, the sailor lurched so violently that he fell head first over the side, where he hung, clutching a fragment of the broken mast. The good Jacques ran to his aid, and helped him to climb back on board, but in the process was himself thrown into the sea under the very eyes of the sailor, who allowed him to drown without even glancing at him. Candide rushed to the rail, and saw his benefactor rise for a moment to the surface, then sink forever. He wanted to dive to his rescue; but the philosopher Pangloss prevented him by proving that the bay of Lisbon had been formed expressly for this Anabaptist to drown in. While he was proving the point *a priori*, the vessel opened up and everyone perished except for Pangloss, Candide, and the brutal sailor who had caused the virtuous Anabaptist to drown; this rascal swam easily to shore, while Pangloss and Candide drifted there on a plank.

When they had recovered a bit of energy, they set out for Lisbon; they still had a little money with which they hoped to stave off hunger after escaping the storm.

Scarcely had they set foot in the town, still bewailing the loss of their benefactor, when they felt the earth quake underfoot; the sea was lashed to a froth, burst into the port, and smashed all the vessels lying at anchor there. Whirlwinds of fire and ash swirled through the streets and public squares; houses crumbled, roofs came crashing down on foundations, foundations split; thirty thousand inhabitants of every age and either sex were crushed in the ruins.[7] The sailor whistled through his teeth, and said with an oath:—There'll be something to pick up here.

—What can be the sufficient reason of this phenomenon? asked Pangloss.

—The Last Judgment is here, cried Candide.

But the sailor ran directly into the middle of the ruins, heedless of danger in his eagerness for gain; he found some money, laid violent hands on it, got drunk, and, having slept off his wine, bought the favors of the first streetwalker he could find amid the ruins of smashed houses, amid corpses and suffering victims on every hand. Pangloss however tugged at his sleeve.

—My friend, said he, this is not good form at all; your behavior falls short of that required by the universal reason; it's untimely, to say the least.

—Bloody hell, said the other, I'm a sailor, born in Batavia; I've been four times to Japan and stamped four times on the crucifix;[8] get out of here with your universal reason.

Some falling stonework had struck Candide; he lay prostrate in the street, covered with rubble, and calling to Pangloss:—For pity's sake bring me a little wine and oil; I'm dying.

—This earthquake is nothing novel, Pangloss replied; the city of Lima, in South America, underwent much the same sort of tremor, last year; same causes, same effects; there is surely a vein of sulphur under the earth's surface reaching from Lima to Lisbon.

—Nothing is more probable, said Candide; but, for God's sake, a little oil and wine.

7. The great Lisbon earthquake and fire occurred on November 1, 1755; between thirty and forty thousand deaths resulted.
8. The Japanese, originally receptive to foreign visitors, grew fearful that priests and proselytizers were merely advance agents of empire and expelled both the Portuguese and Spanish early in the 17th century. Only the Dutch were allowed to retain a small foothold, under humiliating conditions, of which the notion of stamping on the crucifix is symbolic. It was never what Voltaire suggests here, an actual requirement for entering the country.

—What do you mean, probable? replied the philosopher; I regard the case as proved.

Candide fainted and Pangloss brought him some water from a nearby fountain.

Next day, as they wandered amid the ruins, they found a little food which restored some of their strength. Then they fell to work like the others, bringing relief to those of the inhabitants who had escaped death. Some of the citizens whom they rescued gave them a dinner as good as was possible under the circumstances; it is true that the meal was a melancholy one, and the guests watered their bread with tears; but Pangloss consoled them by proving that things could not possibly be otherwise.

—For, said he, all this is for the best, since if there is a volcano at Lisbon, it cannot be somewhere else, since it is unthinkable that things should not be where they are, since everything is well.

A little man in black, an officer of the Inquisition,[9] who was sitting beside him, politely took up the question, and said:—It would seem that the gentleman does not believe in original sin, since if everything is for the best, man has not fallen and is not liable to eternal punishment.

—I most humbly beg pardon of your excellency, Pangloss answered, even more politely, but the fall of man and the curse of original sin entered necessarily into the best of all possible worlds.

—Then you do not believe in free will? said the officer.

—Your excellency must excuse me, said Pangloss; free will agrees very well with absolute necessity, for it was necessary that we should be free, since a will which is determined . . .

Pangloss was in the middle of his sentence, when the officer nodded significantly to the attendant who was pouring him a glass of port, or Oporto, wine.

CHAPTER 6

How They Made a Fine Auto-da-Fé to Prevent Earthquakes, and How Candide Was Whipped

After the earthquake had wiped out three quarters of Lisbon, the learned men of the land could find no more effective way of averting total destruction than to give the people a fine auto-da-fé;[1] the University of Coimbra had established that the spectacle of several persons being roasted over a slow fire with full ceremonial rites is an infallible specific against earthquakes.

In consequence, the authorities had rounded up a Biscayan convicted of marrying a woman who had stood godmother to his child, and two Portuguese who while eating a chicken had set aside a bit of bacon used for seasoning.[2] After dinner, men came with ropes to tie up Doctor Pangloss and his disciple Candide, one for talking and the other for listening with an air of approval; both were taken separately to a set of remarkably cool apartments, where the glare of the sun is

9. Specifically, a *familier* or *poursuivant*, an undercover agent with powers of arrest.

1. Literally, "act of faith," a public ceremony of repentance and humiliation. Such an auto-da-fé was actually held in Lisbon, June 20, 1756.

2. The Biscayan's fault lay in marrying someone within the forbidden bounds of relationship, an act of spiritual incest. The men who declined pork or bacon were understood to be crypto-Jews.

never bothersome; eight days later they were both dressed in *san-benitos* and crowned with paper mitres;[3] Candide's mitre and *san-benito* were decorated with inverted flames and with devils who had neither tails nor claws; but Pangloss's devils had both tails and claws, and his flames stood upright. Wearing these costumes, they marched in a procession, and listened to a very touching sermon, followed by a beautiful concert of plainsong. Candide was flogged in cadence to the music; the Biscayan and the two men who had avoided bacon were burned, and Pangloss was hanged, though hanging is not customary. On the same day there was another earthquake, causing frightful damage.[4]

Candide, stunned, stupefied, despairing, bleeding, trembling, said to himself:—If this is the best of all possible worlds, what are the others like? The flogging is not so bad, I was flogged by the Bulgars. But oh my dear Pangloss, greatest of philosophers, was it necessary for me to watch you being hanged, for no reason that I can see? Oh my dear Anabaptist, best of men, was it necessary that you should be drowned in the port? Oh Miss Cunégonde, pearl of young ladies, was it necessary that you should have your belly slit open?

He was being led away, barely able to stand, lectured, lashed, absolved, and blessed, when an old woman approached and said,—My son, be of good cheer and follow me.

CHAPTER 7

How an Old Woman Took Care of Candide, and How He Regained What He Loved

Candide was of very bad cheer, but he followed the old woman to a shanty; she gave him a jar of ointment to rub himself, left him food and drink; she showed him a tidy little bed; next to it was a suit of clothing.

—Eat, drink, sleep, she said; and may Our Lady of Atocha, Our Lord St. Anthony of Padua, and Our Lord St. James of Compostela watch over you. I will be back tomorrow.

Candide, still completely astonished by everything he had seen and suffered, and even more by the old woman's kindness, offered to kiss her hand.

—It's not *my* hand you should be kissing, said she. I'll be back tomorrow; rub yourself with the ointment, eat and sleep.

In spite of his many sufferings, Candide ate and slept. Next day the old woman returned bringing breakfast; she looked at his back and rubbed it herself with another ointment; she came back with lunch; and then she returned in the evening, bringing supper. Next day she repeated the same routine.

—Who are you? Candide asked continually. Who told you to be so kind to me? How can I ever repay you?

The good woman answered not a word; she returned in the evening, and without food.

—Come with me, says she, and don't speak a word.

Taking him by the hand, she walks out into the countryside with him for about a quarter of a mile; they reach an isolated house, quite surrounded by gardens

3. The cone-shaped paper cap (intended to resemble a bishop's mitre) and flowing yellow cape were customary garb for those pleading before the Inquisition.

4. In fact, the second quake occurred December 21, 1755.

and ditches. The old woman knocks at a little gate, it opens. She takes Candide up a secret stairway to a gilded room furnished with a fine brocaded sofa; there she leaves him, closes the door, disappears. Candide stood as if entranced; his life, which had seemed like a nightmare so far, was now starting to look like a delightful dream.

Soon the old woman returned; on her feeble shoulder leaned a trembling woman, of a splendid figure, glittering in diamonds, and veiled.

—Remove the veil, said the old woman to Candide.

The young man stepped timidly forward, and lifted the veil. What an event! What a surprise! Could it be Miss Cunégonde? Yes, it really was! She herself! His knees give way, speech fails him, he falls at her feet, Cunégonde collapses on the sofa. The old woman plies them with brandy, they return to their senses, they exchange words. At first they could utter only broken phrases, questions and answers at cross purposes, sighs, tears, exclamations. The old woman warned them not to make too much noise, and left them alone.

—Then it's really you, said Candide, you're alive, I've found you again in Portugal. Then you never were raped? You never had your belly ripped open, as the philosopher Pangloss assured me?

—Oh yes, said the lovely Cunégonde, but one doesn't always die of these two accidents.

—But your father and mother were murdered then?

—All too true, said Cunégonde, in tears.

—And your brother?

—Killed too.

—And why are you in Portugal? and how did you know I was here? and by what device did you have me brought to this house?

—I shall tell you everything, the lady replied; but first you must tell me what has happened to you since that first innocent kiss we exchanged and the kicking you got because of it.

Candide obeyed her with profound respect; and though he was overcome, though his voice was weak and hesitant, though he still had twinges of pain from his beating, he described as simply as possible everything that had happened to him since the time of their separation. Cunégonde lifted her eyes to heaven; she wept at the death of the good Anabaptist and at that of Pangloss; after which she told the following story to Candide, who listened to every word while he gazed on her with hungry eyes.

CHAPTER 8

Cunégonde's Story

—I was in my bed and fast asleep when heaven chose to send the Bulgars into our castle of Thunder-Ten-Tronckh. They butchered my father and brother, and hacked my mother to bits. An enormous Bulgar, six feet tall, seeing that I had swooned from horror at the scene, set about raping me; at that I recovered my senses, I screamed and scratched, bit and fought, I tried to tear the eyes out of that big Bulgar—not realizing that everything which had happened in my father's castle was a mere matter of routine. The brute then stabbed me with a knife on my left thigh, where I still bear the scar.

—What a pity! I should very much like to see it, said the simple Candide.

—You shall, said Cunégonde; but shall I go on?

—Please do, said Candide.

So she took up the thread of her tale:—A Bulgar captain appeared, he saw me covered with blood and the soldier too intent to get up. Shocked by the monster's failure to come to attention, the captain killed him on my body. He then had my wound dressed, and took me off to his quarters, as a prisoner of war. I laundered his few shirts and did his cooking; he found me attractive, I confess it, and I won't deny that he was a handsome fellow, with a smooth, white skin; apart from that, however, little wit, little philosophical training; it was evident that he had not been brought up by Doctor Pangloss. After three months, he had lost all his money and grown sick of me; so he sold me to a Jew named Don Issachar, who traded in Holland and Portugal, and who was mad after women. This Jew developed a mighty passion for my person, but he got nowhere with it; I held him off better than I had done with the Bulgar soldier; for though a person of honor may be raped once, her virtue is only strengthened by the experience. In order to keep me hidden, the Jew brought me to his country house, which you see here. Till then I had thought there was nothing on earth so beautiful as the castle of Thunder-Ten-Tronckh; I was now undeceived.

—One day the Grand Inquisitor took notice of me at mass; he ogled me a good deal, and made known that he must talk to me on a matter of secret business. I was taken to his palace; I told him of my rank; he pointed out that it was beneath my dignity to belong to an Israelite. A suggestion was then conveyed to Don Issachar that he should turn me over to My Lord the Inquisitor. Don Issachar, who is court banker and a man of standing, refused out of hand. The inquisitor threatened him with an auto-da-fé. Finally my Jew, fearing for his life, struck a bargain by which the house and I would belong to both of them as joint tenants; the Jew would get Mondays, Wednesdays, and the Sabbath, the inquisitor would get the other days of the week. That has been the arrangement for six months now. There have been quarrels; sometimes it has not been clear whether the night from Saturday to Sunday belonged to the old or the new dispensation. For my part, I have so far been able to hold both of them off; and that, I think, is why they are both still in love with me.

—Finally, in order to avert further divine punishment by earthquake, and to terrify Don Issachar, My Lord the Inquisitor chose to celebrate an auto-da-fé. He did me the honor of inviting me to attend. I had an excellent seat; the ladies were served with refreshments between the mass and the execution. To tell you the truth, I was horrified to see them burn alive those two Jews and that decent Biscayan who had married his child's godmother; but what was my surprise, my terror, my grief, when I saw, huddled in a *san-benito* and wearing a mitre, someone who looked like Pangloss! I rubbed my eyes, I watched his every move, I saw him hanged; and I fell back in a swoon. Scarcely had I come to my senses again, when I saw you stripped for the lash; that was the peak of my horror, consternation, grief, and despair. I may tell you, by the way, that your skin is even whiter and more delicate than that of my Bulgar captain. Seeing you, then, redoubled the torments which were already overwhelming me. I shrieked aloud, I wanted to call out, 'Let him go, you brutes!' but my voice died within me, and my cries would have been useless. When you had been thoroughly thrashed: 'How can it be,' I asked myself, 'that agreeable Candide and wise Pangloss have come to Lisbon, one to receive a hundred whiplashes, the other to be hanged by order of My Lord the Inquisitor, whose mistress I am? Pangloss must have deceived me cruelly when he told me that all is for the best in this world.'

—Frantic, exhausted, half out of my senses, and ready to die of weakness, I felt as if my mind were choked with the massacre of my father, my mother, my brother, with the arrogance of that ugly Bulgar soldier, with the knife slash he inflicted on me, my slavery, my cookery, my Bulgar captain, my nasty Don Issachar, my abominable inquisitor, with the hanging of Doctor Pangloss, with that great plainsong *miserere* which they sang while they flogged you—and above all, my mind was full of the kiss which I gave you behind the screen, on the day I saw you for the last time. I praised God, who had brought you back to me after so many trials. I asked my old woman to look out for you, and to bring you here as soon as she could. She did just as I asked; I have had the indescribable joy of seeing you again, hearing you and talking with you once more. But you must be frightfully hungry; I am, myself; let us begin with a dinner.

So then and there they sat down to table; and after dinner, they adjourned to that fine brocaded sofa, which has already been mentioned; and there they were when the eminent Don Issachar, one of the masters of the house, appeared. It was the day of the Sabbath; he was arriving to assert his rights and express his tender passion.

CHAPTER 9

What Happened to Cunégonde, Candide, the Grand Inquisitor,
and a Jew

This Issachar was the most choleric Hebrew seen in Israel since the Babylonian captivity.

—What's this, says he, you bitch of a Christian, you're not satisfied with the Grand Inquisitor? Do I have to share you with this rascal, too?

So saying, he drew a long dagger, with which he always went armed, and, supposing his opponent defenceless, flung himself on Candide. But our good Westphalian had received from the old woman, along with his suit of clothes, a fine sword. Out it came, and though his manners were of the gentlest, in short order he laid the Israelite stiff and cold on the floor, at the feet of the lovely Cunégonde.

—Holy Virgin! she cried. What will become of me now? A man killed in my house! If the police find out, we're done for.

—If Pangloss had not been hanged, said Candide, he would give us good advice in this hour of need, for he was a great philosopher. Lacking him, let's ask the old woman.

She was a sensible body, and was just starting to give her opinion of the situation, when another little door opened. It was just one o'clock in the morning, Sunday morning. This day belonged to the inquisitor. In he came, and found the whipped Candide with a sword in his hand, a corpse at his feet, Cunégonde in terror, and an old woman giving them both good advice.

Here now is what passed through Candide's mind in this instant of time; this is how he reasoned:—If this holy man calls for help, he will certainly have me burned, and perhaps Cunégonde as well; he has already had me whipped without mercy; he is my rival; I have already killed once; why hesitate?

It was a quick, clear chain of reasoning; without giving the inquisitor time to recover from his surprise, he ran him through, and laid him beside the Jew.

—Here you've done it again, said Cunégonde; there's no hope for us now. We'll be excommunicated, our last hour has come. How is it that you, who were born so gentle, could kill in two minutes a Jew and a prelate?

—My dear girl, replied Candide, when a man is in love, jealous, and just whipped by the Inquisition, he is no longer himself.

The old woman now spoke up and said:—There are three Andalusian steeds in the stable, with their saddles and bridles; our brave Candide must get them ready: my lady has some gold coin and diamonds; let's take to horse at once, though I can only ride on one buttock; we will go to Cadiz. The weather is as fine as can be, and it is pleasant to travel in the cool of the evening.

Promptly, Candide saddled the three horses. Cunégonde, the old woman, and he covered thirty miles without a stop. While they were fleeing, the Holy Brotherhood[5] came to investigate the house; they buried the inquisitor in a fine church, and threw Issachar on the dunghill.

Candide, Cunégonde, and the old woman were already in the little town of Avacena, in the middle of the Sierra Morena; and there, as they sat in a country inn, they had this conversation.

CHAPTER 10

In Deep Distress, Candide, Cunégonde, and the Old Woman Reach Cadiz; They Put to Sea

—Who then could have robbed me of my gold and diamonds? said Cunégonde, in tears. How shall we live? what shall we do? where shall I find other inquisitors and Jews to give me some more?

—Ah, said the old woman, I strongly suspect that reverend Franciscan friar who shared the inn with us yesterday at Badajoz. God save me from judging him unfairly! But he came into our room twice, and he left long before us.

—Alas, said Candide, the good Pangloss often proved to me that the fruits of the earth are a common heritage of all, to which each man has equal right. On these principles, the Franciscan should at least have left us enough to finish our journey. You have nothing at all, my dear Cunégonde?

—Not a maravedi, said she.

—What to do? said Candide.

—We'll sell one of the horses, said the old woman; I'll ride on the croup behind my mistress, though only on one buttock, and so we will get to Cadiz.

There was in the same inn a Benedictine prior; he bought the horse cheap. Candide, Cunégonde, and the old woman passed through Lucena, Chillas, and Lebrixa, and finally reached Cadiz. There a fleet was being fitted out and an army assembled, to reason with the Jesuit fathers in Paraguay, who were accused of fomenting among their flock a revolt against the kings of Spain and Portugal near the town of St. Sacrement.[6] Candide, having served in the Bulgar army, performed the Bulgar manual of arms before the general of the little army with such grace, swiftness, dexterity, fire, and agility, that they gave him a company of infantry to command. So here he is, a captain; and off he sails with Miss Cunégonde, the old woman, two valets, and the two Andalusian steeds which had belonged to My Lord the Grand Inquisitor of Portugal.

---

5. A semireligious order with police powers, very active in 18th-century Spain.
6. Actually, Colonia del Sacramento. Voltaire took great interest in the Jesuit role in Paraguay, which he has much oversimplified and largely misrepresented here in the interests of his satire. In 1750 they did, however, offer armed resistance to an agreement made between Spain and Portugal. They were subdued and expelled in 1769.

Throughout the crossing, they spent a great deal of time reasoning about the philosophy of poor Pangloss.

—We are destined, in the end, for another universe, said Candide; no doubt that is the one where everything is well. For in this one, it must be admitted, there is some reason to grieve over our physical and moral state.

—I love you with all my heart, said Cunégonde; but my soul is still harrowed by thoughts of what I have seen and suffered.

—All will be well, replied Candide; the sea of this new world is already better than those of Europe, calmer and with steadier winds. Surely it is the New World which is the best of all possible worlds.

—God grant it, said Cunégonde; but I have been so horribly unhappy in the world so far, that my heart is almost dead to hope.

—You pity yourselves, the old woman told them; but you have had no such misfortunes as mine.

Cunégonde nearly broke out laughing; she found the old woman comic in pretending to be more unhappy than she.

—Ah, you poor old thing, said she, unless you've been raped by two Bulgars, been stabbed twice in the belly, seen two of your castles destroyed, witnessed the murder of two of your mothers and two of your fathers, and watched two of your lovers being whipped in an auto-da-fé, I do not see how you can have had it worse than me. Besides, I was born a baroness, with seventy-two quarterings, and I have worked in a scullery.

—My lady, replied the old woman, you do not know my birth and rank; and if I showed you my rear end, you would not talk as you do, you might even speak with less assurance.

These words inspired great curiosity in Candide and Cunégonde, which the old woman satisfied with this story.

CHAPTER 11

The Old Woman's Story

—My eyes were not always bloodshot and red-rimmed, my nose did not always touch my chin, and I was not born a servant. I am in fact the daughter of Pope Urban the Tenth and the Princess of Palestrina.[7] Till the age of fourteen, I lived in a palace so splendid that all the castles of all your German barons would not have served it as a stable; a single one of my dresses was worth more than all the assembled magnificence of Westphalia. I grew in beauty, in charm, in talent, surrounded by pleasures, dignities, and glowing visions of the future. Already I was inspiring the young men to love; my breast was formed—and what a breast! white, firm, with the shape of the Venus de Medici;[8] and what eyes! what lashes, what black brows! What fire flashed from my glances and outshone the glitter of the stars, as the local poets used to tell me! The women who helped me dress and undress fell into ecstasies, whether they looked at me from in front or behind; and all the men wanted to be in their place.

7. Voltaire left behind a comment on this passage, a note first published in 1829: "Note the extreme discretion of the author; hitherto there has never been a pope named Urban X; he avoided attributing a bastard to a known pope. What circumspection! what an exquisite conscience!"

8. A famous Roman sculpture of Venus in marble from the 1st century B.C.E. that belonged to the Medici family in Italy; 18th-century Europeans considered it to be one of the best surviving works of art from ancient times.

—I was engaged to the ruling prince of Massa-Carrara; and what a prince he was! as handsome as I, softness and charm compounded, brilliantly witty, and madly in love with me. I loved him in return as one loves for the first time, with a devotion approaching idolatry. The wedding preparations had been made, with a splendor and magnificence never heard of before; nothing but celebrations, masks, and comic operas, uninterruptedly; and all Italy composed in my honor sonnets of which not one was even passable. I had almost attained the very peak of bliss, when an old marquise who had been the mistress of my prince invited him to her house for a cup of chocolate. He died in less than two hours, amid horrifying convulsions. But that was only a trifle. My mother, in complete despair (though less afflicted than I), wished to escape for a while the oppressive atmosphere of grief. She owned a handsome property near Gaeta.[9] We embarked on a papal galley gilded like the altar of St. Peter's in Rome. Suddenly a pirate ship from Salé swept down and boarded us. Our soldiers defended themselves as papal troops usually do; falling on their knees and throwing down their arms, they begged of the corsair absolution *in articulo mortis*.[1]

—They were promptly stripped as naked as monkeys, and so was my mother, and so were our maids of honor, and so was I too. It's a very remarkable thing, the energy these gentlemen put into stripping people. But what surprised me even more was that they stuck their fingers in a place where we women usually admit only a syringe. This ceremony seemed a bit odd to me, as foreign usages always do when one hasn't traveled. They only wanted to see if we didn't have some diamonds hidden there; and I soon learned that it's a custom of long standing among the genteel folk who swarm the seas. I learned that my lords the very religious knights of Malta never overlook this ceremony when they capture Turks, whether male or female; it's one of those international laws which have never been questioned.

—I won't try to explain how painful it is for a young princess to be carried off into slavery in Morocco with her mother. You can imagine everything we had to suffer on the pirate ship. My mother was still very beautiful; our maids of honor, our mere chambermaids, were more charming than anything one could find in all Africa. As for myself, I was ravishing, I was loveliness and grace supreme, and I was a virgin. I did not remain so for long; the flower which had been kept for the handsome prince of Massa-Carrara was plucked by the corsair captain; he was an abominable negro, who thought he was doing me a great favor. My Lady the Princess of Palestrina and I must have been strong indeed to bear what we did during our journey to Morocco. But on with my story; these are such common matters that they are not worth describing.

—Morocco was knee deep in blood when we arrived. Of the fifty sons of the emperor Muley-Ismael,[2] each had his faction, which produced in effect fifty civil wars, of blacks against blacks, of blacks against browns, halfbreeds against halfbreeds; throughout the length and breadth of the empire, nothing but one continual carnage.

—Scarcely had we stepped ashore, when some negroes of a faction hostile to my captor arrived to take charge of his plunder. After the diamonds and gold, we women were the most prized possessions. I was now witness of a struggle such as

9. About halfway between Rome and Naples.
1. Literally, when at the point of death. Absolution from a corsair in the act of murdering one is of very dubious validity.

2. Having reigned for more than fifty years, a potent and ruthless sultan of Morocco, he died in 1727 and left his kingdom in much the condition described.

you never see in the temperate climate of Europe. Northern people don't have hot blood; they don't feel the absolute fury for women which is common in Africa. Europeans seem to have milk in their veins; it is vitriol or liquid fire which pulses through these people around Mount Atlas. The fight for possession of us raged with the fury of the lions, tigers, and poisonous vipers of that land. A Moor snatched my mother by the right arm, the first mate held her by the left; a Moorish soldier grabbed one leg, one of our pirates the other. In a moment's time almost all our girls were being dragged four different ways. My captain held me behind him while with his scimitar he killed everyone who braved his fury. At last I saw all our Italian women, including my mother, torn to pieces, cut to bits, murdered by the monsters who were fighting over them. My captive companions, their captors, soldiers, sailors, blacks, browns, whites, mulattoes, and at last my captain, all were killed, and I remained half dead on a mountain of corpses. Similar scenes were occurring, as is well known, for more than three hundred leagues around, without anyone skimping on the five prayers a day decreed by Mohammed.

—With great pain, I untangled myself from this vast heap of bleeding bodies, and dragged myself under a great orange tree by a neighboring brook, where I collapsed, from terror, exhaustion, horror, despair, and hunger. Shortly, my weary mind surrendered to a sleep which was more of a swoon than a rest. I was in this state of weakness and languor, between life and death, when I felt myself touched by something which moved over my body. Opening my eyes, I saw a white man, rather attractive, who was groaning and saying under his breath: '*O che sciagura d'essere senza coglioni!*'[3]

CHAPTER 12

The Old Woman's Story Continued

—Amazed and delighted to hear my native tongue, and no less surprised by what this man was saying, I told him that there were worse evils than those he was complaining of. In a few words, I described to him the horrors I had undergone, and then fainted again. He carried me to a nearby house, put me to bed, gave me something to eat, served me, flattered me, comforted me, told me he had never seen anyone so lovely, and added that he had never before regretted so much the loss of what nobody could give him back.

'I was born at Naples,' he told me, 'where they caponize two or three thousand children every year; some die of it, others acquire a voice more beautiful than any woman's, still others go on to become governors of kingdoms.[4] The operation was a great success with me, and I became court musician to the Princess of Palestrina . . .'

'Of my mother,' I exclaimed.

'Of your mother,' cried he, bursting into tears; 'then you must be the princess whom I raised till she was six, and who already gave promise of becoming as beautiful as you are now!'

'I am that very princess; my mother lies dead, not a hundred yards from here, buried under a pile of corpses.'

---

3. "Oh what a misfortune to have no testicles!"
4. The castrato Farinelli (1705–1782), originally a singer, came to exercise considerable political influence on the kings of Spain, Philip V and Ferdinand VI.

—I told him my adventures, he told me his: that he had been sent by a Christian power to the King of Morocco, to conclude a treaty granting him gunpowder, cannon, and ships with which to liquidate the traders of the other Christian powers.

'My mission is concluded,' said this honest eunuch; 'I shall take ship at Ceuta and bring you back to Italy. *Ma che sciagura d'essere senza coglioni!*'

—I thanked him with tears of gratitude, and instead of returning me to Italy, he took me to Algiers and sold me to the dey of that country. Hardly had the sale taken place, when that plague which has made the rounds of Africa, Asia, and Europe broke out in full fury at Algiers. You have seen earthquakes; but tell me, young lady, have you ever had the plague?

—Never, replied the baroness.

—If you had had it, said the old woman, you would agree that it is far worse than an earthquake. It is very frequent in Africa, and I had it. Imagine, if you will, the situation of a pope's daughter, fifteen years old, who in three months' time had experienced poverty, slavery, had been raped almost every day, had seen her mother quartered, had suffered from famine and war, and who now was dying of pestilence in Algiers. As a matter of fact, I did not die; but the eunuch and the dey and nearly the entire seraglio of Algiers perished.

—When the first horrors of this ghastly plague had passed, the slaves of the dey were sold. A merchant bought me and took me to Tunis; there he sold me to another merchant, who resold me at Tripoli; from Tripoli I was sold to Alexandria, from Alexandria resold to Smyrna, from Smyrna to Constantinople. I ended by belonging to an aga of janizaries, who was shortly ordered to defend Azov against the besieging Russians.[5]

—The aga, who was a gallant soldier, took his whole seraglio with him, and established us in a little fort amid the Maeotian marshes,[6] guarded by two black eunuchs and twenty soldiers. Our side killed a prodigious number of Russians, but they paid us back nicely. Azov was put to fire and sword without respect for age or sex; only our little fort continued to resist, and the enemy determined to starve us out. The twenty janizaries had sworn never to surrender. Reduced to the last extremities of hunger, they were forced to eat our two eunuchs, lest they violate their oaths. After several more days, they decided to eat the women too.

—We had an imam,[7] very pious and sympathetic, who delivered an excellent sermon, persuading them not to kill us altogether.

'Just cut off a single rumpsteak from each of these ladies,' he said, 'and you'll have a fine meal. Then if you should need another, you can come back in a few days and have as much again; heaven will bless your charitable action, and you will be saved.'

—His eloquence was splendid, and he persuaded them. We underwent this horrible operation. The imam treated us all with the ointment that they use on newly circumcised children. We were at the point of death.

—Scarcely had the janizaries finished the meal for which we furnished the materials, when the Russians appeared in flat-bottomed boats; not a janizary escaped. The Russians paid no attention to the state we were in; but there are French physicians everywhere, and one of them, who knew his trade, took care of

---

5. Azov, near the mouth of the Don, was besieged by the Russians under Peter the Great in 1695–96. "Janizaries": an elite corps of the Ottoman armies.

6. The Roman name of the so-called Sea of Azov, a shallow swampy lake near the town.

7. In effect, a chaplain.

us. He cured us, and I shall remember all my life that when my wounds were healed, he made me a proposition. For the rest, he counselled us simply to have patience, assuring us that the same thing had happened in several other sieges, and that it was according to the laws of war.

—As soon as my companions could walk, we were herded off to Moscow. In the division of booty, I fell to a boyar who made me work in his garden, and gave me twenty whiplashes a day; but when he was broken on the wheel after about two years, with thirty other boyars, over some little court intrigue,[8] I seized the occasion; I ran away; I crossed all Russia; I was for a long time a chambermaid in Riga, then at Rostock, Vismara, Leipzig, Cassel, Utrecht, Leyden, The Hague, Rotterdam; I grew old in misery and shame, having only half a backside and remembering always that I was the daughter of a Pope; a hundred times I wanted to kill myself, but always I loved life more. This ridiculous weakness is perhaps one of our worst instincts; is anything more stupid than choosing to carry a burden that really one wants to cast on the ground? to hold existence in horror, and yet to cling to it? to fondle the serpent which devours us till it has eaten out our heart?

—In the countries through which I have been forced to wander, in the taverns where I have had to work, I have seen a vast number of people who hated their existence; but I never saw more than a dozen who deliberately put an end to their own misery: three negroes, four Englishmen, four Genevans, and a German professor named Robeck.[9] My last post was as servant to the Jew Don Issachar; he attached me to your service, my lovely one; and I attached myself to your destiny, till I have become more concerned with your fate than with my own. I would not even have mentioned my own misfortunes, if you had not irked me a bit, and if it weren't the custom, on shipboard, to pass the time with stories. In a word, my lady, I have had some experience of the world, I know it; why not try this diversion? Ask every passenger on this ship to tell you his story, and if you find a single one who has not often cursed the day of his birth, who has not often told himself that he is the most miserable of men, then you may throw me overboard head first.

CHAPTER 13

How Candide Was Forced to Leave the Lovely Cunégonde and the Old Woman

Having heard out the old woman's story, the lovely Cunégonde paid her the respects which were appropriate to a person of her rank and merit. She took up the wager as well, and got all the passengers, one after another, to tell her their adventures. She and Candide had to agree that the old woman had been right.

—It's certainly too bad, said Candide, that the wise Pangloss was hanged, contrary to the custom of auto-da-fé; he would have admirable things to say of the physical evil and moral evil which cover land and sea, and I might feel within me the impulse to dare to raise several polite objections.

8. Voltaire had in mind an ineffectual conspiracy against Peter the Great known as the "revolt of the streltsy" or musketeers, which took place in 1698. Though easily put down, it provoked from the emperor a massive and atrocious program of reprisals.

9. Johann Robeck (1672–1739) published a treatise advocating suicide and showed his conviction by drowning himself at the age of sixty-seven.

As the passengers recited their stories, the boat made steady progress, and presently landed at Buenos Aires. Cunégonde, Captain Candide, and the old woman went to call on the governor, Don Fernando d'Ibaraa y Figueroa y Mascarenes y Lampourdos y Souza. This nobleman had the pride appropriate to a man with so many names. He addressed everyone with the most aristocratic disdain, pointing his nose so loftily, raising his voice so mercilessly, lording it so splendidly, and assuming so arrogant a pose, that everyone who met him wanted to kick him. He loved women to the point of fury; and Cunégonde seemed to him the most beautiful creature he had ever seen. The first thing he did was to ask directly if she were the captain's wife. His manner of asking this question disturbed Candide; he did not dare say she was his wife, because in fact she was not; he did not dare say she was his sister, because she wasn't that either; and though this polite lie was once common enough among the ancients,[1] and sometimes serves moderns very well, he was too pure of heart to tell a lie.

—Miss Cunégonde, said he, is betrothed to me, and we humbly beg your excellency to perform the ceremony for us.

Don Fernando d'Ibaraa y Figueroa y Mascarenes y Lampourdos y Souza twirled his moustache, smiled sardonically, and ordered Captain Candide to go drill his company. Candide obeyed. Left alone with My Lady Cunégonde, the governor declared his passion, and protested that he would marry her tomorrow, in church or in any other manner, as it pleased her charming self. Cunégonde asked for a quarter-hour to collect herself, consult the old woman, and make up her mind.

The old woman said to Cunégonde:—My lady, you have seventy-two quarterings and not one penny; if you wish, you may be the wife of the greatest lord in South America, who has a really handsome moustache; are you going to insist on your absolute fidelity? You have already been raped by the Bulgars; a Jew and an inquisitor have enjoyed your favors; miseries entitle one to privileges. I assure you that in your position I would make no scruple of marrying My Lord the Governor, and making the fortune of Captain Candide.

While the old woman was talking with all the prudence of age and experience, there came into the harbor a small ship bearing an alcalde and some alguazils.[2] This is what had happened.

As the old woman had very shrewdly guessed, it was a long-sleeved Franciscan who stole Cunégonde's gold and jewels in the town of Badajoz, when she and Candide were in flight. The monk tried to sell some of the gems to a jeweler, who recognized them as belonging to the Grand Inquisitor. Before he was hanged, the Franciscan confessed that he had stolen them, indicating who his victims were and where they were going. The flight of Cunégonde and Candide was already known. They were traced to Cadiz, and a vessel was hastily dispatched in pursuit of them. This vessel was now in the port of Buenos Aires. The rumor spread that an alcalde was aboard, in pursuit of the murderers of My Lord the Grand Inquisitor. The shrewd old woman saw at once what was to be done.

—You cannot escape, she told Cunégonde, and you have nothing to fear. You are not the one who killed my lord, and, besides, the governor, who is in love with you, won't let you be mistreated. Sit tight.

And then she ran straight to Candide:—Get out of town, she said, or you'll be burned within the hour.

---

1. Voltaire has in mind Abraham's adventures with Sarah (Genesis 12) and Isaac's with Rebecca (Genesis 26).
2. Police officers.

There was not a moment to lose; but how to leave Cunégonde, and where to go?

CHAPTER 14

How Candide and Cacambo Were Received by the Jesuits of Paraguay

Candide had brought from Cadiz a valet of the type one often finds in the provinces of Spain and in the colonies. He was one quarter Spanish, son of a half-breed in the Tucuman;[3] he had been choirboy, sacristan, sailor, monk, merchant, soldier, and lackey. His name was Cacambo, and he was very fond of his master because his master was a very good man. In hot haste he saddled the two Andalusian steeds.

—Hurry, master, do as the old woman says; let's get going and leave this town without a backward look.

Candide wept:—O my beloved Cunégonde! must I leave you now, just when the governor is about to marry us! Cunégonde, brought from so far, what will ever become of you?

—She'll become what she can, said Cacambo; women can always find something to do with themselves; God sees to it; let's get going.

—Where are you taking me? where are we going? what will we do without Cunégonde? said Candide.

—By Saint James of Compostela, said Cacambo, you were going to make war against the Jesuits, now we'll go make war for them. I know the roads pretty well, I'll bring you to their country, they will be delighted to have a captain who knows the Bulgar drill; you'll make a prodigious fortune. If you don't get your rights in one world, you will find them in another. And isn't it pleasant to see new things and do new things?

—Then you've already been in Paraguay? said Candide.

—Indeed I have, replied Cacambo; I was cook in the College of the Assumption, and I know the government of Los Padres[4] as I know the streets of Cadiz. It's an admirable thing, this government. The kingdom is more than three hundred leagues across; it is divided into thirty provinces. Los Padres own everything in it, and the people nothing; it's a masterpiece of reason and justice. I myself know nothing so wonderful as Los Padres, who in this hemisphere make war on the kings of Spain and Portugal, but in Europe hear their confessions; who kill Spaniards here, and in Madrid send them to heaven; that really tickles me; let's get moving, you're going to be the happiest of men. Won't Los Padres be delighted when they learn they have a captain who knows the Bulgar drill!

As soon as they reached the first barricade, Cacambo told the frontier guard that a captain wished to speak with My Lord the Commander. A Paraguayan officer ran to inform headquarters by laying the news at the feet of the commander. Candide and Cacambo were first disarmed and deprived of their Andalusian horses. They were then placed between two files of soldiers; the commander was at the end, his three-cornered hat on his head, his cassock drawn up, a sword at his side, and a pike in his hand. He nods, and twenty-four soldiers surround the newcomers. A sergeant then informs them that they must wait, that the commander

---

3. A province of Argentina, to the northwest of Buenos Aires.   4. The Jesuit fathers.

cannot talk to them, since the reverend father provincial has forbidden all Spaniards from speaking, except in his presence, and from remaining more than three hours in the country.

—And where is the reverend father provincial? says Cacambo.

—He is reviewing his troops after having said mass, the sergeant replies, and you'll only be able to kiss his spurs in three hours.

—But, says Cacambo, my master the captain, who, like me, is dying from hunger, is not Spanish at all, he is German; can't we have some breakfast while waiting for his reverence?

The sergeant promptly went off to report this speech to the commander.

—God be praised, said this worthy; since he is German, I can talk to him; bring him into my bower.

Candide was immediately led into a leafy nook surrounded by a handsome colonnade of green and gold marble and trellises amid which sported parrots, hummingbirds,[5] guinea fowl, and all the rarest species of birds. An excellent breakfast was prepared in golden vessels; and while the Paraguayans ate corn out of wooden bowls in the open fields under the glare of the sun, the reverend father commander entered into his bower.

He was a very handsome young man, with an open face, rather blonde in coloring, with ruddy complexion, arched eyebrows, liquid eyes, pink ears, bright red lips, and an air of pride, but a pride somehow different from that of a Spaniard or a Jesuit. Their confiscated weapons were restored to Candide and Cacambo, as well as their Andalusian horses; Cacambo fed them oats alongside the bower, always keeping an eye on them for fear of an ambush.

First Candide kissed the hem of the commander's cassock, then they sat down at the table.

—So you are German? said the Jesuit, speaking in that language.

—Yes, your reverence, said Candide.

As they spoke these words, both men looked at one another with great surprise, and another emotion which they could not control.

—From what part of Germany do you come? said the Jesuit.

—From the nasty province of Westphalia, said Candide; I was born in the castle of Thunder-Ten-Tronckh.

—Merciful heavens! cries the commander. Is it possible?

—What a miracle! exclaims Candide.

—Can it be you? asks the commander.

—It's impossible, says Candide.

They both fall back in their chairs, they embrace, they shed streams of tears.

—What, can it be you, reverend father! you, the brother of the lovely Cunégonde! you, who were killed by the Bulgars! you, the son of My Lord the Baron! you, a Jesuit in Paraguay! It's a mad world, indeed it is. Oh, Pangloss! Pangloss! how happy you would be, if you hadn't been hanged.

The commander dismissed his negro slaves and the Paraguayans who served his drink in crystal goblets. He thanked God and Saint Ignatius a thousand times, he clasped Candide in his arms, their faces were bathed in tears.

---

5. In this passage and several later ones, Voltaire uses in conjunction two words, both of which mean hummingbird. The French system of classifying hummingbirds, based on the work of the celebrated Buffon, distinguishes oiseaux-mouches with straight bills from colibris with curved bills. This distinction is wholly fallacious. Hummingbirds have all manner of shaped bills, and the division of species must be made on other grounds entirely.

—You would be even more astonished, even more delighted, even more beside yourself, said Candide, if I told you that My Lady Cunégonde, your sister, who you thought was disemboweled, is enjoying good health.

—Where?

—Not far from here, in the house of the governor of Buenos Aires; and to think that I came to make war on you!

Each word they spoke in this long conversation added another miracle. Their souls danced on their tongues, hung eagerly at their ears, glittered in their eyes. As they were Germans, they sat a long time at table, waiting for the reverend father provincial; and the commander spoke in these terms to his dear Candide.

CHAPTER 15

How Candide Killed the Brother of His Dear Cunégonde

—All my life long I shall remember the horrible day when I saw my father and mother murdered and my sister raped. When the Bulgars left, that adorable sister of mine was nowhere to be found; so they loaded a cart with my mother, my father, myself, two serving girls, and three little murdered boys, to carry us all off for burial in a Jesuit chapel some two leagues from our ancestral castle. A Jesuit sprinkled us with holy water; it was horribly salty, and a few drops got into my eyes; the father noticed that my lid made a little tremor; putting his hand on my heart, he felt it beat; I was rescued, and at the end of three weeks was as good as new. You know, my dear Candide, that I was a very pretty boy; I became even more so; the reverend father Croust,[6] superior of the abbey, conceived a most tender friendship for me; he accepted me as a novice, and shortly after, I was sent to Rome. The Father General had need of a resupply of young German Jesuits. The rulers of Paraguay accept as few Spanish Jesuits as they can; they prefer foreigners, whom they think they can control better. I was judged fit, by the Father General, to labor in this vineyard. So we set off, a Pole, a Tyrolean, and myself. Upon our arrival, I was honored with the posts of subdeacon and lieutenant; today I am a colonel and a priest. We are giving a vigorous reception to the King of Spain's men; I assure you they will be excommunicated as well as trounced on the battlefield. Providence has sent you to help us. But is it really true that my dear sister, Cunégonde, is in the neighborhood, with the governor of Buenos Aires?

Candide reassured him with a solemn oath that nothing could be more true. Their tears began to flow again.

The baron could not weary of embracing Candide; he called him his brother, his savior.

—Ah, my dear Candide, said he, maybe together we will be able to enter the town as conquerors, and be united with my sister Cunégonde.

—That is all I desire, said Candide; I was expecting to marry her, and I still hope to.

—You insolent dog, replied the baron, you would have the effrontery to marry my sister, who has seventy-two quarterings! It's a piece of presumption for you even to mention such a crazy project in my presence.

Candide, terrified by this speech, answered:—Most reverend father, all the quarterings in the world don't affect this case; I have rescued your sister out of

6. A Jesuit rector at Colmar with whom Voltaire had quarreled in 1754.

the arms of a Jew and an inquisitor; she has many obligations to me, she wants to marry me. Master Pangloss always taught me that men are equal; and I shall certainly marry her.

—We'll see about that, you scoundrel, said the Jesuit baron of Thunder-Ten-Tronckh; and so saying, he gave him a blow across the face with the flat of his sword. Candide immediately drew his own sword and thrust it up to the hilt in the baron's belly; but as he drew it forth all dripping, he began to weep.

—Alas, dear God! said he, I have killed my old master, my friend, my brother-in-law; I am the best man in the world, and here are three men I've killed already, and two of the three were priests.

Cacambo, who was standing guard at the entry of the bower, came running.

—We can do nothing but sell our lives dearly, said his master; someone will certainly come; we must die fighting.

Cacambo, who had been in similar scrapes before, did not lose his head; he took the Jesuit's cassock, which the commander had been wearing, and put it on Candide; he stuck the dead man's square hat on Candide's head, and forced him onto horseback. Everything was done in the wink of an eye.

—Let's ride, master; everyone will take you for a Jesuit on his way to deliver orders; and we will have passed the frontier before anyone can come after us.

Even as he was pronouncing these words, he charged off, crying in Spanish:— Way, make way for the reverend father colonel!

CHAPTER 16

What Happened to the Two Travelers with Two Girls, Two Monkeys, and the Savages Named Biglugs

Candide and his valet were over the frontier before anyone in the camp knew of the death of the German Jesuit. Foresighted Cacambo had taken care to fill his satchel with bread, chocolate, ham, fruit, and several bottles of wine. They pushed their Andalusian horses forward into unknown country, where there were no roads. Finally a broad prairie divided by several streams opened before them. Our two travelers turned their horses loose to graze; Cacambo suggested that they eat too, and promptly set the example. But Candide said:—How can you expect me to eat ham when I have killed the son of My Lord the Baron, and am now condemned never to see the lovely Cunégonde for the rest of my life? Why should I drag out my miserable days, since I must exist far from her in the depths of despair and remorse? And what will the *Journal de Trévoux*[7] say of all this?

Though he talked this way, he did not neglect the food. Night fell. The two wanderers heard a few weak cries which seemed to be voiced by women. They could not tell whether the cries expressed grief or joy; but they leaped at once to their feet, with that uneasy suspicion which one always feels in an unknown country. The outcry arose from two girls, completely naked, who were running swiftly along the edge of the meadow, pursued by two monkeys who snapped at their buttocks. Candide was moved to pity; he had learned marksmanship with the Bulgars, and could have knocked a nut off a bush without touching the leaves. He raised his Spanish rifle, fired twice, and killed the two monkeys.

---

7. A newspaper published by the Jesuit order, founded in 1701 and consistently hostile to Voltaire.

—God be praised, my dear Cacambo! I've saved these two poor creatures from great danger. Though I committed a sin in killing an inquisitor and a Jesuit, I've redeemed myself by saving the lives of two girls. Perhaps they are two ladies of rank, and this good deed may gain us special advantages in the country.

He had more to say, but his mouth shut suddenly when he saw the girls embracing the monkeys tenderly, weeping over their bodies, and filling the air with lamentations.

—I wasn't looking for quite so much generosity of spirit, said he to Cacambo; the latter replied:—You've really fixed things this time, master; you've killed the two lovers of these young ladies.

—Their lovers! Impossible! You must be joking, Cacambo; how can I believe you?

—My dear master, Cacambo replied, you're always astonished by everything. Why do you think it so strange that in some countries monkeys succeed in obtaining the good graces of women? They are one quarter human, just as I am one quarter Spanish.

—Alas, Candide replied, I do remember now hearing Master Pangloss say that such things used to happen, and that from these mixtures there arose pans, fauns, and satyrs, and that these creatures had appeared to various grand figures of antiquity; but I took all that for fables.

—You should be convinced now, said Cacambo; it's true, and you see how people make mistakes who haven't received a measure of education. But what I fear is that these girls may get us into real trouble.

These sensible reflections led Candide to leave the field and to hide in a wood. There he dined with Cacambo; and there both of them, having duly cursed the inquisitor of Portugal, the governor of Buenos Aires, and the baron, went to sleep on a bed of moss. When they woke up, they found themselves unable to move; the reason was that during the night the Biglugs,[8] natives of the country, to whom the girls had complained of them, had tied them down with cords of bark. They were surrounded by fifty naked Biglugs, armed with arrows, clubs, and stone axes. Some were boiling a caldron of water, others were preparing spits, and all cried out:—It's a Jesuit, a Jesuit! We'll be revenged and have a good meal; let's eat some Jesuit, eat some Jesuit!

—I told you, my dear master, said Cacambo sadly, I said those two girls would play us a dirty trick.

Candide, noting the caldron and spits, cried out:—We are surely going to be roasted or boiled. Ah, what would Master Pangloss say if he could see these men in a state of nature? All is for the best, I agree; but I must say it seems hard to have lost Miss Cunégonde and to be stuck on a spit by the Biglugs.

Cacambo did not lose his head.

—Don't give up hope, said he to the disconsolate Candide; I understand a little of the jargon these people speak, and I'm going to talk to them.

—Don't forget to remind them, said Candide, of the frightful inhumanity of eating their fellow men, and that Christian ethics forbid it.

—Gentlemen, said Cacambo, you have a mind to eat a Jesuit today? An excellent idea; nothing is more proper than to treat one's enemies so. Indeed, the law

8. Voltaire's name is "Oreillons" from Spanish "Orejones," a name mentioned in Garcilaso de Vega's *Historia General del Perú* (1609), on which Voltaire drew for many of the details in his picture of South America.

of nature teaches us to kill our neighbor, and that's how men behave the whole world over. Though we Europeans don't exercise our right to eat our neighbors, the reason is simply that we find it easy to get a good meal elsewhere; but you don't have our resources, and we certainly agree that it's better to eat your enemies than to let the crows and vultures have the fruit of your victory. But, gentlemen, you wouldn't want to eat your friends. You think you will be spitting a Jesuit, and it's your defender, the enemy of your enemies, whom you will be roasting. For my part, I was born in your country; the gentleman whom you see is my master, and far from being a Jesuit, he has just killed a Jesuit, the robe he is wearing was stripped from him; that's why you have taken a dislike to him. To prove that I am telling the truth, take his robe and bring it to the nearest frontier of the kingdom of Los Padres; find out for yourselves if my master didn't kill a Jesuit officer. It won't take long; if you find that I have lied, you can still eat us. But if I've told the truth, you know too well the principles of public justice, customs, and laws, not to spare our lives.

The Biglugs found this discourse perfectly reasonable; they appointed chiefs to go posthaste and find out the truth; the two messengers performed their task like men of sense, and quickly returned bringing good news. The Biglugs untied their two prisoners, treated them with great politeness, offered them girls, gave them refreshments, and led them back to the border of their state, crying joyously:—He isn't a Jesuit, he isn't a Jesuit!

Candide could not weary of exclaiming over his preservation.

—What a people! he said. What men! what customs! If I had not had the good luck to run a sword through the body of Miss Cunégonde's brother, I would have been eaten on the spot! But, after all, it seems that uncorrupted nature is good, since these folk, instead of eating me, showed me a thousand kindnesses as soon as they knew I was not a Jesuit.

CHAPTER 17

Arrival of Candide and His Servant at the Country of Eldorado, and What They Saw There

When they were out of the land of the Biglugs, Cacambo said to Candide:— You see that this hemisphere is no better than the other; take my advice, and let's get back to Europe as soon as possible.

—How to get back, asked Candide, and where to go? If I go to my own land, the Bulgars and Abares are murdering everyone in sight; if I go to Portugal, they'll burn me alive; if we stay here, we risk being skewered any day. But how can I ever leave that part of the world where Miss Cunégonde lives?

—Let's go toward Cayenne, said Cacambo, we shall find some Frenchmen there, for they go all over the world; they can help us; perhaps God will take pity on us.

To get to Cayenne was not easy; they knew more or less which way to go, but mountains, rivers, cliffs, robbers, and savages obstructed the way everywhere. Their horses died of weariness; their food was eaten; they subsisted for one whole month on wild fruits, and at last they found themselves by a little river fringed with coconut trees, which gave them both life and hope.

Cacambo, who was as full of good advice as the old woman, said to Candide:—We can go no further, we've walked ourselves out; I see an abandoned canoe on the bank, let's fill it with coconuts, get into the boat, and float with the current; a river always leads to some inhabited spot or other. If we don't find anything pleasant, at least we may find something new.

—Let's go, said Candide, and let Providence be our guide.

They floated some leagues between banks sometimes flowery, sometimes sandy, now steep, now level. The river widened steadily; finally it disappeared into a chasm of frightful rocks that rose high into the heavens. The two travelers had the audacity to float with the current into this chasm. The river, narrowly confined, drove them onward with horrible speed and a fearful roar. After twenty-four hours, they saw daylight once more; but their canoe was smashed on the snags. They had to drag themselves from rock to rock for an entire league; at last they emerged to an immense horizon, ringed with remote mountains. The countryside was tended for pleasure as well as profit; everywhere the useful was joined to the agreeable. The roads were covered, or rather decorated, with elegantly shaped carriages made of a glittering material, carrying men and women of singular beauty, and drawn by great red sheep which were faster than the finest horses of Andalusia, Tetuan, and Mequinez.

—Here now, said Candide, is a country that's better than Westphalia.

Along with Cacambo, he climbed out of the river at the first village he could see. Some children of the town, dressed in rags of gold brocade, were playing quoits at the village gate; our two men from the other world paused to watch them; their quoits were rather large, yellow, red, and green, and they glittered with a singular luster. On a whim, the travelers picked up several; they were of gold, emeralds, and rubies, and the least of them would have been the greatest ornament of the Great Mogul's throne.

—Surely, said Cacambo, these quoit players are the children of the king of the country.

The village schoolmaster appeared at that moment, to call them back to school.

—And there, said Candide, is the tutor of the royal household.

The little rascals quickly gave up their game, leaving on the ground their quoits and playthings. Candide picked them up, ran to the schoolmaster, and presented them to him humbly, giving him to understand by sign language that their royal highnesses had forgotten their gold and jewels. With a smile, the schoolmaster tossed them to the ground, glanced quickly but with great surprise at Candide's face, and went his way.

The travelers did not fail to pick up the gold, rubies, and emeralds.

—Where in the world are we? cried Candide. The children of this land must be well trained, since they are taught contempt for gold and jewels.

Cacambo was as much surprised as Candide. At last they came to the finest house of the village; it was built like a European palace. A crowd of people surrounded the door, and even more were in the entry; delightful music was heard, and a delicious aroma of cooking filled the air. Cacambo went up to the door, listened, and reported that they were talking Peruvian; that was his native language, for every reader must know that Cacambo was born in Tucuman, in a village where they talk that language exclusively.

—I'll act as interpreter, he told Candide; it's an hotel, let's go in.

Promptly two boys and two girls of the staff, dressed in cloth of gold, and wearing ribbons in their hair, invited them to sit at the host's table. The meal consisted of four soups, each one garnished with a brace of parakeets, a boiled condor which weighed two hundred pounds, two roast monkeys of an excellent flavor, three hundred birds of paradise in one dish and six hundred humming-birds in another, exquisite stews, delicious pastries, the whole thing served up in plates of what looked like rock crystal. The boys and girls of the staff poured them various beverages made from sugar cane.

The diners were for the most part merchants and travelers, all extremely polite, who questioned Cacambo with the most discreet circumspection, and answered his questions very directly.

When the meal was over, Cacambo as well as Candide supposed he could set-tle his bill handsomely by tossing onto the table two of those big pieces of gold which they had picked up; but the host and hostess burst out laughing, and for a long time nearly split their sides. Finally they subsided.

—Gentlemen, said the host, we see clearly that you're foreigners; we don't meet many of you here. Please excuse our laughing when you offered us in pay-ment a couple of pebbles from the roadside. No doubt you don't have any of our local currency, but you don't need it to eat here. All the hotels established for the promotion of commerce are maintained by the state. You have had meager enter-tainment here, for we are only a poor town; but everywhere else you will be given the sort of welcome you deserve.

Cacambo translated for Candide all the host's explanations, and Candide lis-tened to them with the same admiration and astonishment that his friend Cacambo showed in reporting them.

—What is this country, then, said they to one another, unknown to the rest of the world, and where nature itself is so different from our own? This probably is the country where everything is for the best; for it's absolutely necessary that such a country should exist somewhere. And whatever Master Pangloss said of the matter, I have often had occasion to notice that things went badly in Westphalia.

CHAPTER 18

What They Saw in the Land of Eldorado

Cacambo revealed his curiosity to the host, and the host told him:—I am an igno-rant man and content to remain so; but we have here an old man, retired from the court, who is the most knowing person in the kingdom, and the most talkative.

Thereupon he brought Cacambo to the old man's house. Candide now played second fiddle, and acted as servant to his own valet. They entered an austere little house, for the door was merely of silver and the paneling of the rooms was only gold, though so tastefully wrought that the finest paneling would not surpass it. If the truth must be told, the lobby was only decorated with rubies and emeralds; but the patterns in which they were arranged atoned for the extreme simplicity.

The old man received the two strangers on a sofa stuffed with bird-of-paradise feathers, and offered them several drinks in diamond carafes; then he satisfied their curiosity in these terms.

—I am a hundred and seventy-two years old, and I heard from my late father, who was liveryman to the king, about the astonishing revolutions in Peru which he had seen. Our land here was formerly part of the kingdom of the Incas, who rashly left it in order to conquer another part of the world, and who were ulti-mately destroyed by the Spaniards. The wisest princes of their house were those who had never left their native valley; they decreed, with the consent of the nation, that henceforth no inhabitant of our little kingdom should ever leave it; and this rule is what has preserved our innocence and our happiness. The

Spaniards heard vague rumors about this land, they called it Eldorado;[9] and an English knight named Raleigh even came somewhere close to it about a hundred years ago; but as we are surrounded by unscalable mountains and precipices, we have managed so far to remain hidden from the rapacity of the European nations, who have an inconceivable rage for the pebbles and mud of our land, and who, in order to get some, would butcher us all to the last man.

The conversation was a long one; it turned on the form of the government, the national customs, on women, public shows, the arts. At last Candide, whose taste always ran to metaphysics, told Cacambo to ask if the country had any religion.

The old man grew a bit red.

—How's that? he said. Can you have any doubt of it? Do you suppose we are altogether thankless scoundrels?

Cacambo asked meekly what was the religion of Eldorado. The old man flushed again.

—Can there be two religions? he asked. I suppose our religion is the same as everyone's, we worship God from morning to evening.

—Then you worship a single deity? said Cacambo, who acted throughout as interpreter of the questions of Candide.

—It's obvious, said the old man, that there aren't two or three or four of them. I must say the people of your world ask very remarkable questions.

Candide could not weary of putting questions to this good old man; he wanted to know how the people of Eldorado prayed to God.

—We don't pray to him at all, said the good and respectable sage; we have nothing to ask him for, since everything we need has already been granted; we thank God continually.

Candide was interested in seeing the priests; he had Cacambo ask where they were. The old gentleman smiled.

—My friends, said he, we are all priests; the king and all the heads of household sing formal psalms of thanksgiving every morning, and five or six thousand voices accompany them.

—What! you have no monks to teach, argue, govern, intrigue, and burn at the stake everyone who disagrees with them?

—We should have to be mad, said the old man; here we are all of the same mind, and we don't understand what you're up to with your monks.

Candide was overjoyed at all these speeches, and said to himself:—This is very different from Westphalia and the castle of My Lord the Baron; if our friend Pangloss had seen Eldorado, he wouldn't have called the castle of Thunder-Ten-Tronckh the finest thing on earth; to know the world one must travel.

After this long conversation, the old gentleman ordered a carriage with six sheep made ready, and gave the two travelers twelve of his servants for their journey to the court.

—Excuse me, said he, if old age deprives me of the honor of accompanying you. The king will receive you after a style which will not altogether displease you, and you will doubtless make allowance for the customs of the country if there are any you do not like.

9. The myth of this land of gold somewhere in Central or South America had been widespread since the 16th century. *The Discovery of Guiana*, published in 1595, described Sir Walter Ralegh's infatuation with the myth of Eldorado and served to spread the story still further.

Candide and Cacambo climbed into the coach; the six sheep flew like the wind, and in less than four hours they reached the king's palace at the edge of the capital. The entryway was two hundred and twenty feet high and a hundred wide; it is impossible to describe all the materials of which it was made. But you can imagine how much finer it was than those pebbles and sand which we call gold and jewels.

Twenty beautiful girls of the guard detail welcomed Candide and Cacambo as they stepped from the carriage, took them to the baths, and dressed them in robes woven of hummingbird feathers; then the high officials of the crown, both male and female, led them to the royal chamber between two long lines, each of a thousand musicians, as is customary. As they approached the throne room, Cacambo asked an officer what was the proper method of greeting his majesty: if one fell to one's knees or on one's belly; if one put one's hands on one's head or on one's rear; if one licked up the dust of the earth—in a word, what was the proper form?[1]

—The ceremony, said the officer, is to embrace the king and kiss him on both cheeks.

Candide and Cacambo fell on the neck of his majesty, who received them with all the dignity imaginable, and asked them politely to dine.

In the interim, they were taken about to see the city, the public buildings rising to the clouds, the public markets and arcades, the fountains of pure water and of rose water, those of sugar cane liquors which flowed perpetually in the great plazas paved with a sort of stone which gave off odors of gilly-flower and rose petals. Candide asked to see the supreme court and the hall of parliament; they told him there was no such thing, that lawsuits were unknown. He asked if there were prisons, and was told there were not. What surprised him more, and gave him most pleasure, was the palace of sciences, in which he saw a gallery two thousand paces long, entirely filled with mathematical and physical instruments.

Having passed the whole afternoon seeing only a thousandth part of the city, they returned to the king's palace. Candide sat down to dinner with his majesty, his own valet Cacambo, and several ladies. Never was better food served, and never did a host preside more jovially than his majesty. Cacambo explained the king's witty sayings to Candide, and even when translated they still seemed witty. Of all the things which astonished Candide, this was not, in his eyes, the least astonishing.

They passed a month in this refuge. Candide never tired of saying to Cacambo:— It's true, my friend, I'll say it again, the castle where I was born does not compare with the land where we now are; but Miss Cunégonde is not here, and you doubtless have a mistress somewhere in Europe. If we stay here, we shall be just like everybody else, whereas if we go back to our own world, taking with us just a dozen sheep loaded with Eldorado pebbles, we shall be richer than all the kings put together, we shall have no more inquisitors to fear, and we shall easily be able to retake Miss Cunégonde.

This harangue pleased Cacambo; wandering is such pleasure, it gives a man such prestige at home to be able to talk of what he has seen abroad, that the two happy men resolved to be so no longer, but to take their leave of his majesty.

---

1. Candide's questions are probably derived from those of Gulliver on a similar occasion, in the third part of *Gulliver's Travels*.

—You are making a foolish mistake, the king told them; I know very well that my kingdom is nothing much; but when you are pretty comfortable somewhere, you had better stay there. Of course I have no right to keep strangers against their will, that sort of tyranny is not in keeping with our laws or our customs; all men are free; depart when you will, but the way out is very difficult. You cannot possibly go up the river by which you miraculously came; it runs too swiftly through its underground caves. The mountains which surround my land are ten thousand feet high, and steep as walls; each one is more than ten leagues across; the only way down is over precipices. But since you really must go, I shall order my engineers to make a machine which can carry you conveniently. When we take you over the mountains, nobody will be able to go with you, for my subjects have sworn never to leave their refuge, and they are too sensible to break their vows. Other than that, ask of me what you please.

—We only request of your majesty, Cacambo said, a few sheep loaded with provisions, some pebbles, and some of the mud of your country.

The king laughed.

—I simply can't understand, said he, the passion you Europeans have for our yellow mud; but take all you want, and much good may it do you.

He promptly gave orders to his technicians to make a machine for lifting these two extraordinary men out of his kingdom. Three thousand good physicists worked at the problem; the machine was ready in two weeks' time, and cost no more than twenty million pounds sterling, in the money of the country. Cacambo and Candide were placed in the machine; there were two great sheep, saddled and bridled to serve them as steeds when they had cleared the mountains, twenty pack sheep with provisions, thirty which carried presents consisting of the rarities of the country, and fifty loaded with gold, jewels, and diamonds. The king bade tender farewell to the two vagabonds.

It made a fine spectacle, their departure, and the ingenious way in which they were hoisted with their sheep up to the top of the mountains. The technicians bade them good-bye after bringing them to safety, and Candide had now no other desire and no other object than to go and present his sheep to Miss Cunégonde.

—We have, said he, enough to pay off the governor of Buenos Aires—if, indeed, a price can be placed on Miss Cunégonde. Let us go to Cayenne, take ship there, and then see what kingdom we can find to buy up.

CHAPTER 19

*What Happened to Them at Surinam, and How Candide
Got to Know Martin*

The first day was pleasant enough for our travelers. They were encouraged by the idea of possessing more treasures than Asia, Europe, and Africa could bring together. Candide, in transports, carved the name of Cunégonde on the trees. On the second day two of their sheep bogged down in a swamp and were lost with their loads; two other sheep died of fatigue a few days later; seven or eight others starved to death in a desert; still others fell, a little after, from precipices. Finally, after a hundred days' march, they had only two sheep left. Candide told Cacambo:— My friend, you see how the riches of this world are fleeting; the only solid things are virtue and the joy of seeing Miss Cunégonde again.

—I agree, said Cacambo, but we still have two sheep, laden with more treasure than the king of Spain will ever have; and I see in the distance a town which

I suspect is Surinam; it belongs to the Dutch. We are at the end of our trials and on the threshold of our happiness.

As they drew near the town, they discovered a negro stretched on the ground with only half his clothes left, that is, a pair of blue drawers; the poor fellow was also missing his left leg and his right hand.

—Good Lord, said Candide in Dutch, what are you doing in that horrible condition, my friend?

—I am waiting for my master, Mr. Vanderdendur,[2] the famous merchant, answered the negro.

—Is Mr. Vanderdendur, Candide asked, the man who treated you this way?

—Yes, sir, said the negro, that's how things are around here. Twice a year we get a pair of linen drawers to wear. If we catch a finger in the sugar mill where we work, they cut off our hand; if we try to run away, they cut off our leg: I have undergone both these experiences. This is the price of the sugar you eat in Europe. And yet, when my mother sold me for ten Patagonian crowns on the coast of Guinea, she said to me: 'My dear child, bless our witch doctors, reverence them always, they will make your life happy; you have the honor of being a slave to our white masters, and in this way you are making the fortune of your father and mother.' Alas! I don't know if I made their fortunes, but they certainly did not make mine. The dogs, monkeys, and parrots are a thousand times less unhappy than we are. The Dutch witch doctors who converted me tell me every Sunday that we are all sons of Adam, black and white alike. I am no genealogist; but if these preachers are right, we must all be remote cousins; and you must admit no one could treat his own flesh and blood in a more horrible fashion.

—Oh Pangloss! cried Candide, you had no notion of these abominations! I'm through, I must give up your optimism after all.

—What's optimism? said Cacambo.

—Alas, said Candide, it is a mania for saying things are well when one is in hell.

And he shed bitter tears as he looked at this negro, and he was still weeping as he entered Surinam.

The first thing they asked was if there was not some vessel in port which could be sent to Buenos Aires. The man they asked was a Spanish merchant who undertook to make an honest bargain with them. They arranged to meet in a café; Candide and the faithful Cacambo, with their two sheep, went there to meet with him.

Candide, who always said exactly what was in his heart, told the Spaniard of his adventures, and confessed that he wanted to recapture Miss Cunégonde.

—I shall take good care *not* to send you to Buenos Aires, said the merchant; I should be hanged, and so would you. The lovely Cunégonde is his lordship's favorite mistress.

This was a thunderstroke for Candide; he wept for a long time; finally he drew Cacambo aside.

—Here, my friend, said he, is what you must do. Each one of us has in his pockets five or six millions' worth of diamonds; you are cleverer than I; go get

2. A name perhaps intended to suggest Van-Duren, a Dutch bookseller with whom Voltaire had quarreled. In particular, the incident of gradually raising one's price recalls Van-Duren, to whom Voltaire had successively offered 1,000, 1,500, 2,000, and 3,000 florins for the return of the manuscript of Frederick the Great's *Anti-Machiavel*.

Miss Cunégonde in Buenos Aires. If the governor makes a fuss, give him a million; if that doesn't convince him, give him two millions; you never killed an inquisitor, nobody will suspect you. I'll fit out another boat and go wait for you in Venice. That is a free country, where one need have no fear either of Bulgars or Abares or Jews or inquisitors.

Cacambo approved of this wise decision. He was in despair at leaving a good master who had become a bosom friend; but the pleasure of serving him overcame the grief of leaving him. They embraced, and shed a few tears; Candide urged him not to forget the good old woman. Cacambo departed that very same day; he was a very good fellow, that Cacambo.

Candide remained for some time in Surinam, waiting for another merchant to take him to Italy, along with the two sheep which were left him. He hired servants and bought everything necessary for the long voyage; finally Mr. Vanderdendur, master of a big ship, came calling.

—How much will you charge, Candide asked this man, to take me to Venice—myself, my servants, my luggage, and those two sheep over there?

The merchant set a price of ten thousand piastres; Candide did not blink an eye.

—Oh, ho, said the prudent Vanderdendur to himself, this stranger pays out ten thousand piastres at once, he must be pretty well fixed.

Then, returning a moment later, he made known that he could not set sail under twenty thousand.

—All right, you shall have them, said Candide.

—Whew, said the merchant softly to himself, this man gives twenty thousand piastres as easily as ten.

He came back again to say he could not go to Venice for less than thirty thousand piastres.

—All right, thirty then, said Candide.

—Ah ha, said the Dutch merchant, again speaking to himself; so thirty thousand piastres mean nothing to this man; no doubt the two sheep are loaded with immense treasures; let's say no more; we'll pick up the thirty thousand piastres first, and then we'll see.

Candide sold two little diamonds, the least of which was worth more than all the money demanded by the merchant. He paid him in advance. The two sheep were taken aboard. Candide followed in a little boat, to board the vessel at its anchorage. The merchant bides his time, sets sail, and makes his escape with a favoring wind. Candide, aghast and stupefied, soon loses him from view.

—Alas, he cries, now there is a trick worthy of the old world!

He returns to shore sunk in misery; for he had lost riches enough to make the fortunes of twenty monarchs.

Now he rushes to the house of the Dutch magistrate, and, being a bit disturbed, he knocks loudly at the door; goes in, tells the story of what happened, and shouts a bit louder than is customary. The judge begins by fining him ten thousand piastres for making such a racket; then he listens patiently to the story, promises to look into the matter as soon as the merchant comes back, and charges another ten thousand piastres as the costs of the hearing.

This legal proceeding completed the despair of Candide. In fact he had experienced miseries a thousand times more painful, but the coldness of the judge, and that of the merchant who had robbed him, roused his bile and plunged him into a black melancholy. The malice of men rose up before his spirit in all its ugliness, and his mind dwelt only on gloomy thoughts. Finally, when a French vessel was ready to leave for Bordeaux, since he had no more diamond-laden sheep to transport, he took a cabin at a fair price, and made it known in the town that he would pay passage and keep, plus two thousand piastres, to any honest man who wanted to make the journey with him, on condition that this man must be the most disgusted with his own condition and the most unhappy man in the province.

This drew such a crowd of applicants as a fleet could not have held. Candide wanted to choose among the leading candidates, so he picked out about twenty who seemed companionable enough, and of whom each pretended to be more miserable than all the others. He brought them together at his inn and gave them a dinner, on condition that each would swear to tell truthfully his entire history. He would select as his companion the most truly miserable and rightly discontented man, and among the others he would distribute various gifts.

The meeting lasted till four in the morning. Candide, as he listened to all the stories, remembered what the old woman had told him on the trip to Buenos Aires, and of the wager she had made, that there was nobody on the boat who had not undergone great misfortunes. At every story that was told him, he thought of Pangloss.

—That Pangloss, he said, would be hard put to prove his system. I wish he was here. Certainly if everything goes well, it is in Eldorado and not in the rest of the world.

At last he decided in favor of a poor scholar who had worked ten years for the booksellers of Amsterdam. He decided that there was no trade in the world with which one should be more disgusted.

This scholar, who was in fact a good man, had been robbed by his wife, beaten by his son, and deserted by his daughter, who had got herself abducted by a Portuguese. He had just been fired from the little job on which he existed; and the preachers of Surinam were persecuting him because they took him for a Socinian.[3] The others, it is true, were at least as unhappy as he, but Candide hoped the scholar would prove more amusing on the voyage. All his rivals declared that Candide was doing them a great injustice, but he pacified them with a hundred piastres apiece.

CHAPTER 20

What Happened to Candide and Martin at Sea

The old scholar, whose name was Martin, now set sail with Candide for Bordeaux. Both men had seen and suffered much; and even if the vessel had been sailing from Surinam to Japan via the Cape of Good Hope, they would have been able to keep themselves amused with instances of moral evil and physical evil during the entire trip.

However, Candide had one great advantage over Martin, that he still hoped to see Miss Cunégonde again, and Martin had nothing to hope for; besides, he had gold and diamonds, and though he had lost a hundred big red sheep loaded with the greatest treasures of the earth, though he had always at his heart a memory of

---

3. A follower of Faustus and Laelius Socinus, 16th-century Polish theologians who proposed a form of "rational" Christianity that exalted the rational conscience and minimized such mysteries as the Trinity. The Socinians, by a special irony, were vigorous optimists.

the Dutch merchant's villainy, yet, when he thought of the wealth that remained in his hands, and when he talked of Cunégonde, especially just after a good dinner, he still inclined to the system of Pangloss.

—But what about you, Monsieur Martin, he asked the scholar, what do you think of all that? What is your idea of moral evil and physical evil?

—Sir, answered Martin, those priests accused me of being a Socinian, but the truth is that I am a Manichee.[4]

—You're joking, said Candide; there aren't any more Manichees in the world.

—There's me, said Martin; I don't know what to do about it, but I can't think otherwise.

—You must be possessed of the devil, said Candide.

—He's mixed up with so many things of this world, said Martin, that he may be in me as well as elsewhere; but I assure you, as I survey this globe, or globule, I think that God has abandoned it to some evil spirit—all of it except Eldorado. I have scarcely seen one town which did not wish to destroy its neighboring town, no family which did not wish to exterminate some other family. Everywhere the weak loathe the powerful, before whom they cringe, and the powerful treat them like brute cattle, to be sold for their meat and fleece. A million regimented assassins roam Europe from one end to the other, plying the trades of murder and robbery in an organized way for a living, because there is no more honest form of work for them; and in the cities which seem to enjoy peace and where the arts are flourishing, men are devoured by more envy, cares, and anxieties than a whole town experiences when it's under siege. Private griefs are worse even than public trials. In a word, I have seen so much and suffered so much, that I am a Manichee.

—Still there is some good, said Candide.

—That may be, said Martin, but I don't know it.

In the middle of this discussion, the rumble of cannon was heard. From minute to minute the noise grew louder. Everyone reached for his spyglass. At a distance of some three miles they saw two vessels fighting; the wind brought both of them so close to the French vessel that they had a pleasantly comfortable seat to watch the fight. Presently one of the vessels caught the other with a broadside so low and so square as to send it to the bottom. Candide and Martin saw clearly a hundred men on the deck of the sinking ship; they all raised their hands to heaven, uttering fearful shrieks; and in a moment everything was swallowed up.

—Well, said Martin, that is how men treat one another.

—It is true, said Candide, there's something devilish in this business.

As they chatted, he noticed something of a striking red color floating near the sunken vessel. They sent out a boat to investigate; it was one of his sheep. Candide was more joyful to recover this one sheep than he had been afflicted to lose a hundred of them, all loaded with big Eldorado diamonds.

The French captain soon learned that the captain of the victorious vessel was Spanish and that of the sunken vessel was a Dutch pirate. It was the same man who had robbed Candide. The enormous riches which this rascal had stolen were sunk beside him in the sea, and nothing was saved but a single sheep.

—You see, said Candide to Martin, crime is punished sometimes; this scoundrel of a Dutch merchant has met the fate he deserved.

4. Mani, a Persian sage and philosopher of the 3rd century, taught (probably under the influence of traditions stemming from Zoroaster and the worshipers of the sun god Mithra) that the earth is a field of dispute between two almost equal powers, one of light and one of darkness, both of which must be propitiated.

—Yes, said Martin; but did the passengers aboard his ship have to perish too? God punished the scoundrel, and the devil drowned the others.

Meanwhile the French and Spanish vessels continued on their journey, and Candide continued his talks with Martin. They disputed for fifteen days in a row, and at the end of that time were just as much in agreement as at the beginning. But at least they were talking, they exchanged their ideas, they consoled one another. Candide caressed his sheep.

—Since I have found you again, said he, I may well rediscover Miss Cunégonde.

CHAPTER 21

Candide and Martin Approach the Coast of France:
They Reason Together

At last the coast of France came in view.

—Have you ever been in France, Monsieur Martin? asked Candide.

—Yes, said Martin, I have visited several provinces. There are some where half the inhabitants are crazy, others where they are too sly, still others where they are quite gentle and stupid, some where they venture on wit; in all of them the principal occupation is love-making, the second is slander, and the third stupid talk.

—But, Monsieur Martin, were you ever in Paris?

—Yes, I've been in Paris; it contains specimens of all these types; it is a chaos, a mob, in which everyone is seeking pleasure and where hardly anyone finds it, at least from what I have seen. I did not live there for long; as I arrived, I was robbed of everything I possessed by thieves at the fair of St. Germain; I myself was taken for a thief, and spent eight days in jail, after which I took a proofreader's job to earn enough money to return on foot to Holland. I knew the writing gang, the intriguing gang, the gang with fits and convulsions.[5] They say there are some very civilized people in that town; I'd like to think so.

—I myself have no desire to visit France, said Candide; you no doubt realize that when one has spent a month in Eldorado, there is nothing else on earth one wants to see, except Miss Cunégonde. I am going to wait for her at Venice; we will cross France simply to get to Italy; wouldn't you like to come with me?

—Gladly, said Martin; they say Venice is good only for the Venetian nobles, but that on the other hand they treat foreigners very well when they have plenty of money. I don't have any; you do, so I'll follow you anywhere.

—By the way, said Candide, do you believe the earth was originally all ocean, as they assure us in that big book belonging to the ship's captain?[6]

—I don't believe that stuff, said Martin, nor any of the dreams which people have been peddling for some time now.

—But why, then, was this world formed at all? asked Candide.

—To drive us mad, answered Martin.

—Aren't you astonished, Candide went on, at the love which those two girls showed for the monkeys in the land of the Biglugs that I told you about?

—Not at all, said Martin, I see nothing strange in these sentiments; I have seen so many extraordinary things that nothing seems extraordinary any more.

5. The Jansenists, a sect of strict Catholics, became notorious for spiritual ecstasies. Their public displays reached a height during the 1720s, and Voltaire described them in *Le* *Siècle de Louis XIV* (chap. 37), as well as in the article "Convulsions" in the *Philosophical Dictionary.*

6. The Bible: Genesis I.

—Do you believe, asked Candide, that men have always massacred one another as they do today? That they have always been liars, traitors, ingrates, thieves, weaklings, sneaks, cowards, backbiters, gluttons, drunkards, misers, climbers, killers, calumniators, sensualists, fanatics, hypocrites, and fools?

—Do you believe, said Martin, that hawks have always eaten pigeons when they could get them?

—Of course, said Candide.

—Well, said Martin, if hawks have always had the same character, why do you suppose that men have changed?

—Oh, said Candide, there's a great deal of difference, because freedom of the will . . .

As they were disputing in this manner, they reached Bordeaux.

CHAPTER 22

What Happened in France to Candide and Martin

Candide paused in Bordeaux only long enough to sell a couple of Eldorado pebbles and to fit himself out with a fine two-seater carriage, for he could no longer do without his philosopher Martin; only he was very unhappy to part with his sheep, which he left to the academy of science in Bordeaux. They proposed, as the theme of that year's prize contest, the discovery of why the wool of the sheep was red; and the prize was awarded to a northern scholar[7] who demonstrated by A plus B minus C divided by Z that the sheep ought to be red and die of sheep rot.

But all the travelers with whom Candide talked in the roadside inns told him:—We are going to Paris.

This general consensus finally inspired in him too a desire to see the capital; it was not much out of his road to Venice.

He entered through the Faubourg Saint-Marceau,[8] and thought he was in the meanest village of Westphalia.

Scarcely was Candide in his hotel, when he came down with a mild illness caused by exhaustion. As he was wearing an enormous diamond ring, and people had noticed among his luggage a tremendously heavy safe, he soon found at his bedside two doctors whom he had not called, several intimate friends who never left him alone, and two pious ladies who helped to warm his broth. Martin said:—I remember that I too was ill on my first trip to Paris; I was very poor; and as I had neither friends, pious ladies, nor doctors, I got well.

However, as a result of medicines and bleedings, Candide's illness became serious. A resident of the neighborhood came to ask him politely to fill out a ticket, to be delivered to the porter of the other world.[9] Candide wanted nothing to do with it. The pious ladies assured him it was a new fashion; Candide replied that he wasn't a man of fashion. Martin wanted to throw the resident out the window.

7. Maupertuis Le Lapon, philosopher and mathematician, whom Voltaire had accused of trying to adduce mathematical proofs of the existence of God.

8. A district on the left bank, notably grubby in the 18th century. "As I entered [Paris] through the Faubourg Saint-Marceau, I saw nothing but dirty stinking little streets, ugly black houses, a general air of squalor and poverty, beggars, carters, menders of clothes, sellers of herb-drinks and old hats." Jean-Jacques Rousseau, Confessions, Book IV.

9. In the middle of the 18th century in France, it became customary to require persons who were grievously ill to sign billets de confession, without which they could not be given absolution, admitted to the last sacraments, or buried in consecrated ground.

The cleric swore that without the ticket they wouldn't bury Candide. Martin swore that he would bury the cleric if he continued to be a nuisance. The quarrel grew heated; Martin took him by the shoulders and threw him bodily out the door; all of which caused a great scandal, from which developed a legal case.

Candide got better; and during his convalescence he had very good company in to dine. They played cards for money; and Candide was quite surprised that none of the aces were ever dealt to him, and Martin was not surprised at all.

Among those who did the honors of the town for Candide there was a little abbé from Perigord, one of those busy fellows, always bright, always useful, assured, obsequious, and obliging, who waylay passing strangers, tell them the scandal of the town, and offer them pleasures at any price they want to pay. This fellow first took Candide and Martin to the theatre. A new tragedy was being played. Candide found himself seated next to a group of wits. That did not keep him from shedding a few tears in the course of some perfectly played scenes. One of the commentators beside him remarked during the intermission:—You are quite mistaken to weep, this actress is very bad indeed; the actor who plays with her is even worse; and the play is even worse than the actors in it. The author knows not a word of Arabic, though the action takes place in Arabia; and besides, he is a man who doesn't believe in innate ideas. Tomorrow I will show you twenty pamphlets written against him.

—Tell me, sir, said Candide to the abbé, how many plays are there for performance in France?

—Five or six thousand, replied the other.

—That's a lot, said Candide; how many of them are any good?

—Fifteen or sixteen, was the answer.

—That's a lot, said Martin.

Candide was very pleased with an actress who took the part of Queen Elizabeth in a rather dull tragedy[1] that still gets played from time to time.

—I like this actress very much, he said to Martin, she bears a slight resemblance to Miss Cunégonde; I should like to meet her.

The abbé from Perigord offered to introduce him. Candide, raised in Germany, asked what was the protocol, how one behaved in France with queens of England.

—You must distinguish, said the abbé; in the provinces, you take them to an inn; at Paris they are respected while still attractive, and thrown on the dunghill when they are dead.[2]

—Queens on the dunghill! said Candide.

—Yes indeed, said Martin, the abbé is right; I was in Paris when Miss Monime herself[3] passed, as they say, from this life to the other; she was refused what these folk call 'the honors of burial,' that is, the right to rot with all the beggars of the district in a dirty cemetery; she was buried all alone by her troupe at the corner of the Rue de Bourgogne; this must have been very disagreeable to her, for she had a noble character.

—That was extremely rude, said Candide.

---

1. *Le Comte d'Essex* by Thomas Corneille.
2. Voltaire engaged in a long and vigorous campaign against the rule that actors and actresses could not be buried in consecrated ground. The superstition probably arose from a feeling that by assuming false identities they drained their own souls.
3. Adrienne Lecouvreur (1690–1730), so called because she made her debut as Monime in Racine's *Mithridate*. Voltaire had assisted at her secret midnight funeral and wrote an indignant poem about it.

—What do you expect? said Martin; that is how these folk are. Imagine all the contradictions, all the incompatibilities you can, and you will see them in the government, the courts, the churches, and the plays of this crazy nation.

—Is it true that they are always laughing in Paris? asked Candide.

—Yes, said the abbé, but with a kind of rage too; when people complain of things, they do so amid explosions of laughter; they even laugh as they perform the most detestable actions.

—Who was that fat swine, said Candide, who spoke so nastily about the play over which I was weeping, and the actors who gave me so much pleasure?

—He is a living illness, answered the abbé, who makes a business of slandering all the plays and books; he hates the successful ones, as eunuchs hate successful lovers; he's one of those literary snakes who live on filth and venom; he's a folliculator . . .

—What's this word *folliculator?* asked Candide.

—It's a folio filler, said the abbé, a Fréron.[4]

It was after this fashion that Candide, Martin, and the abbé from Perigord chatted on the stairway as they watched the crowd leaving the theatre.

—Although I'm in a great hurry to see Miss Cunégonde again, said Candide, I would very much like to dine with Miss Clairon,[5] for she seemed to me admirable.

The abbé was not the man to approach Miss Clairon, who saw only good company.

—She has an engagement tonight, he said; but I shall have the honor of introducing you to a lady of quality, and there you will get to know Paris as if you had lived here for years.

Candide, who was curious by nature, allowed himself to be brought to the lady's house, in the depths of the Faubourg St.-Honoré; they were playing faro;[6] twelve melancholy punters held in their hands a little sheaf of cards, blank summaries of their bad luck. Silence reigned supreme, the punters were pallid, the banker uneasy; and the lady of the house, seated beside the pitiless banker, watched with the eyes of a lynx for the various illegal redoublings and bets at long odds which the players tried to signal by folding the corners of their cards; she had them unfolded with a determination which was severe but polite, and concealed her anger lest she lose her customers. The lady caused herself to be known as the Marquise of Parolignac.[7] Her daughter, fifteen years old, sat among the punters and tipped off her mother with a wink to the sharp practices of these unhappy players when they tried to recoup their losses. The abbé from Perigord, Candide, and Martin came in; nobody arose or greeted them or looked at them; all were lost in the study of their cards.

—My Lady the Baroness of Thunder-Ten-Tronckh was more civil, thought Candide.

However, the abbé whispered in the ear of the marquise, who, half rising, honored Candide with a gracious smile and Martin with a truly noble nod; she gave a

4. A successful and popular journalist who had attacked several of Voltaire's plays, including *Tancrède*.

5. Actually Claire Leris (1723–1803). She had played the lead role in *Tancrède* and was for many years a leading figure on the Paris stage.

6. A game of cards, about which it is necessary to know only that a number of punters play against a banker or dealer. The pack is dealt out two cards at a time, and each player may bet on any card as much as he pleases. The sharp practices of the punters consist essentially of tricks for increasing their winnings without corresponding risks.

7. A *paroli* is an illegal redoubling of one's bet; her name therefore implies a title grounded in cardsharping.

seat and dealt a hand of cards to Candide, who lost fifty thousand francs in two turns; after which they had a very merry supper. Everyone was amazed that Candide was not upset over his losses; the lackeys, talking together in their usual lackey language, said:—He must be some English milord.

The supper was like most Parisian suppers: first silence, then an indistinguishable rush of words; then jokes, mostly insipid, false news, bad logic, a little politics, a great deal of malice. They even talked of new books.

—Have you seen the new novel by Dr. Gauchat, the theologian?[8] asked the abbé from Perigord.

—Oh yes, answered one of the guests; but I couldn't finish it. We have a horde of impudent scribblers nowadays, but all of them put together don't match the impudence of this Gauchat, this doctor of theology. I have been so struck by the enormous number of detestable books which are swamping us that I have taken up punting at faro.

—And the *Collected Essays* of Archdeacon T———[9] asked the abbé, what do you think of them?

—Ah, said Madame de Parolignac, what a frightful bore he is! He takes such pains to tell you what everyone knows; he discourses so learnedly on matters which aren't worth a casual remark! He plunders, and not even wittily, the wit of other people! He spoils what he plunders, he's disgusting! But he'll never disgust me again; a couple of pages of the archdeacon have been enough for me.

There was at table a man of learning and taste, who supported the marquise on this point. They talked next of tragedies; the lady asked why there were tragedies which played well enough but which were wholly unreadable. The man of taste explained very clearly how a play could have a certain interest and yet little merit otherwise; he showed succinctly that it was not enough to conduct a couple of intrigues, such as one can find in any novel, and which never fail to excite the spectator's interest; but that one must be new without being grotesque, frequently touch the sublime but never depart from the natural; that one must know the human heart and give it words; that one must be a great poet without allowing any character in the play to sound like a poet; and that one must know the language perfectly, speak it purely, and maintain a continual harmony without ever sacrificing sense to mere sound.

—Whoever, he added, does not observe all these rules may write one or two tragedies which succeed in the theatre, but he will never be ranked among the good writers; there are very few good tragedies; some are idylls in well-written, well-rhymed dialogue, others are political arguments which put the audience to sleep, or revolting pomposities; still others are the fantasies of enthusiasts, barbarous in style, incoherent in logic, full of long speeches to the gods because the author does not know how to address men, full of false maxims and emphatic commonplaces.

Candide listened attentively to this speech and conceived a high opinion of the speaker; and as the marquise had placed him by her side, he turned to ask her who was this man who spoke so well.

—He is a scholar, said the lady, who never plays cards and whom the abbé sometimes brings to my house for supper; he knows all about tragedies and

8. He had written against Voltaire, and Voltaire suspected him (wrongly) of having written the novel *L'Oracle des nouveaux philosophes*.
9. His name was Trublet, and he had said, among other disagreeable things, that Voltaire's epic poem, the *Henriade*, made him yawn and that Voltaire's genius was "the perfection of mediocrity."

books, and has himself written a tragedy that was hissed from the stage and a book, the only copy of which ever seen outside his publisher's office was dedicated to me.

—What a great man, said Candide, he's Pangloss all over.

Then, turning to him, he said:—Sir, you doubtless think everything is for the best in the physical as well as the moral universe, and that nothing could be otherwise than as it is?

—Not at all, sir, replied the scholar, I believe nothing of the sort. I find that everything goes wrong in our world; that nobody knows his place in society or his duty, what he's doing or what he ought to be doing, and that outside of mealtimes, which are cheerful and congenial enough, all the rest of the day is spent in useless quarrels, as of Jansenists against Molinists,[1] parliament-men against churchmen, literary men against literary men, courtiers against courtiers, financiers against the plebs, wives against husbands, relatives against relatives—it's one unending warfare.

Candide answered:—I have seen worse; but a wise man, who has since had the misfortune to be hanged, taught me that everything was marvelously well arranged. Troubles are just the shadows in a beautiful picture.

—Your hanged philosopher was joking, said Martin; the shadows are horrible ugly blots.

—It is human beings who make the blots, said Candide, and they can't do otherwise.

—Then it isn't their fault, said Martin.

Most of the faro players, who understood this sort of talk not at all, kept on drinking; Martin disputed with the scholar, and Candide told part of his story to the lady of the house.

After supper, the marquise brought Candide into her room and sat him down on a divan.

—Well, she said to him, are you still madly in love with Miss Cunégonde of Thunder-Ten-Tronckh?

—Yes, ma'am, replied Candide. The marquise turned upon him a tender smile.

—You answer like a young man of Westphalia, said she; a Frenchman would have told me: 'It is true that I have been in love with Miss Cunégonde; but since seeing you, madame, I fear that I love her no longer.'

—Alas, ma'am, said Candide, I will answer any way you want.

—Your passion for her, said the marquise, began when you picked up her handkerchief; I prefer that you should pick up my garter.

—Gladly, said Candide, and picked it up.

—But I also want you to put it back on, said the lady; and Candide put it on again.

—Look you now, said the lady, you are a foreigner; my Paris lovers I sometimes cause to languish for two weeks or so, but to you I surrender the very first night, because we must render the honors of the country to a young man from Westphalia.

---

1. The Jansenists (from Corneille Jansen, 1585–1638) were a relatively strict party of religious reform; the Molinists (from Luis Molina) were the party of the Jesuits. Their central issue of controversy was the relative importance of divine grace and human will to the salvation of man.

The beauty, who had seen two enormous diamonds on the two hands of her young friend, praised them so sincerely that from the fingers of Candide they passed over to the fingers of the marquise.

As he returned home with his Perigord abbé, Candide felt some remorse at having been unfaithful to Miss Cunégonde; the abbé sympathized with his grief; he had only a small share in the fifty thousand francs which Candide lost at cards, and in the proceeds of the two diamonds which had been half-given, half-extorted. His scheme was to profit, as much as he could, from the advantage of knowing Candide. He spoke at length of Cunégonde, and Candide told him that he would beg forgiveness for his beloved for his infidelity when he met her at Venice.

The Perigordian overflowed with politeness and unction, taking a tender interest in everything Candide said, everything he did, and everything he wanted to do.

—Well, sir, said he, so you have an assignation at Venice?

—Yes indeed, sir, I do, said Candide; it is absolutely imperative that I go there to find Miss Cunégonde.

And then, carried away by the pleasure of talking about his love, he recounted, as he often did, a part of his adventures with that illustrious lady of Westphalia.

—I suppose, said the abbé, that Miss Cunégonde has a fine wit and writes charming letters.

—I never received a single letter from her, said Candide; for, as you can imagine, after being driven out of the castle for love of her, I couldn't write; shortly I learned that she was dead; then I rediscovered her; then I lost her again, and I have now sent, to a place more than twenty-five hundred leagues from here, a special agent whose return I am expecting.

The abbé listened carefully, and looked a bit dreamy. He soon took his leave of the two strangers, after embracing them tenderly. Next day Candide, when he woke up, received a letter, to the following effect:

—Dear sir, my very dear lover, I have been lying sick in this town for a week, I have just learned that you are here. I would fly to your arms if I could move. I heard that you had passed through Bordeaux; that was where I left the faithful Cacambo and the old woman, who are soon to follow me here. The governor of Buenos Aires took everything, but left me your heart. Come; your presence will either return me to life or cause me to die of joy.

This charming letter, coming so unexpectedly, filled Candide with inexpressible delight, while the illness of his dear Cunégonde covered him with grief. Torn between these two feelings, he took gold and diamonds, and had himself brought, with Martin, to the hotel where Miss Cunégonde was lodging. Trembling with emotion, he enters the room; his heart thumps, his voice breaks. He tries to open the curtains of the bed, he asks to have some lights.

—Absolutely forbidden, says the serving girl; light will be the death of her.

And abruptly she pulls shut the curtain.

—My dear Cunégonde, says Candide in tears, how are you feeling? If you can't see me, won't you at least speak to me?

—She can't talk, says the servant.

But then she draws forth from the bed a plump hand, over which Candide weeps a long time, and which he fills with diamonds, meanwhile leaving a bag of gold on the chair.

Amid his transports, there arrives a bailiff followed by the abbé from Perigord and a strong-arm squad.

—These here are the suspicious foreigners? says the officer; and he has them seized and orders his bullies to drag them off to jail.

—They don't treat visitors like this in Eldorado, says Candide.

—I am more a Manichee than ever, says Martin.

—But, please sir, where are you taking us? says Candide.

—To the lowest hole in the dungeons, says the bailiff.

Martin, having regained his self-possession, decided that the lady who pretended to be Cunégonde was a cheat, the abbé from Perigord was another cheat who had imposed on Candide's innocence, and the bailiff still another cheat, of whom it would be easy to get rid.

Rather than submit to the forms of justice, Candide, enlightened by Martin's advice and eager for his own part to see the real Cunégonde again, offered the bailiff three little diamonds worth about three thousand pistoles apiece.

—Ah, my dear sir! cried the man with the ivory staff, even if you have committed every crime imaginable, you are the most honest man in the world. Three diamonds! each one worth three thousand pistoles! My dear sir! I would gladly die for you, rather than take you to jail. All foreigners get arrested here; but let me manage it; I have a brother at Dieppe in Normandy; I'll take you to him; and if you have a bit of a diamond to give him, he'll take care of you, just like me.

—And why do they arrest all foreigners? asked Candide.

The abbé from Perigord spoke up and said:—It's because a beggar from Atrebatum[2] listened to some stupidities; that made him commit a parricide, not like the one of May, 1610, but like the one of December, 1594, much on the order of several other crimes committed in other years and other months by other beggars who had listened to stupidities.

The bailiff then explained what it was all about.[3]

—Foh! what beasts! cried Candide. What! monstrous behavior of this sort from a people who sing and dance? As soon as I can, let me get out of this country, where the monkeys provoke the tigers. In my own country I've lived with bears; only in Eldorado are there proper men. In the name of God, sir bailiff, get me to Venice where I can wait for Miss Cunégonde.

—I can only get you to Lower Normandy, said the guardsman.

He had the irons removed at once, said there had been a mistake, dismissed his gang, and took Candide and Martin to Dieppe, where he left them with his brother. There was a little Dutch ship at anchor. The Norman, changed by three more diamonds into the most helpful of men, put Candide and his people aboard the vessel, which was bound for Portsmouth in England. It wasn't on the way to Venice, but Candide felt like a man just let out of hell; and he hoped to get back on the road to Venice at the first possible occasion.

---

2. The Latin name for the district of Artois, from which came Robert-François Damiens, who tried to stab Louis XV in 1757. The assassination failed, like that of Châtel, who tried to kill Henri IV in 1594, but unlike that of Ravaillac, who succeeded in killing him in 1610.

3. The point, in fact, is not too clear since arresting foreigners is an indirect way at best to guard against homegrown fanatics, and the position of the abbé from Perigord in the whole transaction remains confused. Has he called in the officer just to get rid of Candide? If so, why is he sardonic about the very suspicions he is trying to foster? Candide's reaction is to the notion that Frenchmen should be capable of political assassination at all; it seems excessive.

CHAPTER 23

Candide and Martin Pass the Shores of England;
What They See There

—Ah, Pangloss! Pangloss! Ah, Martin! Martin! Ah, my darling Cunégonde! What is this world of ours? sighed Candide on the Dutch vessel.

—Something crazy, something abominable, Martin replied.

—You have been in England; are people as crazy there as in France?

—It's a different sort of crazy, said Martin. You know that these two nations have been at war over a few acres of snow near Canada, and that they are spending on this fine struggle more than Canada itself is worth.[4] As for telling you if there are more people in one country or the other who need a strait jacket, that is a judgment too fine for my understanding; I know only that the people we are going to visit are eaten up with melancholy.

As they chatted thus, the vessel touched at Portsmouth. A multitude of people covered the shore, watching closely a rather bulky man who was kneeling, his eyes blindfolded, on the deck of a man-of-war. Four soldiers, stationed directly in front of this man, fired three bullets apiece into his brain, as peaceably as you would want; and the whole assemblage went home, in great satisfaction.[5]

—What's all this about? asked Candide. What devil is everywhere at work?

He asked who was that big man who had just been killed with so much ceremony.

—It was an admiral, they told him.

—And why kill this admiral?

—The reason, they told him, is that he didn't kill enough people; he gave battle to a French admiral, and it was found that he didn't get close enough to him.

—But, said Candide, the French admiral was just as far from the English admiral as the English admiral was from the French admiral.

—That's perfectly true, came the answer; but in this country it is useful from time to time to kill one admiral in order to encourage the others.

Candide was so stunned and shocked at what he saw and heard, that he would not even set foot ashore; he arranged with the Dutch merchant (without even caring if he was robbed, as at Surinam) to be taken forthwith to Venice.

The merchant was ready in two days; they coasted along France, they passed within sight of Lisbon, and Candide quivered. They entered the straits, crossed the Mediterranean, and finally landed at Venice.

—God be praised, said Candide, embracing Martin; here I shall recover the lovely Cunégonde. I trust Cacambo as I would myself. All is well, all goes well, all goes as well as possible.

---

4. The wars of the French and English over Canada dragged intermittently through the 18th century till the peace of Paris sealed England's conquest (1763). Voltaire thought the French should concentrate on developing Louisiana, where the Jesuit influence was less marked.

5. Candide has witnessed the execution of Admiral John Byng, defeated off Minorca by the French fleet under Galisonnière and executed by firing squad on March 14, 1757. Voltaire had intervened to avert the execution.

CHAPTER 24

About Paquette and Brother Giroflée

As soon as he was in Venice, he had a search made for Cacambo in all the inns, all the cafés, all the stews—and found no trace of him. Every day he sent to investigate the vessels and coastal traders; no news of Cacambo.

—How's this? said he to Martin. I have had time to go from Surinam to Bordeaux, from Bordeaux to Paris, from Paris to Dieppe, from Dieppe to Portsmouth, to skirt Portugal and Spain, cross the Mediterranean, and spend several months at Venice—and the lovely Cunégonde has not come yet! In her place, I have met only that impersonator and that abbé from Perigord. Cunégonde is dead, without a doubt; and nothing remains for me too but death. Oh, it would have been better to stay in the earthly paradise of Eldorado than to return to this accursed Europe. How right you are, my dear Martin; all is but illusion and disaster.

He fell into a black melancholy, and refused to attend the fashionable operas or take part in the other diversions of the carnival season; not a single lady tempted him in the slightest. Martin told him:—You're a real simpleton if you think a half-breed valet with five or six millions in his pockets will go to the end of the world to get your mistress and bring her to Venice for you. If he finds her, he'll take her for himself; if he doesn't, he'll take another. I advise you to forget about your servant Cacambo and your mistress Cunégonde.

Martin was not very comforting. Candide's melancholy increased, and Martin never wearied of showing him that there is little virtue and little happiness on this earth, except perhaps in Eldorado, where nobody can go.

While they were discussing this important matter and still waiting for Cunégonde, Candide noticed in St. Mark's Square a young Theatine[6] monk who had given his arm to a girl. The Theatine seemed fresh, plump, and flourishing; his eyes were bright, his manner cocky, his glance brilliant, his step proud. The girl was very pretty, and singing aloud; she glanced lovingly at her Theatine, and from time to time pinched his plump cheeks.

—At least you must admit, said Candide to Martin, that these people are happy. Until now I have not found in the whole inhabited earth, except Eldorado, anything but miserable people. But this girl and this monk, I'd be willing to bet, are very happy creatures.

—I'll bet they aren't, said Martin.

—We have only to ask them to dinner, said Candide, and we'll find out if I'm wrong.

Promptly he approached them, made his compliments, and invited them to his inn for a meal of macaroni, Lombardy partridges, and caviar, washed down with wine from Montepulciano, Cyprus, and Samos, and some Lacrima Christi. The girl blushed but the Theatine accepted gladly, and the girl followed him, watching Candide with an expression of surprise and confusion, darkened by several tears. Scarcely had she entered the room when she said to Candide:—What, can it be that Master Candide no longer knows Paquette?

At these words Candide, who had not yet looked carefully at her because he was preoccupied with Cunégonde, said to her:—Ah, my poor child! so you are the one who put Doctor Pangloss in the fine fix where I last saw him.

6. A Catholic order founded in 1524 by Cardinal Cajetan and G. P. Caraffa, later Pope Paul IV.

—Alas, sir, I was the one, said Paquette; I see you know all about it. I heard of the horrible misfortunes which befell the whole household of My Lady the Baroness and the lovely Cunégonde. I swear to you that my own fate has been just as unhappy. I was perfectly innocent when you knew me. A Franciscan, who was my confessor, easily seduced me. The consequences were frightful; shortly after My Lord the Baron had driven you out with great kicks on the backside, I too was forced to leave the castle. If a famous doctor had not taken pity on me, I would have died. Out of gratitude, I became for some time the mistress of this doctor. His wife, who was jealous to the point of frenzy, beat me mercilessly every day; she was a gorgon. The doctor was the ugliest of men, and I the most miserable creature on earth, being continually beaten for a man I did not love. You will understand, sir, how dangerous it is for a nagging woman to be married to a doctor. This man, enraged by his wife's ways, one day gave her as a cold cure a medicine so potent that in two hours' time she died amid horrible convulsions. Her relatives brought suit against the bereaved husband; he fled the country, and I was put in prison. My innocence would never have saved me if I had not been rather pretty. The judge set me free on condition that he should become the doctor's successor. I was shortly replaced in this post by another girl, dismissed without any payment, and obliged to continue this abominable trade which you men find so pleasant and which for us is nothing but a bottomless pit of misery. I went to ply the trade in Venice. Ah, my dear sir, if you could imagine what it is like to have to caress indiscriminately an old merchant, a lawyer, a monk, a gondolier, an abbé; to be subjected to every sort of insult and outrage; to be reduced, time and again, to borrowing a skirt in order to go have it lifted by some disgusting man; to be robbed by this fellow of what one has gained from that; to be shaken down by the police, and to have before one only the prospect of a hideous old age, a hospital, and a dunghill, you will conclude that I am one of the most miserable creatures in the world.

Thus Paquette poured forth her heart to the good Candide in a hotel room, while Martin sat listening nearby. At last he said to Candide:—You see, I've already won half my bet.

Brother Giroflée[7] had remained in the dining room, and was having a drink before dinner.

—But how's this? said Candide to Paquette. You looked so happy, so joyous, when I met you; you were singing, you caressed the Theatine with such a natural air of delight; you seemed to me just as happy as you now say you are miserable.

—Ah, sir, replied Paquette, that's another one of the miseries of this business; yesterday I was robbed and beaten by an officer, and today I have to seem in good humor in order to please a monk.

Candide wanted no more; he conceded that Martin was right. They sat down to table with Paquette and the Theatine; the meal was amusing enough, and when it was over, the company spoke out among themselves with some frankness.

—Father, said Candide to the monk, you seem to me a man whom all the world might envy; the flower of health glows in your cheek, your features radiate pleasure; you have a pretty girl for your diversion, and you seem very happy with your life as a Theatine.

—Upon my word, sir, said Brother Giroflée, I wish that all the Theatines were at the bottom of the sea. A hundred times I have been tempted to set fire to my

---

7. His name means "carnation" and Paquette means "daisy."

convent, and go turn Turk. My parents forced me, when I was fifteen years old, to put on this detestable robe, so they could leave more money to a cursed older brother of mine, may God confound him! Jealousy, faction, and fury spring up, by natural law, within the walls of convents. It is true, I have preached a few bad sermons which earned me a little money, half of which the prior stole from me; the remainder serves to keep me in girls. But when I have to go back to the monastery at night, I'm ready to smash my head against the walls of my cell; and all my fellow monks are in the same fix.

Martin turned to Candide and said with his customary coolness:

—Well, haven't I won the whole bet?

Candide gave two thousand piastres to Paquette and a thousand to Brother Giroflée.

—I assure you, said he, that with that they will be happy.

—I don't believe so, said Martin; your piastres may make them even more unhappy than they were before.

—That may be, said Candide; but one thing comforts me, I note that people often turn up whom one never expected to see again; it may well be that, having rediscovered my red sheep and Paquette, I will also rediscover Cunégonde.

—I hope, said Martin, that she will some day make you happy; but I very much doubt it.

—You're a hard man, said Candide.

—I've lived, said Martin.

—But look at these gondoliers, said Candide; aren't they always singing?

—You don't see them at home, said Martin, with their wives and squalling children. The doge has his troubles, the gondoliers theirs. It's true that on the whole one is better off as a gondolier than as a doge; but the difference is so slight, I don't suppose it's worth the trouble of discussing.

—There's a lot of talk here, said Candide, of this Senator Pococurante,[8] who has a fine palace on the Brenta and is hospitable to foreigners. They say he is a man who has never known a moment's grief.

—I'd like to see such a rare specimen, said Martin.

Candide promptly sent to Lord Pococurante, asking permission to call on him tomorrow.

CHAPTER 25

Visit to Lord Pococurante, Venetian Nobleman

Candide and Martin took a gondola on the Brenta, and soon reached the palace of the noble Pococurante. The gardens were large and filled with beautiful marble statues; the palace was handsomely designed. The master of the house, sixty years old and very rich, received his two inquisitive visitors perfectly politely, but with very little warmth; Candide was disconcerted and Martin not at all displeased.

First two pretty and neatly dressed girls served chocolate, which they whipped to a froth. Candide could not forbear praising their beauty, their grace, their skill.

—They are pretty good creatures, said Pococurante; I sometimes have them into my bed, for I'm tired of the ladies of the town, with their stupid tricks, quarrels, jealousies, fits of ill humor and petty pride, and all the sonnets one has to make or order for them; but, after all, these two girls are starting to bore me too.

8. His name means "small care."

After lunch, Candide strolled through a long gallery, and was amazed at the beauty of the pictures. He asked who was the painter of the two finest.

—They are by Raphael, said the senator; I bought them for a lot of money, out of vanity, some years ago; people say they're the finest in Italy, but they don't please me at all; the colors have all turned brown, the figures aren't well modeled and don't stand out enough, the draperies bear no resemblance to real cloth. In a word, whatever people may say, I don't find in them a real imitation of nature. I like a picture only when I can see in it a touch of nature itself, and there are none of this sort. I have many paintings, but I no longer look at them.

As they waited for dinner, Pococurante ordered a concerto performed. Candide found the music delightful.

—That noise? said Pococurante. It may amuse you for half an hour, but if it goes on any longer, it tires everybody though no one dares to admit it. Music today is only the art of performing difficult pieces, and what is merely difficult cannot please for long. Perhaps I should prefer the opera, if they had not found ways to make it revolting and monstrous. Anyone who likes bad tragedies set to music is welcome to them; in these performances the scenes serve only to introduce, inappropriately, two or three ridiculous songs designed to show off the actress's sound box. Anyone who wants to, or who can, is welcome to swoon with pleasure at the sight of a castrate wriggling through the role of Caesar or Cato, and strutting awkwardly about the stage. For my part, I have long since given up these paltry trifles which are called the glory of modern Italy, and for which monarchs pay such ruinous prices.

Candide argued a bit, but timidly; Martin was entirely of a mind with the senator.

They sat down to dinner, and after an excellent meal adjourned to the library. Candide, seeing a copy of Homer in a splendid binding, complimented the noble lord on his good taste.

—That is an author, said he, who was the special delight of great Pangloss, the best philosopher in all Germany.

—He's no special delight of mine, said Pococurante coldly. I was once made to believe that I took pleasure in reading him; but that constant recital of fights which are all alike, those gods who are always interfering but never decisively, that Helen who is the cause of the war and then scarcely takes any part in the story, that Troy which is always under siege and never taken—all that bores me to tears. I have sometimes asked scholars if reading it bored them as much as it bores me; everyone who answered frankly told me the book dropped from his hands like lead, but that they had to have it in their libraries as a monument of antiquity, like those old rusty coins which can't be used in real trade.

Your Excellence doesn't hold the same opinion of Virgil? said Candide.

—I concede, said Pococurante, that the second, fourth, and sixth books of his *Aeneid* are fine; but as for his pious Aeneas, and strong Cloanthes, and faithful Achates, and little Ascanius, and that imbecile King Latinus, and middle-class Amata, and insipid Lavinia, I don't suppose there was ever anything so cold and unpleasant. I prefer Tasso and those sleepwalkers' stories of Ariosto.

—Dare I ask, sir, said Candide, if you don't get great enjoyment from reading Horace?

—There are some maxims there, said Pococurante, from which a man of the world can profit, and which, because they are formed into vigorous couplets, are more easily remembered; but I care very little for his trip to Brindisi, his description of a bad dinner, or his account of a quibblers' squabble between some fellow

Pupilus, whose words he says *were full of pus*, and another whose words *were full of vinegar*.[9] I feel nothing but extreme disgust at his verses against old women and witches; and I can't see what's so great in his telling his friend Maecenas that if he is raised by him to the ranks of lyric poets, he will strike the stars with his lofty forehead. Fools admire everything in a well-known author. I read only for my own pleasure; I like only what is in my style.

Candide, who had been trained never to judge for himself, was much astonished by what he heard; and Martin found Pococurante's way of thinking quite rational.

—Oh, here is a copy of Cicero, said Candide. Now this great man I suppose you're never tired of reading.

—I never read him at all, replied the Venetian. What do I care whether he pleaded for Rabirius or Cluentius? As a judge, I have my hands full of lawsuits. I might like his philosophical works better, but when I saw that he had doubts about everything, I concluded that I knew as much as he did, and that I needed no help to be ignorant.

—Ah, here are eighty volumes of collected papers from a scientific academy, cried Martin; maybe there is something good in them.

—There would be indeed, said Pococurante, if one of these silly authors had merely discovered a new way of making pins; but in all those volumes there is nothing but empty systems, not a single useful discovery.

—What a lot of stage plays I see over there, said Candide, some in Italian, some in Spanish and French.

—Yes, said the senator, three thousand of them, and not three dozen good ones. As for those collections of sermons, which all together are not worth a page of Seneca, and all these heavy volumes of theology, you may be sure I never open them, nor does anybody else.

Martin noticed some shelves full of English books.

—I suppose, said he, that a republican must delight in most of these books written in the land of liberty.

—Yes, replied Pococurante, it's a fine thing to write as you think; it is mankind's privilege. In all our Italy, people write only what they do not think; men who inhabit the land of the Caesars and Antonines dare not have an idea without the permission of a Dominican. I would rejoice in the freedom that breathes through English genius, if partisan passions did not corrupt all that is good in that precious freedom.

Candide, noting a Milton, asked if he did not consider this author a great man.

—Who? said Pococurante. That barbarian who made a long commentary on the first chapter of Genesis in ten books of crabbed verse?[1] That clumsy imitator of the Greeks, who disfigures creation itself, and while Moses represents the eternal being as creating the world with a word, has the messiah take a big compass out of a heavenly cupboard in order to design his work? You expect me to admire the man who spoiled Tasso's hell and devil? who disguises Lucifer now as a toad, now as a pigmy? who makes him rehash the same arguments a hundred times

---

9. *Satires* 1.7; Pococurante, with gentlemanly negligence, has corrupted Rupilius to Pupilus. Horace's poems against witches are *Epodes* 5.8, 12; the one about striking the stars with

his lofty forehead is *Odes* 1.1.

1. The first edition of *Paradise Lost* had ten books, which Milton later expanded to twelve.

over? who makes him argue theology? and who, taking seriously Ariosto's comic story of the invention of firearms, has the devils shooting off cannon in heaven? Neither I nor anyone else in Italy has been able to enjoy these gloomy extravagances. The marriage of Sin and Death, and the monster that Sin gives birth to, will nauseate any man whose taste is at all refined; and his long description of a hospital is good only for a gravedigger. This obscure, extravagant, and disgusting poem was despised at its birth; I treat it today as it was treated in its own country by its contemporaries. Anyhow, I say what I think, and care very little whether other people agree with me.

Candide was a little cast down by this speech; he respected Homer, and had a little affection for Milton.

—Alas, he said under his breath to Martin, I'm afraid this man will have a supreme contempt for our German poets.

—No harm in that, said Martin.

—Oh what a superior man, said Candide, still speaking softly, what a great genius this Pococurante must be! Nothing can please him.

Having thus looked over all the books, they went down into the garden. Candide praised its many beauties.

—I know nothing in such bad taste, said the master of the house; we have nothing but trifles here; tomorrow I am going to have one set out on a nobler design.

When the two visitors had taken leave of his excellency:—Well now, said Candide to Martin, you must agree that this was the happiest of all men, for he is superior to everything he possesses.

—Don't you see, said Martin, that he is disgusted with everything he possesses? Plato said, a long time ago, that the best stomachs are not those which refuse all food.

—But, said Candide, isn't there pleasure in criticizing everything, in seeing faults where other people think they see beauties?

—That is to say, Martin replied, that there's pleasure in having no pleasure?

—Oh well, said Candide, then I am the only happy man . . . or will be, when I see Miss Cunégonde again.

—It's always a good thing to have hope, said Martin.

But the days and the weeks slipped past; Cacambo did not come back, and Candide was so buried in his grief, that he did not even notice that Paquette and Brother Giroflée had neglected to come and thank him.

CHAPTER 26

About a Supper that Candide and Martin Had with Six Strangers, and Who They Were

One evening when Candide, accompanied by Martin, was about to sit down for dinner with the strangers staying in his hotel, a man with a soot-colored face came up behind him, took him by the arm, and said:—Be ready to leave with us, don't miss out.

He turned and saw Cacambo. Only the sight of Cunégonde could have astonished and pleased him more. He nearly went mad with joy. He embraced his dear friend.

—Cunégonde is here, no doubt? Where is she? Bring me to her, let me die of joy in her presence.

—Cunégonde is not here at all, said Cacambo, she is at Constantinople.

—Good Heavens, at Constantinople! but if she were in China, I must fly there, let's go.

—We will leave after supper, said Cacambo; I can tell you no more; I am a slave, my owner is looking for me, I must go wait on him at table; mum's the word; eat your supper and be prepared.

Candide, torn between joy and grief, delighted to have seen his faithful agent again, astonished to find him a slave, full of the idea of recovering his mistress, his heart in a turmoil, his mind in a whirl, sat down to eat with Martin, who was watching all these events coolly, and with six strangers who had come to pass the carnival season at Venice.

Cacambo, who was pouring wine for one of the strangers, leaned respectfully over his master at the end of the meal, and said to him:—Sire, Your Majesty may leave when he pleases, the vessel is ready.

Having said these words, he exited. The diners looked at one another in silent amazement, when another servant, approaching his master, said to him:—Sire, Your Majesty's litter is at Padua, and the bark awaits you.

The master nodded, and the servant vanished. All the diners looked at one another again, and the general amazement redoubled. A third servant, approaching a third stranger, said to him:—Sire, take my word for it, Your Majesty must stay here no longer; I shall get everything ready.

Then he too disappeared.

Candide and Martin had no doubt, now, that it was a carnival masquerade. A fourth servant spoke to a fourth master:—Your Majesty will leave when he pleases—and went out like the others. A fifth followed suit. But the sixth servant spoke differently to the sixth stranger, who sat next to Candide. He said:—My word, sire, they'll give no more credit to Your Majesty, nor to me either; we could very well spend the night in the lockup, you and I. I've got to look out for myself, so good-bye to you.

When all the servants had left, the six strangers, Candide, and Martin remained under a pall of silence. Finally Candide broke it.

—Gentlemen, said he, here's a funny kind of joke. Why are you all royalty? I assure you that Martin and I aren't.

Cacambo's master spoke up gravely then, and said in Italian:—This is no joke, my name is Achmet the Third.[2] I was grand sultan for several years; then, as I had dethroned my brother, my nephew dethroned me. My viziers had their throats cut; I was allowed to end my days in the old seraglio. My nephew, the Grand Sultan Mahmoud, sometimes lets me travel for my health; and I have come to spend the carnival season at Venice.

A young man who sat next to Achmet spoke after him, and said:—My name is Ivan; I was once emperor of all the Russias.[3] I was dethroned while still in my cradle; my father and mother were locked up, and I was raised in prison; I sometimes have permission to travel, though always under guard, and I have come to spend the carnival season at Venice.

The third said:—I am Charles Edward, king of England;[4] my father yielded me his rights to the kingdom, and I fought to uphold them; but they tore out the

2. Ottoman ruler (1673–1736); he was deposed in 1730.
3. Ivan VI reigned from his birth in 1740 until 1756, then was confined in the Schlusselberg, and executed in 1764.

4. This is the Young Pretender (1720–1788), known to his supporters as Bonnie Prince Charlie. The defeat so theatrically described took place at Culloden, April 16, 1746.

hearts of eight hundred of my partisans, and flung them in their faces. I have been in prison; now I am going to Rome, to visit the king, my father, dethroned like me and my grandfather; and I have come to pass the carnival season at Venice.

The fourth king then spoke up, and said:—I am a king of the Poles;[5] the luck of war has deprived me of my hereditary estates; my father suffered the same losses; I submit to Providence like Sultan Achmet, Emperor Ivan, and King Charles Edward, to whom I hope heaven grants long lives; and I have come to pass the carnival season at Venice.

The fifth said:—I too am a king of the Poles;[6] I lost my kingdom twice, but Providence gave me another state, in which I have been able to do more good than all the Sarmatian kings ever managed to do on the banks of the Vistula. I too have submitted to Providence, and I have come to pass the carnival season at Venice.

It remained for the sixth monarch to speak.

—Gentlemen, said he, I am no such great lord as you, but I have in fact been a king like any other. I am Theodore; I was elected king of Corsica.[7] People used to call me *Your Majesty*, and now they barely call me *Sir*; I used to coin currency, and now I don't have a cent; I used to have two secretaries of state, and now I scarcely have a valet; I have sat on a throne, and for a long time in London I was in jail, on the straw; and I may well be treated the same way here, though I have come, like your majesties, to pass the carnival season at Venice.

The five other kings listened to his story with noble compassion. Each one of them gave twenty sequins to King Theodore, so that he might buy a suit and some shirts; Candide gave him a diamond worth two thousand sequins.

—Who in the world, said the five kings, is this private citizen who is in a position to give a hundred times as much as any of us, and who actually gives it?[8]

Just as they were rising from dinner, there arrived at the same establishment four most serene highnesses, who had also lost their kingdoms through the luck of war, and who came to spend the rest of the carnival season at Venice. But Candide never bothered even to look at these newcomers because he was only concerned to go find his dear Cunégonde at Constantinople.

CHAPTER 27

Candide's Trip to Constantinople

Faithful Cacambo had already arranged with the Turkish captain who was returning Sultan Achmet to Constantinople to make room for Candide and Martin on board. Both men boarded ship after prostrating themselves before his miserable highness. On the way, Candide said to Martin:—Six dethroned kings that we had dinner with! and yet among those six there was one on whom I had to bestow charity! Perhaps there are other princes even more unfortunate. I myself

---

5. Augustus III (1696–1763), Elector of Saxony and King of Poland, dethroned by Frederick the Great in 1756.

6. Stanislas Leczinski (1677–1766), father-in-law of Louis XV, who abdicated the throne of Poland in 1736, was made Duke of Lorraine and in that capacity befriended Voltaire.

7. Theodore von Neuhof (1690–1756), an authentic Westphalian, an adventurer and a soldier of fortune, who in 1736 was (for about eight months) the elected king of Corsica. He spent time in an Amsterdam as well as a London debtor's prison.

8. Voltaire was very conscious of his situation as a man richer than many princes; in 1758 he had money on loan to no fewer than three highnesses, Charles Eugene, Duke of Wurtemburg; Charles Theodore, Elector Palatine; and the Duke of Saxe-Gotha.

have only lost a hundred sheep, and now I am flying to the arms of Cunégonde. My dear Martin, once again Pangloss is proved right, all is for the best.

—I hope so, said Martin.

—But, said Candide, that was a most unlikely experience we had at Venice. Nobody ever saw, or heard tell of, six dethroned kings eating together at an inn.

—It is no more extraordinary, said Martin, than most of the things that have happened to us. Kings are frequently dethroned; and as for the honor we had from dining with them, that's a trifle which doesn't deserve our notice.[9]

Scarcely was Candide on board than he fell on the neck of his former servant, his friend Cacambo.

—Well! said he, what is Cunégonde doing? Is she still a marvel of beauty? Does she still love me? How is her health? No doubt you have bought her a palace at Constantinople.

—My dear master, answered Cacambo, Cunégonde is washing dishes on the shores of the Propontis, in the house of a prince who has very few dishes to wash; she is a slave in the house of a onetime king named Ragotski,[1] to whom the Great Turk allows three crowns a day in his exile; but, what is worse than all this, she has lost all her beauty and become horribly ugly.

—Ah, beautiful or ugly, said Candide, I am an honest man, and my duty is to love her forever. But how can she be reduced to this wretched state with the five or six millions that you had?

—All right, said Cacambo, didn't I have to give two millions to Señor don Fernando d'Ibaraa y Figueroa y Mascarenes y Lampourdos y Souza, governor of Buenos Aires, for his permission to carry off Miss Cunégonde? And didn't a pirate cleverly strip us of the rest? And didn't this pirate carry us off to Cape Matapan, to Melos, Nicaria, Samos, Petra, to the Dardanelles, Marmora, Scutari? Cunégonde and the old woman are working for the prince I told you about, and I am the slave of the dethroned sultan.

—What a lot of fearful calamities linked one to the other, said Candide. But after all, I still have a few diamonds, I shall easily deliver Cunégonde. What a pity that she's become so ugly!

Then, turning toward Martin, he asked:—Who in your opinion is more to be pitied, the Emperor Achmet, the Emperor Ivan, King Charles Edward, or myself?

—I have no idea, said Martin; I would have to enter your hearts in order to tell.

—Ah, said Candide, if Pangloss were here, he would know and he would tell us.

—I can't imagine, said Martin, what scales your Pangloss would use to weigh out the miseries of men and value their griefs. All I will venture is that the earth holds millions of men who deserve our pity a hundred times more than King Charles Edward, Emperor Ivan, or Sultan Achmet.

—You may well be right, said Candide.

In a few days they arrived at the Black Sea canal. Candide began by repurchasing Cacambo at an exorbitant price; then, without losing an instant, he flung himself and his companions into a galley to go search out Cunégonde on the shores of Propontis, however ugly she might be.

There were in the chain gang two convicts who bent clumsily to the oar, and on whose bare shoulders the Levantine[2] captain delivered from time to time a few

---

9. Another late change adds the following question:—*What does it matter whom you dine with as long as you fare well at table?* I have omitted it, again on literary grounds.
1. Francis Leopold Rakoczy (1676–1735),

who was briefly king of Transylvania in the early 18th century. After 1720 he was interned in Turkey.
2. From the eastern Mediterranean.

lashes with a bullwhip. Candide naturally noticed them more than the other galley slaves, and out of pity came closer to them. Certain features of their disfigured faces seemed to him to bear a slight resemblance to Pangloss and to that wretched Jesuit, that baron, that brother of Miss Cunégonde. The notion stirred and saddened him. He looked at them more closely.

—To tell you the truth, he said to Cacambo, if I hadn't seen Master Pangloss hanged, and if I hadn't been so miserable as to murder the baron, I should think they were rowing in this very galley.

At the names of 'baron' and 'Pangloss' the two convicts gave a great cry, sat still on their bench, and dropped their oars. The Levantine captain came running, and the bullwhip lashes redoubled.

—Stop, stop, captain, cried Candide. I'll give you as much money as you want.

—What, can it be Candide? cried one of the convicts.

—What, can it be Candide? cried the other.

—Is this a dream? said Candide. Am I awake or asleep? Am I in this galley? Is that My Lord the Baron, whom I killed? Is that Master Pangloss, whom I saw hanged?

—It is indeed, they replied.

—What, is that the great philosopher? said Martin.

—Now, sir, Mr. Levantine Captain, said Candide, how much money do you want for the ransom of My Lord Thunder-Ten-Tronckh, one of the first barons of the empire, and Master Pangloss, the deepest metaphysician in all Germany?

—Dog of a Christian, replied the Levantine captain, since these two dogs of Christian convicts are barons and metaphysicians, which is no doubt a great honor in their country, you will give me fifty thousand sequins for them.

—You shall have them, sir, take me back to Constantinople and you shall be paid on the spot. Or no, take me to Miss Cunégonde.

The Levantine captain, at Candide's first word, had turned his bow toward the town, and he had them rowed there as swiftly as a bird cleaves the air.

A hundred times Candide embraced the baron and Pangloss.

—And how does it happen I didn't kill you, my dear baron? and my dear Pangloss, how can you be alive after being hanged? and why are you both rowing in the galleys of Turkey?

—Is it really true that my dear sister is in this country? asked the baron.

—Yes, answered Cacambo.

—And do I really see again my dear Candide? cried Pangloss.

Candide introduced Martin and Cacambo. They all embraced; they all talked at once. The galley flew, already they were back in port. A Jew was called, and Candide sold him for fifty thousand sequins a diamond worth a hundred thousand, while he protested by Abraham that he could not possibly give more for it. Candide immediately ransomed the baron and Pangloss. The latter threw himself at the feet of his liberator, and bathed them with tears; the former thanked him with a nod, and promised to repay this bit of money at the first opportunity.

—But is it really possible that my sister is in Turkey? said he.

—Nothing is more possible, replied Cacambo, since she is a dishwasher in the house of a prince of Transylvania.

At once two more Jews were called; Candide sold some more diamonds; and they all departed in another galley to the rescue of Cunégonde.

CHAPTER 28

What Happened to Candide, Cunégonde, Pangloss, Martin, &c.

—Let me beg your pardon once more, said Candide to the baron, pardon me, reverend father, for having run you through the body with my sword.

—Don't mention it, replied the baron. I was a little too hasty myself, I confess it; but since you want to know the misfortune which brought me to the galleys, I'll tell you. After being cured of my wound by the brother who was apothecary to the college, I was attacked and abducted by a Spanish raiding party; they jailed me in Buenos Aires at the time when my sister had just left. I asked to be sent to Rome, to the father general. Instead, I was named to serve as almoner in Constantinople, under the French ambassador. I had not been a week on this job when I chanced one evening on a very handsome young ichoglan.[3] The evening was hot; the young man wanted to take a swim; I seized the occasion, and went with him. I did not know that it is a capital offense for a Christian to be found naked with a young Moslem. A cadi sentenced me to receive a hundred blows with a cane on the soles of my feet, and then to be sent to the galleys. I don't suppose there was ever such a horrible miscarriage of justice. But I would like to know why my sister is in the kitchen of a Transylvanian king exiled among Turks.

—But how about you, my dear Pangloss, said Candide; how is it possible that we have met again?

—It is true, said Pangloss, that you saw me hanged; in the normal course of things, I should have been burned, but you recall that a cloudburst occurred just as they were about to roast me. So much rain fell that they despaired of lighting the fire; thus I was hanged, for lack of anything better to do with me. A surgeon bought my body, carried me off to his house, and dissected me. First he made a cross-shaped incision in me, from the navel to the clavicle. No one could have been worse hanged than I was. In fact, the executioner of the high ceremonials of the Holy Inquisition, who was a subdeacon, burned people marvelously well, but he was not in the way of hanging them. The rope was wet, and tightened badly; it caught on a knot; in short, I was still breathing. The cross-shaped incision made me scream so loudly that the surgeon fell over backwards; he thought he was dissecting the devil, fled in an agony of fear, and fell downstairs in his flight. His wife ran in, at the noise, from a nearby room; she found me stretched out on the table with my cross-shaped incision, was even more frightened than her husband, fled, and fell over him. When they had recovered a little, I heard her say to him: 'My dear, what were you thinking of, trying to dissect a heretic? Don't you know those people are always possessed of the devil? I'm going to get the priest and have him exorcised.' At these words, I shuddered, and collected my last remaining energies to cry: 'Have mercy on me!' At last the Portuguese barber[4] took courage; he sewed me up again; his wife even nursed me; in two weeks I was up and about. The barber found me a job and made me lackey to a Knight of Malta who was going to Venice; and when this master could no longer pay me, I took service under a Venetian merchant, whom I followed to Constantinople.

—One day it occurred to me to enter a mosque; no one was there but an old imam and a very attractive young worshipper who was saying her prayers. Her bosom was completely bare; and between her two breasts she had a lovely bouquet of tulips, roses, anemones, buttercups, hyacinths, and primroses. She

---

3. A page to the sultan.
4. The two callings of barber and surgeon, since they both involved sharp instruments, were interchangeable in the early days of medicine.

dropped her bouquet, I picked it up, and returned it to her with the most respect-ful attentions. I was so long getting it back in place that the imam grew angry, and, seeing that I was a Christian, he called the guard. They took me before the cadi, who sentenced me to receive a hundred blows with a cane on the soles of my feet, and then to be sent to the galleys. I was chained to the same galley and precisely the same bench as My Lord the Baron. There were in this galley four young fellows from Marseilles, five Neapolitan priests, and two Corfu monks, who assured us that these things happen every day. My Lord the Baron asserted that he had suffered a greater injustice than I; I, on the other hand, proposed that it was much more permissible to replace a bouquet in a bosom than to be found naked with an ichoglan. We were arguing the point continually, and getting twenty lashes a day with the bullwhip, when the chain of events within this uni-verse brought you to our galley, and you ransomed us.

—Well, my dear Pangloss, Candide said to him, now that you have been hanged, dissected, beaten to a pulp, and sentenced to the galleys, do you still think everything is for the best in this world?

—I am still of my first opinion, replied Pangloss; for after all I am a philoso-pher, and it would not be right for me to recant since Leibniz could not possibly be wrong, and besides pre-established harmony is the finest notion in the world, like the plenum and subtle matter.[5]

CHAPTER 29

How Candide Found Cunégonde and the Old Woman Again

While Candide, the baron, Pangloss, Martin, and Cacambo were telling one another their stories, while they were disputing over the contingent or non-contingent events of this universe, while they were arguing over effects and causes, over moral evil and physical evil, over liberty and necessity, and over the consola-tions available to one in a Turkish galley, they arrived at the shores of Propontis and the house of the prince of Transylvania. The first sight to meet their eyes was Cunégonde and the old woman, who were hanging out towels on lines to dry.

The baron paled at what he saw. The tender lover Candide, seeing his lovely Cunégonde with her skin weathered, her eyes bloodshot, her breasts fallen, her cheeks seamed, her arms red and scaly, recoiled three steps in horror, and then advanced only out of politeness. She embraced Candide and her brother; every-one embraced the old woman; Candide ransomed them both.

There was a little farm in the neighborhood; the old woman suggested that Candide occupy it until some better fate should befall the group. Cunégonde did not know she was ugly, no one had told her; she reminded Candide of his prom-ises in so firm a tone that the good Candide did not dare to refuse her. So he went to tell the baron that he was going to marry his sister.

—Never will I endure, said the baron, such baseness on her part, such inso-lence on yours; this shame at least I will not put up with; why, my sister's children would not be able to enter the Chapters in Germany.[6] No, my sister will never marry anyone but a baron of the empire.

---

5. Rigorous determinism requires that there be no empty spaces in the universe, so wher-ever it seems empty, one posits the existence of the "plenum." "Subtle matter" describes the soul, the mind, and all spiritual agencies—which can, therefore, be supposed subject to the influence and control of the great world machine, which is, of course, visibly material. Both are concepts needed to round out the system of optimistic determinism.

6. Knightly assemblies.

Cunégonde threw herself at his feet, and bathed them with her tears; he was inflexible.

—You absolute idiot, Candide told him, I rescued you from the galleys, I paid your ransom, I paid your sister's; she was washing dishes, she is ugly, I am good enough to make her my wife, and you still presume to oppose it! If I followed my impulses, I would kill you all over again.

—You may kill me again, said the baron, but you will not marry my sister while I am alive.

CHAPTER 30

Conclusion

At heart, Candide had no real wish to marry Cunégonde; but the baron's extreme impertinence decided him in favor of the marriage, and Cunégonde was so eager for it that he could not back out. He consulted Pangloss, Martin, and the faithful Cacambo. Pangloss drew up a fine treatise, in which he proved that the baron had no right over his sister and that she could, according to all the laws of the empire, marry Candide morganatically.[7] Martin said they should throw the baron into the sea. Cacambo thought they should send him back to the Levantine captain to finish his time in the galleys, and then send him to the father general in Rome by the first vessel. This seemed the best idea; the old woman approved, and nothing was said to his sister; the plan was executed, at modest expense, and they had the double pleasure of snaring a Jesuit and punishing the pride of a German baron.

It is quite natural to suppose that after so many misfortunes, Candide, married to his mistress, and living with the philosopher Pangloss, the philosopher Martin, the prudent Cacambo, and the old woman—having, besides, brought back so many diamonds from the land of the ancient Incas—must have led the most agreeable life in the world. But he was so cheated by the Jews[8] that nothing was left but his little farm; his wife, growing every day more ugly, became sour-tempered and insupportable; the old woman was ailing and even more ill-humored than Cunégonde. Cacambo, who worked in the garden and went into Constantinople to sell vegetables, was worn out with toil, and cursed his fate. Pangloss was in despair at being unable to shine in some German university. As for Martin, he was firmly persuaded that things are just as bad wherever you are; he endured in patience. Candide, Martin, and Pangloss sometimes argued over metaphysics and morals. Before the windows of the farmhouse they often watched the passage of boats bearing effendis, pashas, and cadis into exile on Lemnos, Mytilene, and Erzeroum; they saw other cadis, other pashas, other effendis coming, to take the place of the exiles and to be exiled in their turn. They saw various heads, neatly impaled, to be set up at the Sublime Porte.[9] These sights gave fresh impetus to their discussions; and when they were not arguing, the boredom was so fierce that one day the old woman ventured to say:—I should like to know which is worse, being raped a hundred times by negro pirates, having a buttock cut off, running the gauntlet in the Bulgar army, being flogged and hanged in an auto-da-fé, being

---

7. A morganatic marriage confers no rights on the partner of lower rank or on the offspring.
8. Voltaire's anti-Semitism, derived from various unhappy experiences with Jewish financiers, is not the most attractive aspect of his personality.

9. The gate of the sultan's palace is often used by extension to describe his government as a whole. But it was in fact a real gate where the heads of traitors and public enemies were gruesomely exposed.

dissected and rowing in the galleys—experiencing, in a word, all the miseries through which we have passed—or else just sitting here and doing nothing?

—It's a hard question, said Candide.

These words gave rise to new reflections, and Martin in particular concluded that man was bound to live either in convulsions of misery or in the lethargy of boredom. Candide did not agree, but expressed no positive opinion. Pangloss asserted that he had always suffered horribly; but having once declared that everything was marvelously well, he continued to repeat the opinion and didn't believe a word of it.

One thing served to confirm Martin in his detestable opinions, to make Candide hesitate more than ever, and to embarrass Pangloss. It was the arrival one day at their farm of Paquette and Brother Giroflée, who were in the last stages of misery. They had quickly run through their three thousand piastres, had split up, made up, quarreled, been jailed, escaped, and finally Brother Giroflée had turned Turk. Paquette continued to ply her trade everywhere, and no longer made any money at it.

—I told you, said Martin to Candide, that your gifts would soon be squandered and would only render them more unhappy. You have spent millions of piastres, you and Cacambo, and you are no more happy than Brother Giroflée and Paquette.

—Ah ha, said Pangloss to Paquette, so destiny has brought you back in our midst, my poor girl! Do you realize you cost me the end of my nose, one eye, and an ear? And look at you now! eh! what a world it is, after all!

This new adventure caused them to philosophize more than ever.

There was in the neighborhood a very famous dervish, who was said to be the best philosopher in Turkey; they went to ask his advice. Pangloss was spokesman, and he said:—Master, we have come to ask you to tell us why such a strange animal as man was created.

—What are you getting into? answered the dervish. Is it any of your business?

—But, reverend father, said Candide, there's a horrible lot of evil on the face of the earth.

—What does it matter, said the dervish, whether there's good or evil? When his highness sends a ship to Egypt, does he worry whether the mice on board are comfortable or not?

—What shall we do then? asked Pangloss.

—Hold your tongue, said the dervish.

—I had hoped, said Pangloss, to reason a while with you concerning effects and causes, the best of possible worlds, the origin of evil, the nature of the soul, and pre-established harmony.

At these words, the dervish slammed the door in their faces.

During this interview, word was spreading that at Constantinople they had just strangled two viziers of the divan,[1] as well as the mufti, and impaled several of their friends. This catastrophe made a great and general sensation for several hours. Pangloss, Candide, and Martin, as they returned to their little farm, passed a good old man who was enjoying the cool of the day at his doorstep under a grove of orange trees. Pangloss, who was as inquisitive as he was explanatory, asked the name of the mufti who had been strangled.

—I know nothing of it, said the good man, and I have never cared to know the name of a single mufti or vizier. I am completely ignorant of the episode you are

---

1. Intimate advisers of the sultan.

discussing. I presume that in general those who meddle in public business sometimes perish miserably, and that they deserve their fate; but I never listen to the news from Constantinople; I am satisfied with sending the fruits of my garden to be sold there.

Having spoken these words, he asked the strangers into his house; his two daughters and two sons offered them various sherbets which they had made themselves, Turkish cream flavored with candied citron, orange, lemon, lime, pineapple, pistachio, and mocha coffee uncontaminated by the inferior coffee of Batavia and the East Indies. After which the two daughters of this good Moslem perfumed the beards of Candide, Pangloss, and Martin.

—You must possess, Candide said to the Turk, an enormous and splendid property?

I have only twenty acres, replied the Turk; I cultivate them with my children, and the work keeps us from three great evils, boredom, vice, and poverty.

Candide, as he walked back to his farm, meditated deeply over the words of the Turk. He said to Pangloss and Martin:—This good old man seems to have found himself a fate preferable to that of the six kings with whom we had the honor of dining.

—Great place, said Pangloss, is very perilous in the judgment of all the philosophers; for, after all, Eglon, king of the Moabites, was murdered by Ehud; Absalom was hung up by the hair and pierced with three darts; King Nadab, son of Jeroboam, was killed by Baasha; King Elah by Zimri; Ahaziah by Jehu; Athaliah by Jehoiada; and Kings Jehoiakim, Jeconiah, and Zedekiah were enslaved. You know how death came to Croesus, Astyages, Darius, Dionysius of Syracuse, Pyrrhus, Perseus, Hannibal, Jugurtha, Ariovistus, Caesar, Pompey, Nero, Otho, Vitellius, Domitian, Richard II of England, Edward II, Henry VI, Richard III, Mary Stuart, Charles I, the three Henrys of France, and the Emperor Henry IV? You know . . .

—I know also, said Candide, that we must cultivate our garden.

—You are perfectly right, said Pangloss; for when man was put into the garden of Eden, he was put there *ut operaretur eum*, so that he should work it; this proves that man was not born to take his ease.

—Let's work without speculation, said Martin; it's the only way of rendering life bearable.

The whole little group entered into this laudable scheme; each one began to exercise his talents. The little plot yielded fine crops. Cunégonde was, to tell the truth, remarkably ugly; but she became an excellent pastry cook. Paquette took up embroidery; the old woman did the laundry. Everyone, down even to Brother Giroflée, did something useful; he became a very adequate carpenter, and even an honest man; and Pangloss sometimes used to say to Candide:—All events are linked together in the best of possible worlds for, after all, if you had not been driven from a fine castle by being kicked in the backside for love of Miss Cunégonde, if you hadn't been sent before the Inquisition, if you hadn't traveled across America on foot, if you hadn't given a good sword thrust to the baron, if you hadn't lost all your sheep from the good land of Eldorado, you wouldn't be sitting here eating candied citron and pistachios.

—That is very well put, said Candide, but we must cultivate our garden.

III

Early Modern Chinese Vernacular Literature

An early twentieth-century version of this anthology would probably not have featured a section on "Chinese Vernacular Literature." Although the vernacular stories and novels in this volume are now regarded as unquestionable masterpieces, the status of vernacular literature was until recently far below that of the ancient and authoritative genres of classical poetry, prose, and tales. The last two dynasties of imperial China, the Ming (1368–1644) and Qing (1644–1911), bristled with artistic and literary creativity, and the classical genres thrived in an intellectual climate of unprecedented variety and sophistication. At the same time, new literatures formed, written not in the scholastic classical language but in the living vernacular of everyday speech. This literature was much more adept at handling themes and topics that had been outside the purview of classical literature, such as sex, violence, corruption, social satire, and slapstick humor. Vernacular literatures in China could lay claim to a richer, or at least more wide-ranging, portrait of the lives of Chinese readers, and thus had a broad appeal across class lines.

From the series *Landscapes after Ancient Masters*, ca. 1675, by Wang Hui (ca. 1632–ca. 1717).

THE MONGOLS AND THE RISE OF VERNACULAR LITERATURE

The beginnings of written vernacular literature in China are intimately connected to the drastic political and social changes during the Yuan Dynasty (1279–1368). Several decades after completing the conquest of North China, Mongol armies crossed the Yangzi River and conquered the Southern Song Dynasty in 1279. Although they assumed a Chinese dynastic title and some of the trappings of Chinese imperial government, the Mongols did not base their state on Confucian principles, for which they often showed contempt. To the great shock of Chinese intellectuals, the Mongols suspended the examination system, by which members of the educated elite had been recruited for government service during previous dynasties. The long-established link among classical literature, an education in the Confucian Classics, and service in the government was temporarily broken. As a consequence, classical literature temporarily lost its place as the core around which public, social, and private life were organized. Instead, literature in the vernacular such as plays, verse romances, and prose fiction emerged, laying the groundwork for their subsequent triumph.

VERNACULAR LITERATURE OF THE MING DYNASTY: PLAYS, STORIES, NOVELS

With the Ming Dynasty the civil service examinations regained their importance as a venue for a political career and thus created again a national culture of shared elite education, leading to a renewal of classical literature. At the same time an emergent urban bourgeoisie, increasingly literate and influential, provided an eager market for literature in the vernacular, such as plays, stories, and prose fiction. The print culture in the urban centers also contributed to a rising level of literacy and education.

One of the new, vernacular genres was drama, since in contrast to Greek culture, for example, China did not have a classical tradition of dramatic literature. It was during the Ming Dynasty that *chuanqi* drama ("records of marvels," also known as "Kunqu Opera") reached its high point. An opulent and sprawling form of romantic drama, performances often spread over several days and attracted increasingly sophisticated crowds of connoisseurs. Chuanqi drama was enjoyed both as theater in performance and as literature to be read. Most famous of all was the playwright Tang Xianzu (1550–1616) and his *Peony Pavilion*, a romantic drama in which the lovers meet in beguiling dream encounters and the heroine is brought back to life for the final reunion. The last great play in this tradition is **Kong Shangren's *Peach Blossom Fan*** (1699), a historical drama that intertwines the love story between a courtesan and an aspiring young exam candidate with the chaotic events surrounding the fall of the Ming Dynasty and the establishment of the Qing Dynasty.

As with drama, vernacular stories, rooted in oral performances presented by storytellers, had already existed during the Mongol Dynasty, but with the Ming Dynasty they gained in complexity and appeal. Master story writers collected and rewrote popular stories. While retaining the storyteller conventions of the genre, they infused their narratives with plots, themes, and language from classical literature and thus successfully elevated the vernacular story to a more respectable literary genre. **Feng Menglong**, a failed exam candidate who was obsessed both with the rarified realms of Confucian scholarship and the popular gossip of low life, was the most versatile writer of vernacular stories during the Ming.

The Ming and the Qing are the age of the great Chinese historical romances and novels, which were often lengthy elaborations of older stories. On some level Chinese popular literature can be described as a vast tapestry of interrelated stories. This was a literature whose strength lay not in inventing new plots but in filling in details and saying what had been omitted in older ones. A dramatist might take one incident from a story cycle and develop it into a play. A fiction writer might spin out a short story in a novel. A number of these historical romances survive, the most famous being *The Romance of the Three Kingdoms* (*Sanguo yanyi*)—attributed to Luo Guanzhong (earliest printed version 1522)—an elaboration of the official history of the struggle between the three kingdoms that succeeded the Han Dynasty (206 B.C.E.–220 C.E.). In

The Romance of the Three Kingdoms, the somewhat dry historical account about remote events of the third century was transformed into a dazzling saga of battles, clever stratagems, and martial heroism. Stories of a famous group of twelfth-century bandits, like Robin Hood representing justice against corrupt authority, developed into the novel *Water Margin* (*Shuihuzhuan*) (early 1500s). One small incident in *Water Margin* was elaborated into the saga of a corrupt sensualist whose greed and sexual escapades give a vivid if skewed portrait of urban life in Ming China in the novel *Golden Lotus* (*Jin Pingmei*) (1617). And the rather prosaic story of the travel of the Tang Dynasty (618–907) monk Xuanzang to India in search for Buddhist scriptures became **Journey to the West** (1592) by **Wu Cheng'en**, a brilliant novel populated with fantastic creatures including a wily monkey, who masters larger-than-life challenges with supernatural powers.

An illustrated page from a 1581 edition of *The Romance of the Three Kingdoms*.

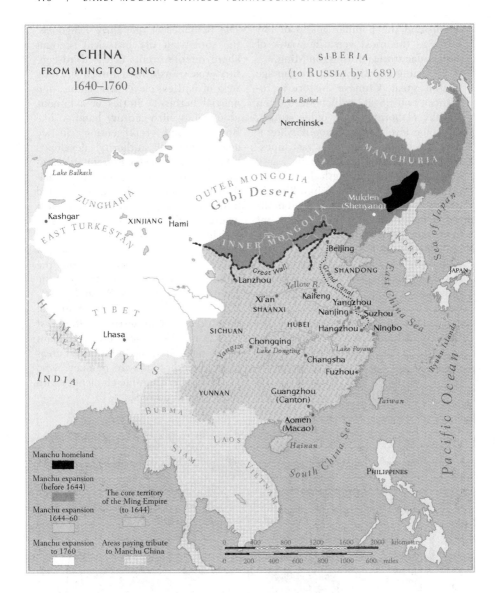

CHINA
FROM MING TO QING
1640–1760

SIBERIA
(to RUSSIA by 1689)

Lake Baikal

Nerchinsk

MANCHURIA

Lake Balkash

ZUNGHARIA

OUTER MONGOLIA
Gobi Desert

Mukden
(Shenyang)

Sea of Japan

Kashgar   XINJIANG   Hami
EAST TURKESTAN

INNER MONGOLIA

KOREA

JAPAN

Beijing

Great Wall

SHANDONG

East China Sea

Lanzhou

Yellow R.

Grand Canal

HIMALAYAS

TIBET

NEPAL

Lhasa

INDIA

Xi'an
SHAANXI

Kaifeng

Yangzhou

Nanjing   Suzhou
Hangzhou   Ningbo

SICHUAN
HUBEI

Chongqing

Ryuku Islands

Yangtze

Lake Dongting

Lake Poyang

Changsha

Fuzhou

BURMA

YUNNAN

Guangzhou
(Canton)

Taiwan

Pacific Ocean

Aomen
(Macao)

LAOS

Hainan

SIAM

VIETNAM

South China Sea

PHILIPPINES

Manchu homeland

Manchu expansion
(before 1644)

Manchu expansion
1644–60

Manchu expansion
to 1760

The core territory
of the Ming Empire
(to 1644)

Areas paying tribute
to Manchu China

0   400   800   1200   1600   2000   kilometers
0   200   400   600   800   1000   600 miles

LITERATURE AND THE INTELLECTUAL CLIMATE DURING THE QING DYNASTY

In 1644 Manchu armies from the Northeast descended into China and established a new dynasty, the Qing, which would rule China until the Republican revolution in 1911. Once again under non-Chinese rule, and forced to wear the Manchu *queue* (a long ponytail) as a mark of submission, many Chinese harbored strong anti-Manchu sentiments. The Manchus, for their part, became very sensitive to native opposition. Censors whose job was to survey current writings for hostility to the regime continually discovered slights, both real and imagined, against the dynasty. The late seventeenth and eighteenth centuries, known as the "literary inquisition," had a chilling effect on writing.

Qing intellectual culture rejected the radical individualism of the later Ming, when personal freedom had been celebrated at the expense of social responsibility. Early Qing intellectuals held this late Ming ethos responsible for the decline of the dynasty. In particular, intellectuals turned away from a brand of Confucianism propagated by the Ming thinker Wang Yangming (1472–1529), who had claimed that humans possessed inborn knowledge that simply needed to be rediscovered, not learned. Accordingly, studies of canonical texts by even the greatest sages like Confucius became little more than aids in the process of subjective rediscovery.

The reaction against Ming subjectivism saw not only a conservative public morality but also a new historical and philological rigor in determining the origin, transformation, and meaning of early canonical texts. This empirical approach to the canon was called "evidential learning" and it was closely analogous to the development of Western historical philology, which treated sacred texts as historical documents. The new emphasis on historical scholarship had profound consequences for both China and the West, each of which had depended to some degree on the authority of received texts. In China, as in the West, empiricism in scholarship became linked to other forms of empiricism, such as natural philosophy and science.

The debates about the interpretation of the Confucian Classics were just one aspect of the complex presence of Confucianism in Qing society. Confucianism was a form of governance, a state cult, a tool of civil service recruitment, a tradition of textual study, and

a system of public morals and personal ethics that was to guide all aspects of life. Its rigid demands for sociopolitical success and stern moral self-cultivation failed in basic ways to address the complexities of human nature and the pressures of living in an increasingly complex world. Except among a very few committed thinkers, it was a philosophical position that invited gross hypocrisy. Vernacular literature, on the other hand, celebrated liberty, violent energy, and passion. Though such works often contained elements of neo-Confucian ethics and were later given pious neo-Confucian interpretations, by and large they either voiced qualities that neo-Confucianism sought to repress or savagely attacked society as a world of false appearances and secret evils. The hypocrisy of Confucian elite values had already been dramatically exposed in plays and stories since the Yuan Dynasty, but two Qing novels contain particularly trenchant representations of the ambiguities of Confucianism's grip on society. Wu Jingzi's (1701–1754) *The Scholars*

Portrait of a Confucian Scholar (late eighteenth century), attributed to the Korean painter Yi Che-gwan.

hovers between satire of petrified Confucian institutions—such as the civil service examination system—and the ideal vision of a true form of Confucianism. **Cao Xueqin's *The Story of the Stone*** (1791), an epic family saga of glamour and decline, conveys an even more ambiguous picture of the ideals and evils of Confucianism in the broader context of intellectual, artistic, and sexual aspirations in life.

The conflict between Confucianism as the dogma of a disingenuous ruling elite and its potential as a vision for a good life in a just society resonated strongly in other East Asian countries, many of which had a Chinese-style ruling elite trained in the Confucian canon. Both Kièu, the heroine of *The Tale of Kièu* by the Vietnamese writer **Nguyễn Du** (1765–1820), and Ch'unhyang, the heroine of the Korean narrative *p'ansori* drama *The Song of Ch'un-hyang*, are heroines whose social status or lifestyle offends official Confucian decorum, but who represent a truer form of Confucianism, effectively teaching the hypocritical guardians of public morality what Confucianism could and should mean at its best.

Vernacular literature is an enthralling and varied body of literature that thrived alongside the classical tradition in early modern China and influenced many later writers. The intellectuals of the first half of the twentieth century, who called for a literary revolution that would abolish classical Chinese and the privileges that were associated with it, propelled this body of literature into the limelight and belligerently declared it to be the "true" tradition of Chinese literature: it spoke the language of the people; it decried hypocrisy, violence, and corruption through money and power; and it celebrated passion, truth, love, and heroic loyalty to oneself and one's principles. At the beginning of the twenty-first century, when China's revolutionary rhetoric has lost its earlier edge, we can recognize vernacular literature as a complementary, equal part to the classical tradition, from which it drew generously while also significantly expanding and enriching its literary themes and expressive power.

WU CHENG'EN

ca. 1500–1582

Nothing is impossible in *The Journey to the West*. People and fantastic creatures are whisked through the universe, a magic monkey can create thousands of companions by blowing on a wisp of his hair, and virgin monks can become pregnant. The novel has won over generations of readers with its unusual blend of a fast-paced, suspenseful martial-arts narrative and religious allegory, as well as its vivid satirical portrait of the workings and failings of human and heavenly bureaucracies.

The Journey to the West was not the work of a single person. First published in 1592, the novel is a product of the cumulative retelling of the story, which circulated orally and was adapted and transformed through the centuries. The final form of these stories in this vast, sprawling compendium of one hundred chapters transformed the traditional material into a great work of literature. Scholars are not entirely certain whether Wu Cheng'en did indeed give final shape to the story and was the author of the 1592 edition of *The Journey to the West*. But a local gazetteer of his home prefecture connects this title to his name. This piece of evidence is further supported by the fact that Wu had a reputation for being a versatile poet (there are over 1,700 poems in the novel), and for writing on mythical and supernatural subjects in a satirical style. Also, he was a native of a region in southeast China, whose dialect appears in the novel. We do not know much more about Wu than that he was a minor official serving under the Ming Dynasty (1368–1644).

The core of the story had a historical basis in the journey of the monk Xuanzang, or Tripitaka (596–664), who traveled from China to India in search of Buddhist scriptures during the reign of Emperor Taizong, one of the most splendid emperors of the Tang Dynasty (618–907). At the time, travel to the Western territories was forbidden and Tripitaka could have faced arrest and execution for his transgression. But when he returned seventeen years later with the coveted scriptures, he earned immediate imperial patronage and was allowed to settle down, translate the new scriptures, and propagate them. He spent the last twenty years of his life in the Tang capital of Chang'an (modern-day Xi'an), translating hundreds of sutras and other Buddhist texts from Sanskrit into Chinese, more than any other person before him had ever done. He did write a brief record of his experience during his travels. The account of the historical Xuanzang had virtually nothing to do with the much-later novel, but it may have served as the early basis from which the story began to be retold. Pilgrimages to India were by no means unique among Chinese monks of this era, but Tripitaka's journey somehow captured the popular imagination; it was retold in stories and plays, until it finally emerged as *The Journey to the West*.

As Xuanzang's journey was retold, the most important addition was his acquisition of a wondrous disciple named Sun Wukong, "Monkey Aware-of-Vacuity." Monkey had already made his appearance in a twelfth-century version of the story and came to so dominate the full novel version that the first major English translation of the novel, published in 1943, was named after this character: *Monkey*. An argument can be made, from a Buddhist point of view, that Tripitaka, however inept and timorous, is the novel's true hero. But for most readers the monkey's splendid vitality and boundless humor remain the center of interest. Tripitaka is also accompanied by the ever-hungry and lustful Bajie (alternately called "Pigsy"), a Daoist immortal who was banned to the human world for flirting with a goddess and who becomes increasingly unsympathetic as the journey progresses. Tripitaka's third disciple and protector is the gentle Sha monk (also called "Sandy"), a former marshal of the hosts of Heaven who was sent to the bottom of a river to expiate the sin of having broken the crystal cup of the Jade Emperor, a powerful Daoist deity.

Throughout their journey, the four travelers are watched over, and sometimes interact with, a number of otherworldly beings: an assortment of benign bodhisattvas (buddhas who linger in this world to help others) and a Daoist pantheon of unruly and sometimes dangerous deities. On the earthly plane the pilgrims move through a landscape of strange kingdoms and monsters, stopping sometimes to help those in need or to protect themselves from harm. Some of the earthly monsters belong to the places where the pilgrims find them, but many of the demons and temptresses that the travelers encounter are either exiles and escapees from the heavenly realm or are sent on purpose to test the pilgrims. Although the story of the Buddhist monk at times shows the traditional hostility of Buddhism against Daoism, Xuanzang's quest has a broader, conciliatory message that sees Confucianism, Buddhism, and Daoism as complementary

truths. As the Buddha says about the scriptures before the monk and his companions set out to India, they "are for the cultivation of immortality and the gate to ultimate virtue." Thus Buddhist scriptures also serve the purpose of fulfilling the Daoist desire for self-preservation and immortality as well as the Confucian quest for moral virtue.

Surrounded by three guardian disciples who are endowed with a more general, allegorical meaning, Tripitaka is the only truly human character in *The Journey to the West*. He is easily frightened, sometimes petulant, and never knows what to do. He is not so much driven on the pilgrimage by determined resolve as merely carried along by it. Yet he alone is the character destined for full Buddhahood at the end, and his apparent lack of concern for the quest and for his disciples has been interpreted as the true manifestation of Buddhist detachment. Although "Pilgrim," the monkey king, grows increasingly devoted to his master through the course of the novel, Tripitaka never fully trusts him, however much he depends on him. If there is a difficult Buddhist lesson in the novel, it is to grasp how Tripitaka, the ordinary man as saint, can be the novel's true hero. He is the empty center of the group, kept alive and carried forward by his more powerful and active disciples, both willing and unwilling. Yet he remains the master, and without him the pilgrimage would not exist.

Both Pilgrim and Bajie are creatures of desire, though the nature of their desires differs greatly. Pilgrim, who had once lived an idyllic life with his monkey subjects in Water Curtain Cave at Flower-Fruit Mountain, is, in the novel's early chapters, driven by a hunger for knowledge and immortality which takes him around the earth and the heavens. In the first stage of his existence, Pilgrim's curiosity is never perfectly directed; it is a turbulence of spirit that always leads to mischief and an urge to create chaos. He acquires skills and magic tools that make him more powerful, but since he uses them unwisely, they only lead him to ever more outrageous escapades. After wreaking havoc in Heaven and being subdued by the god Erlang, he is imprisoned by the Buddha under a mountain for five hundred years. Finally Monkey is given a chance to redeem himself by guarding Tripitaka on his pilgrimage to India as "Pilgrim."

During the course of the pilgrimage, the monkey becomes increasingly bound both to his master and to the quest itself, without ever losing his energy and humor. Despite occasional outbursts of his former mischief making, the quest becomes for Pilgrim a structured series of challenges by which he can focus and discipline his rambunctious intellect. The journey is driven forward by Pilgrim alone, with Tripitaka ever willing to give up in despair and Bajie always ready to be seduced or return to his wife. Monkey understands the world with a comic detachment that is in some ways akin to Buddhist detachment, and this detachment makes him always more resourceful and often wiser than Tripitaka. Yet in his fierce energy and sheer joy in the use of his mind, Monkey falls short of the Buddhist ideal of true tranquility, while remaining the hero for unenlightened mortals.

Pilgrim is a complex character with many contradictions, as is perhaps fitting for a creature that may be seen in some sense as an allegory of the human mind. Bajie, on the other hand, is a straightforward and predictable emblem of human sensual appetites. In his initial domestic setting, as the unwelcome son-in-law on Mr. Gao's farm, Bajie was at least reliable and hardworking. But in the enforced celibacy of the pilgrimage, he grows increasingly slothful and undependable. Now and then on the journey he is permitted to gorge himself, but every time he finds a beautiful woman, something prevents him from satisfying his sexual appetite. Never having freely chosen the quest, Bajie is always distracted by his desire to go home to his wife—or to take another along the way. Yet his preoccupation with food and sex often makes him an endearing character.

The selections printed here treat the monkey's birth and early apprenticeship, and Tripitaka's dispatch to India, which is destined by the Buddha, overseen by the Bodhisattva Guanyin, and endorsed by Emperor Taizong. The next two sequences show the adventures and challenges Tripitaka and his companions encounter in two peculiar countries: one, a Daoist kingdom that suppresses Buddhists, where the Buddhist pilgrims straighten out the record with hilarious interventions for the sake of their brothers in faith; and the other, a kingdom of women in which the monk is erroneously impregnated by the water of a stream crossing its territory. While searching for a cure they have to resist the attack of female charms and a female scorpion monster. Finally, in the last sections of our selection they reach their goal in India and receive the scriptures. Whisked back to China by divine winds, they are rewarded in a solemn ceremony by the emperor back home in the capital of Chang'an, according to their merits.

Critics count *The Journey to the West* among the greatest novels of traditional China, along with **Cao Xueqin's The Story of the Stone**. In the modern period it has inspired films, musicals, television series, comic books, anime adaptations, and computer games. They all capture facets of *The Journey to the West*, whose sprawling imagination and playful esprit make it unlike any other book.

From The Journey to the West[1]

From *Chapter 1*

The divine root being conceived, the origin appears;
The moral nature cultivated, the Great Dao is born.

* * *

There was on top of that very mountain[2] an immortal stone, which measured thirty-six feet and five inches in height and twenty-four feet in circumference. The height of thirty-six feet and five inches corresponded to the three hundred and sixty-five cyclical degrees, while the circumference of twenty-four feet corresponded to the twenty-four solar terms of the calendar. On the stone were also nine perforations and eight holes, which corresponded to the Palaces of the Nine Constellations and the Eight Trigrams. Thought it lacked the shade of trees on all sides, it was set off by epidendrums on the left and right. Since the creation of the world, it had been nourished for a long period by the seeds of Heaven and Earth and by the essences of the sun and the moon, until, quickened by divine inspiration, it became pregnant with a divine embryo. One day, it split open, giving birth to a stone egg about the size of a playing ball. Exposed to the wind, it was transformed into a stone monkey endowed with fully developed features and limbs. Having learned at once to climb and run, this monkey also bowed to the four quarters, while two beams of golden light flashed from his eyes to reach even the Palace of the Polestar. The light disturbed the Great Benevolent Sage of Heaven, the Celestial Jade Emperor[3] of the Most Venerable Deva, who, attended by his divine ministers, was sitting in the Cloud Palace of the Golden Arches, in the Treasure Hall of the Divine Mists. Upon seeing the glimmer of the golden beams, he ordered Thousand-Mile Eye and Fair-Wind Ear to open the South Heaven Gate and to look out. At this command the two captains went out to the gate, and, having looked intently and listened clearly, they returned presently to report. "Your subjects, obeying your command to locate the beams, discovered that they came from the Flower-Fruit Mountain at the border of the small Aolai Country, which lies to the east of the East Pūrvavideha Continent. On this mountain is an immortal stone which has given birth to an egg. Exposed to the wind, it has been transformed into a monkey, who, when bowing to the four quarters, has flashed from his eyes those golden beams that reached the Palace of the Polestar. Now that he is taking some food and drink, the light is about to grow dim." With compassionate mercy the Jade Emperor declared, "These creatures from the world below are born of the essences of Heaven and Earth, and they need not surprise us."

That monkey in the mountain was able to walk, run, and leap about; he fed on grass and shrubs, drank from the brooks and streams, gathered mountain flowers, and searched out fruits from trees. He made his companions the tiger and the lizard, the wolf and the leopard; he befriended the civet and the deer, and he called the gibbon and the baboon his kin. At night he slept beneath stony ridges, and in the morning he sauntered about the caves and the peaks, Truly,

---

1. Translated by Anthony Yu.
2. Flower-Fruit-Mountain.

3. The chief deity in the Daoist pantheon.

In the mountain there is no passing of time;
The cold recedes, but one knows not the year.

One very hot morning, he was playing with a group of monkeys under the shade of some pine trees to escape the heat. Look at them, each amusing himself in his own way by

Swinging from branches to branches,
Searching for flowers and fruits;
They played two games or three
With pebbles and with pellets;
They circled sandy pits;
They built rare pagodas;
They chased the dragonflies;
They ran down small lizards:
Bowing low to the sky,
They worshiped Bodhisattvas;
They pulled the creeping vines;
They plaited mats with grass;
They searched to catch the louse
They bit or crushed with their nails;
They dressed their furry coats;
They scraped their fingernails;
Some leaned and leaned;
Some rubbed and rubbed;
Some pushed and pushed;
Some pressed and pressed;
Some pulled and pulled;
Some tugged and tugged.
Beneath the pine forest they played without a care,
Washing themselves in the green-water stream.

So, after the monkeys had frolicked for a while, they went to bathe in the mountain stream and saw that its currents bounced and splashed like rumbling melons. As the old saying goes,

Fowls have their fowl speech,
And beasts have their beast language.

The monkeys said to each other, "We don't know where this water comes from. Since we have nothing to do today, let us follow the stream up to its source to have some fun." With a shriek of joy, they dragged along males and females, calling out to brothers and sisters, and scrambled up the mountain alongside the stream. Reaching its source, they found a great waterfall. What they saw was

A column of rising white rainbows,
A thousand fathoms of dancing waves—
Which the sea wind buffets but cannot sever,
On which the river moon shines and reposes.

Its cold breath divides the green ranges;
Its tributaries moisten the blue-green hillsides.
This torrential body, its name a cascade,
Seems truly like a hanging curtain.

All the monkeys clapped their hands in acclaim: "Marvelous water! Marvelous water! So this waterfall is distantly connected with the stream at the base of the mountain, and flows directly out, even to the great ocean." They said also, "If any of us had the ability to penetrate the curtain and find out where the water comes from without hurting himself, we would honor him as king." They gave the call three times, when suddenly the stone monkey leaped out from the crowd. He answered the challenge with a loud voice. "I'll go in! I'll go in!" What a monkey! For

Today his fame will spread wide.
His fortune arrives with the time;
He's fated to live in this place,
Sent by a king to this godly palace.

Look at him! He closed his eyes, crouched low, and with one leap he jumped straight through the waterfall. Opening his eyes at once and raising his head to look around, he saw that there was neither water not waves inside, only a gleaming, shining bridge. He paused to collect himself and looked more carefully again: it was a bridge made of sheet iron. The water beneath it surged through a hole in the rock to reach the outside, filling in all the space under the arch. With bent body he climbed on the bridge, looking about as he walked, and discovered a beautiful place that seemed to be some kind of residence. Then he saw

Fresh mosses piling up indigo,
White clouds like jade afloat,
And luminous sheens of mist and smoke;
Empty windows, quiet rooms,
And carved flowers growing smoothly on benches;
Stalactites suspended in milky caves;
Rare blossoms voluminous over the ground.
Pans and stoves near the wall show traces of fire;
Bottles and cups on the table contain leftovers.
The stone seats and beds were truly lovable;
The stone pots and bowls were more praiseworthy.
There were, furthermore, a stalk or two of tall bamboos,
And three or five sprigs of plum flowers.
With a few green pines always draped in rain,
This whole place indeed resembled a home.

After staring at the place for a long time, he jumped across the middle of the bridge and looked left and right. There in the middle was a stone tablet on which was inscribed in regular, large letters:

The Blessed Land of Flower-Fruit Mountain,
The Cave Heaven of Water-Curtain Cave.

Beside himself with delight, the stone monkey quickly turned around to go back out and, closing his eyes and crouching again, leaped out of the water. "A great stroke of luck," he exclaimed with two loud guffaws, "a great stroke of luck." The other monkeys surrounded him and asked, "How is it inside? How deep is the water?" The stone monkey replied, "There isn't any water at all. There's a sheet iron bridge, and beyond it is a piece of Heaven-sent property." "What do you mean that there's property in there?" asked the monkeys.

Laughing, the stone monkey said, "This water splashes through a hole in the rock and fills the space under the bridge. Beside the bridge there is a stone mansion with trees and flowers. Inside are stone ovens and stoves, stone pots and pans, stone beds and benches. A stone tablet in the middle has the inscription,

> "The Blessed Land of the Flower-Fruit Mountain,
> The Cave Heaven of the Water-Curtain Cave.

This is truly the place for us to settle in. It is, moreover, very spacious inside and can hold thousands of the young and old. Let's all go live in there, and spare ourselves from being subject to the whims of Heaven. For we have in there

> A retreat from the wind,
> A shelter from the rain.
> You fear no frost or snow;
> You hear no thunderclap.
> Mist and smoke are brightened,
> Warmed by a holy light—
> The pines are ever green:
> Rare flowers, daily new."

When the monkeys heard that, they were delighted, saying. "You go in first and lead the way." The stone monkey closed his eyes again, crouched low, and jumped inside. "All of you," he cried. "Follow me in! Follow me in!" The braver of the monkeys leaped in at once, but the more timid ones stuck out their heads and then drew them back, scratched their ears, rubbed their jaws, and chattered noisily. After milling around for some time, they too bounded inside. Jumping across the bridge, they were all soon snatching dishes, clutching bowls, or fighting for stoves and beds—shoving and pushing things hither and thither. Befitting their stubbornly prankish nature, the monkeys could not keep still for a moment and stopped only when they were utterly exhausted. The stone monkey then solemnly took a seat above and spoke to them: "Gentlemen! 'If a man lacks trustworthiness, it is difficult to know what he can accomplish!'[4] You yourselves promised just now that whoever could get in here and leave again without hurting himself would be honored as king. Now that I have come in and gone out, gone out and come in, and have found for all of you this Heavenly grotto in which you may reside securely and enjoy the privilege of raising a family, why don't you honor me as your king?" When the monkeys heard this, they all folded their hands on their breasts and obediently prostrated themselves. Each one of them then lined up according to rank and

---

4. From the Confucian *Analects*.

age, and, bowing reverently, they intoned. "Long live our great king!" From that moment, the stone monkey ascended the throne of kingship. He did away with the word "stone" in his name and assumed the title, Handsome Monkey King. There is a testimonial poem which says:

> When triple spring mated to produce all things,
> A divine stone was quickened by the sun and moon.
> The egg changed to a monkey, perfecting the Great Way.
> He took a name, matching elixir's success.
> Formless, his inward shape is thus concealed:
> His outer frame by action is plainly known.
> In every age all persons will yield to him;
> Named a king, a sage, he is free to roam.

The Handsome Monkey King thus led a flock of gibbons and baboons, some of whom were appointed by him as his officers and ministers. They toured the Flower-Fruit Mountain in the morning, and they lived in the Water-Curtain Cave by night. Living in concord and sympathy, they did not mingle with bird or beast but enjoyed their independence in perfect happiness. For such were their activities:

> In the spring they gathered flowers for food and drink.
> In the summer they went in quest of fruits for sustenance.
> In the autumn they amassed taros and chestnuts to ward off time.
> In the winter they searched for yellow-sperms[5] to live out the year.

The Handsome Monkey King had enjoyed this insouciant existence for three or four hundred years when one day, while feasting with the rest of the monkeys, he suddenly grew sad and shed a few tears. Alarmed, the monkeys surrounded him, bowed down, and asked, "What is disturbing the Great King?" The Monkey King replied, "Though I am very happy at the moment, I am a little concerned about the future. Hence I'm distressed." The monkeys all laughed and said, "The Great King indeed does not know contentment! Here we daily have a banquet on an immortal mountain in a blessed land, in an ancient cave on a divine continent. We are not subject to the unicorn or the phoenix, nor are we governed by the rulers of mankind. Such independence and comfort are immeasurable blessings. Why, then, does he worry about the future?" The Monkey King said, "Though we are not subject to the laws of man today, nor need we be threatened by the rule of any bird or beast, old age and physical decay in the future will disclose the secret sovereignty of Yama, King of the Underworld. If we die, shall we not have lived in vain, not being able to rank forever among the Heavenly beings?"

When the monkeys heard this, they all covered their faces and wept mournfully, each one troubled by his own impermanence. But look! From among the ranks a bareback monkey suddenly leaped forth and cried aloud, "If the Great King is so farsighted, it may well indicate the sprouting of his religious inclination. There are, among the five major divisions of all living creatures, only

---

5. Plant whose roots were used for medicinal purposes.

three species that are not subject to Yama, King of the Underworld." The Monkey King said, "Do you know who they are?" The monkey said, "They are the Buddhas, the immortals, and the holy sages; these three alone can avoid the Wheel of Transmigration as well as the process of birth and destruction, and live as long as Heaven and Earth, the mountains and the streams." "Where do they live?" asked the Monkey King. The monkey said, "They do not live beyond the world of the Jambūdvīpa for they dwell within ancient caves on immortal mountains." When the Monkey King heard this, he was filled with delight, saying, "Tomorrow I shall take leave of you all and go down the mountain. Even if I have to wander with the clouds to the corners of the sea or journey to the distant edges of Heaven, I intend to find these three kinds of people. I will learn from them how to be young forever and escape the calamity inflicted by King Yama." Lo, this utterance at once led him

> To leap free of the Transmigration Net,
> And be the Great Sage, Equal to Heaven.

All the monkeys clapped their hands in acclamation, saying, "Wonderful! Wonderful! Tomorrow we shall scour the mountain ranges to gather plenty of fruits, so that we may send the Great King off with a great banquet."

Next day the monkeys duly went to gather immortal peaches, to pick rare fruits, to dig out mountain herbs, and to chop yellow-sperms. They brought in an orderly manner every variety of orchids and epidendrums, exotic plants and strange flowers. They set out the stone chairs and stone tables, covering the tables with immortal wines and food. Look at the

> Golden balls and pearly pellets,
> Red ripeness and yellow plumpness.
> Golden balls and pearly pellets are the cherries,
> Their colors truly luscious.
> Red ripeness and yellow plumpness are the plums,
> Their taste—a fragrant tartness.
> Fresh lungans
> Of sweet pulps and thin skins.
> Fiery lychees
> Of small pits and red sacks.
> Green fruits of the Pyrus are presented by the branches.
> The loquats yellow with buds are held with their leaves.
> Pears like rabbit heads and dates like chicken hearts
> Dispel your thirst, your sorrow, and the effects of wine.
> Fragrant peaches and soft almonds
> Are sweet as the elixir of life:
> Crisply fresh plums and strawberries
> Are sour like cheese and buttermilk.
> Red pulps and black seeds compose the ripe watermelons.
> Four cloves of yellow rind enfold the big persimmons.
> When the pomegranates are split wide,
> Cinnabar grains glisten like specks of ruby:
> When the chestnuts are cracked open,
> Their tough brawns are hard like cornelian.

Walnut and silver almonds fare well with tea.
Coconuts and grapes may be pressed into wine.
Hazelnuts, yews, and crabapples overfill the dishes.
Kumquats, sugarcanes, tangerines, and oranges crowd the tables.
Sweet yams are baked,
Yellow-sperms overboiled,
The tubers minced with seeds of waterlily,
And soup in stone pots simmers on a gentle fire.
Mankind may boast its delicious dainties,
But what can best the pleasure of mountain monkeys.

The monkeys honored the Monkey King with the seat at the head of the table, while they sat below according to their age and rank. They drank for a whole day, each of the monkeys taking a turn to go forward and present the Monkey King with wine, flowers, and fruits. Next day the Monkey King rose early and gave the instruction, "Little ones, cut me some pinewood and make me a raft. Then find me a bamboo for the pole, and gather some fruits and the like. I'm about to leave." When all was ready, he got onto the raft by himself. Pushing off with all his might, he drifted out toward the great ocean and, taking advantage of the wind, set sail for the border of South Jambūdvīpa Continent. Here is the consequence of this journey:

The Heaven-born monkey, strong in magic might,
He left the mount and rode the raft to catch fair wind:
He drifted across the sea to seek immortals' way,
Determined in heart and mind to achieve great things.
It's his lot, his portion, to quit earthly zeals:
Calm and carefree, he'll face a lofty sage.
He'd meet, I think, a true, discerning friend:
The source disclosed, all dharma will be known.

It was indeed his fortune that, after he had boarded the wooden raft, a strong southeast wind which lasted for days sent him to the northwestern coast, the border of the South Jambūdvīpa Continent. He took the pole to test the water, and, finding it shallow one day, he abandoned the raft and jumped ashore. On the beach there were people fishing, hunting wild geese, digging clams, and draining salt. He approached them and, making a weird face and some strange antics, he scared them into dropping their baskets and nets and scattering in all directions. One of them could not run and was caught by the Monkey King, who stripped him of his clothes and put them on himself, aping the way humans wore them. With a swagger he walked through counties and prefectures, imitating human speech and human manners in the marketplaces. He rested by night and dined in the morning, but he was bent on finding the way of the Buddhas, immortals, and holy sages, on discovering the formula for eternal youth. He saw, however, that the people of the world were all seekers after profit and fame: there was not one who showed concern for his appointed end. This is their condition:

When will end this quest for fortune and fame,
This tyrant of early rising and retiring late?

Riding on mules they long for noble steeds;
By now prime ministers, they hope to be kings.
For food and raiment they suffer stress and strain,
Never fearing Yama's call to reckoning.
Seeking wealth and power to give to sons of sons,
There's not one ever willing to turn back.

The Monkey King searched diligently for the way of immortality, but he had no chance of meeting it. Going through big cities and visiting small towns, he unwittingly spent eight or nine years on the South Jambūdvīpa Continent before he suddenly came upon the Great Western Ocean. He thought that there would certainly be immortals living beyond the ocean; so, having built himself a raft like the previous one, he once again drifted across the Western Ocean until he reached the West Aparagodānīya Continent. After landing, he searched for a long time, when all at once he came upon a tall and beautiful mountain with thick forests at its base. Since he was afraid neither of wolves and lizards nor of tigers and leopards, he went straight to the top to look around. It was indeed a magnificent mountain:

A thousand peaks stand like rows of spears,
Like ten thousand cubits of screen widespread.
The sun's beams lightly enclose the azure mist;
In darkening rain, the mount's color turns cool and green.
Dry creepers entwine old trees;
Ancient fords edge secluded paths.
Rare flowers and luxuriant grass.
Tall bamboos and lofty pines.
Tall bamboos and lofty pines
For ten thousand years grow green in this blessed land.
Rare flowers and luxuriant grass
In all seasons bloom as in the Isles of the Blest.
The calls of birds hidden are near.
The sounds of streams rushing are clear.
Deep inside deep canyons the orchids interweave.
On every ridge and crag sprout lichens and mosses.
Rising and falling, the ranges show a fine dragon's pulse.[6]
Here in reclusion must an eminent man reside.

As he was looking about, he suddenly heard the sound of a man speaking deep within the woods. Hurriedly he dashed into the forest and cocked his ear to listen. It was someone singing, and the song went thus:

I watch chess games, my ax handle's rotted.
I crop at wood, zheng zheng the sound.
I walk slowly by the cloud's fringe at the valley's entrance.
Selling my firewood to buy some wine.
I am happy and laugh without restraint.
When the path is frosted in autumn's height,

6. One of the magnetic currents recognized by geomancers.

I face the moon, my pillow the pine root.
Sleeping till dawn
I find my familiar woods.
I climb the plateaus and scale the peaks
To cut dry creepers with my ax.

When I gather enough to make a load,
I stroll singing through the marketplace
And trade it for three pints of rice,
With nary the slightest bickering
Over a price so modest.
Plots and schemes I do not know;
Without vainglory or attaint
My life's prolonged in simplicity.
Those I meet,
If not immortals, would be Daoists,
Seated quietly to expound the Yellow Court.

When the Handsome Monkey King heard this, he was filled with delight, saying, "So the immortals are hiding in this place." He leaped at once into the forest. Looking again carefully, he found a woodcutter chopping firewood with his ax. The man he saw was very strangely attired.

On his head he wore a wide splint hat
Of seed-leaves freshly cast from new bamboos.
On his body he wore a cloth garment
Of gauze woven from the native cotton.
Around his waist he tied a winding sash
Of silk spun from an old silkworm.
On his feet he had a pair of straw sandals,
With laces rolled from withered sedge.
In his hands he held a fine steel ax;
A sturdy rope coiled round and round his load.
In breaking pines or chopping trees
Where's the man to equal him?

The Monkey King drew near and called out: "Reverend immortal! Your disciple raises his hands." The woodcutter was so flustered that he dropped his ax as he turned to return the salutation. "Blasphemy! Blasphemy!" he said, "I, a foolish fellow with hardly enough clothes or food! How can I beat the title of immortal?" The Monkey King said, "If you are not an immortal, how is it that you speak his language?" The woodcutter said, "What did I say that sounded like the language of an immortal?" The Monkey King said, "When I came just now to the forest's edge, I heard you singing, 'Those I meet, if not immortals, would be Daoists, seated quietly to expound the *Yellow Court*.' The *Yellow Court* contains the perfected words of the Way and Virtue.[7] What can you be but an immortal?"

7. Also the title of the ancient Chinese Daoist classic, the *Daodejing* (*The Classic of the Way and Virtue*).

Laughing, the woodcutter said, "I can tell you this much: the tune of that lyric is named 'A Court Full of Blossoms,' and it was taught to me by an immortal, a neighbor of mine. He saw that I had to struggle to make a living and that my days were full of worries: so he told me to recite the poem whenever I was troubled. This, he said, would both comfort me and rid me of my difficulties. It happened that I was anxious about something just now; so I sang the song. It didn't occur to me that I would be overheard."

The Monkey King said, "If you are a neighbor of the immortal, why don't you follow him in the cultivation of the Way? Wouldn't it be nice to learn from him the formula for eternal youth?" The woodcutter said, "My lot has been a hard one all my life. When I was young, I was indebted to my parents' nurture until I was eight or nine. As soon as I began to have some understanding of human affairs, my father unfortunately died, and my mother remained a widow. I had no brothers or sisters; so there was no alternative but for me alone to support and care for my mother. Now that my mother is growing old, all the more I dare not leave her. Moreover, my fields are rather barren and desolate, and we haven't enough food or clothing. I can't do more than chop two bundles of firewood to take to the market in exchange for a few pennies to buy a few pints of rice. I cook that myself, serving it to my mother with the tea that I make. That's why I can't practice austerities."

The Monkey King said, "According to what you have said, you are indeed a gentleman of filial piety, and you will certainly be rewarded in the future. I hope, however, that you will show me the way to the immortal's abode, so that I may reverently call upon him." "It's not far. It's not far," the woodcutter said. "This mountain is called the Mountain of Mind and Heart, and in it is the Cave of Slanting Moon and Three Stars. Inside the cave is an immortal by the name of the Patriarch Subodhi, who has already sent out innumerable disciples. Even now there are thirty or forty persons who are practicing austerities with him. Follow this narrow path and travel south for about seven or eight miles, and you will come to his home." Grabbing at the woodcutter, the Monkey King said. "Honored brother, go with me. If I receive any benefit, I will not forget the favor of your guidance." "What a boneheaded fellow you are!" the woodcutter said, "I have just finished telling you these things, and you still don't understand. If I go with you, won't I be neglecting my livelihood? And who will take care of my mother? I must chop my firewood. You go on by yourself!"

When the Monkey King heard this, he had to take his leave. Emerging from the deep forest, he found the path and went past the slope of a hill. After he had traveled seven or eight miles, a cave dwelling indeed came into sight. He stood up straight to take a better look at this splendid place, and this was what he saw:

> Mist and smoke in diffusive brilliance,
> Flashing lights from the sun and moon,
> A thousand stalks of old cypress,
> Ten thousand stems of tall bamboo.
> A thousand stalks of old cypress
> Draped in rain half fill the air with tender green;
> Ten thousand stems of tall bamboo
> Held in smoke will paint the glen chartreuse.

Strange flowers spread brocades before the door.
Jadelike grass emits fragrance beside the bridge.
On ridges protruding grow moist green lichens;
On hanging cliffs cling the long blue mosses.
The cries of immortal cranes are often heard.
Once in a while a phoenix soars overhead.
When the cranes cry,
Their sounds reach through the marsh to the distant sky.
When the phoenix soars up,
Its plume with five bright colors embroiders the clouds.
Black apes and white deer may come or hide:
Gold lions and jade elephants may leave or hide.
Look with care at this blessed, holy place:
It has the true semblance of Paradise.

He noticed that the door of the cave was tightly shut; all was quiet, and there was no sign of any human inhabitant. He turned around and suddenly perceived, at the top of the clif, a stone slab approximately eight feet wide and over thirty feet tall. On it was written in large letters:

The Mountain of Mind and Heart;
The Cave of Slanting Moon and Three Stars.

Immensely pleased, the Handsome Monkey King said, "People here are truly honest. This mountain and this cave really do exist!" He stared at the place for a long time but dared not knock. Instead, he jumped onto the branch of a pine tree, picked a few pine seeds and ate them, and began to play.

After a moment he heard the door of the cave open with a squeak, and an immortal youth walked out. His bearing was exceedingly graceful; his features were highly refined. This was certainly no ordinary young mortal, for he had

His hair bound with two cords of silk,
A wide robe with two sleeves of wind.
His body and face seemed most distinct,
For visage and mind were both detached.
Long a stranger to all worldly things
He was the mountain's ageless boy.
Untainted even with a speck of dust,
He feared no havoc by the seasons wrought.

After coming through the door, the boy shouted, "Who is causing disturbance here?" With a bound the Monkey King leaped down from the tree, and went up to him bowing. "Immortal boy," he said, "I am a seeker of the way of immortality. I would never dare cause any disturbance." With a chuckle, the immortal youth asked, "Are you a seeker of the Way?" "I am indeed," answered the Monkey King. "My master at the house," the boy said, "has just left his couch to give a lecture on the platform. Before even announcing his theme, however, he told me to go out and open the door, saying, 'There is someone outside who wants to practice austerities. You may go and receive him.' It must be you, I suppose." The Monkey King said, smiling, "It is I, most assuredly!" "Follow me in then," said the boy. With solemnity the Monkey King set his clothes in order and followed the boy into the depths of the cave. They passed rows and rows of lofty towers and huge alcoves, of pearly chambers and carved arches. After walking through innumerable quiet chambers and empty studios, they finally reached the base of the green jade platform. Patriarch Subodhi was seen seated solemnly on the platform, with thirty lesser immortals standing below in rows. He was truly

> *An immortal of great ken and purest mien,*
> *Master Subodhi, whose wondrous form of the West*
> *Had no end or birth for the work of Double Three.*[8]
> *His whole spirit and breath were with mercy filled.*
> *Empty, spontaneous, it could change at will,*
> *His Buddha-nature able to do all things.*
> *The same age as Heaven had his majestic frame.*
> *Fully tried and enlightened was this grand priest.*

As soon as the Handsome Monkey King saw him, he prostrated himself and kowtowed times without number, saying, "Master! Master! I, your pupil, pay you my sincere homage." The Patriarch said, "Where do you come from? Let's hear you state clearly your name and country before you kowtow again." The Monkey King said, "Your pupil came from the Water-Curtain Cave of the Flower-Fruit Mountain, in the Aolai Country of the East Pūrvavideha Continent." "Chase him out of here!" the Patriarch shouted. "He is nothing but a liar and a fabricator of falsehood. How can he possibly be interested in attaining enlightenment?" The Monkey King hastened to kowtow unceasingly and to say, "Your pupil's word is an honest one, without any deceit." The Patriarch said, "If you are telling the truth, how is it that you mention the East Pūrvavideha Continent? Separating that place and mine are two great oceans and the entire region of the South Jambūdvīpa Continent. How could you possibly get here?" Again kowtowing, the Monkey King said, "Your pupil drifted across the oceans and trudged through many regions for more than ten years before finding this place." The Patriarch said, "If you have come on a long journey in many stages, I'll let that pass. What is your *xing*?" The Monkey King again replied, "I have no *xing*.[9] If a man rebukes me, I am not offended; if he hits me, I am not angered. In fact, I simply repay him with a ceremonial greeting and that's all. My whole life's without ill temper." "I'm not speaking of your temper," the Patriarch said, "I'm asking after the name of your parents." "I have no parents either," said the Monkey King. The Patriarch said, "If you have no parents, you must have been born from a tree." "Not from a tree," said the Monkey King, "but from a rock. I recall that there used to be an immortal stone on the Flower-Fruit Mountain. I was born the year the stone split open."

When the Patriarch heard this, he was secretly pleased, and said, "Well, evidently you have been created by Heaven and Earth. Get up and show me how you walk." Snapping erect, the Monkey King scurried around a couple of times. The Patriarch laughed and said. "Though your features are not the most

---

8. A higher form of meditation, reflecting a doubling of the three standard practices.

9. A pun on *xing* meaning both "surname" and "temper."

attractive, you do resemble a monkey (*husun*) that feeds on pine seeds. This gives me the idea of deriving your surname from your appearance. I intended to call you by the name *Hu*. Now, when the accompanying animal radical is dropped from this word, what's left is a compound made up of the two characters, *gu* and *yue*. *Gu* means aged and *yue* means female, but an aged female cannot reproduce. Therefore, it is better to give you the surname of *Sun*. When the accompanying animal radical is dropped from this word, we have the compound of *zi* and *xi*. *Zi* means a boy and *xi* means a baby, so that the name exactly accords with the Doctrine of the Baby. So your surname will be 'Sun.'"

When the Monkey King heard this, he was filled with delight. "Splendid! Splendid!" he cried, kowtowing, "At last I know my surname. May the master be even more gracious! Since I have received the surname, let me be given also a personal name, so that it may facilitate your calling and commanding me." The Patriarch said, "Within my tradition are twelve characters which have been used to name the pupils according to their divisions. You are one who belongs to the tenth generation." "Which twelve characters are they?" asked the Monkey King. The Patriarch said, "They are: wide (*guang*), great (*da*), wise (*zhi*), intelligence (*hui*), true (*zhen*), conforming (*ru*), nature (*xing*), sea (*hai*), sharp (*ying*), wake-to (*wu*), complete (*yuan*), and awakening (*jue*). Your rank falls precisely on the word 'wake-to' (*wu*). You will hence be given the religious name 'Wake-to-Vacuity' (*wukong*). All right?" "Splendid! Splendid!" said the Monkey King, laughing, "henceforth I shall be called Sun Wukong." So it was thus:

> At nebula's first clearing there was no name;
> Smashing stubborn vacuity requires wake-to-vacuity.

We do not know what fruit of Daoist cultivation he succeeded in attaining afterward; let's listen to the explanation in the next chapter.

* * *

From *Chapter 12*

The Tang emperor, firm in sincerity, convenes the Grand Mass;
Guanyin, revealing herself, converts Gold Cicada.[1]

* * *

The work was finished and reported; Taizong[2] was exceedingly pleased. He then gathered many officials together in order that a public notice be issued to invite monks for the celebration of the Grand Mass of Land and Water, so that those orphaned souls in the Region of Darkness might find salvation. The notice went throughout the empire, and officials of all regions were asked to recommend monks illustrious for their holiness to go to Chang'an for the Mass. In less than a month's time, the various monks from the empire had arrived. The Tang emperor ordered the court historian, Fu Yi, to select an illus-

---

1. Guanyin is the Bodhisattva of Mercy. "Gold Cicada" refers to the monk Xuanzang who was considered the reincarnation of the Buddha's second disciple, named Master Gold Cicada. Because he failed to follow the master's teachings, he was banished and reborn in China. His acquisition of the scriptures and adherence to Buddhism allow him in the end to reach Buddhahood.

2. Emperor Taizong of the Tang Dynasty, who ruled from 626 to 649 and dispatched Xuanzang to India.

trious priest to take charge of the ceremonies. When Fu Yi received the order, however, he presented a memorial to the Throne which attempted to dispute the worth of Buddha. The memorial said:

> The teachings of the Western Territory deny the relations of ruler and subject, of father and son.[3] With the doctrines of the Three Ways and the Sixfold Path, they beguile and seduce the foolish and the simpleminded. They emphasize the sins of the past in order to ensure the felicities of the future. By chanting in Sanskrit, they seek a way of escape. We submit, however, that birth, death, and the length of one's life are ordered by nature; but the conditions of public disgrace or honor are determined by human volition. These phenomena are not, as some philistines would now maintain, ordained by Buddha. The teachings of Buddha did not exist in the time of the Three Kings and the Five Emperors,[4] and yet those rulers were wise, their subjects loyal, and their reigns long-lasting. It was not until the period of Emperor Ming in the Han dynasty that the worship of foreign gods was established, but this meant only that priests of the Western Territory were permitted to propagate their faith. The event, in fact, represented a foreign intrusion in China, and the teachings are hardly worthy to be believed.

When Taizong saw the memorial, he had it distributed among the various officials for discussion. At that time the prime minister Xiao Yu came forward and prostrated himself to address the Throne, saying, "The teachings of Buddha, which have flourished in several previous dynasties, seek to exalt the good and to restrain what is evil. In this way they are covertly an aid to the nation, and there is no reason why they should be rejected. For Buddha after all is also a sage, and he who spurns a sage is himself lawless. I urge that the dissenter be severely punished."

Taking up the debate with Xiao Yu, Fu Yi contended that propriety had its foundation in service to one's parents and ruler. Yet Buddha forsook his parents and left his family; indeed, he defied the Son of Heaven[5] all by himself, just as he used an inherited body to rebel against his parents. Xiao Yu, Fu Yi went on to say, was not born in the wilds, but by his adherence to this doctrine of parental denial, he confirmed the saying that an unfilial son had in fact no parents. Xiao Yu, however, folded his hands in front of him and declared, "Hell was established precisely for people of this kind." Taizong thereupon called on the Lord High Chamberlain, Zhang Daoyuan, and the President of the Grand Secretariat, Zhang Shiheng, and asked how efficacious the Buddhist exercises were in the procurement of blessings. The two officials replied, "The emphasis of Buddha is on purity, benevolence, compassion, the proper fruits, and the unreality of things. It was Emperor Wu of the Northern Zhou dynasty who set the Three Religions in order. The Chan Master, Da Hui, also had extolled those concepts of the dark and the distant. Generations of people revered such saints as the Fifth Patriarch, who became man, or the Bodhidharma, who appeared in his sacred form; none of them proved to be inconspicuous in grace and power. Moreover, it has been held since antiquity that the Three Religions are most honorable, not to be destroyed or abolished. We beseech therefore, Your Majesty to exercise your clear and sagacious judgment." Highly pleased,

---

3. "Buddhism denies the principles of our Confucianism." The "teachings of the Western Territory" refer to Buddhism and the "relations of ruler and subject, of father and son" stands for the Confucian emphasis on social hierarchies.
4. Sage rulers of High Antiquity, long before Buddhism reached China from India.
5. The Chinese emperor.

Taizong said, "The words of our worthy subjects are not unreasonable. Anyone who disputes them further will be punished." He thereupon ordered Wei Zheng, Xiao Yu, and Zhang Daoyuan to invite the various Buddhist priests to prepare the site for the Grand Mass and to select from among them someone of great merit and virtue to preside over the ceremonies. All the officials then bowed their heads to the ground to thank the emperor before withdrawing. From that time also came the law that any person who denounces a monk or Buddhism will have his arms broken.

Next day the three court officials began the process of selection at the Mountain-River Platform, and from among the priests gathered there they chose an illustrious monk of great merit. "Who is this person?" you ask.

> Gold Cicada was his former divine name.
> As heedless he was of the Buddha's talk,
> He had to suffer in this world of dust,
> To fall in the net by being born a man.
> He met misfortune as he came to Earth,
> And evildoers even before his birth.
> His father: Chen, a zhuangyuan from Haizhou.
> His mother's sire: chief of this dynasty's court.
> Fated by his natal star to fall in the stream,
> He followed tide and current, chased by mighty waves.
> At Gold Mountain, the island, he had great fortune;
> For the abbot, Qian'an, raised him up.
> He met his true mother at age eighteen,
> And called on her father at the capital.
> A great army was sent by Chief Kaishan
> To stamp out the vicious crew at Hongzhou.
> The zhuangyuan Guangrui escaped his doom:
> Son united with sire—how worthy of praise!
> They saw the king to receive his favor;
> Their names resounded in Lingyan Tower.
> Declining office, he wished to be a monk,
> To seek at Hongfu Temple the Way of Truth,
> A former child of Buddha, nicknamed River Float,
> Had a religious name of Chen Xuanzang.

So that very day the multitude selected the priest Xuanzang, a man who had been a monk since childhood, who maintained a vegetarian diet, and who had received the commandments the moment he left his mother's womb. His maternal grandfather was Yin Kaishan, one of the chief army commanders of the present dynasty. His father, Chen Guangrui, had taken the prize of zhuangyuan and was appointed Grand Secretary of the Wenyuan Chamber. Xuanzang, however, had no love for glory or wealth, being dedicated wholly to the pursuit of Nirvāna. Their investigations revealed that he had an excellent family background and the highest moral character. Not one of the thousands of classics and sūtras had he failed to master; none of the Buddhist chants and hymns was unknown to him. The three officials led Xuanzang before the Throne. After going through elaborate court ritual, they bowed to report, "Your subjects, in obedience to your holy decree, have selected an illustrious monk by the name of Chen Xuanzang." Hearing the name, Taizong thought silently for a long time and said, "Can Xuanzang be the son of Grand Secretary Chen Guangrui?" Child River Float kowtowed and replied, "That is indeed your subject." "This is a most appropriate choice," said Taizong, delighted. "You are truly a monk of great virtue and devotion. We therefore appoint you the Grand Expositor of the Faith, Supreme Vicar of Priests." Xuanzang touched his forehead to the ground to express his gratitude and to receive his appointment. He was given, furthermore, a cassock of knitted gold and five colors, a Vairocana hat, and the instruction diligently to seek out all worthy monks and to rank all these ācāryas[6] in order. They were to follow the imperial decree and proceed to the Temple of Transformation, where they would begin the ceremony after selecting a propitious day and hour.

Xuanzang bowed again to receive the decree and left. He went to the Temple of Transformation and gathered many monks together; they made ready the beds, built the platforms, and rehearsed the music. A total of one thousand two hundred worthy monks, young and old, were chosen, who were further separated into three divisions, occupying the rear, middle, and front portions of the hall. All the preparations were completed and everything was put in order before the Buddhas.

* * *

We shall now tell you about the Bodhisattva Guanyin of the Potalaka Mountain in the South Sea, who, since receiving the command of Tathāgata,[7] was searching in the city of Chang'an for a worthy person to be the seeker of scriptures. For a long time, however, she did not encounter anyone truly virtuous. Then she learned that Taizong was extolling merit and virtue and selecting illustrious monks to hold the Grand Mass. When she discovered, moreover, that the chief priest and celebrant was the monk Child River Float, who was a child of Buddha born from paradise and who happened also to be the very elder whom she had sent to this incarnation, the Bodhisattva was exceedingly pleased. She immediately took the treasures bestowed by Buddha and carried them out with Moksa to sell them on the main streets of the city. "What were these treasures?" you ask. There were the embroidered cassock with rare jewels and the nine-ring priestly staff. But she kept hidden the Golden, the Constrictive, and the Prohibitive Fillets for use in a later time, putting up for sale only the cassock and the priestly staff.

Now in the city of Chang'an there was one of those foolish monks who had not been selected to participate in the Grand Mass but who happened to possess a few strands of pelf. Seeing the Bodhisattva, who had changed herself into a monk covered with scabs and sores, bare-footed and bare-headed, dressed in rags, and holding up for sale the glowing cassock, he approached and asked, "You filthy monk, how much do you want for your cassock?" "The price of the cassock," said the Bodhisattva, "is five thousand taels of silver; for the staff, two thousand." The foolish monk laughed and said, "This filthy monk is mad! A lunatic! You want seven thousand taels of silver for two such common articles? They are not worth that much even if wearing them would make

6. Spiritual masters, another word for Bud-   7. The Buddha.
dhist priests.

you immortal or turn you into a buddha. Take them away! You'll never be able to sell them!" The Bodhisattva did not bother to argue with him; she walked away and proceeded on her journey with Moksa.

After a long while, they came to the Eastern Flower Gate and ran right into the chief minister Xiao Yu, who was just returning from court. His outriders were shouting to clear the streets, but the Bodhisattva boldly refused to step aside. She stood on the street holding the cassock and met the chief minister head on. The chief minister pulled in his reins to look at this bright, luminous cassock, and asked his subordinates to inquire about the price of the garment. "I want five thousand taels for the cassock," said the Bodhisattva, "and two thousand for the staff." "What is so good about them," said Xiao Yu, "that they should be so expensive?" "This cassock," said the Bodhisattva, "has something good about it, and something bad, too. For some people it may be very expensive, but for others it may cost nothing at all."

"What's good about it," asked Xiao Yu, "and what's bad about it?"

"He who wears my cassock," said the Bodhisattva, "will not fall into perdition, will not suffer in Hell, will not encounter violence, and will not meet tigers and wolves. That's how good it is! But if the person happens to be a foolish monk who relishes pleasures and rejoices in iniquities, or a priest who obeys neither the dietary laws nor the commandments, or a worldly fellow who attacks the sūtras and slanders the Buddha, he will never even get to see my cassock. That's what's bad about it!" The chief minister asked again, "What do you mean, it will be expensive for some and not expensive for others?" "He who does not follow the Law of Buddha," said the Bodhisattva, "or revere the Three Jewels will be required to pay seven thousand taels if he insists on buying my cassock and my staff. That's how expensive it'll be! But if he honors the Three Jewels, rejoices in doing good deeds, and obeys our Buddha, he is a person worthy of these things. I shall willingly give him the cassock and the staff to establish an affinity of goodness with him. That's what I meant when I said that for some it would cost nothing."

When Xiao Yu heard these words, his face could not hide his pleasure, for he knew that this was a good person. He dismounted at once and greeted the Bodhisattva ceremoniously, saying, "Your Holy Eminence, please pardon whatever offense Xiao Yu might have caused. Our Great Tang Emperor is a most religious person, and all the officials of his court are like-minded. In fact, we have just begun a Grand Mass of Land and Water, and this cassock will be most appropriate for the use of Chen Xuanzang, the Grand Expositor of the Faith. Let me go with you to have an audience with the Throne."

The Bodhisattva was happy to comply with the suggestion. They turned around and went into the Eastern Flower Gate. The Custodian of the Yellow Door went inside to make the report, and they were summoned to the Treasure Hall, where Xiao Yu and the two monks covered with scabs and sores stood below the steps. "What does Xiao Yu want to report to us?" asked the Tang emperor. Prostrating himself before the steps, Xiao Yu said, "Your subject going out of the Eastern Flower Gate met by chance these two monks, selling a cassock and a priestly staff. I thought of the priest, Xuanzang, who might wear this garment. For this reason, we asked to have an audience with Your Majesty."

Highly pleased, Taizong asked for the price of the cassock. The Bodhisattva and Moksa stood at the foot of the steps but did not bow at all. When asked the price of the cassock, the Bodhisattva replied, "Five thousand taels for the cassock and two thousand for the priestly staff." "What's so good about the cassock," said Taizong, "that it should cost so much?" The Bodhisattva said:

"Of this cassock,
A dragon which wears but one shred
Will miss the woe of being devoured by the great roc;
Or a crane on which one thread is hung
Will transcend this world and reach the place of the gods.
Sit in it:
Ten thousand gods will salute you!
Move with it:
Seven Buddhas will follow you!
This cassock was made of silk drawn from ice silkworm
And threads spun by skilled craftsmen.
Immortal girls did the weaving;
Divine maidens helped at the loom.
Bit by bit, the parts were sewn and embroidered.
Stitch by stitch, it arose—a brocade from the heddle,
Its pellucid weave finer than ornate blooms.
Its colors, brilliant, emit precious light.
Wear it, and crimson mist will surround your frame.
Doff it, and see the colored clouds take flight.
Outside the Three Heavens' door its primal light was seen;
Before the Five Mountains its magic aura grew.
Inlaid are layers of lotus from the West,
And hanging pearls shine like planets and stars.
On four corners are pearls which glow at night;
On top stays fastened an emerald.
Though lacking the all-seeing primal form.
It's held by Eight Treasures all aglow.
This cassock
You keep folded at leisure;
You wear it to meet sages.
When it's kept folded at leisure,
Its rainbowlike hues cut through a thousand wrappings.
When you wear it to meet sages,
All Heaven takes fright—both demons and gods!
On top are the ṛddhi pearl,
The māni pearl,
The dust-clearing pearl,
The wind-stopping pearl.
There are also the red cornelian,
The purple coral,
The luminescent pearl,
The Śāriputra.
They rob the moon of its whiteness;
They match the sun in its redness.
In waves its divine aura imbues the sky;
In flashes its brightness lifts up its perfection.
In waves its divine aura imbues the sky,

> *Flooding the Gate of Heaven.*
> *In flashes its brightness lifts up its perfection,*
> *Lighting up the whole world.*
> *Shining upon the mountains and the streams.*
> *It wakens tigers and leopards;*
> *Lighting up the isles and the seas,*
> *It moves dragons and fishes,*
> *Along its edges hang two chains of melted gold,*
> *And joins the collars a ring of snow-white jade.*
> *The poem says:*
> *The august Three Jewels, this venerable Truth—*
> *It judges all Four Creatures on the Sixfold Path.*
> *The mind enlightened knows and holds God's Law and man's;*
> *The soul illumined can transmit the lamp of wisdom.*
> *The solemn guard of one's body is Vajradhātu;*[8]
> *Like ice in a jade pitcher is the purified mind.*
> *Since Buddha caused this cassock to be made,*
> *Which of ten thousand kalpas can harm a monk?"*

When the Tang emperor, who was up in the Treasure Hall, heard these words, he was highly pleased. "Tell me, priest," he asked again, "What's so good about the nine-ring priestly staff?" "My staff," said the Bodhisattva, "has on it

> *Nine joined-rings made of iron and set in bronze,*
> *And nine joints of vine immortal ever young.*
> *When held, it scorns the sight of aging bones:*
> *It leaves the mount to return with fleecy clouds.*
> *It roamed through Heaven with the Fifth Patriarch:*
> *It broke Hell's gate where Lo Bo sought his Mom.*
> *Not soiled by the fifth of this red-dust world,*
> *It gladly trails the god-monk up Mount Jade."*[9]

When the Tang emperor heard these words, he gave the order to have the cassock spread open so that he might examine it carefully from top to bottom. It was indeed a marvelous thing! "Venerable Elder of the Great Law,"[1] he said, "we shall not deceive you. At this very moment we have exalted the Religion of Mercy and planted abundantly in the fields of blessing. You may see many priests assembled in the Temple of Transformation to perform the Law and the sūtras. In their midst is a man of great merit and virtue, whose religious name is Xuanzang. We wish, therefore, to purchase these two treasure objects from you to give them to him. How much do you really want for these things?" Hearing these words, the Bodhisattva and Moksa folded their hands and gave praise to the Buddha. "If he is a man of virtue and merit," she said to the Throne, bowing, "this humble cleric is willing to give them to him. I shall not accept any money." She finished speaking and turned at once to leave. The Tang emperor quickly asked Xiao Yu to hold her back. Standing up in the Hall, he bowed low before saying, "Previously you claimed that the cassock was worth five thousand

---

8. Golden or diamond element in the universe, signifying the indestructibility wisdom of
a particular Buddha.

9. Abode of the Queen Mother of the West, a
Daoist deity.

1. The "Great Law" of Buddhism.

taels of silver, and the staff two thousand. Now that you see we want to buy them, you refuse to accept payment. Are you implying that we would bank on our position and take your possession by force? That's absurd! We shall pay you according to the original sum you asked for: please do not refuse it."

Raising her hands for a salutation, the Bodhisattva said, "This humble cleric made a vow before, stating that anyone who reveres the Three Treasures, rejoices in virtue, and submits to our Buddha will be given these treasures free. Since it is clear that Your Majesty is eager to magnify virtues to rest in excellence, and to honor our Buddhist faith by having an illustrious monk proclaim the Great Law, it is my duty to present these gifts to you. I shall take no money for them. They will be left here and this humble cleric will take leave of you." When the Tang emperor saw that she was so insistent, he was very pleased. He ordered the Court of Banquets to prepare a huge vegetarian feast to thank the Bodhisattva, who firmly declined that also. She left amiably and went back to her hiding place at the Temple of the Local Spirit, which we shall mention no further.

* * *

Time went by like the snapping of fingers, and the formal celebration of the Grand Mass on the seventh day was to take place. Xuanzang presented the Tang emperor with a memorial, inviting him to raise the incense. News of these good works was circulating throughout the empire. Upon receiving the notice, Taizong sent for his carriage and led many of his officials, both civil and military, as well as his relatives and the ladies of the court, to the temple. All the people of the city—young and old, nobles and commoners—went along also to hear the preaching. At the same time the Bodhisattva said to Moksa, "Today is the formal celebration of the Grand Mass, the first seventh of seven such occasions. It's about time for you and me to join the crowd. First, we want to see how the mass is going; second, we want to find out whether Gold Cicada is worthy of my treasures; and third, we can discover what division of Buddhism he is preaching about."

* * *

On the platform, that Master of the Law recited for a while the *Sūtra of Life and Deliverance for the Dead*; he then lectured for a while on the *Heavenly Treasure Chronicle for Peace in the Nation*, after which he preached for a while on the *Scroll on Merit and Self-Cultivation*. The Bodhisattva drew near and thumped her hands on the platform, calling out in a loud voice, "Hey, monk! You only know how to talk about the teachings of the Little Vehicle. Don't you know anything about the Great Vehicle?"[2] When Xuanzang heard this question, he was filled with delight. He turned and leaped down from the platform, raised his hands and saluted the Bodhisattva, saying, "Venerable Teacher, please pardon your pupil for much disrespect. I only know that the priests who came before me all talk about the teachings of the Little Vehicle. I have no idea what the Great Vehicle teaches." "The doctrines of your Little Vehicle,"

---

2. "Little Vehicle" and "Great Vehicle" refer to two forms of Buddhism. Hīnayāna Buddhism, the "Little Vehicle," is focused more on ascetic practices and individual salvation, while Mahāyāna Buddhism, the "Great Vehicle," which became dominant in East Asia, emphasizes care for others.

said the Bodhisattva, "cannot save the damned by leading them up to Heaven; they can only mislead and confuse mortals. I have in my possession Tripitaka, three collections of the Great Vehicle Laws of Buddha, which are able to send the lost to Heaven, to deliver the afflicted from their sufferings, to fashion ageless bodies, and to break the cycles of coming and going."

As they were speaking, the officer in charge of incense and the inspection of halls went to report to the emperor, saying, "The Master was just in the process of lecturing on the wondrous Law when he was pulled down by two scabby mendicants, babbling some kind of nonsense." The king ordered them to be arrested, and the two monks were taken by many people and pushed into the hall in the rear. When the monk saw Taizong, she neither raised her hands nor made a bow; instead, she lifted her face and said, "What do you want of me, Your Majesty?" Recognizing her, the Tang emperor said, "Aren't you the monk who brought us the cassock the other day?" "I am," said the Bodhisattva. "If you have come to listen to the lecture," said Taizong, "you may as well take some vegetarian food. Why indulge in this wanton discussion with our Master and disturb the lecture hall, delaying our religious service?"

"What that Master of yours was lecturing on," said the Bodhisattva, "happens to be the teachings of the Little Vehicle, which cannot lead the lost up to Heaven. In my possession is the Tripitaka, the Great Vehicle Law of Buddha, which is able to save the damned, deliver the afflicted, and fashion the indestructible body." Delighted, Taizong asked eagerly, "Where is your Great Vehicle Law of Buddha?" "At the place of our lord, Tathāgata," said the Bodhisattva, "in the Great Temple of Thunderclap, located in India of the Great Western Heaven.[3] It can untie the knot of a hundred enmities; it can dispel unexpected misfortunes." "Can you remember any of it?" said Taizong. "Certainly," said the Bodhisattva. Taizong was overjoyed and said, "Let the Master lead this monk to the platform to begin a lecture at once."

Our Bodhisattva led Moksa and flew up onto the high platform. She then trod on the hallowed clouds to rise up into the air and revealed her true salvific form, holding the pure vase with the willow branch. At her left stood the virile figure of Moksa carrying the rod. The Tang emperor was so overcome that he bowed to the sky and worshiped, as civil and military officials all knelt on the ground and burned incense. Throughout the temple, there was not one of the monks, nuns, Taoists, secular persons, scholars, craftsmen, and merchants, who did not bow down and exclaim, "Dear Bodhisattva! Dear Bodhisattva!" We have a song as a testimony. They saw only

> *Auspicious mist in diffusion*
> *And dharmakāya[4] veiled by holy light.*
> *In the bright air of ninefold Heaven*
> *A lady immortal appeared.*
> *That Bodhisattva*
> *Wore on her head a cap*
> *Fastened by leaves of gold*
> *And set with flowers of jade,*
> *With tassels of dangling pearls,*

---

3. Destination of Xuanzang's trip to India.   4. The spiritual form embodying Buddhahood.

All aglow with golden light.
On her body she had
A robe of fine blue silk.
Lightly colored
And simply fretted
By circling dragons
And soaring phoenixes.
Down in front was hung
A pair of fragrant girdle-jade,
Which glowed with the moon
And danced with the wind,
Overlaid with precious pearls
And with imperial jade.
Around her waist was tied
An embroidered velvet skirt
Of ice-worm silk
And piped in gold,
In which she topped the colored clouds
And crossed the jasper sea.
Before her she led
A cockatoo with red beak and yellow plumes,
Which had roamed the Eastern Ocean
And throughout the world
To foster deeds of mercy and filial piety.
She held in her hands
A grace-dispensing and world-sustaining precious vase,
In which was planted
A twig of pliant willow,
That could moisten the blue sky,
And sweep aside all evil—
All clinging fog and smoke.
Her jade rings joined the embroidered loops,
And gold lotus grew thick beneath her feet.
In three days how often she came and went:
This very Guanshiyin[5] who saves from pain and woe.

So pleased by the vision was Tang Taizong that he forgot about his empire; so enthralled were the civil and military officials that they completely ignored court etiquette. Everyone was chanting, "Namo Bodhisattva Guanshiyin!"

Taizong at once gave the order for a skilled painter to sketch the true form of the Bodhisattva. No sooner had he spoken than a certain Wu Daozi was selected, who could portray gods and sages and was a master of the noble perspective and lofty vision. (This man, in fact, was the one who would later paint the portraits of meritorious officials in the Lingyan Tower.) Immediately he opened up his magnificent brush to record the true form. The hallowed clouds of the Bodhisattva gradually drifted away, and in a little while the golden light disappeared. From midair came floating down a slip of paper on which were plainly written several lines in the style of the *gāthā*:[6]

5. Full name of Guanyin, meaning "She who listens to the voices of the world."　　**6.** A verse.

> We greet the great Ruler of Tang
> With scripts most sublime of the West.
> The way: a hundred and eight thousand miles.
> Seek earnestly this Mahāyāna,[7]
> These Books, when they reach your fair state,
> Can redeem damned spirits from Hell.
> If someone is willing to go,
> He'll become a Buddha of gold.

When Taizong saw the *gāthā*, he said to the various monks: "Let's stop the Mass. Wait until I have sent someone to bring back the scriptures of the Great Vehicle. We shall then renew our sincere effort to cultivate the fruits of virtue." Not one of the officials disagreed with the emperor, who then asked in the temple, "Who is willing to accept our commission to seek scriptures from Buddha in the Western Heaven?" Hardly had he finished speaking when the Master of the Law stepped from the side and saluted him, saying, "Though your poor monk has no talents, he is ready to perform the service of a dog and a horse. I shall seek these true scriptures on behalf of Your Majesty, that the empire of our king may be firm and everlasting." Highly pleased, the Tang emperor went forward to raise up the monk with his royal hands, saying, "If the Master is willing to express his loyalty this way, undaunted by the great distance or by the journey over mountains and streams, we are willing to become bond brothers with you." Xuanzang touched his forehead to the ground to express his gratitude. Being indeed a righteous man, the Tang emperor went at once before Buddha's image in the temple and bowed to Xuanzang four times, addressing him as "our brother and holy monk."

Deeply moved, Xuanzang said, "Your Majesty, what ability and what virtue does your poor monk possess that he should merit such affection from your Heavenly Grace? I shall not spare myself in this journey, but I shall proceed with all diligence until I reach the Western Heaven. If I do not attain my goal, or the true scriptures, I shall not return to our land even if I have to die. I would rather fall into eternal perdition in Hell." He thereupon lifted the incense before Buddha and made that his vow. Highly pleased, the Tang emperor ordered his carriage back to the palace to wait for the auspicious day and hour, when official documents could be issued for the journey to begin. And so the Throne withdrew as everyone dispersed.

Xuanzang also went back to the Temple of Great Blessing. The many monks of that temple and his several disciples, who had heard about the quest for the scriptures, all came to see him. They asked, "Is it true that you have vowed to go to the Western Heaven?" "It is," said Xuanzang. "O Master," one of his disciples said, "I have heard people say that the way to the Western Heaven is long, filled with tigers, leopards, and all kinds of monsters. I fear that there will be departure but no return for you, as it will be difficult to safeguard your life."

"I have already made a great vow and a profound promise," said Xuanzang, "that if I do not acquire the true scriptures, I shall fall into eternal perdition in Hell. Since I have received such grace and favor from the king, I have no alternative but to serve my country to the utmost of my loyalty. It is true, of course, that I have no knowledge of how I shall fare on this journey or whether good or

---

7. Again, this refers to Mahāyāna Buddhism common in East Asia.

evil awaits me." He said to them again, "My disciples, after I leave, wait for two or three years, or six or seven years. If you see the branches of the pine trees within our gate pointing eastward, you will know that I am about to return. If not, I shall not be coming back." The disciples all committed his words firmly to memory.

The next morning Taizong held court and gathered all the officials together. They wrote up the formal rescript stating the intent to acquire scriptures and stamped it with the seal of free passage. The President of the Imperial Board of Astronomy then came with the report, "Today the positions of the planets are especially favorable for men to make a journey of great length." The Tang emperor was most delighted. Thereafter the custodian of the Yellow Gate also made a report, saying, "The Master of the Law awaits your pleasure outside the court." The emperor summoned him up to the treasure hall and said, "Royal Brother, today is an auspicious day for the journey, and your rescript for free passage is ready. We also present you with a bowl made of purple gold for you to collect alms on your way. Two attendants have been selected to accompany you, and a horse will be your means of travel. You may begin your journey at once."

Highly pleased, Xuanzang expressed his gratitude and received his gifts, not displaying the least desire to linger. The Tang emperor called for his carriage and led many officials outside the city gate to see him off. The monks in the Temple of Great Blessing and the disciples were already waiting there with Xuanzang's winter and summer clothing. When the emperor saw them, he ordered the bags to be packed on the horses first, and then asked an officer to bring a pitcher of wine. Taizong lifted his cup to toast the pilgrim saying, "What is the byname of our Royal Brother?" "Your poor monk," said Xuanzang, "is a person who has left the family. He dares not assume a byname." "The Bodhisattva said earlier," said Taizong, that there were three collections of scriptures in the Western Heaven. Our Brother can take that as a byname and call himself Tripitaka.[8] How about it?" Thanking him, Xuanzang accepted the wine and said, "Your Majesty, wine is the first prohibition of priesthood. Your poor monk has practiced abstinence since birth." "Today's journey," said Taizong, "is not to be compared with any ordinary event. Please drink one cup of this dietary wine, and accept our good wishes that go along with the toast." Xuanzang dared not refuse; he took the wine and was about to drink, when he saw Taizong stoop down to scoop up a handful of dirt with his fingers and sprinkle it in the wine. Tripitaka had no idea what this gesture meant.

"Dear Brother," said Taizong, laughing, "how long will it take you to come back from this trip to the Western Heaven?" "Probably in three years time," said Tripitaka, "I'll be returning to our noble nation." "The years are long and the journey is great," said Taizong. "Drink this, Royal Brother, and remember: Treasure a handful of dirt from your home, but love not ten thousand taels of foreign gold." Then Tripitaka understood the meaning of the handful of dirt sprinkled in his cup: he thanked the emperor once more and drained the cup. He went out of the gate and left, as the Tang emperor returned in his carriage. We do not know what will happen to him on this journey; let's listen to the explanation in the next chapter.

* * *

8. The monk carries hereafter the name "Buddhist Canon."

From *Chapter 44*

The dharma-body in primary cycle meets the force of the cart;
The mind, righting monstrous deviates, crosses the spine-ridge pass.

* * *

When the monks saw the two Daoists, they were terrified;[1] every one of them redoubled his effort to pull desperately at the cart. "So, that's it!" said Pilgrim, comprehending the situation all at once. "These monks must be awfully afraid of the Daoists, for if not, why should they be tugging so hard at the carts? I have heard someone say that there is a place on the road to the West where Daoism is revered and Buddhism is set for destruction. This must be the place. I would like to go back and report this to Master, but I still don't know the whole truth and he might blame me for bringing him surmises, saying that even a smart person like me can't be counted on for a reliable report. Let me go down there and question them thoroughly before I give Master an answer."

"Whom would he question?" you ask. Dear Great Sage! He lowered his cloud and with a shake of his torso, he changed at the foot of the city into a wandering Daoist of the Completed Authenticity sect, with an exorcist hamper hung on his left arm. Striking a hollow wooden fish with his hands and chanting lyrics of Daoist themes, he walked up to the two Daoists near the city gate. "Masters," he said, bowing, "this humble Daoist raises his hand." Returning his salute, one of the Daoists said, "Sir, where did you come from?" "This disciple," said Pilgrim, "has wandered to the corners of the sea and to the edges of Heaven. I arrived here this morning with the sole purpose of collecting subscriptions for good works. May I ask the two masters which street in this city is favorable towards the Dao, and which alley is inclined towards piety? This humble Daoist would like to go there and beg for some vegetarian food." Smiling, the Daoist said, "O Sir! Why do you speak in such a disgraceful manner?" "What do you mean by disgraceful?" said Pilgrim. "If you want to *beg* for vegetarian food," said the Daoist, "isn't that disgraceful?" Pilgrim said, "Those who have left the family live by begging. If I didn't beg, where would I have money to buy food?"

Chuckling, the Daoist said, "You've come from afar, and you don't know anything about our city. In this city of ours, not only the civil and military officials are fond of the Dao, the rich merchants and men of prominence devoted to piety, but even the ordinary citizens, young and old, will bow to present us food once they see us. It is, in fact, a trivia matter, hardly worth mentioning. What's most important about our city is that His Majesty, the king, is also fond of the Dao and devoted to piety." "This humble cleric is first of all quite young," said Pilgrim, "and second, he is indeed from afar. In truth I'm ignorant of the situation here. May I trouble the two masters to tell me the name of this place and give me a thorough account of how the king has come to be so devoted to the cause of Dao—for the sake of fraternal feelings among us Daoists?" The Daoist said, "This city has the name of the Cart Slow Kingdom, and the ruler on the precious throne is a relative of ours."

---

1. In the intervening chapters Tripitaka, the monk Xuanzang, has gained his three disciples: Pilgrim (the monkey, Sun Wukong), Sha Monk (or Sha Wujing), and Zhu Bajie. Having been subjected to numerous ordeals on the way to India in pursuit of the scriptures, they here enter a land where Buddhists are enslaved by Daoists.

When Pilgrim heard these words, he broke into loud guffaws, saying, "I suppose that a Daoist has become king." "No," said the Daoist. "What happened was that twenty years ago, this region had a drought, so severe that not a single drop of rain fell from the sky and all grains and plants perished. The king and his subjects, the rich as well as the poor—every person was burning incense and praying to Heaven for relief. Just when it seemed that nothing else could preserve their lives, three immortals suddenly descended from the sky and saved us all." "Who were these immortals?" asked Pilgrim. "Our masters," said the Daoist. "What are their names?" said Pilgrim. The Daoist replied, "The eldest master is called the Tiger-Strength Great Immortal; the second master, the Deer-Strength Great Immortal; and the third master, Goat-Strength Great Immortal." "What kinds of magic power do your esteemed teachers possess?" asked Pilgrim. The Daoist said, "Summoning the wind and the rain for my masters would be as easy as flipping over one's palms; they point at water and it will change into oil; they touch stones and change them into gold, as quickly as one turns over in bed. With this kind of magic power, they are thus able to rob the creative genius of Heaven and Earth, to alter the mysteries of the stars and constellations. The king and his subjects have such profound respect for them that all of us Daoists are claimed as royal kin." Pilgrim said, "This ruler is lucky, all right. After all, the proverb says, 'Magic moves ministers!' He certainly can't lose to claim kinship with your old masters, if they possess such powers. Alas! I wonder if I had even that tiniest spark of affinity, such that I could have an audience with the old masters?" Chuckling, the Daoist replied, "If you want to see our masters, it's not difficult at all. The two of us are their bosom disciples. Moreover, our masters are so devoted to the Way and so deferential to the pious that the mere mention of the word 'Dao' would bring them out of the door, full of welcome. If we two were to introduce you, we would need to exert our themselves no more vigorously than to blow away some ashes."

Bowing deeply, Pilgrim said, "I am indebted to you for your introduction. Let us go into the city then." "Let's wait a moment," said one of the Daoists. "You sit here while we two finish our official business first. Then we'll go with you." Pilgrim said, "Those of us who have left the family are without cares or ties; we are completely free. What do you mean by official business?" The Daoist pointed with his finger at the monks on the beach and said, "Their work happens to be the means of livelihood for us. Lest they become indolent, we have come to check them off the roll before we go with you." Smiling, Pilgrim said, "You must be mistaken, Masters. Buddhists and Daoists are all people who have left the family. For what reason are they working for our support? Why are they willing to submit to our roll call?"

The Daoist said, "You have no idea that in the year when we were all praying for rain, the monks bowed to Buddha on one side while the Daoists petitioned the Pole Star on the other, all for the sake of finding some food for the country. The monks, however, were useless, their empty chants of sūtras wholly without efficacy. As soon as our masters arrived on the scene, they summoned the wind and the rain and the bitter affliction was removed from the multitudes. It was then that the Court became terribly vexed at the monks, saying that they were completely ineffective and that they deserved to have their monasteries wrecked and their Buddha images destroyed. Their travel rescripts were revoked and they were not permitted to return to their native regions. His Majesty gave them to us instead and they were to serve as bondsmen: they are the ones who tend the fires in our temple, who sweep the grounds, and who guard the gates. Since we have some buildings in the rear which are not completely finished, we have ordered these monks here to haul bricks, tiles, and timber for the construction. But for fear of their mischief, indolence, and unwillingness to pull the cart, we have come to investigate and make the roll call."

When Pilgrim heard that, he tugged at the Daoist as tears rolled from his eyes. "I said that I might not have the good affinity to see your old masters," he said, "and true enough I don't." "Why not?" asked the Daoist. "This humble Daoist is making a wide tour of the world," said Pilgrim, "both for the sake of eking out a living and for finding a relative." "What sort of relative do you have?" said the Daoist. Pilgrim said, "I have an uncle, who since his youth had left the family and shorn his hair to become a monk. Because of famine some years ago he had to go abroad to beg for alms and hadn't returned since. As I remembered our ancestral benevolence, I decided that I would make a special effort to find him along the way. It's very likely, I suppose, that he is detained here and cannot go home. I must find him somehow and get to see him before I can go inside the city with you." "That's easy," said the Daoist. "The two of us can sit here while you go down to the beach to make the roll call for us. There should be five hundred of them on the roll. Take a look and see if your uncle is among them. If he is, we'll let him go for the sake of the fact that you, too, are a fellow Daoist. Then we'll go inside the city with you. How about that?"

Pilgrim thanked them profusely, and with a deep bow he took leave of the Daoists. Striking up his wooden fish, he headed down to the beach, passing the double passes as he walked down the narrow path from the steep ridge. All those monks knelt down at once and kowtowed, saying in unison, "Father, we have not been indolent. Not even half a person from the five hundred is missing—we are all here pulling the cart." Snickering to himself, Pilgrim thought: "These monks must have been awfully abused by the Daoists. They are terrified even when they see a fake Daoist like me. If a real Daoist goes near them, they will probably die of fear." Waving his hand, Pilgrim said, "Get up, and don't be afraid! I'm not here to inspect your work, I'm here to find a relative." When those monks heard that he was looking for a relative, they surrounded him on all sides, every one of them sticking out his head and coughing, hoping that he would be claimed as kin. "Which of us is his relative?" they said. After he had looked at them for a while, Pilgrim burst into laughter. "Father," said the monks, "you don't seem to have found your relative. Why are you laughing instead?" Pilgrim said, "You want to know why I'm laughing? I'm laughing at how immature you monks are! It was because of your having been born under an unlucky star that your parents, for fear of your bringing misfortune upon them or for not bringing with you additional brothers and sisters, turned you out of the family and made you priests. How could you then not follow the Three Jewels and not revere the law of Buddha? Why aren't you reading the sūtras and chanting the litanies? Why do you serve the Daoists and allow them to exploit you as bondsmen and slaves?" "Venerable Father," said the monks, "are you here to ridicule us? You must have come from abroad, and you have no idea of our plight." "Indeed I'm from abroad," said Pilgrim, "and I truly have no idea of what sort of plight you have."

As they began to weep, the monks said, "The ruler of our country is wicked and partial. All he cares for are those persons like you, Venerable Father, and those whom he hates are us Buddhists." "Why is that?" asked Pilgrim. "Because the need for wind and rain," said one of the monks, "caused three immortal elders to come here. They deceived our ruler and persuaded him to tear down our monasteries and revoke our travel rescripts, forbidding us to return to our native regions. He would not, moreover, permit us to serve even in any secular capacity except as slaves in the household of those immortal elders. Our agony is unbearable! If any Daoist mendicant shows up in this region, they would immediately request the king to grant him an audience and a handsome reward; but if a monk appears, regardless of whether he is from nearby or afar, he will be seized and sent to be a servant in the house of the immortals." Pilgrim said, "Could it be that those Daoists are truly in possession of some mighty magic, potent enough to seduce the king? If it's only a matter of summoning the wind and the rain, then it is merely a trivial trick of heterodoxy. How could it sway a ruler's heart?" The monks said, "They know how to manipulate cinnabar and refine lead, to sit in meditation in order to nourish their spirits. They point to water and it changes into oil; they touch stones and transform them into pieces of gold. Now they are in the process of building a huge temple for the Three Pure Ones, in which they can perform rites to Heaven and Earth and read scriptures night and day, to the end that the king will remain youthful for ten thousand years. Such enterprise undoubtedly pleases the king."

"So that's how it is!" said Pilgrim. "Why don't you all run away and be done with it?" "Father, we can't!" said the monks. "Those immortal elders have obtained permission from the king to have our portraits painted and hung up in all four quarters of the kingdom. Although the territory of this Cart Slow Kingdom is quite large, there is a picture of monks displayed in the marketplace of every village, town, county, and province. It bears on top the royal inscription that any official who catches a monk will be elevated three grades, and any private citizen who does so will receive a reward of fifty taels of white silver. That's why we can never escape. Let's not say monks—but even those who have cut their hair short or are getting bald will find it difficult to get past the officials. They are everywhere, the detectives and the runners! No matter what you do, you simply can't flee. We have no alternative but to remain here and suffer."

* * *

There were three old Daoists resplendent in their ritual robes, and Pilgrim thought they had to be the Tiger-Strength, Deer-Strength, and Goat-Strength Immortals. Below them there was a motley crew of some seven or eight hundred Daoists; lined up on opposite sides, they were beating drums and gongs, offering incense, and saying prayers. Secretly pleased, Pilgrim said to himself, "I would like to go down there and fool with them a bit, but as the proverb says,

> A silk fiber is no thread;
> A single hand cannot clap.

Let me go back and alert Bajie and Sha Monk. Then we can return and have some fun."

He dropped down from the auspicious cloud and went straight back to the abbot's hall, where he found Bajie and Sha Monk asleep head to foot in one bed. Pilgrim tried to wake Wujing first, and as he stirred, Sha Monk said, "Elder Brother, you aren't asleep yet?" "Get up now," said Pilgrim, "for you and I are going to enjoy ourselves." "In the dead of night," said Sha Monk, "how could we enjoy ourselves when our mouths are dried and our eyes won't stay open?" Pilgrim said, "There is indeed in this city a Temple of the Three Pure Ones. Right now the Daoists in the temple are conducting a mass, and their main hall is filled with all kinds of offerings. The buns are big as barrels, and their cakes must weigh fifty or sixty pounds each. There are also countless rice condiments and fresh fruits. Come with me and we'll go enjoy ourselves!" When Zhu Bajie heard in his sleep that there were good things to eat, he immediately woke up, saying, "Elder Brother, aren't you going to take care of me too?" "Brother," said Pilgrim, "if you want to eat, don't make all these noises and wake up Master. Just follow me."

The two of them slipped on their clothes and walked quietly out the door. They trod on the cloud with Pilgrim and rose into the air. When Idiot saw the flare of lights, he wanted immediately to go down there had not Pilgrim pulled him back. "Don't be so impatient," said Pilgrim, "wait till they disperse. Then we can go down there." Bajie said, "But obviously they are having such a good time praying. Why would they want to disperse? "Let me use a little magic," said Pilgrim, "and they will."

Dear Great Sage! He made the magic sign with his fingers and recited a spell before he drew in his breath facing the ground toward the southwest. Then he blew it out and at once a violent whirlwind assailed the Three Pure Ones Hall, smashing flower vases and candle stands and tearing up all the ex-votos hanging on the four walls. As lights and torches were all blown out, the Daoists became terrified. Tiger-Strength Immortal said, "Disciples, let's disperse. Since this divine wind has extinguished all our lamps, torches, and incense, each of us should retire. We can rise earlier tomorrow morning to recite a few more scrolls of scriptures and make up for what we miss tonight." The various Daoists indeed retreated.

Our Pilgrim leading Bajie and Sha Monk lowered the clouds and dashed up to the Three Pure Ones Hall. Without bothering to find out whether it was raw or cooked, Idiot grabbed one of the cakes and gave it a fierce bite. Pilgrim whipped out the iron rod and tried to give his hand a whack. Hastily withdrawing his hand to dodge the blow, Bajie said, "I haven't even found out the taste yet, and you're trying to hit me already?" "Don't be so rude," said Pilgrim. "Let's sit down with proper manners and then we may treat ourselves." "Aren't you embarrassed?" said Bajie. "You are stealing food, you know, and you still want proper manners! If you were invited here, what would you do then?" Pilgrim said, "Who are these bodhisattvas sitting up there?" "What do you mean by who are these bodhisattvas?" chuckled Bajie. "Can't you recognize the Three Pure Ones?" "Which Three Pure Ones?" said Pilgrim. "The one in the middle," said Bajie, "is the Honorable Divine of the Origin; the one on the left is the Enlightened Lord of Spiritual Treasures; and the one on the right is Laozi.²" Pilgrim said, "We have to take on their appearances. Only then can we

2. Famous ancient philosophical master, to whom the book *Laozi* is ascribed, and central deity of the Daoist pantheon.

eat safely and comfortably." When he caught hold of the delicious fragrance coming from the offerings, Idiot could wait no longer. Climbing up onto the tall platform, he gave the figure of Laozi a shove with his snout and pushed it to the floor, saying, "Old fellow, you have sat here long enough! Now let old Hog take your place for a while!" So Bajie changed himself into Laozi, while Pilgrim took on the appearance of the Honorable Divine of the Origin and Sha Monk became the Enlightened Lord of Spiritual Treasures. All the original images were pushed down to the floor. The moment they sat down, Bajie began to gorge himself with the huge buns. "Could you wait one moment?" said Pilgrim. "Elder Brother," said Bajie, "we have changed into their forms. Why wait any longer?"

"Brother," said Pilgrim, "it's small thing to eat, but giving ourselves away is no small matter! These holy images we pushed on the floor could be found by those Daoists who had to rise early to strike the bell or sweep the grounds. If they stumbled over them, wouldn't our secret be revealed? Why don't you see if you can hide them somewhere?" Bajie said, "This is an unfamiliar place, and I don't even know where to begin to look for a hiding spot." "Just now when we entered the hall," Pilgrim said, "I chanced to notice a little door on our right. Judging from the foul stench coming through it, I think it must be a Bureau of Five-Grain Transmigration. Send them in there."

Idiot, in truth, was rather good at crude labor! He leaped down, threw the three images over his shoulder, and carried them out of the hall. When be kicked open the door, he found a huge privy inside. Chuckling to himself he said, "This Bimawen truly has a way with words! He even bestows on a privy a sacred title! The Bureau of Five-Grain Transmigration, what a name!" Still hauling the images on this shoulders, Idiot began to mumble this prayer to them:

"O Pure Ones Three,
I'll confide in thee:
From afar we came,
Staunch foes of bogies.
We'd like a treat,
But nowhere's cozy.
We borrow your seats
For a while only.
You've sat too long,
Now go to the privy.
In times past you've enjoyed countless good things
By being pure and clean Daoists.
Today you can't avoid facing something dirty
When you become Honorable Divines Most Smelly!"

After he had made his supplication, he threw them inside with a splash and half of his robe was soiled by the muck. As he walked back into the hall, Pilgrim said, "Did you hide them well?" "Well enough," said Bajie, "but some of the filth stained my robe. It still stinks. I hope it won't make you retch." "Never mind," said Pilgrim, laughing, "you just come and enjoy yourself. I wonder if we could all make a clean getaway!" After Idiot changed back into the form of Laozi, the three of them took their seats and abandoned themselves to enjoyment. They ate the huge buns first; then they gobbled down the side dishes, the rice condiments, the dumplings, the baked goods, the cakes, the deep-fried dishes, and the steamed pastries—regardless of whether these were hot or cold. Pilgrim Sun, however, was not too fond of anything cooked; all he had were a few pieces of fruit, just to keep the other two company. Meanwhile Bajie and Sha Monk went after the offerings like comets chasing the moon, like wind mopping up the clouds! In no time at all, they were completely devoured. When there was nothing left for them to eat, they, instead of leaving, remained seated there to chat and wait for the food to digest.

* * *

From Chapter 46

Heresy flaunts its strength to make orthodoxy;
Mind Monkey shows his saintliness to slay the deviates.

We were telling you that when the king saw Pilgrim Sun's ability to summon dragons and command sages, he immediately applied his treasure seal to the travel rescript. He was about to hand it back to the Tang monk and permit him to take up the journey once more, when the three Daoists went forward and prostrated themselves before the steps of the Hall of Golden Chimes. The king left his dragon throne hurriedly and tried to raise them with his hands. "National Preceptors," he said, "why do you three go through such a great ceremony with us today?" "Your Majesty," said the Daoists, "we have been upholding your reign and providing security for your people here for these twenty years. Today this priest has made use of some paltry tricks of magic and robbed us of all our credit and ruined our reputation. Just because of one rainstorm, Your Majesty has pardoned even their crime of murder. Are we not being treated lightly? Let Your Majesty withhold their rescript for the moment and allow us brothers to wage another contest with them. We shall see what happens then."

* * *

Just then, the Tiger-Strength Great Immortal walked out from the Pavilion of Cultural Florescence after he had been washed and combed. "Your Majesty," he said as he walked up the hall, "this monk knows the magic of object removal. Give me the chest, and I'll destroy his magic. Then we can have another contest with him." "What do you want to do?" said the king. Tiger-Strength said, "His magic can remove only lifeless objects but not a human body. Put this Daoist youth in the chest, and he'll never be able to remove him." The youth indeed was hidden in the chest, which was then brought down again from the hall to be placed before the steps. "You, monk," said the king, "guess again what sort of treasure we have inside." Tripitaka said, "Here it comes again!" "Let me go and have another look." said Pilgrim. With a buzz, he flew off and crawled inside, where he found a Daoist lad. Marvelous Great Sage! What readiness of mind! Truly

Such agility is rare in the world!
Such cleverness is uncommon indeed!

Shaking his body once, he changed himself into the form of one of those old Daoists, whispering as he entered the chest, "Disciple."

"Master," said the lad, "how did you come in here?" "With the magic of invisibility," said Pilgrim. The lad said, "Do you have some instructions for me?" "The priest saw you enter the chest," said Pilgrim, "and if he made his guess a Daoist lad, wouldn't we lose to him again? That's why I came here to discuss the matter with you. Let's shave your head, and we'll then make them guess that you are a monk." The Daoist lad said, "Do whatever you want, Master, just so that we win. For if we lose to them again, not only our reputation will be ruined, but the court also may no longer revere us." "Exactly," said Pilgrim. "Come over here, my child. When we defeat them, I'll reward you handsomely." He changed his golden-hooped rod into a sharp razor, and hugging the lad, he said, "Darling, try to endure the pain for a moment. Don't make any noise! I'll shave your head." In a little while, the lad's hair was completely shorn, rolled into a ball, and stuffed into one of the corners of the chest. He put away the razor, and rubbing the lad's bald head, he said, "My child, your head looks like a monk's all right, but your clothes don't fit. Take them off and let me change them for you." What the Daoist lad had on was a crane's-down robe of spring-onion white silk, embroidered with the cloud pattern and trimmed with brocade. When he took it off, Pilgrim blew on it his immortal breath, crying, "Change!" It changed instantly into a monk shirt of brown color, which Pilgrim helped him put on. He then pulled off two pieces of hair which he changed into a wooden fish and a tap. "Disciple," said Pilgrim, as he handed over the fish and the tap to the lad, "you must listen carefully. If you hear someone call for the Daoist youth, don't ever leave this chest. If someone calls 'Monk,' then you may push open the chest door, strike up the wooden fish, and walk out chanting a Buddhist sūtra. Then it'll be complete success for us." "I only know," said the lad, "how to recite the *Three Officials Scripture*, the *Northern Dipper Scripture*, or the *Woe-Dispelling Scripture*. I don't know how to recite any Buddhist sūtra." Pilgrim said, "Can you chant the name of Buddha?" "You mean Amitābha,"[1] said the lad. "Who doesn't know that?" "Good enough! Good enough!" said Pilgrim. "You may chant the name of Buddha. It'll spare me from having to teach you anything new. Remember what I've told you. I'm leaving." He changed back into a mole-cricket and crawled out, after which, he flew back to the ear of the Tang monk and said, "Master, just guess it's a monk." Tripitaka said, "This time I know I'll win." "How could you be so sure?" said Pilgrim, and Tripitaka replied, "The sūtras said, 'The Buddha, the Dharma, and the Sangha are the Three Jewels.' A monk therefore is a treasure."

As they were thus talking among themselves, the Tiger-Strength Great Immortal said, "Your Majesty, this third time it is a Daoist youth." He made the declaration several times, but nothing happened nor did anyone make an appearance. Pressing his palms together, Tripitaka said, "It's a monk." With all his might, Bajie screamed: "It's a monk in the chest!" All at once the youth kicked open the chest and walked out, striking the wooden fish and chanting the name of Buddha. So delighted were the two rows of civil and military officials

---

1. "Buddha of Infinite Light," who presides over the Pure Land Paradise in the West, where believers who call his name can be reborn.

that they shouted bravos repeatedly; so astonished were the three Daoists that they could not utter a sound. "These priests must have the assistance from spirits and gods," said the king. "How could a Daoist enter the chest and come out a monk? Even if he had an attendant with him, he might have been able to have his head shaved. How could he know how to take up the chanting of Buddha's name? O Preceptors! Please let them go!"

"Your Majesty," said the Tiger-Strength Great Immortal, "as the proverb says, 'The warrior has found his equal, the chess player his match.' We might as well make use of what we learned in our youth at Zhongnan Mountain and challenge them to a greater competition." "What did you learn?" said the king. Tiger-Strength said, "We three brothers all have acquired some magic abilities: cut off our heads, and we can put them back on our necks; open our chests and gouge out our hearts, and they will grow back again: inside a cauldron of boiling oil, we can take baths." Highly startled the king said, "These three things are all roads leading to certain death!" "Only because we have such magic power," said Tiger-Strength, "do we dare make so bold a claim. We won't quit until we have waged this contest with them." The king said in a loud voice, "You priests from the Land of the East, our National Preceptors are unwilling to let you go. They wish to wage one more contest with you in head cutting, stomach ripping, and going into a cauldron of boiling oil to take a bath."

Pilgrim was still assuming the form of the mole-cricket, flying back and forth to make his secret report. When he heard this, he retrieved his hair, which had been changed into his substitute, and he himself changed at once back into his true form. "Lucky! Lucky!" he cried with loud guffaws. "Business has come to my door!" "These three things," said Bajie, "will certainly make you lose your life. How could you say that business has come to your door?" "You still have no idea of my abilities!" said Pilgrim. "Elder Brother," said Bajie, "you are quite clever, quite capable in those transformations. Aren't those skills something already? What more abilities do you have?" Pilgrim said,

> "Cut off my head and I still can speak.
> Sever my arms, I still can beat you up!
> My legs amputated, I still can walk.
> My belly, ripped open, will heal again,
> Smooth and snug as a wonton people make:
> A tiny pinch and it's completely formed.
> To bathe in boiling oil is easier still;
> It's like warm liquid cleansing me of dirt."

When Bajie and Sha Monk heard these words, they roared with laughter. Pilgrim went forward and said, "Your Majesty, this young priest knows how to have his head cut off." "How did you acquire such an ability?" asked the king. "When I was practicing austerities in a monastery some years ago," said Pilgrim, "I met a mendicant Chan[2] master, who taught me the magic of head cutting. I don't know whether it works or not, and that's why I want to try it out right now." "This priest is so young and ignorant!" said the king, chuckling. "Is head cutting something to try out? The head is, after all, the very fountain of the six kinds of *yang* energies[3] in one's body. If you cut it off. you'll die." "That's

---

2. Also known as Zen (Japanese). A Buddhist sect.

3. According to traditional medicine the body consists of a mixture of *yin* and *yang* energies.

what we want," said Tiger-Strength. "Only then can our feelings be relieved!" Besotted by the Daoist's words, the foolish ruler immediately gave the decree for an execution site to be prepared.

Once the command was given, three thousand imperial guards took up their positions outside the gate of the court. The king said, "Monk, go and cut off your head first." "I'll go first! I'll go first!" said Pilgrim merrily. He folded his hands before his chest and shouted, "National Preceptors, pardon my presumption for taking my turn first!" He turned swiftly and was about to dash out. The Tang monk grabbed him, saying, "O Disciple! Be careful! Where you are going isn't a playground!" "No fear!" said Pilgrim. "Take off your hands! Let me go!"

The Great Sage went straight to the execution site, where he was caught hold of by the executioner and bound with ropes. He was then led to a tall mound and pinned down on top of it. At the cry "Kill," his head came off with a swishing sound. Then the executioner gave the head a kick, and it rolled off like a watermelon to a distance of some forty paces away. No blood, however, spurted from the neck of Pilgrim. Instead, a voice came from inside his stomach, crying, "Come, head!" So alarmed was the Deer-Strength Great Immortal by the sight of such ability that he at once recited a spell and gave this charge to the local spirit and patron deity: "Hold down that head. When I have defeated the monk, I'll persuade the king to turn your little shrines into huge temples, your idols of clay into true bodies of gold." The local spirit and the god, you see, had to serve him since he knew the magic of the five thunders. Secretly, they indeed held Pilgrim's head down. Once more Pilgrim cried, "Come, head!" But the head stayed on the ground as if it had taken root; it would not move at all. Somewhat anxious, Pilgrim rolled his hands into fists and wrenched his body violently. The ropes all snapped and fell off; at the cry "Grow," a head sprang up instantly from his neck. Every one of the executioners and every member of the imperial guards became terrified, while the officer in charge of the execution dashed inside the court to make this report: "Your Majesty, that young priest had his head cut off, but another head has grown up." "Sha Monk," said Bajie, giggling, "we truly had no idea that Elder Brother has this kind of talent!" "If he knows seventy-two ways of transformation," said Sha Monk, "he may have altogether seventy-two heads!"

Hardly had he finished speaking when Pilgrim came walking back, saying, "Master." Exceedingly pleased, Tripitaka said, "Disciple, did it hurt?" "Hardly," said Pilgrim, "it's sort of fun!" "Elder Brother," said Bajie, "do you need ointment for the scar?" "Touch me," said Pilgrim, "and see if there's any scar." Idiot touched him and he was dumbfounded. "Marvelous! Marvelous!" he giggled. "It healed perfectly. You can't feel even the slightest scar!"

As the brothers were chatting happily among themselves, they heard the king say, "Receive your rescript. We give you a complete pardon. Go away!" Pilgrim said, "We'll take the rescript all right, but we want the National Preceptor to go there and cut his head off too! He should try something new!" "Great National Preceptor," said the king, "the priest is not willing to pass you up. If you want to compete with him, please try not to frighten us." Tiger-Strength had no choice but to go up to the site, where he was bound and pinned to the ground by several executioners. One of them lifted the sword and cut off his head, which was then kicked some thirty paces away. Blood did not spurt from his trunk either, and he, too, gave a cry, "Come, head!" Hurriedly pulling off a piece of hair, Pilgrim blew on it his immortal breath, crying, "Change!" It

458 | WU CHENG'EN

changed into a yellow hound, which dashed into the execution site, picked up the Daoist's head with its mouth, and ran to drop it into the imperial moat. The Daoist, meanwhile, called for his head three times without success. He did not, you see, have the ability of Pilgrim, and there was no possibility that he could produce another head. All at once, bright crimson gushed out from his trunk. Alas!

> *Though he could send for wind and call for rain,*
> *How could he match an immortal of the right fruit?*

In a moment, he fell to the dust, and those gathered about him discovered that he was actually a headless tiger with yellow fur.

* * *

We tell you now instead about those monks who succeeded in escaping with their lives. When they heard of the decree that was promulgated, every one of them was delighted and began to return to the city to search for the Great Sage Sun,[4] to thank him, and to return his hairs. Meanwhile, the elder, after the banquet was over, obtained the rescript from the king, who led the queen, the concubines, and two rows of civil and military officials out the gate of the court to see the priests off, As they came out, they found many monks kneeling on both sides of the road, saying "Father Great Sage, Equal to Heaven, we are the monks who escaped with our lives on the beach. When we heard that Father had wiped out the demons and rescued us, and when we further heard that our king had issued a decree commanding our return, we came here to present to you the hairs and to thank you for your Heavenly grace." "How many of you came back?" asked Pilgrim, chuckling, and they replied, "All five hundred. None's missing." Pilgrim shook his body once and immediately retrieved his hairs. Then he said to the king and the laypeople, "These monks indeed were released by old Monkey. The cart was smashed after old Monkey tossed it through the double passes and up the steep ridge, and it was Monkey also who beat to death those two perverse Daoists. After such pestilence has been exterminated this day, you should realize that the true way is the gate of Chan. Hereafter you should never believe in false doctrines. I hope you will honor the unity of the Three Religions: revere the monks, revere also the Daoists, and take care to nurture the talented. Your kingdom, I assure you, will be secure forever." The king gave his assent and his thanks repeatedly before he escorted the Tang monk out of the city. And so, this was the purpose of their journey:

> *A diligent search for the three canons;*
> *A strenuous quest for the primal light.*

We do not know what will happen to master and disciples; let's listen to the explanation in the next chapter.

* * *

4. Sun Wukong, the monkey.

From *Chapter 53*

The Chan¹ Master, taking food, is demonically conceived;
Yellow Hag brings water to dissolve the perverse pregnancy.

* * *

Walking to the side of the boat, Pilgrim said, "You are the one ferrying the boat?" "Yes," said the woman. "Why is the ferryman not here?" asked Pilgrim. "Why is the ferrywoman punting the boat?" The woman smiled and did not reply; she pulled out the gangplank instead and set it up. Sha Monk then poled the luggage into the boat, followed by the master holding onto Pilgrim. Then they moved the boat sideways so that Bajie could lead the horse to step into it. After the gangplank was put away, the woman punted the boat away from shore and, in a moment, rowed it across the river.

After they reached the western shore, the elder asked Sha Monk to untie one of the wraps and take out a few pennies for the woman. Without disputing the price, the woman tied the boat to a wooden pillar by the water and walked into one of the village huts nearby, giggling loudly all the time. When Tripitaka saw how clear the water was, he felt thirsty and told Bajie: "Get the almsbowl and fetch some water for me to drink." "I was just about to drink some myself," said Idiot, who took out the almsbowl and bailed out a full bowl of water to hand over to the master. The master drank less than half of the water, and when Idiot took the bowl back, he drank the rest of it in one gulp before he helped his master to mount the horse once more.

After master and disciples resumed their journey to the West, they had hardly traveled half an hour when the elder began to groan as he rode. "Stomachache!" he said, and Bajie behind him also said, "I have a stomachache, too." Sha Monk said, "It must be the cold water you drank." But before he even finished speaking, the elder cried out: "The pain's awful!" Bajie also screamed: "The pain's awful!" As the two of them struggled with this unbearable pain, their bellies began to swell in size steadily. Inside their abdomens, there seemed to be a clot of blood or a lump of flesh, which could be felt clearly by the hand, kicking and jumping wildly about. Tripitaka was in great discomfort when they came upon a small village by the road; two bundles of hay were tied to some branches on a tall tree nearby. "Master, that's good!" said Pilgrim. "The house over there must be an inn. Let me go over there to beg some hot liquid for you. I'll ask them also whether there is an apothecary around, so that I can get some ointment for your stomachache."

Delighted by what he heard, Tripitaka whipped his white horse and soon arrived at the village. As he dismounted, he saw an old woman sitting on a grass mound outside the village gate and knitting hemp. Pilgrim went forward and bowed to her with palms pressed together saying, "Popo,² this poor monk has come from the Great Tang in the Land of the East. My master is the royal brother of the Tang court. Because he drank some water from the river back there after we crossed it, he is having a stomachache." Breaking into loud guffaws, the woman said, "You people drank some water from the river?" "Yes," replied Pilgrim, "we drank some of the clean river water east of here." Giggling

1. Again, Zen (Japanese), a Buddhist sect.　　2. Granny.

loudly, the old woman said, "What a joke! What a joke! Come in, all of you. I'll explain to you."

Pilgrim went to take hold of Tang monk while Sha Monk held up Bajie; moaning with every step the two sick men walked into the thatched hut to take a seat, their stomachs protruding and their faces turning yellow from the pain. "Popo," Pilgrim kept saying, "please make some hot liquid for my master. We'll thank you." Instead of boiling water, however, the old woman dashed inside, laughing and yelling, "Come and look, all of you!"

With loud clip-clops, several middle-aged women ran out from within to stare at the Tang monk, grinning stupidly all the time. Enraged, Pilgrim gave a yell and ground his teeth together, so frightening the whole crowd of them that they turned to flee, stumbling all over. Pilgrim darted forward and caught hold of the old woman, crying, "Boil some water quick and I'll spare you!" "O Father!" said the old woman, shaking violently, "boiling water is useless, because it won't cure their stomachaches. Let me go, and I'll tell you." Pilgrim released her, and she said, "This is the Nation of Women of Western Liang.[3] There are only women in our country, and not even a single male can be found here. That's why we were amused when we saw you. That water your master drank is not the best, for the river is called Child-and-Mother River. Outside our capital we also have a Male Reception Post-house, by the side of which there is also a Pregnancy Reflection Stream. Only after reaching her twentieth year would someone from this region dare go and drink that river's water, for she would feel the pain of conception soon after she took a drink. After three days, she would go to the Male Reception Post-house and look at her reflection in the stream. If a double reflection appears, it means that she will give birth to a child. Since your master drank some water from the Child-and-Mother River, he too has become pregnant and will give birth to a child. How could hot water cure him?"

When Tripitaka heard this, he paled with fright. "O disciple," he cried, "what shall we do?" "O father!" groaned Bajie as he twisted to spread his legs further apart, "we are men, and we have to give birth to babies? Where can we find a birth canal? How could the fetus come out?" With a chuckle Pilgrim said, "According to the ancients, 'A ripe melon will fall by itself.' When the time comes, you may have a gaping hole at your armpit and the baby will crawl out."

When Bajie heard this, he shook with fright, and that made the pain all the more unbearable. "Finished! Finished!" he cried. "I'm dead! I'm dead!" "Second Elder Brother," said Sha Monk, laughing, "stop writhing! Stop writhing! You may hurt the umbilical cord and end up with some sort of prenatal sickness." Our Idiot became more alarmed than ever. Tears welling up in his eyes, he tugged at Pilgrim and said, "Elder Brother, please ask the Popo to see if they have some midwives here who are not too heavy-handed. Let's find a few right away. The movement inside is becoming more frequent now. It must be labor pain. It's coming! It's coming!" Again Sha Monk said chuckling, "Second Elder Brother, if it's labor pain, you'd better sit still. I fear you may puncture the water bag."

"O Popo," said Tripitaka with a moan, "do you have a physician here? I'll ask my disciple to go there and ask for a prescription. We'll take the drug and have

---

3. In the *Record of the Western Territories of the Great Tang*, a diary by the historical Xuanzang, he mentions a Western kingdom of women.

an abortion." "Even drugs are useless," said the old woman, "but due south of here there is a Male-Undoing Mountain. In it there is a Child Destruction Cave, and inside the cave there is an Abortion Stream. You must drink a mouthful of water from the stream before the pregnancy can be terminated. But nowadays, it's not easy to get that water. Last year, a Daoist by the name of True Immortal Compliant came on the scene and he changed the name of the Child Destruction Cave to the Shrine of Immortal Assembly. Claiming the water from the Abortion Stream as his possession, he refused to give it out freely. Anyone who wants the water must present monetary offerings together with meats, wines, and fruit baskets. After bowing to him in complete reverence, you will receive a tiny bowl of the water. But all of you are mendicants. Where could you find the kind of money you need to spend for something like this? You might as well suffer here and wait for the births." When Pilgrim heard this, he was filled with delight. "Popo," he said, "how far is it from here to the Male-Undoing Mountain?" "About three thousand miles," replied the old woman. "Excellent! Excellent!" said Pilgrim. "Relax, Master! Let old Monkey go and fetch some of that water for you to drink."

* * *

When Pilgrim saw him, he pressed his palms together before him and bowed, saying, "This poor monk is Sun Wukong." "Are you the real Sun Wukong," said the master with a laugh, "or are you merely assuming his name and surname?" "Look at the way the master speaks!" said Pilgrim. "As the proverb says, 'A gentleman changes neither his name when he stands, nor his surname when he sits.' What would be the reason for me to assume someone else's name?" The master asked, "Do you recognize me?" "Since I made repentance in the Buddhist gate and embraced with all sincerity the teaching of the monks," said Pilgrim, "I have only been climbing mountains and fording waters. I have lost contact with all the friends of my youth. Because I have never been able to visit you, I have never beheld your honorable countenance before. When we asked for our way in a village household west of the Child-and-Mother River, they told me that the master is called the True Immortal Compliant. That's how I know your name." The master said, "You are walking on your way, and I'm cultivating my realized immortality. Why did you come to visit me?" "Because my master drank by mistake the water of the Child-and-Mother River," replied Pilgrim, "and his stomachache turned into a pregnancy. I came especially to your immortal mansion to beg you for a bowl of water from the Abortion Stream, in order that my master might be freed from this ordeal."

"Is your master Tripitaka Tang?" asked the master, his eyes glowering. "Yes, indeed!" answered Pilgrim. Grinding his teeth together, the master said spitefully, "Have you run into a Great King Holy Child?" "That's the nickname of the fiend, Red Boy," said Pilgrim, "who lived in the Fiery Cloud Cave by the Dried Pine Stream, in the Roaring Mountain. Why does the True Immortal ask after him?" "He happens to be my nephew," replied the master, "and the Bull Demon King is my brother. Some time ago my elder brother told me in a letter that Sun Wukong, the eldest disciple of Tripitaka Tang, was such a rascal that he brought his son great harm. I didn't know where to find you for vengeance, but you came instead to seek me out. And you're asking me for water?" Trying to placate him with a smile, Pilgrim said, "You are wrong, Sir. Your elder brother used to be my friend, for both of us belonged to a league of seven bond brothers when we were young. I just didn't know about you, and so I did not come to pay my respect in your mansion. Your nephew is very well off, for he is now the attendant of the Bodhisattva Guanyin. He has become the Boy of Goodly Wealth, with whom even we cannot compare. Why do you blame me instead?"

"You brazen monkey!" shouted the master. "Still waxing your tongue! Is my nephew better off being a king by himself, or being a slave to someone? Stop this insolence and have a taste of my hook!" Using the iron rod to parry the blow, the Great Sage said, "Please don't use the language of war, Sir. Give me some water and I'll leave." "Brazen monkey!" scolded the master. "You don't know any better! If you can withstand me for three rounds, I'll give you the water. If not, I'll chop you up as meat sauce to avenge my nephew." "You damned fool!" scolded Pilgrim. "You don't know what's good for you! If you want to fight, get up here and watch my rod!" The master at once countered with his compliant hook, and the two of them had quite a fight before the Shrine of Immortal Assembly.

> The sage monk drinks from this procreant stream,
> And Pilgrim must th' Immortal Compliant seek.
> Who knows the True Immortal is a fiend,
> Who safeguards by force the Abortion Stream?
> When these two meet, they speak as enemies
> Feuding, and resolved not to give one whit.
> The words thus traded engender distress;
> Rancor and malice so bent on revenge.
> This one, whose master's life is threatened, comes seeking water;
> That one for losing his nephew refuses to yield.
> Fierce as a scorpion's the compliant hook;
> Wild like a dragon's the golden-hooped rod.
> Madly it stabs the chest, what savagery!
> Aslant, it hooks the legs, what subtlety!
> The rod aiming down there[4] inflicts grave wounds;
> The hook, passing shoulders, will whip the head.
> The rod slaps the waist—"a hawk holds a bird."
> The hook swipes the head—"a mantis hits its prey."
> They move here and there, both striving to win;
> They turn and close in again and again.
> The hook hooks, the rod strikes, without letup—
> On either side victory cannot be seen.

* * *

The two of them began their fighting outside the shrine, and as they struggled and danced together, they gradually moved to the mountain slope below. We shall leave this bitter contest for a moment.

We tell you instead about our Sha Monk, who crashed inside the door, holding the bucket. He was met by the Daoist, who barred the way at the well and said, "Who are you that you dare come to get our water?" Dropping the bucket, Sha Monk took out his fiend-routing treasure staff and, without a word, brought it down on the Daoist's head. The Daoist was unable to dodge fast enough, and

4. I.e., the genitals.

his left arm and shoulder were broken by this one blow. Falling to the ground, he lay there struggling for his life. "I wanted to slaughter you, cursed beast," scolded Sha Monk, "but you are, after all, a human being. I still have some pity for you, and I'll spare you. Let me bail out the water." Crying for Heaven and Earth to help him, the Daoist crawled slowly to the rear, while Sha Monk lowered the bucket into the well and filled it to the brim. He then walked out of the shrine and mounted the cloud and fog before he shouted to Pilgrim, "Big Brother, I have gotten the water and I'm leaving. Spare him! Spare him!" When the Great Sage heard this, he stopped the hook with his iron rod and said, "I was about to exterminate you, but you have not committed a crime. Moreover, I still have regard for the feelings of your brother, the Bull Demon King. When I first came here, I was hooked by you twice and didn't get my water. When I returned, I came with the trick of enticing the tiger to leave the mountain and deceived you into fighting me, so that my brother could go inside to get the water. If old Monkey is willing to use his real abilities to fight with you, don't say there is only one of you so-called True Immortal Compliants; even if there were several of you, I would beat you all to death. But to kill is not as good as to let live, and so I'm going to spare you and permit you to have a few more years. From now on if anyone wishes to obtain the water, you must not blackmail the person."

Not knowing anything better, that bogus immortal brandished his hook and once more attempted to catch Pilgrim's legs. The Great Sage evaded the blade of his hook and then rushed forward, crying, "Don't run!" The bogus immortal was caught unprepared and he was pushed head over heels to the ground, unable to get up. Grabbing the compliant hook the Great Sage snapped it in two; then he bundled the pieces together and, with another bend, broke them into four segments. Throwing them on the ground, he said, "Brazen, cursed beast! Still dare to be unruly?" Trembling all over, the bogus immortal took the insult and dared not utter a word. Our Great Sage, in peals of laughter, mounted the cloud to rise into the air, and we have a testimonial poem. The poem says:

> You need true water to smelt true lead;
> With dried mercury true water mixes well.
> True mercury and lead have no maternal breath;
> Elixir is divine drug and cinnabar.
> In vain the child conceived attains a form;
> Earth Mother has achieved merit with ease.
> Heresy pushed down, right faith's affirmed;
> The lord of the mind, all smiles, now goes back.

Mounting the auspicious luminosity, the Great Sage caught up with Sha Monk. Having acquired the true water, they were filled with delight as they returned to where they belonged. After they lowered the clouds and went up to the village hut, they found Zhu Bajie leaning on the door post and groaning, his belly huge and protruding. Walking quietly up to him, Pilgrim said, "Idiot, when did you enter the delivery room?" Horrified, Idiot said, "Elder Brother, don't make fun of me. Did you bring the water?" Pilgrim was about to tease him some more when Sha Monk followed him in, laughing as he said, "Water's coming! Water's coming!" Enduring the pain, Tripitaka rose slightly and said, "O disciples, I've caused you a lot of trouble." That old woman, too, was most delighted, and all of her relatives came out to kowtow, crying, "O bodhisattva! This is our luck! This is our luck!" She took a goblet of flowered porcelain, filled it half full, and handed it to Tripitaka, saying, "Old master, drink it slowly. All you need is a mouthful and the pregnancy will dissolve." "I don't need any goblet," said Bajie, "I'll just finish the bucket." "O Venerable Father, don't scare people to death!" said the old woman. "If you drink this bucket of water, your stomach and your intestines will all be dissolved."

Idiot was so taken aback that he dared not misbehave; he drank only half a goblet. In less than the time of a meal, the two of them experienced sharp pain and cramps in their bellies, and then their intestines growled four or five times. After that, Idiot could no longer contain himself: both waste and urine poured out of him. The Tang monk, too, felt the urge to relieve himself and wanted to go to a quiet place. "Master," said Pilgrim, "you mustn't go out to a place where there is a draft. If you are exposed to the wind, I fear that you may catch some postnatal illness." At once the old woman brought to them two night pots so that the two of them could find relief. After several bowel movements, the pain stopped and the swelling of their bellies gradually subsided as the lump of blood and flesh dissolved. The relatives of the old woman also boiled some white rice congee and presented it to them to strengthen their postnatal weakness.

"Popo," said Bajie, "I have a healthy constitution, and I have no need to strengthen any postnatal weakness. You go and boil me some water, so that I can take a bath before I eat the congee." "Second Elder Brother," said Sha Monk, "you can't take a bath. If water gets inside someone within a month after birth, the person will be sick." Bajie said, "But I have not given proper birth to anything; at most, I only have had a miscarriage. What's there to be afraid of? I must wash and clean up." Indeed, the old woman prepared some hot water for them to clean their hands and feet. The Tang monk then ate about two bowls of congee, but Bajie consumed over fifteen bowls and he still wanted more. "Coolie," chuckled Pilgrim, "don't eat so much. If you get a sandbag belly, you'll look quite awful." "Don't worry, don't worry," replied Bajie. "I'm no female hog. So, what's there to be afraid of?" The family members indeed went to prepare some more rice.

The old woman then said to the Tang monk, "Old master, please bestow this water on me." Pilgrim said, "Idiot, you are not drinking the water anymore?" "My stomachache is gone," said Bajie, "and the pregnancy, I suppose, must be dissolved. I'm quite fine now. Why should I drink any more water?" "Since the two of them have recovered," said Pilgrim, "we'll give this water to your family." After thanking Pilgrim, the old woman poured what was left of the water into a porcelain jar, which she buried in the rear garden. She said to the rest of the family, "This jar of water will take care of my funeral expenses." Everyone in that family, young and old, was delighted. A vegetarian meal was prepared and tables were set out to serve to the Tang monk. He and his disciples had a leisurely dinner and then rested.

*　*　*

From *Chapter 54*

Dharma-nature, going west, reaches the Women Nation;
Mind Monkey devises a plan to flee the fair sex.

We tell you now about Tripitaka and his disciples, who left the household at the village and followed the road westward. In less than forty miles, they came upon the boundary of Western Liang. Pointing ahead as he rode along, the Tang monk said, "Wukong, we are approaching a city, and from the noise and hubbub coming from the markets, I suppose it must be the Nation of Women. All of you must take care to behave properly. Keep your desires under control and don't let them violate the teachings of our gate of Law." When the three disciples heard this, they obeyed the strict admonition. Soon they reached the head of the street that opened to the eastern gate. The people there, with long skirts and short blouses, powdered faces and oily heads, were all women regardless of whether they were young or old. Many of them were doing business on the streets, and when they saw the four of them walking by, they all clapped their hands in acclaim and laughed aloud, crying happily, "Human seeds are coming! Human seeds are coming!" Tripitaka was so startled that he reined in his horse; all at once the street was blocked, completely filled with women, and all you could hear were laughter and chatter. Bajie began to holler wildly: "I'm a pig for sale! I'm a pig for sale!" "Idiot," said Pilgrim, "stop this nonsense. Bring out your old features, that's all!" Indeed, Bajie shook his head a couple of times and stuck up his two rush-leaf fan ears; then he wriggled his lips like two hanging lotus roots and gave a yell, so frightening those women that they all fell and stumbled. We have a testimonial poem, and the poem says:

> The sage monk, seeking Buddha, reached Western Liang,
> A land full of females but without one male.
> Farmers, scholars, workers, and those in trade,
> The fishers and plowers were women all.
> Maidens lined the streets, crying "Human seeds!"
> Young girls filled the roads to greet the comely men.
> If Wuneng did not show his ugly face,
> The siege by the fair sex would be pain indeed.

In this way, the people became frightened and none dared go forward; everyone was rubbing her hands and squatting down. They shook their heads, bit their fingers, and crowded both sides of the street, trembling all over but still eager to stare at the Tang monk. The Great Sage Sun had to display his hideous face in order to open up the road, while Sha Monk, too, played monster to keep order. Leading the horse, Bajie stuck out his snout and waved his ears. As the whole entourage proceeded, the pilgrims discovered that the houses in the city were built in orderly rows while the shops had lavish displays. There were merchants selling rice and salt; there were wine and tea houses.

> There were bell and drum towers with goods piled high;
> Bannered pavilions with screens hung low.

As master and disciples followed the street through its several turns, they came upon a woman official standing in the street and crying, "Visitors from afar should not enter the city gate without permission. Please go to the post-house and enter your names on the register. Allow this humble official to announce you to the Throne. After your rescript is certified, you will be permitted to pass through." Hearing this, Tripitaka dismounted; then he saw a horizontal plaque hung over the gate of an official mansion nearby, and on the plaque were the three words, Male Reception Post-house. "Wukong," said the elder; "what that family in the village said is true. There is indeed a Male Reception Post-house." "Second Elder Brother," said Sha Monk, laughing, "go and show yourself at the Pregnancy Reflection Stream and see if there's a double reflection." Bajie replied, "Don't play with me! Since I drank that cup of water from the Abortion Stream, the pregnancy has been dissolved. Why should I show myself?" Turning around, Tripitaka said to him, "Wuneng, be careful with your words." He then went forward to greet the woman official, who led them inside the post-house.

* * *

They had hardly finished speaking when the two women officials arrived and bowed deeply to the elder, who returned their salutations one by one, saying, "This humble cleric is someone who has left the family. What virtue or talent do I have that I dare let you bow to me?" When the Grand Preceptor saw how impressive the elder looked, she was delighted and thought to herself: "Our nation is truly quite lucky! Such a man is most worthy to be the husband of our ruler." After the officials made their greetings, they stood on either side of the Tang monk and said, "Father royal brother, we wish you ten thousand happinesses!" "I'm someone who has left the family," replied Tripitaka. "Where do those happinesses come from?" Again bending low, the Grand Preceptor said, "This is the Nation of Women in the Western Liang, and since time immemorial, there is not a single male in our country. We are lucky at this time to have the arrival of father royal brother. Your subject, by the decree of my ruler, has come especially to offer a proposal of marriage." "My goodness! My goodness!" said Tripitaka. "This poor monk has arrived at your esteemed region all by himself, without the attendance of either son or daughter. I have with me only three mischievous disciples, and I wonder to which of us is offered this marriage proposal." The post-house clerk said, "Your lowly official just now went into court to present my report, and my ruler, in great delight, told us of an auspicious dream she had last night. She dreamed that

> Luminous hues grew from the screens of gold,
> Refulgent rays spread from the mirrors of jade.

When she learned that the royal brother is a man from the noble nation of China, she was willing to use the wealth of her entire nation to ask you to be her live-in husband. You would take the royal seat facing south to be called the man set apart from others,[1] and our ruler would be the queen. That was why she gave the decree for the Grand Preceptor to serve as the marriage go-between and this lowly official to officiate at the wedding. We came especially to offer you this proposal." When Tripitaka heard these words, he bowed his head and fell into complete silence. "When a man finds the time propitious,"

---

1. The "man set apart from others" is an elevated expression for the emperor.

said the Grand Preceptor, "he should not pass up such an opportunity. Though there is, to be sure, such a thing in the world as asking a husband to live in the wife's family, the dowry of a nation's wealth is rare indeed. May we ask the royal brother to give his quick consent, so that we may report to our ruler." The elder, however, became more dumb and deaf than ever.

Sticking out his pestlelike snout, Bajie shouted, "Grand Preceptor, go back and tell your ruler that my master happens to be an arhat who has attained the Way after a long process of cultivation. He will never fall in love with the dowry of a nation's wealth, nor will he be enamored with even beauty that can topple an empire. You may as well certify the travel rescript quickly and send them off to the West. Let me stay here to be the live-in husband. How's that?" When the Grand Preceptor heard this, her heart quivered and her gall shook, unable to answer at all. The clerk of the post-house said, "Though you may be a male, your looks are hideous. Our ruler will not find you attractive." "You are much too inflexible," said Bajie, laughing. "As the proverb says,

> The thick willow's a basket, the thin, a barrel—
> Who in the world will take a man as an ugly fellow?"

Pilgrim said, "Idiot, stop this foolish talk. Let Master make up his mind: if he wants to leave, let him leave, and if he wants to stay, let him stay. Let's not waste the time of the marriage go-between."

"Wukong," said Tripitaka, "What do you think I ought to do?" "In old Monkey's opinion," replied Pilgrim, "perhaps it's good that you stay here. As the ancients said, 'One thread can tie up a distant marriage.' Where will you ever find such a marvelous opportunity?" Tripitaka said, "Disciple, if we remain here to dote on riches and glory, who will go to acquire scriptures in the Western Heaven? Won't the waiting kill my emperor of the Great Tang?" The Grand Preceptor said, "In the presence of the royal brother, your humble official dares not hide the truth. The wish of our ruler is only to offer you the proposal of marriage. After your disciples have attended the wedding banquet, provisions will be given them and the travel rescript will be certified, so that they may proceed to the Western Heaven to acquire the scriptures." "What the Grand Preceptor said is most reasonable," said Pilgrim, "and we need not be difficult about this. We are willing to let our master remain here to become the husband of your mistress. Certify our rescript quickly and send us off to the West. When we have acquired the scriptures, we will return here to visit father and mother and ask for travel expenses so that we may go back to the Great Tang." Both the Grand Preceptor and the clerk of the post-house bowed to Pilgrim as they said, "We thank this teacher for his kind assistance in concluding this marriage." Bajie said, "Grand Preceptor, don't use only your mouth to set the table! Since we have given our consent, tell your mistress to prepare us a banquet first. Let us have an engagement drink. How about it?" "Of course! Of course!" said the Grand Preceptor. "We'll send you a feast at once." In great delight, the Grand Preceptor left with the clerk of the post-house.

We tell you now about our elder Tang, who caught hold of Pilgrim immediately and berated him, crying, "Monkey head! Your tricks are killing me! How could you say such things and ask me to get married here while you people go to the Western Heaven to see Buddha? Even if I were to die, I would not dare do this." "Relax, Master," said Pilgrim, "old Monkey's not ignorant of how you feel.

But since we have reached this place and met this kind of people, we have no alternative but to meet plot with plot." "What do you mean by that?" asked Tripitaka.

Pilgrim said, "If you persist in refusing them, they will not certify our travel rescript nor will they permit us to pass through. If they grow vicious and order many people to cut you up and use your flesh to make those so-called fragrant bags, do you think that we will treat them with kindness? We will, of course, bring out our abilities which are meant to subdue demons and dispel fiends. Our hands and feet are quite heavy, you know, and our weapons ferocious. Once we lift our hands, the people of this entire nation will be wiped out. But you must think of this, however. Although they are now blocking our path, they are no fiendish creatures or monster-spirits; all of them in this country are humans. And you have always been a man committed to kindness and compassion, refusing to hurt even one sentient being on our way. If we slaughter all these common folk here, can you bear it? That would be true wickedness."

When Tripitaka heard this, he said, "Wukong, what you have just said is most virtuous. But I fear that if the queen asks me to enter the palace, she will want me to perform the conjugal rite with her. How could I consent to lose my original *yang* and destroy the virtue of Buddhism, to leak my true sperm and fall from the humanity of our faith?" "Once we have agreed to the marriage," said Pilgrim, "she will no doubt follow royal etiquette and send her carriage out of the capital to receive you. Don't refuse her. Take a ride in her phoenix carriage and dragon chariot to go up to the treasure hall, and then sit down on the throne facing south. Ask the queen to take out her imperial seal and summon us brothers to go into court. After you have stamped the seal on the rescript, tell the queen to sign the document also and give it back to us. Meanwhile, you can also tell them to prepare a huge banquet; call it a wedding feast as well as a farewell party for us. After the banquet, ask for the chariot once more on the excuse that you want to see us off outside the capital before you return to consummate the marriage with the queen. In this way, both ruler and subjects will be duped into false happiness; they will no longer try to block our way, nor will they have any cause to become vicious. Once we reach the outskirts of the capital, you will come down from the dragon chariot and Sha Monk will help you to mount the white horse immediately. Old Monkey will then use his magic of immobility to make all of them, ruler and subjects, unable to move. We can then follow the main road to the West. After one day and one night, I will recite a spell to recall the magic and release all of them, so that they can wake up and return to the city. For one thing, their lives will be preserved, and for another, your primal soul will not be hurt. This is a plot called Fleeing the Net by a False Marriage. Isn't it a doubly advantageous act?" When Tripitaka heard these words, he seemed as if he were snapping out of a stupor or waking up from a dream. So delighted was he that he forgot all his worries and thanked Pilgrim profusely, saying, "I'm deeply grateful for my worthy disciple's lofty intelligence." And so, the four of them were united in their decision, and we shall leave them for the moment.

*   *   *

After putting everything in order, Pilgrim, Bajie, and Sha Monk faced the imperial carriage and cried out in unison, "The queen need not go any further. We shall take our leave now." Descending slowly from the dragon chariot, the elder raised his hands toward the queen and said, "Please go back, Your Majesty, and let this poor monk go to acquire scriptures." When the queen heard this, she paled with fright and tugged at the Tang monk. "Royal brother darling," she cried, "I'm willing to use the wealth of my entire nation to ask you to be my husband. Tomorrow you shall ascend the tall treasure throne to call yourself king, and I am to be your queen. You have even eaten the wedding feast. Why are you changing your mind now?" When Bajie heard what she said, he became slightly mad. Pouting his snout and flapping his ears wildly, he charged up to the carriage, shouting, "How could we monks marry a powdered skeleton like you? Let my master go on his journey!" When the queen saw that hideous face and ugly behavior, she was scared out of her wits and fell back into the carriage. Sha Monk pulled Tripitaka out of the crowd and was just helping him to mount the horse when another girl dashed out from somewhere and shouted, "Royal brother Tang, where are you going? Let's you and I make some love!" "You stupid hussy!" cried Sha Monk and, whipping out his treasure staff, brought it down hard on the head of the girl. Suddenly calling up a cyclone, the girl carried away the Tang monk with a loud whoosh and both of them vanished without a trace. Alas! Thus it was that

> Having just left the fair sex net,
> Then the demon of love he met.

We do not know whether that girl is a human or a fiend, or whether the old master will die or live; let's listen to the explanation in the next chapter.

From Chapter 55

Deviant form makes lustful play for Tripitaka Tang;
Upright nature safeguards the uncorrupted self.

* * *

We now tell you about Sha Monk, who was grazing the horse before the mountain slope when he heard some hog-grunting. As he raised his head, he saw Bajie dashing back, lips pouted and grunting as he ran. "What in the world . . . ?" said Sha Monk, and our Idiot blurted out: "It's awful! It's awful! This pain! This pain!" Hardly had he finished speaking when Pilgrim also arrived. "Dear Idiot!" he chuckled. "Yesterday you said I had a brain tumor, but now you are suffering from the plague of the swollen lip!" "I can't bear it!" cried Bajie. "The pain's acute! It's terrible! It's terrible!"

The three of them were thus in sad straits when they saw an old woman approaching from the south on the mountain road, her left hand carrying a little bamboo basket with vegetables in it. "Big Brother," said Sha Monk, "look at that old lady approaching. Let me find out from her what sort of a monster-spirit this is and what kind of weapon she has that can inflict a wound like this." "You stay where you are," said Pilgrim, "and let old Monkey question her." When Pilgrim stared at the old woman carefully, he saw that there were auspicious clouds covering her head and fragrant mists encircling her body. Recognizing all at once who she was, Pilgrim shouted. "Brothers, kowtow quickly! The lady is Bodhisattva!" Ignoring his pain, Bajie hurriedly went to his knees while Sha Monk bent low, still holding the reins of the horse. The Great Sage Sun, too, pressed his palms together and knelt down, all crying. "We submit to the great and compassionate, the efficacious savior, Bodhisattva Guanshiyin."

When the Bodhisattva saw that they recognized her primal light, she at once trod on the auspicious clouds and rose to midair to reveal her true form, the one which carried the fish basket. Pilgrim rushed up there also to say to her, bowing. "Bodhisattva, pardon us for not receiving you properly. We were desperately trying to rescue our master and we had no idea that the Bodhisattva was descending to earth. Our present demonic ordeal is hard to overcome indeed, and we beg the Bodhisattva to help us." "This monster-spirit," said the Bodhisattva. "is most formidable. Those tridents of hers happen to be two front claws, and what gave you such a painful stab is actually a stinger on her tail. It's called the Horse-Felling Poison, for she herself is a scorpion spirit. Once upon a time she happened to be listening to a lecture in the Thunderclap Monastery. When Tathāgata[1] saw her, he wanted to push her away with his hand, but she turned around and gave the left thumb of the Buddha a stab. Even Tathāgata found the pain unbearable! When he ordered the arhats to seize her, she fled here. If you want to rescue the Tang monk, you must find a special friend of mine for even I cannot go near her." Bowing again, Pilgrim said, "I beg the Bodhisattva to reveal to whom it is that your disciple should go to ask for assistance." "Go to the East Heaven Gate," replied the Bodhisattva, "and ask for help from the Star Lord Orionis in the Luminescent Palace. He is the one to subdue this monster-spirit." When she finished speaking, she changed into a beam of golden light to return to South Sea.

Dropping down from the clouds, the Great Sage Sun said to Bajie and Sha Monk, "Relax, Brothers, we've found someone to rescue Master." "From where?" asked Sha Monk, and Pilgrim replied, "Just now the Bodhisattva told me to seek the assistance of the Star Lord Orionis. Old Monkey will go immediately." With swollen lips, Bajie grunted: "Elder Brother, please ask the god for some medicine for the pain." "No need for medicine," said Pilgrim with a laugh. "After one night, the pain will go away like mine." "Stop talking," said Sha Monk. "Go quickly!"

Dear Pilgrim! Mounting his cloud-somersault, he arrived instantly at the East Heaven Gate, where he was met by the Devarāja Virūḍhaka. "Great Sage," said the devarāja, bowing, "where are you going?" "On our way to acquire scriptures in the West," replied Pilgrim, "the Tang monk ran into another demonic obstacle. I must go to the Luminescent Palace to find the Star God of the Rising Sun." As he spoke, Tao, Zhang, Xin, and Deng, the four Grand Marshals, also approached him to ask where he was going. "I have to find the Star Lord Orionis," said Pilgrim, "and ask him to rescue my master from a monster-spirit." One of the grand marshals said, "By the decree of the Jade Emperor this morning, the god went to patrol the Star-Gazing Terrace." "Is that true?" asked Pilgrim. "All of us humble warriors," replied Grand Marshal Xin, "left the Dipper Palace with him at the same time. Would we dare speak falsehood?" "It has been a long time," said Grand Marshal Tao, "and he might be back already. The Great Sage should go to the Luminescent Palace first, and if he's not there, then you can go to the Star-Gazing Terrace."

Delighted, the Great Sage took leave of them and arrived at the gate of the Luminescent Palace. Indeed, there was no one in sight, and as he turned to

1. Again, the Buddha.

leave, he saw a troop of soldiers approaching, followed by the god, who still had on his court regalia made of golden threads. Look at

> *His cap of five folds ablaze with gold;*
> *His court tablet of most lustrous jade.*
> *A seven-star sword, cloud patterned, hung from his robe;*
> *An eight-treasure belt, lucent, wrapped around his waist.*
> *His pendant jangled as if striking a tune;*
> *It rang like a bell in a strong gust of wind.*
> *Kingfisher fans parted and Orionis came*
> *As celestial fragrance the courtyard filled.*

Those soldiers walking in front saw Pilgrim standing outside the Luminescent Palace, and they turned quickly to report: "My lord, the Great Sage Sun is here." Stopping his cloud and straightening his court attire, the god ordered the soldiers to stand on both sides in two rows while he went forward to salute his visitor, saying, "Why has the Great Sage come here?"

"I have come here," replied Pilgrim, "especially to ask you to save my master from an ordeal." "Which ordeal," asked the god, "and where?" "In the Cave of the Lute at the Toxic Foe Mountain," Pilgrim answered "which is located in the State of Western Liang." "What sort of monster is there in the cave," asked the god again, "that has made it necessary for you to call on this humble deity?"

Pilgrim said, "Just now the Bodhisattva Guanyin, in her epiphany, revealed to us that it was a scorpion spirit. She told us further that only you, sir, could overcome it. That is why I have come to call on you." "I should first go back and report to the Jade Emperor," said the god, "but the Great Sage is already here, and you have, moreover, the Bodhisattva's recommendation. Since I don't want to cause you delay, I dare not ask you for tea. I shall go with you to subdue the monster-spirit first before I report to the Throne."

When the Great Sage heard this, he at once went out of the East Heaven Gate with the god and sped to the State of Western Liang. Seeing the mountain ahead, Pilgrim pointed at it and said, "This is it." The god lowered his cloud and walked with Pilgrim up to the stone screen beneath the mountain slope. When Sha Monk saw them, he said, "Second Elder Brother, please rise. Big Brother has brought back the star god." His lips still pouting, Idiot said, "Pardon! Pardon! I'm ill, and I cannot salute you." "You are a man who practices self-cultivation," said the star god. "What kind of sickness do you have?" "Earlier in the morning," replied Bajie, "we fought with the monster-spirit, who gave me a stab on my lip. It still hurts."

The star god said, "Come up here, and I'll cure it for you." Taking his hand away from his snout, Idiot said, "I beg you to cure it, and I'll thank you most heartily." The star god used his hand to give Bajie's lip a stroke before blowing a mouthful of breath on it. At once, the pain ceased. In great delight, our Idiot went to his knees, crying, "Marvelous! Marvelous!" "May I trouble the star god to touch the top of my head also?" said Pilgrim with a grin. "You weren't poisoned," said the star god. "Why should I touch you?" Pilgrim replied, "Yesterday, I was poisoned, but after one night the pain is gone. The spot, however, still feels somewhat numb and itchy, and I fear that it may act up when the weather changes. Please cure it for me." The star god indeed touched the top of his head and blew a mouthful of breath on it. The remaining poison was thus eliminated, and Pilgrim no longer felt the numbness or the itch. "Elder Brother," said Bajie, growing ferocious, "let's go and beat up that bitch!" "Exactly!" said the star god. "You provoke her to come out, the two of you, and I'll subdue her."

Leaping up the mountain slope, Pilgrim and Bajie again went behind the stone screen. With his mouth spewing abuses and his hands working like a pair of fuel-gatherer hooks, our Idiot used his rake to remove the rocks piled up in front of the cave in no time at all. He then dashed up to the second-level door, and one blow of his rake reduced it to powder. The little fiends inside were so terrified that they fled inside to report: "Madam, those two ugly men have destroyed even our second-level door!" The fiend was just about to untie the Tang monk so that he could be fed some tea and rice. When she heard that the door had been broken down, she jumped out of the flower arbor and stabbed Bajie with the trident. Bajie met her with the rake, while Pilgrim assisted him with his iron rod. Rushing at her opponents, the fiend wanted to use her poisonous trick again, but Pilgrim and Bajie perceived her intentions and retreated immediately.

The fiend chased them beyond the stone screen, and Pilgrim shouted: "Orionis, where are you?" Standing erect on the mountain slope, the star god revealed his true form. He was, you see, actually a huge, double-combed rooster, about seven feet tall when he held up his head. He faced the fiend and crowed once: immediately the fiend revealed her true form, which was that of a scorpion about the size of a lute. The star god crowed again, and the fiend, whose whole body became paralyzed, died before the slope. We have a testimonial poem for you, and the poem says:

> Like tasseled balls his embroidered neck and comb,
> With long, hard claws and angry, bulging eyes,
> He perfects the Five Virtues forcefully;
> His three crows are done heroically.
> No common, clucking fowl about the hut,
> He's Heaven's star showing his holy name.
> In vain the scorpion seeks the human ways;
> She now her true, original form displays.

Bajie went forward and placed one foot on the back of the creature, saying, "Cursed beast! You can't use your Horse-Felling Poison this time!" Unable to make even a twitch, the fiend was pounded into a paste by the rake of the Idiot. Gathering up again his golden beams, the star god mounted the clouds and left, while Pilgrim led Bajie and Sha Monk to bow to the sky, saying, "Sorry for all your inconvenience! In another day, we shall go to your palace to thank you in person."

* * *

From *Chapter 98*

> *Only when ape and horse are tamed will shells be cast;*
> *With merit and work perfected, they see the Real.*

We shall now tell you about the Tang monk and his three disciples, who set out on the main road.

In truth the land of Buddha in the West[1] was quite different from other regions. What they saw everywhere were gemlike flowers and jasperlike grasses, aged cypresses and hoary pines. In the regions they passed through, every family was devoted to good works, and every household would feed the monks.

> They met people in cultivation beneath the hills
> And saw travellers reciting sūtras in the woods.

Resting at night and journeying at dawn, master and disciples proceeded for some six or seven days when they suddenly caught sight of a row of tall buildings and noble lofts. Truly

> They soar skyward a hundred feet,
> Tall and towering in the air.
> You look down to see the setting sun
> And reach out to pluck the shooting stars.
> Spacious windows engulf the universe;
> Lofty pillars join with the cloudy screens.
> Yellow cranes bring letters[2] as autumn trees age;
> Phoenix-sheets come with the cool evening breeze.
> These are the treasure arches of a spirit palace,
> The pearly courts and jeweled edifices,
> The immortal hall where the Way is preached,
> The cosmos where sūtras are taught.
> The flowers bloom in the spring;
> Pines grow green after the rain.
> Purple agaric and divine fruits, fresh every year.
> Phoenixes gambol, potent in every manner.

Lifting his whip to point ahead, Tripitaka said, "Wukong, what a lovely place!"

"Master," said Pilgrim, "you insisted on bowing down even in a specious region, before false images of Buddha. Today you have arrived at a true region with real images of Buddha, and you still haven't dismounted. What's your excuse?"

So taken aback was Tripitaka when he heard these words that he leaped down from the horse. Soon they arrived at the entrance to the buildings. A Daoist lad, standing before the gate, called out, "Are you the scripture seeker from the Land of the East?" Hurriedly tidying his clothes, the elder raised his head and looked at his interrogator.

> He wore a robe of silk
> And held a jade duster.
> He wore a robe of silk
> Often to feast at treasure lofts and jasper pools;
> He held a jade yak's-tail

---

1. The pilgrims have now reached India, the destination of their trip.
2. Immortals are thought to send their communications through magic birds like yellow cranes and blue phoenixes.

> *To wave and dust in the purple mansions.*
> *From his arm hangs a sacred register,*
> *And his feet are shod in sandals.*
> *He floats—a true feathered-one;*[3]
> *He's winsome—indeed uncanny!*
> *Long life attained, he lives in this fine place;*
> *Immortal, he can leave the world of dust.*
> *The sage monk knows not our Mount Spirit guest:*
> *The Immortal Golden Head of former years.*

The Great Sage, however, recognized the person. "Master," he cried, "this is the Great Immortal of the Golden Head, who resides in the Yuzhen Daoist Temple at the foot of the Spirit Mountain."

Only then did Tripitaka realize the truth, and he walked forward to make his bow. With laughter, the great immortal said, "So the sage monk has finally arrived this year. I have been deceived by the Bodhisattva Guanyin. When she received the gold decree from Buddha over ten years ago to find a scripture seeker in the Land of the East, she told me that he would be here after two or three years. I waited year after year for you, but no news came at all. Hardly have I anticipated that I would meet you this year!"

Pressing his palms together, Tripitaka said, "I'm greatly indebted to the great immortal's kindness. Thank you! Thank you!" The four pilgrims, leading the horse and toting the luggage, all went inside the temple before each of them greeted the great immortal once more. Tea and a vegetarian meal were ordered. The immortal also asked the lads to heat some scented liquid for the sage monk to bathe, so that he could ascend the land of Buddha. Truly,

> *It's good to bathe when merit and work are done,*
> *When nature's tamed and the natural state is won.*
> *All toils and labors are now at rest;*
> *Law and obedience have renewed their zest.*
> *At māra's end they reach indeed Buddha-land;*
> *Their woes dispelled, before Śramana*[4] *they stand.*
> *Unstained, they are washed of all filth and dust.*
> *To a diamond body*[5] *return they must.*

After master and disciples had bathed, it became late and they rested in the Yuzhen Temple.

Next morning the Tang monk changed his clothing and put on his brocade cassock and his Vairocana hat. Holding the priestly staff, he ascended the main hall to take leave of the great immortal. "Yesterday you seemed rather dowdy," said the great immortal, chuckling, "but today everything is fresh and bright. As I look at you now, you are a true of son of Buddha!" After a bow, Tripitaka wanted to set out at once.

"Wait a moment," said the great immortal. "Allow me to escort you." "There's no need for that," said Pilgrim. "Old Monkey knows the way."

---

3. Immortal or transcendent being.
4. Wandering ascetic.

5. The incorruptible body of Buddhahood.

"What you know happens to be the way in the clouds," said the great immortal, "a means of travel to which the sage monk has not yet been elevated. You must still stick to the main road."

"What you say is quite right," replied Pilgrim. "Though old Monkey has been to this place several times, he has always come and gone on the clouds and he has never stepped on the ground. If we must stick to the main road, we must trouble you to escort us a distance. My master's most eager to bow to Buddha. Let's not dally." Smiling broadly, the great immortal held the Tang monk's hand

To lead Candana up the gate of Law.

The way that they had to go, you see, did not lead back to the front gate. Instead, they had to go through the central hall of the temple to go out the rear door. Immediately behind the temple, in fact, was the Spirit Mountain, to which the great immortal pointed and said, "Sage Monk, look at the spot half-way up the sky, shrouded by auspicious luminosity of five colors and a thousand folds of hallowed mists. That's the tall Spirit Vulture Peak, the holy region of the Buddhist Patriarch."

The moment the Tang monk saw it, he began to bend low. With a chuckle, Pilgrim said, "Master, you haven't reached that place where you should bow down. As the proverb says, 'Even within sight of a mountain you can ride a horse to death!' You are still quite far from that principality. Why do you want to bow down now? How many times does your head need to touch the ground if you kowtow all the way to the summit?"

"Sage Monk," said the great immortal, "you, along with the Great Sage, Heavenly Reeds, and Curtain-Raising, have arrived at the blessed land when you can see Mount Spirit. I'm going back." Thereupon Tripitaka bowed to take leave of him.

*   *   *

Highly pleased, the elder said, "Disciples, stop your frivolity! There's a boat coming." The three of them leaped up and stood still to stare at the boat. When it drew near, they found that it was a bottomless one. With his fiery eyes and diamond pupils, Pilgrim at once recognized that the ferryman was in fact the Conductor Buddha, also named the Light of Ratnadhvaja. Without revealing the Buddha's identity, however, Pilgrim simply said, "Over here! Punt it this way!"

Immediately the boatman punted it up to the shore. "Ahoy! Ahoy!" he cried. Terrified by what he saw, Tripitaka said, "How could this bottomless boat of yours carry anybody?" The Buddhist Patriarch said, "This boat of mine

Since creation's dawn has achieved great fame;
Punted by me, it has e'er been the same.
Upon the wind and wave it's still secure:
With no end or beginning its joy is sure.
It can return to One, completely clean,
Through ten thousand kalpas a sail serene.
Though bottomless boats may ne'er cross the sea,
This ferries all souls through eternity."

Pressing his palms together to thank him, the Great Sage Sun said, "I thank you for your great kindness in coming to receive and lead my master. Master, get on the boat. Though it is bottomless, it is safe. Even if there are wind and waves, it will not capsize."

The elder still hesistated, but Pilgrim took him by the shoulder and gave him a shove. With nothing to stand on, that master tumbled straight into the water, but the boatman swiftly pulled him out. As he stood on the side of the boat, the master kept shaking out his clothes and stamping his feet as he grumbled at Pilgrim. Pilgrim, however, helped Sha Monk and Bajie to lead the horse and tote the luggage into the boat. As they all stood on the gunwale, the Buddhist Patriarch gently punted the vessel away from shore. All at once they saw a corpse floating down the upstream, the sight of which filled the elder with terror.

"Don't be afraid, Master," said Pilgrim, laughing. "It's actually you!"

"It's you! It's you!" said Bajie also.

Clapping his hands, Sha Monk also said, "It's you! It's you!"

Adding his voice to the chorus, the boatman also said, "That's you! Congratulations! Congratulations!" Then the three disciples repeated this chanting in unison as the boat was punted across the water. In no time at all, they crossed the Divine Cloud-Transcending Stream all safe and sound. Only then did Tripitaka turn and skip lightly onto the other shore. We have here a testimonial poem, which says:

> Delivered from their mortal flesh and bone,
> A primal spirit of mutual love has grown.
> Their work done, they become Buddhas this day,
> Free of their former six-six senses[6] sway.

Truly this is what is meant by the profound wisdom and the boundless dharma which enable a person to reach the other shore.

The moment the four pilgrims went ashore and turned around, the boatman and even the bottomless boat had disappeared. Only then did Pilgrim point out that it was the Conductor Buddha, and immediately Tripitaka awoke to the truth. Turning quickly, he thanked his three disciples instead.

* * *

Highly pleased, Holy Father Buddha at once asked the Eight Bodhisattvas, the Four Vajra Guardians, the Five Hundred Arhats, the Three Thousand Guardians, the Eleven Great Orbs, and the Eighteen Guardians of Monasteries to form two rows for the reception. Then he issued the golden decree to summon in the Tang monk. Again the word was passed from section to section, from gate to gate: "Let the sage monk enter." Meticulously observing the rules of ritual propriety, our Tang monk walked through the monastery gate with Wukong, Wuneng, and Wujing, still leading the horse and toting the luggage. Thus it was that

> Commissioned that year, a resolve he made
> To leave with rescript the royal steps of jade.

6. Intensive form of the six impure qualities engendered by the objects and organs of sense: sight, sound, smell, taste, touch, and idea.

The hills he'd climb to face the morning dew
Or rest on a boulder when the twilight fades.
He totes his faith to ford three thousand streams,
His staff trailing o'er endless palisades.
His every thought's on seeking the right fruit.
Homage to Buddha will this day be paid.

The four pilgrims, on reaching the Great Hero Treasure Hall, prostrated themselves before Tathāgata. Thereafter, they bowed to all the attendants of Buddha on the left and right. This they repeated three times before kneeling again before the Buddhist Patriarch to present their traveling rescript to him. After reading it carefully, Tathāgata handed it back to Tripitaka, who touched his head to the ground once more to say, "By the decree of the Great Tang Emperor in the Land of the East, your disciple Xuanzang has come to this treasure monastery to beg you for the true scriptures for the redemption of the multitude. I implore the Buddhist Patriarch to vouchsafe his grace and grant me my wish, so that I may soon return to my country."

To express the compassion of his heart, Tathāgata opened his mouth of mercy and said to Tripitaka, "Your Land of the East belongs to the South Jambūdvīpa Continent. Because of your size and your fertile land, your prosperity and population, there is a great deal of greed and killing, lust and lying, oppression and deceit. People neither honor the teachings of Buddha nor cultivate virtuous karma; they neither revere the three lights nor respect the five grains. They are disloyal and unfilial, unrighteous and unkind, unscrupulous and self-deceiving. Through all manners of injustice and taking of lives, they have committed boundless transgressions. The fullness of their iniquities therefore has brought on them the ordeal of hell and sent them into eternal darkness and perdition to suffer the pains of pounding and grinding and of being transformed into beasts. Many of them will assume the forms of creatures with fur and horns; in this manner they will repay their debts by having their flesh made for food for mankind. These are the reasons for their eternal perdition in Avīci without deliverance.

"Though Confucius had promoted his teachings of benevolence, righteousness, ritual, and wisdom, and though a succession of kings and emperors had established such penalties as transportation, banishment, hanging, and beheading, these institutions had little effect on the foolish and the blind, the reckless and the antinomian.

"Now, I have here three baskets of scriptures which can deliver humanity from its afflictions and dispel its calamities. There is one basket of vinaya, which speak of Heaven; a basket of śāstras, which tell of the Earth; and a basket of sūtras, which redeem the damned. Altogether these three baskets of scriptures contain thirty-five titles written in fifteen thousand one hundred and forty-four scrolls. They are truly the pathway to the realization of immortality and the gate to ultimate virtue. Every concern of astronomy, geography, biography, flora and fauna, utensils, and human affairs within the Four Great Continents of this world is recorded therein. Since all of you have traveled such a great distance to come here, I would have liked to give the entire set to you. Unfortunately, the people of your region are both stupid and headstrong. Mocking the true words, they refuse to recognize the profound significance of our teachings of Śramana."

Then Buddha turned to call out: "Ānanda[7] and Kāśyapa, take the four of them to the space beneath the precious tower. Give them a vegetarian meal first. After the maigre, open our treasure loft for them and select a few scrolls from each of the thirty-five divisions of our three canons, so that they may take them back to the Land of the East as a perpetual token of grace."

The two Honored Ones obeyed and took the four pilgrims to the space beneath the tower, where countless rare dainties and exotic treasures were laid out in a seemingly endless spread. Those deities in charge of offerings and sacrifices began to serve a magnificent feast of divine food, tea, and fruit—viands of a hundred flavors completely different from those of the mortal world. After master and disciples had bowed to give thanks to Buddha, they abandoned themselves to enjoyment. In truth

> Treasure flames, gold beams on their eyes have shined;
> Strange fragrance and feed even more refined.
> Boundlessly fair the tow'r of gold appears;
> There's immortal music that clears the ears.
> Such divine fare and flower humans rarely see;
> Long life's attained through strange food and fragrant tea.
> Long have they endured a thousand forms of pain.
> This day in glory the Way they're glad to gain.

This time it was Bajie who was in luck and Sha Monk who had the advantage, for what the Buddhist Patriarch had provided for their complete enjoyment was nothing less than such viands as could grant them longevity and health and enable them to transform their mortal substance into immortal flesh and bones.

When the four pilgrims had finished their meal, the two Honored Ones who had kept them company led them up to the treasure loft. The moment the door was opened, they found the room enveloped in a thousand layers of auspicious air and magic beams, in ten thousand folds of colored fog and hallowed clouds. On the sūtra cases and jeweled chests red labels were attached, on which the titles of the books were written in clerkly script. After Ānanda and Kāśyapa had shown all the titles to the Tang monk, they said to him, "Sage Monk, having come all this distance from the Land of the East, what sort of small gifts have you brought for us? Take them out quickly! We'll be pleased to hand over the scriptures to you."

On hearing this, Tripitaka said, "Because of the great distance, your disciple, Xuanzang, has not been able to make such preparation."

"How nice! How nice!" said the two Honored Ones, snickering. "If we imparted the scriptures to you gratis, our posterity would starve to death!"

When Pilgrim saw them fidgeting and fussing, refusing to hand over the scriptures, he could not refrain from yelling, "Master, let's go tell Tathāgata about this! Let's make him come himself and hand over the scriptures to old Monkey!"

"Stop shouting!" said Ānanda. "Where do you think you are that you dare indulge in such mischief and waggery? Get over here and receive the scriptures!" Controlling their annoyance, Bajie and Sha Monk managed to restrain

7. Devout disciple of the Buddha.

Pilgrim before they turned to receive the books. Scroll after scroll were wrapped and laid on the horse. Four additional luggage wraps were bundled up for Bajie and Sha Monk to tote, after which the pilgrims went before the jeweled throne again to kowtow and thank Tathāgata. As they walked out the gates of the monastery, they bowed twice whenever they came upon a Buddhist Patriarch or a Bodhisattva. When they reached the main gate, they also bowed to take leave of the priests and nuns, the upāsakas and upāsikās, before descending the mountain. We shall now leave them for the moment.

We tell you now that there was up in the treasure loft the aged Dīpamkara, also named the Buddha of the Past, who overheard everything and understood immediately that Ānanda and Kāśyapa had handed over to the pilgrims scrolls of scriptures that were actually wordless. Chuckling to himself, he said, "Most of the priests in the Land of the East are so stupid and blind that they will not recognize the value of these wordless scriptures. When that happens, won't it have made this long trek of our sage monk completely worthless?"

* * *

In a little while they reached the temple gates, where they were met by the multitude with hands folded in their sleeves. "Has the sage monk returned to ask for an exchange of scriptures?" they asked, laughing. Tripitaka nodded his affirmation, and the Vajra Guardians permitted them to go straight inside. When they arrived before the Great Hero Hall, Pilgrim shouted, "Tathāgata, we master and disciples had to experience ten thousand stings and a thousand demons in order to come bowing from the Land of the East. After you had specifically ordered the scriptures to be given to us, Ānanda and Kāśyapa sought a bribe from us; when they didn't succeed, they conspired in fraud and deliberately handed over wordless texts to us. Even if we took them, what good would they do? Pardon me, Tathāgata, but you must deal with this matter!"

"Stop shouting!" said the Buddhist Patriarch with a chuckle. "I knew already that the two of them would ask you for a little present. After all, the holy scriptures are not to be given lightly, nor are they to be received gratis. Some time ago, in fact, a few of our sage priests went down the mountain and recited these scriptures in the house of one Elder Zhao in the Kingdom of Śrāvastī, so that the living in his family would all be protected from harm and the deceased redeemed from perdition. For all that service they managed to charge him only three pecks and three pints of rice. I told them that they had made far too cheap a sale and that their posterity would have no money to spend. Since you people came with empty hands to acquire scriptures, blank texts were handed over to you. But these blank texts are actually true, wordless scriptures, and they are just as good as those with words. However, those creatures in your Land of the East are so foolish and unenlightened that I have no choice but to impart to you now the texts with words."

"Ānanda and Kāśyapa," he then called out, "quickly select for them a few scrolls from each of the titles of true scriptures with words, and then come back to me to report the total number."

The two Honored Ones again led the four pilgrims to the treasure loft, where they once more demanded a gift from the Tang monk. Since he had virtually nothing to offer, Tripitaka told Sha Monk to take out the alms bowl of purple gold. With both hands he presented it to the Honored Ones, saying, "Your disciple in truth has not brought with him any gift, owing to the great distance and my own poverty. This alms bowl, however, was bestowed by the Tang emperor in person, in order that I could use it to beg for my maigre, throughout the journey. As the humblest token of my gratitude, I am presenting it to you now, and I beg the Honored Ones to accept it. When I return to the court and make my report to the Tang emperor, a generous reward will certainly be forthcoming. Only grant us the true scriptures with words, so that His Majesty's goodwill will not be thwarted nor the labor of this lengthy journey be wasted." With a gentle smile, Ānanda took the alms bowl. All those vīra who guarded the precious towers, the kitchen helpers in charge of sacrifices and incense, and the Honored Ones who worked in the treasure loft began to clap one another on the back and tickle one another on the face. Snapping their fingers and curling their lips, every one of them said, "How shameless! How shameless! Asking the scripture seeker for a present!"

After a while, the two Honored Ones became rather embarrassed, though Ānanda continued to clutch firmly at the alms bowl. Kāśyapa, however, went into the loft to select the scrolls and handed them item by item to Tripitaka. "Disciples," said Tripitaka, "take a good look at these, and make sure that they are not like the earlier ones."

The three disciples examined each scroll as they received it, and this time all the scrolls had words written on them. Altogether they were given five thousand and forty-eight scrolls, making up the number of a single canon. After being properly packed, the scriptures were loaded onto the horse. An additional load was made for Bajie to tote, while their own luggage was toted by Sha Monk. As Pilgrim led the horse, the Tang monk took up his priestly staff and gave his Vairocana hat a press and his brocade cassock a shake.

*　*　*

From Chapter 99

Nine times nine ends the count and Māra's all destroyed;
The work of three times three[1] done, the Dao reverts to its root.

We shall not speak of the Eight Vajra Guardians escorting the Tang monk back to his nation. We turn instead to those Guardians of the Five Quarters, the Four Sentinels, the Six Gods of Darkness and the Six Gods of Light, and the Guardians of Monasteries, who appeared before the triple gates and said to the Bodhisattva Guanyin, "Your disciples had received the Bodhisattva's dharma decree to give secret protection to the sage monk. Now that the work of the sage monk is completed, and the Bodhisattva has returned the Buddhist Patriarch's golden decree to him, we too request permission from the Bodhisattva to return your dharma decree to you."

Highly pleased also, the Bodhisattva said, "Yes, yes! You have my permission." Then she asked, "What was the disposition of the four pilgrims during their journey?"

"They showed genuine devotion and determination," replied the various deities, "which could hardly have escaped the penetrating observation of the

---

1. Work of advanced meditation. Double three, equaling nine, is an auspicious number. "*Māra's*": of the evil demon who tried to tempt the Buddha.

Bodhisattva. The Tang monk, after all, had endured unspeakable sufferings. Indeed, all the ordeals which he had to undergo throughout his journey have been recorded by your disciples. Here is the complete account." The Bodhisattva started to read the registry from its beginning, and this was the content:

> The Guardians in obedience to your decree
> Record with care the Tang monk's calamities.
> Gold Cicada banished is the first ordeal;
> Being almost killed after birth is the second ordeal;
> Delivered of mortal stock at Cloud-Transcending Stream
>   is the eightieth ordeal;
> The journey: one hundred and eight thousand miles.
> The sage monk's ordeals are clearly on file.

After the Bodhisattva had read through the entire registry of ordeals, she said hurriedly, "Within our order of Buddhism, nine times nine is the crucial means by which one returns to immortality. The sage monk has undergone eighty ordeals. Because one ordeal, therefore, is still lacking, the sacred number is not yet complete."

At once she gave this order to one of the Guardians: "Catch the Vajra Guardians and create one more ordeal." Having received this command, the Guardian soared toward the east astride the clouds. After a night and a day he caught the Vajra Guardians and whispered in their ears, "Do this and this . . . ! Don't fail to obey the dharma decree of the Bodhisattva." On hearing these words, the Eight Vajra Guardians immediately retrieved the wind that had borne aloft the four pilgrims, dropping them and the horse bearing the scriptures to the ground. Alas! Truly such is

> Nine times nine, hard task of immortality!
> Firmness of will yields the mysterious key.
> By bitter toil you must the demons spurn;
> Cultivation will the proper way return.
> Regard not the scriptures as easy things.
> So many are the sage monk's sufferings!
> Learn of the old, wondrous Kinship of the Three:[2]
> Elixir won't gel if there's slight errancy.

When his feet touched profane ground, Tripitaka became terribly frightened. Bajie, however, roared with laughter, saying, "Good! Good! Good! This is exactly a case of 'More haste, less speed'!"

"Good! Good! Good!" said Sha Monk. "Because we've speeded up too much, they want us to take a little rest here." "Have no worry," said the Great Sage. "As the proverb says,

> For ten days you sit on the shore;
> In one day you may pass nine beaches."

2. Reputedly the earliest book on alchemy; from the 2nd century C.E.

"Stop matching your wits, you three!" said Tripitaka. "Let's see if we can tell where we are." Looking all around, Sha Monk said, "I know the place! I know the place! Master, listen to the sound of water!"

Pilgrim said, "The sound of water, I suppose, reminds you of your ancestral home." "Which is the Flowing-Sand River," said Bajie. "No! No!" said Sha Monk. "This happens to be the Heaven-Reaching River." Tripitaka said, "O Disciples! Take a careful look and see which side of the river we're on."

Vaulting into the air, Pilgrim shielded his eyes with his hand and took a careful survey of the place before dropping down once more. "Master," he said, "this is the west bank of the Heaven-Reaching River."

"Now I remember,"[4] said Tripitaka. "There was a Chen Village on the east bank. When we arrived here that year, you rescued their son and daughter. In their gratitude to us, they wanted to make a boat to take us across. Eventually we were fortunate enough to get across on the back of a white turtle. I recall, too, that there was no human habitation whatever on the west bank. What shall we do this time?"

"I thought that only profane people would practice this sort of fraud," said Bajie. "Now I know that even the Vajra Guardians before the face of Buddha can practice fraud! Buddha commanded them to take us back east. How could they just abandon us in mid-journey? Now we're in quite a bind! How are we going to get across?" "Stop grumbling, Second Elder Brother!" said Sha Monk. "Our master has already attained the Way, for he had already been delivered from his mortal frame previously at the Cloud-Transcending Stream. This time he can't possibly sink in water. Let's all of us exercise our magic of Displacement and take Master across."

"You can't take him over! You can't take him over!" said Pilgrim, chuckling to himself. Now, why did he say that? If he were willing to exercise his magic powers and reveal the mystery of flight, master and disciples could cross even a thousand rivers. He knew, however, that the Tang monk had not yet perfected the sacred number of nine times nine. That one remaining ordeal made it necessary for them to be detained at the spot.

As master and disciples conversed and walked slowly up to the edge of the water, they suddenly heard someone calling, "Tang Sage Monk! Tang Sage Monk! Come this way! Come this way!" Startled, the four of them looked all around but could not see any sign of a human being or a boat. Then they caught sight of a huge, white, scabby-headed turtle at the shoreline. "Old Master," he cried with outstretched neck, "I have waited for you for so many years! Have you returned only at this time?"

"Old Turtle," replied Pilgrim, smiling, "we troubled you in a year past, and today we meet again." Tripitaka, Bajie, and Sha Monk could not have been more pleased. "If indeed you want to serve us," said Pilgrim, "come up on the shore." The turtle crawled up the bank. Pilgrim told his companions to guide the horse onto the turtle's back. As before, Bajie squatted at the rear of the horse, while the Tang monk and Sha Monk took up positions to the left and to the right of the horse. With one foot on the turtle's head and another on his neck, Pilgrim said, "Old Turtle, go steadily."

His four legs outstretched, the old turtle moved through the water as if he were on dry level ground, carrying all five of them—master, disciples, and the horse—straight toward the eastern shore. Thus it is that

In Advaya's[3] *gate the dharma profound*
Reveals Heav'n and Earth and demons confounds.
The original visage now they see;
Causes find perfection in one body.
Freely they move when Triyāna's *won,*
And when the elixir's nine turns are done.
The luggage and the staff there's no need to tote,
Glad to return on old turtle afloat.

Carrying the pilgrims on his back, the old turtle trod on the waves and proceeded for more than half a day. Late in the afternoon they were near the eastern shore when he suddenly asked this question: "Old Master, in that year when I took you across, I begged you to question Tathāgata, once you got to see him, when I would find my sought-after refuge and how much longer would I live. Did you do that?"

Now, that elder, since his arrival at the Western Heaven, had been preoccupied with bathing in the Yuzhen Temple, being renewed at Cloud-Transcending Stream, and bowing to the various sage monks, Bodhisattvas, and Buddhas. When he walked up the Spirit Mountain, he fixed his thought on the worship of Buddha and on the acquisition of scriptures, completely banishing from his mind all other concerns. He did not, of course, ask about the allotted age of the old turtle. Not daring to lie, however, he fell silent and did not answer the question for a long time. Perceiving that Tripitaka had not asked the Buddha for him, the old turtle shook his body once and dove with a splash into the depths. The four pilgrims, the horse, and the scriptures all fell into the water as well. Ah! It was fortunate that the Tang monk had cast off his mortal frame and attained the Way. If he were like the person he had been before, he would have sunk straight to the bottom. The white horse, moreover, was originally a dragon, while Bajie and Sha Monk both were quite at home in the water. Smiling broadly, Pilgrim made a great display of his magic powers by hauling the Tang monk right out of the water and onto the eastern shore. But the scriptures, the clothing, and the saddle were completely soaked.

* * *

From *Chapter 100*

They return to the Land of the East;
The five sages attain immortality.

* * *

We tell you now instead about the Eight Vajra Guardians, who employed the second gust of fragrant wind to carry the four pilgrims back to the Land of the East. In less than a day, the capital, Chang'an, gradually came into view. That Emperor Taizong, you see, had escorted the Tang monk out of the city three days before the full moon in the ninth month of the thirteenth year of the Zhenguan reign period. By the sixteenth year, he had already asked the Bureau of Labor to erect a Scripture-Watch Tower outside the Western-Peace Pass to receive the holy books. Each year Taizong would go personally to that place for

---

3. Gateway to Buddha-nature.

a visit. It so happened that he had gone again to the tower that day when he caught sight of a skyful of auspicious mists drifting near from the West, and he noticed at the same time strong gusts of fragrant wind.

Halting in midair, the Vajra Guardians cried, "Sage Monk, this is the city Chang'an. It's not convenient for us to go down there, for the people of this region are quite intelligent, and our true identity may become known to them. Even the Great Sage Sun and his two companions needn't go; you yourself can go, hand over the scriptures, and return at once. We'll wait for you in the air so that we may all go back to report to Buddha."

"What the Honored Ones say may be most appropriate," said the Great Sage, "but how could my master tote all those scriptures? How could he lead the horse at the same time? We will have to escort him down there. May we trouble you to wait a while in the air? We dare not tarry."

"When the Bodhisattva Guanyin spoke to Tathāgata the other day," said the Vajra Guardians, "she assured him that the whole trip should take only eight days, so that the canonical number would be fulfilled. It's already more than four days now. We fear that Bajie might become so enamored of the riches down below that we will not be able to meet our appointed schedule."

"When Master attains Buddhahood," said Bajie, chuckling, "I, too, will attain Buddhahood. How could I become enamored of riches down below? Stupid old ruffians! Wait for me here, all of you! As soon as we have handed over the scriptures, I'll return with you and be canonized." Idiot took up the pole, Sha Monk led the horse, and Pilgrim supported the sage monk. Lowering their cloud, they dropped down beside the Scripture-Watch Tower.

When Taizong and his officials saw them, they all descended the tower to receive them. "Has the royal brother returned?" said the emperor. The Tang monk immediately prostrated himself, but he was raised by the emperor's own hands. "Who are these three persons?" asked the emperor once more.

"They are my disciples made during our journey," replied the Tang monk. Highly pleased, Taizong at once ordered his attendants, "Saddle one of our chariot horses for our royal brother to ride. We'll go back to the court together." The Tang monk thanked him and mounted the horse, closely followed by the Great Sage wielding his golden-hooped rod and by Bajie and Sha Monk toting the luggage and supporting the other horse. The entire entourage thus entered together the city of Chang'an. Truly

> A banquet of peace was held years ago.
> When lords, civil and martial, made a grand show.
> A priest preached the law in a great event;
> From Golden Chimes the king his subject sent.
> Tripitaka was given a royal rescript,
> For Five Phases matched the cause of holy script.
> Through bitter smelting all demons were purged.
> Merit done, they now on the court converged.

The Tang monk and his three disciples followed the Throne into the court, and soon there was not a single person in the city of Chang'an who had not learned of the scripture seekers' return.

We tell you now about those priests, young and old, of the Temple of Great Blessing, which was also the old residence of the Tang monk in Chang'an. That day they suddenly discovered that the branches of a few pine trees within the temple gate were pointing eastward. Astonished, they cried, "Strange! Strange! There was no strong wind to speak of last night. Why are all the tops of these trees twisted in this manner?"

One of the former disciples of Tripitaka said, "Quickly, let's get our proper clerical garb. The old master who went away to acquire scriptures must have returned."

"How do you know that?" asked the other priests.

"At the time of his departure," the old disciple said, "he made the remark that he might be away for two or three years, or for six or seven years. Whenever we noticed that these pine-tree tops were pointing to the east, it would mean that he has returned. Since my master spoke the holy words of a true Buddha, I know that the truth has been confirmed this day."

They put on their clothing hurriedly and left; by the time they reached the street to the west, people were already saying that the scripture seeker had just arrived and been received into the city by His Majesty. When they heard the news, the various monks dashed forward and ran right into the imperial chariot. Not daring to approach the emperor, they followed the entourage instead to the gate of the court. The Tang monk dismounted and entered the court with the emperor. The dragon horse, the scripture packs, Pilgrim, Bajie, and Sha Monk were all placed beneath the steps of jade, while Taizong commanded the royal brother to ascend the hall and take a seat.

After thanking the emperor and taking his seat, the Tang monk asked that the scripture scrolls be brought up. Pilgrim and his companions handed them over to the imperial attendants, who presented them in turn to the emperor for inspection. "How many scrolls of scriptures are there," asked Taizong, "and how did you acquire them?"

"When your subject arrived at the Spirit Mountain and bowed to the Buddhist Patriarch," replied Tripitaka, "he was kind enough to ask Ānanda and Kāśyapa, the two Honored Ones, to lead us to the precious tower first for a meal. Then we were brought to the treasure loft, where the scriptures were bestowed on us. Those Honored Ones asked for a gift, but we were not prepared and did not give them any. They gave us some scriptures anyway, and after thanking the Buddhist Patriarch, we headed east, but a monstrous wind snatched away the scriptures. My humble disciple fortunately had a little magic power; he gave chase at once, and the scriptures were thrown and scattered all over. When we unrolled the scrolls, we saw that they were all wordless, blank texts. Your subjects in great fear went again to bow and plead before Buddha. The Buddhist Patriarch said, 'When these scriptures were created, some Bhikṣu sage monks left the monastery and recited some scrolls for one Elder Zhao in the Śrāvastī Kingdom. As a result, the living members of that family were granted safety and protection, while the deceased attained redemption. For such great service they only managed to ask the elder for three pecks and three pints of rice and a little gold. I told them that it was too cheap a sale, and that their descendants would have no money to spend.' Since we learned that even the Buddhist Patriarch anticipated that the two Honored Ones would demand a gift, we had little choice but to offer them that alms bowl of purple gold which Your Majesty had bestowed on me. Only then did they willingly turn over the true scriptures with writing to us. There are thirty-five titles of these scriptures, and several scrolls were selected from each title. Altogether, there are now five thousand and forty-eight scrolls, the number of which makes up one canonical sum."

More delighted than ever, Taizong gave this command: "Let the Court of Imperial Entertainments prepare a banquet in the East Hall so that we may thank our royal brother." Then he happened to notice Tripitaka's three disciples standing beneath the steps, all with extraordinary looks, and he therefore asked, "Are your noble disciples foreigners?"

Prostrating himself, the elder said, "My eldest disciple has the surname of Sun, and his religious name is Wukong. Your subject also addresses him as Pilgrim Sun. He comes from the Water Curtain Cave of the Flower-Fruit Mountain, located in the Aolai Country in the East Pūrvavideha Continent. Because he caused great disturbance in the Celestial Palace, he was imprisoned in a stone box by the Buddhist Patriarch and pressed beneath the Mountain of Two Frontiers in the region of the Western barbarians. Thanks to the admonitions of the Bodhisattva Guanyin, he was converted to Buddhism and became my disciple when I freed him. Throughout my journey I relied heavily on his protection.

"My second disciple has the surname of Zhu, and his religious name is Wuneng. Your subject also addresses him as Zhu Bajie. He comes from the Cloudy Paths Cave of Fuling Mountain. He was playing the fiend at the Old Gao Village of Tibet when the admonitions of the Bodhisattva and the power of the Pilgrim caused him to become my disciple. He made his merit on our journey by toting the luggage and helping us to ford the waters.

"My third disciple has the surname of Sha, and his religious name is Wujing. Your subject also addresses him as Sha Monk. Originally he was a fiend at the Flowing-Sand River. Again the admonitions of the Bodhisattva persuaded him to take the vows of Buddhism. By the way, the horse is not the one my Lord bestowed on me."

Taizong said, "The color and the coat seem all the same. Why isn't it the same horse?"

"When your subject reached the Eagle Grief Stream in the Serpent Coil Mountain and tried to cross it," replied Tripitaka, "the original horse was devoured by this horse. Pilgrim managed to learn from the Bodhisattva that this horse was originally the prince of the Dragon King of the Western Ocean. Convicted of a crime, he would have been executed had it not been for the intervention of the Bodhisattva, who ordered him to be the steed of your subject. It was then that he changed into a horse with exactly the same coat as that of my original mount. I am greatly indebted to him for taking me over mountains and summits and through the most treacherous passages. Whether it be carrying me on my way there or bearing the scriptures upon our return, we are much beholden to his strength."

On hearing these words, Taizong complimented him profusely before asking again, "This long trek to the Western Region, exactly how far is it?"

Tripitaka said, "I recall that the Bodhisattva told us that the distance was a hundred and eight thousand miles. I did not make a careful record on the way. All I know is that we have experienced fourteen seasons of heat and cold. We encountered mountains and ridges daily; the forests we came upon were not small, and the waters we met were wide and swift. We also went through many kingdoms, whose rulers had affixed their seals and signatures on our document." Then he called out: "Disciples, bring up the travel rescript and present it to our Lord."

It was handed over immediately. Taizong took a look and realized that the document had been issued on the third day before the full moon, in the ninth month of the thirteenth year during the Zhenguan reign period. Smiling, Taizong said, "We have caused you the trouble of taking a long journey. This is now the twenty-seventh year of the Zhenguan period!" The travel rescript bore the seals of the Precious Image Kingdom, the Black Rooster Kingdom, the Cart Slow Kingdom, the Kingdom of Women in Western Liang, the Sacrifice Kingdom, the Scarlet-Purple Kingdom, the Bhikṣu Kingdom, the Dharma-Destroying Kingdom. There were also the seals of the Phoenix-Immortal Prefecture, the Jade-Flower County, and the Gold-Level Prefecture. After reading through the document, Taizong put it away.

Soon the officer in attendance to the Throne arrived to invite them to the banquet. As the emperor took the hand of Tripitaka and walked down the steps of the hall, he asked once more, "Are your noble disciples familiar with the etiquette of the court?"

"My humble disciples," replied Tripitaka, "all began their careers as monsters deep in the wilds or a mountain village, and they have never been instructed in the etiquette of China's sage court. I beg my Lord to pardon them."

Smiling, Taizong said, "We won't blame them! We won't blame them! Let's all go to the feast set up in the East Hall." Tripitaka thanked him once more before calling for his three disciples to join them. Upon their arrival at the hall, they saw that the opulence of the great nation of China was indeed different from all ordinary kingdoms. You see

> *The doorway o'erhung with brocade.*
> *The floor adorned with red carpets,*
> *The whirls of exotic incense,*
> *And fresh victuals most rare.*
> *The amber cups*
> *And crystal goblets*
> *Are gold-trimmed and jade-set;*
> *The gold platters*
> *And white-jade bowls*
> *Are patterned and silver-rimmed.*
> *The tubers thoroughly cooked,*
> *The taros sugar-coated;*
> *Sweet, lovely button mushrooms,*
> *Unusual, pure seaweeds.*
> *Bamboo shoots, ginger-spiced, are served a few times;*
> *Malva leafs, honey-drenched, are mixed several ways.*
> *Wheat-glutens fried with xiangchun leaves:*[1]
> *Wood-ears cooked with bean-curd skins.*

1. From a fragrant, slightly spicy plant.

Rock ferns and fairy plants;
Fern flour and dried wei-leaves.
Radishes cooked with Sichuan peppercorns;
Melon strands stirred with mustard powder.
These few vegetarian dishes are so-so,
But the many rare fruits quite steal the show!
Walnuts and persimmons,
Lung-ans and lychees.
The chestnuts of Yizhou and Shandong's dates;
The South's ginko fruits and hare-head pears.
Pine-seeds, lotus-seeds, and giant grapes;
Fei-nuts, melon seeds, and water chestnuts.
"Chinese olives"and wild apples;
Crabapples and Pyrus-pears;
Tender stalks and young lotus roots;
Crisp plums and "Chinese strawberries."
Not one species is missing;
Not one kind is wanting.
There are, moreover, the steamed mille-feuilles, honeyed pastries, and
*   fine viands;*
And there are also the lovely wines, fragrant teas, and strange dainties.
An endless spread of a hundred flavors, true noble fare.
Western barbarians with great China can never compare!

Master and three disciples were grouped together with the officials, both civil and military, on both sides of the emperor Taizong, who took the seat in the middle. The dancing and the music proceeded in an orderly and solemn manner, and in this way they enjoyed themselves thoroughly for one whole day. Truly

The royal banquet rivals the sage kings':
True scriptures acquired excess blessings bring.
Forever these will prosper and remain
As Buddha's light shines on the king's domain.

When it became late, the officials thanked the emperor; while Taizong withdrew into his palace, the various officials returned to their residences. The Tang monk and his disciples, however, went to the Temple of Great Blessing, where they were met by the resident priests kowtowing. As they entered the temple gate, the priests said, "Master, the top of these trees were all suddenly pointing eastward this morning. We remembered your words and hurried out to the city to meet you. Indeed, you did arrive!" The elder could not have been more pleased as they were ushered into the abbot's quarters. By then, Bajie was not clamoring at all for food or tea, nor did he indulge in any mischief. Both Pilgrim and Sha Monk behaved most properly, for they had become naturally quiet and reserved since the Dao in them had come to fruition. They rested that night.

Taizong held court next morning and said to the officials, "We did not sleep the whole night when we reflected on how great and profound has been the merit of our brother, such that no compensation is quite adequate. We finally

composed in our head several homely sentences as a mere token of our gratitude, but they have not yet been written down." Calling for one of the secretaries from the Central Drafting Office, he said, "Come, let us recite our
composition for you, and you take it down sentence by sentence." The composition was as follows:

> We have heard how the Two Primary Forces[2] which manifest themselves in
> Heaven and Earth in the production of life are represented by images, whereas the
> invisible powers of the four seasons bring about transformation of things through
> the hidden action of heat and cold. By scanning Heaven and Earth, even the
> most ignorant may perceive their rudimentary laws. Even the thorough under-
> standing of yin and yang, however, has seldom enabled the worthy and wise to
> comprehend fully their ultimate principle. It is easy to recognize that Heaven and
> Earth do contain yin and yang because there are images. It is difficult to compre-
> hend fully how yin and yang pervade Heaven and Earth because the forces them-
> selves are invisible. That images may manifest the minute is a fact that does not
> perplex even the foolish, whereas forms hidden in what is invisible are what con-
> fuse even the learned.
>
> How much more difficult it is, therefore, to understand the way of Buddhism,
> which exalts the void, uses the dark, and exploits the silent in order to succor the
> myriad grades of living things and exercise control over the entire world. Its spiri-
> tual authority is the highest, and its divine potency has no equal. Its magnitude
> impregnates the entire cosmos; there is no space so tiny that it does not permeate
> it. Birthless and deathless, it does not age after a thousand kalpas; half-hidden and
> half-manifest, it brings a hundred blessings even now. A wondrous way most mys-
> terious, those who follow it cannot know its limit. A law flowing silent and deep,
> those who draw on it cannot fathom its source. How, therefore, could those
> benighted ordinary mortals not be perplexed if they tried to plumb its depths?
>
> Now, this great Religion arose in the Land of the West. It soared to the court
> of the Han period in the form of a radiant dream,[3] which flowed with its mercy to
> enlighten the Eastern territory. In antiquity, during the time when form and
> abstraction were clearly distinguished, the words of the Buddha, even before
> spreading, had already established their goodly influence. In a generation when
> he was both frequently active in and withdrawn from the world, the people
> beheld his virtue and honored it. But when he returned to Nirvāṇa and genera-
> tions passed by, the golden images concealed his true form and did not reflect the
> light of the universe. The beautiful paintings, though unfolding lovely portraits,
> vainly held up the figure of thirty-two marks.[4] Nonetheless his subtle doctrines
> spread far and wide to save men and beasts from the three unhappy paths, and
> his traditions were widely proclaimed to lead all creatures through the ten stages
> toward Buddhahood. Moreover, the Buddha made scriptures, which could be
> divided into the Great and the Small Vehicles. He also possessed the Law, which
> could be transmitted either in the correct or in the deviant method.

2. Probably forces of darkness and light, of
yin and yang.
3. Reference to a famous legend about China's first contact with Buddhism. Emperor
Ming of the Han (r. 58–75 B.C.E.) dreamed
that a golden deity was flying in front of his
palace. The next morning one minister identified the deity in the dream as the flying Buddha from India.
4. Special physical marks on the body of the
Buddha.

Our priest Xuanzang, a Master of the Law, is a leader within the Gate of Law. Devoted and intelligent as a youth, he realized at an early age the merit of the three forms of immateriality. When grown he comprehended the principles of the spiritual, including first the practice of the four forms of patience.[5] Neither the pine in the wind nor the moon mirrored in water can compare with his purity and radiance. Even the dew of Heaven and luminous gems cannot surpass the clarity and refinement of his person. His intelligence encompassed even those elements which seemingly had no relations, and his spirit could perceive that which had yet to take visible forms. Having transcended the lure of the six senses, he was such an outstanding figure that in all the past he had no rival. He concentrated his mind on the internal verities, mourning all the time the mutilation of the correct doctrines. Worrying over the mysteries, he lamented that even the most profound treatises had errors.

He thought of revising the teachings and reviving certain arguments, so as to disseminate what he had received to a wider audience. He would, moreover, strike out the erroneous and preserve the true to enlighten the students. For this reason he longed for the Pure Land and a pilgrimage to the Western Territories. Risking dangers he set out on a long journey, with only his staff for his companion on this solitary expedition. Snow drifts in the morning would blanket his roadway; sand storms at dusk would blot out the horizon. Over ten thousand miles of mountains and streams he proceeded, pushing aside mist and smoke. Through a thousand alternations of heat and cold he advanced amidst frost and rain. As his zeal was great, he considered his task a light one, for he was determined to succeed.

He toured throughout the Western World for fourteen years,[6] going to all the foreign nations in quest of the proper doctrines. He led the life of an ascetic beneath twin śāla trees[7] and by the eight rivers of India. At the Deer Park and on the Vulture Peak he beheld the strange and searched out the different. He received ultimate truths from the senior sages and was taught the true doctrines by the highest worthies. Penetrating into the mysteries, he mastered the most profound lessons. The way of the Triyāna and Six Commandments he learned by heart; a hundred cases of scriptures forming the canon flowed like waves from his lips.

Though the countries he visited were innumerable, the scriptures he succeeded in acquiring had a definite number. Of those important texts of the Mahāyāna he received, there are thirty-five titles in altogether five thousand and forty-eight scrolls. When they are translated and spread through China, they will proclaim the surpassing merit of Buddhism, drawing the cloud of mercy from the Western extremity to shower the dharma-rain on the Eastern region. The Holy Religion, once incomplete, is now returned to perfection. The multitudes, once full of sins, are now brought back to blessing. Like that which quenches the fire in a burning house, Buddhism works to save humanity lost on its way to perdition. Like a golden beam shining on darkened waters, it leads the voyagers to climb the other shore safely.

---

5. Four forms of patience: endurance under shame, hatred, physical hardship, and in pursuit of faith [translator's Note].
6. Perhaps a deliberate deviation from the nearly seventeen years of the pilgrimage indicated in the historical sources.
7. Trees under which the Buddha died and passed into nirvana.

Thus we know that the wicked will fall because of their iniquities, but the virtuous will rise because of their affinities. The causes of such rise and fall are all self-made by man. Consider the cinnamon flourishing high on the mountain, its flowers nourished by cloud and mist, or the lotus growing atop the green waves, its leaves unsoiled by dust. This is not because the lotus is by nature clean or because the cinnamon itself is chaste, but because what the cinnamon depends on for its existence is lofty, and thus it will not be weighed down by trivia; and because what the lotus relies on is pure, and thus impurity cannot stain it. Since even the vegetable kingdom, which is itself without intelligence, knows that excellence comes from an environment of excellence, how can humans who understand the great relations not search for well-being by following well-being?

May these scriptures abide forever as the sun and moon and may the blessings they confer spread throughout the universe!

After the secretary had finished writing this treatise, the sage monk was summoned. At the time, the elder was already waiting outside the gate of the court. When he heard the summons, he hurried inside and prostrated himself to pay homage to the emperor.

Taizong asked him to ascend the hall and handed him the document. When he had finished reading it, the priest went to his knees again to express his gratitude. "The style and rhetoric of my Lord," said the priest, "are lofty and classical, while the reasoning in the treatise is both profound and subtle. I would like to know, however, whether a title has been chosen for this composition."

"We composed it orally last night,"[8] replied Taizong, "as a token of thanks to our royal brother. Will it be acceptable if I title this 'Preface to the Holy Religion'?" The elder kowtowed and thanked him profusely. Once more Taizong said,

> "Our talents pale before the imperial tablets,
> And our words cannot match the bronze and stone inscriptions.
> As for the esoteric texts,
> Our ignorance thereof is even greater.
> Our treatise orally composed
> Is actually quite unpolished—
> Like mere spilled ink on tablets of gold.
> Or broken tiles in a forest of pearls.
> Writing it in self-interest,
> We have quite ignored even embarrassment.
> It is not worth your notice,
> And you should not thank us."

All the officials present, however, congratulated the emperor and made arrangements immediately to promulgate the royal essay on Holy Religion inside and outside the capital.

Taizong said, "We would like to ask the royal brother to recite the true scriptures for us. How about it?"

"My Lord," said the elder, "if you want me to recite the true scriptures, we must find the proper religious site. The treasure palace is no place for recitation."

---

8. The emperor's declaration here was actually a note written in reply to a formal memorial of thanks submitted to the historical Xuanzang [translator's note].

Exceedingly pleased, Taizong asked his attendants, "Among the monasteries of Chang'an, which is the purest one?"

From among the ranks stepped forth the Grand Secretary, Xiao Yu, who said, "The Wild-Goose Pagoda Temple in the city is purest of all." At once Taizong gave this command to the various officials: "Each of you take several scrolls of these true scriptures and go reverently with us to the Wild-Goose Pagoda Temple. We want to ask our royal brother to expound the scriptures to us." Each of the officials indeed took up several scrolls and followed the emperor's carriage to the temple. A lofty platform with proper appointments was then erected. As before, the elder told Bajie and Sha Monk to hold the dragon horse and mind the luggage, while Pilgrim was to serve him by his side. Then he said to Taizong, "If my Lord would like to circulate the true scriptures throughout his empire, copies should be made before they are dispersed. We should treasure the originals and not handle them lightly."

Smiling, Taizong said, "The words of our royal brother are most appropriate! Most appropriate!" He thereupon ordered the officials in the Hanlin Academy and the Central Drafting Office to make copies of the true scriptures. For them he also erected another temple east of the capital and named it the Temple for Imperial Transcription.

*　　*　　*

We must tell you now about those Eight Great Vajra Guardians, who mounted the fragrant wind to lead the elder, his three disciples, and the white horse back to Spirit Mountain. The round trip was made precisely within a period of eight days. At that time the various divinities of Spirit Mountain were all assembled before Buddha to listen to his lecture. Ushering master and disciples before his presence, the Eight Vajra Guardians said, "Your disciples by your golden decree have escorted the sage monk and his companions back to the Tang nation. The scriptures have been handed over. We now return to surrender your decree." The Tang monk and his disciples were then told to approach the throne of Buddha to receive their appointments.

"Sage Monk," said Tathāgata, "in your previous incarnation you were originally my second disciple named Master Gold Cicada. Because you failed to listen to my exposition of the law and slighted my great teaching, your true spirit was banished to find another incarnation in the Land of the East. Happily you submitted and, by remaining faithful to our teaching, succeeded in acquiring the true scriptures. For such magnificent merit, you will receive a great promotion to become the Buddha of Candana Merit.

"Sun Wukong, when you caused great disturbance at the Celestial Palace, I had to exercise enormous dharma power to have you pressed beneath the Mountain of Five Phases. Fortunately your Heaven-sent calamity came to an end, and you embraced the Buddhist religion. I am pleased even more by the fact that you were devoted to the scourging of evil and the exaltation of good. Throughout your journey you made great merit by smelting the demons and defeating the fiends. For being faithful in the end as you were in the beginning, I hereby give you the grand promotion and appoint you the Buddha Victorious in Strife.

"Zhu Wuneng, you were originally an aquatic deity of the Heavenly River, the Marshal of Heavenly Reeds. For getting drunk during the Festival of Immortal Peaches and insulting the divine maiden, you were banished to an incarnation in the Region Below which would give you the body of a beast. Fortunately you still cherished and loved the human form, so that even when you sinned at the Cloudy Paths Cave in Fuling Mountain, you eventually submitted to our great religion and embraced our vows. Although you protected the sage monk on his way, you were still quite mischievous, for greed and lust were never wholly extinguished in you. For the merit of toting the luggage, however, I hereby grant you promotion and appoint you Janitor of the Altars."

"They have all become Buddhas!" shouted Bajie. "Why am I alone made Janitor of the Altars?"

"Because you are still talkative and lazy," replied Tathāgata, "and you retain an enormous appetite. Within the four great continents of the world, there are many people who observe our religion. Whenever there are Buddhist services, you will be asked to clear the altars. That's an appointment which offers you plenty of enjoyment. How could it be bad?

"Sha Wujing, you were originally the Great Curtain-Raising Captain. Because you broke a crystal chalice during the Festival of Immortal Peaches, you were banished to the Region Below, where at the River of Flowing-Sand you sinned by devouring humans. Fortunately you submitted to our religion and remained firm in your faith. As you escorted the sage monk, you made merit by leading his horse over all those mountains. I hereby grant you promotion and appoint you the Golden-Bodied Arhat."

Then he said to the white horse, "You were originally the prince of Dragon King Guangjin of the Western Ocean. Because you disobeyed your father's command and committed the crime of unfiliality, you were to be executed. Fortunately you made submission to the Law and accepted our vows. Because you carried the sage monk daily on your back during his journey to the West and because you also took the holy scriptures back to the East, you too have made merit. I hereby grant you promotion and appoint you one of the dragons belonging to the Eight Classes of Supernatural Beings."

The elder, his three disciples, and the horse all kowtowed to thank the Buddha, who ordered some of the guardians to take the horse to the Dragon-Transforming Pool at the back of the Spirit Mountain. After being pushed into the pool, the horse stretched himself, and in a little while he shed his coat, horns began to grow on his head, golden scales appeared all over his body, and silver whiskers emerged on his cheeks. His whole body shrouded in auspicious air and his four paws wrapped in hallowed clouds, he soared out of the pool and circled inside the monastery gate, on top of one of the Pillars that Support Heaven.

As the various Buddhas gave praise to the great dharma of Tathāgata, Pilgrim Sun said also to the Tang monk, "Master, I've become a Buddha now, just like you. It can't be that I still must wear a golden fillet! And you wouldn't want to clamp my head still by reciting that so-called Tight-Fillet Spell, would you? Recite the Loose-Fillet Spell quickly and get it off my head. I'm going to smash it to pieces, so that that so-called Bodhisattva can't use it anymore to play tricks on other people."

"Because you were difficult to control previously," said the Tang monk, "this method had to be used to keep you in hand. Now that you have become a Buddha, naturally it will be gone. How could it be still on your head? Try touching your head and see." Pilgrim raised his hand and felt along his head, and indeed the fillet had vanished. So at that time, Buddha Candana, Buddha Victorious in Strife, Janitor of the Altars, and Golden-Bodied Arhat all assumed the position of their own rightful fruition. The Heavenly dragon-horse too returned to immortality, and we have a testimonial poem for them. The poem says:

> One reality fallen to the dusty plain
> Fuses with Four Signs and cultivates self again.
> In Five Phases terms forms are but silent and void;
> The hundred fiends' false names one should all avoid.
> The great Bodhi's the right Candana fruition;
> Appointments complete their rise from perdition.
> When scriptures spread throughout the world the gracious light,
> Henceforth five sages live within Advaya's heights.

At the time when these five sages assumed their positions, the various Buddhist Patriarchs, Bodhisattvas, sage priests, arhats, guardians, bhikṣus, upāsakas and upāsikās, the immortals of various mountains and caves, the grand divinities, the Gods of Darkness and Light, the Sentinels, the Guardians of Monasteries, and all the immortals and preceptors who had attained the Way all came to listen to the proclamation before retiring to their proper stations. Look now at

> Colored mists crowding the Spirit Vulture Peak,
> And hallowed clouds gathered in the world of bliss.
> Gold dragons safely sleeping,
> Jade tigers resting in peace;
> Black hares scampering freely,
> Snakes and turtles circling at will.
> Phoenixes, red and blue, gambol pleasantly;
> Black apes and white deer saunter happily.
> Strange flowers of eight periods,
> Divine fruits of four seasons,
> Hoary pines and old junipers,
> Jade cypresses and aged bamboos.
> Five-colored plums often blossoming and bearing fruit;
> Millennial peaches frequently ripening and fresh.
> A thousand flowers and fruits vying for beauty;
> A whole sky full of auspicious mists.

Pressing their palms together to indicate their devotion, the holy congregation all chanted:

I submit to Dipamkara, the Buddha of Antiquity.
I submit to Bhaiṣajya-vaidūrya-prabhāṣa, the Physician and Buddha
    of Crystal Lights.

I submit to the Buddha Śākyamuni.
I submit to the Buddha of the Past, Present, and Future.
I submit to the Buddha of Pure Joy.
I submit to the Buddha Vairocana.
I submit to the Buddha, King of the Precious Banner.
I submit to the Maitreya, the Honored Buddha.
I submit to the Buddha Amitābha.
I submit to Sukhāvativyūha, the Buddha of Infinite Life.
I submit to the Buddha who Receives and Leads to Immorality.
I submit to the Buddha of Diamond Indestructibility.
I submit to Sūrya, the Buddha of Precious Light.
I submit to Mañjuśrī, the Buddha of the Race of Honorable Dragon
    Kings.
I submit to the Buddha of Zealous Progress and Virtue.
I submit to Candraprabha, the Buddha of Precious Moonlight.
I submit to the Buddha of Presence without Ignorance.
I submit to Varuna, the Buddha of Sky and Water.
I submit to the Buddha Nārāyaṇa.
I submit to the Buddha of Radiant Meritorious Works.
I submit to the Buddha of Talented Meritorious Works.
I submit to Svāgata, the Buddha of the Well-Departed.
I submit to the Buddha of Candana Light.
I submit to the Buddha of Jeweled Banner.
I submit to the Buddha of the Light of Wisdom Torch.
I submit to the Buddha of the Light of Sea-Virtue.
I submit to the Buddha of Great Mercy Light.
I submit to the Buddha, King of Compassion-Power.
I submit to the Buddha, Leader of the Sages.
I submit to the Buddha of Vast Solemnity.
I submit to the Buddha of Golden Radiance.
I submit to the Buddha of Luminous Gifts.
I submit to the Buddha Victorious in Wisdom.
I submit to the Buddha, Quiescent Light of the World.
I submit to the Buddha, Light of the Sun and Moon.
I submit to the Buddha, Light of the Sun-and-Moon Pearl.
I submit to the Buddha, King of the Victorious Banner.
I submit to the Buddha of Wondrous Tone and Sound.
I submit to the Buddha, Banner of Permanent Light.
I submit to the Buddha, Lamp that Scans the World.
I submit to the Buddha, King of Surpassing Dharma.
I submit to the Buddha of Sumeru Light.
I submit to the Buddha, King of Great Wisdom.
I submit to the Buddha of Golden Sea Light.
I submit to the Buddha of Great Perfect Light.
I submit to the Buddha of the Gift of Light.
I submit to the Buddha of Candana Merit.
I submit to the Buddha Victorious in Strife.
I submit to the Bodhisattva Guanshiyin.
I submit to the Bodhisattva, Great Power-Coming.
I submit to the Bodhisattva Mañjuśrī.

I submit to the Bodhisattva Viśvabhadra and other Bodhisattvas.
I submit to the various Bodhisattvas of the Great Pure Ocean.
I submit to the Bodhisattva, the Buddha of Lotus Pool and Ocean
    Assembly.
I submit to the various Bodhisattvas in the Western Heaven of
    Ultimate Bliss.
I submit to the Great Bodhisattvas, the Three Thousand Guardians.
I submit to the Great Bodhisattvas, the Five Hundred Arhats.
I submit to the Bodhisattva, Bhikṣu-īkṣṇi.
I submit to the Bodhisattva of Boundless and Limitless Dharma.
I submit to the Bodhisattva, Diamond Great Scholar-Sage.
I submit to the Bodhisattva, Janitor of the Altars.
I submit to the Bodhisattva, Golden-Bodied Arhat of Eight Jewels.
I submit to the Bodhisattva of Vast Strength, the Heavenly Dragon
    of Eight Divisions of Supernatural Beings.

Such are these various Buddhas in all the worlds.

> *I wish to use these merits*
> *To adorn Buddha's pure land—*
> *To repay fourfold grace above*
> *And save those on three paths below.*
> *If there are those who see and hear,*
> *Their minds will find enlightenment.*
> *Their births with us in paradise*
> *Will be this body's recompense.*
> *All the Buddhas of past, present, future in all the world,*
> *The various Honored Bodhisattvas and Mahāsattvas,*
> *Mahā-prajñā-pāramitā!*[9]

---

9. The Great Perfection of Wisdom.

FENG MENGLONG
1574–1646

Feng Menglong was one of the most versatile writers of early modern China. An ardent scholar of the Confucian Classics, he was also enthralled by village gossip and genuinely interested in the small dramas of everyday life. That he enjoyed capturing the high points and low ends of human pursuits all at once made him an unusual figure in his time. But for him both ends of the spectrum were complementary rather than contradictory. As he explains in the preface to the story collection *Common Words to Warn the World*, "Because peasants, children, ordinary women, and peddlers are easily stirred to feelings of joy or wrath by what others do rightly or wrongly, because they let stories about the operations of karma guide their actions, and gain knowledge from rumors and gossip, popular historical romances can well serve to supplement what the Classics and the Histories omit." Poised between the elite values of Confucian high culture and the truths of common people, he turned vernacular stories into a respectable literary genre. This practice also allowed him to unmask the hypocritical values of the ruling elites and give a moral voice to his low-class heroes and heroines.

Feng Menglong was born in 1574 into a prosperous and well-educated family in Suzhou, one of the cultural centers of the Ming Dynasty (1368–1644) in the wealthy South. Despite his talent and growing literary fame he repeatedly failed the highest level of the civil service examination, the one goal to which many Ming intellectuals aspired and which allowed them to serve in the large Ming bureaucracy. Finally around 1630, in his mid-fifties, Feng gave up on his dream and accepted minor offices, including an appointment as county magistrate in Fujian Province in the Southeast. He felt strongly about his participation in political life, and when the Ming Dynasty crumbled and the Manchus, non-Chinese conquerors from the Northeast, established the Qing Dynasty in 1644, he threw in his lot with the unsuccessful Ming resistance and wrote patriotic tracts for their national cause. He died two years after the Qing takeover, probably still hopeful that the doomed Ming could reestablish themselves against the foreign invaders.

Feng Menglong's work has a broad scope. As a passionate reader of popular literature and observer of commoner culture, Feng compiled collections of jokes and folk songs. His notorious love affair with a famous Suzhou courtesan fostered his image as a bohemian libertine. This stood in delicate contrast with Feng the scholar, who produced at least three handbooks on *The Spring and Autumn Annals*, attributed to the great master Confucius (551–479 B.C.E.) and one of the Confucian Classics that scholars had been carefully discussing and annotating for almost two millennia. His greatest achievement, however, are three collections of vernacular stories.

Vernacular stories, which thrived from the Song (960–1279) to the Qing Dynasty, originated as transcriptions of storyteller performances in the colloquial language of their illiterate audiences. In this they differed considerably from classical stories of the Tang Dynasty (618–907) such as Yuan Zhen's *The Story of Yingying*, which were written in the classical language of educated literati. Vernacular literature gained acceptance during the Yuan Dynasty (1279–1368), when the Mongols ruled China and Chinese literati were despised by the foreign invaders. This change in rule loosened the grip of classical language on literature so that vernacular stories became suddenly worthy of dissemination in print. Unlike the long novels that became popular during the Ming Dynasty, vernacular stories are short and have a unified plotline. They often draw on older stories from the classical Tang tales, including themes like the supernatural and romance. But the new urban culture during the Ming Dynasty soon contributed new topics: sex, money, crimes, and court cases.

Feng had an anthropological interest in vernacular stories. He avidly collected and edited them, also adding creations of his own that read like popular stories. Out of the one-hundred-and-twenty stories in his three story collections, about thirty-seven were probably written entirely by himself. For a highly educated writer like Feng the vernacular language had many attractions: it allowed the inclusion of nuances in expressing social differences, local color, and expressive suspense, which could not easily be rendered in the classical language. Feng deeply believed in the educational value of the stories and at one point even claimed boldly that vernacular stories were more conducive to moral education than even the *Analects* that contained the canonical words of Confucius. For this purpose he retained the pose of the storyteller, who directly addresses his readers, noisily drives home his moral message, quotes popular verse and folk wisdom, and inserts lengthy prologues into his stories to give his audience time to settle in before starting his performance. Feng was instrumental in making this pretense of being an oral storyteller the hallmark of the new literary form of vernacular story.

"Du Tenth Sinks the Jewel Box in Anger," our selection, comes from *Common Words to Warn the World* (1624). It is a story of romantic love and loyalty repeatedly put to the test and a story about the exploitation of class anxieties. The remarkable and resourceful courtesan Du, a renowned beauty, meets the deplorably spineless Li Jia, who is sent by his father, a prominent local official, to take the exams in the Ming capital Nanjing. He soon loses himself in the pleasure quarters and exhausts his resources in his passionate desire for Du. The story is based on a classical tale and stands in a long tradition of romances about courtesans and aspiring exam candidates, but Ming commercial culture creeps into the plotline and painfully spells out the economic costs and debts of the relationship, dramatizing the human losses that lead to a tragic end and ultimately showing what money cannot buy.

Although the tradition of vernacular stories had lost vitality by the nineteenth century, Feng Menglong and other seventeenth-century vernacular story writers were still eagerly read and provided inspiration for new novels and other genres. Feng Menglong's ability to vividly portray human nature at its best and worst easily crosses boundaries of genre and time.

Du Tenth Sinks the Jewel Box in Anger[1]

The last barbarians swept away, the imperial seat is established;
    soaring dragons and dancing phoenixes—a majestic scene!
To the left, encircled in a sash of east-sea sky;
    to the right, hugged by Taihang's ten-thousand-mountain walls.[2]
Halberd and spear: the nine frontiers held in sway to the utmost passes;
    gown and cap: the myriad fiefdoms look up in reverence to the serene
      robes of state.
In a peaceful age, the people rejoice in the realm of Huaxu;
    for ever and ever, a golden jar gleaming in the sun.[3]

This poem is devoted to the praise of our dynasty's founding of the capital at
Yan.[4] As for the situation of the Yan capital, it is guarded to the north by towering passes, and commands the region of central China to the south. It is truly
a golden citadel, a heavenly mansion, a foundation not to be toppled in ten
thousand years! In the beginning, Granddad Hongwu swept away the barbarian dust and established his reign at Jinling.[5] This is the capital known as Nanjing. When Granddad Yongle led his troops out of Beiping to pacify the turmoil,
the capital was removed to Yan. This is the capital known as Beijing. And all as
a result of this removal, what had been a region of bleak chill was transformed
into a realm of flowered brocade. From Granddad Yongle the throne passed
down through nine generations to Granddad Wanli, the eleventh Son of
Heaven of our dynasty. He was wise and strong, perfect in both virtue and good
fortune. He succeeded to the kingdom at the age of ten and ruled for forty-
eight years, during which time he put down three armed uprisings. Which
three were they?

The Prime Minister Toyotomi Hideyoshi of Japan, Bei Cheng'en of the Xixia,
and Yang Yinglong of Bozhou.[6]

Toyotomi Hideyoshi invaded Korea, and Bei Cheng'en and Yang Yinglong
were native officials[7] who plotted revolt; they were put down one after the other.
There were none among the distant tribes who were not frightened into submission, and they strove with one another to pay homage and tribute. Truly,

    One man's blessed fortune brings content to all;
    No trouble within the four seas mars the nation's peace.

1. Translated by and with notes adapted from
Robert Ashmore.
2. The Bohai Gulf and the Taihang Mountain
Range formed parts of the eastern and southwestern borders of the northern capital zone
in the Ming. The directions "left" and "right"
here, as in old Chinese maps, assume a viewer
facing south.
3. Huaxu was a utopian state characterized by
social harmony. "Golden jar" is a poetic figure
for the solidity and permanence of a nation's
borders.
4. Ancient name for the Beijing region.

5. The Hongwu emperor (1328–1398) defeated the Mongol Yuan Dynasty and founded
the Ming Dynasty (1368–1644).
6. Toyotomi Hideyoshi (1536–1598), military
ruler of Japan, attempted invasions of Korea in
1592 and 1597.
7. Bo Cheng'en led a military uprising on the
northwestern frontier of the Ming Empire in
1591, while Yang Yinglong, a leader of the
Miao ethnic minority under the Ming in the
Southwest, led sporadic raids, which eventually escalated into revolt against the Ming.

Our story picks up during the twentieth year of the Wanli period, when the Japanese Prime Minister created discord by invading Korea. The King of Korea submitted a missive requesting assistance, and our celestial court dispatched troops to traverse the sea and go to the rescue. Around this time, a proposal by a Bureau of Households official was granted approval, to this effect:

In view of the present armed strife, our logistical supplies are insufficient. Let us provisionally adopt the precedent of accepting payment in exchange for positions in the imperial academy. . . .

Now it turns out that there were several types of advantage for those who bought academy scholar status in this way: it made it easier to study, easier to participate in the civil service exams, and easier to pass. All in all, it added up to a nice little prospect for career advancement. For this reason, the young masters of official families and the scions of wealthy houses became unwilling to take the ordinary licentiates' exam, preferring to take advantage of the quota and become academy scholars. Following the implementation of this practice, the number of scholars at the academies at each of the two capitals rose to over a thousand.

Among this number there was a young man surnamed Li, named Jia, with the cognomen Ganxian, a native of Shaoxing Prefecture in Zhejiang. He was the eldest of the three sons of his father, Provincial Commissioner Li. From childhood he had been studying in the local school, but had not yet passed the district licentiates' examination. At this time he entered the academy at the Northern capital under the new provision. When he had been enrolled as an academy scholar, he would pass the time in the compound of the Ministry of Music along with his townsman the academy scholar Liu Yuchun. There he encountered a famous courtesan. She was surnamed Du, named Mei, and was tenth-born of her generation, so in the quarters everyone called her Du Tenth.
She was

> High-toned allure from head to toe;
>   every inch coy scent.
> Two arcs of eyebrow traced with green of distant hills;
>   a pair of eyes bright with welling autumn floods.
> Face like a lotus bud—just like Wenjun of the Zhuo clan;
>   lips like cherries—not a jot inferior to Fansu[8] of the Bai household.
> Pity this slip of flawless jade
>   that fell by mistake amid whoredom's flowers and willows!

Du Tenth had lost her maidenhead at the age of thirteen, and was at this time nineteen. During those seven years there is no telling how many lordlings and ducal heirs she had gone through, leaving each of them wanton and besotted with passion—they wrecked households and squandered fortunes without the least regret. A jingle circulated around the quarters that went:

> When Tenth attends a drinking bout
> abstainers quaff till the wine runs out.

8. A singing girl in the household of the Tang poet Bai Juyi. "Wenjun": Zhuo Wenjun, the wife of the bohemian Han Dynasty writer Sima Xiangru.

When dandies meet Mei on their rounds,
They swear the rest all look like hounds.

Now our young master Li was a dashing fellow who had never before encountered real womanly charms. When he ran into Du Tenth, his happiness exceeded all expectation. He took the whole burden of his youthful passion and loaded it on her alone. Our young master had a handsome face and a tender disposition, besides being a big spender and quick to say the right thing. So he and Du Tenth became an inseparable couple who got along in everything. Tenth, knowing how greedy and unjust her madam was, had long been meaning to go straight. Furthermore, when she noticed how sincere and earnest young master Li was toward her, she was very much inclined to throw in her lot with him. The thing was that master Li was deathly afraid of his old man, and did not dare take her up on her proposal. Nonetheless, the two grew ever more devoted to one another, and happily spent both day and night in each other's company, just like a married couple. They swore by seas and vowed by mountains that they would never have thoughts of another. Truly,

Affection as deep as an unfathomed sea;
Loyalty as heavy as mountains, but higher.

Now as for Tenth's madam, what she saw was her girl being monopolized by Master Li—none of those other worthy heirs and lordlings who were drawn by Tenth's reputation could get so much as a peek. In the beginning, when Master Li was spending in grand style, the madam would hunch up her shoulders and laugh ingratiatingly, playing up to him for all she was worth. But days and months went by, and before they knew it, it had been over a year. Master Li's coffers gradually grew empty, and he was unable to spend according to his heart's desires. Then the madam began to snub him. And when old Commissioner Li back home heard that his son was passing his time whoring in the pleasure district, he repeatedly sent letters calling him back home. But Master Li was befuddled with Tenth's charms, and was forever putting off his departure. Later on he heard that his old man was in a towering rage at home, and he became more unwilling than ever to go back. The ancients said, "friendship based on profit grows cold when profit runs dry." But that Du Tenth had a real affection for Master Li, and the more she saw the hard financial straits he was in, the warmer she grew toward him. Her madam told her repeatedly to send Li Jia away from the premises, and when the madam saw that her girl was paying her no mind, she began herself making verbal attacks on Master Li, in hopes of angering him and thus provoking him to take his leave. But the young master was mannerly and subdued by nature, and only became ever more accommodating in his tone.

The madam had nothing for it, and could only browbeat Tenth day in and day out, saying, "In our profession we rely on our guests for both food and clothing. We 'see off the old at the back gate and welcome the new at the front.' Our forecourt stays as lively as a house on fire, and money piles up in a heap. That Li Jia has been hanging around here for over a year now. Forget about new guests, even our old patrons have been cut out of the picture. It's clear as clear can be that it's a ghost-catcher you've brought in here—not even a little ghost would dare set foot in this door! It's to the point where your old lady's household is running on nothing but wind. What way is this to do business?"

Du Tenth could not remain silent in the face of this dressing-down, and answered, "Master Li didn't show up here empty-handed. He's spent big money." The madam said, "That was then; this is now. You just tell him to go and spend some little money to keep your old lady and you in rice and firewood, and that'll do. Those girls in the other houses are all money trees—it's just like magic. Why does it have to be my place that's got all the bad luck? I've raised a money-losing white tiger. Every one of the seven necessities has to be seen to by my poor old self.[9] And it's to the point where I have to see to the upkeep of this bum of yours, you lousy slut! Where are my clothes and food supposed to come from? You go and tell that bum: if he's worth anything let him give me a few ounces of silver and buy you out so you can go off with him. Then I can find another girl to support me. How about that?"

Tenth said, "Mama, do you mean that or are you just kidding?" The madam knew that Li Jia had not a penny to his name, and had even pawned all his clothes. She figured he'd never be able to bring it off. So she replied, "When has your old lady ever told a lie? Of course I mean it." Tenth said, "Ma, how much money do you want from him?" The madam said, "If it were anyone else, I'd ask for a thousand or so. But I know that bum can't afford it, so I'll just ask for three hundred. Then I can go find another tart to take your place. But there's just one thing: he's got to give me the money within three days. I'll hand you over to him as soon as he hands me the cash. But if he hasn't got it within three days, then I'm not going to trouble my old self about any 'Master' this or 'Master' that—I'll cudgel his footsoles, and drive that vagrant right out the door. And when that day comes, don't you go finding fault with poor old me!"

Tenth said, "Though the young master may be a little strapped for cash here this far from home, I'm sure he can raise three hundred. But three days is such a short time. Give him ten, and you've got a deal." The madam thought to herself, "This bum has got nothing but a pair of empty hands. Even if I gave him a hundred days, where would he ever get the money? And if he can't raise the money, then no matter how shameless he may be, I'll bet he won't have the nerve to show his face at this door again. Then I can put this house back in style, and Mei won't have a thing to say about it." She answered, "For your sake, then, I'll give him ten days. But if the tenth day comes and he hasn't got the money, don't go trying to blame it on me."

Tenth said, "If he hasn't raised the money inside of ten days, then I'll bet he won't have the gall to come back here. I'm just afraid that if he gets the three hundred taels of silver, Mama may have second thoughts." The madam said, "My poor old self is now fifty-one years old, and I carefully keep the ten fast-days.[1] How should I dare to tell a lie? If you don't believe me, we can slap hands and swear on it. If I go back on my word, let me be reborn as a pig or a dog."

> The ocean's water can't be guessed in cups;
> that farcical old bawd has no goodwill.

9. Generally referring to everyday household expenses, the "seven necessities" were firewood, rice, cooking oil, salt, soybean paste, vinegar, and tea.

1. Ten days during each month when lay Buddhists were forbidden to eat meat or kill animals.

She's sure the struggling scholar's purse is dry,
and speaks of marriage gifts to trick the girl.

That night, Tenth and the young master discussed their future as they lay in bed. The young master said, "It's not that I don't want this to work out. But getting a girl's name off the courtesans' register is extremely expensive. Nothing less than a thousand taels will do the trick. My purse is empty, down to the last speck. What can I do about it?" Tenth said, "I've already got Ma to agree to only three hundred, but it's got to be raised within ten days. I know you've used up all your traveling funds, but don't you have any friends or relatives in the capital who might lend you some? If you can raise the set amount, then I shall be yours alone, and we can be spared the overbearing behavior of that evil woman." The young master said, "My relations and friends have had nothing to do with me since I began spending all my time in the pleasure quarters. Tomorrow I'll pack up my things and set out, going to each house as if to take my leave. Then I'll bring up the topic of borrowing some money for traveling expenses. If I pool it all together, perhaps I could reach that figure."

He got up and dressed, said goodbye to Tenth, and set out. Tenth said, "Be sure to be quick about it. I will be waiting here for good news." The young master said, "I need no reminding about that." He set out from the gate of the quarters and went in turn to the places of his various relatives and friends, pretending that he was setting off for home and had come to take his leave. When they heard he was headed home, they were in fact glad to hear it. But then he came to the part about lacking traveling money and hoping to borrow some. The adage has it that "the mention of money dissolves predestined ties." His friends and relatives did not respond to his pitch, and, to tell the truth, they had good reason. They thought to themselves, "Here is this Master Li, a big-spending wastrel, enchanted with high living. He's been dallying here a year or so, and his father at home is sick with fury. And today he suddenly wants to set off on his return? There is no telling if this is real or an act. And what if it should turn out that the money he collects as 'traveling expenses' ends up being paid out on whoring debts? If his father should get wind of it, he'd take our good intentions as bad ones . . . One way or another we're sure to end up on somebody's bad side, so when all is said and done, it's cleaner just to turn him down." And so they answered, "It just happens we're a little short at the moment, and unfortunately can't help you out. It's really most embarrassing. . . ." And it was the same with each and every one of them; there was not a single man of noble sentiment to agree to spot him ten or twenty.

Master Li rushed about for three days in a row without a thing to show for it. He did not dare go back to tell Tenth it was no good, so he just made equivocal replies to buy time. When the fourth day came and he still hadn't come up with a plan, he felt too embarrassed to return to the quarters. And since he'd been staying at Du Mei's place lately, he did not even have lodgings of his own. So at this point he found himself with no place to spend the night. All he could do was go to the lodgings of his townsman, the academy scholar Liu, to stay over. When Liu Yuchun saw the worry clouding the young master's face, he asked him what he had been up to. The young master told him all about how Du Tenth wanted to marry him. Yuchun shook his head, saying, "I wouldn't be so sure about that. That Du Mei is the number-one courtesan in the pleasure district. If she wanted to go straight, wouldn't there have to be a marriage gift of ten measures of pearls and a good thousand in silver? How could that madam just ask for three hundred? I bet the madam is just down on you for having no money to spend, and taking up her girl's time for nothing. She's made up a plan to get you out of her house. As for the girl herself, she's been with you for a long time, and feels too much compunction to say it outright. She knows good and well you're empty-handed. But by setting this price of three hundred taels, and giving you ten days, she makes it seem like she's doing you a favor. And if you don't have the money in ten days, you won't very well be able to show your face at their door. Even if you did, she'd make fun of you and put you down. You'd end up with a good dose of humiliation, and would natu-rally find it impossible to settle down there again. This is an old brothel trick for getting rid of unwanted guests. My good friend, I hope you'll consider carefully—don't be taken in! If you want my advice, I'd say your best plan is to make a clean break right away."

On hearing this, the young master sat a long while in silence, not knowing what to think. Yuchun continued, "My friend, make no mistake. If you really return home, the travel expenses won't come to that much, and there will still be people to help you out. But if it's three hundred you want, well then, forget ten days, in even ten months you could scarcely raise that amount. In this day and age, who do you expect will show understanding for your situation? That mist-and-flowers woman knows you've got nowhere to go to raise that kind of money, and is only telling you all this to put you in an impossible position."

The young master said, "Worthy brother, what you say is quite true." But though he said this, he was unable to fully resign himself to it in his heart. He continued as before to run about here and there looking for help—but at night he did not return to the quarters. The young master lodged for three days run-ning in the rooms of academy scholar Liu, which made six all together. When Du Tenth saw that the master had gone several days without returning, she grew quite anxious, and sent her little servant boy Number Four to go out on the streets looking for him. When Number Four went out, it just happened that he ran into Master Li. Number Four called out to him, "Brother-in-law Li, the mistress is looking for you at home." The young master felt too ashamed to go, and answered, "I haven't got time today. I'll go tomorrow." But Number Four had received strict orders from Tenth, and grabbed hold of the young master and would not let go for anything. He said, "The mistress told me to find you. You've got to come along."

Now the young master was secretly missing that whore, so there was nothing for it but to give in and follow Number Four to the quarters. When he saw Tenth, he just stood there dumbly. Tenth asked him, "How is our plan pro-gressing?" The young master began to shed tears. Tenth said, "Can it be that people have grown so unfeeling that you cannot raise the three hundred?" The young master, with tears in his eyes, said,

> "Catching tigers cannot be considered easy,
> but begging favors is what's truly hard.

"I've been rushing about for six days in a row, and haven't a penny to show for it. With this pair of empty hands I've been ashamed to see you, so these few days I have not dared come here. Today I received your command, and come bearing up under shame. It is not that I haven't tried. But human feelings have in fact come to this pass." Tenth said, "Don't let that wicked crone hear any of this. Stay here tonight, my love—I have another idea." Tenth prepared food and drink, and shared a happy banquet with the young master.

When they'd slept half the night, Tenth said, "My love, can you really not come up with even a single coin? What is to become of the plan for my future?" The young master just wept, unable to answer a single word. Around the fifth watch, it gradually grew light. Tenth said, "The padded quilt I sleep on contains a hundred fifty taels in odd change. This is my private savings. My love, you may take it. I will take care of half of the three hundred, and you can take care of the other half. That should make things easier. But there are only four days left before our time is up. Be sure not to be late."

Tenth got up and gave the quilt to the young master, who was pleased beyond his wildest expectations. He called the servant boy to take the quilt away and took his leave. He went straight to Liu Yuchun's place, and told him all that had happened the night before. When they opened up the quilt and looked inside, there were odd coins wrapped inside the stuffing. When they took them to exchange, the amount really did come out to one hundred and fifty taels. Yuchun said, astounded, "This is truly a woman with sincere intentions. Since she has real feeling, she should not be let down. I will see to this on your behalf." The young master said, "If our dream is fulfilled, I promise not to forget you."

Then Liu Yuchun, leaving Master Li at his place, set out himself to borrow money. Within two days, he had put together the one hundred and fifty taels, and handed them over the master, saying, "It was not for your sake that I borrowed this money, but rather because I am moved by the sincere feeling of Du Tenth."

When Li Jia had the three hundred in hand, it was like a gift dropped from Heaven, and he went off, beaming with joy, to see Tenth. It was only the ninth day, so he had not even used all ten of the allotted days. Tenth asked him, "A few days ago you had a hard time borrowing even the least bit. How is it that now you have suddenly got a hundred fifty taels?" The young master related to her the business with academy scholar Liu. Tenth raised her hands to her forehead, saying, "It is all thanks to the efforts of Mr. Liu that our desires have been fulfilled." The two of them were overcome with happiness, and spent another evening in the quarters.

The next day, Tenth rose early and said to Li Jia, "Once I've handed over this silver, I will be able to follow you. We should prepare the necessary carriages and boats. I have recently borrowed twenty taels of white silver, which you may take to cover our traveling expenses." The young master had just then been worrying that he had no source of traveling money, but had not dared speak of it. When he received this money, he was extremely happy. Before they'd done speaking, the madam came knocking at the door, saying, "Mei, today is the tenth day." When the master heard her call, he opened the door and asked her in, saying, "We have benefited from your kindness, and were just going to invite you here." With this he put the three hundred taels on the table.

The madam had not expected the young master to have money, and stood silently, her expression suddenly changing. She seemed to have it in mind to go back on her promise. Tenth said, "I have been in Mama's house for eight years, and the gold and treasures I have brought in are nothing short of a thousand talents. The happy occasion of my reformation today was granted from Mama's own lips. There is not one jot lacking of the three hundred taels, nor have we passed the time limit. If Mama should go back on her word and prevent us, my husband will take the silver away, and I will make an end of myself this very instant. I fear that then you will have lost both person and profit, and it will be too late for regrets." The madam had no reply to make to this, and pondered it over for a while to herself. In the end, all she could do was bring out a scale to weigh out the silver. She said, "Since it has come to this, I guess I won't be able to stop you. But if you mean to go then go at once. Don't imagine you'll take one bit of your clothes and jewelry along with you."

When she'd done saying this, she pushed the young master and Tenth out the chamber door, found a lock, and locked it right up. It was around November at this time, and Tenth, who had just got out of bed, had not even had time to dress. Wearing the old robe she happened to have on at the time, she bowed twice to her "Mama." Master Li also made a bow. With this they departed, husband and wife, from the door of that old crone.

> The carp slips off the iron hook
> and glides off without looking back.

The young master asked Tenth to wait up a moment. "I will go and call a sedan chair to carry you. For the time being we can go to Liu Rongqing's lodgings, and make further plans from there." Tenth said, "All my sisters in the quarters have stood by me through thick and thin. By rights I should go and take my leave of them. What's more it was from them that I got the loan of that traveling money. It would not do to go without thanking them." Thereupon she went with the young master to the homes of all her sisters to thank them and to take leave of them. Of the sisters it was Xie Yuelang and Xu Susu who lived closest by, and they were also on especially good terms with Tenth. Tenth went first to Xie Yuelang's house. When Yuelang saw Tenth going about in a bare hairknot and old worn robe, she asked in bewilderment what had happened. Tenth told her the whole story, and led Li Jia in to see her. Tenth pointed to Yuelang, saying, "The travel money I received the other day was the loan of this elder sister. My lord ought to thank her." Li Jia bowed again and again. Then Yuelang asked Tenth to dress, going in the meanwhile to invite over Xu Susu.

When Tenth had done making herself up, the two beauties Xie and Xu brought out their whole store—emerald brooches and gold bracelets, jade hairpins and precious earrings, patterned skirts and brocade-sleeved blouses, phoenix sashes and embroidered slippers, and they did up Tenth all over again, so that she looked like a completely different person. They also prepared wine for a celebratory banquet. Yuelang gave up her own chamber to Li Jia and Du Mei to spend the night.

The next day, they had another big banquet and invited all the sisters from the quarters. None of those who were good friends with Tenth failed to appear, and they all drank to the health and happiness of bride and groom. With pipes and strings, song and dance, each made the most of her talents, intent on making it a joyful gathering. They kept at it right up until midnight. Then Tenth thanked each of the sisters in turn. The assembled sisters said, "Tenth is commander in the legion of glamour. She is now setting out with her man, and we will have no more chance of seeing her. On the day you choose to leave for good, we sisters should once more come to see you off." Yuelang said to them, "When the time is fixed, I will come and notify you. Our sister will be journeying hundreds of miles over hill and dale along with her husband. Yet her savings are scanty, and she is not in the least prepared. This is a matter that should concern all of us. We should work together to ensure that our sister does not have to worry about being left without resources." All the sisters voiced their assent to this and went their separate ways.

That evening, the master and Tenth lodged once more at the Xie house. At the fifth watch, Tenth said to the young master, "After this departure of ours, where will we settle? Have you come up with some solid plan?" The master said, "My aged father is in the height of rage. If he learns that I've returned home along with a prostitute as my wife, he is sure to make trouble, and I may end up more trouble than help to you. I've thought over this again and again, and I still have no perfect plan." Tenth said, "How could the Heaven-ordained relation of father and son be permanently cut off? But since it is not a good idea to provoke him by a sudden confrontation, it would be better to take up temporary residence in the scenic region of Suzhou and Hangzhou. You can return first, and ask friends and relatives to intercede on your behalf before your reverend father and convince him to relent. Then you can come and take me home with you. In this way all will be well on both sides." The young master said, "This is well said."

The next day the two set out, taking leave of Xie Yuelang, and went for a time to the lodgings of academy scholar Liu to get their luggage ready. When Du Tenth saw Liu Yuchun, she prostrated herself before him and thanked him for the kind service which had allowed things to work out. "On some future day I swear that we will worthily repay your kindness." Yuchun hurriedly returned her bow, saying, "You were stirred to true love for your favorite, and did not change your feelings on account of poverty. This makes you a hero among women. All your servant has done amounts to 'blowing a flame along with the wind'—really, what need is there to mention my insignificant efforts!"

The three of them spent another day drinking. The next morning, they selected an auspicious day for their departure and hired the necessary sedan chairs and horses. Tenth once more dispatched her servant boy to take a message to say goodbye to Xie Yuelang. When it came time to leave, bearers and palanquins began arriving in great numbers. It was Xie Yuelang and Xu Susu, who had brought along all the sisters to say goodbye. Yuelang said, "Tenth sister is following her husband into distant parts, yet their traveling purse is barren. We are by no means able to put aside our sisterly concern, and have raised a meager sum among ourselves. Tenth sister, you may take it under your care. It may be that in your long journey you fall short, and even this may be of some small use." When she had done speaking, she commanded the others to bring forward a gold-inlaid stationery box, which was locked up most securely so that there was no guessing what it might contain. Tenth neither refused it nor opened it to look inside. All she did was to thank them earnestly. In a short while carriage and horses were in readiness, and the attendant urged them to set out at once. Academy scholar Liu poured out three cups of parting wine, and saw them off as far as the outside of Chongwen Gate, along with the troop of beauties. One by one they tearfully took their leave. Truly,

> None can predict a future meeting date
> This moment of parting is most hard to bear.

Now when Master Li and Du Tenth had traveled as far as the Lu Canal,[2] they left the land and took to boats. By good luck they were able to take advantage of the envoy boat from Guazhou, which was about to set out on its return journey. They agreed on a price and reserved a cabin. When it came time to board, Master Li's purse had not the least bit of cash left in it. Now you may be asking, if Du Tenth gave the young master twenty taels of silver, how came it that he suddenly had nothing left? Well, the young master had been whoring in the quarters till his clothes were all bedraggled. When he got his hands on some money, he couldn't help but go to the pawnbroker's to redeem some clothes, and have a set of quilts and bedding made. What was left over was just enough to cover the carriage and horses.

Just as the young master was growing worried, Tenth said, "My husband, don't be troubled. The collection made by all my sisters will surely help us out." With this, she took out the key and opened up the case. The young master, who was standing to one side, felt ashamed, and did not venture to peek at what was inside the box. Tenth pulled out a red silk pouch and tossed it onto the table, saying, "Why don't you open that up and take a look?" The young master lifted it up in his hand and felt that it was quite heavy. When he opened it up and took a look, he saw it was all white silver, together all of fifty taels. Tenth locked up the box once more without saying what else might be inside. She merely told the young master, "Thanks to the noble feelings of all my sisters, we will not only lack nothing on our journey, but there should be a little something to help with our household expenses while we pass the time in the South." The young master, startled and pleased all at once, said, "If I had not encountered you, my dear benefactress, I, Li Jia, would have been left without even a place to be buried. I will never dare forget this debt of gratitude as long as I live." From this time on, whenever their talk turned to events of the past, the young master would always be moved to tears, and Tenth would try gently to console him. And so they traveled on.

Before they knew it, they had reached Guazhou, and the big boat moored at the bank. The young master hired another boat, loaded their luggage onto it, and arranged that they should set out across the river at dawn. It was now around the beginning of January, and the moon was as bright as water as the young master and Tenth sat at the bow of the boat. The young master said, "Ever since we left the capital gate we've been penned up in one little cabin with people all around us, and have been unable to speak freely. Now we've got this whole boat to ourselves, and have no further cause for restraint. Furthermore, we've left the North behind us and are just now drawing near Jiangnan. It is fitting that we should set ourselves at ease and drink as much as we please, so as to relieve our cooped-up feelings. Dear benefactress, what do you say to

2. Northern section of the Grand Canal, which linked the northern and mid-southern regions of China.

that?" Tenth said, "I have grown long unused to conversation and laughter, and I share this feeling of yours. That you should speak of it now is proof of our fellow nature."

Then the young master brought out drinking vessels and arrayed them on the deck, and spread out a felt mat for the two of them to sit on. The cups passed back and forth between them. When they were half-giddy with the wine, the young master, clutching his cup, said to Tenth, "Dear benefactress, your wondrous voice was counted finest among the quarters at the time when my unworthy self first made your acquaintance. Each time I heard one of your incomparable songs, I was unable to restrain the flight of my soul. Much has gone awry since then, and both of us have long been anxious and ill at ease. The simurgh's cry and the phoenix's song have long been silent. Now on this clear river under the bright moon, in the still of the night with no one else to hear, will you deign to sing me a song?"

Tenth as well felt a sudden stirring, and she unleashed her voice and varied her tone, tapping out the time with a fan. Crooning and murmuring, she sang from the scene "The Exam Champion Holds the Cup to Chanjuan" from the opera *Bowing to Moon Pavilion* by the Yuan writer Shi Junmei, to the tune of "Little Red Peach." Truly,

> The tone flies up to the Milky Way—clouds stop in their tracks;
> the echo sinks into the deep pool—fish come up to play.

Now on a neighboring boat there was a young man surnamed Sun, named Fu, with the cognomen Shanlai, who was a native of Xin'an County in Huizhou. His family had been in the salt trade at Yangzhou for generations and had amassed an immense fortune. Sun Fu was just twenty years old at this time, and was also a fellow of the Nanjing Imperial Academy. He was glamorous by nature, accustomed to buying smiles in the "blue houses," seeking happiness in rouge and powder just as if on a jaunt to enjoy breeze and moonlight. He was a commander in the legion of loverboys. Well, coincidences will happen, and it came about that on that evening he was also moored at the ferry dock at Guazhou, drinking alone in boredom. Suddenly he heard the bright sound of a singing voice—chanting phoenix and piping simurgh could not compare to it in beauty. He rose and stood at the prow, listening raptly for a while.

Soon he divined that the sound was coming from the neighboring boat. Just as he was making ready to inquire, the resounding tones grew suddenly still. Thereupon he dispatched a servant to ask the boatmen what it was. All they knew was that the boat had been hired by his excellency Li, but they did not know the background of the singer. Sun Fu thought to himself, "This singer is certainly not of respectable background. Now, how can I get a look at her?" He mused over this, staying awake all night. When he'd stuck it out to the fifth watch, he suddenly heard the wind on the river kicking up fiercely. By dawn the sky was packed with dusky clouds, and snow swirled wildly about. How can we know about this scene? There is a poem bearing witness:

> A thousand hills wiped clean of clouds and trees;
> the tracks on countless human paths swept clear.

> In poncho and rainhat, an old man on a skiff
> fishes alone in the snow of the cold river.[3]

With this snowstorm enveloping the ford, the boats were unable to set out. Sun Fu commanded his helmsman to move the boat, mooring it by the side of Li Jia's boat. Sun Fu, in ermine cap and foxfur coat, opened the window and looked out, pretending to be enjoying the snowy scene. Du Tenth had just then finished washing. With her slender jade white hands, she lifted up the short curtain at the side of the boat and emptied the washbasin into the river. Her powdered face shone out for a moment, and Sun Fu got a peek. Sure enough, she was a heavenly beauty, and his soul was shaken and his heart went wild. He stared intently at the spot, waiting for another chance to see her, but he had no such luck. He sat long in a funk, and then loudly chanted these two lines of Scholar Gao's[4] "Poem of Plum Blossoms":

> Snow fills the mountain slopes, the recluse lies at ease;
> moonlight shines beneath the forest's eaves—the lovely one
> approaches.

When Li Jia heard someone chanting poetry in the neighboring boat, he stretched his head out of the cabin to see who it was. And with this he fell right into Sun Fu's trap. Sun Fu was chanting that poem precisely in order to entice Master Li to poke his head out, so there would be a chance to start up a conversation. Right away Sun raised his hand in greeting and asked, "Respected friend, what is your surname and given name?" Master Li told him his name and native place, and of course it would not do not to ask Sun Fu in turn. Sun Fu introduced himself as well. Then they exchanged some idle talk of the academy, gradually growing more cordial as they chatted. Then Sun Fu said, "This snowstorm which has delayed our boats was Heaven's way of granting me the chance to meet you—this is truly a stroke of good fortune for me! Lodging on board a boat is tiresome and monotonous. It is my sincere wish to go ashore with you for a drink in the wineshop, so as to receive some small portion of your wise instruction. I earnestly beg that you not refuse me!" The young master said, "We have met like drifting duckweed on the water. What right have I to put you to such trouble?" Sun Fu said, "What can you possibly mean? 'Within the four seas all are brothers.'"[5]

He barked out an order to the boatmen to leap over and to the servant boy to hold open an umbrella and receive the young master on board his boat. Sun Fu came right up to the bow of his boat to greet him. Then, making room for the young master to lead the way, Sun followed up as they went ashore. Before they'd walked more than a few steps, they came upon a wineshop. The two walked upstairs and sought out a clean spot beside the window. The steward laid out wine and snacks before them. Sun Fu raised his cup and urged Master

---

3. With minor alterations, this is a poem by the Tang poet Liu Zongyuan (773–819).
4. A poet of the early Ming Dynasty, under

which Feng Menglong lived.
5. Well-known saying from the Confucian *Analects*.

Li not to stand on ceremony, and the two of them sat drinking and enjoying the snowy scene. First they exchanged a few polite commonplaces, but soon the conversation turned toward affairs of the heart. The two of them were both men of the world, and found in each other sympathetic listeners.

As their talk became relaxed and unrestrained, they grew ever more confidential. Sun Fu sent away all the attendants and asked in a low voice, "Who was the clear-voiced singer on your boat last night?" Li Jia was just then anxious to play the man of the world, and he blurted out, "That was Du Tenth, the famous courtesan from Beijing." Sun Fu said, "If she is a sister from the quarters, how is it she has become part of your household?" Then the young master told all about how he first met Du Tenth, how they became lovers, and how later she wanted to marry him and how he borrowed money to win her, from beginning to end in full detail.

Sun Fu said, "My dear friend, your return home with this beauty is certainly a happy event. What I wonder is, will your family be able to accept her?" The young master said, "My humble mate is no cause for concern. What worries me is my old father, who is by nature strict and unyielding. This is still causing me some hesitation." Sun Fu, adapting his strategy to the circumstances, asked, "If you fear your reverend father may not accept her, where do you plan to settle this lovely whom you are escorting? Have you spoken to her of this and made plans together?" The young master wrinkled up his brows and answered, "I have in fact discussed this matter with my unworthy consort." Sun Fu asked with a smile, "Surely your esteemed pet has a splendid strategem." The young master said, "It is her intention to take up temporary residence in Suzhou or Hangzhou, to linger for a while among the hills and lakes. She would have me return first and ask relations and friends to put things delicately before the head of my family. At such time as he shall change his ire to pleasure, we will consider how we may best return. But what do you make of this?"

Sun Fu sat murmuring to himself for a while, and put on an anxious expression. He said, "I made your acquaintance only a short time ago. If I presume on such a brief friendship to speak frankly to you, I truly fear that you will be offended." The young master said, "I find myself just now in need of your wise instruction. Why need you stand on ceremony like this?" Sun Fu said, "Your esteemed parent holds the keys of the provincial government, and is sure to be strict about maintaining propriety in the affairs of his household. From the beginning, he has been displeased that you frequented houses of ill fame. How then can he be expected to accept your marriage to an unchaste woman? Furthermore, which of your noble friends and relations will not be solicitous of the wishes of your esteemed parent? If you vainly ask them for favors, they are sure to refuse. And even supposing that some tactless one among them puts in a word on your behalf, once he sees that your esteemed parent does not mean to give in, he will surely change his tune. You will find yourself unable either to restore harmony to your family or to answer to your esteemed pet. Even whiling away the time amid the scenery of hills and lakes is no long-term solution. If some day your savings should run out, will you not be left with nowhere to turn?"

The young master knew that all he had left was the fifty taels of silver, and by now even that had largely been spent. When he heard this part about being left with no place to turn, he unconsciously began nodding his assent. Sun Fu continued, "I have one thing further to say. Will you indulge me by listening?" The young master said, "You are too kind. I beg you say everything that is on your mind." Sun Fu said, "'Distant relations should not come between close ones.' On second thought, I think it is better not to say it." The young master said, "Just say it, what harm can there be in that?" Sun Fu said, "Of old it has been said, 'woman's nature is water, devoid of constancy.' How much more so of the league of mist and flowers, who lack truth and abound in artifice? Given that she is a famed courtesan of the pleasure districts, she must have acquaintances everywhere under the sun. It may just be that she has a previous engagement in the South, and is making use of you to bring her there, to run off with someone else." The young master said, "As for that, I really don't think that that is the case." Sun Fu said, "Even if it isn't, the young men of Jiangnan are champion womanizers. If you keep such a lovely alone there, it is hard to be sure there won't be some 'fence-climbing and wall-tunneling.' And if you take her along home with you, it is certain you will further inflame your esteemed parent's anger against you. There really seems to be no good way out of your present situation. Moreover, the relation of father and son is sanctioned by Heaven, and is by no means to be abrogated. If you offend your father on account of a concubine, if you abandon your family due to a prostitute, everyone in the world will surely agree that you are a reckless and outlandish person. In the future your wife will not treat you as a husband, your brother will not treat you as brother, and your colleagues will not treat you as a colleague. How will you find a place to stand between Heaven and Earth? My friend, you really cannot but consider this carefully."

When the young master heard all this, he was dazed and at a loss for words. He edged his seat closer and asked, "As you see it, what advice would you give me?" Sun Fu said, "Your servant has one plan which could be most advantageous. I only fear that you, enamored as you are of the joys of pillow and mat, will not necessarily be able to carry it out, in which case it would be a mere waste of words to tell you." The young master said, "If you have a plan that can allow me once more to know the joy of a harmonious family, you are truly my benefactor. What need have you to be fearful of telling me?" Sun Fu said, "You have been roaming away from home for over a year, and your stern parent has become enraged. Chamber and tower are set at odds. Imagining myself in your position, it seems this must be a time when there can be no peace of mind in sleep or at table. However, the cause of your esteemed parent's anger with you is nothing more than your fondness for the land of 'flowers and willows,' for which you spend money like dirt. You must seem sure to turn out a homeless wastrel, and thus not suited to inherit the family fortune. To go home empty-handed at such a time would be just the thing to set him off. But if you are willing to set aside the affections of quilt and mattress, and act decisively when opportunity presents itself, I would be willing to present you with a thousand taels. With these thousand taels to placate your esteemed parent, you can claim that you kept to your chambers at the capital and have not wasted the least bit. Your esteemed parent is sure to believe this. From then on your family will be at peace, and there should be no further grumbling. In no time at all you could change disaster into good fortune. Please think this over carefully. It is not that I am covetous of the charms of the lovely one. The truth is that I am eager to give some small expression of my devotion to your welfare."

Now Li Jia had always been a man with no backbone who, when all was said and done, was terrified of his dad. Sun Fu's little talk went right to the heart of his fears. He rose and bowed, saying, "On hearing this instruction from you, the scales have fallen from my eyes. But my little consort has stood by me through a journey of hundreds of miles; I cannot in justice cut her off all at once. Allow me to return and discuss it with her. When I have received her earnest assent, I will come back and present my reply." Sun Fu said, "When you talk to her, you ought to put it delicately. But if she is really motivated by sincere loyalty to you, she's sure to be unwilling to cause father and son to split. She'll certainly do her part to bring about your successful return home."

The two of them drank a while longer, and when the wind settled and the snow stopped, it was already quite late. Sun Fu told his servant boy to settle the bill, and he led the young master by the hand down toward the boats. Truly,

> With strangers, say a third of what you think;
> don't throw out all your heart's designs at once.

Now we turn to Du Tenth in the boat. She set out wine and dainties, meaning to share a small banquet with the young master. When he failed to return all day, she trimmed a lamp and sat up waiting for him. When the young master came aboard, Tenth rose to greet him. He had a flustered expression and seemed to have something unhappy on his mind, so she poured out a full cup of warm wine and tried to console him. But the young master shook his head and refused to drink. Without uttering a single word, he went right to bed alone and lay down. Tenth was worried by this, and, after gathering up the cups and trays, she came and helped Master Li undress and make ready to sleep. She asked him, "What has happened that has put you in such a gloomy mood?" The young master just sighed, still not opening his mouth to speak. She asked him the same thing three or four times, but in the end she noticed he had already nodded off. Tenth could not resolve it in her mind, and sat at the side of the bed, unable to sleep.

In the middle of the night, the young master woke up and sighed once more. Tenth said, "My lord, what difficult matter do you have in your mind, that you sigh so?" The young master sat up, clutching the blankets about him, and made as if to speak, but stopped short several times. And then streams of tears began running down his cheeks. Tenth clasped the young master in her bosom and spoke softly to comfort him, saying, "You and I have been lovers for two years now, and we have held out to this day through innumerable trials and reversals, and every manner of difficulty. But through all the hundreds of miles of our journey together I have never seen you grieve like this. Now we are preparing to cross the river, on the verge of a new lifetime of happiness. How is it that you instead grow sad and troubled? There must surely be some reason. Husband and wife share all equally between them, in life and death. If any problem arises it can surely be talked over. Do not be afraid to say whatever is on your mind."

The young master, thus repeatedly egged on, could not hold out, and at last said tearfully, "I was left destitute and without recourse at the ends of the earth. I undeservingly received your forbearing indulgence, and you consented to follow me to this place. It is truly an incomparable favor that you have done me.

But I have pondered it over and over; my father, in his position of local prominence, is subject to strict standards of propriety. Furthermore, he himself is stern and inflexible by nature. I fear that if I add to his ire, he is sure to run me out of the house. If you and I are forced to wander rootlessly, where shall we come to rest? The joys of husband and wife will be hard to preserve intact, while the relation of father and son will be broken. During the day, I received an invitation to drink from my new friend Mr. Sun of Xin'an. He considered this problem on my behalf . . . yet my poor heart feels as if it is being cut!"

Tenth said in great alarm, "What is it you mean to do?" The young master said, "Being as I was personally involved in the situation, I was unable to grasp it clearly. Now my friend Sun has devised a plan for me which seems quite good. My only fear is that you, my love, will not give your assent to it." Tenth said, "Who is this friend Sun? If the plan is a good one, what can there be against following it?" The young master said, "My friend Sun is named Fu, a salt merchant from Xin'an. He is a stylish young fellow. During the night he heard the clear tones of your voice, and thus inquired about you. I told him your background, as well as the reasons making my return home difficult. He has it in mind to take you in for one thousand taels. With that thousand taels I will have a pretext on which to call on my parents, and you, my dear benefactress, will also have someone to rely on. But I cannot bear to give up the affection I feel for you. It is for this reason that I am grieved and weep." When he had said this his tears fell like rain.

Tenth removed her hands from him and laughed coldly, saying, "The man who devised this plan for you is truly a great hero. The fortune of the thousand taels will enable you to restore your position in your family, and I will go to another man so as not to be a burden to you. 'Originating in feeling and stopping in accordance with propriety'[6]—truly this can be called a strategy with advantage on all sides. Where are the thousand taels?" The young master dried his tears and said, "Since I had not received your approval, the money has not yet been exchanged. It is still over at his boat." Tenth said, "Go first thing in the morning to settle it with him. You mustn't let this opportunity slip by. But a thousand taels of silver is a serious matter. You must be sure to have it counted out in full and securely in your hands before I go over to his boat—do not fall victim to an unscrupulous trader." By this time it was nearly the fourth watch, and Tenth got up and lit a lamp and made herself up, saying, "Today's dressing is for the purpose of 'welcoming the new and seeing off the old.' It's no ordinary occasion."

Having said this, she attentively made herself up with powder and perfume. In her ornate bracelets and embroidered jacket, she looked splendid. A fragrant breeze seemed to play about her, and she radiated a brilliance that dazzled all who saw her. By the time she was done dressing, it was just beginning to grow light outside. Sun Fu's servant boy came to the bow of their boat to await news. Tenth looked in at the young master, smiling as though pleased with how things were going, and urged him to go and give his reply, and to quickly count out the silver in full. The young master went in person to Sun Fu's boat, and

---

6. Direct quotation from the "Great Preface" to the *Classic of Poetry*, which shows how Du can use her erudition for sarcastic purposes.

replied that he agreed to everything. Sun Fu said, "Counting out the silver is not a problem. But I would like to have the lovely's make-up stand as security." The young master went back once more to pass this reply on to Tenth. She pointed to the gold-inlaid stationery box, saying, "Go on and take it."

Sun Fu was greatly pleased. He then took one thousand taels of white silver, and sent it off to the young master's boat. Tenth counted it out herself and found to that it was sufficient in both purity and amount, without the least error. Thereupon she grasped the gunwale and waved to Sun Fu, and as soon as Sun Fu saw her, his soul flew out of him. Tenth opened her crimson lips, exposing gleaming teeth, saying, "Please send back that box I sent over just now. In it are some travel documents of Master Li's which should be picked out and returned to him." Sun Fu already regarded Tenth as a turtle in his trap, and without hesitation ordered his servant to carry that gold-inlaid stationery box right over and place it at the prow of Li Jia's boat. Tenth took out the key and opened the lock. Inside the box were many small drawers. Tenth asked the young master to pull out the first drawer to look, and there was all kingfisher feathers and bright pendants, jade hairpins and jeweled earrings filling it up inside, probably worth several hundred taels.

Tenth threw it all right into the river. Li Jia and Sun Fu and the rest of the people on the boats were all astonished. She then told the young master to open another drawer. It was filled with jade whistles and golden pipes. He opened another drawer full of antique knicknacks of ancient jade and purple gold, probably worth several thousand. Tenth threw all this into the great river. People began gathering on the bank, until they packed the entire shoreline. They said with one voice, "What a shame!" and were left standing there, wondering what it was all about.

Finally Li Jia opened one more drawer. Inside this drawer there was another box. When he opened the box and looked, there were handfuls of priceless pearls, and all sorts of sapphires, cat's-eyes, and rare treasures such as they had never seen before, There was no guessing at their worth. The crowd of people all cheered lustily, and the noise of their commotion was like thunder. Tenth made as if to throw these things as well into the river. In that instant Li Jia was overcome with remorse. He clasped Tenth and wailed aloud. Then Sun Fu came over as well and tried to reason with her. Tenth pushed the young master to one side and cursed Sun Fu, saying, "Mr. Li and I have endured every kind of hardship. It was no easy thing for us to come this far. But you with your lecherous intentions hatched a cunning plot that has dissolved all our destined life together in a single day, and destroyed the love and affection between us. You are my sworn enemy. If I have consciousness after death, I swear I will take my grievance against you to the clear-eyed gods. And you dream of sharing the joy of pillow and mat with me!"

Then she said to Li Jia, "I languished in a fallen life for several years, during which time I amassed some private savings. This was meant as a provision against old age. I did not intend for those mountain vows and ocean oaths that we exchanged to be broken even in our declining years. That day as we were leaving the capital, I used the pretext of my sisters' parting gifts to store these hundred treasures in this box. There is no less than ten thousand taels here. I meant to use this to set you up in such style that you could return to see your parents without shame. Perhaps they might have taken pity on me for my sincerity and allowed me to assist your wife in the duties of the household, so that I could live out my life relying on you, with no regrets to my dying day. How could I have guessed that your trust in me was so shallow that you could be confused by groundless counsel? You have abandoned me at midjourney and betrayed my earnest heart. Today, before these many eyes, I open this box to reveal its contents, so that you may learn that a thousand taels is no great thing. In my jewel case there is true jade; I regret that you lack eyes in your head to see it. Born in an ill-fated hour, I fell into the bonds of a shameful life. And just as I made good my escape, I have been cast aside once more. Today every person who has ears and eyes can witness that it is not I who have betrayed you, but rather you who have betrayed me!"

At this the crowd that had gathered to watch all shed tears, every last one of them, and they all cursed Master Li for a heartless deceiver. The young master was both ashamed and grieved. He wept with remorse, and was just beginning to beg for her forgiveness when, clutching the treasure box, she plunged right into the heart of the river. The crowd cried out in alarm for someone to save her. But all that could be seen were dark clouds over the river, and the restless waves—there was no trace of her. Alas, a famed courtesan, beautiful as flowers or jade, left all at once to be entombed in fishes' bellies!

> The three souls settle to the water-kingdom's trackless depths;
> the seven spirits set off on the distant road of darkness.

At the time, the people who were watching gnashed their teeth in fury, climbing over one another in their desire to thrash Li Jia and Sun Fu, which startled these two so badly they didn't know what to do. They hurriedly called out to the boatmen to set out, and went off in separate directions. Li Jia sat in his boat looking at the thousand taels and thinking back on Tenth, brooding day in and day out on his shame. These oppressive feelings eventually drove him crazy, and he never recovered as long as he lived. As for Sun Fu, after the shock of that day he fell ill and was bedridden for over a month. All day he would see Du Tenth beside him, cursing him. In time, he died. People said it was revenge exacted from the depths of the river.

And now we speak of that Liu Yuchun. When his stint in the academy at the capital was up, he packed up his things to return home, and moored at Guabu. He happened to drop a bronze washbasin in the river as he was washing his face over the water, and he sought out a fisherman to fish it up with his net. When the net came out, what was inside was a little case. Yuchun opened the case to look, and in it were bright pearls and rare treasures, precious things of inestimable price. Yuchun richly rewarded the fisherman, and kept the things by his bedside to play with them. That night in a dream he saw a woman out in the river, striding toward him over the waves. When he looked closely, it was Du Tenth. She approached him and greeted him, and complained to him of Mr. Li's unfeeling behavior. She also said, "I was the recipient of your gracious assistance, when you helped us out with that hundred and fifty taels. I originally meant to seek out a way to repay you when we came to the end of our journey. Little did I know that there was to be no constancy from beginning to end. Yet I often bear your noble favor in mind, unable to forget it. This morning I presented you a small case by way of the fisherman as a small token of my heartfelt thanks. From this time on, we shall never meet." When she had done speaking, he awoke all at once in alarm. Only then did he realize that Tenth had died, and he sighed with pity for several days.

Those who later assessed the merits of this case felt that Sun Fu, who thought nothing of throwing away a thousand taels in a plot to steal away a lovely woman, was certainly no gentleman, while Li Jia, who failed to recognize Du Tenth's sincere devotion, was a vulgar person not even worth talking about. But most of all they wondered why a rare hero among women like Tenth could not find a mate worthy of her, to ride away together on a Qin Terrace phoenix.[7] Yet she mistakenly took up with Master Li, casting bright pearls and lovely jade before a blind man. The result was that gratitude was made enmity, and their ten thousand feelings of affection were changed to flowing water. This is most pitifull A poem lamenting this event says:

> Do not talk idly of romance if you don't know the game;
> a world is hidden there within love's name.
> If one knew all of love that was in love to know,
> the epithet "romantic" should be thought no cause for shame.

7. An image of romantic happiness, this is a reference to the story of Xiao Shi and Nong Yu, daughter of Duke Mu of the state of Qin. Xiao Shi was an expert player of the *xiao*, a whistle-like instrument, and could imitate the call of phoenixes. Eventually a phoenix descended to the couple at the terrace that Duke Mu built for them and carried them off to Heaven.

CAO XUEQIN
ca. 1715–1763

Of the world's great novels perhaps only **Don Quixote** rivals *The Story of the Stone* as the embodiment of a modern nation's cultural identity, much as the epic once embodied cultural identity in the ancient world. For Chinese readers of the past two centuries, *The Story of the Stone* (also known as *The Dream of the Red Chamber*) has come to represent the best and worst of traditional China in its final phase. It is the story of an extended family, centered around its women, maids, and outside relations, that asks tantalizing questions about the nature of love and lust, the differences between male and female sensibilities, the corrupting effects of money and power, and the reality of truth and illusion. Even after the twentieth century, a century of war, revolution, and social experiment that saw the dissolution of the traditional extended family, *The Story of the Stone* has retained its power to move people's hearts and minds. It is generally considered the greatest Chinese novel of all time.

THE CAO CLAN AND CAO XUEQIN

Cao Xueqin came from a Han Chinese family, the dominant ethnic group in China, but his ancestors had been captured and forced into service by the Manchus, a people from the northeastern border of the Ming Empire (1368–1644), who had conquered China and set up their own Chinese-style Manchu empire, the Qing (1644–1911). Having fought on the victors' side certainly added to the family's fortunes with the first Qing emperors, and several generations of the Cao family served in a prominent and lucrative official position as Imperial Textile Commissioner in Nanjing, the old southern capital. Given the fame of the Cao family, it is surprising how little we know about Cao Xueqin's life. We do know of the sudden demise of the family when Cao was in his teens. A new emperor suddenly confiscated their opulent mansion and properties, probably due to political intrigues. The family was reduced to poverty and forced to relocate to Beijing. Cao Xueqin may have passed a low-level civil service examination and served in minor offices. Between 1740 and 1750 he was at work on *The Story of the Stone*, and toward the end of his life he lived in the suburbs of Beijing, struggling to support himself by selling his paintings—painting being a typical pastime of Chinese literati and writers.

THE ORIGIN OF
THE STORY OF THE STONE

The novel itself has a peculiar genesis. The first eighty chapters are the work of Cao Xueqin, who probably wrote the novel, in at least five drafts, between 1740 and 1750. There is another figure in the process of the novel's composition, however, someone who used the pseudonym "Red Inkstone" (or more properly "He of the Red Inkstone Studio") and who added commentary and made corrections to the manuscript. He was obviously a close friend or relative of Cao Xueqin and his comments suggest that the characters in the main portion of the novel are based on real people. This remark and the lack of information about Cao's life has inspired scholars and lovers of *The Story of the Stone* to identify historical figures and events in the novel. Biographical readings of the novel are often far-fetched and clearly born from the desire to get an inch closer to the masterful mind behind this epic novel. Still, the demise of Cao's own family in young age certainly resonates with the novel's minute chronicling of a grand family's glory and doom.

The novel was unfinished when Cao died and he probably never intended it for publication. But it did circulate widely in Beijing in manuscript copies, whose many variations show a complex process of revision. One version of the manuscript came into the hands of the writer Gao E (ca. 1740–ca. 1815), who probably completed the story by adding another forty chapters, finally publishing a full 120–chapter version in 1791, about a half century after Cao Xueqin had begun to write it. Due to the supreme status of *The Story of the Stone* and its complicated textual history, the novel has given birth to a separate field in Chinese literary studies. The transformations of the novel in its manuscript versions, the role of the mysterious Red Inkstone (and of another early commentator who calls himself "Odd Tablet"), and the relation of the characters to Cao's life are questions that continue to engage professional and amateur scholars of "Redology" or "Red Studies" (named after the novel's alternative title).

THE WORLDS OF
THE STORY OF THE STONE

Chinese novels are, as a rule, very long, and *The Story of the Stone* is longer than most, taking up five substantial volumes in its complete English translation. The narrative is impossible to summarize and difficult to excerpt. It has a cast of about four hundred characters, both major and minor, who appear and disappear in intricately interwoven incidents and interspersed sequences of episodes. The novel's opulent cast of characters plays out its social dramas in equally opulent surroundings. The daily life in the Jia household is spent with birthday parties, poetry contests, opera performances, and artistic pastimes, and these aristocratic pursuits are captured in a vocabulary of luxurious abundance, detailing the charms of buildings, the exotic recipes of expensive medicines, the texture of exquisite clothes, makeup, and features of sophisticated landscape gardening.

This ornate world of splendor that is described in lovingly realist detail and fills a large part of the novel comes, literally, out of nowhere, out of the cosmic void. As the title tells us, the novel is the story of a magical and conscious stone, the one block left over when the goddess Nü-wa repaired the damaged vault of the sky in the mythic past. Transported into the mortal world by a pair of priests, a Buddhist and a Daoist, the stone is destined to find enlightenment by suffering the pains of love, loss, and disillusion as a human being. It does so when it is incarnated as the sole legitimate male heir of the powerful household of the Jias, which is about to pass from the height of prosperity into decline. The novel unfolds in an unnamed city, which blends features of Beijing and Nanjing. Miraculously, the baby is born with an inscribed piece of jade in his mouth, from which he is given his name Baoyu ("Precious Jade") and which he wears always. In a novel filled with ominous puns and double entendres, "yu" ("jade") puns on "desire." Baoyu has a delicate prefer-

ence for girls, once claiming that "girls are made of water, boys are made of mud." He has a remarkable sensibility for the world of lyrical poetry, artistic reverie and rarified intellectual pleasures. And he is said to possess a "lust of the mind." His grandmother dotes on him and often protects him from the callous attacks of his stern father who considers him a n'er-do-well dreamer, pampered by the weak women around him. The father is disgusted with Baoyu's lack of interest in serious Confucian studies, which would prepare him for the civil service examinations and a successful career in the Qing bureaucracy. The strident conflict between father and heir unmasks the hypocrisy of Confucian scholasticism and its creatures, such as the sycophant "literary gentlemen" surrounding Baoyu's father. Beyond the father-son conflict, the darker sides of Qing Confucianism surface in briberies, corruption and outrageous cover-ups of murders perpetrated by Confucian magistrates at the expense of people of lower social status.

In addition to Baoyu, the human metamorphosis of the Stone, one other central character originates in the supernatural frame story and its fanciful landscape: the Crimson Pearl Flower, a semidivine plant. While Stone is serving at the court of the goddess Disenchantment before being born into the human world as Baoyu, he takes a fancy to this flower and waters it with sweet dew. This eventually brings the flower to life in the form of a fairy girl, who is obsessed with repaying the kindness of Stone, and for his gift of sweet dew she owes him the "debt of tears." The girl is born as Baoyu's cousin, the delicate and high-strung Lin Daiyu (*Daiyu* means "Black Jade"). The early chapters of the novel are devoted to the supernatural frame story and to bringing the characters together in the household of the all too human Jia family. In chapters seventeen and eighteen, Baoyu's elder sister, an imperial concubine, has been permitted to pay a visit to her home—an unusual break with court protocol that displays the emperor's favor to her and her family. In her honor a huge garden ("Prospect Garden") is constructed on the grounds of the family compound. After the imperial concubine's departure, the adolescent girls of the extended family are allowed to take up residence in the various buildings in the garden, and by special permission Baoyu is also permitted to live there with his maids. The world of the garden is one of adolescent love in full flower, though we never forget the violent and ugly world outside, a world that can barely be held at bay.

The love between Baoyu and Daiyu forms the core of the novel. Each is intensely sensitive to the other, and neither can express what he or she feels. Communication between them often depends on subtle gestures with implicit meanings that are inevitably misunderstood. Both believe in a perfect understanding of hearts, but even in the charmed world of the garden, closeness eludes them. The novel often juxtaposes brutish characters (usually male) with those possessed of a finer sensibility; but in the case of Daiyu, sensibility is carried to the extreme. Daiyu's relation to Baoyu is balanced out by that of another distant relation, Xue Baochai, whose plump good looks and gentle common sense are the very opposite of Daiyu's frailty and histrionic morbidity. Baochai ("Precious Hairpin") has a golden locket with an inscription that matches Baoyu's jade, and the marriage of "jade and gold" is being seriously considered by older members of the family. Eventually, in Gao E's ending for the novel, as Daiyu is dying of consumption, Baoyu will be tricked into marrying Baochai, falling dangerously ill as he realizes the plot. In passing the grueling civil service examination Baoyu finally carries out

his obligation toward the family line, although the novel ends on a twist.

Although the triangle of Baoyu, Daiyu, and Baochai stands at the center of the novel, scores of subplots involve characters of all types. The reader easily becomes absorbed in the intensity of the family's internal relationships, always to be reminded of how those relationships touch and are touched by the world outside. There is a vast establishment of close and distant family members, personal maids, and servants, each with his or her own status. Although personal maids have some responsibilities, the number of maids attached to each family member is primarily a mark of status, while for a girl from a poor family, the position of personal maid is very desirable, providing room, board, and income to send to her own family. Because the Jias have social power, the actions taken by family members to serve its interests and loyalties can also be seen as corruption. In some cases the corruption is obvious, but the reader is also induced to identify with the family and to take many acts of power and privilege for granted. At the same time, the outside world has the capacity to impinge on the protected space of the family, and the reader sees these forces from the point of view of the insider, as intrusions. It is a world of concentric circles of proximity, both of kinship and affinity. Petty details and private loves and hates grow larger and larger as they approach the center. And above all this hovers the Buddhist and Daoist lesson about the illusory nature of a world driven by emotions that cause only suffering, both to one's self and others.

The lesson of illusion is underscored by the family name Jia, a real Chinese surname that can mean "false" or "feigned." Puns ominously underlie many proper names in the novel. The names of Zhen Shiyin and Jia Yucun, who introduce the Jia household in the first chapters from the sidelines, can alternatively mean "true things are hidden" and "false words remain." The most emblematic statement of the novel's play with truth and illusion stands on a tablet over the entrance to the "Land of Illusion": "Truth becomes fiction when the fiction's true. Real becomes not-real when the unreal's real."

The selections printed here include the opening frame story, the first few chapters of the novel that gradually introduce the reader into the Jia household. We then move to the building of the Prospect Garden for the visit of the imperial concubine, which becomes a space of poetic passions, artistic pursuits and almost metaphysical realm of blissful love for Baoyu and the adolescent women around him. We pick up the story again much later, with chapters 96 through 98, when the family fortunes have declined and Daiyu enters a final bout of illness when she learns that Baoyu is to be married to Baochai. With the final selections, from chapters 119 and 120, we witness Baoyu's triumphant success in the civil service examinations, as well as the novel's sudden and surprising ending. At the end, Stone is whisked from the stage of his human incarnation by the Buddhist and Daoist monks.

Although nothing can replace the experience of reading the whole novel, the selective glimpses of Stone's world and story presented here make for a contagious experience with the greatest and last novel of traditional China. A few decades after the publication of the novel, Western powers forced China into wars, carved out colonial enclaves, and helped bring down the Qing Dynasty. Stone is a full-fledged creature of traditional China, but the metaphor of fateful decline that pervades his trials in the human world came to resonate differently for readers who witnessed the painful end of twenty-two centuries of imperial China in the twentieth century.

From The Story of the Stone[1]

CHARACTERS

AROMA, NIGHTINGALE, *Snowgoose, Tealeaf, Crimson etc.: Maids in the Jia Household*

AUNT XUE: *widowed sister of Lady Wang and mother of Xue Pan and Xue Baochai*

FENG YUAN: *Caltrop's first purchaser, murdered by Xue Pan's servants*

GRANDMOTHER JIA: *née Shi; widow of Baoyu's paternal grandfather and head of the Rongguo branch of the Jia family*

GRANNY LIU: *old countrywoman patronized by Wang Xifeng and the Rongguo Jias*

JIA BAOYU: *incarnation of Stone; the eldest surviving son of Jia Zheng and Lady Wang of Rongguo House*

JIA LAN: *Baoyu's deceased elder brother*

JIA RONG: *son of Cousin Zhen and Youshi*

JIA SHE: *Jia Zheng's elder brother, Baoyu's uncle*

JIA TANCHUN: *daughter of Jia Zheng and "Aunt" Zhao; half-sister of Baoyu*

JIA YINGCHUN: *daughter of Jia She by a concubine*

JIA YUANCHUN: *daughter of Jia Zheng and Lady Wang and elder sister of Baoyu; the Imperial Concubine*

1. Chapters 1–17 are translated by David Hawkes.

JIA YUCUN: *careerist claiming relation-
ship with the Rongguo family*
JIA ZHEN: *also "Cousin Zhen"; son of
Jia Jing; acting head of the senior
(Ningguo) branch of the Jia family*
JIAN ZHENG: *Baoyu's father; the
younger of Grandmother Jia's
two sons*
LADY XING: *wife of Jia She and mother
of Jia Lian*
LENG ZIXING: *an antique dealer;
friend of Jia Yucun*
LIN DAIYU: *incarnation of the
Crimson Pearl Flower; daughter
of Lin Ruhai and Jia Zheng's
sister, Jia Min*

LIN RUHAI: *Daiyu's father; the Salt
Commissioner of Yangchow*
QINSHI (OR KEQING): *wife of
Jia Rong*
WANG XIFENG: *wife of Jia Lan and
niece of Lady Wang and
Aunt Xue*
XUE BAOCHAI: *daughter of Aunt Xue*
XUE PAN: *son of Aunt Xue and
reckless elder brother of Baochai*
ZHEN SHIYIN: *retired gentleman of
Soochow; father of Caltrop*
ZHEN YINGLIAN: *daughter of Zhen
Shiyin, later know as Caltrop*

GENEALOGY OF THE NINGGUO AND RONGGUO HOUSES OF THE JIA CLAN

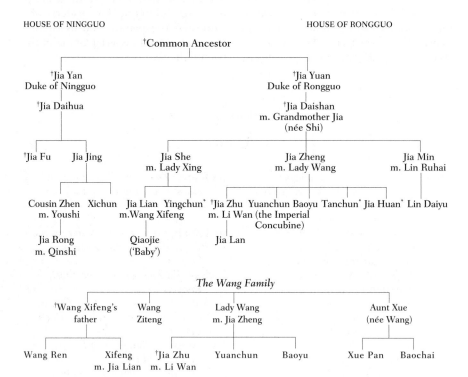

m. married   †dead before the beginning of the novel   *son or daughter by a concubine

FROM **CHAPTER 1**

Zhen Shiyin makes the Stone's acquaintance in a dream
And Jia Yu-cun finds that poverty is not incompatible with romantic feelings

GENTLE READER,

What, you may ask, was the origin of this book?

Though the answer to this question may at first seem to border on the absurd, reflection will show that there is a good deal more in it than meets the eye.

Long ago, when the goddess Nü-wa was repairing the sky, she melted down a great quantity of rock and, on the Incredible Crags of the Great Fable Mountains, moulded the amalgam into thirty-six thousand, five hundred and one large building blocks, each measuring seventy-two feet by a hundred and forty-four feet square. She used thirty-six thousand five hundred of these blocks in the course of her building operations, leaving a single odd block unused, which lay, all on its own, at the foot of Greensickness Peak in the aforementioned mountains.

Now this block of stone, having undergone the melting and moulding of a goddess, possessed magic powers. It could move about at will and could grow or shrink to any size it wanted. Observing that all the other blocks had been used for celestial repairs and that it was the only one to have been rejected as unworthy, it became filled with shame and resentment and passed its days in sorrow and lamentation.

One day, in the midst of its lamentings, it saw a monk and a Taoist approaching from a great distance, each of them remarkable for certain eccentricities of manner and appearance. When they arrived at the foot of Greensickness Peak, they sat down on the ground and began to talk. The monk, catching sight of a lustrous, translucent stone—it was in fact the rejected building block which had now shrunk itself to the size of a fan-pendant[2] and looked very attractive in its new shape—took it up on the palm of his hand and addressed it with a smile:

'Ha, I see you have magical properties! But nothing to recommend you. I shall have to cut a few words on you so that anyone seeing you will know at once that you are something special. After that I shall take you to a certain

> brilliant
> successful
> poetical
> cultivated
> aristocratic
> elegant
> delectable
> luxurious
> opulent
> locality on a little trip'.

The stone was delighted.

'What words will you cut? Where is this place you will take me to? I beg to be enlightened.'

---

2. Jade decoration strung from the bottom of a fan.

'Do not ask,' replied the monk with a laugh. 'You will know soon enough when the time comes.'

And with that he slipped the stone into his sleeve and set off at a great pace with the Taoist. But where they both went to I have no idea.

Countless aeons went by and a certain Taoist called Vanitas in quest of the secret of immortality chanced to be passing below that same Greensickness Peak in the Incredible Crags of the Great Fable Mountains when he caught sight of a large stone standing there, on which the characters of a long inscription were clearly discernible.

Vanitas read the inscription through from beginning to end and learned that this was a once lifeless stone block which had been found unworthy to repair the sky, but which had magically transformed its shape and been taken down by the Buddhist mahāsattva[3] Impervioso and the Taoist illuminate Mysterioso into the world of mortals, where it had lived out the life of a man before finally attaining nirvana and returning to the other shore.[4] The inscription named the country where it had been born, and went into considerable detail about its domestic life, youthful amours, and even the verses, mottoes and riddles it had written. All it lacked was the authentication of a dynasty and date. On the back of the stone was inscribed the following quatrain:

> Found unfit to repair the azure sky
> Long years a foolish mortal man was I.
> My life in both worlds on this stone is writ:
> Pray who will copy out and publish it?

From his reading of the inscription Vanitas realized that this was a stone of some consequence. Accordingly he addressed himself to it in the following manner:

'Brother Stone, according to what you yourself seem to imply in these verses, this story of yours contains matter of sufficient interest to merit publication and has been carved here with that end in view. But as far as I can see (a) it has no discoverable dynastic period, and (b) it contains no examples of moral grandeur among its characters—no statesmanship, no social message of any kind. All I can find in it, in fact, are a number of females, conspicuous, if at all, only for their passion or folly or for some trifling talent or insignificant virtue. Even if I were to copy all this out, I cannot see that it would make a very remarkable book.'

'Come, your reverence,' said the stone (for Vanitas had been correct in assuming that it could speak) 'must you be so obtuse? All the romances ever written have an artificial period setting—Han or Tang for the most part. In refusing to make use of that stale old convention and telling my *Story of the Stone* exactly as it occurred, it seems to me that, far from *depriving* it of anything, I have given it a freshness these other books do not have.

'Your so-called "historical romances", consisting, as they do, of scandalous anecdotes about statesmen and emperors of bygone days and scabrous attacks

---

3. Wise man.
4. That is, achieving enlightenment and passing beyond the cycles of rebirth.

on the reputations of long-dead gentlewomen, contain more wickedness and immorality than I care to mention. Still worse is the "erotic novel", by whose filthy obscenities our young folk are all too easily corrupted. And the "boudoir romances", those dreary stereotypes with their volume after volume all pitched on the same note and their different characters undistinguishable except by name (all those ideally beautiful young ladies and ideally eligible young bachelors)—even they seem unable to avoid descending sooner or later into indecency.

'The trouble with this last kind of romance is that it only gets written in the first place because the author requires a framework in which to show off his love-poems. He goes about constructing this framework quite mechanically, beginning with the names of his pair of young lovers and invariably adding a third character, a servant or the like, to make mischief between them, like the *chou*[5] in a comedy.

'What makes these romances even more detestable is the stilted, bombastic language—inanities dressed in pompous rhetoric, remote alike from nature and common sense and teeming with the grossest absurdities.

'Surely my "number of females", whom I spent half a lifetime studying with my own eyes and ears, are preferable to this kind of stuff? I do not claim that they are better people than the ones who appear in books written before my time; I am only saying that the contemplation of their actions and motives may prove a more effective antidote to boredom and melancholy. And even the inelegant verses with which my story is interlarded could serve to entertain and amuse on those convivial occasions when rhymes and riddles are in demand.

'All that my story narrates, the meetings and partings, the joys and sorrows, the ups and downs of fortune, are recorded exactly as they happened. I have not dared to add the tiniest bit of touching-up, for fear of losing the true picture.

'My only wish is that men in the world below may sometimes pick up this tale when they are recovering from sleep or drunkenness, or when they wish to escape from business worries or a fit of the dumps, and in doing so find not only mental refreshment but even perhaps, if they will heed its lesson and abandon their vain and frivolous pursuits, some small arrest in the deterioration of their vital forces. What does your reverence say to that?'

For a long time Vanitas stood lost in thought, pondering this speech. He then subjected the *Story of the Stone* to a careful second reading. He could see that its main theme was love; that it consisted quite simply of a true record of real events; and that it was entirely free from any tendency to deprave and corrupt. He therefore copied it all out from beginning to end and took it back with him to look for a publisher.

As a consequence of all this, Vanitas, starting off in the Void (which is Truth) came to the contemplation of Form (which is Illusion); and from Form engendered Passion; and by communicating Passion, entered again into Form; and from Form awoke to the Void (which is Truth). He therefore changed his name from Vanitas to Brother Amor, or the Passionate Monk, (because he had approached Truth by way of Passion), and changed the title of the book from *The Story of the Stone* to *The Tale of Brother Amor*.

---

5. The stock role of the clown in a play.

Old Kong Meixi from the homeland of Confucius called the book *A Mirror for the Romantic*. Wu Yufeng called it *A Dream of Golden Days*. Cao Xueqin in his Nostalgia Studio worked on it for ten years, in the course of which he rewrote it no less than five times, dividing it into chapters, composing chapter headings, renaming it *The Twelve Beauties of Jinling*, and adding an introductory quatrain. Red Inkstone restored the original title when he recopied the book and added his second set of annotations to it.

This, then, is a true account of how *The Story of the Stone* came to be written.

> Pages full of idle words
> Penned with hot and bitter tears:
> All men call the author fool;
> None his secret message hears.

The origin of *The Story of the Stone* has now been made clear. The same cannot, however, be said of the characters and events which it recorded. Gentle reader, have patience! This is how the inscription began:

Long, long ago the world was tilted downwards towards the south-east; and in that lower-lying south-easterly part of the earth there is a city called Soochow; and in Soochow the district around the Chang-men Gate is reckoned one of the two or three wealthiest and most fashionable quarters in the world of men. Outside the Chang-men Gate is a wide thoroughfare called Worldly Way; and somewhere off Worldly Way is an area called Carnal Lane. There is an old temple in the Carnal Lane area which, because of the way it is bottled up inside a narrow *cul-de-sac*, is referred to locally as Bottle-gourd Temple. Next door to Bottle-gourd Temple lived a gentleman of private means called Zhen Shiyin and his wife Fengshi, a kind, good woman with a profound sense of decency and decorum. The household was not a particularly wealthy one, but they were nevertheless looked up to by all and sundry as the leading family in the neighbourhood.

Zhen Shiyin himself was by nature a quiet and totally unambitious person. He devoted his time to his garden and to the pleasures of wine and poetry. Except for a single flaw, his existence could, indeed, have been described as an idyllic one. The flaw was that, although already past fifty, he had no son, only a little girl, just two years old, whose name was Yinglian.

Once, during the tedium of a burning summer's day, Shiyin was sitting idly in his study. The book had slipped from his nerveless grasp and his head had nodded down onto the desk in a doze. While in this drowsy state he seemed to drift off to some place he could not identify, where he became aware of a monk and a Taoist walking along and talking as they went.

'Where do you intend to take that thing you are carrying?' the Taoist was asking.

'Don't you worry about him!' replied the monk with a laugh. 'There is a batch of lovesick souls awaiting incarnation in the world below whose fate is due to be decided this very day. I intend to take advantage of this opportunity to slip our little friend in amongst them and let him have a taste of human life along with the rest.'

'Well, well, so another lot of these amorous wretches is about to enter the vale of tears,' said the Taoist. 'How did all this begin? And where are the souls to be reborn?'

'You will laugh when I tell you,' said the monk. 'When this stone was left unused by the goddess, he found himself at a loose end and took to wandering about all over the place for want of better to do, until one day his wanderings took him to the place where the fairy Disenchantment lives.

'Now Disenchantment could tell that there was something unusual about this stone, so she kept him there in her Sunset Glow Palace and gave him the honorary title of Divine Luminescent Stone-in-Waiting in the Court of Sunset Glow.

'But most of his time he spent west of Sunset Glow exploring the banks of the Magic River. There, by the Rock of Rebirth, he found the beautiful Crimson Pearl Flower, for which he conceived such a fancy that he took to watering her every day with sweet dew, thereby conferring on her the gift of life.

'Crimson Pearl's substance was composed of the purest cosmic essences, so she was already half-divine; and now, thanks to the vitalizing effect of the sweet dew, she was able to shed her vegetable shape and assume the form of a girl.

'This fairy girl wandered about outside the Realm of Separation, eating the Secret Passion Fruit when she was hungry and drinking from the Pool of Sadness when she was thirsty. The consciousness that she owed the stone something for his kindness in watering her began to prey on her mind and ended by becoming an obsession.

'"I have no sweet dew here that I can repay him with," she would say to herself. "The only way in which I could perhaps repay him would be with the tears shed during the whole of a mortal lifetime if he and I were ever to be reborn as humans in the world below."

'Because of this strange affair, Disenchantment has got together a group of amorous young souls, of which Crimson Pearl is one, and intends to send them down into the world to take part in the great illusion of human life. And as today happens to be the day on which this stone is fated to go into the world too, I am taking him with me to Disenchantment's tribunal for the purpose of getting him registered and sent down to earth with the rest of these romantic creatures.'

'How very amusing!' said the Taoist. 'I have certainly never heard of a debt of tears before. Why shouldn't the two of us take advantage of this opportunity to go down into the world ourselves and save a few souls? It would be a work of merit.'

'That is exactly what I was thinking,' said the monk. 'Come with me to Disenchantment's palace to get this absurd creature cleared. Then, when this last batch of romantic idiots goes down, you and I can go down with them. At present about half have already been born. They await this last batch to make up the number.'

'Very good, I will go with you then,' said the Taoist. Shiyin heard all this conversation quite clearly, and curiosity impelled him to go forward and greet the two reverend gentlemen. They returned his greeting and asked him what he wanted.

'It is not often that one has the opportunity of listening to a discussion of the operations of *karma*[6] such as the one I have just been privileged to overhear,' said Shiyin. 'Unfortunately I am a man of very limited understanding and have

---

6. The accumulation of good and bad deeds that determines a soul's future lives.

not been able to derive the full benefit from your conversation. If you would have the very great kindness to enlighten my benighted understanding with a somewhat fuller account of what you were discussing, I can promise you the most devout attention. I feel sure that your teaching would have a salutary effect on me and—who knows—might save me from the pains of hell.'

The reverend gentlemen laughed. 'These are heavenly mysteries and may not be divulged. But if you wish to escape from the fiery pit, you have only to remember us when the time comes, and all will be well.'

Shi-yin saw that it would be useless to press them. 'Heavenly mysteries must not, of course, be revealed. But might one perhaps inquire what the "absurd creature" is that you were talking about? Is it possible that I might be allowed to see it?'

'Oh, as for that,' said the monk: 'I think it is on the cards for you to have a look at *him*,' and he took the object from his sleeve and handed it to Shiyin.

Shi-yin took the object from him and saw that it was a clear, beautiful jade on one side of which were carved the words 'Magic Jade'. There were several columns of smaller characters on the back, which Shiyin was just going to examine more closely when the monk, with a cry of 'Here we are, at the frontier of Illusion', snatched the stone from him and disappeared, with the Taoist, through a big stone archway above which

THE LAND OF ILLUSION

was written in large characters. A couplet in smaller characters was inscribed vertically on either side of the arch:

> Truth becomes fiction when the fiction's true;
> Real becomes not-real where the unreal's real.

Shiyin was on the point of following them through the archway when suddenly a great clap of thunder seemed to shake the earth to its very foundations, making him cry out in alarm.

And there he was sitting in his study, the contents of his dream already half forgotten, with the sun still blazing on the ever-rustling plantains outside, and the wet-nurse at the door with his little daughter Yinglian in her arms. Her delicate little pink-and-white face seemed dearer to him than ever at that moment, and he stretched out his arms to take her and hugged her to him.

After playing with her for a while at his desk, he carried her out to the front of the house to watch the bustle in the street. He was about to go in again when he saw a monk and a Taoist approaching, the monk scabby-headed and barefoot, the Taoist tousle-haired and limping. They were behaving like madmen, shouting with laughter and gesticulating wildly as they walked along.

When this strange pair reached Shiyin's door and saw him standing there holding Yinglian, the monk burst into loud sobs. 'Patron,' he said, addressing Shiyin, 'what are you doing, holding in your arms that ill-fated creature who is destined to involve both her parents in her own misfortune?'

Shiyin realized that he was listening to the words of a madman and took no notice. But the monk persisted:

'Give her to me! Give her to me!'

Shiyin was beginning to lose patience and, clasping his little girl more tightly to him, turned on his heel and was about to re-enter the house when the monk pointed his finger at him, roared with laughter, and then proceeded to intone the following verses:

'Fond man, your pampered child to cherish so—
That caltrop-glass which shines on melting snow!
Beware the high feast of the fifteenth day,
When all in smoke and fire shall pass away!'

Shiyin heard all this quite plainly and was a little worried by it. He was thinking of asking the monk what lay behind these puzzling words when he heard the Taoist say, 'We don't need to stay together. Why don't we part company here and each go about his own business? Three *kalpas*[7] from now I shall wait for you on Beimang Hill. Having joined forces again there, we can go together to the Land of Illusion to sign off.'

'Excellent!' said the other. And the two of them went off and soon were both lost to sight.

'There must have been something behind all this,' thought Shiyin to himself. 'I really ought to have asked him what he meant, but now it is too late.'

He was still standing outside his door brooding when Jia Yucun, the poor student who lodged at the Bottle-gourd Temple next door, came up to him. Yucun was a native of Huzhou and came from a family of scholars and bureaucrats which had, however, fallen on bad times when Yucun was born. The family fortunes on both his father's and mother's side had all been spent, and the members of the family had themselves gradually died off until only Yucun was left. There were no prospects for him in his home town, so he had set off for the capital, in search of fame and fortune. Unfortunately he had got no further than Soochow when his funds ran out, and he had now been living there in poverty for a year, lodging in this temple and keeping himself alive by working as a copyist. For this reason Shiyin saw a great deal of his company.

As soon as he caught sight of Shiyin, Yucun clasped his hands in greeting and smiled ingratiatingly. 'I could see you standing there gazing, sir. Has anything been happening in the street?'

'No, no,' said Shiyin. 'It just happened that my little girl was crying, so I brought her out here to amuse her. Your coming is most opportune, dear boy. I was beginning to feel most dreadfully bored. Won't you come into my little den, and we can help each other to while away this tedious hot day?'

So saying, he called for a servant to take the child indoors, while he himself took Yucun by the hand and led him into his study, where his boy served them both with tea. But they had not exchanged half-a-dozen words before one of the servants rushed in to say that 'Mr Yan had come to pay a call.' Shiyin hurriedly rose up and excused himself: 'I seem to have brought you here under false pretences. I do hope you will forgive me. If you don't mind sitting on your own here for a moment, I shall be with you directly.'

---

7. An aeon, an extraordinarily long span of cosmic time.

Yucun rose to his feet too. 'Please do not distress yourself on my account, sir. I am a regular visitor here and can easily wait a bit.' But by the time he had finished saying this, Shiyin was already out of the study and on his way to the guestroom.

Left to himself, Yucun was flicking through some of Shiyin's books of poetry in order to pass the time, when he heard a woman's cough outside the window. Immediately he jumped up and peered out to see who it was. The cough appeared to have come from a maid who was picking flowers in the garden. She was an unusually good-looking girl with a rather refined face: not a great beauty, by any means, but with something striking about her. Yucun gazed at her spellbound.

Having now finished picking her flowers, this anonymous member of the Zhen household was about to go in again when, on some sudden impulse, she raised her head and caught sight of a man standing in the window. His hat was frayed and his clothing threadbare; yet, though obviously poor, he had a fine, manly physique and handsome, well-proportioned features.

The maid hastened to remove herself from this male presence; but as she went she thought to herself, 'What a fine-looking man! But so shabby! The family hasn't got any friends or relations as poor as that. It must be that Jia Yucun the master is always on about. No wonder he says that he won't stay poor long. I remember hearing him say that he's often wanted to help him but hasn't yet found an opportunity.' And thinking these thoughts she could not forbear to turn back for another peep or two.

Yucun saw her turn back and, at once assuming that she had taken a fancy to him, was beside himself with delight. What a perceptive young woman she must be, he thought, to have seen the genius underneath the rags! A real friend in trouble!

After a while the boy came in again and Yucun elicited from him that the visitor in the front room was now staying to dinner. It was obviously out of the question to wait much longer, so he slipped down the passage-way at the side of the house and let himself out by the back gate. Nor did Shiyin invite him round again when, having at last seen off his visitor, he learned that Yucun had already left.

But then the Mid Autumn festival arrived and, after the family convivialities were over, Shiyin had a little dinner for two laid out in his study and went in person to invite Yucun, walking to his temple lodgings in the moonlight.

Ever since the day the Zhens' maid had, by looking back twice over her shoulder, convinced him that she was a friend, Yucun had had the girl very much on his mind, and now that it was festival time, the full moon of Mid Autumn lent an inspiration to his romantic impulses which finally resulted in the following octet:

'Ere on ambition's path my feet are set,
Sorrow comes often this poor heart to fret.
Yet, as my brow contracted with new care,
Was there not one who, parting, turned to stare?
Dare I, that grasp at shadows in the wind,
Hope, underneath the moon, a friend to find?
Bright orb, if with my plight you sympathize,
Shine first upon the chamber where she lies.'

Having delivered himself of this masterpiece, Yucun's thoughts began to run on his unrealized ambitions and, after much head-scratching and many heavenward glances accompanied by heavy sighs, he produced the following couplet, reciting it in a loud, ringing voice which caught the ear of Shiyin, who chanced at that moment to be arriving:

> 'The jewel in the casket bides till one shall come to buy.
> The jade pin in the drawer hides, waiting its time to fly.'[8]

Shi-yin smiled. 'You are a man of no mean ambition, Yucun.'

'Oh no!' Yucun smiled back deprecatingly. 'You are too flattering. I was merely reciting at random from the lines of some old poet. But what brings you here, sir?'

'Tonight is Mid Autumn night,'[9] said Shiyin. 'People call it the Festival of Reunion. It occurred to me that you might be feeling rather lonely here in your monkery, so I have arranged for the two of us to take a little wine together in my study. I hope you will not refuse to join me.'

Yucun made no polite pretence of declining. 'Your kindness is more than I deserve,' he said. 'I accept gratefully.' And he accompanied Shiyin back to the study next door.

Soon they had finished their tea. Wine and various choice dishes were brought in and placed on the table, already laid out with cups, plates, and so forth, and the two men took their places and began to drink. At first they were rather slow and ceremonious; but gradually, as the conversation grew more animated, their potations too became more reckless and uninhibited. The sounds of music and singing which could now be heard from every house in the neighbourhood and the full moon which shone with cold brilliance overhead seemed to increase their elation, so that the cups were emptied almost as soon as they touched their lips, and Yucun, who was already a sheet or so in the wind, was seized with an irrepressible excitement to which he presently gave expression in the form of a quatrain, ostensibly on the subject of the moon, but really about the ambition he had hitherto been at some pains to conceal:

> 'In thrice five nights her perfect O is made,
> Whose cold light bathes each marble balustrade.
> As her bright wheel starts on its starry ways,
> On earth ten thousand heads look up and gaze.'

'Bravo!' said Shiyin loudly. 'I have always insisted that you were a young fellow who would go up in the world, and now, in these verses you have just recited, I see an augury of your ascent. In no time at all we shall see you up among the clouds! This calls for a drink!' And, saying this, he poured Yucun a large cup of wine.

Yucun drained the cup, then, surprisingly, sighed:

8. Yucun is thinking of the jade hairpin given by a visiting fairy to an early Chinese emperor; the hairpin later turned into a white swallow and flew away into the sky. Metaphors of flying were frequently used to hint at success in the civil service examinations.
9. The fifteenth day of the eighth month, when, according to the lunar calendar, the moon is at its brightest.

'Don't imagine the drink is making me boastful, but I really do believe that if it were just a question of having the sort of qualifications now in demand, I should stand as good a chance as any of getting myself on to the list of candidates. The trouble is that I simply have no means of laying my hands on the money that would be needed for lodgings and travel expenses. The journey to the capital is a long one, and the sort of money I can earn from my copying is not enough—'

'Why ever didn't you say this before?' said Shiyin interrupting him. 'I have long wanted to do something about this, but on all the occasions I have met you previously, the conversation has never got round to this subject, and I haven't liked to broach it for fear of offending you. Well, now we know where we are. I am not a very clever man, but at least I know the right thing to do when I see it. Luckily, the next Triennial is only a few months ahead. You must go to the capital without delay. A spring examination triumph will make you feel that all your studying has been worthwhile. I shall take care of all your expenses. It is the least return I can make for your friendship.' And there and then he instructed his boy to go with all speed and make up a parcel of fifty taels of the best refined silver and two suits of winter clothes.

'The almanac gives the nineteenth as a good day for travelling,' he went on, addressing Yucun again. 'You can set about hiring a boat for the journey straight away. How delightful it will be to meet again next winter when you have distinguished yourself by soaring to the top over all the other candidates!'

Yucun accepted the silver and the clothes with only the most perfunctory word of thanks and without, apparently, giving them a further moment's thought, for he continued to drink and laugh and talk as if nothing had happened. It was well after midnight before they broke up.

After seeing Yucun off, Shiyin went to bed and slept without a break until the sun was high in the sky next morning. When he awoke, his mind was still running on the conversation of the previous night. He thought he would write a couple of introductory letters for Yucun to take with him to the capital, and arrange for him to call on the family of an official he was acquainted with who might be able to put him up; but when he sent a servant to invite him over, the servant brought back word from the temple as follows:

'The monk says that Mr Jia set out for the capital at five o'clock this morning, sir. He says he left a message to pass on to you. He said to tell you, "A scholar should not concern himself with almanacs, but should act as the situation demands," and he said there wasn't time to say good-bye.'

So Shiyin was obliged to let the matter drop.

* * *

FROM CHAPTER 2

A daughter of the Jias ends her days in Yangchow City
And Leng Zixing discourses on the Jias of Rongguo House.

* * *

[Yucun] now thought that in order to give the full rural flavour to his outing he would treat himself to a few cups of wine in a little country inn and accordingly directed his steps towards the near-by village. He had scarcely set foot inside the door of the village inn when one of the men drinking at separate tables inside rose up and advanced to meet him with a broad smile.

'Fancy meeting you!'

It was an antique dealer called Leng Zixing whom Yucun had got to know some years previously when he was staying in the capital. Yucun had a great admiration for Zixing as a practical man of business, whilst Zixing for his part was tickled to claim acquaintanceship with a man of Yucun's great learning and culture. On the basis of this mutual admiration the two of them had got on wonderfully well, and Yucun now returned the other's greeting with a pleased smile.

'My dear fellow! How long have you been here? I really had no idea you were in these parts. It was quite an accident that I came here today at all. What an extraordinary coincidence!'

'I went home at the end of last year to spend New Year with the family,' said Zixing. 'On my way back to the capital I thought I would stop off and have a few words with a friend of mine who lives hereabouts, and he very kindly invited me to spend a few days with him. I hadn't got any urgent business waiting for me, so I thought I might as well stay on a bit and leave at the middle of the month. I came out here on my own because my friend has an engagement today. I certainly didn't expect to run into *you* here.'

Zixing conducted Yucun to his table as he spoke and ordered more wine and some fresh dishes to be brought. The two men then proceeded, between leisurely sips of wine, to relate what each had been doing in the years that had elapsed since their last meeting.

Presently Yucun asked Zixing if anything of interest had happened recently in the capital.

'I can't think of anything particularly deserving of mention,' said Zixing. 'Except, perhaps, for a very small but very unusual event that took place in your own clan there.'

'What makes you say that?' said Yucun, 'I have no family connections in the capital.'

'Well, it's the same name,' said Zixing. 'They must be the same clan.'

Yucun asked him what family he could be referring to.

'I fancy you wouldn't disown the Jias of the Rongguo mansion as unworthy of you.'

'Oh, you mean them,' said Yucun. 'There are so many members of my clan, it's hard to keep up with them all. Since the time of Jia Fu of the Eastern Han dynasty there have been branches of the Jia clan in every province of the empire. The Rongguo branch is, as a matter of fact, on the same clan register as my own; but since they are exalted so far above us socially, we don't normally claim the connection, and nowadays we are completely out of touch with them.'

Zixing sighed. 'You shouldn't speak about them in that way, you know. Nowadays both the Rong and Ning mansions are in a greatly reduced state compared with what they used to be.'

'When I was last that way the Rong and Ning mansions both seemed to be fairly humming with life. Surely nothing could have happened to reduce their prosperity in so short a time?'

'Ah, you may well ask. But it's a long story.'

'Last time I was in Jinling,' went on Yucun, 'I passed by their two houses one day on my way to Shitoucheng to visit the ruins. The Ningguo mansion along the eastern half of the road and the Rongguo mansion along the western half must between them have occupied the greater part of the north side frontage of that street. It's true that there wasn't much activity outside the main entrances, but looking up over the outer walls I had a glimpse of the most magnificent and imposing halls and pavilions, and even the rocks and trees of the gardens beyond seemed to have a sleekness and luxuriance that were certainly not suggestive of a family whose fortunes were in a state of decline.'

'Well! For a Palace Graduate Second Class, you ought to know better than that! Haven't you ever heard the old saying, "The beast with a hundred legs is a long time dying"? Although I say they are not as prosperous as they used to be in years past, of course I don't mean to say that there is not still a world of difference between *their* circumstances and those you would expect to find in the household of your average government official. At the moment the numbers of their establishment and the activities they engage in are, if anything, on the increase. Both masters and servants all lead lives of luxury and magnificence. And they still have plenty of plans and projects under way. But they can't bring themselves to economize or make any adjustment in their accustomed style of living. Consequently, though outwardly they still manage to keep up appearances, inwardly they are beginning to feel the pinch. But that's a small matter. There's something much more seriously wrong with them than that. They are not able to turn out good sons, those stately houses, for all their pomp and show. The males in the family get more degenerate from one generation to the next.'

'Surely,' said Yucun with surprise, 'it is inconceivable that such highly cultured households should not give their children the best education possible? I say nothing of other families, but the Jias of the Ning and Rong households used to be famous for the way in which they brought up their sons. How could they come to be as you describe?'

'I assure you, it is precisely those families I am speaking of. Let me tell you something of their history. The Duke of Ningguo and the Duke of Rongguo were two brothers by the same mother. Ningguo was the elder of the two. When he died, his eldest son, Jia Daihua, inherited his post. Daihua had two sons. The elder, Jia Fu, died at the age of eight or nine, leaving only the second son, Jia Jing, to inherit. Nowadays Jia Jing's only interest in life is Taoism. He spends all his time over retorts and crucibles concocting elixirs, and refuses to be bothered with anything else.

'Fortunately he had already provided himself with a son, Jia Zhen, long before he took up this hobby. So, having set his mind on turning himself into an immortal, he has given up his post in favour of this son. And what's more he refuses outright to live at home and spends his time fooling around with a pack of Taoists somewhere outside the city walls.

'This Jia Zhen has got a son of his own, a lad called Jia Rong, just turned sixteen. With old Jia Jing out of the way and refusing to exercise any authority, Jia Zhen has thrown his responsibilities to the winds and given himself up to a life of pleasure. He has turned that Ningguo mansion upside down, but there is no one around who dares gainsay him.

'Now I come to the Rong household—it was there that this strange event occurred that I was telling you about. When the old Duke of Rongguo died, his eldest son, Jia Daishan, inherited his emoluments. He married a girl from a very old Nanking family, the daughter of Marquis Shi, who bore him two sons, Jia She and Jia Zheng.

'Daishan has been dead this many a year, but the old lady is still alive. The elder son, Jia She, inherited; but he's only a very middling sort of person and doesn't play much part in running the family. The second son, though, Jia Zheng, has been mad keen on study ever since he was a lad. He is a very upright sort of person, straight as a die. He was his grandfather's favourite. He would have sat for the examinations, but when the emperor saw Daishan's testamentary memorial that he wrote on his death bed, he was so moved, thinking what a faithful servant the old man had been, that he not only ordered the elder son to inherit his father's position, but also gave instructions that any other sons of his were to be presented to him at once, and on seeing Jia Zheng he gave him the post of Supernumerary Executive Officer, brevet rank, with instructions to continue his studies while on the Ministry's payroll. From there he has now risen to the post of Under Secretary.

'Sir Zheng's lady was formerly a Miss Wang. Her first child was a boy called Jia Zhu. He was already a Licensed Scholar at the age of fourteen. Then he married and had a son. But he died of an illness before he was twenty. The second child she bore him was a little girl, rather remarkable because she was born on New Year's day. Then after an interval of twelve years or more she suddenly had another son. He was even more remarkable, because at the moment of his birth he had a piece of beautiful, clear, coloured jade in his mouth with a lot of writing on it. They gave him the name "Baoyu" as a consequence. Now tell me if you don't think that is an extraordinary thing.'

'It certainly is,' Yucun agreed. 'I should not be at all surprised to find that there was something very unusual in the heredity of that child.'

'Humph,' said Zixing. 'A great many people have said that. That is the reason why his old grandmother thinks him such a treasure. But when they celebrated the First Twelve-month and Sir Zheng tested his disposition by putting a lot of objects in front of him and seeing which he would take hold of, he stretched out his little hand and started playing with some women's things—combs, bracelets, pots of rouge and powder and the like—completely ignoring all the other objects. Sir Zheng was very displeased. He said he would grow up to be a rake, and ever since then he hasn't felt much affection for the child. But to the old lady he's the very apple of her eye.

'But there's more that's unusual about him than that. He's now rising ten and unusually mischievous, yet his mind is as sharp as a needle. You wouldn't find one in a hundred to match him. Some of the childish things he says are most extraordinary. He'll say, "Girls are made of water and boys are made of mud. When I am with girls I feel fresh and clean, but when I am with boys I feel stupid and nasty." Now isn't that priceless! He'll be a lady-killer when he grows up, no question of that.'

Yucun's face assumed an expression of unwonted severity. 'Not so. By no means. It is a pity that none of you seem to understand this child's heredity. Most likely even my esteemed kinsman Sir Jia Zheng is mistaken in treating the boy as a future libertine. This is something that no one but a widely read person, and one moreover well-versed in moral philosophy and in the subtle arcana of metaphysical science could possibly understand.'

Observing the weighty tone in which these words were uttered, Zixing hurriedly asked to be instructed, and Yucun proceeded as follows:

'The generative processes operating in the universe provide the great majority of mankind with natures in which good and evil are commingled in more or less equal proportions. Instances of exceptional goodness and exceptional badness are produced by the operation of beneficent or noxious ethereal influences, of which the former are symptomatized by the equilibrium of society and the latter by its disequilibrium.

'*Thus*,

> Yao,
> Shun,
> Yu,
> Tang,
> King Wen,
> King Wu,
> the Duke of Zhou,
> the Duke of Shao,
> Confucius,
> Mencius,
> Dong Zhongshu,
> Han Yu,
> Zhou Dunyi,
> the Cheng brothers,
> Zhu Xi and
> Zhang Zai[1]

—all instances of exceptional goodness—were born under the influence of benign forces, and all sought to promote the well-being of the societies in which they lived; whilst

> Chi You,
> Gong Gong,
> Jie,
> Zhou,
> the First Qin Emperor,
> Wang Mang,
> Cao Cao,
> Huan Wen,
> An Lushan and
> Qin Kuai[2]

—all instances of exceptional badness—were born under the influence of harmful forces, and all sought to disrupt the societies in which they lived.

'*Now*,[3] the good cosmic fluid with which the natures of the exceptionally good are compounded is a pure, quintessential humour; whilst the evil fluid which infuses the natures of the exceptionally bad is a cruel, perverse humour.

'*Therefore*, our age being one in which beneficent ethereal influences are in the ascendant, in which the reigning dynasty is well-established and society both peaceful and prosperous, innumerable instances are to be found, from

1. List of most virtuous figures in Chinese history, ranging from sage kings and philosophical masters to scholar-officials.
2. List of archetypal villains in Chinese history, ranging from rulers, to ministers, to rebels.

3. The translator highlights the particularly dry, scholastic line of argument in these few paragraphs by italicizing the cumbersome connective words.

the palace down to the humblest cottage, of individuals endowed with the pure, quintessential humour.

'*Moreover*, an unused surplus of this pure, quintessential humour, unable to find corporeal lodgement, circulates freely abroad until it manifests itself in the form of sweet dews and balmy winds, asperged and effused for the enrichment and refreshment of all terrestial life.

'*Consequently*, the cruel and perverse humours, unable to circulate freely in the air and sunlight, subside, by a process of incrassation and coagulation, into the bottoms of ditches and ravines.

'*Now*, should these incrassate humours chance to be stirred or provoked by wind or weather into a somewhat more volatile and active condition, it sometimes happens that a stray wisp or errant flocculus may escape from the fissure or concavity in which they are contained; and if some of the pure, quintessential humour should chance to be passing overhead at that same moment, the two will become locked in irreconcilable conflict, the good refusing to yield to the evil, the evil persisting in its hatred of the good. And just as wind, water, thunder and lightning meeting together over the earth can neither dissipate nor yield one to another but produce an explosive shock resulting in the downward emission of rain, so does this clash of humours result in the forcible downward expulsion of the evil humour, which, being thus forced downwards, will find its way into some human creature.

'Such human recipients, whether they be male or female, since they are already amply endowed with the benign humour before the evil humour is injected, are incapable of becoming either greatly good or greatly bad; but place them in the company of ten thousand others and you will find that they are superior to all the rest in sharpness and intelligence and inferior to all the rest in perversity, wrongheadedness and eccentricity. Born into a rich or noble household they are likely to become great lovers or the occasion of great love in others; in a poor but well-educated household they will become literary rebels or eccentric aesthetes; even if they are born in the lowest stratum of society they are likely to become great actors or famous *hetaerae*. Under no circumstances will you find them in servile or menial positions, content to be at the beck and call of mediocrities.

'For examples I might cite:

> Xu You,
> Tao Yuanming,
> Ruan Ji,
> Ji Kang,
> Liu Ling,
> the Wang and Xie clans of the Jin period,
> Gu Kaizhi,
> the last ruler of Chen,
> the emperor Minghuang of the Tang dynasty,
> the emperor Huizong of the Song dynasty,
> Liu Tingzhi,
> Wen Tingyun,
> Mi Fei,
> Shi Yannian,

Liu Yong and
Qin Guan;

or, from more recent centuries:

Ni Zan,
Tang Yin and
Zhu Yunming;

or again, for examples of the last type:

Li Guinian,
Huang Fanchuo,
Jing Xinmo,
Zhuo Wenjun,
Little Red Duster,
Xue Tao,
Cui Yingying and
Morning Cloud.[4]

All of these, though their circumstances differed, were essentially the same.'
'You mean,' Zixing interposed,

'Zhang victorious is a hero,
Zhang beaten is a lousy knave?'

'Precisely so,' said Yucun. 'I should have told you that during the two years after I was cashiered I travelled extensively in every province of the empire and saw quite a few remarkable children in the course of my travels; so that just now when you mentioned this Baoyu I felt pretty certain what type of boy he must be. But one doesn't need to go very far afield for another example. There is one in the Zhen family in Nanking—I am referring to the family of the Zhen who is Imperial Deputy Director-General of the Nanking Secretariat. Perhaps you know who I mean?'

'Who doesn't?' said Zixing. 'There is an old family connection between the Zhen family and the Jias of whom we have just been speaking, and they are still on very close terms with each other. I've done business with them myself for longer than I'd care to mention.'

'Last year when I was in Nanking,' said Yucun, smiling at the recollection, 'I was recommended for the post of tutor in their household. I could tell at a glance, as soon as I got inside the place, that for all the ducal splendour this was a family "though rich yet given to courtesy", in the words of the Sage, and that it was a rare piece of luck to have got a place in it. But when I came to teach my pupil, though he was only at the first year primary stage, he gave me more trouble than an examination candidate.

'He was indeed a comedy. He once said, "I must have two girls to do my lessons with me if I am to remember the words and understand the sense. Other-

4. Lists of eccentric and extraordinary individuals from the Chinese tradition, including figures such as recluses, poets, emperors, painters, and courtesans.

wise my mind will simply not work." And he would often tell the little pages who waited on him, "The word 'girl' is very precious and very pure. It is much more rare and precious than all the rarest beasts and birds and plants in the world. So it is most extremely important that you should never, never violate it with your coarse mouths and stinking breath. Whenever you need to say it, you should first rinse your mouths out with clean water and scented tea. And if ever I catch you slipping up, I shall have holes drilled through your teeth and lace them up together."

'There was simply no end to his violence and unruliness. Yet as soon as his lessons were over and he went inside to visit the girls of the family, he became a completely different person—all gentleness and calm, and as intelligent and well-bred as you please.

'His father gave him several severe beatings but it made no difference. Whenever the pain became too much for him he would start yelling "Girls! girls!" Afterwards, when the girls in the family got to hear about it, they made fun of him. "Why do you always call to us when you are hurt? I suppose you think we shall come and plead for you to be let off. You ought to be ashamed of yourself!" But you should have heard his answer. He said, "Once when the pain was very bad, I thought that perhaps if I shouted the word 'girls' it might help to ease it. Well," he said, "I just called out once, and the pain really was quite a bit better. So now that I have found this secret remedy, I just keep on shouting 'Girls! girls! girls!' whenever the pain is at its worst." I could not help laughing.

'But because his grandmother doted on him so much, she was always taking the child's part against me and his father. In the end I had to hand in my notice. A boy like that will never be able to keep up the family traditions or listen to the advice of his teachers and friends. The pity of it is, though, that the girls in that family are all exceptionally good.'

'The three at present in the Jia household are also very fine girls,' said Zixing. 'Sir Jia Zheng's eldest girl, Yuanchun, was chosen for her exceptional virtue and cleverness to be a Lady Secretary in the Imperial Palace.[5] The next in age after her and eldest of the three still at home is called Yingchun. She is the daughter of Sir Jia She by one of his secondary wives. After her comes another daughter of Sir Zheng's, also a concubine's child, called Tanchun. The youngest, Xichun, is sister-german to Mr Jia Zhen of the Ningguo mansion. Old Lady Jia is very fond of her granddaughters and keeps them all in her own apartments on the Rongguo side. They all study together, and I have been told that they are doing very well.'

'One of the things I liked about the Zhen family,' said Yucun, 'was their custom of giving the girls the same sort of names as the boys, unlike the majority of families who invariably use fancy words like "*chun*", "*hong*", "*xiang*", "*yu*", and so forth. How comes it that the Jias should have followed the vulgar practice in this respect?'

'They didn't,' said Zixing. 'The eldest girl was called "Yuanchun" because she was in fact born on the first day of spring. The others were given names with "*chun*" in them to match hers. But if you go back a generation, you will find that among the Jias too the girls had names exactly like the boys'.

5. Baoyu's sister became an imperial concubine.

'I can give you proof. Your present employer's good lady is sister-german to Sir She and Sir Zheng of the Rong household. Her name, before she married, was Jia Min. If you don't believe me, you make a few inquiries when you get home and you'll find it is so.'

Yucun clapped his hands with a laugh. 'Of course! I have often wondered why it is that my pupil Daiyu always pronounces "*min*" as "*mi*" when she is reading and, if she has to write it, always makes the character with one or two strokes missing. Now I understand. No wonder her speech and behaviour are so unlike those of ordinary children! I always supposed that there must have been something remarkable about the mother for her to have produced so remarkable a daughter. Now I know that she was related to the Jias of the Rong household, I am not surprised.

'By the way, I am sorry to say that last month the mother passed away.'

Zixing sighed. 'Fancy her dying so soon! She was the youngest of the three. And the generation before them are all gone, every one. We shall have to see what sort of husbands they manage to find for the younger generation!'

'Yes, indeed,' said Yucun. 'Just now you mentioned that Sir Zheng had this boy with the jade in his mouth and you also mentioned a little grandson left behind by his elder son. What about old Sir She? Surely he must have a son?'

'Since Sir Zheng had the boy with the jade, he has had another son by a concubine,' said Zixing, 'but I couldn't tell you what he's like. So at present he has two sons and one grandson. Of course, we don't know what the future may bring.

'But you were asking about Sir She. Yes, he has a son too, called Jia Lian. He's already a young man in his early twenties. He married his own kin, the niece of his Uncle Zheng's wife, Lady Wang. He's been married now for four or five years. Holds the rank of a Sub-prefect by purchase. He's another member of the family who doesn't find responsibilities congenial. He knows his way around, though, and has a great gift of the gab, so at present he stays at home with his Uncle Zheng and helps him manage the family's affairs. However, ever since he married this young lady I mentioned, everyone high and low has joined in praising *her*, and he has been put into the shade rather. She is not only a *very* handsome young woman, she also has a very ready tongue and a very good head—more than a match for most men, I can tell you.'

'You see, I was not mistaken,' said Yucun. 'All these people you and I have been talking about are probably examples of that mixture of good and evil humours I was describing to you.'

'Well, I don't know about that,' said Zixing. 'Instead of sitting here setting other people's accounts to rights, let's have another drink!'

* * *

FROM CHAPTER 3

*Lin Ruhai recommends a private tutor to his brother-in-law
And old Lady Jia extends a compassionate welcome to the motherless child*

* * *

On the day of her arrival in the capital, Daiyu stepped ashore to find covered chairs from the Rong mansion for her and her women and a cart for the luggage ready, waiting on the quay.

She had often heard her mother say that her Grandmother Jia's home was not like other people's houses. The servants she had been in contact with during the past few days were comparatively low-ranking ones in the domestic hierarchy, yet the food they ate, the clothes they wore, and everything about them was quite out of the ordinary. Daiyu tried to imagine what the people who employed these superior beings must be like. When she arrived at their house she would have to watch every step she took and weigh every word she said, for if she put a foot wrong they would surely laugh her to scorn.

Daiyu got into her chair and was soon carried through the city walls. Peeping through the gauze panel which served as a window, she could see streets and buildings more rich and elegant and throngs of people more lively and numerous than she had ever seen in her life before. After being carried for what seemed a very great length of time, she saw, on the north front of the east-west street through which they were passing, two great stone lions crouched one on each side of a triple gateway whose doors were embellished with animal-heads. In front of the gateway ten or so splendidly dressed flunkeys sat in a row. The centre of the three gates was closed, but people were going in and out of the two side ones. There was a board above the centre gate on which were written in large characters the words:

NINGGUO HOUSE

Founded and Constructed by
Imperial Command

Daiyu realized that this must be where the elder branch of her grandmother's family lived. The chair proceeded some distance more down the street and presently there was another triple gate, this time with the legend

RONGGUO HOUSE

above it.

Ignoring the central gate, her bearers went in by the western entrance and after traversing the distance of a bow-shot inside, half turned a corner and set the chair down. The chairs of her female attendants which were following behind were set down simultaneously and the old women got out. The places of Daiyu's bearers were taken by four handsome, fresh-faced pages of seventeen or eighteen. They shouldered her chair and, with the old women now following on foot, carried it as far as an ornamental inner gate. There they set it down again and then retired in respectful silence. The old women came forward to the front of the chair, held up the curtain, and helped Daiyu to get out.

Each hand resting on the outstretched hand of an elderly attendant, Daiyu passed through the ornamental gate into a courtyard which had balustraded loggias running along its sides and a covered passage-way through the centre. The foreground of the courtyard beyond was partially hidden by a screen of polished marble set in an elaborate red sandalwood frame. Passing round the screen and through a small reception hall beyond it, they entered the large courtyard of the mansion's principal apartments. These were housed in an imposing five-frame building resplendent with carved and painted beams and rafters which faced them across the courtyard. Running along either side of the courtyard were galleries hung with cages containing a variety of different-coloured parrots, cockatoos, white-eyes, and other birds. Some gaily-dressed maids were sitting on the steps of the main building opposite. At the appearance of the visitors they rose to their feet and came forward with smiling faces to welcome them.

'You've come just at the right time! Lady Jia[1] was only this moment asking about you.'

Three or four of them ran to lift up the door-curtain, while another of them announced in loud tones,

'Miss Lin is here!'

As Daiyu entered the room she saw a silver-haired old lady advancing to meet her, supported on either side by a servant. She knew that this must be her Grandmother Jia and would have fallen on her knees and made her kotow, but before she could do so her grandmother had caught her in her arms and pressing her to her bosom with cries of 'My pet!' and 'My poor lamb!' burst into loud sobs, while all those present wept in sympathy, and Daiyu felt herself crying as though she would never stop. It was some time before those present succeeded in calming them both down and Daiyu was at last able to make her kotow.

Grandmother Jia now introduced those present.

'This is your elder uncle's wife, Aunt Xing. This is your Uncle Zheng's wife, Aunt Wang. This is Li Wan, the wife of your Cousin Zhu, who died.'

Daiyu kotowed to each of them in turn.

'Call the girls!' said Grandmother Jia. 'Tell them that we have a very special visitor and that they need not do their lessons today.'

There was a cry of 'Yes ma'am' from the assembled maids, and two of them went off to do her bidding.

Presently three girls arrived, attended by three nurses and five or six maids.

The first girl was of medium height and slightly plumpish, with cheeks as white and firm as a fresh lychee and a nose as white and shiny as soap made from the whitest goose-fat. She had a gentle, sweet, reserved manner. To look at her was to love her.

The second girl was rather tall, with sloping shoulders and a slender waist. She had an oval face under whose well-formed brows large, expressive eyes shot out glances that sparkled with animation. To look at her was to forget all that was mean or vulgar.

The third girl was undersized and her looks were still somewhat babyish and unformed.

All three were dressed in identical skirts and dresses and wore identical sets of bracelets and hair ornaments.

Daiyu rose to meet them and exchanged curtseys and introductions. When she was seated once more, a maid served tea, and a conversation began on the subject of her mother: how her illness had started, what doctors had been called in, what medicines prescribed, what arrangements had been made for the funeral, and how the mourning had been observed. This conversation had the foreseeable effect of upsetting the old lady all over again.

---

1. Baoyu's grandmother.

'Of all my girls your mother was the one I loved the best,' she said, 'and now she's been the first to go, and without my even being able to see her again before the end. I can't help being upset!' And holding fast to Daiyu's hand, she once more burst into tears. The rest of the company did their best to comfort her, until at last she had more or less recovered.

Everyone's attention now centred on Daiyu. They observed that although she was still young, her speech and manner already showed unusual refinement. They also noticed the frail body which seemed scarcely strong enough to bear the weight of its clothes, but which yet had an inexpressible grace about it, and realizing that she must be suffering from some deficiency, asked her what medicine she took for it and why it was still not better.

'I have always been like this,' said Daiyu. 'I have been taking medicine ever since I could eat and been looked at by ever so many well-known doctors, but it has never done me any good. Once, when I was only three, I can remember a scabby-headed old monk came and said he wanted to take me away and have me brought up as a nun; but of course, Mother and Father wouldn't hear of it. So he said, "Since you are not prepared to give her up, I am afraid her illness will never get better as long as she lives. The only way it might get better would be if she were never to hear the sound of weeping from this day onwards and never to see any relations other than her own mother and father. Only in those conditions could she get through her life without trouble." Of course, he was quite crazy, and no one took any notice of the things he said. I'm still taking Ginseng Tonic Pills.'

'Well, that's handy,' said Grandmother Jia. 'I take the Pills myself. We can easily tell them to make up a few more each time.'

She had scarcely finished speaking when someone could be heard talking and laughing in a very loud voice in the inner courtyard behind them.

'Oh dear! I'm late,' said the voice. 'I've missed the arrival of our guest.'

'Everyone else around here seems to go about with bated breath,' thought Daiyu. 'Who can this new arrival be who is so brash and unmannerly?'

Even as she wondered, a beautiful young woman entered from the room behind the one they were sitting in, surrounded by a bevy of serving women and maids. She was dressed quite differently from the others present, gleaming like some fairy princess with sparkling jewels and gay embroideries.

Her chignon was enclosed in a circlet of gold filigree and clustered pearls. It was fastened with a pin embellished with flying phoenixes, from whose beaks pearls were suspended on tiny chains.

Her necklet was of red gold in the form of a coiling dragon.

Her dress had a fitted bodice and was made of dark red silk damask with a pattern of flowers and butterflies in raised gold thread.

Her jacket was lined with ermine. It was of a slate-blue stuff with woven insets in coloured silks.

Her under-skirt was of a turquoise-coloured imported silk crêpe embroidered with flowers.

She had, moreover,

> eyes like a painted phoenix,
> eyebrows like willow-leaves,
> a slender form,

> seductive grace;
> the ever-smiling summer face
> of hidden thunders showed no trace;
> the ever-bubbling laughter started
> almost before the lips were parted.

'You don't know her,' said Grandmother Jia merrily. 'She's a holy terror this one. What we used to call in Nanking a "peppercorn". You just call her "Peppercorn Feng".[2] She'll know who you mean!'

Daiyu was at a loss to know how she was to address this Peppercorn Feng until one of the cousins whispered that it was 'Cousin Lian's wife', and she remembered having heard her mother say that her elder uncle, Uncle She, had a son called Jia Lian who was married to the niece of her Uncle Zheng's wife, Lady Wang. She had been brought up from earliest childhood just like a boy, and had acquired in the schoolroom the somewhat boyish-sounding name of Wang Xifeng. Daiyu accordingly smiled and curtseyed, greeting her by her correct name as she did so.

Xifeng took Daiyu by the hand and for a few moments scrutinized her carefully from top to toe before conducting her back to her seat beside Grandmother Jia.

'She's a beauty, Grannie dear! If I hadn't set eyes on her today, I shouldn't have believed that such a beautiful creature could exist! And everything about her so *distingué*! She doesn't take after your side of the family, Grannie. She's more like a Jia. I don't blame you for having gone on so about her during the past few days—but poor little thing! What a cruel fate to have lost Auntie like that!' and she dabbed at her eyes with a handkerchief.

'I've only just recovered,' laughed Grandmother Jia. 'Don't you go trying to start me off again! Besides, your little cousin is not very strong, and we've only just managed to get *her* cheered up. So let's have no more of this!'

In obedience to the command Xifeng at once exchanged her grief for merriment.

'Yes, of course. It was just that seeing my little cousin here put everything else out of my mind. It made me want to laugh and cry all at the same time. I'm afraid I quite forgot about you, Grannie dear. I deserve to be spanked, don't I?'

She grabbed Daiyu by the hand.

'How old are you dear? Have you begun school yet? You musn't feel homesick here. If there's anything you want to eat or anything you want to play with, just come and tell me. And you must tell me if any of the maids or the old nannies are nasty to you.'

Daiyu made appropriate responses to all of these questions and injunctions.

Xifeng turned to the servants.

'Have Miss Lin's things been brought in yet? How many people did she bring with her? You'd better hurry up and get a couple of rooms swept out for them to rest in.'

While Xifeng was speaking, the servants brought in tea and various plates of food, the distribution of which she proceeded to supervise in person.

Daiyu noticed her Aunt Wang questioning Xifeng on the side:

'Have this month's allowances been paid out yet?'

---

2. Nickname for Wang Xifeng.

'Yes. By the way, just now I went with some of the women to the upstairs store-room at the back to look for that satin. We looked and looked, but we couldn't find any like the one you described yesterday. Perhaps you misremembered.'

'Oh well, if you can't find it, it doesn't really matter,' said Lady Wang. Then, after a moment's reflection, 'You'd better pick out a couple of lengths presently to have made up into clothes for your little cousin here. If you think of it, send someone round in the evening to fetch them!'

'It's already been seen to. I knew she was going to arrive within a day or two, so I had some brought out in readiness. They are waiting back at your place for your approval. If you think they are all right, they can be sent over straight away.'

Lady Wang merely smiled and nodded her head without saying anything.

The tea things and dishes were now cleared away, and Grandmother Jia ordered two old nurses to take Daiyu round to see her uncles; but Uncle She's wife, Lady Xing, hurriedly rose to her feet and suggested that it would be more convenient if she were to take her niece round herself.

'Very well,' said Grandmother Jia. 'You go now, then. There is no need for you to come back afterwards.'

So having, together with Lady Wang, who was also returning to her quarters, taken leave of the old lady, Lady Xing went off with Daiyu, attended across the courtyard as far as the covered way by the rest of the company.

A carriage painted dark blue and hung with kingfisher-blue curtains had been drawn up in front of the ornamental gateway by some pages. Into this Aunt Xing ascended hand in hand with Daiyu. The old women pulled down the carriage blind and ordered the pages to take up the shafts, the pages drew the carriage into an open space and harnessed mules to it, and Daiyu and her aunt were driven out of the west gate, eastwards past the main gate of the Rong mansion, in again through a big black-lacquered gate, and up to an inner gate, where they were set down again.

Holding Daiyu by the hand, Aunt Xing led her into a courtyard in the middle of what she imagined must once have been part of the mansion's gardens. This impression was strengthened when they passed through a third gateway into the quarters occupied by her uncle and aunt; for here the smaller scale and quiet elegance of the halls, galleries and loggias were quite unlike the heavy magnificence and imposing grandeur they had just come from, and ornamental trees and artificial rock formations, all in exquisite taste, were to be seen on every hand.

As they entered the main reception hall, a number of heavily made-up and expensively dressed maids and concubines, who had been waiting in readiness, came forward to greet them.

Aunt Xing asked Daiyu to be seated while she sent a servant to call Uncle She. After a considerable wait the servant returned with the following message:

'The Master says he hasn't been well these last few days, and as it would only upset them both if he were to see Miss Lin now, he doesn't feel up to it for the time being. He says, tell Miss Lin not to grieve and not to feel homesick. She must think of her grandmother and her aunts as her own family now. He says that her cousins may not be very clever girls, but at least they should be company for her and help to take her mind off things. If she finds anything at all here to distress her, she is to speak up at once. She mustn't feel like an out-sider. She is to make herself completely at home.'

Daiyu stood up throughout this recital and murmured polite assent when-ever assent seemed indicated. She then sat for about another quarter of an hour before rising to take her leave. Her Aunt Xing was very pressing that she should have a meal with her before she went, but Daiyu smilingly replied that though it was very kind of her aunt to offer, and though she ought really not to refuse, nevertheless she still had to pay her respects to her Uncle Zheng, and feared that it would be disrespectful if she were to arrive late. She hoped that she might accept on another occasion and begged her aunt to excuse her.

'In that case, never mind,' said Lady Xing, and instructed the old nurses to see her to her Uncle Zheng's in the same carriage she had come by. Daiyu for-mally took her leave, and Lady Xing saw her as far as the inner gate, where she issued a few more instructions to the servants and watched her niece's carriage out of sight before returning to her rooms.

Presently they re-entered the Rong mansion proper and Daiyu got down from the carriage. There was a raised stone walk running all the way up to the main gate, along which the old nurses now conducted her. Turning right, they led her down a roofed passage-way along the back of a south-facing hall, then through an inner gate into a large courtyard.

The big building at the head of the courtyard was connected at each end to galleries running through the length of the side buildings by means of 'stag's head' roofing over the corners. The whole formed an architectural unit of greater sumptuousness and magnificence than anything Daiyu had yet seen that day, from which she concluded that this must be the main inner hall of the whole mansion.

High overhead on the wall facing her as she entered the hall was a great blue board framed in gilded dragons, on which was written in large gold characters

THE HALL OF EXALTED FELICITY

with a column of smaller characters at the side giving a date and the words '. . . written for Our beloved Subject, Jia Yuan, Duke of Rongguo', followed by the Emperor's private seal, a device containing the words 'kingly cares' and 'royal brush' in archaic seal-script.

A long, high table of carved red sandalwood, ornamented with dragons, stood against the wall underneath. In the centre of this was a huge antique bronze *ding*, fully a yard high, covered with a green patina. On the wall above the *ding* hung a long vertical scroll with an ink-painting of a dragon emerging from clouds and waves, of the kind often presented to high court officials in token of their office. The *ding* was flanked on one side by a smaller antique bronze ves-sel with a pattern of gold inlay and on the other by a crystal bowl. At each side of the table stood a row of eight yellow cedar-wood armchairs with their backs to the wall; and above the chairs hung, one on each side, a pair of vertical ebony boards inlaid with a couplet in characters of gold:

(on the right-hand one)

May the jewel of learning shine in this house more effulgently than the sun and moon.

(on the left-hand one)

May the insignia of honour glitter in these halls more brilliantly than the
    starry sky.

This was followed by a colophon in smaller characters:

    With the Respectful Compliments of your Fellow-
    Student, Mu Shi, Hereditary Prince of Dongan.

Lady Wang did not, however, normally spend her leisure hours in this
main reception hall, but in a smaller room on the east side of the same building. Accordingly the nurses conducted Daiyu through the door into this side
apartment.

Here there was a large kang[3] underneath the window, covered with a scarlet
Kashmir rug. In the middle of the kang was a dark-red bolster with a pattern of
medallions in the form of tiny dragons, and a long russet-green seating strip in the
same pattern. A low rose-shaped table of coloured lacquer-work stood at each side.
On the left-hand one was a small, square, four-legged *ding*, together with a bronze
ladle, metal chopsticks, and an incense container. On the right-hand one was a
narrow-waisted Ru-ware imitation *gu*[4] with a spray of freshly cut flowers in it.

In the part of the room below the kang there was a row of four big chairs
against the east wall. All had footstools in front of them and chair-backs and
seat-covers in old rose brocade sprigged with flowers. There were also narrow
side-tables on which tea things and vases of flowers were arranged, besides
other furnishings which it would be superfluous to enumerate.

The old nurses invited Daiyu to get up on the kang; but guessing that the
brocade cushions arranged one on each side near the edge of it must be her
uncle's and aunt's places, she deemed it more proper to sit on one of the chairs
against the wall below. The maids in charge of the apartment served tea, and as
she sipped it Daiyu observed that their clothing, makeup, and deportment were
quite different from those of the maids she had seen so far in other parts of the
mansion.

Before she had time to finish her tea, a smiling maid came in wearing a dress
of red damask and a black silk sleeveless jacket which had scalloped borders of
some coloured material.

'The Mistress says will Miss Lin come over to the other side, please.'

The old nurses now led Daiyu down the east gallery to a reception room at
the side of the courtyard. This too had a kang. It was bisected by a long, low
table piled with books and tea things. A much-used black satin back-rest was
pushed up against the east wall. Lady Wang was seated on a black satin cush-
ion and leaning against another comfortable-looking back-rest of black satin
somewhat farther forward on the opposite side.

Seeing her niece enter, she motioned her to sit opposite her on the kang, but
Daiyu felt sure that this must be her Uncle Zheng's place. So, having observed
a row of three chairs near the kang with covers of flower-sprigged brocade
which looked as though they were in fairly constant use, she sat upon one of
those instead. Only after much further pressing from her aunt would she get
up on the kang, and even then she would only sit beside her and not in the
position of honour opposite.

---

3. A heated bed-stove.   4. *Ding* and *gu* are vessel types.

'Your uncle is in retreat today,' said Lady Wang. 'He will see you another time. There is, however, something I have got to talk to you about. The three girls are very well-behaved children, and in future, when you are studying or sewing together, even if once in a while they may grow a bit high-spirited, I can depend on them not to go too far. There is only one thing that worries me. I have a little monster of a son who tyrannizes over all the rest of this household. He has gone off to the temple today in fulfilment of a vow and is not yet back; but you will see what I mean this evening. The thing to do is never to take any notice of him. None of your cousins dare provoke him.'

Daiyu had long ago been told by her mother that she had a boy cousin who was born with a piece of jade in his mouth and who was exceptionally wild and naughty. He hated study and liked to spend all his time in the women's apartments with the girls; but because Grandmother Jia doted on him so much, no one ever dared to correct him. She realized that it must be this cousin her aunt was now referring to.

'Do you mean the boy born with the jade, Aunt?' she asked. 'Mother often told me about him at home. She told me that he was one year older than me and that his name was Baoyu. But she said that though he was very wilful, he always behaved very nicely to girls. Now that I am here, I suppose I shall be spending all my time with my girl cousins and not in the same part of the house as the boys. Surely there will be no danger of *my* provoking him?'

Lady Wang gave a rueful smile. 'You little know how things are here! Baoyu is a law unto himself. Because your grandmother is so fond of him she has thoroughly spoiled him. When he was little he lived with the girls, so with the girls he remains now. As long as they take no notice of him, things run quietly enough. But if they give him the least encouragement, he at once becomes excitable, and then there is no end to the mischief he may get up to. That is why I counsel you to ignore him. He can be all honey-sweet words one minute and ranting and raving like a lunatic the next. So don't believe anything he says.'

Daiyu promised to follow her aunt's advice.

Just then a maid came in with a message that 'Lady Jia said it was time for dinner', whereupon Lady Wang took Daiyu by the hand and hurried her out through a back door. Passing along a verandah which ran beneath the rear eaves of the hall they came to a corner gate through which they passed into an alley-way running north and south. At the south end it was traversed by a narrow little building with a short passage-way running through its middle. At the north end was a white-painted screen wall masking a medium-sized gateway leading to a small courtyard in which stood a very little house.

'That,' said Lady Wang, pointing to the little house, 'is where your Cousin Lian's wife, Wang Xifeng, lives, in case you want to see her later on. She is the person to talk to if there is anything you need.'

There were a few young pages at the gate of the courtyard who, when they saw Lady Wang coming, all stood to attention with their hands at their sides.

Lady Wang now led Daiyu along a gallery, running from east to west, which brought them out into the courtyard behind Grandmother Jia's apartments. Entering these by a back entrance, they found a number of servants waiting there who, as soon as they saw Lady Wang, began to arrange the table and chairs for dinner. The ladies of the house themselves took part in the service. Li Wan brought in the cups, Xifeng laid out the chopsticks, and Lady Wang brought in the soup.

The table at which Grandmother Jia presided, seated alone on a couch, had two empty chairs on either side. Xifeng tried to seat Daiyu in the one on the left nearer to her grandmother—an honour which she strenuously resisted until her grandmother explained that her aunt and her elder cousins' wives would not be eating with them, so that, since she was a guest, the place was properly hers. Only then did she ask permission to sit, as etiquette prescribed. Grandmother Jia then ordered Lady Wang to be seated. This was the cue for the three girls to ask permission to sit. Yingchun sat in the first place on the right opposite Daiyu, Tanchun sat second on the left, and Xichun sat second on the right.

While Li Wan and Xifeng stood by the table helping to distribute food from the dishes, maids holding fly-whisks, spittoons, and napkins ranged themselves on either side. In addition to these, there were numerous other maids and serving-women in attendance in the outer room, yet not so much as a cough was heard throughout the whole of the meal.

When they had finished eating, a maid served each diner with tea on a little tray. Daiyu's parents had brought their daughter up to believe that good health was founded on careful habits, and in pursuance of this principle, had always insisted that after a meal one should allow a certain interval to elapse before taking tea in order to avoid indigestion. However, she could see that many of the rules in this household were different from the ones she had been used to at home; so, being anxious to conform as much as possible, she accepted the tea. But as she did so, another maid proferred a spittoon, from which she inferred that the tea was for rinsing her mouth with. And it was not, in fact, until they had all rinsed out their mouths and washed their hands that another lot of tea was served, this time for drinking.

Grandmother Jia now dismissed her lady servers, observing that she wished to enjoy a little chat with her young grandchildren without the restraint of their grown-up presence.

Lady Wang obediently rose to her feet and, after exchanging a few pleasant-ries, went out, taking Li Wan and Wang Xifeng with her.

Grandmother Jia asked Daiyu what books she was studying.

'The Four Books,'[5] said Daiyu, and inquired in turn what books her cousins were currently engaged on.

'Gracious, child, they don't study books,' said her grandmother; 'they can barely read and write!'

While they were speaking, a flurry of footsteps could be heard outside and a maid came in to say that Baoyu was back.

'I wonder,' thought Daiyu, 'just what sort of graceless creature this Baoyu is going to be!'

The young gentleman who entered in answer to her unspoken question had a small jewel-encrusted gold coronet on the top of his head and a golden headband low down over his brow in the form of two dragons playing with a large pearl.

He was wearing a narrow-sleeved, full-skirted robe of dark red material with a pattern of flowers and butterflies in two shades of gold. It was confined at the waist with a court girdle of coloured silks braided at regular intervals into elaborate clusters of knotwork and terminating in long tassels.

---

5. The Neoconfucian canon: *Analects, Mencius, Doctrine of the Mean*, and *The Great Learning*.

Over the upper part of his robe he wore a jacket of slate-blue Japanese silk damask with a raised pattern of eight large medallions on the front and with tasselled borders.

On his feet he had half-length dress boots of black satin with thick white soles.

As to his person, he had:
a face like the moon of Mid-Autumn,
a complexion like flowers at dawn,
a hairline straight as a knife-cut,
eyebrows that might have been painted by an artist's brush,
a shapely nose, and
eyes clear as limpid pools,
    that even in anger seemed to smile,
    and, as they glared, beamed tenderness the while.

Around his neck he wore a golden torque in the likeness of a dragon and a woven cord of coloured silks to which the famous jade was attached.

Daiyu looked at him with astonishment. How strange! How very strange! It was as though she had seen him somewhere before, he was so extraordinarily familiar. Baoyu went straight past her and saluted his grandmother, who told him to come after he had seen his mother, whereupon he turned round and walked straight out again.

Quite soon he was back once more, this time dressed in a completely different outfit.

The crown and circlet had gone. She could now see that his side hair was dressed in a number of small braids plaited with red silk, which were drawn round to join the long hair at the back in a single large queue of glistening jet black, fastened at intervals from the nape downwards with four enormous pearls and ending in a jewelled gold clasp. He had changed his robe and jacket for a rather more worn-looking rose-coloured gown, sprigged with flowers. He wore the gold torque and his jade as before, and she observed that the collection of objects round his neck had been further augmented by a padlock-shaped amulet and a lucky charm. A pair of ivy-coloured embroidered silk trousers were partially visible beneath his gown, thrust into black and white socks trimmed with brocade. In place of the formal boots he was wearing thick-soled crimson slippers.

She was even more struck than before by his fresh complexion. The cheeks might have been brushed with powder and the lips touched with rouge, so bright was their natural colour.

His glance was soulful,
yet from his lips the laughter often leaped;
    a world of charm upon that brow was heaped;
    a world of feeling from those dark eyes peeped.

In short, his outward appearance was very fine. But appearances can be misleading. A perceptive poet has supplied two sets of verses, to be sung to the tune of *Moon On West River*, which contain a more accurate appraisal of our hero than the foregoing descriptions.

I

Oft-times he sought out what would make him sad;
Sometimes an idiot seemed and sometimes mad.
Though outwardly a handsome sausage-skin,
He proved to have but sorry meat within.
A harum-scarum, to all duty blind,
A doltish mule, to study disinclined;
His acts outlandish and his nature queer;
Yet not a whit cared he how folk might jeer!

2

Prosperous, he could not play his part with grace,
Nor, poor, bear hardship with a smiling face.
So shamefully the precious hours he'd waste
That both indoors and out he was disgraced.
For uselessness the world's prize he might bear;
His gracelessness in history has no peer.
Let gilded youths who every dainty sample
Not imitate this rascal's dite example!

'Fancy changing your clothes before you have welcomed the visitor!' Grand-mother Jia chided indulgently on seeing Baoyu back again. 'Aren't you going to pay your respects to your cousin?'

Baoyu had already caught sight of a slender, delicate girl whom he surmised to be his Aunt Lin's daughter and quickly went over to greet her. Then, return-ing to his place and taking a seat, he studied her attentively. How different she seemed from the other girls he knew!

Her mist-wreathed brows at first seemed to frown, yet were
    not frowning;
Her passionate eyes at first seemed to smile, yet were not
    merry.
Habit had given a melancholy cast to her tender face;
Nature had bestowed a sickly constitution on her delicate
    frame.
Often the eyes swam with glistening tears;
Often the breath came in gentle gasps.
In stillness she made one think of a graceful flower reflected
    in the water;
In motion she called to mind tender willow shoots caressed by
    the wind.
She had more chambers in her heart than the martyred Bi Gan;
And suffered a tithe more pain in it than the beautiful Xi Shi.[6]

6. A famous beauty from early China known for a slight frown. "More chambers . . . Bi Gan": When Bi Gan tried to restrain the behavior of the last tyrannical ruler of the Shang Dynasty (ca. 1500–1045 B.C.E.), the ruler retorted that he had heard that a sage had a heart with seven openings and that he would have to tear his heart out to ascertain this truth.

Having completed his survey, Baoyu gave a laugh.

'I have seen this cousin before.'

'Nonsense!' said Grandmother Jia. 'How could you possibly have done?'

'Well, perhaps not,' said Baoyu, 'but her face seems so familiar that I have the impression of meeting her again after a long separation.'

'All the better,' said Grandmother Jia. 'That means that you should get on well together.'

Baoyu moved over again and, drawing a chair up beside Daiyu, recommenced his scrutiny.

Presently: 'Do you study books yet, cousin?'

'No,' said Daiyu. 'I have only been taking lessons for a year or so. I can barely read and write.'

'What's your name?'

Daiyu told him.

'What's your school-name?'

'I haven't got one.'

Baoyu laughed. 'I'll give you one, cousin. I think "Frowner" would suit you perfectly.'

'Where's your reference?' said Tanchun.

'In the *Encyclopedia of Men and Objects Ancient and Modern* it says that somewhere in the West there is a mineral called "dai" which can be used instead of eye-black for painting the eyebrows with. She has this "dai" in her name and she knits her brows together in a little frown. I think it's a splendid name for her!'

'I expect you made it up,' said Tanchun scornfully.

'What if I did?' said Baoyu. 'There are lots of made-up things in books—apart from the *Four Books*, of course.'

He returned to his interrogation of Daiyu.

'Have you got a jade?'

The rest of the company were puzzled, but Daiyu at once divined that he was asking her if she too had a jade like the one he was born with.

'No,' said Daiyu. 'That jade of yours is a very rare object. You can't expect everybody to have one.'

This sent Baoyu off instantly into one of his mad fits. Snatching the jade from his neck he hurled it violently on the floor as if to smash it and began abusing it passionately.

'Rare object! Rare object! What's so lucky about a stone that can't even tell which people are better than others? Beastly thing! I don't want it!'

The maids all seemed terrified and rushed forward to pick it up, while Grandmother Jia clung to Baoyu in alarm.

'Naughty, naughty boy! Shout at someone or strike them if you like when you are in a nasty temper, but why go smashing that precious thing that your very life depends on?'

'None of the girls has got one,' said Baoyu, his face streaming with tears and sobbing hysterically. 'Only I have got one. It always upsets me. And now this new cousin comes here who is as beautiful as an angel and she hasn't got one either, so I *know* it can't be any good.'

'Your cousin did have a jade once,' said Grandmother Jia, coaxing him like a little child, 'but because when Auntie died she couldn't bear to leave her little girl behind, they had to let her take the jade with her instead. In that way your cousin could show her mamma how much she loved her by letting the jade be buried with her; and at the same time, whenever Auntie's spirit looked at the jade, it would be just like looking at her own little girl again.

'So when your cousin said she hadn't got one, it was only because she didn't want to boast about the good, kind thing she did when she gave it to her mamma. Now you put yours on again like a good boy, and mind your mother doesn't find out how naughty you have been.'

So saying, she took the jade from the hands of one of the maids and hung it round his neck for him. And Baoyu, after reflecting for a moment or two on what she had said, offered no further resistance.

*   *   *

FROM CHAPTER 17

The inspection of the new garden becomes a test of talent
And Rongguo House makes itself ready for an important visitor

*   *   *

One day Cousin Zhen came to Jia Zheng with his team of helpers to report that work on the new garden had been completed.

'Uncle She has already had a look,' said Cousin Zhen. 'Now we are only waiting for you to look round it to tell us if there is anything you think will need altering and also to decide what inscriptions ought to be used on the boards everywhere.'

Jia Zheng reflected a while in silence.

'These inscriptions are going to be difficult,' he said eventually. 'By rights, of course, Her Grace should have the privilege of doing them herself; but she can scarcely be expected to make them up out of her head without having seen any of the views which they are to describe. On the other hand, if we wait until she has already visited the garden before asking her, half the pleasure of the visit will be lost. All those prospects and pavilions—even the rocks and trees and flowers will seem somehow incomplete without that touch of poetry which only the written word can lend a scene.'

'My dear patron, you are so right,' said one of the literary gentlemen who sat with him. 'But we have had an idea. The inscriptions for the various parts of the garden obviously cannot be dispensed with; nor, equally obviously, can they be decided in advance. Our suggestion is that we should compose provisional names and couplets to suit the places where inscriptions are required, and have them painted on rectangular paper lanterns which can be hung up temporarily—either horizontally or vertically as the case may be—when Her Grace comes to visit. We can ask her to decide on the permanent names after she has inspected the garden. Is not this a solution of the dilemma?'

'It is indeed,' said Jia Zheng. 'When we look round the garden presently, we must all try to think of words that can be used. If they seem suitable, we can keep them for the lanterns. If not, we can call for Yucun to come and help us out.'

'Your own suggestions are sure to be admirable, Sir Zheng,' said the literary gentlemen ingratiatingly. 'There will be no need to call in Yucun.'

Jia Zheng smiled deprecatingly.

'I am afraid it is not as you imagine. In my youth I had at best only indifferent skill in the art of writing verses about natural objects—birds and flowers and scenery and the like; and now that I am older and have to devote all my energies to official documents and government papers, I am even more out of touch with this sort of thing than I was then; so that even if I were to try my hand at it, I fear that my efforts would be rather dull and pedantic ones. Instead of enhancing the interest and beauty of the garden, they would probably have a deadening effect upon both.'

'That doesn't matter,' the literary gentlemen replied. 'We can *all* try our hands at composing. If each of us contributes what he is best at, and if we then select the better attempts and reject the ones that are not so good, we should be able to manage all right.'

'That seems to me a very good suggestion,' said Jia Zheng. 'As the weather today is so warm and pleasant, let us all go and take a turn round the garden now!'

So saying he rose to his feet and conducted his little retinue of literary luminaries towards the garden. Cousin Zhen hurried on ahead to warn those in charge that they were coming.

As Baoyu was still in very low spirits these days because of his grief for Qin Zhong, Grandmother Jia had hit on the idea of sending him into the newly made garden to play. By unlucky chance she had selected this very day on which to try out her antidote. He had in fact only just entered the garden when Cousin Zhen came hurrying towards him.

'Better get out of here!' said Cousin Zhen with an amused smile. 'Your father will be here directly!'

Baoyu streaked back towards the gate, a string of nurses and pages hurrying at his heels. But he had only just turned the corner on coming out of it when he almost ran into the arms of Jia Zheng and his party coming from the opposite direction. Escape was impossible. He simply had to stand meekly to one side and await instructions.

Jia Zheng had recently received a favourable report on Baoyu from his teacher Jia Dairu in which mention had been made of his skill in composing couplets. Although the boy showed no aptitude for serious study, Dairu had said, he nevertheless possessed a certain meretricious talent for versification not undeserving of commendation. Because of this report, Jia Zheng ordered Baoyu to accompany him into the garden, intending to put his aptitude to the test. Baoyu, who knew nothing either of Dairu's report or of his father's intentions, followed with trepidation.

As soon as they reached the gate they found Cousin Zhen at the head of a group of overseers waiting to learn Jia Zheng's wishes.

'I want you to close the gate,' said Jia Zheng, 'so that we can see what it looks like from outside before we go in.'

Cousin Zhen ordered the gate to be closed, and Jia Zheng stood back and studied it gravely.

It was a five-frame gate-building with a hump-backed roof of half-cylinder tiles. The wooden lattice-work of the doors and windows was finely carved and ingeniously patterned. The whole gatehouse was quite unadorned by colour or gilding, yet all was of the most exquisite workmanship. Its walls stood on a terrace of white marble carved with a pattern of passion-flowers in relief, and the garden's whitewashed circumference wall to left and right of it had a footing made of black-and-white striped stone blocks arranged so that the stripes formed a simple pattern. Jia Zheng found the unostentatious simplicity of this entrance greatly to his liking, and after ordering the gates to be opened, passed on inside.

A cry of admiration escaped them as they entered, for there, immediately in front of them, screening everything else from their view, rose a steep, verdure-clad hill.

'Without this hill,' Jia Zheng somewhat otiosely observed, 'the whole garden would be visible as one entered, and all its mystery would be lost.'

The literary gentlemen concurred. 'Only a master of the art of landscape could have conceived so bold a stroke,' said one of them.

As they gazed at this miniature mountain, they observed a great number of large white rocks in all kinds of grotesque and monstrous shapes, rising course above course up one of its sides, some recumbent, some upright or leaning at angles, their surfaces streaked and spotted with moss and lichen or half concealed by creepers, and with a narrow, zig-zag path only barely discernible to the eye winding up between them.

'Let us begin our tour by following this path,' said Jia Zheng. 'If we work our way round towards the other side of the hill on our way back, we shall have made a complete circuit of the garden.'

He ordered Cousin Zhen to lead the way, and leaning on Baoyu's shoulder, began the winding ascent of the little mountain. Suddenly on the mountain-side above his head, he noticed a white rock whose surface had been polished to mirror smoothness and realized that this must be one of the places which had been prepared for an inscription.

'Aha, gentlemen!' said Jia Zheng, turning back to address the others who were climbing up behind him. 'What name are we going to choose for this mountain?'

'Emerald Heights,' said one.

'Embroidery Hill,' said another.

Another proposed that they should call it 'Little Censer' after the famous Censer Peak in Kiangsi. Another proposed 'Little Zhongnan'. Altogether some twenty or thirty names were suggested—none of them very seriously, since the literary gentlemen were aware that Jia Zheng intended to test Baoyu and were anxious not to make the boy's task too difficult. Baoyu understood and was duly grateful.

When no more names were forthcoming Jia Zheng turned to Baoyu and asked him to propose something himself.

'I remember reading in some old book,' said Baoyu, 'that "to recall old things is better than to invent new ones; and to recut an ancient text is better than to engrave a modern". We ought, then, to choose something old. But as this is not the garden's principal "mountain" or its chief vista, strictly speaking there is no justification for having an inscription here at all—unless it is to be something which implies that this is merely a first step towards more important things ahead. I suggest we should call it "Pathway to Mysteries" after the line in Chang Jian's poem about the mountain temple:

A path winds upwards to mysterious places.

A name like that would be more distinguished.'

There was a chorus of praise from the literary gentlemen:

'Exactly right! Wonderful! Our young friend with his natural talent and youthful imagination succeeds immediately where we old pedants fail!'

Jia Zheng gave a deprecatory laugh:

'You mustn't flatter the boy! People of his age are adept at making a little knowledge go a long way. I only asked him as a joke, to see what he would say. We shall have to think of a better name later on.'

As he spoke, they passed through a tunnel of rock in the mountain's shoulder into an artificial ravine ablaze with the vari-coloured flowers and foliage of many varieties of tree and shrub which grew there in great profusion. Down below, where the trees were thickest, a clear stream gushed between the rocks. After they had advanced a few paces in a somewhat northerly direction, the ravine broadened into a little flat-bottomed valley and the stream widened out to form a pool. Gaily painted and carved pavilions rose from the slopes on either side, their lower halves concealed amidst the trees, their tops reaching into the blue. In the midst of the prospect below them was a handsome bridge:

> In a green ravine
> A jade stream sped.
> A stair of stone
> Plunged to the brink.
> Where the water widened
> To a placid pool,
> A marble baluster
> Ran round about.
> A marble bridge crossed it
> With triple span,
> And a marble lion's maw
> Crowned each of the arches.

Over the centre of the bridge there was a little pavilion, which Jia Zheng and the others entered and sat down in.

'Well, gentlemen!' said Jia Zheng. 'What are we going to call it?'

'Ou-yang Xiu[1] in his *Pavilion of the Old Drunkard* speaks of "a pavilion poised above the water",' said one of them. 'What about "Poised Pavilion"?'

'"Poised Pavilion" is good,' said Jia Zheng, 'but *this* pavilion was put here in order to dominate the water it stands over, and I think there ought to be some reference to water in its name. I seem to recollect that in that same essay you mention Ou-yang Xiu speaks of the water "gushing between twin peaks". Could we not use the word "gushing" in some way?'

'Yes, yes!' said one of the literary gentlemen. '"Gushing Jade" would do splendidly.'

Jia Zheng fondled his beard meditatively, then turned to Baoyu and asked him for *his* suggestion.

'I agreed with what you said just now, Father,' said Baoyu, 'but on second thought it seems to me that though it may have been all right for Ou-yang Xiu

---

1. A well-known scholar-official of the 11th century.

to use the word "gushing" in describing the source of the river Rang, it doesn't really suit the water round this pavilion. Then again, as this is a Separate Residence specially designed for the reception of a royal personage, it seems to me that something rather formal is called for, and that an expression taken from the *Drunkard's Pavilion* might seem a bit improper. I think we should try to find a rather more imaginative, less obvious sort of name.'

'I hope you gentlemen are all taking this in!' said Jia Zheng sarcastically. 'You will observe that when we suggest something original we are recommended to prefer the old to the new, but that when we *do* make use of an old text we are "improper" and "unimaginative"!—Well, carry on then! Let's have your suggestion!'

'I think "Drenched Blossoms" would be more original and more tasteful than "Gushing Jade".'

Jia Zheng stroked his beard and nodded silently. The literary gentlemen could see that he was pleased and hastened to commend Baoyu's remarkable ability.

'That's the two words for the framed board on top,' said Jia Zheng. '*Not* a very difficult task. But what about the seven-word lines for the sides?'

Baoyu glanced quickly round, seeking inspiration from the scene, and presently came up with the following couplet:

> 'Three pole-thrust lengths of bankside willows green,
> One fragrant breath of bankside flowers sweet.'

Jia Zheng nodded and a barely perceptible smile played over his features. The literary gentlemen redoubled their praises.

They now left the pavilion and crossed to the other side of the pool. For a while they walked on, stopping from time to time to admire the various rocks and flowers and trees which they passed on their way, until suddenly they found themselves at the foot of a range of whitewashed walls enclosing a small retreat almost hidden among the hundreds and hundreds of green bamboos which grew in a dense thicket behind them. With cries of admiration they went inside. A cloister-like covered walk ran round the walls from the entrance to the back of the forecourt and a cobbled pathway led up to the steps of the terrace. The house was a tiny three-frame one, two parts latticed, the third part windowless. The tables, chairs and couches which furnished it seemed to have been specially made to fit the interior. A door in the rear wall opened onto a garden of broad-leaved plantains dominated by a large flowering pear-tree and overlooked on either side by two diminutive lodges built at right angles to the back of the house. A stream gushed through an opening at the foot of the garden wall into a channel barely a foot wide which ran to the foot of the rear terrace and thence round the side of the house to the front, where it meandered through the bamboos of the forecourt before finally disappearing through another opening in the surrounding wall.

'This must be a pleasant enough place at any time,' said Jia Zheng with a smile. 'But just imagine what it would be like to sit studying beside the window here on a moonlight night! It is pleasures like that which make a man feel he has not lived in vain!'

As he spoke, his glance happened to fall on Baoyu, who instantly became so embarrassed that he hung his head in shame. He was rescued by the timely intervention of the literary gentlemen who changed the subject from that of study to a less dangerous topic. Two of them suggested that the name given to this retreat should be a four-word one. Jia Zheng asked them what four words they proposed.

'"Where Bends the Qi"' said one of them, no doubt having in mind the song in the *Poetry Classic*[2] which begins with the words

> See in that nook where bends the Qi,
> The green bamboos, how graceful grown!

'No,' said Jia Zheng. 'Too obvious!'

'"North of the Sui",' said the other, evidently thinking of the ancient Rabbit Garden of the Prince of Liang in Suiyang—also famous for its bamboos and running water.

'No,' said Jia Zheng. 'Still too obvious!'

'You'd better ask Cousin Bao again,' said Cousin Zhen, who stood by listening.

'He always insists on criticizing everyone else's suggestions before he will deign to make one of his own,' said Jia Zheng. 'He is a worthless creature.'

'That's all right,' said the others. 'His criticisms are very good ones. He is in no way to blame for making them.'

'You shouldn't let him get away with it!' said Jia Zheng. 'All right!' he went on, turning to Baoyu. 'Today we will indulge you up to the hilt. Let's have your criticisms, and after that we'll hear your own proposal. What about the two suggestions that have just been made? Do you think either of them could be used?'

'Neither of them seems quite right to me,' said Baoyu in answer to the question.

'In what way "not quite right"?' said Jia Zheng with a scornful smile.

'Well,' said Baoyu, 'This is the first building our visitor will enter when she looks over the garden, so there ought to be some word of praise for the Emperor at this point. If we want a classical reference with imperial symbolism, I suggest "The Phoenix Dance", alluding to that passage in the *History Classic* about the male and female phoenixes alighting "with measured gambollings" in the Emperor's courtyard.'

'What about "Bend of the Qi" and "North of the Sui"?' said Jia Zheng. 'Aren't they classical allusions? If not, I should like to know what they are!'

'Yes,' said Baoyu, 'but they are too contrived. "The Phoenix Dance" is more fitting.'

There was a loud murmur of assent from the literary gentlemen. Jia Zhong nodded and tried not to look pleased.

'Young idiot!—A "small capacity but a great self-conceit", gentlemen—All right!' he ordered: 'now the couplet!'

So Baoyu recited the following couplet:

> 'From the empty cauldron the steam still rises after the brewing of tea.

---

2. The *Classic of Poetry*.

By the darkening window the fingers are still cold after the game
of Go.'

Jia Zheng shook his head:
'Nothing very remarkable about *that*!'

*　*　*

They had been moving on meanwhile, and he now led them into the largest of
the little thatched buildings, from whose simple interior with its paper win-
dows and plain deal furniture all hint of urban refinement had been banished.
Jia Zheng was inwardly pleased. He stared hard at Baoyu:
'How do you like *this* place, then?'
With secret winks and nods the literary gentlemen urged Baoyu to make a
favourable reply, but he wilfully ignored their promptings.
'Not nearly as much as "The Phoenix Dance".'
His father snorted disgustedly.
'Ignoramus! You have eyes only for painted halls and gaudy pavilions—the
rubbishy trappings of wealth. What can *you* know of the beauty that lies in
quietness and natural simplicity? This is a consequence of your refusal to
study properly.'
'Your rebuke is, of course, justified, Father,' Baoyu replied promptly, 'but then
I have never really understood what it was the ancients *meant* by "natural".'
The literary gentlemen, who had observed a vein of mulishness in Baoyu
which boded trouble, were surprised by the seeming naïveté of this reply.
'Why, fancy not knowing what "natural" means—you who have such a good
understanding of so much else! "Natural" is that which is *of nature*, that is to
say, that which is produced by nature as opposed to that which is produced by
human artifice.'
'There you are, you see!' said Baoyu. 'A farm set down in the middle of a
place like this is obviously the product of human artifice. There are no neighbouring villages, no distant prospects of city walls; the mountain at the back
doesn't belong to any system; there is no pagoda rising from some tree-hid
monastery in the hills above; there is no bridge below leading to a near-by
market town. It sticks up out of nowhere, in total isolation from everything
else. It isn't even a particularly remarkable view—not nearly so "natural" in
either form or spirit as those other places we have seen. The bamboos in those
other places may have been planted by human hand and the streams diverted
out of their natural courses, but there was no *appearance* of artifice. That's
why, when the ancients use the term "natural" I have my doubts about what
they really meant. For example, when they speak of a "natural painting", I can't
help wondering if they are not referring to precisely that forcible interference
with the landscape to which I object: putting hills where they are not meant to
be, and that sort of thing. However great the skill with which this is done; the
results are never quite . . .'
His discourse was cut short by an outburst of rage from Jia Zheng.
'Take that boy out of here!'
Baoyu fled.
'Come back!'
He returned.

'You still have to make a couplet on this place. If it isn't satisfactory, you will find yourself reciting it to the tune of a slapped face!'

Baoyu stood quivering with fright and for some moments was unable to say anything. At last he recited the following couplet:

'Emergent buds swell where the washerwoman soaks her cloth.
A fresh tang rises where the cress-gatherer fills his pannier.'

Jia Zheng shook his head:
'Worse and worse.'
He led them out of the 'village' and round the foot of the hill:

through flowers and foliage,
by rock and rivulet,
past rose-crowned pergolas
and rose-twined trellises,
through small pavillions
embowered in peonies,
where scent of sweet-briers stole,
or pliant plantains waved—

until they came to a place where a musical murmur of water issued from a cave in the rock. The cave was half-veiled by a green curtain of creeper, and the water below was starred with bobbing blossoms.

'What a delightful spot!' the literary gentlemen exclaimed.

'Very well, gentlemen. What are you going to call it?' said Jia Zheng.

Inevitably the literary gentlemen thought of Tao Yuanming's fisherman of Wuling and his Peach-blossom Stream.[3]

'"The Wuling Stream",' said one of them. 'The name is ready-made for this place. No need to look further than that.'

Jia Zheng laughed:

'The same trouble again, I am afraid. It is the name of a real place. In any case, it is too hackneyed.'

'All right,' said the others good-humouredly. 'In that case simply call it "Refuge of the Qins".'[4] Their minds still ran on the Peach-blossom Stream and its hidden paradise.

'That's even more inappropriate!' said Baoyu. '"Refuge of the Qins" would imply that the people here were fugitives from tyranny. How can we possibly call it that? I suggest "Smartweed Bank and Flowery Harbour".'

'Rubbish!' said Jia Zheng.

*　*　*

---

3. Allusion to Tao Qian's (or Tao Yuanming's) vision of a utopian society, the *Peach Blossom Spring*.

4. In Tao Qian's *Peach Blossom Spring* the inhabitants were said to have fled political upheavals and the draconian rule of the Qin Dynasty (221–206 B.C.E.), China's first empire.

Baoyu was now longing to get back to the girls, but as no dismissal was forth-coming from his father, he followed him along with the others into his study. Fortunately Jia Zheng suddenly recollected that Baoyu was still with him:

'Well, run along then! Your grandmother will be worrying about you. I take it you're not still waiting for more?'

At last Baoyu could withdraw. But as soon as he was in the courtyard out-side, he was waylaid by a group of Jia Zheng's pages who laid hands on him and prevented him from going.

'You've done well today, haven't you, coming out top with all those poems? You have *us* to thank for that! Her Old Ladyship sent round several times ask-ing about you, but because the Master was so pleased with you, we told her not to worry. If we hadn't done that, you wouldn't have had the chance to show off your poems! Everyone says they were better than all the others. What about sharing your good luck with us?'

Baoyu laughed good-naturedly.

'All right. A string of cash each.'

'Who wants a measly string of cash? Give us that little purse you're wearing!' And without a 'by your leave' they began to despoil him, beginning with the purse and his fan-case, of all his trinkets, until every one of the objects he car-ried about him had been taken from him.

'Now,' they said, 'we'll see you back in style!'

And closing round him, they marched him back to Grandmother Jia's apart-ment in triumphal procession.

Grandmother Jia had been waiting for him with some anxiety, and was natu-rally delighted to see him come in apparently none the worse for his experience.

Soon after, when he was back in his own room, Aroma came in to pour him some tea and noticed that all the little objects he usually carried about his waist had disappeared.

'Where have the things from your belt gone?' she said. 'I suppose those worthless pages have taken them again.'

Daiyu overheard her and came up to inspect. Sure enough, not one of the things was there.

'So you've given away that little purse I gave you? Very well, then. You needn't expect me to give you anything in future, however much you want it!'

With these words she went off to her own room in a temper, and taking up a still unfinished perfume sachet which she was making for him at his own request, she began to cut it up with her embroidery scissors. Baoyu, observing that she was angry, had hurried after her—but it was too late. The sachet was already cut to pieces.

Although it had not been finished, Baoyu could see that the embroidery was very fine, and it made him angry to think of the hours and hours of work so wantonly destroyed. Tearing open his collar he took out the little embroidered purse which had all along been hanging round his neck and held it out for her to see.

'Look! What's that? When have I ever given anything of yours to someone else?'

Daiyu knew that he must have treasured her gift to have worn it inside his clothing where there was no risk of its being taken from him. She regretted her over-hasty destruction of the sachet and hung her head in silence.

'You needn't have cut it up,' said Baoyu. 'I know it's only because you hate giving things away. Here, you can have this back too since you're so stingy!'

He tossed the purse into her lap and turned to go. Daiyu burst into tears of rage, and picking up the little purse, attacked that too with her scissors. Baoyu hurried back and caught her by the wrist.

'Come, cuzzy dear!' he said with a laugh. 'Have mercy on it!'

Daiyu threw down the scissors and wiped her streaming eyes.

'You shouldn't blow hot and cold by turns. If you want to quarrel, let's quarrel properly and have nothing to do with each other!'

She got up on the kang in a great huff, and turning her back on him, sobbed into her handkerchief and affected to ignore his presence. But Bao-yu got up beside her, and with many soothing words and affectionate endearments humbly entreated her forgiveness.

*   *   *

FROM CHAPTER 96[1]

Xifeng conceives an ingenious plan of deception
And Frowner[2] is deranged by an inadvertent disclosure

*   *   *

The time had come round for the triennial review of civil servants stationed in the capital. Jia Zheng's Board gave him a high commendation, and in the second month the Board of Civil Office presented him for an audience with the Emperor. His Majesty, in view of Jia Zheng's record as a 'diligent, frugal, conscientious and prudent servant of the Throne', appointed him immediately to the post of Grain Intendant for the province of Kiangsi. The same day, Jia Zheng offered his humble acceptance and gratitude for the honour, and suggested a day for his departure. Friends and relatives were all eager to celebrate, but he was not in festive mood. He was loth to leave the capital at a time when things were so unsettled at home, although at the same time he knew that he could not delay his departure.

He was pondering this dilemma, when a message came to summon him to Grandmother Jia's presence. He made his way promptly to her apartment, where he found Lady Wang also present, despite her illness. He paid his respects to Grandmother Jia, who told him to be seated and then began:

'In a few days, you will be leaving us to take up your post. There is something I should like to discuss with you, if you are willing.'

The old lady's eyes were wet with tears. Jia Zheng rose swiftly to his feet, and said:

'Whatever you have to say, Mother, please speak: your word is my command.'

'I shall be eighty-one this year,' said Grandmother Jia, sobbing as she spoke. 'You are going away to a post in the provinces, and with your elder brother still at home, you will not be able to apply for early retirement to come and look after me. When you are gone, of the ones closest to my heart I shall only have

---

1. Chapters 96–120 are translated by John Minford.   2. Lin Daiyu's nickname.

Baoyu left to me. And he, poor darling, is in such a wretched state, I don't know what we can do for him! The other day I sent out Lai Sheng's wife to have the boy's fortune told. The man's reading was uncanny. What he said was: "This person must marry a lady with a destiny of gold, to help him and support him. He must be given a marriage as soon as possible to turn his luck. If not, he may not live." Now I know you don't believe in such things, which is why I sent for you, to talk it over with you. You and his mother must discuss it among yourselves. Are we to save him, or are we to do nothing and watch him fade away?'

Jia Zheng smiled anxiously.

'Could I, who as a child received such tender love and care from you, Mother, not have fatherly feelings myself? It is just that I have been exasperated by his repeated failure to make progress in his studies, and have perhaps been too ambitious for him. You are perfectly right in wanting to see him married. How could I possibly wish to oppose you? I am concerned for the boy, and his recent illness has caused me great anxiety. But as you have kept him from me, I have not ventured to say anything. I should like to see him now for myself, and form my own impression of his condition.'

Lady Wang saw that his eyes were moist, and knew that he was genuinely concerned. She told Aroma to fetch Baoyu and help him into the room. He walked in, and when Aroma told him to pay his respects to his father, did exactly as she said. Jia Zheng saw how emaciated his face had grown, how lifeless his eyes were. His son was like some pathetic simpleton. He told them to take him back to his room.

* * *

A day or two after these events, Daiyu, having eaten her breakfast, decided to take Nightingale with her to visit Grandmother Jia. She wanted to pay her respects, and also thought the visit might provide some sort of distraction for herself. She had hardly left the Naiad's House, when she remembered that she had left her handkerchief at home, and sent Nightingale back to fetch it, saying that she would walk ahead slowly and wait for her to catch up. She had just reached the corner behind the rockery at Drenched Blossoms Bridge—the very spot where she had once buried the flowers with Baoyu—when all of a sudden she heard the sound of sobbing. She stopped at once and listened. She could not tell whose voice it was, nor could she distinguish what it was that the voice was complaining of, so tearfully and at such length. It really was most puzzling. She moved forward again cautiously and as she turned the corner, saw before her the source of the sobbing, a maid with large eyes and thick-set eyebrows.

Before setting eyes on this girl, Daiyu had guessed that one of the many maids in the Jia household must have had an unhappy love-affair, and had come here to cry her heart out in secret. But now she laughed at the very idea. 'How could such an ungainly creature as this know the meaning of love?' she thought to herself. 'This must be one of the odd-job girls, who has probably been scolded by one of the senior maids.' She looked more closely, but still could not place the girl. Seeing Daiyu, the maid ceased her weeping, wiped her cheeks, and rose to her feet.

'Come now, what are you so upset about?' inquired Daiyu.

'Oh Miss Lin!' replied the maid, amid fresh tears. 'Tell me if you think it fair. *They* were talking about it, and how was I to know better? Just because I say one thing wrong, is that a reason for sister to start hitting me?'

Daiyu did not know what she was talking about. She smiled, and asked again:

'Who is your sister?'

'Pearl,' answered the maid.

From this, Daiyu concluded that she must work in Grandmother Jia's apartment.

'And what is your name?'

'Simple.'

Daiyu laughed. Then:

'Why did she hit you? What did you say that was so wrong?'

'That's what I'd like to know! It was only to do with Master Bao marrying Miss Chai!'

The words struck Daiyu's ears like a clap of thunder. Her heart started thumping fiercely. She tried to calm herself for a moment, and told the maid to come with her. The maid followed her to the secluded corner of the garden, where the Flower Burial Mound was situated. Here Daiyu asked her:

'Why should she hit you for mentioning Master Bao's marriage to Miss Chai?'

'Her Old Ladyship, Her Ladyship and Mrs Lian,' replied Simple, 'have decided that as the Master is leaving soon, they are going to arrange with Mrs Xue to marry Master Bao and Miss Chai as quickly as possible. They want the wedding to turn his luck, and then . . .'

Her voice tailed off. She stared at Daiyu, laughed and continued:

'Then, as soon as those two are married, they are going to find a husband for you, Miss Lin.'

Daiyu was speechless with horror. The maid went on regardless:

'But how was I to know that they'd decided to keep it quiet, for fear of embarrassing Miss Chai? All I did was say to Aroma, that serves in Master Bao's room: "Won't it be a fine to-do here soon, when Miss Chai comes over, or Mrs Bao . . . what *will* we have to call her?" That's all I said. What was there in that to hurt sister Pearl? Can *you* see, Miss Lin? She came across and hit me straight in the face and said I was talking rubbish and disobeying orders, and would be dismissed from service! How was I to know their Ladyships didn't want us to mention it? Nobody told me, and she just hit me!'

She started sobbing again. Daiyu's heart felt as though oil, soy-sauce, sugar and vinegar had all been poured into it at once. She could not tell which flavour predominated, the sweet, the sour, the bitter or the salty. After a few moments' silence, she said in a trembling voice:

'Don't talk such rubbish. Any more of that, and you'll be beaten again. Off you go!'

She herself turned back in the direction of the Naiad's House. Her body felt as though it weighed a hundred tons, her feet were as wobbly as if she were walking on cotton-floss. She could only manage one step at a time. After an age, she still had not reached the bank by Drenched Blossoms Bridge. She was going so slowly, with her feet about to collapse beneath her, and in her giddiness and confusion had wandered off course and increased the distance by about a hundred yards. She reached Drenched Blossoms Bridge only to start drifting back again along the bank in the direction she had just come from, quite unaware of what she was doing.

Nightingale had by now returned with the handkerchief, but could not find Daiyu anywhere. She finally saw her, pale as snow, tottering along, her eyes staring straight in front of her, meandering in circles. Nightingale also caught sight of a maid disappearing in the distance beyond Daiyu, but could not make out who it was. She was most bewildered, and quickened her step.

'Why are you turning back again, Miss?' she asked softly. 'Where are you heading for?'

Daiyu only heard the blurred outline of this question. She replied:

'I want to ask Baoyu something.'

Nightingale could not fathom what was going on, and could only try to guide her on her way to Grandmother Jia's apartment. When they came to the entrance, Daiyu seemed to feel clearer in mind. She turned, saw Nightingale supporting her, stopped for a moment, and asked:

'What are you doing here?'

'I went to fetch your handkerchief,' replied Nightingale, smiling anxiously. 'I saw you over by the bridge and hurried across. I asked you where you were going, but you took no notice.'

'Oh!' said Daiyu with a smile. 'I thought you had come to see Baoyu. What else did we come here for?'

Nightingale could see that her mind was utterly confused. She guessed that it was something that the maid had said in the garden, and only nodded with a faint smile in reply to Daiyu's question. But to herself she was trying to imagine what sort of an encounter this was going to be, between the young master who had already lost his wits, and her young mistress who was now herself a little touched. Despite her apprehensions, she dared not prevent the meeting, and helped Daiyu into the room. The funny thing was that Daiyu now seemed to have recovered her strength. She did not wait for Nightingale but raised the portière herself, and walked into the room. It was very quiet inside. Grandmother Jia had retired for her afternoon nap. Some of the maids had sneaked off to play, some were having forty winks themselves and others had gone to wait on Grandmother Jia in her bedroom. It was Aroma who came out to see who was there, when she heard the swish of the portière. Seeing that it was Dai-yu, she greeted her politely:

'Please come in and sit down, Miss.'

'Is Master Bao at home?' asked Daiyu with a smile.

Aroma did not know that anything was amiss, and was about to answer, when she saw Nightingale make an urgent movement with her lips from behind Daiyu's back, pointing to her mistress and making a warning gesture with her hand. Aroma had no idea what she meant and dared not ask. Undeterred, Daiyu walked on into Baoyu's room. He was sitting up in bed, and when she came in made no move to get up or welcome her, but remained where he was, staring at her and giving a series of silly laughs. Daiyu sat down uninvited, and she too began to smile and stare back at Baoyu. There were no greetings exchanged, no courtesies, in fact no words of any kind. They just sat there staring into each other's faces and smiling like a pair of half-wits. Aroma stood watching, completely at a loss.

Suddenly Daiyu said:

'Baoyu, why are you sick?'

Baoyu laughed.

'I'm sick because of Miss Lin.'

Aroma and Nightingale grew pale with fright. They tried to change the subject, but their efforts only met with silence and more senseless smiles. By now it was clear to Aroma that Daiyu's mind was as disturbed as Baoyu's.

'Miss Lin has only just recovered from her illness,' she whispered to Nightingale. 'I'll ask Ripple to help you take her back. She should go home and lie down.' Turning to Ripple, she said: 'Go with Nightingale and accompany Miss Lin home. And no stupid chattering on the way, mind.'

Ripple smiled, and without a word came over to help Nightingale. The two of them began to help Daiyu to her feet. Daiyu stood up at once, unassisted, still staring fixedly at Baoyu, smiling and nodding her head.

'Come on, Miss!' urged Nightingale. 'It's time to go home and rest.'

'Of course!' exclaimed Daiyu. 'It's time!'

She turned to go. Still smiling and refusing any assistance from the maids, she strode out at twice her normal speed. Ripple and Nightingale hurried after her. On leaving Grandmother Jia's apartment, Daiyu kept on walking, in quite the wrong direction. Nightingale hurried up to her and took her by the hand.

'This is the way, Miss.'

Still smiling, Daiyu allowed herself to be led, and followed Nightingale towards the Naiad's House. When they were nearly there, Nightingale exclaimed:

'Lord Buddha be praised! Home at last!'

She had no sooner uttered these words when she saw Daiyu stumble forwards onto the ground, and give a loud cry. A stream of blood came gushing from her mouth.

To learn if she survived this crisis, please read the next chapter.

FROM CHAPTER 97

Lin Daiyu burns her poems to signal the end of her heart's folly
And Xue Baochai leaves home to take part in a solemn rite

* * *

Next day, Xifeng came over after breakfast. Wishing to sound out Baoyu according to her plan, she advanced into his room and said:

'Congratulations, Cousin Bao! Uncle Zheng has already chosen a lucky day for your wedding! Isn't that good news?'

Baoyu stared at her with a blank smile, and nodded his head faintly.

'He is marrying you,' went on Xifeng, with a studied smile, 'to your cousin Lin. Are you happy?'

Baoyu burst out laughing. Xifeng watched him carely, but could not make out whether he had understood her, or was simply raving. She went on:

'Uncle Zheng says, you are to marry Miss Lin, *if* you get better. But not if you carry on behaving like a half-wit.'

Baoyu's expression suddenly changed to one of utter seriousness, as he said:

'I'm not a half-wit. You're the half-wit.'

He stood up.

'I am going to see Cousin Lin, to set her mind at rest.'

Xifeng quickly put out a hand to stop him.

'She knows already. And, as your bride-to-be, she would be much too embarrassed to receive you now.'

'What about when we're married? Will she see me then?'

Xifeng found this both comic and somewhat disturbing.

'Aroma was right,' she thought to herself. 'Mention Daiyu, and while he still talks like an idiot, he at least seems to understand what's going on. I can see we shall be in real trouble, if he sees through our scheme and finds out that his bride is not to be Daiyu after all.'

In reply to his question, she said, suppressing a smile:

'If you behave, she will see you. But not if you continue to act like an imbecile.'

To which Baoyu replied:

'I have given my heart to Cousin Lin. If she marries me, she will bring it with her and put it back in its proper place.'

Now this was madman's talk if ever, thought Xifeng, She left him, and walked back into the outer room, glancing with a smile in Grandmother Jia's direction. The old lady too found Baoyu's words both funny and distressing.

'I heard you both myself,' she said to Xifeng. 'For the present, we must ignore it. Tell Aroma to do her best to calm him down. Come, let us go.'

Lady Wang joined them, and the three ladies went across to Aunt Xue's. On arrival there, they pretended to be concerned about the course of Xue Pan's affair. Aunt Xue expressed her profound gratitude for this concern, and gave them the latest news. After they had all taken tea, Aunt Xue was about to send for Baochai, when Xifeng stopped her, saying:

'There is no need to tell Cousin Chai that we are here, Auntie.'

With a diplomatic smile, she continued:

'Grandmother's visit today is not purely a social one. She has something of importance to say, and would like you to come over later so that we can all discuss it together.'

Aunt Xue nodded.

'Of course.'

After a little more chat, the three ladies returned.

That evening Aunt Xue came over as arranged, and after paying her respects to Grandmother Jia, went to her sister's apartment. First there was the inevitable scene of sisterly commiseration over Wang Ziteng's death. Then Aunt Xue said:

'Just now when I was at Lady Jia's, young Bao came out to greet me and seemed quite well. A little thin perhaps, but certainly not as ill as I had been led to expect from your description and Xifeng's.'

'No, it is really not that serious,' said Xifeng. 'It's only Grandmother who will worry so. Her idea is that it would be reassuring for Sir Zheng to see Baoyu married before he leaves, as who knows when he will be able to come home from his new posting. And then from Baoyu's own point of view, it might be just the thing to turn his luck. With Cousin Chai's golden locket to counteract the evil influence, he should make a good recovery.'

Aunt Xue was willing enough to go along with the idea, but was concerned that Baochai might feel rather hard done by.

'I see nothing against it,' she said. 'But I think we should all take time to think it over properly.'

In accordance with Xifeng's plan, Lady Wang went on:

'As you have no head of family present, we should like you to dispense with the usual trousseau. Tomorrow you should send Ke to let Pan know that while we proceed with the wedding, we shall continue to do our utmost to settle his court-case.'

She made no mention of Baoyu's feelings for Daiyu, but continued:

'Since you have given your consent, the sooner they are married, the sooner things will look up for everyone.'

At this point, Faithful came in to take back a report to Grandmother Jia. Though Aunt Xue was still concerned about Baochai's feelings, she saw that in the circumstances she had no choice, and agreed to everything they had suggested. Faithful reported this to Grandmother Jia, who was delighted and sent her back again to ask Mrs Xue to explain to Baochai why it was that things were being done in this way, so that she would not feel unfairly treated. Aunt Xue agreed to do this, and it was settled that Xifeng and Jia Lian would act as official go-betweens. Xifeng retired to her apartment, while Aunt Xue and Lady Wang stayed up talking together well into the night.

Next day, Aunt Xue returned to her apartment and told Baochai the details of the proposal, adding:

'I have already given my consent.'

At first Baochai hung her head in silence. Then she began to cry. Aunt Xue said all that she could to comfort her, and went to great lengths to explain the reasoning behind the decision. Baochai retired to her room, and Baoqin went in to keep her company and cheer her up. Aunt Xue also spoke to Ke, instructing him as follows:

'You must leave tomorrow. Find out the latest news of Pan's judgement, and then convey this message to him. Return as soon as you possibly can.'

* * *

Daiyu meanwhile, for all the medicine she took, continued to grow iller with every day that passed. Nightingale did her utmost to raise her spirits. Our story finds her standing once more by Daiyu's bedside, earnestly beseeching her:

'Miss, now that things have come to this pass, I simply must speak my mind. We know what it is that's eating your heart out. But can't you see that your fears are groundless? Why, look at the state Baoyu is in! How can he possibly get married, when he's so ill? You must ignore these silly rumours, stop fretting and let yourself get better.'

Daiyu gave a wraithlike smile, but said nothing. She started coughing again and brought up a lot more blood. Nightingale and Snowgoose came closer and watched her feebly struggling for breath. They knew that any further attempt to rally her would be to no avail, and could do nothing but stand there watching and weeping. Each day Nightingale went over three or four times to tell Grandmother Jia, but Faithful, judging the old lady's attitude towards Daiyu to have hardened of late, intercepted her reports and hardly mentioned Daiyu to her mistress. Grandmother Jia was preoccupied with the wedding arrangements, and in the absence of any particular news of Daiyu, did not show a great deal of interest in the girl's fate, considering it sufficient that she should be receiving medical attention.

Previously, when she had been ill, Daiyu had always received frequent visits from everyone in the household, from Grandmother Jia down to the humblest maidservant. But now not a single person came to see her. The only face she saw looking down at her was that of Nightingale. She began to feel her end drawing near, and struggled to say a few words to her:

'Dear Nightingale! Dear sister! Closest friend! Though you were Grandmother's maid before you came to serve me, over the years you have become as a sister to me . . .'

She had to stop for breath. Nightingale felt a pang of pity, was reduced to tears and could say nothing. After a long silence, Daiyu began to speak again, searching for breath between words:

'Dear sister! I am so uncomfortable lying down like this. Please help me up and sit next to me.'

'I don't think you should sit up, Miss, in your condition. You might get cold in the draught.'

Daiyu closed her eyes in silence. A little later she asked to sit up again. Nightingale and Snowgoose felt they could no longer deny her request. They propped her up on both sides with soft pillows, while Nightingale sat by her on the bed to give further support. Daiyu was not equal to the effort. The bed where she sat on it seemed to dig into her, and she struggled with all her remaining strength to lift herself up and ease the pain. She told Snowgoose to come closer.

'My poems . . .'

Her voice failed, and she fought for breath again. Snowgoose guessed that she meant the manuscripts she had been revising a few days previously, went to fetch them and laid them on Daiyu's lap. Daiyu nodded, then raised her eyes and gazed in the direction of a chest that stood on a stand close by. Snowgoose did not know how to interpret this and stood there at a loss. Daiyu stared at her now with feverish impatience. She began to cough again and brought up another mouthful of blood. Snowgoose went to fetch some water, and Daiyu rinsed her mouth and spat into the spittoon. Nightingale wiped her lips with a handkerchief. Daiyu took the handkerchief from her and pointed to the chest. She tried to speak, but was again seized with an attack of breathlessness and closed her eyes.

'Lie down, Miss,' said Nightingale. Daiyu shook her head. Nightingale thought she must want one of her handkerchiefs, and told Snowgoose to open the chest and bring her a plain white silk one. Daiyu looked at it, and dropped it on the bed. Making a supreme effort, she gasped out:

'The ones with the writing on . . .'

Nightingale finally realized that she meant the handkerchiefs Baoyu had sent her, the ones she had inscribed with her own poems. She told Snowgoose to fetch them, and herself handed them to Daiyu, with these words of advice:

'You must lie down and rest, Miss. Don't start wearing yourself out. You can look at these another time, when you are feeling better.'

Daiyu took the handkerchiefs in one hand and without even looking at them, brought round her other hand (which cost her a great effort) and tried with all her might to tear them in two. But she was so weak that all she could achieve was a pathetic trembling motion. Nightingale knew that Baoyu was the object of all this bitterness but dared not mention his name, saying instead:

'Miss, there is no sense in working yourself up again.'

Daiyu nodded faintly, and slipped the handkerchiefs into her sleeve.

'Light the lamp,' she ordered.

Snowgoose promptly obeyed. Daiyu looked into the lamp, then closed her eyes and sat in silence. Another fit of breathlessness. Then:

'Make up the fire in the brazier.'

Thinking she wanted it for the extra warmth, Nightingale protested:

'You should lie down, Miss, and have another cover on. And the fumes from the brazier might be bad for you.'

Daiyu shook her head, and Snowgoose reluctantly made up the brazier, placing it on its stand on the floor. Daiyu made a motion with her hand, indicating that she wanted it moved up onto the kang. Snowgoose lifted it and placed it there, temporarily using the floor-stand, while she went out to fetch the special stand they used on the kang. Daiyu, far from resting back in the warmth, now inclined her body slightly forward—Nightingale had to support her with both hands as she did so. Daiyu took the handkerchiefs in one hand. Staring into the flames and nodding thoughtfully to herself, she dropped them into the brazier. Nightingale was horrified, but much as she would have liked to snatch them from the flames, she did not dare move her hands and leave Daiyu unsupported. Snowgoose was out of the room, fetching the brazier-stand, and by now the handkerchiefs were all ablaze.

'Miss!' cried Nightingale. 'What are you doing?'

As if she had not heard, Daiyu reached over for her manuscripts, glanced at them and let them fall again onto the kang. Nightingale, anxious lest she burn these too, leaned up against Daiyu and freeing one hand, reached out with it to take hold of them. But before she could do so, Daiyu had picked them up again and dropped them in the flames. The brazier was out of Nightingale's reach, and there was nothing she could do but look on helplessly.

Just at that moment Snowgoose came in with the stand. She saw Daiyu drop something into the fire, and without knowing what it was, rushed forward to try and save it. The manuscripts had caught at once and were already ablaze. Heedless of the danger to her hands, Snowgoose reached into the flames and pulled out what she could, throwing the paper on the floor and stamping frantically on it. But the fire had done its work, and only a few charred fragments remained.

Daiyu closed her eyes and slumped back, almost causing Nightingale to topple over with her. Nightingale, her heart thumping in great agitation, called Snowgoose over to help her settle Daiyu down again. It was too late now to send for anyone. And yet, what if Daiyu should die during the night, and the only people there were Snowgoose, herself and the one or two other junior maids in the Naiad's House? They passed a restless night. Morning came at last, and Daiyu seemed a little more comfortable. But after breakfast she suddenly began coughing and vomiting, and became tense and feverish again. Nightingale could see that she had reached a crisis.

* * *

FROM **CHAPTER 98**

Crimson Pearl's suffering spirit returns to the Realm of Separation
And the convalescent Stone-in-waiting weeps at the scene of past affection

On his return from seeing his father, Baoyu, as we have seen, regressed into a worse state of stupor and depression than ever. He was too lacking in energy to move, and could eat nothing, but fell straight into a heavy slumber. Once more the doctor was called, once more he took Baoyu's pulses and made out a prescription, which was administered to no effect. He could not even recognize the people around him. And yet, if helped into a sitting position, he could still pass for someone in normal health. Provided he was not called upon to do anything, there were no external symptoms to indicate how seriously ill he was. He continued like this for several days, to the increasing anxiety of the family, until the Ninth Day after the wedding, when according to tradition the newly-married couple should visit the bride's family. If they did not go, Aunt Xue would be most offended. But if they went with Baoyu in his present state, whatever were they to say? Knowing that his illness was caused by his attachment to Daiyu, Grandmother Jia would have liked to make a clean breast of it and tell Aunt Xue. But she feared that this too might cause offence and ill-feeling. It was also difficult for her to be of any comfort to Baochai, who was in a delicate position as a new member of the Jia family. Such comfort could only be rendered by a visit from the girl's mother, which would be difficult if they had already offended her by not celebrating the Ninth Day. It must be gone through with. Grandmother Jia imparted her views on the matter to Lady Wang and Xifeng:

'It is only Baoyu's mind that has been temporarily affected. I don't think a little excursion would do him any harm. We must prepare two small sedan-chairs, and send a maid to support him. They can go through the Garden. Once the Ninth Day has been properly celebrated, we can ask Mrs Xue to come over and comfort Baochai, while we do our utmost to restore Baoyu to health. They will both benefit.'

Lady Wang agreed and immediately began making the necessary preparations. Baochai acquiesced in the charade out of a sense of conjugal duty, while Baoyu in his moronic state was easily manipulated. Baochai now knew the full truth, and in her own mind blamed her mother for making a foolish decision. But now that things had gone this far she said nothing. Aunt Xue herself, when she witnessed Baoyu's pitiful condition, began to regret having ever given her consent, and could only bring herself to play a perfunctory part in the proceedings.

When they returned home, Baoyu's condition seemed to grow worse. By the next day he could not even sit up in bed. This deterioration continued daily, until he could no longer swallow medicine or water. Aunt Xue was there, and she and the other ladies in their frantic despair scoured the city for eminent physicians, without finding one that could diagnose the illness. Finally they discovered, lodging in a broken-down temple outside the city, a down-and-out practitioner by the name of Bi Zhian, who diagnosed it as a case of severe emotional shock, aggravated by a failure to dress in accordance with the seasons and by irregular eating habits, with consequent accumulation of choler and obstruction of the humours. In short, an internal disorder made worse by external factors. He made out a prescription in accordance with this diagnosis, which was administered that evening. At about ten o'clock it began to take effect. Baoyu began to show signs of consciousness and asked for water to drink. Grandmother Jia, Lady Wang and all the other ladies congregated round the sick-bed felt that they could at last have a brief respite from their vigil, and Aunt Xue was invited to bring Baochai with her to Grandmother Jia's apartment to rest for a while.

His brief access of clarity enabled Baoyu to understand the gravity of his illness. When the others had gone and he was left alone with Aroma, he called her over to his side and taking her by the hand said tearfully:

'Please tell me how Cousin Chai came to be here? I remember Father marrying me to Cousin Lin. Why has *she* been made to go? Why has Cousin Chai taken her place? She has no right to be here! I'd like to tell her so, but I don't want to offend her. How has Cousin Lin taken it? Is she very upset?'

Aroma did not dare tell him the truth, but merely said:

'Miss Lin is ill.'

'I must go and see her,' insisted Baoyu. He wanted to get up, but days of going without food and drink had so sapped his strength that he could no longer move, but could only weep bitterly and say:

'I know I am going to die! There's something on my mind, something very important, that I want you to tell Grannie for me, Cousin Lin and I are both ill. We are both dying. It will be too late to help us when we are dead: but if they prepare a room for us now and if we are taken there before it is too late, we can at least be cared for together while we are still alive, and be laid out together when we die. Do this for me, for friendship's sake!'

Aroma found this plea at once disturbing, comical and moving. Baochai, who happened to be passing with Oriole, heard every word and took him to task straight away.

'Instead of resting and trying to get well, you make yourself iller with all this gloomy talk! Grandmother has scarcely stopped worrying about you for a moment, and here you are causing more trouble for her. She is over eighty now and may not live to acquire a title because of your achievements; but at least, by leading a good life, you can repay her a little for all that she has suffered for your sake. And I hardly need mention the agonies Mother has endured in bringing you up. You are the only son she has left. If you were to die, think how she would suffer! As for me, I am wretched enough as it is; you don't need to make a widow of me. Three good reasons why even if you want to die, the powers above will not let you and you will not be able to. After four or five days of proper rest and care, your illness will pass, your strength will be restored and you will be yourself again.'

For a while Baoyu could think of no reply to this homily. Finally he gave a silly laugh and said:

'After not speaking to me for so long, here you are lecturing me. You are wasting your breath.'

Encouraged by this response to go a step further, Baochai said:

'Let me tell you the plain truth, then. Some days ago, while you were unconscious, Cousin Lin passed away.'

With a sudden movement, Baoyu sat up and cried out in horror:

'It can't be true!'

'It is. Would I lie about such a thing? Grandmother and Mother knew how fond you were of each other, and wouldn't tell you because they were afraid that if they did, you would die too.'

Baoyu began howling unrestrainedly and slumped back in his bed. Suddenly all was pitch black before his eyes. He could not tell where he was and was beginning to feel very lost, when he thought he saw a man walking towards him and asked in a bewildered tone of voice:

'Would you be so kind as to tell me where I am?'

'This,' replied the stranger, 'is the road to the Springs of the Nether World. Your time is not yet come. What brings you here?'

'I have just learned of the death of a friend and have come to find her. But I seem to have lost my way.'

'Who is this friend of yours?'

'Lin Daiyu of Soochow.'

The man gave a chilling smile:

'In life Lin Daiyu was no ordinary mortal, and in death she has become no ordinary shade. An ordinary mortal has two souls which coalesce at birth to vitalize the physical frame, and disperse at death to rejoin the cosmic flux. If you consider the impossibility of tracing even such ordinary human entities in the Nether World, you will realize what a futile task it is to look for Lin Daiyu. You had better return at once.'

After standing for a moment lost in thought, Baoyu asked again:

'But if as you say, death is a dispersion, how can there be such a place as the Nether World?'

'There is,' replied the man with a superior smile, 'and yet there is not, such a place. It is a teaching, devised to warn mankind in its blind attachment to the idea of life and death. The Supreme Wrath is aroused by human folly in all forms—whether it be excessive ambition, premature death self-sought, or futile self-destruction through debauchery and a life of overweening violence. Hell is the place where souls such as these are imprisoned and made to suffer countless torments in expiation of their sins. This search of yours for Lin Daiyu is a case of futile self-delusion. Daiyu has already returned to the Land of Illusion and if you really want to find her you must cultivate your mind and strengthen your spiritual nature. Then one day you will see her again. But if you throw your life away, you will be guilty of premature death self-sought and will be confined to Hell. And then, although you may be allowed to see your parents, you will certainly never see Daiyu again.'

When he had finished speaking, the man took a stone from within his sleeve and threw it at Baoyu's chest. The words he had spoken and the impact of the stone as it landed on his chest combined to give Baoyu such a fright that he would have returned home at once, if he had only known which way to turn. In his confusion he suddenly heard a voice, and turning, saw the figures of Grandmother Jia, Lady Wang, Baochai, Aroma and his other maids standing in a circle around him, weeping and calling his name. He was lying on his own bed. The red lamp was on the table. The moon was shining brilliantly through the window. He was back among the elegant comforts of his own home.

A moment's reflection told him that what he had just experienced had been a dream. He was in a cold sweat. Though his mind felt strangely lucid, thinking only intensified his feeling of helpless desolation, and he uttered several profound sighs.

Baochai had known of Daiyu's death for several days. While Grandmother Jia had forbidden the maids to tell him for fear of further complicating his illness, she felt she knew better. Aware that it was Daiyu who lay at the root of his illness and that the loss of his jade was only a secondary factor, she took the opportunity of breaking the news of her death to him in this abrupt manner, hoping that by severing his attachment once and for all she would enable his sanity and health to be restored. Grandmother Jia, Lady Wang and company were not aware of her intentions and at first reproached her for her lack of caution. But when they saw Baoyu regain consciousness, they were all greatly relieved and went at once to the library to ask doctor Bi to come in and examine his patient again. The doctor carefully took his pulses.

'How odd!' he exclaimed. 'His pulses are deep and still, his spirit calm, the oppression quite dispersed. Tomorrow he must take a regulative draught, which I shall prescribe, and he should make a prompt and complete recovery.'

The doctor left and the ladies all returned to their apartments in much improved spirits.

Although at first Aroma greatly resented the way in which Baochai had broken the news, she did not dare say so. Oriole, on the other hand, reproved her mistress in private for having been, as she put it, too hasty.

'What do you know about such things?' retorted Baochai. 'Leave this to me. I take full responsibility.'

Baochai ignored the opinions and criticisms of those around her and continued to keep a close watch on Baoyu's progress, probing him judiciously, like an acupunturist with a needle.

A day or two later, he began to feel a slight improvement in himself, though his mental equilibrium was still easily disturbed by the least thought of Daiyu. Aroma was constantly at his side, with such words of consolation as:

'The Master chose Miss Chai as your bride for her more dependable nature. He thought Miss Lin too difficult and temperamental for you, and besides there was always the fear that she would not live long. Then later Her Old Ladyship thought you were not in a fit state to know what was best for you and would only be upset and make yourself iller if you knew the truth, so she made Snowgoose come over, to try and make things easier for you.'

This did nothing to lessen his grief, and he often wept inconsolably. But each time he thought of putting an end to his life, he remembered the words of the stranger in his dream; and then he thought of the distress his death would cause his mother and grandmother and knew that he could not tear himself away from them. He also reflected that Daiyu was dead, and that Baochai was a fine lady in her own right; there must after all have been some truth in the bond of gold and jade. This thought eased his mind a little. Baochai could see that things were improving, and herself felt calmer as a result. Every day she scrupulously performed her duties towards Grandmother Jia and Lady Wang, and when these were completed, did all she could to cure Baoyu of his grief. He was still not able to sit up for long periods, but often when he saw her sitting by his bedside he would succumb to his old weakness for the fairer sex. She tried to rally him in an earnest manner, saying:

'The important thing is to take care of your health. Now that we are married, we have a whole lifetime ahead of us.'

He was reluctant to listen to her advice. But since his grandmother, his mother, Aunt Xue and all the others took it in turns to watch over him during the day, and since Baochai slept on her own in an adjoining room, and he was waited on at night by one or two maids of Grandmother Jia's, he found himself left with little choice but to rest and get well again. And as time went by and Baochai proved herself a gentle and devoted companion, he found that a small part of his love for Daiyu began to transfer itself to her. But this belongs to a later part of our story.

*　*　*

FROM CHAPTER 119

Baoyu becomes a Provincial Graduate and severs worldly ties
The House of Jia receives Imperial favour and renews ancestral glory

*　*　*

The time drew near for the examination. All the family were full of eager anticipation, hoping that the two boys would write creditable compositions and bring the family honour. All except for Baochai; while it was true that Baoyu had prepared well, she had also on occasions noticed a strange indifference in his behaviour. Her first concern was that the two boys, for both of whom this was the first venture of its kind, might get hurt or have some accident in the crush of men and vehicles around the examination halls. She was more particularly worried for Baoyu, who had not been out at all since his encounter with the monk. His delight in studying seemed to her the result of a somewhat too hasty and not altogether convincing conversion, and she had a premonition that something untoward was going to happen. So, on the day before the big event, she dispatched Aroma and a few of the junior maids to go with Candida and her helpers and make sure that the candidates were both properly prepared. She herself inspected their things and put them out in readiness, and then went over with Li Wan to Lady Wang's apartment, where she selected a few of the more trusty family retainers to accompany them the next day, for fear they might be jolted or trampled on in the crowds.

The big day finally arrived, and Baoyu and Jia Lan changed into smart but unostentatious clothes. They came over in high spirits to bid farewell to Lady Wang, who gave them a few parting words of advice:

'This is the first examination for both of you, and although you are such big boys now, it will still be the first time either of you has been away from me for a whole day. You may have gone out in the past, but you were always surrounded by your maids and nurses. You have never spent the night away on your own like this. Today, when you both go into the examination, you are bound to feel rather lonely with none of the family by you. You must take special care. Finish your papers and come out as early as possible, and then be sure to find one of the family servants and come home as soon as you can. We shall be worrying about you.'

As she spoke, Lady Wang herself was greatly moved by the occasion. Jia Lan made all the appropriate responses, but Baoyu remained silent until his mother had quite finished speaking. Then he walked up to her, knelt at her feet and with tears streaming down his cheeks kowtowed to her three times and said:

'I could never repay you adequately for all you have done for me, Mother. But if I can do this one thing successfully, if I can do my very best and pass this examination, then perhaps I can bring you a little pleasure. Then my worldly duty will be accomplished and I will at least have made some small return for all the trouble I have caused you.'

Lady Wang was still more deeply moved by this:

'It is a very fine thing, what you are setting out to do. It is only a shame that your grandmother couldn't be here to witness it.'

She wept as she spoke and put her arms around him to draw him to her. Baoyu remained kneeling however and would not rise.

'Even though Grandmother is not here,' he said, 'I am sure she knows about it and is happy. So really it is just as if she were present. What separates us is only matter. We are together in spirit.'

* * *

At last came the day when the examinations were due to be concluded and the students released from their cells.[1] Lady Wang was eagerly awaiting the return of Baoyu and Jia Lan, and when midday came and there was still no sign of either of them, she, Li Wan and Baochai all began to worry and sent one servant after another to find out what had become of them. The servants could obtain no news, and not one of them dared to return empty handed. Later another batch was dispatched on the same mission, with the same result. The three ladies were beside themselves with anxiety.

When evening came, someone returned at last: it was Jia Lan. They were delighted to see him, and immediately asked:

'Where is Baoyu?'

He did not even greet them but burst into tears.

'Lost!' he sobbed.

For several minutes Lady Wang was struck dumb. Then she collapsed senseless onto her couch. Luckily Suncloud and one or two other maids were at hand to support her, and they brought her round, themselves sobbing hysterically the while. Baochai stared in front of her with a glazed expression in her eyes, while Arorna sobbed her heart out. The only thing they could find time to do between their fits of sobbing was to scold Jia Lan:

'Fool! You were with Baoyu—how could he get lost?'

'Before the examinations we stayed in the same room, we ate together and slept together. Even when we went in we were never far apart, we were always within sight of each other. This morning Uncle Bao finished his paper early and waited for me. We handed in our papers at the same time and left together. When we reached the Dragon Gate outside there was a big crowd and I lost sight of him. The servants who had come to fetch us asked me where he was

1. During the several days of the examinations, candidates were sequestered in individual exam cells.

and Li Gui told them: "One minute he was just over there clear as daylight, the next minute he was gone. How can he have disappeared so suddenly in the crowd?" I told Li Gui and the others to split up into search parties, while I took some men and looked in all the cubicles. But there was no sign of him. That's why I'm so late back.'

Lady Wang had been sobbing throughout this, without saying a word. Baochai had already more or less guessed the truth. Aroma continued to weep inconsolably. Jia Qiang and the other men needed no further orders but set off immediately in several directions to join in the search. It was a sad sight, with everyone in the lowest of spirits and the welcome-home party prepared in vain. Jia Lan forgot his own exhaustion and wanted to go out with the others. But Lady Wang kept him back:

'My child! Your uncle is lost; if we lost you as well, it would be more than we could bear! You have a rest now, there's a good boy!'

He was reluctant to stay behind, but acquiesced when Youshi added her entreaties to Lady Wang's.

The only person present who seemed unsurprised was Xichun. She did not feel free to express her thoughts, but instead inquired of Baochai:

'Did Baoyu have his jade with him when he left?'

'Of course he did,' she replied. 'He never goes anywhere without it.'

Xichun was silent. Aroma remembered how they had had to waylay Baoyu and snatch the jade from his hands, and she had an overwhelming suspicion that today's mishap was that monk's doing too. Her heart ached with grief, tears poured down her cheeks and she began wailing despondently. Memories flooded back of the affection Baoyu had shown her. 'I annoyed him sometimes, I know, and then he'd be cross. But he always had a way of making it up. He was so kind to me, and so thoughtful. In heated moments he often would vow to become a monk. I never believed him. And now he's gone!'

It was two o'clock in the morning by now, and still there was no sign of Baoyu. Li Wan, afraid that Lady Wang would injure herself through excess of grief, did her best to console her and advised her to retire to bed. The rest of the family accompanied her to her room, except for Lady Xing who returned to her own apartment, and Jia Huan, who was still lying low and had not dared to make an appearance at all. Lady Wang told Jia Lan to go back to his room, and herself spent a sleepless night. Next day at dawn some of the servants dispatched the previous day returned, to report that they had searched everywhere and failed to find the slightest trace of Baoyu. During the morning a stream of relations including Aunt Xue, Xue Ke, Shi Xiangyun, Baoqin and old Mrs Li came to enquire after Lady Wang's health and to ask for news of Baoyu.

After several days of this, Lady Wang was so consumed with grief that she could neither eat nor drink, and her very life seemed in danger. Then suddenly a servant announced a messenger from the Commandant of the Haimen Coastal Region, who brought news that Tanchun was due to arrive in the capital the following day. Although this could not totally dispel her grief at Baoyu's disappearance, Lady Wang felt some slight comfort at the thought of seeing Tanchun again. The next day, Tanchun arrived at Rongguo House and they all went out to the front to greet her, finding her lovelier than ever and most prettily dressed. When Tanchun saw how Lady Wang had aged, and how red-eyed everyone in the family was, tears sprang to her eyes, and it was a while before she could stop weeping and greet them all properly. She was also distressed to see Xichun in a nun's habit, and wept again to learn of Baoyu's strange disappearance and the many other family misfortunes. But she had always been gifted with a knack of finding the right thing to say, and her natural equanimity restored a degree of calm to the gathering and gave some real comfort to Lady Wang and the rest of the family. The next day her husband came to visit, and when he learned how things stood he begged her to stay at home and console her family. The maids and old serving-women who had accompanied her to her new home were thus granted a welcome reunion with their old friends.

The entire household, masters and servants alike, still waited anxiously day and night for news of Baoyu. Very late one night, during the fifth watch, some servants came as far as the inner gate, announcing that they had indeed wonderful news to report, and a couple of the junior maids hurried in to the inner apartments, without stopping to inform the senior maids.

'Ma'am, ladies!' they announced. 'Wonderful news!'

Lady Wang thought that Baoyu must at last have been found and rising from her bed she exclaimed with delight:

'Where did they find him? Send him in at once to see me!'

'He has been placed seventh on the roll of successful candidates!' the maid cried.

'But has he been *found?*'

The maid was silent. Lady Wang sat down again.

'*Who* came seventh?' asked Tanchun.

'Mr Bao.'

As they were talking they heard a voice outside shouting:

'Master Lan has passed too!'

A servant went hurrying out to receive the official notice, on which it was written that Jia Lan had been placed one hundred and thirtieth on the roll.

Since there was still no news of Baoyu's whereabouts, Li Wan did not feel free to express her feelings of pride and joy; and Lady Wang, delighted as she was that Jia Lan had passed, could not help thinking to herself:

'If only Baoyu were here too, what a happy celebration it would be!'

Baochai alone was still plunged in gloom, though she felt it inappropriate to weep. The others were busy offering their congratulations and trying to look on the cheerful side:

'Since it was Baoyu's fate to pass, he cannot remain lost for long. In a day or two he is sure to be found.'

This plausible suggestion brought a momentary smile to Lady Wang's cheeks, and the family seized on this opportunity to persuade her to eat and drink a little. A moment later Tealeaf's voice could be heard calling excitedly from the inner gate:

'Now that Mr Bao has passed, he is sure to be found soon!'

'What makes you so sure of that?' they asked him.

'There's a saying: "If a man once passes the examination, the whole world learns his name." Now everyone will know Mr Bao's name wherever he goes, and someone will be sure to bring him home.'

'That Tealeaf may be a cheeky little devil, but there's something in what he says,' agreed the maids.

Xichun differed:

'How could a grown man like Baoyu be lost? If you ask me, he has deliberately severed his ties with the world and chosen the life of a monk. And in that case he *will* be hard to find.'

This set the ladies weeping all over again.

'It is certainly true,' said Li Wan, 'that since ancient times many men have renounced worldly rank and riches to become Buddhas or Saints.'

'But if he rejects his own mother and father,' sobbed Lady Wang, 'then he's failing in his duty as a son. And in that case how can he ever hope to become a Saint or a Buddha?'

'It is best to be ordinary,' commented Tanchun. 'Baoyu was always different. He had that jade of his ever since he was born, and everyone always thought it lucky. But looking back, I can see that it's brought him nothing but bad luck. If a few more days go by and we still cannot find him I don't want to upset you, Mother—but I think in that case we must resign ourselves to the fact that this is something decreed by fate and beyond our understanding. It would be better not to think of him as having ever been born from your womb. His destiny is after all the fruit of karma, the result of your accumulated merit in several lifetimes.'

Baochai listened to this in silence. Aroma could bear it no longer; her heart ached, she felt dizzy and sank to the ground in a faint. Lady Wang seemed most concerned for her, and told one of the maids to help her up.

Jia Huan was feeling extremely out of sorts. On top of his disgrace in the Qiao-jie affair, there was now the added humiliation of having to watch both his brother and nephew pass their examinations. He cursed Qiang and Yun for having dragged him into this trouble. Tanchun was sure to take him to task now that she was back. And yet he dared not try to hide. He was altogether in a state of abject misery.

The next day Jia Lan had to attend court to give thanks for his successful graduation. There he met Zhen Baoyu[2] and discovered that he too had passed. So now all three of them belonged to the same 'class'. When Lan mentioned Baoyu's strange disappearance, Zhen Baoyu sighed and offered a few words of consolation.

The Chief Examiner presented the successful candidates' compositions to the throne, and His Majesty read them through one by one and found them all to be well balanced and cogent, displaying both breadth of learning and soundness of judgement. When he noticed two Nanking Jias in seventh and one hundred and thirtieth place, he asked if they were any relation of the late Jia Concubine. One of his ministers went to summon Jia Baoyu and Jia Lan for questioning on this matter. Jia Lan, on arrival, explained the circumstances of his uncle's disappearance and gave a full account of the three preceding generations of the family, all of which was transmitted to the throne by the minister. His Majesty, as a consequence of this information, being a monarch of exceptional enlightenment and compassion, instructed his minister, in consideration of the family's distinguished record of service, to submit a full report on their case. This the minister

---

2. Son of a friend of Baoyu's father. The Zhens, also a wealthy southern family, had close ties with the Jias.

did and drafted a detailed memorial on the subject. His Majesty's concern was such that on reading this memorial he ordered the minister to re-examine the facts that had led to Jia She's conviction. Subsequently the Imperial eye lighted upon yet another memorial describing the success of the recent campaign to quell the coastal disturbances, 'causing the seas to be at peace and the rivers to be cleansed, and leaving the honest citizenry free to pursue their livelihood unmolested once more'. His Majesty was overjoyed at this good news and ordered his council of ministers to deliberate on suitable rewards and also to pronounce a general amnesty throughout the Empire.

When Jia Lan had left court and had gone to pay his respects to his examiner, he learned of the amnesty and hurried home to tell Lady Wang and the rest of the family. They all seemed delighted, though their pleasure was marred by Baoyu's continued absence. Aunt Xue was particularly happy at the news, and set about making preparations for the payment of Xue Pan's fine, since his death sentence would now be commuted as part of the amnesty.

A few days later it was announced that Zhen Baoyu and his father had called to offer their congratulations, and Lady Wang sent Jia Lan out to receive them. Shortly afterwards Jia Lan returned with a broad smile on his face:

'Good news, Grandmother! Uncle Zhen Baoyu's father has heard at court of an edict pardoning both Great-uncle She and Uncle Zhen from Ningguo House, and restoring the hereditary Ningguo rank to Uncle Zhen. Grandfather is to keep the hereditary Rongguo rank and after his period of mourning will be reinstated as a Permanent Secretary in the Board of Works. All the family's confiscated property is to be restored. His Majesty has read Uncle Bao's composition and was extremely struck by it. When he discovered that the candidate concerned was Her Late Grace's younger brother, and when the Prince of Beijing added a few words of commendation, His Majesty expressed a desire to summon him to court for an audience. The ministers then told him that Uncle Bao had disappeared after the examination (it was I who informed them of this in the first place), and that he was at present being looked for everywhere, without success, whereupon His Majesty issued another edict, ordering all the garrisons in the capital to make a thorough search for him. You can set your mind at rest now, Grandmother. With His Majesty taking a personal interest in the matter, Uncle Bao is sure to be found!'

Lady Wang and the rest of the family were delighted and congratulated each other on this new turn of events.

*　*　*

FROM CHAPTER 120

Zhen Shiyin expounds the Nature of Passion and Illusion
And Jia Yucun concludes the Dream of Golden Days

*　*　*

Jia Zheng had arrived in Nanking with Grandmother Jia's coffin, accompanied by Jia Rong and the coffins of Qinshi, Xifeng, Daiyu and Faithful. They made arrangements for the Jia family members to be interred, and then Jia Rong took

Daiyu's coffin to her own family graveyard to be buried there, while Jia Zheng saw to the construction of the tombs. Then one day a letter arrived from home, in which he read of the success achieved by Baoyu and Jia Lan in their examinations—which gave him great pleasure—and of Baoyu's disappearance, which disturbed him greatly and made him decide to cut short his stay and hurry home. On his return journey he learned of the amnesty decreed by the Emperor, and received another letter from home telling him that Jia She and Cousin Zhen had been pardoned, and their titles restored. Much cheered by this news, he pressed on towards home, travelling by day and night.

On the day when his boat reached the post-station at Piling, there was a sudden cold turn in the weather and it began to snow. He moored in a quiet, lonely stretch of the canal and sent his servants ashore to deliver a few visiting-cards and to apologize to his friends in the locality, saying that since his boat was due to set off again at any moment he would not be able to call on them in person or entertain them aboard. Only one page-boy remained to wait on him while he sat in the cabin writing a letter home (to be sent on ahead by land). When he came to write about Baoyu, he paused for a moment and looked up. There, up on deck, standing in the very entrance to his cabin and silhouetted dimly against the snow, was the figure of a man with shaven head and bare feet, wrapped in a large cape made of crimson felt. The figure knelt down and bowed to Jia Zheng, who did not recognize the features and hurried out on deck, intending to raise him up and ask him his name. The man bowed four times, and now stood upright, pressing his palms together in monkish greeting. Jia Zheng was about to reciprocate with a respectful bow of the head when he looked into the man's eyes and with a sudden shock recognized him as Baoyu.

'Are you not my son?' he asked.

The man was silent and an expression that seemed to contain both joy and sorrow played on his face. Jia Zheng asked again:

'If you are Baoyu, why are you dressed like this? And what brings you to this place?'

Before Baoyu could reply two other men appeared on the deck, a Buddhist monk and a Taoist, and holding him between them they said:

'Come, your earthly karma is complete. Tarry no longer.'

The three of them mounted the bank and strode off into the snow. Jia Zheng went chasing after them along the slippery track, but although he could spy them ahead of him, somehow they always remained just out of reach. He could hear all three of them singing some sort of a song:

> 'On Greensickness Peak
> I dwell;
> In the Cosmic Void
> I roam.
> Who will pass over,
> Who will go with me,
> Who will explore
> The supremely ineffable

> Vastly mysterious
> Wilderness
> To which I return!'

Jia Zheng listened to the song and continued to follow them until they rounded the slope of a small hill and suddenly vanished from sight. He was weak and out of breath by now with the exertion of the chase, and greatly mystified by what he had seen. Looking back he saw his page-boy, hurrying up behind him.

'Did you see those three men just now?' he questioned him.

'Yes, sir, I did,' replied the page. 'I saw you following them, so I came too. Then they disappeared and I could see no one but you.'

Jia Zheng wanted to continue, but all he could see before him was a vast expanse of white, with not a soul anywhere. He knew there was more to this strange occurrence than he could understand, and reluctantly he turned back and began to retrace his steps.

The other servants had returned to their master's boat to find the cabin empty and were told by the boatman that Jia Zheng had gone on shore in pursuit of two monks and a Taoist. They followed his footsteps through the snow and when they saw him coming towards them in the distance hurried forward to meet him, and then all returned to the boat together. Jia Zheng sat down to regain his breath and told them what had happened. They sought his authority to mount a search for Baoyu in the area, but Jia Zheng dismissed the idea.

'You do not understand,' he said with a sigh. 'This was indeed no supernatural apparition; I saw these men with my own eyes. I heard them singing, and the words of their song held a most profound and mysterious meaning. Baoyu came into the world with his jade, and there was always something strange about it. I knew it for an ill omen. But because his grandmother doted on him so, we nurtured him and brought him up until now. That monk and that Taoist I have seen before, three times altogether. The first time was when they came to extol the virtues of the jade; the second was when Baoyu was seriously ill and the monk came and said a prayer over the jade, which seemed to cure Baoyu at once; the third time was when he restored the jade to us after it had been lost. He was sitting in the hall one minute, and the next he had vanished completely. I thought it strange at the time and could only conclude that perhaps Baoyu was in some way blessed and that these two holy men had come to protect him. But the truth of the matter must be that he himself is a being from a higher realm who has descended into the world to experience the trials of this human life. For these past nineteen years he has been doted on in vain by his poor grandmother! Now at last I understand!'

As he said these words, tears came to his eyes.

'But surely,' protested one of the servants, 'if Mr Bao was really a Buddhist Immortal, what need was there for him to bother with passing his exams before disappearing?'

'How can you ever hope to understand these things?' replied Jia Zheng with a sigh. 'The constellations in the heavens, the hermits in their hills, the spirits in their caves, each has a particular configuration, a unique temperament. When did you ever see Baoyu willingly work at his books? And yet if once he applied himself, nothing was beyond his reach. His temperament was certainly unique.'

In an effort to restore his spirits, the servants turned the conversation to Jia Lan's success in the exams and the revival of the family fortunes. Then Jia Zheng completed and sealed his letter, in which he related his encounter with Baoyu and instructed the family not to brood over their loss too much, and dispatched one of the servants to deliver it to Rongguo House while he himself continued his journey by boat. But of this no more.

* * *

IV
Early Modern Japanese Popular Literature

Japan's transition from the late medieval age of civil wars to an early modern world of peace and order is one of the most dramatic turning points in Japanese history. The new military rulers of the Tokugawa shogunate (1603–1868) created peace and order, imposed strict social hierarchies and forceful policies, and laid the foundations for economic prosperity and a new cultural flourishing. As the traditional elites and great military clans lost their influence and power, they also witnessed the rise of social newcomers. Commoners, a crucial driving force in Japan's commercial revolution, made their fortune in the rapidly growing great cities. Even the lower social classes, for the first time in Japanese history, had broader access to education under the Tokugawa. The new social prominence of the commoners and the great leap in literacy gave birth to a new type of literature: popular fiction, haikai poetry, and popular theater such as kabuki and puppet theater. This literature captured the pleasures and challenges of the lives of the new commoner class and their vibrant urban milieu.

A portrait of the seventeenth-century Japanese poet Bashō, with the text of one of his most famous haikus: "An old pond— / A frog leaps in, / The sound of water." (See p. 614.)

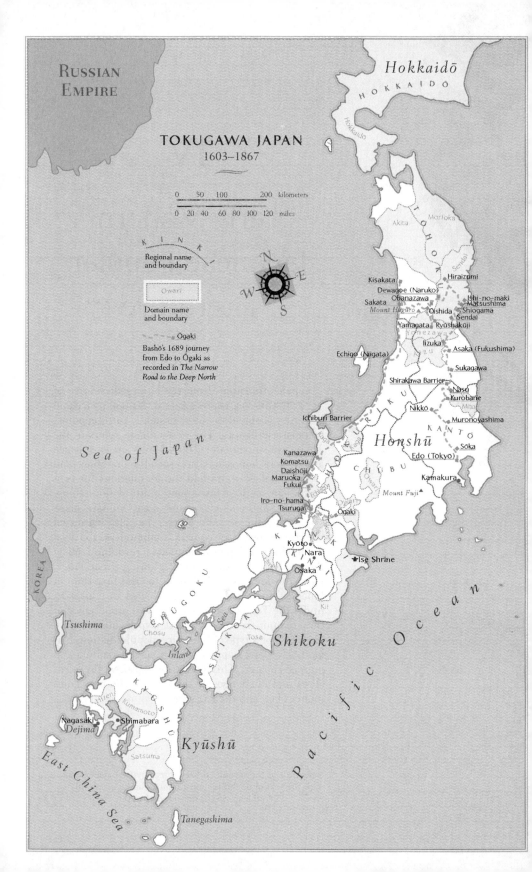

RUSSIAN
EMPIRE

Hokkaidō

HOKKAIDŌ

TOKUGAWA JAPAN
1603–1867

| 0 | 50 | 100 | | 200 kilometers |

| 0 | 20 | 40 | 60 | 80 | 100 | 120 miles |

K I N K I

Regional name
and boundary

Owari

Domain name
and boundary

Ōgaki

Bashō's 1689 journey
from Edo to Ōgaki as
recorded in *The Narrow
Road to the Deep North*

Akita

TŌHOKU

Morioka

Sendai

Kisakata ● Hiraizumi
Dewagoe (Naruko)
Obanazawa ● Ishi-no-maki
Sakata Matsushima
Mount Haguro Ōishida Shiogama
Yamagata Ryūshakuji Sendai
Echigo (Niigata) Iizuka Asaka (Fukushima)
Yonezawa
Aizu Sukagawa
Shirakawa Barrier
Nasu
Ichiburi Barrier Kurobane
Nikkō
Muronoyashima

Kanazawa *Honshū* Sōka
Komatsu KANTŌ
Daishōji CHŪBU Edo (Tokyo)
Maruoka Owari
Fukui Kamakura
Iro-no-hama *Mount Fuji* ▲
Tsuruga Ōgaki

Sea of Japan

HOKURIKU

Kyoto
Nara
Osaka ★ Ise Shrine

K I N A I

Kii

KOREA

Tsushima

CHŪGOKU
Chōsu
Inland Sea SHIKOKU Tosa *Shikoku*

Pacific Ocean

Nagasaki
Dejima ● Shimabara
Buzen Kumamoto
KYŪSHŪ

Satsuma

Kyūshū

East China Sea

Tanegashima

THE TOKUGAWA CLAN

Since the late twelfth century, in the wake of the civil wars chronicled in *The Tales of the Heike*, Japan had been governed by a series of military clans who held de facto power on behalf of politically impotent emperors. The first military government, the Kamakura shogunate (1185–1333) ruled from Kamakura near modern-day Tokyo. The Ashikaga shogunate (1336–1573) ruled from Muromachi, a quarter in Kyoto. But after 1467 Japan descended into 150 years of chaos and bloodshed until the beginning of the seventeenth century, when one clan, the Tokugawa, managed to reunify Japan and to set up a new military government in Edo, modern-day Tokyo.

The Tokugawa shoguns created a rigid class society, consisting of samurai, farmers, artisans, and merchants. The old aristocracy and Buddhist and Shintō priests stood outside of this hierarchy, although priests ranked equal to the samurai class. The shoguns' vast bureaucracy was staffed by samurai retainers. With no more wars to fight, these former soldiers became bureaucrats, and with a government to run they clustered in the cities. Removed from the land and their previous mili-

tary and agricultural pursuits, the urban samurai developed new needs, which were promptly met by enterprising urban commoners—such as merchants and artisans—whose numbers swelled in response to economic opportunity. Even the traditional ways of commerce evolved under the Tokugawa. Because rice, which had long been the traditional standard of exchange, was unwieldy and inconvenient in an urban setting, coined money took its place in business transactions. The growth of a money economy had a slow but irreversible effect on every aspect of Japanese life.

Cities grew into bustling centers of commercial activity and changed under the impact of new policies. To prevent power challenges from the provinces, the shogun required his most prestigious retainers, the so-called "domain lords," to keep estates in Edo in addition to their castles in the provinces. Their women and children were held as hostages of sorts in Edo, while the domain lords lived in alternating years in the provinces and in Edo. This policy changed the face of Edo, as wealth from the provinces flooded into the city and commercial and cultural exchange between the provinces and the political center increased. The shoguns were

This late eighteenth-century woodblock print by Katsukawa Shunshō depicts a street scene in Edo's Yoshiwara pleasure quarter.

also worried about public morals. To control prostitution, they consolidated brothels that were previously spread out into "officially licensed pleasure quarters." The pleasure quarters were surrounded by a moat and only accessible through a main gate, to monitor entering clients and to prevent courtesans from leaving at their own will. The largest pleasure quarters—Yoshiwara in Edo, Shimabara in Kyoto, and Shinmachi in Osaka—quickly became proverbial. They appear again and again in popular literature as sites where fortunes were spent on music, dance, songs, and sex; purses and families ruined; hearts broken, and double love suicides planned.

Connected to the pleasure quarters both geographically and in spirit, the theater districts embodied the heartbeat of the early modern era. Although medieval Noh theater continued to thrive as an elegant, courtly entertainment for the upper classes that was sponsored by the Tokugawa shoguns, commoners crowded into the urban theater districts to witness the new forms of theater—*kabuki* and puppet plays—that emerged in the seventeenth century. Both kabuki—an opulent form of dance-drama with live actors—and puppet theater—narrative chanting (*jōruri*) performed by one chanter accompanied by a banjō-like *shamisen* and the miming with large puppets—dramatized issues of contemporary Edo society. They often staged current events. Whether in the guise of "historical dramas" or of "contemporary-life dramas" such as **Chikamatsu Monzaemon's *Love Suicides at Amijima***, popular theater touched upon hot issues of the day: the repressive class system which led to clashes between people's individual desires and societal expectations; grisly acts of desperation, in particular double suicides of lovers

A detail from an early seventeenth-century folding screen showing Portuguese merchants in Japan.

whose union was unacceptable to Tokugawa society; or the hypocrisy of authority figures who propagated the values of Confucian virtue and honor but were actually driven by vanity, greed, and pettiness. Although actors and courtesans were considered outcasts, together with entertainers and beggars, they were the heroes of their age, darlings of an early modern celebrity cult. The newly popular *ukiyo-e* woodblock prints ("pictures of the floating world") depicted the world of the pleasure quarters and the world of theater: Mass-produced portraits of courtesans and actors show the faces of the giddy and voluptuous creativity of early modern Japan. It is therefore not surprising that the pleasure quarters and the theater district were at times subject to censorship and repression by the authorities.

The Tokugawa shoguns were also worried about outside threats. Portuguese traders had first reached Japan in 1543 when blown ashore by a typhoon. European merchants brought a few products that would have a major impact on Japan: firearms and New World crops such as corn, sweet potatoes, and tobacco. Catholic missionaries who were seeking converts outside of Europe to combat the reformation movements in Rome followed in the wake of these merchants and traders. Francis Xavier, a priest of the recently founded Jesuit order, reached Japan in 1549 and, like many missionaries who followed him, had a keen interest in Asian cultures and was sensitive to indigenous beliefs and practices. But ultimately quarrels between different Catholic orders over how to present Christianity in East Asia and how to accommodate their radically different cultural values and religious traditions damaged the credibility of the missionaries in the eyes of East Asian rulers. Repressions against Christianity began in Japan in 1587, and the Tokugawa shoguns quickly decided that the foreigners must go. By 1639 the shoguns had forbidden the practice of

Christianity, overseas travel, and the importation of foreign books. European traders and Christian missionaries were expelled under threat of execution. Japanese converts were sometimes tortured or killed if they refused to abjure their Christian beliefs.

Although the period when Christian missionaries worked in Japan was relatively brief, they helped inspire a development that altered the face of Japan within a century: mass printing. Japanese had imported printed texts from China as early as the eighth century and had subsequently used the technology of woodblock printing to print Buddhist sutras. But until the late sixteenth century all books except for Buddhist texts circulated in extremely small, restricted numbers in manuscript format. Manuscripts were expensive, because they had to be copied by an expert hand; therefore access to book knowledge was limited to those few who owned copies as members of elite families or who had the means to have them copied. After Christian missionaries set up a printing press with movable type and published among others a Japanese translation of Aesop's Fables (*Isoho monogatari* or "Tales of Isoho") in 1594, the first shogun, Tokugawa Ieyasu, had prominent Confucian texts, along with administrative and military works, printed with movable type in the early 1600s. Classical works of vernacular literature, such as an abridged version of *The Tale of Genji* and *Essays in Idleness*, followed soon in luxury editions. In the 1630s movable type printing was replaced with woodblock printing, which was more suitable to print the cursive Japanese *kana* syllabary, and commercial publishing houses opened. Seventeenth-century Japan underwent a printing revolution. Classical Chinese and Japanese texts were printed quickly and sold to the urban population in the dozens of bookstores that sprung up in response.

As a result, literacy levels soared. Until 1600 only aristocrats and the Buddhist clergy received an extensive education, while peasants and many samurai could not read or write. By the mid-seventeenth century, most of the samurai, artisans, merchants, and even some farmers had gained basic literacy. A growing network of private schools for the merchant class and domain schools for the samurai class made this drastic change possible. **Ihara Saikaku's** *Life of a Sensuous Woman* (1686), an example of the new "Books about the Floating World" that depicted the pleasure quarters, was a national bestseller partly because there was a substantial literate audience able and eager to read the confessions of this highly promiscuous lady.

The advent of mass printing fuelled the speed of both reading and writing. At one point, for example, on a single day in 1680, Saikaku composed in a frenzied single sitting a four-thousand-verse sequence. But not everybody followed the acceleration of the printing revolution. The entire oeuvre of **Matsuo Bashō** (1644–1694), generally considered the most famous haiku writer of all time, contains only about a thousand verses and Bashō seems to have disdained Saikaku's prolific literary output as well as the commercialization of literature he saw happening around him.

Despite their different outlook, both Bashō and Saikaku belonged to the new world of early modern popular literature. There was a strong awareness of the polar dynamic between popular (*zoku*) literature and refined or elegant (*ga*) literature. Refined literature was rooted in the classical traditions. Chinese-style poetry and classical *waka* poetry continued to stress aristocratic topics and relied on a fixed vocabulary of acceptable themes and diction—romantic love (in the case of waka), the seasons, spring warblers, or cherry blossoms. Popular literature, in turn, became expert in depicting bad places such as the theater districts and

the pleasure quarters in vulgar language or celebrating themes and earthy expressions of simple commoner life—courtesans, potatoes, or piss. Popular linked verse (*haikai no renga*), which gave birth to the genre of haiku, became a major ground for experimenting with novel combinations of high and low diction, classical and popular themes, and Chinese and Japanese styles. Bashō's *The Narrow Road to the Deep North*, a poetic diary of his travels through northeastern Japan, is a brilliant example of how the literary tradition could be recaptured and recast through a new poetic language that preserved all the rich resonances of that tradition.

Early modern popular literature was one part of the revolution in lifestyles and forms of entertainment of this era. Actors, courtesans, adventurers, shopkeepers, rice brokers, moneylenders, fashion-plate wives, and precocious sons and daughters all created their own new cosmopolitan customs. *Kabuki* playwrights, haiku poets, woodblock artists, and best-selling novelists all captured in their own genres an intimate glimpse of kinetic bourgeois life—blunt, expansive, iconoclastic, irrepressibly playful. For the first time ordinary people became standard literary characters, and the material and sexual aspects of life were deemed worthy subjects of literature. We should note that the rich and varied spectrum of literary production in the early modern period also included sophisticated debates about the philological and historical interpretation of the Chinese Confucian Classics and the canonical works of Japan such as *The Man'yōshū* (*Collection of Myriad Leaves*) and *The Tale of Genji*, and thus the classical genres never went completely out of style, but popular literary forms—popular theater, fiction, and haiku—were the truly novel genres that emerged from the great transformations of early modern Japan.

IHARA SAIKAKU

1642–1693

No writer caught the substance of seventeenth-century Japanese city life with as much sparkle as Ihara Saikaku. Born in Osaka, when the city was the commercial epicenter of Japan, he knew the preoccupations and foibles of the merchant class inside out because he was one of them. At the time, money, love, and sex, the major themes of his voluminous work, were radically new topics for Japanese literature. The subject matter alone would have guaranteed Saikaku some measure of popularity, but his wit and sly inventiveness made him an icon in his time, and an author still widely read and enjoyed today.

Ihara Saikaku was born into a wealthy merchant family as Hirayama Tōgo. Ihara is thought to have been his mother's surname, and Saikaku is the pen name he took when he became a writer. At age fifteen he inherited the family business, but his new responsibilities did not keep him from devoting himself to his passion: composing *haikai*, a popular form of linked verse consisting of sequences of haiku poems (of 5-7-5 or 5-7-7 syllables). By the time he was in his early twenties, he had established himself as a renowned haikai master, attracting students and leading groups of poets in large-scale composition sessions of poetry sequences. When his wife died suddenly at age twenty-five, Saikaku left the family business in the hands of trusted clerks, shaved his head to become a lay monk, and spent the rest of his life as a haikai master and a prolific writer of vernacular fiction.

As his fame grew Saikaku wrote at an increasingly vertiginous speed. He had always worked quickly, even under emotionally trying circumstances (for example, upon the death of his wife, he composed an emotional thousand-verse mourning sequence for her in twelve hours, leaving him less than half a minute per poem), but by his midlife, Saikaku's output was startlingly prolific. In 1687–88 alone he published twelve books. He became one of Japan's first professional writers.

Saikaku's early work in poetry informed and influenced his later work in fiction. He learned both classical linked verse (*renga*) and the new genre of popular linked verse (*haikai*) with masters who emphasized wordplay and inventive association, and who encouraged parody of the classical poetic tradition. This playfulness and irreverence would serve him well in his vernacular fiction, as would the skills he learned in linking short haiku into longer narratives. His injection of everyday language, visceral humor, and snapshots from contemporary commoner life into poetry brought a new edge to these genres, and each of these was easily exported to fiction.

Life of a Sensuous Woman (published in 1686), excerpted below, belongs to the genre of "Books of the Floating World" (*ukiyo zōshi*)—vernacular fiction that depicted the pleasure quarters of the flourishing urban centers of Osaka, Kyoto, and Edo (today's Tokyo) and flourished from Saikaku's time to the end of the eighteenth century. In 1682 Saikaku had established the genre with the publication of *Life of a Sensuous Man*, a picaresque tale of the amorous exploits of a sexually precocious and ultimately insatiable hero. The development of the "Books of the Floating World" was also linked to the emerging art of Japanese wood-block printing (*ukiyo-e* or "Pictures of the Floating World"), which began to enchant Western audiences in the nineteenth century: Hishikawa Moronobu, the earliest wood-block print artist, produced the illustrations for a pirated version of *Life of a Sensuous Man* printed for the Tokyo market.

Life of a Sensuous Woman is unique in Saikaku's oeuvre, because he wrote it in the voice of an aging woman who tells the story of her life—lived in pursuit of love and lust—to two young men who come to visit her in her meditation hut in the reclusive outskirts of Kyoto. Just as the protagonist of *Life of a Sensuous Man* is a satire of Genji, the classical aristocratic lover par excellence from the eleventh-century *The Tale of Genji*, the heroine of *Life of a Sensuous Woman* is a popular early modern refashioning of Ono no Komachi, the most beautiful and gifted Heian poet. Legend had it that Komachi, once surrounded by countless suitors, ended her life as an ugly old hag. Saikaku's old heroine begins her reminiscences about her love-filled life with a confession: "with this single body of mine I have slept with more than ten thousand men." This echoes the well-known genre of the Buddhist confession narrative, in which an aged narrator, now repentant, confesses to sins and depravities in order to secure favorable rebirth as a human rather than a hungry ghost or animal. The line between the serious intention of the Buddhist genre—the old woman ends her confession with an emphasis on her regained purity—and Saikaku's indulgence in lustful storytelling is fine and adds to the attraction of Saikaku's book.

By having the heroine move through all walks of life—from professions such as a lady-in-waiting at the imperial palace, or a domain mistress, to an obsessive monk's wife, and finally a streetwalker—Saikaku exposes the unsavory underside of the lives of the privileged classes of society, including domain lords, greedy monks, presumptuous samurai, and rich merchants. The resourcefulness of Saikaku's heroine allows her to prevail over them all, while also helping her to gratify her insatiable sexual desire.

During Saikaku's lifetime, his sprawling oeuvre of vernacular fiction was considered entertainment, not literature in any serious sense. But he was one of the first writers to enjoy a broad readership among urban commoners, and he is now considered the greatest fiction writer of the Edo period. His works continue to be read with gusto and have had great impact on modern Japanese writers, regardless of whether they appreciate Saikaku the social realist, the fine chronicler of manners, the sexual libertine, or the grotesque satirist.

From Life of a Sensuous Woman[1]

An Old Woman's Hermitage

A beautiful woman, many ages have agreed, is an ax that cuts down a man's life. No one, of course, escapes death. The invisible blossoms of the mind finally fall and scatter;[2] the soul leaves; and the body is fed like kindling into a crematorium fire in the night. But for the blossoms to fall all too soon in a morning storm—ah, how foolish are the men who die young of overindulgence in the way of sensuous love. Yet there is no end of them.

On the seventh of the First Month, the day people go out to have their fortunes told, I had to visit Saga[3] in northwest Kyoto. As if to show that spring had truly come, the plums at Umezu Crossing were just breaking into blossom. On the eastbound ferry to Saga I saw an attractive young man dressed in the latest style but unmistakably disheveled. His face was pale, and he was thin and worn, obviously from too much lovemaking. He looked as if he didn't have much time left and was getting ready to leave his inheritance to his own parents.

"I've never lacked anything at all," he said to the man with him. "But there's one thing I really would like. I wish my pledging liquid could keep flowing on and on like this river and never stop."

His friend was startled. "What I'd like," he said, "is a country without women. I'd go there and find a quiet place to live, far from any town. There I'd take good care of myself, so I could live to a decent old age. The world keeps changing, and I'd really like to see a lot of different things."

The two men had opposite attitudes toward life and death. One sought as much sensual pleasure as he could get, even though he knew that it was shortening his life, and the other wanted to give up love altogether and live many more years. Both longed for the impossible, and they talked in a dazed way, halfway between dreaming and waking.

After we reached the other side, the men joked and horsed around, staggering along the path on the bank and stamping without a thought on the parsley and thistles that were coming into leaf. Finally they turned away from the river, left the last houses behind, and entered the shadows of the mountains to the north. I felt curious about them and followed at a distance. Eventually we came to a grove of red pines and, within it, an old fence made of bundled bush-clover stalks that were beginning to come apart. Beside the braided bamboo gate a gap had been opened so a dog could pass through. Inside the fence, in deep silence, stood a meditation hut, its front roof sloping down from a boulder above the mouth of a natural cave. Ferns grew in its thatched eaves, and vines clung to the roof, their leaves still tinted with last fall's colors.

To the east stood a willow tree, and from below it came a soft sound. Clear, pure water was flowing naturally through a raised pipe of split bamboo from a source nearby. I looked around for the venerable monk that I assumed must live there and was surprised to see an old woman, one whose face the years had given a refined beauty. Her back was bent, but her frost-touched hair was well combed. Her eyes were as soft and hazy as the moon low on the western horizon. Over an

1. Translated by and with notes adapted from Chris Drake.
2. Alludes to a poem by the female poet Ono no Komachi from the *Kokinshū*: "They fade invisibly and change, these blossoms of the mind in our human world."
3. A wooded area of temples and huts of recluses.

old-style sky blue wadded-silk robe embroidered with gold thread, she wore another splashed with a dappled pattern of thickly petaled chrysanthemums. Her medium-width sash, with flowers in a lozenge design, was tied in front—stylish even at her age. To the crossbeam above the front of what seemed to be her bedroom was attached a weathered plaque that read "Hut of a Sensuous Hermit." A scent of incense lingered in the air. I think it must have been First Warbler's Cry, a very fine aloeswood.[4]

I found a place outside a window and stood there, so overcome with curiosity that my mind strained to leap out of myself and into the hermitage. As I watched, the two men, looking thoroughly at home, went right inside without even announcing themselves.

"So, you've come again today," the woman said smiling. "There are so many pleasures in the world to captivate you men. Why have you come all the way here to see me, like wind visiting a rotting old tree? My ears are bad, and words no longer come easily. It's just too difficult for me now to keep up relationships properly, the way I'd need to do if I wanted to stay in the world. I've been living in this place for seven years already, and the plum trees are my calendar. When they bloom, I know spring's come. When the mountains are white with snow, I know it's winter. I almost never see anyone any more. Why do you keep coming here?"

"He's being tortured by love," said one of the men. "And I get very depressed. Neither of us understands the way of sensuous love deeply enough yet. We've heard many things about you, and we've followed the same path you've traveled. Right here to your door. You're so very experienced, won't you please tell us the story of your life in the words people use now? Please do it in a way that will help us understand more about life and the world today."

One of the men poured some fine saké into a beautiful gold wine cup and strongly urged the old woman to drink. She relented and gradually lost her reserve and began to play on her koto. She was so skillful it was obvious she played it often. For a while she sang a short song about deep love. Then overcome with emotion, she began to relate, as if in a dream, all the loves in her own life and the various things that had happened to her.

I didn't come from a low-class family, she began. My mother was a commoner, but my father was descended from middle-ranking aristocrats who mixed with high officials at the court of Emperor GoHanazono. Families, like everything else in the world, go up and down. Mine came down very hard, and we were so miserable we didn't want to go on living. But I happened to be born with a beautiful face, so I went to Kyoto to serve a court lady of the highest rank, and I learned most of those elegant, refined ways of aristocrats. If I'd continued to serve there for a few more years, I'm sure I would have had a very happy future.

From the beginning of the summer when I was eleven, I became very loose and forgot I was supposed to concentrate on serving my employer. When people did my hair, I wouldn't be satisfied and I'd redo it myself. I was the one, you know, who invented the version of the Shimada hairstyle that has the hair swept up behind and the chignon tied and folded flat in back. It became quite stylish. I also created that way of tying the topknot without showing the cord that became so popular. I'm sure you know the white silk robes with colorful Gosho-dyed patterns. Well, in the beginning only court ladies wore them. But I spent all my time

---

4. Temple incense chosen to match the early spring season.

and energy making new patterns and colors for them, and soon they became quite popular with ordinary women.

Aristocrats, you know, are always thinking about love, whether they're composing poems or playing kickball. Those women's pillows, why, they're always in use. Whenever I saw women and men lying together, I'd feel excited, and when I'd hear them in the dark, my heart pounded. Naturally I began to want to make love myself. Just when I was beginning to feel love was the most important thing in my life, I also began to get love letters from a lot of men. They all were full of deep feelings and tender thoughts, but I got so many I had no way to get rid of them all. I had to ask a guard to burn them for me. Of course I made him promise to keep it secret. Later, you know, he told me something strange. The places in the letters where the men swore by their patron gods that their love for me was true and would never change, those places, he said, didn't burn. They rose up with the smoke and came down in the Yoshida Shrine, where all the gods of Japan gather together. There's nothing as strange as love. Every one of the men who longed for me was handsome and knew how to look attractive, but I didn't have special feelings for any of them. I was interested in a young samurai who was working for one of the aristocrats. He was of low rank and wasn't good-looking, but his writing, even in his very first letter, sent me into another world. He kept on writing more and more letters, and before I knew it I was beginning to suffer and yearn for him, too.

It was hard for us to meet, but I managed to arrange things sometimes, and we were able to make love. Rumors started, but I couldn't stop myself. In the faint light early one morning, someone saw both of us together out in the shifting mist, as they say, and while the mist swirled ever more thickly, my employer secretly fired me and had me discreetly left beside the road at the end of Uji Bridge.[5] I was merely punished, but the man—how cruel they were! He lost his life for what we'd done.

For four or five days I couldn't tell whether I was sleeping or awake. I couldn't sleep, but I couldn't get up either. Several times I was terrified when I saw the man's resentful-looking shape in front of me. It refused to even speak. I was in complete shock, and I thought about killing myself. But the days went by, and you know, I completely forgot about that man. It's amazing how quickly a woman's mind can change. But I was thirteen at the time, and people looked on me leniently. Ridiculous, they'd think, surely she hasn't done *that* already. And what could have been more ridiculous than their own thoughts!

In the old days, when it came time for a bride to leave for the groom's house, she would grieve at leaving her parents' house and cry at the gate until her sleeves were all wet. But these days young women know a lot more about lovemaking. They grow impatient with the slow bargaining of the go-between woman, rush to get their trousseaus ready, and can't wait for the fancy palanquin to come and take them away. When it arrives, they practically leap in, excitement glowing everywhere, to the tips of their noses. Until forty years ago, young women used to play horse outside their front doors until they were eighteen or nineteen. And young men didn't have their coming-of-age ceremonies until they were twenty-five. My goodness, the world certainly does change quickly!

I was very young when I learned about love. I was still a flower in bud, you could say. And after that I had so many experiences that the pure water of my

5. The woman was born in Uji, just south of Kyoto.

mind turned completely the color of sensuous love, like the water in the Uji River where it turns yellow from all the mountain roses on the banks. I just followed my desires wherever they went—and I ruined myself. The water will never be clear again. There's no use regretting it now, though. I certainly have managed to live a long time, but my life, well, it wasn't what you'd call exemplary.

Mistress of a Domain Lord

The land was at peace, and calm breezes drifted through the pines of Edo. One year the daimyō lord[6] of a certain rural domain was in Edo spending his obligatory year living near the castle of the shōgun. There he was able to be with his wife, who was required to live permanently in Edo, but during the year she died. Since she'd left no male heir, the lord's worried retainers gathered more than forty beautiful young women from leading warrior families in Edo, hoping one of them would bear a boy baby for the lord and ensure the continued rule of the lord's clan over the domain—and the retainers' own employment. The head chambermaid was resourceful, and whenever she saw the lord feeling good, she brought a young woman near his sleeping chamber and did her best to put him in the mood. All the women were fresh as budding cherry blossoms, ready to burst into full bloom if wet by the slightest rain. Most men would have gazed at any of these women and never grown tired, yet not a single one suited the lord, and his retainers began to grow anxious.[7]

The retainers didn't bother to look for other women among the commoners in Edo. Ordinary women raised in the eastern provinces, you know, they're rough and insensitive.[8] They have flat feet and thick necks, and their skin is hard. They're honest and straightforward, but they don't feel deep passion and don't know how to express their desire to men or attract them by acting afraid. Their minds are sincere, but they're ignorant of the way of sensuous love and can't share it with a man who knows it.

I've never heard of any women more attractive than those in Kyoto. For one thing, Kyoto women have a beautiful way of speaking. It's not something they study. They pick it up naturally living in the capital, where women have talked that way for centuries. Just look at how different Kyoto is from Izumo Province. In Izumo they have an ancient tradition of love and courtship going back to the days of the gods, but the men and women there slur their words so badly it's hard to understand them. But then just go offshore from Izumo to Oki Island. The islanders there look like country people, but they speak the way people do in the capital. And Oki women are gentle and know how to play the koto, play go, distinguish fine incense, and compose and appreciate waka poems. That's because long ago Emperor GoDaigo was exiled to Oki with his entourage,[9] and the islanders maintain the customs from that time even now.

So the daimyō's councillors thought that in Kyoto, at least, there must be a woman their lord would like. To look for one, they sent the lord's old and trusted retainer, the overseer of the inner chambers. The overseer was more than seventy.

---

6. Domain lord.

7. If a domain lord died without a male heir, the domain administration was transferred to a new clan and his samurai retainers lost their employment.

8. Edo, the old name for Tokyo, was located in the eastern provinces, an area that Kyoto people considered rustic and unrefined.

9. In 1332.

He couldn't see a thing without glasses and had only few front teeth. He'd forgotten what octopus tasted like, and the only pickled vegetables he could still eat were finely grated radishes. Day after day he lived without any pleasure, and as for sensuous love, well, he did wear a loincloth, but he might as well have been a woman. The best he could do was excitedly tell a few sexy stories. As a samurai, he wore formal divided skirts and robes with starched, high shoulders, but since he served in his lord's wife's private chambers and in the women's quarters, he wasn't allowed to wear either a long or a short sword. Too old to be a warrior, he was put in charge of watching the silver lock on the doors to the inner chambers. That's why the councillors chose him to go to Kyoto to find a mistress—and to chaperon her all the way back to Edo. It would be like putting a precious buddha statue in front of a puzzled cat. You just can't let a young man alone with a woman, you know, even if he's Shakyamuni Buddha.

The old retainer finally arrived in the capital, which looked to him like the Pure Land paradise on earth. He went directly to one of the exclusive Sasaya clothiers on Muromachi Avenue that caters to aristocrats and warrior lords. There he announced himself and was led to a private room.

"I cannot discuss my business with any of the young clerks," he told the person who received him. "I need to talk very confidentially with the owner's retired parents."

The old retainer, who knew nothing of how things worked, felt uneasy as he waited. Finally the retired shop owner and his wife appeared. With a grave expression on his face, the old retainer said, "I've come to choose a mistress for my lord." "But of course," the retired owner said. "All the daimyō lords have them. Exactly what kind of woman are you looking for?"

The retainer opened a paulownia-wood scroll box and took out a painting of a woman. "We want to find someone," he said, "who looks like this."

The retired couple saw a woman between fifteen and eighteen with a full, oval face of the kind so popular then, skin the light color of cherry blossoms, and perfect facial features. The lord's councillors wanted round eyes; thick eyebrows with plenty of space between them; a gradually rising nose; a small month with large, even white teeth; ears a bit long but not fleshy and with clearly formed earlobes; a natural forehead and unaltered hairline; as well as a long, slender nape with no loose hairs. Her fingers were to be long and delicate with thin nails, and her feet, about seven inches long, with the large toes naturally curved the way a truly sensuous woman's are and with arched soles. Her torso was to be longer than most women's, her waist firm and slim, and her hips full. She should move and wear her clothes gracefully, and her figure should show dignity and refinement. She was to have a gentle personality, be skilled at all the arts that women learn, and know something about everything. The old retainer added that she was not to have a single mole on her body.

"The capital is a big place," the retired owner said, "and a lot of women live here. Even so, it won't be easy to find a woman who meets all these requirements. But it's for a domain lord, and expense is no concern. If the woman exists, we'll find her for you." The retired couple then went to see an experienced employment agent named Hanaya Kakuemon on Takeyamachi Street. They discreetly explained all the conditions and asked him to search for suitable candidates.

Employment agencies live off commissions. If an employer pays one hundred large gold coins as a down payment, the agency takes ten. This is broken down into silver coins, and even the errand woman gets 2 percent. An applicant for a mistress job has to have an interview, and if she has no proper clothes, she has to rent what she wants. For two and a half ounces of silver a day, she can rent a white silk robe or one of figured black satin, a dapple-dyed robe to wear over that, a wide brocade sash, a scarlet crepe underskirt, a colorful dye-pattern shawl to cover her head like an elegant lady, and even a mat to sit on in her hired palanquin. If the young woman makes a good impression and is hired, she has to pay the agency a large silver coin as its fee.

A woman from a poor family needs to have a new set of foster parents who own property and will vouch for her. The agency negotiates with the owners of a small house, and the young woman formally becomes their daughter. In return, the foster parents receive money and gifts from the lord or rich merchant who employs their new daughter. If the woman works for a lord and bears a baby boy, she becomes an official domain retainer, and the lord gives a regular rice stipend to her foster parents.

Competition is intense, and candidates try very hard to make a good impression at the interview. In addition to renting clothes, they have to spend half an ounce of silver for a palanquin and two carriers—no matter how short the ride is, the rate is the same to anywhere in Kyoto. And the woman needs a girl helper at two grams of silver a day and an older maid at three. She also has to pay for their two meals. After all this, if the woman is not hired, not only does she still have no job, but she's lost well over three ounces of silver. It's a very hard way to make a living.

And that's not the only thing the woman has to worry about. Well-off merchants from Osaka and Sakai constantly come to Kyoto to visit the Shimabara licensed quarter or party with boy kabuki actors near the theaters along the river by the Fourth Avenue Bridge. Sometimes these men have some free time and prey on women applicants to amuse themselves. The merchant pays a jester with a shaved head to pretend to be a wealthy visitor from the western provinces and has him ask women from all over Kyoto to come interview to be his mistress. The merchant attends the interview, and if a woman catches his eye, he asks her to stay and secretly negotiates with the owner of the house for a secluded room. Then he asks the woman to sleep with him for just that one time. The surprised woman is terribly angry and disappointed, but when she tries to leave, he says all sorts of things to persuade her. Finally he mentions money, and since the woman has paid so much for the interview, she gives in. For selling herself, she gets two small gold pieces. There's nothing else she can do. But women who aren't from poor families don't do that.

The employment agency carefully chose more than 170 attractive young women and sent them to the old retainer for interviews, but he wasn't satisfied with a single one. Desperately, the agency kept on searching, and when they heard about me, they contacted someone in the village of Kohata on the Uji River. Together they came to see me at my parents' house in an out-of-the-way part of Uji, where we were trying to live inconspicuously away from the world until people had forgotten what I'd done. But I agreed to an interview, and I went right back to Kyoto with the anxious agents just as I was, without putting on good clothes or makeup. When I got there, the old retainer thought I was even better than the woman in the painting, so the search was called off. Everything was decided on the spot, and I got to set the conditions myself. I became an official domain mistress.

And so I went with the retainer all the way to Edo, far off in Musashi Province in the east. There I lived very happily day and night in the lord's third mansion in Asakusa, on the outskirts of the city. Everything was so luxurious, well, in the day

I couldn't believe my eyes. I felt I must be seeing the most beautiful cherry blossoms in the world on the Mount Yoshino in China[1] that people talk about. And at night they had top kabuki actors from Sakai-chō come, and we'd watch their plays and variety shows and laugh hour after hour. Everything was so luxurious you couldn't imagine anything else you'd want.

But women, you know, are very basic creatures. They just can't forget about physical love, even though warriors have very strict rules keeping women and men apart. The serving women who live in the inner rooms of those mansions almost never even see a man and don't have the slightest idea what the scent of a man's loincloth is like. Whenever they look at one of Moronobu's suggestive prints, they'll feel a rush and go dizzy with desire. Without even imagining they're really making love, they'll twist and push their own heels or middle fingers way around and move their implements. And when they're finished, they still feel unsatisfied. They want to make love with a flesh-and-blood man all the more.

Daimyō lords usually spend most of their time in the front rooms of their mansions overseeing domain business, and without knowing it, they become attracted to the young pages with long hair who are constantly waiting on them. The love a lord feels for a page is deeper than anything he feels for a woman. His wife is definitely in second place. In my opinion, this is because a lord's wife isn't allowed to show her jealousy the way commoner women do. Men, high or low, fear a jealous woman more anything else in the world, and those warriors take strict precautions.

I've always been an unlucky woman, but with the lord I was fortunate. He was tender to me, and we enjoyed our lovemaking. But things didn't work out. Before I could get pregnant, he started taking herbal pills. They didn't do much good, though. He was still young, but in bed he just couldn't do anything anymore. It was just extremely bad luck. I couldn't talk about it with anyone, so I spent all my time regretting what had happened. The lord kept losing weight, and finally he became so weak and haggard he was just awful to look at.

I was amazed to discover that the councillors thought it was my fault. They said I was a woman from the capital who liked fancy sex and had worn out their lord. Those old men didn't know the first thing about love, but they made the decisions. I was suddenly dismissed and sent all the way back to my parents—again. If you look closely at the world, you'll see that a man who's born sexually weak is a very sad thing for a woman.

A Monk's Wife in a Worldly Temple

I have a small build, so I unstitched the sewn-up openings under the arms of the robes I'd worn as a girl and put them on again.[2] I looked so young people called me a female version of the Daoist wizard Tieguai.[3]

---

1. Mount Yoshino is famous for its cherry blossoms. There is no Mount Yoshino in China, but there was apparently a belief that there was such a place and that its beauty exceeded that of Japan's famous site.
2. Girls wore long, loose sleeves with an opening under the arms that was sewn up when they became adults. In this chapter the woman is about twenty-five years old.
3. Li Tieguai, or "Iron-Crutched Li," was one of the Eight Daoist Immortals. Although usually depicted as an old infirm beggar, he is seen here as an embodiment of eternal youth and immortality.

In those days Buddhism was at its proverbial high noon, and truly, even in broad daylight, women dressed as temple pages[4] would walk right into temple precincts and visit the monks there. I, too, finally overcame my shame and had my hair done up like a boy, with thick, long hair in front and the top of my head shaved. I learned to speak like a boy and move my body almost like one, too. When I put on a loincloth, I was surprised to see how much like a boy I looked! I also changed to a boy's narrow sash, but the first time I stuck long and short swords through it, they were so heavy I couldn't keep my waist and legs steady. And when I put on a boy's cloak and wide-rimmed sedge hat, I began to wonder whether I was really myself.

I hired a young man with a long ink moustache painted on his face to carry my spare sandals and other things, and I set out together with a professional jester from the licensed quarter who knew a lot about how things worked in Kyoto. We asked around and found a temple known to have wealth and a sex-loving head monk. We walked right through the gate in the earth walls surrounding the temple, pretending we were going inside to see the small cherry tree in the temple garden. Then the jester went to the head monk's quarters and began whispering with the monk, who seemed to have a lot of free time on his hands. Soon I was called into the reception room, where the jester introduced me to the monk.

"This young warrior," the jester said, "has lost his lord, and he has no one to depend on. He's been able to make some contacts, but while he's waiting for an offer from another lord, he'll drop in here from time to time for a little recreation. I most sincerely ask you to take care of him to the best of your ability." He went on and on about a lot of similar things.

The head monk was flushed with excitement. "Just last night," he blurted out, "I got someone to teach me how to make an herbal mixture to induce abortions. It's something you women really need to . . ." Then he clapped his hand on his mouth. It was all quite amusing.

Later we drank some saké and spoke more freely. As we savored the smells of meat and fish coming from the temple kitchen, my fee was set at two small gold coins per night. Later, the jester and I went around to temples of every persuasion suggesting they switch to the Woman-Loving sect, and we didn't find a single monk who didn't convert.

Eventually the head priest of one temple fell in love with me, and I agreed to become his temporary wife for three years in exchange for twenty-five pounds of silver. I became what people call an "oven god."[5] As the days went by, I was more and more amazed by what I saw and heard at this floating-world temple. In the past, a group of monk friends who lived in various halls around the temple compound had gotten together on the six days a month when special purifications and austerities are required. They all solemnly pledged that on days except for these six, they would strictly obey their abstentions. And they vowed to rigorously limit their fish and poultry and their sex with women to the nights of these six days, except, of course, when the days fell on the memorial days for various buddhas and the sect founder. To pursue their pleasures, they went all the way to

4. Boy assistants to high-ranking monks. They often were sexual partners of the older men, but in the 17th century, women were able to enter temples more easily, and a new type of "page" flourished.

5. One of the seven gods of fortune, "oven god" was also a euphemism for a woman living and cooking in a temple, a custom that was widespread but officially forbidden.

Third Avenue in downtown Kyoto and visited places like the Koiya Inn.[6] On other days, the men acted like model monks. The buddhas, who know all, looked on them leniently, and everything went smoothly.

But in the last few years, this large temple had been growing very prosperous, and the monks were losing all restraint. At night they replaced their black robes with long cloaks and went to the licensed quarter pretending to be shaven-headed herbal doctors. And the head priest would bring his secret wife of the moment right into the monks' living quarters. He'd had his monks dig far down below one corner of the main living room and built a secret underground room for the wife. Between the ground and the raised floor of the quarters, they'd constructed a narrow window in a place that no one could see from the outside. That way the woman could have a little light. They'd also filled the space between the ceiling of the underground room and the quarters floor with earth and constructed sound-proof walls more than a foot thick all the way around to the back of the room. During the day the head priest forced me down into this underground cell. When the sun went down, I was allowed up and could go as far as his bedroom.

Living like this was depressing enough, but sleeping with the priest made me even sadder. It was just a job, and there was no love in it. I had to give myself to that disgusting priest day and night, whenever he wanted to have sex, and I began to lose interest in living. Nothing gave me pleasure any more, and I gradually lost weight and grew weaker. But the priest didn't let up in the least. His expression showed that as far as he was concerned, if I died he'd just have me secretly buried somewhere on the temple grounds without even a proper cremation. And that would be that. It was frightening.

Later I got used to the situation, and I even came to enjoy it. When the priest went out to chant sutras at a parishioner's house on the night after a death or on a memorial day, I found myself waiting up late, wishing he would come back. And when he went out at dawn to pray over the ashes of a cremated person, I felt as if we were saying good-bye to each other, and I hated for him to be away, no matter how short a time it was. Even the smell of incense on his white robe clung to my body and seemed dear to me. After a while I forgot my loneliness, and I started to like the sounds of gongs and cymbals at the ceremonies. At first, you know, I would hold my hands over my ears whenever I heard them. And my nose got used to the smell from the crematory. The more deaths there were, well, the happier I was, since they meant more offerings for the temple. Early each evening, I called in fish peddlers and made suppers of duck meat with and without bones, blowfish soup, cedar-broiled fish, and other fine seafood.[7] I did take one small precaution, though. I always put a cover on the brazier so the nice smells wouldn't escape.

The young monks in training saw our loose way of living and imitated us. They hid salted red herrings in their sleeve pockets and wrapped them in pieces of old calligraphy practice paper covered with half-written buddha names. After soaking the papers, they would place them in warm ashes to bake and would eat herrings from morning until night. It gave them wonderful complexions and lustrous skin and kept them vigorous and healthy. Some monks go off for long periods to a mountain or forest where they eat only berries and plants. Other monks are so

---

6. A popular restaurant with private rooms where monks could meet women.   7. All prohibited foods.

poor they have no choice but to eat only vegetables. You can spot these kinds of monks right away from their lifeless expressions. They look like rotting trees.

I'd worked at the temple from spring until early fall. At first the priest was terribly afraid I would run away, and while I was up out of my underground room, he would lock the living quarters each time he went out. But later he came to trust me and just glanced in at me from the kitchen from time to time. Gradually I became bolder, and when parishioners came to visit the priest I no longer rushed underground but simply slipped out of sight into another room.

One evening I went out onto the bamboo verandah to get some fresh air, and a strong wind was moaning in the trees and ripping the thin leaves of the plantains in the garden. It was an eerie sight. Everything in the world really does change, I felt, just as they preach. I lay down on the porch with my head on my arm and was soon very drowsy. Then I saw what looked like a phantom shape. Her hair was completely gray, and her face was covered with wrinkles. Her pathetic arms and legs were thin as tongs, and she was bent over with a crooked back. She came toward me crawling on all fours.

"I've lived in this temple for many, many years," she said in a voice so full of sorrow I could hardly bear to listen. "The priest told people I was his mother. I'm not from a low-class family, but I decided to do a disgraceful thing, and I came here. I was twenty years older than he was, and I'm ashamed to say I was so poor I couldn't get by any more, and I began to sleep with him. Later we became close and exchanged many pledges, but they. . . . For him, all those pledges were nothing, nothing at all. When I got old like this, he pushed me into a dark corner of the temple. He gives me nothing but old rice offerings he's taken down from the altars. And now he sees I'm not about to die eating only that, so he glares resentfully at me. He's treated me terribly, but still, you know, it isn't really so bad. There's something else that gnaws at me until I can't stand it. Every single day. It's you! You don't know anything about me, but whenever I hear you and the priest saying little things to each other in bed, well, you see, even at my age I just can't forget sex. So I've decided to get rid of this terrible longing I have and feel good again. I'm going to bite right into you. Tonight!"

I was completely shaken. I knew I had no business being in that temple a minute longer. Finally I devised a method of escape that impressed even me. I stuffed a lot of cotton wadding between the outer and inner layers in the front part of my robe. That made me look quite heavy. Then I went to see the head priest.

"I haven't told you until now," I said, "but I'm several months pregnant. I'm not sure exactly when, but the baby could come any time now."

The priest lost his usual composure. "Please go back to your parents' house," he said. "Have a safe delivery and then come back here." He gathered up a lot of offertory coins from different places and gave them to me, swearing he was very worried about all the needs I'd have at home. Then he gave me some tiny silk robes that grief-stricken parents had left as offerings after their babies died. The priest said he couldn't stand to look at them any more, and he gave me all he had, telling me to sew them into things for his baby instead. Then he began celebrating and named the child Ishijiyo—Everlasting Rock—a boy's name, even though it hadn't been born yet.

I'd had enough of that temple. There was a lot of time left on my contract, but I never went back. The priest must have been very upset, but in a situation like that, well, there was no legal action he could take.

A Teacher of Calligraphy and Manners

"The irises you sent are exquisite.[8] Watching them gives me endless pleasure in ways too many to begin to count." This is the kind of thing a woman has to write to begin a respectable thank-you letter in early summer.

In Kyoto, ordinary women can learn to write in a flowing woman's hand from women calligraphy teachers, who also sell their skills transcribing letters. These commoner teachers start their careers when they're young, serving for several years in the mansion of an aristocrat and learning from experience all the proper ways of elegant comportment, writing, and speech as well as the various traditional ceremonies that mark off the year. When they finish their service, most of these women are models of respectability and make a decent living teaching what they've learned. Parents tell their daughters to emulate these teachers and send their girls to study under them.

I, too, had once worked for a high-ranking aristocratic family. Although I'd been through a lot since then, some very kind people thought it would be a shame for me to waste my experience and knowledge, and they helped me establish my own calligraphy school for girls. It consisted of a single room, which served as my bedroom at night, but it was a pleasant place, and I was extremely happy to finally have a house of my own. I pasted a notice on the doorpost announcing that I taught calligraphy to women, and to help me, I hired a young woman from the country who'd just arrived in Kyoto.

Taking care of other people's daughters isn't an easy job. Day after day you continually have to exert yourself correcting brush strokes on the girls' practice papers and generally act as an example, demonstrating and explaining to them the cultured manners and decorum they're expected to learn. To avoid rumors, I completely gave up relationships with men and managed to overcome every temptation to meet them.

Then one day an obviously vigorous young man in a state of extreme passion came to me and asked me to write a letter to a certain woman with whom he fervently wished to become intimate. Since I'd worked in the licensed quarter, I knew how to compose love letters that would reach their readers' hearts. I could make a woman reader want to fly together with a man, sharing the same wings and eyes, or make her desire to become one with him, like two trees linked by a shared limb. Choosing precisely the right expressions, I could make the woman who read one of my letters fall deeply in love with the man who'd asked me to write it. I could see directly into the feelings of young women still living with their parents and persuade even the most experienced woman who knew everything about men. I used different ways of affecting each woman, but there was none my letters didn't move.

Nothing shows a person's feelings better than a letter. No matter how far away the person you're thinking of is, you can communicate your thoughts with your brush. You may write at length, using phrase after polished phrase, but if your letter is filled with falsehoods, it will show and soon be forgotten. Truthful brush strokes go straight to the heart. As you read, you will feel as if you're meeting the writer, who's right there with you.

---

8. Sending flowers in tune with the seasons was a sign of good taste expected from upper-class women. Commoners increasingly adopted these manners in the 17th century.

When I was working in the licensed quarter, there was one man among my many customers whom I loved very much. Whenever I met him I forgot I was performing and opened my heart completely to him. I trusted him and told him everything. The man also opened himself to me, but when his parents discovered our relationship, they forced him to stop his visits. I was so sad I wrote him every day and had the letter secretly delivered to him at home.

Later he told me that while he was confined in his parents' house he felt as if we were still together—as if I were right there with him. After reading each of my letters several times, he would go to sleep at night with it pressed against his skin. Sooner or later the same dream would come. In it, the letter would take on my shape, and we would talk and hold each other all night. The people guarding the man slept near him, and they would hear two voices coming from the place where he was sleeping. They certainly had a hard time believing what they heard!

Eventually the man's parents relented, and when we met again he told me about everything he'd experienced. I discovered that the thoughts I'd been thinking each day had also reached his mind—exactly as I'd thought them. Actually, though, there's nothing strange about that. When you spend a long time writing a letter, you forget about everything else. If you put your whole mind into thinking something, it will always reach the other person.

I turned to the young man who'd visited my school. "Since I'm taking on the full responsibility for writing your letters," I said, "I can assure you that sooner or later the woman will respond to your love, no matter how uninterested she seems now." I put all of myself into composing the best letters I possibly could. But as I wrote more and more letters, I found I'd lost control. The man who'd asked me to write the letters had become very, very dear to me.

During one of the man's visits, I was unable to continue writing. I sat there holding my brush and thinking only about him. Then I abandoned all shame. "What an incredibly coldhearted woman she is," I said. "She's torturing you and not showing the slightest sensitivity to your feelings. You're just not getting anywhere with her. Why don't you love me instead? We'd have to talk about it, of course, and we'd have to set looks aside. But I'm kindhearted, and with me you can realize your love without even waiting. You've got a lot to gain with me right now."

The man looked surprised, and he remained silent for some time. He didn't know whether the woman he was writing to so often to would ever agree to meet him, and he realized it would be a lot quicker with me. He didn't seem to think I was a bad substitute, either. Judging from my wavy hair, curving large toes, and small mouth, he thought I must be a very passionate woman.

"Please let me be frank," he finally said. "Even in relationships I begin myself, money's out of the question. I won't be able to give you even one new sash. And after we've known each other a short time, if you start inquiring whether I know any dry goods dealers and ask me for two rolls of ordinary silk or a roll of crimson silk, I just won't be able to promise you that. I've got to make that absolutely clear right from the beginning."

How insensitive and mean, I thought to myself, to say an arrogant thing like that to someone he wants to make love with! There was no shortage of nice men in the capital, and I decided I'd have to look somewhere else.

It was the rainy season, and just then a soft rain began to come down. Suddenly it became very quiet outside. A sparrow flew in through the window, and the flame in the lamp went out. Taking advantage of the darkness, the man threw himself on me and grabbed me tightly. He was breathing heavily as he forced himself on me, and as he began, he took some expensive tissue paper out of his robe and placed it near the pillow. After he finished, he slapped me gently on the small of the back, apparently thinking I'd enjoyed it. He even sang an old wedding song, saying he'd love me till I was a hundred and he was ninety-nine.

What an idiot, I thought. You have no idea how fragile life is. Do you really think life is an old song and you're going to live to be ninety-nine? You said some pretty disrespectful things just now. You won't last even one year. Pretty soon you'll have a sunken jaw and be walking with a stick. And then you'll leave the floating world altogether.

I made love with the man day and night. When he lost his desire, I strengthened him with loach broth, eggs, and yams, and we continued. Gradually, as I expected, he ran dry. It was pitiful to see him shivering in the Fourth Month of the next year, still wearing thick winter robes when everyone else had changed into early summer things. Every doctor he'd seen had given up on him. His beard was long and unkempt; his nails lengthened unclipped; and he had to cup his hand to his ear in order to hear. At the slightest mention of an attractive woman, he turned his head away with a look of endless regret.

A Stylish Woman Who Brought Disaster

Kickball has long been a sport for aristocratic men and warriors, but I discovered that women play it, too. At the time, I was working as the outside messenger for the wife of a daimyō domain lord in the lord's main mansion in Edo.[9] My job was running errands and dealing with people outside the women's quarters, and once I went with the lord's wife to their third mansion in Asakusa, where she sometimes went to relax. In the large garden inside the mansion, azaleas were beginning to bloom, turning all the small fields and hills a bright crimson. Nearby I saw some waiting women wearing long divided skirts of a matching crimson. Their long sleeves were fluttering and swaying as they played kickball inside a high, rectangular fence. They lifted the deerskin ball almost noiselessly with special shoes, and using only their feet, they strained to keep it moving in the air for as long as they could. They were extremely good and used the Multiple Cherry, the Mountain Crossing, and other difficult kicks. I was amazed that women were doing this. It was the first time I'd seen anything like it.

Earlier, in Kyoto, I'd been quite surprised to see court ladies practicing indoor archery, but people at court said it was quite natural. The women were following a venerable tradition begun in China by the imperial consort Yang Guifei.[1] Still, I'd never heard of women in Japan playing football in all the centuries since it was first played here by Prince Shōtoku.[2] But the wife of a domain lord is free to do any thing she wants. How magnificent she was!

---

9. The domain lord's wife and children were required to live in Edo, Tokyo, as virtual hostages of the Tokugawa shōguns, the de facto rulers of Japan during the so-called Tokugawa or Edo Period (1600–1867).
1. The favorite consort of Emperor Xuanzong of the Tang Dynasty. Her seductive talents and eventual execution during a rebellion are recounted in the "Song of Everlasting Sorrow" of the Tang poet Bo Juyi.
2. Prince Shōtoku (574–622), a founding figure of the early Japanese state, is associated with the introduction of Buddhism from China and Korea into Japan. One of the many legends that grew around him claims that he played kickball.

Later, as evening approached, a strong wind began to blow, bending the trees in the garden. The kickers had a hard time controlling the ball, which wouldn't spin and constantly swerved off course, and soon everyone lost interest in the game. The lord's wife had just taken off her kickball robes and put them away when her face suddenly took on a fierce expression as if she'd remembered something. Nothing her attendants said cheered her up, so finally they stopped speaking and tried not to move or make any noise. Then a lady in waiting named Kasai, who'd served for many years, spoke up in an obsequious tone of voice. Her head moved back and forth and her knees trembled with excitement.

"Tonight," she said, "please honor us by holding another jealousy meeting.[3] Until the tall candle burns itself out!"

The lord's wife's face suddenly took on a pleasant expression. "Yes," she said. "Yes indeed!"

An older woman named Yoshioka, the head waiting woman, pulled on a brocade-tufted cord that ran along the wall of a corridor. At the far end a bell rang, and soon even the cooks and bath maids appeared and sat without the slightest hesitation in a circle around the lord's wife. There must have been thirty-four or thirty-five women in all. I also joined them.

"You may speak about anything at all," Yoshioka told us. "Don't hold anything back. Confess something you yourself did. How you blocked another woman's love for a man and hated her. How you were jealous of a man going to see another woman and spoke badly of him. Or the pleasure you felt when a man and woman broke up. Stories like these will bring great joy to our mistress." This certainly was an extraordinary kind of meeting, I thought, but I couldn't laugh, since it was being held at the command of the lord's wife.

Soon they opened a wooden door with a painting of a weeping willow on it and brought out a life-size doll that looked exactly like a real woman. The artisan who made it must have been a master. It had a graceful figure and a face more beautiful than any blossom in full bloom. I myself am a woman, but I was entranced and couldn't stop gazing at it.

One by one, each woman spoke what she felt. Among them was a lady in waiting named Iwahashi who had a face so classically unattractive it invited disaster. No man would want to make love with her in the daytime, and she hadn't slept with a man at night for a very long time. In fact, during all that time she hadn't even seen a man. Now she ostentatiously pushed her way through the other women and volunteered.

"I was born and raised in Tōchi in Yamato," she said, "where I also married and lived with my husband. But that damn man started making trips to Nara. Then people began to tell me he was seeing the daughter of one of the lower priests at the Kasuga Shrine[4] there. She was exceptionally beautiful, they said. So one night I secretly followed my husband. My heart pounded loudly as I went, and when he arrived, I stood nearby and listened while the woman opened the small back gate and pulled him inside.

"'Tonight,' the woman says, 'my eyebrows kept on itching and itching. No matter how hard I rubbed them. I just knew something good was going to

---

3. Such meetings, where women shared their resentments and repressed desires, were commonly held in the 7th century by women of the upper merchant and warrior classes, who were particularly restricted.
4. One of the largest shrines in Japan.

happen.' And then, with no shame at all, she calmly rests her slender little waist against his.

"I couldn't bear any more of that and ran right over to them. 'Hey,' I shouted, 'that's my husband!' I opened my mouth wide to show her my blackened teeth and prove I was married, and before I knew it, I'd bitten into her as hard as I could!" Then Iwahashi fastened her teeth around the beautiful doll and refused to let go. The way she did it made me feel that right there in front of me, with my own eyes, I was seeing exactly what had happened that night long ago. I was terrified.

The jealousy meeting had begun. The next woman walked very slowly out in front of us as if she hardly knew where she was. She was a typical woman who lets her emotions run away with her. I don't know how she was able to say the things she did.

"When I was young," she confessed, "I lived in Akashi in Harima Province. My niece got married and took in her husband as part of her own family.[5] What a tramp he turned out to be. And a complete lecher! He slept with every single maid and with the helping women, too. It was perfectly obvious—they were dozing off all the time. My niece tried to keep up appearances, you know, so she let things go and didn't criticize him. Inside, though, she was very upset at not being able to do anything. So every night I would go and try to help her. I got someone to nail iron fasteners to her bedroom door, and after asking my niece and her husband to go inside, I'd shout, 'Please sleep together tonight!' Before I'd go back to my own room, I'd lock their door from the outside.

"Soon my niece was looking thin and exhausted. She didn't even want to see her husband's face any more. 'If he keeps on like this,' she told me, 'I'm not going to live much longer.' Her body was shaking when she said that. She was born in the year of the fiery horse,[6] so she should have caused her husband to die young, but he was the one who was wearing her down. She got very sick because of that despicable man and his endless urges. I'd like to make him do it again and again right now with this doll here. Until he falls over dead!" She hit the doll and knocked it over, and then she screamed at it for some time.

Then another lady in waiting named Sodegaki got up. She was from Kuwana in Ise Province. She told us she'd been a jealous person even before she got married. She was so jealous of her parents' maids she wouldn't let them put on makeup or use mirrors when they did their hair or put white powder on their skin. If a maid had a pretty face, she forced the woman to make herself look as unattractive as she could. Stories about how she acted got around, though, and people began avoiding her. No men in her hometown or for miles around would think of marrying her. So she came all the way to Edo to look for work.

"Hey, beautiful doll," the woman yelled. "Yes, you're so very, very smart, aren't you. You even know how to make another woman's husband stay overnight at your house!" Then she began to disfigure the innocent doll.

Each woman tried to speak more jealously than the rest, but none of their stories satisfied the lord's wife. When my turn came, I went directly to the doll and pulled it down onto the floor. Then I got on top of it.

---

5. Among commoners, a groom often took his wife's name and legally became a family member.
6. A "double fire" year in the sixty-year zodia-

cal cycle. It was believed that a woman born in such a year would be so passionate she would wear out her husband. Such years occurred in 1606 and 1666.

"You!" I said. "You're just a mistress. But the lord likes you, so you act as if you're more important than his wife, sleeping with him on the same long pillow, just as you like without thinking anything about it. Listen, you, I'm not going to let you get away with it!" I glared at the doll, ground my teeth, and acted as if I truly hated the doll from the bottom of my heart.

What I'd said turned out to be what the lord's wife herself had been thinking. "Exactly," she said, "exactly! Let me tell you about this doll. You see, the lord treats me now as if I hardly existed. He's had his beautiful mistress from the domain brought all the way here to Edo, and he doesn't think about anyone but her day and night. It's very sad being a woman—complaining does no good at all. But I did have this doll made to look like her. At least I can cause pain to it."

Before the lord's wife had finished, something strange happened. First the doll opened her eyes and extended her arms. She looked around the room for a while, and then she seemed to stand up, although by that time no one was watching closely anymore. All the frightened women were scrambling away as fast as they could. Then the doll grabbed the front of the lord's wife's outer robe and wouldn't let go. I only barely managed to separate them. After that, nothing more happened.

Perhaps because of this incident, a few days later the lord's wife fell ill and began to speak deliriously of terrible things. The waiting women thought she must be possessed by the doll's soul. If they didn't stop the resentful doll, it might cause even more serious harm, so they secretly decided to get rid of it. In a far corner of the mansion they burned the doll so completely that nothing at all remained, but they showed their respect and buried the ashes in a formal grave. After that, people began to fear the burial mound, and they claimed that every evening they could clearly hear a woman's wailing voice coming from inside it. The rumor spread beyond the mansion walls, and the lord's wife became the object of widespread ridicule.

Word of the affair eventually reached the lord, who was at his second Edo mansion with his mistress from his home domain. Astounded, he started an investigation and ordered the outside messenger to report to him. Since that was my job, I had to appear. I couldn't hide what I knew, and I related everything about the doll, just as it had happened. The people who heard me clapped their hands together in amazement.

"There's nothing as nasty as a woman's vengeance," the lord told his aides. "I have no doubt at all that very soon my mistress won't be safe from my wife's avenging soul. Her life is in danger here. Explain the situation to her and have her return to the domain."

When the woman appeared and sat nervously on her knees before the lord, I saw she was far more graceful and beautiful than the doll had been. I was a bit proud of my own looks, you know, and we both were women, but I was so overwhelmed I could hardly bear to look at her. Such great beauty, I thought to myself, and yet the lord's wife, out of jealousy, is trying to kill her with curses. The lord declared that women were fearsome creatures, and he never again entered the women's quarters of his main mansion in Edo. His wife became a virtual widow while her husband was still alive.

I had to watch all this and try to take messages between them. Soon I grew very weary of my job, prestigious as it was, and I submitted my resignation. It was accepted, and I returned to Kyoto feeling so disappointed with the world I thought I might become a nun. Jealously is something you must never, never give in to. Women should be very careful to resist it.

Five Hundred Disciples of the Buddha—I'd Known Them All

In winter the mountains sleep beneath leafless trees, and the bare limbs of the cherries turn white only with snow at dusk. Then spring dawns come once more, filled with blossoms. Only humans get old as the years pass and lose all pleasure in living. I especially. When I recalled my own life, I felt thoroughly ashamed.

I thought I at least ought to pray for the one thing I could still wish for—to be reborn in Amida Buddha's Pure Land paradise.[7] So I went back to Kyoto one more time and made a pilgrimage to the Daiunji temple in the northern hills. It was supposed to be a visible Pure Land right here in this world. My mind was filled with pious feelings, and I'd chosen a good time to visit. It was the end of the Twelfth Month, when people gathered to chant the names of all the buddhas and to confess the bad deeds they'd done during the year and ask for forgiveness. I joined in their chanting.

Afterward, as I walked down the steps of the main hall, I noticed a smaller hall devoted to the Five Hundred Disciples of Shakyamuni Buddha. All were wise and worthy men who had achieved enlightenment, and I went over and looked inside. Each virtuous disciple was distinctly individual and differed from all the others. I wondered what marvelous sculptor could have carved all these many unique statues.

People say there are so many disciples that if you search hard enough, you're bound to find someone you know. Wondering if it might be true, I looked over the wooden statues and saw disciples who obviously were men with whom I'd shared my pillow when I was younger. I began to examine them more closely and found a statue that looked like Yoshi from Chōjamachi in Kyoto. When I was working in the Shimabara quarter, we exchanged very deep vows, and he tattooed my name on his wrist where no one would notice. I was beginning to remember all the things that had happened between us when I saw another disciple sitting under a large rock. He looked exactly like the owner of the house in uptown Kyoto where I worked as a parlor maid. He loved me in so many ways that even after all those years I couldn't forget him.

On the other side of the hall I saw Gohei. Even the disciple's high-ridged nose was exactly his. I once lived together with him. We loved each other from the bottoms of our hearts for several years, and he was especially dear to me. Then, closer to me, I saw a wide-bodied disciple in a blue green robe with one shoulder bared. He was working very hard—and he looked familiar. Yes, yes, it was definitely Danpei, the man who did odd jobs for a warrior mansion in Kōjimachi. While I was working in Edo, I used to meet him secretly six nights a month.

Up on some rocks in back was a handsome man with light skin and the soft, gentle face of a buddha. Finally I remembered. He was a kabuki actor from the theaters down along the riverbank near the Fourth Avenue in Kyoto who'd started out as a boy actor selling himself to men on the side. We met while I was working at a teahouse, and I was the first woman with whom he'd ever made love. I taught him all the different styles women and men use, and he learned well, but pretty soon he just folded up. He grew weaker and weaker, like a flame in a lantern, and then he was gone. He was only twenty-four when they took his body to the crematory at Toribe Mountain. The disciple I saw had just his hollow jaw and sunken eyes. There was no doubt about it.

---

7. According to the Pure Land sect of Buddhism, people hoped to be reborn in the Pure Land Paradise presided over by Amida, the "Buddha of Infinite Light."

Farther on was a ruddy-faced disciple with a mustache and bald head. Except for the mustache, he looked just like the old chief priest who'd kept me in his temple as his mistress and treated me so badly. By the time I met him I was used to every kind of sex, but he came at me day and night until I was so worn down I lost weight and had fevers and coughs and my period stopped. But even he had died. Endless storehouse of desire that he was, he, too, finally went up in crematory smoke.

And there, under a withered tree, a disciple with a fairly intelligent face and prominent forehead was shaving the top of his head. He seemed to be on the verge of saying something, and his legs and arms looked as though they were beginning to move. As I gazed at him, I gradually realized he, too, resembled someone I'd loved. While I was going around dressed up like a singing nun, I would meet a new man every day, but there was one who became very attached to me. He'd been sent from a western domain to help oversee the domain's rice warehouse sales in Osaka, and he loved me so much he risked his life for me. I could still remember everything about him. The sad things as well as the happy ones. He was very generous with what people begrudge the most,[8] and I was able to pay back everything I owed my manager.

Calmly I examined all five hundred disciples and found I recognized every single one! They all were men I'd known intimately. I began to remember event after event from the painful years when I was forced to work getting money from men. Women who sold themselves, I was sure, were the most fearful of all women, and I began to grow frightened of myself. With this single body of mine I'd slept with more than ten thousand men. It made me feel low and ashamed to go on living so long. My heart roared in my chest like a burning wagon in hell,[9] and hot tears poured from my eyes and scattered in every direction like water from one of hell's cauldrons. Suddenly I went into a sort of trance and no longer knew where I was. I collapsed on the ground, got up, and fell down again and again.

Many monks had apparently come to where I was, and they were telling me that the sun was going down. Then the booming of the big temple bell finally returned my soul to my body and startled me back to my senses.

"Old woman, what grieves you so?"

"Does one of these five hundred disciples resemble your dead child?"

"Is one your husband?"

"Why were you crying so hard?"

Their gentle voices made me feel even more ashamed. Without replying, I walked quickly out the temple gate. As I did, I suddenly realized the most important thing there is to know in life. It was all actually true![1] The Pure Land, I was sure then, really does exist. And our bodies really do disappear completely. Only our names stay behind in the world. Our bones turn to ash and end up buried in wild grass near some swamp.

Some time later I found myself standing in the grass at the edge of Hirosawa Pond.[2] And there, beyond it, stood Narutaki Mountain. There was no longer

---

8. Money.
9. The woman fears that she will go to Buddhist hell, not to the Pure Land Paradise. Fiery carts were believed to carry condemned souls to the assigned part of hell.
1. The woman cites the Noh play *Tomonaga*, in which a monk prays for the soul of the dead warrior Tomonaga. His soul returns and exclaims that the Pure Land and various other Buddhist beliefs are all "actually true!"
2. Large pond in Saga, where the woman's hut is located.

anything at all keeping me from entering the mountain of enlightenment on the far side. I would leave all my worldly attachments behind and ride the Boat of the Buddhist Dharma[3] across the waters of worldly passions all the way to the Other Shore. I made up my mind to pray, enter the water, and be reborn in the Pure Land.[4]

I ran toward the pond as fast as I could. But just then someone grabbed me and held me back. It was a person who'd known me well many years before. He persuaded me not to end my own life and fixed up this hermitage for me.

"Let your death come when it comes," he said. "Free yourself from all your false words and actions and return to your original mind. Meditate and enter the way of the Buddha."

I was very grateful for this advice, and I've devoted myself to meditation ever since. From morning to night I concentrate my mind and do nothing but chant Amida Buddha's name. Then you two men came to my old door, and I felt drawn to you. I have so few visitors here. Then I let you pour me some saké and it confused my mind. I actually do realize how short life is, you know, though I've gone on and on, boring you with the long story of my own.

Well, no matter. Think of it as my sincere confession of all the bad things I've ever done. It's cleared the clouds of attachment from me, and I feel my mind now shining bright as the moon. I hope I've also managed to make this spring night pass more pleasantly for you. I didn't hide anything, you know. With no husband or children, I had no reason to. The lotus flower in my heart[5] opened for you, and before it closed it told everything, from beginning to end. I've certainly worked in some dirty professions, but is my heart not pure?

---

3. The Buddhist Law is often compared to a boat that transports its believers to a realm of enlightenment.
4. Many people believed that they could reach the Pure Land by drowning themselves from a boat in the sea or ponds and rivers while meditating on Amida Buddha. It was a form of religious suicide.
5. A common Buddhist metaphor for purity amidst depravity. Just as the lotus blossom rises from the mud, the pure mind is capable of enlightenment amidst the delusions of the world.

THE WORLD OF HAIKU

Haiku is the best-known form of Japanese poetry and a testament to the importance of poetry within Japanese culture even today. With its evocative power and ability to surprise with unexpected juxtapositions, haiku is also the only Japanese genre to have spread beyond the Japanese archipelago. Haiku written in English have become a part of Anglophone literature and are used for elementary education in poetry. And poets throughout Europe, India, and the world bring the genre to life in many different languages. Today haiku is without doubt the shortest poetic form of world literature with a truly global reach.

Haikai, which can mean "comic" or "unorthodox" poetry and is the origin of haiku, was both a literary genre and a distinctive attitude towards language, the literary tradition, and life. Haikai poets wrote not only popular linked verse; they also pioneered a new style in writing prose essays (*haibun*) such as travelogues, and they produced striking ink paintings (*haiga*), which are as sparsely and poignantly sketched in ink as haikus are sketched in words. Although there were many different schools of haikai with competing claims about their craft, they shared a basic spirit: they all venerated novelty produced against the backdrop of the classical past. They enjoyed collages of high and low culture, relished the clashes resulting from inserting every-

day, vulgar expressions of the new popular culture into the nuanced vocabulary of previous elite traditions, or blending Chinese and Japanese elements, which had previously been carefully kept apart. Enamored of puns, wit, and parody, haikai poets thus rewrote the tradition in often playful and humorous ways. Haiku became more than simply another form of poetry: it became an expression of modern life.

The seventeenth century, when haikai became popular, was a period of drastic change. After a prolonged period of civil wars, the military clan of the Tokugawa brought back order and prosperity when they established themselves as shoguns in Edo, modern-day Tokyo, on behalf of the emperors, the symbolical heads of state residing in Kyoto. A new class of urban commoners, including merchants and samurai, became a driving economic and cultural force. Commercial printing took off and bookstores selling popular literature targeting the new commoner class dotted the alleys of the expanding urban centers of Osaka, Edo, and Kyoto. Thanks to domain and temple schools, the literacy rate among samurai, merchants, and even peasants increased dramatically within the short span of half a century. Copies of Chinese and Japanese classics were now affordable to almost all classes of society, and a vibrant popular culture of vernacular literature, which often parodied classical models, thrived alongside Neo-Confucian studies and classical scholarship. Haikai had a large share in this new commercial book culture: during

Woman Admiring Plum Blossoms at Night (mid-eighteenth century), by Suzuki Harunobu.

the second half of the seventeenth century 650 separate haikai titles were published in Kyoto alone. They represented the second most popular category of printed books after Buddhist devotional texts.

Originally haiku was the "hokku," the "opening verse" in a longer sequence of linked poems, which typically included a greeting to the host of a poetry session. The "opening verse," with a 5-7-5 syllable pattern, was followed by a verse with a 7-7 pattern, and capped by a third verse, again in 5-7-5 patterns continuing in alternation until the completion of the sequence. Sequences of 36, 100, or even 1,000 poems, composed alone or in a group, were the most common forms of linked verse. Haiku stood at the end of a long process of gradual shrinking of traditional verse forms. After the capacious "long verse poems" (*chōka*) in the eighth-century *Man'yōshū* (*Collection of Myriad Leaves*), the much shorter waka form, in a 5-7-5-7-7 pattern (also called *tanka* or "short poem") became the classical verse form since the tenth-century *Kokinshū* (*Collection of Ancient and Modern Poems*). Beginning with the fourteenth century, classical linked verse, the forerunner of popular linked verse, cut the waka pattern further down into alternating units of 5-7-5 and 7-7. Hokku appeared independently in prose texts and paintings in the seventeenth century. These short poems were not called haiku until the 1890s when the poet and critic Masaoka Shiki (1867–1902) coined the term "haiku" for poems in the 5-7-5 pattern.

Haiku typically contains a "seasonal word" (*kigo*), which evokes a host of associations relating landscape to mood (for example autumn wind to desolation), and a "cutting word" (*kireji*), which usually stands at the end of the first or second line and divides the haiku into two parts. A good example is a haiku by the haiku master **Matsuo Bashō** (1644–1694). On one of his travels, ghosts of fallen warriors appeared to Bashō along the shore of Akashi, where troops of the aristocratic Heike clan were massacred in the civil wars at the end of the twelfth century (described in *The Tales of the Heike*). Bashō captured the tragic spirit of the site in this humorous haiku:

> Octopus traps—
> fleeting dreams under
> a summer moon

Bashō must have seen local fishermen at Akashi lowering their octopus traps in the afternoon and hoping for a good catch the next morning. Tragic memory, traditional imagery, and the vignette of the simple fisherman life experienced by the poet-traveler clash in these few syllables. The classical image of the "summer moon," suggesting brevity of life and impermanence of all things, is juxtaposed with the all-too-real octopus traps. But the vulgar traps of the poet's actual experience are also the traps which once captured the Heike warriors, putting an end to their short-lived glory, short like a summer night.

Haikai exponentially expanded the topics on which one could write. If a poem introduced a word on which previous poets could never seriously compose, this "haikai word" was elevated to the status of the poetic, infusing literary language with the earthy, unrefined presence of contemporary commoner life.

The excitement over novelty was not directed only against the classic tradition, but also against the haikai tradition itself. Bashō's famous haiku of 1686 shook up the firm convictions of what "frogs" were expected to do in a classical poem:

> An old pond—
> A frog leaps in,
> The sound of water

Frogs appeared in spring, calling out to their mates with their beautiful voices, next to the bright yellow blossoms of the globeflower that typically grew next to a crystal-clear murmuring mountain stream. Bashō's haikai creature could hardly be more different from the "poetic essence" of the classical frog: not singing in spring, not in love, not enjoying its sparkling mountain stream, but stuck in a stagnant pond associated with the dead season of winter. As Bashō shook up classical frog poems, later haiku poets kept shaking up Bashō's poem:

> Jumping in,
> Washing off an old poem—
> A frog
>
> (Yosa Buson, 1716–1783)

> A new pond—
> Without the sound of
> A frog jumping in
>
> (Ryōkan, 1758–1831)

Both in today's Japan and in the West, haiku has become a different genre. It is no longer devoted to the rewriting of classical Chinese and Japanese poetry, as knowledge of these traditions has declined. But newer forms of haiku are thriving. As it is one of the few poetic genres of truly global reach, its fate lies in the hands of poets who write in many different languages and live in diverse locales. But haiku is still a poetry of small things and of everyday experience that preserves the sparkles of the particular in its universal appeal.

KITAMURA KIGIN

Kitamura Kigin (1624–1705) was a prominent member of the Teimon school of haikai. He emphasized the importance of classical waka poetry and Heian vernacular literature such as *The Tale of Genji* and *The Pillow Book*, on which he wrote commentaries. In his youth the future haikai master **Bashō** studied with him for a while.

"Fireflies" comes from a haikai manual Kigin wrote in 1648. This how-to manual is an early example of the poetic almanacs sold in Japanese bookstores today. In the entry on the topic of "fireflies," the reader can experience the quick-witted jumps between traditional poetic associations and funny new meanings.

From The Mountain Well

Fireflies[1]

In composing haikai about fireflies, those that mingle among the wild pinks are said to share the feelings of Prince Hyōbukyō and the ones that jump at the lilies are said to be like the amorous Minamoto Itaru.[2] The ones that fly on Mount

1. Translated by and with notes adapted from Haruo Shirane.
2. Situations in which fireflies helped lovers glimpse their object of desire: In the "Fireflies" chapter of *The Tale of Genji*, Prince Hyōbukyō, Genji's brother, sees the young Tamakazura in the light of fireflies, which Genji

cleverly releases behind the screen where she is sitting, and the prince falls instantly in love. The "wild pinks" refer to Tamakazura. In another romantic tale from the Heian Period, Minamoto Itaru peers into a woman's carriage aided by the light from fireflies.

Hiyoshi are compared to the red buttocks of monkeys, and the ones that glitter on Mount Inari are thought to be fox fires.³ Fireflies are also said to be the soul of China's Baosi or the fire that shone in our country's Tamamo no mae.⁴ Furthermore, poetry reveals the way in which the fireflies remain still on a moonlit night while wagging their rear ends in the darkness, or the way they light up the water's edge as if camphor or moxa were in the river, or the way they look like stars—like the Pleiades or shooting stars.

> At Mount Kōya
> Even the fireflies in the valley
> are holy men⁵

3. The messenger to the god of the Hiyoshi Shrine on Mount Hiei, northeast of Kyoto, was said to be a monkey. Inari Shrine, also near Kyoto, was associated with both foxes and "fox fires," strange lights appearing in the hills and fields at night.
4. A nine-tailed golden fox that bewitched Emperor Toba by disguising itself as a beautiful woman. The emperor loved Tamamo no mae, but the light she radiated was so painful to him that he had to have her exorcised. Tamamo no mae was believed to be a reincarnation of the Chinese beauty Baosi.
5. The headquarters of the Buddhist esoteric sect and an area with numerous monasteries and temples. The poem puns on *hijiri*, which means both "holy men" and "fire buttock" (lower part of a hearth), and implies homosexuality, not uncommon for Buddhist priests in the medieval period.

MATSUO BASHŌ

During his lifetime Matsuo Bashō (1644–1694) was only one of many haikai masters. He was not even part of the prominent haikai circles in the major cities of Kyoto, Osaka, or Edo, but spent much time on the road and eventually settled on the outskirts of Edo, supported by patrons and friends. Although Bashō was a socially marginal figure, like the travelers, outcasts, beggars, and old people who feature in his poetry, he and his school of haikai came to embody the art of haiku.

Bashō was born into a former samurai family that had fallen low in a small castle town thirty miles southeast of Kyoto. After serving the lord of the local castle, where he also developed his tastes for haikai poetry, he moved to Edo at the age of twenty-nine and installed himself as a haikai master, making his living from teaching poetry. A few years later, in 1680, Bashō retreated to a "Banana plant hut" (Bashō-an), from which he took his pen-name, on the Sumida River in the outskirts of Edo. For the next four years he would write in a style heavily tinged by Chinese recluse poetry, before setting out on travels in 1684, during which he wrote poetic travel diaries.

In 1689 he set out with his travel companion Sora on a five-month journey to explore the Northeast, a trip which resulted in *The Narrow Road to the Deep North*, included in the selections here. The journey depicted in *Narrow Road* is a pilgrimage through nature, but it is also a very conscious emulation of the conventions of the past as Bashō seeks inspiration from famous poetic sites. It is also a travel through language. Some places evoke the frail aesthetics of Heian waka, while others are tinged with reminiscences of Chinese poets, such as Du Fu and Li Bo. Both Bashō and his travel companion Sora kept a travel diary of sorts. Sora's diary, not published until 1943, shows that the majority of the fifty haiku in Bashō's travelogue were actually written after the journey or were revisions of earlier poems, and that Bashō made himself look far more ascetic and contemplative in the process of revision. *The Narrow Road to the Deep North* is thus not a diary but an idealized version of his travels.

Bashō was always on the move in search for new poetic themes, new languages, and new objects. In his travel diaries he accomplished nothing less than influencing how people saw some of the most defining sites of Japanese identity. He gave the haikai movement a distinctive prose style. Previous classical linked verse had always stayed in the aristocratic realm of waka, never developing a prose language of its own. But with the innovations of haikai prose, haikai poetry reached a new degree of freedom, where poetry, prose, painting, and lifestyle flowed seamlessly into one another.

From The Narrow Road to the Deep North[1]

* * *

The months and days, the travelers of a hundred ages;
the years that come and go, voyagers too.
floating away their lives on boats,
growing old as they lead horses by the bit,
for them, each day a journey, travel their home.
Many, too, are the ancients who perished on the road.
Some years ago, seized by wanderlust, I wandered along the shores
    of the sea.

Then, last autumn, I swept away the old cobwebs in my dilapidated dwelling on the river's edge. As the year gradually came to an end and spring arrived, filling the sky with mist, I longed to cross the Shirakawa Barrier, the most revered of poetic places. Somehow or other, I became possessed by a spirit, which crazed my soul. Unable to sit still, I accepted the summons of the Deity of the Road. No sooner had I repaired the holes in my trousers, attached a new cord to my rain hat, and cauterized my legs with moxa than my thoughts were on the famous moon at Matsushima. I turned my dwelling over to others and moved to Sanpū's villa.

> Time even for the grass hut
> to change owners—
> house of dolls[2]

I left a sheet of eight linked verses on the pillar of the hermitage.

I started out on the twenty-seventh day of the Third Month.

1. Translated by Haruo Shirane. For the route of Bashō's travels, see the map on p. 586.
2. It is the time of the Doll Festival, in the Third Month, when dolls representing the emperor, the empress, and their attendants are displayed in every household.

The dawn sky was misting over; the moon lingered, giving off a pale light; the peak of Mount Fuji appeared faintly in the distance. I felt uncertain, wondering whether I would see again the cherry blossoms on the boughs at Ueno and Yanaka. My friends had gathered the night before to see me off and joined me on the boat. When I disembarked at a place called Senju, my breast was overwhelmed by thoughts of the "three thousand leagues ahead," and standing at the crossroads of the illusory world, I wept at the parting.

> Spring going—
> birds crying and tears
> in the eyes of the fish

Making this my first journal entry, we set off but made little progress. People lined the sides of the street, seeing us off, it seemed, as long as they could see our backs.

Was it the second year of Genroku?[3] On a mere whim, I had resolved that I would make a long journey to the Deep North. Although I knew I would probably suffer, my hair growing white under the distant skies of Wu, I wanted to view those places that I had heard of but never seen and placed my faith in an uncertain future, not knowing if I would return alive. We barely managed to reach the Sōka post station that night. The luggage that I carried over my bony shoulders began to cause me pain. I had departed on the journey thinking that I need bring only myself, but I ended up carrying a coat to keep me warm at night, a night robe, rain gear, inkstone, brush, and the like, as well as the farewell presents that I could not refuse. All these became a burden on the road.

We paid our respects to the shrine at Muro-no-yashima, Eight Islands of the Sealed Room. Sora, my travel companion, noted: "This deity is called the Goddess of the Blooming Cherry Tree and is the same as that worshiped at Mount Fuji. Since the goddess entered a sealed hut and burned herself giving birth to Hohodemi, the God of Emitting Fire, and proving her vow, they call the place Eight Islands of the Sealed Room. The custom of including smoke in poems on this place also derives from this story. It is forbidden to consume a fish called *konoshiro*, or shad, which is thought to smell like flesh when burned. The essence of this shrine history is already known to the world."

On the thirtieth, we stopped at the foot of Nikkō Mountain. The owner said, "My name is Buddha Gozaemon. People have given me this name because I make honesty my first concern in all matters. As a consequence, you can relax for one night on the road. Please stay here." I wondered what kind of buddha had manifested itself in this soiled world to help someone like me, traveling like a beggar priest on a pilgrimage. I observed the actions of the innkeeper carefully and saw that he was neither clever nor calculating. He was nothing but honesty—the type of person that Confucius referred to when he said, "Those who are strong in will and without pretension are close to humanity." I had nothing but respect for the purity of his character.

On the first of the Fourth Month, we paid our respects to the holy mountain. In the distant past, the name of this sacred mountain was written with the characters Nikkōzan, Two Rough Mountain, but when Priest Kūkai[4] established a

---

3. 1689.
4. Famous 9th-century priest and calligrapher who studied in China and introduced esoteric Buddhism into Japan.

temple here, he changed the name to Nikkō, Light of the Sun. Perhaps he was able to see a thousand years into the future. Now this venerable light shines throughout the land, and its benevolence flows to the eight corners of the earth, and the four classes—warrior, samurai, artisan, and merchant—all live in peace. Out of a sense of reverence and awe, I put my brush down here.

> Awe inspiring!
> on the green leaves, budding leaves
> light of the sun

Black Hair Mountain, enshrouded in mist, the snow still white.

> Shaving my head
> at Black Hair Mountain—
> time for summer clothes
>
> Sora

Sora's family name is Kawai; his personal name is Sōgoro. He lived near me, helping me gather wood and heat water, and was delighted at the thought of sharing with me the sights of Matsushima and Kisagata. At the same time, he wanted to help me overcome the hardships of travel. On the morning of the departure, he shaved his hair, changed to dark black robes, and took on the Buddhist name of Sōgo. That is why he wrote the Black Hair Mountain poem. I thought that the words "time for summer clothes"[5] were particularly effective.

Climbing more than a mile up a mountain, we came to a waterfall. From the top of the cavern, the water flew down a hundred feet, falling into a blue pool of a thousand rocks. I squeezed into a hole in the rocks and entered the cavern: they say that this is called Back-View Falls because you can see the waterfall from the back, from inside the cavern.

> Secluded for a while
> in a waterfall—
> beginning of summer austerities[6]

. . .

There is a mountain-priest temple called Kōmyōji. We were invited there and prayed at the Hall of Gyōja.

> Summer mountains—
> praying to the tall clogs
> at journey's start[7]

. . .

---

5. The first day of the Fourth Month was the date for changing from winter to summer clothing.

6. Period in which Buddhist practitioners remained indoors, fasting, reciting scripture, and practicing austerities.

7. At the beginning of the journey, the traveler bows before the high clogs, a prayer for the foot strength of En no Gyōja, the founder of a mountain priest sect believed to have gained superhuman powers from rigorous mountain training.

The willow that was the subject of Saigyō's[8] poem, "Where a Crystal Stream Flows," still stood in the village of Ashino, on a footpath in a rice field. The lord of the manor of this village had repeatedly said, "I would like to show you this willow," and I had wondered where it was. Today I was able to stand in its very shade.

> Whole field of
> rice seedlings planted—I part
> from the willow

The days of uncertainty piled one on the other, and when we came upon the Shirakawa Barrier, I finally felt as if I had settled into the journey. I can understand why that poet had written, "Had I a messenger, I would send a missive to the capital!" One of three noted barriers, the Shirakawa Barrier captured the hearts of poets. With the sound of the autumn wind in my ears and the image of the autumn leaves in my mind, I was moved all the more by the tops of the green-leafed trees. The flowering of the wild rose amid the white deutzia clusters made me feel as if I were crossing over snow. . . .

At the Sukagawa post station, we visited a man named Tōkyū. He insisted that we stay for four or five days and asked me how I had found the Shirakawa Barrier. I replied, "My body and spirit were tired from the pain of the long journey; my heart overwhelmed by the landscape. The thoughts of the distant past tore through me, and I couldn't think straight." But feeling it would be a pity to cross the barrier without producing a single verse, I wrote:

> Beginnings of poetry—
> rice-planting songs
> of the Deep North

This opening verse was followed by a second verse and then a third; before we knew it, three sequences. . . .

The next day we went to Shinobu[9] Village and visited Shinobu Mottling Rock. The rock was in a small village, half buried, deep in the shade of the mountain. A child from the village came and told us, "In the distant past, the rock was on top of this mountain, but the villagers, angered by the visitors who had been tearing up the barley grass to test the rock, pushed it down into the valley, where it lies face down." Perhaps that was the way it had to be.

> Planting rice seedlings
> the hands—in the distant past pressing
> the grass of longing

> . . .

8. Celebrated 12th-century poet. Bashō thinks here of the following poem: "I thought to pause on the roadside where a crystal stream flows beneath a willow and stood rooted to the spot."

9. One of the place names with the longest poetic history in the Deep North. The "Mottling Rock" was thought to have been used to imprint cloth with patterns of *Shinobugusa*, literally "longing grass," a typical local product. The plant was associated with wild and uncontrollable longing.

The Courtyard Inscribed-Stone was in Taga Castle in the village of Ichikawa. More than six feet high and about three feet wide; the moss had eaten away the rock, and the letters were faint. On the memorial, which listed the number of miles to the four borders of the province: "This castle was built in 724 by Lord Ono no Azumabito, the Provincial Governor and General of the Barbarian-Subduing Headquarters. In 762, on the first of the Twelfth Month, it was rebuilt by the Councillor and Military Commander of the Eastern Seaboard, Lord Emi Asakari." The memorial belonged to the era of the sovereign Shōmu. Famous places in poetry have been collected and preserved; but mountains crumble, rivers shift, roads change, rock are buried in dirt; trees age, saplings replace them; times change, generations come and go. But here, without a doubt, was a memorial of a thousand years: I was peering into the heart of the ancients. The virtues of travel, the joys of life, forgetting the weariness of travel, I shed only tears. . . .

It was already close to noon when we borrowed a boat and crossed over to Matsushima. The distance was more than two leagues, and we landed on the shore of Ojima. It has been said many times, but Matsushima is the most beautiful place in all of Japan. First of all, it can hold its head up to Dongting Lake or West Lake. Letting in the sea from the southeast, it fills the bay, three leagues wide, with the tide of Zhejiang.[1] Matsushima has gathered countless islands: the high ones point their fingers to heaven; those lying down crawl over the waves. Some are piled two deep; some, three deep. To the left, the islands are separated from one another; to the right, they are linked. Some seem to be carrying islands on their backs; others, to be embracing them like a person caressing a child. The green of the pine is dark and dense, the branches and leaves bent by the salty sea breeze—as if they were deliberately twisted. A soft, tranquil landscape, like a beautiful lady powdering her face. Did the god of the mountain create this long ago, in the age of the gods? Is this the work of the Creator? What words to describe this?

The rocky shore of Ojima extended out from the coast and became an island protruding into the sea. Here were the remains of Priest Ungo's dwelling and the rock on which he meditated. Again, one could see, scattered widely in the shadow of the pines, people who had turned their backs on the world. They lived quietly in grass huts, the smoke from burning rice ears and pinecones rising from the huts. I didn't know what kind of people they were, but I was drawn to them, and when I approached, the moon was reflected on the sea, and the scenery changed again, different from the afternoon landscape. When we returned to the shore and took lodgings, I opened the window. It was a two-story building, and I felt like a traveler sleeping amid the wind and the clouds: to a strange degree it was a good feeling.

> Matsushima—
> borrow the body of a crane
> cuckoo!![2]

> Sora

---

1. Flattering comparisons to well-known scenic sites in China. The tidal bore in Hangzhou, Zhejiang Province, was already famous in ancient China.

2. Typical summer bird. The gist of the poem is: "Your song is appealing, cuckoo, but the stately white crane is the bird we expect to see at Matsushima [Pine Isles]." Pines and cranes were a conventional pair, both symbols of longevity.

I closed my mouth and tried to sleep but couldn't. When I left my old hermitage, Sodō had given me a Chinese poem on Matsushima, and Hara Anteki had sent me a waka on Matsugaurashima. Opening my knapsack, I made those poems my friends for the night. There also were hokku by Sanpū and Jokushi.[3]

* * *

On the twelfth we headed for Hiraizumi. We had heard of such places as the Pine at Anewa and the Thread-Broken Bridge, but there were few human traces, and finding it difficult to recognize the path normally used by the rabbit hunters and woodcutters, we ended up losing our way and came out at a harbor called Ishi no maki. Across the water we could see Kinkazan the Golden Flower Mountain, where the "Blooming of the Golden Flower"[4] poem had been composed as an offering to the emperor. Several hundred ferry boats gathered in the inlet; human dwellings fought for space on the shore; and the smoke from the ovens rose high. It never occurred to me that I would come across such a prosperous place. We attempted to find a lodging, but no one gave us a place for the night. Finally, we spent the night in an impoverished hovel and, at dawn, wandered off again onto an unknown road. Looking afar at Sode no watari, Obuchi no maki, Mano no kayahara, and other famous places, we made our way over a dike that extended into the distance. We followed the edge of a lonely and narrow marsh, lodged for the night at a place called Toima, and then arrived at Hiraizumi: a distance, I think, of more than twenty leagues.

The glory of three generations of Fujiwara[5] vanished in the space of a dream; the remains of the Great Gate stood two miles in the distance. Hidehira's headquarters had turned into rice paddies and wild fields. Only Kinkeizan, Golden Fowl Hill, remained as it was. First, we climbed Takadachi, Castle-on-the-Heights, from where we could see the Kitakami, a broad river that flowed from the south. The Koromo River rounded Izumi Castle, and at a point beneath Castle-on-the-Heights, it dropped into the broad river. The ancient ruins of Yasuhira[6] and others, lying behind Koromo Barrier, appear to close off the southern entrance and guard against the Ainu barbarians. Selecting his loyal retainers, Yoshitsune fortified himself in the castle, but his glory quickly turned to grass. "The state is destroyed; rivers and hills remain. The city walls turn to spring; grasses and trees are green." With these lines from Du Fu[7] in my head, I lay down my bamboo hat, letting the time and tears flow.

3. Bashō's disciples. "Hokku": the first three lines of a linked-verse sequence, from which haiku evolved.
4. Ōtomo no Yakamochi, an important poet in the *Man'yōshū*, composed a poem for the emperor when gold was discovered in the area: "For our sovereign's reign, / an auspicious augury: / among the mountains of the Deep North / in the east, / golden flowers have blossomed."
5. In the 12th century, members of a local branch of the powerful Fujiwara family—Kiyohira, Motohira, and Hidehira—had built up a flourishing power base in the north. Hiraizumi was the tragic site of the forced suicide of Minamoto no Yoshitsune, a heroic warrior of the Genpei Wars (1180–85) fought between the Taira/Heike and the Minamoto/Genji.

6. Son of Fujiwara Hidehira, whose fight with his brother destroyed the clan's prosperity in the region. After killing his brother, Yasuhira was in turn killed by the Minamoto/Genji chieftain Yoritomo, the founder of the Kamakura shogunate in 1185.
7. Minamoto no Yoshitsune won the crucial battles in the Genpei Wars, chronicled in *The Tales of the Heike*, and gave the Heike/Taira their death blow in 1185. Since his half-brother Yoritomo had become ever more suspicious of him, he sought refuge with the Fujiwara in Hiraizumi. Fujiwara no Yasuhira eventually betrayed him to Yoritomo and Yoshitsune was forced into suicide in 1189. Bashō compares Yoshitsune's tragedy to Du Fu's poem "View in Spring," written in a tragic moment when the Chinese capital was taken by rebels.

Summer grasses—
the traces of dreams
of ancient warriors

In the deutzia
Kanefusa[8] appears
white haired

Sora

The two halls about which we had heard such wonderful things were open. The Sutra Hall held the statues of the three chieftains, and the Hall of Light contained the coffins of three generations, preserving three sacred images.[9] The seven precious substances were scattered and lost; the doors of jewels, torn by the wind; the pillars of gold, rotted in the snow. The hall should have turned into a mound of empty, abandoned grass, but the four sides were enclosed, covering the roof with shingles, surviving the snow and rain. For a while, it became a memorial to a thousand years.

Have the summer rains
come and gone, sparing
the Hall of Light?

Gazing afar at the road that extended to the south, we stopped at the village of Iwade. We passed Ogurazaki and Mizu no ojima, and from Narugo Hot Springs we proceeded to Passing-Water Barrier and attempted to cross into Dewa Province. Since there were few travelers on this road, we were regarded with suspicion by the barrier guards, and it was only after considerable effort that we were able to cross the barrier. We climbed a large mountain, and since it had already grown dark, we caught sight of a house of a border guard and asked for lodging. For three days, the wind and rain were severe, forcing us to stay in the middle of a boring mountain.

Fleas, lice—
a horse passes water
by my pillow

. . .

I visited a person named Seifū at Obanazawa. Though wealthy, he had the spirit of a recluse. Having traveled repeatedly to the capital, he understood the tribulations of travel and gave me shelter for a number of days. He eased the pain of the long journey.

Taking coolness
for my lodging
I relax

. . .

8. A loyal retainer of Yoshitsune. Some legends claim that he helped Yoshitsune's wife and children commit suicide and also saw his master to his end, before himself dying. "Deutzia": a white summer flower.

9. Of Amida Buddha, the Buddha presiding over the Pure Land Paradise in the West, and his attendants Kannon and Seishi. The coffins contained the mummified remains of Hidehira, his father, and his grandfather.

In Yamagata there was a mountain temple, the Ryūshaku-ji, founded by the high priest Jikaku,[1] an especially pure and tranquil place. People had urged us to see this place at least once, so we backtracked from Obanazawa, a distance of about seven leagues. It was still light when we arrived. We borrowed a room at a temple at the mountain foot and climbed to the Buddha hall at the top. Boulders were piled on boulders; the pines and cypress had grown old; the soil and rocks were aged, covered with smooth moss. The doors to the temple buildings at the top were closed, not a sound to be heard. I followed the edge of the cliff, crawling over the boulders, and then prayed at the Buddhist hall. It was a stunning scene wrapped in quiet—I felt my spirit being purified.

> Stillness—
> sinking deep into the rocks
> cries of the cicada

The Mogami River originates in the Deep North; its upper reaches are in Yamagata. As we descended, we encountered frightening rapids with names like Scattered Go Stones and Flying Eagle. The river skirts the north side of Mount Itajiki and then finally pours into the sea at Sakata. As I descended, passing through the dense foliage, I felt as if the mountains were covering the river on both sides. When filled with rice, these boats are apparently called "rice boats." Through the green leaves, I could see the falling waters of White-Thread Cascade. Sennindō, Hall of the Wizard, stood on the banks, directly facing the water. The river was swollen with rain, making the boat journey perilous.

> Gathering the rains
> of the wet season—swift
> the Mogami River

. . .

Haguroyama, Gassan, and Yudono are called the Three Mountains of Dewa. At Haguroyama, Feather Black Mountain—which belongs to the Tōeizan Temple in Edo, in Musashi Province—the moon of Tendai[2] concentration and contemplation shines, and the lamp of the Buddhist Law of instant enlightenment glows. The temple quarters stand side by side, and the ascetics devote themselves to their calling. The efficacy of the divine mountain, whose prosperity will last forever, fills people with awe and fear.

On the eighth, we climbed Gassan, Moon Mountain. With purification cords around our necks and white cloth wrapped around our heads, we were led up the mountain by a person called a strongman. Surrounded by clouds and mist, we walked over ice and snow and climbed for twenty miles. Wondering if we had passed Cloud Barrier, beyond which the sun and moon move back and forth, I ran out of breath, my body frozen. By the time we reached the top, the sun had set and the moon had come out. We spread bamboo grass on the ground and lay down, waiting for the dawn. When the sun emerged and the clouds cleared away, we descended to Yudono, Bathhouse Mountain.

---

1. Better known as Ennin (794–864), a famous Japanese priest who studied in China and helped establish Tendai Buddhism in Japan.

2. A Buddhist sect that originated from Tiantai (Japanese Tendai) Mountain in southern China and was established in Japan in the 9th century.

On the side of the valley were the so-called Blacksmith Huts. Here blacksmiths collect divine water, purify their bodies and minds, forge swords admired by the world, and engrave them with "Moon Mountain." I hear that in China they harden swords in the sacred water at Dragon Spring, and I was reminded of the ancient story of Gan Jiang and Mo Ye, the two Chinese who crafted famous swords.[3] The devotion of these masters to the art was extraordinary. Sitting down on a large rock for a short rest, I saw a cherry tree about three feet high, its buds half open. The tough spirit of the late-blooming cherry tree, buried beneath the accumulated snow, remembering the spring, moved me. It was as if I could smell the "plum blossom in the summer heat," and I remembered the pathos of the poem by Priest Gyōson.[4] Forbidden to speak of the details of this sacred mountain, I put down my brush.

When we returned to the temple quarters, at Priest Egaku's behest, we wrote down verses about our pilgrimage to the Three Mountains.

> Coolness—
> faintly a crescent moon over
> Feather Black Mountain

> Cloud peaks
> crumbling one after another—
> Moon Mountain

> Forbidden to speak—
> wetting my sleeves
> at Bathhouse Mountain!

Left Haguro and at the castle town of Tsurugaoka were welcomed by the samurai Nagayama Shigeyuki. Composed a round of haikai. Sakichi accompanied us this far. Boarded a boat and went down to the port of Sakata. Stayed at the house of a doctor named En'an Fugyoku.

> From Hot Springs Mountain
> to the Bay of Breezes,
> the evening cool

> Pouring the hot day
> into the sea—
> Mogami River

Having seen all the beautiful landscapes—rivers, mountains, seas, and coasts—I now prepared my heart for Kisagata. From the port at Sakata moving northeast, we crossed over a mountain, followed the rocky shore, and walked across the

---

3. Gan Jiang was a Chinese swordsmith who forged two famous swords with his wife, Moye.
4. "Plum blossoms in summer heat" is a Zen phrase for the unusual ability to achieve enlightenment. The plum tree blossoms open in early spring and never last until the sum- mer. The poem by Gyōson (1055–1135), com- posed when he discovered cherries blooming out of season, reads: "Let us sympathize / with one another, / cherry tree on the mountain: / were it not for your blossoms, / I would have no friend at all."

sand—all for a distance of ten miles. The sun was on the verge of setting when we arrived. The sea wind blew sand into the air; the rain turned everything to mist, hiding Chōkai Mountain. I groped in the darkness. Having heard that the landscape was exceptional in the rain,[5] I decided that it must also be worth seeing after the rain, too, and squeezed into a fisherman's thatched hut to wait for the rain to pass.

By the next morning the skies had cleared, and with the morning sun shining brightly, we took a boat to Kisagata. Our first stop was Nōin Island, where we visited the place where Nōin had secluded himself for three years. We docked our boat on the far shore and visited the old cherry tree on which Saigyō had written the poem about "a fisherman's boat rowing over the flowers."[6] On the shore of the river was an imperial mausoleum, the gravestone of Empress Jingū.[7] The temple was called Kanmanju Temple. I wondered why I had yet to hear of an imperial procession to this place.

We sat down in the front room of the temple and raised the blinds, taking in the entire landscape at one glance. To the south, Chōkai Mountain held up the heavens, its shadow reflected on the bay of Kisagata; to the west, the road came to an end at Muyamuya Barrier; and to the east, there was a dike. The road to Akita stretched into the distance. To the north was the sea, the waves pounding into the bay at Shiogoshi, Tide-Crossing. The face of the bay, about two and a half miles in width and length, resembled Matsushima but with a different mood. If Matsushima was like someone laughing, Kisagata resembled a resentful person filled with sorrow and loneliness. The land was as if in a state of anguish.

> Kisagata—
> Xi Shi[8] asleep in the rain
> flowers of the silk tree

> In the shallows—
> cranes wetting their legs
> coolness of the sea

> . . .

Reluctant to leave Sakata, the days piled up; now I turn my gaze to the far-off clouds of the northern provinces. Thoughts of the distant road ahead fill me with anxiety; I hear it is more than 325 miles to the castle town in Kaga. After we crossed Nezu-no-seki, Mouse Barrier, we hurried toward Echigo and came to Ichiburi, in Etchū Province. Over these nine days, I suffered from the extreme heat, fell ill, and did not record anything.

---

5. Bashō compares Kisakata to the famous West Lake in China, of which the Chinese poet Su Shi (or Su Dongpo, 1037–1101) wrote: "The sparkling, brimming waters are beautiful in sunshine; / The view when a misty rain veils the mountains is exceptional too."
6. From a poem attributed to Saigyō: "The cherry trees at Kisakata are buried in waves—a fisherman's boat rowing over the flowers."
7. Legendary empress said to have ruled in the second half of the 4th century.
8. A legendary beauty of early China, whose charms were used to bring down an enemy state. Xi Shi was known for a constant frown, which enhanced her beauty.

The Seventh Month—
the sixth day, too, is different
from the usual night[9]

A wild sea—
stretching to Sado Isle
the River of Heaven

Today, exhausted from crossing the most dangerous places in the north country—places with names like Children Forget Parents, Parents Forget Children, Dogs Turn Back, Horses Sent Back—I drew up my pillow and lay down to sleep, only to hear in the adjoining room the voices of two young women. An elderly man joined in the conversation, and I gathered that they were women of pleasure from a place called Niigata in Echigo Province. They were on a pilgrimage to Ise Shrine, and the man was seeing them off as far as the barrier here at Ichiburi. They seemed to be writing letters and giving him other trivial messages to take back to Niigata tomorrow. Like "the daughters of the fishermen, passing their lives on the shore where the white waves roll in,"[1] they had fallen low in this world, exchanging vows with every passerby. What terrible lives they must have had in their previous existence for this to occur. I fell asleep as I listened to them talk. The next morning, they came up to us as we departed. "The difficulties of road, not knowing our destination, the uncertainty and sorrow—it makes us want to follow your tracks. We'll be inconspicuous. Please bless us with your robes of compassion, link us to the Buddha," they said tearfully.

"We sympathize with you, but we have many stops on the way. Just follow the others. The gods will make sure that no harm occurs to you." Shaking them off with these remarks, we left, but the pathos of their situation lingered with us.

Under the same roof
women of pleasure also sleep—
bush clover and moon[2]

I dictated this to Sora, who wrote it down. . . .

We visited Tada Shrine where Sanemori's helmet and a piece of his brocade robe were stored. They say that long ago when Sanemori belonged to the Genji clan, Lord Yoshitomo offered him the helmet. Indeed, it was not the armor of a common soldier. A chrysanthemum and vine carved design inlaid with gold extended from the visor to the ear flaps, and a two-horn frontpiece was attached

---

9. Because people were preparing for the Tanabata Festival, which was held on the seventh day of the Seventh Month in honor of the stars Altair (the herd boy) and Vega (the weaver maiden). Legend held that the two lovers were separated by the Milky Way, except for this one night, when they would meet for their annual rendezvous.

1. From an anonymous poem: "Since I am the daughter of a fisherman, passing my life on the shore where the white waves roll in, I have no home."

2. Bashō shows surprise that two very different parties—the young prostitutes and the male priest-travelers—have something in common. The bush clover, the object of love in classical poetry, suggests the prostitutes, while the moon, associated with enlightenment and clarity, implies Bashō and his priest friend.

to the dragon head. After Sanemori died in battle, Kiso Yoshinaka attached a prayer sheet to the helmet and offered it to the shrine. Higuchi Jirō acted as Kiso's messenger. It was as if the past were appearing before my very eyes.

> "How pitiful!"
> beneath the warrior helmet
> cries of a cricket[3]

> . . .

The sixteenth. The skies had cleared, and we decided to gather little red shells at Iro-no-hama, Color Beach, seven leagues across the water. A man named Ten'ya made elaborate preparations—lunch boxes, wine flasks, and the like—and ordered a number of servants to go with us on the boat. Enjoying a tailwind, we arrived quickly. The beach was dotted with a few fisherman's huts and a dilapidated Lotus Flower temple. We drank tea, warmed up saké, and were overwhelmed by the loneliness of the evening.

> Loneliness—
> an autumn beach judged
> superior to Suma's[4]

> Between the waves—
> mixed with small shells
> petals of bush clover

I had Tōsai write down the main events of that day and left it at the temple.

Rotsū came as far as the Tsuruga harbor to greet me, and together we went to Mino Province. With the aid of horses, we traveled to Ōgaki. Sora joined us from Ise. Etsujin galloped in on horseback, and we gathered at the house of Jokō. Zensenshi, Keiko, Keiko's sons, and other intimate acquaintances visited day and night. For them, it was like meeting someone who had returned from the dead. They were both overjoyed and sympathetic. Although I had not yet recovered from the weariness of the journey, we set off again on the sixth of the Ninth Month. Thinking to pay our respects to the great shrine at Ise, we boarded a boat.

> Autumn going—
> parting for Futami
> a clam pried from its shell

---

3. An allusion to a scene from *The Tales of the Heike*, in which the warrior Sanemori, who did not want other soldiers to realize his advanced age, dyed his white hair black and fought valiantly to death, slain by retainers of Yoshinaka. A Noh play connects the washing and identification of Sanemori's head, which occurred at the place Bashō is visiting here, to the cry of a cricket, a poetic image of autumn, decline, and loneliness.

4. A coastal town well-known for people who spent their time in exile, such as the poet Ariwara no Yukihira (ca. 893) and Genji, the protagonist of *The Tale of Genji*.

MORIKAWA KYORIKU

orikawa Kyoriku (1656–1715) was one of the most important disciples of **Bashō**. In his treatise *Haikai Dialogue* (1697), he argues that the "combination poem," which combines two unexpected elements in a single haiku, is the central technique of Bashō's school. In this short extract from his treatise, we have the privilege of glancing into the poet's mind at work, as he tries to find the perfect words to link an unlikely couple of things: "scent of plum blossoms" and "blue lacquer bowl."

From Haikai Dialogue[1]

Recently, I thought that "scent of plum blossoms" would make a good combination with "blue lacquer bowl" and tried various middle phrases, but none of them felt right.

> Scent of plum blossoms—
> pickled vegetables and
> a blue lacquer bowl

> Scent of plum blossoms—
> arranged in a row
> blue lacquer bowls

> Scent of plum blossoms
> from somewhere or other
> a blue lacquer bowl

I tried these various possibilities, but none of them was successful. When the subject matter and the combination are excellent but a good hokku[2] does not materialize, it means that the necessary intermediary has yet to be found. After more searching, I came up with the following:

> Scent of plum blossoms—
> beneath the guest's nose
> a blue lacquer bowl

---

1. Translated by Haruo Shirane.
2. Again, the first three lines of a linked-verse sequence, now usually called "haiku."

YOSA BUSON

Unlike many other haikai poets, Yosa Buson (1716–1783) came from a peasant family living outside of Osaka. Around the age of twenty he studied haikai poetry in Edo with a student of one of Bashō's students. He moved to Kyoto in his mid-thirties and devoted himself to Chinese-style literati painting. He ultimately became the head of his own school, succeeding his previous teacher. While **Bashō** sought novelty mostly in the everyday, Buson favored a "departure from the common," the pursuit of another, imaginary world inspired mostly by classical Chinese literature. In "Preface to Shōha's Haiku Collection," which he wrote in 1777 for Shōha, a wealthy merchant who studied Chinese-style poetry with well-known poets in Edo, Buson explains the attraction of mixing popular haikai with highbrow Chinese poetry. *New Flower Gathering* (1784, published 1797), his own collection, is a series of haiku and prose anecdotes that captures his infatuation with the strange and curious. One of the anecdotes, "The Badger," shows the serious, spiritual purposes that haiku could be put to by the eighteenth century.

Preface to Shōha's Haiku Collection[1]

I once met with Shōha at his villa in western Kyoto. When Shōha asked me about haikai, I said, "Although haikai greatly values the use of common language, it nonetheless departs from the common. That is, haikai departs from the common while using the common. The doctrine of departure from the common [*rizoku*] is most difficult to understand. It is like the famous Zen master who said, 'Listen to the sound of one hand clapping.'[2] The principle of departure from the common is the zen of haikai." Shōha was immediately enlightened.

He asked again, "Your explanation of departure from the common is, in its essence, profound and mysterious. Doesn't it mean finding a way to accomplish the deed by oneself? Isn't there another way? Isn't there a quicker way to change naturally, to depart from the common without others knowing it, without knowing it oneself?" I answered, "There is: Chinese poetry. From the beginning you've been very skilled at Chinese poetry. You needn't look elsewhere."

Shōha had doubts and asked again, "Now Chinese poetry and haikai differ in character. And yet you tell me to disregard haikai and discuss Chinese poetry—isn't this a roundabout approach?" I answered, "Painters assume that there is only one method for departing from the common, that if one reads many books, one's literary inclinations will increase and one's common or vulgar inclinations will decrease. Students must pay attention to this. To depart from the common in painting, they must throw away their brushes and read books. In this case, how can there be a distance between Chinese poetry and haikai?" Shōha immediately understood.

---

1. Translated by Jack Stoneman.　　　　2. A well-known Zen paradox.

From New Flower Gathering

The Badger[1]

Jōu of Yūki acquired a second house and had an old man stay there as a caretaker. Even though it was in the middle of town, it was surrounded by trees and luxuriant with plants, and because it was a place where one could escape the hustle and bustle of the world, I myself stayed there for quite some time.

The old man had nothing to do there other than keep the place clean. One time he spent the long autumn night praying over his beads in the light of a single lamp while I stayed in the back room, working on my haikai and my Chinese poetry. Eventually I grew tired, and I spread out the blankets and pulled them over my head. But just as I was drifting off to sleep, there was a tapping sound on the shutters by the veranda. There must have been some twenty or thirty taps. My heart beat faster, and I thought, "How strange!" But when I got out of bed and quietly slid open the shutter to take a look, there was nothing. When I went back to bed and pretended to be asleep, there was the same tapping sound. Once again I got out of bed and looked outside, but found nothing. "How very strange," I thought, and consulted the old caretaker: "What should we do?" The caretaker responded, "It's that badger again. The next time it starts tapping like that, quickly open the shutter and chase after it. I'll come around from the back door, and it will probably be hiding under the fence." I saw that he was holding a switch.

I went back to bed and once more pretended to be asleep. Again there was the sound of tapping. When I shouted, "Aha!" opened the shutter, and ran out, the old man came out too, yelling, "Gotcha!" But there was nothing there, so we both got very angry. Even though we looked in every corner of the property, we couldn't find a thing.

This went on for some five nights running. Wearied by it all, I finally came to the conclusion that I could no longer stay there. But then a servant of Jōu's house came and said, "You will not be disturbed tonight, sir. This morning one of the villagers shot an old badger in a place called Yabushita. I know for sure that all that fuss and trouble was the work of this badger. Rest well tonight."

And indeed, from that night on, all the noises ceased. I began to think sadly that the animal that I had thought of as a nuisance had really offered me some comfort from the loneliness of my lodging. I felt pity for the badger's soul and wondered whether we had formed a karmic bond. For that reason I called on a cleric named Priest Zenku, made a donation, and for one night chanted the *nen-butsu*[2] in order that the badger might eventually achieve buddhahood.

> Late in autumn
> transformed into a buddha
> —the badger

A badger had come to the door to visit, and people said he made tapping sounds with his tail, but that was not the case. In fact, he had pressed his back against the door.

---

1. Translated by Cheryl Crowley. There is a rich popular lore associated with the Japanese *tanuki*, here translated as "badger" (sometimes also called "raccoon dog").

2. "Calling the name of Amida Buddha," who presided over the Pure Land Paradise in the West, helped people attain Buddhahood.

Selected Bibliographies

I. East Asian Drama

The *Cambridge Guide to Asian Theater* (1993), ed. James R. Brandon, provides introductions to the major dramatic forms of East Asia.

Chikamatsu Monzaemon

To explore the world of Japanese puppet theater, Barbara Curtis Adachi's *Backstage at Bunraku: A Behind the Scenes Look at Japan's Traditional Puppet Theater* (1985), Adachi's *The Voices and Hands of Bunraku* (1978), Donald Keene's *Bunraku: The Art of the Japanese Puppet Theatre* (1965), and C. U. Dunn's *The Early Japanese Puppet Drama* (1966) are recommended.

To read other plays by Chikamatsu, see Andrew C. Gerstle's *Chikamatsu: Five Late Plays* (2001), Donald Keene's *Four Major Plays of Chikamatsu* (1969) and his *Major Plays of Chikamatsu* (1961). Gerstle's *Circles of Fantasy: Convention in the Plays of Chikamatsu* (1986) discusses Chikamatsu's art and craft as a playwright.

To read some of the greatest puppet plays by authors other than Chikamatsu, consult Stanleigh H. Jones's *Sugawara and the Secrets of Calligraphy* (1985) (a puppet play revolving around the tenth-century poet-official Sugawara no Michizane), Stanleigh H. Jones's *Yoshitsune and the Thousand Cherry Trees: A Masterpiece of the Eighteenth-Century Japanese Puppet Theater* (1993), and Donald Keene's *Chūshingura: The Treasury of Loyal Retainers* (1971), a play about the forty-seven samurai who avenged the humiliation of their lord and then committed ritual suicide.

Kong Shangren

For an introduction to Chinese drama in general, see Siu Wang-Ngai and Peter Lovrick, *Chinese Opera: Images and Stories* (1997) and Colin Mackerras, *Peking Opera* (1997). Siu Leung Li discusses the importance of gender change in Chinese drama in *Cross-Dressing in*

Chinese Opera (2003). Richard E. Strassberg's *The World of K'ung Shang-jen: A Man of Letters in Early Ch'ing China* (1985) contains a biography of Kong Shangren. Jing Shen's *Playwrights and Literary Games in Seventeenth-Century China: Plays by Tang Xianzu, Mei Dingzuo, Wu Bing, Li Yu, and Kong Shangren* (2010) puts *The Peach Blossom Fan* into the broader context of drama during the seventeenth century. Wai-yee Li, "The Representation of History in *The Peach Blossom Fan*," *Journal of the American Oriental Society* 115.3 (1995): 421–33 and Lynn A. Struve, "History and *The Peach Blossom Fan*," *Chinese Literature: Essays, Articles, Reviews* 2.1 (Jan. 1980): 55–72 are thought-provoking explorations of the relation between history and drama in *The Peach Blossom Fan*.

The Song of Ch'un-hyang

A complete translation with introduction to *The Tale of Ch'un-hyang* is included in Richard Rutt and Kim Chong-un's *Virtuous Women: Three Masterpieces of Traditional Korean Fiction* (1974). A discussion of p'ansori as performance art and as integral part of Korean oral song traditions appears in Chan E. Park's *Voices from the Straw Mat: Toward an Ethnography of Korean Story Singing* (2003) and Kim Hunggyu's *Understanding Korean Literature* (1997). For an introduction in particular to the genre of p'ansori see Marshall Pihl's *The Korean Singer of Tales* (2003). An overview of the history of *The Song of Ch'un-hyang* and its appearance in modern literature and film can be found in Jinsoo An's *Popular Reasoning of South Korean Melodrama Films (1953–1972)* (2005). Im Kwon-tack's successful movie *Ch'un-hyang* (2000) tells the story through a compelling mix of p'ansori performance and realistic cinematic depiction.

For an overview of classical Korean literature see Kichung Kim's *An Introduction to Classical Korean Literature: From Hyangga to Pansori* (1996).

Zeami Motokiyo

A basic introduction to the dramatic genres of Japan and important pieces of the repertoire can be found in Karen Brazell and James T. Araki's *Traditional Japanese Theater: An Anthology of Plays* (1998). A valuable introduction to Noh is Donald Keene's *Nō: The Classical Theatre of Japan* (1973). Zeami's theories of drama are available in English in J. Thomas Rimer and Yamazaki Masakazu's *On the Art of Nō Drama:*

The Major Treatises of Zeami (1894); they are discussed by Makoto Ueda in "Zeami and the Art of the Nō Drama: Imitation, Yugen and Sublimity," in Nancy G. Hulme, ed., *Japanese Aesthetics and Culture: A Reader* (1998) and Benito Ortolani and Samuel L. Leiter, eds., *Zeami and the Nō Theatre in the World* (1998). Two excellent technical works are P. G. O'Neill's *Early Nō Drama* (1974) and Thomas Blenman Hare's *Zeami's Style: The Noh Plays of Zeami Motokiyo* (1986). Other collections of translations include Arthur Waley's *The Nō Plays of Japan* (1921); Donald Keene's *Twenty Plays of the Nō Theatre* (1970); Nippon Gakujutsu Shinkōkai, *The Noh Drama* (1973); Kenneth Yasuda's *Masterworks of the Nō Theatre* (1989); and Royall Tyler's *Japanese Nō Dramas* (1992).

II. The Enlightenment in Europe and the Americas

Peter Gay, *Age of Enlightenment* (1966) is the classic work on the subject. Two other good historical introductions are Dorinda Outram, *The Enlightenment* (1995; 2nd ed. 2005) and Roy Porter, *The Enlightenment* (2001). See also Porter's *Creation of the Modern World: The Untold Story of the British Enlightenment* (2001). Studies of women in the period include Carla Hesse, *The Other Enlightenment: How French Women Became Modern* (2003), Karen O'Brien, *Women and Enlightenment in Eighteenth-Century Britain* (2009), and M. Williamson, *Raising Their Voices, 1650–1750* (1990). For excellent studies of Enlightenment philosophical thinking, see F. C. Beiser, *The Sovereignty of Reason: The Defense of Rationality in the Early English Enlightenment* (1996); L. Crocker, *An Age of Crisis: Man and World in Eighteenth-Century French Thought* (1959); Knud Haakonssen, *Natural Law and Moral Philosophy: From Grotius to the Scottish Enlightenment* (1996); and Jonathan Israel, *Enlightenment Contested: Philosophy, Modernity, and the Emancipation of Man* (2006). A brilliant survey of literature, art, and history can be found in John Brewer, *The Pleasures of the Imagination: English Culture in the Eighteenth Century* (1998). Useful works for considering the literature of the period include M. Price, *To the Palace of Wisdom: Studies in Order and Energy from Dryden to Blake* (1964); L. Gossman, *French Society and Culture: Background for Eighteenth-Century Literature* (1972); S. Gearhart, *The Open Boundary of History and Fiction: A Critical Approach to the French Enlightenment* (1984); J. Sambrook, *The Eighteenth Century: The Intellectual and Cultural Context of English Literature, 1700–1789* (1986); and T. M. Kavanaugh, *Esthetics of the Moment: Literature and Art in the French Enlightenment* (1996).

Aphra Behn

Janet Todd, *The Secret Life of Aphra Behn* (1996) delves into the contradictions of Behn's biography. *Rereading Aphra Behn: History, Theory and Criticism* (1993), a collection of essays edited by Heidi Hutner, locates Behn in the larger literary culture of the Restoration. Laura Brown's *Ends of Empire: Women and*

Ideology in Early Eighteenth-Century English Literature (1993) discusses *Oroonoko*, gender, and the slave trade. Recent years have seen an explosion of new work on race and colonialism in *Oroonoko*. Important essays include Srinivas Aravamudan, "Petting Oroonoko," *Tropicopolitans* (1999) and Elliott Visconsi, "A Degenerate Race: English Barbarism in Behn's

Oroonoko and *The Widow Ranter*," *ELH* (2002). Thomas Southerne's theatrical adaptation of Behn's novella, first performed in 1695, is also available in print.

Sor Juana Inés de la Cruz
Gerard Flynn's *Sor Juana Inés de la Cruz* (1971) provides a biographical, critical, and bibliographical introduction. Octavio Paz's *Sor Juana; Or, The Traps of Faith* (1988) is a famous study by the Mexican writer and Nobel Prize winner. Other important studies include Pamela Kirk, *Sor Juana Inés de la Cruz: Religion, Art, and Feminism* (1998); Stephanie Merrim, *Early Modern Women's Writing and Sor Juana Inés de la Cruz* (1999); and Frederick Luciani, *Literary Self-Fashioning in Sor Juana Inés de la Cruz* (2004). *Feminist Perspectives on Sor Juana Inés de la Cruz*, ed. Stephanie Merrim (1991), is a useful collection of essays.

Molière
H. Walker, *Molière* (1990), provides a general biographical and critical introduction to the playwright. Useful critical studies include L. Gossman, *Men and Masks: A Study of Molière* (1963); Jacques Guicharnaud, ed., *Molière: A Collection of Critical Essays* (1964); N. Gross, *From Gesture to Idea: Esthetics and Ethics in Molière's Comedy* (1982); J. F. Gaines, *Social Structures in Molière's Theater* (1984); and L. F. Norman, *The Public Mirror: Molière and the Social Commerce of Depiction* (1999). An excellent treatment of Molière in his historical context is W. D. Howarth, *Molière: A Playwright and His Audience* (1984). Harold C. Knutson, *The Triumph of Wit* (1988) examines Molière in relation to Shakespeare and Ben Jonson. Martin Turnell, *The Classical Moment: Studies of Corneille, Molière, and Racine* (1975) offers useful insight into the French dramatic tradition.

Alexander Pope
The standard edition of Pope's poetry is the eleven-volume *Poems of Alexander Pope*, ed. John Butt et al. (1938–1969). Maynard Mack's *Alexander Pope: A Life* (1985) is a fascinating read, joining insightful criticism of the poetry with the poet's life. Brean Hammond's *Pope Among the Satirists* (2005) provides wonderful contextual material and is concise and well written. Leo Damrosch's *The World of Alexander Pope* (1987) includes perceptive criticism, and for a reading that focuses on the relationship between Pope's work and his disabled body, see

Helen Deutsch, *Resemblance and Disgrace* (1996). Pope's relationship to the changing marketplace is brilliantly captured in Catherine Ingrassia's concise essay, "Money," in *The Cambridge Companion to Alexander Pope*, ed. Pat Rogers (2007): 175–85. David Foxon's illustrated *Pope and the Early Eighteenth-Century Book Trade* (1991) gives a rich picture of the complex relationship between Pope and his printers, including questions of typography and design.

Jonathan Swift
The most comprehensive biography is Irvin Ehrenpreis's three-volume *Swift: The Man, His Works, and the Age* (1962–1983). Joseph McMinn has a fine shorter biography called *Jonathan Swift: A Literary Life* (1991), and Victoria Glendinning gives a vivid but somewhat impressionistic picture of Swift's character in *Jonathan Swift* (1999). Paul J. Degategno and R. Jay Stubblefield have put together a usefully concise introduction to Swift's life and works in their *Critical Companion to Jonathan Swift* (2006). Gary Weiner's *Readings on Gulliver's Travels* (2000) is an excellent collection of responses to the text from Swift's time to ours, and a number of interesting essays by prominent scholars are included in Frederick N. Smith's *The Genres of Gulliver's Travels* (1990). For a look at the image of cannibalism in *A Modest Proposal*, see Ahsan Chowdhury, "Splenetic Ogres and Heroic Cannibals in Jonathan Swift's *A Modest Proposal*," *English Studies in Canada* (2008).

Voltaire
Roger Pearson has a lively biography called *Voltaire Almighty: A Life in Pursuit of Freedom* (2005). Theodore Besterman's *Voltaire* (1969) is longer and more detailed. Nicholas Cronk's collection of essays in *The Cambridge Companion to Voltaire* (2009) provides both excellent readings and helpful contextual material. Haydn Mason's *Candide, Optimism Demolished* (1992) considers the ideas, the reception, and the form of the text. For a series of competing interpretations of the Eldorado section of *Candide*, see Thomas Walsh, ed., *Readings on Candide* (2001).

What Is Enlightenment?
For general introductions to Enlightenment thought, see Ernst Cassirer, *The Philosophy of the Enlightenment*, trans. Fritz Koelln and James Pettegrove (1951); Peter Gay, *The Enlightenment: The Science of Freedom* (1996); and Roy Porter, *The Enlightenment* (2001).

The Portable Enlightenment Reader, ed. Isaac Kramnick (1995), provides a good range of short readings. Those interested in scientific developments during the period will enjoy Thomas L. Hankins, *Science and the Enlightenment* (1985). For the influence of Enlightenment thinkers on the emerging form of modern democracy, see Jonathan Yisrael, *A Revolution of the Mind* (2009). For a bleaker take on the legacy of Enlightenment power and authority, see Michel Foucault, *Discipline and Punish*, trans. Alan Sheridan (1977). Foucault also responds to Kant in his own essay, "What is Enlightenment?" in *The Foucault Reader*, ed. Paul Rabinow (1984). Robert Darnton's *The Business of Enlightenment: A Publishing History of the Encyclopédie* (1986) tells a fascinating story about the dissemination of the encyclopedia after its initial publication. Emmanuel Chukwudi Eze has published an excellent reader called *Race and the Enlightenment* (1997). There is a lively debate among scholars concerning the relation between Enlightenment thinkers and European imperial expansion. See, for example, Uday Singh Mehta, *Liberalism and Empire* (1999), Sankar Muthu, *Enlightenment against Empire* (2003), and Jennifer Pitts, *A Turn to Empire* (2006).

III. Early Modern Chinese Literature

For an introduction to Chinese vernacular literature, including drama, stories, and novels, see the relevant chapters in Victor H. Mair's *The Columbia History of Chinese Literature* (2001) and Stephen Owen and Kang-i Sun Chang's *The Cambridge History of Chinese Literature* (2010). To further explore women's writing in the early modern period, the second half of Wilt Idema and Beata Grant's *The Red Brush: Writing Women of Imperial China* (2004) and the relevant parts of Kang-i Sun Chang and Haun Saussy's *Women Writers of Traditional China: An Anthology of Poetry and Criticism* (1999) are a treasure trove with introductions to major female authors and sample works.

A basic survey of the history of Chinese drama can be found in William Dolby, *A History of Chinese Drama* (1976). C. T. Hsia's *The Classic Chinese Novel: A Critical Introduction* (1968) remains one of the most readable introductions to the major novels. Patrick Hanan, *The Chinese Vernacular Story* (1981) provides an insightful study of the cultural background of vernacular fiction. To explore how writers of China's literary revolution during the first half of the twentieth century discovered vernacular literature and elevated it to its central place in the Chinese literary canon, see the tremendously popular *A Brief History of Chinese Fiction* (1959, originally published 1925) by Lu Xun, one of China's first and foremost modern writers, whose works are included in the last volume of this anthology.

Cao Xueqin

There is a complete translation of *The Story of the Stone* in five volumes (1973–1982), the first three volumes by David Hawkes and the last two by John Minford. Selections of this have also appeared in a bilingual version in 2005. Andrew Plaks, *Archetype and Allegory in the Dream of the Red Chamber* (1976); Anthony C. Yu, *Rereading the Stone: Desire and the Making of Fiction in Dream of the Red Chamber* (1997); and Dore J. Levy, *Ideal and Actual in The Story of the Stone* (1999) are useful studies. C. T. Hsia's *The Classic Chinese Novel: A Critical Introduction* (1968) has chapters on China's great novels. For comparisons of the pursuit of enlightenment and the role of magic stones in *The Story of the Stone* and *The Journey to the West* see Li Qiancheng's *Fictions of Enlightenment: Journey to the West, Tower of Myriad Mirrors, and Dream of the Red Chamber* (2004) and Jing Wang's *Story of Stone: Intertextuality, Ancient Chinese Stone Lore, and the Stone Symbolism in Dream of the Red Chamber, Water Margin, and The Journey to the West* (1992). On the significance of the garden scenes in the novel, see Xiao Chi's *The Chinese Garden as Lyric Enclave: A Generic Study of the Story of the Stone* (2001).

Feng Menglong

Shuhui Yang and Yunqin Yang have produced good annotated translations of all three of Feng Menglong's story collections: *Stories Old and New* (2000), *Stories to Caution the World* (2005), and *Stories to Awaken the World* (2009). Shuhui Yang's *Appropriation and Representation: Feng Menglong and the Chinese Vernacular Story* (1998) is an interesting study of Feng Menglong's promotion of vernacular stories as a genre appealing to the literati class.

Wu Cheng'en

Arthur Waley's translation *Monkey* (1943) is an abridged adaptation of thirty of the original hundred chapters, but Waley's gifts as a translator and the nature of his abridgement make this version still a delight to read. There is a complete translation in four volumes by Anthony C. Yu, *The Journey to the West* (1977).

The translation of the selections here comes from Anthony C. Yu's abridged version *Monkey & the Monk: A Revised Abridgment of The Journey to the West* (2006). There is an excellent chapter on the novel in C. T. Hsia, *The Classic Chinese Novel: A Critical Introduction* (1968). Glen Dudbridge's *The Hsi-yu-chi: A Study of the Antecedents to the Sixteenth-Century Chinese Novel* (1970) examines the development of Xuanzang's story before the novel. For comparisons of the pursuit of enlightenment and the role of magic stones in *The Journey to the West* and *The Story of the Stone*, see Li Qiancheng's *Fictions of Enlightenment: Journey to the West, Tower of Myriad Mirrors, and Dream of the Red Chamber* (2004) and Jing Wang's *Story of Stone: Intertextuality, Ancient Chinese Stone Lore, and the Stone Symbolism in Dream of the Red Chamber, Water Margin, and The Journey to the West* (1992).

IV. Early Modern Japanese Popular Literature

For a close-up of Tokugawa culture and society see Andrew C. Gerstle's *Eighteenth-Century Japan: Culture and Society* (1989), Matsunosuke Nishiyama's *Edo Culture: Daily Life and Diversions in Urban Japan 1600–1868* (1997), and Chie Nakane and Shinzaburō Ōishi's *Tokugawa Japan: The Social and Economic Antecedents of Modern Japan* (1991).

To read more of early modern Japanese literature, Haruo Shirane's *Early Modern Japanese Literature: An Anthology 1600–1900* (2002) is a treasure trove of texts with excellent introductions. On Tokugawa wood prints and urban culture see Christine Guth's *Art of Edo Japan: The Artist and the City, 1615–1868* (1996). On the Japanese printing revolution in the context of the development of book culture Peter Kornicki's *The Book in Japan: A Cultural History from the Beginnings to the Nineteenth Century* (1998) is highly recommended. To further explore the pleasure quarters there is Cecilia Segawa's *Yoshiwara: The Glittering World of the Japanese Courtesan* (1993) and Elizabeth Swinton's *The Women of the Pleasure Quarter: Japanese Paintings and Prints of the Floating World* (1995).

Ihara Saikaku

For a sampling from Saikaku's many works of fiction with introductions see chapter 3 ("Ihara Saikaku and the Books of the Floating World") of Haruo Shirane's *Early Modern Japanese Literature: An Anthology 1600–1900* (2002). There is a complete translation of *The Life of an Amorous Woman* by Ivan Morris (1963). Complete translations of Saikaku's other works are numerous and include Kengi Hamada, *The Life of an Amorous Man* (1964); William Theodore de Bary, *Five Women Who Loved Love* (1956); G. W. Sargent, *The Japanese Family Storehouse* (1959); Thomas M. Kondo and

Alfred H. Marks, *Tales of Japanese Justice* (1980); E. Powys Mathers, *Comrade Loves of the Samurai* (1972); Masanori Takatsuka and David C. Stubbs, *This Scheming World* (1965); Peter Nosco, *Some Final Words of Advice* (1980); and Paul Gordon Schalow, *The Great Mirror of Male Love* (1990). For an introduction to Saikaku and his times, see Howard Hibbett, *The Floating World in Japanese Fiction* (1959).

The World of Haiku

For compelling introductions into the world of Japanese haiku see Haruo Shirane, *Traces of*

Dreams: Landscape, Cultural Memory, and the Poetry of Bashō (1998); Kenneth Yasuda, *The Japanese Haiku: Its Essential Nature, History, and Possibilities in English* (1957); Harold G. Henderson, *An Introduction to Haiku* (1958); Koji Kawamoto's *The Poetics of Japanese Verse: Imagery, Structure, Meter* (2000); Stephen Addiss, Fumiko Yamamoto, and Akira Yamamoto, *Haiku: An Anthology of Japanese Poems* (2009); and Michael F. Marra's *Seasons and Landscapes in Japanese Poetry: An Introduction to Haiku and Waka* (2009). Nippon Gakujutsu Shinkokai, ed., *Haikai and Haiku* (1958) is a basic reference.

To explore haiku movements beyond Japan, see Bruce Ross's *Haiku Moment: An Anthology of Contemporary North American Haiku* (1993); John Brandi and Dennis Maloney, *The Unswept Path: Contemporary American Haiku* (2005); and Hiroaki Sato's *One Hundred Frogs: From Renga to Haiku in English* (1983). Yoshinobu Hakutani's *Haiku and Modernist Poetics* (2009) explores the impact of haiku on modernist literature in the West.

For Bashō's poetry see Jane Reichhold, *Bashō: The Complete Haiku* (2008); Sam Hamill, *The Essential Bashō* (1999). All five of Bashō's travel journals are found in Nobuyuki Yuasa's *The Narrow Road to the Deep North and Other Travel Sketches* (1966). For Bashō's linked verse see Earl Miner and Hiroko Odagiri, *The Monkey's Straw Raincoat* (1981) and, more generally, Earl Miner's *Japanese Linked Poetry* (1979). The following translations of *Narrow Road of the Interior* are recommended: Cid Corman and Kamaike Susumu, *Back Roads to Far Towns* (1986); Donald Keene, *The Narrow Road to Oku* (1996); Dorothy Britton, *A Haiku Journey: Bashō's "Narrow Road to a Far Province"* (1980). There are two interesting studies of Bashō, both by Makoto Ueda: *Matsuo Bashō* (1982) and *Bashō and His Interpreters* (1991).

On the painter literatus and haiku poet Yosa Buson, see Makoto Ueda's study *The Path of Flowering Thorn: The Life and Poetry of Yosa Buson* (1998) and Yuki Sawa and Eith M. Shiffert's *Haiku Master Buson* (1978).

Timeline

Contexts | Texts

1368
The Ming Dynasty is established, with the capital at Nanjing

Timeline spans 250 years on these two pages

1350 C.E.   1400 C.E.   1450 C.E.

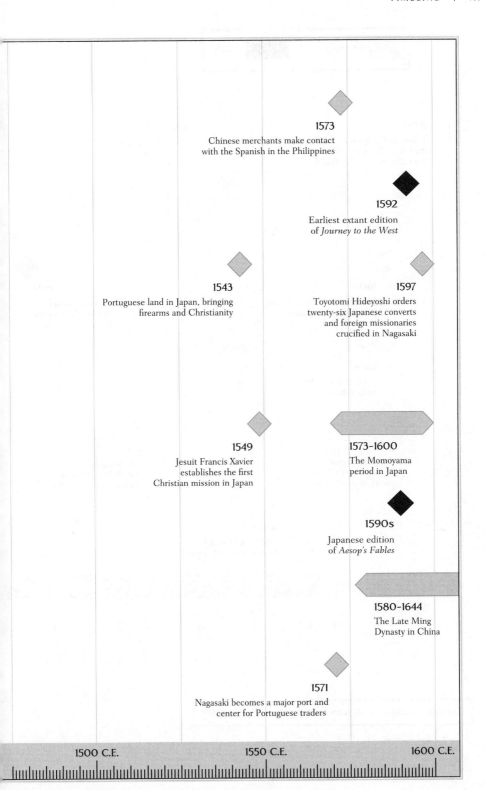

1573

Chinese merchants make contact
with the Spanish in the Philippines

1592

Earliest extant edition
of *Journey to the West*

1543

Portuguese land in Japan, bringing
firearms and Christianity

1597

Toyotomi Hideyoshi orders
twenty-six Japanese converts
and foreign missionaries
crucified in Nagasaki

1549

Jesuit Francis Xavier
establishes the first
Christian mission in Japan

1573-1600

The Momoyama
period in Japan

1590s

Japanese edition
of *Aesop's Fables*

1580-1644

The Late Ming
Dynasty in China

1571

Nagasaki becomes a major port and
center for Portuguese traders

1500 C.E.   1550 C.E.   1600 C.E.

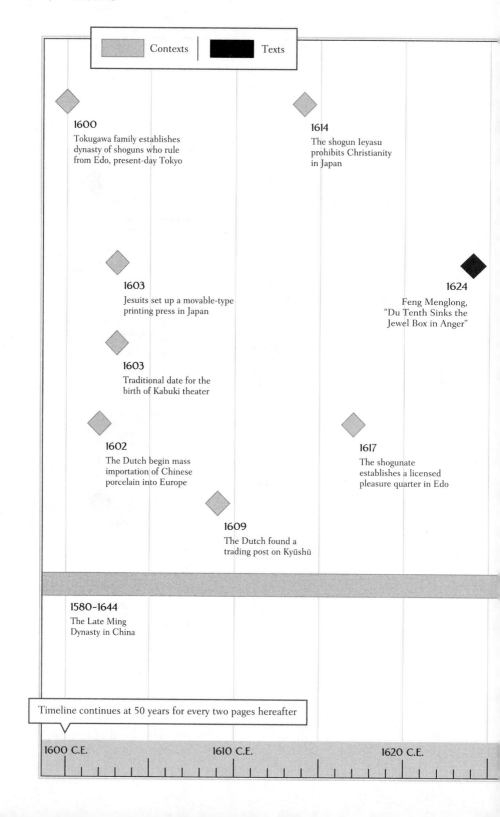

Contexts | Texts

1600
Tokugawa family establishes
dynasty of shoguns who rule
from Edo, present-day Tokyo

1614
The shogun Ieyasu
prohibits Christianity
in Japan

1603
Jesuits set up a movable-type
printing press in Japan

1624
Feng Menglong,
"Du Tenth Sinks the
Jewel Box in Anger"

1603
Traditional date for the
birth of Kabuki theater

1602
The Dutch begin mass
importation of Chinese
porcelain into Europe

1617
The shogunate
establishes a licensed
pleasure quarter in Edo

1609
The Dutch found a
trading post on Kyūshū

1580–1644
The Late Ming
Dynasty in China

Timeline continues at 50 years for every two pages hereafter

1600 C.E.   1610 C.E.   1620 C.E.

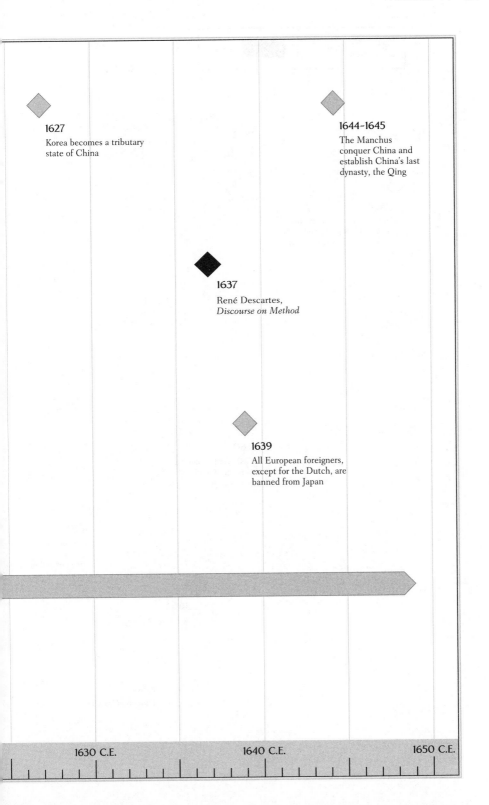

1627
Korea becomes a tributary
state of China

1644-1645
The Manchus
conquer China and
establish China's last
dynasty, the Qing

1637
René Descartes,
Discourse on Method

1639
All European foreigners,
except for the Dutch, are
banned from Japan

1630 C.E.   1640 C.E.   1650 C.E.

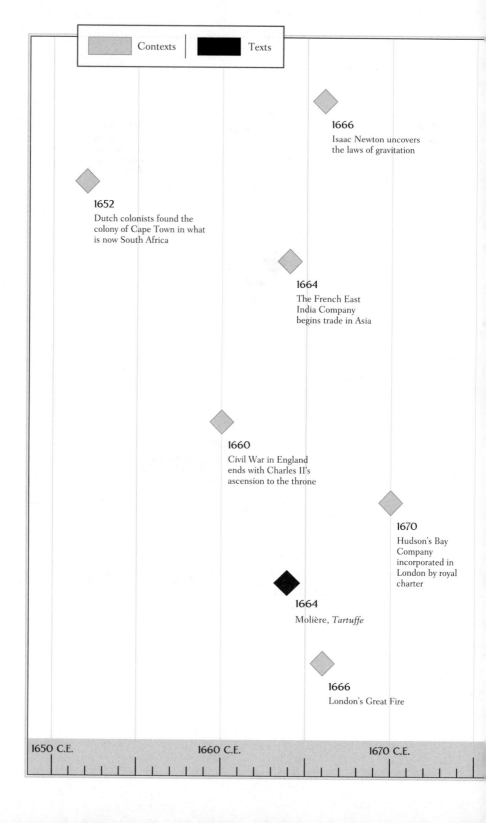

Contexts | Texts

1666
Isaac Newton uncovers the laws of gravitation

1652
Dutch colonists found the colony of Cape Town in what is now South Africa

1664
The French East India Company begins trade in Asia

1660
Civil War in England ends with Charles II's ascension to the throne

1670
Hudson's Bay Company incorporated in London by royal charter

1664
Molière, *Tartuffe*

1666
London's Great Fire

1650 C.E.   1660 C.E.   1670 C.E.

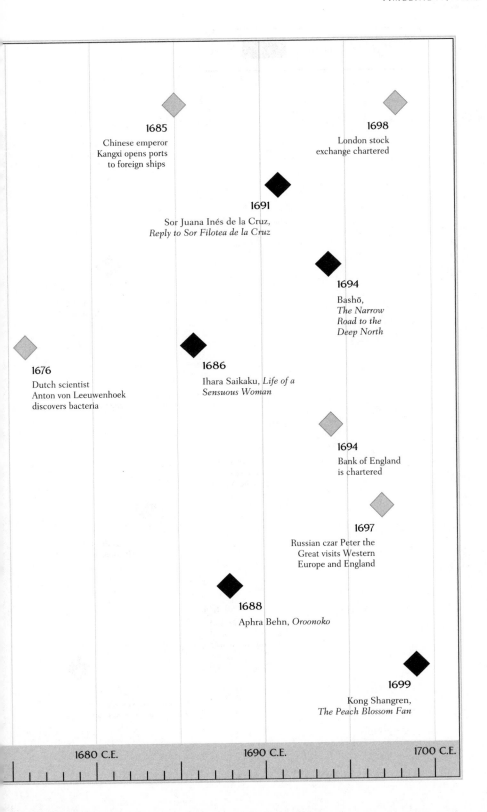

1685
Chinese emperor
Kangxi opens ports
to foreign ships

1698
London stock
exchange chartered

1691
Sor Juana Inés de la Cruz,
Reply to Sor Filotea de la Cruz

1694
Bashō,
*The Narrow
Road to the
Deep North*

1676
Dutch scientist
Anton von Leeuwenhoek
discovers bacteria

1686
Ihara Saikaku, *Life of a
Sensuous Woman*

1694
Bank of England
is chartered

1697
Russian czar Peter the
Great visits Western
Europe and England

1688
Aphra Behn, *Oroonoko*

1699
Kong Shangren,
The Peach Blossom Fan

1680 C.E.   1690 C.E.   1700 C.E.

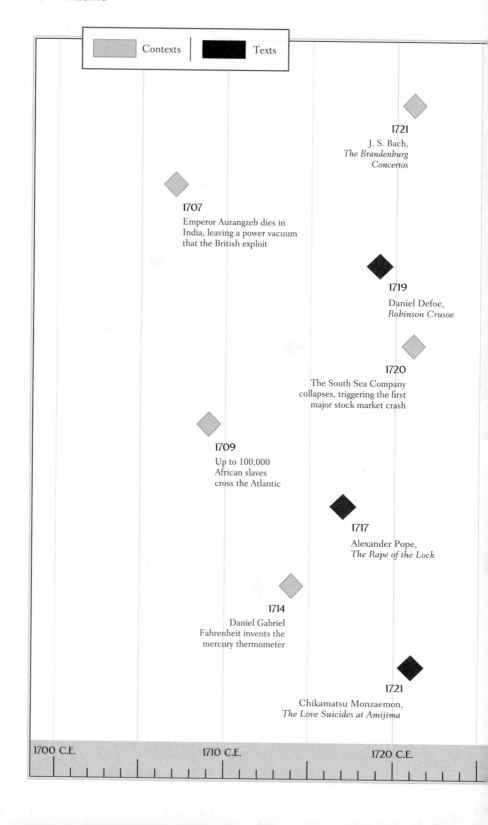

Contexts | Texts

1721
J. S. Bach,
*The Brandenburg
Concertos*

1707
Emperor Aurangzeb dies in
India, leaving a power vacuum
that the British exploit

1719
Daniel Defoe,
Robinson Crusoe

1720
The South Sea Company
collapses, triggering the first
major stock market crash

1709
Up to 100,000
African slaves
cross the Atlantic

1717
Alexander Pope,
The Rape of the Lock

1714
Daniel Gabriel
Fahrenheit invents the
mercury thermometer

1721
Chikamatsu Monzaemon,
The Love Suicides at Amijima

1700 C.E.   1710 C.E.   1720 C.E.

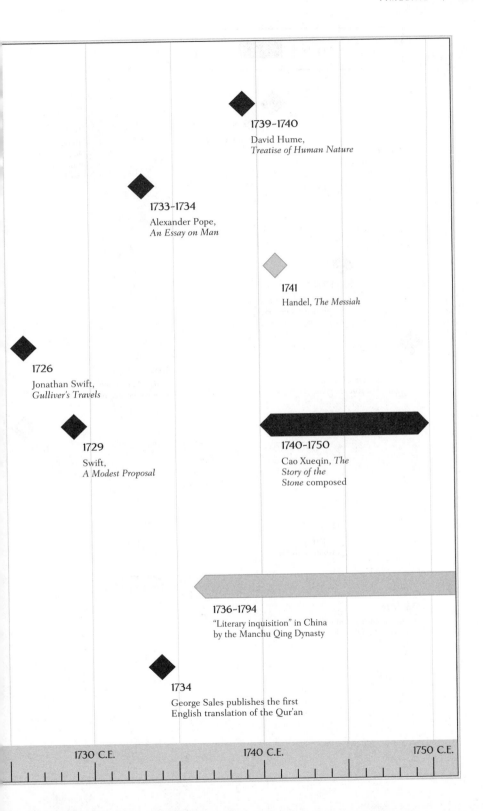

1739–1740
David Hume,
Treatise of Human Nature

1733–1734
Alexander Pope,
An Essay on Man

1741
Handel, *The Messiah*

1726
Jonathan Swift,
Gulliver's Travels

1729
Swift,
A Modest Proposal

1740–1750
Cao Xueqin, *The
Story of the
Stone* composed

1736–1794
"Literary inquisition" in China
by the Manchu Qing Dynasty

1734
George Sales publishes the first
English translation of the Qur'an

1730 C.E.   1740 C.E.   1750 C.E.

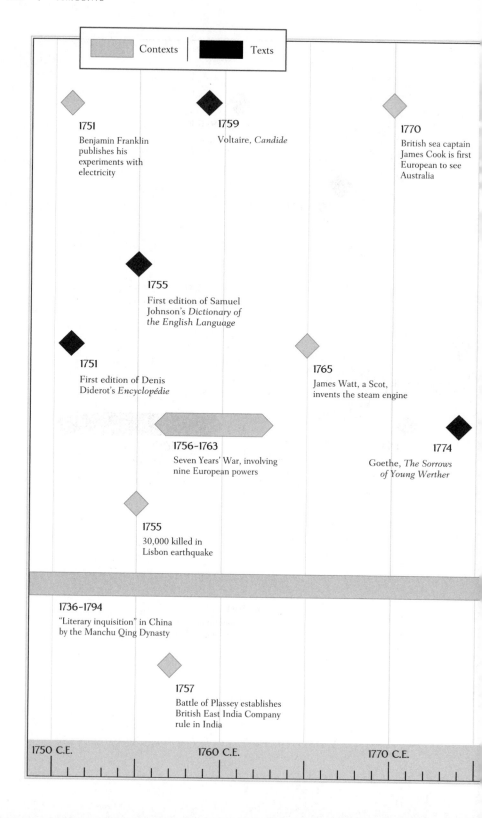

Contexts   Texts

1751
Benjamin Franklin
publishes his
experiments with
electricity

1759
Voltaire, *Candide*

1770
British sea captain
James Cook is first
European to see
Australia

1755
First edition of Samuel
Johnson's *Dictionary of
the English Language*

1751
First edition of Denis
Diderot's *Encyclopédie*

1765
James Watt, a Scot,
invents the steam engine

1756–1763
Seven Years' War, involving
nine European powers

1774
Goethe, *The Sorrows
of Young Werther*

1755
30,000 killed in
Lisbon earthquake

1736–1794
"Literary inquisition" in China
by the Manchu Qing Dynasty

1757
Battle of Plassey establishes
British East India Company
rule in India

1750 C.E.   1760 C.E.   1770 C.E.

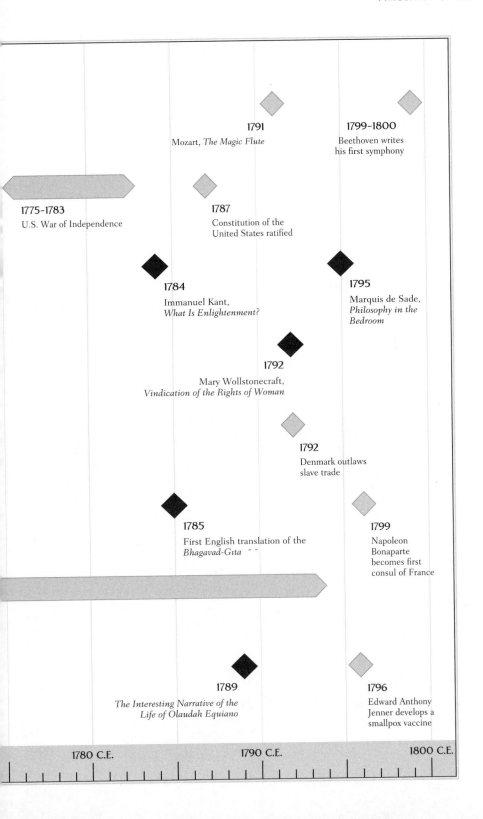

1791
Mozart, *The Magic Flute*

1799–1800
Beethoven writes
his first symphony

1775–1783
U.S. War of Independence

1787
Constitution of the
United States ratified

1784
Immanuel Kant,
What Is Enlightenment?

1795
Marquis de Sade,
*Philosophy in the
Bedroom*

1792
Mary Wollstonecraft,
Vindication of the Rights of Woman

1792
Denmark outlaws
slave trade

1785
First English translation of the
Bhagavad-Gita

1799
Napoleon
Bonaparte
becomes first
consul of France

1789
*The Interesting Narrative of the
Life of Olaudah Equiano*

1796
Edward Anthony
Jenner develops a
smallpox vaccine

1780 C.E.   1790 C.E.   1800 C.E.

Permissions Acknowledgments

Matsuo Bashō: From "The Narrow Road to the Deep North," trans. by Haruo Shirane, from EARLY MODERN JAPANESE LITERATURE: AN ANTHOLOGY 1600–1900, ed. by Haruo Shirane. Copyright © 2002 by Columbia University Press. Reprinted by permission of the publisher.

Cao Xueqin: From THE STORY OF THE STONE, Vol. 1: THE GOLDEN DAYS, trans. with an introduction by David Hawkes (Penguin Classics 1973). Copyright © 1973 David Hawkes. From Vol. 4: THE DEBT OF TEARS, ed. by Gao E, trans. by John Minford (Penguin Classics 1982). Translation copyright © 1982 John Minford. From Vol. 5: THE DREAMER WAKES, ed. by Gao E, trans. by John Minford (Penguin Classics 1982). Translation copyright © 1982 John Minford. Genealogy Charts "The Wang Family" and "Genealogy of the Ningguo and Rongguo Houses of the Jian Clan" from THE STORY OF THE STONE, vol. 1: THE GOLDEN DAYS, trans. with an introduction by David Hawkes (Penguin Classics 1973). Copyright © 1973 by David Hawkes. Reproduced by permission of Penguin Books Ltd.

Sor Juana Inés de la Cruz: From THE ANSWER/LA RESPUESTA, ed. and trans. by Electa Arenal and Amanda Powell. Translation copyright © 1994. Reprinted with the permission of the Feminist Press, www.feministpress.org. All rights reserved.

Marquis de Sade: Excerpts from JUSTINE, PHILOSOPHY IN THE BEDROOM AND OTHER WRITINGS by the Marquis de Sade, copyright © 1965 by Richard Seaver and Austryn Wainhouse. Used by permission of Grove/Atlantic, Inc.

René Descartes: "I think therefore I am . . ." from "The Discourse on Method" from THE PORTABLE ENLIGHTENMENT READER, ed. by Isaac Kramnick, copyright © 1995 by Penguin Books USA, Inc. Used by permission of Viking Penguin, a division of Penguin Group (USA), Inc.

Denis Diderot: From DENIS DIDEROT'S THE ENCYCLOPEDIA, SELECTIONS (1967), ed. and trans. by Stephen J. Gendzier. Reprinted by permission of the translator.

Feng Menglong: From "Common Words to Warn the World" and "Du Tenth Sinks the Jewel Box in Anger," trans. by Robert Ashmore from AN ANTHOLOGY OF CHINESE LITERATURE: BEGINNINGS TO 1911, ed. by Stephen Owen. Copyright © 1996 by Stephen Owen and the Council for Cultural Planning and Development of the Executive Yuan of the Republic of China. Used by permission of W. W. Norton & Company, Inc.

Ihara Saikaku: From "Life of a Sensuous Woman," trans. by Chris Drake from EARLY MODERN JAPANESE LITERATURE: AN ANTHOLOGY 1600–1900, ed. by Haruo Shirane. Copyright © 2002 by Columbia University Press. Reprinted by permission of the publisher.

Immanuel Kant: "What Is Enlightenment," trans. Lewis White Beck, rev. edition, 1990, FOUNDATIONS OF THE METAPHYSICS OF MORALS AND WHAT IS ENLIGHTENMENT, copyright © 1990. Reprinted by permission of Pearson Education, Inc., Upper Saddle River, NJ.

Kitamura Kigin: "Fireflies" from "The Mountain Well," trans. by Haruo Shirane, from EARLY MODERN JAPANESE LITERATURE: AN ANTHOLOGY 1600–1900, ed. by Haruo Shirane. Copyright © 2002 by Columbia University Press. Reprinted by permission of the publisher.

Molière: *Tartuffe*, trans. by Constance Congdon. Copyright © 2008 by Constance Congdon, from TARTUFFE: A NORTON CRITICAL EDITION, ed. by Constance Congdon and Virginia Scott. Used by permission of W. W. Norton & Company, Inc.

Morikawa Kyoriku: From "Haikai Dialogue," trans. by Haruo Shirane, from EARLY MODERN JAPANESE LITERATURE: AN ANTHOLOGY 1600–1900, ed. by Haruo Shirane. Copyright © 2002 by Columbia University Press. Reprinted by permission of the publisher.

Alexander Pope: "The Rape of the Lock" with notes by Samuel Holt Monk from THE NORTON ANTHOLOGY OF ENGLISH LITERATURE, Revised, Vol. 1, ed. by M. H. Abrams et al. Copyright © 1968, 1962 by W. W. Norton & Company, Inc. Used by permission of W. W. Norton & Company, Inc.

Voltaire: From CANDIDE: A NORTON CRITICAL EDITION, second ed., trans. by Robert M. Adams. Copyright © 1991, 1966 by W. W. Norton & Company, Inc. Used by permission of W. W. Norton & Company, Inc.

Wu Cheng'en: From THE MONKEY AND THE MONK: A REVISED ABRIDGMENT OF JOURNEY TO THE WEST, trans. by Anthony Yu. Copyright © 2006 by the University of Chicago. Reprinted by permission of the University of Chicago Press.

Yosa Busōn: Preface to Shōha's Haiku Collection, trans. by Jack Stoneman, and "The Badger" from NEW FLOWER GATHERING, trans. by Cheryl Crowley, from EARLY MODERN JAPANESE LITERATURE: AN ANTHOLOGY 1600–1900, ed. by Haruo Shirane. Copyright © 2002 by Columbia University Press. Reprinted by permission of the publisher.

IMAGES

2–3 Swim Ink / Corbis; **6** Digital Image © 2009 Museum Associates / LACMA / Art Resource, NY; **17** Photo by China Photos / Getty Images; **47** Werner Foreman / Art Resource, NY; **90–91** Erich Lessing / Art Resource, NY; **92** SSPL / Science Museum / Art Resource, NY; **93** Courtesy of Historical Collections & Services, Claude Moore Health Sciences Library, University of Virginia; **94** Erich Lessing / Art Resource, NY; **96** Réunion des Musées Nationaux / Art Resource, NY; **98** Hulton Archive / Getty Images; **100** bpk, Berlin / Art Resource, NY; **414–15** © The Metropolitan Museum of Art. Image source: Art Resource, NY; **417** Wikimedia Commons; **419** © The Trustees of the British Museum / Art Resource, NY; **584–85** HIP / Art Resource, NY; **587** Réunion des Musées Nationaux / Art Resource, NY; **588** Werner Forman / Art Resource, NY; **612–13** © The Metropolitan Museum of Art / Art Resource, NY.

COLOR INSERT

Dushi Wang. Réunion des Musée Nationaux / Art Resource, NY; **Calligraphy by Matsuo Bashō.** Werner Forman / Art Resource, NY; **The Peddler.** Réunion des Musée Nationaux / Art Resource, NY; **Commonplace Book.** Wikimedia Commons / Yale University, Beinecke Library; **Gulliver's Travels.** The Pierpont Morgan Library / Art Resource, NY; **Daytime in the Gay Quarters.** Brooklyn Museum / Corbis; **Sister Juana Ines de la Cruz.** Schalkwijk / Art Resource, NY; **Wedgewood antislavery medallion.** Trustees of the British Museum / Art Resource, NY.

Index

At Mount Kōya, 616
Atsumori (Zeami), 7, 8

Bashō, Matsuo, 616
Beattie, James, 130
Behn, Aphra, 198
Buson, Yosa, 630

Candide, or Optimism (Voltaire), 355
Cao Xuequin, 517

D'Alembert, Jean le Rond, 113
de la Cruz, Sor Juana Inés, 246
de Sade, Marquis, 137
Descartes, René, 110
Dictionary of the English Language,
    A (Johnson), 104
Diderot, Denis, 113
Discourse on Method, The (Descartes), 110
Du Tenth Sinks the Jewel Box in Anger
    (Feng), 499

Encyclopédie, The (Diderot and
    D'Alembert), 114
Essay on Man, An (Pope), 344
Essay on Truth, An (Beattie), 131

Feng Menglong, 497
Franklin, Benjamin, 128

Gulliver's Travels (Swift), 269

Haikai Dialogue (Kyoriku), 629
Hume, David, 129

Johnson, Samuel, 104
Journey to the West, The (Wu), 421, 424

Kant, Immanuel, 105
Kigin, Kitamura, 615
Kong Shangren, 16
Kyoriku, Morikawa, 629

Letter to Joseph Priestley (Franklin), 128
Life of a Sensuous Woman (Saikaku), 593

Love Suicides at Amijima, The (Monzaemon),
    47, 48

Modest Proposal, A (Swift), 315
Molière, Jean-Baptiste (Poquelin),
    141
Monzaemon, Chikamatsu, 45
Mountain Well, The (Kigin), 615

Narrow Road to the Deep North, The
    (Bashō), 617
New Flower Gathering (Buson), 631

Of National Characters (Hume), 129
Optimism (Voltaire), 355
Oroonoko; or, The Royal Slave
    (Behn), 200

Peach Blossom Fan, The (Kong), 17, 19
Philosophical Satire (de la Cruz), 263
Philosophy in the Bedroom (de Sade), 137
Poet's Answer to the Most Illustrious
    Sor Filotea de la Cruz (de la
    Cruz), 248
Pope, Alexander, 321
Preface to Shōha's Haiku Collection
    (Buson), 630

Rape of the Lock, The (Pope), 325

Saikaku, Ihara, 591
Scent of plum blossoms—, 629
Song of Ch'un-hyang, The, 74, 76
Story of the Stone, The (Cao), 518, 521
Swift, Jonathan, 265

Tartuffe (Molière), 142, 144
The last barbarians swept away, the imperial
    seat is established, 499
The months and days, the travelers of a
    hundred ages, 617
[This afternoon, my darling, when we spoke]
    (de la Cruz), 262
[This object which you see—a painted snare]
    (de la Cruz), 262

Vindication of the Rights of Women, A (Wollstonecraft), 134
Voltaire (François-Marie Arouet), 352

What dire offense from amorous causes springs, 326
What Is Enlightenment? (Kant), 105

Wollstonecraft, Mary, 133
Wu Cheng'en, 421

You foolish and unreasoning men, 263

Zeami Motokiyo, 5